Seven Jack London Novels

By

Jack London

Cover Photograph: mybulldog

ISBN: 978-1-78139-339-0

Contents

THE CALL OF THE WILD

WHITE FANG

PART I

PART II

PART III

PART IV

PART V

THE SCARLET PLAGUE

THE SEA-WOLF

THE IRON HEEL

MARTIN EDEN

THE VALLEY OF THE MOON

BOOK I

BOOK II

BOOK III

THE CALL OF THE WILD

CHAPTER I. INTO THE PRIMITIVE

"Old longings nomadic leap,
Chafing at custom's chain;
Again from its brumal sleep
Wakens the ferine strain."

Buck did not read the newspapers, or he would have known that trouble was brewing, not alone for himself, but for every tide-water dog, strong of muscle and with warm, long hair, from Puget Sound to San Diego. Because men, groping in the Arctic darkness, had found a yellow metal, and because steamship and transportation companies were booming the find, thousands of men were rushing into the Northland. These men wanted dogs, and the dogs they wanted were heavy dogs, with strong muscles by which to toil, and furry coats to protect them from the frost.

Buck lived at a big house in the sun-kissed Santa Clara Valley. Judge Miller's place, it was called. It stood back from the road, half hidden among the trees, through which glimpses could be caught of the wide cool veranda that ran around its four sides. The house was approached by gravelled driveways which wound about through wide-spreading lawns and under the interlacing boughs of tall poplars. At the rear things were on even a more spacious scale than at the front. There were great stables, where a dozen grooms and boys held forth, rows of vine-clad servants' cottages, an endless and orderly array of outhouses, long grape arbors, green pastures, orchards, and berry patches. Then there was the pumping plant for the artesian well, and the big cement tank where Judge Miller's boys took their morning plunge and kept cool in the hot afternoon.

And over this great demesne Buck ruled. Here he was born, and here he had lived the four years of his life. It was true, there were other dogs, There could not but be other dogs on so vast a place, but they did not count. They came and went, resided in the populous kennels, or lived obscurely in the recesses of the house after the fashion of Toots, the Japanese pug, or Ysabel, the Mexican hairless,—strange creatures that rarely put nose out of doors or set foot to ground. On the other hand, there were the fox terriers, a score of them at least, who yelped fearful promises at Toots and Ysabel looking out of the windows at them and protected by a legion of housemaids armed with brooms and mops.

But Buck was neither house-dog nor kennel-dog. The whole realm was his. He plunged into the swimming tank or went hunting with the Judge's sons; he escorted Mollie and Alice, the Judge's daughters, on long twilight or early morning rambles;

on wintry nights he lay at the Judge's feet before the roaring library fire; he carried the Judge's grandsons on his back, or rolled them in the grass, and guarded their footsteps through wild adventures down to the fountain in the stable yard, and even beyond, where the paddocks were, and the berry patches. Among the terriers he stalked imperiously, and Toots and Ysabel he utterly ignored, for he was king,—king over all creeping, crawling, flying things of Judge Miller's place, humans included.

His father, Elmo, a huge St. Bernard, had been the Judge's inseparable companion, and Buck bid fair to follow in the way of his father. He was not so large,—he weighed only one hundred and forty pounds,—for his mother, Shep, had been a Scotch shepherd dog. Nevertheless, one hundred and forty pounds, to which was added the dignity that comes of good living and universal respect, enabled him to carry himself in right royal fashion. During the four years since his puppyhood he had lived the life of a sated aristocrat; he had a fine pride in himself, was even a trifle egotistical, as country gentlemen sometimes become because of their insular situation. But he had saved himself by not becoming a mere pampered house-dog. Hunting and kindred outdoor delights had kept down the fat and hardened his muscles; and to him, as to the cold-tubbing races, the love of water had been a tonic and a health preserver.

And this was the manner of dog Buck was in the fall of 1897, when the Klondike strike dragged men from all the world into the frozen North. But Buck did not read the newspapers, and he did not know that Manuel, one of the gardener's helpers, was an undesirable acquaintance. Manuel had one besetting sin. He loved to play Chinese lottery. Also, in his gambling, he had one besetting weakness—faith in a system; and this made his damnation certain. For to play a system requires money, while the wages of a gardener's helper do not lap over the needs of a wife and numerous progeny.

The Judge was at a meeting of the Raisin Growers' Association, and the boys were busy organizing an athletic club, on the memorable night of Manuel's treachery. No one saw him and Buck go off through the orchard on what Buck imagined was merely a stroll. And with the exception of a solitary man, no one saw them arrive at the little flag station known as College Park. This man talked with Manuel, and money chinked between them.

"You might wrap up the goods before you deliver 'm," the stranger said gruffly, and Manuel doubled a piece of stout rope around Buck's neck under the collar.

"Twist it, an' you'll choke 'm plentee," said Manuel, and the stranger grunted a ready affirmative.

Buck had accepted the rope with quiet dignity. To be sure, it was an unwonted performance: but he had learned to trust in men he knew, and to give them credit for a wisdom that outreached his own. But when the ends of the rope were placed in the stranger's hands, he growled menacingly. He had merely intimated his displeasure, in his pride believing that to intimate was to command. But to his surprise the rope tightened around his neck, shutting off his breath. In quick rage he sprang at the man, who met him halfway, grappled him close by the throat, and with a deft twist threw him over on his back. Then the rope tightened mercilessly, while Buck struggled in a fury, his tongue lolling out of his mouth and his great chest panting futilely. Never in all his life had he been so vilely treated, and never in all his life had he been so angry. But his strength ebbed, his eyes glazed, and he knew nothing when the train was flagged and the two men threw him into the baggage car.

CHAPTER I. INTO THE PRIMITIVE

The next he knew, he was dimly aware that his tongue was hurting and that he was being jolted along in some kind of a conveyance. The hoarse shriek of a locomotive whistling a crossing told him where he was. He had travelled too often with the Judge not to know the sensation of riding in a baggage car. He opened his eyes, and into them came the unbridled anger of a kidnapped king. The man sprang for his throat, but Buck was too quick for him. His jaws closed on the hand, nor did they relax till his senses were choked out of him once more.

"Yep, has fits," the man said, hiding his mangled hand from the baggageman, who had been attracted by the sounds of struggle. "I'm takin' 'm up for the boss to 'Frisco. A crack dog-doctor there thinks that he can cure 'm."

Concerning that night's ride, the man spoke most eloquently for himself, in a little shed back of a saloon on the San Francisco water front.

"All I get is fifty for it," he grumbled; "an' I wouldn't do it over for a thousand, cold cash."

His hand was wrapped in a bloody handkerchief, and the right trouser leg was ripped from knee to ankle.

"How much did the other mug get?" the saloon-keeper demanded.

"A hundred," was the reply. "Wouldn't take a sou less, so help me."

"That makes a hundred and fifty," the saloon-keeper calculated; "and he's worth it, or I'm a squarehead."

The kidnapper undid the bloody wrappings and looked at his lacerated hand. "If I don't get the hydrophoby—"

"It'll be because you was born to hang," laughed the saloon-keeper. "Here, lend me a hand before you pull your freight," he added.

Dazed, suffering intolerable pain from throat and tongue, with the life half throttled out of him, Buck attempted to face his tormentors. But he was thrown down and choked repeatedly, till they succeeded in filing the heavy brass collar from off his neck. Then the rope was removed, and he was flung into a cagelike crate.

There he lay for the remainder of the weary night, nursing his wrath and wounded pride. He could not understand what it all meant. What did they want with him, these strange men? Why were they keeping him pent up in this narrow crate? He did not know why, but he felt oppressed by the vague sense of impending calamity. Several times during the night he sprang to his feet when the shed door rattled open, expecting to see the Judge, or the boys at least. But each time it was the bulging face of the saloon-keeper that peered in at him by the sickly light of a tallow candle. And each time the joyful bark that trembled in Buck's throat was twisted into a savage growl.

But the saloon-keeper let him alone, and in the morning four men entered and picked up the crate. More tormentors, Buck decided, for they were evil-looking creatures, ragged and unkempt; and he stormed and raged at them through the bars. They only laughed and poked sticks at him, which he promptly assailed with his teeth till he realized that that was what they wanted. Whereupon he lay down sullenly and allowed the crate to be lifted into a wagon. Then he, and the crate in which he was imprisoned, began a passage through many hands. Clerks in the express office took charge of him; he was carted about in another wagon; a truck carried him, with an assortment of boxes and parcels, upon a ferry steamer; he was trucked off the steamer into a great railway depot, and finally he was deposited in an express car.

For two days and nights this express car was dragged along at the tail of shrieking locomotives; and for two days and nights Buck neither ate nor drank. In his anger he had met the first advances of the express messengers with growls, and they had retaliated by teasing him. When he flung himself against the bars, quivering and frothing, they laughed at him and taunted him. They growled and barked like detestable dogs, mewed, and flapped their arms and crowed. It was all very silly, he knew; but therefore the more outrage to his dignity, and his anger waxed and waxed. He did not mind the hunger so much, but the lack of water caused him severe suffering and fanned his wrath to fever-pitch. For that matter, high-strung and finely sensitive, the ill treatment had flung him into a fever, which was fed by the inflammation of his parched and swollen throat and tongue.

He was glad for one thing: the rope was off his neck. That had given them an unfair advantage; but now that it was off, he would show them. They would never get another rope around his neck. Upon that he was resolved. For two days and nights he neither ate nor drank, and during those two days and nights of torment, he accumulated a fund of wrath that boded ill for whoever first fell foul of him. His eyes turned blood-shot, and he was metamorphosed into a raging fiend. So changed was he that the Judge himself would not have recognized him; and the express messengers breathed with relief when they bundled him off the train at Seattle.

Four men gingerly carried the crate from the wagon into a small, high-walled back yard. A stout man, with a red sweater that sagged generously at the neck, came out and signed the book for the driver. That was the man, Buck divined, the next tormentor, and he hurled himself savagely against the bars. The man smiled grimly, and brought a hatchet and a club.

"You ain't going to take him out now?" the driver asked.

"Sure," the man replied, driving the hatchet into the crate for a pry.

There was an instantaneous scattering of the four men who had carried it in, and from safe perches on top the wall they prepared to watch the performance.

Buck rushed at the splintering wood, sinking his teeth into it, surging and wrestling with it. Wherever the hatchet fell on the outside, he was there on the inside, snarling and growling, as furiously anxious to get out as the man in the red sweater was calmly intent on getting him out.

"Now, you red-eyed devil," he said, when he had made an opening sufficient for the passage of Buck's body. At the same time he dropped the hatchet and shifted the club to his right hand.

And Buck was truly a red-eyed devil, as he drew himself together for the spring, hair bristling, mouth foaming, a mad glitter in his blood-shot eyes. Straight at the man he launched his one hundred and forty pounds of fury, surcharged with the pent passion of two days and nights. In mid air, just as his jaws were about to close on the man, he received a shock that checked his body and brought his teeth together with an agonizing clip. He whirled over, fetching the ground on his back and side. He had never been struck by a club in his life, and did not understand. With a snarl that was part bark and more scream he was again on his feet and launched into the air. And again the shock came and he was brought crushingly to the ground. This time he was aware that it was the club, but his madness knew no caution. A dozen times he charged, and as often the club broke the charge and smashed him down.

After a particularly fierce blow, he crawled to his feet, too dazed to rush. He staggered limply about, the blood flowing from nose and mouth and ears, his beautiful coat sprayed and flecked with bloody slaver. Then the man advanced and deliberately dealt him a frightful blow on the nose. All the pain he had endured was as nothing compared with the exquisite agony of this. With a roar that was almost lionlike in its ferocity, he again hurled himself at the man. But the man, shifting the club from right to left, coolly caught him by the under jaw, at the same time wrenching downward and backward. Buck described a complete circle in the air, and half of another, then crashed to the ground on his head and chest.

For the last time he rushed. The man struck the shrewd blow he had purposely withheld for so long, and Buck crumpled up and went down, knocked utterly senseless.

"He's no slouch at dog-breakin', that's wot I say," one of the men on the wall cried enthusiastically.

"Druther break cayuses any day, and twice on Sundays," was the reply of the driver, as he climbed on the wagon and started the horses.

Buck's senses came back to him, but not his strength. He lay where he had fallen, and from there he watched the man in the red sweater.

"'Answers to the name of Buck,'" the man soliloquized, quoting from the saloon-keeper's letter which had announced the consignment of the crate and contents. "Well, Buck, my boy," he went on in a genial voice, "we've had our little ruction, and the best thing we can do is to let it go at that. You've learned your place, and I know mine. Be a good dog and all 'll go well and the goose hang high. Be a bad dog, and I'll whale the stuffin' outa you. Understand?"

As he spoke he fearlessly patted the head he had so mercilessly pounded, and though Buck's hair involuntarily bristled at touch of the hand, he endured it without protest. When the man brought him water he drank eagerly, and later bolted a generous meal of raw meat, chunk by chunk, from the man's hand.

He was beaten (he knew that); but he was not broken. He saw, once for all, that he stood no chance against a man with a club. He had learned the lesson, and in all his after life he never forgot it. That club was a revelation. It was his introduction to the reign of primitive law, and he met the introduction halfway. The facts of life took on a fiercer aspect; and while he faced that aspect uncowed, he faced it with all the latent cunning of his nature aroused. As the days went by, other dogs came, in crates and at the ends of ropes, some docilely, and some raging and roaring as he had come; and, one and all, he watched them pass under the dominion of the man in the red sweater. Again and again, as he looked at each brutal performance, the lesson was driven home to Buck: a man with a club was a lawgiver, a master to be obeyed, though not necessarily conciliated. Of this last Buck was never guilty, though he did see beaten dogs that fawned upon the man, and wagged their tails, and licked his hand. Also he saw one dog, that would neither conciliate nor obey, finally killed in the struggle for mastery.

Now and again men came, strangers, who talked excitedly, wheedlingly, and in all kinds of fashions to the man in the red sweater. And at such times that money passed between them the strangers took one or more of the dogs away with them. Buck wondered where they went, for they never came back; but the fear of the future was strong upon him, and he was glad each time when he was not selected.

Yet his time came, in the end, in the form of a little weazened man who spat broken English and many strange and uncouth exclamations which Buck could not understand.

"Sacredam!" he cried, when his eyes lit upon Buck. "Dat one dam bully dog! Eh? How moch?"

"Three hundred, and a present at that," was the prompt reply of the man in the red sweater. "And seem' it's government money, you ain't got no kick coming, eh, Perrault?"

Perrault grinned. Considering that the price of dogs had been boomed skyward by the unwonted demand, it was not an unfair sum for so fine an animal. The Canadian Government would be no loser, nor would its despatches travel the slower. Perrault knew dogs, and when he looked at Buck he knew that he was one in a thousand—"One in ten t'ousand," he commented mentally.

Buck saw money pass between them, and was not surprised when Curly, a good-natured Newfoundland, and he were led away by the little weazened man. That was the last he saw of the man in the red sweater, and as Curly and he looked at receding Seattle from the deck of the Narwhal, it was the last he saw of the warm Southland. Curly and he were taken below by Perrault and turned over to a black-faced giant called Francois. Perrault was a French-Canadian, and swarthy; but Francois was a French-Canadian half-breed, and twice as swarthy. They were a new kind of men to Buck (of which he was destined to see many more), and while he developed no affection for them, he none the less grew honestly to respect them. He speedily learned that Perrault and Francois were fair men, calm and impartial in administering justice, and too wise in the way of dogs to be fooled by dogs.

In the 'tween-decks of the Narwhal, Buck and Curly joined two other dogs. One of them was a big, snow-white fellow from Spitzbergen who had been brought away by a whaling captain, and who had later accompanied a Geological Survey into the Barrens. He was friendly, in a treacherous sort of way, smiling into one's face the while he meditated some underhand trick, as, for instance, when he stole from Buck's food at the first meal. As Buck sprang to punish him, the lash of Francois's whip sang through the air, reaching the culprit first; and nothing remained to Buck but to recover the bone. That was fair of Francois, he decided, and the half-breed began his rise in Buck's estimation.

The other dog made no advances, nor received any; also, he did not attempt to steal from the newcomers. He was a gloomy, morose fellow, and he showed Curly plainly that all he desired was to be left alone, and further, that there would be trouble if he were not left alone. "Dave" he was called, and he ate and slept, or yawned between times, and took interest in nothing, not even when the Narwhal crossed Queen Charlotte Sound and rolled and pitched and bucked like a thing possessed. When Buck and Curly grew excited, half wild with fear, he raised his head as though annoyed, favored them with an incurious glance, yawned, and went to sleep again.

Day and night the ship throbbed to the tireless pulse of the propeller, and though one day was very like another, it was apparent to Buck that the weather was steadily growing colder. At last, one morning, the propeller was quiet, and the Narwhal was pervaded with an atmosphere of excitement. He felt it, as did the other dogs, and knew that a change was at hand. Francois leashed them and brought them on deck. At the first step upon the cold surface, Buck's feet sank into a white mushy something very like mud. He sprang back with a snort. More of this white stuff was falling through the air. He shook himself, but more of it fell upon him. He sniffed it curiously, then licked some up on his tongue. It bit like fire, and the next instant was gone. This puzzled him. He tried it again, with the same result. The onlookers laughed uproariously, and he felt ashamed, he knew not why, for it was his first snow.

CHAPTER II. THE LAW OF CLUB AND FANG

Buck's first day on the Dyea beach was like a nightmare. Every hour was filled with shock and surprise. He had been suddenly jerked from the heart of civilization and flung into the heart of things primordial. No lazy, sun-kissed life was this, with nothing to do but loaf and be bored. Here was neither peace, nor rest, nor a moment's safety. All was confusion and action, and every moment life and limb were in peril. There was imperative need to be constantly alert; for these dogs and men were not town dogs and men. They were savages, all of them, who knew no law but the law of club and fang.

He had never seen dogs fight as these wolfish creatures fought, and his first experience taught him an unforgetable lesson. It is true, it was a vicarious experience, else he would not have lived to profit by it. Curly was the victim. They were camped near the log store, where she, in her friendly way, made advances to a husky dog the size of a full-grown wolf, though not half so large as she. There was no warning, only a leap in like a flash, a metallic clip of teeth, a leap out equally swift, and Curly's face was ripped open from eye to jaw.

It was the wolf manner of fighting, to strike and leap away; but there was more to it than this. Thirty or forty huskies ran to the spot and surrounded the combatants in an intent and silent circle. Buck did not comprehend that silent intentness, nor the eager way with which they were licking their chops. Curly rushed her antagonist, who struck again and leaped aside. He met her next rush with his chest, in a peculiar fashion that tumbled her off her feet. She never regained them, This was what the onlooking huskies had waited for. They closed in upon her, snarling and yelping, and she was buried, screaming with agony, beneath the bristling mass of bodies.

So sudden was it, and so unexpected, that Buck was taken aback. He saw Spitz run out his scarlet tongue in a way he had of laughing; and he saw Francois, swinging an axe, spring into the mess of dogs. Three men with clubs were helping him to scatter them. It did not take long. Two minutes from the time Curly went down, the last of her assailants were clubbed off. But she lay there limp and lifeless in the bloody, trampled snow, almost literally torn to pieces, the swart half-breed standing over her and cursing horribly. The scene often came back to Buck to trouble him in his sleep. So that was the way. No fair play. Once down, that was the end of you. Well, he would see to it that he never went down. Spitz ran out his tongue and laughed again, and from that moment Buck hated him with a bitter and deathless hatred.

CHAPTER II. THE LAW OF CLUB AND FANG

Before he had recovered from the shock caused by the tragic passing of Curly, he received another shock. Francois fastened upon him an arrangement of straps and buckles. It was a harness, such as he had seen the grooms put on the horses at home. And as he had seen horses work, so he was set to work, hauling Francois on a sled to the forest that fringed the valley, and returning with a load of firewood. Though his dignity was sorely hurt by thus being made a draught animal, he was too wise to rebel. He buckled down with a will and did his best, though it was all new and strange. Francois was stern, demanding instant obedience, and by virtue of his whip receiving instant obedience; while Dave, who was an experienced wheeler, nipped Buck's hind quarters whenever he was in error. Spitz was the leader, likewise experienced, and while he could not always get at Buck, he growled sharp reproof now and again, or cunningly threw his weight in the traces to jerk Buck into the way he should go. Buck learned easily, and under the combined tuition of his two mates and Francois made remarkable progress. Ere they returned to camp he knew enough to stop at "ho," to go ahead at "mush," to swing wide on the bends, and to keep clear of the wheeler when the loaded sled shot downhill at their heels.

"T'ree vair' good dogs," Francois told Perrault. "Dat Buck, heem pool lak hell. I tich heem queek as anyt'ing."

By afternoon, Perrault, who was in a hurry to be on the trail with his despatches, returned with two more dogs. "Billee" and "Joe" he called them, two brothers, and true huskies both. Sons of the one mother though they were, they were as different as day and night. Billee's one fault was his excessive good nature, while Joe was the very opposite, sour and introspective, with a perpetual snarl and a malignant eye. Buck received them in comradely fashion, Dave ignored them, while Spitz proceeded to thrash first one and then the other. Billee wagged his tail appeasingly, turned to run when he saw that appeasement was of no avail, and cried (still appeasingly) when Spitz's sharp teeth scored his flank. But no matter how Spitz circled, Joe whirled around on his heels to face him, mane bristling, ears laid back, lips writhing and snarling, jaws clipping together as fast as he could snap, and eyes diabolically gleaming—the incarnation of belligerent fear. So terrible was his appearance that Spitz was forced to forego disciplining him; but to cover his own discomfiture he turned upon the inoffensive and wailing Billee and drove him to the confines of the camp.

By evening Perrault secured another dog, an old husky, long and lean and gaunt, with a battle-scarred face and a single eye which flashed a warning of prowess that commanded respect. He was called Sol-leks, which means the Angry One. Like Dave, he asked nothing, gave nothing, expected nothing; and when he marched slowly and deliberately into their midst, even Spitz left him alone. He had one peculiarity which Buck was unlucky enough to discover. He did not like to be approached on his blind side. Of this offence Buck was unwittingly guilty, and the first knowledge he had of his indiscretion was when Sol-leks whirled upon him and slashed his shoulder to the bone for three inches up and down. Forever after Buck avoided his blind side, and to the last of their comradeship had no more trouble. His only apparent ambition, like Dave's, was to be left alone; though, as Buck was afterward to learn, each of them possessed one other and even more vital ambition.

That night Buck faced the great problem of sleeping. The tent, illumined by a candle, glowed warmly in the midst of the white plain; and when he, as a matter of course, entered it, both Perrault and Francois bombarded him with curses and cooking utensils, till he recovered from his consternation and fled ignominiously into the outer cold. A chill wind was blowing that nipped him sharply and bit with especial venom into his wounded shoulder. He lay down on the snow and attempted to sleep, but the frost soon drove him shivering to his feet. Miserable and disconsolate, he wandered about among the many tents, only to find that one place was as cold as another. Here and there savage dogs rushed upon him, but he bristled his neck-hair and snarled (for he was learning fast), and they let him go his way unmolested.

Finally an idea came to him. He would return and see how his own team-mates were making out. To his astonishment, they had disappeared. Again he wandered about through the great camp, looking for them, and again he returned. Were they in the tent? No, that could not be, else he would not have been driven out. Then where could they possibly be? With drooping tail and shivering body, very forlorn indeed, he aimlessly circled the tent. Suddenly the snow gave way beneath his fore legs and he sank down. Something wriggled under his feet. He sprang back, bristling and snarling, fearful of the unseen and unknown. But a friendly little yelp reassured him, and he went back to investigate. A whiff of warm air ascended to his nostrils, and there, curled up under the snow in a snug ball, lay Billee. He whined placatingly, squirmed and wriggled to show his good will and intentions, and even ventured, as a bribe for peace, to lick Buck's face with his warm wet tongue.

Another lesson. So that was the way they did it, eh? Buck confidently selected a spot, and with much fuss and waste effort proceeded to dig a hole for himself. In a trice the heat from his body filled the confined space and he was asleep. The day had been long and arduous, and he slept soundly and comfortably, though he growled and barked and wrestled with bad dreams.

Nor did he open his eyes till roused by the noises of the waking camp. At first he did not know where he was. It had snowed during the night and he was completely buried. The snow walls pressed him on every side, and a great surge of fear swept through him—the fear of the wild thing for the trap. It was a token that he was harking back through his own life to the lives of his forebears; for he was a civilized dog, an unduly civilized dog, and of his own experience knew no trap and so could not of himself fear it. The muscles of his whole body contracted spasmodically and instinctively, the hair on his neck and shoulders stood on end, and with a ferocious snarl he bounded straight up into the blinding day, the snow flying about him in a flashing cloud. Ere he landed on his feet, he saw the white camp spread out before him and knew where he was and remembered all that had passed from the time he went for a stroll with Manuel to the hole he had dug for himself the night before.

A shout from Francois hailed his appearance. "Wot I say?" the dog-driver cried to Perrault. "Dat Buck for sure learn queek as anyt'ing."

Perrault nodded gravely. As courier for the Canadian Government, bearing important despatches, he was anxious to secure the best dogs, and he was particularly gladdened by the possession of Buck.

Three more huskies were added to the team inside an hour, making a total of nine, and before another quarter of an hour had passed they were in harness and swinging up the trail toward the Dyea Canon. Buck was glad to be gone, and though the work was hard he found he did not particularly despise it. He was surprised at the eagerness which animated the whole team and which was communicated to him; but still more surprising was the change wrought in Dave and Sol-leks. They were new dogs, utterly transformed by the harness. All passiveness and unconcern had dropped from them. They were alert and active, anxious that the work should go well, and fiercely irritable with whatever, by delay or confusion, retarded that work. The toil of the traces seemed the supreme expression of their being, and all that they lived for and the only thing in which they took delight.

Dave was wheeler or sled dog, pulling in front of him was Buck, then came Solleks; the rest of the team was strung out ahead, single file, to the leader, which position was filled by Spitz.

Buck had been purposely placed between Dave and Sol-leks so that he might receive instruction. Apt scholar that he was, they were equally apt teachers, never allowing him to linger long in error, and enforcing their teaching with their sharp teeth. Dave was fair and very wise. He never nipped Buck without cause, and he never failed to nip him when he stood in need of it. As Francois's whip backed him up, Buck found it to be cheaper to mend his ways than to retaliate. Once, during a brief halt, when he got tangled in the traces and delayed the start, both Dave and Solleks flew at him and administered a sound trouncing. The resulting tangle was even worse, but Buck took good care to keep the traces clear thereafter; and ere the day was done, so well had he mastered his work, his mates about ceased nagging him. Francois's whip snapped less frequently, and Perrault even honored Buck by lifting up his feet and carefully examining them.

It was a hard day's run, up the Canon, through Sheep Camp, past the Scales and the timber line, across glaciers and snowdrifts hundreds of feet deep, and over the great Chilcoot Divide, which stands between the salt water and the fresh and guards forbiddingly the sad and lonely North. They made good time down the chain of lakes which fills the craters of extinct volcanoes, and late that night pulled into the huge camp at the head of Lake Bennett, where thousands of goldseekers were building boats against the break-up of the ice in the spring. Buck made his hole in the snow and slept the sleep of the exhausted just, but all too early was routed out in the cold darkness and harnessed with his mates to the sled.

That day they made forty miles, the trail being packed; but the next day, and for many days to follow, they broke their own trail, worked harder, and made poorer time. As a rule, Perrault travelled ahead of the team, packing the snow with webbed shoes to make it easier for them. Francois, guiding the sled at the gee-pole, sometimes exchanged places with him, but not often. Perrault was in a hurry, and he prided himself on his knowledge of ice, which knowledge was indispensable, for the fall ice was very thin, and where there was swift water, there was no ice at all.

Day after day, for days unending, Buck toiled in the traces. Always, they broke camp in the dark, and the first gray of dawn found them hitting the trail with fresh miles reeled off behind them. And always they pitched camp after dark, eating their bit of fish, and crawling to sleep into the snow. Buck was ravenous. The pound and a half of sun-dried salmon, which was his ration for each day, seemed to go nowhere. He never had enough, and suffered from perpetual hunger pangs. Yet the other dogs, because they weighed less and were born to the life, received a pound only of the fish and managed to keep in good condition.

He swiftly lost the fastidiousness which had characterized his old life. A dainty eater, he found that his mates, finishing first, robbed him of his unfinished ration. There was no defending it. While he was fighting off two or three, it was disappearing down the throats of the others. To remedy this, he ate as fast as they; and, so greatly did hunger compel him, he was not above taking what did not belong to him. He watched and learned. When he saw Pike, one of the new dogs, a clever malingerer and thief, slyly steal a slice of bacon when Perrault's back was turned, he duplicated the performance the following day, getting away with the whole chunk. A great uproar was raised, but he was unsuspected; while Dub, an awkward blunderer who was always getting caught, was punished for Buck's misdeed.

This first theft marked Buck as fit to survive in the hostile Northland environment. It marked his adaptability, his capacity to adjust himself to changing conditions, the lack of which would have meant swift and terrible death. It marked, further, the decay or going to pieces of his moral nature, a vain thing and a handicap in the ruthless struggle for existence. It was all well enough in the Southland, under the law of love and fellowship, to respect private property and personal feelings; but in the Northland, under the law of club and fang, whoso took such things into account was a fool, and in so far as he observed them he would fail to prosper.

Not that Buck reasoned it out. He was fit, that was all, and unconsciously he accommodated himself to the new mode of life. All his days, no matter what the odds, he had never run from a fight. But the club of the man in the red sweater had beaten into him a more fundamental and primitive code. Civilized, he could have died for a moral consideration, say the defence of Judge Miller's riding-whip; but the completeness of his decivilization was now evidenced by his ability to flee from the defence of a moral consideration and so save his hide. He did not steal for joy of it, but because of the clamor of his stomach. He did not rob openly, but stole secretly and cunningly, out of respect for club and fang. In short, the things he did were done because it was easier to do them than not to do them.

His development (or retrogression) was rapid. His muscles became hard as iron, and he grew callous to all ordinary pain. He achieved an internal as well as external economy. He could eat anything, no matter how loathsome or indigestible; and, once eaten, the juices of his stomach extracted the last least particle of nutriment; and his blood carried it to the farthest reaches of his body, building it into the toughest and stoutest of tissues. Sight and scent became remarkably keen, while his hearing developed such acuteness that in his sleep he heard the faintest sound and knew whether it heralded peace or peril. He learned to bite the ice out with his teeth when it collected between his toes; and when he was thirsty and there was a thick scum of ice over the water hole, he would break it by rearing and striking it with stiff fore legs. His most conspicuous trait was an ability to scent the wind and forecast it a night in advance. No matter how breathless the air when he dug his nest by tree or bank, the wind that later blew inevitably found him to leeward, sheltered and snug.

And not only did he learn by experience, but instincts long dead became alive again. The domesticated generations fell from him. In vague ways he remembered back to the youth of the breed, to the time the wild dogs ranged in packs through the primeval forest and killed their meat as they ran it down. It was no task for him to learn to fight with cut and slash and the quick wolf snap. In this manner had fought forgotten ancestors. They quickened the old life within him, and the old tricks which they had stamped into the heredity of the breed were his tricks. They came to him without effort or discovery, as though they had been his always. And when, on the still cold nights, he pointed his nose at a star and howled long and wolflike, it was his ancestors, dead and dust, pointing nose at star and howling down through the centuries and through him. And his cadences were their cadences, the cadences which voiced their woe and what to them was the meaning of the stiffness, and the cold, and dark.

Thus, as token of what a puppet thing life is, the ancient song surged through him and he came into his own again; and he came because men had found a yellow metal in the North, and because Manuel was a gardener's helper whose wages did not lap over the needs of his wife and divers small copies of himself.

CHAPTER III. THE DOMINANT PRIMORDIAL BEAST

The dominant primordial beast was strong in Buck, and under the fierce conditions of trail life it grew and grew. Yet it was a secret growth. His newborn cunning gave him poise and control. He was too busy adjusting himself to the new life to feel at ease, and not only did he not pick fights, but he avoided them whenever possible. A certain deliberateness characterized his attitude. He was not prone to rashness and precipitate action; and in the bitter hatred between him and Spitz he betrayed no impatience, shunned all offensive acts.

On the other hand, possibly because he divined in Buck a dangerous rival, Spitz never lost an opportunity of showing his teeth. He even went out of his way to bully Buck, striving constantly to start the fight which could end only in the death of one or the other. Early in the trip this might have taken place had it not been for an unwonted accident. At the end of this day they made a bleak and miserable camp on the shore of Lake Le Barge. Driving snow, a wind that cut like a white-hot knife, and darkness had forced them to grope for a camping place. They could hardly have fared worse. At their backs rose a perpendicular wall of rock, and Perrault and Francois were compelled to make their fire and spread their sleeping robes on the ice of the lake itself. The tent they had discarded at Dyea in order to travel light. A few sticks of driftwood furnished them with a fire that thawed down through the ice and left them to eat supper in the dark.

Close in under the sheltering rock Buck made his nest. So snug and warm was it, that he was loath to leave it when Francois distributed the fish which he had first thawed over the fire. But when Buck finished his ration and returned, he found his nest occupied. A warning snarl told him that the trespasser was Spitz. Till now Buck had avoided trouble with his enemy, but this was too much. The beast in him roared. He sprang upon Spitz with a fury which surprised them both, and Spitz particularly, for his whole experience with Buck had gone to teach him that his rival was an unusually timid dog, who managed to hold his own only because of his great weight and size.

Francois was surprised, too, when they shot out in a tangle from the disrupted nest and he divined the cause of the trouble. "A-a-ah!" he cried to Buck. "Gif it to heem, by Gar! Gif it to heem, the dirty t'eef!"

Spitz was equally willing. He was crying with sheer rage and eagerness as he circled back and forth for a chance to spring in. Buck was no less eager, and no less cautious, as he likewise circled back and forth for the advantage. But it was then that the unexpected happened, the thing which projected their struggle for supremacy far into the future, past many a weary mile of trail and toil.

An oath from Perrault, the resounding impact of a club upon a bony frame, and a shrill yelp of pain, heralded the breaking forth of pandemonium. The camp was suddenly discovered to be alive with skulking furry forms,—starving huskies, four or five score of them, who had scented the camp from some Indian village. They had crept in while Buck and Spitz were fighting, and when the two men sprang among them with stout clubs they showed their teeth and fought back. They were crazed by the smell of the food. Perrault found one with head buried in the grub-box. His club landed heavily on the gaunt ribs, and the grub-box was capsized on the ground. On the instant a score of the famished brutes were scrambling for the bread and bacon. The clubs fell upon them unheeded. They yelped and howled under the rain of blows, but struggled none the less madly till the last crumb had been devoured.

In the meantime the astonished team-dogs had burst out of their nests only to be set upon by the fierce invaders. Never had Buck seen such dogs. It seemed as though their bones would burst through their skins. They were mere skeletons, draped loosely in draggled hides, with blazing eyes and slavered fangs. But the hunger-madness made them terrifying, irresistible. There was no opposing them. The team-dogs were swept back against the cliff at the first onset. Buck was beset by three huskies, and in a trice his head and shoulders were ripped and slashed. The din was frightful. Billee was crying as usual. Dave and Sol-leks, dripping blood from a score of wounds, were fighting bravely side by side. Joe was snapping like a demon. Once, his teeth closed on the fore leg of a husky, and he crunched down through the bone. Pike, the malingerer, leaped upon the crippled animal, breaking its neck with a quick flash of teeth and a jerk, Buck got a frothing adversary by the throat, and was sprayed with blood when his teeth sank through the jugular. The warm taste of it in his mouth goaded him to greater fierceness. He flung himself upon another, and at the same time felt teeth sink into his own throat. It was Spitz, treacherously attacking from the side.

Perrault and Francois, having cleaned out their part of the camp, hurried to save their sled-dogs. The wild wave of famished beasts rolled back before them, and Buck shook himself free. But it was only for a moment. The two men were compelled to run back to save the grub, upon which the huskies returned to the attack on the team. Billee, terrified into bravery, sprang through the savage circle and fled away over the ice. Pike and Dub followed on his heels, with the rest of the team behind. As Buck drew himself together to spring after them, out of the tail of his eye he saw Spitz rush upon him with the evident intention of overthrowing him. Once off his feet and under that mass of huskies, there was no hope for him. But he braced himself to the shock of Spitz's charge, then joined the flight out on the lake.

Later, the nine team-dogs gathered together and sought shelter in the forest. Though unpursued, they were in a sorry plight. There was not one who was not wounded in four or five places, while some were wounded grievously. Dub was badly injured in a hind leg; Dolly, the last husky added to the team at Dyea, had a badly torn throat; Joe had lost an eye; while Billee, the good-natured, with an ear chewed and rent to ribbons, cried and whimpered throughout the night. At daybreak they limped warily back to camp, to find the marauders gone and the two men in bad tempers. Fully half their grub supply was gone. The huskies had chewed through the sled lashings and canvas coverings. In fact, nothing, no matter how remotely eatable, had escaped them. They had eaten a pair of Perrault's moose-hide moccasins, chunks out of the leather traces, and even two feet of lash from the end of Francois's whip. He broke from a mournful contemplation of it to look over his wounded dogs.

"Ah, my frien's," he said softly, "mebbe it mek you mad dog, dose many bites. Mebbe all mad dog, sacredam! Wot you t'ink, eh, Perrault?"

The courier shook his head dubiously. With four hundred miles of trail still between him and Dawson, he could ill afford to have madness break out among his dogs. Two hours of cursing and exertion got the harnesses into shape, and the wound-stiffened team was under way, struggling painfully over the hardest part of the trail they had yet encountered, and for that matter, the hardest between them and Dawson.

The Thirty Mile River was wide open. Its wild water defied the frost, and it was in the eddies only and in the quiet places that the ice held at all. Six days of exhausting toil were required to cover those thirty terrible miles. And terrible they were, for every foot of them was accomplished at the risk of life to dog and man. A dozen times, Perrault, nosing the way broke through the ice bridges, being saved by the long pole he carried, which he so held that it fell each time across the hole made by his body. But a cold snap was on, the thermometer registering fifty below zero, and each time he broke through he was compelled for very life to build a fire and dry his garments.

Nothing daunted him. It was because nothing daunted him that he had been chosen for government courier. He took all manner of risks, resolutely thrusting his little weazened face into the frost and struggling on from dim dawn to dark. He skirted the frowning shores on rim ice that bent and crackled under foot and upon which they dared not halt. Once, the sled broke through, with Dave and Buck, and they were half-frozen and all but drowned by the time they were dragged out. The usual fire was necessary to save them. They were coated solidly with ice, and the two men kept them on the run around the fire, sweating and thawing, so close that they were singed by the flames.

At another time Spitz went through, dragging the whole team after him up to Buck, who strained backward with all his strength, his fore paws on the slippery edge and the ice quivering and snapping all around. But behind him was Dave, likewise straining backward, and behind the sled was Francois, pulling till his tendons cracked.

Again, the rim ice broke away before and behind, and there was no escape except up the cliff. Perrault scaled it by a miracle, while Francois prayed for just that miracle; and with every thong and sled lashing and the last bit of harness rove into a long rope, the dogs were hoisted, one by one, to the cliff crest. Francois came up last, after the sled and load. Then came the search for a place to descend, which descent was ultimately made by the aid of the rope, and night found them back on the river with a quarter of a mile to the day's credit.

By the time they made the Hootalinqua and good ice, Buck was played out. The rest of the dogs were in like condition; but Perrault, to make up lost time, pushed them late and early. The first day they covered thirty-five miles to the Big Salmon; the next day thirty-five more to the Little Salmon; the third day forty miles, which brought them well up toward the Five Fingers.

Buck's feet were not so compact and hard as the feet of the huskies. His had softened during the many generations since the day his last wild ancestor was tamed by a cave-dweller or river man. All day long he limped in agony, and camp once made, lay down like a dead dog. Hungry as he was, he would not move to receive his ration of fish, which Francois had to bring to him. Also, the dog-driver rubbed Buck's feet for half an hour each night after supper, and sacrificed the tops of his own moccasins to make four moccasins for Buck. This was a great relief, and Buck caused even the weazened face of Perrault to twist itself into a grin one morning, when Francois forgot the moccasins and Buck lay on his back, his four feet waving appealingly in the air, and refused to budge without them. Later his feet grew hard to the trail, and the worn-out foot-gear was thrown away.

At the Pelly one morning, as they were harnessing up, Dolly, who had never been conspicuous for anything, went suddenly mad. She announced her condition by a long, heartbreaking wolf howl that sent every dog bristling with fear, then sprang straight for Buck. He had never seen a dog go mad, nor did he have any reason to fear madness; yet he knew that here was horror, and fled away from it in a panic. Straight away he raced, with Dolly, panting and frothing, one leap behind; nor could she gain on him, so great was his terror, nor could he leave her, so great was her madness. He plunged through the wooded breast of the island, flew down to the lower end, crossed a back channel filled with rough ice to another island, gained a third island, curved back to the main river, and in desperation started to cross it. And all the time, though he did not look, he could hear her snarling just one leap behind. Francois called to him a quarter of a mile away and he doubled back, still one leap ahead, gasping painfully for air and putting all his faith in that Francois would save him. The dog-driver held the axe poised in his hand, and as Buck shot past him the axe crashed down upon mad Dolly's head.

Buck staggered over against the sled, exhausted, sobbing for breath, helpless. This was Spitz's opportunity. He sprang upon Buck, and twice his teeth sank into his unresisting foe and ripped and tore the flesh to the bone. Then Francois's lash descended, and Buck had the satisfaction of watching Spitz receive the worst whipping as yet administered to any of the teams.

"One devil, dat Spitz," remarked Perrault. "Some dam day heem keel dat Buck."

"Dat Buck two devils," was Francois's rejoinder. "All de tam I watch dat Buck I know for sure. Lissen: some dam fine day heem get mad lak hell an' den heem chew dat Spitz all up an' spit heem out on de snow. Sure. I know."

From then on it was war between them. Spitz, as lead-dog and acknowledged master of the team, felt his supremacy threatened by this strange Southland dog. And strange Buck was to him, for of the many Southland dogs he had known, not one had shown up worthily in camp and on trail. They were all too soft, dying under the toil, the frost, and starvation. Buck was the exception. He alone endured and prospered, matching the husky in strength, savagery, and cunning. Then he was a masterful dog, and what made him dangerous was the fact that the club of the man in the red sweater had knocked all blind pluck and rashness out of his desire for mastery. He was preeminently cunning, and could bide his time with a patience that was nothing less than primitive.

It was inevitable that the clash for leadership should come. Buck wanted it. He wanted it because it was his nature, because he had been gripped tight by that nameless, incomprehensible pride of the trail and trace—that pride which holds dogs in the toil to the last gasp, which lures them to die joyfully in the harness, and breaks their hearts if they are cut out of the harness. This was the pride of Dave as wheel-dog, of

Sol-leks as he pulled with all his strength; the pride that laid hold of them at break of camp, transforming them from sour and sullen brutes into straining, eager, ambitious creatures; the pride that spurred them on all day and dropped them at pitch of camp at night, letting them fall back into gloomy unrest and uncontent. This was the pride that bore up Spitz and made him thrash the sled-dogs who blundered and shirked in the traces or hid away at harness-up time in the morning. Likewise it was this pride that made him fear Buck as a possible lead-dog. And this was Buck's pride, too.

He openly threatened the other's leadership. He came between him and the shirks he should have punished. And he did it deliberately. One night there was a heavy snowfall, and in the morning Pike, the malingerer, did not appear. He was securely hidden in his nest under a foot of snow. Francois called him and sought him in vain. Spitz was wild with wrath. He raged through the camp, smelling and digging in every likely place, snarling so frightfully that Pike heard and shivered in his hiding-place.

But when he was at last unearthed, and Spitz flew at him to punish him, Buck flew, with equal rage, in between. So unexpected was it, and so shrewdly managed, that Spitz was hurled backward and off his feet. Pike, who had been trembling abjectly, took heart at this open mutiny, and sprang upon his overthrown leader. Buck, to whom fair play was a forgotten code, likewise sprang upon Spitz. But Francois, chuckling at the incident while unswerving in the administration of justice, brought his lash down upon Buck with all his might. This failed to drive Buck from his prostrate rival, and the butt of the whip was brought into play. Half-stunned by the blow, Buck was knocked backward and the lash laid upon him again and again, while Spitz soundly punished the many times offending Pike.

In the days that followed, as Dawson grew closer and closer, Buck still continued to interfere between Spitz and the culprits; but he did it craftily, when Francois was not around, With the covert mutiny of Buck, a general insubordination sprang up and increased. Dave and Sol-leks were unaffected, but the rest of the team went from bad to worse. Things no longer went right. There was continual bickering and jangling. Trouble was always afoot, and at the bottom of it was Buck. He kept Francois busy, for the dog-driver was in constant apprehension of the life-and-death struggle between the two which he knew must take place sooner or later; and on more than one night the sounds of quarrelling and strife among the other dogs turned him out of his sleeping robe, fearful that Buck and Spitz were at it.

But the opportunity did not present itself, and they pulled into Dawson one dreary afternoon with the great fight still to come. Here were many men, and countless dogs, and Buck found them all at work. It seemed the ordained order of things that dogs should work. All day they swung up and down the main street in long teams, and in the night their jingling bells still went by. They hauled cabin logs and firewood, freighted up to the mines, and did all manner of work that horses did in the Santa Clara Valley. Here and there Buck met Southland dogs, but in the main they were the wild wolf husky breed. Every night, regularly, at nine, at twelve, at three, they lifted a nocturnal song, a weird and eerie chant, in which it was Buck's delight to join.

With the aurora borealis flaming coldly overhead, or the stars leaping in the frost dance, and the land numb and frozen under its pall of snow, this song of the huskies might have been the defiance of life, only it was pitched in minor key, with long-drawn wailings and half-sobs, and was more the pleading of life, the articulate travail of existence. It was an old song, old as the breed itself—one of the first songs of the younger world in a day when songs were sad. It was invested with the woe of unnumbered generations, this plaint by which Buck was so strangely stirred. When he moaned and sobbed, it was with the pain of living that was of old the pain of his wild fathers, and the fear and mystery of the cold and dark that was to them fear and mystery. And that he should be stirred by it marked the completeness with which he harked back through the ages of fire and roof to the raw beginnings of life in the howling ages.

Seven days from the time they pulled into Dawson, they dropped down the steep bank by the Barracks to the Yukon Trail, and pulled for Dyea and Salt Water. Perrault was carrying despatches if anything more urgent than those he had brought in; also, the travel pride had gripped him, and he purposed to make the record trip of the year. Several things favored him in this. The week's rest had recuperated the dogs and put them in thorough trim. The trail they had broken into the country was packed hard by later journeyers. And further, the police had arranged in two or three places deposits of grub for dog and man, and he was travelling light.

They made Sixty Mile, which is a fifty-mile run, on the first day; and the second day saw them booming up the Yukon well on their way to Pelly. But such splendid running was achieved not without great trouble and vexation on the part of Francois. The insidious revolt led by Buck had destroyed the solidarity of the team. It no longer was as one dog leaping in the traces. The encouragement Buck gave the rebels led them into all kinds of petty misdemeanors. No more was Spitz a leader greatly to be feared. The old awe departed, and they grew equal to challenging his authority. Pike robbed him of half a fish one night, and gulped it down under the protection of Buck. Another night Dub and Joe fought Spitz and made him forego the punishment they deserved. And even Billee, the good-natured, was less good-natured, and whined not half so placatingly as in former days. Buck never came near Spitz without snarling and bristling menacingly. In fact, his conduct approached that of a bully, and he was given to swaggering up and down before Spitz's very nose.

The breaking down of discipline likewise affected the dogs in their relations with one another. They quarrelled and bickered more than ever among themselves, till at times the camp was a howling bedlam. Dave and Sol-leks alone were unaltered, though they were made irritable by the unending squabbling. Francois swore strange barbarous oaths, and stamped the snow in futile rage, and tore his hair. His lash was always singing among the dogs, but it was of small avail. Directly his back was turned they were at it again. He backed up Spitz with his whip, while Buck backed up the remainder of the team. Francois knew he was behind all the trouble, and Buck knew he knew; but Buck was too clever ever again to be caught red-handed. He worked faithfully in the harness, for the toil had become a delight to him; yet it was a greater delight slyly to precipitate a fight amongst his mates and tangle the traces.

At the mouth of the Tahkeena, one night after supper, Dub turned up a snowshoe rabbit, blundered it, and missed. In a second the whole team was in full cry. A hundred yards away was a camp of the Northwest Police, with fifty dogs, huskies all, who joined the chase. The rabbit sped down the river, turned off into a small creek, up the frozen bed of which it held steadily. It ran lightly on the surface of the snow, while the dogs ploughed through by main strength. Buck led the pack, sixty strong, around bend after bend, but he could not gain. He lay down low to the race, whining eagerly, his splendid body flashing forward, leap by leap, in the wan white moonlight. And leap by leap, like some pale frost wraith, the snowshoe rabbit flashed on ahead.

All that stirring of old instincts which at stated periods drives men out from the sounding cities to forest and plain to kill things by chemically propelled leaden pellets, the blood lust, the joy to kill—all this was Buck's, only it was infinitely more intimate. He was ranging at the head of the pack, running the wild thing down, the living meat, to kill with his own teeth and wash his muzzle to the eyes in warm blood.

There is an ecstasy that marks the summit of life, and beyond which life cannot rise. And such is the paradox of living, this ecstasy comes when one is most alive, and it comes as a complete forgetfulness that one is alive. This ecstasy, this forgetfulness of living, comes to the artist, caught up and out of himself in a sheet of flame; it comes to the soldier, war-mad on a stricken field and refusing quarter; and it came to Buck, leading the pack, sounding the old wolf-cry, straining after the food that was alive and that fled swiftly before him through the moonlight. He was sounding the deeps of his nature, and of the parts of his nature that were deeper than he, going back into the womb of Time. He was mastered by the sheer surging of life, the tidal wave of being, the perfect joy of each separate muscle, joint, and sinew in that it was everything that was not death, that it was aglow and rampant, expressing itself in movement, flying exultantly under the stars and over the face of dead matter that did not move.

But Spitz, cold and calculating even in his supreme moods, left the pack and cut across a narrow neck of land where the creek made a long bend around. Buck did not know of this, and as he rounded the bend, the frost wraith of a rabbit still flitting before him, he saw another and larger frost wraith leap from the overhanging bank into the immediate path of the rabbit. It was Spitz. The rabbit could not turn, and as the white teeth broke its back in mid air it shrieked as loudly as a stricken man may shriek. At sound of this, the cry of Life plunging down from Life's apex in the grip of Death, the fall pack at Buck's heels raised a hell's chorus of delight.

Buck did not cry out. He did not check himself, but drove in upon Spitz, shoulder to shoulder, so hard that he missed the throat. They rolled over and over in the powdery snow. Spitz gained his feet almost as though he had not been overthrown, slashing Buck down the shoulder and leaping clear. Twice his teeth clipped together, like the steel jaws of a trap, as he backed away for better footing, with lean and lifting lips that writhed and snarled.

In a flash Buck knew it. The time had come. It was to the death. As they circled about, snarling, ears laid back, keenly watchful for the advantage, the scene came to Buck with a sense of familiarity. He seemed to remember it all,—the white woods, and earth, and moonlight, and the thrill of battle. Over the whiteness and silence brooded a ghostly calm. There was not the faintest whisper of air—nothing moved, not a leaf quivered, the visible breaths of the dogs rising slowly and lingering in the frosty air. They had made short work of the snowshoe rabbit, these dogs that were ill-tamed wolves; and they were now drawn up in an expectant circle. They, too, were silent, their eyes only gleaming and their breaths drifting slowly upward. To Buck it was nothing new or strange, this scene of old time. It was as though it had always been, the wonted way of things.

Spitz was a practised fighter. From Spitzbergen through the Arctic, and across Canada and the Barrens, he had held his own with all manner of dogs and achieved to mastery over them. Bitter rage was his, but never blind rage. In passion to rend and destroy, he never forgot that his enemy was in like passion to rend and destroy. He never rushed till he was prepared to receive a rush; never attacked till he had first defended that attack.

In vain Buck strove to sink his teeth in the neck of the big white dog. Wherever his fangs struck for the softer flesh, they were countered by the fangs of Spitz. Fang clashed fang, and lips were cut and bleeding, but Buck could not penetrate his enemy's guard. Then he warmed up and enveloped Spitz in a whirlwind of rushes. Time and time again he tried for the snow-white throat, where life bubbled near to the surface, and each time and every time Spitz slashed him and got away. Then Buck took to rushing, as though for the throat, when, suddenly drawing back his head and curving in from the side, he would drive his shoulder at the shoulder of Spitz, as a ram by which to overthrow him. But instead, Buck's shoulder was slashed down each time as Spitz leaped lightly away.

Spitz was untouched, while Buck was streaming with blood and panting hard. The fight was growing desperate. And all the while the silent and wolfish circle waited to finish off whichever dog went down. As Buck grew winded, Spitz took to rushing, and he kept him staggering for footing. Once Buck went over, and the whole circle of sixty dogs started up; but he recovered himself, almost in mid air, and the circle sank down again and waited.

But Buck possessed a quality that made for greatness—imagination. He fought by instinct, but he could fight by head as well. He rushed, as though attempting the old shoulder trick, but at the last instant swept low to the snow and in. His teeth closed on Spitz's left fore leg. There was a crunch of breaking bone, and the white dog faced him on three legs. Thrice he tried to knock him over, then repeated the trick and broke the right fore leg. Despite the pain and helplessness, Spitz struggled madly to keep up. He saw the silent circle, with gleaming eyes, lolling tongues, and silvery breaths drifting upward, closing in upon him as he had seen similar circles close in upon beaten antagonists in the past. Only this time he was the one who was beaten.

There was no hope for him. Buck was inexorable. Mercy was a thing reserved for gentler climes. He manoeuvred for the final rush. The circle had tightened till he could feel the breaths of the huskies on his flanks. He could see them, beyond Spitz and to either side, half crouching for the spring, their eyes fixed upon him. A pause seemed to fall. Every animal was motionless as though turned to stone. Only Spitz quivered and bristled as he staggered back and forth, snarling with horrible menace, as though to frighten off impending death. Then Buck sprang in and out; but while he was in, shoulder had at last squarely met shoulder. The dark circle became a dot on the moon-flooded snow as Spitz disappeared from view. Buck stood and looked on, the successful champion, the dominant primordial beast who had made his kill and found it good.

CHAPTER IV. WHO HAS WON TO MASTERSHIP

"Eh? Wot I say? I spik true w'en I say dat Buck two devils." This was Francois's speech next morning when he discovered Spitz missing and Buck covered with wounds. He drew him to the fire and by its light pointed them out.

"Dat Spitz fight lak hell," said Perrault, as he surveyed the gaping rips and cuts.

"An' dat Buck fight lak two hells," was Francois's answer. "An' now we make good time. No more Spitz, no more trouble, sure."

While Perrault packed the camp outfit and loaded the sled, the dog-driver proceeded to harness the dogs. Buck trotted up to the place Spitz would have occupied as leader; but Francois, not noticing him, brought Sol-leks to the coveted position. In his judgment, Sol-leks was the best lead-dog left. Buck sprang upon Sol-leks in a fury, driving him back and standing in his place.

"Eh? eh?" Francois cried, slapping his thighs gleefully. "Look at dat Buck. Heem keel dat Spitz, heem t'ink to take de job."

"Go 'way, Chook!" he cried, but Buck refused to budge.

He took Buck by the scruff of the neck, and though the dog growled threateningly, dragged him to one side and replaced Sol-leks. The old dog did not like it, and showed plainly that he was afraid of Buck. Francois was obdurate, but when he turned his back Buck again displaced Sol-leks, who was not at all unwilling to go.

Francois was angry. "Now, by Gar, I feex you!" he cried, coming back with a heavy club in his hand.

Buck remembered the man in the red sweater, and retreated slowly; nor did he attempt to charge in when Sol-leks was once more brought forward. But he circled just beyond the range of the club, snarling with bitterness and rage; and while he circled he watched the club so as to dodge it if thrown by Francois, for he was become wise in the way of clubs. The driver went about his work, and he called to Buck when he was ready to put him in his old place in front of Dave. Buck retreated two or three steps. Francois followed him up, whereupon he again retreated. After some time of this, Francois threw down the club, thinking that Buck feared a thrashing. But Buck was in open revolt. He wanted, not to escape a clubbing, but to have the leadership. It was his by right. He had earned it, and he would not be content with less.

Perrault took a hand. Between them they ran him about for the better part of an hour. They threw clubs at him. He dodged. They cursed him, and his fathers and mothers before him, and all his seed to come after him down to the remotest generation, and every hair on his body and drop of blood in his veins; and he answered curse with snarl and kept out of their reach. He did not try to run away, but retreated around and around the camp, advertising plainly that when his desire was met, he would come in and be good.

Francois sat down and scratched his head. Perrault looked at his watch and swore. Time was flying, and they should have been on the trail an hour gone. Francois scratched his head again. He shook it and grinned sheepishly at the courier, who shrugged his shoulders in sign that they were beaten. Then Francois went up to where Sol-leks stood and called to Buck. Buck laughed, as dogs laugh, yet kept his distance. Francois unfastened Sol-leks's traces and put him back in his old place. The team stood harnessed to the sled in an unbroken line, ready for the trail. There was no place for Buck save at the front. Once more Francois called, and once more Buck laughed and kept away.

"T'row down de club," Perrault commanded.

Francois complied, whereupon Buck trotted in, laughing triumphantly, and swung around into position at the head of the team. His traces were fastened, the sled broken out, and with both men running they dashed out on to the river trail.

Highly as the dog-driver had forevalued Buck, with his two devils, he found, while the day was yet young, that he had undervalued. At a bound Buck took up the duties of leadership; and where judgment was required, and quick thinking and quick acting, he showed himself the superior even of Spitz, of whom Francois had never seen an equal.

But it was in giving the law and making his mates live up to it, that Buck excelled. Dave and Sol-leks did not mind the change in leadership. It was none of their business. Their business was to toil, and toil mightily, in the traces. So long as that were not interfered with, they did not care what happened. Billee, the good-natured, could lead for all they cared, so long as he kept order. The rest of the team, however, had grown unruly during the last days of Spitz, and their surprise was great now that Buck proceeded to lick them into shape.

Pike, who pulled at Buck's heels, and who never put an ounce more of his weight against the breast-band than he was compelled to do, was swiftly and repeatedly shaken for loafing; and ere the first day was done he was pulling more than ever before in his life. The first night in camp, Joe, the sour one, was punished roundly—a thing that Spitz had never succeeded in doing. Buck simply smothered him by virtue of superior weight, and cut him up till he ceased snapping and began to whine for mercy.

The general tone of the team picked up immediately. It recovered its old-time solidarity, and once more the dogs leaped as one dog in the traces. At the Rink Rapids two native huskies, Teek and Koona, were added; and the celerity with which Buck broke them in took away Francois's breath.

"Nevaire such a dog as dat Buck!" he cried. "No, nevaire! Heem worth one t'ousan' dollair, by Gar! Eh? Wot you say, Perrault?"

And Perrault nodded. He was ahead of the record then, and gaining day by day. The trail was in excellent condition, well packed and hard, and there was no new-fallen snow with which to contend. It was not too cold. The temperature dropped to fifty below zero and remained there the whole trip. The men rode and ran by turn, and the dogs were kept on the jump, with but infrequent stoppages.

The Thirty Mile River was comparatively coated with ice, and they covered in one day going out what had taken them ten days coming in. In one run they made a sixty-mile dash from the foot of Lake Le Barge to the White Horse Rapids. Across Marsh, Tagish, and Bennett (seventy miles of lakes), they flew so fast that the man whose turn it was to run towed behind the sled at the end of a rope. And on the last night of the second week they topped White Pass and dropped down the sea slope with the lights of Skaguay and of the shipping at their feet.

It was a record run. Each day for fourteen days they had averaged forty miles. For three days Perrault and Francois threw chests up and down the main street of Skaguay and were deluged with invitations to drink, while the team was the constant centre of a worshipful crowd of dog-busters and mushers. Then three or four western bad men aspired to clean out the town, were riddled like pepper-boxes for their pains, and public interest turned to other idols. Next came official orders. Francois called Buck to him, threw his arms around him, wept over him. And that was the last of Francois and Perrault. Like other men, they passed out of Buck's life for good.

A Scotch half-breed took charge of him and his mates, and in company with a dozen other dog-teams he started back over the weary trail to Dawson. It was no light running now, nor record time, but heavy toil each day, with a heavy load behind; for this was the mail train, carrying word from the world to the men who sought gold under the shadow of the Pole.

Buck did not like it, but he bore up well to the work, taking pride in it after the manner of Dave and Sol-leks, and seeing that his mates, whether they prided in it or not, did their fair share. It was a monotonous life, operating with machine-like regularity. One day was very like another. At a certain time each morning the cooks turned out, fires were built, and breakfast was eaten. Then, while some broke camp, others harnessed the dogs, and they were under way an hour or so before the darkness fell which gave warning of dawn. At night, camp was made. Some pitched the flies, others cut firewood and pine boughs for the beds, and still others carried water or ice for the cooks. Also, the dogs were fed. To them, this was the one feature of the day, though it was good to loaf around, after the fish was eaten, for an hour or so with the other dogs, of which there were fivescore and odd. There were fierce fighters among them, but three battles with the fiercest brought Buck to mastery, so that when he bristled and showed his teeth they got out of his way.

Best of all, perhaps, he loved to lie near the fire, hind legs crouched under him, fore legs stretched out in front, head raised, and eyes blinking dreamily at the flames. Sometimes he thought of Judge Miller's big house in the sun-kissed Santa Clara Valley, and of the cement swimming-tank, and Ysabel, the Mexican hairless, and Toots, the Japanese pug; but oftener he remembered the man in the red sweater, the death of Curly, the great fight with Spitz, and the good things he had eaten or would like to eat. He was not homesick. The Sunland was very dim and distant, and such memories had no power over him. Far more potent were the memories of his heredity that gave things he had never seen before a seeming familiarity; the instincts (which were but the memories of his ancestors become habits) which had lapsed in later days, and still later, in him, quickened and become alive again.

Sometimes as he crouched there, blinking dreamily at the flames, it seemed that the flames were of another fire, and that as he crouched by this other fire he saw another and different man from the half-breed cook before him. This other man was shorter of leg and longer of arm, with muscles that were stringy and knotty rather than rounded and swelling. The hair of this man was long and matted, and his head slanted back under it from the eyes. He uttered strange sounds, and seemed very much afraid of the darkness, into which he peered continually, clutching in his hand, which hung midway between knee and foot, a stick with a heavy stone made fast to the end. He was all but naked, a ragged and fire-scorched skin hanging part way down his back, but on his body there was much hair. In some places, across the chest and shoulders and down the outside of the arms and thighs, it was matted into almost a thick fur. He did not stand erect, but with trunk inclined forward from the hips, on legs that bent at the knees. About his body there was a peculiar springiness, or resiliency, almost cat-like, and a quick alertness as of one who lived in perpetual fear of things seen and unseen.

At other times this hairy man squatted by the fire with head between his legs and slept. On such occasions his elbows were on his knees, his hands clasped above his head as though to shed rain by the hairy arms. And beyond that fire, in the circling darkness, Buck could see many gleaming coals, two by two, always two by two, which he knew to be the eyes of great beasts of prey. And he could hear the crashing of their bodies through the undergrowth, and the noises they made in the night. And dreaming there by the Yukon bank, with lazy eyes blinking at the fire, these sounds and sights of another world would make the hair to rise along his back and stand on end across his shoulders and up his neck, till he whimpered low and suppressedly, or growled softly, and the half-breed cook shouted at him, "Hey, you Buck, wake up!" Whereupon the other world would vanish and the real world come into his eyes, and he would get up and yawn and stretch as though he had been asleep.

It was a hard trip, with the mail behind them, and the heavy work wore them down. They were short of weight and in poor condition when they made Dawson, and should have had a ten days' or a week's rest at least. But in two days' time they dropped down the Yukon bank from the Barracks, loaded with letters for the outside. The dogs were tired, the drivers grumbling, and to make matters worse, it snowed every day. This meant a soft trail, greater friction on the runners, and heavier pulling for the dogs; yet the drivers were fair through it all, and did their best for the animals.

Each night the dogs were attended to first. They ate before the drivers ate, and no man sought his sleeping-robe till he had seen to the feet of the dogs he drove. Still, their strength went down. Since the beginning of the winter they had travelled eighteen hundred miles, dragging sleds the whole weary distance; and eighteen hundred miles will tell upon life of the toughest. Buck stood it, keeping his mates up to their work and maintaining discipline, though he, too, was very tired. Billee cried and whimpered regularly in his sleep each night. Joe was sourer than ever, and Sol-leks was unapproachable, blind side or other side.

But it was Dave who suffered most of all. Something had gone wrong with him. He became more morose and irritable, and when camp was pitched at once made his nest, where his driver fed him. Once out of the harness and down, he did not get on his feet again till harness-up time in the morning. Sometimes, in the traces, when jerked by a sudden stoppage of the sled, or by straining to start it, he would cry out with pain. The driver examined him, but could find nothing. All the drivers became interested in his case. They talked it over at meal-time, and over their last pipes before going to bed, and one night they held a consultation. He was brought from his nest to the fire and was pressed and prodded till he cried out many times. Something was wrong inside, but they could locate no broken bones, could not make it out.

By the time Cassiar Bar was reached, he was so weak that he was falling repeatedly in the traces. The Scotch half-breed called a halt and took him out of the team, making the next dog, Sol-leks, fast to the sled. His intention was to rest Dave, letting him run free behind the sled. Sick as he was, Dave resented being taken out, grunting and growling while the traces were unfastened, and whimpering broken-heartedly when he saw Sol-leks in the position he had held and served so long. For the pride of trace and trail was his, and, sick unto death, he could not bear that another dog should do his work.

When the sled started, he floundered in the soft snow alongside the beaten trail, attacking Sol-leks with his teeth, rushing against him and trying to thrust him off into the soft snow on the other side, striving to leap inside his traces and get between him and the sled, and all the while whining and yelping and crying with grief and pain. The half-breed tried to drive him away with the whip; but he paid no heed to the stinging lash, and the man had not the heart to strike harder. Dave refused to run quietly on the trail behind the sled, where the going was easy, but continued to flounder alongside in the soft snow, where the going was most difficult, till exhausted. Then he fell, and lay where he fell, howling lugubriously as the long train of sleds churned by.

With the last remnant of his strength he managed to stagger along behind till the train made another stop, when he floundered past the sleds to his own, where he stood alongside Sol-leks. His driver lingered a moment to get a light for his pipe from the man behind. Then he returned and started his dogs. They swung out on the trail with remarkable lack of exertion, turned their heads uneasily, and stopped in surprise. The driver was surprised, too; the sled had not moved. He called his comrades to witness the sight. Dave had bitten through both of Sol-leks's traces, and was standing directly in front of the sled in his proper place.

He pleaded with his eyes to remain there. The driver was perplexed. His comrades talked of how a dog could break its heart through being denied the work that killed it, and recalled instances they had known, where dogs, too old for the toil, or injured, had died because they were cut out of the traces. Also, they held it a mercy, since Dave was to die anyway, that he should die in the traces, heart-easy and content. So he was harnessed in again, and proudly he pulled as of old, though more than once he cried out involuntarily from the bite of his inward hurt. Several times he fell down and was dragged in the traces, and once the sled ran upon him so that he limped thereafter in one of his hind legs.

But he held out till camp was reached, when his driver made a place for him by the fire. Morning found him too weak to travel. At harness-up time he tried to crawl to his driver. By convulsive efforts he got on his feet, staggered, and fell. Then he wormed his way forward slowly toward where the harnesses were being put on his mates. He would advance his fore legs and drag up his body with a sort of hitching movement, when he would advance his fore legs and hitch ahead again for a few more inches. His strength left him, and the last his mates saw of him he lay gasping in the snow and yearning toward them. But they could hear him mournfully howling till they passed out of sight behind a belt of river timber.

Here the train was halted. The Scotch half-breed slowly retraced his steps to the camp they had left. The men ceased talking. A revolver-shot rang out. The man came back hurriedly. The whips snapped, the bells tinkled merrily, the sleds churned along the trail; but Buck knew, and every dog knew, what had taken place behind the belt of river trees.

CHAPTER V. THE TOIL OF TRACE AND TRAIL

Thirty days from the time it left Dawson, the Salt Water Mail, with Buck and his mates at the fore, arrived at Skaguay. They were in a wretched state, worn out and worn down. Buck's one hundred and forty pounds had dwindled to one hundred and fifteen. The rest of his mates, though lighter dogs, had relatively lost more weight than he. Pike, the malingerer, who, in his lifetime of deceit, had often successfully feigned a hurt leg, was now limping in earnest. Sol-leks was limping, and Dub was suffering from a wrenched shoulder-blade.

They were all terribly footsore. No spring or rebound was left in them. Their feet fell heavily on the trail, jarring their bodies and doubling the fatigue of a day's travel. There was nothing the matter with them except that they were dead tired. It was not the dead-tiredness that comes through brief and excessive effort, from which recovery is a matter of hours; but it was the dead-tiredness that comes through the slow and prolonged strength drainage of months of toil. There was no power of recuperation left, no reserve strength to call upon. It had been all used, the last least bit of it. Every muscle, every fibre, every cell, was tired, dead tired. And there was reason for it. In less than five months they had travelled twenty-five hundred miles, during the last eighteen hundred of which they had had but five days' rest. When they arrived at Skaguay they were apparently on their last legs. They could barely keep the traces taut, and on the down grades just managed to keep out of the way of the sled.

"Mush on, poor sore feets," the driver encouraged them as they tottered down the main street of Skaguay. "Dis is de las'. Den we get one long res'. Eh? For sure. One bully long res'."

The drivers confidently expected a long stopover. Themselves, they had covered twelve hundred miles with two days' rest, and in the nature of reason and common justice they deserved an interval of loafing. But so many were the men who had rushed into the Klondike, and so many were the sweethearts, wives, and kin that had not rushed in, that the congested mail was taking on Alpine proportions; also, there were official orders. Fresh batches of Hudson Bay dogs were to take the places of those worthless for the trail. The worthless ones were to be got rid of, and, since dogs count for little against dollars, they were to be sold.

Three days passed, by which time Buck and his mates found how really tired and weak they were. Then, on the morning of the fourth day, two men from the States came along and bought them, harness and all, for a song. The men addressed each other as "Hal" and "Charles." Charles was a middle-aged, lightish-colored man, with weak and watery eyes and a mustache that twisted fiercely and vigorously up, giving the lie to the limply drooping lip it concealed. Hal was a youngster of nineteen or twenty, with a big Colt's revolver and a hunting-knife strapped about him on a belt that fairly bristled with cartridges. This belt was the most salient thing about him. It advertised his callowness—a callowness sheer and unutterable. Both men were manifestly out of place, and why such as they should adventure the North is part of the mystery of things that passes understanding.

Buck heard the chaffering, saw the money pass between the man and the Government agent, and knew that the Scotch half-breed and the mail-train drivers were passing out of his life on the heels of Perrault and Francois and the others who had gone before. When driven with his mates to the new owners' camp, Buck saw a slipshod and slovenly affair, tent half stretched, dishes unwashed, everything in disorder; also, he saw a woman. "Mercedes" the men called her. She was Charles's wife and Hal's sister—a nice family party.

Buck watched them apprehensively as they proceeded to take down the tent and load the sled. There was a great deal of effort about their manner, but no businesslike method. The tent was rolled into an awkward bundle three times as large as it should have been. The tin dishes were packed away unwashed. Mercedes continually fluttered in the way of her men and kept up an unbroken chattering of remonstrance and advice. When they put a clothes-sack on the front of the sled, she suggested it should go on the back; and when they had put it on the back, and covered it over with a couple of other bundles, she discovered overlooked articles which could abide nowhere else but in that very sack, and they unloaded again.

Three men from a neighboring tent came out and looked on, grinning and winking at one another.

"You've got a right smart load as it is," said one of them; "and it's not me should tell you your business, but I wouldn't tote that tent along if I was you."

"Undreamed of!" cried Mercedes, throwing up her hands in dainty dismay. "However in the world could I manage without a tent?"

"It's springtime, and you won't get any more cold weather," the man replied.

She shook her head decidedly, and Charles and Hal put the last odds and ends on top the mountainous load.

"Think it'll ride?" one of the men asked.

"Why shouldn't it?" Charles demanded rather shortly.

"Oh, that's all right, that's all right," the man hastened meekly to say. "I was just a-wonderin', that is all. It seemed a mite top-heavy."

Charles turned his back and drew the lashings down as well as he could, which was not in the least well.

"An' of course the dogs can hike along all day with that contraption behind them," affirmed a second of the men.

"Certainly," said Hal, with freezing politeness, taking hold of the gee-pole with one hand and swinging his whip from the other. "Mush!" he shouted. "Mush on there!"

The dogs sprang against the breast-bands, strained hard for a few moments, then relaxed. They were unable to move the sled.

"The lazy brutes, I'll show them," he cried, preparing to lash out at them with the whip.

But Mercedes interfered, crying, "Oh, Hal, you mustn't," as she caught hold of the whip and wrenched it from him. "The poor dears! Now you must promise you won't be harsh with them for the rest of the trip, or I won't go a step."

"Precious lot you know about dogs," her brother sneered; "and I wish you'd leave me alone. They're lazy, I tell you, and you've got to whip them to get anything out of them. That's their way. You ask any one. Ask one of those men."

Mercedes looked at them imploringly, untold repugnance at sight of pain written in her pretty face.

"They're weak as water, if you want to know," came the reply from one of the men. "Plum tuckered out, that's what's the matter. They need a rest."

"Rest be blanked," said Hal, with his beardless lips; and Mercedes said, "Oh!" in pain and sorrow at the oath.

But she was a clannish creature, and rushed at once to the defence of her brother. "Never mind that man," she said pointedly. "You're driving our dogs, and you do what you think best with them."

Again Hal's whip fell upon the dogs. They threw themselves against the breast-bands, dug their feet into the packed snow, got down low to it, and put forth all their strength. The sled held as though it were an anchor. After two efforts, they stood still, panting. The whip was whistling savagely, when once more Mercedes interfered. She dropped on her knees before Buck, with tears in her eyes, and put her arms around his neck.

"You poor, poor dears," she cried sympathetically, "why don't you pull hard?—then you wouldn't be whipped." Buck did not like her, but he was feeling too miserable to resist her, taking it as part of the day's miserable work.

One of the onlookers, who had been clenching his teeth to suppress hot speech, now spoke up:—

"It's not that I care a whoop what becomes of you, but for the dogs' sakes I just want to tell you, you can help them a mighty lot by breaking out that sled. The runners are froze fast. Throw your weight against the gee-pole, right and left, and break it out."

A third time the attempt was made, but this time, following the advice, Hal broke out the runners which had been frozen to the snow. The overloaded and unwieldy sled forged ahead, Buck and his mates struggling frantically under the rain of blows. A hundred yards ahead the path turned and sloped steeply into the main street. It would have required an experienced man to keep the top-heavy sled upright, and Hal was not such a man. As they swung on the turn the sled went over, spilling half its load through the loose lashings. The dogs never stopped. The lightened sled bounded on its side behind them. They were angry because of the ill treatment they had received and the unjust load. Buck was raging. He broke into a run, the team following his lead. Hal cried "Whoa! whoa!" but they gave no heed. He tripped and was pulled off his feet. The capsized sled ground over him, and the dogs dashed on up the street, adding to the gayety of Skaguay as they scattered the remainder of the outfit along its chief thoroughfare.

Kind-hearted citizens caught the dogs and gathered up the scattered belongings. Also, they gave advice. Half the load and twice the dogs, if they ever expected to reach Dawson, was what was said. Hal and his sister and brother-in-law listened unwillingly, pitched tent, and overhauled the outfit. Canned goods were turned out that made men laugh, for canned goods on the Long Trail is a thing to dream about. "Blankets for a hotel" quoth one of the men who laughed and helped. "Half as many is too much; get rid of them. Throw away that tent, and all those dishes,—who's going to wash them, anyway? Good Lord, do you think you're travelling on a Pullman?"

And so it went, the inexorable elimination of the superfluous. Mercedes cried when her clothes-bags were dumped on the ground and article after article was thrown out. She cried in general, and she cried in particular over each discarded thing. She clasped hands about knees, rocking back and forth broken-heartedly. She averred she would not go an inch, not for a dozen Charleses. She appealed to everybody and to everything, finally wiping her eyes and proceeding to cast out even articles of apparel that were imperative necessaries. And in her zeal, when she had finished with her own, she attacked the belongings of her men and went through them like a tornado.

This accomplished, the outfit, though cut in half, was still a formidable bulk. Charles and Hal went out in the evening and bought six Outside dogs. These, added to the six of the original team, and Teek and Koona, the huskies obtained at the Rink Rapids on the record trip, brought the team up to fourteen. But the Outside dogs, though practically broken in since their landing, did not amount to much. Three were short-haired pointers, one was a Newfoundland, and the other two were mongrels of indeterminate breed. They did not seem to know anything, these newcomers. Buck and his comrades looked upon them with disgust, and though he speedily taught them their places and what not to do, he could not teach them what to do. They did not take kindly to trace and trail. With the exception of the two mongrels, they were bewildered and spirit-broken by the strange savage environment in which they found themselves and by the ill treatment they had received. The two mongrels were without spirit at all; bones were the only things breakable about them.

With the newcomers hopeless and forlorn, and the old team worn out by twenty-five hundred miles of continuous trail, the outlook was anything but bright. The two men, however, were quite cheerful. And they were proud, too. They were doing the thing in style, with fourteen dogs. They had seen other sleds depart over the Pass for Dawson, or come in from Dawson, but never had they seen a sled with so many as fourteen dogs. In the nature of Arctic travel there was a reason why fourteen dogs should not drag one sled, and that was that one sled could not carry the food for fourteen dogs. But Charles and Hal did not know this. They had worked the trip out with a pencil, so much to a dog, so many dogs, so many days, Q.E.D. Mercedes looked over their shoulders and nodded comprehensively, it was all so very simple.

Late next morning Buck led the long team up the street. There was nothing lively about it, no snap or go in him and his fellows. They were starting dead weary. Four times he had covered the distance between Salt Water and Dawson, and the knowledge that, jaded and tired, he was facing the same trail once more, made him bitter. His heart was not in the work, nor was the heart of any dog. The Outsides were timid and frightened, the Insides without confidence in their masters.

Buck felt vaguely that there was no depending upon these two men and the woman. They did not know how to do anything, and as the days went by it became apparent that they could not learn. They were slack in all things, without order or discipline. It took them half the night to pitch a slovenly camp, and half the morning to break that camp and get the sled loaded in fashion so slovenly that for the rest of the day they were occupied in stopping and rearranging the load. Some days they did not make ten miles. On other days they were unable to get started at all. And on no day did they succeed in making more than half the distance used by the men as a basis in their dog-food computation.

It was inevitable that they should go short on dog-food. But they hastened it by overfeeding, bringing the day nearer when underfeeding would commence. The Outside dogs, whose digestions had not been trained by chronic famine to make the most of little, had voracious appetites. And when, in addition to this, the worn-out huskies pulled weakly, Hal decided that the orthodox ration was too small. He doubled it. And to cap it all, when Mercedes, with tears in her pretty eyes and a quaver in her throat, could not cajole him into giving the dogs still more, she stole from the fish-sacks and fed them slyly. But it was not food that Buck and the huskies needed, but rest. And though they were making poor time, the heavy load they dragged sapped their strength severely.

Then came the underfeeding. Hal awoke one day to the fact that his dog-food was half gone and the distance only quarter covered; further, that for love or money no additional dog-food was to be obtained. So he cut down even the orthodox ration and tried to increase the day's travel. His sister and brother-in-law seconded him; but they were frustrated by their heavy outfit and their own incompetence. It was a simple matter to give the dogs less food; but it was impossible to make the dogs travel faster, while their own inability to get under way earlier in the morning prevented them from travelling longer hours. Not only did they not know how to work dogs, but they did not know how to work themselves.

The first to go was Dub. Poor blundering thief that he was, always getting caught and punished, he had none the less been a faithful worker. His wrenched shoulder-blade, untreated and unrested, went from bad to worse, till finally Hal shot him with the big Colt's revolver. It is a saying of the country that an Outside dog starves to death on the ration of the husky, so the six Outside dogs under Buck could do no less than die on half the ration of the husky. The Newfoundland went first, followed by the three short-haired pointers, the two mongrels hanging more grittily on to life, but going in the end.

By this time all the amenities and gentlenesses of the Southland had fallen away from the three people. Shorn of its glamour and romance, Arctic travel became to them a reality too harsh for their manhood and womanhood. Mercedes ceased weeping over the dogs, being too occupied with weeping over herself and with quarrelling with her husband and brother. To quarrel was the one thing they were never too weary to do. Their irritability arose out of their misery, increased with it, doubled upon it, outdistanced it. The wonderful patience of the trail which comes to men who toil hard and suffer sore, and remain sweet of speech and kindly, did not come to these two men and the woman. They had no inkling of such a patience. They were stiff and in pain; their muscles ached, their bones ached, their very hearts ached; and because of this they became sharp of speech, and hard words were first on their lips in the morning and last at night.

Charles and Hal wrangled whenever Mercedes gave them a chance. It was the cherished belief of each that he did more than his share of the work, and neither forbore to speak this belief at every opportunity. Sometimes Mercedes sided with her husband, sometimes with her brother. The result was a beautiful and unending family quarrel. Starting from a dispute as to which should chop a few sticks for the fire (a dispute which concerned only Charles and Hal), presently would be lugged in the rest of the family, fathers, mothers, uncles, cousins, people thousands of miles away, and some of them dead. That Hal's views on art, or the sort of society plays his mother's brother wrote, should have anything to do with the chopping of a few sticks of fire-wood, passes comprehension; nevertheless the quarrel was as likely to tend in that direction as in the direction of Charles's political prejudices. And that Charles's sister's tale-bearing tongue should be relevant to the building of a Yukon fire, was apparent only to Mercedes, who disburdened herself of copious opinions upon that topic, and incidentally upon a few other traits unpleasantly peculiar to her husband's family. In the meantime the fire remained unbuilt, the camp half pitched, and the dogs unfed.

Mercedes nursed a special grievance—the grievance of sex. She was pretty and soft, and had been chivalrously treated all her days. But the present treatment by her husband and brother was everything save chivalrous. It was her custom to be helpless. They complained. Upon which impeachment of what to her was her most essential sex-prerogative, she made their lives unendurable. She no longer considered the dogs, and because she was sore and tired, she persisted in riding on the sled. She was pretty and soft, but she weighed one hundred and twenty pounds—a lusty last straw to the load dragged by the weak and starving animals. She rode for days, till they fell in the traces and the sled stood still. Charles and Hal begged her to get off and walk, pleaded with her, entreated, the while she wept and importuned Heaven with a recital of their brutality.

On one occasion they took her off the sled by main strength. They never did it again. She let her legs go limp like a spoiled child, and sat down on the trail. They went on their way, but she did not move. After they had travelled three miles they unloaded the sled, came back for her, and by main strength put her on the sled again.

In the excess of their own misery they were callous to the suffering of their animals. Hal's theory, which he practised on others, was that one must get hardened. He had started out preaching it to his sister and brother-in-law. Failing there, he hammered it into the dogs with a club. At the Five Fingers the dog-food gave out, and a toothless old squaw offered to trade them a few pounds of frozen horse-hide for the Colt's revolver that kept the big hunting-knife company at Hal's hip. A poor substitute for food was this hide, just as it had been stripped from the starved horses of the cattlemen six months back. In its frozen state it was more like strips of galvanized iron, and when a dog wrestled it into his stomach it thawed into thin and innutritious leathery strings and into a mass of short hair, irritating and indigestible.

And through it all Buck staggered along at the head of the team as in a nightmare. He pulled when he could; when he could no longer pull, he fell down and remained down till blows from whip or club drove him to his feet again. All the stiffness and gloss had gone out of his beautiful furry coat. The hair hung down, limp and draggled, or matted with dried blood where Hal's club had bruised him. His muscles had wasted away to knotty strings, and the flesh pads had disappeared, so that each rib and every bone in his frame were outlined cleanly through the loose hide that was wrinkled in folds of emptiness. It was heartbreaking, only Buck's heart was unbreakable. The man in the red sweater had proved that.

As it was with Buck, so was it with his mates. They were perambulating skeletons. There were seven all together, including him. In their very great misery they had become insensible to the bite of the lash or the bruise of the club. The pain of the beat-beating was dull and distant, just as the things their eyes saw and their ears heard seemed dull and distant. They were not half living, or quarter living. They were simply so many bags of bones in which sparks of life fluttered faintly. When a halt was made, they dropped down in the traces like dead dogs, and the spark dimmed and paled and seemed to go out. And when the club or whip fell upon them, the spark fluttered feebly up, and they tottered to their feet and staggered on.

There came a day when Billee, the good-natured, fell and could not rise. Hal had traded off his revolver, so he took the axe and knocked Billee on the head as he lay in the traces, then cut the carcass out of the harness and dragged it to one side. Buck saw, and his mates saw, and they knew that this thing was very close to them. On the next day Koona went, and but five of them remained: Joe, too far gone to be malignant; Pike, crippled and limping, only half conscious and not conscious enough longer to malinger; Sol-leks, the one-eyed, still faithful to the toil of trace and trail, and mournful in that he had so little strength with which to pull; Teek, who had not travelled so far that winter and who was now beaten more than the others because he was fresher; and Buck, still at the head of the team, but no longer enforcing discipline or striving to enforce it, blind with weakness half the time and keeping the trail by the loom of it and by the dim feel of his feet.

It was beautiful spring weather, but neither dogs nor humans were aware of it. Each day the sun rose earlier and set later. It was dawn by three in the morning, and twilight lingered till nine at night. The whole long day was a blaze of sunshine. The ghostly winter silence had given way to the great spring murmur of awakening life. This murmur arose from all the land, fraught with the joy of living. It came from the things that lived and moved again, things which had been as dead and which had not moved during the long months of frost. The sap was rising in the pines. The willows and aspens were bursting out in young buds. Shrubs and vines were putting on fresh garbs of green. Crickets sang in the nights, and in the days all manner of creeping, crawling things rustled forth into the sun. Partridges and woodpeckers were booming and knocking in the forest. Squirrels were chattering, birds singing, and overhead honked the wild-fowl driving up from the south in cunning wedges that split the air.

From every hill slope came the trickle of running water, the music of unseen fountains. All things were thawing, bending, snapping. The Yukon was straining to break loose the ice that bound it down. It ate away from beneath; the sun ate from above. Air-holes formed, fissures sprang and spread apart, while thin sections of ice fell through bodily into the river. And amid all this bursting, rending, throbbing of awakening life, under the blazing sun and through the soft-sighing breezes, like wayfarers to death, staggered the two men, the woman, and the huskies.

With the dogs falling, Mercedes weeping and riding, Hal swearing innocuously, and Charles's eyes wistfully watering, they staggered into John Thornton's camp at the mouth of White River. When they halted, the dogs dropped down as though they had all been struck dead. Mercedes dried her eyes and looked at John Thornton. Charles sat down on a log to rest. He sat down very slowly and painstakingly what of his great stiffness. Hal did the talking. John Thornton was whittling the last touches on an axe-handle he had made from a stick of birch. He whittled and listened, gave monosyllabic replies, and, when it was asked, terse advice. He knew the breed, and he gave his advice in the certainty that it would not be followed.

"They told us up above that the bottom was dropping out of the trail and that the best thing for us to do was to lay over," Hal said in response to Thornton's warning to take no more chances on the rotten ice. "They told us we couldn't make White River, and here we are." This last with a sneering ring of triumph in it.

"And they told you true," John Thornton answered. "The bottom's likely to drop out at any moment. Only fools, with the blind luck of fools, could have made it. I tell you straight, I wouldn't risk my carcass on that ice for all the gold in Alaska."

"That's because you're not a fool, I suppose," said Hal. "All the same, we'll go on to Dawson." He uncoiled his whip. "Get up there, Buck! Hi! Get up there! Mush on!"

Thornton went on whittling. It was idle, he knew, to get between a fool and his folly; while two or three fools more or less would not alter the scheme of things.

But the team did not get up at the command. It had long since passed into the stage where blows were required to rouse it. The whip flashed out, here and there, on its merciless errands. John Thornton compressed his lips. Sol-leks was the first to crawl to his feet. Teek followed. Joe came next, yelping with pain. Pike made painful efforts. Twice he fell over, when half up, and on the third attempt managed to rise. Buck made no effort. He lay quietly where he had fallen. The lash bit into him again and again, but he neither whined nor struggled. Several times Thornton started, as though to speak, but changed his mind. A moisture came into his eyes, and, as the whipping continued, he arose and walked irresolutely up and down.

This was the first time Buck had failed, in itself a sufficient reason to drive Hal into a rage. He exchanged the whip for the customary club. Buck refused to move under the rain of heavier blows which now fell upon him. Like his mates, he was barely able to get up, but, unlike them, he had made up his mind not to get up. He had a vague feeling of impending doom. This had been strong upon him when he pulled in to the bank, and it had not departed from him. What of the thin and rotten ice he had felt under his feet all day, it seemed that he sensed disaster close at hand, out there ahead on the ice where his master was trying to drive him. He refused to stir. So greatly had he suffered, and so far gone was he, that the blows did not hurt much. And as they continued to fall upon him, the spark of life within flickered and went down. It was nearly out. He felt strangely numb. As though from a great distance, he was aware that he was being beaten. The last sensations of pain left him. He no longer felt anything, though very faintly he could hear the impact of the club upon his body. But it was no longer his body, it seemed so far away.

And then, suddenly, without warning, uttering a cry that was inarticulate and more like the cry of an animal, John Thornton sprang upon the man who wielded the club. Hal was hurled backward, as though struck by a falling tree. Mercedes screamed. Charles looked on wistfully, wiped his watery eyes, but did not get up because of his stiffness.

John Thornton stood over Buck, struggling to control himself, too convulsed with rage to speak.

"If you strike that dog again, I'll kill you," he at last managed to say in a choking voice.

"It's my dog," Hal replied, wiping the blood from his mouth as he came back. "Get out of my way, or I'll fix you. I'm going to Dawson."

Thornton stood between him and Buck, and evinced no intention of getting out of the way. Hal drew his long hunting-knife. Mercedes screamed, cried, laughed, and manifested the chaotic abandonment of hysteria. Thornton rapped Hal's knuckles with the axe-handle, knocking the knife to the ground. He rapped his knuckles again as he tried to pick it up. Then he stooped, picked it up himself, and with two strokes cut Buck's traces.

Hal had no fight left in him. Besides, his hands were full with his sister, or his arms, rather; while Buck was too near dead to be of further use in hauling the sled. A few minutes later they pulled out from the bank and down the river. Buck heard them go and raised his head to see, Pike was leading, Sol-leks was at the wheel, and between were Joe and Teek. They were limping and staggering. Mercedes was riding the loaded sled. Hal guided at the gee-pole, and Charles stumbled along in the rear.

As Buck watched them, Thornton knelt beside him and with rough, kindly hands searched for broken bones. By the time his search had disclosed nothing more than many bruises and a state of terrible starvation, the sled was a quarter of a mile away. Dog and man watched it crawling along over the ice. Suddenly, they saw its back end drop down, as into a rut, and the gee-pole, with Hal clinging to it, jerk into the air. Mercedes's scream came to their ears. They saw Charles turn and make one step to run back, and then a whole section of ice give way and dogs and humans disappear. A yawning hole was all that was to be seen. The bottom had dropped out of the trail.

John Thornton and Buck looked at each other.

"You poor devil," said John Thornton, and Buck licked his hand.

CHAPTER VI. FOR THE LOVE OF A MAN

When John Thornton froze his feet in the previous December his partners had made him comfortable and left him to get well, going on themselves up the river to get out a raft of saw-logs for Dawson. He was still limping slightly at the time he rescued Buck, but with the continued warm weather even the slight limp left him. And here, lying by the river bank through the long spring days, watching the running water, listening lazily to the songs of birds and the hum of nature, Buck slowly won back his strength.

A rest comes very good after one has travelled three thousand miles, and it must be confessed that Buck waxed lazy as his wounds healed, his muscles swelled out, and the flesh came back to cover his bones. For that matter, they were all loafing,—Buck, John Thornton, and Skeet and Nig,—waiting for the raft to come that was to carry them down to Dawson. Skeet was a little Irish setter who early made friends with Buck, who, in a dying condition, was unable to resent her first advances. She had the doctor trait which some dogs possess; and as a mother cat washes her kittens, so she washed and cleansed Buck's wounds. Regularly, each morning after he had finished his breakfast, she performed her self-appointed task, till he came to look for her ministrations as much as he did for Thornton's. Nig, equally friendly, though less demonstrative, was a huge black dog, half bloodhound and half deerhound, with eyes that laughed and a boundless good nature.

To Buck's surprise these dogs manifested no jealousy toward him. They seemed to share the kindliness and largeness of John Thornton. As Buck grew stronger they enticed him into all sorts of ridiculous games, in which Thornton himself could not forbear to join; and in this fashion Buck romped through his convalescence and into a new existence. Love, genuine passionate love, was his for the first time. This he had never experienced at Judge Miller's down in the sun-kissed Santa Clara Valley. With the Judge's sons, hunting and tramping, it had been a working partnership; with the Judge's grandsons, a sort of pompous guardianship; and with the Judge himself, a stately and dignified friendship. But love that was feverish and burning, that was adoration, that was madness, it had taken John Thornton to arouse.

This man had saved his life, which was something; but, further, he was the ideal master. Other men saw to the welfare of their dogs from a sense of duty and business expediency; he saw to the welfare of his as if they were his own children, because he could not help it. And he saw further. He never forgot a kindly greeting or a cheering word, and to sit down for a long talk with them ("gas" he called it) was as much his delight as theirs. He had a way of taking Buck's head roughly between his hands, and resting his own head upon Buck's, of shaking him back and forth, the while calling him ill names that to Buck were love names. Buck knew no greater joy than that rough embrace and the sound of murmured oaths, and at each jerk back and forth it seemed that his heart would be shaken out of his body so great was its ecstasy. And when, released, he sprang to his feet, his mouth laughing, his eyes eloquent, his throat vibrant with unuttered sound, and in that fashion remained without movement, John Thornton would reverently exclaim, "God! you can all but speak!"

Buck had a trick of love expression that was akin to hurt. He would often seize Thornton's hand in his mouth and close so fiercely that the flesh bore the impress of his teeth for some time afterward. And as Buck understood the oaths to be love words, so the man understood this feigned bite for a caress.

For the most part, however, Buck's love was expressed in adoration. While he went wild with happiness when Thornton touched him or spoke to him, he did not seek these tokens. Unlike Skeet, who was wont to shove her nose under Thornton's hand and nudge and nudge till petted, or Nig, who would stalk up and rest his great head on Thornton's knee, Buck was content to adore at a distance. He would lie by the hour, eager, alert, at Thornton's feet, looking up into his face, dwelling upon it, studying it, following with keenest interest each fleeting expression, every movement or change of feature. Or, as chance might have it, he would lie farther away, to the side or rear, watching the outlines of the man and the occasional movements of his body. And often, such was the communion in which they lived, the strength of Buck's gaze would draw John Thornton's head around, and he would return the gaze, without speech, his heart shining out of his eyes as Buck's heart shone out.

For a long time after his rescue, Buck did not like Thornton to get out of his sight. From the moment he left the tent to when he entered it again, Buck would follow at his heels. His transient masters since he had come into the Northland had bred in him a fear that no master could be permanent. He was afraid that Thornton would pass out of his life as Perrault and Francois and the Scotch half-breed had passed out. Even in the night, in his dreams, he was haunted by this fear. At such times he would shake off sleep and creep through the chill to the flap of the tent, where he would stand and listen to the sound of his master's breathing.

But in spite of this great love he bore John Thornton, which seemed to bespeak the soft civilizing influence, the strain of the primitive, which the Northland had aroused in him, remained alive and active. Faithfulness and devotion, things born of fire and roof, were his; yet he retained his wildness and wiliness. He was a thing of the wild, come in from the wild to sit by John Thornton's fire, rather than a dog of the soft Southland stamped with the marks of generations of civilization. Because of his very great love, he could not steal from this man, but from any other man, in any other camp, he did not hesitate an instant; while the cunning with which he stole enabled him to escape detection.

His face and body were scored by the teeth of many dogs, and he fought as fiercely as ever and more shrewdly. Skeet and Nig were too good-natured for quarrelling,—besides, they belonged to John Thornton; but the strange dog, no matter what the breed or valor, swiftly acknowledged Buck's supremacy or found himself struggling for life with a terrible antagonist. And Buck was merciless. He had learned well the law of club and fang, and he never forewent an advantage or drew back from a foe he had started on the way to Death. He had lessoned from Spitz, and from the chief fighting dogs of the police and mail, and knew there was no middle course. He must master or be mastered; while to show mercy was a weakness. Mercy did not exist in the primordial life. It was misunderstood for fear, and such misunderstandings made for death. Kill or be killed, eat or be eaten, was the law; and this mandate, down out of the depths of Time, he obeyed.

He was older than the days he had seen and the breaths he had drawn. He linked the past with the present, and the eternity behind him throbbed through him in a mighty rhythm to which he swayed as the tides and seasons swayed. He sat by John Thornton's fire, a broad-breasted dog, white-fanged and long-furred; but behind him were the shades of all manner of dogs, half-wolves and wild wolves, urgent and prompting, tasting the savor of the meat he ate, thirsting for the water he drank, scenting the wind with him, listening with him and telling him the sounds made by the wild life in the forest, dictating his moods, directing his actions, lying down to sleep with him when he lay down, and dreaming with him and beyond him and becoming themselves the stuff of his dreams.

So peremptorily did these shades beckon him, that each day mankind and the claims of mankind slipped farther from him. Deep in the forest a call was sounding, and as often as he heard this call, mysteriously thrilling and luring, he felt compelled to turn his back upon the fire and the beaten earth around it, and to plunge into the forest, and on and on, he knew not where or why; nor did he wonder where or why, the call sounding imperiously, deep in the forest. But as often as he gained the soft unbroken earth and the green shade, the love for John Thornton drew him back to the fire again.

Thornton alone held him. The rest of mankind was as nothing. Chance travellers might praise or pet him; but he was cold under it all, and from a too demonstrative man he would get up and walk away. When Thornton's partners, Hans and Pete, arrived on the long-expected raft, Buck refused to notice them till he learned they were close to Thornton; after that he tolerated them in a passive sort of way, accepting favors from them as though he favored them by accepting. They were of the same large type as Thornton, living close to the earth, thinking simply and seeing clearly; and ere they swung the raft into the big eddy by the saw-mill at Dawson, they understood Buck and his ways, and did not insist upon an intimacy such as obtained with Skeet and Nig.

For Thornton, however, his love seemed to grow and grow. He, alone among men, could put a pack upon Buck's back in the summer travelling. Nothing was too great for Buck to do, when Thornton commanded. One day (they had grub-staked themselves from the proceeds of the raft and left Dawson for the head-waters of the Tanana) the men and dogs were sitting on the crest of a cliff which fell away, straight down, to naked bed-rock three hundred feet below. John Thornton was sitting near the edge, Buck at his shoulder. A thoughtless whim seized Thornton, and he drew the attention of Hans and Pete to the experiment he had in mind. "Jump, Buck!" he commanded, sweeping his arm out and over the chasm. The next instant he was grappling with Buck on the extreme edge, while Hans and Pete were dragging them back into safety.

"It's uncanny," Pete said, after it was over and they had caught their speech.

Thornton shook his head. "No, it is splendid, and it is terrible, too. Do you know, it sometimes makes me afraid."

"I'm not hankering to be the man that lays hands on you while he's around," Pete announced conclusively, nodding his head toward Buck.

"Py Jingo!" was Hans's contribution. "Not mineself either."

It was at Circle City, ere the year was out, that Pete's apprehensions were realized. "Black" Burton, a man evil-tempered and malicious, had been picking a quarrel with a tenderfoot at the bar, when Thornton stepped good-naturedly between. Buck, as was his custom, was lying in a corner, head on paws, watching his master's every action. Burton struck out, without warning, straight from the shoulder. Thornton was sent spinning, and saved himself from falling only by clutching the rail of the bar.

Those who were looking on heard what was neither bark nor yelp, but a something which is best described as a roar, and they saw Buck's body rise up in the air as he left the floor for Burton's throat. The man saved his life by instinctively throwing out his arm, but was hurled backward to the floor with Buck on top of him. Buck loosed his teeth from the flesh of the arm and drove in again for the throat. This time the man succeeded only in partly blocking, and his throat was torn open. Then the crowd was upon Buck, and he was driven off; but while a surgeon checked the bleeding, he prowled up and down, growling furiously, attempting to rush in, and being forced back by an array of hostile clubs. A "miners' meeting," called on the spot, decided that the dog had sufficient provocation, and Buck was discharged. But his reputation was made, and from that day his name spread through every camp in Alaska.

Later on, in the fall of the year, he saved John Thornton's life in quite another fashion. The three partners were lining a long and narrow poling-boat down a bad stretch of rapids on the Forty-Mile Creek. Hans and Pete moved along the bank, snubbing with a thin Manila rope from tree to tree, while Thornton remained in the boat, helping its descent by means of a pole, and shouting directions to the shore. Buck, on the bank, worried and anxious, kept abreast of the boat, his eyes never off his master.

At a particularly bad spot, where a ledge of barely submerged rocks jutted out into the river, Hans cast off the rope, and, while Thornton poled the boat out into the stream, ran down the bank with the end in his hand to snub the boat when it had cleared the ledge. This it did, and was flying down-stream in a current as swift as a mill-race, when Hans checked it with the rope and checked too suddenly. The boat flirted over and snubbed in to the bank bottom up, while Thornton, flung sheer out of it, was carried down-stream toward the worst part of the rapids, a stretch of wild water in which no swimmer could live.

Buck had sprung in on the instant; and at the end of three hundred yards, amid a mad swirl of water, he overhauled Thornton. When he felt him grasp his tail, Buck headed for the bank, swimming with all his splendid strength. But the progress shoreward was slow; the progress down-stream amazingly rapid. From below came the fatal roaring where the wild current went wilder and was rent in shreds and spray by the rocks which thrust through like the teeth of an enormous comb. The suck of the water as it took the beginning of the last steep pitch was frightful, and Thornton knew that the shore was impossible. He scraped furiously over a rock, bruised across a second, and struck a third with crushing force. He clutched its slippery top with both hands, releasing Buck, and above the roar of the churning water shouted: "Go, Buck! Go!"

Buck could not hold his own, and swept on down-stream, struggling desperately, but unable to win back. When he heard Thornton's command repeated, he partly reared out of the water, throwing his head high, as though for a last look, then turned obediently toward the bank. He swam powerfully and was dragged ashore by Pete and Hans at the very point where swimming ceased to be possible and destruction began.

They knew that the time a man could cling to a slippery rock in the face of that driving current was a matter of minutes, and they ran as fast as they could up the bank to a point far above where Thornton was hanging on. They attached the line with which they had been snubbing the boat to Buck's neck and shoulders, being careful that it should neither strangle him nor impede his swimming, and launched him into the stream. He struck out boldly, but not straight enough into the stream. He discovered the mistake too late, when Thornton was abreast of him and a bare half-dozen strokes away while he was being carried helplessly past.

Hans promptly snubbed with the rope, as though Buck were a boat. The rope thus tightening on him in the sweep of the current, he was jerked under the surface, and under the surface he remained till his body struck against the bank and he was hauled out. He was half drowned, and Hans and Pete threw themselves upon him, pounding the breath into him and the water out of him. He staggered to his feet and fell down. The faint sound of Thornton's voice came to them, and though they could not make out the words of it, they knew that he was in his extremity. His master's voice acted on Buck like an electric shock, He sprang to his feet and ran up the bank ahead of the men to the point of his previous departure.

Again the rope was attached and he was launched, and again he struck out, but this time straight into the stream. He had miscalculated once, but he would not be guilty of it a second time. Hans paid out the rope, permitting no slack, while Pete kept it clear of coils. Buck held on till he was on a line straight above Thornton; then he turned, and with the speed of an express train headed down upon him. Thornton saw him coming, and, as Buck struck him like a battering ram, with the whole force of the current behind him, he reached up and closed with both arms around the shaggy neck. Hans snubbed the rope around the tree, and Buck and Thornton were jerked under the water. Strangling, suffocating, sometimes one uppermost and sometimes the other, dragging over the jagged bottom, smashing against rocks and snags, they veered in to the bank.

Thornton came to, belly downward and being violently propelled back and forth across a drift log by Hans and Pete. His first glance was for Buck, over whose limp and apparently lifeless body Nig was setting up a howl, while Skeet was licking the wet face and closed eyes. Thornton was himself bruised and battered, and he went carefully over Buck's body, when he had been brought around, finding three broken ribs.

"That settles it," he announced. "We camp right here." And camp they did, till Buck's ribs knitted and he was able to travel.

That winter, at Dawson, Buck performed another exploit, not so heroic, perhaps, but one that put his name many notches higher on the totem-pole of Alaskan fame. This exploit was particularly gratifying to the three men; for they stood in need of the outfit which it furnished, and were enabled to make a long-desired trip into the virgin

East, where miners had not yet appeared. It was brought about by a conversation in the Eldorado Saloon, in which men waxed boastful of their favorite dogs. Buck, because of his record, was the target for these men, and Thornton was driven stoutly to defend him. At the end of half an hour one man stated that his dog could start a sled with five hundred pounds and walk off with it; a second bragged six hundred for his dog; and a third, seven hundred.

"Pooh! pooh!" said John Thornton; "Buck can start a thousand pounds."

"And break it out? and walk off with it for a hundred yards?" demanded Matthewson, a Bonanza King, he of the seven hundred vaunt.

"And break it out, and walk off with it for a hundred yards," John Thornton said coolly.

"Well," Matthewson said, slowly and deliberately, so that all could hear, "I've got a thousand dollars that says he can't. And there it is." So saying, he slammed a sack of gold dust of the size of a bologna sausage down upon the bar.

Nobody spoke. Thornton's bluff, if bluff it was, had been called. He could feel a flush of warm blood creeping up his face. His tongue had tricked him. He did not know whether Buck could start a thousand pounds. Half a ton! The enormousness of it appalled him. He had great faith in Buck's strength and had often thought him capable of starting such a load; but never, as now, had he faced the possibility of it, the eyes of a dozen men fixed upon him, silent and waiting. Further, he had no thousand dollars; nor had Hans or Pete.

"I've got a sled standing outside now, with twenty fiftypound sacks of flour on it," Matthewson went on with brutal directness; "so don't let that hinder you."

Thornton did not reply. He did not know what to say. He glanced from face to face in the absent way of a man who has lost the power of thought and is seeking somewhere to find the thing that will start it going again. The face of Jim O'Brien, a Mastodon King and old-time comrade, caught his eyes. It was as a cue to him, seeming to rouse him to do what he would never have dreamed of doing.

"Can you lend me a thousand?" he asked, almost in a whisper.

"Sure," answered O'Brien, thumping down a plethoric sack by the side of Matthewson's. "Though it's little faith I'm having, John, that the beast can do the trick."

The Eldorado emptied its occupants into the street to see the test. The tables were deserted, and the dealers and gamekeepers came forth to see the outcome of the wager and to lay odds. Several hundred men, furred and mittened, banked around the sled within easy distance. Matthewson's sled, loaded with a thousand pounds of flour, had been standing for a couple of hours, and in the intense cold (it was sixty below zero) the runners had frozen fast to the hard-packed snow. Men offered odds of two to one that Buck could not budge the sled. A quibble arose concerning the phrase "break out." O'Brien contended it was Thornton's privilege to knock the runners loose, leaving Buck to "break it out" from a dead standstill. Matthewson insisted that the phrase included breaking the runners from the frozen grip of the snow. A majority of the men who had witnessed the making of the bet decided in his favor, whereat the odds went up to three to one against Buck.

There were no takers. Not a man believed him capable of the feat. Thornton had been hurried into the wager, heavy with doubt; and now that he looked at the sled itself, the concrete fact, with the regular team of ten dogs curled up in the snow before it, the more impossible the task appeared. Matthewson waxed jubilant.

"Three to one!" he proclaimed. "I'll lay you another thousand at that figure, Thornton. What d'ye say?"

Thornton's doubt was strong in his face, but his fighting spirit was aroused—the fighting spirit that soars above odds, fails to recognize the impossible, and is deaf to all save the clamor for battle. He called Hans and Pete to him. Their sacks were slim, and with his own the three partners could rake together only two hundred dollars. In the ebb of their fortunes, this sum was their total capital; yet they laid it unhesitatingly against Matthewson's six hundred.

The team of ten dogs was unhitched, and Buck, with his own harness, was put into the sled. He had caught the contagion of the excitement, and he felt that in some way he must do a great thing for John Thornton. Murmurs of admiration at his splendid appearance went up. He was in perfect condition, without an ounce of superfluous flesh, and the one hundred and fifty pounds that he weighed were so many pounds of grit and virility. His furry coat shone with the sheen of silk. Down the neck and across the shoulders, his mane, in repose as it was, half bristled and seemed to lift with every movement, as though excess of vigor made each particular hair alive and active. The great breast and heavy fore legs were no more than in proportion with the rest of the body, where the muscles showed in tight rolls underneath the skin. Men felt these muscles and proclaimed them hard as iron, and the odds went down to two to one.

"Gad, sir! Gad, sir!" stuttered a member of the latest dynasty, a king of the Skookum Benches. "I offer you eight hundred for him, sir, before the test, sir; eight hundred just as he stands."

Thornton shook his head and stepped to Buck's side.

"You must stand off from him," Matthewson protested. "Free play and plenty of room."

The crowd fell silent; only could be heard the voices of the gamblers vainly offering two to one. Everybody acknowledged Buck a magnificent animal, but twenty fifty-pound sacks of flour bulked too large in their eyes for them to loosen their pouch-strings.

Thornton knelt down by Buck's side. He took his head in his two hands and rested cheek on cheek. He did not playfully shake him, as was his wont, or murmur soft love curses; but he whispered in his ear. "As you love me, Buck. As you love me," was what he whispered. Buck whined with suppressed eagerness.

The crowd was watching curiously. The affair was growing mysterious. It seemed like a conjuration. As Thornton got to his feet, Buck seized his mittened hand between his jaws, pressing in with his teeth and releasing slowly, half-reluctantly. It was the answer, in terms, not of speech, but of love. Thornton stepped well back.

"Now, Buck," he said.

Buck tightened the traces, then slacked them for a matter of several inches. It was the way he had learned.

"Gee!" Thornton's voice rang out, sharp in the tense silence.

Buck swung to the right, ending the movement in a plunge that took up the slack and with a sudden jerk arrested his one hundred and fifty pounds. The load quivered, and from under the runners arose a crisp crackling.

"Haw!" Thornton commanded.

Buck duplicated the manoeuvre, this time to the left. The crackling turned into a snapping, the sled pivoting and the runners slipping and grating several inches to the side. The sled was broken out. Men were holding their breaths, intensely unconscious of the fact.

"Now, MUSH!"

Thornton's command cracked out like a pistol-shot. Buck threw himself forward, tightening the traces with a jarring lunge. His whole body was gathered compactly together in the tremendous effort, the muscles writhing and knotting like live things under the silky fur. His great chest was low to the ground, his head forward and down, while his feet were flying like mad, the claws scarring the hard-packed snow in parallel grooves. The sled swayed and trembled, half-started forward. One of his feet slipped, and one man groaned aloud. Then the sled lurched ahead in what appeared a rapid succession of jerks, though it never really came to a dead stop again...half an inch...an inch... two inches... The jerks perceptibly diminished; as the sled gained momentum, he caught them up, till it was moving steadily along.

Men gasped and began to breathe again, unaware that for a moment they had ceased to breathe. Thornton was running behind, encouraging Buck with short, cheery words. The distance had been measured off, and as he neared the pile of firewood which marked the end of the hundred yards, a cheer began to grow and grow, which burst into a roar as he passed the firewood and halted at command. Every man was tearing himself loose, even Matthewson. Hats and mittens were flying in the air. Men were shaking hands, it did not matter with whom, and bubbling over in a general incoherent babel.

But Thornton fell on his knees beside Buck. Head was against head, and he was shaking him back and forth. Those who hurried up heard him cursing Buck, and he cursed him long and fervently, and softly and lovingly.

"Gad, sir! Gad, sir!" spluttered the Skookum Bench king. "I'll give you a thousand for him, sir, a thousand, sir—twelve hundred, sir."

Thornton rose to his feet. His eyes were wet. The tears were streaming frankly down his cheeks. "Sir," he said to the Skookum Bench king, "no, sir. You can go to hell, sir. It's the best I can do for you, sir."

Buck seized Thornton's hand in his teeth. Thornton shook him back and forth. As though animated by a common impulse, the onlookers drew back to a respectful distance; nor were they again indiscreet enough to interrupt.

CHAPTER VII. THE SOUNDING OF THE CALL

When Buck earned sixteen hundred dollars in five minutes for John Thornton, he made it possible for his master to pay off certain debts and to journey with his partners into the East after a fabled lost mine, the history of which was as old as the history of the country. Many men had sought it; few had found it; and more than a few there were who had never returned from the quest. This lost mine was steeped in tragedy and shrouded in mystery. No one knew of the first man. The oldest tradition stopped before it got back to him. From the beginning there had been an ancient and ramshackle cabin. Dying men had sworn to it, and to the mine the site of which it marked, clinching their testimony with nuggets that were unlike any known grade of gold in the Northland.

But no living man had looted this treasure house, and the dead were dead; wherefore John Thornton and Pete and Hans, with Buck and half a dozen other dogs, faced into the East on an unknown trail to achieve where men and dogs as good as themselves had failed. They sledded seventy miles up the Yukon, swung to the left into the Stewart River, passed the Mayo and the McQuestion, and held on until the Stewart itself became a streamlet, threading the upstanding peaks which marked the backbone of the continent.

John Thornton asked little of man or nature. He was unafraid of the wild. With a handful of salt and a rifle he could plunge into the wilderness and fare wherever he pleased and as long as he pleased. Being in no haste, Indian fashion, he hunted his dinner in the course of the day's travel; and if he failed to find it, like the Indian, he kept on travelling, secure in the knowledge that sooner or later he would come to it. So, on this great journey into the East, straight meat was the bill of fare, ammunition and tools principally made up the load on the sled, and the time-card was drawn upon the limitless future.

To Buck it was boundless delight, this hunting, fishing, and indefinite wandering through strange places. For weeks at a time they would hold on steadily, day after day; and for weeks upon end they would camp, here and there, the dogs loafing and the men burning holes through frozen muck and gravel and washing countless pans of dirt by the heat of the fire. Sometimes they went hungry, sometimes they feasted riotously, all according to the abundance of game and the fortune of hunting. Summer arrived, and dogs and men packed on their backs, rafted across blue mountain lakes, and descended or ascended unknown rivers in slender boats whipsawed from the standing forest.

The months came and went, and back and forth they twisted through the uncharted vastness, where no men were and yet where men had been if the Lost Cabin were true. They went across divides in summer blizzards, shivered under the midnight sun on naked mountains between the timber line and the eternal snows, dropped into summer valleys amid swarming gnats and flies, and in the shadows of glaciers picked strawberries and flowers as ripe and fair as any the Southland could boast. In the fall of the year they penetrated a weird lake country, sad and silent, where wildfowl had been, but where then there was no life nor sign of life—only the blowing of chill winds, the forming of ice in sheltered places, and the melancholy rippling of waves on lonely beaches.

And through another winter they wandered on the obliterated trails of men who had gone before. Once, they came upon a path blazed through the forest, an ancient path, and the Lost Cabin seemed very near. But the path began nowhere and ended nowhere, and it remained mystery, as the man who made it and the reason he made it remained mystery. Another time they chanced upon the time-graven wreckage of a hunting lodge, and amid the shreds of rotted blankets John Thornton found a long-barrelled flint-lock. He knew it for a Hudson Bay Company gun of the young days in the Northwest, when such a gun was worth its height in beaver skins packed flat, And that was all—no hint as to the man who in an early day had reared the lodge and left the gun among the blankets.

Spring came on once more, and at the end of all their wandering they found, not the Lost Cabin, but a shallow placer in a broad valley where the gold showed like yellow butter across the bottom of the washing-pan. They sought no farther. Each day they worked earned them thousands of dollars in clean dust and nuggets, and they worked every day. The gold was sacked in moose-hide bags, fifty pounds to the bag, and piled like so much firewood outside the spruce-bough lodge. Like giants they toiled, days flashing on the heels of days like dreams as they heaped the treasure up.

There was nothing for the dogs to do, save the hauling in of meat now and again that Thornton killed, and Buck spent long hours musing by the fire. The vision of the short-legged hairy man came to him more frequently, now that there was little work to be done; and often, blinking by the fire, Buck wandered with him in that other world which he remembered.

The salient thing of this other world seemed fear. When he watched the hairy man sleeping by the fire, head between his knees and hands clasped above, Buck saw that he slept restlessly, with many starts and awakenings, at which times he would peer fearfully into the darkness and fling more wood upon the fire. Did they walk by the beach of a sea, where the hairy man gathered shellfish and ate them as he gathered, it was with eyes that roved everywhere for hidden danger and with legs prepared to run like the wind at its first appearance. Through the forest they crept noiselessly, Buck at the hairy man's heels; and they were alert and vigilant, the pair of them, ears twitching and moving and nostrils quivering, for the man heard and smelled as keenly as Buck. The hairy man could spring up into the trees and travel ahead as fast as on the ground, swinging by the arms from limb to limb, sometimes a dozen feet apart, letting go and catching, never falling, never missing his grip. In fact, he seemed as much at home among the trees as on the ground; and Buck had memories of nights of vigil spent beneath trees wherein the hairy man roosted, holding on tightly as he slept.

CHAPTER VII. THE SOUNDING OF THE CALL

And closely akin to the visions of the hairy man was the call still sounding in the depths of the forest. It filled him with a great unrest and strange desires. It caused him to feel a vague, sweet gladness, and he was aware of wild yearnings and stirrings for he knew not what. Sometimes he pursued the call into the forest, looking for it as though it were a tangible thing, barking softly or defiantly, as the mood might dictate. He would thrust his nose into the cool wood moss, or into the black soil where long grasses grew, and snort with joy at the fat earth smells; or he would crouch for hours, as if in concealment, behind fungus-covered trunks of fallen trees, wide-eyed and wide-eared to all that moved and sounded about him. It might be, lying thus, that he hoped to surprise this call he could not understand. But he did not know why he did these various things. He was impelled to do them, and did not reason about them at all.

Irresistible impulses seized him. He would be lying in camp, dozing lazily in the heat of the day, when suddenly his head would lift and his ears cock up, intent and listening, and he would spring to his feet and dash away, and on and on, for hours, through the forest aisles and across the open spaces where the niggerheads bunched. He loved to run down dry watercourses, and to creep and spy upon the bird life in the woods. For a day at a time he would lie in the underbrush where he could watch the partridges drumming and strutting up and down. But especially he loved to run in the dim twilight of the summer midnights, listening to the subdued and sleepy murmurs of the forest, reading signs and sounds as man may read a book, and seeking for the mysterious something that called—called, waking or sleeping, at all times, for him to come.

One night he sprang from sleep with a start, eager-eyed, nostrils quivering and scenting, his mane bristling in recurrent waves. From the forest came the call (or one note of it, for the call was many noted), distinct and definite as never before,—a long-drawn howl, like, yet unlike, any noise made by husky dog. And he knew it, in the old familiar way, as a sound heard before. He sprang through the sleeping camp and in swift silence dashed through the woods. As he drew closer to the cry he went more slowly, with caution in every movement, till he came to an open place among the trees, and looking out saw, erect on haunches, with nose pointed to the sky, a long, lean, timber wolf.

He had made no noise, yet it ceased from its howling and tried to sense his presence. Buck stalked into the open, half crouching, body gathered compactly together, tail straight and stiff, feet falling with unwonted care. Every movement advertised commingled threatening and overture of friendliness. It was the menacing truce that marks the meeting of wild beasts that prey. But the wolf fled at sight of him. He followed, with wild leapings, in a frenzy to overtake. He ran him into a blind channel, in the bed of the creek where a timber jam barred the way. The wolf whirled about, pivoting on his hind legs after the fashion of Joe and of all cornered husky dogs, snarling and bristling, clipping his teeth together in a continuous and rapid succession of snaps.

Buck did not attack, but circled him about and hedged him in with friendly advances. The wolf was suspicious and afraid; for Buck made three of him in weight, while his head barely reached Buck's shoulder. Watching his chance, he darted away, and the chase was resumed. Time and again he was cornered, and the thing repeated, though he was in poor condition, or Buck could not so easily have overtaken him. He would run till Buck's head was even with his flank, when he would whirl around at bay, only to dash away again at the first opportunity.

But in the end Buck's pertinacity was rewarded; for the wolf, finding that no harm was intended, finally sniffed noses with him. Then they became friendly, and played about in the nervous, half-coy way with which fierce beasts belie their fierceness. After some time of this the wolf started off at an easy lope in a manner that plainly showed he was going somewhere. He made it clear to Buck that he was to come, and they ran side by side through the sombre twilight, straight up the creek bed, into the gorge from which it issued, and across the bleak divide where it took its rise.

On the opposite slope of the watershed they came down into a level country where were great stretches of forest and many streams, and through these great stretches they ran steadily, hour after hour, the sun rising higher and the day growing warmer. Buck was wildly glad. He knew he was at last answering the call, running by the side of his wood brother toward the place from where the call surely came. Old memories were coming upon him fast, and he was stirring to them as of old he stirred to the realities of which they were the shadows. He had done this thing before, somewhere in that other and dimly remembered world, and he was doing it again, now, running free in the open, the unpacked earth underfoot, the wide sky overhead.

They stopped by a running stream to drink, and, stopping, Buck remembered John Thornton. He sat down. The wolf started on toward the place from where the call surely came, then returned to him, sniffing noses and making actions as though to encourage him. But Buck turned about and started slowly on the back track. For the better part of an hour the wild brother ran by his side, whining softly. Then he sat down, pointed his nose upward, and howled. It was a mournful howl, and as Buck held steadily on his way he heard it grow faint and fainter until it was lost in the distance.

John Thornton was eating dinner when Buck dashed into camp and sprang upon him in a frenzy of affection, overturning him, scrambling upon him, licking his face, biting his hand—"playing the general tom-fool," as John Thornton characterized it, the while he shook Buck back and forth and cursed him lovingly.

For two days and nights Buck never left camp, never let Thornton out of his sight. He followed him about at his work, watched him while he ate, saw him into his blankets at night and out of them in the morning. But after two days the call in the forest began to sound more imperiously than ever. Buck's restlessness came back on him, and he was haunted by recollections of the wild brother, and of the smiling land beyond the divide and the run side by side through the wide forest stretches. Once again he took to wandering in the woods, but the wild brother came no more; and though he listened through long vigils, the mournful howl was never raised.

He began to sleep out at night, staying away from camp for days at a time; and once he crossed the divide at the head of the creek and went down into the land of timber and streams. There he wandered for a week, seeking vainly for fresh sign of the wild brother, killing his meat as he travelled and travelling with the long, easy lope that seems never to tire. He fished for salmon in a broad stream that emptied somewhere into the sea, and by this stream he killed a large black bear, blinded by the mosquitoes while likewise fishing, and raging through the forest helpless and terrible. Even so, it was a hard fight, and it aroused the last latent remnants of Buck's ferocity. And two days later, when he returned to his kill and found a dozen wolverenes quarrelling over the spoil, he scattered them like chaff; and those that fled left two behind who would quarrel no more.

The blood-longing became stronger than ever before. He was a killer, a thing that preyed, living on the things that lived, unaided, alone, by virtue of his own strength and prowess, surviving triumphantly in a hostile environment where only the strong survived. Because of all this he became possessed of a great pride in himself, which communicated itself like a contagion to his physical being. It advertised itself in all his movements, was apparent in the play of every muscle, spoke plainly as speech in the way he carried himself, and made his glorious furry coat if anything more glorious. But for the stray brown on his muzzle and above his eyes, and for the splash of white hair that ran midmost down his chest, he might well have been mistaken for a gigantic wolf, larger than the largest of the breed. From his St. Bernard father he had inherited size and weight, but it was his shepherd mother who had given shape to that size and weight. His muzzle was the long wolf muzzle, save that it was larger than the muzzle of any wolf; and his head, somewhat broader, was the wolf head on a massive scale.

His cunning was wolf cunning, and wild cunning; his intelligence, shepherd intelligence and St. Bernard intelligence; and all this, plus an experience gained in the fiercest of schools, made him as formidable a creature as any that roamed the wild. A carnivorous animal living on a straight meat diet, he was in full flower, at the high tide of his life, overspilling with vigor and virility. When Thornton passed a caressing hand along his back, a snapping and crackling followed the hand, each hair discharging its pent magnetism at the contact. Every part, brain and body, nerve tissue and fibre, was keyed to the most exquisite pitch; and between all the parts there was a perfect equilibrium or adjustment. To sights and sounds and events which required action, he responded with lightning-like rapidity. Quickly as a husky dog could leap to defend from attack or to attack, he could leap twice as quickly. He saw the movement, or heard sound, and responded in less time than another dog required to compass the mere seeing or hearing. He perceived and determined and responded in the same instant. In point of fact the three actions of perceiving, determining, and responding were sequential; but so infinitesimal were the intervals of time between them that they appeared simultaneous. His muscles were surcharged with vitality, and snapped into play sharply, like steel springs. Life streamed through him in splendid flood, glad and rampant, until it seemed that it would burst him asunder in sheer ecstasy and pour forth generously over the world.

"Never was there such a dog," said John Thornton one day, as the partners watched Buck marching out of camp.

"When he was made, the mould was broke," said Pete.

"Py jingo! I t'ink so mineself," Hans affirmed.

They saw him marching out of camp, but they did not see the instant and terrible transformation which took place as soon as he was within the secrecy of the forest. He no longer marched. At once he became a thing of the wild, stealing along softly, cat-footed, a passing shadow that appeared and disappeared among the shadows. He knew how to take advantage of every cover, to crawl on his belly like a snake, and like a snake to leap and strike. He could take a ptarmigan from its nest, kill a rabbit as it slept, and snap in mid air the little chipmunks fleeing a second too late for the trees. Fish, in open pools, were not too quick for him; nor were beaver, mending their dams, too wary. He killed to eat, not from wantonness; but he preferred to eat what he killed himself. So a lurking humor ran through his deeds, and it was his delight to steal upon the squirrels, and, when he all but had them, to let them go, chattering in mortal fear to the treetops.

As the fall of the year came on, the moose appeared in greater abundance, moving slowly down to meet the winter in the lower and less rigorous valleys. Buck had already dragged down a stray part-grown calf; but he wished strongly for larger and more formidable quarry, and he came upon it one day on the divide at the head of the creek. A band of twenty moose had crossed over from the land of streams and timber, and chief among them was a great bull. He was in a savage temper, and, standing over six feet from the ground, was as formidable an antagonist as even Buck could desire. Back and forth the bull tossed his great palmated antlers, branching to fourteen points and embracing seven feet within the tips. His small eyes burned with a vicious and bitter light, while he roared with fury at sight of Buck.

From the bull's side, just forward of the flank, protruded a feathered arrow-end, which accounted for his savageness. Guided by that instinct which came from the old hunting days of the primordial world, Buck proceeded to cut the bull out from the herd. It was no slight task. He would bark and dance about in front of the bull, just out of reach of the great antlers and of the terrible splay hoofs which could have stamped his life out with a single blow. Unable to turn his back on the fanged danger and go on, the bull would be driven into paroxysms of rage. At such moments he charged Buck, who retreated craftily, luring him on by a simulated inability to escape. But when he was thus separated from his fellows, two or three of the younger bulls would charge back upon Buck and enable the wounded bull to rejoin the herd.

There is a patience of the wild—dogged, tireless, persistent as life itself—that holds motionless for endless hours the spider in its web, the snake in its coils, the panther in its ambuscade; this patience belongs peculiarly to life when it hunts its living food; and it belonged to Buck as he clung to the flank of the herd, retarding its march, irritating the young bulls, worrying the cows with their half-grown calves, and driving the wounded bull mad with helpless rage. For half a day this continued. Buck multiplied himself, attacking from all sides, enveloping the herd in a whirlwind of menace, cutting out his victim as fast as it could rejoin its mates, wearing out the patience of creatures preyed upon, which is a lesser patience than that of creatures preying.

As the day wore along and the sun dropped to its bed in the northwest (the darkness had come back and the fall nights were six hours long), the young bulls retraced their steps more and more reluctantly to the aid of their beset leader. The down-coming winter was harrying them on to the lower levels, and it seemed they could never shake off this tireless creature that held them back. Besides, it was not the life of the herd, or of the young bulls, that was threatened. The life of only one member was demanded, which was a remoter interest than their lives, and in the end they were content to pay the toll.

As twilight fell the old bull stood with lowered head, watching his mates—the cows he had known, the calves he had fathered, the bulls he had mastered—as they shambled on at a rapid pace through the fading light. He could not follow, for before his nose leaped the merciless fanged terror that would not let him go. Three hundred-weight more than half a ton he weighed; he had lived a long, strong life, full of fight and struggle, and at the end he faced death at the teeth of a creature whose head did not reach beyond his great knuckled knees.

From then on, night and day, Buck never left his prey, never gave it a moment's rest, never permitted it to browse the leaves of trees or the shoots of young birch and willow. Nor did he give the wounded bull opportunity to slake his burning thirst in the slender trickling streams they crossed. Often, in desperation, he burst into long stretches of flight. At such times Buck did not attempt to stay him, but loped easily at his heels, satisfied with the way the game was played, lying down when the moose stood still, attacking him fiercely when he strove to eat or drink.

The great head drooped more and more under its tree of horns, and the shambling trot grew weak and weaker. He took to standing for long periods, with nose to the ground and dejected ears dropped limply; and Buck found more time in which to get water for himself and in which to rest. At such moments, panting with red lolling tongue and with eyes fixed upon the big bull, it appeared to Buck that a change was coming over the face of things. He could feel a new stir in the land. As the moose were coming into the land, other kinds of life were coming in. Forest and stream and air seemed palpitant with their presence. The news of it was borne in upon him, not by sight, or sound, or smell, but by some other and subtler sense. He heard nothing, saw nothing, yet knew that the land was somehow different; that through it strange things were afoot and ranging; and he resolved to investigate after he had finished the business in hand.

At last, at the end of the fourth day, he pulled the great moose down. For a day and a night he remained by the kill, eating and sleeping, turn and turn about. Then, rested, refreshed and strong, he turned his face toward camp and John Thornton. He broke into the long easy lope, and went on, hour after hour, never at loss for the tangled way, heading straight home through strange country with a certitude of direction that put man and his magnetic needle to shame.

As he held on he became more and more conscious of the new stir in the land. There was life abroad in it different from the life which had been there throughout the summer. No longer was this fact borne in upon him in some subtle, mysterious way. The birds talked of it, the squirrels chattered about it, the very breeze whispered of it. Several times he stopped and drew in the fresh morning air in great sniffs, reading a message which made him leap on with greater speed. He was oppressed with a sense of calamity happening, if it were not calamity already happened; and as he crossed the last watershed and dropped down into the valley toward camp, he proceeded with greater caution.

Three miles away he came upon a fresh trail that sent his neck hair rippling and bristling, It led straight toward camp and John Thornton. Buck hurried on, swiftly and stealthily, every nerve straining and tense, alert to the multitudinous details which told a story—all but the end. His nose gave him a varying description of the passage of the life on the heels of which he was travelling. He remarked the pregnant silence of the forest. The bird life had flitted. The squirrels were in hiding. One only he saw,—a sleek gray fellow, flattened against a gray dead limb so that he seemed a part of it, a woody excrescence upon the wood itself.

As Buck slid along with the obscureness of a gliding shadow, his nose was jerked suddenly to the side as though a positive force had gripped and pulled it. He followed the new scent into a thicket and found Nig. He was lying on his side, dead where he had dragged himself, an arrow protruding, head and feathers, from either side of his body.

A hundred yards farther on, Buck came upon one of the sled-dogs Thornton had bought in Dawson. This dog was thrashing about in a death-struggle, directly on the trail, and Buck passed around him without stopping. From the camp came the faint sound of many voices, rising and falling in a sing-song chant. Bellying forward to the edge of the clearing, he found Hans, lying on his face, feathered with arrows like a porcupine. At the same instant Buck peered out where the spruce-bough lodge had been and saw what made his hair leap straight up on his neck and shoulders. A gust of overpowering rage swept over him. He did not know that he growled, but he growled aloud with a terrible ferocity. For the last time in his life he allowed passion to usurp cunning and reason, and it was because of his great love for John Thornton that he lost his head.

The Yeehats were dancing about the wreckage of the spruce-bough lodge when they heard a fearful roaring and saw rushing upon them an animal the like of which they had never seen before. It was Buck, a live hurricane of fury, hurling himself upon them in a frenzy to destroy. He sprang at the foremost man (it was the chief of the Yeehats), ripping the throat wide open till the rent jugular spouted a fountain of blood. He did not pause to worry the victim, but ripped in passing, with the next bound tearing wide the throat of a second man. There was no withstanding him. He plunged about in their very midst, tearing, rending, destroying, in constant and terrific motion which defied the arrows they discharged at him. In fact, so inconceivably rapid were his movements, and so closely were the Indians tangled together, that they shot one another with the arrows; and one young hunter, hurling a spear at Buck in mid air, drove it through the chest of another hunter with such force that the point broke through the skin of the back and stood out beyond. Then a panic seized the Yeehats, and they fled in terror to the woods, proclaiming as they fled the advent of the Evil Spirit.

And truly Buck was the Fiend incarnate, raging at their heels and dragging them down like deer as they raced through the trees. It was a fateful day for the Yeehats. They scattered far and wide over the country, and it was not till a week later that the last of the survivors gathered together in a lower valley and counted their losses. As for Buck, wearying of the pursuit, he returned to the desolated camp. He found Pete where he had been killed in his blankets in the first moment of surprise. Thornton's desperate struggle was fresh-written on the earth, and Buck scented every detail of it down to the edge of a deep pool. By the edge, head and fore feet in the water, lay Skeet, faithful to the last. The pool itself, muddy and discolored from the sluice boxes, effectually hid what it contained, and it contained John Thornton; for Buck followed his trace into the water, from which no trace led away.

All day Buck brooded by the pool or roamed restlessly about the camp. Death, as a cessation of movement, as a passing out and away from the lives of the living, he knew, and he knew John Thornton was dead. It left a great void in him, somewhat akin to hunger, but a void which ached and ached, and which food could not fill, At times, when he paused to contemplate the carcasses of the Yeehats, he forgot the pain of it; and at such times he was aware of a great pride in himself,—a pride greater than any he had yet experienced. He had killed man, the noblest game of all, and he had killed in the face of the law of club and fang. He sniffed the bodies curiously. They had died so easily. It was harder to kill a husky dog than them. They were no match at all, were it not for their arrows and spears and clubs. Thenceforward he would be unafraid of them except when they bore in their hands their arrows, spears, and clubs.

Night came on, and a full moon rose high over the trees into the sky, lighting the land till it lay bathed in ghostly day. And with the coming of the night, brooding and mourning by the pool, Buck became alive to a stirring of the new life in the forest other than that which the Yeehats had made, He stood up, listening and scenting. From far away drifted a faint, sharp yelp, followed by a chorus of similar sharp yelps. As the moments passed the yelps grew closer and louder. Again Buck knew them as things heard in that other world which persisted in his memory. He walked to the centre of the open space and listened. It was the call, the many-noted call, sounding more luringly and compellingly than ever before. And as never before, he was ready to obey. John Thornton was dead. The last tie was broken. Man and the claims of man no longer bound him.

Hunting their living meat, as the Yeehats were hunting it, on the flanks of the migrating moose, the wolf pack had at last crossed over from the land of streams and timber and invaded Buck's valley. Into the clearing where the moonlight streamed, they poured in a silvery flood; and in the centre of the clearing stood Buck, motionless as a statue, waiting their coming. They were awed, so still and large he stood, and a moment's pause fell, till the boldest one leaped straight for him. Like a flash Buck struck, breaking the neck. Then he stood, without movement, as before, the stricken wolf rolling in agony behind him. Three others tried it in sharp succession; and one after the other they drew back, streaming blood from slashed throats or shoulders.

This was sufficient to fling the whole pack forward, pell-mell, crowded together, blocked and confused by its eagerness to pull down the prey. Buck's marvellous quickness and agility stood him in good stead. Pivoting on his hind legs, and snapping and gashing, he was everywhere at once, presenting a front which was apparently unbroken so swiftly did he whirl and guard from side to side. But to prevent them from getting behind him, he was forced back, down past the pool and into the creek bed, till he brought up against a high gravel bank. He worked along to a right angle in the bank which the men had made in the course of mining, and in this angle he came to bay, protected on three sides and with nothing to do but face the front.

And so well did he face it, that at the end of half an hour the wolves drew back discomfited. The tongues of all were out and lolling, the white fangs showing cruelly white in the moonlight. Some were lying down with heads raised and ears pricked forward; others stood on their feet, watching him; and still others were lapping water from the pool. One wolf, long and lean and gray, advanced cautiously, in a friendly manner, and Buck recognized the wild brother with whom he had run for a night and a day. He was whining softly, and, as Buck whined, they touched noses.

Then an old wolf, gaunt and battle-scarred, came forward. Buck writhed his lips into the preliminary of a snarl, but sniffed noses with him, Whereupon the old wolf sat down, pointed nose at the moon, and broke out the long wolf howl. The others sat down and howled. And now the call came to Buck in unmistakable accents. He, too, sat down and howled. This over, he came out of his angle and the pack crowded around him, sniffing in half-friendly, half-savage manner. The leaders lifted the yelp of the pack and sprang away into the woods. The wolves swung in behind, yelping in chorus. And Buck ran with them, side by side with the wild brother, yelping as he ran.

And here may well end the story of Buck. The years were not many when the Yeehats noted a change in the breed of timber wolves; for some were seen with splashes of brown on head and muzzle, and with a rift of white centring down the chest. But more remarkable than this, the Yeehats tell of a Ghost Dog that runs at the head of the pack. They are afraid of this Ghost Dog, for it has cunning greater than they, stealing from their camps in fierce winters, robbing their traps, slaying their dogs, and defying their bravest hunters.

Nay, the tale grows worse. Hunters there are who fail to return to the camp, and hunters there have been whom their tribesmen found with throats slashed cruelly open and with wolf prints about them in the snow greater than the prints of any wolf. Each fall, when the Yeehats follow the movement of the moose, there is a certain valley which they never enter. And women there are who become sad when the word goes over the fire of how the Evil Spirit came to select that valley for an abiding-place.

In the summers there is one visitor, however, to that valley, of which the Yeehats do not know. It is a great, gloriously coated wolf, like, and yet unlike, all other wolves. He crosses alone from the smiling timber land and comes down into an open space among the trees. Here a yellow stream flows from rotted moose-hide sacks and sinks into the ground, with long grasses growing through it and vegetable mould over-running it and hiding its yellow from the sun; and here he muses for a time, howling once, long and mournfully, ere he departs.

But he is not always alone. When the long winter nights come on and the wolves follow their meat into the lower valleys, he may be seen running at the head of the pack through the pale moonlight or glimmering borealis, leaping gigantic above his fellows, his great throat a-bellow as he sings a song of the younger world, which is the song of the pack.

WHITE FANG

PART I

CHAPTER I—THE TRAIL OF THE MEAT

Dark spruce forest frowned on either side the frozen waterway. The trees had been stripped by a recent wind of their white covering of frost, and they seemed to lean towards each other, black and ominous, in the fading light. A vast silence reigned over the land. The land itself was a desolation, lifeless, without movement, so lone and cold that the spirit of it was not even that of sadness. There was a hint in it of laughter, but of a laughter more terrible than any sadness—a laughter that was mirthless as the smile of the sphinx, a laughter cold as the frost and partaking of the grimness of infallibility. It was the masterful and incommunicable wisdom of eternity laughing at the futility of life and the effort of life. It was the Wild, the savage, frozen-hearted Northland Wild.

But there *was* life, abroad in the land and defiant. Down the frozen waterway toiled a string of wolfish dogs. Their bristly fur was rimed with frost. Their breath froze in the air as it left their mouths, spouting forth in spumes of vapour that settled upon the hair of their bodies and formed into crystals of frost. Leather harness was on the dogs, and leather traces attached them to a sled which dragged along behind. The sled was without runners. It was made of stout birch-bark, and its full surface rested on the snow. The front end of the sled was turned up, like a scroll, in order to force down and under the bore of soft snow that surged like a wave before it. On the sled, securely lashed, was a long and narrow oblong box. There were other things on the sled—blankets, an axe, and a coffee-pot and frying-pan; but prominent, occupying most of the space, was the long and narrow oblong box.

In advance of the dogs, on wide snowshoes, toiled a man. At the rear of the sled toiled a second man. On the sled, in the box, lay a third man whose toil was over,—a man whom the Wild had conquered and beaten down until he would never move nor struggle again. It is not the way of the Wild to like movement. Life is an offence to it, for life is movement; and the Wild aims always to destroy movement. It freezes the water to prevent it running to the sea; it drives the sap out of the trees till they are frozen to their mighty hearts; and most ferociously and terribly of all does the Wild harry and crush into submission man—man who is the most restless of life, ever in revolt against the dictum that all movement must in the end come to the cessation of movement.

But at front and rear, unawed and indomitable, toiled the two men who were not yet dead. Their bodies were covered with fur and soft-tanned leather. Eyelashes and cheeks and lips were so coated with the crystals from their frozen breath that their faces were not discernible. This gave them the seeming of ghostly masques, undertakers in a spectral world at the funeral of some ghost. But under it all they were men, penetrating the land of desolation and mockery and silence, puny adventurers bent on colossal adventure, pitting themselves against the might of a world as remote and alien and pulseless as the abysses of space.

They travelled on without speech, saving their breath for the work of their bodies. On every side was the silence, pressing upon them with a tangible presence. It affected their minds as the many atmospheres of deep water affect the body of the diver. It crushed them with the weight of unending vastness and unalterable decree. It crushed them into the remotest recesses of their own minds, pressing out of them, like juices from the grape, all the false ardours and exaltations and undue self-values of the human soul, until they perceived themselves finite and small, specks and motes, moving with weak cunning and little wisdom amidst the play and inter-play of the great blind elements and forces.

An hour went by, and a second hour. The pale light of the short sunless day was beginning to fade, when a faint far cry arose on the still air. It soared upward with a swift rush, till it reached its topmost note, where it persisted, palpitant and tense, and then slowly died away. It might have been a lost soul wailing, had it not been invested with a certain sad fierceness and hungry eagerness. The front man turned his head until his eyes met the eyes of the man behind. And then, across the narrow oblong box, each nodded to the other.

A second cry arose, piercing the silence with needle-like shrillness. Both men located the sound. It was to the rear, somewhere in the snow expanse they had just traversed. A third and answering cry arose, also to the rear and to the left of the second cry.

"They're after us, Bill," said the man at the front.

His voice sounded hoarse and unreal, and he had spoken with apparent effort.

"Meat is scarce," answered his comrade. "I ain't seen a rabbit sign for days."

Thereafter they spoke no more, though their ears were keen for the hunting-cries that continued to rise behind them.

At the fall of darkness they swung the dogs into a cluster of spruce trees on the edge of the waterway and made a camp. The coffin, at the side of the fire, served for seat and table. The wolf-dogs, clustered on the far side of the fire, snarled and bickered among themselves, but evinced no inclination to stray off into the darkness.

"Seems to me, Henry, they're stayin' remarkable close to camp," Bill commented.

Henry, squatting over the fire and settling the pot of coffee with a piece of ice, nodded. Nor did he speak till he had taken his seat on the coffin and begun to eat.

"They know where their hides is safe," he said. "They'd sooner eat grub than be grub. They're pretty wise, them dogs."

Bill shook his head. "Oh, I don't know."

His comrade looked at him curiously. "First time I ever heard you say anything about their not bein' wise."

"Henry," said the other, munching with deliberation the beans he was eating, "did you happen to notice the way them dogs kicked up when I was a-feedin' 'em?"

"They did cut up more'n usual," Henry acknowledged.

"How many dogs 've we got, Henry?"

"Six."

CHAPTER I—THE TRAIL OF THE MEAT

"Well, Henry . . . " Bill stopped for a moment, in order that his words might gain greater significance. "As I was sayin', Henry, we've got six dogs. I took six fish out of the bag. I gave one fish to each dog, an', Henry, I was one fish short."

"You counted wrong."

"We've got six dogs," the other reiterated dispassionately. "I took out six fish. One Ear didn't get no fish. I came back to the bag afterward an' got 'm his fish."

"We've only got six dogs," Henry said.

"Henry," Bill went on. "I won't say they was all dogs, but there was seven of 'm that got fish."

Henry stopped eating to glance across the fire and count the dogs.

"There's only six now," he said.

"I saw the other one run off across the snow," Bill announced with cool positiveness. "I saw seven."

Henry looked at him commiseratingly, and said, "I'll be almighty glad when this trip's over."

"What d'ye mean by that?" Bill demanded.

"I mean that this load of ourn is gettin' on your nerves, an' that you're beginnin' to see things."

"I thought of that," Bill answered gravely. "An' so, when I saw it run off across the snow, I looked in the snow an' saw its tracks. Then I counted the dogs an' there was still six of 'em. The tracks is there in the snow now. D'ye want to look at 'em? I'll show 'em to you."

Henry did not reply, but munched on in silence, until, the meal finished, he topped it with a final cup of coffee. He wiped his mouth with the back of his hand and said:

"Then you're thinkin' as it was—"

A long wailing cry, fiercely sad, from somewhere in the darkness, had interrupted him. He stopped to listen to it, then he finished his sentence with a wave of his hand toward the sound of the cry, "—one of them?"

Bill nodded. "I'd a blame sight sooner think that than anything else. You noticed yourself the row the dogs made."

Cry after cry, and answering cries, were turning the silence into a bedlam. From every side the cries arose, and the dogs betrayed their fear by huddling together and so close to the fire that their hair was scorched by the heat. Bill threw on more wood, before lighting his pipe.

"I'm thinking you're down in the mouth some," Henry said.

"Henry . . . " He sucked meditatively at his pipe for some time before he went on. "Henry, I was a-thinkin' what a blame sight luckier he is than you an' me'll ever be."

He indicated the third person by a downward thrust of the thumb to the box on which they sat.

"You an' me, Henry, when we die, we'll be lucky if we get enough stones over our carcases to keep the dogs off of us."

"But we ain't got people an' money an' all the rest, like him," Henry rejoined. "Long-distance funerals is somethin' you an' me can't exactly afford."

"What gets me, Henry, is what a chap like this, that's a lord or something in his own country, and that's never had to bother about grub nor blankets; why he comes a-buttin' round the Godforsaken ends of the earth—that's what I can't exactly see."

"He might have lived to a ripe old age if he'd stayed at home," Henry agreed.

Bill opened his mouth to speak, but changed his mind. Instead, he pointed towards the wall of darkness that pressed about them from every side. There was no suggestion of form in the utter blackness; only could be seen a pair of eyes gleaming like live coals. Henry indicated with his head a second pair, and a third. A circle of the gleaming eyes had drawn about their camp. Now and again a pair of eyes moved, or disappeared to appear again a moment later.

The unrest of the dogs had been increasing, and they stampeded, in a surge of sudden fear, to the near side of the fire, cringing and crawling about the legs of the men. In the scramble one of the dogs had been overturned on the edge of the fire, and it had yelped with pain and fright as the smell of its singed coat possessed the air. The commotion caused the circle of eyes to shift restlessly for a moment and even to withdraw a bit, but it settled down again as the dogs became quiet.

"Henry, it's a blame misfortune to be out of ammunition."

Bill had finished his pipe and was helping his companion to spread the bed of fur and blanket upon the spruce boughs which he had laid over the snow before supper. Henry grunted, and began unlacing his mocassins.

"How many cartridges did you say you had left?" he asked.

"Three," came the answer. "An' I wisht 'twas three hundred. Then I'd show 'em what for, damn 'em!"

He shook his fist angrily at the gleaming eyes, and began securely to prop his moccasins before the fire.

"An' I wisht this cold snap'd break," he went on. "It's ben fifty below for two weeks now. An' I wisht I'd never started on this trip, Henry. I don't like the looks of it. I don't feel right, somehow. An' while I'm wishin', I wisht the trip was over an' done with, an' you an' me a-sittin' by the fire in Fort McGurry just about now an' playing cribbage—that's what I wisht."

Henry grunted and crawled into bed. As he dozed off he was aroused by his comrade's voice.

"Say, Henry, that other one that come in an' got a fish—why didn't the dogs pitch into it? That's what's botherin' me."

"You're botherin' too much, Bill," came the sleepy response. "You was never like this before. You jes' shut up now, an' go to sleep, an' you'll be all hunkydory in the mornin'. Your stomach's sour, that's what's botherin' you."

The men slept, breathing heavily, side by side, under the one covering. The fire died down, and the gleaming eyes drew closer the circle they had flung about the camp. The dogs clustered together in fear, now and again snarling menacingly as a pair of eyes drew close. Once their uproar became so loud that Bill woke up. He got out of bed carefully, so as not to disturb the sleep of his comrade, and threw more wood on the fire. As it began to flame up, the circle of eyes drew farther back. He glanced casually at the huddling dogs. He rubbed his eyes and looked at them more sharply. Then he crawled back into the blankets.

"Henry," he said. "Oh, Henry."

Henry groaned as he passed from sleep to waking, and demanded, "What's wrong now?"

"Nothin'," came the answer; "only there's seven of 'em again. I just counted."

Henry acknowledged receipt of the information with a grunt that slid into a snore as he drifted back into sleep.

CHAPTER I—THE TRAIL OF THE MEAT

In the morning it was Henry who awoke first and routed his companion out of bed. Daylight was yet three hours away, though it was already six o'clock; and in the darkness Henry went about preparing breakfast, while Bill rolled the blankets and made the sled ready for lashing.

"Say, Henry," he asked suddenly, "how many dogs did you say we had?"

"Six."

"Wrong," Bill proclaimed triumphantly.

"Seven again?" Henry queried.

"No, five; one's gone."

"The hell!" Henry cried in wrath, leaving the cooking to come and count the dogs.

"You're right, Bill," he concluded. "Fatty's gone."

"An' he went like greased lightnin' once he got started. Couldn't 've seen 'm for smoke."

"No chance at all," Henry concluded. "They jes' swallowed 'm alive. I bet he was yelpin' as he went down their throats, damn 'em!"

"He always was a fool dog," said Bill.

"But no fool dog ought to be fool enough to go off an' commit suicide that way." He looked over the remainder of the team with a speculative eye that summed up instantly the salient traits of each animal. "I bet none of the others would do it."

"Couldn't drive 'em away from the fire with a club," Bill agreed. "I always did think there was somethin' wrong with Fatty anyway."

And this was the epitaph of a dead dog on the Northland trail—less scant than the epitaph of many another dog, of many a man.

CHAPTER II—THE SHE-WOLF

Breakfast eaten and the slim camp-outfit lashed to the sled, the men turned their backs on the cheery fire and launched out into the darkness. At once began to rise the cries that were fiercely sad—cries that called through the darkness and cold to one another and answered back. Conversation ceased. Daylight came at nine o'clock. At midday the sky to the south warmed to rose-colour, and marked where the bulge of the earth intervened between the meridian sun and the northern world. But the rose-colour swiftly faded. The grey light of day that remained lasted until three o'clock, when it, too, faded, and the pall of the Arctic night descended upon the lone and silent land.

As darkness came on, the hunting-cries to right and left and rear drew closer—so close that more than once they sent surges of fear through the toiling dogs, throwing them into short-lived panics.

At the conclusion of one such panic, when he and Henry had got the dogs back in the traces, Bill said:

"I wisht they'd strike game somewheres, an' go away an' leave us alone."

"They do get on the nerves horrible," Henry sympathised.

They spoke no more until camp was made.

Henry was bending over and adding ice to the babbling pot of beans when he was startled by the sound of a blow, an exclamation from Bill, and a sharp snarling cry of pain from among the dogs. He straightened up in time to see a dim form disappearing across the snow into the shelter of the dark. Then he saw Bill, standing amid the dogs, half triumphant, half crestfallen, in one hand a stout club, in the other the tail and part of the body of a sun-cured salmon.

"It got half of it," he announced; "but I got a whack at it jes' the same. D'ye hear it squeal?"

"What'd it look like?" Henry asked.

"Couldn't see. But it had four legs an' a mouth an' hair an' looked like any dog."

"Must be a tame wolf, I reckon."

"It's damned tame, whatever it is, comin' in here at feedin' time an' gettin' its whack of fish."

That night, when supper was finished and they sat on the oblong box and pulled at their pipes, the circle of gleaming eyes drew in even closer than before.

"I wisht they'd spring up a bunch of moose or something, an' go away an' leave us alone," Bill said.

CHAPTER II—THE SHE-WOLF

Henry grunted with an intonation that was not all sympathy, and for a quarter of an hour they sat on in silence, Henry staring at the fire, and Bill at the circle of eyes that burned in the darkness just beyond the firelight.

"I wisht we was pullin' into McGurry right now," he began again.

"Shut up your wishin' and your croakin'," Henry burst out angrily. "Your stomach's sour. That's what's ailin' you. Swallow a spoonful of sody, an' you'll sweeten up wonderful an' be more pleasant company."

In the morning Henry was aroused by fervid blasphemy that proceeded from the mouth of Bill. Henry propped himself up on an elbow and looked to see his comrade standing among the dogs beside the replenished fire, his arms raised in objurgation, his face distorted with passion.

"Hello!" Henry called. "What's up now?"

"Frog's gone," came the answer.

"No."

"I tell you yes."

Henry leaped out of the blankets and to the dogs. He counted them with care, and then joined his partner in cursing the power of the Wild that had robbed them of another dog.

"Frog was the strongest dog of the bunch," Bill pronounced finally.

"An' he was no fool dog neither," Henry added.

And so was recorded the second epitaph in two days.

A gloomy breakfast was eaten, and the four remaining dogs were harnessed to the sled. The day was a repetition of the days that had gone before. The men toiled without speech across the face of the frozen world. The silence was unbroken save by the cries of their pursuers, that, unseen, hung upon their rear. With the coming of night in the mid-afternoon, the cries sounded closer as the pursuers drew in according to their custom; and the dogs grew excited and frightened, and were guilty of panics that tangled the traces and further depressed the two men.

"There, that'll fix you fool critters," Bill said with satisfaction that night, standing erect at completion of his task.

Henry left the cooking to come and see. Not only had his partner tied the dogs up, but he had tied them, after the Indian fashion, with sticks. About the neck of each dog he had fastened a leather thong. To this, and so close to the neck that the dog could not get his teeth to it, he had tied a stout stick four or five feet in length. The other end of the stick, in turn, was made fast to a stake in the ground by means of a leather thong. The dog was unable to gnaw through the leather at his own end of the stick. The stick prevented him from getting at the leather that fastened the other end.

Henry nodded his head approvingly.

"It's the only contraption that'll ever hold One Ear," he said. "He can gnaw through leather as clean as a knife an' jes' about half as quick. They all'll be here in the mornin' hunkydory."

"You jes' bet they will," Bill affirmed. "If one of em' turns up missin', I'll go without my coffee."

"They jes' know we ain't loaded to kill," Henry remarked at bed-time, indicating the gleaming circle that hemmed them in. "If we could put a couple of shots into 'em, they'd be more respectful. They come closer every night. Get the firelight out of your eyes an' look hard—there! Did you see that one?"

For some time the two men amused themselves with watching the movement of vague forms on the edge of the firelight. By looking closely and steadily at where a pair of eyes burned in the darkness, the form of the animal would slowly take shape. They could even see these forms move at times.

A sound among the dogs attracted the men's attention. One Ear was uttering quick, eager whines, lunging at the length of his stick toward the darkness, and desisting now and again in order to make frantic attacks on the stick with his teeth.

"Look at that, Bill," Henry whispered.

Full into the firelight, with a stealthy, sidelong movement, glided a doglike animal. It moved with commingled mistrust and daring, cautiously observing the men, its attention fixed on the dogs. One Ear strained the full length of the stick toward the intruder and whined with eagerness.

"That fool One Ear don't seem scairt much," Bill said in a low tone.

"It's a she-wolf," Henry whispered back, "an' that accounts for Fatty an' Frog. She's the decoy for the pack. She draws out the dog an' then all the rest pitches in an' eats 'm up."

The fire crackled. A log fell apart with a loud spluttering noise. At the sound of it the strange animal leaped back into the darkness.

"Henry, I'm a-thinkin'," Bill announced.

"Thinkin' what?"

"I'm a-thinkin' that was the one I lambasted with the club."

"Ain't the slightest doubt in the world," was Henry's response.

"An' right here I want to remark," Bill went on, "that that animal's familyarity with campfires is suspicious an' immoral."

"It knows for certain more'n a self-respectin' wolf ought to know," Henry agreed. "A wolf that knows enough to come in with the dogs at feedin' time has had experiences."

"Ol' Villan had a dog once that run away with the wolves," Bill cogitates aloud. "I ought to know. I shot it out of the pack in a moose pasture over 'on Little Stick. An' Ol' Villan cried like a baby. Hadn't seen it for three years, he said. Ben with the wolves all that time."

"I reckon you've called the turn, Bill. That wolf's a dog, an' it's eaten fish many's the time from the hand of man."

"An if I get a chance at it, that wolf that's a dog'll be jes' meat," Bill declared. "We can't afford to lose no more animals."

"But you've only got three cartridges," Henry objected.

"I'll wait for a dead sure shot," was the reply.

In the morning Henry renewed the fire and cooked breakfast to the accompaniment of his partner's snoring.

"You was sleepin' jes' too comfortable for anything," Henry told him, as he routed him out for breakfast. "I hadn't the heart to rouse you."

Bill began to eat sleepily. He noticed that his cup was empty and started to reach for the pot. But the pot was beyond arm's length and beside Henry.

"Say, Henry," he chided gently, "ain't you forgot somethin'?"

Henry looked about with great carefulness and shook his head. Bill held up the empty cup.

"You don't get no coffee," Henry announced.

"Ain't run out?" Bill asked anxiously.

"Nope."

"Ain't thinkin' it'll hurt my digestion?"

"Nope."

A flush of angry blood pervaded Bill's face.

"Then it's jes' warm an' anxious I am to be hearin' you explain yourself," he said.

"Spanker's gone," Henry answered.

Without haste, with the air of one resigned to misfortune Bill turned his head, and from where he sat counted the dogs.

"How'd it happen?" he asked apathetically.

Henry shrugged his shoulders. "Don't know. Unless One Ear gnawed 'm loose. He couldn't a-done it himself, that's sure."

"The darned cuss." Bill spoke gravely and slowly, with no hint of the anger that was raging within. "Jes' because he couldn't chew himself loose, he chews Spanker loose."

"Well, Spanker's troubles is over anyway; I guess he's digested by this time an' cavortin' over the landscape in the bellies of twenty different wolves," was Henry's epitaph on this, the latest lost dog. "Have some coffee, Bill."

But Bill shook his head.

"Go on," Henry pleaded, elevating the pot.

Bill shoved his cup aside. "I'll be ding-dong-danged if I do. I said I wouldn't if ary dog turned up missin', an' I won't."

"It's darn good coffee," Henry said enticingly.

But Bill was stubborn, and he ate a dry breakfast washed down with mumbled curses at One Ear for the trick he had played.

"I'll tie 'em up out of reach of each other to-night," Bill said, as they took the trail.

They had travelled little more than a hundred yards, when Henry, who was in front, bent down and picked up something with which his snowshoe had collided. It was dark, and he could not see it, but he recognised it by the touch. He flung it back, so that it struck the sled and bounced along until it fetched up on Bill's snowshoes.

"Mebbe you'll need that in your business," Henry said.

Bill uttered an exclamation. It was all that was left of Spanker—the stick with which he had been tied.

"They ate 'm hide an' all," Bill announced. "The stick's as clean as a whistle. They've ate the leather offen both ends. They're damn hungry, Henry, an' they'll have you an' me guessin' before this trip's over."

Henry laughed defiantly. "I ain't been trailed this way by wolves before, but I've gone through a whole lot worse an' kept my health. Takes more'n a handful of them pesky critters to do for yours truly, Bill, my son."

"I don't know, I don't know," Bill muttered ominously.

"Well, you'll know all right when we pull into McGurry."

"I ain't feelin' special enthusiastic," Bill persisted.

"You're off colour, that's what's the matter with you," Henry dogmatised. "What you need is quinine, an' I'm goin' to dose you up stiff as soon as we make McGurry."

Bill grunted his disagreement with the diagnosis, and lapsed into silence. The day was like all the days. Light came at nine o'clock. At twelve o'clock the southern horizon was warmed by the unseen sun; and then began the cold grey of afternoon that would merge, three hours later, into night.

It was just after the sun's futile effort to appear, that Bill slipped the rifle from under the sled-lashings and said:

"You keep right on, Henry, I'm goin' to see what I can see."

"You'd better stick by the sled," his partner protested. "You've only got three cartridges, an' there's no tellin' what might happen."

"Who's croaking now?" Bill demanded triumphantly.

Henry made no reply, and plodded on alone, though often he cast anxious glances back into the grey solitude where his partner had disappeared. An hour later, taking advantage of the cut-offs around which the sled had to go, Bill arrived.

"They're scattered an' rangin' along wide," he said: "keeping up with us an' lookin' for game at the same time. You see, they're sure of us, only they know they've got to wait to get us. In the meantime they're willin' to pick up anything eatable that comes handy."

"You mean they *think* they're sure of us," Henry objected pointedly.

But Bill ignored him. "I seen some of them. They're pretty thin. They ain't had a bite in weeks I reckon, outside of Fatty an' Frog an' Spanker; an' there's so many of 'em that that didn't go far. They're remarkable thin. Their ribs is like wash-boards, an' their stomachs is right up against their backbones. They're pretty desperate, I can tell you. They'll be goin' mad, yet, an' then watch out."

A few minutes later, Henry, who was now travelling behind the sled, emitted a low, warning whistle. Bill turned and looked, then quietly stopped the dogs. To the rear, from around the last bend and plainly into view, on the very trail they had just covered, trotted a furry, slinking form. Its nose was to the trail, and it trotted with a peculiar, sliding, effortless gait. When they halted, it halted, throwing up its head and regarding them steadily with nostrils that twitched as it caught and studied the scent of them.

"It's the she-wolf," Bill answered.

The dogs had lain down in the snow, and he walked past them to join his partner in the sled. Together they watched the strange animal that had pursued them for days and that had already accomplished the destruction of half their dog-team.

After a searching scrutiny, the animal trotted forward a few steps. This it repeated several times, till it was a short hundred yards away. It paused, head up, close by a clump of spruce trees, and with sight and scent studied the outfit of the watching men. It looked at them in a strangely wistful way, after the manner of a dog; but in its wistfulness there was none of the dog affection. It was a wistfulness bred of hunger, as cruel as its own fangs, as merciless as the frost itself.

It was large for a wolf, its gaunt frame advertising the lines of an animal that was among the largest of its kind.

"Stands pretty close to two feet an' a half at the shoulders," Henry commented. "An' I'll bet it ain't far from five feet long."

"Kind of strange colour for a wolf," was Bill's criticism. "I never seen a red wolf before. Looks almost cinnamon to me."

The animal was certainly not cinnamon-coloured. Its coat was the true wolf-coat. The dominant colour was grey, and yet there was to it a faint reddish hue—a hue that was baffling, that appeared and disappeared, that was more like an illusion of the vision, now grey, distinctly grey, and again giving hints and glints of a vague redness of colour not classifiable in terms of ordinary experience.

"Looks for all the world like a big husky sled-dog," Bill said. "I wouldn't be s'prised to see it wag its tail."

"Hello, you husky!" he called. "Come here, you whatever-your-name-is."

"Ain't a bit scairt of you," Henry laughed.

Bill waved his hand at it threateningly and shouted loudly; but the animal betrayed no fear. The only change in it that they could notice was an accession of alertness. It still regarded them with the merciless wistfulness of hunger. They were meat, and it was hungry; and it would like to go in and eat them if it dared.

"Look here, Henry," Bill said, unconsciously lowering his voice to a whisper because of what he imitated. "We've got three cartridges. But it's a dead shot. Couldn't miss it. It's got away with three of our dogs, an' we oughter put a stop to it. What d'ye say?"

Henry nodded his consent. Bill cautiously slipped the gun from under the sled-lashing. The gun was on the way to his shoulder, but it never got there. For in that instant the she-wolf leaped sidewise from the trail into the clump of spruce trees and disappeared.

The two men looked at each other. Henry whistled long and comprehendingly.

"I might have knowed it," Bill chided himself aloud as he replaced the gun. "Of course a wolf that knows enough to come in with the dogs at feedin' time, 'd know all about shooting-irons. I tell you right now, Henry, that critter's the cause of all our trouble. We'd have six dogs at the present time, 'stead of three, if it wasn't for her. An' I tell you right now, Henry, I'm goin' to get her. She's too smart to be shot in the open. But I'm goin' to lay for her. I'll bushwhack her as sure as my name is Bill."

"You needn't stray off too far in doin' it," his partner admonished. "If that pack ever starts to jump you, them three cartridges'd be wuth no more'n three whoops in hell. Them animals is damn hungry, an' once they start in, they'll sure get you, Bill."

They camped early that night. Three dogs could not drag the sled so fast nor for so long hours as could six, and they were showing unmistakable signs of playing out. And the men went early to bed, Bill first seeing to it that the dogs were tied out of gnawing-reach of one another.

But the wolves were growing bolder, and the men were aroused more than once from their sleep. So near did the wolves approach, that the dogs became frantic with terror, and it was necessary to replenish the fire from time to time in order to keep the adventurous marauders at safer distance.

"I've hearn sailors talk of sharks followin' a ship," Bill remarked, as he crawled back into the blankets after one such replenishing of the fire. "Well, them wolves is land sharks. They know their business better'n we do, an' they ain't a-holdin' our trail this way for their health. They're goin' to get us. They're sure goin' to get us, Henry."

"They've half got you a'ready, a-talkin' like that," Henry retorted sharply. "A man's half licked when he says he is. An' you're half eaten from the way you're goin' on about it."

"They've got away with better men than you an' me," Bill answered.

"Oh, shet up your croakin'. You make me all-fired tired."

Henry rolled over angrily on his side, but was surprised that Bill made no similar display of temper. This was not Bill's way, for he was easily angered by sharp words. Henry thought long over it before he went to sleep, and as his eyelids fluttered down and he dozed off, the thought in his mind was: "There's no mistakin' it, Bill's almighty blue. I'll have to cheer him up to-morrow."

CHAPTER III—THE HUNGER CRY

The day began auspiciously. They had lost no dogs during the night, and they swung out upon the trail and into the silence, the darkness, and the cold with spirits that were fairly light. Bill seemed to have forgotten his forebodings of the previous night, and even waxed facetious with the dogs when, at midday, they overturned the sled on a bad piece of trail.

It was an awkward mix-up. The sled was upside down and jammed between a tree-trunk and a huge rock, and they were forced to unharness the dogs in order to straighten out the tangle. The two men were bent over the sled and trying to right it, when Henry observed One Ear sidling away.

"Here, you, One Ear!" he cried, straightening up and turning around on the dog.

But One Ear broke into a run across the snow, his traces trailing behind him. And there, out in the snow of their back track, was the she-wolf waiting for him. As he neared her, he became suddenly cautious. He slowed down to an alert and mincing walk and then stopped. He regarded her carefully and dubiously, yet desirefully. She seemed to smile at him, showing her teeth in an ingratiating rather than a menacing way. She moved toward him a few steps, playfully, and then halted. One Ear drew near to her, still alert and cautious, his tail and ears in the air, his head held high.

He tried to sniff noses with her, but she retreated playfully and coyly. Every advance on his part was accompanied by a corresponding retreat on her part. Step by step she was luring him away from the security of his human companionship. Once, as though a warning had in vague ways flitted through his intelligence, he turned his head and looked back at the overturned sled, at his team-mates, and at the two men who were calling to him.

But whatever idea was forming in his mind, was dissipated by the she-wolf, who advanced upon him, sniffed noses with him for a fleeting instant, and then resumed her coy retreat before his renewed advances.

In the meantime, Bill had bethought himself of the rifle. But it was jammed beneath the overturned sled, and by the time Henry had helped him to right the load, One Ear and the she-wolf were too close together and the distance too great to risk a shot.

Too late One Ear learned his mistake. Before they saw the cause, the two men saw him turn and start to run back toward them. Then, approaching at right angles to the trail and cutting off his retreat they saw a dozen wolves, lean and grey, bounding across the snow. On the instant, the she-wolf's coyness and playfulness disappeared.

With a snarl she sprang upon One Ear. He thrust her off with his shoulder, and, his retreat cut off and still intent on regaining the sled, he altered his course in an attempt to circle around to it. More wolves were appearing every moment and joining in the chase. The she-wolf was one leap behind One Ear and holding her own.

"Where are you goin'?" Henry suddenly demanded, laying his hand on his partner's arm.

Bill shook it off. "I won't stand it," he said. "They ain't a-goin' to get any more of our dogs if I can help it."

Gun in hand, he plunged into the underbrush that lined the side of the trail. His intention was apparent enough. Taking the sled as the centre of the circle that One Ear was making, Bill planned to tap that circle at a point in advance of the pursuit. With his rifle, in the broad daylight, it might be possible for him to awe the wolves and save the dog.

"Say, Bill!" Henry called after him. "Be careful! Don't take no chances!"

Henry sat down on the sled and watched. There was nothing else for him to do. Bill had already gone from sight; but now and again, appearing and disappearing amongst the underbrush and the scattered clumps of spruce, could be seen One Ear. Henry judged his case to be hopeless. The dog was thoroughly alive to its danger, but it was running on the outer circle while the wolf-pack was running on the inner and shorter circle. It was vain to think of One Ear so outdistancing his pursuers as to be able to cut across their circle in advance of them and to regain the sled.

The different lines were rapidly approaching a point. Somewhere out there in the snow, screened from his sight by trees and thickets, Henry knew that the wolf-pack, One Ear, and Bill were coming together. All too quickly, far more quickly than he had expected, it happened. He heard a shot, then two shots, in rapid succession, and he knew that Bill's ammunition was gone. Then he heard a great outcry of snarls and yelps. He recognised One Ear's yell of pain and terror, and he heard a wolf-cry that bespoke a stricken animal. And that was all. The snarls ceased. The yelping died away. Silence settled down again over the lonely land.

He sat for a long while upon the sled. There was no need for him to go and see what had happened. He knew it as though it had taken place before his eyes. Once, he roused with a start and hastily got the axe out from underneath the lashings. But for some time longer he sat and brooded, the two remaining dogs crouching and trembling at his feet.

At last he arose in a weary manner, as though all the resilience had gone out of his body, and proceeded to fasten the dogs to the sled. He passed a rope over his shoulder, a man-trace, and pulled with the dogs. He did not go far. At the first hint of darkness he hastened to make a camp, and he saw to it that he had a generous supply of firewood. He fed the dogs, cooked and ate his supper, and made his bed close to the fire.

But he was not destined to enjoy that bed. Before his eyes closed the wolves had drawn too near for safety. It no longer required an effort of the vision to see them. They were all about him and the fire, in a narrow circle, and he could see them plainly in the firelight lying down, sitting up, crawling forward on their bellies, or slinking back and forth. They even slept. Here and there he could see one curled up in the snow like a dog, taking the sleep that was now denied himself.

CHAPTER III—THE HUNGER CRY

He kept the fire brightly blazing, for he knew that it alone intervened between the flesh of his body and their hungry fangs. His two dogs stayed close by him, one on either side, leaning against him for protection, crying and whimpering, and at times snarling desperately when a wolf approached a little closer than usual. At such moments, when his dogs snarled, the whole circle would be agitated, the wolves coming to their feet and pressing tentatively forward, a chorus of snarls and eager yelps rising about him. Then the circle would lie down again, and here and there a wolf would resume its broken nap.

But this circle had a continuous tendency to draw in upon him. Bit by bit, an inch at a time, with here a wolf bellying forward, and there a wolf bellying forward, the circle would narrow until the brutes were almost within springing distance. Then he would seize brands from the fire and hurl them into the pack. A hasty drawing back always resulted, accompanied by angry yelps and frightened snarls when a well-aimed brand struck and scorched a too daring animal.

Morning found the man haggard and worn, wide-eyed from want of sleep. He cooked breakfast in the darkness, and at nine o'clock, when, with the coming of daylight, the wolf-pack drew back, he set about the task he had planned through the long hours of the night. Chopping down young saplings, he made them cross-bars of a scaffold by lashing them high up to the trunks of standing trees. Using the sled-lashing for a heaving rope, and with the aid of the dogs, he hoisted the coffin to the top of the scaffold.

"They got Bill, an' they may get me, but they'll sure never get you, young man," he said, addressing the dead body in its tree-sepulchre.

Then he took the trail, the lightened sled bounding along behind the willing dogs; for they, too, knew that safety lay open in the gaining of Fort McGurry. The wolves were now more open in their pursuit, trotting sedately behind and ranging along on either side, their red tongues lolling out, their lean sides showing the undulating ribs with every movement. They were very lean, mere skin-bags stretched over bony frames, with strings for muscles—so lean that Henry found it in his mind to marvel that they still kept their feet and did not collapse forthright in the snow.

He did not dare travel until dark. At midday, not only did the sun warm the southern horizon, but it even thrust its upper rim, pale and golden, above the sky-line. He received it as a sign. The days were growing longer. The sun was returning. But scarcely had the cheer of its light departed, than he went into camp. There were still several hours of grey daylight and sombre twilight, and he utilised them in chopping an enormous supply of fire-wood.

With night came horror. Not only were the starving wolves growing bolder, but lack of sleep was telling upon Henry. He dozed despite himself, crouching by the fire, the blankets about his shoulders, the axe between his knees, and on either side a dog pressing close against him. He awoke once and saw in front of him, not a dozen feet away, a big grey wolf, one of the largest of the pack. And even as he looked, the brute deliberately stretched himself after the manner of a lazy dog, yawning full in his face and looking upon him with a possessive eye, as if, in truth, he were merely a delayed meal that was soon to be eaten.

This certitude was shown by the whole pack. Fully a score he could count, staring hungrily at him or calmly sleeping in the snow. They reminded him of children gathered about a spread table and awaiting permission to begin to eat. And he was the food they were to eat! He wondered how and when the meal would begin.

As he piled wood on the fire he discovered an appreciation of his own body which he had never felt before. He watched his moving muscles and was interested in the cunning mechanism of his fingers. By the light of the fire he crooked his fingers slowly and repeatedly now one at a time, now all together, spreading them wide or making quick gripping movements. He studied the nail-formation, and prodded the finger-tips, now sharply, and again softly, gauging the while the nerve-sensations produced. It fascinated him, and he grew suddenly fond of this subtle flesh of his that worked so beautifully and smoothly and delicately. Then he would cast a glance of fear at the wolf-circle drawn expectantly about him, and like a blow the realisation would strike him that this wonderful body of his, this living flesh, was no more than so much meat, a quest of ravenous animals, to be torn and slashed by their hungry fangs, to be sustenance to them as the moose and the rabbit had often been sustenance to him.

He came out of a doze that was half nightmare, to see the red-hued she-wolf before him. She was not more than half a dozen feet away sitting in the snow and wistfully regarding him. The two dogs were whimpering and snarling at his feet, but she took no notice of them. She was looking at the man, and for some time he returned her look. There was nothing threatening about her. She looked at him merely with a great wistfulness, but he knew it to be the wistfulness of an equally great hunger. He was the food, and the sight of him excited in her the gustatory sensations. Her mouth opened, the saliva drooled forth, and she licked her chops with the pleasure of anticipation.

A spasm of fear went through him. He reached hastily for a brand to throw at her. But even as he reached, and before his fingers had closed on the missile, she sprang back into safety; and he knew that she was used to having things thrown at her. She had snarled as she sprang away, baring her white fangs to their roots, all her wistfulness vanishing, being replaced by a carnivorous malignity that made him shudder. He glanced at the hand that held the brand, noticing the cunning delicacy of the fingers that gripped it, how they adjusted themselves to all the inequalities of the surface, curling over and under and about the rough wood, and one little finger, too close to the burning portion of the brand, sensitively and automatically writhing back from the hurtful heat to a cooler gripping-place; and in the same instant he seemed to see a vision of those same sensitive and delicate fingers being crushed and torn by the white teeth of the she-wolf. Never had he been so fond of this body of his as now when his tenure of it was so precarious.

All night, with burning brands, he fought off the hungry pack. When he dozed despite himself, the whimpering and snarling of the dogs aroused him. Morning came, but for the first time the light of day failed to scatter the wolves. The man waited in vain for them to go. They remained in a circle about him and his fire, displaying an arrogance of possession that shook his courage born of the morning light.

He made one desperate attempt to pull out on the trail. But the moment he left the protection of the fire, the boldest wolf leaped for him, but leaped short. He saved himself by springing back, the jaws snapping together a scant six inches from his thigh. The rest of the pack was now up and surging upon him, and a throwing of firebrands right and left was necessary to drive them back to a respectful distance.

CHAPTER III—THE HUNGER CRY

Even in the daylight he did not dare leave the fire to chop fresh wood. Twenty feet away towered a huge dead spruce. He spent half the day extending his campfire to the tree, at any moment a half dozen burning faggots ready at hand to fling at his enemies. Once at the tree, he studied the surrounding forest in order to fell the tree in the direction of the most firewood.

The night was a repetition of the night before, save that the need for sleep was becoming overpowering. The snarling of his dogs was losing its efficacy. Besides, they were snarling all the time, and his benumbed and drowsy senses no longer took note of changing pitch and intensity. He awoke with a start. The she-wolf was less than a yard from him. Mechanically, at short range, without letting go of it, he thrust a brand full into her open and snarling mouth. She sprang away, yelling with pain, and while he took delight in the smell of burning flesh and hair, he watched her shaking her head and growling wrathfully a score of feet away.

But this time, before he dozed again, he tied a burning pine-knot to his right hand. His eyes were closed but few minutes when the burn of the flame on his flesh awakened him. For several hours he adhered to this programme. Every time he was thus awakened he drove back the wolves with flying brands, replenished the fire, and rearranged the pine-knot on his hand. All worked well, but there came a time when he fastened the pine-knot insecurely. As his eyes closed it fell away from his hand.

He dreamed. It seemed to him that he was in Fort McGurry. It was warm and comfortable, and he was playing cribbage with the Factor. Also, it seemed to him that the fort was besieged by wolves. They were howling at the very gates, and sometimes he and the Factor paused from the game to listen and laugh at the futile efforts of the wolves to get in. And then, so strange was the dream, there was a crash. The door was burst open. He could see the wolves flooding into the big living-room of the fort. They were leaping straight for him and the Factor. With the bursting open of the door, the noise of their howling had increased tremendously. This howling now bothered him. His dream was merging into something else—he knew not what; but through it all, following him, persisted the howling.

And then he awoke to find the howling real. There was a great snarling and yelping. The wolves were rushing him. They were all about him and upon him. The teeth of one had closed upon his arm. Instinctively he leaped into the fire, and as he leaped, he felt the sharp slash of teeth that tore through the flesh of his leg. Then began a fire fight. His stout mittens temporarily protected his hands, and he scooped live coals into the air in all directions, until the campfire took on the semblance of a volcano.

But it could not last long. His face was blistering in the heat, his eyebrows and lashes were singed off, and the heat was becoming unbearable to his feet. With a flaming brand in each hand, he sprang to the edge of the fire. The wolves had been driven back. On every side, wherever the live coals had fallen, the snow was sizzling, and every little while a retiring wolf, with wild leap and snort and snarl, announced that one such live coal had been stepped upon.

Flinging his brands at the nearest of his enemies, the man thrust his smouldering mittens into the snow and stamped about to cool his feet. His two dogs were missing, and he well knew that they had served as a course in the protracted meal which had begun days before with Fatty, the last course of which would likely be himself in the days to follow.

"You ain't got me yet!" he cried, savagely shaking his fist at the hungry beasts; and at the sound of his voice the whole circle was agitated, there was a general snarl, and the she-wolf slid up close to him across the snow and watched him with hungry wistfulness.

He set to work to carry out a new idea that had come to him. He extended the fire into a large circle. Inside this circle he crouched, his sleeping outfit under him as a protection against the melting snow. When he had thus disappeared within his shelter of flame, the whole pack came curiously to the rim of the fire to see what had become of him. Hitherto they had been denied access to the fire, and they now settled down in a close-drawn circle, like so many dogs, blinking and yawning and stretching their lean bodies in the unaccustomed warmth. Then the she-wolf sat down, pointed her nose at a star, and began to howl. One by one the wolves joined her, till the whole pack, on haunches, with noses pointed skyward, was howling its hunger cry.

Dawn came, and daylight. The fire was burning low. The fuel had run out, and there was need to get more. The man attempted to step out of his circle of flame, but the wolves surged to meet him. Burning brands made them spring aside, but they no longer sprang back. In vain he strove to drive them back. As he gave up and stumbled inside his circle, a wolf leaped for him, missed, and landed with all four feet in the coals. It cried out with terror, at the same time snarling, and scrambled back to cool its paws in the snow.

The man sat down on his blankets in a crouching position. His body leaned forward from the hips. His shoulders, relaxed and drooping, and his head on his knees advertised that he had given up the struggle. Now and again he raised his head to note the dying down of the fire. The circle of flame and coals was breaking into segments with openings in between. These openings grew in size, the segments diminished.

"I guess you can come an' get me any time," he mumbled. "Anyway, I'm goin' to sleep."

Once he awakened, and in an opening in the circle, directly in front of him, he saw the she-wolf gazing at him.

Again he awakened, a little later, though it seemed hours to him. A mysterious change had taken place—so mysterious a change that he was shocked wider awake. Something had happened. He could not understand at first. Then he discovered it. The wolves were gone. Remained only the trampled snow to show how closely they had pressed him. Sleep was welling up and gripping him again, his head was sinking down upon his knees, when he roused with a sudden start.

There were cries of men, and churn of sleds, the creaking of harnesses, and the eager whimpering of straining dogs. Four sleds pulled in from the river bed to the camp among the trees. Half a dozen men were about the man who crouched in the centre of the dying fire. They were shaking and prodding him into consciousness. He looked at them like a drunken man and maundered in strange, sleepy speech.

"Red she-wolf. . . . Come in with the dogs at feedin' time. . . . First she ate the dog-food. . . . Then she ate the dogs. . . . An' after that she ate Bill. . . . "

"Where's Lord Alfred?" one of the men bellowed in his ear, shaking him roughly.

He shook his head slowly. "No, she didn't eat him. . . . He's roostin' in a tree at the last camp."

"Dead?" the man shouted.

"An' in a box," Henry answered. He jerked his shoulder petulantly away from the grip of his questioner. "Say, you lemme alone. . . . I'm jes' plump tuckered out. . . . Goo' night, everybody."

His eyes fluttered and went shut. His chin fell forward on his chest. And even as they eased him down upon the blankets his snores were rising on the frosty air.

But there was another sound. Far and faint it was, in the remote distance, the cry of the hungry wolf-pack as it took the trail of other meat than the man it had just missed.

PART II

CHAPTER I—THE BATTLE OF THE FANGS

It was the she-wolf who had first caught the sound of men's voices and the whining of the sled-dogs; and it was the she-wolf who was first to spring away from the cornered man in his circle of dying flame. The pack had been loath to forego the kill it had hunted down, and it lingered for several minutes, making sure of the sounds, and then it, too, sprang away on the trail made by the she-wolf.

Running at the forefront of the pack was a large grey wolf—one of its several leaders. It was he who directed the pack's course on the heels of the she-wolf. It was he who snarled warningly at the younger members of the pack or slashed at them with his fangs when they ambitiously tried to pass him. And it was he who increased the pace when he sighted the she-wolf, now trotting slowly across the snow.

She dropped in alongside by him, as though it were her appointed position, and took the pace of the pack. He did not snarl at her, nor show his teeth, when any leap of hers chanced to put her in advance of him. On the contrary, he seemed kindly disposed toward her—too kindly to suit her, for he was prone to run near to her, and when he ran too near it was she who snarled and showed her teeth. Nor was she above slashing his shoulder sharply on occasion. At such times he betrayed no anger. He merely sprang to the side and ran stiffly ahead for several awkward leaps, in carriage and conduct resembling an abashed country swain.

This was his one trouble in the running of the pack; but she had other troubles. On her other side ran a gaunt old wolf, grizzled and marked with the scars of many battles. He ran always on her right side. The fact that he had but one eye, and that the left eye, might account for this. He, also, was addicted to crowding her, to veering toward her till his scarred muzzle touched her body, or shoulder, or neck. As with the running mate on the left, she repelled these attentions with her teeth; but when both bestowed their attentions at the same time she was roughly jostled, being compelled, with quick snaps to either side, to drive both lovers away and at the same time to maintain her forward leap with the pack and see the way of her feet before her. At such times her running mates flashed their teeth and growled threateningly across at each other. They might have fought, but even wooing and its rivalry waited upon the more pressing hunger-need of the pack.

After each repulse, when the old wolf sheered abruptly away from the sharp-toothed object of his desire, he shouldered against a young three-year-old that ran on his blind right side. This young wolf had attained his full size; and, considering the weak and famished condition of the pack, he possessed more than the average vigour and spirit. Nevertheless, he ran with his head even with the shoulder of his one-eyed elder. When he ventured to run abreast of the older wolf (which was seldom), a snarl and a snap sent him back even with the shoulder again. Sometimes, however, he dropped cautiously and slowly behind and edged in between the old leader and the she-wolf. This was doubly resented, even triply resented. When she snarled her displeasure, the old leader would whirl on the three-year-old. Sometimes she whirled with him. And sometimes the young leader on the left whirled, too.

At such times, confronted by three sets of savage teeth, the young wolf stopped precipitately, throwing himself back on his haunches, with fore-legs stiff, mouth menacing, and mane bristling. This confusion in the front of the moving pack always caused confusion in the rear. The wolves behind collided with the young wolf and expressed their displeasure by administering sharp nips on his hind-legs and flanks. He was laying up trouble for himself, for lack of food and short tempers went together; but with the boundless faith of youth he persisted in repeating the manoeuvre every little while, though it never succeeded in gaining anything for him but discomfiture.

Had there been food, love-making and fighting would have gone on apace, and the pack-formation would have been broken up. But the situation of the pack was desperate. It was lean with long-standing hunger. It ran below its ordinary speed. At the rear limped the weak members, the very young and the very old. At the front were the strongest. Yet all were more like skeletons than full-bodied wolves. Nevertheless, with the exception of the ones that limped, the movements of the animals were effortless and tireless. Their stringy muscles seemed founts of inexhaustible energy. Behind every steel-like contraction of a muscle, lay another steel-like contraction, and another, and another, apparently without end.

They ran many miles that day. They ran through the night. And the next day found them still running. They were running over the surface of a world frozen and dead. No life stirred. They alone moved through the vast inertness. They alone were alive, and they sought for other things that were alive in order that they might devour them and continue to live.

They crossed low divides and ranged a dozen small streams in a lower-lying country before their quest was rewarded. Then they came upon moose. It was a big bull they first found. Here was meat and life, and it was guarded by no mysterious fires nor flying missiles of flame. Splay hoofs and palmated antlers they knew, and they flung their customary patience and caution to the wind. It was a brief fight and fierce. The big bull was beset on every side. He ripped them open or split their skulls with shrewdly driven blows of his great hoofs. He crushed them and broke them on his large horns. He stamped them into the snow under him in the wallowing struggle. But he was foredoomed, and he went down with the she-wolf tearing savagely at his throat, and with other teeth fixed everywhere upon him, devouring him alive, before ever his last struggles ceased or his last damage had been wrought.

There was food in plenty. The bull weighed over eight hundred pounds—fully twenty pounds of meat per mouth for the forty-odd wolves of the pack. But if they could fast prodigiously, they could feed prodigiously, and soon a few scattered bones were all that remained of the splendid live brute that had faced the pack a few hours before.

CHAPTER I—THE BATTLE OF THE FANGS

There was now much resting and sleeping. With full stomachs, bickering and quarrelling began among the younger males, and this continued through the few days that followed before the breaking-up of the pack. The famine was over. The wolves were now in the country of game, and though they still hunted in pack, they hunted more cautiously, cutting out heavy cows or crippled old bulls from the small moose-herds they ran across.

There came a day, in this land of plenty, when the wolf-pack split in half and went in different directions. The she-wolf, the young leader on her left, and the one-eyed elder on her right, led their half of the pack down to the Mackenzie River and across into the lake country to the east. Each day this remnant of the pack dwindled. Two by two, male and female, the wolves were deserting. Occasionally a solitary male was driven out by the sharp teeth of his rivals. In the end there remained only four: the she-wolf, the young leader, the one-eyed one, and the ambitious three-year-old.

The she-wolf had by now developed a ferocious temper. Her three suitors all bore the marks of her teeth. Yet they never replied in kind, never defended themselves against her. They turned their shoulders to her most savage slashes, and with wagging tails and mincing steps strove to placate her wrath. But if they were all mildness toward her, they were all fierceness toward one another. The three-year-old grew too ambitious in his fierceness. He caught the one-eyed elder on his blind side and ripped his ear into ribbons. Though the grizzled old fellow could see only on one side, against the youth and vigour of the other he brought into play the wisdom of long years of experience. His lost eye and his scarred muzzle bore evidence to the nature of his experience. He had survived too many battles to be in doubt for a moment about what to do.

The battle began fairly, but it did not end fairly. There was no telling what the outcome would have been, for the third wolf joined the elder, and together, old leader and young leader, they attacked the ambitious three-year-old and proceeded to destroy him. He was beset on either side by the merciless fangs of his erstwhile comrades. Forgotten were the days they had hunted together, the game they had pulled down, the famine they had suffered. That business was a thing of the past. The business of love was at hand—ever a sterner and crueller business than that of food-getting.

And in the meanwhile, the she-wolf, the cause of it all, sat down contentedly on her haunches and watched. She was even pleased. This was her day—and it came not often—when manes bristled, and fang smote fang or ripped and tore the yielding flesh, all for the possession of her.

And in the business of love the three-year-old, who had made this his first adventure upon it, yielded up his life. On either side of his body stood his two rivals. They were gazing at the she-wolf, who sat smiling in the snow. But the elder leader was wise, very wise, in love even as in battle. The younger leader turned his head to lick a wound on his shoulder. The curve of his neck was turned toward his rival. With his one eye the elder saw the opportunity. He darted in low and closed with his fangs. It was a long, ripping slash, and deep as well. His teeth, in passing, burst the wall of the great vein of the throat. Then he leaped clear.

The young leader snarled terribly, but his snarl broke midmost into a tickling cough. Bleeding and coughing, already stricken, he sprang at the elder and fought while life faded from him, his legs going weak beneath him, the light of day dulling on his eyes, his blows and springs falling shorter and shorter.

And all the while the she-wolf sat on her haunches and smiled. She was made glad in vague ways by the battle, for this was the love-making of the Wild, the sex-tragedy of the natural world that was tragedy only to those that died. To those that survived it was not tragedy, but realisation and achievement.

When the young leader lay in the snow and moved no more, One Eye stalked over to the she-wolf. His carriage was one of mingled triumph and caution. He was plainly expectant of a rebuff, and he was just as plainly surprised when her teeth did not flash out at him in anger. For the first time she met him with a kindly manner. She sniffed noses with him, and even condescended to leap about and frisk and play with him in quite puppyish fashion. And he, for all his grey years and sage experience, behaved quite as puppyishly and even a little more foolishly.

Forgotten already were the vanquished rivals and the love-tale red-written on the snow. Forgotten, save once, when old One Eye stopped for a moment to lick his stiffening wounds. Then it was that his lips half writhed into a snarl, and the hair of his neck and shoulders involuntarily bristled, while he half crouched for a spring, his claws spasmodically clutching into the snow-surface for firmer footing. But it was all forgotten the next moment, as he sprang after the she-wolf, who was coyly leading him a chase through the woods.

After that they ran side by side, like good friends who have come to an understanding. The days passed by, and they kept together, hunting their meat and killing and eating it in common. After a time the she-wolf began to grow restless. She seemed to be searching for something that she could not find. The hollows under fallen trees seemed to attract her, and she spent much time nosing about among the larger snow-piled crevices in the rocks and in the caves of overhanging banks. Old One Eye was not interested at all, but he followed her good-naturedly in her quest, and when her investigations in particular places were unusually protracted, he would lie down and wait until she was ready to go on.

They did not remain in one place, but travelled across country until they regained the Mackenzie River, down which they slowly went, leaving it often to hunt game along the small streams that entered it, but always returning to it again. Sometimes they chanced upon other wolves, usually in pairs; but there was no friendliness of intercourse displayed on either side, no gladness at meeting, no desire to return to the pack-formation. Several times they encountered solitary wolves. These were always males, and they were pressingly insistent on joining with One Eye and his mate. This he resented, and when she stood shoulder to shoulder with him, bristling and showing her teeth, the aspiring solitary ones would back off, turn-tail, and continue on their lonely way.

One moonlight night, running through the quiet forest, One Eye suddenly halted. His muzzle went up, his tail stiffened, and his nostrils dilated as he scented the air. One foot also he held up, after the manner of a dog. He was not satisfied, and he continued to smell the air, striving to understand the message borne upon it to him. One careless sniff had satisfied his mate, and she trotted on to reassure him. Though he followed her, he was still dubious, and he could not forbear an occasional halt in order more carefully to study the warning.

She crept out cautiously on the edge of a large open space in the midst of the trees. For some time she stood alone. Then One Eye, creeping and crawling, every sense on the alert, every hair radiating infinite suspicion, joined her. They stood side by side, watching and listening and smelling.

To their ears came the sounds of dogs wrangling and scuffling, the guttural cries of men, the sharper voices of scolding women, and once the shrill and plaintive cry of a child. With the exception of the huge bulks of the skin-lodges, little could be seen save the flames of the fire, broken by the movements of intervening bodies, and the smoke rising slowly on the quiet air. But to their nostrils came the myriad smells of an Indian camp, carrying a story that was largely incomprehensible to One Eye, but every detail of which the she-wolf knew.

She was strangely stirred, and sniffed and sniffed with an increasing delight. But old One Eye was doubtful. He betrayed his apprehension, and started tentatively to go. She turned and touched his neck with her muzzle in a reassuring way, then regarded the camp again. A new wistfulness was in her face, but it was not the wistfulness of hunger. She was thrilling to a desire that urged her to go forward, to be in closer to that fire, to be squabbling with the dogs, and to be avoiding and dodging the stumbling feet of men.

One Eye moved impatiently beside her; her unrest came back upon her, and she knew again her pressing need to find the thing for which she searched. She turned and trotted back into the forest, to the great relief of One Eye, who trotted a little to the fore until they were well within the shelter of the trees.

As they slid along, noiseless as shadows, in the moonlight, they came upon a runway. Both noses went down to the footprints in the snow. These footprints were very fresh. One Eye ran ahead cautiously, his mate at his heels. The broad pads of their feet were spread wide and in contact with the snow were like velvet. One Eye caught sight of a dim movement of white in the midst of the white. His sliding gait had been deceptively swift, but it was as nothing to the speed at which he now ran. Before him was bounding the faint patch of white he had discovered.

They were running along a narrow alley flanked on either side by a growth of young spruce. Through the trees the mouth of the alley could be seen, opening out on a moonlit glade. Old One Eye was rapidly overhauling the fleeing shape of white. Bound by bound he gained. Now he was upon it. One leap more and his teeth would be sinking into it. But that leap was never made. High in the air, and straight up, soared the shape of white, now a struggling snowshoe rabbit that leaped and bounded, executing a fantastic dance there above him in the air and never once returning to earth.

One Eye sprang back with a snort of sudden fright, then shrank down to the snow and crouched, snarling threats at this thing of fear he did not understand. But the she-wolf coolly thrust past him. She poised for a moment, then sprang for the dancing rabbit. She, too, soared high, but not so high as the quarry, and her teeth clipped emptily together with a metallic snap. She made another leap, and another.

Her mate had slowly relaxed from his crouch and was watching her. He now evinced displeasure at her repeated failures, and himself made a mighty spring upward. His teeth closed upon the rabbit, and he bore it back to earth with him. But at the same time there was a suspicious crackling movement beside him, and his astonished eye saw a young spruce sapling bending down above him to strike him. His jaws let go their grip, and he leaped backward to escape this strange danger, his lips drawn back from his fangs, his throat snarling, every hair bristling with rage and fright. And in that moment the sapling reared its slender length upright and the rabbit soared dancing in the air again.

The she-wolf was angry. She sank her fangs into her mate's shoulder in reproof; and he, frightened, unaware of what constituted this new onslaught, struck back ferociously and in still greater fright, ripping down the side of the she-wolf's muzzle. For him to resent such reproof was equally unexpected to her, and she sprang upon him in snarling indignation. Then he discovered his mistake and tried to placate her. But she proceeded to punish him roundly, until he gave over all attempts at placation, and whirled in a circle, his head away from her, his shoulders receiving the punishment of her teeth.

In the meantime the rabbit danced above them in the air. The she-wolf sat down in the snow, and old One Eye, now more in fear of his mate than of the mysterious sapling, again sprang for the rabbit. As he sank back with it between his teeth, he kept his eye on the sapling. As before, it followed him back to earth. He crouched down under the impending blow, his hair bristling, but his teeth still keeping tight hold of the rabbit. But the blow did not fall. The sapling remained bent above him. When he moved it moved, and he growled at it through his clenched jaws; when he remained still, it remained still, and he concluded it was safer to continue remaining still. Yet the warm blood of the rabbit tasted good in his mouth.

It was his mate who relieved him from the quandary in which he found himself. She took the rabbit from him, and while the sapling swayed and teetered threateningly above her she calmly gnawed off the rabbit's head. At once the sapling shot up, and after that gave no more trouble, remaining in the decorous and perpendicular position in which nature had intended it to grow. Then, between them, the she-wolf and One Eye devoured the game which the mysterious sapling had caught for them.

There were other run-ways and alleys where rabbits were hanging in the air, and the wolf-pair prospected them all, the she-wolf leading the way, old One Eye following and observant, learning the method of robbing snares—a knowledge destined to stand him in good stead in the days to come.

CHAPTER II—THE LAIR

For two days the she-wolf and One Eye hung about the Indian camp. He was worried and apprehensive, yet the camp lured his mate and she was loath to depart. But when, one morning, the air was rent with the report of a rifle close at hand, and a bullet smashed against a tree trunk several inches from One Eye's head, they hesitated no more, but went off on a long, swinging lope that put quick miles between them and the danger.

They did not go far—a couple of days' journey. The she-wolf's need to find the thing for which she searched had now become imperative. She was getting very heavy, and could run but slowly. Once, in the pursuit of a rabbit, which she ordinarily would have caught with ease, she gave over and lay down and rested. One Eye came to her; but when he touched her neck gently with his muzzle she snapped at him with such quick fierceness that he tumbled over backward and cut a ridiculous figure in his effort to escape her teeth. Her temper was now shorter than ever; but he had become more patient than ever and more solicitous.

And then she found the thing for which she sought. It was a few miles up a small stream that in the summer time flowed into the Mackenzie, but that then was frozen over and frozen down to its rocky bottom—a dead stream of solid white from source to mouth. The she-wolf was trotting wearily along, her mate well in advance, when she came upon the overhanging, high clay-bank. She turned aside and trotted over to it. The wear and tear of spring storms and melting snows had underwashed the bank and in one place had made a small cave out of a narrow fissure.

She paused at the mouth of the cave and looked the wall over carefully. Then, on one side and the other, she ran along the base of the wall to where its abrupt bulk merged from the softer-lined landscape. Returning to the cave, she entered its narrow mouth. For a short three feet she was compelled to crouch, then the walls widened and rose higher in a little round chamber nearly six feet in diameter. The roof barely cleared her head. It was dry and cosey. She inspected it with painstaking care, while One Eye, who had returned, stood in the entrance and patiently watched her. She dropped her head, with her nose to the ground and directed toward a point near to her closely bunched feet, and around this point she circled several times; then, with a tired sigh that was almost a grunt, she curled her body in, relaxed her legs, and dropped down, her head toward the entrance. One Eye, with pointed, interested ears, laughed at her, and beyond, outlined against the white light, she could see the brush of his tail waving good-naturedly. Her own ears, with a snuggling movement, laid their sharp points backward and down against the head for a moment, while her mouth opened and her tongue lolled peaceably out, and in this way she expressed that she was pleased and satisfied.

One Eye was hungry. Though he lay down in the entrance and slept, his sleep was fitful. He kept awaking and cocking his ears at the bright world without, where the April sun was blazing across the snow. When he dozed, upon his ears would steal the faint whispers of hidden trickles of running water, and he would rouse and listen intently. The sun had come back, and all the awakening Northland world was calling to him. Life was stirring. The feel of spring was in the air, the feel of growing life under the snow, of sap ascending in the trees, of buds bursting the shackles of the frost.

He cast anxious glances at his mate, but she showed no desire to get up. He looked outside, and half a dozen snow-birds fluttered across his field of vision. He started to get up, then looked back to his mate again, and settled down and dozed. A shrill and minute singing stole upon his heating. Once, and twice, he sleepily brushed his nose with his paw. Then he woke up. There, buzzing in the air at the tip of his nose, was a lone mosquito. It was a full-grown mosquito, one that had lain frozen in a dry log all winter and that had now been thawed out by the sun. He could resist the call of the world no longer. Besides, he was hungry.

He crawled over to his mate and tried to persuade her to get up. But she only snarled at him, and he walked out alone into the bright sunshine to find the snow-surface soft under foot and the travelling difficult. He went up the frozen bed of the stream, where the snow, shaded by the trees, was yet hard and crystalline. He was gone eight hours, and he came back through the darkness hungrier than when he had started. He had found game, but he had not caught it. He had broken through the melting snow crust, and wallowed, while the snowshoe rabbits had skimmed along on top lightly as ever.

He paused at the mouth of the cave with a sudden shock of suspicion. Faint, strange sounds came from within. They were sounds not made by his mate, and yet they were remotely familiar. He bellied cautiously inside and was met by a warning snarl from the she-wolf. This he received without perturbation, though he obeyed it by keeping his distance; but he remained interested in the other sounds—faint, muffled sobbings and slubberings.

His mate warned him irritably away, and he curled up and slept in the entrance. When morning came and a dim light pervaded the lair, he again sought after the source of the remotely familiar sounds. There was a new note in his mate's warning snarl. It was a jealous note, and he was very careful in keeping a respectful distance. Nevertheless, he made out, sheltering between her legs against the length of her body, five strange little bundles of life, very feeble, very helpless, making tiny whimpering noises, with eyes that did not open to the light. He was surprised. It was not the first time in his long and successful life that this thing had happened. It had happened many times, yet each time it was as fresh a surprise as ever to him.

His mate looked at him anxiously. Every little while she emitted a low growl, and at times, when it seemed to her he approached too near, the growl shot up in her throat to a sharp snarl. Of her own experience she had no memory of the thing happening; but in her instinct, which was the experience of all the mothers of wolves, there lurked a memory of fathers that had eaten their new-born and helpless progeny.

It manifested itself as a fear strong within her, that made her prevent One Eye from more closely inspecting the cubs he had fathered.

But there was no danger. Old One Eye was feeling the urge of an impulse, that was, in turn, an instinct that had come down to him from all the fathers of wolves. He did not question it, nor puzzle over it. It was there, in the fibre of his being; and it was the most natural thing in the world that he should obey it by turning his back on his new-born family and by trotting out and away on the meat-trail whereby he lived.

Five or six miles from the lair, the stream divided, its forks going off among the mountains at a right angle. Here, leading up the left fork, he came upon a fresh track. He smelled it and found it so recent that he crouched swiftly, and looked in the direction in which it disappeared. Then he turned deliberately and took the right fork. The footprint was much larger than the one his own feet made, and he knew that in the wake of such a trail there was little meat for him.

Half a mile up the right fork, his quick ears caught the sound of gnawing teeth. He stalked the quarry and found it to be a porcupine, standing upright against a tree and trying his teeth on the bark. One Eye approached carefully but hopelessly. He knew the breed, though he had never met it so far north before; and never in his long life had porcupine served him for a meal. But he had long since learned that there was such a thing as Chance, or Opportunity, and he continued to draw near. There was never any telling what might happen, for with live things events were somehow always happening differently.

The porcupine rolled itself into a ball, radiating long, sharp needles in all directions that defied attack. In his youth One Eye had once sniffed too near a similar, apparently inert ball of quills, and had the tail flick out suddenly in his face. One quill he had carried away in his muzzle, where it had remained for weeks, a rankling flame, until it finally worked out. So he lay down, in a comfortable crouching position, his nose fully a foot away, and out of the line of the tail. Thus he waited, keeping perfectly quiet. There was no telling. Something might happen. The porcupine might unroll. There might be opportunity for a deft and ripping thrust of paw into the tender, unguarded belly.

But at the end of half an hour he arose, growled wrathfully at the motionless ball, and trotted on. He had waited too often and futilely in the past for porcupines to unroll, to waste any more time. He continued up the right fork. The day wore along, and nothing rewarded his hunt.

The urge of his awakened instinct of fatherhood was strong upon him. He must find meat. In the afternoon he blundered upon a ptarmigan. He came out of a thicket and found himself face to face with the slow-witted bird. It was sitting on a log, not a foot beyond the end of his nose. Each saw the other. The bird made a startled rise, but he struck it with his paw, and smashed it down to earth, then pounced upon it, and caught it in his teeth as it scuttled across the snow trying to rise in the air again. As his teeth crunched through the tender flesh and fragile bones, he began naturally to eat. Then he remembered, and, turning on the back-track, started for home, carrying the ptarmigan in his mouth.

A mile above the forks, running velvet-footed as was his custom, a gliding shadow that cautiously prospected each new vista of the trail, he came upon later imprints of the large tracks he had discovered in the early morning. As the track led his way, he followed, prepared to meet the maker of it at every turn of the stream.

He slid his head around a corner of rock, where began an unusually large bend in the stream, and his quick eyes made out something that sent him crouching swiftly down. It was the maker of the track, a large female lynx. She was crouching as he had crouched once that day, in front of her the tight-rolled ball of quills. If he had been a gliding shadow before, he now became the ghost of such a shadow, as he crept and circled around, and came up well to leeward of the silent, motionless pair.

He lay down in the snow, depositing the ptarmigan beside him, and with eyes peering through the needles of a low-growing spruce he watched the play of life before him—the waiting lynx and the waiting porcupine, each intent on life; and, such was the curiousness of the game, the way of life for one lay in the eating of the other, and the way of life for the other lay in being not eaten. While old One Eye, the wolf crouching in the covert, played his part, too, in the game, waiting for some strange freak of Chance, that might help him on the meat-trail which was his way of life.

Half an hour passed, an hour; and nothing happened. The balls of quills might have been a stone for all it moved; the lynx might have been frozen to marble; and old One Eye might have been dead. Yet all three animals were keyed to a tenseness of living that was almost painful, and scarcely ever would it come to them to be more alive than they were then in their seeming petrifaction.

One Eye moved slightly and peered forth with increased eagerness. Something was happening. The porcupine had at last decided that its enemy had gone away. Slowly, cautiously, it was unrolling its ball of impregnable armour. It was agitated by no tremor of anticipation. Slowly, slowly, the bristling ball straightened out and lengthened. One Eye watching, felt a sudden moistness in his mouth and a drooling of saliva, involuntary, excited by the living meat that was spreading itself like a repast before him.

Not quite entirely had the porcupine unrolled when it discovered its enemy. In that instant the lynx struck. The blow was like a flash of light. The paw, with rigid claws curving like talons, shot under the tender belly and came back with a swift ripping movement. Had the porcupine been entirely unrolled, or had it not discovered its enemy a fraction of a second before the blow was struck, the paw would have escaped unscathed; but a side-flick of the tail sank sharp quills into it as it was withdrawn.

Everything had happened at once—the blow, the counter-blow, the squeal of agony from the porcupine, the big cat's squall of sudden hurt and astonishment. One Eye half arose in his excitement, his ears up, his tail straight out and quivering behind him. The lynx's bad temper got the best of her. She sprang savagely at the thing that had hurt her. But the porcupine, squealing and grunting, with disrupted anatomy trying feebly to roll up into its ball-protection, flicked out its tail again, and again the big cat squalled with hurt and astonishment. Then she fell to backing away and sneezing, her nose bristling with quills like a monstrous pin-cushion. She brushed her nose with her paws, trying to dislodge the fiery darts, thrust it into the snow, and rubbed it against twigs and branches, and all the time leaping about, ahead, sidewise, up and down, in a frenzy of pain and fright.

She sneezed continually, and her stub of a tail was doing its best toward lashing about by giving quick, violent jerks. She quit her antics, and quieted down for a long minute. One Eye watched. And even he could not repress a start and an involuntary bristling of hair along his back when she suddenly leaped, without warning, straight up in the air, at the same time emitting a long and most terrible squall. Then she sprang away, up the trail, squalling with every leap she made.

It was not until her racket had faded away in the distance and died out that One Eye ventured forth. He walked as delicately as though all the snow were carpeted with porcupine quills, erect and ready to pierce the soft pads of his feet. The porcupine met his approach with a furious squealing and a clashing of its long teeth. It had managed to roll up in a ball again, but it was not quite the old compact ball; its muscles were too much torn for that. It had been ripped almost in half, and was still bleeding profusely.

One Eye scooped out mouthfuls of the blood-soaked snow, and chewed and tasted and swallowed. This served as a relish, and his hunger increased mightily; but he was too old in the world to forget his caution. He waited. He lay down and waited, while the porcupine grated its teeth and uttered grunts and sobs and occasional sharp little squeals. In a little while, One Eye noticed that the quills were drooping and that a great quivering had set up. The quivering came to an end suddenly. There was a final defiant clash of the long teeth. Then all the quills drooped quite down, and the body relaxed and moved no more.

With a nervous, shrinking paw, One Eye stretched out the porcupine to its full length and turned it over on its back. Nothing had happened. It was surely dead. He studied it intently for a moment, then took a careful grip with his teeth and started off down the stream, partly carrying, partly dragging the porcupine, with head turned to the side so as to avoid stepping on the prickly mass. He recollected something, dropped the burden, and trotted back to where he had left the ptarmigan. He did not hesitate a moment. He knew clearly what was to be done, and this he did by promptly eating the ptarmigan. Then he returned and took up his burden.

When he dragged the result of his day's hunt into the cave, the she-wolf inspected it, turned her muzzle to him, and lightly licked him on the neck. But the next instant she was warning him away from the cubs with a snarl that was less harsh than usual and that was more apologetic than menacing. Her instinctive fear of the father of her progeny was toning down. He was behaving as a wolf-father should, and manifesting no unholy desire to devour the young lives she had brought into the world.

CHAPTER III—THE GREY CUB

He was different from his brothers and sisters. Their hair already betrayed the reddish hue inherited from their mother, the she-wolf; while he alone, in this particular, took after his father. He was the one little grey cub of the litter. He had bred true to the straight wolf-stock—in fact, he had bred true to old One Eye himself, physically, with but a single exception, and that was he had two eyes to his father's one.

The grey cub's eyes had not been open long, yet already he could see with steady clearness. And while his eyes were still closed, he had felt, tasted, and smelled. He knew his two brothers and his two sisters very well. He had begun to romp with them in a feeble, awkward way, and even to squabble, his little throat vibrating with a queer rasping noise (the forerunner of the growl), as he worked himself into a passion. And long before his eyes had opened he had learned by touch, taste, and smell to know his mother—a fount of warmth and liquid food and tenderness. She possessed a gentle, caressing tongue that soothed him when it passed over his soft little body, and that impelled him to snuggle close against her and to doze off to sleep.

Most of the first month of his life had been passed thus in sleeping; but now he could see quite well, and he stayed awake for longer periods of time, and he was coming to learn his world quite well. His world was gloomy; but he did not know that, for he knew no other world. It was dim-lighted; but his eyes had never had to adjust themselves to any other light. His world was very small. Its limits were the walls of the lair; but as he had no knowledge of the wide world outside, he was never oppressed by the narrow confines of his existence.

But he had early discovered that one wall of his world was different from the rest. This was the mouth of the cave and the source of light. He had discovered that it was different from the other walls long before he had any thoughts of his own, any conscious volitions. It had been an irresistible attraction before ever his eyes opened and looked upon it. The light from it had beat upon his sealed lids, and the eyes and the optic nerves had pulsated to little, sparklike flashes, warm-coloured and strangely pleasing. The life of his body, and of every fibre of his body, the life that was the very substance of his body and that was apart from his own personal life, had yearned toward this light and urged his body toward it in the same way that the cunning chemistry of a plant urges it toward the sun.

Always, in the beginning, before his conscious life dawned, he had crawled toward the mouth of the cave. And in this his brothers and sisters were one with him. Never, in that period, did any of them crawl toward the dark corners of the back-wall.

The light drew them as if they were plants; the chemistry of the life that composed them demanded the light as a necessity of being; and their little puppet-bodies crawled blindly and chemically, like the tendrils of a vine. Later on, when each developed individuality and became personally conscious of impulsions and desires, the attraction of the light increased. They were always crawling and sprawling toward it, and being driven back from it by their mother.

It was in this way that the grey cub learned other attributes of his mother than the soft, soothing, tongue. In his insistent crawling toward the light, he discovered in her a nose that with a sharp nudge administered rebuke, and later, a paw, that crushed him down and rolled him over and over with swift, calculating stroke. Thus he learned hurt; and on top of it he learned to avoid hurt, first, by not incurring the risk of it; and second, when he had incurred the risk, by dodging and by retreating. These were conscious actions, and were the results of his first generalisations upon the world. Before that he had recoiled automatically from hurt, as he had crawled automatically toward the light. After that he recoiled from hurt because he *knew* that it was hurt.

He was a fierce little cub. So were his brothers and sisters. It was to be expected. He was a carnivorous animal. He came of a breed of meat-killers and meat-eaters. His father and mother lived wholly upon meat. The milk he had sucked with his first flickering life, was milk transformed directly from meat, and now, at a month old, when his eyes had been open for but a week, he was beginning himself to eat meat—meat half-digested by the she-wolf and disgorged for the five growing cubs that already made too great demand upon her breast.

But he was, further, the fiercest of the litter. He could make a louder rasping growl than any of them. His tiny rages were much more terrible than theirs. It was he that first learned the trick of rolling a fellow-cub over with a cunning paw-stroke. And it was he that first gripped another cub by the ear and pulled and tugged and growled through jaws tight-clenched. And certainly it was he that caused the mother the most trouble in keeping her litter from the mouth of the cave.

The fascination of the light for the grey cub increased from day to day. He was perpetually departing on yard-long adventures toward the cave's entrance, and as perpetually being driven back. Only he did not know it for an entrance. He did not know anything about entrances—passages whereby one goes from one place to another place. He did not know any other place, much less of a way to get there. So to him the entrance of the cave was a wall—a wall of light. As the sun was to the outside dweller, this wall was to him the sun of his world. It attracted him as a candle attracts a moth. He was always striving to attain it. The life that was so swiftly expanding within him, urged him continually toward the wall of light. The life that was within him knew that it was the one way out, the way he was predestined to tread. But he himself did not know anything about it. He did not know there was any outside at all.

There was one strange thing about this wall of light. His father (he had already come to recognise his father as the one other dweller in the world, a creature like his mother, who slept near the light and was a bringer of meat)—his father had a way of walking right into the white far wall and disappearing. The grey cub could not understand this. Though never permitted by his mother to approach that wall, he had approached the other walls, and encountered hard obstruction on the end of his tender nose. This hurt. And after several such adventures, he left the walls alone. Without thinking about it, he accepted this disappearing into the wall as a peculiarity of his father, as milk and half-digested meat were peculiarities of his mother.

In fact, the grey cub was not given to thinking—at least, to the kind of thinking customary of men. His brain worked in dim ways. Yet his conclusions were as sharp and distinct as those achieved by men. He had a method of accepting things, without questioning the why and wherefore. In reality, this was the act of classification. He was never disturbed over why a thing happened. How it happened was sufficient for him. Thus, when he had bumped his nose on the back-wall a few times, he accepted that he would not disappear into walls. In the same way he accepted that his father could disappear into walls. But he was not in the least disturbed by desire to find out the reason for the difference between his father and himself. Logic and physics were no part of his mental make-up.

Like most creatures of the Wild, he early experienced famine. There came a time when not only did the meat-supply cease, but the milk no longer came from his mother's breast. At first, the cubs whimpered and cried, but for the most part they slept. It was not long before they were reduced to a coma of hunger. There were no more spats and squabbles, no more tiny rages nor attempts at growling; while the adventures toward the far white wall ceased altogether. The cubs slept, while the life that was in them flickered and died down.

One Eye was desperate. He ranged far and wide, and slept but little in the lair that had now become cheerless and miserable. The she-wolf, too, left her litter and went out in search of meat. In the first days after the birth of the cubs, One Eye had journeyed several times back to the Indian camp and robbed the rabbit snares; but, with the melting of the snow and the opening of the streams, the Indian camp had moved away, and that source of supply was closed to him.

When the grey cub came back to life and again took interest in the far white wall, he found that the population of his world had been reduced. Only one sister remained to him. The rest were gone. As he grew stronger, he found himself compelled to play alone, for the sister no longer lifted her head nor moved about. His little body rounded out with the meat he now ate; but the food had come too late for her. She slept continuously, a tiny skeleton flung round with skin in which the flame flickered lower and lower and at last went out.

Then there came a time when the grey cub no longer saw his father appearing and disappearing in the wall nor lying down asleep in the entrance. This had happened at the end of a second and less severe famine. The she-wolf knew why One Eye never came back, but there was no way by which she could tell what she had seen to the grey cub. Hunting herself for meat, up the left fork of the stream where lived the lynx, she had followed a day-old trail of One Eye. And she had found him, or what remained of him, at the end of the trail. There were many signs of the battle that had been fought, and of the lynx's withdrawal to her lair after having won the victory. Before she went away, the she-wolf had found this lair, but the signs told her that the lynx was inside, and she had not dared to venture in.

After that, the she-wolf in her hunting avoided the left fork. For she knew that in the lynx's lair was a litter of kittens, and she knew the lynx for a fierce, bad-tempered creature and a terrible fighter. It was all very well for half a dozen wolves to drive a lynx, spitting and bristling, up a tree; but it was quite a different matter for a lone wolf to encounter a lynx—especially when the lynx was known to have a litter of hungry kittens at her back.

But the Wild is the Wild, and motherhood is motherhood, at all times fiercely protective whether in the Wild or out of it; and the time was to come when the she-wolf, for her grey cub's sake, would venture the left fork, and the lair in the rocks, and the lynx's wrath.

CHAPTER IV—THE WALL OF THE WORLD

By the time his mother began leaving the cave on hunting expeditions, the cub had learned well the law that forbade his approaching the entrance. Not only had this law been forcibly and many times impressed on him by his mother's nose and paw, but in him the instinct of fear was developing. Never, in his brief cave-life, had he encountered anything of which to be afraid. Yet fear was in him. It had come down to him from a remote ancestry through a thousand thousand lives. It was a heritage he had received directly from One Eye and the she-wolf; but to them, in turn, it had been passed down through all the generations of wolves that had gone before. Fear!—that legacy of the Wild which no animal may escape nor exchange for pottage.

So the grey cub knew fear, though he knew not the stuff of which fear was made. Possibly he accepted it as one of the restrictions of life. For he had already learned that there were such restrictions. Hunger he had known; and when he could not appease his hunger he had felt restriction. The hard obstruction of the cave-wall, the sharp nudge of his mother's nose, the smashing stroke of her paw, the hunger unappeased of several famines, had borne in upon him that all was not freedom in the world, that to life there was limitations and restraints. These limitations and restraints were laws. To be obedient to them was to escape hurt and make for happiness.

He did not reason the question out in this man fashion. He merely classified the things that hurt and the things that did not hurt. And after such classification he avoided the things that hurt, the restrictions and restraints, in order to enjoy the satisfactions and the remunerations of life.

Thus it was that in obedience to the law laid down by his mother, and in obedience to the law of that unknown and nameless thing, fear, he kept away from the mouth of the cave. It remained to him a white wall of light. When his mother was absent, he slept most of the time, while during the intervals that he was awake he kept very quiet, suppressing the whimpering cries that tickled in his throat and strove for noise.

Once, lying awake, he heard a strange sound in the white wall. He did not know that it was a wolverine, standing outside, all a-trembling with its own daring, and cautiously scenting out the contents of the cave. The cub knew only that the sniff was strange, a something unclassified, therefore unknown and terrible—for the unknown was one of the chief elements that went into the making of fear.

The hair bristled upon the grey cub's back, but it bristled silently. How was he to know that this thing that sniffed was a thing at which to bristle? It was not born of any knowledge of his, yet it was the visible expression of the fear that was in him, and for which, in his own life, there was no accounting. But fear was accompanied by another instinct—that of concealment. The cub was in a frenzy of terror, yet he lay without movement or sound, frozen, petrified into immobility, to all appearances dead. His mother, coming home, growled as she smelt the wolverine's track, and bounded into the cave and licked and nozzled him with undue vehemence of affection. And the cub felt that somehow he had escaped a great hurt.

But there were other forces at work in the cub, the greatest of which was growth. Instinct and law demanded of him obedience. But growth demanded disobedience. His mother and fear impelled him to keep away from the white wall. Growth is life, and life is for ever destined to make for light. So there was no damming up the tide of life that was rising within him—rising with every mouthful of meat he swallowed, with every breath he drew. In the end, one day, fear and obedience were swept away by the rush of life, and the cub straddled and sprawled toward the entrance.

Unlike any other wall with which he had had experience, this wall seemed to recede from him as he approached. No hard surface collided with the tender little nose he thrust out tentatively before him. The substance of the wall seemed as permeable and yielding as light. And as condition, in his eyes, had the seeming of form, so he entered into what had been wall to him and bathed in the substance that composed it.

It was bewildering. He was sprawling through solidity. And ever the light grew brighter. Fear urged him to go back, but growth drove him on. Suddenly he found himself at the mouth of the cave. The wall, inside which he had thought himself, as suddenly leaped back before him to an immeasurable distance. The light had become painfully bright. He was dazzled by it. Likewise he was made dizzy by this abrupt and tremendous extension of space. Automatically, his eyes were adjusting themselves to the brightness, focusing themselves to meet the increased distance of objects. At first, the wall had leaped beyond his vision. He now saw it again; but it had taken upon itself a remarkable remoteness. Also, its appearance had changed. It was now a variegated wall, composed of the trees that fringed the stream, the opposing mountain that towered above the trees, and the sky that out-towered the mountain.

A great fear came upon him. This was more of the terrible unknown. He crouched down on the lip of the cave and gazed out on the world. He was very much afraid. Because it was unknown, it was hostile to him. Therefore the hair stood up on end along his back and his lips wrinkled weakly in an attempt at a ferocious and intimidating snarl. Out of his puniness and fright he challenged and menaced the whole wide world.

Nothing happened. He continued to gaze, and in his interest he forgot to snarl. Also, he forgot to be afraid. For the time, fear had been routed by growth, while growth had assumed the guise of curiosity. He began to notice near objects—an open portion of the stream that flashed in the sun, the blasted pine-tree that stood at the base of the slope, and the slope itself, that ran right up to him and ceased two feet beneath the lip of the cave on which he crouched.

Now the grey cub had lived all his days on a level floor. He had never experienced the hurt of a fall. He did not know what a fall was. So he stepped boldly out upon the air. His hind-legs still rested on the cave-lip, so he fell forward head downward. The earth struck him a harsh blow on the nose that made him yelp. Then he began rolling down the slope, over and over. He was in a panic of terror. The unknown had caught him at last. It had gripped savagely hold of him and was about to wreak upon him some terrific hurt. Growth was now routed by fear, and he ki-yi'd like any frightened puppy.

The unknown bore him on he knew not to what frightful hurt, and he yelped and ki-yi'd unceasingly. This was a different proposition from crouching in frozen fear while the unknown lurked just alongside. Now the unknown had caught tight hold of him. Silence would do no good. Besides, it was not fear, but terror, that convulsed him.

But the slope grew more gradual, and its base was grass-covered. Here the cub lost momentum. When at last he came to a stop, he gave one last agonised yell and then a long, whimpering wail. Also, and quite as a matter of course, as though in his life he had already made a thousand toilets, he proceeded to lick away the dry clay that soiled him.

After that he sat up and gazed about him, as might the first man of the earth who landed upon Mars. The cub had broken through the wall of the world, the unknown had let go its hold of him, and here he was without hurt. But the first man on Mars would have experienced less unfamiliarity than did he. Without any antecedent knowledge, without any warning whatever that such existed, he found himself an explorer in a totally new world.

Now that the terrible unknown had let go of him, he forgot that the unknown had any terrors. He was aware only of curiosity in all the things about him. He inspected the grass beneath him, the moss-berry plant just beyond, and the dead trunk of the blasted pine that stood on the edge of an open space among the trees. A squirrel, running around the base of the trunk, came full upon him, and gave him a great fright. He cowered down and snarled. But the squirrel was as badly scared. It ran up the tree, and from a point of safety chattered back savagely.

This helped the cub's courage, and though the woodpecker he next encountered gave him a start, he proceeded confidently on his way. Such was his confidence, that when a moose-bird impudently hopped up to him, he reached out at it with a playful paw. The result was a sharp peck on the end of his nose that made him cower down and ki-yi. The noise he made was too much for the moose-bird, who sought safety in flight.

But the cub was learning. His misty little mind had already made an unconscious classification. There were live things and things not alive. Also, he must watch out for the live things. The things not alive remained always in one place, but the live things moved about, and there was no telling what they might do. The thing to expect of them was the unexpected, and for this he must be prepared.

He travelled very clumsily. He ran into sticks and things. A twig that he thought a long way off, would the next instant hit him on the nose or rake along his ribs. There were inequalities of surface. Sometimes he overstepped and stubbed his nose. Quite as often he understepped and stubbed his feet. Then there were the pebbles and stones that turned under him when he trod upon them; and from them he came to know that the things not alive were not all in the same state of stable equilibrium as was his cave—also, that small things not alive were more liable than large things to fall down or turn over. But with every mishap he was learning. The longer he walked, the better he walked. He was adjusting himself. He was learning to calculate his own muscular movements, to know his physical limitations, to measure distances between objects, and between objects and himself.

CHAPTER IV—THE WALL OF THE WORLD

His was the luck of the beginner. Born to be a hunter of meat (though he did not know it), he blundered upon meat just outside his own cave-door on his first foray into the world. It was by sheer blundering that he chanced upon the shrewdly hidden ptarmigan nest. He fell into it. He had essayed to walk along the trunk of a fallen pine. The rotten bark gave way under his feet, and with a despairing yelp he pitched down the rounded crescent, smashed through the leafage and stalks of a small bush, and in the heart of the bush, on the ground, fetched up in the midst of seven ptarmigan chicks.

They made noises, and at first he was frightened at them. Then he perceived that they were very little, and he became bolder. They moved. He placed his paw on one, and its movements were accelerated. This was a source of enjoyment to him. He smelled it. He picked it up in his mouth. It struggled and tickled his tongue. At the same time he was made aware of a sensation of hunger. His jaws closed together. There was a crunching of fragile bones, and warm blood ran in his mouth. The taste of it was good. This was meat, the same as his mother gave him, only it was alive between his teeth and therefore better. So he ate the ptarmigan. Nor did he stop till he had devoured the whole brood. Then he licked his chops in quite the same way his mother did, and began to crawl out of the bush.

He encountered a feathered whirlwind. He was confused and blinded by the rush of it and the beat of angry wings. He hid his head between his paws and yelped. The blows increased. The mother ptarmigan was in a fury. Then he became angry. He rose up, snarling, striking out with his paws. He sank his tiny teeth into one of the wings and pulled and tugged sturdily. The ptarmigan struggled against him, showering blows upon him with her free wing. It was his first battle. He was elated. He forgot all about the unknown. He no longer was afraid of anything. He was fighting, tearing at a live thing that was striking at him. Also, this live thing was meat. The lust to kill was on him. He had just destroyed little live things. He would now destroy a big live thing. He was too busy and happy to know that he was happy. He was thrilling and exulting in ways new to him and greater to him than any he had known before.

He held on to the wing and growled between his tight-clenched teeth. The ptarmigan dragged him out of the bush. When she turned and tried to drag him back into the bush's shelter, he pulled her away from it and on into the open. And all the time she was making outcry and striking with her free wing, while feathers were flying like a snow-fall. The pitch to which he was aroused was tremendous. All the fighting blood of his breed was up in him and surging through him. This was living, though he did not know it. He was realising his own meaning in the world; he was doing that for which he was made—killing meat and battling to kill it. He was justifying his existence, than which life can do no greater; for life achieves its summit when it does to the uttermost that which it was equipped to do.

After a time, the ptarmigan ceased her struggling. He still held her by the wing, and they lay on the ground and looked at each other. He tried to growl threateningly, ferociously. She pecked on his nose, which by now, what of previous adventures was sore. He winced but held on. She pecked him again and again. From wincing he went to whimpering. He tried to back away from her, oblivious to the fact that by his hold on her he dragged her after him. A rain of pecks fell on his ill-used nose. The flood of fight ebbed down in him, and, releasing his prey, he turned tail and scampered on across the open in inglorious retreat.

He lay down to rest on the other side of the open, near the edge of the bushes, his tongue lolling out, his chest heaving and panting, his nose still hurting him and causing him to continue his whimper. But as he lay there, suddenly there came to him a feeling as of something terrible impending. The unknown with all its terrors rushed upon him, and he shrank back instinctively into the shelter of the bush. As he did so, a draught of air fanned him, and a large, winged body swept ominously and silently past. A hawk, driving down out of the blue, had barely missed him.

While he lay in the bush, recovering from his fright and peering fearfully out, the mother-ptarmigan on the other side of the open space fluttered out of the ravaged nest. It was because of her loss that she paid no attention to the winged bolt of the sky. But the cub saw, and it was a warning and a lesson to him—the swift downward swoop of the hawk, the short skim of its body just above the ground, the strike of its talons in the body of the ptarmigan, the ptarmigan's squawk of agony and fright, and the hawk's rush upward into the blue, carrying the ptarmigan away with it.

It was a long time before the cub left its shelter. He had learned much. Live things were meat. They were good to eat. Also, live things when they were large enough, could give hurt. It was better to eat small live things like ptarmigan chicks, and to let alone large live things like ptarmigan hens. Nevertheless he felt a little prick of ambition, a sneaking desire to have another battle with that ptarmigan hen—only the hawk had carried her away. May be there were other ptarmigan hens. He would go and see.

He came down a shelving bank to the stream. He had never seen water before. The footing looked good. There were no inequalities of surface. He stepped boldly out on it; and went down, crying with fear, into the embrace of the unknown. It was cold, and he gasped, breathing quickly. The water rushed into his lungs instead of the air that had always accompanied his act of breathing. The suffocation he experienced was like the pang of death. To him it signified death. He had no conscious knowledge of death, but like every animal of the Wild, he possessed the instinct of death. To him it stood as the greatest of hurts. It was the very essence of the unknown; it was the sum of the terrors of the unknown, the one culminating and unthinkable catastrophe that could happen to him, about which he knew nothing and about which he feared everything.

He came to the surface, and the sweet air rushed into his open mouth. He did not go down again. Quite as though it had been a long-established custom of his he struck out with all his legs and began to swim. The near bank was a yard away; but he had come up with his back to it, and the first thing his eyes rested upon was the opposite bank, toward which he immediately began to swim. The stream was a small one, but in the pool it widened out to a score of feet.

Midway in the passage, the current picked up the cub and swept him downstream. He was caught in the miniature rapid at the bottom of the pool. Here was little chance for swimming. The quiet water had become suddenly angry. Sometimes he was under, sometimes on top. At all times he was in violent motion, now being turned over or around, and again, being smashed against a rock. And with every rock he struck, he yelped. His progress was a series of yelps, from which might have been adduced the number of rocks he encountered.

CHAPTER IV—THE WALL OF THE WORLD

Below the rapid was a second pool, and here, captured by the eddy, he was gently borne to the bank, and as gently deposited on a bed of gravel. He crawled frantically clear of the water and lay down. He had learned some more about the world. Water was not alive. Yet it moved. Also, it looked as solid as the earth, but was without any solidity at all. His conclusion was that things were not always what they appeared to be. The cub's fear of the unknown was an inherited distrust, and it had now been strengthened by experience. Thenceforth, in the nature of things, he would possess an abiding distrust of appearances. He would have to learn the reality of a thing before he could put his faith into it.

One other adventure was destined for him that day. He had recollected that there was such a thing in the world as his mother. And then there came to him a feeling that he wanted her more than all the rest of the things in the world. Not only was his body tired with the adventures it had undergone, but his little brain was equally tired. In all the days he had lived it had not worked so hard as on this one day. Furthermore, he was sleepy. So he started out to look for the cave and his mother, feeling at the same time an overwhelming rush of loneliness and helplessness.

He was sprawling along between some bushes, when he heard a sharp intimidating cry. There was a flash of yellow before his eyes. He saw a weasel leaping swiftly away from him. It was a small live thing, and he had no fear. Then, before him, at his feet, he saw an extremely small live thing, only several inches long, a young weasel, that, like himself, had disobediently gone out adventuring. It tried to retreat before him. He turned it over with his paw. It made a queer, grating noise. The next moment the flash of yellow reappeared before his eyes. He heard again the intimidating cry, and at the same instant received a sharp blow on the side of the neck and felt the sharp teeth of the mother-weasel cut into his flesh.

While he yelped and ki-yi'd and scrambled backward, he saw the mother-weasel leap upon her young one and disappear with it into the neighbouring thicket. The cut of her teeth in his neck still hurt, but his feelings were hurt more grievously, and he sat down and weakly whimpered. This mother-weasel was so small and so savage. He was yet to learn that for size and weight the weasel was the most ferocious, vindictive, and terrible of all the killers of the Wild. But a portion of this knowledge was quickly to be his.

He was still whimpering when the mother-weasel reappeared. She did not rush him, now that her young one was safe. She approached more cautiously, and the cub had full opportunity to observe her lean, snakelike body, and her head, erect, eager, and snake-like itself. Her sharp, menacing cry sent the hair bristling along his back, and he snarled warningly at her. She came closer and closer. There was a leap, swifter than his unpractised sight, and the lean, yellow body disappeared for a moment out of the field of his vision. The next moment she was at his throat, her teeth buried in his hair and flesh.

At first he snarled and tried to fight; but he was very young, and this was only his first day in the world, and his snarl became a whimper, his fight a struggle to escape. The weasel never relaxed her hold. She hung on, striving to press down with her teeth to the great vein where his life-blood bubbled. The weasel was a drinker of blood, and it was ever her preference to drink from the throat of life itself.

The grey cub would have died, and there would have been no story to write about him, had not the she-wolf come bounding through the bushes. The weasel let go the cub and flashed at the she-wolf's throat, missing, but getting a hold on the jaw instead. The she-wolf flirted her head like the snap of a whip, breaking the weasel's hold and flinging it high in the air. And, still in the air, the she-wolf's jaws closed on the lean, yellow body, and the weasel knew death between the crunching teeth.

The cub experienced another access of affection on the part of his mother. Her joy at finding him seemed even greater than his joy at being found. She nozzled him and caressed him and licked the cuts made in him by the weasel's teeth. Then, between them, mother and cub, they ate the blood-drinker, and after that went back to the cave and slept.

CHAPTER V—THE LAW OF MEAT

The cub's development was rapid. He rested for two days, and then ventured forth from the cave again. It was on this adventure that he found the young weasel whose mother he had helped eat, and he saw to it that the young weasel went the way of its mother. But on this trip he did not get lost. When he grew tired, he found his way back to the cave and slept. And every day thereafter found him out and ranging a wider area.

He began to get accurate measurement of his strength and his weakness, and to know when to be bold and when to be cautious. He found it expedient to be cautious all the time, except for the rare moments, when, assured of his own intrepidity, he abandoned himself to petty rages and lusts.

He was always a little demon of fury when he chanced upon a stray ptarmigan. Never did he fail to respond savagely to the chatter of the squirrel he had first met on the blasted pine. While the sight of a moose-bird almost invariably put him into the wildest of rages; for he never forgot the peck on the nose he had received from the first of that ilk he encountered.

But there were times when even a moose-bird failed to affect him, and those were times when he felt himself to be in danger from some other prowling meat hunter. He never forgot the hawk, and its moving shadow always sent him crouching into the nearest thicket. He no longer sprawled and straddled, and already he was developing the gait of his mother, slinking and furtive, apparently without exertion, yet sliding along with a swiftness that was as deceptive as it was imperceptible.

In the matter of meat, his luck had been all in the beginning. The seven ptarmigan chicks and the baby weasel represented the sum of his killings. His desire to kill strengthened with the days, and he cherished hungry ambitions for the squirrel that chattered so volubly and always informed all wild creatures that the wolf-cub was approaching. But as birds flew in the air, squirrels could climb trees, and the cub could only try to crawl unobserved upon the squirrel when it was on the ground.

The cub entertained a great respect for his mother. She could get meat, and she never failed to bring him his share. Further, she was unafraid of things. It did not occur to him that this fearlessness was founded upon experience and knowledge. Its effect on him was that of an impression of power. His mother represented power; and as he grew older he felt this power in the sharper admonishment of her paw; while the reproving nudge of her nose gave place to the slash of her fangs. For this, likewise, he respected his mother. She compelled obedience from him, and the older he grew the shorter grew her temper.

Famine came again, and the cub with clearer consciousness knew once more the bite of hunger. The she-wolf ran herself thin in the quest for meat. She rarely slept any more in the cave, spending most of her time on the meat-trail, and spending it vainly. This famine was not a long one, but it was severe while it lasted. The cub found no more milk in his mother's breast, nor did he get one mouthful of meat for himself.

Before, he had hunted in play, for the sheer joyousness of it; now he hunted in deadly earnestness, and found nothing. Yet the failure of it accelerated his development. He studied the habits of the squirrel with greater carefulness, and strove with greater craft to steal upon it and surprise it. He studied the wood-mice and tried to dig them out of their burrows; and he learned much about the ways of moose-birds and woodpeckers. And there came a day when the hawk's shadow did not drive him crouching into the bushes. He had grown stronger and wiser, and more confident. Also, he was desperate. So he sat on his haunches, conspicuously in an open space, and challenged the hawk down out of the sky. For he knew that there, floating in the blue above him, was meat, the meat his stomach yearned after so insistently. But the hawk refused to come down and give battle, and the cub crawled away into a thicket and whimpered his disappointment and hunger.

The famine broke. The she-wolf brought home meat. It was strange meat, different from any she had ever brought before. It was a lynx kitten, partly grown, like the cub, but not so large. And it was all for him. His mother had satisfied her hunger elsewhere; though he did not know that it was the rest of the lynx litter that had gone to satisfy her. Nor did he know the desperateness of her deed. He knew only that the velvet-furred kitten was meat, and he ate and waxed happier with every mouthful.

A full stomach conduces to inaction, and the cub lay in the cave, sleeping against his mother's side. He was aroused by her snarling. Never had he heard her snarl so terribly. Possibly in her whole life it was the most terrible snarl she ever gave. There was reason for it, and none knew it better than she. A lynx's lair is not despoiled with impunity. In the full glare of the afternoon light, crouching in the entrance of the cave, the cub saw the lynx-mother. The hair rippled up along his back at the sight. Here was fear, and it did not require his instinct to tell him of it. And if sight alone were not sufficient, the cry of rage the intruder gave, beginning with a snarl and rushing abruptly upward into a hoarse screech, was convincing enough in itself.

The cub felt the prod of the life that was in him, and stood up and snarled valiantly by his mother's side. But she thrust him ignominiously away and behind her. Because of the low-roofed entrance the lynx could not leap in, and when she made a crawling rush of it the she-wolf sprang upon her and pinned her down. The cub saw little of the battle. There was a tremendous snarling and spitting and screeching. The two animals threshed about, the lynx ripping and tearing with her claws and using her teeth as well, while the she-wolf used her teeth alone.

Once, the cub sprang in and sank his teeth into the hind leg of the lynx. He clung on, growling savagely. Though he did not know it, by the weight of his body he clogged the action of the leg and thereby saved his mother much damage. A change in the battle crushed him under both their bodies and wrenched loose his hold. The next moment the two mothers separated, and, before they rushed together again, the lynx lashed out at the cub with a huge fore-paw that ripped his shoulder open to the bone and sent him hurtling sidewise against the wall. Then was added to the uproar the cub's shrill yelp of pain and fright. But the fight lasted so long that he had time to cry himself out and to experience a second burst of courage; and the end of the battle found him again clinging to a hind-leg and furiously growling between his teeth.

The lynx was dead. But the she-wolf was very weak and sick. At first she caressed the cub and licked his wounded shoulder; but the blood she had lost had taken with it her strength, and for all of a day and a night she lay by her dead foe's side, without movement, scarcely breathing. For a week she never left the cave, except for water, and then her movements were slow and painful. At the end of that time the lynx was devoured, while the she-wolf's wounds had healed sufficiently to permit her to take the meat-trail again.

The cub's shoulder was stiff and sore, and for some time he limped from the terrible slash he had received. But the world now seemed changed. He went about in it with greater confidence, with a feeling of prowess that had not been his in the days before the battle with the lynx. He had looked upon life in a more ferocious aspect; he had fought; he had buried his teeth in the flesh of a foe; and he had survived. And because of all this, he carried himself more boldly, with a touch of defiance that was new in him. He was no longer afraid of minor things, and much of his timidity had vanished, though the unknown never ceased to press upon him with its mysteries and terrors, intangible and ever-menacing.

He began to accompany his mother on the meat-trail, and he saw much of the killing of meat and began to play his part in it. And in his own dim way he learned the law of meat. There were two kinds of life—his own kind and the other kind. His own kind included his mother and himself. The other kind included all live things that moved. But the other kind was divided. One portion was what his own kind killed and ate. This portion was composed of the non-killers and the small killers. The other portion killed and ate his own kind, or was killed and eaten by his own kind. And out of this classification arose the law. The aim of life was meat. Life itself was meat. Life lived on life. There were the eaters and the eaten. The law was: EAT OR BE EATEN. He did not formulate the law in clear, set terms and moralise about it. He did not even think the law; he merely lived the law without thinking about it at all.

He saw the law operating around him on every side. He had eaten the ptarmigan chicks. The hawk had eaten the ptarmigan-mother. The hawk would also have eaten him. Later, when he had grown more formidable, he wanted to eat the hawk. He had eaten the lynx kitten. The lynx-mother would have eaten him had she not herself been killed and eaten. And so it went. The law was being lived about him by all live things, and he himself was part and parcel of the law. He was a killer. His only food was meat, live meat, that ran away swiftly before him, or flew into the air, or climbed trees, or hid in the ground, or faced him and fought with him, or turned the tables and ran after him.

Had the cub thought in man-fashion, he might have epitomised life as a voracious appetite and the world as a place wherein ranged a multitude of appetites, pursuing and being pursued, hunting and being hunted, eating and being eaten, all in blindness and confusion, with violence and disorder, a chaos of gluttony and slaughter, ruled over by chance, merciless, planless, endless.

But the cub did not think in man-fashion. He did not look at things with wide vision. He was single-purposed, and entertained but one thought or desire at a time. Besides the law of meat, there were a myriad other and lesser laws for him to learn and obey. The world was filled with surprise. The stir of the life that was in him, the play of his muscles, was an unending happiness. To run down meat was to experience thrills and elations. His rages and battles were pleasures. Terror itself, and the mystery of the unknown, led to his living.

And there were easements and satisfactions. To have a full stomach, to doze lazily in the sunshine—such things were remuneration in full for his ardours and toils, while his ardours and tolls were in themselves self-remunerative. They were expressions of life, and life is always happy when it is expressing itself. So the cub had no quarrel with his hostile environment. He was very much alive, very happy, and very proud of himself.

PART III

CHAPTER I—THE MAKERS OF FIRE

The cub came upon it suddenly. It was his own fault. He had been careless. He had left the cave and run down to the stream to drink. It might have been that he took no notice because he was heavy with sleep. (He had been out all night on the meat-trail, and had but just then awakened.) And his carelessness might have been due to the familiarity of the trail to the pool. He had travelled it often, and nothing had ever happened on it.

He went down past the blasted pine, crossed the open space, and trotted in amongst the trees. Then, at the same instant, he saw and smelt. Before him, sitting silently on their haunches, were five live things, the like of which he had never seen before. It was his first glimpse of mankind. But at the sight of him the five men did not spring to their feet, nor show their teeth, nor snarl. They did not move, but sat there, silent and ominous.

Nor did the cub move. Every instinct of his nature would have impelled him to dash wildly away, had there not suddenly and for the first time arisen in him another and counter instinct. A great awe descended upon him. He was beaten down to movelessness by an overwhelming sense of his own weakness and littleness. Here was mastery and power, something far and away beyond him.

The cub had never seen man, yet the instinct concerning man was his. In dim ways he recognised in man the animal that had fought itself to primacy over the other animals of the Wild. Not alone out of his own eyes, but out of the eyes of all his ancestors was the cub now looking upon man—out of eyes that had circled in the darkness around countless winter camp-fires, that had peered from safe distances and from the hearts of thickets at the strange, two-legged animal that was lord over living things. The spell of the cub's heritage was upon him, the fear and the respect born of the centuries of struggle and the accumulated experience of the generations. The heritage was too compelling for a wolf that was only a cub. Had he been full-grown, he would have run away. As it was, he cowered down in a paralysis of fear, already half proffering the submission that his kind had proffered from the first time a wolf came in to sit by man's fire and be made warm.

One of the Indians arose and walked over to him and stooped above him. The cub cowered closer to the ground. It was the unknown, objectified at last, in concrete flesh and blood, bending over him and reaching down to seize hold of him. His hair bristled involuntarily; his lips writhed back and his little fangs were bared. The hand, poised like doom above him, hesitated, and the man spoke laughing, "*Wabam wabisca ip pit tah.*" ("Look! The white fangs!")

The other Indians laughed loudly, and urged the man on to pick up the cub. As the hand descended closer and closer, there raged within the cub a battle of the instincts. He experienced two great impulsions—to yield and to fight. The resulting action was a compromise. He did both. He yielded till the hand almost touched him. Then he fought, his teeth flashing in a snap that sank them into the hand. The next moment he received a clout alongside the head that knocked him over on his side. Then all fight fled out of him. His puppyhood and the instinct of submission took charge of him. He sat up on his haunches and ki-yi'd. But the man whose hand he had bitten was angry. The cub received a clout on the other side of his head. Whereupon he sat up and ki-yi'd louder than ever.

The four Indians laughed more loudly, while even the man who had been bitten began to laugh. They surrounded the cub and laughed at him, while he wailed out his terror and his hurt. In the midst of it, he heard something. The Indians heard it too. But the cub knew what it was, and with a last, long wail that had in it more of triumph than grief, he ceased his noise and waited for the coming of his mother, of his ferocious and indomitable mother who fought and killed all things and was never afraid. She was snarling as she ran. She had heard the cry of her cub and was dashing to save him.

She bounded in amongst them, her anxious and militant motherhood making her anything but a pretty sight. But to the cub the spectacle of her protective rage was pleasing. He uttered a glad little cry and bounded to meet her, while the man-animals went back hastily several steps. The she-wolf stood over against her cub, facing the men, with bristling hair, a snarl rumbling deep in her throat. Her face was distorted and malignant with menace, even the bridge of the nose wrinkling from tip to eyes so prodigious was her snarl.

Then it was that a cry went up from one of the men. "Kiche!" was what he uttered. It was an exclamation of surprise. The cub felt his mother wilting at the sound.

"Kiche!" the man cried again, this time with sharpness and authority.

And then the cub saw his mother, the she-wolf, the fearless one, crouching down till her belly touched the ground, whimpering, wagging her tail, making peace signs. The cub could not understand. He was appalled. The awe of man rushed over him again. His instinct had been true. His mother verified it. She, too, rendered submission to the man-animals.

The man who had spoken came over to her. He put his hand upon her head, and she only crouched closer. She did not snap, nor threaten to snap. The other men came up, and surrounded her, and felt her, and pawed her, which actions she made no attempt to resent. They were greatly excited, and made many noises with their mouths. These noises were not indication of danger, the cub decided, as he crouched near his mother still bristling from time to time but doing his best to submit.

"It is not strange," an Indian was saying. "Her father was a wolf. It is true, her mother was a dog; but did not my brother tie her out in the woods all of three nights in the mating season? Therefore was the father of Kiche a wolf."

"It is a year, Grey Beaver, since she ran away," spoke a second Indian.

"It is not strange, Salmon Tongue," Grey Beaver answered. "It was the time of the famine, and there was no meat for the dogs."

"She has lived with the wolves," said a third Indian.

"So it would seem, Three Eagles," Grey Beaver answered, laying his hand on the cub; "and this be the sign of it."

The cub snarled a little at the touch of the hand, and the hand flew back to administer a clout. Whereupon the cub covered its fangs, and sank down submissively, while the hand, returning, rubbed behind his ears, and up and down his back.

"This be the sign of it," Grey Beaver went on. "It is plain that his mother is Kiche. But his father was a wolf. Wherefore is there in him little dog and much wolf. His fangs be white, and White Fang shall be his name. I have spoken. He is my dog. For was not Kiche my brother's dog? And is not my brother dead?"

The cub, who had thus received a name in the world, lay and watched. For a time the man-animals continued to make their mouth-noises. Then Grey Beaver took a knife from a sheath that hung around his neck, and went into the thicket and cut a stick. White Fang watched him. He notched the stick at each end and in the notches fastened strings of raw-hide. One string he tied around the throat of Kiche. Then he led her to a small pine, around which he tied the other string.

White Fang followed and lay down beside her. Salmon Tongue's hand reached out to him and rolled him over on his back. Kiche looked on anxiously. White Fang felt fear mounting in him again. He could not quite suppress a snarl, but he made no offer to snap. The hand, with fingers crooked and spread apart, rubbed his stomach in a playful way and rolled him from side to side. It was ridiculous and ungainly, lying there on his back with legs sprawling in the air. Besides, it was a position of such utter helplessness that White Fang's whole nature revolted against it. He could do nothing to defend himself. If this man-animal intended harm, White Fang knew that he could not escape it. How could he spring away with his four legs in the air above him? Yet submission made him master his fear, and he only growled softly. This growl he could not suppress; nor did the man-animal resent it by giving him a blow on the head. And furthermore, such was the strangeness of it, White Fang experienced an unaccountable sensation of pleasure as the hand rubbed back and forth. When he was rolled on his side he ceased to growl, when the fingers pressed and prodded at the base of his ears the pleasurable sensation increased; and when, with a final rub and scratch, the man left him alone and went away, all fear had died out of White Fang. He was to know fear many times in his dealing with man; yet it was a token of the fearless companionship with man that was ultimately to be his.

After a time, White Fang heard strange noises approaching. He was quick in his classification, for he knew them at once for man-animal noises. A few minutes later the remainder of the tribe, strung out as it was on the march, trailed in. There were more men and many women and children, forty souls of them, and all heavily burdened with camp equipage and outfit. Also there were many dogs; and these, with the exception of the part-grown puppies, were likewise burdened with camp outfit. On their backs, in bags that fastened tightly around underneath, the dogs carried from twenty to thirty pounds of weight.

White Fang had never seen dogs before, but at sight of them he felt that they were his own kind, only somehow different. But they displayed little difference from the wolf when they discovered the cub and his mother. There was a rush. White Fang bristled and snarled and snapped in the face of the open-mouthed oncoming wave of dogs, and went down and under them, feeling the sharp slash of teeth in his body, himself biting and tearing at the legs and bellies above him. There was a great uproar. He could hear the snarl of Kiche as she fought for him; and he could hear the cries of the man-animals, the sound of clubs striking upon bodies, and the yelps of pain from the dogs so struck.

Only a few seconds elapsed before he was on his feet again. He could now see the man-animals driving back the dogs with clubs and stones, defending him, saving him from the savage teeth of his kind that somehow was not his kind. And though there was no reason in his brain for a clear conception of so abstract a thing as justice, nevertheless, in his own way, he felt the justice of the man-animals, and he knew them for what they were—makers of law and executors of law. Also, he appreciated the power with which they administered the law. Unlike any animals he had ever encountered, they did not bite nor claw. They enforced their live strength with the power of dead things. Dead things did their bidding. Thus, sticks and stones, directed by these strange creatures, leaped through the air like living things, inflicting grievous hurts upon the dogs.

To his mind this was power unusual, power inconceivable and beyond the natural, power that was godlike. White Fang, in the very nature of him, could never know anything about gods; at the best he could know only things that were beyond knowing—but the wonder and awe that he had of these man-animals in ways resembled what would be the wonder and awe of man at sight of some celestial creature, on a mountain top, hurling thunderbolts from either hand at an astonished world.

The last dog had been driven back. The hubbub died down. And White Fang licked his hurts and meditated upon this, his first taste of pack-cruelty and his introduction to the pack. He had never dreamed that his own kind consisted of more than One Eye, his mother, and himself. They had constituted a kind apart, and here, abruptly, he had discovered many more creatures apparently of his own kind. And there was a subconscious resentment that these, his kind, at first sight had pitched upon him and tried to destroy him. In the same way he resented his mother being tied with a stick, even though it was done by the superior man-animals. It savoured of the trap, of bondage. Yet of the trap and of bondage he knew nothing. Freedom to roam and run and lie down at will, had been his heritage; and here it was being infringed upon. His mother's movements were restricted to the length of a stick, and by the length of that same stick was he restricted, for he had not yet got beyond the need of his mother's side.

He did not like it. Nor did he like it when the man-animals arose and went on with their march; for a tiny man-animal took the other end of the stick and led Kiche captive behind him, and behind Kiche followed White Fang, greatly perturbed and worried by this new adventure he had entered upon.

They went down the valley of the stream, far beyond White Fang's widest ranging, until they came to the end of the valley, where the stream ran into the Mackenzie River. Here, where canoes were cached on poles high in the air and where stood fish-racks for the drying of fish, camp was made; and White Fang looked on with wondering eyes. The superiority of these man-animals increased with every moment. There was their mastery over all these sharp-fanged dogs. It breathed of power. But greater than that, to the wolf-cub, was their mastery over things not alive; their capacity to communicate motion to unmoving things; their capacity to change the very face of the world.

It was this last that especially affected him. The elevation of frames of poles caught his eye; yet this in itself was not so remarkable, being done by the same creatures that flung sticks and stones to great distances. But when the frames of poles were made into tepees by being covered with cloth and skins, White Fang was astounded. It was the colossal bulk of them that impressed him. They arose around him, on every side, like some monstrous quick-growing form of life. They occupied nearly the whole circumference of his field of vision. He was afraid of them. They loomed ominously above him; and when the breeze stirred them into huge movements, he cowered down in fear, keeping his eyes warily upon them, and prepared to spring away if they attempted to precipitate themselves upon him.

But in a short while his fear of the tepees passed away. He saw the women and children passing in and out of them without harm, and he saw the dogs trying often to get into them, and being driven away with sharp words and flying stones. After a time, he left Kiche's side and crawled cautiously toward the wall of the nearest tepee. It was the curiosity of growth that urged him on—the necessity of learning and living and doing that brings experience. The last few inches to the wall of the tepee were crawled with painful slowness and precaution. The day's events had prepared him for the unknown to manifest itself in most stupendous and unthinkable ways. At last his nose touched the canvas. He waited. Nothing happened. Then he smelled the strange fabric, saturated with the man-smell. He closed on the canvas with his teeth and gave a gentle tug. Nothing happened, though the adjacent portions of the tepee moved. He tugged harder. There was a greater movement. It was delightful. He tugged still harder, and repeatedly, until the whole tepee was in motion. Then the sharp cry of a squaw inside sent him scampering back to Kiche. But after that he was afraid no more of the looming bulks of the tepees.

A moment later he was straying away again from his mother. Her stick was tied to a peg in the ground and she could not follow him. A part-grown puppy, somewhat larger and older than he, came toward him slowly, with ostentatious and belligerent importance. The puppy's name, as White Fang was afterward to hear him called, was Lip-lip. He had had experience in puppy fights and was already something of a bully.

Lip-lip was White Fang's own kind, and, being only a puppy, did not seem dangerous; so White Fang prepared to meet him in a friendly spirit. But when the strangers walk became stiff-legged and his lips lifted clear of his teeth, White Fang stiffened too, and answered with lifted lips. They half circled about each other, tentatively, snarling and bristling. This lasted several minutes, and White Fang was beginning to enjoy it, as a sort of game. But suddenly, with remarkable swiftness, Lip-lip leaped in, delivering a slashing snap, and leaped away again. The snap had taken effect on the shoulder that had been hurt by the lynx and that was still sore deep down near the bone. The surprise and hurt of it brought a yelp out of White Fang; but the next moment, in a rush of anger, he was upon Lip-lip and snapping viciously.

But Lip-lip had lived his life in camp and had fought many puppy fights. Three times, four times, and half a dozen times, his sharp little teeth scored on the newcomer, until White Fang, yelping shamelessly, fled to the protection of his mother. It was the first of the many fights he was to have with Lip-lip, for they were enemies from the start, born so, with natures destined perpetually to clash.

Kiche licked White Fang soothingly with her tongue, and tried to prevail upon him to remain with her. But his curiosity was rampant, and several minutes later he was venturing forth on a new quest. He came upon one of the man-animals, Grey Beaver, who was squatting on his hams and doing something with sticks and dry moss spread before him on the ground. White Fang came near to him and watched. Grey Beaver made mouth-noises which White Fang interpreted as not hostile, so he came still nearer.

Women and children were carrying more sticks and branches to Grey Beaver. It was evidently an affair of moment. White Fang came in until he touched Grey Beaver's knee, so curious was he, and already forgetful that this was a terrible man-animal. Suddenly he saw a strange thing like mist beginning to arise from the sticks and moss beneath Grey Beaver's hands. Then, amongst the sticks themselves, appeared a live thing, twisting and turning, of a colour like the colour of the sun in the sky. White Fang knew nothing about fire. It drew him as the light, in the mouth of the cave had drawn him in his early puppyhood. He crawled the several steps toward the flame. He heard Grey Beaver chuckle above him, and he knew the sound was not hostile. Then his nose touched the flame, and at the same instant his little tongue went out to it.

For a moment he was paralysed. The unknown, lurking in the midst of the sticks and moss, was savagely clutching him by the nose. He scrambled backward, bursting out in an astonished explosion of ki-yi's. At the sound, Kiche leaped snarling to the end of her stick, and there raged terribly because she could not come to his aid. But Grey Beaver laughed loudly, and slapped his thighs, and told the happening to all the rest of the camp, till everybody was laughing uproariously. But White Fang sat on his haunches and ki-yi'd and ki-yi'd, a forlorn and pitiable little figure in the midst of the man-animals.

It was the worst hurt he had ever known. Both nose and tongue had been scorched by the live thing, sun-coloured, that had grown up under Grey Beaver's hands. He cried and cried interminably, and every fresh wail was greeted by bursts of laughter on the part of the man-animals. He tried to soothe his nose with his tongue, but the tongue was burnt too, and the two hurts coming together produced greater hurt; whereupon he cried more hopelessly and helplessly than ever.

And then shame came to him. He knew laughter and the meaning of it. It is not given us to know how some animals know laughter, and know when they are being laughed at; but it was this same way that White Fang knew it. And he felt shame that the man-animals should be laughing at him. He turned and fled away, not from the hurt of the fire, but from the laughter that sank even deeper, and hurt in the spirit of him. And he fled to Kiche, raging at the end of her stick like an animal gone mad—to Kiche, the one creature in the world who was not laughing at him.

Twilight drew down and night came on, and White Fang lay by his mother's side. His nose and tongue still hurt, but he was perplexed by a greater trouble. He was homesick. He felt a vacancy in him, a need for the hush and quietude of the stream and the cave in the cliff. Life had become too populous. There were so many of the man-animals, men, women, and children, all making noises and irritations. And there were the dogs, ever squabbling and bickering, bursting into uproars and creating confusions. The restful loneliness of the only life he had known was gone. Here the very air was palpitant with life. It hummed and buzzed unceasingly. Continually changing its intensity and abruptly variant in pitch, it impinged on his nerves and senses, made him nervous and restless and worried him with a perpetual imminence of happening.

CHAPTER I—THE MAKERS OF FIRE

He watched the man-animals coming and going and moving about the camp. In fashion distantly resembling the way men look upon the gods they create, so looked White Fang upon the man-animals before him. They were superior creatures, of a verity, gods. To his dim comprehension they were as much wonder-workers as gods are to men. They were creatures of mastery, possessing all manner of unknown and impossible potencies, overlords of the alive and the not alive—making obey that which moved, imparting movement to that which did not move, and making life, sun-coloured and biting life, to grow out of dead moss and wood. They were fire-makers! They were gods.

CHAPTER II—THE BONDAGE

The days were thronged with experience for White Fang. During the time that Kiche was tied by the stick, he ran about over all the camp, inquiring, investigating, learning. He quickly came to know much of the ways of the man-animals, but familiarity did not breed contempt. The more he came to know them, the more they vindicated their superiority, the more they displayed their mysterious powers, the greater loomed their god-likeness.

To man has been given the grief, often, of seeing his gods overthrown and his altars crumbling; but to the wolf and the wild dog that have come in to crouch at man's feet, this grief has never come. Unlike man, whose gods are of the unseen and the overguessed, vapours and mists of fancy eluding the garmenture of reality, wandering wraiths of desired goodness and power, intangible out-croppings of self into the realm of spirit—unlike man, the wolf and the wild dog that have come in to the fire find their gods in the living flesh, solid to the touch, occupying earth-space and requiring time for the accomplishment of their ends and their existence. No effort of faith is necessary to believe in such a god; no effort of will can possibly induce disbelief in such a god. There is no getting away from it. There it stands, on its two hind-legs, club in hand, immensely potential, passionate and wrathful and loving, god and mystery and power all wrapped up and around by flesh that bleeds when it is torn and that is good to eat like any flesh.

And so it was with White Fang. The man-animals were gods unmistakable and unescapable. As his mother, Kiche, had rendered her allegiance to them at the first cry of her name, so he was beginning to render his allegiance. He gave them the trail as a privilege indubitably theirs. When they walked, he got out of their way. When they called, he came. When they threatened, he cowered down. When they commanded him to go, he went away hurriedly. For behind any wish of theirs was power to enforce that wish, power that hurt, power that expressed itself in clouts and clubs, in flying stones and stinging lashes of whips.

He belonged to them as all dogs belonged to them. His actions were theirs to command. His body was theirs to maul, to stamp upon, to tolerate. Such was the lesson that was quickly borne in upon him. It came hard, going as it did, counter to much that was strong and dominant in his own nature; and, while he disliked it in the learning of it, unknown to himself he was learning to like it. It was a placing of his destiny in another's hands, a shifting of the responsibilities of existence. This in itself was compensation, for it is always easier to lean upon another than to stand alone.

CHAPTER II—THE BONDAGE

But it did not all happen in a day, this giving over of himself, body and soul, to the man-animals. He could not immediately forego his wild heritage and his memories of the Wild. There were days when he crept to the edge of the forest and stood and listened to something calling him far and away. And always he returned, restless and uncomfortable, to whimper softly and wistfully at Kiche's side and to lick her face with eager, questioning tongue.

White Fang learned rapidly the ways of the camp. He knew the injustice and greediness of the older dogs when meat or fish was thrown out to be eaten. He came to know that men were more just, children more cruel, and women more kindly and more likely to toss him a bit of meat or bone. And after two or three painful adventures with the mothers of part-grown puppies, he came into the knowledge that it was always good policy to let such mothers alone, to keep away from them as far as possible, and to avoid them when he saw them coming.

But the bane of his life was Lip-lip. Larger, older, and stronger, Lip-lip had selected White Fang for his special object of persecution. While Fang fought willingly enough, but he was outclassed. His enemy was too big. Lip-lip became a nightmare to him. Whenever he ventured away from his mother, the bully was sure to appear, trailing at his heels, snarling at him, picking upon him, and watchful of an opportunity, when no man-animal was near, to spring upon him and force a fight. As Lip-lip invariably won, he enjoyed it hugely. It became his chief delight in life, as it became White Fang's chief torment.

But the effect upon White Fang was not to cow him. Though he suffered most of the damage and was always defeated, his spirit remained unsubdued. Yet a bad effect was produced. He became malignant and morose. His temper had been savage by birth, but it became more savage under this unending persecution. The genial, playful, puppyish side of him found little expression. He never played and gambolled about with the other puppies of the camp. Lip-lip would not permit it. The moment White Fang appeared near them, Lip-lip was upon him, bullying and hectoring him, or fighting with him until he had driven him away.

The effect of all this was to rob White Fang of much of his puppyhood and to make him in his comportment older than his age. Denied the outlet, through play, of his energies, he recoiled upon himself and developed his mental processes. He became cunning; he had idle time in which to devote himself to thoughts of trickery. Prevented from obtaining his share of meat and fish when a general feed was given to the camp-dogs, he became a clever thief. He had to forage for himself, and he foraged well, though he was oft-times a plague to the squaws in consequence. He learned to sneak about camp, to be crafty, to know what was going on everywhere, to see and to hear everything and to reason accordingly, and successfully to devise ways and means of avoiding his implacable persecutor.

It was early in the days of his persecution that he played his first really big crafty game and got there from his first taste of revenge. As Kiche, when with the wolves, had lured out to destruction dogs from the camps of men, so White Fang, in manner somewhat similar, lured Lip-lip into Kiche's avenging jaws. Retreating before Lip-lip, White Fang made an indirect flight that led in and out and around the various tepees of the camp. He was a good runner, swifter than any puppy of his size, and swifter than Lip-lip. But he did not run his best in this chase. He barely held his own, one leap ahead of his pursuer.

Lip-lip, excited by the chase and by the persistent nearness of his victim, forgot caution and locality. When he remembered locality, it was too late. Dashing at top speed around a tepee, he ran full tilt into Kiche lying at the end of her stick. He gave one yelp of consternation, and then her punishing jaws closed upon him. She was tied, but he could not get away from her easily. She rolled him off his legs so that he could not run, while she repeatedly ripped and slashed him with her fangs.

When at last he succeeded in rolling clear of her, he crawled to his feet, badly dishevelled, hurt both in body and in spirit. His hair was standing out all over him in tufts where her teeth had mauled. He stood where he had arisen, opened his mouth, and broke out the long, heart-broken puppy wail. But even this he was not allowed to complete. In the middle of it, White Fang, rushing in, sank his teeth into Lip-lip's hind leg. There was no fight left in Lip-lip, and he ran away shamelessly, his victim hot on his heels and worrying him all the way back to his own tepee. Here the squaws came to his aid, and White Fang, transformed into a raging demon, was finally driven off only by a fusillade of stones.

Came the day when Grey Beaver, deciding that the liability of her running away was past, released Kiche. White Fang was delighted with his mother's freedom. He accompanied her joyfully about the camp; and, so long as he remained close by her side, Lip-lip kept a respectful distance. White-Fang even bristled up to him and walked stiff-legged, but Lip-lip ignored the challenge. He was no fool himself, and whatever vengeance he desired to wreak, he could wait until he caught White Fang alone.

Later on that day, Kiche and White Fang strayed into the edge of the woods next to the camp. He had led his mother there, step by step, and now when she stopped, he tried to inveigle her farther. The stream, the lair, and the quiet woods were calling to him, and he wanted her to come. He ran on a few steps, stopped, and looked back. She had not moved. He whined pleadingly, and scurried playfully in and out of the underbrush. He ran back to her, licked her face, and ran on again. And still she did not move. He stopped and regarded her, all of an intentness and eagerness, physically expressed, that slowly faded out of him as she turned her head and gazed back at the camp.

There was something calling to him out there in the open. His mother heard it too. But she heard also that other and louder call, the call of the fire and of man—the call which has been given alone of all animals to the wolf to answer, to the wolf and the wild-dog, who are brothers.

Kiche turned and slowly trotted back toward camp. Stronger than the physical restraint of the stick was the clutch of the camp upon her. Unseen and occultly, the gods still gripped with their power and would not let her go. White Fang sat down in the shadow of a birch and whimpered softly. There was a strong smell of pine, and subtle wood fragrances filled the air, reminding him of his old life of freedom before the days of his bondage. But he was still only a part-grown puppy, and stronger than the call either of man or of the Wild was the call of his mother. All the hours of his short life he had depended upon her. The time was yet to come for independence. So he arose and trotted forlornly back to camp, pausing once, and twice, to sit down and whimper and to listen to the call that still sounded in the depths of the forest.

In the Wild the time of a mother with her young is short; but under the dominion of man it is sometimes even shorter. Thus it was with White Fang. Grey Beaver was in the debt of Three Eagles. Three Eagles was going away on a trip up the Mackenzie to the Great Slave Lake. A strip of scarlet cloth, a bearskin, twenty cartridges, and Kiche, went to pay the debt. White Fang saw his mother taken aboard Three Eagles' canoe, and tried to follow her. A blow from Three Eagles knocked him backward to the land. The canoe shoved off. He sprang into the water and swam after it, deaf to the sharp cries of Grey Beaver to return. Even a man-animal, a god, White Fang ignored, such was the terror he was in of losing his mother.

But gods are accustomed to being obeyed, and Grey Beaver wrathfully launched a canoe in pursuit. When he overtook White Fang, he reached down and by the nape of the neck lifted him clear of the water. He did not deposit him at once in the bottom of the canoe. Holding him suspended with one hand, with the other hand he proceeded to give him a beating. And it *was* a beating. His hand was heavy. Every blow was shrewd to hurt; and he delivered a multitude of blows.

Impelled by the blows that rained upon him, now from this side, now from that, White Fang swung back and forth like an erratic and jerky pendulum. Varying were the emotions that surged through him. At first, he had known surprise. Then came a momentary fear, when he yelped several times to the impact of the hand. But this was quickly followed by anger. His free nature asserted itself, and he showed his teeth and snarled fearlessly in the face of the wrathful god. This but served to make the god more wrathful. The blows came faster, heavier, more shrewd to hurt.

Grey Beaver continued to beat, White Fang continued to snarl. But this could not last for ever. One or the other must give over, and that one was White Fang. Fear surged through him again. For the first time he was being really man-handled. The occasional blows of sticks and stones he had previously experienced were as caresses compared with this. He broke down and began to cry and yelp. For a time each blow brought a yelp from him; but fear passed into terror, until finally his yelps were voiced in unbroken succession, unconnected with the rhythm of the punishment.

At last Grey Beaver withheld his hand. White Fang, hanging limply, continued to cry. This seemed to satisfy his master, who flung him down roughly in the bottom of the canoe. In the meantime the canoe had drifted down the stream. Grey Beaver picked up the paddle. White Fang was in his way. He spurned him savagely with his foot. In that moment White Fang's free nature flashed forth again, and he sank his teeth into the moccasined foot.

The beating that had gone before was as nothing compared with the beating he now received. Grey Beaver's wrath was terrible; likewise was White Fang's fright. Not only the hand, but the hard wooden paddle was used upon him; and he was bruised and sore in all his small body when he was again flung down in the canoe. Again, and this time with purpose, did Grey Beaver kick him. White Fang did not repeat his attack on the foot. He had learned another lesson of his bondage. Never, no matter what the circumstance, must he dare to bite the god who was lord and master over him; the body of the lord and master was sacred, not to be defiled by the teeth of such as he. That was evidently the crime of crimes, the one offence there was no condoning nor overlooking.

When the canoe touched the shore, White Fang lay whimpering and motionless, waiting the will of Grey Beaver. It was Grey Beaver's will that he should go ashore, for ashore he was flung, striking heavily on his side and hurting his bruises afresh. He crawled tremblingly to his feet and stood whimpering. Lip-lip, who had watched the whole proceeding from the bank, now rushed upon him, knocking him over and sinking his teeth into him. White Fang was too helpless to defend himself, and it would have gone hard with him had not Grey Beaver's foot shot out, lifting Lip-lip into the air with its violence so that he smashed down to earth a dozen feet away. This was the man-animal's justice; and even then, in his own pitiable plight, White Fang experienced a little grateful thrill. At Grey Beaver's heels he limped obediently through the village to the tepee. And so it came that White Fang learned that the right to punish was something the gods reserved for themselves and denied to the lesser creatures under them.

That night, when all was still, White Fang remembered his mother and sorrowed for her. He sorrowed too loudly and woke up Grey Beaver, who beat him. After that he mourned gently when the gods were around. But sometimes, straying off to the edge of the woods by himself, he gave vent to his grief, and cried it out with loud whimperings and wailings.

It was during this period that he might have harkened to the memories of the lair and the stream and run back to the Wild. But the memory of his mother held him. As the hunting man-animals went out and came back, so she would come back to the village some time. So he remained in his bondage waiting for her.

But it was not altogether an unhappy bondage. There was much to interest him. Something was always happening. There was no end to the strange things these gods did, and he was always curious to see. Besides, he was learning how to get along with Grey Beaver. Obedience, rigid, undeviating obedience, was what was exacted of him; and in return he escaped beatings and his existence was tolerated.

Nay, Grey Beaver himself sometimes tossed him a piece of meat, and defended him against the other dogs in the eating of it. And such a piece of meat was of value. It was worth more, in some strange way, then a dozen pieces of meat from the hand of a squaw. Grey Beaver never petted nor caressed. Perhaps it was the weight of his hand, perhaps his justice, perhaps the sheer power of him, and perhaps it was all these things that influenced White Fang; for a certain tie of attachment was forming between him and his surly lord.

Insidiously, and by remote ways, as well as by the power of stick and stone and clout of hand, were the shackles of White Fang's bondage being riveted upon him. The qualities in his kind that in the beginning made it possible for them to come in to the fires of men, were qualities capable of development. They were developing in him, and the camp-life, replete with misery as it was, was secretly endearing itself to him all the time. But White Fang was unaware of it. He knew only grief for the loss of Kiche, hope for her return, and a hungry yearning for the free life that had been his.

CHAPTER III—THE OUTCAST

Lip-lip continued so to darken his days that White Fang became wickeder and more ferocious than it was his natural right to be. Savageness was a part of his make-up, but the savageness thus developed exceeded his make-up. He acquired a reputation for wickedness amongst the man-animals themselves. Wherever there was trouble and uproar in camp, fighting and squabbling or the outcry of a squaw over a bit of stolen meat, they were sure to find White Fang mixed up in it and usually at the bottom of it. They did not bother to look after the causes of his conduct. They saw only the effects, and the effects were bad. He was a sneak and a thief, a mischief-maker, a fomenter of trouble; and irate squaws told him to his face, the while he eyed them alert and ready to dodge any quick-flung missile, that he was a wolf and worthless and bound to come to an evil end.

He found himself an outcast in the midst of the populous camp. All the young dogs followed Lip-lip's lead. There was a difference between White Fang and them. Perhaps they sensed his wild-wood breed, and instinctively felt for him the enmity that the domestic dog feels for the wolf. But be that as it may, they joined with Lip-lip in the persecution. And, once declared against him, they found good reason to continue declared against him. One and all, from time to time, they felt his teeth; and to his credit, he gave more than he received. Many of them he could whip in single fight; but single fight was denied him. The beginning of such a fight was a signal for all the young dogs in camp to come running and pitch upon him.

Out of this pack-persecution he learned two important things: how to take care of himself in a mass-fight against him—and how, on a single dog, to inflict the greatest amount of damage in the briefest space of time. To keep one's feet in the midst of the hostile mass meant life, and this he learnt well. He became cat-like in his ability to stay on his feet. Even grown dogs might hurtle him backward or sideways with the impact of their heavy bodies; and backward or sideways he would go, in the air or sliding on the ground, but always with his legs under him and his feet downward to the mother earth.

When dogs fight, there are usually preliminaries to the actual combat—snarlings and bristlings and stiff-legged struttings. But White Fang learned to omit these preliminaries. Delay meant the coming against him of all the young dogs. He must do his work quickly and get away. So he learnt to give no warning of his intention. He rushed in and snapped and slashed on the instant, without notice, before his foe could prepare to meet him. Thus he learned how to inflict quick and severe damage. Also he learned the value of surprise. A dog, taken off its guard, its shoulder slashed open or its ear ripped in ribbons before it knew what was happening, was a dog half whipped.

Furthermore, it was remarkably easy to overthrow a dog taken by surprise; while a dog, thus overthrown, invariably exposed for a moment the soft underside of its neck—the vulnerable point at which to strike for its life. White Fang knew this point. It was a knowledge bequeathed to him directly from the hunting generation of wolves. So it was that White Fang's method when he took the offensive, was: first to find a young dog alone; second, to surprise it and knock it off its feet; and third, to drive in with his teeth at the soft throat.

Being but partly grown his jaws had not yet become large enough nor strong enough to make his throat-attack deadly; but many a young dog went around camp with a lacerated throat in token of White Fang's intention. And one day, catching one of his enemies alone on the edge of the woods, he managed, by repeatedly overthrowing him and attacking the throat, to cut the great vein and let out the life. There was a great row that night. He had been observed, the news had been carried to the dead dog's master, the squaws remembered all the instances of stolen meat, and Grey Beaver was beset by many angry voices. But he resolutely held the door of his tepee, inside which he had placed the culprit, and refused to permit the vengeance for which his tribespeople clamoured.

White Fang became hated by man and dog. During this period of his development he never knew a moment's security. The tooth of every dog was against him, the hand of every man. He was greeted with snarls by his kind, with curses and stones by his gods. He lived tensely. He was always keyed up, alert for attack, wary of being attacked, with an eye for sudden and unexpected missiles, prepared to act precipitately and coolly, to leap in with a flash of teeth, or to leap away with a menacing snarl.

As for snarling he could snarl more terribly than any dog, young or old, in camp. The intent of the snarl is to warn or frighten, and judgment is required to know when it should be used. White Fang knew how to make it and when to make it. Into his snarl he incorporated all that was vicious, malignant, and horrible. With nose serrulated by continuous spasms, hair bristling in recurrent waves, tongue whipping out like a red snake and whipping back again, ears flattened down, eyes gleaming hatred, lips wrinkled back, and fangs exposed and dripping, he could compel a pause on the part of almost any assailant. A temporary pause, when taken off his guard, gave him the vital moment in which to think and determine his action. But often a pause so gained lengthened out until it evolved into a complete cessation from the attack. And before more than one of the grown dogs White Fang's snarl enabled him to beat an honourable retreat.

An outcast himself from the pack of the part-grown dogs, his sanguinary methods and remarkable efficiency made the pack pay for its persecution of him. Not permitted himself to run with the pack, the curious state of affairs obtained that no member of the pack could run outside the pack. White Fang would not permit it. What of his bushwhacking and waylaying tactics, the young dogs were afraid to run by themselves. With the exception of Lip-lip, they were compelled to hunch together for mutual protection against the terrible enemy they had made. A puppy alone by the river bank meant a puppy dead or a puppy that aroused the camp with its shrill pain and terror as it fled back from the wolf-cub that had waylaid it.

CHAPTER III—THE OUTCAST

But White Fang's reprisals did not cease, even when the young dogs had learned thoroughly that they must stay together. He attacked them when he caught them alone, and they attacked him when they were bunched. The sight of him was sufficient to start them rushing after him, at which times his swiftness usually carried him into safety. But woe the dog that outran his fellows in such pursuit! White Fang had learned to turn suddenly upon the pursuer that was ahead of the pack and thoroughly to rip him up before the pack could arrive. This occurred with great frequency, for, once in full cry, the dogs were prone to forget themselves in the excitement of the chase, while White Fang never forgot himself. Stealing backward glances as he ran, he was always ready to whirl around and down the overzealous pursuer that outran his fellows.

Young dogs are bound to play, and out of the exigencies of the situation they realised their play in this mimic warfare. Thus it was that the hunt of White Fang became their chief game—a deadly game, withal, and at all times a serious game. He, on the other hand, being the fastest-footed, was unafraid to venture anywhere. During the period that he waited vainly for his mother to come back, he led the pack many a wild chase through the adjacent woods. But the pack invariably lost him. Its noise and outcry warned him of its presence, while he ran alone, velvet-footed, silently, a moving shadow among the trees after the manner of his father and mother before him. Further he was more directly connected with the Wild than they; and he knew more of its secrets and stratagems. A favourite trick of his was to lose his trail in running water and then lie quietly in a near-by thicket while their baffled cries arose around him.

Hated by his kind and by mankind, indomitable, perpetually warred upon and himself waging perpetual war, his development was rapid and one-sided. This was no soil for kindliness and affection to blossom in. Of such things he had not the faintest glimmering. The code he learned was to obey the strong and to oppress the weak. Grey Beaver was a god, and strong. Therefore White Fang obeyed him. But the dog younger or smaller than himself was weak, a thing to be destroyed. His development was in the direction of power. In order to face the constant danger of hurt and even of destruction, his predatory and protective faculties were unduly developed. He became quicker of movement than the other dogs, swifter of foot, craftier, deadlier, more lithe, more lean with ironlike muscle and sinew, more enduring, more cruel, more ferocious, and more intelligent. He had to become all these things, else he would not have held his own nor survive the hostile environment in which he found himself.

CHAPTER IV—THE TRAIL OF THE GODS

In the fall of the year, when the days were shortening and the bite of the frost was coming into the air, White Fang got his chance for liberty. For several days there had been a great hubbub in the village. The summer camp was being dismantled, and the tribe, bag and baggage, was preparing to go off to the fall hunting. White Fang watched it all with eager eyes, and when the tepees began to come down and the canoes were loading at the bank, he understood. Already the canoes were departing, and some had disappeared down the river.

Quite deliberately he determined to stay behind. He waited his opportunity to slink out of camp to the woods. Here, in the running stream where ice was beginning to form, he hid his trail. Then he crawled into the heart of a dense thicket and waited. The time passed by, and he slept intermittently for hours. Then he was aroused by Grey Beaver's voice calling him by name. There were other voices. White Fang could hear Grey Beaver's squaw taking part in the search, and Mit-sah, who was Grey Beaver's son.

White Fang trembled with fear, and though the impulse came to crawl out of his hiding-place, he resisted it. After a time the voices died away, and some time after that he crept out to enjoy the success of his undertaking. Darkness was coming on, and for a while he played about among the trees, pleasuring in his freedom. Then, and quite suddenly, he became aware of loneliness. He sat down to consider, listening to the silence of the forest and perturbed by it. That nothing moved nor sounded, seemed ominous. He felt the lurking of danger, unseen and unguessed. He was suspicious of the looming bulks of the trees and of the dark shadows that might conceal all manner of perilous things.

Then it was cold. Here was no warm side of a tepee against which to snuggle. The frost was in his feet, and he kept lifting first one fore-foot and then the other. He curved his bushy tail around to cover them, and at the same time he saw a vision. There was nothing strange about it. Upon his inward sight was impressed a succession of memory-pictures. He saw the camp again, the tepees, and the blaze of the fires. He heard the shrill voices of the women, the gruff basses of the men, and the snarling of the dogs. He was hungry, and he remembered pieces of meat and fish that had been thrown him. Here was no meat, nothing but a threatening and inedible silence.

His bondage had softened him. Irresponsibility had weakened him. He had forgotten how to shift for himself. The night yawned about him. His senses, accustomed to the hum and bustle of the camp, used to the continuous impact of sights and sounds, were now left idle. There was nothing to do, nothing to see nor hear. They strained to catch some interruption of the silence and immobility of nature. They were appalled by inaction and by the feel of something terrible impending.

He gave a great start of fright. A colossal and formless something was rushing across the field of his vision. It was a tree-shadow flung by the moon, from whose face the clouds had been brushed away. Reassured, he whimpered softly; then he suppressed the whimper for fear that it might attract the attention of the lurking dangers.

A tree, contracting in the cool of the night, made a loud noise. It was directly above him. He yelped in his fright. A panic seized him, and he ran madly toward the village. He knew an overpowering desire for the protection and companionship of man. In his nostrils was the smell of the camp-smoke. In his ears the camp-sounds and cries were ringing loud. He passed out of the forest and into the moonlit open where were no shadows nor darknesses. But no village greeted his eyes. He had forgotten. The village had gone away.

His wild flight ceased abruptly. There was no place to which to flee. He slunk forlornly through the deserted camp, smelling the rubbish-heaps and the discarded rags and tags of the gods. He would have been glad for the rattle of stones about him, flung by an angry squaw, glad for the hand of Grey Beaver descending upon him in wrath; while he would have welcomed with delight Lip-lip and the whole snarling, cowardly pack.

He came to where Grey Beaver's tepee had stood. In the centre of the space it had occupied, he sat down. He pointed his nose at the moon. His throat was afflicted by rigid spasms, his mouth opened, and in a heart-broken cry bubbled up his loneliness and fear, his grief for Kiche, all his past sorrows and miseries as well as his apprehension of sufferings and dangers to come. It was the long wolf-howl, full-throated and mournful, the first howl he had ever uttered.

The coming of daylight dispelled his fears but increased his loneliness. The naked earth, which so shortly before had been so populous; thrust his loneliness more forcibly upon him. It did not take him long to make up his mind. He plunged into the forest and followed the river bank down the stream. All day he ran. He did not rest. He seemed made to run on for ever. His iron-like body ignored fatigue. And even after fatigue came, his heritage of endurance braced him to endless endeavour and enabled him to drive his complaining body onward.

Where the river swung in against precipitous bluffs, he climbed the high mountains behind. Rivers and streams that entered the main river he forded or swam. Often he took to the rim-ice that was beginning to form, and more than once he crashed through and struggled for life in the icy current. Always he was on the lookout for the trail of the gods where it might leave the river and proceed inland.

White Fang was intelligent beyond the average of his kind; yet his mental vision was not wide enough to embrace the other bank of the Mackenzie. What if the trail of the gods led out on that side? It never entered his head. Later on, when he had travelled more and grown older and wiser and come to know more of trails and rivers, it might be that he could grasp and apprehend such a possibility. But that mental power was yet in the future. Just now he ran blindly, his own bank of the Mackenzie alone entering into his calculations.

All night he ran, blundering in the darkness into mishaps and obstacles that delayed but did not daunt. By the middle of the second day he had been running continuously for thirty hours, and the iron of his flesh was giving out. It was the endurance of his mind that kept him going. He had not eaten in forty hours, and he was weak with hunger. The repeated drenchings in the icy water had likewise had their effect on him. His handsome coat was draggled. The broad pads of his feet were bruised and bleeding. He had begun to limp, and this limp increased with the hours. To make it worse, the light of the sky was obscured and snow began to fall—a raw, moist, melting, clinging snow, slippery under foot, that hid from him the landscape he traversed, and that covered over the inequalities of the ground so that the way of his feet was more difficult and painful.

Grey Beaver had intended camping that night on the far bank of the Mackenzie, for it was in that direction that the hunting lay. But on the near bank, shortly before dark, a moose coming down to drink, had been espied by Kloo-kooch, who was Grey Beaver's squaw. Now, had not the moose come down to drink, had not Mit-sah been steering out of the course because of the snow, had not Kloo-kooch sighted the moose, and had not Grey Beaver killed it with a lucky shot from his rifle, all subsequent things would have happened differently. Grey Beaver would not have camped on the near side of the Mackenzie, and White Fang would have passed by and gone on, either to die or to find his way to his wild brothers and become one of them—a wolf to the end of his days.

Night had fallen. The snow was flying more thickly, and White Fang, whimpering softly to himself as he stumbled and limped along, came upon a fresh trail in the snow. So fresh was it that he knew it immediately for what it was. Whining with eagerness, he followed back from the river bank and in among the trees. The camp-sounds came to his ears. He saw the blaze of the fire, Kloo-kooch cooking, and Grey Beaver squatting on his hams and mumbling a chunk of raw tallow. There was fresh meat in camp!

White Fang expected a beating. He crouched and bristled a little at the thought of it. Then he went forward again. He feared and disliked the beating he knew to be waiting for him. But he knew, further, that the comfort of the fire would be his, the protection of the gods, the companionship of the dogs—the last, a companionship of enmity, but none the less a companionship and satisfying to his gregarious needs.

He came cringing and crawling into the firelight. Grey Beaver saw him, and stopped munching the tallow. White Fang crawled slowly, cringing and grovelling in the abjectness of his abasement and submission. He crawled straight toward Grey Beaver, every inch of his progress becoming slower and more painful. At last he lay at the master's feet, into whose possession he now surrendered himself, voluntarily, body and soul. Of his own choice, he came in to sit by man's fire and to be ruled by him. White Fang trembled, waiting for the punishment to fall upon him. There was a movement of the hand above him. He cringed involuntarily under the expected blow. It did not fall. He stole a glance upward. Grey Beaver was breaking the lump of tallow in half! Grey Beaver was offering him one piece of the tallow! Very gently and somewhat suspiciously, he first smelled the tallow and then proceeded to eat it. Grey Beaver ordered meat to be brought to him, and guarded him from the other dogs while he ate. After that, grateful and content, White Fang lay at Grey Beaver's feet, gazing at the fire that warmed him, blinking and dozing, secure in the knowledge that the morrow would find him, not wandering forlorn through bleak forest-stretches, but in the camp of the man-animals, with the gods to whom he had given himself and upon whom he was now dependent.

CHAPTER V—THE COVENANT

When December was well along, Grey Beaver went on a journey up the Mackenzie. Mit-sah and Kloo-kooch went with him. One sled he drove himself, drawn by dogs he had traded for or borrowed. A second and smaller sled was driven by Mit-sah, and to this was harnessed a team of puppies. It was more of a toy affair than anything else, yet it was the delight of Mit-sah, who felt that he was beginning to do a man's work in the world. Also, he was learning to drive dogs and to train dogs; while the puppies themselves were being broken in to the harness. Furthermore, the sled was of some service, for it carried nearly two hundred pounds of outfit and food.

White Fang had seen the camp-dogs toiling in the harness, so that he did not resent overmuch the first placing of the harness upon himself. About his neck was put a moss-stuffed collar, which was connected by two pulling-traces to a strap that passed around his chest and over his back. It was to this that was fastened the long rope by which he pulled at the sled.

There were seven puppies in the team. The others had been born earlier in the year and were nine and ten months old, while White Fang was only eight months old. Each dog was fastened to the sled by a single rope. No two ropes were of the same length, while the difference in length between any two ropes was at least that of a dog's body. Every rope was brought to a ring at the front end of the sled. The sled itself was without runners, being a birch-bark toboggan, with upturned forward end to keep it from ploughing under the snow. This construction enabled the weight of the sled and load to be distributed over the largest snow-surface; for the snow was crystal-powder and very soft. Observing the same principle of widest distribution of weight, the dogs at the ends of their ropes radiated fan-fashion from the nose of the sled, so that no dog trod in another's footsteps.

There was, furthermore, another virtue in the fan-formation. The ropes of varying length prevented the dogs attacking from the rear those that ran in front of them. For a dog to attack another, it would have to turn upon one at a shorter rope. In which case it would find itself face to face with the dog attacked, and also it would find itself facing the whip of the driver. But the most peculiar virtue of all lay in the fact that the dog that strove to attack one in front of him must pull the sled faster, and that the faster the sled travelled, the faster could the dog attacked run away. Thus, the dog behind could never catch up with the one in front. The faster he ran, the faster ran the one he was after, and the faster ran all the dogs. Incidentally, the sled went faster, and thus, by cunning indirection, did man increase his mastery over the beasts.

CHAPTER V—THE COVENANT

Mit-sah resembled his father, much of whose grey wisdom he possessed. In the past he had observed Lip-lip's persecution of White Fang; but at that time Lip-lip was another man's dog, and Mit-sah had never dared more than to shy an occasional stone at him. But now Lip-lip was his dog, and he proceeded to wreak his vengeance on him by putting him at the end of the longest rope. This made Lip-lip the leader, and was apparently an honour! but in reality it took away from him all honour, and instead of being bully and master of the pack, he now found himself hated and persecuted by the pack.

Because he ran at the end of the longest rope, the dogs had always the view of him running away before them. All that they saw of him was his bushy tail and fleeing hind legs—a view far less ferocious and intimidating than his bristling mane and gleaming fangs. Also, dogs being so constituted in their mental ways, the sight of him running away gave desire to run after him and a feeling that he ran away from them.

The moment the sled started, the team took after Lip-lip in a chase that extended throughout the day. At first he had been prone to turn upon his pursuers, jealous of his dignity and wrathful; but at such times Mit-sah would throw the stinging lash of the thirty-foot cariboo-gut whip into his face and compel him to turn tail and run on. Lip-lip might face the pack, but he could not face that whip, and all that was left him to do was to keep his long rope taut and his flanks ahead of the teeth of his mates.

But a still greater cunning lurked in the recesses of the Indian mind. To give point to unending pursuit of the leader, Mit-sah favoured him over the other dogs. These favours aroused in them jealousy and hatred. In their presence Mit-sah would give him meat and would give it to him only. This was maddening to them. They would rage around just outside the throwing-distance of the whip, while Lip-lip devoured the meat and Mit-sah protected him. And when there was no meat to give, Mit-sah would keep the team at a distance and make believe to give meat to Lip-lip.

White Fang took kindly to the work. He had travelled a greater distance than the other dogs in the yielding of himself to the rule of the gods, and he had learned more thoroughly the futility of opposing their will. In addition, the persecution he had suffered from the pack had made the pack less to him in the scheme of things, and man more. He had not learned to be dependent on his kind for companionship. Besides, Kiche was well-nigh forgotten; and the chief outlet of expression that remained to him was in the allegiance he tendered the gods he had accepted as masters. So he worked hard, learned discipline, and was obedient. Faithfulness and willingness characterised his toil. These are essential traits of the wolf and the wild-dog when they have become domesticated, and these traits White Fang possessed in unusual measure.

A companionship did exist between White Fang and the other dogs, but it was one of warfare and enmity. He had never learned to play with them. He knew only how to fight, and fight with them he did, returning to them a hundred-fold the snaps and slashes they had given him in the days when Lip-lip was leader of the pack. But Lip-lip was no longer leader—except when he fled away before his mates at the end of his rope, the sled bounding along behind. In camp he kept close to Mit-sah or Grey Beaver or Kloo-kooch. He did not dare venture away from the gods, for now the fangs of all dogs were against him, and he tasted to the dregs the persecution that had been White Fang's.

With the overthrow of Lip-lip, White Fang could have become leader of the pack. But he was too morose and solitary for that. He merely thrashed his team-mates. Otherwise he ignored them. They got out of his way when he came along; nor did the boldest of them ever dare to rob him of his meat. On the contrary, they devoured their own meat hurriedly, for fear that he would take it away from them. White Fang knew the law well: *to oppress the weak and obey the strong*. He ate his share of meat as rapidly as he could. And then woe the dog that had not yet finished! A snarl and a flash of fangs, and that dog would wail his indignation to the uncomforting stars while White Fang finished his portion for him.

Every little while, however, one dog or another would flame up in revolt and be promptly subdued. Thus White Fang was kept in training. He was jealous of the isolation in which he kept himself in the midst of the pack, and he fought often to maintain it. But such fights were of brief duration. He was too quick for the others. They were slashed open and bleeding before they knew what had happened, were whipped almost before they had begun to fight.

As rigid as the sled-discipline of the gods, was the discipline maintained by White Fang amongst his fellows. He never allowed them any latitude. He compelled them to an unremitting respect for him. They might do as they pleased amongst themselves. That was no concern of his. But it *was* his concern that they leave him alone in his isolation, get out of his way when he elected to walk among them, and at all times acknowledge his mastery over them. A hint of stiff-leggedness on their part, a lifted lip or a bristle of hair, and he would be upon them, merciless and cruel, swiftly convincing them of the error of their way.

He was a monstrous tyrant. His mastery was rigid as steel. He oppressed the weak with a vengeance. Not for nothing had he been exposed to the pitiless struggles for life in the day of his cubhood, when his mother and he, alone and unaided, held their own and survived in the ferocious environment of the Wild. And not for nothing had he learned to walk softly when superior strength went by. He oppressed the weak, but he respected the strong. And in the course of the long journey with Grey Beaver he walked softly indeed amongst the full-grown dogs in the camps of the strange man-animals they encountered.

The months passed by. Still continued the journey of Grey Beaver. White Fang's strength was developed by the long hours on trail and the steady toil at the sled; and it would have seemed that his mental development was well-nigh complete. He had come to know quite thoroughly the world in which he lived. His outlook was bleak and materialistic. The world as he saw it was a fierce and brutal world, a world without warmth, a world in which caresses and affection and the bright sweetnesses of the spirit did not exist.

He had no affection for Grey Beaver. True, he was a god, but a most savage god. White Fang was glad to acknowledge his lordship, but it was a lordship based upon superior intelligence and brute strength. There was something in the fibre of White Fang's being that made his lordship a thing to be desired, else he would not have come back from the Wild when he did to tender his allegiance. There were deeps in his nature which had never been sounded. A kind word, a caressing touch of the hand, on the part of Grey Beaver, might have sounded these deeps; but Grey Beaver did not caress, nor speak kind words. It was not his way. His primacy was savage, and savagely he ruled, administering justice with a club, punishing transgression with the pain of a blow, and rewarding merit, not by kindness, but by withholding a blow.

So White Fang knew nothing of the heaven a man's hand might contain for him. Besides, he did not like the hands of the man-animals. He was suspicious of them. It was true that they sometimes gave meat, but more often they gave hurt. Hands were things to keep away from. They hurled stones, wielded sticks and clubs and whips, administered slaps and clouts, and, when they touched him, were cunning to hurt with pinch and twist and wrench. In strange villages he had encountered the hands of the children and learned that they were cruel to hurt. Also, he had once nearly had an eye poked out by a toddling papoose. From these experiences he became suspicious of all children. He could not tolerate them. When they came near with their ominous hands, he got up.

It was in a village at the Great Slave Lake, that, in the course of resenting the evil of the hands of the man-animals, he came to modify the law that he had learned from Grey Beaver: namely, that the unpardonable crime was to bite one of the gods. In this village, after the custom of all dogs in all villages, White Fang went foraging, for food. A boy was chopping frozen moose-meat with an axe, and the chips were flying in the snow. White Fang, sliding by in quest of meat, stopped and began to eat the chips. He observed the boy lay down the axe and take up a stout club. White Fang sprang clear, just in time to escape the descending blow. The boy pursued him, and he, a stranger in the village, fled between two tepees to find himself cornered against a high earth bank.

There was no escape for White Fang. The only way out was between the two tepees, and this the boy guarded. Holding his club prepared to strike, he drew in on his cornered quarry. White Fang was furious. He faced the boy, bristling and snarling, his sense of justice outraged. He knew the law of forage. All the wastage of meat, such as the frozen chips, belonged to the dog that found it. He had done no wrong, broken no law, yet here was this boy preparing to give him a beating. White Fang scarcely knew what happened. He did it in a surge of rage. And he did it so quickly that the boy did not know either. All the boy knew was that he had in some unaccountable way been overturned into the snow, and that his club-hand had been ripped wide open by White Fang's teeth.

But White Fang knew that he had broken the law of the gods. He had driven his teeth into the sacred flesh of one of them, and could expect nothing but a most terrible punishment. He fled away to Grey Beaver, behind whose protecting legs he crouched when the bitten boy and the boy's family came, demanding vengeance. But they went away with vengeance unsatisfied. Grey Beaver defended White Fang. So did Mit-sah and Kloo-kooch. White Fang, listening to the wordy war and watching the angry gestures, knew that his act was justified. And so it came that he learned there were gods and gods. There were his gods, and there were other gods, and between them there was a difference. Justice or injustice, it was all the same, he must take all things from the hands of his own gods. But he was not compelled to take injustice from the other gods. It was his privilege to resent it with his teeth. And this also was a law of the gods.

Before the day was out, White Fang was to learn more about this law. Mit-sah, alone, gathering firewood in the forest, encountered the boy that had been bitten. With him were other boys. Hot words passed. Then all the boys attacked Mit-sah. It was going hard with him. Blows were raining upon him from all sides. White Fang looked on at first. This was an affair of the gods, and no concern of his. Then he realised that this was Mit-sah, one of his own particular gods, who was being maltreated. It was no reasoned impulse that made White Fang do what he then did. A mad rush of anger sent him leaping in amongst the combatants. Five minutes later the landscape was covered with fleeing boys, many of whom dripped blood upon the snow in token that White Fang's teeth had not been idle. When Mit-sah told the story in camp, Grey Beaver ordered meat to be given to White Fang. He ordered much meat to be given, and White Fang, gorged and sleepy by the fire, knew that the law had received its verification.

It was in line with these experiences that White Fang came to learn the law of property and the duty of the defence of property. From the protection of his god's body to the protection of his god's possessions was a step, and this step he made. What was his god's was to be defended against all the world—even to the extent of biting other gods. Not only was such an act sacrilegious in its nature, but it was fraught with peril. The gods were all-powerful, and a dog was no match against them; yet White Fang learned to face them, fiercely belligerent and unafraid. Duty rose above fear, and thieving gods learned to leave Grey Beaver's property alone.

One thing, in this connection, White Fang quickly learnt, and that was that a thieving god was usually a cowardly god and prone to run away at the sounding of the alarm. Also, he learned that but brief time elapsed between his sounding of the alarm and Grey Beaver coming to his aid. He came to know that it was not fear of him that drove the thief away, but fear of Grey Beaver. White Fang did not give the alarm by barking. He never barked. His method was to drive straight at the intruder, and to sink his teeth in if he could. Because he was morose and solitary, having nothing to do with the other dogs, he was unusually fitted to guard his master's property; and in this he was encouraged and trained by Grey Beaver. One result of this was to make White Fang more ferocious and indomitable, and more solitary.

The months went by, binding stronger and stronger the covenant between dog and man. This was the ancient covenant that the first wolf that came in from the Wild entered into with man. And, like all succeeding wolves and wild dogs that had done likewise, White Fang worked the covenant out for himself. The terms were simple. For the possession of a flesh-and-blood god, he exchanged his own liberty. Food and fire, protection and companionship, were some of the things he received from the god. In return, he guarded the god's property, defended his body, worked for him, and obeyed him.

The possession of a god implies service. White Fang's was a service of duty and awe, but not of love. He did not know what love was. He had no experience of love. Kiche was a remote memory. Besides, not only had he abandoned the Wild and his kind when he gave himself up to man, but the terms of the covenant were such that if ever he met Kiche again he would not desert his god to go with her. His allegiance to man seemed somehow a law of his being greater than the love of liberty, of kind and kin.

CHAPTER VI—THE FAMINE

The spring of the year was at hand when Grey Beaver finished his long journey. It was April, and White Fang was a year old when he pulled into the home villages and was loosed from the harness by Mit-sah. Though a long way from his full growth, White Fang, next to Lip-lip, was the largest yearling in the village. Both from his father, the wolf, and from Kiche, he had inherited stature and strength, and already he was measuring up alongside the full-grown dogs. But he had not yet grown compact. His body was slender and rangy, and his strength more stringy than massive, His coat was the true wolf-grey, and to all appearances he was true wolf himself. The quarter-strain of dog he had inherited from Kiche had left no mark on him physically, though it had played its part in his mental make-up.

He wandered through the village, recognising with staid satisfaction the various gods he had known before the long journey. Then there were the dogs, puppies growing up like himself, and grown dogs that did not look so large and formidable as the memory pictures he retained of them. Also, he stood less in fear of them than formerly, stalking among them with a certain careless ease that was as new to him as it was enjoyable.

There was Baseek, a grizzled old fellow that in his younger days had but to uncover his fangs to send White Fang cringing and crouching to the right about. From him White Fang had learned much of his own insignificance; and from him he was now to learn much of the change and development that had taken place in himself. While Baseek had been growing weaker with age, White Fang had been growing stronger with youth.

It was at the cutting-up of a moose, fresh-killed, that White Fang learned of the changed relations in which he stood to the dog-world. He had got for himself a hoof and part of the shin-bone, to which quite a bit of meat was attached. Withdrawn from the immediate scramble of the other dogs—in fact out of sight behind a thicket—he was devouring his prize, when Baseek rushed in upon him. Before he knew what he was doing, he had slashed the intruder twice and sprung clear. Baseek was surprised by the other's temerity and swiftness of attack. He stood, gazing stupidly across at White Fang, the raw, red shin-bone between them.

Baseek was old, and already he had come to know the increasing valour of the dogs it had been his wont to bully. Bitter experiences these, which, perforce, he swallowed, calling upon all his wisdom to cope with them. In the old days he would have sprung upon White Fang in a fury of righteous wrath. But now his waning powers would not permit such a course. He bristled fiercely and looked ominously across the shin-bone at White Fang. And White Fang, resurrecting quite a deal of the old awe, seemed to wilt and to shrink in upon himself and grow small, as he cast about in his mind for a way to beat a retreat not too inglorious.

And right here Baseek erred. Had he contented himself with looking fierce and ominous, all would have been well. White Fang, on the verge of retreat, would have retreated, leaving the meat to him. But Baseek did not wait. He considered the victory already his and stepped forward to the meat. As he bent his head carelessly to smell it, White Fang bristled slightly. Even then it was not too late for Baseek to retrieve the situation. Had he merely stood over the meat, head up and glowering, White Fang would ultimately have slunk away. But the fresh meat was strong in Baseek's nostrils, and greed urged him to take a bite of it.

This was too much for White Fang. Fresh upon his months of mastery over his own team-mates, it was beyond his self-control to stand idly by while another devoured the meat that belonged to him. He struck, after his custom, without warning. With the first slash, Baseek's right ear was ripped into ribbons. He was astounded at the suddenness of it. But more things, and most grievous ones, were happening with equal suddenness. He was knocked off his feet. His throat was bitten. While he was struggling to his feet the young dog sank teeth twice into his shoulder. The swiftness of it was bewildering. He made a futile rush at White Fang, clipping the empty air with an outraged snap. The next moment his nose was laid open, and he was staggering backward away from the meat.

The situation was now reversed. White Fang stood over the shin-bone, bristling and menacing, while Baseek stood a little way off, preparing to retreat. He dared not risk a fight with this young lightning-flash, and again he knew, and more bitterly, the enfeeblement of oncoming age. His attempt to maintain his dignity was heroic. Calmly turning his back upon young dog and shin-bone, as though both were beneath his notice and unworthy of his consideration, he stalked grandly away. Nor, until well out of sight, did he stop to lick his bleeding wounds.

The effect on White Fang was to give him a greater faith in himself, and a greater pride. He walked less softly among the grown dogs; his attitude toward them was less compromising. Not that he went out of his way looking for trouble. Far from it. But upon his way he demanded consideration. He stood upon his right to go his way unmolested and to give trail to no dog. He had to be taken into account, that was all. He was no longer to be disregarded and ignored, as was the lot of puppies, and as continued to be the lot of the puppies that were his team-mates. They got out of the way, gave trail to the grown dogs, and gave up meat to them under compulsion. But White Fang, uncompanionable, solitary, morose, scarcely looking to right or left, redoubtable, forbidding of aspect, remote and alien, was accepted as an equal by his puzzled elders. They quickly learned to leave him alone, neither venturing hostile acts nor making overtures of friendliness. If they left him alone, he left them alone—a state of affairs that they found, after a few encounters, to be pre-eminently desirable.

In midsummer White Fang had an experience. Trotting along in his silent way to investigate a new tepee which had been erected on the edge of the village while he was away with the hunters after moose, he came full upon Kiche. He paused and looked at her. He remembered her vaguely, but he *remembered* her, and that was more than could be said for her. She lifted her lip at him in the old snarl of menace, and his memory became clear. His forgotten cubhood, all that was associated with that familiar snarl, rushed back to him. Before he had known the gods, she had been to him the centre-pin of the universe. The old familiar feelings of that time came back upon him, surged up within him. He bounded towards her joyously, and she met him with shrewd fangs that laid his cheek open to the bone. He did not understand. He backed away, bewildered and puzzled.

But it was not Kiche's fault. A wolf-mother was not made to remember her cubs of a year or so before. So she did not remember White Fang. He was a strange animal, an intruder; and her present litter of puppies gave her the right to resent such intrusion.

One of the puppies sprawled up to White Fang. They were half-brothers, only they did not know it. White Fang sniffed the puppy curiously, whereupon Kiche rushed upon him, gashing his face a second time. He backed farther away. All the old memories and associations died down again and passed into the grave from which they had been resurrected. He looked at Kiche licking her puppy and stopping now and then to snarl at him. She was without value to him. He had learned to get along without her. Her meaning was forgotten. There was no place for her in his scheme of things, as there was no place for him in hers.

He was still standing, stupid and bewildered, the memories forgotten, wondering what it was all about, when Kiche attacked him a third time, intent on driving him away altogether from the vicinity. And White Fang allowed himself to be driven away. This was a female of his kind, and it was a law of his kind that the males must not fight the females. He did not know anything about this law, for it was no generalisation of the mind, not a something acquired by experience of the world. He knew it as a secret prompting, as an urge of instinct—of the same instinct that made him howl at the moon and stars of nights, and that made him fear death and the unknown.

The months went by. White Fang grew stronger, heavier, and more compact, while his character was developing along the lines laid down by his heredity and his environment. His heredity was a life-stuff that may be likened to clay. It possessed many possibilities, was capable of being moulded into many different forms. Environment served to model the clay, to give it a particular form. Thus, had White Fang never come in to the fires of man, the Wild would have moulded him into a true wolf. But the gods had given him a different environment, and he was moulded into a dog that was rather wolfish, but that was a dog and not a wolf.

And so, according to the clay of his nature and the pressure of his surroundings, his character was being moulded into a certain particular shape. There was no escaping it. He was becoming more morose, more uncompanionable, more solitary, more ferocious; while the dogs were learning more and more that it was better to be at peace with him than at war, and Grey Beaver was coming to prize him more greatly with the passage of each day.

White Fang, seeming to sum up strength in all his qualities, nevertheless suffered from one besetting weakness. He could not stand being laughed at. The laughter of men was a hateful thing. They might laugh among themselves about anything they pleased except himself, and he did not mind. But the moment laughter was turned upon him he would fly into a most terrible rage. Grave, dignified, sombre, a laugh made him frantic to ridiculousness. It so outraged him and upset him that for hours he would behave like a demon. And woe to the dog that at such times ran foul of him. He knew the law too well to take it out of Grey Beaver; behind Grey Beaver were a club and godhead. But behind the dogs there was nothing but space, and into this space they flew when White Fang came on the scene, made mad by laughter.

In the third year of his life there came a great famine to the Mackenzie Indians. In the summer the fish failed. In the winter the cariboo forsook their accustomed track. Moose were scarce, the rabbits almost disappeared, hunting and preying animals perished. Denied their usual food-supply, weakened by hunger, they fell upon and devoured one another. Only the strong survived. White Fang's gods were always hunting animals. The old and the weak of them died of hunger. There was wailing in the village, where the women and children went without in order that what little they had might go into the bellies of the lean and hollow-eyed hunters who trod the forest in the vain pursuit of meat.

To such extremity were the gods driven that they ate the soft-tanned leather of their mocassins and mittens, while the dogs ate the harnesses off their backs and the very whip-lashes. Also, the dogs ate one another, and also the gods ate the dogs. The weakest and the more worthless were eaten first. The dogs that still lived, looked on and understood. A few of the boldest and wisest forsook the fires of the gods, which had now become a shambles, and fled into the forest, where, in the end, they starved to death or were eaten by wolves.

In this time of misery, White Fang, too, stole away into the woods. He was better fitted for the life than the other dogs, for he had the training of his cubhood to guide him. Especially adept did he become in stalking small living things. He would lie concealed for hours, following every movement of a cautious tree-squirrel, waiting, with a patience as huge as the hunger he suffered from, until the squirrel ventured out upon the ground. Even then, White Fang was not premature. He waited until he was sure of striking before the squirrel could gain a tree-refuge. Then, and not until then, would he flash from his hiding-place, a grey projectile, incredibly swift, never failing its mark—the fleeing squirrel that fled not fast enough.

Successful as he was with squirrels, there was one difficulty that prevented him from living and growing fat on them. There were not enough squirrels. So he was driven to hunt still smaller things. So acute did his hunger become at times that he was not above rooting out wood-mice from their burrows in the ground. Nor did he scorn to do battle with a weasel as hungry as himself and many times more ferocious.

In the worst pinches of the famine he stole back to the fires of the gods. But he did not go into the fires. He lurked in the forest, avoiding discovery and robbing the snares at the rare intervals when game was caught. He even robbed Grey Beaver's snare of a rabbit at a time when Grey Beaver staggered and tottered through the forest, sitting down often to rest, what of weakness and of shortness of breath.

One day While Fang encountered a young wolf, gaunt and scrawny, loose-jointed with famine. Had he not been hungry himself, White Fang might have gone with him and eventually found his way into the pack amongst his wild brethren. As it was, he ran the young wolf down and killed and ate him.

Fortune seemed to favour him. Always, when hardest pressed for food, he found something to kill. Again, when he was weak, it was his luck that none of the larger preying animals chanced upon him. Thus, he was strong from the two days' eating a lynx had afforded him when the hungry wolf-pack ran full tilt upon him. It was a long, cruel chase, but he was better nourished than they, and in the end outran them.

And not only did he outrun them, but, circling widely back on his track, he gathered in one of his exhausted pursuers.

After that he left that part of the country and journeyed over to the valley wherein he had been born. Here, in the old lair, he encountered Kiche. Up to her old tricks, she, too, had fled the inhospitable fires of the gods and gone back to her old refuge to give birth to her young. Of this litter but one remained alive when White Fang came upon the scene, and this one was not destined to live long. Young life had little chance in such a famine.

Kiche's greeting of her grown son was anything but affectionate. But White Fang did not mind. He had outgrown his mother. So he turned tail philosophically and trotted on up the stream. At the forks he took the turning to the left, where he found the lair of the lynx with whom his mother and he had fought long before. Here, in the abandoned lair, he settled down and rested for a day.

During the early summer, in the last days of the famine, he met Lip-lip, who had likewise taken to the woods, where he had eked out a miserable existence.

White Fang came upon him unexpectedly. Trotting in opposite directions along the base of a high bluff, they rounded a corner of rock and found themselves face to face. They paused with instant alarm, and looked at each other suspiciously.

White Fang was in splendid condition. His hunting had been good, and for a week he had eaten his fill. He was even gorged from his latest kill. But in the moment he looked at Lip-lip his hair rose on end all along his back. It was an involuntary bristling on his part, the physical state that in the past had always accompanied the mental state produced in him by Lip-lip's bullying and persecution. As in the past he had bristled and snarled at sight of Lip-lip, so now, and automatically, he bristled and snarled. He did not waste any time. The thing was done thoroughly and with despatch. Lip-lip essayed to back away, but White Fang struck him hard, shoulder to shoulder. Lip-lip was overthrown and rolled upon his back. White Fang's teeth drove into the scrawny throat. There was a death-struggle, during which White Fang walked around, stiff-legged and observant. Then he resumed his course and trotted on along the base of the bluff.

One day, not long after, he came to the edge of the forest, where a narrow stretch of open land sloped down to the Mackenzie. He had been over this ground before, when it was bare, but now a village occupied it. Still hidden amongst the trees, he paused to study the situation. Sights and sounds and scents were familiar to him. It was the old village changed to a new place. But sights and sounds and smells were different from those he had last had when he fled away from it. There was no whimpering nor wailing. Contented sounds saluted his ear, and when he heard the angry voice of a woman he knew it to be the anger that proceeds from a full stomach. And there was a smell in the air of fish. There was food. The famine was gone. He came out boldly from the forest and trotted into camp straight to Grey Beaver's tepee. Grey Beaver was not there; but Kloo-kooch welcomed him with glad cries and the whole of a fresh-caught fish, and he lay down to wait Grey Beaver's coming.

PART IV

CHAPTER I—THE ENEMY OF HIS KIND

Had there been in White Fang's nature any possibility, no matter how remote, of his ever coming to fraternise with his kind, such possibility was irretrievably destroyed when he was made leader of the sled-team. For now the dogs hated him—hated him for the extra meat bestowed upon him by Mit-sah; hated him for all the real and fancied favours he received; hated him for that he fled always at the head of the team, his waving brush of a tail and his perpetually retreating hind-quarters for ever maddening their eyes.

And White Fang just as bitterly hated them back. Being sled-leader was anything but gratifying to him. To be compelled to run away before the yelling pack, every dog of which, for three years, he had thrashed and mastered, was almost more than he could endure. But endure it he must, or perish, and the life that was in him had no desire to perish out. The moment Mit-sah gave his order for the start, that moment the whole team, with eager, savage cries, sprang forward at White Fang.

There was no defence for him. If he turned upon them, Mit-sah would throw the stinging lash of the whip into his face. Only remained to him to run away. He could not encounter that howling horde with his tail and hind-quarters. These were scarcely fit weapons with which to meet the many merciless fangs. So run away he did, violating his own nature and pride with every leap he made, and leaping all day long.

One cannot violate the promptings of one's nature without having that nature recoil upon itself. Such a recoil is like that of a hair, made to grow out from the body, turning unnaturally upon the direction of its growth and growing into the body—a rankling, festering thing of hurt. And so with White Fang. Every urge of his being impelled him to spring upon the pack that cried at his heels, but it was the will of the gods that this should not be; and behind the will, to enforce it, was the whip of cariboo-gut with its biting thirty-foot lash. So White Fang could only eat his heart in bitterness and develop a hatred and malice commensurate with the ferocity and indomitability of his nature.

If ever a creature was the enemy of its kind, White Fang was that creature. He asked no quarter, gave none. He was continually marred and scarred by the teeth of the pack, and as continually he left his own marks upon the pack. Unlike most leaders, who, when camp was made and the dogs were unhitched, huddled near to the gods for protection, White Fang disdained such protection. He walked boldly about the camp, inflicting punishment in the night for what he had suffered in the day. In the time before he was made leader of the team, the pack had learned to get out of his way. But now it was different. Excited by the day-long pursuit of him, swayed subconsciously by the insistent iteration on their brains of the sight of him fleeing away, mastered by the feeling of mastery enjoyed all day, the dogs could not bring themselves to give way to him. When he appeared amongst them, there was always a squabble. His progress was marked by snarl and snap and growl. The very atmosphere he breathed was surcharged with hatred and malice, and this but served to increase the hatred and malice within him.

When Mit-sah cried out his command for the team to stop, White Fang obeyed. At first this caused trouble for the other dogs. All of them would spring upon the hated leader only to find the tables turned. Behind him would be Mit-sah, the great whip singing in his hand. So the dogs came to understand that when the team stopped by order, White Fang was to be let alone. But when White Fang stopped without orders, then it was allowed them to spring upon him and destroy him if they could. After several experiences, White Fang never stopped without orders. He learned quickly. It was in the nature of things, that he must learn quickly if he were to survive the unusually severe conditions under which life was vouchsafed him.

But the dogs could never learn the lesson to leave him alone in camp. Each day, pursuing him and crying defiance at him, the lesson of the previous night was erased, and that night would have to be learned over again, to be as immediately forgotten. Besides, there was a greater consistence in their dislike of him. They sensed between themselves and him a difference of kind—cause sufficient in itself for hostility. Like him, they were domesticated wolves. But they had been domesticated for generations. Much of the Wild had been lost, so that to them the Wild was the unknown, the terrible, the ever-menacing and ever warring. But to him, in appearance and action and impulse, still clung the Wild. He symbolised it, was its personification: so that when they showed their teeth to him they were defending themselves against the powers of destruction that lurked in the shadows of the forest and in the dark beyond the camp-fire.

But there was one lesson the dogs did learn, and that was to keep together. White Fang was too terrible for any of them to face single-handed. They met him with the mass-formation, otherwise he would have killed them, one by one, in a night. As it was, he never had a chance to kill them. He might roll a dog off its feet, but the pack would be upon him before he could follow up and deliver the deadly throat-stroke. At the first hint of conflict, the whole team drew together and faced him. The dogs had quarrels among themselves, but these were forgotten when trouble was brewing with White Fang.

On the other hand, try as they would, they could not kill White Fang. He was too quick for them, too formidable, too wise. He avoided tight places and always backed out of it when they bade fair to surround him. While, as for getting him off his feet, there was no dog among them capable of doing the trick. His feet clung to the earth with the same tenacity that he clung to life. For that matter, life and footing were synonymous in this unending warfare with the pack, and none knew it better than White Fang.

So he became the enemy of his kind, domesticated wolves that they were, softened by the fires of man, weakened in the sheltering shadow of man's strength. White Fang was bitter and implacable. The clay of him was so moulded. He declared a vendetta against all dogs. And so terribly did he live this vendetta that Grey Beaver, fierce savage himself, could not but marvel at White Fang's ferocity. Never, he swore, had there been the like of this animal; and the Indians in strange villages swore likewise when they considered the tale of his killings amongst their dogs.

When White Fang was nearly five years old, Grey Beaver took him on another great journey, and long remembered was the havoc he worked amongst the dogs of the many villages along the Mackenzie, across the Rockies, and down the Porcupine to the Yukon. He revelled in the vengeance he wreaked upon his kind. They were ordinary, unsuspecting dogs. They were not prepared for his swiftness and directness, for his attack without warning. They did not know him for what he was, a lightning-flash of slaughter. They bristled up to him, stiff-legged and challenging, while he, wasting no time on elaborate preliminaries, snapping into action like a steel spring, was at their throats and destroying them before they knew what was happening and while they were yet in the throes of surprise.

He became an adept at fighting. He economised. He never wasted his strength, never tussled. He was in too quickly for that, and, if he missed, was out again too quickly. The dislike of the wolf for close quarters was his to an unusual degree. He could not endure a prolonged contact with another body. It smacked of danger. It made him frantic. He must be away, free, on his own legs, touching no living thing. It was the Wild still clinging to him, asserting itself through him. This feeling had been accentuated by the Ishmaelite life he had led from his puppyhood. Danger lurked in contacts. It was the trap, ever the trap, the fear of it lurking deep in the life of him, woven into the fibre of him.

In consequence, the strange dogs he encountered had no chance against him. He eluded their fangs. He got them, or got away, himself untouched in either event. In the natural course of things there were exceptions to this. There were times when several dogs, pitching on to him, punished him before he could get away; and there were times when a single dog scored deeply on him. But these were accidents. In the main, so efficient a fighter had he become, he went his way unscathed.

Another advantage he possessed was that of correctly judging time and distance. Not that he did this consciously, however. He did not calculate such things. It was all automatic. His eyes saw correctly, and the nerves carried the vision correctly to his brain. The parts of him were better adjusted than those of the average dog. They worked together more smoothly and steadily. His was a better, far better, nervous, mental, and muscular co-ordination. When his eyes conveyed to his brain the moving image of an action, his brain without conscious effort, knew the space that limited that action and the time required for its completion. Thus, he could avoid the leap of another dog, or the drive of its fangs, and at the same moment could seize the infinitesimal fraction of time in which to deliver his own attack. Body and brain, his was a more perfected mechanism. Not that he was to be praised for it. Nature had been more generous to him than to the average animal, that was all.

It was in the summer that White Fang arrived at Fort Yukon. Grey Beaver had crossed the great watershed between Mackenzie and the Yukon in the late winter, and spent the spring in hunting among the western outlying spurs of the Rockies. Then, after the break-up of the ice on the Porcupine, he had built a canoe and paddled down that stream to where it effected its junction with the Yukon just under the Arctic circle. Here stood the old Hudson's Bay Company fort; and here were many Indians, much food, and unprecedented excitement. It was the summer of 1898, and thousands of gold-hunters were going up the Yukon to Dawson and the Klondike. Still hundreds of miles from their goal, nevertheless many of them had been on the way for a year, and the least any of them had travelled to get that far was five thousand miles, while some had come from the other side of the world.

Here Grey Beaver stopped. A whisper of the gold-rush had reached his ears, and he had come with several bales of furs, and another of gut-sewn mittens and moccasins. He would not have ventured so long a trip had he not expected generous profits. But what he had expected was nothing to what he realised. His wildest dreams had not exceeded a hundred per cent. profit; he made a thousand per cent. And like a true Indian, he settled down to trade carefully and slowly, even if it took all summer and the rest of the winter to dispose of his goods.

It was at Fort Yukon that White Fang saw his first white men. As compared with the Indians he had known, they were to him another race of beings, a race of superior gods. They impressed him as possessing superior power, and it is on power that godhead rests. White Fang did not reason it out, did not in his mind make the sharp generalisation that the white gods were more powerful. It was a feeling, nothing more, and yet none the less potent. As, in his puppyhood, the looming bulks of the tepees, man-reared, had affected him as manifestations of power, so was he affected now by the houses and the huge fort all of massive logs. Here was power. Those white gods were strong. They possessed greater mastery over matter than the gods he had known, most powerful among which was Grey Beaver. And yet Grey Beaver was as a child-god among these white-skinned ones.

To be sure, White Fang only felt these things. He was not conscious of them. Yet it is upon feeling, more often than thinking, that animals act; and every act White Fang now performed was based upon the feeling that the white men were the superior gods. In the first place he was very suspicious of them. There was no telling what unknown terrors were theirs, what unknown hurts they could administer. He was curious to observe them, fearful of being noticed by them. For the first few hours he was content with slinking around and watching them from a safe distance. Then he saw that no harm befell the dogs that were near to them, and he came in closer.

In turn he was an object of great curiosity to them. His wolfish appearance caught their eyes at once, and they pointed him out to one another. This act of pointing put White Fang on his guard, and when they tried to approach him he showed his teeth and backed away. Not one succeeded in laying a hand on him, and it was well that they did not.

White Fang soon learned that very few of these gods—not more than a dozen—lived at this place. Every two or three days a steamer (another and colossal manifestation of power) came into the bank and stopped for several hours. The white men came from off these steamers and went away on them again. There seemed untold numbers of these white men. In the first day or so, he saw more of them than he had seen Indians in all his life; and as the days went by they continued to come up the river, stop, and then go on up the river out of sight.

But if the white gods were all-powerful, their dogs did not amount to much. This White Fang quickly discovered by mixing with those that came ashore with their masters. They were irregular shapes and sizes. Some were short-legged—too short; others were long-legged—too long. They had hair instead of fur, and a few had very little hair at that. And none of them knew how to fight.

CHAPTER I—THE ENEMY OF HIS KIND

As an enemy of his kind, it was in White Fang's province to fight with them. This he did, and he quickly achieved for them a mighty contempt. They were soft and helpless, made much noise, and floundered around clumsily trying to accomplish by main strength what he accomplished by dexterity and cunning. They rushed bellowing at him. He sprang to the side. They did not know what had become of him; and in that moment he struck them on the shoulder, rolling them off their feet and delivering his stroke at the throat.

Sometimes this stroke was successful, and a stricken dog rolled in the dirt, to be pounced upon and torn to pieces by the pack of Indian dogs that waited. White Fang was wise. He had long since learned that the gods were made angry when their dogs were killed. The white men were no exception to this. So he was content, when he had overthrown and slashed wide the throat of one of their dogs, to drop back and let the pack go in and do the cruel finishing work. It was then that the white men rushed in, visiting their wrath heavily on the pack, while White Fang went free. He would stand off at a little distance and look on, while stones, clubs, axes, and all sorts of weapons fell upon his fellows. White Fang was very wise.

But his fellows grew wise in their own way; and in this White Fang grew wise with them. They learned that it was when a steamer first tied to the bank that they had their fun. After the first two or three strange dogs had been downed and destroyed, the white men hustled their own animals back on board and wrecked savage vengeance on the offenders. One white man, having seen his dog, a setter, torn to pieces before his eyes, drew a revolver. He fired rapidly, six times, and six of the pack lay dead or dying—another manifestation of power that sank deep into White Fang's consciousness.

White Fang enjoyed it all. He did not love his kind, and he was shrewd enough to escape hurt himself. At first, the killing of the white men's dogs had been a diversion. After a time it became his occupation. There was no work for him to do. Grey Beaver was busy trading and getting wealthy. So White Fang hung around the landing with the disreputable gang of Indian dogs, waiting for steamers. With the arrival of a steamer the fun began. After a few minutes, by the time the white men had got over their surprise, the gang scattered. The fun was over until the next steamer should arrive.

But it can scarcely be said that White Fang was a member of the gang. He did not mingle with it, but remained aloof, always himself, and was even feared by it. It is true, he worked with it. He picked the quarrel with the strange dog while the gang waited. And when he had overthrown the strange dog the gang went in to finish it. But it is equally true that he then withdrew, leaving the gang to receive the punishment of the outraged gods.

It did not require much exertion to pick these quarrels. All he had to do, when the strange dogs came ashore, was to show himself. When they saw him they rushed for him. It was their instinct. He was the Wild—the unknown, the terrible, the ever-menacing, the thing that prowled in the darkness around the fires of the primeval world when they, cowering close to the fires, were reshaping their instincts, learning to fear the Wild out of which they had come, and which they had deserted and betrayed. Generation by generation, down all the generations, had this fear of the Wild been stamped into their natures. For centuries the Wild had stood for terror and destruction. And during all this time free licence had been theirs, from their masters, to kill the things of the Wild. In doing this they had protected both themselves and the gods whose companionship they shared.

And so, fresh from the soft southern world, these dogs, trotting down the gang-plank and out upon the Yukon shore had but to see White Fang to experience the irresistible impulse to rush upon him and destroy him. They might be town-reared dogs, but the instinctive fear of the Wild was theirs just the same. Not alone with their own eyes did they see the wolfish creature in the clear light of day, standing before them. They saw him with the eyes of their ancestors, and by their inherited memory they knew White Fang for the wolf, and they remembered the ancient feud.

All of which served to make White Fang's days enjoyable. If the sight of him drove these strange dogs upon him, so much the better for him, so much the worse for them. They looked upon him as legitimate prey, and as legitimate prey he looked upon them.

Not for nothing had he first seen the light of day in a lonely lair and fought his first fights with the ptarmigan, the weasel, and the lynx. And not for nothing had his puppyhood been made bitter by the persecution of Lip-lip and the whole puppy pack. It might have been otherwise, and he would then have been otherwise. Had Lip-lip not existed, he would have passed his puppyhood with the other puppies and grown up more doglike and with more liking for dogs. Had Grey Beaver possessed the plummet of affection and love, he might have sounded the deeps of White Fang's nature and brought up to the surface all manner of kindly qualities. But these things had not been so. The clay of White Fang had been moulded until he became what he was, morose and lonely, unloving and ferocious, the enemy of all his kind.

CHAPTER II—THE MAD GOD

A small number of white men lived in Fort Yukon. These men had been long in the country. They called themselves Sour-doughs, and took great pride in so classifying themselves. For other men, new in the land, they felt nothing but disdain. The men who came ashore from the steamers were newcomers. They were known as *chechaquos*, and they always wilted at the application of the name. They made their bread with baking-powder. This was the invidious distinction between them and the Sour-doughs, who, forsooth, made their bread from sour-dough because they had no baking-powder.

All of which is neither here nor there. The men in the fort disdained the newcomers and enjoyed seeing them come to grief. Especially did they enjoy the havoc worked amongst the newcomers' dogs by White Fang and his disreputable gang. When a steamer arrived, the men of the fort made it a point always to come down to the bank and see the fun. They looked forward to it with as much anticipation as did the Indian dogs, while they were not slow to appreciate the savage and crafty part played by White Fang.

But there was one man amongst them who particularly enjoyed the sport. He would come running at the first sound of a steamboat's whistle; and when the last fight was over and White Fang and the pack had scattered, he would return slowly to the fort, his face heavy with regret. Sometimes, when a soft southland dog went down, shrieking its death-cry under the fangs of the pack, this man would be unable to contain himself, and would leap into the air and cry out with delight. And always he had a sharp and covetous eye for White Fang.

This man was called "Beauty" by the other men of the fort. No one knew his first name, and in general he was known in the country as Beauty Smith. But he was anything save a beauty. To antithesis was due his naming. He was pre-eminently unbeautiful. Nature had been niggardly with him. He was a small man to begin with; and upon his meagre frame was deposited an even more strikingly meagre head. Its apex might be likened to a point. In fact, in his boyhood, before he had been named Beauty by his fellows, he had been called "Pinhead."

Backward, from the apex, his head slanted down to his neck and forward it slanted uncompromisingly to meet a low and remarkably wide forehead. Beginning here, as though regretting her parsimony, Nature had spread his features with a lavish hand. His eyes were large, and between them was the distance of two eyes. His face, in relation to the rest of him, was prodigious. In order to discover the necessary area,

Nature had given him an enormous prognathous jaw. It was wide and heavy, and protruded outward and down until it seemed to rest on his chest. Possibly this appearance was due to the weariness of the slender neck, unable properly to support so great a burden.

This jaw gave the impression of ferocious determination. But something lacked. Perhaps it was from excess. Perhaps the jaw was too large. At any rate, it was a lie. Beauty Smith was known far and wide as the weakest of weak-kneed and snivelling cowards. To complete his description, his teeth were large and yellow, while the two eye-teeth, larger than their fellows, showed under his lean lips like fangs. His eyes were yellow and muddy, as though Nature had run short on pigments and squeezed together the dregs of all her tubes. It was the same with his hair, sparse and irregular of growth, muddy-yellow and dirty-yellow, rising on his head and sprouting out of his face in unexpected tufts and bunches, in appearance like clumped and wind-blown grain.

In short, Beauty Smith was a monstrosity, and the blame of it lay elsewhere. He was not responsible. The clay of him had been so moulded in the making. He did the cooking for the other men in the fort, the dish-washing and the drudgery. They did not despise him. Rather did they tolerate him in a broad human way, as one tolerates any creature evilly treated in the making. Also, they feared him. His cowardly rages made them dread a shot in the back or poison in their coffee. But somebody had to do the cooking, and whatever else his shortcomings, Beauty Smith could cook.

This was the man that looked at White Fang, delighted in his ferocious prowess, and desired to possess him. He made overtures to White Fang from the first. White Fang began by ignoring him. Later on, when the overtures became more insistent, White Fang bristled and bared his teeth and backed away. He did not like the man. The feel of him was bad. He sensed the evil in him, and feared the extended hand and the attempts at soft-spoken speech. Because of all this, he hated the man.

With the simpler creatures, good and bad are things simply understood. The good stands for all things that bring easement and satisfaction and surcease from pain. Therefore, the good is liked. The bad stands for all things that are fraught with discomfort, menace, and hurt, and is hated accordingly. White Fang's feel of Beauty Smith was bad. From the man's distorted body and twisted mind, in occult ways, like mists rising from malarial marshes, came emanations of the unhealth within. Not by reasoning, not by the five senses alone, but by other and remoter and uncharted senses, came the feeling to White Fang that the man was ominous with evil, pregnant with hurtfulness, and therefore a thing bad, and wisely to be hated.

White Fang was in Grey Beaver's camp when Beauty Smith first visited it. At the faint sound of his distant feet, before he came in sight, White Fang knew who was coming and began to bristle. He had been lying down in an abandon of comfort, but he arose quickly, and, as the man arrived, slid away in true wolf-fashion to the edge of the camp. He did not know what they said, but he could see the man and Grey Beaver talking together. Once, the man pointed at him, and White Fang snarled back as though the hand were just descending upon him instead of being, as it was, fifty feet away. The man laughed at this; and White Fang slunk away to the sheltering woods, his head turned to observe as he glided softly over the ground.

Grey Beaver refused to sell the dog. He had grown rich with his trading and stood in need of nothing. Besides, White Fang was a valuable animal, the strongest sled-dog he had ever owned, and the best leader. Furthermore, there was no dog like him on the Mackenzie nor the Yukon. He could fight. He killed other dogs as easily as men killed mosquitoes. (Beauty Smith's eyes lighted up at this, and he licked his thin lips with an eager tongue). No, White Fang was not for sale at any price.

But Beauty Smith knew the ways of Indians. He visited Grey Beaver's camp often, and hidden under his coat was always a black bottle or so. One of the potencies of whisky is the breeding of thirst. Grey Beaver got the thirst. His fevered membranes and burnt stomach began to clamour for more and more of the scorching fluid; while his brain, thrust all awry by the unwonted stimulant, permitted him to go any length to obtain it. The money he had received for his furs and mittens and moccasins began to go. It went faster and faster, and the shorter his money-sack grew, the shorter grew his temper.

In the end his money and goods and temper were all gone. Nothing remained to him but his thirst, a prodigious possession in itself that grew more prodigious with every sober breath he drew. Then it was that Beauty Smith had talk with him again about the sale of White Fang; but this time the price offered was in bottles, not dollars, and Grey Beaver's ears were more eager to hear.

"You ketch um dog you take um all right," was his last word.

The bottles were delivered, but after two days. "You ketch um dog," were Beauty Smith's words to Grey Beaver.

White Fang slunk into camp one evening and dropped down with a sigh of content. The dreaded white god was not there. For days his manifestations of desire to lay hands on him had been growing more insistent, and during that time White Fang had been compelled to avoid the camp. He did not know what evil was threatened by those insistent hands. He knew only that they did threaten evil of some sort, and that it was best for him to keep out of their reach.

But scarcely had he lain down when Grey Beaver staggered over to him and tied a leather thong around his neck. He sat down beside White Fang, holding the end of the thong in his hand. In the other hand he held a bottle, which, from time to time, was inverted above his head to the accompaniment of gurgling noises.

An hour of this passed, when the vibrations of feet in contact with the ground foreran the one who approached. White Fang heard it first, and he was bristling with recognition while Grey Beaver still nodded stupidly. White Fang tried to draw the thong softly out of his master's hand; but the relaxed fingers closed tightly and Grey Beaver roused himself.

Beauty Smith strode into camp and stood over White Fang. He snarled softly up at the thing of fear, watching keenly the deportment of the hands. One hand extended outward and began to descend upon his head. His soft snarl grew tense and harsh. The hand continued slowly to descend, while he crouched beneath it, eyeing it malignantly, his snarl growing shorter and shorter as, with quickening breath, it approached its culmination. Suddenly he snapped, striking with his fangs like a snake. The hand was jerked back, and the teeth came together emptily with a sharp click. Beauty Smith was frightened and angry. Grey Beaver clouted White Fang alongside the head, so that he cowered down close to the earth in respectful obedience.

White Fang's suspicious eyes followed every movement. He saw Beauty Smith go away and return with a stout club. Then the end of the thong was given over to him by Grey Beaver. Beauty Smith started to walk away. The thong grew taut.

White Fang resisted it. Grey Beaver clouted him right and left to make him get up and follow. He obeyed, but with a rush, hurling himself upon the stranger who was dragging him away. Beauty Smith did not jump away. He had been waiting for this. He swung the club smartly, stopping the rush midway and smashing White Fang down upon the ground. Grey Beaver laughed and nodded approval. Beauty Smith tightened the thong again, and White Fang crawled limply and dizzily to his feet.

He did not rush a second time. One smash from the club was sufficient to convince him that the white god knew how to handle it, and he was too wise to fight the inevitable. So he followed morosely at Beauty Smith's heels, his tail between his legs, yet snarling softly under his breath. But Beauty Smith kept a wary eye on him, and the club was held always ready to strike.

At the fort Beauty Smith left him securely tied and went in to bed. White Fang waited an hour. Then he applied his teeth to the thong, and in the space of ten seconds was free. He had wasted no time with his teeth. There had been no useless gnawing. The thong was cut across, diagonally, almost as clean as though done by a knife. White Fang looked up at the fort, at the same time bristling and growling. Then he turned and trotted back to Grey Beaver's camp. He owed no allegiance to this strange and terrible god. He had given himself to Grey Beaver, and to Grey Beaver he considered he still belonged.

But what had occurred before was repeated—with a difference. Grey Beaver again made him fast with a thong, and in the morning turned him over to Beauty Smith. And here was where the difference came in. Beauty Smith gave him a beating. Tied securely, White Fang could only rage futilely and endure the punishment. Club and whip were both used upon him, and he experienced the worst beating he had ever received in his life. Even the big beating given him in his puppyhood by Grey Beaver was mild compared with this.

Beauty Smith enjoyed the task. He delighted in it. He gloated over his victim, and his eyes flamed dully, as he swung the whip or club and listened to White Fang's cries of pain and to his helpless bellows and snarls. For Beauty Smith was cruel in the way that cowards are cruel. Cringing and snivelling himself before the blows or angry speech of a man, he revenged himself, in turn, upon creatures weaker than he. All life likes power, and Beauty Smith was no exception. Denied the expression of power amongst his own kind, he fell back upon the lesser creatures and there vindicated the life that was in him. But Beauty Smith had not created himself, and no blame was to be attached to him. He had come into the world with a twisted body and a brute intelligence. This had constituted the clay of him, and it had not been kindly moulded by the world.

White Fang knew why he was being beaten. When Grey Beaver tied the thong around his neck, and passed the end of the thong into Beauty Smith's keeping, White Fang knew that it was his god's will for him to go with Beauty Smith. And when Beauty Smith left him tied outside the fort, he knew that it was Beauty Smith's will that he should remain there. Therefore, he had disobeyed the will of both the gods, and earned the consequent punishment. He had seen dogs change owners in the past, and he had seen the runaways beaten as he was being beaten. He was wise, and yet in the nature of him there were forces greater than wisdom. One of these was fidelity. He did not love Grey Beaver, yet, even in the face of his will and his anger, he was faithful to him. He could not help it. This faithfulness was a quality of the clay that composed him. It was the quality that was peculiarly the possession of his kind; the quality that set apart his species from all other species; the quality that has enabled the wolf and the wild dog to come in from the open and be the companions of man.

After the beating, White Fang was dragged back to the fort. But this time Beauty Smith left him tied with a stick. One does not give up a god easily, and so with White Fang. Grey Beaver was his own particular god, and, in spite of Grey Beaver's will, White Fang still clung to him and would not give him up. Grey Beaver had betrayed and forsaken him, but that had no effect upon him. Not for nothing had he surrendered himself body and soul to Grey Beaver. There had been no reservation on White Fang's part, and the bond was not to be broken easily.

So, in the night, when the men in the fort were asleep, White Fang applied his teeth to the stick that held him. The wood was seasoned and dry, and it was tied so closely to his neck that he could scarcely get his teeth to it. It was only by the severest muscular exertion and neck-arching that he succeeded in getting the wood between his teeth, and barely between his teeth at that; and it was only by the exercise of an immense patience, extending through many hours, that he succeeded in gnawing through the stick. This was something that dogs were not supposed to do. It was unprecedented. But White Fang did it, trotting away from the fort in the early morning, with the end of the stick hanging to his neck.

He was wise. But had he been merely wise he would not have gone back to Grey Beaver who had already twice betrayed him. But there was his faithfulness, and he went back to be betrayed yet a third time. Again he yielded to the tying of a thong around his neck by Grey Beaver, and again Beauty Smith came to claim him. And this time he was beaten even more severely than before.

Grey Beaver looked on stolidly while the white man wielded the whip. He gave no protection. It was no longer his dog. When the beating was over White Fang was sick. A soft southland dog would have died under it, but not he. His school of life had been sterner, and he was himself of sterner stuff. He had too great vitality. His clutch on life was too strong. But he was very sick. At first he was unable to drag himself along, and Beauty Smith had to wait half-an-hour for him. And then, blind and reeling, he followed at Beauty Smith's heels back to the fort.

But now he was tied with a chain that defied his teeth, and he strove in vain, by lunging, to draw the staple from the timber into which it was driven. After a few days, sober and bankrupt, Grey Beaver departed up the Porcupine on his long journey to the Mackenzie. White Fang remained on the Yukon, the property of a man more than half mad and all brute. But what is a dog to know in its consciousness of madness? To White Fang, Beauty Smith was a veritable, if terrible, god. He was a mad god at best, but White Fang knew nothing of madness; he knew only that he must submit to the will of this new master, obey his every whim and fancy.

CHAPTER III—THE REIGN OF HATE

Under the tutelage of the mad god, White Fang became a fiend. He was kept chained in a pen at the rear of the fort, and here Beauty Smith teased and irritated and drove him wild with petty torments. The man early discovered White Fang's susceptibility to laughter, and made it a point after painfully tricking him, to laugh at him. This laughter was uproarious and scornful, and at the same time the god pointed his finger derisively at White Fang. At such times reason fled from White Fang, and in his transports of rage he was even more mad than Beauty Smith.

Formerly, White Fang had been merely the enemy of his kind, withal a ferocious enemy. He now became the enemy of all things, and more ferocious than ever. To such an extent was he tormented, that he hated blindly and without the faintest spark of reason. He hated the chain that bound him, the men who peered in at him through the slats of the pen, the dogs that accompanied the men and that snarled malignantly at him in his helplessness. He hated the very wood of the pen that confined him. And, first, last, and most of all, he hated Beauty Smith.

But Beauty Smith had a purpose in all that he did to White Fang. One day a number of men gathered about the pen. Beauty Smith entered, club in hand, and took the chain off from White Fang's neck. When his master had gone out, White Fang turned loose and tore around the pen, trying to get at the men outside. He was magnificently terrible. Fully five feet in length, and standing two and one-half feet at the shoulder, he far outweighed a wolf of corresponding size. From his mother he had inherited the heavier proportions of the dog, so that he weighed, without any fat and without an ounce of superfluous flesh, over ninety pounds. It was all muscle, bone, and sinew-fighting flesh in the finest condition.

The door of the pen was being opened again. White Fang paused. Something unusual was happening. He waited. The door was opened wider. Then a huge dog was thrust inside, and the door was slammed shut behind him. White Fang had never seen such a dog (it was a mastiff); but the size and fierce aspect of the intruder did not deter him. Here was some thing, not wood nor iron, upon which to wreak his hate. He leaped in with a flash of fangs that ripped down the side of the mastiff's neck. The mastiff shook his head, growled hoarsely, and plunged at White Fang. But White Fang was here, there, and everywhere, always evading and eluding, and always leaping in and slashing with his fangs and leaping out again in time to escape punishment.

The men outside shouted and applauded, while Beauty Smith, in an ecstasy of delight, gloated over the ripping and mangling performed by White Fang. There was no hope for the mastiff from the first. He was too ponderous and slow. In the end, while Beauty Smith beat White Fang back with a club, the mastiff was dragged out by its owner. Then there was a payment of bets, and money clinked in Beauty Smith's hand.

White Fang came to look forward eagerly to the gathering of the men around his pen. It meant a fight; and this was the only way that was now vouchsafed him of expressing the life that was in him. Tormented, incited to hate, he was kept a prisoner so that there was no way of satisfying that hate except at the times his master saw fit to put another dog against him. Beauty Smith had estimated his powers well, for he was invariably the victor. One day, three dogs were turned in upon him in succession. Another day a full-grown wolf, fresh-caught from the Wild, was shoved in through the door of the pen. And on still another day two dogs were set against him at the same time. This was his severest fight, and though in the end he killed them both he was himself half killed in doing it.

In the fall of the year, when the first snows were falling and mush-ice was running in the river, Beauty Smith took passage for himself and White Fang on a steamboat bound up the Yukon to Dawson. White Fang had now achieved a reputation in the land. As "the Fighting Wolf" he was known far and wide, and the cage in which he was kept on the steam-boat's deck was usually surrounded by curious men. He raged and snarled at them, or lay quietly and studied them with cold hatred. Why should he not hate them? He never asked himself the question. He knew only hate and lost himself in the passion of it. Life had become a hell to him. He had not been made for the close confinement wild beasts endure at the hands of men. And yet it was in precisely this way that he was treated. Men stared at him, poked sticks between the bars to make him snarl, and then laughed at him.

They were his environment, these men, and they were moulding the clay of him into a more ferocious thing than had been intended by Nature. Nevertheless, Nature had given him plasticity. Where many another animal would have died or had its spirit broken, he adjusted himself and lived, and at no expense of the spirit. Possibly Beauty Smith, arch-fiend and tormentor, was capable of breaking White Fang's spirit, but as yet there were no signs of his succeeding.

If Beauty Smith had in him a devil, White Fang had another; and the two of them raged against each other unceasingly. In the days before, White Fang had had the wisdom to cower down and submit to a man with a club in his hand; but this wisdom now left him. The mere sight of Beauty Smith was sufficient to send him into transports of fury. And when they came to close quarters, and he had been beaten back by the club, he went on growling and snarling, and showing his fangs. The last growl could never be extracted from him. No matter how terribly he was beaten, he had always another growl; and when Beauty Smith gave up and withdrew, the defiant growl followed after him, or White Fang sprang at the bars of the cage bellowing his hatred.

When the steamboat arrived at Dawson, White Fang went ashore. But he still lived a public life, in a cage, surrounded by curious men. He was exhibited as "the Fighting Wolf," and men paid fifty cents in gold dust to see him. He was given no rest. Did he lie down to sleep, he was stirred up by a sharp stick—so that the audience might get its money's worth. In order to make the exhibition interesting, he was kept in a rage most of the time. But worse than all this, was the atmosphere in which he lived. He was regarded as the most fearful of wild beasts, and this was borne in to him through the bars of the cage. Every word, every cautious action, on the part of the men, impressed upon him his own terrible ferocity. It was so much added fuel to the flame of his fierceness. There could be but one result, and that was that his ferocity fed upon itself and increased. It was another instance of the plasticity of his clay, of his capacity for being moulded by the pressure of environment.

In addition to being exhibited he was a professional fighting animal. At irregular intervals, whenever a fight could be arranged, he was taken out of his cage and led off into the woods a few miles from town. Usually this occurred at night, so as to avoid interference from the mounted police of the Territory. After a few hours of waiting, when daylight had come, the audience and the dog with which he was to fight arrived. In this manner it came about that he fought all sizes and breeds of dogs. It was a savage land, the men were savage, and the fights were usually to the death.

Since White Fang continued to fight, it is obvious that it was the other dogs that died. He never knew defeat. His early training, when he fought with Lip-lip and the whole puppy-pack, stood him in good stead. There was the tenacity with which he clung to the earth. No dog could make him lose his footing. This was the favourite trick of the wolf breeds—to rush in upon him, either directly or with an unexpected swerve, in the hope of striking his shoulder and overthrowing him. Mackenzie hounds, Eskimo and Labrador dogs, huskies and Malemutes—all tried it on him, and all failed. He was never known to lose his footing. Men told this to one another, and looked each time to see it happen; but White Fang always disappointed them.

Then there was his lightning quickness. It gave him a tremendous advantage over his antagonists. No matter what their fighting experience, they had never encountered a dog that moved so swiftly as he. Also to be reckoned with, was the immediateness of his attack. The average dog was accustomed to the preliminaries of snarling and bristling and growling, and the average dog was knocked off his feet and finished before he had begun to fight or recovered from his surprise. So often did this happen, that it became the custom to hold White Fang until the other dog went through its preliminaries, was good and ready, and even made the first attack.

But greatest of all the advantages in White Fang's favour, was his experience. He knew more about fighting than did any of the dogs that faced him. He had fought more fights, knew how to meet more tricks and methods, and had more tricks himself, while his own method was scarcely to be improved upon.

As the time went by, he had fewer and fewer fights. Men despaired of matching him with an equal, and Beauty Smith was compelled to pit wolves against him. These were trapped by the Indians for the purpose, and a fight between White Fang and a wolf was always sure to draw a crowd. Once, a full-grown female lynx was secured, and this time White Fang fought for his life. Her quickness matched his; her ferocity equalled his; while he fought with his fangs alone, and she fought with her sharp-clawed feet as well.

But after the lynx, all fighting ceased for White Fang. There were no more animals with which to fight—at least, there was none considered worthy of fighting with him. So he remained on exhibition until spring, when one Tim Keenan, a faro-dealer, arrived in the land. With him came the first bull-dog that had ever entered the Klondike. That this dog and White Fang should come together was inevitable, and for a week the anticipated fight was the mainspring of conversation in certain quarters of the town.

CHAPTER IV—THE CLINGING DEATH

Beauty Smith slipped the chain from his neck and stepped back.

For once White Fang did not make an immediate attack. He stood still, ears pricked forward, alert and curious, surveying the strange animal that faced him. He had never seen such a dog before. Tim Keenan shoved the bull-dog forward with a muttered "Go to it." The animal waddled toward the centre of the circle, short and squat and ungainly. He came to a stop and blinked across at White Fang.

There were cries from the crowd of, "Go to him, Cherokee! Sick 'm, Cherokee! Eat 'm up!"

But Cherokee did not seem anxious to fight. He turned his head and blinked at the men who shouted, at the same time wagging his stump of a tail good-naturedly. He was not afraid, but merely lazy. Besides, it did not seem to him that it was intended he should fight with the dog he saw before him. He was not used to fighting with that kind of dog, and he was waiting for them to bring on the real dog.

Tim Keenan stepped in and bent over Cherokee, fondling him on both sides of the shoulders with hands that rubbed against the grain of the hair and that made slight, pushing-forward movements. These were so many suggestions. Also, their effect was irritating, for Cherokee began to growl, very softly, deep down in his throat. There was a correspondence in rhythm between the growls and the movements of the man's hands. The growl rose in the throat with the culmination of each forward-pushing movement, and ebbed down to start up afresh with the beginning of the next movement. The end of each movement was the accent of the rhythm, the movement ending abruptly and the growling rising with a jerk.

This was not without its effect on White Fang. The hair began to rise on his neck and across the shoulders. Tim Keenan gave a final shove forward and stepped back again. As the impetus that carried Cherokee forward died down, he continued to go forward of his own volition, in a swift, bow-legged run. Then White Fang struck. A cry of startled admiration went up. He had covered the distance and gone in more like a cat than a dog; and with the same cat-like swiftness he had slashed with his fangs and leaped clear.

The bull-dog was bleeding back of one ear from a rip in his thick neck. He gave no sign, did not even snarl, but turned and followed after White Fang. The display on both sides, the quickness of the one and the steadiness of the other, had excited the partisan spirit of the crowd, and the men were making new bets and increasing original bets. Again, and yet again, White Fang sprang in, slashed, and got away untouched, and still his strange foe followed after him, without too great haste, not slowly, but deliberately and determinedly, in a businesslike sort of way. There was purpose in his method—something for him to do that he was intent upon doing and from which nothing could distract him.

His whole demeanour, every action, was stamped with this purpose. It puzzled White Fang. Never had he seen such a dog. It had no hair protection. It was soft, and bled easily. There was no thick mat of fur to baffle White Fang's teeth as they were often baffled by dogs of his own breed. Each time that his teeth struck they sank easily into the yielding flesh, while the animal did not seem able to defend itself. Another disconcerting thing was that it made no outcry, such as he had been accustomed to with the other dogs he had fought. Beyond a growl or a grunt, the dog took its punishment silently. And never did it flag in its pursuit of him.

Not that Cherokee was slow. He could turn and whirl swiftly enough, but White Fang was never there. Cherokee was puzzled, too. He had never fought before with a dog with which he could not close. The desire to close had always been mutual. But here was a dog that kept at a distance, dancing and dodging here and there and all about. And when it did get its teeth into him, it did not hold on but let go instantly and darted away again.

But White Fang could not get at the soft underside of the throat. The bull-dog stood too short, while its massive jaws were an added protection. White Fang darted in and out unscathed, while Cherokee's wounds increased. Both sides of his neck and head were ripped and slashed. He bled freely, but showed no signs of being disconcerted. He continued his plodding pursuit, though once, for the moment baffled, he came to a full stop and blinked at the men who looked on, at the same time wagging his stump of a tail as an expression of his willingness to fight.

In that moment White Fang was in upon him and out, in passing ripping his trimmed remnant of an ear. With a slight manifestation of anger, Cherokee took up the pursuit again, running on the inside of the circle White Fang was making, and striving to fasten his deadly grip on White Fang's throat. The bull-dog missed by a hair's-breadth, and cries of praise went up as White Fang doubled suddenly out of danger in the opposite direction.

The time went by. White Fang still danced on, dodging and doubling, leaping in and out, and ever inflicting damage. And still the bull-dog, with grim certitude, toiled after him. Sooner or later he would accomplish his purpose, get the grip that would win the battle. In the meantime, he accepted all the punishment the other could deal him. His tufts of ears had become tassels, his neck and shoulders were slashed in a score of places, and his very lips were cut and bleeding—all from these lightning snaps that were beyond his foreseeing and guarding.

Time and again White Fang had attempted to knock Cherokee off his feet; but the difference in their height was too great. Cherokee was too squat, too close to the ground. White Fang tried the trick once too often. The chance came in one of his quick doublings and counter-circlings. He caught Cherokee with head turned away as he whirled more slowly. His shoulder was exposed. White Fang drove in upon it: but his own shoulder was high above, while he struck with such force that his momentum carried him on across over the other's body. For the first time in his fighting history, men saw White Fang lose his footing. His body turned a half-somersault in the air, and he would have landed on his back had he not twisted, catlike, still in the air, in the effort to bring his feet to the earth. As it was, he struck heavily on his side. The next instant he was on his feet, but in that instant Cherokee's teeth closed on his throat.

It was not a good grip, being too low down toward the chest; but Cherokee held on. White Fang sprang to his feet and tore wildly around, trying to shake off the bull-dog's body. It made him frantic, this clinging, dragging weight. It bound his movements, restricted his freedom. It was like the trap, and all his instinct resented it and revolted against it. It was a mad revolt. For several minutes he was to all intents insane. The basic life that was in him took charge of him. The will to exist of his body surged over him. He was dominated by this mere flesh-love of life. All intelligence was gone. It was as though he had no brain. His reason was unseated by the blind yearning of the flesh to exist and move, at all hazards to move, to continue to move, for movement was the expression of its existence.

Round and round he went, whirling and turning and reversing, trying to shake off the fifty-pound weight that dragged at his throat. The bull-dog did little but keep his grip. Sometimes, and rarely, he managed to get his feet to the earth and for a moment to brace himself against White Fang. But the next moment his footing would be lost and he would be dragging around in the whirl of one of White Fang's mad gyrations. Cherokee identified himself with his instinct. He knew that he was doing the right thing by holding on, and there came to him certain blissful thrills of satisfaction. At such moments he even closed his eyes and allowed his body to be hurled hither and thither, willy-nilly, careless of any hurt that might thereby come to it. That did not count. The grip was the thing, and the grip he kept.

White Fang ceased only when he had tired himself out. He could do nothing, and he could not understand. Never, in all his fighting, had this thing happened. The dogs he had fought with did not fight that way. With them it was snap and slash and get away, snap and slash and get away. He lay partly on his side, panting for breath. Cherokee still holding his grip, urged against him, trying to get him over entirely on his side. White Fang resisted, and he could feel the jaws shifting their grip, slightly relaxing and coming together again in a chewing movement. Each shift brought the grip closer to his throat. The bull-dog's method was to hold what he had, and when opportunity favoured to work in for more. Opportunity favoured when White Fang remained quiet. When White Fang struggled, Cherokee was content merely to hold on.

The bulging back of Cherokee's neck was the only portion of his body that White Fang's teeth could reach. He got hold toward the base where the neck comes out from the shoulders; but he did not know the chewing method of fighting, nor were his jaws adapted to it. He spasmodically ripped and tore with his fangs for a space. Then a change in their position diverted him. The bull-dog had managed to roll him over on his back, and still hanging on to his throat, was on top of him. Like a cat, White Fang bowed his hind-quarters in, and, with the feet digging into his enemy's abdomen above him, he began to claw with long tearing-strokes. Cherokee might well have been disembowelled had he not quickly pivoted on his grip and got his body off of White Fang's and at right angles to it.

There was no escaping that grip. It was like Fate itself, and as inexorable. Slowly it shifted up along the jugular. All that saved White Fang from death was the loose skin of his neck and the thick fur that covered it. This served to form a large roll in Cherokee's mouth, the fur of which well-nigh defied his teeth. But bit by bit, whenever the chance offered, he was getting more of the loose skin and fur in his mouth. The result was that he was slowly throttling White Fang. The latter's breath was drawn with greater and greater difficulty as the moments went by.

It began to look as though the battle were over. The backers of Cherokee waxed jubilant and offered ridiculous odds. White Fang's backers were correspondingly depressed, and refused bets of ten to one and twenty to one, though one man was rash enough to close a wager of fifty to one. This man was Beauty Smith. He took a step into the ring and pointed his finger at White Fang. Then he began to laugh derisively and scornfully. This produced the desired effect. White Fang went wild with rage. He called up his reserves of strength, and gained his feet. As he struggled around the ring, the fifty pounds of his foe ever dragging on his throat, his anger passed on into panic. The basic life of him dominated him again, and his intelligence fled before the will of his flesh to live. Round and round and back again, stumbling and falling and rising, even uprearing at times on his hind-legs and lifting his foe clear of the earth, he struggled vainly to shake off the clinging death.

At last he fell, toppling backward, exhausted; and the bull-dog promptly shifted his grip, getting in closer, mangling more and more of the fur-folded flesh, throttling White Fang more severely than ever. Shouts of applause went up for the victor, and there were many cries of "Cherokee!" "Cherokee!" To this Cherokee responded by vigorous wagging of the stump of his tail. But the clamour of approval did not distract him. There was no sympathetic relation between his tail and his massive jaws. The one might wag, but the others held their terrible grip on White Fang's throat.

It was at this time that a diversion came to the spectators. There was a jingle of bells. Dog-mushers' cries were heard. Everybody, save Beauty Smith, looked apprehensively, the fear of the police strong upon them. But they saw, up the trail, and not down, two men running with sled and dogs. They were evidently coming down the creek from some prospecting trip. At sight of the crowd they stopped their dogs and came over and joined it, curious to see the cause of the excitement. The dog-musher wore a moustache, but the other, a taller and younger man, was smooth-shaven, his skin rosy from the pounding of his blood and the running in the frosty air.

White Fang had practically ceased struggling. Now and again he resisted spasmodically and to no purpose. He could get little air, and that little grew less and less under the merciless grip that ever tightened. In spite of his armour of fur, the great vein of his throat would have long since been torn open, had not the first grip of the bull-dog been so low down as to be practically on the chest. It had taken Cherokee a long time to shift that grip upward, and this had also tended further to clog his jaws with fur and skin-fold.

In the meantime, the abysmal brute in Beauty Smith had been rising into his brain and mastering the small bit of sanity that he possessed at best. When he saw White Fang's eyes beginning to glaze, he knew beyond doubt that the fight was lost. Then he broke loose. He sprang upon White Fang and began savagely to kick him. There were hisses from the crowd and cries of protest, but that was all. While this went on, and Beauty Smith continued to kick White Fang, there was a commotion in the crowd. The tall young newcomer was forcing his way through, shouldering men right and left without ceremony or gentleness. When he broke through into the ring, Beauty Smith was just in the act of delivering another kick. All his weight was on one foot, and he was in a state of unstable equilibrium. At that moment the newcomer's fist landed a smashing blow full in his face. Beauty Smith's remaining leg left the ground, and his whole body seemed to lift into the air as he turned over backward and struck the snow. The newcomer turned upon the crowd.

"You cowards!" he cried. "You beasts!"

He was in a rage himself—a sane rage. His grey eyes seemed metallic and steel-like as they flashed upon the crowd. Beauty Smith regained his feet and came toward him, sniffling and cowardly. The new-comer did not understand. He did not know how abject a coward the other was, and thought he was coming back intent on fighting. So, with a "You beast!" he smashed Beauty Smith over backward with a second blow in the face. Beauty Smith decided that the snow was the safest place for him, and lay where he had fallen, making no effort to get up.

"Come on, Matt, lend a hand," the newcomer called the dog-musher, who had followed him into the ring.

Both men bent over the dogs. Matt took hold of White Fang, ready to pull when Cherokee's jaws should be loosened. This the younger man endeavoured to accomplish by clutching the bulldog's jaws in his hands and trying to spread them. It was a vain undertaking. As he pulled and tugged and wrenched, he kept exclaiming with every expulsion of breath, "Beasts!"

The crowd began to grow unruly, and some of the men were protesting against the spoiling of the sport; but they were silenced when the newcomer lifted his head from his work for a moment and glared at them.

"You damn beasts!" he finally exploded, and went back to his task.

"It's no use, Mr. Scott, you can't break 'm apart that way," Matt said at last.

The pair paused and surveyed the locked dogs.

"Ain't bleedin' much," Matt announced. "Ain't got all the way in yet."

"But he's liable to any moment," Scott answered. "There, did you see that! He shifted his grip in a bit."

The younger man's excitement and apprehension for White Fang was growing. He struck Cherokee about the head savagely again and again. But that did not loosen the jaws. Cherokee wagged the stump of his tail in advertisement that he understood the meaning of the blows, but that he knew he was himself in the right and only doing his duty by keeping his grip.

"Won't some of you help?" Scott cried desperately at the crowd.

But no help was offered. Instead, the crowd began sarcastically to cheer him on and showered him with facetious advice.

"You'll have to get a pry," Matt counselled.

The other reached into the holster at his hip, drew his revolver, and tried to thrust its muzzle between the bull-dog's jaws. He shoved, and shoved hard, till the grating of the steel against the locked teeth could be distinctly heard. Both men were on their knees, bending over the dogs. Tim Keenan strode into the ring. He paused beside Scott and touched him on the shoulder, saying ominously:

"Don't break them teeth, stranger."

"Then I'll break his neck," Scott retorted, continuing his shoving and wedging with the revolver muzzle.

"I said don't break them teeth," the faro-dealer repeated more ominously than before.

But if it was a bluff he intended, it did not work. Scott never desisted from his efforts, though he looked up coolly and asked:

"Your dog?"

The faro-dealer grunted.

"Then get in here and break this grip."

"Well, stranger," the other drawled irritatingly, "I don't mind telling you that's something I ain't worked out for myself. I don't know how to turn the trick."

"Then get out of the way," was the reply, "and don't bother me. I'm busy."

Tim Keenan continued standing over him, but Scott took no further notice of his presence. He had managed to get the muzzle in between the jaws on one side, and was trying to get it out between the jaws on the other side. This accomplished, he pried gently and carefully, loosening the jaws a bit at a time, while Matt, a bit at a time, extricated White Fang's mangled neck.

"Stand by to receive your dog," was Scott's peremptory order to Cherokee's owner.

The faro-dealer stooped down obediently and got a firm hold on Cherokee.

"Now!" Scott warned, giving the final pry.

The dogs were drawn apart, the bull-dog struggling vigorously.

"Take him away," Scott commanded, and Tim Keenan dragged Cherokee back into the crowd.

White Fang made several ineffectual efforts to get up. Once he gained his feet, but his legs were too weak to sustain him, and he slowly wilted and sank back into the snow. His eyes were half closed, and the surface of them was glassy. His jaws were apart, and through them the tongue protruded, draggled and limp. To all appearances he looked like a dog that had been strangled to death. Matt examined him.

"Just about all in," he announced; "but he's breathin' all right."

Beauty Smith had regained his feet and come over to look at White Fang.

"Matt, how much is a good sled-dog worth?" Scott asked.

The dog-musher, still on his knees and stooped over White Fang, calculated for a moment.

"Three hundred dollars," he answered.

"And how much for one that's all chewed up like this one?" Scott asked, nudging White Fang with his foot.

"Half of that," was the dog-musher's judgment. Scott turned upon Beauty Smith.

"Did you hear, Mr. Beast? I'm going to take your dog from you, and I'm going to give you a hundred and fifty for him."

He opened his pocket-book and counted out the bills.

Beauty Smith put his hands behind his back, refusing to touch the proffered money.

"I ain't a-sellin'," he said.

"Oh, yes you are," the other assured him. "Because I'm buying. Here's your money. The dog's mine."

Beauty Smith, his hands still behind him, began to back away.

Scott sprang toward him, drawing his fist back to strike. Beauty Smith cowered down in anticipation of the blow.

"I've got my rights," he whimpered.

"You've forfeited your rights to own that dog," was the rejoinder. "Are you going to take the money? or do I have to hit you again?"

"All right," Beauty Smith spoke up with the alacrity of fear. "But I take the money under protest," he added. "The dog's a mint. I ain't a-goin' to be robbed. A man's got his rights."

"Correct," Scott answered, passing the money over to him. "A man's got his rights. But you're not a man. You're a beast."

"Wait till I get back to Dawson," Beauty Smith threatened. "I'll have the law on you."

"If you open your mouth when you get back to Dawson, I'll have you run out of town. Understand?"

Beauty Smith replied with a grunt.

"Understand?" the other thundered with abrupt fierceness.

"Yes," Beauty Smith grunted, shrinking away.

"Yes what?"

"Yes, sir," Beauty Smith snarled.

"Look out! He'll bite!" some one shouted, and a guffaw of laughter went up.

Scott turned his back on him, and returned to help the dog-musher, who was working over White Fang.

Some of the men were already departing; others stood in groups, looking on and talking. Tim Keenan joined one of the groups.

"Who's that mug?" he asked.

"Weedon Scott," some one answered.

"And who in hell is Weedon Scott?" the faro-dealer demanded.

"Oh, one of them crackerjack minin' experts. He's in with all the big bugs. If you want to keep out of trouble, you'll steer clear of him, that's my talk. He's all hunky with the officials. The Gold Commissioner's a special pal of his."

"I thought he must be somebody," was the faro-dealer's comment. "That's why I kept my hands offen him at the start."

CHAPTER V—THE INDOMITABLE

"It's hopeless," Weedon Scott confessed.

He sat on the step of his cabin and stared at the dog-musher, who responded with a shrug that was equally hopeless.

Together they looked at White Fang at the end of his stretched chain, bristling, snarling, ferocious, straining to get at the sled-dogs. Having received sundry lessons from Matt, said lessons being imparted by means of a club, the sled-dogs had learned to leave White Fang alone; and even then they were lying down at a distance, apparently oblivious of his existence.

"It's a wolf and there's no taming it," Weedon Scott announced.

"Oh, I don't know about that," Matt objected. "Might be a lot of dog in 'm, for all you can tell. But there's one thing I know sure, an' that there's no gettin' away from."

The dog-musher paused and nodded his head confidentially at Moosehide Mountain.

"Well, don't be a miser with what you know," Scott said sharply, after waiting a suitable length of time. "Spit it out. What is it?"

The dog-musher indicated White Fang with a backward thrust of his thumb.

"Wolf or dog, it's all the same—he's ben tamed 'ready."

"No!"

"I tell you yes, an' broke to harness. Look close there. D'ye see them marks across the chest?"

"You're right, Matt. He was a sled-dog before Beauty Smith got hold of him."

"And there's not much reason against his bein' a sled-dog again."

"What d'ye think?" Scott queried eagerly. Then the hope died down as he added, shaking his head, "We've had him two weeks now, and if anything he's wilder than ever at the present moment."

"Give 'm a chance," Matt counselled. "Turn 'm loose for a spell."

The other looked at him incredulously.

"Yes," Matt went on, "I know you've tried to, but you didn't take a club."

"You try it then."

The dog-musher secured a club and went over to the chained animal. White Fang watched the club after the manner of a caged lion watching the whip of its trainer.

"See 'm keep his eye on that club," Matt said. "That's a good sign. He's no fool. Don't dast tackle me so long as I got that club handy. He's not clean crazy, sure."

As the man's hand approached his neck, White Fang bristled and snarled and crouched down. But while he eyed the approaching hand, he at the same time contrived to keep track of the club in the other hand, suspended threateningly above him. Matt unsnapped the chain from the collar and stepped back.

White Fang could scarcely realise that he was free. Many months had gone by since he passed into the possession of Beauty Smith, and in all that period he had never known a moment of freedom except at the times he had been loosed to fight with other dogs. Immediately after such fights he had always been imprisoned again.

He did not know what to make of it. Perhaps some new devilry of the gods was about to be perpetrated on him. He walked slowly and cautiously, prepared to be assailed at any moment. He did not know what to do, it was all so unprecedented. He took the precaution to sheer off from the two watching gods, and walked carefully to the corner of the cabin. Nothing happened. He was plainly perplexed, and he came back again, pausing a dozen feet away and regarding the two men intently.

"Won't he run away?" his new owner asked.

Matt shrugged his shoulders. "Got to take a gamble. Only way to find out is to find out."

"Poor devil," Scott murmured pityingly. "What he needs is some show of human kindness," he added, turning and going into the cabin.

He came out with a piece of meat, which he tossed to White Fang. He sprang away from it, and from a distance studied it suspiciously.

"Hi-yu, Major!" Matt shouted warningly, but too late.

Major had made a spring for the meat. At the instant his jaws closed on it, White Fang struck him. He was overthrown. Matt rushed in, but quicker than he was White Fang. Major staggered to his feet, but the blood spouting from his throat reddened the snow in a widening path.

"It's too bad, but it served him right," Scott said hastily.

But Matt's foot had already started on its way to kick White Fang. There was a leap, a flash of teeth, a sharp exclamation. White Fang, snarling fiercely, scrambled backward for several yards, while Matt stooped and investigated his leg.

"He got me all right," he announced, pointing to the torn trousers and undercloths, and the growing stain of red.

"I told you it was hopeless, Matt," Scott said in a discouraged voice. "I've thought about it off and on, while not wanting to think of it. But we've come to it now. It's the only thing to do."

As he talked, with reluctant movements he drew his revolver, threw open the cylinder, and assured himself of its contents.

"Look here, Mr. Scott," Matt objected; "that dog's ben through hell. You can't expect 'm to come out a white an' shinin' angel. Give 'm time."

"Look at Major," the other rejoined.

The dog-musher surveyed the stricken dog. He had sunk down on the snow in the circle of his blood and was plainly in the last gasp.

"Served 'm right. You said so yourself, Mr. Scott. He tried to take White Fang's meat, an' he's dead-O. That was to be expected. I wouldn't give two whoops in hell for a dog that wouldn't fight for his own meat."

"But look at yourself, Matt. It's all right about the dogs, but we must draw the line somewhere."

"Served me right," Matt argued stubbornly. "What'd I want to kick 'm for? You said yourself that he'd done right. Then I had no right to kick 'm."

"It would be a mercy to kill him," Scott insisted. "He's untamable."

"Now look here, Mr. Scott, give the poor devil a fightin' chance. He ain't had no chance yet. He's just come through hell, an' this is the first time he's ben loose. Give 'm a fair chance, an' if he don't deliver the goods, I'll kill 'm myself. There!"

"God knows I don't want to kill him or have him killed," Scott answered, putting away the revolver. "We'll let him run loose and see what kindness can do for him. And here's a try at it."

He walked over to White Fang and began talking to him gently and soothingly.

"Better have a club handy," Matt warned.

Scott shook his head and went on trying to win White Fang's confidence.

White Fang was suspicious. Something was impending. He had killed this god's dog, bitten his companion god, and what else was to be expected than some terrible punishment? But in the face of it he was indomitable. He bristled and showed his teeth, his eyes vigilant, his whole body wary and prepared for anything. The god had no club, so he suffered him to approach quite near. The god's hand had come out and was descending upon his head. White Fang shrank together and grew tense as he crouched under it. Here was danger, some treachery or something. He knew the hands of the gods, their proved mastery, their cunning to hurt. Besides, there was his old antipathy to being touched. He snarled more menacingly, crouched still lower, and still the hand descended. He did not want to bite the hand, and he endured the peril of it until his instinct surged up in him, mastering him with its insatiable yearning for life.

Weedon Scott had believed that he was quick enough to avoid any snap or slash. But he had yet to learn the remarkable quickness of White Fang, who struck with the certainty and swiftness of a coiled snake.

Scott cried out sharply with surprise, catching his torn hand and holding it tightly in his other hand. Matt uttered a great oath and sprang to his side. White Fang crouched down, and backed away, bristling, showing his fangs, his eyes malignant with menace. Now he could expect a beating as fearful as any he had received from Beauty Smith.

"Here! What are you doing?" Scott cried suddenly.

Matt had dashed into the cabin and come out with a rifle.

"Nothin'," he said slowly, with a careless calmness that was assumed, "only goin' to keep that promise I made. I reckon it's up to me to kill 'm as I said I'd do."

"No you don't!"

"Yes I do. Watch me."

As Matt had pleaded for White Fang when he had been bitten, it was now Weedon Scott's turn to plead.

"You said to give him a chance. Well, give it to him. We've only just started, and we can't quit at the beginning. It served me right, this time. And—look at him!"

White Fang, near the corner of the cabin and forty feet away, was snarling with blood-curdling viciousness, not at Scott, but at the dog-musher.

"Well, I'll be everlastingly gosh-swoggled!" was the dog-musher's expression of astonishment.

"Look at the intelligence of him," Scott went on hastily. "He knows the meaning of firearms as well as you do. He's got intelligence and we've got to give that intelligence a chance. Put up the gun."

"All right, I'm willin'," Matt agreed, leaning the rifle against the woodpile.

"But will you look at that!" he exclaimed the next moment.

White Fang had quieted down and ceased snarling. "This is worth investigatin'. Watch."

Matt, reached for the rifle, and at the same moment White Fang snarled. He stepped away from the rifle, and White Fang's lifted lips descended, covering his teeth.

"Now, just for fun."

Matt took the rifle and began slowly to raise it to his shoulder. White Fang's snarling began with the movement, and increased as the movement approached its culmination. But the moment before the rifle came to a level on him, he leaped sidewise behind the corner of the cabin. Matt stood staring along the sights at the empty space of snow which had been occupied by White Fang.

The dog-musher put the rifle down solemnly, then turned and looked at his employer.

"I agree with you, Mr. Scott. That dog's too intelligent to kill."

CHAPTER VI—THE LOVE-MASTER

As White Fang watched Weedon Scott approach, he bristled and snarled to advertise that he would not submit to punishment. Twenty-four hours had passed since he had slashed open the hand that was now bandaged and held up by a sling to keep the blood out of it. In the past White Fang had experienced delayed punishments, and he apprehended that such a one was about to befall him. How could it be otherwise? He had committed what was to him sacrilege, sunk his fangs into the holy flesh of a god, and of a white-skinned superior god at that. In the nature of things, and of intercourse with gods, something terrible awaited him.

The god sat down several feet away. White Fang could see nothing dangerous in that. When the gods administered punishment they stood on their legs. Besides, this god had no club, no whip, no firearm. And furthermore, he himself was free. No chain nor stick bound him. He could escape into safety while the god was scrambling to his feet. In the meantime he would wait and see.

The god remained quiet, made no movement; and White Fang's snarl slowly dwindled to a growl that ebbed down in his throat and ceased. Then the god spoke, and at the first sound of his voice, the hair rose on White Fang's neck and the growl rushed up in his throat. But the god made no hostile movement, and went on calmly talking. For a time White Fang growled in unison with him, a correspondence of rhythm being established between growl and voice. But the god talked on interminably. He talked to White Fang as White Fang had never been talked to before. He talked softly and soothingly, with a gentleness that somehow, somewhere, touched White Fang. In spite of himself and all the pricking warnings of his instinct, White Fang began to have confidence in this god. He had a feeling of security that was belied by all his experience with men.

After a long time, the god got up and went into the cabin. White Fang scanned him apprehensively when he came out. He had neither whip nor club nor weapon. Nor was his uninjured hand behind his back hiding something. He sat down as before, in the same spot, several feet away. He held out a small piece of meat. White Fang pricked his ears and investigated it suspiciously, managing to look at the same time both at the meat and the god, alert for any overt act, his body tense and ready to spring away at the first sign of hostility.

Still the punishment delayed. The god merely held near to his nose a piece of meat. And about the meat there seemed nothing wrong. Still White Fang suspected; and though the meat was proffered to him with short inviting thrusts of the hand, he refused to touch it. The gods were all-wise, and there was no telling what masterful treachery lurked behind that apparently harmless piece of meat. In past experience, especially in dealing with squaws, meat and punishment had often been disastrously related.

In the end, the god tossed the meat on the snow at White Fang's feet. He smelled the meat carefully; but he did not look at it. While he smelled it he kept his eyes on the god. Nothing happened. He took the meat into his mouth and swallowed it. Still nothing happened. The god was actually offering him another piece of meat. Again he refused to take it from the hand, and again it was tossed to him. This was repeated a number of times. But there came a time when the god refused to toss it. He kept it in his hand and steadfastly proffered it.

The meat was good meat, and White Fang was hungry. Bit by bit, infinitely cautious, he approached the hand. At last the time came that he decided to eat the meat from the hand. He never took his eyes from the god, thrusting his head forward with ears flattened back and hair involuntarily rising and cresting on his neck. Also a low growl rumbled in his throat as warning that he was not to be trifled with. He ate the meat, and nothing happened. Piece by piece, he ate all the meat, and nothing happened. Still the punishment delayed.

He licked his chops and waited. The god went on talking. In his voice was kindness—something of which White Fang had no experience whatever. And within him it aroused feelings which he had likewise never experienced before. He was aware of a certain strange satisfaction, as though some need were being gratified, as though some void in his being were being filled. Then again came the prod of his instinct and the warning of past experience. The gods were ever crafty, and they had unguessed ways of attaining their ends.

Ah, he had thought so! There it came now, the god's hand, cunning to hurt, thrusting out at him, descending upon his head. But the god went on talking. His voice was soft and soothing. In spite of the menacing hand, the voice inspired confidence. And in spite of the assuring voice, the hand inspired distrust. White Fang was torn by conflicting feelings, impulses. It seemed he would fly to pieces, so terrible was the control he was exerting, holding together by an unwonted indecision the counter-forces that struggled within him for mastery.

He compromised. He snarled and bristled and flattened his ears. But he neither snapped nor sprang away. The hand descended. Nearer and nearer it came. It touched the ends of his upstanding hair. He shrank down under it. It followed down after him, pressing more closely against him. Shrinking, almost shivering, he still managed to hold himself together. It was a torment, this hand that touched him and violated his instinct. He could not forget in a day all the evil that had been wrought him at the hands of men. But it was the will of the god, and he strove to submit.

The hand lifted and descended again in a patting, caressing movement. This continued, but every time the hand lifted, the hair lifted under it. And every time the hand descended, the ears flattened down and a cavernous growl surged in his throat. White Fang growled and growled with insistent warning. By this means he announced that he was prepared to retaliate for any hurt he might receive. There was no telling when the god's ulterior motive might be disclosed. At any moment that soft, confidence-inspiring voice might break forth in a roar of wrath, that gentle and caressing hand transform itself into a vice-like grip to hold him helpless and administer punishment.

But the god talked on softly, and ever the hand rose and fell with non-hostile pats. White Fang experienced dual feelings. It was distasteful to his instinct. It restrained him, opposed the will of him toward personal liberty. And yet it was not physically painful. On the contrary, it was even pleasant, in a physical way. The patting movement slowly and carefully changed to a rubbing of the ears about their bases, and the physical pleasure even increased a little. Yet he continued to fear, and he stood on guard, expectant of unguessed evil, alternately suffering and enjoying as one feeling or the other came uppermost and swayed him.

"Well, I'll be gosh-swoggled!"

So spoke Matt, coming out of the cabin, his sleeves rolled up, a pan of dirty dishwater in his hands, arrested in the act of emptying the pan by the sight of Weedon Scott patting White Fang.

At the instant his voice broke the silence, White Fang leaped back, snarling savagely at him.

Matt regarded his employer with grieved disapproval.

"If you don't mind my expressin' my feelin's, Mr. Scott, I'll make free to say you're seventeen kinds of a damn fool an' all of 'em different, an' then some."

Weedon Scott smiled with a superior air, gained his feet, and walked over to White Fang. He talked soothingly to him, but not for long, then slowly put out his hand, rested it on White Fang's head, and resumed the interrupted patting. White Fang endured it, keeping his eyes fixed suspiciously, not upon the man that patted him, but upon the man that stood in the doorway.

"You may be a number one, tip-top minin' expert, all right all right," the dog-musher delivered himself oracularly, "but you missed the chance of your life when you was a boy an' didn't run off an' join a circus."

White Fang snarled at the sound of his voice, but this time did not leap away from under the hand that was caressing his head and the back of his neck with long, soothing strokes.

It was the beginning of the end for White Fang—the ending of the old life and the reign of hate. A new and incomprehensibly fairer life was dawning. It required much thinking and endless patience on the part of Weedon Scott to accomplish this. And on the part of White Fang it required nothing less than a revolution. He had to ignore the urges and promptings of instinct and reason, defy experience, give the lie to life itself.

Life, as he had known it, not only had had no place in it for much that he now did; but all the currents had gone counter to those to which he now abandoned himself. In short, when all things were considered, he had to achieve an orientation far vaster than the one he had achieved at the time he came voluntarily in from the Wild and accepted Grey Beaver as his lord. At that time he was a mere puppy, soft from the making, without form, ready for the thumb of circumstance to begin its work upon him. But now it was different. The thumb of circumstance had done its work only too well. By it he had been formed and hardened into the Fighting Wolf, fierce and implacable, unloving and unlovable. To accomplish the change was like a reflux of being, and this when the plasticity of youth was no longer his; when the fibre of him had become tough and knotty; when the warp and the woof of him had made of him an adamantine texture, harsh and unyielding; when the face of his spirit had become iron and all his instincts and axioms had crystallised into set rules, cautions, dislikes, and desires.

Yet again, in this new orientation, it was the thumb of circumstance that pressed and prodded him, softening that which had become hard and remoulding it into fairer form. Weedon Scott was in truth this thumb. He had gone to the roots of White Fang's nature, and with kindness touched to life potencies that had languished and well-nigh perished. One such potency was *love*. It took the place of *like*, which latter had been the highest feeling that thrilled him in his intercourse with the gods.

But this love did not come in a day. It began with *like* and out of it slowly developed. White Fang did not run away, though he was allowed to remain loose, because he liked this new god. This was certainly better than the life he had lived in the cage of Beauty Smith, and it was necessary that he should have some god. The lordship of man was a need of his nature. The seal of his dependence on man had been set upon him in that early day when he turned his back on the Wild and crawled to Grey Beaver's feet to receive the expected beating. This seal had been stamped upon him again, and ineradicably, on his second return from the Wild, when the long famine was over and there was fish once more in the village of Grey Beaver.

And so, because he needed a god and because he preferred Weedon Scott to Beauty Smith, White Fang remained. In acknowledgment of fealty, he proceeded to take upon himself the guardianship of his master's property. He prowled about the cabin while the sled-dogs slept, and the first night-visitor to the cabin fought him off with a club until Weedon Scott came to the rescue. But White Fang soon learned to differentiate between thieves and honest men, to appraise the true value of step and carriage. The man who travelled, loud-stepping, the direct line to the cabin door, he let alone—though he watched him vigilantly until the door opened and he received the endorsement of the master. But the man who went softly, by circuitous ways, peering with caution, seeking after secrecy—that was the man who received no suspension of judgment from White Fang, and who went away abruptly, hurriedly, and without dignity.

Weedon Scott had set himself the task of redeeming White Fang—or rather, of redeeming mankind from the wrong it had done White Fang. It was a matter of principle and conscience. He felt that the ill done White Fang was a debt incurred by man and that it must be paid. So he went out of his way to be especially kind to the Fighting Wolf. Each day he made it a point to caress and pet White Fang, and to do it at length.

At first suspicious and hostile, White Fang grew to like this petting. But there was one thing that he never outgrew—his growling. Growl he would, from the moment the petting began till it ended. But it was a growl with a new note in it. A stranger could not hear this note, and to such a stranger the growling of White Fang was an exhibition of primordial savagery, nerve-racking and blood-curdling. But White Fang's throat had become harsh-fibred from the making of ferocious sounds through the many years since his first little rasp of anger in the lair of his cubhood, and he could not soften the sounds of that throat now to express the gentleness he felt. Nevertheless, Weedon Scott's ear and sympathy were fine enough to catch the new note all but drowned in the fierceness—the note that was the faintest hint of a croon of content and that none but he could hear.

CHAPTER VI—THE LOVE-MASTER

As the days went by, the evolution of *like* into *love* was accelerated. White Fang himself began to grow aware of it, though in his consciousness he knew not what love was. It manifested itself to him as a void in his being—a hungry, aching, yearning void that clamoured to be filled. It was a pain and an unrest; and it received easement only by the touch of the new god's presence. At such times love was joy to him, a wild, keen-thrilling satisfaction. But when away from his god, the pain and the unrest returned; the void in him sprang up and pressed against him with its emptiness, and the hunger gnawed and gnawed unceasingly.

White Fang was in the process of finding himself. In spite of the maturity of his years and of the savage rigidity of the mould that had formed him, his nature was undergoing an expansion. There was a burgeoning within him of strange feelings and unwonted impulses. His old code of conduct was changing. In the past he had liked comfort and surcease from pain, disliked discomfort and pain, and he had adjusted his actions accordingly. But now it was different. Because of this new feeling within him, he ofttimes elected discomfort and pain for the sake of his god. Thus, in the early morning, instead of roaming and foraging, or lying in a sheltered nook, he would wait for hours on the cheerless cabin-stoop for a sight of the god's face. At night, when the god returned home, White Fang would leave the warm sleeping-place he had burrowed in the snow in order to receive the friendly snap of fingers and the word of greeting. Meat, even meat itself, he would forego to be with his god, to receive a caress from him or to accompany him down into the town.

Like had been replaced by *love*. And love was the plummet dropped down into the deeps of him where like had never gone. And responsive out of his deeps had come the new thing—love. That which was given unto him did he return. This was a god indeed, a love-god, a warm and radiant god, in whose light White Fang's nature expanded as a flower expands under the sun.

But White Fang was not demonstrative. He was too old, too firmly moulded, to become adept at expressing himself in new ways. He was too self-possessed, too strongly poised in his own isolation. Too long had he cultivated reticence, aloofness, and moroseness. He had never barked in his life, and he could not now learn to bark a welcome when his god approached. He was never in the way, never extravagant nor foolish in the expression of his love. He never ran to meet his god. He waited at a distance; but he always waited, was always there. His love partook of the nature of worship, dumb, inarticulate, a silent adoration. Only by the steady regard of his eyes did he express his love, and by the unceasing following with his eyes of his god's every movement. Also, at times, when his god looked at him and spoke to him, he betrayed an awkward self-consciousness, caused by the struggle of his love to express itself and his physical inability to express it.

He learned to adjust himself in many ways to his new mode of life. It was borne in upon him that he must let his master's dogs alone. Yet his dominant nature asserted itself, and he had first to thrash them into an acknowledgment of his superiority and leadership. This accomplished, he had little trouble with them. They gave trail to him when he came and went or walked among them, and when he asserted his will they obeyed.

In the same way, he came to tolerate Matt—as a possession of his master. His master rarely fed him. Matt did that, it was his business; yet White Fang divined that it was his master's food he ate and that it was his master who thus fed him vicariously. Matt it was who tried to put him into the harness and make him haul sled with the other dogs. But Matt failed. It was not until Weedon Scott put the harness on White Fang and worked him, that he understood. He took it as his master's will that Matt should drive him and work him just as he drove and worked his master's other dogs.

Different from the Mackenzie toboggans were the Klondike sleds with runners under them. And different was the method of driving the dogs. There was no fan-formation of the team. The dogs worked in single file, one behind another, hauling on double traces. And here, in the Klondike, the leader was indeed the leader. The wisest as well as strongest dog was the leader, and the team obeyed him and feared him. That White Fang should quickly gain this post was inevitable. He could not be satisfied with less, as Matt learned after much inconvenience and trouble. White Fang picked out the post for himself, and Matt backed his judgment with strong language after the experiment had been tried. But, though he worked in the sled in the day, White Fang did not forego the guarding of his master's property in the night. Thus he was on duty all the time, ever vigilant and faithful, the most valuable of all the dogs.

"Makin' free to spit out what's in me," Matt said one day, "I beg to state that you was a wise guy all right when you paid the price you did for that dog. You clean swindled Beauty Smith on top of pushin' his face in with your fist."

A recrudescence of anger glinted in Weedon Scott's grey eyes, and he muttered savagely, "The beast!"

In the late spring a great trouble came to White Fang. Without warning, the love-master disappeared. There had been warning, but White Fang was unversed in such things and did not understand the packing of a grip. He remembered afterwards that his packing had preceded the master's disappearance; but at the time he suspected nothing. That night he waited for the master to return. At midnight the chill wind that blew drove him to shelter at the rear of the cabin. There he drowsed, only half asleep, his ears keyed for the first sound of the familiar step. But, at two in the morning, his anxiety drove him out to the cold front stoop, where he crouched, and waited.

But no master came. In the morning the door opened and Matt stepped outside. White Fang gazed at him wistfully. There was no common speech by which he might learn what he wanted to know. The days came and went, but never the master. White Fang, who had never known sickness in his life, became sick. He became very sick, so sick that Matt was finally compelled to bring him inside the cabin. Also, in writing to his employer, Matt devoted a postscript to White Fang.

Weedon Scott reading the letter down in Circle City, came upon the following:

"That dam wolf won't work. Won't eat. Aint got no spunk left. All the dogs is licking him. Wants to know what has become of you, and I don't know how to tell him. Mebbe he is going to die."

It was as Matt had said. White Fang had ceased eating, lost heart, and allowed every dog of the team to thrash him. In the cabin he lay on the floor near the stove, without interest in food, in Matt, nor in life. Matt might talk gently to him or swear at him, it was all the same; he never did more than turn his dull eyes upon the man, then drop his head back to its customary position on his fore-paws.

And then, one night, Matt, reading to himself with moving lips and mumbled sounds, was startled by a low whine from White Fang. He had got upon his feet, his ears cocked towards the door, and he was listening intently. A moment later, Matt heard a footstep. The door opened, and Weedon Scott stepped in. The two men shook hands. Then Scott looked around the room.

"Where's the wolf?" he asked.

Then he discovered him, standing where he had been lying, near to the stove. He had not rushed forward after the manner of other dogs. He stood, watching and waiting.

"Holy smoke!" Matt exclaimed. "Look at 'm wag his tail!"

Weedon Scott strode half across the room toward him, at the same time calling him. White Fang came to him, not with a great bound, yet quickly. He was awakened from self-consciousness, but as he drew near, his eyes took on a strange expression. Something, an incommunicable vastness of feeling, rose up into his eyes as a light and shone forth.

"He never looked at me that way all the time you was gone!" Matt commented.

Weedon Scott did not hear. He was squatting down on his heels, face to face with White Fang and petting him—rubbing at the roots of the ears, making long caressing strokes down the neck to the shoulders, tapping the spine gently with the balls of his fingers. And White Fang was growling responsively, the crooning note of the growl more pronounced than ever.

But that was not all. What of his joy, the great love in him, ever surging and struggling to express itself, succeeding in finding a new mode of expression. He suddenly thrust his head forward and nudged his way in between the master's arm and body. And here, confined, hidden from view all except his ears, no longer growling, he continued to nudge and snuggle.

The two men looked at each other. Scott's eyes were shining.

"Gosh!" said Matt in an awe-stricken voice.

A moment later, when he had recovered himself, he said, "I always insisted that wolf was a dog. Look at 'm!"

With the return of the love-master, White Fang's recovery was rapid. Two nights and a day he spent in the cabin. Then he sallied forth. The sled-dogs had forgotten his prowess. They remembered only the latest, which was his weakness and sickness. At the sight of him as he came out of the cabin, they sprang upon him.

"Talk about your rough-houses," Matt murmured gleefully, standing in the doorway and looking on.

"Give 'm hell, you wolf! Give 'm hell!—an' then some!"

White Fang did not need the encouragement. The return of the love-master was enough. Life was flowing through him again, splendid and indomitable. He fought from sheer joy, finding in it an expression of much that he felt and that otherwise was without speech. There could be but one ending. The team dispersed in ignominious defeat, and it was not until after dark that the dogs came sneaking back, one by one, by meekness and humility signifying their fealty to White Fang.

Having learned to snuggle, White Fang was guilty of it often. It was the final word. He could not go beyond it. The one thing of which he had always been particularly jealous was his head. He had always disliked to have it touched. It was the Wild in him, the fear of hurt and of the trap, that had given rise to the panicky impulses to avoid contacts. It was the mandate of his instinct that that head must be free. And now, with the love-master, his snuggling was the deliberate act of putting himself into a position of hopeless helplessness. It was an expression of perfect confidence, of absolute self-surrender, as though he said: "I put myself into thy hands. Work thou thy will with me."

One night, not long after the return, Scott and Matt sat at a game of cribbage preliminary to going to bed. "Fifteen-two, fifteen-four an' a pair makes six," Mat was pegging up, when there was an outcry and sound of snarling without. They looked at each other as they started to rise to their feet.

"The wolf's nailed somebody," Matt said.

A wild scream of fear and anguish hastened them.

"Bring a light!" Scott shouted, as he sprang outside.

Matt followed with the lamp, and by its light they saw a man lying on his back in the snow. His arms were folded, one above the other, across his face and throat. Thus he was trying to shield himself from White Fang's teeth. And there was need for it. White Fang was in a rage, wickedly making his attack on the most vulnerable spot. From shoulder to wrist of the crossed arms, the coat-sleeve, blue flannel shirt and undershirt were ripped in rags, while the arms themselves were terribly slashed and streaming blood.

All this the two men saw in the first instant. The next instant Weedon Scott had White Fang by the throat and was dragging him clear. White Fang struggled and snarled, but made no attempt to bite, while he quickly quieted down at a sharp word from the master.

Matt helped the man to his feet. As he arose he lowered his crossed arms, exposing the bestial face of Beauty Smith. The dog-musher let go of him precipitately, with action similar to that of a man who has picked up live fire. Beauty Smith blinked in the lamplight and looked about him. He caught sight of White Fang and terror rushed into his face.

At the same moment Matt noticed two objects lying in the snow. He held the lamp close to them, indicating them with his toe for his employer's benefit—a steel dog-chain and a stout club.

Weedon Scott saw and nodded. Not a word was spoken. The dog-musher laid his hand on Beauty Smith's shoulder and faced him to the right about. No word needed to be spoken. Beauty Smith started.

In the meantime the love-master was patting White Fang and talking to him.

"Tried to steal you, eh? And you wouldn't have it! Well, well, he made a mistake, didn't he?"

"Must 'a' thought he had hold of seventeen devils," the dog-musher sniggered.

White Fang, still wrought up and bristling, growled and growled, the hair slowly lying down, the crooning note remote and dim, but growing in his throat.

PART V

CHAPTER I—THE LONG TRAIL

It was in the air. White Fang sensed the coming calamity, even before there was tangible evidence of it. In vague ways it was borne in upon him that a change was impending. He knew not how nor why, yet he got his feel of the oncoming event from the gods themselves. In ways subtler than they knew, they betrayed their intentions to the wolf-dog that haunted the cabin-stoop, and that, though he never came inside the cabin, knew what went on inside their brains.

"Listen to that, will you!" the dug-musher exclaimed at supper one night.

Weedon Scott listened. Through the door came a low, anxious whine, like a sobbing under the breath that had just grown audible. Then came the long sniff, as White Fang reassured himself that his god was still inside and had not yet taken himself off in mysterious and solitary flight.

"I do believe that wolf's on to you," the dog-musher said.

Weedon Scott looked across at his companion with eyes that almost pleaded, though this was given the lie by his words.

"What the devil can I do with a wolf in California?" he demanded.

"That's what I say," Matt answered. "What the devil can you do with a wolf in California?"

But this did not satisfy Weedon Scott. The other seemed to be judging him in a non-committal sort of way.

"White man's dogs would have no show against him," Scott went on. "He'd kill them on sight. If he didn't bankrupt me with damaged suits, the authorities would take him away from me and electrocute him."

"He's a downright murderer, I know," was the dog-musher's comment.

Weedon Scott looked at him suspiciously.

"It would never do," he said decisively.

"It would never do!" Matt concurred. "Why you'd have to hire a man 'specially to take care of 'm."

The other suspicion was allayed. He nodded cheerfully. In the silence that followed, the low, half-sobbing whine was heard at the door and then the long, questing sniff.

"There's no denyin' he thinks a hell of a lot of you," Matt said.

The other glared at him in sudden wrath. "Damn it all, man! I know my own mind and what's best!"

"I'm agreein' with you, only . . . "

"Only what?" Scott snapped out.

"Only . . . " the dog-musher began softly, then changed his mind and betrayed a rising anger of his own. "Well, you needn't get so all-fired het up about it. Judgin' by your actions one'd think you didn't know your own mind."

Weedon Scott debated with himself for a while, and then said more gently: "You are right, Matt. I don't know my own mind, and that's what's the trouble."

"Why, it would be rank ridiculousness for me to take that dog along," he broke out after another pause.

"I'm agreein' with you," was Matt's answer, and again his employer was not quite satisfied with him.

"But how in the name of the great Sardanapolis he knows you're goin' is what gets me," the dog-musher continued innocently.

"It's beyond me, Matt," Scott answered, with a mournful shake of the head.

Then came the day when, through the open cabin door, White Fang saw the fatal grip on the floor and the love-master packing things into it. Also, there were comings and goings, and the erstwhile placid atmosphere of the cabin was vexed with strange perturbations and unrest. Here was indubitable evidence. White Fang had already scented it. He now reasoned it. His god was preparing for another flight. And since he had not taken him with him before, so, now, he could look to be left behind.

That night he lifted the long wolf-howl. As he had howled, in his puppy days, when he fled back from the Wild to the village to find it vanished and naught but a rubbish-heap to mark the site of Grey Beaver's tepee, so now he pointed his muzzle to the cold stars and told to them his woe.

Inside the cabin the two men had just gone to bed.

"He's gone off his food again," Matt remarked from his bunk.

There was a grunt from Weedon Scott's bunk, and a stir of blankets.

"From the way he cut up the other time you went away, I wouldn't wonder this time but what he died."

The blankets in the other bunk stirred irritably.

"Oh, shut up!" Scott cried out through the darkness. "You nag worse than a woman."

"I'm agreein' with you," the dog-musher answered, and Weedon Scott was not quite sure whether or not the other had snickered.

The next day White Fang's anxiety and restlessness were even more pronounced. He dogged his master's heels whenever he left the cabin, and haunted the front stoop when he remained inside. Through the open door he could catch glimpses of the luggage on the floor. The grip had been joined by two large canvas bags and a box. Matt was rolling the master's blankets and fur robe inside a small tarpaulin. White Fang whined as he watched the operation.

Later on two Indians arrived. He watched them closely as they shouldered the luggage and were led off down the hill by Matt, who carried the bedding and the grip. But White Fang did not follow them. The master was still in the cabin. After a time, Matt returned. The master came to the door and called White Fang inside.

"You poor devil," he said gently, rubbing White Fang's ears and tapping his spine. "I'm hitting the long trail, old man, where you cannot follow. Now give me a growl—the last, good, good-bye growl."

But White Fang refused to growl. Instead, and after a wistful, searching look, he snuggled in, burrowing his head out of sight between the master's arm and body.

"There she blows!" Matt cried. From the Yukon arose the hoarse bellowing of a river steamboat. "You've got to cut it short. Be sure and lock the front door. I'll go out the back. Get a move on!"

The two doors slammed at the same moment, and Weedon Scott waited for Matt to come around to the front. From inside the door came a low whining and sobbing. Then there were long, deep-drawn sniffs.

"You must take good care of him, Matt," Scott said, as they started down the hill. "Write and let me know how he gets along."

"Sure," the dog-musher answered. "But listen to that, will you!"

Both men stopped. White Fang was howling as dogs howl when their masters lie dead. He was voicing an utter woe, his cry bursting upward in great heart-breaking rushes, dying down into quavering misery, and bursting upward again with a rush upon rush of grief.

The *Aurora* was the first steamboat of the year for the Outside, and her decks were jammed with prosperous adventurers and broken gold seekers, all equally as mad to get to the Outside as they had been originally to get to the Inside. Near the gang-plank, Scott was shaking hands with Matt, who was preparing to go ashore. But Matt's hand went limp in the other's grasp as his gaze shot past and remained fixed on something behind him. Scott turned to see. Sitting on the deck several feet away and watching wistfully was White Fang.

The dog-musher swore softly, in awe-stricken accents. Scott could only look in wonder.

"Did you lock the front door?" Matt demanded. The other nodded, and asked, "How about the back?"

"You just bet I did," was the fervent reply.

White Fang flattened his ears ingratiatingly, but remained where he was, making no attempt to approach.

"I'll have to take 'm ashore with me."

Matt made a couple of steps toward White Fang, but the latter slid away from him. The dog-musher made a rush of it, and White Fang dodged between the legs of a group of men. Ducking, turning, doubling, he slid about the deck, eluding the other's efforts to capture him.

But when the love-master spoke, White Fang came to him with prompt obedience.

"Won't come to the hand that's fed 'm all these months," the dog-musher muttered resentfully. "And you—you ain't never fed 'm after them first days of gettin' acquainted. I'm blamed if I can see how he works it out that you're the boss."

Scott, who had been patting White Fang, suddenly bent closer and pointed out fresh-made cuts on his muzzle, and a gash between the eyes.

Matt bent over and passed his hand along White Fang's belly.

"We plump forgot the window. He's all cut an' gouged underneath. Must 'a' butted clean through it, b'gosh!"

But Weedon Scott was not listening. He was thinking rapidly. The *Aurora's* whistle hooted a final announcement of departure. Men were scurrying down the gang-plank to the shore. Matt loosened the bandana from his own neck and started to put it around White Fang's. Scott grasped the dog-musher's hand.

"Good-bye, Matt, old man. About the wolf—you needn't write. You see, I've . . . !"

"What!" the dog-musher exploded. "You don't mean to say . . .?"

"The very thing I mean. Here's your bandana. I'll write to you about him."

Matt paused halfway down the gang-plank.

"He'll never stand the climate!" he shouted back. "Unless you clip 'm in warm weather!"

The gang-plank was hauled in, and the *Aurora* swung out from the bank. Weedon Scott waved a last good-bye. Then he turned and bent over White Fang, standing by his side.

"Now growl, damn you, growl," he said, as he patted the responsive head and rubbed the flattening ears.

CHAPTER II—THE SOUTHLAND

White Fang landed from the steamer in San Francisco. He was appalled. Deep in him, below any reasoning process or act of consciousness, he had associated power with godhead. And never had the white men seemed such marvellous gods as now, when he trod the slimy pavement of San Francisco. The log cabins he had known were replaced by towering buildings. The streets were crowded with perils—waggons, carts, automobiles; great, straining horses pulling huge trucks; and monstrous cable and electric cars hooting and clanging through the midst, screeching their insistent menace after the manner of the lynxes he had known in the northern woods.

All this was the manifestation of power. Through it all, behind it all, was man, governing and controlling, expressing himself, as of old, by his mastery over matter. It was colossal, stunning. White Fang was awed. Fear sat upon him. As in his cubhood he had been made to feel his smallness and puniness on the day he first came in from the Wild to the village of Grey Beaver, so now, in his full-grown stature and pride of strength, he was made to feel small and puny. And there were so many gods! He was made dizzy by the swarming of them. The thunder of the streets smote upon his ears. He was bewildered by the tremendous and endless rush and movement of things. As never before, he felt his dependence on the love-master, close at whose heels he followed, no matter what happened never losing sight of him.

But White Fang was to have no more than a nightmare vision of the city—an experience that was like a bad dream, unreal and terrible, that haunted him for long after in his dreams. He was put into a baggage-car by the master, chained in a corner in the midst of heaped trunks and valises. Here a squat and brawny god held sway, with much noise, hurling trunks and boxes about, dragging them in through the door and tossing them into the piles, or flinging them out of the door, smashing and crashing, to other gods who awaited them.

And here, in this inferno of luggage, was White Fang deserted by the master. Or at least White Fang thought he was deserted, until he smelled out the master's canvas clothes-bags alongside of him, and proceeded to mount guard over them.

"'Bout time you come," growled the god of the car, an hour later, when Weedon Scott appeared at the door. "That dog of yourn won't let me lay a finger on your stuff."

White Fang emerged from the car. He was astonished. The nightmare city was gone. The car had been to him no more than a room in a house, and when he had entered it the city had been all around him. In the interval the city had disappeared. The roar of it no longer dinned upon his ears. Before him was smiling country, streaming with sunshine, lazy with quietude. But he had little time to marvel at the transformation. He accepted it as he accepted all the unaccountable doings and manifestations of the gods. It was their way.

There was a carriage waiting. A man and a woman approached the master. The woman's arms went out and clutched the master around the neck—a hostile act! The next moment Weedon Scott had torn loose from the embrace and closed with White Fang, who had become a snarling, raging demon.

"It's all right, mother," Scott was saying as he kept tight hold of White Fang and placated him. "He thought you were going to injure me, and he wouldn't stand for it. It's all right. It's all right. He'll learn soon enough."

"And in the meantime I may be permitted to love my son when his dog is not around," she laughed, though she was pale and weak from the fright.

She looked at White Fang, who snarled and bristled and glared malevolently.

"He'll have to learn, and he shall, without postponement," Scott said.

He spoke softly to White Fang until he had quieted him, then his voice became firm.

"Down, sir! Down with you!"

This had been one of the things taught him by the master, and White Fang obeyed, though he lay down reluctantly and sullenly.

"Now, mother."

Scott opened his arms to her, but kept his eyes on White Fang.

"Down!" he warned. "Down!"

White Fang, bristling silently, half-crouching as he rose, sank back and watched the hostile act repeated. But no harm came of it, nor of the embrace from the strange man-god that followed. Then the clothes-bags were taken into the carriage, the strange gods and the love-master followed, and White Fang pursued, now running vigilantly behind, now bristling up to the running horses and warning them that he was there to see that no harm befell the god they dragged so swiftly across the earth.

At the end of fifteen minutes, the carriage swung in through a stone gateway and on between a double row of arched and interlacing walnut trees. On either side stretched lawns, their broad sweep broken here and there by great sturdy-limbed oaks. In the near distance, in contrast with the young-green of the tended grass, sunburnt hay-fields showed tan and gold; while beyond were the tawny hills and upland pastures. From the head of the lawn, on the first soft swell from the valley-level, looked down the deep-porched, many-windowed house.

Little opportunity was given White Fang to see all this. Hardly had the carriage entered the grounds, when he was set upon by a sheep-dog, bright-eyed, sharp-muzzled, righteously indignant and angry. It was between him and the master, cutting him off. White Fang snarled no warning, but his hair bristled as he made his silent and deadly rush. This rush was never completed. He halted with awkward abruptness, with stiff fore-legs bracing himself against his momentum, almost sitting down on his haunches, so desirous was he of avoiding contact with the dog he was in the act of attacking. It was a female, and the law of his kind thrust a barrier between. For him to attack her would require nothing less than a violation of his instinct.

But with the sheep-dog it was otherwise. Being a female, she possessed no such instinct. On the other hand, being a sheep-dog, her instinctive fear of the Wild, and especially of the wolf, was unusually keen. White Fang was to her a wolf, the hereditary marauder who had preyed upon her flocks from the time sheep were first herded and guarded by some dim ancestor of hers. And so, as he abandoned his rush at her and braced himself to avoid the contact, she sprang upon him. He snarled involuntarily as he felt her teeth in his shoulder, but beyond this made no offer to hurt her. He backed away, stiff-legged with self-consciousness, and tried to go around her. He dodged this way and that, and curved and turned, but to no purpose. She remained always between him and the way he wanted to go.

"Here, Collie!" called the strange man in the carriage.

Weedon Scott laughed.

"Never mind, father. It is good discipline. White Fang will have to learn many things, and it's just as well that he begins now. He'll adjust himself all right."

The carriage drove on, and still Collie blocked White Fang's way. He tried to outrun her by leaving the drive and circling across the lawn but she ran on the inner and smaller circle, and was always there, facing him with her two rows of gleaming teeth. Back he circled, across the drive to the other lawn, and again she headed him off.

The carriage was bearing the master away. White Fang caught glimpses of it disappearing amongst the trees. The situation was desperate. He essayed another circle. She followed, running swiftly. And then, suddenly, he turned upon her. It was his old fighting trick. Shoulder to shoulder, he struck her squarely. Not only was she overthrown. So fast had she been running that she rolled along, now on her back, now on her side, as she struggled to stop, clawing gravel with her feet and crying shrilly her hurt pride and indignation.

White Fang did not wait. The way was clear, and that was all he had wanted. She took after him, never ceasing her outcry. It was the straightaway now, and when it came to real running, White Fang could teach her things. She ran frantically, hysterically, straining to the utmost, advertising the effort she was making with every leap: and all the time White Fang slid smoothly away from her silently, without effort, gliding like a ghost over the ground.

As he rounded the house to the *porte-cochère*, he came upon the carriage. It had stopped, and the master was alighting. At this moment, still running at top speed, White Fang became suddenly aware of an attack from the side. It was a deer-hound rushing upon him. White Fang tried to face it. But he was going too fast, and the hound was too close. It struck him on the side; and such was his forward momentum and the unexpectedness of it, White Fang was hurled to the ground and rolled clear over. He came out of the tangle a spectacle of malignancy, ears flattened back, lips writhing, nose wrinkling, his teeth clipping together as the fangs barely missed the hound's soft throat.

The master was running up, but was too far away; and it was Collie that saved the hound's life. Before White Fang could spring in and deliver the fatal stroke, and just as he was in the act of springing in, Collie arrived. She had been out-manoeuvred and out-run, to say nothing of her having been unceremoniously tumbled in the gravel, and her arrival was like that of a tornado—made up of offended dignity, justifiable wrath, and instinctive hatred for this marauder from the Wild. She struck White Fang at right angles in the midst of his spring, and again he was knocked off his feet and rolled over.

The next moment the master arrived, and with one hand held White Fang, while the father called off the dogs.

"I say, this is a pretty warm reception for a poor lone wolf from the Arctic," the master said, while White Fang calmed down under his caressing hand. "In all his life he's only been known once to go off his feet, and here he's been rolled twice in thirty seconds."

The carriage had driven away, and other strange gods had appeared from out the house. Some of these stood respectfully at a distance; but two of them, women, perpetrated the hostile act of clutching the master around the neck. White Fang, however, was beginning to tolerate this act. No harm seemed to come of it, while the noises the gods made were certainly not threatening. These gods also made overtures to White Fang, but he warned them off with a snarl, and the master did likewise with word of mouth. At such times White Fang leaned in close against the master's legs and received reassuring pats on the head.

The hound, under the command, "Dick! Lie down, sir!" had gone up the steps and lain down to one side of the porch, still growling and keeping a sullen watch on the intruder. Collie had been taken in charge by one of the woman-gods, who held arms around her neck and petted and caressed her; but Collie was very much perplexed and worried, whining and restless, outraged by the permitted presence of this wolf and confident that the gods were making a mistake.

All the gods started up the steps to enter the house. White Fang followed closely at the master's heels. Dick, on the porch, growled, and White Fang, on the steps, bristled and growled back.

"Take Collie inside and leave the two of them to fight it out," suggested Scott's father. "After that they'll be friends."

"Then White Fang, to show his friendship, will have to be chief mourner at the funeral," laughed the master.

The elder Scott looked incredulously, first at White Fang, then at Dick, and finally at his son.

"You mean . . .?"

Weedon nodded his head. "I mean just that. You'd have a dead Dick inside one minute—two minutes at the farthest."

He turned to White Fang. "Come on, you wolf. It's you that'll have to come inside."

White Fang walked stiff-legged up the steps and across the porch, with tail rigidly erect, keeping his eyes on Dick to guard against a flank attack, and at the same time prepared for whatever fierce manifestation of the unknown that might pounce out upon him from the interior of the house. But no thing of fear pounced out, and when he had gained the inside he scouted carefully around, looking at it and finding it not. Then he lay down with a contented grunt at the master's feet, observing all that went on, ever ready to spring to his feet and fight for life with the terrors he felt must lurk under the trap-roof of the dwelling.

CHAPTER III—THE GOD'S DOMAIN

Not only was White Fang adaptable by nature, but he had travelled much, and knew the meaning and necessity of adjustment. Here, in Sierra Vista, which was the name of Judge Scott's place, White Fang quickly began to make himself at home. He had no further serious trouble with the dogs. They knew more about the ways of the Southland gods than did he, and in their eyes he had qualified when he accompanied the gods inside the house. Wolf that he was, and unprecedented as it was, the gods had sanctioned his presence, and they, the dogs of the gods, could only recognise this sanction.

Dick, perforce, had to go through a few stiff formalities at first, after which he calmly accepted White Fang as an addition to the premises. Had Dick had his way, they would have been good friends. All but White Fang was averse to friendship. All he asked of other dogs was to be let alone. His whole life he had kept aloof from his kind, and he still desired to keep aloof. Dick's overtures bothered him, so he snarled Dick away. In the north he had learned the lesson that he must let the master's dogs alone, and he did not forget that lesson now. But he insisted on his own privacy and self-seclusion, and so thoroughly ignored Dick that that good-natured creature finally gave him up and scarcely took as much interest in him as in the hitching-post near the stable.

Not so with Collie. While she accepted him because it was the mandate of the gods, that was no reason that she should leave him in peace. Woven into her being was the memory of countless crimes he and his had perpetrated against her ancestry. Not in a day nor a generation were the ravaged sheepfolds to be forgotten. All this was a spur to her, pricking her to retaliation. She could not fly in the face of the gods who permitted him, but that did not prevent her from making life miserable for him in petty ways. A feud, ages old, was between them, and she, for one, would see to it that he was reminded.

So Collie took advantage of her sex to pick upon White Fang and maltreat him. His instinct would not permit him to attack her, while her persistence would not permit him to ignore her. When she rushed at him he turned his fur-protected shoulder to her sharp teeth and walked away stiff-legged and stately. When she forced him too hard, he was compelled to go about in a circle, his shoulder presented to her, his head turned from her, and on his face and in his eyes a patient and bored expression. Sometimes, however, a nip on his hind-quarters hastened his retreat and made it anything but stately. But as a rule he managed to maintain a dignity that was almost solemnity. He ignored her existence whenever it was possible, and made it a point to keep out of her way. When he saw or heard her coming, he got up and walked off.

There was much in other matters for White Fang to learn. Life in the Northland was simplicity itself when compared with the complicated affairs of Sierra Vista. First of all, he had to learn the family of the master. In a way he was prepared to do this. As Mit-sah and Kloo-kooch had belonged to Grey Beaver, sharing his food, his fire, and his blankets, so now, at Sierra Vista, belonged to the love-master all the denizens of the house.

But in this matter there was a difference, and many differences. Sierra Vista was a far vaster affair than the tepee of Grey Beaver. There were many persons to be considered. There was Judge Scott, and there was his wife. There were the master's two sisters, Beth and Mary. There was his wife, Alice, and then there were his children, Weedon and Maud, toddlers of four and six. There was no way for anybody to tell him about all these people, and of blood-ties and relationship he knew nothing whatever and never would be capable of knowing. Yet he quickly worked it out that all of them belonged to the master. Then, by observation, whenever opportunity offered, by study of action, speech, and the very intonations of the voice, he slowly learned the intimacy and the degree of favour they enjoyed with the master. And by this ascertained standard, White Fang treated them accordingly. What was of value to the master he valued; what was dear to the master was to be cherished by White Fang and guarded carefully.

Thus it was with the two children. All his life he had disliked children. He hated and feared their hands. The lessons were not tender that he had learned of their tyranny and cruelty in the days of the Indian villages. When Weedon and Maud had first approached him, he growled warningly and looked malignant. A cuff from the master and a sharp word had then compelled him to permit their caresses, though he growled and growled under their tiny hands, and in the growl there was no crooning note. Later, he observed that the boy and girl were of great value in the master's eyes. Then it was that no cuff nor sharp word was necessary before they could pat him.

Yet White Fang was never effusively affectionate. He yielded to the master's children with an ill but honest grace, and endured their fooling as one would endure a painful operation. When he could no longer endure, he would get up and stalk determinedly away from them. But after a time, he grew even to like the children. Still he was not demonstrative. He would not go up to them. On the other hand, instead of walking away at sight of them, he waited for them to come to him. And still later, it was noticed that a pleased light came into his eyes when he saw them approaching, and that he looked after them with an appearance of curious regret when they left him for other amusements.

All this was a matter of development, and took time. Next in his regard, after the children, was Judge Scott. There were two reasons, possibly, for this. First, he was evidently a valuable possession of the master's, and next, he was undemonstrative. White Fang liked to lie at his feet on the wide porch when he read the newspaper, from time to time favouring White Fang with a look or a word—untroublesome tokens that he recognised White Fang's presence and existence. But this was only when the master was not around. When the master appeared, all other beings ceased to exist so far as White Fang was concerned.

CHAPTER III—THE GOD'S DOMAIN

White Fang allowed all the members of the family to pet him and make much of him; but he never gave to them what he gave to the master. No caress of theirs could put the love-croon into his throat, and, try as they would, they could never persuade him into snuggling against them. This expression of abandon and surrender, of absolute trust, he reserved for the master alone. In fact, he never regarded the members of the family in any other light than possessions of the love-master.

Also White Fang had early come to differentiate between the family and the servants of the household. The latter were afraid of him, while he merely refrained from attacking them. This because he considered that they were likewise possessions of the master. Between White Fang and them existed a neutrality and no more. They cooked for the master and washed the dishes and did other things just as Matt had done up in the Klondike. They were, in short, appurtenances of the household.

Outside the household there was even more for White Fang to learn. The master's domain was wide and complex, yet it had its metes and bounds. The land itself ceased at the county road. Outside was the common domain of all gods—the roads and streets. Then inside other fences were the particular domains of other gods. A myriad laws governed all these things and determined conduct; yet he did not know the speech of the gods, nor was there any way for him to learn save by experience. He obeyed his natural impulses until they ran him counter to some law. When this had been done a few times, he learned the law and after that observed it.

But most potent in his education was the cuff of the master's hand, the censure of the master's voice. Because of White Fang's very great love, a cuff from the master hurt him far more than any beating Grey Beaver or Beauty Smith had ever given him. They had hurt only the flesh of him; beneath the flesh the spirit had still raged, splendid and invincible. But with the master the cuff was always too light to hurt the flesh. Yet it went deeper. It was an expression of the master's disapproval, and White Fang's spirit wilted under it.

In point of fact, the cuff was rarely administered. The master's voice was sufficient. By it White Fang knew whether he did right or not. By it he trimmed his conduct and adjusted his actions. It was the compass by which he steered and learned to chart the manners of a new land and life.

In the Northland, the only domesticated animal was the dog. All other animals lived in the Wild, and were, when not too formidable, lawful spoil for any dog. All his days White Fang had foraged among the live things for food. It did not enter his head that in the Southland it was otherwise. But this he was to learn early in his residence in Santa Clara Valley. Sauntering around the corner of the house in the early morning, he came upon a chicken that had escaped from the chicken-yard. White Fang's natural impulse was to eat it. A couple of bounds, a flash of teeth and a frightened squawk, and he had scooped in the adventurous fowl. It was farm-bred and fat and tender; and White Fang licked his chops and decided that such fare was good.

Later in the day, he chanced upon another stray chicken near the stables. One of the grooms ran to the rescue. He did not know White Fang's breed, so for weapon he took a light buggy-whip. At the first cut of the whip, White Fang left the chicken for the man. A club might have stopped White Fang, but not a whip. Silently, without flinching, he took a second cut in his forward rush, and as he leaped for the throat the groom cried out, "My God!" and staggered backward. He dropped the whip and shielded his throat with his arms. In consequence, his forearm was ripped open to the bone.

The man was badly frightened. It was not so much White Fang's ferocity as it was his silence that unnerved the groom. Still protecting his throat and face with his torn and bleeding arm, he tried to retreat to the barn. And it would have gone hard with him had not Collie appeared on the scene. As she had saved Dick's life, she now saved the groom's. She rushed upon White Fang in frenzied wrath. She had been right. She had known better than the blundering gods. All her suspicions were justified. Here was the ancient marauder up to his old tricks again.

The groom escaped into the stables, and White Fang backed away before Collie's wicked teeth, or presented his shoulder to them and circled round and round. But Collie did not give over, as was her wont, after a decent interval of chastisement. On the contrary, she grew more excited and angry every moment, until, in the end, White Fang flung dignity to the winds and frankly fled away from her across the fields.

"He'll learn to leave chickens alone," the master said. "But I can't give him the lesson until I catch him in the act."

Two nights later came the act, but on a more generous scale than the master had anticipated. White Fang had observed closely the chicken-yards and the habits of the chickens. In the night-time, after they had gone to roost, he climbed to the top of a pile of newly hauled lumber. From there he gained the roof of a chicken-house, passed over the ridgepole and dropped to the ground inside. A moment later he was inside the house, and the slaughter began.

In the morning, when the master came out on to the porch, fifty white Leghorn hens, laid out in a row by the groom, greeted his eyes. He whistled to himself, softly, first with surprise, and then, at the end, with admiration. His eyes were likewise greeted by White Fang, but about the latter there were no signs of shame nor guilt. He carried himself with pride, as though, forsooth, he had achieved a deed praiseworthy and meritorious. There was about him no consciousness of sin. The master's lips tightened as he faced the disagreeable task. Then he talked harshly to the unwitting culprit, and in his voice there was nothing but godlike wrath. Also, he held White Fang's nose down to the slain hens, and at the same time cuffed him soundly.

White Fang never raided a chicken-roost again. It was against the law, and he had learned it. Then the master took him into the chicken-yards. White Fang's natural impulse, when he saw the live food fluttering about him and under his very nose, was to spring upon it. He obeyed the impulse, but was checked by the master's voice. They continued in the yards for half an hour. Time and again the impulse surged over White Fang, and each time, as he yielded to it, he was checked by the master's voice. Thus it was he learned the law, and ere he left the domain of the chickens, he had learned to ignore their existence.

"You can never cure a chicken-killer." Judge Scott shook his head sadly at luncheon table, when his son narrated the lesson he had given White Fang. "Once they've got the habit and the taste of blood . . ." Again he shook his head sadly.

But Weedon Scott did not agree with his father. "I'll tell you what I'll do," he challenged finally. "I'll lock White Fang in with the chickens all afternoon."

"But think of the chickens," objected the judge.

"And furthermore," the son went on, "for every chicken he kills, I'll pay you one dollar gold coin of the realm."

"But you should penalise father, too," interpose Beth.

Her sister seconded her, and a chorus of approval arose from around the table. Judge Scott nodded his head in agreement.

"All right." Weedon Scott pondered for a moment. "And if, at the end of the afternoon White Fang hasn't harmed a chicken, for every ten minutes of the time he has spent in the yard, you will have to say to him, gravely and with deliberation, just as if you were sitting on the bench and solemnly passing judgment, 'White Fang, you are smarter than I thought.'"

From hidden points of vantage the family watched the performance. But it was a fizzle. Locked in the yard and there deserted by the master, White Fang lay down and went to sleep. Once he got up and walked over to the trough for a drink of water. The chickens he calmly ignored. So far as he was concerned they did not exist. At four o'clock he executed a running jump, gained the roof of the chicken-house and leaped to the ground outside, whence he sauntered gravely to the house. He had learned the law. And on the porch, before the delighted family, Judge Scott, face to face with White Fang, said slowly and solemnly, sixteen times, "White Fang, you are smarter than I thought."

But it was the multiplicity of laws that befuddled White Fang and often brought him into disgrace. He had to learn that he must not touch the chickens that belonged to other gods. Then there were cats, and rabbits, and turkeys; all these he must let alone. In fact, when he had but partly learned the law, his impression was that he must leave all live things alone. Out in the back-pasture, a quail could flutter up under his nose unharmed. All tense and trembling with eagerness and desire, he mastered his instinct and stood still. He was obeying the will of the gods.

And then, one day, again out in the back-pasture, he saw Dick start a jackrabbit and run it. The master himself was looking on and did not interfere. Nay, he encouraged White Fang to join in the chase. And thus he learned that there was no taboo on jackrabbits. In the end he worked out the complete law. Between him and all domestic animals there must be no hostilities. If not amity, at least neutrality must obtain. But the other animals—the squirrels, and quail, and cottontails, were creatures of the Wild who had never yielded allegiance to man. They were the lawful prey of any dog. It was only the tame that the gods protected, and between the tame deadly strife was not permitted. The gods held the power of life and death over their subjects, and the gods were jealous of their power.

Life was complex in the Santa Clara Valley after the simplicities of the Northland. And the chief thing demanded by these intricacies of civilisation was control, restraint—a poise of self that was as delicate as the fluttering of gossamer wings and at the same time as rigid as steel. Life had a thousand faces, and White Fang found he must meet them all—thus, when he went to town, in to San Jose, running behind the carriage or loafing about the streets when the carriage stopped. Life flowed past him, deep and wide and varied, continually impinging upon his senses, demanding of him instant and endless adjustments and correspondences, and compelling him, almost always, to suppress his natural impulses.

There were butcher-shops where meat hung within reach. This meat he must not touch. There were cats at the houses the master visited that must be let alone. And there were dogs everywhere that snarled at him and that he must not attack. And then, on the crowded sidewalks there were persons innumerable whose attention he attracted. They would stop and look at him, point him out to one another, examine him, talk of him, and, worst of all, pat him. And these perilous contacts from all these strange hands he must endure. Yet this endurance he achieved. Furthermore, he got over being awkward and self-conscious. In a lofty way he received the attentions of the multitudes of strange gods. With condescension he accepted their condescension. On the other hand, there was something about him that prevented great familiarity. They patted him on the head and passed on, contented and pleased with their own daring.

But it was not all easy for White Fang. Running behind the carriage in the outskirts of San Jose, he encountered certain small boys who made a practice of flinging stones at him. Yet he knew that it was not permitted him to pursue and drag them down. Here he was compelled to violate his instinct of self-preservation, and violate it he did, for he was becoming tame and qualifying himself for civilisation.

Nevertheless, White Fang was not quite satisfied with the arrangement. He had no abstract ideas about justice and fair play. But there is a certain sense of equity that resides in life, and it was this sense in him that resented the unfairness of his being permitted no defence against the stone-throwers. He forgot that in the covenant entered into between him and the gods they were pledged to care for him and defend him. But one day the master sprang from the carriage, whip in hand, and gave the stone-throwers a thrashing. After that they threw stones no more, and White Fang understood and was satisfied.

One other experience of similar nature was his. On the way to town, hanging around the saloon at the cross-roads, were three dogs that made a practice of rushing out upon him when he went by. Knowing his deadly method of fighting, the master had never ceased impressing upon White Fang the law that he must not fight. As a result, having learned the lesson well, White Fang was hard put whenever he passed the cross-roads saloon. After the first rush, each time, his snarl kept the three dogs at a distance but they trailed along behind, yelping and bickering and insulting him. This endured for some time. The men at the saloon even urged the dogs on to attack White Fang. One day they openly sicked the dogs on him. The master stopped the carriage.

"Go to it," he said to White Fang.

But White Fang could not believe. He looked at the master, and he looked at the dogs. Then he looked back eagerly and questioningly at the master.

The master nodded his head. "Go to them, old fellow. Eat them up."

White Fang no longer hesitated. He turned and leaped silently among his enemies. All three faced him. There was a great snarling and growling, a clashing of teeth and a flurry of bodies. The dust of the road arose in a cloud and screened the battle. But at the end of several minutes two dogs were struggling in the dirt and the third was in full flight. He leaped a ditch, went through a rail fence, and fled across a field. White Fang followed, sliding over the ground in wolf fashion and with wolf speed, swiftly and without noise, and in the centre of the field he dragged down and slew the dog.

With this triple killing his main troubles with dogs ceased. The word went up and down the valley, and men saw to it that their dogs did not molest the Fighting Wolf.

CHAPTER IV—THE CALL OF KIND

The months came and went. There was plenty of food and no work in the Southland, and White Fang lived fat and prosperous and happy. Not alone was he in the geographical Southland, for he was in the Southland of life. Human kindness was like a sun shining upon him, and he flourished like a flower planted in good soil.

And yet he remained somehow different from other dogs. He knew the law even better than did the dogs that had known no other life, and he observed the law more punctiliously; but still there was about him a suggestion of lurking ferocity, as though the Wild still lingered in him and the wolf in him merely slept.

He never chummed with other dogs. Lonely he had lived, so far as his kind was concerned, and lonely he would continue to live. In his puppyhood, under the persecution of Lip-lip and the puppy-pack, and in his fighting days with Beauty Smith, he had acquired a fixed aversion for dogs. The natural course of his life had been diverted, and, recoiling from his kind, he had clung to the human.

Besides, all Southland dogs looked upon him with suspicion. He aroused in them their instinctive fear of the Wild, and they greeted him always with snarl and growl and belligerent hatred. He, on the other hand, learned that it was not necessary to use his teeth upon them. His naked fangs and writhing lips were uniformly efficacious, rarely failing to send a bellowing on-rushing dog back on its haunches.

But there was one trial in White Fang's life—Collie. She never gave him a moment's peace. She was not so amenable to the law as he. She defied all efforts of the master to make her become friends with White Fang. Ever in his ears was sounding her sharp and nervous snarl. She had never forgiven him the chicken-killing episode, and persistently held to the belief that his intentions were bad. She found him guilty before the act, and treated him accordingly. She became a pest to him, like a policeman following him around the stable and the hounds, and, if he even so much as glanced curiously at a pigeon or chicken, bursting into an outcry of indignation and wrath. His favourite way of ignoring her was to lie down, with his head on his forepaws, and pretend sleep. This always dumfounded and silenced her.

With the exception of Collie, all things went well with White Fang. He had learned control and poise, and he knew the law. He achieved a staidness, and calmness, and philosophic tolerance. He no longer lived in a hostile environment. Danger and hurt and death did not lurk everywhere about him. In time, the unknown, as a thing of terror and menace ever impending, faded away. Life was soft and easy. It flowed along smoothly, and neither fear nor foe lurked by the way.

He missed the snow without being aware of it. "An unduly long summer," would have been his thought had he thought about it; as it was, he merely missed the snow in a vague, subconscious way. In the same fashion, especially in the heat of summer when he suffered from the sun, he experienced faint longings for the Northland. Their only effect upon him, however, was to make him uneasy and restless without his knowing what was the matter.

White Fang had never been very demonstrative. Beyond his snuggling and the throwing of a crooning note into his love-growl, he had no way of expressing his love. Yet it was given him to discover a third way. He had always been susceptible to the laughter of the gods. Laughter had affected him with madness, made him frantic with rage. But he did not have it in him to be angry with the love-master, and when that god elected to laugh at him in a good-natured, bantering way, he was nonplussed. He could feel the pricking and stinging of the old anger as it strove to rise up in him, but it strove against love. He could not be angry; yet he had to do something. At first he was dignified, and the master laughed the harder. Then he tried to be more dignified, and the master laughed harder than before. In the end, the master laughed him out of his dignity. His jaws slightly parted, his lips lifted a little, and a quizzical expression that was more love than humour came into his eyes. He had learned to laugh.

Likewise he learned to romp with the master, to be tumbled down and rolled over, and be the victim of innumerable rough tricks. In return he feigned anger, bristling and growling ferociously, and clipping his teeth together in snaps that had all the seeming of deadly intention. But he never forgot himself. Those snaps were always delivered on the empty air. At the end of such a romp, when blow and cuff and snap and snarl were last and furious, they would break off suddenly and stand several feet apart, glaring at each other. And then, just as suddenly, like the sun rising on a stormy sea, they would begin to laugh. This would always culminate with the master's arms going around White Fang's neck and shoulders while the latter crooned and growled his love-song.

But nobody else ever romped with White Fang. He did not permit it. He stood on his dignity, and when they attempted it, his warning snarl and bristling mane were anything but playful. That he allowed the master these liberties was no reason that he should be a common dog, loving here and loving there, everybody's property for a romp and good time. He loved with single heart and refused to cheapen himself or his love.

The master went out on horseback a great deal, and to accompany him was one of White Fang's chief duties in life. In the Northland he had evidenced his fealty by toiling in the harness; but there were no sleds in the Southland, nor did dogs pack burdens on their backs. So he rendered fealty in the new way, by running with the master's horse. The longest day never played White Fang out. His was the gait of the wolf, smooth, tireless and effortless, and at the end of fifty miles he would come in jauntily ahead of the horse.

It was in connection with the riding, that White Fang achieved one other mode of expression—remarkable in that he did it but twice in all his life. The first time occurred when the master was trying to teach a spirited thoroughbred the method of opening and closing gates without the rider's dismounting. Time and again and many times he ranged the horse up to the gate in the effort to close it and each time the horse became frightened and backed and plunged away. It grew more nervous and excited every moment. When it reared, the master put the spurs to it and made it drop its fore-legs back to earth, whereupon it would begin kicking with its hind-legs. White Fang watched the performance with increasing anxiety until he could contain himself no longer, when he sprang in front of the horse and barked savagely and warningly.

Though he often tried to bark thereafter, and the master encouraged him, he succeeded only once, and then it was not in the master's presence. A scamper across the pasture, a jackrabbit rising suddenly under the horse's feet, a violent sheer, a stumble, a fall to earth, and a broken leg for the master, was the cause of it. White Fang sprang in a rage at the throat of the offending horse, but was checked by the master's voice.

"Home! Go home!" the master commanded when he had ascertained his injury.

White Fang was disinclined to desert him. The master thought of writing a note, but searched his pockets vainly for pencil and paper. Again he commanded White Fang to go home.

The latter regarded him wistfully, started away, then returned and whined softly. The master talked to him gently but seriously, and he cocked his ears, and listened with painful intentness.

"That's all right, old fellow, you just run along home," ran the talk. "Go on home and tell them what's happened to me. Home with you, you wolf. Get along home!"

White Fang knew the meaning of "home," and though he did not understand the remainder of the master's language, he knew it was his will that he should go home. He turned and trotted reluctantly away. Then he stopped, undecided, and looked back over his shoulder.

"Go home!" came the sharp command, and this time he obeyed.

The family was on the porch, taking the cool of the afternoon, when White Fang arrived. He came in among them, panting, covered with dust.

"Weedon's back," Weedon's mother announced.

The children welcomed White Fang with glad cries and ran to meet him. He avoided them and passed down the porch, but they cornered him against a rocking-chair and the railing. He growled and tried to push by them. Their mother looked apprehensively in their direction.

"I confess, he makes me nervous around the children," she said. "I have a dread that he will turn upon them unexpectedly some day."

Growling savagely, White Fang sprang out of the corner, overturning the boy and the girl. The mother called them to her and comforted them, telling them not to bother White Fang.

"A wolf is a wolf!" commented Judge Scott. "There is no trusting one."

"But he is not all wolf," interposed Beth, standing for her brother in his absence.

"You have only Weedon's opinion for that," rejoined the judge. "He merely surmises that there is some strain of dog in White Fang; but as he will tell you himself, he knows nothing about it. As for his appearance—"

He did not finish his sentence. White Fang stood before him, growling fiercely.

"Go away! Lie down, sir!" Judge Scott commanded.

White Fang turned to the love-master's wife. She screamed with fright as he seized her dress in his teeth and dragged on it till the frail fabric tore away. By this time he had become the centre of interest.

He had ceased from his growling and stood, head up, looking into their faces. His throat worked spasmodically, but made no sound, while he struggled with all his body, convulsed with the effort to rid himself of the incommunicable something that strained for utterance.

"I hope he is not going mad," said Weedon's mother. "I told Weedon that I was afraid the warm climate would not agree with an Arctic animal."

"He's trying to speak, I do believe," Beth announced.

At this moment speech came to White Fang, rushing up in a great burst of barking.

"Something has happened to Weedon," his wife said decisively.

They were all on their feet now, and White Fang ran down the steps, looking back for them to follow. For the second and last time in his life he had barked and made himself understood.

After this event he found a warmer place in the hearts of the Sierra Vista people, and even the groom whose arm he had slashed admitted that he was a wise dog even if he was a wolf. Judge Scott still held to the same opinion, and proved it to everybody's dissatisfaction by measurements and descriptions taken from the encyclopaedia and various works on natural history.

The days came and went, streaming their unbroken sunshine over the Santa Clara Valley. But as they grew shorter and White Fang's second winter in the Southland came on, he made a strange discovery. Collie's teeth were no longer sharp. There was a playfulness about her nips and a gentleness that prevented them from really hurting him. He forgot that she had made life a burden to him, and when she disported herself around him he responded solemnly, striving to be playful and becoming no more than ridiculous.

One day she led him off on a long chase through the back-pasture land into the woods. It was the afternoon that the master was to ride, and White Fang knew it. The horse stood saddled and waiting at the door. White Fang hesitated. But there was that in him deeper than all the law he had learned, than the customs that had moulded him, than his love for the master, than the very will to live of himself; and when, in the moment of his indecision, Collie nipped him and scampered off, he turned and followed after. The master rode alone that day; and in the woods, side by side, White Fang ran with Collie, as his mother, Kiche, and old One Eye had run long years before in the silent Northland forest.

CHAPTER V—THE SLEEPING WOLF

It was about this time that the newspapers were full of the daring escape of a convict from San Quentin prison. He was a ferocious man. He had been ill-made in the making. He had not been born right, and he had not been helped any by the moulding he had received at the hands of society. The hands of society are harsh, and this man was a striking sample of its handiwork. He was a beast—a human beast, it is true, but nevertheless so terrible a beast that he can best be characterised as carnivorous.

In San Quentin prison he had proved incorrigible. Punishment failed to break his spirit. He could die dumb-mad and fighting to the last, but he could not live and be beaten. The more fiercely he fought, the more harshly society handled him, and the only effect of harshness was to make him fiercer. Straight-jackets, starvation, and beatings and clubbings were the wrong treatment for Jim Hall; but it was the treatment he received. It was the treatment he had received from the time he was a little pulpy boy in a San Francisco slum—soft clay in the hands of society and ready to be formed into something.

It was during Jim Hall's third term in prison that he encountered a guard that was almost as great a beast as he. The guard treated him unfairly, lied about him to the warden, lost his credits, persecuted him. The difference between them was that the guard carried a bunch of keys and a revolver. Jim Hall had only his naked hands and his teeth. But he sprang upon the guard one day and used his teeth on the other's throat just like any jungle animal.

After this, Jim Hall went to live in the incorrigible cell. He lived there three years. The cell was of iron, the floor, the walls, the roof. He never left this cell. He never saw the sky nor the sunshine. Day was a twilight and night was a black silence. He was in an iron tomb, buried alive. He saw no human face, spoke to no human thing. When his food was shoved in to him, he growled like a wild animal. He hated all things. For days and nights he bellowed his rage at the universe. For weeks and months he never made a sound, in the black silence eating his very soul. He was a man and a monstrosity, as fearful a thing of fear as ever gibbered in the visions of a maddened brain.

And then, one night, he escaped. The warders said it was impossible, but nevertheless the cell was empty, and half in half out of it lay the body of a dead guard. Two other dead guards marked his trail through the prison to the outer walls, and he had killed with his hands to avoid noise.

He was armed with the weapons of the slain guards—a live arsenal that fled through the hills pursued by the organised might of society. A heavy price of gold was upon his head. Avaricious farmers hunted him with shot-guns. His blood might pay off a mortgage or send a son to college. Public-spirited citizens took down their rifles and went out after him. A pack of bloodhounds followed the way of his bleeding feet. And the sleuth-hounds of the law, the paid fighting animals of society, with telephone, and telegraph, and special train, clung to his trail night and day.

Sometimes they came upon him, and men faced him like heroes, or stampeded through barbed-wire fences to the delight of the commonwealth reading the account at the breakfast table. It was after such encounters that the dead and wounded were carted back to the towns, and their places filled by men eager for the man-hunt.

And then Jim Hall disappeared. The bloodhounds vainly quested on the lost trail. Inoffensive ranchers in remote valleys were held up by armed men and compelled to identify themselves. While the remains of Jim Hall were discovered on a dozen mountain-sides by greedy claimants for blood-money.

In the meantime the newspapers were read at Sierra Vista, not so much with interest as with anxiety. The women were afraid. Judge Scott pooh-poohed and laughed, but not with reason, for it was in his last days on the bench that Jim Hall had stood before him and received sentence. And in open court-room, before all men, Jim Hall had proclaimed that the day would come when he would wreak vengeance on the Judge that sentenced him.

For once, Jim Hall was right. He was innocent of the crime for which he was sentenced. It was a case, in the parlance of thieves and police, of "rail-roading." Jim Hall was being "rail-roaded" to prison for a crime he had not committed. Because of the two prior convictions against him, Judge Scott imposed upon him a sentence of fifty years.

Judge Scott did not know all things, and he did not know that he was party to a police conspiracy, that the evidence was hatched and perjured, that Jim Hall was guiltless of the crime charged. And Jim Hall, on the other hand, did not know that Judge Scott was merely ignorant. Jim Hall believed that the judge knew all about it and was hand in glove with the police in the perpetration of the monstrous injustice. So it was, when the doom of fifty years of living death was uttered by Judge Scott, that Jim Hall, hating all things in the society that misused him, rose up and raged in the court-room until dragged down by half a dozen of his blue-coated enemies. To him, Judge Scott was the keystone in the arch of injustice, and upon Judge Scott he emptied the vials of his wrath and hurled the threats of his revenge yet to come. Then Jim Hall went to his living death . . . and escaped.

Of all this White Fang knew nothing. But between him and Alice, the master's wife, there existed a secret. Each night, after Sierra Vista had gone to bed, she rose and let in White Fang to sleep in the big hall. Now White Fang was not a house-dog, nor was he permitted to sleep in the house; so each morning, early, she slipped down and let him out before the family was awake.

On one such night, while all the house slept, White Fang awoke and lay very quietly. And very quietly he smelled the air and read the message it bore of a strange god's presence. And to his ears came sounds of the strange god's movements. White Fang burst into no furious outcry. It was not his way. The strange god walked softly, but more softly walked White Fang, for he had no clothes to rub against the flesh of his body. He followed silently. In the Wild he had hunted live meat that was infinitely timid, and he knew the advantage of surprise.

The strange god paused at the foot of the great staircase and listened, and White Fang was as dead, so without movement was he as he watched and waited. Up that staircase the way led to the love-master and to the love-master's dearest possessions. White Fang bristled, but waited. The strange god's foot lifted. He was beginning the ascent.

Then it was that White Fang struck. He gave no warning, with no snarl anticipated his own action. Into the air he lifted his body in the spring that landed him on the strange god's back. White Fang clung with his fore-paws to the man's shoulders, at the same time burying his fangs into the back of the man's neck. He clung on for a moment, long enough to drag the god over backward. Together they crashed to the floor. White Fang leaped clear, and, as the man struggled to rise, was in again with the slashing fangs.

Sierra Vista awoke in alarm. The noise from downstairs was as that of a score of battling fiends. There were revolver shots. A man's voice screamed once in horror and anguish. There was a great snarling and growling, and over all arose a smashing and crashing of furniture and glass.

But almost as quickly as it had arisen, the commotion died away. The struggle had not lasted more than three minutes. The frightened household clustered at the top of the stairway. From below, as from out an abyss of blackness, came up a gurgling sound, as of air bubbling through water. Sometimes this gurgle became sibilant, almost a whistle. But this, too, quickly died down and ceased. Then naught came up out of the blackness save a heavy panting of some creature struggling sorely for air.

Weedon Scott pressed a button, and the staircase and downstairs hall were flooded with light. Then he and Judge Scott, revolvers in hand, cautiously descended. There was no need for this caution. White Fang had done his work. In the midst of the wreckage of overthrown and smashed furniture, partly on his side, his face hidden by an arm, lay a man. Weedon Scott bent over, removed the arm and turned the man's face upward. A gaping throat explained the manner of his death.

"Jim Hall," said Judge Scott, and father and son looked significantly at each other.

Then they turned to White Fang. He, too, was lying on his side. His eyes were closed, but the lids slightly lifted in an effort to look at them as they bent over him, and the tail was perceptibly agitated in a vain effort to wag. Weedon Scott patted him, and his throat rumbled an acknowledging growl. But it was a weak growl at best, and it quickly ceased. His eyelids drooped and went shut, and his whole body seemed to relax and flatten out upon the floor.

"He's all in, poor devil," muttered the master.

"We'll see about that," asserted the Judge, as he started for the telephone.

"Frankly, he has one chance in a thousand," announced the surgeon, after he had worked an hour and a half on White Fang.

Dawn was breaking through the windows and dimming the electric lights. With the exception of the children, the whole family was gathered about the surgeon to hear his verdict.

"One broken hind-leg," he went on. "Three broken ribs, one at least of which has pierced the lungs. He has lost nearly all the blood in his body. There is a large likelihood of internal injuries. He must have been jumped upon. To say nothing of three bullet holes clear through him. One chance in a thousand is really optimistic. He hasn't a chance in ten thousand."

"But he mustn't lose any chance that might be of help to him," Judge Scott exclaimed. "Never mind expense. Put him under the X-ray—anything. Weedon, telegraph at once to San Francisco for Doctor Nichols. No reflection on you, doctor, you understand; but he must have the advantage of every chance."

The surgeon smiled indulgently. "Of course I understand. He deserves all that can be done for him. He must be nursed as you would nurse a human being, a sick child. And don't forget what I told you about temperature. I'll be back at ten o'clock again."

White Fang received the nursing. Judge Scott's suggestion of a trained nurse was indignantly clamoured down by the girls, who themselves undertook the task. And White Fang won out on the one chance in ten thousand denied him by the surgeon.

The latter was not to be censured for his misjudgment. All his life he had tended and operated on the soft humans of civilisation, who lived sheltered lives and had descended out of many sheltered generations. Compared with White Fang, they were frail and flabby, and clutched life without any strength in their grip. White Fang had come straight from the Wild, where the weak perish early and shelter is vouchsafed to none. In neither his father nor his mother was there any weakness, nor in the generations before them. A constitution of iron and the vitality of the Wild were White Fang's inheritance, and he clung to life, the whole of him and every part of him, in spirit and in flesh, with the tenacity that of old belonged to all creatures.

Bound down a prisoner, denied even movement by the plaster casts and bandages, White Fang lingered out the weeks. He slept long hours and dreamed much, and through his mind passed an unending pageant of Northland visions. All the ghosts of the past arose and were with him. Once again he lived in the lair with Kiche, crept trembling to the knees of Grey Beaver to tender his allegiance, ran for his life before Lip-lip and all the howling bedlam of the puppy-pack.

He ran again through the silence, hunting his living food through the months of famine; and again he ran at the head of the team, the gut-whips of Mit-sah and Grey Beaver snapping behind, their voices crying "Ra! Raa!" when they came to a narrow passage and the team closed together like a fan to go through. He lived again all his days with Beauty Smith and the fights he had fought. At such times he whimpered and snarled in his sleep, and they that looked on said that his dreams were bad.

But there was one particular nightmare from which he suffered—the clanking, clanging monsters of electric cars that were to him colossal screaming lynxes. He would lie in a screen of bushes, watching for a squirrel to venture far enough out on the ground from its tree-refuge. Then, when he sprang out upon it, it would transform itself into an electric car, menacing and terrible, towering over him like a mountain, screaming and clanging and spitting fire at him. It was the same when he challenged the hawk down out of the sky. Down out of the blue it would rush, as it dropped upon him changing itself into the ubiquitous electric car. Or again, he would be in the pen of Beauty Smith. Outside the pen, men would be gathering, and he knew that a fight was on. He watched the door for his antagonist to enter. The door would open, and thrust in upon him would come the awful electric car. A thousand times this occurred, and each time the terror it inspired was as vivid and great as ever.

CHAPTER V—THE SLEEPING WOLF

Then came the day when the last bandage and the last plaster cast were taken off. It was a gala day. All Sierra Vista was gathered around. The master rubbed his ears, and he crooned his love-growl. The master's wife called him the "Blessed Wolf," which name was taken up with acclaim and all the women called him the Blessed Wolf.

He tried to rise to his feet, and after several attempts fell down from weakness. He had lain so long that his muscles had lost their cunning, and all the strength had gone out of them. He felt a little shame because of his weakness, as though, forsooth, he were failing the gods in the service he owed them. Because of this he made heroic efforts to arise and at last he stood on his four legs, tottering and swaying back and forth.

"The Blessed Wolf!" chorused the women.

Judge Scott surveyed them triumphantly.

"Out of your own mouths be it," he said. "Just as I contended right along. No mere dog could have done what he did. He's a wolf."

"A Blessed Wolf," amended the Judge's wife.

"Yes, Blessed Wolf," agreed the Judge. "And henceforth that shall be my name for him."

"He'll have to learn to walk again," said the surgeon; "so he might as well start in right now. It won't hurt him. Take him outside."

And outside he went, like a king, with all Sierra Vista about him and tending on him. He was very weak, and when he reached the lawn he lay down and rested for a while.

Then the procession started on, little spurts of strength coming into White Fang's muscles as he used them and the blood began to surge through them. The stables were reached, and there in the doorway, lay Collie, a half-dozen pudgy puppies playing about her in the sun.

White Fang looked on with a wondering eye. Collie snarled warningly at him, and he was careful to keep his distance. The master with his toe helped one sprawling puppy toward him. He bristled suspiciously, but the master warned him that all was well. Collie, clasped in the arms of one of the women, watched him jealously and with a snarl warned him that all was not well.

The puppy sprawled in front of him. He cocked his ears and watched it curiously. Then their noses touched, and he felt the warm little tongue of the puppy on his jowl. White Fang's tongue went out, he knew not why, and he licked the puppy's face.

Hand-clapping and pleased cries from the gods greeted the performance. He was surprised, and looked at them in a puzzled way. Then his weakness asserted itself, and he lay down, his ears cocked, his head on one side, as he watched the puppy. The other puppies came sprawling toward him, to Collie's great disgust; and he gravely permitted them to clamber and tumble over him. At first, amid the applause of the gods, he betrayed a trifle of his old self-consciousness and awkwardness. This passed away as the puppies' antics and mauling continued, and he lay with half-shut patient eyes, drowsing in the sun.

THE SCARLET PLAGUE

I

THE way led along upon what had once been the embankment of a railroad. But no train had run upon it for many years. The forest on either side swelled up the slopes of the embankment and crested across it in a green wave of trees and bushes. The trail was as narrow as a man's body, and was no more than a wild-animal runway. Occasionally, a piece of rusty iron, showing through the forest-mould, advertised that the rail and the ties still remained. In one place, a ten-inch tree, bursting through at a connection, had lifted the end of a rail clearly into view. The tie had evidently followed the rail, held to it by the spike long enough for its bed to be filled with gravel and rotten leaves, so that now the crumbling, rotten timber thrust itself up at a curious slant. Old as the road was, it was manifest that it had been of the mono-rail type.

An old man and a boy travelled along this runway. They moved slowly, for the old man was very old, a touch of palsy made his movements tremulous, and he leaned heavily upon his staff. A rude skull-cap of goat-skin protected his head from the sun. From beneath this fell a scant fringe of stained and dirty-white hair. A visor, ingeniously made from a large leaf, shielded his eyes, and from under this he peered at the way of his feet on the trail. His beard, which should have been snow-white but which showed the same weather-wear and camp-stain as his hair, fell nearly to his waist in a great tangled mass. About his chest and shoulders hung a single, mangy garment of goat-skin. His arms and legs, withered and skinny, betokened extreme age, as well as did their sunburn and scars and scratches betoken long years of exposure to the elements.

The boy, who led the way, checking the eagerness of his muscles to the slow progress of the elder, likewise wore a single garment—a ragged-edged piece of bear-skin, with a hole in the middle through which he had thrust his head. He could not have been more than twelve years old. Tucked coquettishly over one ear was the freshly severed tail of a pig. In one hand he carried a medium-sized bow and an arrow.

On his back was a quiverful of arrows. From a sheath hanging about his neck on a thong, projected the battered handle of a hunting knife. He was as brown as a berry, and walked softly, with almost a catlike tread. In marked contrast with his sunburned skin were his eyes—blue, deep blue, but keen and sharp as a pair of gimlets. They seemed to bore into aft about him in a way that was habitual. As he went along he smelled things, as well, his distended, quivering nostrils carrying to his brain an endless series of messages from the outside world. Also, his hearing was acute, and had been so trained that it operated automatically. Without conscious effort, he heard all the slight sounds in the apparent quiet—heard, and differentiated, and classified these sounds—whether they were of the wind rustling the leaves, of the humming of bees and gnats, of the distant rumble of the sea that drifted to him only in lulls, or of the gopher, just under his foot, shoving a pouchful of earth into the entrance of his hole.

Suddenly he became alertly tense. Sound, sight, and odor had given him a simultaneous warning. His hand went back to the old man, touching him, and the pair stood still. Ahead, at one side of the top of the embankment, arose a crackling sound, and the boy's gaze was fixed on the tops of the agitated bushes. Then a large bear, a grizzly, crashed into view, and likewise stopped abruptly, at sight of the humans. He did not like them, and growled querulously. Slowly the boy fitted the arrow to the bow, and slowly he pulled the bowstring taut. But he never removed his eyes from the bear.

The old man peered from under his green leaf at the danger, and stood as quietly as the boy. For a few seconds this mutual scrutinizing went on; then, the bear betraying a growing irritability, the boy, with a movement of his head, indicated that the old man must step aside from the trail and go down the embankment. The boy followed, going backward, still holding the bow taut and ready. They waited till a crashing among the bushes from the opposite side of the embankment told them the bear had gone on. The boy grinned as he led back to the trail.

"A big un, Granser," he chuckled.

The old man shook his head.

"They get thicker every day," he complained in a thin, undependable falsetto. "Who'd have thought I'd live to see the time when a man would be afraid of his life on the way to the Cliff House. When I was a boy, Edwin, men and women and little babies used to come out here from San Francisco by tens of thousands on a nice day. And there weren't any bears then. No, sir. They used to pay money to look at them in cages, they were that rare."

"What is money, Granser?"

Before the old man could answer, the boy recollected and triumphantly shoved his hand into a pouch under his bear-skin and pulled forth a battered and tarnished silver dollar. The old man's eyes glistened, as he held the coin close to them.

"I can't see," he muttered. "You look and see if you can make out the date, Edwin."

The boy laughed.

"You're a great Granser," he cried delightedly, "always making believe them little marks mean something."

The old man manifested an accustomed chagrin as he brought the coin back again close to his own eyes.

"2012," he shrilled, and then fell to cackling grotesquely. "That was the year Morgan the Fifth was appointed President of the United States by the Board of Magnates. It must have been one of the last coins minted, for the Scarlet Death came in 2013. Lord! Lord!—think of it! Sixty years ago, and I am the only person alive to-day that lived in those times. Where did you find it, Edwin?"

The boy, who had been regarding him with the tolerant curiousness one accords to the prattlings of the feeble-minded, answered promptly.

"I got it off of Hoo-Hoo. He found it when we was herdin' goats down near San José last spring. Hoo-Hoo said it was *money*. Ain't you hungry, Granser?"

I

The ancient caught his staff in a tighter grip and urged along the trail, his old eyes shining greedily.

"I hope Har-Lip 's found a crab... or two," he mumbled. "They're good eating, crabs, mighty good eating when you've no more teeth and you've got grandsons that love their old grandsire and make a point of catching crabs for him. When I was a boy—"

But Edwin, suddenly stopped by what he saw, was drawing the bowstring on a fitted arrow. He had paused on the brink of a crevasse in the embankment. An ancient culvert had here washed out, and the stream, no longer confined, had cut a passage through the fill. On the opposite side, the end of a rail projected and overhung. It showed rustily through the creeping vines which overran it. Beyond, crouching by a bush, a rabbit looked across at him in trembling hesitancy. Fully fifty feet was the distance, but the arrow flashed true; and the transfixed rabbit, crying out in sudden fright and hurt, struggled painfully away into the brush. The boy himself was a flash of brown skin and flying fur as he bounded down the steep wall of the gap and up the other side. His lean muscles were springs of steel that released into graceful and efficient action. A hundred feet beyond, in a tangle of bushes, he overtook the wounded creature, knocked its head on a convenient tree-trunk, and turned it over to Granser to carry.

"Rabbit is good, very good," the ancient quavered, "but when it comes to a toothsome delicacy I prefer crab. When I was a boy—"

"Why do you say so much that ain't got no sense?" Edwin impatiently interrupted the other's threatened garrulousness.

The boy did not exactly utter these words, but something that remotely resembled them and that was more guttural and explosive and economical of qualifying phrases. His speech showed distant kinship with that of the old man, and the latter's speech was approximately an English that had gone through a bath of corrupt usage.

"What I want to know," Edwin continued, "is why you call crab 'toothsome delicacy'? Crab is crab, ain't it? No one I never heard calls it such funny things."

The old man sighed but did not answer, and they moved on in silence. The surf grew suddenly louder, as they emerged from the forest upon a stretch of sand dunes bordering the sea. A few goats were browsing among the sandy hillocks, and a skin-clad boy, aided by a wolfish-looking dog that was only faintly reminiscent of a collie, was watching them. Mingled with the roar of the surf was a continuous, deep-throated barking or bellowing, which came from a cluster of jagged rocks a hundred yards out from shore. Here huge sea-lions hauled themselves up to lie in the sun or battle with one another. In the immediate foreground arose the smoke of a fire, tended by a third savage-looking boy. Crouched near him were several wolfish dogs similar to the one that guarded the goats.

The old man accelerated his pace, sniffing eagerly as he neared the fire.

"Mussels!" he muttered ecstatically. "Mussels! And ain't that a crab, Hoo-Hoo? Ain't that a crab? My, my, you boys are good to your old grandsire."

Hoo-Hoo, who was apparently of the same age as Edwin, grinned.

"All you want, Granser. I got four."

The old man's palsied eagerness was pitiful. Sitting down in the sand as quickly as his stiff limbs would let him, he poked a large rock-mussel from out of the coals. The heat had forced its shells apart, and the meat, salmon-colored, was thoroughly cooked.

Between thumb and forefinger, in trembling haste, he caught the morsel and carried it to his mouth. But it was too hot, and the next moment was violently ejected. The old man spluttered with the pain, and tears ran out of his eyes and down his cheeks.

The boys were true savages, possessing only the cruel humor of the savage. To them the incident was excruciatingly funny, and they burst into loud laughter. Hoo-Hoo danced up and down, while Edwin rolled gleefully on the ground. The boy with the goats came running to join in the fun.

"Set 'em to cool, Edwin, set 'em to cool," the old man besought, in the midst of his grief, making no attempt to wipe away the tears that still flowed from his eyes. "And cool a crab, Edwin, too. You know your grandsire likes crabs."

From the coals arose a great sizzling, which proceeded from the many mussels bursting open their shells and exuding their moisture. They were large shellfish, running from three to six inches in length. The boys raked them out with sticks and placed them on a large piece of driftwood to cool.

"When I was a boy, we did not laugh at our elders; we respected them."

The boys took no notice, and Granser continued to babble an incoherent flow of complaint and censure. But this time he was more careful, and did not burn his mouth. All began to eat, using nothing but their hands and making loud mouth-noises and lip-smackings. The third boy, who was called Hare-Lip, slyly deposited a pinch of sand on a mussel the ancient was carrying to his mouth; and when the grit of it bit into the old fellow's mucous membrane and gums, the laughter was again uproarious. He was unaware that a joke had been played on him, and spluttered and spat until Edwin, relenting, gave him a gourd of fresh water with which to wash out his mouth.

"Where's them crabs, Hoo-Hoo?" Edwin demanded. "Granser's set upon having a snack."

Again Granser's eyes burned with greediness as a large crab was handed to him. It was a shell with legs and all complete, but the meat had long since departed. With shaky fingers and babblings of anticipation, the old man broke off a leg and found it filled with emptiness.

"The crabs, Hoo-Hoo?" he wailed. "The crabs?"

"I was fooling Granser. They ain't no crabs! I never found one."

The boys were overwhelmed with delight at sight of the tears of senile disappointment that dribbled down the old man's cheeks. Then, unnoticed, Hoo-Hoo replaced the empty shell with a fresh-cooked crab. Already dismembered, from the cracked legs the white meat sent forth a small cloud of savory steam. This attracted the old man's nostrils, and he looked down in amazement.

The change of his mood to one of joy was immediate. He snuffled and muttered and mumbled, making almost a croon of delight, as he began to eat. Of this the boys took little notice, for it was an accustomed spectacle. Nor did they notice his occasional exclamations and utterances of phrases which meant nothing to them, as, for instance, when he smacked his lips and champed his gums while muttering: "Mayonnaise! Just think—mayonnaise! And it's sixty years since the last was ever made! Two generations and never a smell of it! Why, in those days it was served in every restaurant with crab."

When he could eat no more, the old man sighed, wiped his hands on his naked legs, and gazed out over the sea. With the content of a full stomach, he waxed reminiscent.

I

"To think of it! I've seen this beach alive with men, women, and children on a pleasant Sunday. And there weren't any bears to eat them up, either. And right up there on the cliff was a big restaurant where you could get anything you wanted to eat. Four million people lived in San Francisco then. And now, in the whole city and county there aren't forty all told. And out there on the sea were ships and ships always to be seen, going in for the Golden Gate or coming out. And airships in the air—dirigibles and flying machines. They could travel two hundred miles an hour. The mail contracts with the New York and San Francisco Limited demanded that for the minimum. There was a chap, a Frenchman, I forget his name, who succeeded in making three hundred; but the thing was risky, too risky for conservative persons. But he was on the right clew, and he would have managed it if it hadn't been for the Great Plague. When I was a boy, there were men alive who remembered the coming of the first aeroplanes, and now I have lived to see the last of them, and that sixty years ago."

The old man babbled on, unheeded by the boys, who were long accustomed to his garrulousness, and whose vocabularies, besides, lacked the greater portion of the words he used. It was noticeable that in these rambling soliloquies his English seemed to recrudesce into better construction and phraseology. But when he talked directly with the boys it lapsed, largely, into their own uncouth and simpler forms.

"But there weren't many crabs in those days," the old man wandered on. "They were fished out, and they were great delicacies. The open season was only a month long, too. And now crabs are accessible the whole year around. Think of it—catching all the crabs you want, any time you want, in the surf of the Cliff House beach!"

A sudden commotion among the goats brought the boys to their feet. The dogs about the fire rushed to join their snarling fellow who guarded the goats, while the goats themselves stampeded in the direction of their human protectors. A half dozen forms, lean and gray, glided about on the sand hillocks and faced the bristling dogs. Edwin arched an arrow that fell short. But Hare-Lip, with a sling such as David carried into battle against Goliath, hurled a stone through the air that whistled from the speed of its flight. It fell squarely among the wolves and caused them to slink away toward the dark depths of the eucalyptus forest.

The boys laughed and lay down again in the sand, while Granser sighed ponderously. He had eaten too much, and, with hands clasped on his paunch, the fingers interlaced, he resumed his maunderings.

"'The fleeting systems lapse like foam,'" he mumbled what was evidently a quotation. "That's it—foam, and fleeting. All man's toil upon the planet was just so much foam. He domesticated the serviceable animals, destroyed the hostile ones, and cleared the land of its wild vegetation. And then he passed, and the flood of primordial life rolled back again, sweeping his handiwork away—the weeds and the forest inundated his fields, the beasts of prey swept over his flocks, and now there are wolves on the Cliff House beach." He was appalled by the thought. "Where four million people disported themselves, the wild wolves roam to-day, and the savage progeny of our loins, with prehistoric weapons, defend themselves against the fanged despoilers. Think of it! And all because of the Scarlet Death—"

The adjective had caught Hare-Lip's ear.

"He's always saying that," he said to Edwin. "What is *scarlet?*"

"'The scarlet of the maples can shake me like the cry of bugles going by,'" the old man quoted.

"It's red," Edwin answered the question. "And you don't know it because you come from the Chauffeur Tribe. They never did know nothing, none of them. Scarlet is red—I know that."

"Red is red, ain't it?" Hare-Lip grumbled. "Then what's the good of gettin' cocky and calling it scarlet?"

"Granser, what for do you always say so much what nobody knows?" he asked. "Scarlet ain't anything, but red is red. Why don't you say red, then?"

"Red is not the right word," was the reply. "The plague was scarlet. The whole face and body turned scarlet in an hour's time. Don't I know? Didn't I see enough of it? And I am telling you it was scarlet because—well, because it *was* scarlet. There is no other word for it."

"Red is good enough for me," Hare-Lip muttered obstinately. "My dad calls red red, and he ought to know. He says everybody died of the Red Death."

"Your dad is a common fellow, descended from a common fellow," Granser retorted heatedly. "Don't I know the beginnings of the Chauffeurs? Your grandsire was a chauffeur, a servant, and without education. He worked for other persons. But your grandmother was of good stock, only the children did not take after her. Don't I remember when I first met them, catching fish at Lake Temescal?"

"What is *education?*" Edwin asked.

"Calling red scarlet," Hare-Lip sneered, then returned to the attack on Granser. "My dad told me, an' he got it from his dad afore he croaked, that your wife was a Santa Rosan, an' that she was sure no account. He said she was a *hash-slinger* before the Red Death, though I don't know what a *hash-slinger* is. You can tell me, Edwin."

But Edwin shook his head in token of ignorance.

"It is true, she was a waitress," Granser acknowledged. "But she was a good woman, and your mother was her daughter. Women were very scarce in the days after the Plague. She was the only wife I could find, even if she was a *hash-slinger*, as your father calls it. But it is not nice to talk about our progenitors that way."

"Dad says that the wife of the first Chauffeur was a *lady*—"

"What's a *lady?*" Hoo-Hoo demanded.

"A *lady* 's a Chauffeur squaw," was the quick reply of Hare-Lip.

"The first Chauffeur was Bill, a common fellow, as I said before," the old man expounded; "but his wife was a lady, a great lady. Before the Scarlet Death she was the wife of Van Worden. He was President of the Board of Industrial Magnates, and was one of the dozen men who ruled America. He was worth one billion, eight hundred millions of dollars—coins like you have there in your pouch, Edwin. And then came the Scarlet Death, and his wife became the wife of Bill, the first Chauffeur. He used to beat her, too. I have seen it myself."

Hoo-Hoo, lying on his stomach and idly digging his toes in the sand, cried out and investigated, first, his toe-nail, and next, the small hole he had dug. The other two boys joined him, excavating the sand rapidly with their hands till there lay three skeletons exposed. Two were of adults, the third being that of a part-grown child. The old man hudged along on the ground and peered at the find.

"Plague victims," he announced. "That's the way they died everywhere in the last days. This must have been a family, running away from the contagion and perishing here on the Cliff House beach. They—what are you doing, Edwin?"

This question was asked in sudden dismay, as Edwin, using the back of his hunting knife, began to knock out the teeth from the jaws of one of the skulls.

"Going to string 'em," was the response.

The three boys were now hard at it; and quite a knocking and hammering arose, in which Granser babbled on unnoticed.

"You are true savages. Already has begun the custom of wearing human teeth. In another generation you will be perforating your noses and ears and wearing ornaments of bone and shell. I know. The human race is doomed to sink back farther and farther into the primitive night ere again it begins its bloody climb upward to civilization. When we increase and feel the lack of room, we will proceed to kill one another. And then I suppose you will wear human scalp-locks at your waist, as well—as you, Edwin, who are the gentlest of my grandsons, have already begun with that vile pigtail. Throw it away, Edwin, boy; throw it away."

"What a gabble the old geezer makes," Hare-Lip remarked, when, the teeth all extracted, they began an attempt at equal division.

They were very quick and abrupt in their actions, and their speech, in moments of hot discussion over the allotment of the choicer teeth, was truly a gabble. They spoke in monosyllables and short jerky sentences that was more a gibberish than a language. And yet, through it ran hints of grammatical construction, and appeared vestiges of the conjugation of some superior culture. Even the speech of Granser was so corrupt that were it put down literally it would be almost so much nonsense to the reader. This, however, was when he talked with the boys.

When he got into the full swing of babbling to himself, it slowly purged itself into pure English. The sentences grew longer and were enunciated with a rhythm and ease that was reminiscent of the lecture platform.

"Tell us about the Red Death, Granser," Hare-Lip demanded, when the teeth affair had been satisfactorily concluded.

"The Scarlet Death," Edwin corrected.

"An' don't work all that funny lingo on us," Hare-Lip went on. "Talk sensible, Granser, like a Santa Rosan ought to talk. Other Santa Rosans don't talk like you."

II

THE old man showed pleasure in being thus called upon. He cleared his throat and began.

"Twenty or thirty years ago my story was in great demand. But in these days nobody seems interested—"

"There you go!" Hare-Lip cried hotly. "Cut out the funny stuff and talk sensible. What's *interested?* You talk like a baby that don't know how."

"Let him alone," Edwin urged, "or he'll get mad and won't talk at all. Skip the funny places. We'll catch on to some of what he tells us."

"Let her go, Granser," Hoo-Hoo encouraged; for the old man was already maundering about the disrespect for elders and the reversion to cruelty of all humans that fell from high culture to primitive conditions.

The tale began.

"There were very many people in the world in those days. San Francisco alone held four millions—"

"What is millions?" Edwin interrupted.

Granser looked at him kindly.

"I know you cannot count beyond ten, so I will tell you. Hold up your two hands. On both of them you have altogether ten fingers and thumbs. Very well. I now take this grain of sand—you hold it, Hoo-Hoo." He dropped the grain of sand into the lad's palm and went on. "Now that grain of sand stands for the ten fingers of Edwin. I add another grain. That's ten more fingers. And I add another, and another, and another, until I have added as many grains as Edwin has fingers and thumbs. That makes what I call one hundred. Remember that word—one hundred. Now I put this pebble in Hare-Lip's hand. It stands for ten grains of sand, or ten tens of fingers, or one hundred fingers. I put in ten pebbles. They stand for a thousand fingers. I take a mussel-shell, and it stands for ten pebbles, or one hundred grains of sand, or one thousand fingers...." And so on, laboriously, and with much reiteration, he strove to build up in their minds a crude conception of numbers. As the quantities increased, he had the boys holding different magnitudes in each of their hands. For still higher sums, he laid the symbols on the log of driftwood; and for symbols he was hard put, being compelled to use the teeth from the skulls for millions, and the crab-shells for billions. It was here that he stopped, for the boys were showing signs of becoming tired.

"There were four million people in San Francisco—four teeth."

II

The boys' eyes ranged along from the teeth and from hand to hand, down through the pebbles and sand-grains to Edwin's fingers. And back again they ranged along the ascending series in the effort to grasp such inconceivable numbers.

"That was a lot of folks, Granser," Edwin at last hazarded.

"Like sand on the beach here, like sand on the beach, each grain of sand a man, or woman, or child. Yes, my boy, all those people lived right here in San Francisco. And at one time or another all those people came out on this very beach—more people than there are grains of sand. More—more—more. And San Francisco was a noble city. And across the bay—where we camped last year, even more people lived, clear from Point Richmond, on the level ground and on the hills, all the way around to San Leandro—one great city of seven million people.—Seven teeth... there, that's it, seven millions."

Again the boys' eyes ranged up and down from Edwin's fingers to the teeth on the log.

"The world was full of people. The census of 2010 gave eight billions for the whole world—eight crab-shells, yes, eight billions. It was not like to-day. Mankind knew a great deal more about getting food. And the more food there was, the more people there were. In the year 1800, there were one hundred and seventy millions in Europe alone. One hundred years later—a grain of sand, Hoo-Hoo—one hundred years later, at 1900, there were five hundred millions in Europe—five grains of sand, Hoo-Hoo, and this one tooth. This shows how easy was the getting of food, and how men increased. And in the year 2000 there were fifteen hundred millions in Europe. And it was the same all over the rest of the world. Eight crab-shells there, yes, eight billion people were alive on the earth when the Scarlet Death began.

"I was a young man when the Plague came—twenty-seven years old; and I lived on the other side of San Francisco Bay, in Berkeley. You remember those great stone houses, Edwin, when we came down the hills from Contra Costa? That was where I lived, in those stone houses. I was a professor of English literature."

Much of this was over the heads of the boys, but they strove to comprehend dimly this tale of the past.

"What was them stone houses for?" Hare-Lip queried.

"You remember when your dad taught you to swim?" The boy nodded. "Well, in the University of California—that is the name we had for the houses—we taught young men and women how to think, just as I have taught you now, by sand and pebbles and shells, to know how many people lived in those days. There was very much to teach. The young men and women we taught were called students. We had large rooms in which we taught. I talked to them, forty or fifty at a time, just as I am talking to you now. I told them about the books other men had written before their time, and even, sometimes, in their time—"

"Was that all you did?—just talk, talk, talk?" Hoo-Hoo demanded. "Who hunted your meat for you? and milked the goats? and caught the fish?"

"A sensible question, Hoo-Hoo, a sensible question. As I have told you, in those days food-getting was easy. We were very wise. A few men got the food for many men. The other men did other things. As you say, I talked. I talked all the time, and for this food was given me—much food, fine food, beautiful food, food that I have not tasted in sixty years and shall never taste again. I sometimes think the most wonderful achievement of our tremendous civilization was food—its inconceivable abundance, its infinite variety, its marvellous delicacy. O my grandsons, life was life in those days, when we had such wonderful things to eat."

This was beyond the boys, and they let it slip by, words and thoughts, as a mere senile wandering in the narrative.

"Our food-getters were called *freemen.* This was a joke. We of the ruling classes owned all the land, all the machines, everything. These food-getters were our slaves. We took almost all the food they got, and left them a little so that they might eat, and work, and get us more food—"

"I'd have gone into the forest and got food for myself," Hare-Lip announced; "and if any man tried to take it away from me, I'd have killed him."

The old man laughed.

"Did I not tell you that we of the ruling class owned all the land, all the forest, everything? Any food-getter who would not get food for us, him we punished or compelled to starve to death. And very few did that. They preferred to get food for us, and make clothes for us, and prepare and administer to us a thousand—a mussel-shell, Hoo-Hoo—a thousand satisfactions and delights. And I was Professor Smith in those days—Professor James Howard Smith. And my lecture courses were very popular—that is, very many of the young men and women liked to hear me talk about the books other men had written.

"And I was very happy, and I had beautiful things to eat. And my hands were soft, because I did no work with them, and my body was clean all over and dressed in the softest garments—

"He surveyed his mangy goat-skin with disgust.

"We did not wear such things in those days. Even the slaves had better garments. And we were most clean. We washed our faces and hands often every day. You boys never wash unless you fall into the water or go swimming."

"Neither do you Granzer," Hoo-Hoo retorted.

"I know, I know, I am a filthy old man, but times have changed. Nobody washes these days, there are no conveniences. It is sixty years since I have seen a piece of soap.

"You do not know what soap is, and I shall not tell you, for I am telling the story of the Scarlet Death. You know what sickness is. We called it a disease. Very many of the diseases came from what we called germs. Remember that word—germs. A germ is a very small thing. It is like a woodtick, such as you find on the dogs in the spring of the year when they run in the forest. Only the germ is very small. It is so small that you cannot see it—"

Hoo-Hoo began to laugh.

"You're a queer un, Granser, talking about things you can't see. If you can't see 'em, how do you know they are? That's what I want to know. How do you know anything you can't see?"

"A good question, a very good question, Hoo-Hoo. But we did see—some of them. We had what we called microscopes and ultramicroscopes, and we put them to our eyes and looked through them, so that we saw things larger than they really were, and many things we could not see without the microscopes at all. Our best ultramicroscopes could make a germ look forty thousand times larger. A mussel-shell is a thousand fingers like Edwin's. Take forty mussel-shells, and by as many times larger was the germ when we looked at it through a microscope. And after that, we had other ways, by using what we called moving pictures, of making the forty-thousand-times germ many, many thousand times larger still. And thus we saw all these things which our eyes of themselves could not see. Take a grain of sand. Break it into ten pieces. Take one piece and break it into ten. Break one of those pieces into ten, and one of those into ten, and one of those into ten, and one of those into ten, and do it all day, and maybe, by sunset, you will have a piece as small as one of the germs." The boys were openly incredulous. Hare-Lip sniffed and sneered and Hoo-Hoo snickered, until Edwin nudged them to be silent.

"The woodtick sucks the blood of the dog, but the germ, being so very small, goes right into the blood of the body, and there it has many children. In those days there would be as many as a billion—a crab-shell, please—as many as that crab-shell in one man's body. We called germs micro-organisms. When a few million, or a billion, of them were in a man, in all the blood of a man, he was sick. These germs were a disease. There were many different kinds of them—more different kinds than there are grains of sand on this beach. We knew only a few of the kinds. The micro-organic world was an invisible world, a world we could not see, and we knew very little about it. Yet we did know something. There was the *bacillus anthracis*; there was the *micrococcus*; there was the *Bacterium termo*, and the *Bacterium lactis*—that's what turns the goat milk sour even to this day, Hare-Lip; and there were *Schizomycetes* without end. And there were many others...."

Here the old man launched into a disquisition on germs and their natures, using words and phrases of such extraordinary length and meaninglessness, that the boys grinned at one another and looked out over the deserted ocean till they forgot the old man was babbling on.

"But the Scarlet Death, Granser," Edwin at last suggested.

Granser recollected himself, and with a start tore himself away from the rostrum of the lecture-hall, where, to another world audience, he had been expounding the latest theory, sixty years gone, of germs and germ-diseases.

"Yes, yes, Edwin; I had forgotten. Sometimes the memory of the past is very strong upon me, and I forget that I am a dirty old man, clad in goat-skin, wandering with my savage grandsons who are goatherds in the primeval wilderness. 'The fleeting systems lapse like foam,' and so lapsed our glorious, colossal civilization. I am Granser, a tired old man. I belong to the tribe of Santa Rosans. I married into that tribe. My sons and daughters married into the Chauffeurs, the Sacramentos, and the Palo-Altos. You, Hare-Lip, are of the Chauffeurs. You, Edwin, are of the Sacramentos. And you, Hoo-Hoo, are of the Palo-Altos. Your tribe takes its name from a town that was near the seat of another great institution of learning. It was called Stanford University. Yes, I remember now. It is perfectly clear. I was telling you of the Scarlet Death. Where was I in my story?"

"You was telling about germs, the things you can't see but which make men sick," Edwin prompted.

"Yes, that's where I was. A man did not notice at first when only a few of these germs got into his body. But each germ broke in half and became two germs, and they kept doing this very rapidly so that in a short time there were many millions of them in the body. Then the man was sick. He had a disease, and the disease was named after the kind of a germ that was in him. It might be measles, it might be influenza, it might be yellow fever; it might be any of thousands and thousands of kinds of diseases.

"Now this is the strange thing about these germs. There were always new ones coming to live in men's bodies. Long and long and long ago, when there were only a few men in the world, there were few diseases. But as men increased and lived closely together in great cities and civilizations, new diseases arose, new kinds of germs entered their bodies. Thus were countless millions and billions of human beings killed. And the more thickly men packed together, the more terrible were the new diseases that came to be. Long before my time, in the middle ages, there was the Black Plague that swept across Europe. It swept across Europe many times. There was tuberculosis, that entered into men wherever they were thickly packed. A hundred years before my time there was the bubonic plague. And in Africa was the sleeping sickness. The bacteriologists fought all these sicknesses and destroyed them, just as you boys fight the wolves away from your goats, or squash the mosquitoes that light on you. The bacteriologists—"

"But, Granser, what is a what-you-call-it?" Edwin interrupted.

"You, Edwin, are a goatherd. Your task is to watch the goats. You know a great deal about goats. A bacteriologist watches germs. That's his task, and he knows a great deal about them. So, as I was saying, the bacteriologists fought with the germs and destroyed them—sometimes. There was leprosy, a horrible disease. A hundred years before I was born, the bacteriologists discovered the germ of leprosy. They knew all about it. They made pictures of it. I have seen those pictures. But they never found a way to kill it. But in 1984, there was the Pantoblast Plague, a disease that broke out in a country called Brazil and that killed millions of people. But the bacteriologists found it out, and found the way to kill it, so that the Pantoblast Plague went no farther. They made what they called a serum, which they put into a man's body and which killed the pantoblast germs without killing the man. And in 1910, there was Pellagra, and also the hookworm. These were easily killed by the bacteriologists. But in 1947 there arose a new disease that had never been seen before. It got into the bodies of babies of only ten months old or less, and it made them unable to move their hands and feet, or to eat, or anything; and the bacteriologists were eleven years in discovering how to kill that particular germ and save the babies.

"In spite of all these diseases, and of all the new ones that continued to arise, there were more and more men in the world. This was because it was easy to get food. The easier it was to get food, the more men there were; the more men there were, the more thickly were they packed together on the earth; and the more thickly they were packed, the more new kinds of germs became diseases. There were warnings. Soldervetzsky, as early as 1929, told the bacteriologists that they had no guaranty against some new disease, a thousand times more deadly than any they knew, arising and killing by the hundreds of millions and even by the billion. You see, the micro-organic world remained a mystery to the end. They knew there was such a world, and that from time to time armies of new germs emerged from it to kill men.

"And that was all they knew about it. For all they knew, in that invisible micro-organic world there might be as many different kinds of germs as there are grains of sand on this beach. And also, in that same invisible world it might well be that new kinds of germs came to be. It might be there that life originated—the 'abysmal fecundity,' Soldervetzsky called it, applying the words of other men who had written before him...."

It was at this point that Hare-Lip rose to his feet, an expression of huge contempt on his face.

"Granser," he announced, "you make me sick with your gabble. Why don't you tell about the Red Death? If you ain't going to, say so, an' we'll start back for camp."

The old man looked at him and silently began to cry. The weak tears of age rolled down his cheeks and all the feebleness of his eighty-seven years showed in his grief-stricken countenance.

"Sit down," Edwin counselled soothingly. "Granser's all right. He's just gettin' to the Scarlet Death, ain't you, Granser? He's just goin' to tell us about it right now. Sit down, Hare-Lip. Go ahead, Granser."

III

THE old man wiped the tears away on his grimy knuckles and took up the tale in a tremulous, piping voice that soon strengthened as he got the swing of the narrative.

"It was in the summer of 2013 that the Plague came. I was twenty-seven years old, and well do I remember it. Wireless despatches—"

Hare-Lip spat loudly his disgust, and Granser hastened to make amends.

"We talked through the air in those days, thousands and thousands of miles. And the word came of a strange disease that had broken out in New York. There were seventeen millions of people living then in that noblest city of America. Nobody thought anything about the news. It was only a small thing. There had been only a few deaths. It seemed, though, that they had died very quickly, and that one of the first signs of the disease was the turning red of the face and all the body. Within twenty-four hours came the report of the first case in Chicago. And on the same day, it was made public that London, the greatest city in the world, next to Chicago, had been secretly fighting the plague for two weeks and censoring the news despatches—that is, not permitting the word to go forth to the rest of the world that London had the plague.

"It looked serious, but we in California, like everywhere else, were not alarmed. We were sure that the bacteriologists would find a way to overcome this new germ, just as they had overcome other germs in the past. But the trouble was the astonishing quickness with which this germ destroyed human beings, and the fact that it inevitably killed any human body it entered. No one ever recovered. There was the old Asiatic cholera, when you might eat dinner with a well man in the evening, and the next morning, if you got up early enough, you would see him being hauled by your window in the death-cart. But this new plague was quicker than that—much quicker.

"From the moment of the first signs of it, a man would be dead in an hour. Some lasted for several hours. Many died within ten or fifteen minutes of the appearance of the first signs.

"The heart began to beat faster and the heat of the body to increase. Then came the scarlet rash, spreading like wildfire over the face and body. Most persons never noticed the increase in heat and heart-beat, and the first they knew was when the scarlet rash came out. Usually, they had convulsions at the time of the appearance of the rash. But these convulsions did not last long and were not very severe. If one lived through them, he became perfectly quiet, and only did he feel a numbness swiftly creeping up his body from the feet. The heels became numb first, then the legs, and hips, and when the numbness reached as high as his heart he died. They did not rave or sleep. Their minds always remained cool and calm up to the moment their heart numbed and stopped. And another strange thing was the rapidity of decomposition. No sooner was a person dead than the body seemed to fall to pieces, to fly apart, to melt away even as you looked at it. That was one of the reasons the plague spread so rapidly. All the billions of germs in a corpse were so immediately released.

"And it was because of all this that the bacteriologists had so little chance in fighting the germs. They were killed in their laboratories even as they studied the germ of the Scarlet Death. They were heroes. As fast as they perished, others stepped forth and took their places. It was in London that they first isolated it. The news was telegraphed everywhere. Trask was the name of the man who succeeded in this, but within thirty hours he was dead. Then came the struggle in all the laboratories to find something that would kill the plague germs. All drugs failed. You see, the problem was to get a drug, or serum, that would kill the germs in the body and not kill the body. They tried to fight it with other germs, to put into the body of a sick man germs that were the enemies of the plague germs—"

"And you can't see these germ-things, Granser," Hare-Lip objected, "and here you gabble, gabble, gabble about them as if they was anything, when they're nothing at all. Anything you can't see, ain't, that's what. Fighting things that ain't with things that ain't! They must have been all fools in them days. That's why they croaked. I ain't goin' to believe in such rot, I tell you that."

Granser promptly began to weep, while Edwin hotly took up his defence.

"Look here, Hare-Lip, you believe in lots of things you can't see."

Hare-Lip shook his head.

"You believe in dead men walking about. You never seen one dead man walk about."

"I tell you I seen 'em, last winter, when I was wolf-hunting with dad."

"Well, you always spit when you cross running water," Edwin challenged.

"That's to keep off bad luck," was Hare-Lip's defence.

"You believe in bad luck?"

"Sure."

"An' you ain't never seen bad luck," Edwin concluded triumphantly. "You're just as bad as Granser and his germs. You believe in what you don't see. Go on, Granser."

Hare-Lip, crushed by this metaphysical defeat, remained silent, and the old man went on. Often and often, though this narrative must not be clogged by the details, was Granser's tale interrupted while the boys squabbled among themselves. Also, among themselves they kept up a constant, low-voiced exchange of explanation and conjecture, as they strove to follow the old man into his unknown and vanished world.

"The Scarlet Death broke out in San Francisco. The first death came on a Monday morning. By Thursday they were dying like flies in Oakland and San Francisco. They died everywhere—in their beds, at their work, walking along the street. It was on Tuesday that I saw my first death—Miss Collbran, one of my students, sitting right there before my eyes, in my lecture-room. I noticed her face while I was talking. It had suddenly turned scarlet. I ceased speaking and could only look at her, for the first fear of the plague was already on all of us and we knew that it had come. The young women screamed and ran out of the room. So did the young men run out, all but two. Miss Collbran's convulsions were very mild and lasted less than a minute. One of the young men fetched her a glass of water. She drank only a little of it, and cried out:

"'My feet! All sensation has left them.'

"After a minute she said, 'I have no feet. I am unaware that I have any feet. And my knees are cold. I can scarcely feel that I have knees.'

"She lay on the floor, a bundle of notebooks under her head. And we could do nothing. The coldness and the numbness crept up past her hips to her heart, and when it reached her heart she was dead. In fifteen minutes, by the clock—I timed it—she was dead, there, in my own classroom, dead. And she was a very beautiful, strong, healthy young woman. And from the first sign of the plague to her death only fifteen minutes elapsed. That will show you how swift was the Scarlet Death.

"Yet in those few minutes I remained with the dying woman in my classroom, the alarm had spread over the university; and the students, by thousands, all of them, had deserted the lecture-room and laboratories. When I emerged, on my way to make report to the President of the Faculty, I found the university deserted. Across the campus were several stragglers hurrying for their homes. Two of them were running.

"President Hoag, I found in his office, all alone, looking very old and very gray, with a multitude of wrinkles in his face that I had never seen before. At the sight of me, he pulled himself to his feet and tottered away to the inner office, banging the door after him and locking it. You see, he knew I had been exposed, and he was afraid. He shouted to me through the door to go away. I shall never forget my feelings as I walked down the silent corridors and out across that deserted campus. I was not afraid. I had been exposed, and I looked upon myself as already dead. It was not that, but a feeling of awful depression that impressed me. Everything had stopped. It was like the end of the world to me—my world. I had been born within sight and sound of the university. It had been my predestined career. My father had been a professor there before me, and his father before him. For a century and a half had this university, like a splendid machine, been running steadily on. And now, in an instant, it had stopped. It was like seeing the sacred flame die down on some thrice-sacred altar. I was shocked, unutterably shocked.

"When I arrived home, my housekeeper screamed as I entered, and fled away. And when I rang, I found the housemaid had likewise fled. I investigated. In the kitchen I found the cook on the point of departure. But she screamed, too, and in her haste dropped a suitcase of her personal belongings and ran out of the house and across the grounds, still screaming. I can hear her scream to this day. You see, we did not act in this way when ordinary diseases smote us. We were always calm over such things, and sent for the doctors and nurses who knew just what to do. But this was different. It struck so suddenly, and killed so swiftly, and never missed a stroke. When the scarlet rash appeared on a person's face, that person was marked by death. There was never a known case of a recovery.

"I was alone in my big house. As I have told you often before, in those days we could talk with one another over wires or through the air. The telephone bell rang, and I found my brother talking to me. He told me that he was not coming home for fear of catching the plague from me, and that he had taken our two sisters to stop at Professor Bacon's home. He advised me to remain where I was, and wait to find out whether or not I had caught the plague.

"To all of this I agreed, staying in my house and for the first time in my life attempting to cook. And the plague did not come out on me. By means of the telephone I could talk with whomsoever I pleased and get the news. Also, there were the newspapers, and I ordered all of them to be thrown up to my door so that I could know what was happening with the rest of the world.

"New York City and Chicago were in chaos. And what happened with them was happening in all the large cities. A third of the New York police were dead. Their chief was also dead, likewise the mayor. All law and order had ceased. The bodies were lying in the streets un-buried. All railroads and vessels carrying food and such things into the great city had ceased runnings and mobs of the hungry poor were pillaging the stores and warehouses. Murder and robbery and drunkenness were everywhere. Already the people had fled from the city by millions—at first the rich, in their private motor-cars and dirigibles, and then the great mass of the population, on foot, carrying the plague with them, themselves starving and pillaging the farmers and all the towns and villages on the way.

"The man who sent this news, the wireless operator, was alone with his instrument on the top of a lofty building. The people remaining in the city—he estimated them at several hundred thousand—had gone mad from fear and drink, and on all sides of him great fires were raging. He was a hero, that man who staid by his post—an obscure newspaperman, most likely.

"For twenty-four hours, he said, no transatlantic airships had arrived, and no more messages were coming from England. He did state, though, that a message from Berlin—that's in Germany—announced that Hoffmeyer, a bacteriologist of the Metchnikoff School, had discovered the serum for the plague. That was the last word, to this day, that we of America ever received from Europe. If Hoffmeyer discovered the serum, it was too late, or otherwise, long ere this, explorers from Europe would have come looking for us. We can only conclude that what happened in America happened in Europe, and that, at the best, some several score may have survived the Scarlet Death on that whole continent.

"For one day longer the despatches continued to come from New York. Then they, too, ceased. The man who had sent them, perched in his lofty building, had either died of the plague or been consumed in the great conflagrations he had described as raging around him. And what had occurred in New York had been duplicated in all the other cities. It was the same in San Francisco, and Oakland, and Berkeley. By Thursday the people were dying so rapidly that their corpses could not be handled, and dead bodies lay everywhere. Thursday night the panic outrush for the country began. Imagine, my grandsons, people, thicker than the salmon-run you have seen on the Sacramento river, pouring out of the cities by millions, madly over the country, in vain attempt to escape the ubiquitous death. You see, they carried the germs with them. Even the airships of the rich, fleeing for mountain and desert fastnesses, carried the germs.

"Hundreds of these airships escaped to Hawaii, and not only did they bring the plague with them, but they found the plague already there before them. This we learned, by the despatches, until all order in San Francisco vanished, and there were no operators left at their posts to receive or send. It was amazing, astounding, this loss of communication with the world. It was exactly as if the world had ceased, been blotted out. For sixty years that world has no longer existed for me. I know there must be such places as New York, Europe, Asia, and Africa; but not one word has been heard of them—not in sixty years. With the coming of the Scarlet Death the world fell apart, absolutely, irretrievably. Ten thousand years of culture and civilization passed in the twinkling of an eye, 'lapsed like foam.'

"I was telling about the airships of the rich. They carried the plague with them and no matter where they fled, they died. I never encountered but one survivor of any of them—Mungerson. He was afterwards a Santa Rosan, and he married my eldest daughter. He came into the tribe eight years after the plague. He was then nineteen years old, and he was compelled to wait twelve years more before he could marry. You see, there were no unmarried women, and some of the older daughters of the Santa Rosans were already bespoken. So he was forced to wait until my Mary had grown to sixteen years. It was his son, Gimp-Leg, who was killed last year by the mountain lion.

"Mungerson was eleven years old at the time of the plague. His father was one of the Industrial Magnates, a very wealthy, powerful man. It was on his airship, the Condor, that they were fleeing, with all the family, for the wilds of British Columbia, which is far to the north of here. But there was some accident, and they were wrecked near Mount Shasta. You have heard of that mountain. It is far to the north. The plague broke out amongst them, and this boy of eleven was the only survivor. For eight years he was alone, wandering over a deserted land and looking vainly for his own kind. And at last, travelling south, he picked up with us, the Santa Rosans.

"But I am ahead of my story. When the great exodus from the cities around San Francisco Bay began, and while the telephones were still working, I talked with my brother. I told him this flight from the cities was insanity, that there were no symptoms of the plague in me, and that the thing for us to do was to isolate ourselves and our relatives in some safe place. We decided on the Chemistry Building, at the university, and we planned to lay in a supply of provisions, and by force of arms to prevent any other persons from forcing their presence upon us after we had retired to our refuge.

"All this being arranged, my brother begged me to stay in my own house for at least twenty-four hours more, on the chance of the plague developing in me. To this I agreed, and he promised to come for me next day. We talked on over the details of the provisioning and the defending of the Chemistry Building until the telephone died. It died in the midst of our conversation. That evening there were no electric lights, and I was alone in my house in the darkness. No more newspapers were being printed, so I had no knowledge of what was taking place outside.

"I heard sounds of rioting and of pistol shots, and from my windows I could see the glare of the sky of some conflagration in the direction of Oakland. It was a night of terror. I did not sleep a wink. A man—why and how I do not know—was killed on the sidewalk in front of the house. I heard the rapid reports of an automatic pistol, and a few minutes later the wounded wretch crawled up to my door, moaning and crying out for help. Arming myself with two automatics, I went to him. By the light of a match I ascertained that while he was dying of the bullet wounds, at the same time the plague was on him. I fled indoors, whence I heard him moan and cry out for half an hour longer.

"In the morning, my brother came to me. I had gathered into a handbag what things of value I purposed taking, but when I saw his face I knew that he would never accompany me to the Chemistry Building. The plague was on him. He intended shaking my hand, but I went back hurriedly before him.

"'Look at yourself in the mirror,' I commanded.

III

"He did so, and at sight of his scarlet face, the color deepening as he looked at it, he sank down nervelessly in a chair.

"'My God!' he said. 'I've got it. Don't come near me. I am a dead man.'

"Then the convulsions seized him. He was two hours in dying, and he was conscious to the last, complaining about the coldness and loss of sensation in his feet, his calves, his thighs, until at last it was his heart and he was dead.

"That was the way the Scarlet Death slew. I caught up my handbag and fled. The sights in the streets were terrible. One stumbled on bodies everywhere. Some were not yet dead. And even as you looked, you saw men sink down with the death fastened upon them. There were numerous fires burning in Berkeley, while Oakland and San Francisco were apparently being swept by vast conflagrations. The smoke of the burning filled the heavens, so that the midday was as a gloomy twilight, and, in the shifts of wind, sometimes the sun shone through dimly, a dull red orb. Truly, my grandsons, it was like the last days of the end of the world.

"There were numerous stalled motor cars, showing that the gasoline and the engine supplies of the garages had given out. I remember one such car. A man and a woman lay back dead in the seats, and on the pavement near it were two more women and a child. Strange and terrible sights there were on every hand. People slipped by silently, furtively, like ghosts—white-faced women carrying infants in their arms; fathers leading children by the hand; singly, and in couples, and in families—all fleeing out of the city of death. Some carried supplies of food, others blankets and valuables, and there were many who carried nothing.

"There was a grocery store—a place where food was sold. The man to whom it belonged—I knew him well—a quiet, sober, but stupid and obstinate fellow, was defending it. The windows and doors had been broken in, but he, inside, hiding behind a counter, was discharging his pistol at a number of men on the sidewalk who were breaking in. In the entrance were several bodies—of men, I decided, whom he had killed earlier in the day. Even as I looked on from a distance, I saw one of the robbers break the windows of the adjoining store, a place where shoes were sold, and deliberately set fire to it. I did not go to the groceryman's assistance. The time for such acts had already passed. Civilization was crumbling, and it was each for himself."

IV

I WENT away hastily, down a cross-street, and at the first corner I saw another tragedy. Two men of the working class had caught a man and a woman with two children, and were robbing them. I knew the man by sight, though I had never been introduced to him. He was a poet whose verses I had long admired. Yet I did not go to his help, for at the moment I came upon the scene there was a pistol shot, and I saw him sinking to the ground. The woman screamed, and she was felled with a fist-blow by one of the brutes. I cried out threateningly, whereupon they discharged their pistols at me and I ran away around the corner. Here I was blocked by an advancing conflagration. The buildings on both sides were burning, and the street was filled with smoke and flame. From somewhere in that murk came a woman's voice calling shrilly for help. But I did not go to her. A man's heart turned to iron amid such scenes, and one heard all too many appeals for help.

"Returning to the corner, I found the two robbers were gone. The poet and his wife lay dead on the pavement. It was a shocking sight. The two children had vanished—whither I could not tell. And I knew, now, why it was that the fleeing persons I encountered slipped along so furtively and with such white faces. In the midst of our civilization, down in our slums and labor-ghettos, we had bred a race of barbarians, of savages; and now, in the time of our calamity, they turned upon us like the wild beasts they were and destroyed us. And they destroyed themselves as well.

"They inflamed themselves with strong drink and committed a thousand atrocities, quarreling and killing one another in the general madness. One group of workingmen I saw, of the better sort, who had banded together, and, with their women and children in their midst, the sick and aged in litters and being carried, and with a number of horses pulling a truck-load of provisions, they were fighting their way out of the city. They made a fine spectacle as they came down the street through the drifting smoke, though they nearly shot me when I first appeared in their path. As they went by, one of their leaders shouted out to me in apologetic explanation. He said they were killing the robbers and looters on sight, and that they had thus banded together as the only-means by which to escape the prowlers.

"It was here that I saw for the first time what I was soon to see so often. One of the marching men had suddenly shown the unmistakable mark of the plague. Immediately those about him drew away, and he, without a remonstrance, stepped out of his place to let them pass on. A woman, most probably his wife, attempted to follow him. She was leading a little boy by the hand. But the husband commanded her sternly to go on, while others laid hands on her and restrained her from following him. This I saw, and I saw the man also, with his scarlet blaze of face, step into a doorway on the opposite side of the street. I heard the report of his pistol, and saw him sink lifeless to the ground.

"After being turned aside twice again by advancing fires, I succeeded in getting through to the university. On the edge of the campus I came upon a party of university folk who were going in the direction of the Chemistry Building. They were all family men, and their families were with them, including the nurses and the servants. Professor Badminton greeted me, I had difficulty in recognizing him. Somewhere he had gone through flames, and his beard was singed off. About his head was a bloody bandage, and his clothes were filthy.

"He told me he had prowlers, and that his brother had been killed the previous night, in the defence of their dwelling.

"Midway across the campus, he pointed suddenly to Mrs. Swinton's face. The unmistakable scarlet was there. Immediately all the other women set up a screaming and began to run away from her. Her two children were with a nurse, and these also ran with the women. But her husband, Doctor Swinton, remained with her.

"'Go on, Smith,' he told me. 'Keep an eye on the children. As for me, I shall stay with my wife. I know she is as already dead, but I can't leave her. Afterwards, if I escape, I shall come to the Chemistry Building, and do you watch for me and let me in.'

"I left him bending over his wife and soothing her last moments, while I ran to overtake the party. We were the last to be admitted to the Chemistry Building. After that, with our automatic rifles we maintained our isolation. By our plans, we had arranged for a company of sixty to be in this refuge. Instead, every one of the number originally planned had added relatives and friends and whole families until there were over four hundred souls. But the Chemistry Building was large, and, standing by itself, was in no danger of being burned by the great fires that raged everywhere in the city.

"A large quantity of provisions had been gathered, and a food committee took charge of it, issuing rations daily to the various families and groups that arranged themselves into messes. A number of committees were appointed, and we developed a very efficient organization. I was on the committee of defence, though for the first day no prowlers came near. We could see them in the distance, however, and by the smoke of their fires knew that several camps of them were occupying the far edge of the campus. Drunkenness was rife, and often we heard them singing ribald songs or insanely shouting. While the world crashed to ruin about them and all the air was filled with the smoke of its burning, these low creatures gave rein to their bestiality and fought and drank and died. And after all, what did it matter? Everybody died anyway, the good and the bad, the efficients and the weaklings, those that loved to live and those that scorned to live. They passed. Everything passed.

"When twenty-four hours had gone by and no signs of the plague were apparent, we congratulated ourselves and set about digging a well. You have seen the great iron pipes which in those days carried water to all the city-dwellers. We feared that the fires in the city would burst the pipes and empty the reservoirs. So we tore up the cement floor of the central court of the Chemistry Building and dug a well. There were many young men, undergraduates, with us, and we worked night and day on the well.

And our fears were confirmed. Three hours before we reached water, the pipes went dry.

"A second twenty-four hours passed, and still the plague did not appear among us. We thought we were saved. But we did not know what I afterwards decided to be true, namely, that the period of the incubation of the plague germs in a human's body was a matter of a number of days. It slew so swiftly when once it manifested itself, that we were led to believe that the period of incubation was equally swift. So, when two days had left us unscathed, we were elated with the idea that we were free of the contagion.

"But the third day disillusioned us. I can never forget the night preceding it. I had charge of the night guards from eight to twelve, and from the roof of the building I watched the passing of all man's glorious works. So terrible were the local conflagrations that all the sky was lighted up. One could read the finest print in the red glare. All the world seemed wrapped in flames. San Francisco spouted smoke and fire from a score of vast conflagrations that were like so many active volcanoes. Oakland, San Leandro, Haywards—all were burning; and to the northward, clear to Point Richmond, other fires were at work. It was an awe-inspiring spectacle. Civilization, my grandsons, civilization was passing in a sheet of flame and a breath of death. At ten o'clock that night, the great powder magazines at Point Pinole exploded in rapid succession. So terrific were the concussions that the strong building rocked as in an earthquake, while every pane of glass was broken. It was then that I left the roof and went down the long corridors, from room to room, quieting the alarmed women and telling them what had happened.

"An hour later, at a window on the ground floor, I heard pandemonium break out in the camps of the prowlers. There were cries and screams, and shots from many pistols. As we afterward conjectured, this fight had been precipitated by an attempt on the part of those that were well to drive out those that were sick. At any rate, a number of the plague-stricken prowlers escaped across the campus and drifted against our doors. We warned them back, but they cursed us and discharged a fusillade from their pistols. Professor Merryweather, at one of the windows, was instantly killed, the bullet striking him squarely between the eyes. We opened fire in turn, and all the prowlers fled away with the exception of three. One was a woman. The plague was on them and they were reckless. Like foul fiends, there in the red glare from the skies, with faces blazing, they continued to curse us and fire at us. One of the men I shot with my own hand. After that the other man and the woman, still cursing us, lay down under our windows, where we were compelled to watch them die of the plague.

"The situation was critical. The explosions of the powder magazines had broken all the windows of the Chemistry Building, so that we were exposed to the germs from the corpses. The sanitary committee was called upon to act, and it responded nobly. Two men were required to go out and remove the corpses, and this meant the probable sacrifice of their own lives, for, having performed the task, they were not to be permitted to reenter the building. One of the professors, who was a bachelor, and one of the undergraduates volunteered. They bade good-bye to us and went forth. They were heroes. They gave up their lives that four hundred others might live. After they had performed their work, they stood for a moment, at a distance, looking at us wistfully. Then they waved their hands in farewell and went away slowly across the campus toward the burning city.

IV

"And yet it was all useless. The next morning the first one of us was smitten with the plague—a little nurse-girl in the family of Professor Stout. It was no time for weak-kneed, sentimental policies. On the chance that she might be the only one, we thrust her forth from the building and commanded her to be gone.

"She went away slowly across the campus, wringing her hands and crying pitifully. We felt like brutes, but what were we to do? There were four hundred of us, and individuals had to be sacrificed.

"In one of the laboratories three families had domiciled themselves, and that afternoon we found among them no less than four corpses and seven cases of the plague in all its different stages.

"Then it was that the horror began. Leaving the dead lie, we forced the living ones to segregate themselves in another room. The plague began to break out among the rest of us, and as fast as the symptoms appeared, we sent the stricken ones to these segregated rooms. We compelled them to walk there by themselves, so as to avoid laying hands on them. It was heartrending. But still the plague raged among us, and room after room was filled with the dead and dying. And so we who were yet clean retreated to the next floor and to the next, before this sea of the dead, that, room by room and floor by floor, inundated the building.

"The place became a charnel house, and in the middle of the night the survivors fled forth, taking nothing with them except arms and ammunition and a heavy store of tinned foods. We camped on the opposite side of the campus from the prowlers, and, while some stood guard, others of us volunteered to scout into the city in quest of horses, motor cars, carts, and wagons, or anything that would carry our provisions and enable us to emulate the banded workingmen I had seen fighting their way out to the open country.

"I was one of these scouts; and Doctor Hoyle, remembering that his motor car had been left behind in his home garage, told me to look for it. We scouted in pairs, and Dombey, a young undergraduate, accompanied me. We had to cross half a mile of the residence portion of the city to get to Doctor Hoyle's home. Here the buildings stood apart, in the midst of trees and grassy lawns, and here the fires had played freaks, burning whole blocks, skipping blocks and often skipping a single house in a block. And here, too, the prowlers were still at their work. We carried our automatic pistols openly in our hands, and looked desperate enough, forsooth, to keep them from attacking us. But at Doctor Hoyle's house the thing happened. Untouched by fire, even as we came to it the smoke of flames burst forth.

"The miscreant who had set fire to it staggered down the steps and out along the driveway. Sticking out of his coat pockets were bottles of whiskey, and he was very drunk. My first impulse was to shoot him, and I have never ceased regretting that I did not. Staggering and maundering to himself, with bloodshot eyes, and a raw and bleeding slash down one side of his bewhiskered face, he was altogether the most nauseating specimen of degradation and filth I had ever encountered. I did not shoot him, and he leaned against a tree on the lawn to let us go by. It was the most absolute, wanton act. Just as we were opposite him, he suddenly drew a pistol and shot Dombey through the head. The next instant I shot him. But it was too late. Dombey expired without a groan, immediately. I doubt if he even knew what had happened to him.

"Leaving the two corpses, I hurried on past the burning house to the garage, and there found Doctor Hoyle's motor car. The tanks were filled with gasoline, and it was ready for use. And it was in this car that I threaded the streets of the ruined city and came back to the survivors on the campus. The other scouts returned, but none had been so fortunate. Professor Fairmead had found a Shetland pony, but the poor creature, tied in a stable and abandoned for days, was so weak from want of food and water that it could carry no burden at all. Some of the men were for turning it loose, but I insisted that we should lead it along with us, so that, if we got out of food, we would have it to eat.

"There were forty-seven of us when we started, many being women and children. The President of the Faculty, an old man to begin with, and now hopelessly broken by the awful happenings of the past week, rode in the motor car with several young children and the aged mother of Professor Fairmead. Wathope, a young professor of English, who had a grievous bullet-wound in his leg, drove the car. The rest of us walked, Professor Fairmead leading the pony.

"It was what should have been a bright summer day, but the smoke from the burning world filled the sky, through which the sun shone murkily, a dull and lifeless orb, blood-red and ominous. But we had grown accustomed to that blood-red sun. With the smoke it was different. It bit into our nostrils and eyes, and there was not one of us whose eyes were not bloodshot. We directed our course to the southeast through the endless miles of suburban residences, travelling along where the first swells of low hills rose from the flat of the central city. It was by this way, only, that we could expect to gain the country.

"Our progress was painfully slow. The women and children could not walk fast. They did not dream of walking, my grandsons, in the way all people walk to-day. In truth, none of us knew how to walk. It was not until after the plague that I learned really to walk. So it was that the pace of the slowest was the pace of all, for we dared not separate on account of the prowlers. There were not so many now of these human beasts of prey. The plague had already well diminished their numbers, but enough still lived to be a constant menace to us. Many of the beautiful residences were untouched by fire, yet smoking ruins were everywhere. The prowlers, too, seemed to have got over their insensate desire to burn, and it was more rarely that we saw houses freshly on fire.

"Several of us scouted among the private garages in search of motor cars and gasoline. But in this we were unsuccessful. The first great flights from the cities had swept all such utilities away. Calgan, a fine young man, was lost in this work. He was shot by prowlers while crossing a lawn. Yet this was our only casualty, though, once, a drunken brute deliberately opened fire on all of us. Luckily, he fired wildly, and we shot him before he had done any hurt.

"At Fruitvale, still in the heart of the magnificent residence section of the city, the plague again smote us. Professor Fair-mead was the victim. Making signs to us that his mother was not to know, he turned aside into the grounds of a beautiful mansion. He sat down forlornly on the steps of the front veranda, and I, having lingered, waved him a last farewell. That night, several miles beyond Fruitvale and still in the city, we made camp. And that night we shifted camp twice to get away from our dead. In the morning there were thirty of us. I shall never forget the President of the Faculty. During the morning's march his wife, who was walking, betrayed the fatal symptoms, and when she drew aside to let us go on, he insisted on leaving the motor car and remaining with her. There was quite a discussion about this, but in the end we gave in. It was just as well, for we knew not which ones of us, if any, might ultimately escape.

"That night, the second of our march, we camped beyond Haywards in the first stretches of country. And in the morning there were eleven of us that lived. Also, during the night, Wathope, the professor with the wounded leg, deserted us in the motor car. He took with him his sister and his mother and most of our tinned provisions. It was that day, in the afternoon, while resting by the wayside, that I saw the last airship I shall ever see. The smoke was much thinner here in the country, and I first sighted the ship drifting and veering helplessly at an elevation of two thousand feet. What had happened I could not conjecture, but even as we looked we saw her bow dip down lower and lower. Then the bulkheads of the various gas-chambers must have burst, for, quite perpendicular, she fell like a plummet to the earth.

"And from that day to this I have not seen another airship. Often and often, during the next few years, I scanned the sky for them, hoping against hope that somewhere in the world civilization had survived. But it was not to be. What happened with us in California must have happened with everybody everywhere.

"Another day, and at Niles there were three of us. Beyond Niles, in the middle of the highway, we found Wathope. The motor car had broken down, and there, on the rugs which they had spread on the ground, lay the bodies of his sister, his mother, and himself.

"Wearied by the unusual exercise of continual walking, that night I slept heavily. In the morning I was alone in the world. Canfield and Parsons, my last companions, were dead of the plague. Of the four hundred that sought shelter in the Chemistry Building, and of the forty-seven that began the march, I alone remained—I and the Shetland pony. Why this should be so there is no explaining. I did not catch the plague, that is all. I was immune. I was merely the one lucky man in a million—just as every survivor was one in a million, or, rather, in several millions, for the proportion was at least that."

V

"FOR two days I sheltered in a pleasant grove where there had been no deaths. In those two days, while badly depressed and believing that my turn would come at any moment, nevertheless I rested and recuperated. So did the pony. And on the third day, putting what small store of tinned provisions I possessed on the pony's back, I started on across a very lonely land. Not a live man, woman, or child, did I encounter, though the dead were everywhere. Food, however, was abundant. The land then was not as it is now. It was all cleared of trees and brush, and it was cultivated. The food for millions of mouths was growing, ripening, and going to waste. From the fields and orchards I gathered vegetables, fruits, and berries. Around the deserted farmhouses I got eggs and caught chickens. And frequently I found supplies of tinned provisions in the store-rooms.

"A strange thing was what was taking place with all the domestic animals. Everywhere they were going wild and preying on one another. The chickens and ducks were the first to be destroyed, while the pigs were the first to go wild, followed by the cats. Nor were the dogs long in adapting themselves to the changed conditions. There was a veritable plague of dogs. They devoured the corpses, barked and howled during the nights, and in the daytime slunk about in the distance. As the time went by, I noticed a change in their behavior. At first they were apart from one another, very suspicious and very prone to fight. But after a not very long while they began to come together and run in packs. The dog, you see, always was a social animal, and this was true before ever he came to be domesticated by man. In the last days of the world before the plague, there were many many very different kinds of dogs—dogs without hair and dogs with warm fur, dogs so small that they would make scarcely a mouthful for other dogs that were as large as mountain lions. Well, all the small dogs, and the weak types, were killed by their fellows. Also, the very large ones were not adapted for the wild life and bred out. As a result, the many different kinds of dogs disappeared, and there remained, running in packs, the medium-sized wolfish dogs that you know to-day."

"But the cats don't run in packs, Granser," Hoo-Hoo objected.

"The cat was never a social animal. As one writer in the nineteenth century said, the cat walks by himself. He always walked by himself, from before the time he was tamed by man, down through the long ages of domestication, to to-day when once more he is wild.

V

"The horses also went wild, and all the fine breeds we had degenerated into the small mustang horse you know to-day. The cows likewise went wild, as did the pigeons and the sheep. And that a few of the chickens survived you know yourself. But the wild chicken of to-day is quite a different thing from the chickens we had in those days.

"But I must go on with my story. I travelled through a deserted land. As the time went by I began to yearn more and more for human beings. But I never found one, and I grew lonelier and lonelier. I crossed Livermore Valley and the mountains between it and the great valley of the San Joaquin. You have never seen that valley, but it is very large and it is the home of the wild horse. There are great droves there, thousands and tens of thousands. I revisited it thirty years after, so I know. You think there are lots of wild horses down here in the coast valleys, but they are as nothing compared with those of the San Joaquin. Strange to say, the cows, when they went wild, went back into the lower mountains. Evidently they were better able to protect themselves there.

"In the country districts the ghouls and prowlers had been less in evidence, for I found many villages and towns untouched by fire. But they were filled by the pestilential dead, and I passed by without exploring them. It was near Lathrop that, out of my loneliness, I picked up a pair of collie dogs that were so newly free that they were urgently willing to return to their allegiance to man. These collies accompanied me for many years, and the strains of them are in those very dogs there that you boys have to-day. But in sixty years the collie strain has worked out. These brutes are more like domesticated wolves than anything else."

Hare-Lip rose to his feet, glanced to see that the goats were safe, and looked at the sun's position in the afternoon sky, advertising impatience at the prolixity of the old man's tale. Urged to hurry by Edwin, Granser went on.

"There is little more to tell. With my two dogs and my pony, and riding a horse I had managed to capture, I crossed the San Joaquin and went on to a wonderful valley in the Sierras called Yosemite. In the great hotel there I found a prodigious supply of tinned provisions. The pasture was abundant, as was the game, and the river that ran through the valley was full of trout. I remained there three years in an utter loneliness that none but a man who has once been highly civilized can understand. Then I could stand it no more. I felt that I was going crazy. Like the dog, I was a social animal and I needed my kind. I reasoned that since I had survived the plague, there was a possibility that others had survived. Also, I reasoned that after three years the plague germs must all be gone and the land be clean again.

"With my horse and dogs and pony, I set out. Again I crossed the San Joaquin Valley, the mountains beyond, and came down into Livermore Valley. The change in those three years was amazing. All the land had been splendidly tilled, and now I could scarcely recognize it, 'such was the sea of rank vegetation that had overrun the agricultural handiwork of man. You see, the wheat, the vegetables, and orchard trees had always been cared for and nursed by man, so that they were soft and tender. The weeds and wild bushes and such things, on the contrary, had always been fought by man, so that they were tough and resistant. As a result, when the hand of man was removed, the wild vegetation smothered and destroyed practically all the domesticated vegetation. The coyotes were greatly increased, and it was at this time that I first encountered wolves, straying in twos and threes and small packs down from the regions where they had always persisted.

"It was at Lake Temescal, not far from the one-time city of Oakland, that I came upon the first live human beings. Oh, my grandsons, how can I describe to you my emotion, when, astride my horse and dropping down the hillside to the lake, I saw the smoke of a campfire rising through the trees. Almost did my heart stop beating. I felt that I was going crazy. Then I heard the cry of a babe—a human babe. And dogs barked, and my dogs answered. I did not know but what I was the one human alive in the whole world. It could not be true that here were others—smoke, and the cry of a babe.

"Emerging on the lake, there, before my eyes, not a hundred yards away, I saw a man, a large man. He was standing on an outjutting rock and fishing. I was overcome. I stopped my horse. I tried to call out but could not. I waved my hand. It seemed to me that the man looked at me, but he did not appear to wave. Then I laid my head on my arms there in the saddle. I was afraid to look again, for I knew it was an hallucination, and I knew that if I looked the man would be gone. And so precious was the hallucination, that I wanted it to persist yet a little while. I knew, too, that as long as I did not look it would persist.

"Thus I remained, until I heard my dogs snarling, and a man's voice. What do you think the voice said? I will tell you. It said: '*Where in hell did you come from??*'

"Those were the words, the exact words. That was what your other grandfather said to me, Hare-Lip, when he greeted me there on the shore of Lake Temescal fifty-seven years ago. And they were the most ineffable words I have ever heard. I opened my eyes, and there he stood before me, a large, dark, hairy man, heavy-jawed, slant-browed, fierce-eyed. How I got off my horse I do not know. But it seemed that the next I knew I was clasping his hand with both of mine and crying. I would have embraced him, but he was ever a narrow-minded, suspicious man, and he drew away from me. Yet did I cling to his hand and cry."

Granser's voice faltered and broke at the recollection, and the weak tears streamed down his cheeks while the boys looked on and giggled.

"Yet did I cry," he continued, "and desire to embrace him, though the Chauffeur was a brute, a perfect brute—the most abhorrent man I have ever known. His name was... strange, how I have forgotten his name. Everybody called him Chauffeur—it was the name of his occupation, and it stuck. That is how, to this day, the tribe he founded is called the Chauffeur Tribe.

"He was a violent, unjust man. Why the plague germs spared him I can never understand. It would seem, in spite of our old metaphysical notions about absolute justice, that there is no justice in the universe. Why did he live?—an iniquitous, moral monster, a blot on the face of nature, a cruel, relentless, bestial cheat as well. All he could talk about was motor cars, machinery, gasoline, and garages—and especially, and with huge delight, of his mean pilferings and sordid swindlings of the persons who had employed him in the days before the coming of the plague. And yet he was spared, while hundreds of millions, yea, billions, of better men were destroyed.

"I went on with him to his camp, and there I saw her, Vesta, the one woman. It was glorious and... pitiful. There she was, Vesta Van Warden, the young wife of John Van Warden, clad in rags, with marred and scarred and toil-calloused hands, bending over the campfire and doing scullion work—she, Vesta, who had been born to the purple of the greatest baronage of wealth the world had ever known. John Van Warden, her husband, worth one billion, eight hundred millions and President of the Board of Industrial Magnates, had been the ruler of America. Also, sitting on the International Board of Control, he had been one of the seven men who ruled the world. And she herself had come of equally noble stock. Her father, Philip Saxon, had been President of the Board of Industrial Magnates up to the time of his death. This office was in process of becoming hereditary, and had Philip Saxon had a son that son would have succeeded him. But his only child was Vesta, the perfect flower of generations of the highest culture this planet has ever produced. It was not until the engagement between Vesta and Van Warden took place, that Saxon indicated the latter as his successor. It was, I am sure, a political marriage. I have reason to believe that Vesta never really loved her husband in the mad passionate way of which the poets used to sing. It was more like the marriages that obtained among crowned heads in the days before they were displaced by the Magnates.

"And there she was, boiling fish-chowder in a soot-covered pot, her glorious eyes inflamed by the acrid smoke of the open fire. Hers was a sad story. She was the one survivor in a million, as I had been, as the Chauffeur had been. On a crowning eminence of the Alameda Hills, overlooking San Francisco Bay, Van Warden had built a vast summer palace. It was surrounded by a park of a thousand acres. When the plague broke out, Van Warden sent her there. Armed guards patrolled the boundaries of the park, and nothing entered in the way of provisions or even mail matter that was not first fumigated. And yet did the plague enter, killing the guards at their posts, the servants at their tasks, sweeping away the whole army of retainers—or, at least, all of them who did not flee to die elsewhere. So it was that Vesta found herself the sole living person in the palace that had become a charnel house.

"Now the Chauffeur had been one of the servants that ran away. Returning, two months afterward, he discovered Vesta in a little summer pavilion where there had been no deaths and where she had established herself. He was a brute. She was afraid, and she ran away and hid among the trees. That night, on foot, she fled into the mountains—she, whose tender feet and delicate body had never known the bruise of stones nor the scratch of briars. He followed, and that night he caught her. He struck her. Do you understand? He beat her with those terrible fists of his and made her his slave. It was she who had to gather the firewood, build the fires, cook, and do all the degrading camp-labor—she, who had never performed a menial act in her life. These things he compelled her to do, while he, a proper savage, elected to lie around camp and look on. He did nothing, absolutely nothing, except on occasion to hunt meat or catch fish."

"Good for Chauffeur," Hare-Lip commented in an undertone to the other boys. "I remember him before he died. He was a corker. But he did things, and he made things go. You know, Dad married his daughter, an' you ought to see the way he knocked the spots outa Dad. The Chauffeur was a son-of-a-gun. He made us kids stand around. Even when he was croaking he reached out for me, once, an' laid my head open with that long stick he kept always beside him."

Hare-Lip rubbed his bullet head reminiscently, and the boys returned to the old man, who was maundering ecstatically about Vesta, the squaw of the founder of the Chauffeur Tribe.

"And so I say to you that you cannot understand the awfulness of the situation. The Chauffeur was a servant, understand, a servant. And he cringed, with bowed head, to such as she. She was a lord of life, both by birth and by marriage. The destinies of millions, such as he, she carried in the hollow of her pink-white hand. And, in the days before the plague, the slightest contact with such as he would have been pollution. Oh, I have seen it. Once, I remember, there was Mrs. Goldwin, wife of one of the great magnates. It was on a landing stage, just as she was embarking in her private dirigible, that she dropped her parasol. A servant picked it up and made the mistake of handing it to her—to her, one of the greatest royal ladies of the land! She shrank back, as though he were a leper, and indicated her secretary to receive it. Also, she ordered her secretary to ascertain the creature's name and to see that he was immediately discharged from service. And such a woman was Vesta Van Warden. And her the Chauffeur beat and made his slave.

"—Bill—that was it; Bill, the Chauffeur. That was his name. He was a wretched, primitive man, wholly devoid of the finer instincts and chivalrous promptings of a cultured soul. No, there is no absolute justice, for to him fell that wonder of womanhood, Vesta Van Warden. The grievous-ness of this you will never understand, my grandsons; for you are yourselves primitive little savages, unaware of aught else but savagery. Why should Vesta not have been mine? I was a man of culture and refinement, a professor in a great university. Even so, in the time before the plague, such was her exalted position, she would not have deigned to know that I existed. Mark, then, the abysmal degradation to which she fell at the hands of the Chauffeur. Nothing less than the destruction of all mankind had made it possible that I should know her, look in her eyes, converse with her, touch her hand—ay, and love her and know that her feelings toward me were very kindly. I have reason to believe that she, even she, would have loved me, there being no other man in the world except the Chauffeur. Why, when it destroyed eight billions of souls, did not the plague destroy just one more man, and that man the Chauffeur?

"Once, when the Chauffeur was away fishing, she begged me to kill him. With tears in her eyes she begged me to kill him. But he was a strong and violent man, and I was afraid. Afterwards, I talked with him. I offered him my horse, my pony, my dogs, all that I possessed, if he would give Vesta to me. And he grinned in my face and shook his head. He was very insulting. He said that in the old days he had been a servant, had been dirt under the feet of men like me and of women like Vesta, and that now he had the greatest lady in the land to be servant to him and cook his food and nurse his brats. 'You had your day before the plague,' he said; 'but this is my day, and a damned good day it is. I wouldn't trade back to the old times for anything.' Such words he spoke, but they are not his words. He was a vulgar, low-minded man, and vile oaths fell continually from his lips.

"Also, he told me that if he caught me making eyes at his woman he'd wring my neck and give her a beating as well. What was I to do? I was afraid. He was a brute. That first night, when I discovered the camp, Vesta and I had great talk about the things of our vanished world. We talked of art, and books, and poetry; and the Chauffeur listened and grinned and sneered. He was bored and angered by our way of speech which he did not comprehend, and finally he spoke up and said: 'And this is Vesta Van Warden, one-time wife of Van Warden the Magnate—a high and stuck-up beauty, who is now my squaw. Eh, Professor Smith, times is changed, times is changed. Here, you, woman, take off my moccasins, and lively about it. I want Professor Smith to see how well I have you trained.'

"I saw her clench her teeth, and the flame of revolt rise in her face. He drew back his gnarled fist to strike, and I was afraid, and sick at heart. I could do nothing to prevail against him. So I got up to go, and not be witness to such indignity. But the Chauffeur laughed and threatened me with a beating if I did not stay and behold. And I sat there, perforce, by the campfire on the shore of Lake Temescal, and saw Vesta, Vesta Van Warden, kneel and remove the moccasins of that grinning, hairy, apelike human brute.

"—Oh, you do not understand, my grandsons. You have never known anything else, and you do not understand.

"'Halter-broke and bridle-wise,' the Chauffeur gloated, while she performed that dreadful, menial task. 'A trifle balky at times, Professor, a trifle balky; but a clout alongside the jaw makes her as meek and gentle as a lamb.'

"And another time he said: 'We've got to start all over and replenish the earth and multiply. You're handicapped, Professor. You ain't got no wife, and we're up against a regular Garden-of-Eden proposition. But I ain't proud. I'll tell you what, Professor.' He pointed at their little infant, barely a year old. 'There's your wife, though you'll have to wait till she grows up. It's rich, ain't it? We're all equals here, and I'm the biggest toad in the splash. But I ain't stuck up—not I. I do you the honor, Professor Smith, the very great honor of betrothing to you my and Vesta Van Warden's daughter. Ain't it cussed bad that Van Warden ain't here to see?'"

VI

"I LIVED three weeks of infinite torment there in the Chauffeur's camp. And then, one day, tiring of me, or of what to him was my bad effect on Vesta, he told me that the year before, wandering through the Contra Costa Hills to the Straits of Carquinez, across the Straits he had seen a smoke. This meant that there were still other human beings,' and that for three weeks he had kept this inestimably precious information from me. I departed at once, with my dogs and horses, and journeyed across the Contra Costa Hills to the Straits. I saw no smoke on the other side, but at Port Costa discovered a small steel barge on which I was able to embark my animals. Old canvas which I found served me for a sail, and a southerly breeze fanned me across the Straits and up to the ruins of Vallejo. Here, on the outskirts of the city, I found evidences of a recently occupied camp.

"Many clam-shells showed me why these humans had come to the shores of the Bay. This was the Santa Rosa Tribe, and I followed its track along the old railroad right of way across the salt marshes to Sonoma Valley. Here, at the old brickyard at Glen Ellen, I came upon the camp. There were eighteen souls all told. Two were old men, one of whom was Jones, a banker. The other was Harrison, a retired pawnbroker, who had taken for wife the matron of the State Hospital for the Insane at Napa. Of all the persons of the city of Napa, and of all the other towns and villages in that rich and populous valley, she had been the only-survivor. Next, there were the three young men—Cardiff and Hale, who had been farmers, and Wainwright, a common day-laborer. All three had found wives. To Hale, a crude, illiterate farmer, had fallen Isadore, the greatest prize, next to Vesta, of the women who came through the plague. She was one of the world's most noted singers, and the plague had caught her at San Francisco. She has talked with me for hours at a time, telling me of her adventures, until, at last, rescued by Hale in the Mendocino Forest Reserve, there had remained nothing for her to do but become his wife. But Hale was a good fellow, in spite of his illiteracy. He had a keen sense of justice and right-dealing, and she was far happier with him than was Vesta with the Chauffeur.

"The wives of Cardiff and Wainwright were ordinary women, accustomed to toil with strong constitutions—just the type for the wild new life which they were compelled to live. In addition were two adult idiots from the feeble-minded home at Eldredge, and five or six young children and infants born after the formation of the Santa Rosa Tribe. Also, there was Bertha. She was a good woman, Hare-Lip, in spite of the sneers of your father. Her I took for wife. She was the mother of your father, Edwin, and of yours, Hoo-Hoo. And it was our daughter, Vera, who married your father, Hare-Lip—your father, Sandow, who was the oldest son of Vesta Van Warden and the Chauffeur.

"And so it was that I became the nineteenth member of the Santa Rosa Tribe. There were only two outsiders added after me. One was Mungerson, descended from the Magnates, who wandered alone in the wilds of Northern California for eight years before he came south and joined us. He it was who waited twelve years more before he married my daughter, Mary. The other was Johnson, the man who founded the Utah Tribe. That was where he came from, Utah, a country that lies very far away from here, across the great deserts, to the east. It was not until twenty-seven years after the plague that Johnson reached California. In all that Utah region he reported but three survivors, himself one, and all men. For many years these three men lived and hunted together, until, at last, desperate, fearing that with them the human race would perish utterly from the planet, they headed westward on the possibility of finding women survivors in California. Johnson alone came through the great desert, where his two companions died. He was forty-six years old when he joined us, and he married the fourth daughter of Isadore and Hale, and his eldest son married your aunt, Hare-Lip, who was the third daughter of Vesta and the Chauffeur. Johnson was a strong man, with a will of his own. And it was because of this that he seceded from the Santa Rosans and formed the Utah Tribe at San José. It is a small tribe—there are only nine in it; but, though he is dead, such was his influence and the strength of his breed, that it will grow into a strong tribe and play a leading part in the recivilization of the planet.

"There are only two other tribes that we know of—the Los Angelitos and the Carmelitos. The latter started from one man and woman. He was called Lopez, and he was descended from the ancient Mexicans and was very black. He was a cowherd in the ranges beyond Carmel, and his wife was a maidservant in the great Del Monte Hotel. It was seven years before we first got in touch with the Los Angelitos. They have a good country down there, but it is too warm. I estimate the present population of the world at between three hundred and fifty and four hundred—provided, of course, that there are no scattered little tribes elsewhere in the world. If there be such, we have not heard from them. Since Johnson crossed the desert from Utah, no word nor sign has come from the East or anywhere else. The great world which I knew in my boyhood and early manhood is gone. It has ceased to be. I am the last man who was alive in the days of the plague and who knows the wonders of that far-off time. We, who mastered the planet—its earth, and sea, and sky—and who were as very gods, now live in primitive savagery along the water courses of this California country.

"But we are increasing rapidly—your sister, Hare-Lip, already has four children. We are increasing rapidly and making ready for a new climb toward civilization. In time, pressure of population will compel us to spread out, and a hundred generations from now we may expect our descendants to start across the Sierras, oozing slowly along, generation by generation, over the great continent to the colonization of the East—a new Aryan drift around the world.

"But it will be slow, very slow; we have so far to climb. We fell so hopelessly far. If only one physicist or one chemist had survived! But it was not to be, and we have forgotten everything. The Chauffeur started working in iron. He made the forge which we use to this day. But he was a lazy man, and when he died he took with him all he knew of metals and machinery. What was I to know of such things? I was a classical scholar, not a chemist.. The other men who survived were not educated. Only two things did the Chauffeur accomplish—the brewing of strong drink and the growing of tobacco. It was while he was drunk, once, that he killed Vesta. I firmly believe that he killed Vesta in a fit of drunken cruelty though he always maintained that she fell into the lake and was drowned.

"And, my grandsons, let me warn you against the medicine-men. They call themselves *doctors*, travestying what was once a noble profession, but in reality they are medicine-men, devil-devil men, and they make for superstition and darkness. They are cheats and liars. But so debased and degraded are we, that we believe their lies. They, too, will increase in numbers as we increase, and they will strive to rule us. Yet are they liars and charlatans. Look at young Cross-Eyes, posing as a doctor, selling charms against sickness, giving good hunting, exchanging promises of fair weather for good meat and skins, sending the death-stick, performing a thousand abominations. Yet I say to you, that when he says he can do these things, he lies. I, Professor Smith, Professor James Howard Smith, say that he lies. I have told him so to his teeth. Why has he not sent me the death-stick? Because he knows that with me it is without avail. But you, Hare-Lip, so deeply are you sunk in black superstition that did you awake this night and find the death-stick beside you, you would surely die. And you would die, not because of any virtues in the stick, but because you are a savage with the dark and clouded mind of a savage.

"The doctors must be destroyed, and all that was lost must be discovered over again. Wherefore, earnestly, I repeat unto you certain things which you must remember and tell to your children after you. You must tell them that when water is made hot by fire, there resides in it a wonderful thing called steam, which is stronger than ten thousand men and which can do all man's work for him. There are other very useful things. In the lightning flash resides a similarly strong servant of man, which was of old his slave and which some day will be his slave again.

"Quite a different thing is the alphabet. It is what enables me to know the meaning of fine markings, whereas you boys know only rude picture-writing. In that dry cave on Telegraph Hill, where you see me often go when the tribe is down by the sea, I have stored many books. In them is great wisdom. Also, with them, I have placed a key to the alphabet, so that one who knows picture-writing may also know print. Some day men will read again; and then, if no accident has befallen my cave, they will know that Professor James Howard Smith once lived and saved for them the knowledge of the ancients.

"There is another little device that men inevitably will rediscover. It is called gunpowder. It was what enabled us to kill surely and at long distances. Certain things which are found in the ground, when combined in the right proportions, will make this gunpowder. What these things are, I have forgotten, or else I never knew. But I wish I did know. Then would I make powder, and then would I certainly kill Cross-Eyes and rid the land of superstition—"

"After I am man-grown I am going to give Cross-Eyes all the goats, and meat, and skins I can get, so that he'll teach me to be a doctor," Hoo-Hoo asserted. "And when I know, I'll make everybody else sit up and take notice. They'll get down in the dirt to me, you bet."

VI

The old man nodded his head solemnly, and murmured:

"Strange it is to hear the vestiges and remnants of the complicated Aryan speech falling from the lips of a filthy little skin-clad savage. All the world is topsy-turvy. And it has been topsy-turvy ever since the plague."

"You won't make me sit up," Hare-Lip boasted to the would-be medicine-man. "If I paid you for a sending of the death-stick and it didn't work, I'd bust in your head—understand, you Hoo-Hoo, you?"

"I'm going to get Granser to remember this here gunpowder stuff," Edwin said softly, "and then I'll have you all on the run. You, Hare-Lip, will do my fighting for me and get my meat for me, and you, Hoo-Hoo, will send the death-stick for me and make everybody afraid. And if I catch Hare-Lip trying to bust your head, Hoo-Hoo, I'll fix him with that same gunpowder. Granser ain't such a fool as you think, and I'm going to listen to him and some day I'll be boss over the whole bunch of you."

The old man shook his head sadly, and said:

"The gunpowder will come. Nothing can stop it—the same old story over and over. Man will increase, and men will fight. The gunpowder will enable men to kill millions of men, and in this way only, by fire and blood, will a new civilization, in some remote day, be evolved. And of what profit will it be? Just as the old civilization passed, so will the new. It may take fifty thousand years to build, but it will pass. All things pass. Only remain cosmic force and matter, ever in flux, ever acting and reacting and realizing the eternal types—the priest, the soldier, and the king. Out of the mouths of babes comes the wisdom of all the ages. Some will fight, some will rule, some will pray; and all the rest will toil and suffer sore while on their bleeding carcasses is reared again, and yet again, without end, the amazing beauty and surpassing wonder of the civilized state. It were just as well that I destroyed those cave-stored books—whether they remain or perish, all their old truths will be discovered, their old lies lived and handed down. What is the profit—"

Hare-Lip leaped to his feet, giving a quick glance at the pasturing goats and the afternoon sun.

"Gee!" he muttered to Edwin, "The old geezer gets more long-winded every day. Let's pull for camp."

While the other two, aided by the dogs, assembled the goats and started them for the trail through the forest, Edwin stayed by the old man and guided him in the same direction. When they reached the old right of way, Edwin stopped suddenly and looked back. Hare-Lip and Hoo-Hoo and the dogs and the goats passed on. Edwin was looking at a small herd of wild horses which had come down on the hard sand. There were at least twenty of them, young colts and yearlings and mares, led by a beautiful stallion which stood in the foam at the edge of the surf, with arched neck and bright wild eyes, sniffing the salt air from off the sea.

"What is it?" Granser queried.

"Horses," was the answer. "First time I ever seen 'em on the beach. It's the mountain lions getting thicker and thicker and driving 'em down."

The low sun shot red shafts of light, fan-shaped, up from a cloud-tumbled horizon. And close at hand, in the white waste of shore-lashed waters, the sea-lions, bellowing their old primeval chant, hauled up out of the sea on the black rocks and fought and loved.

"Come on, Granser," Edwin prompted. And old man and boy, skin-clad and barbaric, turned and went along the right of way into the forest in the wake of the goats.

THE END

THE SEA-WOLF

CHAPTER I

I scarcely know where to begin, though I sometimes facetiously place the cause of it all to Charley Furuseth's credit. He kept a summer cottage in Mill Valley, under the shadow of Mount Tamalpais, and never occupied it except when he loafed through the winter months and read Nietzsche and Schopenhauer to rest his brain. When summer came on, he elected to sweat out a hot and dusty existence in the city and to toil incessantly. Had it not been my custom to run up to see him every Saturday afternoon and to stop over till Monday morning, this particular January Monday morning would not have found me afloat on San Francisco Bay.

Not but that I was afloat in a safe craft, for the *Martinez* was a new ferry-steamer, making her fourth or fifth trip on the run between Sausalito and San Francisco. The danger lay in the heavy fog which blanketed the bay, and of which, as a landsman, I had little apprehension. In fact, I remember the placid exaltation with which I took up my position on the forward upper deck, directly beneath the pilot-house, and allowed the mystery of the fog to lay hold of my imagination. A fresh breeze was blowing, and for a time I was alone in the moist obscurity—yet not alone, for I was dimly conscious of the presence of the pilot, and of what I took to be the captain, in the glass house above my head.

I remember thinking how comfortable it was, this division of labour which made it unnecessary for me to study fogs, winds, tides, and navigation, in order to visit my friend who lived across an arm of the sea. It was good that men should be specialists, I mused. The peculiar knowledge of the pilot and captain sufficed for many thousands of people who knew no more of the sea and navigation than I knew. On the other hand, instead of having to devote my energy to the learning of a multitude of things, I concentrated it upon a few particular things, such as, for instance, the analysis of Poe's place in American literature—an essay of mine, by the way, in the current *Atlantic*. Coming aboard, as I passed through the cabin, I had noticed with greedy eyes a stout gentleman reading the *Atlantic*, which was open at my very essay. And there it was again, the division of labour, the special knowledge of the pilot and captain which permitted the stout gentleman to read my special knowledge on Poe while they carried him safely from Sausalito to San Francisco.

A red-faced man, slamming the cabin door behind him and stumping out on the deck, interrupted my reflections, though I made a mental note of the topic for use in a projected essay which I had thought of calling "The Necessity for Freedom: A Plea for the Artist." The red-faced man shot a glance up at the pilot-house, gazed around at the fog, stumped across the deck and back (he evidently had artificial legs), and stood still by my side, legs wide apart, and with an expression of keen enjoyment on his face. I was not wrong when I decided that his days had been spent on the sea.

"It's nasty weather like this here that turns heads grey before their time," he said, with a nod toward the pilot-house.

"I had not thought there was any particular strain," I answered. "It seems as simple as A, B, C. They know the direction by compass, the distance, and the speed. I should not call it anything more than mathematical certainty."

"Strain!" he snorted. "Simple as A, B, C! Mathematical certainty!"

He seemed to brace himself up and lean backward against the air as he stared at me. "How about this here tide that's rushin' out through the Golden Gate?" he demanded, or bellowed, rather. "How fast is she ebbin'? What's the drift, eh? Listen to that, will you? A bell-buoy, and we're a-top of it! See 'em alterin' the course!"

From out of the fog came the mournful tolling of a bell, and I could see the pilot turning the wheel with great rapidity. The bell, which had seemed straight ahead, was now sounding from the side. Our own whistle was blowing hoarsely, and from time to time the sound of other whistles came to us from out of the fog.

"That's a ferry-boat of some sort," the new-comer said, indicating a whistle off to the right. "And there! D'ye hear that? Blown by mouth. Some scow schooner, most likely. Better watch out, Mr. Schooner-man. Ah, I thought so. Now hell's a poppin' for somebody!"

The unseen ferry-boat was blowing blast after blast, and the mouth-blown horn was tooting in terror-stricken fashion.

"And now they're payin' their respects to each other and tryin' to get clear," the red-faced man went on, as the hurried whistling ceased.

His face was shining, his eyes flashing with excitement as he translated into articulate language the speech of the horns and sirens. "That's a steam-siren a-goin' it over there to the left. And you hear that fellow with a frog in his throat—a steam schooner as near as I can judge, crawlin' in from the Heads against the tide."

A shrill little whistle, piping as if gone mad, came from directly ahead and from very near at hand. Gongs sounded on the *Martinez*. Our paddle-wheels stopped, their pulsing beat died away, and then they started again. The shrill little whistle, like the chirping of a cricket amid the cries of great beasts, shot through the fog from more to the side and swiftly grew faint and fainter. I looked to my companion for enlightenment.

"One of them dare-devil launches," he said. "I almost wish we'd sunk him, the little rip! They're the cause of more trouble. And what good are they? Any jackass gets aboard one and runs it from hell to breakfast, blowin' his whistle to beat the band and tellin' the rest of the world to look out for him, because he's comin' and can't look out for himself! Because he's comin'! And you've got to look out, too! Right of way! Common decency! They don't know the meanin' of it!"

I felt quite amused at his unwarranted choler, and while he stumped indignantly up and down I fell to dwelling upon the romance of the fog. And romantic it certainly was—the fog, like the grey shadow of infinite mystery, brooding over the whirling speck of earth; and men, mere motes of light and sparkle, cursed with an insane relish for work, riding their steeds of wood and steel through the heart of the mystery, groping their way blindly through the Unseen, and clamouring and clanging in confident speech the while their hearts are heavy with incertitude and fear.

The voice of my companion brought me back to myself with a laugh. I too had been groping and floundering, the while I thought I rode clear-eyed through the mystery.

"Hello! somebody comin' our way," he was saying. "And d'ye hear that? He's comin' fast. Walking right along. Guess he don't hear us yet. Wind's in wrong direction."

The fresh breeze was blowing right down upon us, and I could hear the whistle plainly, off to one side and a little ahead.

"Ferry-boat?" I asked.

He nodded, then added, "Or he wouldn't be keepin' up such a clip." He gave a short chuckle. "They're gettin' anxious up there."

I glanced up. The captain had thrust his head and shoulders out of the pilot-house, and was staring intently into the fog as though by sheer force of will he could penetrate it. His face was anxious, as was the face of my companion, who had stumped over to the rail and was gazing with a like intentness in the direction of the invisible danger.

Then everything happened, and with inconceivable rapidity. The fog seemed to break away as though split by a wedge, and the bow of a steamboat emerged, trailing fog-wreaths on either side like seaweed on the snout of Leviathan. I could see the pilot-house and a white-bearded man leaning partly out of it, on his elbows. He was clad in a blue uniform, and I remember noting how trim and quiet he was. His quietness, under the circumstances, was terrible. He accepted Destiny, marched hand in hand with it, and coolly measured the stroke. As he leaned there, he ran a calm and speculative eye over us, as though to determine the precise point of the collision, and took no notice whatever when our pilot, white with rage, shouted, "Now you've done it!"

On looking back, I realize that the remark was too obvious to make rejoinder necessary.

"Grab hold of something and hang on," the red-faced man said to me. All his bluster had gone, and he seemed to have caught the contagion of preternatural calm. "And listen to the women scream," he said grimly—almost bitterly, I thought, as though he had been through the experience before.

The vessels came together before I could follow his advice. We must have been struck squarely amidships, for I saw nothing, the strange steamboat having passed beyond my line of vision. The *Martinez* heeled over, sharply, and there was a crashing and rending of timber. I was thrown flat on the wet deck, and before I could scramble to my feet I heard the scream of the women. This it was, I am certain,—the most indescribable of blood-curdling sounds,—that threw me into a panic. I remembered the life-preservers stored in the cabin, but was met at the door and swept backward by a wild rush of men and women. What happened in the next few minutes I do not recollect, though I have a clear remembrance of pulling down life-preservers from the overhead racks, while the red-faced man fastened them about the bodies of an hysterical group of women. This memory is as distinct and sharp as that of any picture I have seen. It is a picture, and I can see it now,—the jagged edges of the hole in the side of the cabin, through which the grey fog swirled and eddied; the empty upholstered seats, littered with all the evidences of sudden flight, such as packages, hand satchels, umbrellas, and wraps; the stout gentleman who had been reading my essay, encased in cork and canvas, the magazine still in his hand, and asking me with monotonous insistence if I thought there was any danger; the red-faced man, stumping gallantly around on his artificial legs and buckling life-preservers on all comers; and finally, the screaming bedlam of women.

This it was, the screaming of the women, that most tried my nerves. It must have tried, too, the nerves of the red-faced man, for I have another picture which will never fade from my mind. The stout gentleman is stuffing the magazine into his overcoat pocket and looking on curiously. A tangled mass of women, with drawn, white faces and open mouths, is shrieking like a chorus of lost souls; and the red-faced man, his face now purplish with wrath, and with arms extended overhead as in the act of hurling thunderbolts, is shouting, "Shut up! Oh, shut up!"

I remember the scene impelled me to sudden laughter, and in the next instant I realized I was becoming hysterical myself; for these were women of my own kind, like my mother and sisters, with the fear of death upon them and unwilling to die. And I remember that the sounds they made reminded me of the squealing of pigs under the knife of the butcher, and I was struck with horror at the vividness of the analogy. These women, capable of the most sublime emotions, of the tenderest sympathies, were open-mouthed and screaming. They wanted to live, they were helpless, like rats in a trap, and they screamed.

The horror of it drove me out on deck. I was feeling sick and squeamish, and sat down on a bench. In a hazy way I saw and heard men rushing and shouting as they strove to lower the boats. It was just as I had read descriptions of such scenes in books. The tackles jammed. Nothing worked. One boat lowered away with the plugs out, filled with women and children and then with water, and capsized. Another boat had been lowered by one end, and still hung in the tackle by the other end, where it had been abandoned. Nothing was to be seen of the strange steamboat which had caused the disaster, though I heard men saying that she would undoubtedly send boats to our assistance.

I descended to the lower deck. The *Martinez* was sinking fast, for the water was very near. Numbers of the passengers were leaping overboard. Others, in the water, were clamouring to be taken aboard again. No one heeded them. A cry arose that we were sinking. I was seized by the consequent panic, and went over the side in a surge of bodies. How I went over I do not know, though I did know, and instantly, why those in the water were so desirous of getting back on the steamer. The water was cold—so cold that it was painful. The pang, as I plunged into it, was as quick and sharp as that of fire. It bit to the marrow. It was like the grip of death. I gasped with the anguish and shock of it, filling my lungs before the life-preserver popped me to the surface. The taste of the salt was strong in my mouth, and I was strangling with the acrid stuff in my throat and lungs.

But it was the cold that was most distressing. I felt that I could survive but a few minutes. People were struggling and floundering in the water about me. I could hear them crying out to one another. And I heard, also, the sound of oars. Evidently the strange steamboat had lowered its boats. As the time went by I marvelled that I was still alive. I had no sensation whatever in my lower limbs, while a chilling numbness was wrapping about my heart and creeping into it. Small waves, with spiteful foaming crests, continually broke over me and into my mouth, sending me off into more strangling paroxysms.

The noises grew indistinct, though I heard a final and despairing chorus of screams in the distance, and knew that the *Martinez* had gone down. Later,—how much later I have no knowledge,—I came to myself with a start of fear. I was alone. I could hear no calls or cries—only the sound of the waves, made weirdly hollow and reverberant by the fog. A panic in a crowd, which partakes of a sort of community of interest, is not so terrible as a panic when one is by oneself; and such a panic I now suffered. Whither was I drifting? The red-faced man had said that the tide was ebbing through the Golden Gate. Was I, then, being carried out to sea? And the life-preserver in which I floated? Was it not liable to go to pieces at any moment? I had heard of such things being made of paper and hollow rushes which quickly became saturated and lost all buoyancy. And I could not swim a stroke. And I was alone, floating, apparently, in the midst of a grey primordial vastness. I confess that a madness seized me, that I shrieked aloud as the women had shrieked, and beat the water with my numb hands.

How long this lasted I have no conception, for a blankness intervened, of which I remember no more than one remembers of troubled and painful sleep. When I aroused, it was as after centuries of time; and I saw, almost above me and emerging from the fog, the bow of a vessel, and three triangular sails, each shrewdly lapping the other and filled with wind. Where the bow cut the water there was a great foaming and gurgling, and I seemed directly in its path. I tried to cry out, but was too exhausted. The bow plunged down, just missing me and sending a swash of water clear over my head. Then the long, black side of the vessel began slipping past, so near that I could have touched it with my hands. I tried to reach it, in a mad resolve to claw into the wood with my nails, but my arms were heavy and lifeless. Again I strove to call out, but made no sound.

The stern of the vessel shot by, dropping, as it did so, into a hollow between the waves; and I caught a glimpse of a man standing at the wheel, and of another man who seemed to be doing little else than smoke a cigar. I saw the smoke issuing from his lips as he slowly turned his head and glanced out over the water in my direction. It was a careless, unpremeditated glance, one of those haphazard things men do when they have no immediate call to do anything in particular, but act because they are alive and must do something.

But life and death were in that glance. I could see the vessel being swallowed up in the fog; I saw the back of the man at the wheel, and the head of the other man turning, slowly turning, as his gaze struck the water and casually lifted along it toward me. His face wore an absent expression, as of deep thought, and I became afraid that if his eyes did light upon me he would nevertheless not see me. But his eyes did light upon me, and looked squarely into mine; and he did see me, for he sprang to the wheel, thrusting the other man aside, and whirled it round and round, hand over hand, at the same time shouting orders of some sort. The vessel seemed to go off at a tangent to its former course and leapt almost instantly from view into the fog.

I felt myself slipping into unconsciousness, and tried with all the power of my will to fight above the suffocating blankness and darkness that was rising around me. A little later I heard the stroke of oars, growing nearer and nearer, and the calls of a man. When he was very near I heard him crying, in vexed fashion, "Why in hell don't you sing out?" This meant me, I thought, and then the blankness and darkness rose over me.

CHAPTER II

I seemed swinging in a mighty rhythm through orbit vastness. Sparkling points of light spluttered and shot past me. They were stars, I knew, and flaring comets, that peopled my flight among the suns. As I reached the limit of my swing and prepared to rush back on the counter swing, a great gong struck and thundered. For an immeasurable period, lapped in the rippling of placid centuries, I enjoyed and pondered my tremendous flight.

But a change came over the face of the dream, for a dream I told myself it must be. My rhythm grew shorter and shorter. I was jerked from swing to counter swing with irritating haste. I could scarcely catch my breath, so fiercely was I impelled through the heavens. The gong thundered more frequently and more furiously. I grew to await it with a nameless dread. Then it seemed as though I were being dragged over rasping sands, white and hot in the sun. This gave place to a sense of intolerable anguish. My skin was scorching in the torment of fire. The gong clanged and knelled. The sparkling points of light flashed past me in an interminable stream, as though the whole sidereal system were dropping into the void. I gasped, caught my breath painfully, and opened my eyes. Two men were kneeling beside me, working over me. My mighty rhythm was the lift and forward plunge of a ship on the sea. The terrific gong was a frying-pan, hanging on the wall, that rattled and clattered with each leap of the ship. The rasping, scorching sands were a man's hard hands chafing my naked chest. I squirmed under the pain of it, and half lifted my head. My chest was raw and red, and I could see tiny blood globules starting through the torn and inflamed cuticle.

"That'll do, Yonson," one of the men said. "Carn't yer see you've bloomin' well rubbed all the gent's skin orf?"

The man addressed as Yonson, a man of the heavy Scandinavian type, ceased chafing me, and arose awkwardly to his feet. The man who had spoken to him was clearly a Cockney, with the clean lines and weakly pretty, almost effeminate, face of the man who has absorbed the sound of Bow Bells with his mother's milk. A draggled muslin cap on his head and a dirty gunny-sack about his slim hips proclaimed him cook of the decidedly dirty ship's galley in which I found myself.

"An' 'ow yer feelin' now, sir?" he asked, with the subservient smirk which comes only of generations of tip-seeking ancestors.

For reply, I twisted weakly into a sitting posture, and was helped by Yonson to my feet. The rattle and bang of the frying-pan was grating horribly on my nerves. I could not collect my thoughts. Clutching the woodwork of the galley for support,—and I confess the grease with which it was scummed put my teeth on edge,—I reached across a hot cooking-range to the offending utensil, unhooked it, and wedged it securely into the coal-box.

The cook grinned at my exhibition of nerves, and thrust into my hand a steaming mug with an "'Ere, this'll do yer good." It was a nauseous mess,—ship's coffee,—but the heat of it was revivifying. Between gulps of the molten stuff I glanced down at my raw and bleeding chest and turned to the Scandinavian.

"Thank you, Mr. Yonson," I said; "but don't you think your measures were rather heroic?"

It was because he understood the reproof of my action, rather than of my words, that he held up his palm for inspection. It was remarkably calloused. I passed my hand over the horny projections, and my teeth went on edge once more from the horrible rasping sensation produced.

"My name is Johnson, not Yonson," he said, in very good, though slow, English, with no more than a shade of accent to it.

There was mild protest in his pale blue eyes, and withal a timid frankness and manliness that quite won me to him.

"Thank you, Mr. Johnson," I corrected, and reached out my hand for his.

He hesitated, awkward and bashful, shifted his weight from one leg to the other, then blunderingly gripped my hand in a hearty shake.

"Have you any dry clothes I may put on?" I asked the cook.

"Yes, sir," he answered, with cheerful alacrity. "I'll run down an' tyke a look over my kit, if you've no objections, sir, to wearin' my things."

He dived out of the galley door, or glided rather, with a swiftness and smoothness of gait that struck me as being not so much cat-like as oily. In fact, this oiliness, or greasiness, as I was later to learn, was probably the most salient expression of his personality.

"And where am I?" I asked Johnson, whom I took, and rightly, to be one of the sailors. "What vessel is this, and where is she bound?"

"Off the Farallones, heading about sou-west," he answered, slowly and methodically, as though groping for his best English, and rigidly observing the order of my queries. "The schooner *Ghost*, bound seal-hunting to Japan."

"And who is the captain? I must see him as soon as I am dressed."

Johnson looked puzzled and embarrassed. He hesitated while he groped in his vocabulary and framed a complete answer. "The cap'n is Wolf Larsen, or so men call him. I never heard his other name. But you better speak soft with him. He is mad this morning. The mate—"

But he did not finish. The cook had glided in.

"Better sling yer 'ook out of 'ere, Yonson," he said. "The old man'll be wantin' yer on deck, an' this ayn't no d'y to fall foul of 'im."

Johnson turned obediently to the door, at the same time, over the cook's shoulder, favouring me with an amazingly solemn and portentous wink as though to emphasize his interrupted remark and the need for me to be soft-spoken with the captain.

Hanging over the cook's arm was a loose and crumpled array of evil-looking and sour-smelling garments.

"They was put aw'y wet, sir," he vouchsafed explanation. "But you'll 'ave to make them do till I dry yours out by the fire."

Clinging to the woodwork, staggering with the roll of the ship, and aided by the cook, I managed to slip into a rough woollen undershirt. On the instant my flesh was creeping and crawling from the harsh contact. He noticed my involuntary twitching and grimacing, and smirked:

"I only 'ope yer don't ever 'ave to get used to such as that in this life, 'cos you've got a bloomin' soft skin, that you 'ave, more like a lydy's than any I know of. I was bloomin' well sure you was a gentleman as soon as I set eyes on yer."

I had taken a dislike to him at first, and as he helped to dress me this dislike increased. There was something repulsive about his touch. I shrank from his hand; my flesh revolted. And between this and the smells arising from various pots boiling and bubbling on the galley fire, I was in haste to get out into the fresh air. Further, there was the need of seeing the captain about what arrangements could be made for getting me ashore.

A cheap cotton shirt, with frayed collar and a bosom discoloured with what I took to be ancient blood-stains, was put on me amid a running and apologetic fire of comment. A pair of workman's brogans encased my feet, and for trousers I was furnished with a pair of pale blue, washed-out overalls, one leg of which was fully ten inches shorter than the other. The abbreviated leg looked as though the devil had there clutched for the Cockney's soul and missed the shadow for the substance.

"And whom have I to thank for this kindness?" I asked, when I stood completely arrayed, a tiny boy's cap on my head, and for coat a dirty, striped cotton jacket which ended at the small of my back and the sleeves of which reached just below my elbows.

The cook drew himself up in a smugly humble fashion, a deprecating smirk on his face. Out of my experience with stewards on the Atlantic liners at the end of the voyage, I could have sworn he was waiting for his tip. From my fuller knowledge of the creature I now know that the posture was unconscious. An hereditary servility, no doubt, was responsible.

"Mugridge, sir," he fawned, his effeminate features running into a greasy smile. "Thomas Mugridge, sir, an' at yer service."

"All right, Thomas," I said. "I shall not forget you—when my clothes are dry."

A soft light suffused his face and his eyes glistened, as though somewhere in the deeps of his being his ancestors had quickened and stirred with dim memories of tips received in former lives.

"Thank you, sir," he said, very gratefully and very humbly indeed.

Precisely in the way that the door slid back, he slid aside, and I stepped out on deck. I was still weak from my prolonged immersion. A puff of wind caught me,—and I staggered across the moving deck to a corner of the cabin, to which I clung for support. The schooner, heeled over far out from the perpendicular, was bowing and plunging into the long Pacific roll. If she were heading south-west as Johnson had said, the wind, then, I calculated, was blowing nearly from the south. The fog was gone, and in its place the sun sparkled crisply on the surface of the water, I turned to the east, where I knew California must lie, but could see nothing save low-lying fog-banks—the same fog, doubtless, that had brought about the disaster to the *Martinez* and placed me in my present situation. To the north, and not far away, a group of naked rocks thrust above the sea, on one of which I could distinguish a lighthouse. In the south-west, and almost in our course, I saw the pyramidal loom of some vessel's sails.

Having completed my survey of the horizon, I turned to my more immediate surroundings. My first thought was that a man who had come through a collision and rubbed shoulders with death merited more attention than I received. Beyond a sailor at the wheel who stared curiously across the top of the cabin, I attracted no notice whatever.

Everybody seemed interested in what was going on amid ships. There, on a hatch, a large man was lying on his back. He was fully clothed, though his shirt was ripped open in front. Nothing was to be seen of his chest, however, for it was covered with a mass of black hair, in appearance like the furry coat of a dog. His face and neck were hidden beneath a black beard, intershot with grey, which would have been stiff and bushy had it not been limp and draggled and dripping with water. His eyes were closed, and he was apparently unconscious; but his mouth was wide open, his breast, heaving as though from suffocation as he laboured noisily for breath. A sailor, from time to time and quite methodically, as a matter of routine, dropped a canvas bucket into the ocean at the end of a rope, hauled it in hand under hand, and sluiced its contents over the prostrate man.

Pacing back and forth the length of the hatchways and savagely chewing the end of a cigar, was the man whose casual glance had rescued me from the sea. His height was probably five feet ten inches, or ten and a half; but my first impression, or feel of the man, was not of this, but of his strength. And yet, while he was of massive build, with broad shoulders and deep chest, I could not characterize his strength as massive. It was what might be termed a sinewy, knotty strength, of the kind we ascribe to lean and wiry men, but which, in him, because of his heavy build, partook more of the enlarged gorilla order. Not that in appearance he seemed in the least gorilla-like. What I am striving to express is this strength itself, more as a thing apart from his physical semblance. It was a strength we are wont to associate with things primitive, with wild animals, and the creatures we imagine our tree-dwelling prototypes to have been—a strength savage, ferocious, alive in itself, the essence of life in that it is the potency of motion, the elemental stuff itself out of which the many forms of life have been moulded; in short, that which writhes in the body of a snake when the head is cut off, and the snake, as a snake, is dead, or which lingers in the shapeless lump of turtle-meat and recoils and quivers from the prod of a finger.

Such was the impression of strength I gathered from this man who paced up and down. He was firmly planted on his legs; his feet struck the deck squarely and with surety; every movement of a muscle, from the heave of the shoulders to the tightening of the lips about the cigar, was decisive, and seemed to come out of a strength that was excessive and overwhelming. In fact, though this strength pervaded every action of his, it seemed but the advertisement of a greater strength that lurked within, that lay dormant and no more than stirred from time to time, but which might arouse, at any moment, terrible and compelling, like the rage of a lion or the wrath of a storm.

The cook stuck his head out of the galley door and grinned encouragingly at me, at the same time jerking his thumb in the direction of the man who paced up and down by the hatchway. Thus I was given to understand that he was the captain, the "Old Man," in the cook's vernacular, the individual whom I must interview and put to the trouble of somehow getting me ashore. I had half started forward, to get over with what I was certain would be a stormy five minutes, when a more violent suffocating paroxysm seized the unfortunate person who was lying on his back. He wrenched and writhed about convulsively. The chin, with the damp black beard, pointed higher in the air as the back muscles stiffened and the chest swelled in an unconscious and instinctive effort to get more air. Under the whiskers, and all unseen, I knew that the skin was taking on a purplish hue.

The captain, or Wolf Larsen, as men called him, ceased pacing and gazed down at the dying man. So fierce had this final struggle become that the sailor paused in the act of flinging more water over him and stared curiously, the canvas bucket partly tilted and dripping its contents to the deck. The dying man beat a tattoo on the hatch with his heels, straightened out his legs, and stiffened in one great tense effort, and rolled his head from side to side. Then the muscles relaxed, the head stopped rolling, and a sigh, as of profound relief, floated upward from his lips. The jaw dropped, the upper lip lifted, and two rows of tobacco-discoloured teeth appeared. It seemed as though his features had frozen into a diabolical grin at the world he had left and outwitted.

Then a most surprising thing occurred. The captain broke loose upon the dead man like a thunderclap. Oaths rolled from his lips in a continuous stream. And they were not namby-pamby oaths, or mere expressions of indecency. Each word was a blasphemy, and there were many words. They crisped and crackled like electric sparks. I had never heard anything like it in my life, nor could I have conceived it possible. With a turn for literary expression myself, and a penchant for forcible figures and phrases, I appreciated, as no other listener, I dare say, the peculiar vividness and strength and absolute blasphemy of his metaphors. The cause of it all, as near as I could make out, was that the man, who was mate, had gone on a debauch before leaving San Francisco, and then had the poor taste to die at the beginning of the voyage and leave Wolf Larsen short-handed.

It should be unnecessary to state, at least to my friends, that I was shocked. Oaths and vile language of any sort had always been repellent to me. I felt a wilting sensation, a sinking at the heart, and, I might just as well say, a giddiness. To me, death had always been invested with solemnity and dignity. It had been peaceful in its occurrence, sacred in its ceremonial. But death in its more sordid and terrible aspects was a thing with which I had been unacquainted till now. As I say, while I appreciated the power of the terrific denunciation that swept out of Wolf Larsen's mouth, I was inexpressibly shocked. The scorching torrent was enough to wither the face of the corpse. I should not have been surprised if the wet black beard had frizzled and curled and flared up in smoke and flame. But the dead man was unconcerned. He continued to grin with a sardonic humour, with a cynical mockery and defiance. He was master of the situation.

CHAPTER III

Wolf Larsen ceased swearing as suddenly as he had begun. He relighted his cigar and glanced around. His eyes chanced upon the cook.

"Well, Cooky?" he began, with a suaveness that was cold and of the temper of steel.

"Yes, sir," the cook eagerly interpolated, with appeasing and apologetic servility.

"Don't you think you've stretched that neck of yours just about enough? It's unhealthy, you know. The mate's gone, so I can't afford to lose you too. You must be very, very careful of your health, Cooky. Understand?"

His last word, in striking contrast with the smoothness of his previous utterance, snapped like the lash of a whip. The cook quailed under it.

"Yes, sir," was the meek reply, as the offending head disappeared into the galley.

At this sweeping rebuke, which the cook had only pointed, the rest of the crew became uninterested and fell to work at one task or another. A number of men, however, who were lounging about a companion-way between the galley and hatch, and who did not seem to be sailors, continued talking in low tones with one another. These, I afterward learned, were the hunters, the men who shot the seals, and a very superior breed to common sailor-folk.

"Johansen!" Wolf Larsen called out. A sailor stepped forward obediently. "Get your palm and needle and sew the beggar up. You'll find some old canvas in the sail-locker. Make it do."

"What'll I put on his feet, sir?" the man asked, after the customary "Ay, ay, sir."

"We'll see to that," Wolf Larsen answered, and elevated his voice in a call of "Cooky!"

Thomas Mugridge popped out of his galley like a jack-in-the-box.

"Go below and fill a sack with coal."

"Any of you fellows got a Bible or Prayer-book?" was the captain's next demand, this time of the hunters lounging about the companion-way.

They shook their heads, and some one made a jocular remark which I did not catch, but which raised a general laugh.

Wolf Larsen made the same demand of the sailors. Bibles and Prayer-books seemed scarce articles, but one of the men volunteered to pursue the quest amongst the watch below, returning in a minute with the information that there was none.

The captain shrugged his shoulders. "Then we'll drop him over without any palavering, unless our clerical-looking castaway has the burial service at sea by heart."

CHAPTER III

By this time he had swung fully around and was facing me. "You're a preacher, aren't you?" he asked.

The hunters,—there were six of them,—to a man, turned and regarded me. I was painfully aware of my likeness to a scarecrow. A laugh went up at my appearance,—a laugh that was not lessened or softened by the dead man stretched and grinning on the deck before us; a laugh that was as rough and harsh and frank as the sea itself; that arose out of coarse feelings and blunted sensibilities, from natures that knew neither courtesy nor gentleness.

Wolf Larsen did not laugh, though his grey eyes lighted with a slight glint of amusement; and in that moment, having stepped forward quite close to him, I received my first impression of the man himself, of the man as apart from his body, and from the torrent of blasphemy I had heard him spew forth. The face, with large features and strong lines, of the square order, yet well filled out, was apparently massive at first sight; but again, as with the body, the massiveness seemed to vanish, and a conviction to grow of a tremendous and excessive mental or spiritual strength that lay behind, sleeping in the deeps of his being. The jaw, the chin, the brow rising to a goodly height and swelling heavily above the eyes,—these, while strong in themselves, unusually strong, seemed to speak an immense vigour or virility of spirit that lay behind and beyond and out of sight. There was no sounding such a spirit, no measuring, no determining of metes and bounds, nor neatly classifying in some pigeon-hole with others of similar type.

The eyes—and it was my destiny to know them well—were large and handsome, wide apart as the true artist's are wide, sheltering under a heavy brow and arched over by thick black eyebrows. The eyes themselves were of that baffling protean grey which is never twice the same; which runs through many shades and colourings like intershot silk in sunshine; which is grey, dark and light, and greenish-grey, and sometimes of the clear azure of the deep sea. They were eyes that masked the soul with a thousand guises, and that sometimes opened, at rare moments, and allowed it to rush up as though it were about to fare forth nakedly into the world on some wonderful adventure,—eyes that could brood with the hopeless sombreness of leaden skies; that could snap and crackle points of fire like those which sparkle from a whirling sword; that could grow chill as an arctic landscape, and yet again, that could warm and soften and be all a-dance with love-lights, intense and masculine, luring and compelling, which at the same time fascinate and dominate women till they surrender in a gladness of joy and of relief and sacrifice.

But to return. I told him that, unhappily for the burial service, I was not a preacher, when he sharply demanded:

"What do you do for a living?"

I confess I had never had such a question asked me before, nor had I ever canvassed it. I was quite taken aback, and before I could find myself had sillily stammered, "I—I am a gentleman."

His lip curled in a swift sneer.

"I have worked, I do work," I cried impetuously, as though he were my judge and I required vindication, and at the same time very much aware of my arrant idiocy in discussing the subject at all.

"For your living?"

There was something so imperative and masterful about him that I was quite beside myself—"rattled," as Furuseth would have termed it, like a quaking child before a stern school-master.

"Who feeds you?" was his next question.

"I have an income," I answered stoutly, and could have bitten my tongue the next instant. "All of which, you will pardon my observing, has nothing whatsoever to do with what I wish to see you about."

But he disregarded my protest.

"Who earned it? Eh? I thought so. Your father. You stand on dead men's legs. You've never had any of your own. You couldn't walk alone between two sunrises and hustle the meat for your belly for three meals. Let me see your hand."

His tremendous, dormant strength must have stirred, swiftly and accurately, or I must have slept a moment, for before I knew it he had stepped two paces forward, gripped my right hand in his, and held it up for inspection. I tried to withdraw it, but his fingers tightened, without visible effort, till I thought mine would be crushed. It is hard to maintain one's dignity under such circumstances. I could not squirm or struggle like a schoolboy. Nor could I attack such a creature who had but to twist my arm to break it. Nothing remained but to stand still and accept the indignity. I had time to notice that the pockets of the dead man had been emptied on the deck, and that his body and his grin had been wrapped from view in canvas, the folds of which the sailor, Johansen, was sewing together with coarse white twine, shoving the needle through with a leather contrivance fitted on the palm of his hand.

Wolf Larsen dropped my hand with a flirt of disdain.

"Dead men's hands have kept it soft. Good for little else than dish-washing and scullion work."

"I wish to be put ashore," I said firmly, for I now had myself in control. "I shall pay you whatever you judge your delay and trouble to be worth."

He looked at me curiously. Mockery shone in his eyes.

"I have a counter proposition to make, and for the good of your soul. My mate's gone, and there'll be a lot of promotion. A sailor comes aft to take mate's place, cabin-boy goes for'ard to take sailor's place, and you take the cabin-boy's place, sign the articles for the cruise, twenty dollars per month and found. Now what do you say? And mind you, it's for your own soul's sake. It will be the making of you. You might learn in time to stand on your own legs, and perhaps to toddle along a bit."

But I took no notice. The sails of the vessel I had seen off to the south-west had grown larger and plainer. They were of the same schooner-rig as the *Ghost*, though the hull itself, I could see, was smaller. She was a pretty sight, leaping and flying toward us, and evidently bound to pass at close range. The wind had been momentarily increasing, and the sun, after a few angry gleams, had disappeared. The sea had turned a dull leaden grey and grown rougher, and was now tossing foaming whitecaps to the sky. We were travelling faster, and heeled farther over. Once, in a gust, the rail dipped under the sea, and the decks on that side were for the moment awash with water that made a couple of the hunters hastily lift their feet.

"That vessel will soon be passing us," I said, after a moment's pause. "As she is going in the opposite direction, she is very probably bound for San Francisco."

"Very probably," was Wolf Larsen's answer, as he turned partly away from me and cried out, "Cooky! Oh, Cooky!"

CHAPTER III

The Cockney popped out of the galley.

"Where's that boy? Tell him I want him."

"Yes, sir;" and Thomas Mugridge fled swiftly aft and disappeared down another companion-way near the wheel. A moment later he emerged, a heavy-set young fellow of eighteen or nineteen, with a glowering, villainous countenance, trailing at his heels.

"'Ere 'e is, sir," the cook said.

But Wolf Larsen ignored that worthy, turning at once to the cabin-boy.

"What's your name, boy?"

"George Leach, sir," came the sullen answer, and the boy's bearing showed clearly that he divined the reason for which he had been summoned.

"Not an Irish name," the captain snapped sharply. "O'Toole or McCarthy would suit your mug a damn sight better. Unless, very likely, there's an Irishman in your mother's woodpile."

I saw the young fellow's hands clench at the insult, and the blood crawl scarlet up his neck.

"But let that go," Wolf Larsen continued. "You may have very good reasons for forgetting your name, and I'll like you none the worse for it as long as you toe the mark. Telegraph Hill, of course, is your port of entry. It sticks out all over your mug. Tough as they make them and twice as nasty. I know the kind. Well, you can make up your mind to have it taken out of you on this craft. Understand? Who shipped you, anyway?"

"McCready and Swanson."

"Sir!" Wolf Larsen thundered.

"McCready and Swanson, sir," the boy corrected, his eyes burning with a bitter light.

"Who got the advance money?"

"They did, sir."

"I thought as much. And damned glad you were to let them have it. Couldn't make yourself scarce too quick, with several gentlemen you may have heard of looking for you."

The boy metamorphosed into a savage on the instant. His body bunched together as though for a spring, and his face became as an infuriated beast's as he snarled, "It's a—"

"A what?" Wolf Larsen asked, a peculiar softness in his voice, as though he were overwhelmingly curious to hear the unspoken word.

The boy hesitated, then mastered his temper. "Nothin', sir. I take it back."

"And you have shown me I was right." This with a gratified smile. "How old are you?"

"Just turned sixteen, sir,"

"A lie. You'll never see eighteen again. Big for your age at that, with muscles like a horse. Pack up your kit and go for'ard into the fo'c'sle. You're a boat-puller now. You're promoted; see?"

Without waiting for the boy's acceptance, the captain turned to the sailor who had just finished the gruesome task of sewing up the corpse. "Johansen, do you know anything about navigation?"

"No, sir,"

"Well, never mind; you're mate just the same. Get your traps aft into the mate's berth."

"Ay, ay, sir," was the cheery response, as Johansen started forward.

In the meantime the erstwhile cabin-boy had not moved. "What are you waiting for?" Wolf Larsen demanded.

"I didn't sign for boat-puller, sir," was the reply. "I signed for cabin-boy. An' I don't want no boat-pullin' in mine."

"Pack up and go for'ard."

This time Wolf Larsen's command was thrillingly imperative. The boy glowered sullenly, but refused to move.

Then came another stirring of Wolf Larsen's tremendous strength. It was utterly unexpected, and it was over and done with between the ticks of two seconds. He had sprung fully six feet across the deck and driven his fist into the other's stomach. At the same moment, as though I had been struck myself, I felt a sickening shock in the pit of my stomach. I instance this to show the sensitiveness of my nervous organization at the time, and how unused I was to spectacles of brutality. The cabin-boy—and he weighed one hundred and sixty-five at the very least—crumpled up. His body wrapped limply about the fist like a wet rag about a stick. He lifted into the air, described a short curve, and struck the deck alongside the corpse on his head and shoulders, where he lay and writhed about in agony.

"Well?" Larsen asked of me. "Have you made up your mind?"

I had glanced occasionally at the approaching schooner, and it was now almost abreast of us and not more than a couple of hundred yards away. It was a very trim and neat little craft. I could see a large, black number on one of its sails, and I had seen pictures of pilot-boats.

"What vessel is that?" I asked.

"The pilot-boat *Lady Mine*," Wolf Larsen answered grimly. "Got rid of her pilots and running into San Francisco. She'll be there in five or six hours with this wind."

"Will you please signal it, then, so that I may be put ashore."

"Sorry, but I've lost the signal book overboard," he remarked, and the group of hunters grinned.

I debated a moment, looking him squarely in the eyes. I had seen the frightful treatment of the cabin-boy, and knew that I should very probably receive the same, if not worse. As I say, I debated with myself, and then I did what I consider the bravest act of my life. I ran to the side, waving my arms and shouting:

"*Lady Mine* ahoy! Take me ashore! A thousand dollars if you take me ashore!"

I waited, watching two men who stood by the wheel, one of them steering. The other was lifting a megaphone to his lips. I did not turn my head, though I expected every moment a killing blow from the human brute behind me. At last, after what seemed centuries, unable longer to stand the strain, I looked around. He had not moved. He was standing in the same position, swaying easily to the roll of the ship and lighting a fresh cigar.

"What is the matter? Anything wrong?"

This was the cry from the *Lady Mine*.

"Yes!" I shouted, at the top of my lungs. "Life or death! One thousand dollars if you take me ashore!"

CHAPTER III

"Too much 'Frisco tanglefoot for the health of my crew!" Wolf Larsen shouted after. "This one"—indicating me with his thumb—"fancies sea-serpents and monkeys just now!"

The man on the *Lady Mine* laughed back through the megaphone. The pilot-boat plunged past.

"Give him hell for me!" came a final cry, and the two men waved their arms in farewell.

I leaned despairingly over the rail, watching the trim little schooner swiftly increasing the bleak sweep of ocean between us. And she would probably be in San Francisco in five or six hours! My head seemed bursting. There was an ache in my throat as though my heart were up in it. A curling wave struck the side and splashed salt spray on my lips. The wind puffed strongly, and the *Ghost* heeled far over, burying her lee rail. I could hear the water rushing down upon the deck.

When I turned around, a moment later, I saw the cabin-boy staggering to his feet. His face was ghastly white, twitching with suppressed pain. He looked very sick.

"Well, Leach, are you going for'ard?" Wolf Larsen asked.

"Yes, sir," came the answer of a spirit cowed.

"And you?" I was asked.

"I'll give you a thousand—" I began, but was interrupted.

"Stow that! Are you going to take up your duties as cabin-boy? Or do I have to take you in hand?"

What was I to do? To be brutally beaten, to be killed perhaps, would not help my case. I looked steadily into the cruel grey eyes. They might have been granite for all the light and warmth of a human soul they contained. One may see the soul stir in some men's eyes, but his were bleak, and cold, and grey as the sea itself.

"Well?"

"Yes," I said.

"Say 'yes, sir.'"

"Yes, sir," I corrected.

"What is your name?"

"Van Weyden, sir."

"First name?"

"Humphrey, sir; Humphrey Van Weyden."

"Age?"

"Thirty-five, sir."

"That'll do. Go to the cook and learn your duties."

And thus it was that I passed into a state of involuntary servitude to Wolf Larsen. He was stronger than I, that was all. But it was very unreal at the time. It is no less unreal now that I look back upon it. It will always be to me a monstrous, inconceivable thing, a horrible nightmare.

"Hold on, don't go yet."

I stopped obediently in my walk toward the galley.

"Johansen, call all hands. Now that we've everything cleaned up, we'll have the funeral and get the decks cleared of useless lumber."

While Johansen was summoning the watch below, a couple of sailors, under the captain's direction, laid the canvas-swathed corpse upon a hatch-cover. On either side the deck, against the rail and bottoms up, were lashed a number of small boats.

Several men picked up the hatch-cover with its ghastly freight, carried it to the lee side, and rested it on the boats, the feet pointing overboard. To the feet was attached the sack of coal which the cook had fetched.

I had always conceived a burial at sea to be a very solemn and awe-inspiring event, but I was quickly disillusioned, by this burial at any rate. One of the hunters, a little dark-eyed man whom his mates called "Smoke," was telling stories, liberally intersprinkled with oaths and obscenities; and every minute or so the group of hunters gave mouth to a laughter that sounded to me like a wolf-chorus or the barking of hell-hounds. The sailors trooped noisily aft, some of the watch below rubbing the sleep from their eyes, and talked in low tones together. There was an ominous and worried expression on their faces. It was evident that they did not like the outlook of a voyage under such a captain and begun so inauspiciously. From time to time they stole glances at Wolf Larsen, and I could see that they were apprehensive of the man.

He stepped up to the hatch-cover, and all caps came off. I ran my eyes over them—twenty men all told; twenty-two including the man at the wheel and myself. I was pardonably curious in my survey, for it appeared my fate to be pent up with them on this miniature floating world for I knew not how many weeks or months. The sailors, in the main, were English and Scandinavian, and their faces seemed of the heavy, stolid order. The hunters, on the other hand, had stronger and more diversified faces, with hard lines and the marks of the free play of passions. Strange to say, and I noted it all once, Wolf Larsen's features showed no such evil stamp. There seemed nothing vicious in them. True, there were lines, but they were the lines of decision and firmness. It seemed, rather, a frank and open countenance, which frankness or openness was enhanced by the fact that he was smooth-shaven. I could hardly believe—until the next incident occurred—that it was the face of a man who could behave as he had behaved to the cabin-boy.

At this moment, as he opened his mouth to speak, puff after puff struck the schooner and pressed her side under. The wind shrieked a wild song through the rigging. Some of the hunters glanced anxiously aloft. The lee rail, where the dead man lay, was buried in the sea, and as the schooner lifted and righted the water swept across the deck wetting us above our shoe-tops. A shower of rain drove down upon us, each drop stinging like a hailstone. As it passed, Wolf Larsen began to speak, the bare-headed men swaying in unison, to the heave and lunge of the deck.

"I only remember one part of the service," he said, "and that is, 'And the body shall be cast into the sea.' So cast it in."

He ceased speaking. The men holding the hatch-cover seemed perplexed, puzzled no doubt by the briefness of the ceremony. He burst upon them in a fury.

"Lift up that end there, damn you! What the hell's the matter with you?"

They elevated the end of the hatch-cover with pitiful haste, and, like a dog flung overside, the dead man slid feet first into the sea. The coal at his feet dragged him down. He was gone.

"Johansen," Wolf Larsen said briskly to the new mate, "keep all hands on deck now they're here. Get in the topsails and jibs and make a good job of it. We're in for a sou'-easter. Better reef the jib and mainsail too, while you're about it."

In a moment the decks were in commotion, Johansen bellowing orders and the men pulling or letting go ropes of various sorts—all naturally confusing to a landsman such as myself. But it was the heartlessness of it that especially struck me. The dead man was an episode that was past, an incident that was dropped, in a canvas covering with a sack of coal, while the ship sped along and her work went on. Nobody had been affected. The hunters were laughing at a fresh story of Smoke's; the men pulling and hauling, and two of them climbing aloft; Wolf Larsen was studying the clouding sky to windward; and the dead man, dying obscenely, buried sordidly, and sinking down, down—

Then it was that the cruelty of the sea, its relentlessness and awfulness, rushed upon me. Life had become cheap and tawdry, a beastly and inarticulate thing, a soulless stirring of the ooze and slime. I held on to the weather rail, close by the shrouds, and gazed out across the desolate foaming waves to the low-lying fog-banks that hid San Francisco and the California coast. Rain-squalls were driving in between, and I could scarcely see the fog. And this strange vessel, with its terrible men, pressed under by wind and sea and ever leaping up and out, was heading away into the south-west, into the great and lonely Pacific expanse.

CHAPTER IV

What happened to me next on the sealing-schooner *Ghost*, as I strove to fit into my new environment, are matters of humiliation and pain. The cook, who was called "the doctor" by the crew, "Tommy" by the hunters, and "Cooky" by Wolf Larsen, was a changed person. The difference worked in my status brought about a corresponding difference in treatment from him. Servile and fawning as he had been before, he was now as domineering and bellicose. In truth, I was no longer the fine gentleman with a skin soft as a "lydy's," but only an ordinary and very worthless cabin-boy.

He absurdly insisted upon my addressing him as Mr. Mugridge, and his behaviour and carriage were insufferable as he showed me my duties. Besides my work in the cabin, with its four small state-rooms, I was supposed to be his assistant in the galley, and my colossal ignorance concerning such things as peeling potatoes or washing greasy pots was a source of unending and sarcastic wonder to him. He refused to take into consideration what I was, or, rather, what my life and the things I was accustomed to had been. This was part of the attitude he chose to adopt toward me; and I confess, ere the day was done, that I hated him with more lively feelings than I had ever hated any one in my life before.

This first day was made more difficult for me from the fact that the *Ghost*, under close reefs (terms such as these I did not learn till later), was plunging through what Mr. Mugridge called an "'owlin' sou'-easter." At half-past five, under his directions, I set the table in the cabin, with rough-weather trays in place, and then carried the tea and cooked food down from the galley. In this connection I cannot forbear relating my first experience with a boarding sea.

"Look sharp or you'll get doused," was Mr. Mugridge's parting injunction, as I left the galley with a big tea-pot in one hand, and in the hollow of the other arm several loaves of fresh-baked bread. One of the hunters, a tall, loose-jointed chap named Henderson, was going aft at the time from the steerage (the name the hunters facetiously gave their midships sleeping quarters) to the cabin. Wolf Larsen was on the poop, smoking his everlasting cigar.

"'Ere she comes. Sling yer 'ook!" the cook cried.

I stopped, for I did not know what was coming, and saw the galley door slide shut with a bang. Then I saw Henderson leaping like a madman for the main rigging, up which he shot, on the inside, till he was many feet higher than my head. Also I saw a great wave, curling and foaming, poised far above the rail. I was directly under it.

CHAPTER IV

My mind did not work quickly, everything was so new and strange. I grasped that I was in danger, but that was all. I stood still, in trepidation. Then Wolf Larsen shouted from the poop:

"Grab hold something, you—you Hump!"

But it was too late. I sprang toward the rigging, to which I might have clung, and was met by the descending wall of water. What happened after that was very confusing. I was beneath the water, suffocating and drowning. My feet were out from under me, and I was turning over and over and being swept along I knew not where. Several times I collided against hard objects, once striking my right knee a terrible blow. Then the flood seemed suddenly to subside and I was breathing the good air again. I had been swept against the galley and around the steerage companion-way from the weather side into the lee scuppers. The pain from my hurt knee was agonizing. I could not put my weight on it, or, at least, I thought I could not put my weight on it; and I felt sure the leg was broken. But the cook was after me, shouting through the lee galley door:

"'Ere, you! Don't tyke all night about it! Where's the pot? Lost overboard? Serve you bloody well right if yer neck was broke!"

I managed to struggle to my feet. The great tea-pot was still in my hand. I limped to the galley and handed it to him. But he was consumed with indignation, real or feigned.

"Gawd blime me if you ayn't a slob. Wot 're you good for anyw'y, I'd like to know? Eh? Wot 're you good for any'wy? Cawn't even carry a bit of tea aft without losin' it. Now I'll 'ave to boil some more.

"An' wot 're you snifflin' about?" he burst out at me, with renewed rage. "'Cos you've 'urt yer pore little leg, pore little mamma's darlin'."

I was not sniffling, though my face might well have been drawn and twitching from the pain. But I called up all my resolution, set my teeth, and hobbled back and forth from galley to cabin and cabin to galley without further mishap. Two things I had acquired by my accident: an injured knee-cap that went undressed and from which I suffered for weary months, and the name of "Hump," which Wolf Larsen had called me from the poop. Thereafter, fore and aft, I was known by no other name, until the term became a part of my thought-processes and I identified it with myself, thought of myself as Hump, as though Hump were I and had always been I.

It was no easy task, waiting on the cabin table, where sat Wolf Larsen, Johansen, and the six hunters. The cabin was small, to begin with, and to move around, as I was compelled to, was not made easier by the schooner's violent pitching and wallowing. But what struck me most forcibly was the total lack of sympathy on the part of the men whom I served. I could feel my knee through my clothes, swelling, and swelling, and I was sick and faint from the pain of it. I could catch glimpses of my face, white and ghastly, distorted with pain, in the cabin mirror. All the men must have seen my condition, but not one spoke or took notice of me, till I was almost grateful to Wolf Larsen, later on (I was washing the dishes), when he said:

"Don't let a little thing like that bother you. You'll get used to such things in time. It may cripple you some, but all the same you'll be learning to walk.

"That's what you call a paradox, isn't it?" he added.

He seemed pleased when I nodded my head with the customary "Yes, sir."

"I suppose you know a bit about literary things? Eh? Good. I'll have some talks with you some time."

And then, taking no further account of me, he turned his back and went up on deck.

That night, when I had finished an endless amount of work, I was sent to sleep in the steerage, where I made up a spare bunk. I was glad to get out of the detestable presence of the cook and to be off my feet. To my surprise, my clothes had dried on me and there seemed no indications of catching cold, either from the last soaking or from the prolonged soaking from the foundering of the *Martinez*. Under ordinary circumstances, after all that I had undergone, I should have been fit for bed and a trained nurse.

But my knee was bothering me terribly. As well as I could make out, the kneecap seemed turned up on edge in the midst of the swelling. As I sat in my bunk examining it (the six hunters were all in the steerage, smoking and talking in loud voices), Henderson took a passing glance at it.

"Looks nasty," he commented. "Tie a rag around it, and it'll be all right."

That was all; and on the land I would have been lying on the broad of my back, with a surgeon attending on me, and with strict injunctions to do nothing but rest. But I must do these men justice. Callous as they were to my suffering, they were equally callous to their own when anything befell them. And this was due, I believe, first, to habit; and second, to the fact that they were less sensitively organized. I really believe that a finely-organized, high-strung man would suffer twice and thrice as much as they from a like injury.

Tired as I was,—exhausted, in fact,—I was prevented from sleeping by the pain in my knee. It was all I could do to keep from groaning aloud. At home I should undoubtedly have given vent to my anguish; but this new and elemental environment seemed to call for a savage repression. Like the savage, the attitude of these men was stoical in great things, childish in little things. I remember, later in the voyage, seeing Kerfoot, another of the hunters, lose a finger by having it smashed to a jelly; and he did not even murmur or change the expression on his face. Yet I have seen the same man, time and again, fly into the most outrageous passion over a trifle.

He was doing it now, vociferating, bellowing, waving his arms, and cursing like a fiend, and all because of a disagreement with another hunter as to whether a seal pup knew instinctively how to swim. He held that it did, that it could swim the moment it was born. The other hunter, Latimer, a lean, Yankee-looking fellow with shrewd, narrow-slitted eyes, held otherwise, held that the seal pup was born on the land for no other reason than that it could not swim, that its mother was compelled to teach it to swim as birds were compelled to teach their nestlings how to fly.

For the most part, the remaining four hunters leaned on the table or lay in their bunks and left the discussion to the two antagonists. But they were supremely interested, for every little while they ardently took sides, and sometimes all were talking at once, till their voices surged back and forth in waves of sound like mimic thunder-rolls in the confined space. Childish and immaterial as the topic was, the quality of their reasoning was still more childish and immaterial. In truth, there was very little reasoning or none at all. Their method was one of assertion, assumption, and denunciation. They proved that a seal pup could swim or not swim at birth by stating the proposition very bellicosely and then following it up with an attack on the opposing man's judgment, common sense, nationality, or past history. Rebuttal was precisely similar. I have related this in order to show the mental calibre of the men with whom I was thrown in contact. Intellectually they were children, inhabiting the physical forms of men.

And they smoked, incessantly smoked, using a coarse, cheap, and offensive-smelling tobacco. The air was thick and murky with the smoke of it; and this, combined with the violent movement of the ship as she struggled through the storm, would surely have made me sea-sick had I been a victim to that malady. As it was, it made me quite squeamish, though this nausea might have been due to the pain of my leg and exhaustion.

As I lay there thinking, I naturally dwelt upon myself and my situation. It was unparalleled, undreamed-of, that I, Humphrey Van Weyden, a scholar and a dilettante, if you please, in things artistic and literary, should be lying here on a Bering Sea seal-hunting schooner. Cabin-boy! I had never done any hard manual labour, or scullion labour, in my life. I had lived a placid, uneventful, sedentary existence all my days—the life of a scholar and a recluse on an assured and comfortable income. Violent life and athletic sports had never appealed to me. I had always been a book-worm; so my sisters and father had called me during my childhood. I had gone camping but once in my life, and then I left the party almost at its start and returned to the comforts and conveniences of a roof. And here I was, with dreary and endless vistas before me of table-setting, potato-peeling, and dish-washing. And I was not strong. The doctors had always said that I had a remarkable constitution, but I had never developed it or my body through exercise. My muscles were small and soft, like a woman's, or so the doctors had said time and again in the course of their attempts to persuade me to go in for physical-culture fads. But I had preferred to use my head rather than my body; and here I was, in no fit condition for the rough life in prospect.

These are merely a few of the things that went through my mind, and are related for the sake of vindicating myself in advance in the weak and helpless *rôle* I was destined to play. But I thought, also, of my mother and sisters, and pictured their grief. I was among the missing dead of the *Martinez* disaster, an unrecovered body. I could see the head-lines in the papers; the fellows at the University Club and the Bibelot shaking their heads and saying, "Poor chap!" And I could see Charley Furuseth, as I had said good-bye to him that morning, lounging in a dressing-gown on the be-pillowed window couch and delivering himself of oracular and pessimistic epigrams.

And all the while, rolling, plunging, climbing the moving mountains and falling and wallowing in the foaming valleys, the schooner *Ghost* was fighting her way farther and farther into the heart of the Pacific—and I was on her. I could hear the wind above. It came to my ears as a muffled roar. Now and again feet stamped overhead. An endless creaking was going on all about me, the woodwork and the fittings groaning and squeaking and complaining in a thousand keys. The hunters were still arguing and roaring like some semi-human amphibious breed. The air was filled with oaths and indecent expressions. I could see their faces, flushed and angry, the brutality distorted and emphasized by the sickly yellow of the sea-lamps which rocked back and forth with the ship. Through the dim smoke-haze the bunks looked like the sleeping dens of animals in a menagerie. Oilskins and sea-boots were hanging from the walls, and here and there rifles and shotguns rested securely in the racks. It was a sea-fitting for the buccaneers and pirates of by-gone years. My imagination ran riot, and still I could not sleep. And it was a long, long night, weary and dreary and long.

CHAPTER V

But my first night in the hunters' steerage was also my last. Next day Johansen, the new mate, was routed from the cabin by Wolf Larsen, and sent into the steerage to sleep thereafter, while I took possession of the tiny cabin state-room, which, on the first day of the voyage, had already had two occupants. The reason for this change was quickly learned by the hunters, and became the cause of a deal of grumbling on their part. It seemed that Johansen, in his sleep, lived over each night the events of the day. His incessant talking and shouting and bellowing of orders had been too much for Wolf Larsen, who had accordingly foisted the nuisance upon his hunters.

After a sleepless night, I arose weak and in agony, to hobble through my second day on the *Ghost*. Thomas Mugridge routed me out at half-past five, much in the fashion that Bill Sykes must have routed out his dog; but Mr. Mugridge's brutality to me was paid back in kind and with interest. The unnecessary noise he made (I had lain wide-eyed the whole night) must have awakened one of the hunters; for a heavy shoe whizzed through the semi-darkness, and Mr. Mugridge, with a sharp howl of pain, humbly begged everybody's pardon. Later on, in the galley, I noticed that his ear was bruised and swollen. It never went entirely back to its normal shape, and was called a "cauliflower ear" by the sailors.

The day was filled with miserable variety. I had taken my dried clothes down from the galley the night before, and the first thing I did was to exchange the cook's garments for them. I looked for my purse. In addition to some small change (and I have a good memory for such things), it had contained one hundred and eighty-five dollars in gold and paper. The purse I found, but its contents, with the exception of the small silver, had been abstracted. I spoke to the cook about it, when I went on deck to take up my duties in the galley, and though I had looked forward to a surly answer, I had not expected the belligerent harangue that I received.

"Look 'ere, 'Ump," he began, a malicious light in his eyes and a snarl in his throat; "d'ye want yer nose punched? If you think I'm a thief, just keep it to yerself, or you'll find 'ow bloody well mistyken you are. Strike me blind if this ayn't gratitude for yer! 'Ere you come, a pore mis'rable specimen of 'uman scum, an' I tykes yer into my galley an' treats yer 'ansom, an' this is wot I get for it. Nex' time you can go to 'ell, say I, an' I've a good mind to give you what-for anyw'y."

So saying, he put up his fists and started for me. To my shame be it, I cowered away from the blow and ran out the galley door. What else was I to do? Force, nothing but force, obtained on this brute-ship. Moral suasion was a thing unknown.

Picture it to yourself: a man of ordinary stature, slender of build, and with weak, undeveloped muscles, who has lived a peaceful, placid life, and is unused to violence of any sort—what could such a man possibly do? There was no more reason that I should stand and face these human beasts than that I should stand and face an infuriated bull.

So I thought it out at the time, feeling the need for vindication and desiring to be at peace with my conscience. But this vindication did not satisfy. Nor, to this day can I permit my manhood to look back upon those events and feel entirely exonerated. The situation was something that really exceeded rational formulas for conduct and demanded more than the cold conclusions of reason. When viewed in the light of for-formal logic, there is not one thing of which to be ashamed; but nevertheless a shame rises within me at the recollection, and in the pride of my manhood I feel that my manhood has in unaccountable ways been smirched and sullied.

All of which is neither here nor there. The speed with which I ran from the galley caused excruciating pain in my knee, and I sank down helplessly at the break of the poop. But the Cockney had not pursued me.

"Look at 'im run! Look at 'im run!" I could hear him crying. "An' with a gyme leg at that! Come on back, you pore little mamma's darling. I won't 'it yer; no, I won't."

I came back and went on with my work; and here the episode ended for the time, though further developments were yet to take place. I set the breakfast-table in the cabin, and at seven o'clock waited on the hunters and officers. The storm had evidently broken during the night, though a huge sea was still running and a stiff wind blowing. Sail had been made in the early watches, so that the *Ghost* was racing along under everything except the two topsails and the flying jib. These three sails, I gathered from the conversation, were to be set immediately after breakfast. I learned, also, that Wolf Larsen was anxious to make the most of the storm, which was driving him to the south-west into that portion of the sea where he expected to pick up with the north-east trades. It was before this steady wind that he hoped to make the major portion of the run to Japan, curving south into the tropics and north again as he approached the coast of Asia.

After breakfast I had another unenviable experience. When I had finished washing the dishes, I cleaned the cabin stove and carried the ashes up on deck to empty them. Wolf Larsen and Henderson were standing near the wheel, deep in conversation. The sailor, Johnson, was steering. As I started toward the weather side I saw him make a sudden motion with his head, which I mistook for a token of recognition and good-morning. In reality, he was attempting to warn me to throw my ashes over the lee side. Unconscious of my blunder, I passed by Wolf Larsen and the hunter and flung the ashes over the side to windward. The wind drove them back, and not only over me, but over Henderson and Wolf Larsen. The next instant the latter kicked me, violently, as a cur is kicked. I had not realized there could be so much pain in a kick. I reeled away from him and leaned against the cabin in a half-fainting condition. Everything was swimming before my eyes, and I turned sick. The nausea overpowered me, and I managed to crawl to the side of the vessel. But Wolf Larsen did not follow me up. Brushing the ashes from his clothes, he had resumed his conversation with Henderson. Johansen, who had seen the affair from the break of the poop, sent a couple of sailors aft to clean up the mess.

CHAPTER V

Later in the morning I received a surprise of a totally different sort. Following the cook's instructions, I had gone into Wolf Larsen's state-room to put it to rights and make the bed. Against the wall, near the head of the bunk, was a rack filled with books. I glanced over them, noting with astonishment such names as Shakespeare, Tennyson, Poe, and De Quincey. There were scientific works, too, among which were represented men such as Tyndall, Proctor, and Darwin. Astronomy and physics were represented, and I remarked Bulfinch's *Age of Fable*, Shaw's *History of English and American Literature*, and Johnson's *Natural History* in two large volumes. Then there were a number of grammars, such as Metcalf's, and Reed and Kellogg's; and I smiled as I saw a copy of *The Dean's English*.

I could not reconcile these books with the man from what I had seen of him, and I wondered if he could possibly read them. But when I came to make the bed I found, between the blankets, dropped apparently as he had sunk off to sleep, a complete Browning, the Cambridge Edition. It was open at "In a Balcony," and I noticed, here and there, passages underlined in pencil. Further, letting drop the volume during a lurch of the ship, a sheet of paper fell out. It was scrawled over with geometrical diagrams and calculations of some sort.

It was patent that this terrible man was no ignorant clod, such as one would inevitably suppose him to be from his exhibitions of brutality. At once he became an enigma. One side or the other of his nature was perfectly comprehensible; but both sides together were bewildering. I had already remarked that his language was excellent, marred with an occasional slight inaccuracy. Of course, in common speech with the sailors and hunters, it sometimes fairly bristled with errors, which was due to the vernacular itself; but in the few words he had held with me it had been clear and correct.

This glimpse I had caught of his other side must have emboldened me, for I resolved to speak to him about the money I had lost.

"I have been robbed," I said to him, a little later, when I found him pacing up and down the poop alone.

"Sir," he corrected, not harshly, but sternly.

"I have been robbed, sir," I amended.

"How did it happen?" he asked.

Then I told him the whole circumstance, how my clothes had been left to dry in the galley, and how, later, I was nearly beaten by the cook when I mentioned the matter.

He smiled at my recital. "Pickings," he concluded; "Cooky's pickings. And don't you think your miserable life worth the price? Besides, consider it a lesson. You'll learn in time how to take care of your money for yourself. I suppose, up to now, your lawyer has done it for you, or your business agent."

I could feel the quiet sneer through his words, but demanded, "How can I get it back again?"

"That's your look-out. You haven't any lawyer or business agent now, so you'll have to depend on yourself. When you get a dollar, hang on to it. A man who leaves his money lying around, the way you did, deserves to lose it. Besides, you have sinned. You have no right to put temptation in the way of your fellow-creatures. You tempted Cooky, and he fell. You have placed his immortal soul in jeopardy. By the way, do you believe in the immortal soul?"

His lids lifted lazily as he asked the question, and it seemed that the deeps were opening to me and that I was gazing into his soul. But it was an illusion. Far as it might have seemed, no man has ever seen very far into Wolf Larsen's soul, or seen it at all,—of this I am convinced. It was a very lonely soul, I was to learn, that never unmasked, though at rare moments it played at doing so.

"I read immortality in your eyes," I answered, dropping the "sir,"—an experiment, for I thought the intimacy of the conversation warranted it.

He took no notice. "By that, I take it, you see something that is alive, but that necessarily does not have to live for ever."

"I read more than that," I continued boldly.

"Then you read consciousness. You read the consciousness of life that it is alive; but still no further away, no endlessness of life."

How clearly he thought, and how well he expressed what he thought! From regarding me curiously, he turned his head and glanced out over the leaden sea to windward. A bleakness came into his eyes, and the lines of his mouth grew severe and harsh. He was evidently in a pessimistic mood.

"Then to what end?" he demanded abruptly, turning back to me. "If I am immortal—why?"

I halted. How could I explain my idealism to this man? How could I put into speech a something felt, a something like the strains of music heard in sleep, a something that convinced yet transcended utterance?

"What do you believe, then?" I countered.

"I believe that life is a mess," he answered promptly. "It is like yeast, a ferment, a thing that moves and may move for a minute, an hour, a year, or a hundred years, but that in the end will cease to move. The big eat the little that they may continue to move, the strong eat the weak that they may retain their strength. The lucky eat the most and move the longest, that is all. What do you make of those things?"

He swept his arm in an impatient gesture toward a number of the sailors who were working on some kind of rope stuff amidships.

"They move, so does the jelly-fish move. They move in order to eat in order that they may keep moving. There you have it. They live for their belly's sake, and the belly is for their sake. It's a circle; you get nowhere. Neither do they. In the end they come to a standstill. They move no more. They are dead."

"They have dreams," I interrupted, "radiant, flashing dreams—"

"Of grub," he concluded sententiously.

"And of more—"

"Grub. Of a larger appetite and more luck in satisfying it." His voice sounded harsh. There was no levity in it. "For, look you, they dream of making lucky voyages which will bring them more money, of becoming the mates of ships, of finding fortunes—in short, of being in a better position for preying on their fellows, of having all night in, good grub and somebody else to do the dirty work. You and I are just like them. There is no difference, except that we have eaten more and better. I am eating them now, and you too. But in the past you have eaten more than I have. You have slept in soft beds, and worn fine clothes, and eaten good meals. Who made those beds? and those clothes? and those meals? Not you. You never made anything in your own sweat. You live on an income which your father earned. You are like a frigate bird swooping down upon the boobies and robbing them of the fish they have caught. You are one with a crowd of men who have made what they call a government, who are masters of all the other men, and who eat the food the other men get and would like to eat themselves. You wear the warm clothes. They made the clothes, but they shiver in rags and ask you, the lawyer, or business agent who handles your money, for a job."

"But that is beside the matter," I cried.

"Not at all." He was speaking rapidly now, and his eyes were flashing. "It is piggishness, and it is life. Of what use or sense is an immortality of piggishness? What is the end? What is it all about? You have made no food. Yet the food you have eaten or wasted might have saved the lives of a score of wretches who made the food but did not eat it. What immortal end did you serve? or did they? Consider yourself and me. What does your boasted immortality amount to when your life runs foul of mine? You would like to go back to the land, which is a favourable place for your kind of piggishness. It is a whim of mine to keep you aboard this ship, where my piggishness flourishes. And keep you I will. I may make or break you. You may die to-day, this week, or next month. I could kill you now, with a blow of my fist, for you are a miserable weakling. But if we are immortal, what is the reason for this? To be piggish as you and I have been all our lives does not seem to be just the thing for immortals to be doing. Again, what's it all about? Why have I kept you here?—"

"Because you are stronger," I managed to blurt out.

"But why stronger?" he went on at once with his perpetual queries. "Because I am a bigger bit of the ferment than you? Don't you see? Don't you see?"

"But the hopelessness of it," I protested.

"I agree with you," he answered. "Then why move at all, since moving is living? Without moving and being part of the yeast there would be no hopelessness. But,—and there it is,—we want to live and move, though we have no reason to, because it happens that it is the nature of life to live and move, to want to live and move. If it were not for this, life would be dead. It is because of this life that is in you that you dream of your immortality. The life that is in you is alive and wants to go on being alive for ever. Bah! An eternity of piggishness!"

He abruptly turned on his heel and started forward. He stopped at the break of the poop and called me to him.

"By the way, how much was it that Cooky got away with?" he asked.

"One hundred and eighty-five dollars, sir," I answered.

He nodded his head. A moment later, as I started down the companion stairs to lay the table for dinner, I heard him loudly cursing some men amidships.

CHAPTER VI

By the following morning the storm had blown itself quite out and the *Ghost* was rolling slightly on a calm sea without a breath of wind. Occasional light airs were felt, however, and Wolf Larsen patrolled the poop constantly, his eyes ever searching the sea to the north-eastward, from which direction the great trade-wind must blow.

The men were all on deck and busy preparing their various boats for the season's hunting. There are seven boats aboard, the captain's dingey, and the six which the hunters will use. Three, a hunter, a boat-puller, and a boat-steerer, compose a boat's crew. On board the schooner the boat-pullers and steerers are the crew. The hunters, too, are supposed to be in command of the watches, subject, always, to the orders of Wolf Larsen.

All this, and more, I have learned. The *Ghost* is considered the fastest schooner in both the San Francisco and Victoria fleets. In fact, she was once a private yacht, and was built for speed. Her lines and fittings—though I know nothing about such things—speak for themselves. Johnson was telling me about her in a short chat I had with him during yesterday's second dog-watch. He spoke enthusiastically, with the love for a fine craft such as some men feel for horses. He is greatly disgusted with the outlook, and I am given to understand that Wolf Larsen bears a very unsavoury reputation among the sealing captains. It was the *Ghost* herself that lured Johnson into signing for the voyage, but he is already beginning to repent.

As he told me, the *Ghost* is an eighty-ton schooner of a remarkably fine model. Her beam, or width, is twenty-three feet, and her length a little over ninety feet. A lead keel of fabulous but unknown weight makes her very stable, while she carries an immense spread of canvas. From the deck to the truck of the maintopmast is something over a hundred feet, while the foremast with its topmast is eight or ten feet shorter. I am giving these details so that the size of this little floating world which holds twenty-two men may be appreciated. It is a very little world, a mote, a speck, and I marvel that men should dare to venture the sea on a contrivance so small and fragile.

Wolf Larsen has, also, a reputation for reckless carrying on of sail. I overheard Henderson and another of the hunters, Standish, a Californian, talking about it. Two years ago he dismasted the *Ghost* in a gale on Bering Sea, whereupon the present masts were put in, which are stronger and heavier in every way. He is said to have remarked, when he put them in, that he preferred turning her over to losing the sticks.

CHAPTER VI

Every man aboard, with the exception of Johansen, who is rather overcome by his promotion, seems to have an excuse for having sailed on the *Ghost*. Half the men forward are deep-water sailors, and their excuse is that they did not know anything about her or her captain. And those who do know, whisper that the hunters, while excellent shots, were so notorious for their quarrelsome and rascally proclivities that they could not sign on any decent schooner.

I have made the acquaintance of another one of the crew,—Louis he is called, a rotund and jovial-faced Nova Scotia Irishman, and a very sociable fellow, prone to talk as long as he can find a listener. In the afternoon, while the cook was below asleep and I was peeling the everlasting potatoes, Louis dropped into the galley for a "yarn." His excuse for being aboard was that he was drunk when he signed. He assured me again and again that it was the last thing in the world he would dream of doing in a sober moment. It seems that he has been seal-hunting regularly each season for a dozen years, and is accounted one of the two or three very best boat-steerers in both fleets.

"Ah, my boy," he shook his head ominously at me, "'tis the worst schooner ye could iv selected, nor were ye drunk at the time as was I. 'Tis sealin' is the sailor's paradise—on other ships than this. The mate was the first, but mark me words, there'll be more dead men before the trip is done with. Hist, now, between you an' meself and the stanchion there, this Wolf Larsen is a regular devil, an' the *Ghost'll* be a hell-ship like she's always ben since he had hold iv her. Don't I know? Don't I know? Don't I remember him in Hakodate two years gone, when he had a row an' shot four iv his men? Wasn't I a-layin' on the *Emma L.*, not three hundred yards away? An' there was a man the same year he killed with a blow iv his fist. Yes, sir, killed 'im dead-oh. His head must iv smashed like an eggshell. An' wasn't there the Governor of Kura Island, an' the Chief iv Police, Japanese gentlemen, sir, an' didn't they come aboard the *Ghost* as his guests, a-bringin' their wives along—wee an' pretty little bits of things like you see 'em painted on fans. An' as he was a-gettin' under way, didn't the fond husbands get left astern-like in their sampan, as it might be by accident? An' wasn't it a week later that the poor little ladies was put ashore on the other side of the island, with nothin' before 'em but to walk home acrost the mountains on their weeny-teeny little straw sandals which wouldn't hang together a mile? Don't I know? 'Tis the beast he is, this Wolf Larsen—the great big beast mentioned iv in Revelation; an' no good end will he ever come to. But I've said nothin' to ye, mind ye. I've whispered never a word; for old fat Louis'll live the voyage out if the last mother's son of yez go to the fishes."

"Wolf Larsen!" he snorted a moment later. "Listen to the word, will ye! Wolf—'tis what he is. He's not black-hearted like some men. 'Tis no heart he has at all. Wolf, just wolf, 'tis what he is. D'ye wonder he's well named?"

"But if he is so well-known for what he is," I queried, "how is it that he can get men to ship with him?"

"An' how is it ye can get men to do anything on God's earth an' sea?" Louis demanded with Celtic fire. "How d'ye find me aboard if 'twasn't that I was drunk as a pig when I put me name down? There's them that can't sail with better men, like the hunters, and them that don't know, like the poor devils of wind-jammers for'ard there. But they'll come to it, they'll come to it, an' be sorry the day they was born. I could weep for the poor creatures, did I but forget poor old fat Louis and the troubles before him. But 'tis not a whisper I've dropped, mind ye, not a whisper."

"Them hunters is the wicked boys," he broke forth again, for he suffered from a constitutional plethora of speech. "But wait till they get to cutting up iv jinks and rowin' 'round. He's the boy'll fix 'em. 'Tis him that'll put the fear of God in their rotten black hearts. Look at that hunter iv mine, Horner. 'Jock' Horner they call him, so quiet-like an' easy-goin', soft-spoken as a girl, till ye'd think butter wouldn't melt in the mouth iv him. Didn't he kill his boat-steerer last year? 'Twas called a sad accident, but I met the boat-puller in Yokohama an' the straight iv it was given me. An' there's Smoke, the black little devil—didn't the Roosians have him for three years in the salt mines of Siberia, for poachin' on Copper Island, which is a Roosian preserve? Shackled he was, hand an' foot, with his mate. An' didn't they have words or a ruction of some kind?—for 'twas the other fellow Smoke sent up in the buckets to the top of the mine; an' a piece at a time he went up, a leg to-day, an' to-morrow an arm, the next day the head, an' so on."

"But you can't mean it!" I cried out, overcome with the horror of it.

"Mean what!" he demanded, quick as a flash. "'Tis nothin' I've said. Deef I am, and dumb, as ye should be for the sake iv your mother; an' never once have I opened me lips but to say fine things iv them an' him, God curse his soul, an' may he rot in purgatory ten thousand years, and then go down to the last an' deepest hell iv all!"

Johnson, the man who had chafed me raw when I first came aboard, seemed the least equivocal of the men forward or aft. In fact, there was nothing equivocal about him. One was struck at once by his straightforwardness and manliness, which, in turn, were tempered by a modesty which might be mistaken for timidity. But timid he was not. He seemed, rather, to have the courage of his convictions, the certainty of his manhood. It was this that made him protest, at the commencement of our acquaintance, against being called Yonson. And upon this, and him, Louis passed judgment and prophecy.

"'Tis a fine chap, that squarehead Johnson we've for'ard with us," he said. "The best sailorman in the fo'c'sle. He's my boat-puller. But it's to trouble he'll come with Wolf Larsen, as the sparks fly upward. It's meself that knows. I can see it brewin' an' comin' up like a storm in the sky. I've talked to him like a brother, but it's little he sees in takin' in his lights or flyin' false signals. He grumbles out when things don't go to suit him, and there'll be always some tell-tale carryin' word iv it aft to the Wolf. The Wolf is strong, and it's the way of a wolf to hate strength, an' strength it is he'll see in Johnson—no knucklin' under, and a 'Yes, sir, thank ye kindly, sir,' for a curse or a blow. Oh, she's a-comin'! She's a-comin'! An' God knows where I'll get another boat-puller! What does the fool up an' say, when the old man calls him Yonson, but 'Me name is Johnson, sir,' an' then spells it out, letter for letter. Ye should iv seen the old man's face! I thought he'd let drive at him on the spot. He didn't, but he will, an' he'll break that squarehead's heart, or it's little I know iv the ways iv men on the ships iv the sea."

Thomas Mugridge is becoming unendurable. I am compelled to Mister him and to Sir him with every speech. One reason for this is that Wolf Larsen seems to have taken a fancy to him. It is an unprecedented thing, I take it, for a captain to be chummy with the cook; but this is certainly what Wolf Larsen is doing. Two or three times he put his head into the galley and chaffed Mugridge good-naturedly, and once, this afternoon, he stood by the break of the poop and chatted with him for fully fifteen minutes. When it was over, and Mugridge was back in the galley, he became greasily radiant, and went about his work, humming coster songs in a nerve-racking and discordant falsetto.

"I always get along with the officers," he remarked to me in a confidential tone. "I know the w'y, I do, to myke myself uppreci-yted. There was my last skipper—w'y I thought nothin' of droppin' down in the cabin for a little chat and a friendly glass. 'Mugridge,' sez 'e to me, 'Mugridge,' sez 'e, 'you've missed yer vokytion.' 'An' 'ow's that?' sez I. 'Yer should 'a been born a gentleman, an' never 'ad to work for yer livin'.' God strike me dead, 'Ump, if that ayn't wot 'e sez, an' me a-sittin' there in 'is own cabin, jolly-like an' comfortable, a-smokin' 'is cigars an' drinkin' 'is rum."

This chitter-chatter drove me to distraction. I never heard a voice I hated so. His oily, insinuating tones, his greasy smile and his monstrous self-conceit grated on my nerves till sometimes I was all in a tremble. Positively, he was the most disgusting and loathsome person I have ever met. The filth of his cooking was indescribable; and, as he cooked everything that was eaten aboard, I was compelled to select what I ate with great circumspection, choosing from the least dirty of his concoctions.

My hands bothered me a great deal, unused as they were to work. The nails were discoloured and black, while the skin was already grained with dirt which even a scrubbing-brush could not remove. Then blisters came, in a painful and never-ending procession, and I had a great burn on my forearm, acquired by losing my balance in a roll of the ship and pitching against the galley stove. Nor was my knee any better. The swelling had not gone down, and the cap was still up on edge. Hobbling about on it from morning till night was not helping it any. What I needed was rest, if it were ever to get well.

Rest! I never before knew the meaning of the word. I had been resting all my life and did not know it. But now, could I sit still for one half-hour and do nothing, not even think, it would be the most pleasurable thing in the world. But it is a revelation, on the other hand. I shall be able to appreciate the lives of the working people hereafter. I did not dream that work was so terrible a thing. From half-past five in the morning till ten o'clock at night I am everybody's slave, with not one moment to myself, except such as I can steal near the end of the second dog-watch. Let me pause for a minute to look out over the sea sparkling in the sun, or to gaze at a sailor going aloft to the gaff-topsails, or running out the bowsprit, and I am sure to hear the hateful voice, "'Ere, you, 'Ump, no sodgerin'. I've got my peepers on yer."

There are signs of rampant bad temper in the steerage, and the gossip is going around that Smoke and Henderson have had a fight. Henderson seems the best of the hunters, a slow-going fellow, and hard to rouse; but roused he must have been, for Smoke had a bruised and discoloured eye, and looked particularly vicious when he came into the cabin for supper.

A cruel thing happened just before supper, indicative of the callousness and brutishness of these men. There is one green hand in the crew, Harrison by name, a clumsy-looking country boy, mastered, I imagine, by the spirit of adventure, and making his first voyage. In the light baffling airs the schooner had been tacking about a great deal, at which times the sails pass from one side to the other and a man is sent aloft to shift over the fore-gaff-topsail. In some way, when Harrison was aloft, the sheet jammed in the block through which it runs at the end of the gaff. As I understood it, there were two ways of getting it cleared,—first, by lowering the foresail, which was comparatively easy and without danger; and second, by climbing out the peak-halyards to the end of the gaff itself, an exceedingly hazardous performance.

Johansen called out to Harrison to go out the halyards. It was patent to everybody that the boy was afraid. And well he might be, eighty feet above the deck, to trust himself on those thin and jerking ropes. Had there been a steady breeze it would not have been so bad, but the *Ghost* was rolling emptily in a long sea, and with each roll the canvas flapped and boomed and the halyards slacked and jerked taut. They were capable of snapping a man off like a fly from a whip-lash.

Harrison heard the order and understood what was demanded of him, but hesitated. It was probably the first time he had been aloft in his life. Johansen, who had caught the contagion of Wolf Larsen's masterfulness, burst out with a volley of abuse and curses.

"That'll do, Johansen," Wolf Larsen said brusquely. "I'll have you know that I do the swearing on this ship. If I need your assistance, I'll call you in."

"Yes, sir," the mate acknowledged submissively.

In the meantime Harrison had started out on the halyards. I was looking up from the galley door, and I could see him trembling, as if with ague, in every limb. He proceeded very slowly and cautiously, an inch at a time. Outlined against the clear blue of the sky, he had the appearance of an enormous spider crawling along the tracery of its web.

It was a slight uphill climb, for the foresail peaked high; and the halyards, running through various blocks on the gaff and mast, gave him separate holds for hands and feet. But the trouble lay in that the wind was not strong enough nor steady enough to keep the sail full. When he was half-way out, the *Ghost* took a long roll to windward and back again into the hollow between two seas. Harrison ceased his progress and held on tightly. Eighty feet beneath, I could see the agonized strain of his muscles as he gripped for very life. The sail emptied and the gaff swung amid-ships. The halyards slackened, and, though it all happened very quickly, I could see them sag beneath the weight of his body. Then the gag swung to the side with an abrupt swiftness, the great sail boomed like a cannon, and the three rows of reef-points slatted against the canvas like a volley of rifles. Harrison, clinging on, made the giddy rush through the air. This rush ceased abruptly. The halyards became instantly taut. It was the snap of the whip. His clutch was broken. One hand was torn loose from its hold. The other lingered desperately for a moment, and followed. His body pitched out and down, but in some way he managed to save himself with his legs. He was hanging by them, head downward. A quick effort brought his hands up to the halyards again; but he was a long time regaining his former position, where he hung, a pitiable object.

"I'll bet he has no appetite for supper," I heard Wolf Larsen's voice, which came to me from around the corner of the galley. "Stand from under, you, Johansen! Watch out! Here she comes!"

In truth, Harrison was very sick, as a person is sea-sick; and for a long time he clung to his precarious perch without attempting to move. Johansen, however, continued violently to urge him on to the completion of his task.

"It is a shame," I heard Johnson growling in painfully slow and correct English. He was standing by the main rigging, a few feet away from me. "The boy is willing enough. He will learn if he has a chance. But this is—" He paused awhile, for the word "murder" was his final judgment.

"Hist, will ye!" Louis whispered to him, "For the love iv your mother hold your mouth!"

But Johnson, looking on, still continued his grumbling.

"Look here," the hunter Standish spoke to Wolf Larsen, "that's my boat-puller, and I don't want to lose him."

"That's all right, Standish," was the reply. "He's your boat-puller when you've got him in the boat; but he's my sailor when I have him aboard, and I'll do what I damn well please with him."

"But that's no reason—" Standish began in a torrent of speech.

"That'll do, easy as she goes," Wolf Larsen counselled back. "I've told you what's what, and let it stop at that. The man's mine, and I'll make soup of him and eat it if I want to."

There was an angry gleam in the hunter's eye, but he turned on his heel and entered the steerage companion-way, where he remained, looking upward. All hands were on deck now, and all eyes were aloft, where a human life was at grapples with death. The callousness of these men, to whom industrial organization gave control of the lives of other men, was appalling. I, who had lived out of the whirl of the world, had never dreamed that its work was carried on in such fashion. Life had always seemed a peculiarly sacred thing, but here it counted for nothing, was a cipher in the arithmetic of commerce. I must say, however, that the sailors themselves were sympathetic, as instance the case of Johnson; but the masters (the hunters and the captain) were heartlessly indifferent. Even the protest of Standish arose out of the fact that he did not wish to lose his boat-puller. Had it been some other hunter's boat-puller, he, like them, would have been no more than amused.

But to return to Harrison. It took Johansen, insulting and reviling the poor wretch, fully ten minutes to get him started again. A little later he made the end of the gaff, where, astride the spar itself, he had a better chance for holding on. He cleared the sheet, and was free to return, slightly downhill now, along the halyards to the mast. But he had lost his nerve. Unsafe as was his present position, he was loath to forsake it for the more unsafe position on the halyards.

He looked along the airy path he must traverse, and then down to the deck. His eyes were wide and staring, and he was trembling violently. I had never seen fear so strongly stamped upon a human face. Johansen called vainly for him to come down. At any moment he was liable to be snapped off the gaff, but he was helpless with fright. Wolf Larsen, walking up and down with Smoke and in conversation, took no more notice of him, though he cried sharply, once, to the man at the wheel:

"You're off your course, my man! Be careful, unless you're looking for trouble!"

"Ay, ay, sir," the helmsman responded, putting a couple of spokes down.

He had been guilty of running the *Ghost* several points off her course in order that what little wind there was should fill the foresail and hold it steady. He had striven to help the unfortunate Harrison at the risk of incurring Wolf Larsen's anger.

The time went by, and the suspense, to me, was terrible. Thomas Mugridge, on the other hand, considered it a laughable affair, and was continually bobbing his head out the galley door to make jocose remarks. How I hated him! And how my hatred for him grew and grew, during that fearful time, to cyclopean dimensions. For the first time in my life I experienced the desire to murder—"saw red," as some of our picturesque writers phrase it. Life in general might still be sacred, but life in the particular case of Thomas Mugridge had become very profane indeed. I was frightened when I became conscious that I was seeing red, and the thought flashed through my mind: was I, too, becoming tainted by the brutality of my environment?—I, who even in the most flagrant crimes had denied the justice and righteousness of capital punishment?

Fully half-an-hour went by, and then I saw Johnson and Louis in some sort of altercation. It ended with Johnson flinging off Louis's detaining arm and starting forward. He crossed the deck, sprang into the fore rigging, and began to climb. But the quick eye of Wolf Larsen caught him.

"Here, you, what are you up to?" he cried.

Johnson's ascent was arrested. He looked his captain in the eyes and replied slowly:

"I am going to get that boy down."

"You'll get down out of that rigging, and damn lively about it! D'ye hear? Get down!"

Johnson hesitated, but the long years of obedience to the masters of ships overpowered him, and he dropped sullenly to the deck and went on forward.

At half after five I went below to set the cabin table, but I hardly knew what I did, for my eyes and my brain were filled with the vision of a man, white-faced and trembling, comically like a bug, clinging to the thrashing gaff. At six o'clock, when I served supper, going on deck to get the food from the galley, I saw Harrison, still in the same position. The conversation at the table was of other things. Nobody seemed interested in the wantonly imperilled life. But making an extra trip to the galley a little later, I was gladdened by the sight of Harrison staggering weakly from the rigging to the forecastle scuttle. He had finally summoned the courage to descend.

Before closing this incident, I must give a scrap of conversation I had with Wolf Larsen in the cabin, while I was washing the dishes.

"You were looking squeamish this afternoon," he began. "What was the matter?"

I could see that he knew what had made me possibly as sick as Harrison, that he was trying to draw me, and I answered, "It was because of the brutal treatment of that boy."

He gave a short laugh. "Like sea-sickness, I suppose. Some men are subject to it, and others are not."

"Not so," I objected.

"Just so," he went on. "The earth is as full of brutality as the sea is full of motion. And some men are made sick by the one, and some by the other. That's the only reason."

"But you, who make a mock of human life, don't you place any value upon it whatever?" I demanded.

"Value? What value?" He looked at me, and though his eyes were steady and motionless, there seemed a cynical smile in them. "What kind of value? How do you measure it? Who values it?"

"I do," I made answer.

"Then what is it worth to you? Another man's life, I mean. Come now, what is it worth?"

CHAPTER VI

The value of life? How could I put a tangible value upon it? Somehow, I, who have always had expression, lacked expression when with Wolf Larsen. I have since determined that a part of it was due to the man's personality, but that the greater part was due to his totally different outlook. Unlike other materialists I had met and with whom I had something in common to start on, I had nothing in common with him. Perhaps, also, it was the elemental simplicity of his mind that baffled me. He drove so directly to the core of the matter, divesting a question always of all superfluous details, and with such an air of finality, that I seemed to find myself struggling in deep water, with no footing under me. Value of life? How could I answer the question on the spur of the moment? The sacredness of life I had accepted as axiomatic. That it was intrinsically valuable was a truism I had never questioned. But when he challenged the truism I was speechless.

"We were talking about this yesterday," he said. "I held that life was a ferment, a yeasty something which devoured life that it might live, and that living was merely successful piggishness. Why, if there is anything in supply and demand, life is the cheapest thing in the world. There is only so much water, so much earth, so much air; but the life that is demanding to be born is limitless. Nature is a spendthrift. Look at the fish and their millions of eggs. For that matter, look at you and me. In our loins are the possibilities of millions of lives. Could we but find time and opportunity and utilize the last bit and every bit of the unborn life that is in us, we could become the fathers of nations and populate continents. Life? Bah! It has no value. Of cheap things it is the cheapest. Everywhere it goes begging. Nature spills it out with a lavish hand. Where there is room for one life, she sows a thousand lives, and it's life eats life till the strongest and most piggish life is left."

"You have read Darwin," I said. "But you read him misunderstandingly when you conclude that the struggle for existence sanctions your wanton destruction of life."

He shrugged his shoulders. "You know you only mean that in relation to human life, for of the flesh and the fowl and the fish you destroy as much as I or any other man. And human life is in no wise different, though you feel it is and think that you reason why it is. Why should I be parsimonious with this life which is cheap and without value? There are more sailors than there are ships on the sea for them, more workers than there are factories or machines for them. Why, you who live on the land know that you house your poor people in the slums of cities and loose famine and pestilence upon them, and that there still remain more poor people, dying for want of a crust of bread and a bit of meat (which is life destroyed), than you know what to do with. Have you ever seen the London dockers fighting like wild beasts for a chance to work?"

He started for the companion stairs, but turned his head for a final word. "Do you know the only value life has is what life puts upon itself? And it is of course overestimated since it is of necessity prejudiced in its own favour. Take that man I had aloft. He held on as if he were a precious thing, a treasure beyond diamonds or rubies. To you? No. To me? Not at all. To himself? Yes. But I do not accept his estimate. He sadly overrates himself. There is plenty more life demanding to be born. Had he fallen and dripped his brains upon the deck like honey from the comb, there would have been no loss to the world. He was worth nothing to the world. The supply is too large. To himself only was he of value, and to show how fictitious even this value was, being dead he is unconscious that he has lost himself. He alone rated himself beyond diamonds and rubies. Diamonds and rubies are gone, spread out on the deck to be washed away by a bucket of sea-water, and he does not even know that the diamonds and rubies are gone. He does not lose anything, for with the loss of himself he loses the knowledge of loss. Don't you see? And what have you to say?"

"That you are at least consistent," was all I could say, and I went on washing the dishes.

CHAPTER VII

At last, after three days of variable winds, we have caught the north-east trades. I came on deck, after a good night's rest in spite of my poor knee, to find the *Ghost* foaming along, wing-and-wing, and every sail drawing except the jibs, with a fresh breeże astern. Oh, the wonder of the great trade-wind! All day we sailed, and all night, and the next day, and the next, day after day, the wind always astern and blowing steadily and strong. The schooner sailed herself. There was no pulling and hauling on sheets and tackles, no shifting of topsails, no work at all for the sailors to do except to steer. At night when the sun went down, the sheets were slackened; in the morning, when they yielded up the damp of the dew and relaxed, they were pulled tight again—and that was all.

Ten knots, twelve knots, eleven knots, varying from time to time, is the speed we are making. And ever out of the north-east the brave wind blows, driving us on our course two hundred and fifty miles between the dawns. It saddens me and gladdens me, the gait with which we are leaving San Francisco behind and with which we are foaming down upon the tropics. Each day grows perceptibly warmer. In the second dog-watch the sailors come on deck, stripped, and heave buckets of water upon one another from overside. Flying-fish are beginning to be seen, and during the night the watch above scrambles over the deck in pursuit of those that fall aboard. In the morning, Thomas Mugridge being duly bribed, the galley is pleasantly areek with the odour of their frying; while dolphin meat is served fore and aft on such occasions as Johnson catches the blazing beauties from the bowsprit end.

Johnson seems to spend all his spare time there or aloft at the crosstrees, watching the *Ghost* cleaving the water under press of sail. There is passion, adoration, in his eyes, and he goes about in a sort of trance, gazing in ecstasy at the swelling sails, the foaming wake, and the heave and the run of her over the liquid mountains that are moving with us in stately procession.

The days and nights are "all a wonder and a wild delight," and though I have little time from my dreary work, I steal odd moments to gaze and gaze at the unending glory of what I never dreamed the world possessed. Above, the sky is stainless blue—blue as the sea itself, which under the forefoot is of the colour and sheen of azure satin. All around the horizon are pale, fleecy clouds, never changing, never moving, like a silver setting for the flawless turquoise sky.

I do not forget one night, when I should have been asleep, of lying on the forecastle-head and gazing down at the spectral ripple of foam thrust aside by the *Ghost's* forefoot. It sounded like the gurgling of a brook over mossy stones in some quiet dell, and the crooning song of it lured me away and out of myself till I was no longer Hump the cabin-boy, nor Van Weyden, the man who had dreamed away thirty-five years among books. But a voice behind me, the unmistakable voice of Wolf Larsen, strong with the invincible certitude of the man and mellow with appreciation of the words he was quoting, aroused me.

> *"'O the blazing tropic night, when the wake's a welt of light*
> *That holds the hot sky tame,*
> *And the steady forefoot snores through the planet-powdered floors*
> *Where the scared whale flukes in flame.*
> *Her plates are scarred by the sun, dear lass,*
> *And her ropes are taut with the dew,*
> *For we're booming down on the old trail, our own trail, the out trail,*
> *We're sagging south on the Long Trail—the trail that is always new.'"*

"Eh, Hump? How's it strike you?" he asked, after the due pause which words and setting demanded.

I looked into his face. It was aglow with light, as the sea itself, and the eyes were flashing in the starshine.

"It strikes me as remarkable, to say the least, that you should show enthusiasm," I answered coldly.

"Why, man, it's living! it's life!" he cried.

"Which is a cheap thing and without value." I flung his words at him.

He laughed, and it was the first time I had heard honest mirth in his voice.

"Ah, I cannot get you to understand, cannot drive it into your head, what a thing this life is. Of course life is valueless, except to itself. And I can tell you that my life is pretty valuable just now—to myself. It is beyond price, which you will acknowledge is a terrific overrating, but which I cannot help, for it is the life that is in me that makes the rating."

He appeared waiting for the words with which to express the thought that was in him, and finally went on.

"Do you know, I am filled with a strange uplift; I feel as if all time were echoing through me, as though all powers were mine. I know truth, divine good from evil, right from wrong. My vision is clear and far. I could almost believe in God. But," and his voice changed and the light went out of his face,—"what is this condition in which I find myself? this joy of living? this exultation of life? this inspiration, I may well call it? It is what comes when there is nothing wrong with one's digestion, when his stomach is in trim and his appetite has an edge, and all goes well. It is the bribe for living, the champagne of the blood, the effervescence of the ferment—that makes some men think holy thoughts, and other men to see God or to create him when they cannot see him. That is all, the drunkenness of life, the stirring and crawling of the yeast, the babbling of the life that is insane with consciousness that it is alive. And—bah! To-morrow I shall pay for it as the drunkard pays. And I shall know that I must die, at sea most likely, cease crawling of myself to be all a-crawl with the corruption of the sea; to be fed upon, to be carrion, to yield up all the strength and movement of my muscles that it may become strength and movement in fin and scale and the guts of fishes. Bah! And bah! again. The champagne is already flat. The sparkle and bubble has gone out and it is a tasteless drink."

He left me as suddenly as he had come, springing to the deck with the weight and softness of a tiger. The *Ghost* ploughed on her way. I noted the gurgling forefoot was very like a snore, and as I listened to it the effect of Wolf Larsen's swift rush from sublime exultation to despair slowly left me. Then some deep-water sailor, from the waist of the ship, lifted a rich tenor voice in the "Song of the Trade Wind":

"Oh, I am the wind the seamen love—
I am steady, and strong, and true;
They follow my track by the clouds above,
O'er the fathomless tropic blue.

* * * * *

Through daylight and dark I follow the bark
I keep like a hound on her trail;
I'm strongest at noon, yet under the moon,
I stiffen the bunt of her sail."

CHAPTER VIII

Sometimes I think Wolf Larsen mad, or half-mad at least, what of his strange moods and vagaries. At other times I take him for a great man, a genius who has never arrived. And, finally, I am convinced that he is the perfect type of the primitive man, born a thousand years or generations too late and an anachronism in this culminating century of civilization. He is certainly an individualist of the most pronounced type. Not only that, but he is very lonely. There is no congeniality between him and the rest of the men aboard ship. His tremendous virility and mental strength wall him apart. They are more like children to him, even the hunters, and as children he treats them, descending perforce to their level and playing with them as a man plays with puppies. Or else he probes them with the cruel hand of a vivisectionist, groping about in their mental processes and examining their souls as though to see of what soul-stuff is made.

I have seen him a score of times, at table, insulting this hunter or that, with cool and level eyes and, withal, a certain air of interest, pondering their actions or replies or petty rages with a curiosity almost laughable to me who stood onlooker and who understood. Concerning his own rages, I am convinced that they are not real, that they are sometimes experiments, but that in the main they are the habits of a pose or attitude he has seen fit to take toward his fellow-men. I know, with the possible exception of the incident of the dead mate, that I have not seen him really angry; nor do I wish ever to see him in a genuine rage, when all the force of him is called into play.

While on the question of vagaries, I shall tell what befell Thomas Mugridge in the cabin, and at the same time complete an incident upon which I have already touched once or twice. The twelve o'clock dinner was over, one day, and I had just finished putting the cabin in order, when Wolf Larsen and Thomas Mugridge descended the companion stairs. Though the cook had a cubby-hole of a state-room opening off from the cabin, in the cabin itself he had never dared to linger or to be seen, and he flitted to and fro, once or twice a day, a timid spectre.

"So you know how to play 'Nap,'" Wolf Larsen was saying in a pleased sort of voice. "I might have guessed an Englishman would know. I learned it myself in English ships."

Thomas Mugridge was beside himself, a blithering imbecile, so pleased was he at chumming thus with the captain. The little airs he put on and the painful striving to assume the easy carriage of a man born to a dignified place in life would have been sickening had they not been ludicrous. He quite ignored my presence, though I credited him with being simply unable to see me. His pale, wishy-washy eyes were swimming like lazy summer seas, though what blissful visions they beheld were beyond my imagination.

"Get the cards, Hump," Wolf Larsen ordered, as they took seats at the table. "And bring out the cigars and the whisky you'll find in my berth."

I returned with the articles in time to hear the Cockney hinting broadly that there was a mystery about him, that he might be a gentleman's son gone wrong or something or other; also, that he was a remittance man and was paid to keep away from England—"p'yed 'ansomely, sir," was the way he put it; "p'yed 'ansomely to sling my 'ook an' keep slingin' it."

I had brought the customary liquor glasses, but Wolf Larsen frowned, shook his head, and signalled with his hands for me to bring the tumblers. These he filled two-thirds full with undiluted whisky—"a gentleman's drink?" quoth Thomas Mugridge,—and they clinked their glasses to the glorious game of "Nap," lighted cigars, and fell to shuffling and dealing the cards.

They played for money. They increased the amounts of the bets. They drank whisky, they drank it neat, and I fetched more. I do not know whether Wolf Larsen cheated or not,—a thing he was thoroughly capable of doing,—but he won steadily. The cook made repeated journeys to his bunk for money. Each time he performed the journey with greater swagger, but he never brought more than a few dollars at a time. He grew maudlin, familiar, could hardly see the cards or sit upright. As a preliminary to another journey to his bunk, he hooked Wolf Larsen's buttonhole with a greasy forefinger and vacuously proclaimed and reiterated, "I got money, I got money, I tell yer, an' I'm a gentleman's son."

Wolf Larsen was unaffected by the drink, yet he drank glass for glass, and if anything his glasses were fuller. There was no change in him. He did not appear even amused at the other's antics.

In the end, with loud protestations that he could lose like a gentleman, the cook's last money was staked on the game—and lost. Whereupon he leaned his head on his hands and wept. Wolf Larsen looked curiously at him, as though about to probe and vivisect him, then changed his mind, as from the foregone conclusion that there was nothing there to probe.

"Hump," he said to me, elaborately polite, "kindly take Mr. Mugridge's arm and help him up on deck. He is not feeling very well."

"And tell Johnson to douse him with a few buckets of salt water," he added, in a lower tone for my ear alone.

I left Mr. Mugridge on deck, in the hands of a couple of grinning sailors who had been told off for the purpose. Mr. Mugridge was sleepily spluttering that he was a gentleman's son. But as I descended the companion stairs to clear the table I heard him shriek as the first bucket of water struck him.

Wolf Larsen was counting his winnings.

"One hundred and eighty-five dollars even," he said aloud. "Just as I thought. The beggar came aboard without a cent."

"And what you have won is mine, sir," I said boldly.

He favoured me with a quizzical smile. "Hump, I have studied some grammar in my time, and I think your tenses are tangled. 'Was mine,' you should have said, not 'is mine.'"

"It is a question, not of grammar, but of ethics," I answered.

It was possibly a minute before he spoke.

"D'ye know, Hump," he said, with a slow seriousness which had in it an indefinable strain of sadness, "that this is the first time I have heard the word 'ethics' in the mouth of a man. You and I are the only men on this ship who know its meaning."

"At one time in my life," he continued, after another pause, "I dreamed that I might some day talk with men who used such language, that I might lift myself out of the place in life in which I had been born, and hold conversation and mingle with men who talked about just such things as ethics. And this is the first time I have ever heard the word pronounced. Which is all by the way, for you are wrong. It is a question neither of grammar nor ethics, but of fact."

"I understand," I said. "The fact is that you have the money."

His face brightened. He seemed pleased at my perspicacity. "But it is avoiding the real question," I continued, "which is one of right."

"Ah," he remarked, with a wry pucker of his mouth, "I see you still believe in such things as right and wrong."

"But don't you?—at all?" I demanded.

"Not the least bit. Might is right, and that is all there is to it. Weakness is wrong. Which is a very poor way of saying that it is good for oneself to be strong, and evil for oneself to be weak—or better yet, it is pleasurable to be strong, because of the profits; painful to be weak, because of the penalties. Just now the possession of this money is a pleasurable thing. It is good for one to possess it. Being able to possess it, I wrong myself and the life that is in me if I give it to you and forego the pleasure of possessing it."

"But you wrong me by withholding it," I objected.

"Not at all. One man cannot wrong another man. He can only wrong himself. As I see it, I do wrong always when I consider the interests of others. Don't you see? How can two particles of the yeast wrong each other by striving to devour each other? It is their inborn heritage to strive to devour, and to strive not to be devoured. When they depart from this they sin."

"Then you don't believe in altruism?" I asked.

He received the word as if it had a familiar ring, though he pondered it thoughtfully. "Let me see, it means something about coöperation, doesn't it?"

"Well, in a way there has come to be a sort of connection," I answered unsurprised by this time at such gaps in his vocabulary, which, like his knowledge, was the acquirement of a self-read, self-educated man, whom no one had directed in his studies, and who had thought much and talked little or not at all. "An altruistic act is an act performed for the welfare of others. It is unselfish, as opposed to an act performed for self, which is selfish."

He nodded his head. "Oh, yes, I remember it now. I ran across it in Spencer."

"Spencer!" I cried. "Have you read him?"

"Not very much," was his confession. "I understood quite a good deal of *First Principles*, but his *Biology* took the wind out of my sails, and his *Psychology* left me butting around in the doldrums for many a day. I honestly could not understand what he was driving at. I put it down to mental deficiency on my part, but since then I have decided that it was for want of preparation. I had no proper basis. Only Spencer and myself know how hard I hammered. But I did get something out of his *Data of Ethics*. There's where I ran across 'altruism,' and I remember now how it was used."

I wondered what this man could have got from such a work. Spencer I remembered enough to know that altruism was imperative to his ideal of highest conduct. Wolf Larsen, evidently, had sifted the great philosopher's teachings, rejecting and selecting according to his needs and desires.

"What else did you run across?" I asked.

His brows drew in slightly with the mental effort of suitably phrasing thoughts which he had never before put into speech. I felt an elation of spirit. I was groping into his soul-stuff as he made a practice of groping in the soul-stuff of others. I was exploring virgin territory. A strange, a terribly strange, region was unrolling itself before my eyes.

"In as few words as possible," he began, "Spencer puts it something like this: First, a man must act for his own benefit—to do this is to be moral and good. Next, he must act for the benefit of his children. And third, he must act for the benefit of his race."

"And the highest, finest, right conduct," I interjected, "is that act which benefits at the same time the man, his children, and his race."

"I wouldn't stand for that," he replied. "Couldn't see the necessity for it, nor the common sense. I cut out the race and the children. I would sacrifice nothing for them. It's just so much slush and sentiment, and you must see it yourself, at least for one who does not believe in eternal life. With immortality before me, altruism would be a paying business proposition. I might elevate my soul to all kinds of altitudes. But with nothing eternal before me but death, given for a brief spell this yeasty crawling and squirming which is called life, why, it would be immoral for me to perform any act that was a sacrifice. Any sacrifice that makes me lose one crawl or squirm is foolish,—and not only foolish, for it is a wrong against myself and a wicked thing. I must not lose one crawl or squirm if I am to get the most out of the ferment. Nor will the eternal movelessness that is coming to me be made easier or harder by the sacrifices or selfishnesses of the time when I was yeasty and acrawl."

"Then you are an individualist, a materialist, and, logically, a hedonist."

"Big words," he smiled. "But what is a hedonist?"

He nodded agreement when I had given the definition. "And you are also," I continued, "a man one could not trust in the least thing where it was possible for a selfish interest to intervene?"

"Now you're beginning to understand," he said, brightening.

"You are a man utterly without what the world calls morals?"

"That's it."

"A man of whom to be always afraid—"

"That's the way to put it."

"As one is afraid of a snake, or a tiger, or a shark?"

"Now you know me," he said. "And you know me as I am generally known. Other men call me 'Wolf.'"

"You are a sort of monster," I added audaciously, "a Caliban who has pondered Setebos, and who acts as you act, in idle moments, by whim and fancy."

His brow clouded at the allusion. He did not understand, and I quickly learned that he did not know the poem.

"I'm just reading Browning," he confessed, "and it's pretty tough. I haven't got very far along, and as it is I've about lost my bearings."

Not to be tiresome, I shall say that I fetched the book from his state-room and read "Caliban" aloud. He was delighted. It was a primitive mode of reasoning and of looking at things that he understood thoroughly. He interrupted again and again with comment and criticism. When I finished, he had me read it over a second time, and a third. We fell into discussion—philosophy, science, evolution, religion. He betrayed the inaccuracies of the self-read man, and, it must be granted, the sureness and directness of the primitive mind. The very simplicity of his reasoning was its strength, and his materialism was far more compelling than the subtly complex materialism of Charley Furuseth. Not that I—a confirmed and, as Furuseth phrased it, a temperamental idealist—was to be compelled; but that Wolf Larsen stormed the last strongholds of my faith with a vigour that received respect, while not accorded conviction.

Time passed. Supper was at hand and the table not laid. I became restless and anxious, and when Thomas Mugridge glared down the companion-way, sick and angry of countenance, I prepared to go about my duties. But Wolf Larsen cried out to him:

"Cooky, you've got to hustle to-night. I'm busy with Hump, and you'll do the best you can without him."

And again the unprecedented was established. That night I sat at table with the captain and the hunters, while Thomas Mugridge waited on us and washed the dishes afterward—a whim, a Caliban-mood of Wolf Larsen's, and one I foresaw would bring me trouble. In the meantime we talked and talked, much to the disgust of the hunters, who could not understand a word.

CHAPTER IX

Three days of rest, three blessed days of rest, are what I had with Wolf Larsen, eating at the cabin table and doing nothing but discuss life, literature, and the universe, the while Thomas Mugridge fumed and raged and did my work as well as his own.

"Watch out for squalls, is all I can say to you," was Louis's warning, given during a spare half-hour on deck while Wolf Larsen was engaged in straightening out a row among the hunters.

"Ye can't tell what'll be happenin'," Louis went on, in response to my query for more definite information. "The man's as contrary as air currents or water currents. You can never guess the ways iv him. 'Tis just as you're thinkin' you know him and are makin' a favourable slant along him, that he whirls around, dead ahead and comes howlin' down upon you and a-rippin' all iv your fine-weather sails to rags."

So I was not altogether surprised when the squall foretold by Louis smote me. We had been having a heated discussion,—upon life, of course,—and, grown over-bold, I was passing stiff strictures upon Wolf Larsen and the life of Wolf Larsen. In fact, I was vivisecting him and turning over his soul-stuff as keenly and thoroughly as it was his custom to do it to others. It may be a weakness of mine that I have an incisive way of speech; but I threw all restraint to the winds and cut and slashed until the whole man of him was snarling. The dark sun-bronze of his face went black with wrath, his eyes were ablaze. There was no clearness or sanity in them—nothing but the terrific rage of a madman. It was the wolf in him that I saw, and a mad wolf at that.

He sprang for me with a half-roar, gripping my arm. I had steeled myself to brazen it out, though I was trembling inwardly; but the enormous strength of the man was too much for my fortitude. He had gripped me by the biceps with his single hand, and when that grip tightened I wilted and shrieked aloud. My feet went out from under me. I simply could not stand upright and endure the agony. The muscles refused their duty. The pain was too great. My biceps was being crushed to a pulp.

He seemed to recover himself, for a lucid gleam came into his eyes, and he relaxed his hold with a short laugh that was more like a growl. I fell to the floor, feeling very faint, while he sat down, lighted a cigar, and watched me as a cat watches a mouse. As I writhed about I could see in his eyes that curiosity I had so often noted, that wonder and perplexity, that questing, that everlasting query of his as to what it was all about.

I finally crawled to my feet and ascended the companion stairs. Fair weather was over, and there was nothing left but to return to the galley. My left arm was numb, as though paralysed, and days passed before I could use it, while weeks went by before the last stiffness and pain went out of it. And he had done nothing but put his hand upon my arm and squeeze. There had been no wrenching or jerking. He had just closed his hand with a steady pressure. What he might have done I did not fully realize till next day, when he put his head into the galley, and, as a sign of renewed friendliness, asked me how my arm was getting on.

"It might have been worse," he smiled.

I was peeling potatoes. He picked one up from the pan. It was fair-sized, firm, and unpeeled. He closed his hand upon it, squeezed, and the potato squirted out between his fingers in mushy streams. The pulpy remnant he dropped back into the pan and turned away, and I had a sharp vision of how it might have fared with me had the monster put his real strength upon me.

But the three days' rest was good in spite of it all, for it had given my knee the very chance it needed. It felt much better, the swelling had materially decreased, and the cap seemed descending into its proper place. Also, the three days' rest brought the trouble I had foreseen. It was plainly Thomas Mugridge's intention to make me pay for those three days. He treated me vilely, cursed me continually, and heaped his own work upon me. He even ventured to raise his fist to me, but I was becoming animal-like myself, and I snarled in his face so terribly that it must have frightened him back. It is no pleasant picture I can conjure up of myself, Humphrey Van Weyden, in that noisome ship's galley, crouched in a corner over my task, my face raised to the face of the creature about to strike me, my lips lifted and snarling like a dog's, my eyes gleaming with fear and helplessness and the courage that comes of fear and helplessness. I do not like the picture. It reminds me too strongly of a rat in a trap. I do not care to think of it; but it was elective, for the threatened blow did not descend.

Thomas Mugridge backed away, glaring as hatefully and viciously as I glared. A pair of beasts is what we were, penned together and showing our teeth. He was a coward, afraid to strike me because I had not quailed sufficiently in advance; so he chose a new way to intimidate me. There was only one galley knife that, as a knife, amounted to anything. This, through many years of service and wear, had acquired a long, lean blade. It was unusually cruel-looking, and at first I had shuddered every time I used it. The cook borrowed a stone from Johansen and proceeded to sharpen the knife. He did it with great ostentation, glancing significantly at me the while. He whetted it up and down all day long. Every odd moment he could find he had the knife and stone out and was whetting away. The steel acquired a razor edge. He tried it with the ball of his thumb or across the nail. He shaved hairs from the back of his hand, glanced along the edge with microscopic acuteness, and found, or feigned that he found, always, a slight inequality in its edge somewhere. Then he would put it on the stone again and whet, whet, whet, till I could have laughed aloud, it was so very ludicrous.

It was also serious, for I learned that he was capable of using it, that under all his cowardice there was a courage of cowardice, like mine, that would impel him to do the very thing his whole nature protested against doing and was afraid of doing. "Cooky's sharpening his knife for Hump," was being whispered about among the sailors, and some of them twitted him about it. This he took in good part, and was really pleased, nodding his head with direful foreknowledge and mystery, until George Leach, the erstwhile cabin-boy, ventured some rough pleasantry on the subject.

Now it happened that Leach was one of the sailors told off to douse Mugridge after his game of cards with the captain. Leach had evidently done his task with a thoroughness that Mugridge had not forgiven, for words followed and evil names involving smirched ancestries. Mugridge menaced with the knife he was sharpening for me. Leach laughed and hurled more of his Telegraph Hill Billingsgate, and before either he or I knew what had happened, his right arm had been ripped open from elbow to wrist by a quick slash of the knife. The cook backed away, a fiendish expression on his face, the knife held before him in a position of defence. But Leach took it quite calmly, though blood was spouting upon the deck as generously as water from a fountain.

"I'm goin' to get you, Cooky," he said, "and I'll get you hard. And I won't be in no hurry about it. You'll be without that knife when I come for you."

So saying, he turned and walked quietly forward. Mugridge's face was livid with fear at what he had done and at what he might expect sooner or later from the man he had stabbed. But his demeanour toward me was more ferocious than ever. In spite of his fear at the reckoning he must expect to pay for what he had done, he could see that it had been an object-lesson to me, and he became more domineering and exultant. Also there was a lust in him, akin to madness, which had come with sight of the blood he had drawn. He was beginning to see red in whatever direction he looked. The psychology of it is sadly tangled, and yet I could read the workings of his mind as clearly as though it were a printed book.

Several days went by, the *Ghost* still foaming down the trades, and I could swear I saw madness growing in Thomas Mugridge's eyes. And I confess that I became afraid, very much afraid. Whet, whet, whet, it went all day long. The look in his eyes as he felt the keen edge and glared at me was positively carnivorous. I was afraid to turn my shoulder to him, and when I left the galley I went out backwards—to the amusement of the sailors and hunters, who made a point of gathering in groups to witness my exit. The strain was too great. I sometimes thought my mind would give way under it—a meet thing on this ship of madmen and brutes. Every hour, every minute of my existence was in jeopardy. I was a human soul in distress, and yet no soul, fore or aft, betrayed sufficient sympathy to come to my aid. At times I thought of throwing myself on the mercy of Wolf Larsen, but the vision of the mocking devil in his eyes that questioned life and sneered at it would come strong upon me and compel me to refrain. At other times I seriously contemplated suicide, and the whole force of my hopeful philosophy was required to keep me from going over the side in the darkness of night.

Several times Wolf Larsen tried to inveigle me into discussion, but I gave him short answers and eluded him. Finally, he commanded me to resume my seat at the cabin table for a time and let the cook do my work. Then I spoke frankly, telling him what I was enduring from Thomas Mugridge because of the three days of favouritism which had been shown me. Wolf Larsen regarded me with smiling eyes.

"So you're afraid, eh?" he sneered.

"Yes," I said defiantly and honestly, "I am afraid."

"That's the way with you fellows," he cried, half angrily, "sentimentalizing about your immortal souls and afraid to die. At sight of a sharp knife and a cowardly Cockney the clinging of life to life overcomes all your fond foolishness. Why, my dear fellow, you will live for ever. You are a god, and God cannot be killed. Cooky cannot hurt you. You are sure of your resurrection. What's there to be afraid of?

"You have eternal life before you. You are a millionaire in immortality, and a millionaire whose fortune cannot be lost, whose fortune is less perishable than the stars and as lasting as space or time. It is impossible for you to diminish your principal. Immortality is a thing without beginning or end. Eternity is eternity, and though you die here and now you will go on living somewhere else and hereafter. And it is all very beautiful, this shaking off of the flesh and soaring of the imprisoned spirit. Cooky cannot hurt you. He can only give you a boost on the path you eternally must tread.

"Or, if you do not wish to be boosted just yet, why not boost Cooky? According to your ideas, he, too, must be an immortal millionaire. You cannot bankrupt him. His paper will always circulate at par. You cannot diminish the length of his living by killing him, for he is without beginning or end. He's bound to go on living, somewhere, somehow. Then boost him. Stick a knife in him and let his spirit free. As it is, it's in a nasty prison, and you'll do him only a kindness by breaking down the door. And who knows?—it may be a very beautiful spirit that will go soaring up into the blue from that ugly carcass. Boost him along, and I'll promote you to his place, and he's getting forty-five dollars a month."

It was plain that I could look for no help or mercy from Wolf Larsen. Whatever was to be done I must do for myself; and out of the courage of fear I evolved the plan of fighting Thomas Mugridge with his own weapons. I borrowed a whetstone from Johansen. Louis, the boat-steerer, had already begged me for condensed milk and sugar. The lazarette, where such delicacies were stored, was situated beneath the cabin floor. Watching my chance, I stole five cans of the milk, and that night, when it was Louis's watch on deck, I traded them with him for a dirk as lean and cruel-looking as Thomas Mugridge's vegetable knife. It was rusty and dull, but I turned the grindstone while Louis gave it an edge. I slept more soundly than usual that night.

Next morning, after breakfast, Thomas Mugridge began his whet, whet, whet. I glanced warily at him, for I was on my knees taking the ashes from the stove. When I returned from throwing them overside, he was talking to Harrison, whose honest yokel's face was filled with fascination and wonder.

"Yes," Mugridge was saying, "an' wot does 'is worship do but give me two years in Reading. But blimey if I cared. The other mug was fixed plenty. Should 'a seen 'im. Knife just like this. I stuck it in, like into soft butter, an' the w'y 'e squealed was better'n a tu-penny gaff." He shot a glance in my direction to see if I was taking it in, and went on. "'I didn't mean it Tommy,' 'e was snifflin'; 'so 'elp me Gawd, I didn't mean it!' 'I'll fix yer bloody well right,' I sez, an' kept right after 'im. I cut 'im in ribbons, that's wot I did, an' 'e a-squealin' all the time. Once 'e got 'is 'and on the knife an' tried to 'old it. 'Ad 'is fingers around it, but I pulled it through, cuttin' to the bone. O, 'e was a sight, I can tell yer."

A call from the mate interrupted the gory narrative, and Harrison went aft. Mugridge sat down on the raised threshold to the galley and went on with his knife-sharpening. I put the shovel away and calmly sat down on the coal-box facing him.

He favoured me with a vicious stare. Still calmly, though my heart was going pitapat, I pulled out Louis's dirk and began to whet it on the stone. I had looked for almost any sort of explosion on the Cockney's part, but to my surprise he did not appear aware of what I was doing. He went on whetting his knife. So did I. And for two hours we sat there, face to face, whet, whet, whet, till the news of it spread abroad and half the ship's company was crowding the galley doors to see the sight.

Encouragement and advice were freely tendered, and Jock Horner, the quiet, self-spoken hunter who looked as though he would not harm a mouse, advised me to leave the ribs alone and to thrust upward for the abdomen, at the same time giving what he called the "Spanish twist" to the blade. Leach, his bandaged arm prominently to the fore, begged me to leave a few remnants of the cook for him; and Wolf Larsen paused once or twice at the break of the poop to glance curiously at what must have been to him a stirring and crawling of the yeasty thing he knew as life.

And I make free to say that for the time being life assumed the same sordid values to me. There was nothing pretty about it, nothing divine—only two cowardly moving things that sat whetting steel upon stone, and a group of other moving things, cowardly and otherwise, that looked on. Half of them, I am sure, were anxious to see us shedding each other's blood. It would have been entertainment. And I do not think there was one who would have interfered had we closed in a death-struggle.

On the other hand, the whole thing was laughable and childish. Whet, whet, whet,—Humphrey Van Weyden sharpening his knife in a ship's galley and trying its edge with his thumb! Of all situations this was the most inconceivable. I know that my own kind could not have believed it possible. I had not been called "Sissy" Van Weyden all my days without reason, and that "Sissy" Van Weyden should be capable of doing this thing was a revelation to Humphrey Van Weyden, who knew not whether to be exultant or ashamed.

But nothing happened. At the end of two hours Thomas Mugridge put away knife and stone and held out his hand.

"Wot's the good of mykin' a 'oly show of ourselves for them mugs?" he demanded. "They don't love us, an' bloody well glad they'd be a-seein' us cuttin' our throats. Yer not 'arf bad, 'Ump! You've got spunk, as you Yanks s'y, an' I like yer in a w'y. So come on an' shyke."

Coward that I might be, I was less a coward than he. It was a distinct victory I had gained, and I refused to forego any of it by shaking his detestable hand.

"All right," he said pridelessly, "tyke it or leave it, I'll like yer none the less for it." And to save his face he turned fiercely upon the onlookers. "Get outa my galley-doors, you bloomin' swabs!"

This command was reinforced by a steaming kettle of water, and at sight of it the sailors scrambled out of the way. This was a sort of victory for Thomas Mugridge, and enabled him to accept more gracefully the defeat I had given him, though, of course, he was too discreet to attempt to drive the hunters away.

"I see Cooky's finish," I heard Smoke say to Horner.

"You bet," was the reply. "Hump runs the galley from now on, and Cooky pulls in his horns."

Mugridge heard and shot a swift glance at me, but I gave no sign that the conversation had reached me. I had not thought my victory was so far-reaching and complete, but I resolved to let go nothing I had gained. As the days went by, Smoke's prophecy was verified. The Cockney became more humble and slavish to me than even to Wolf Larsen. I mistered him and sirred him no longer, washed no more greasy pots, and peeled no more potatoes. I did my own work, and my own work only, and when and in what fashion I saw fit. Also I carried the dirk in a sheath at my hip, sailor-fashion, and maintained toward Thomas Mugridge a constant attitude which was composed of equal parts of domineering, insult, and contempt.

CHAPTER X

My intimacy with Wolf Larsen increases—if by intimacy may be denoted those relations which exist between master and man, or, better yet, between king and jester. I am to him no more than a toy, and he values me no more than a child values a toy. My function is to amuse, and so long as I amuse all goes well; but let him become bored, or let him have one of his black moods come upon him, and at once I am relegated from cabin table to galley, while, at the same time, I am fortunate to escape with my life and a whole body.

The loneliness of the man is slowly being borne in upon me. There is not a man aboard but hates or fears him, nor is there a man whom he does not despise. He seems consuming with the tremendous power that is in him and that seems never to have found adequate expression in works. He is as Lucifer would be, were that proud spirit banished to a society of soulless, Tomlinsonian ghosts.

This loneliness is bad enough in itself, but, to make it worse, he is oppressed by the primal melancholy of the race. Knowing him, I review the old Scandinavian myths with clearer understanding. The white-skinned, fair-haired savages who created that terrible pantheon were of the same fibre as he. The frivolity of the laughter-loving Latins is no part of him. When he laughs it is from a humour that is nothing else than ferocious. But he laughs rarely; he is too often sad. And it is a sadness as deep-reaching as the roots of the race. It is the race heritage, the sadness which has made the race sober-minded, clean-lived and fanatically moral, and which, in this latter connection, has culminated among the English in the Reformed Church and Mrs. Grundy.

In point of fact, the chief vent to this primal melancholy has been religion in its more agonizing forms. But the compensations of such religion are denied Wolf Larsen. His brutal materialism will not permit it. So, when his blue moods come on, nothing remains for him, but to be devilish. Were he not so terrible a man, I could sometimes feel sorry for him, as instance three mornings ago, when I went into his stateroom to fill his water-bottle and came unexpectedly upon him. He did not see me. His head was buried in his hands, and his shoulders were heaving convulsively as with sobs. He seemed torn by some mighty grief. As I softly withdrew I could hear him groaning, "God! God! God!" Not that he was calling upon God; it was a mere expletive, but it came from his soul.

At dinner he asked the hunters for a remedy for headache, and by evening, strong man that he was, he was half-blind and reeling about the cabin.

"I've never been sick in my life, Hump," he said, as I guided him to his room. "Nor did I ever have a headache except the time my head was healing after having been laid open for six inches by a capstan-bar."

For three days this blinding headache lasted, and he suffered as wild animals suffer, as it seemed the way on ship to suffer, without plaint, without sympathy, utterly alone.

This morning, however, on entering his state-room to make the bed and put things in order, I found him well and hard at work. Table and bunk were littered with designs and calculations. On a large transparent sheet, compass and square in hand, he was copying what appeared to be a scale of some sort or other.

"Hello, Hump," he greeted me genially. "I'm just finishing the finishing touches. Want to see it work?"

"But what is it?" I asked.

"A labour-saving device for mariners, navigation reduced to kindergarten simplicity," he answered gaily. "From to-day a child will be able to navigate a ship. No more long-winded calculations. All you need is one star in the sky on a dirty night to know instantly where you are. Look. I place the transparent scale on this star-map, revolving the scale on the North Pole. On the scale I've worked out the circles of altitude and the lines of bearing. All I do is to put it on a star, revolve the scale till it is opposite those figures on the map underneath, and presto! there you are, the ship's precise location!"

There was a ring of triumph in his voice, and his eyes, clear blue this morning as the sea, were sparkling with light.

"You must be well up in mathematics," I said. "Where did you go to school?"

"Never saw the inside of one, worse luck," was the answer. "I had to dig it out for myself."

"And why do you think I have made this thing?" he demanded, abruptly. "Dreaming to leave footprints on the sands of time?" He laughed one of his horrible mocking laughs. "Not at all. To get it patented, to make money from it, to revel in piggishness with all night in while other men do the work. That's my purpose. Also, I have enjoyed working it out."

"The creative joy," I murmured.

"I guess that's what it ought to be called. Which is another way of expressing the joy of life in that it is alive, the triumph of movement over matter, of the quick over the dead, the pride of the yeast because it is yeast and crawls."

I threw up my hands with helpless disapproval of his inveterate materialism and went about making the bed. He continued copying lines and figures upon the transparent scale. It was a task requiring the utmost nicety and precision, and I could not but admire the way he tempered his strength to the fineness and delicacy of the need.

When I had finished the bed, I caught myself looking at him in a fascinated sort of way. He was certainly a handsome man—beautiful in the masculine sense. And again, with never-failing wonder, I remarked the total lack of viciousness, or wickedness, or sinfulness in his face. It was the face, I am convinced, of a man who did no wrong. And by this I do not wish to be misunderstood. What I mean is that it was the face of a man who either did nothing contrary to the dictates of his conscience, or who had no conscience. I am inclined to the latter way of accounting for it. He was a magnificent atavism, a man so purely primitive that he was of the type that came into the world before the development of the moral nature. He was not immoral, but merely unmoral.

As I have said, in the masculine sense his was a beautiful face. Smooth-shaven, every line was distinct, and it was cut as clear and sharp as a cameo; while sea and sun had tanned the naturally fair skin to a dark bronze which bespoke struggle and battle and added both to his savagery and his beauty. The lips were full, yet possessed of the firmness, almost harshness, which is characteristic of thin lips. The set of his mouth, his chin, his jaw, was likewise firm or harsh, with all the fierceness and indomitableness of the male—the nose also. It was the nose of a being born to conquer and command. It just hinted of the eagle beak. It might have been Grecian, it might have been Roman, only it was a shade too massive for the one, a shade too delicate for the other. And while the whole face was the incarnation of fierceness and strength, the primal melancholy from which he suffered seemed to greaten the lines of mouth and eye and brow, seemed to give a largeness and completeness which otherwise the face would have lacked.

And so I caught myself standing idly and studying him. I cannot say how greatly the man had come to interest me. Who was he? What was he? How had he happened to be? All powers seemed his, all potentialities—why, then, was he no more than the obscure master of a seal-hunting schooner with a reputation for frightful brutality amongst the men who hunted seals?

My curiosity burst from me in a flood of speech.

"Why is it that you have not done great things in this world? With the power that is yours you might have risen to any height. Unpossessed of conscience or moral instinct, you might have mastered the world, broken it to your hand. And yet here you are, at the top of your life, where diminishing and dying begin, living an obscure and sordid existence, hunting sea animals for the satisfaction of woman's vanity and love of decoration, revelling in a piggishness, to use your own words, which is anything and everything except splendid. Why, with all that wonderful strength, have you not done something? There was nothing to stop you, nothing that could stop you. What was wrong? Did you lack ambition? Did you fall under temptation? What was the matter? What was the matter?"

He had lifted his eyes to me at the commencement of my outburst, and followed me complacently until I had done and stood before him breathless and dismayed. He waited a moment, as though seeking where to begin, and then said:

"Hump, do you know the parable of the sower who went forth to sow? If you will remember, some of the seed fell upon stony places, where there was not much earth, and forthwith they sprung up because they had no deepness of earth. And when the sun was up they were scorched, and because they had no root they withered away. And some fell among thorns, and the thorns sprung up and choked them."

"Well?" I said.

"Well?" he queried, half petulantly. "It was not well. I was one of those seeds."

He dropped his head to the scale and resumed the copying. I finished my work and had opened the door to leave, when he spoke to me.

"Hump, if you will look on the west coast of the map of Norway you will see an indentation called Romsdal Fiord. I was born within a hundred miles of that stretch of water. But I was not born Norwegian. I am a Dane. My father and mother were Danes, and how they ever came to that bleak bight of land on the west coast I do not know. I never heard. Outside of that there is nothing mysterious. They were poor people and unlettered. They came of generations of poor unlettered people—peasants of the sea who sowed their sons on the waves as has been their custom since time began. There is no more to tell."

"But there is," I objected. "It is still obscure to me."

"What can I tell you?" he demanded, with a recrudescence of fierceness. "Of the meagreness of a child's life? of fish diet and coarse living? of going out with the boats from the time I could crawl? of my brothers, who went away one by one to the deep-sea farming and never came back? of myself, unable to read or write, cabin-boy at the mature age of ten on the coastwise, old-country ships? of the rough fare and rougher usage, where kicks and blows were bed and breakfast and took the place of speech, and fear and hatred and pain were my only soul-experiences? I do not care to remember. A madness comes up in my brain even now as I think of it. But there were coastwise skippers I would have returned and killed when a man's strength came to me, only the lines of my life were cast at the time in other places. I did return, not long ago, but unfortunately the skippers were dead, all but one, a mate in the old days, a skipper when I met him, and when I left him a cripple who would never walk again."

"But you who read Spencer and Darwin and have never seen the inside of a school, how did you learn to read and write?" I queried.

"In the English merchant service. Cabin-boy at twelve, ship's boy at fourteen, ordinary seamen at sixteen, able seaman at seventeen, and cock of the fo'c'sle, infinite ambition and infinite loneliness, receiving neither help nor sympathy, I did it all for myself—navigation, mathematics, science, literature, and what not. And of what use has it been? Master and owner of a ship at the top of my life, as you say, when I am beginning to diminish and die. Paltry, isn't it? And when the sun was up I was scorched, and because I had no root I withered away."

"But history tells of slaves who rose to the purple," I chided.

"And history tells of opportunities that came to the slaves who rose to the purple," he answered grimly. "No man makes opportunity. All the great men ever did was to know it when it came to them. The Corsican knew. I have dreamed as greatly as the Corsican. I should have known the opportunity, but it never came. The thorns sprung up and choked me. And, Hump, I can tell you that you know more about me than any living man, except my own brother."

"And what is he? And where is he?"

"Master of the steamship *Macedonia*, seal-hunter," was the answer. "We will meet him most probably on the Japan coast. Men call him 'Death' Larsen."

"Death Larsen!" I involuntarily cried. "Is he like you?"

"Hardly. He is a lump of an animal without any head. He has all my—my—"

"Brutishness," I suggested.

"Yes,—thank you for the word,—all my brutishness, but he can scarcely read or write."

"And he has never philosophized on life," I added.

"No," Wolf Larsen answered, with an indescribable air of sadness. "And he is all the happier for leaving life alone. He is too busy living it to think about it. My mistake was in ever opening the books."

CHAPTER XI

The *Ghost* has attained the southernmost point of the arc she is describing across the Pacific, and is already beginning to edge away to the west and north toward some lone island, it is rumoured, where she will fill her water-casks before proceeding to the season's hunt along the coast of Japan. The hunters have experimented and practised with their rifles and shotguns till they are satisfied, and the boat-pullers and steerers have made their spritsails, bound the oars and rowlocks in leather and sennit so that they will make no noise when creeping on the seals, and put their boats in apple-pie order—to use Leach's homely phrase.

His arm, by the way, has healed nicely, though the scar will remain all his life. Thomas Mugridge lives in mortal fear of him, and is afraid to venture on deck after dark. There are two or three standing quarrels in the forecastle. Louis tells me that the gossip of the sailors finds its way aft, and that two of the telltales have been badly beaten by their mates. He shakes his head dubiously over the outlook for the man Johnson, who is boat-puller in the same boat with him. Johnson has been guilty of speaking his mind too freely, and has collided two or three times with Wolf Larsen over the pronunciation of his name. Johansen he thrashed on the amidships deck the other night, since which time the mate has called him by his proper name. But of course it is out of the question that Johnson should thrash Wolf Larsen.

Louis has also given me additional information about Death Larsen, which tallies with the captain's brief description. We may expect to meet Death Larsen on the Japan coast. "And look out for squalls," is Louis's prophecy, "for they hate one another like the wolf whelps they are." Death Larsen is in command of the only sealing steamer in the fleet, the *Macedonia*, which carries fourteen boats, whereas the rest of the schooners carry only six. There is wild talk of cannon aboard, and of strange raids and expeditions she may make, ranging from opium smuggling into the States and arms smuggling into China, to blackbirding and open piracy. Yet I cannot but believe for I have never yet caught him in a lie, while he has a cyclopædic knowledge of sealing and the men of the sealing fleets.

As it is forward and in the galley, so it is in the steerage and aft, on this veritable hell-ship. Men fight and struggle ferociously for one another's lives. The hunters are looking for a shooting scrape at any moment between Smoke and Henderson, whose old quarrel has not healed, while Wolf Larsen says positively that he will kill the survivor of the affair, if such affair comes off. He frankly states that the position he takes is based on no moral grounds, that all the hunters could kill and eat one another so far as he is concerned, were it not that he needs them alive for the hunting. If they will only hold their hands until the season is over, he promises them a royal carnival, when all grudges can he settled and the survivors may toss the non-survivors overboard and arrange a story as to how the missing men were lost at sea. I think even the hunters are appalled at his cold-bloodedness. Wicked men though they be, they are certainly very much afraid of him.

Thomas Mugridge is cur-like in his subjection to me, while I go about in secret dread of him. His is the courage of fear,—a strange thing I know well of myself,—and at any moment it may master the fear and impel him to the taking of my life. My knee is much better, though it often aches for long periods, and the stiffness is gradually leaving the arm which Wolf Larsen squeezed. Otherwise I am in splendid condition, feel that I am in splendid condition. My muscles are growing harder and increasing in size. My hands, however, are a spectacle for grief. They have a parboiled appearance, are afflicted with hang-nails, while the nails are broken and discoloured, and the edges of the quick seem to be assuming a fungoid sort of growth. Also, I am suffering from boils, due to the diet, most likely, for I was never afflicted in this manner before.

I was amused, a couple of evenings back, by seeing Wolf Larsen reading the Bible, a copy of which, after the futile search for one at the beginning of the voyage, had been found in the dead mate's sea-chest. I wondered what Wolf Larsen could get from it, and he read aloud to me from Ecclesiastes. I could imagine he was speaking the thoughts of his own mind as he read to me, and his voice, reverberating deeply and mournfully in the confined cabin, charmed and held me. He may be uneducated, but he certainly knows how to express the significance of the written word. I can hear him now, as I shall always hear him, the primal melancholy vibrant in his voice as he read:

> "I gathered me also silver and gold, and the peculiar treasure of kings and of the provinces; I gat me men singers and women singers, and the delights of the sons of men, as musical instruments, and that of all sorts.
>
> "So I was great, and increased more than all that were before me in Jerusalem; also my wisdom returned with me.
>
> "Then I looked on all the works that my hands had wrought and on the labour that I had laboured to do; and behold, all was vanity and vexation of spirit, and there was no profit under the sun.
>
> "All things come alike to all; there is one event to the righteous and to the wicked; to the good and to the clean, and to the unclean; to him that sacrificeth, and to him that sacrificeth not; as is the good, so is the sinner; and he that sweareth, as he that feareth an oath.
>
> "This is an evil among all things that are done under the sun, that there is one event unto all; yea, also the heart of the sons of men is full of evil, and madness is in their heart while they live, and after that they go to the dead.
>
> "For to him that is joined to all the living there is hope; for a living dog is better than a dead lion.

CHAPTER XI

> "For the living know that they shall die; but the dead know not anything, neither have they any more a reward; for the memory of them is forgotten.
>
> "Also their love, and their hatred, and their envy, is now perished; neither have they any more a portion for ever in anything that is done under the sun."

"There you have it, Hump," he said, closing the book upon his finger and looking up at me. "The Preacher who was king over Israel in Jerusalem thought as I think. You call me a pessimist. Is not this pessimism of the blackest?—'All is vanity and vexation of spirit,' 'There is no profit under the sun,' 'There is one event unto all,' to the fool and the wise, the clean and the unclean, the sinner and the saint, and that event is death, and an evil thing, he says. For the Preacher loved life, and did not want to die, saying, 'For a living dog is better than a dead lion.' He preferred the vanity and vexation to the silence and unmovableness of the grave. And so I. To crawl is piggish; but to not crawl, to be as the clod and rock, is loathsome to contemplate. It is loathsome to the life that is in me, the very essence of which is movement, the power of movement, and the consciousness of the power of movement. Life itself is unsatisfaction, but to look ahead to death is greater unsatisfaction."

"You are worse off than Omar," I said. "He, at least, after the customary agonizing of youth, found content and made of his materialism a joyous thing."

"Who was Omar?" Wolf Larsen asked, and I did no more work that day, nor the next, nor the next.

In his random reading he had never chanced upon the Rubáiyát, and it was to him like a great find of treasure. Much I remembered, possibly two-thirds of the quatrains, and I managed to piece out the remainder without difficulty. We talked for hours over single stanzas, and I found him reading into them a wail of regret and a rebellion which, for the life of me, I could not discover myself. Possibly I recited with a certain joyous lilt which was my own, for—his memory was good, and at a second rendering, very often the first, he made a quatrain his own—he recited the same lines and invested them with an unrest and passionate revolt that was well-nigh convincing.

I was interested as to which quatrain he would like best, and was not surprised when he hit upon the one born of an instant's irritability, and quite at variance with the Persian's complacent philosophy and genial code of life:

> *"What, without asking, hither hurried Whence?*
> *And, without asking, Whither hurried hence!*
> *Oh, many a Cup of this forbidden Wine*
> *Must drown the memory of that insolence!"*

"Great!" Wolf Larsen cried. "Great! That's the keynote. Insolence! He could not have used a better word."

In vain I objected and denied. He deluged me, overwhelmed me with argument.

"It's not the nature of life to be otherwise. Life, when it knows that it must cease living, will always rebel. It cannot help itself. The Preacher found life and the works of life all a vanity and vexation, an evil thing; but death, the ceasing to be able to be vain and vexed, he found an eviler thing. Through chapter after chapter he is worried by the one event that cometh to all alike. So Omar, so I, so you, even you, for you rebelled against dying when Cooky sharpened a knife for you. You were afraid to die; the life that was in you, that composes you, that is greater than you, did not want to die. You have talked of the instinct of immortality. I talk of the instinct of life, which is to live, and which, when death looms near and large, masters the instinct, so called, of immortality. It mastered it in you (you cannot deny it), because a crazy Cockney cook sharpened a knife.

"You are afraid of him now. You are afraid of me. You cannot deny it. If I should catch you by the throat, thus,"—his hand was about my throat and my breath was shut off,—"and began to press the life out of you thus, and thus, your instinct of immortality will go glimmering, and your instinct of life, which is longing for life, will flutter up, and you will struggle to save yourself. Eh? I see the fear of death in your eyes. You beat the air with your arms. You exert all your puny strength to struggle to live. Your hand is clutching my arm, lightly it feels as a butterfly resting there. Your chest is heaving, your tongue protruding, your skin turning dark, your eyes swimming. 'To live! To live! To live!' you are crying; and you are crying to live here and now, not hereafter. You doubt your immortality, eh? Ha! ha! You are not sure of it. You won't chance it. This life only you are certain is real. Ah, it is growing dark and darker. It is the darkness of death, the ceasing to be, the ceasing to feel, the ceasing to move, that is gathering about you, descending upon you, rising around you. Your eyes are becoming set. They are glazing. My voice sounds faint and far. You cannot see my face. And still you struggle in my grip. You kick with your legs. Your body draws itself up in knots like a snake's. Your chest heaves and strains. To live! To live! To live—"

I heard no more. Consciousness was blotted out by the darkness he had so graphically described, and when I came to myself I was lying on the floor and he was smoking a cigar and regarding me thoughtfully with that old familiar light of curiosity in his eyes.

"Well, have I convinced you?" he demanded. "Here take a drink of this. I want to ask you some questions."

I rolled my head negatively on the floor. "Your arguments are too—er—forcible," I managed to articulate, at cost of great pain to my aching throat.

"You'll be all right in half-an-hour," he assured me. "And I promise I won't use any more physical demonstrations. Get up now. You can sit on a chair."

And, toy that I was of this monster, the discussion of Omar and the Preacher was resumed. And half the night we sat up over it.

CHAPTER XII

The last twenty-four hours have witnessed a carnival of brutality. From cabin to forecastle it seems to have broken out like a contagion. I scarcely know where to begin. Wolf Larsen was really the cause of it. The relations among the men, strained and made tense by feuds, quarrels and grudges, were in a state of unstable equilibrium, and evil passions flared up in flame like prairie-grass.

Thomas Mugridge is a sneak, a spy, an informer. He has been attempting to curry favour and reinstate himself in the good graces of the captain by carrying tales of the men forward. He it was, I know, that carried some of Johnson's hasty talk to Wolf Larsen. Johnson, it seems, bought a suit of oilskins from the slop-chest and found them to be of greatly inferior quality. Nor was he slow in advertising the fact. The slop-chest is a sort of miniature dry-goods store which is carried by all sealing schooners and which is stocked with articles peculiar to the needs of the sailors. Whatever a sailor purchases is taken from his subsequent earnings on the sealing grounds; for, as it is with the hunters so it is with the boat-pullers and steerers—in the place of wages they receive a "lay," a rate of so much per skin for every skin captured in their particular boat.

But of Johnson's grumbling at the slop-chest I knew nothing, so that what I witnessed came with a shock of sudden surprise. I had just finished sweeping the cabin, and had been inveigled by Wolf Larsen into a discussion of Hamlet, his favourite Shakespearian character, when Johansen descended the companion stairs followed by Johnson. The latter's cap came off after the custom of the sea, and he stood respectfully in the centre of the cabin, swaying heavily and uneasily to the roll of the schooner and facing the captain.

"Shut the doors and draw the slide," Wolf Larsen said to me.

As I obeyed I noticed an anxious light come into Johnson's eyes, but I did not dream of its cause. I did not dream of what was to occur until it did occur, but he knew from the very first what was coming and awaited it bravely. And in his action I found complete refutation of all Wolf Larsen's materialism. The sailor Johnson was swayed by idea, by principle, and truth, and sincerity. He was right, he knew he was right, and he was unafraid. He would die for the right if needs be, he would be true to himself, sincere with his soul. And in this was portrayed the victory of the spirit over the flesh, the indomitability and moral grandeur of the soul that knows no restriction and rises above time and space and matter with a surety and invincibleness born of nothing else than eternity and immortality.

But to return. I noticed the anxious light in Johnson's eyes, but mistook it for the native shyness and embarrassment of the man. The mate, Johansen, stood away several feet to the side of him, and fully three yards in front of him sat Wolf Larsen on one of the pivotal cabin chairs. An appreciable pause fell after I had closed the doors and drawn the slide, a pause that must have lasted fully a minute. It was broken by Wolf Larsen.

"Yonson," he began.

"My name is Johnson, sir," the sailor boldly corrected.

"Well, Johnson, then, damn you! Can you guess why I have sent for you?"

"Yes, and no, sir," was the slow reply. "My work is done well. The mate knows that, and you know it, sir. So there cannot be any complaint."

"And is that all?" Wolf Larsen queried, his voice soft, and low, and purring.

"I know you have it in for me," Johnson continued with his unalterable and ponderous slowness. "You do not like me. You—you—"

"Go on," Wolf Larsen prompted. "Don't be afraid of my feelings."

"I am not afraid," the sailor retorted, a slight angry flush rising through his sunburn. "If I speak not fast, it is because I have not been from the old country as long as you. You do not like me because I am too much of a man; that is why, sir."

"You are too much of a man for ship discipline, if that is what you mean, and if you know what I mean," was Wolf Larsen's retort.

"I know English, and I know what you mean, sir," Johnson answered, his flush deepening at the slur on his knowledge of the English language.

"Johnson," Wolf Larsen said, with an air of dismissing all that had gone before as introductory to the main business in hand, "I understand you're not quite satisfied with those oilskins?"

"No, I am not. They are no good, sir."

"And you've been shooting off your mouth about them."

"I say what I think, sir," the sailor answered courageously, not failing at the same time in ship courtesy, which demanded that "sir" be appended to each speech he made.

It was at this moment that I chanced to glance at Johansen. His big fists were clenching and unclenching, and his face was positively fiendish, so malignantly did he look at Johnson. I noticed a black discoloration, still faintly visible, under Johansen's eye, a mark of the thrashing he had received a few nights before from the sailor. For the first time I began to divine that something terrible was about to be enacted,—what, I could not imagine.

"Do you know what happens to men who say what you've said about my slop-chest and me?" Wolf Larsen was demanding.

"I know, sir," was the answer.

"What?" Wolf Larsen demanded, sharply and imperatively.

"What you and the mate there are going to do to me, sir."

"Look at him, Hump," Wolf Larsen said to me, "look at this bit of animated dust, this aggregation of matter that moves and breathes and defies me and thoroughly believes itself to be compounded of something good; that is impressed with certain human fictions such as righteousness and honesty, and that will live up to them in spite of all personal discomforts and menaces. What do you think of him, Hump? What do you think of him?"

"I think that he is a better man than you are," I answered, impelled, somehow, with a desire to draw upon myself a portion of the wrath I felt was about to break upon his head. "His human fictions, as you choose to call them, make for nobility and manhood. You have no fictions, no dreams, no ideals. You are a pauper."

He nodded his head with a savage pleasantness. "Quite true, Hump, quite true. I have no fictions that make for nobility and manhood. A living dog is better than a dead lion, say I with the Preacher. My only doctrine is the doctrine of expediency, and it makes for surviving. This bit of the ferment we call 'Johnson,' when he is no longer a bit of the ferment, only dust and ashes, will have no more nobility than any dust and ashes, while I shall still be alive and roaring."

"Do you know what I am going to do?" he questioned.

I shook my head.

"Well, I am going to exercise my prerogative of roaring and show you how fares nobility. Watch me."

Three yards away from Johnson he was, and sitting down. Nine feet! And yet he left the chair in full leap, without first gaining a standing position. He left the chair, just as he sat in it, squarely, springing from the sitting posture like a wild animal, a tiger, and like a tiger covered the intervening space. It was an avalanche of fury that Johnson strove vainly to fend off. He threw one arm down to protect the stomach, the other arm up to protect the head; but Wolf Larsen's fist drove midway between, on the chest, with a crushing, resounding impact. Johnson's breath, suddenly expelled, shot from his mouth and as suddenly checked, with the forced, audible expiration of a man wielding an axe. He almost fell backward, and swayed from side to side in an effort to recover his balance.

I cannot give the further particulars of the horrible scene that followed. It was too revolting. It turns me sick even now when I think of it. Johnson fought bravely enough, but he was no match for Wolf Larsen, much less for Wolf Larsen and the mate. It was frightful. I had not imagined a human being could endure so much and still live and struggle on. And struggle on Johnson did. Of course there was no hope for him, not the slightest, and he knew it as well as I, but by the manhood that was in him he could not cease from fighting for that manhood.

It was too much for me to witness. I felt that I should lose my mind, and I ran up the companion stairs to open the doors and escape on deck. But Wolf Larsen, leaving his victim for the moment, and with one of his tremendous springs, gained my side and flung me into the far corner of the cabin.

"The phenomena of life, Hump," he girded at me. "Stay and watch it. You may gather data on the immortality of the soul. Besides, you know, we can't hurt Johnson's soul. It's only the fleeting form we may demolish."

It seemed centuries—possibly it was no more than ten minutes that the beating continued. Wolf Larsen and Johansen were all about the poor fellow. They struck him with their fists, kicked him with their heavy shoes, knocked him down, and dragged him to his feet to knock him down again. His eyes were blinded so that he could not see, and the blood running from ears and nose and mouth turned the cabin into a shambles. And when he could no longer rise they still continued to beat and kick him where he lay.

"Easy, Johansen; easy as she goes," Wolf Larsen finally said.

But the beast in the mate was up and rampant, and Wolf Larsen was compelled to brush him away with a back-handed sweep of the arm, gentle enough, apparently, but which hurled Johansen back like a cork, driving his head against the wall with a crash. He fell to the floor, half stunned for the moment, breathing heavily and blinking his eyes in a stupid sort of way.

"Jerk open the doors,—Hump," I was commanded.

I obeyed, and the two brutes picked up the senseless man like a sack of rubbish and hove him clear up the companion stairs, through the narrow doorway, and out on deck. The blood from his nose gushed in a scarlet stream over the feet of the helmsman, who was none other than Louis, his boat-mate. But Louis took and gave a spoke and gazed imperturbably into the binnacle.

Not so was the conduct of George Leach, the erstwhile cabin-boy. Fore and aft there was nothing that could have surprised us more than his consequent behaviour. He it was that came up on the poop without orders and dragged Johnson forward, where he set about dressing his wounds as well as he could and making him comfortable. Johnson, as Johnson, was unrecognizable; and not only that, for his features, as human features at all, were unrecognizable, so discoloured and swollen had they become in the few minutes which had elapsed between the beginning of the beating and the dragging forward of the body.

But of Leach's behaviour—By the time I had finished cleansing the cabin he had taken care of Johnson. I had come up on deck for a breath of fresh air and to try to get some repose for my overwrought nerves. Wolf Larsen was smoking a cigar and examining the patent log which the *Ghost* usually towed astern, but which had been hauled in for some purpose. Suddenly Leach's voice came to my ears. It was tense and hoarse with an overmastering rage. I turned and saw him standing just beneath the break of the poop on the port side of the galley. His face was convulsed and white, his eyes were flashing, his clenched fists raised overhead.

"May God damn your soul to hell, Wolf Larsen, only hell's too good for you, you coward, you murderer, you pig!" was his opening salutation.

I was thunderstruck. I looked for his instant annihilation. But it was not Wolf Larsen's whim to annihilate him. He sauntered slowly forward to the break of the poop, and, leaning his elbow on the corner of the cabin, gazed down thoughtfully and curiously at the excited boy.

And the boy indicted Wolf Larsen as he had never been indicted before. The sailors assembled in a fearful group just outside the forecastle scuttle and watched and listened. The hunters piled pell-mell out of the steerage, but as Leach's tirade continued I saw that there was no levity in their faces. Even they were frightened, not at the boy's terrible words, but at his terrible audacity. It did not seem possible that any living creature could thus beard Wolf Larsen in his teeth. I know for myself that I was shocked into admiration of the boy, and I saw in him the splendid invincibleness of immortality rising above the flesh and the fears of the flesh, as in the prophets of old, to condemn unrighteousness.

And such condemnation! He haled forth Wolf Larsen's soul naked to the scorn of men. He rained upon it curses from God and High Heaven, and withered it with a heat of invective that savoured of a mediæval excommunication of the Catholic Church. He ran the gamut of denunciation, rising to heights of wrath that were sublime and almost Godlike, and from sheer exhaustion sinking to the vilest and most indecent abuse.

His rage was a madness. His lips were flecked with a soapy froth, and sometimes he choked and gurgled and became inarticulate. And through it all, calm and impassive, leaning on his elbow and gazing down, Wolf Larsen seemed lost in a great curiosity. This wild stirring of yeasty life, this terrific revolt and defiance of matter that moved, perplexed and interested him.

Each moment I looked, and everybody looked, for him to leap upon the boy and destroy him. But it was not his whim. His cigar went out, and he continued to gaze silently and curiously.

Leach had worked himself into an ecstasy of impotent rage.

"Pig! Pig! Pig!" he was reiterating at the top of his lungs. "Why don't you come down and kill me, you murderer? You can do it! I ain't afraid! There's no one to stop you! Damn sight better dead and outa your reach than alive and in your clutches! Come on, you coward! Kill me! Kill me! Kill me!"

It was at this stage that Thomas Mugridge's erratic soul brought him into the scene. He had been listening at the galley door, but he now came out, ostensibly to fling some scraps over the side, but obviously to see the killing he was certain would take place. He smirked greasily up into the face of Wolf Larsen, who seemed not to see him. But the Cockney was unabashed, though mad, stark mad. He turned to Leach, saying:

"Such langwidge! Shockin'!"

Leach's rage was no longer impotent. Here at last was something ready to hand. And for the first time since the stabbing the Cockney had appeared outside the galley without his knife. The words had barely left his mouth when he was knocked down by Leach. Three times he struggled to his feet, striving to gain the galley, and each time was knocked down.

"Oh, Lord!" he cried. "'Elp! 'Elp! Tyke 'im aw'y, carn't yer? Tyke 'im aw'y!"

The hunters laughed from sheer relief. Tragedy had dwindled, the farce had begun. The sailors now crowded boldly aft, grinning and shuffling, to watch the pummelling of the hated Cockney. And even I felt a great joy surge up within me. I confess that I delighted in this beating Leach was giving to Thomas Mugridge, though it was as terrible, almost, as the one Mugridge had caused to be given to Johnson. But the expression of Wolf Larsen's face never changed. He did not change his position either, but continued to gaze down with a great curiosity. For all his pragmatic certitude, it seemed as if he watched the play and movement of life in the hope of discovering something more about it, of discerning in its maddest writhings a something which had hitherto escaped him,—the key to its mystery, as it were, which would make all clear and plain.

But the beating! It was quite similar to the one I had witnessed in the cabin. The Cockney strove in vain to protect himself from the infuriated boy. And in vain he strove to gain the shelter of the cabin. He rolled toward it, grovelled toward it, fell toward it when he was knocked down. But blow followed blow with bewildering rapidity. He was knocked about like a shuttlecock, until, finally, like Johnson, he was beaten and kicked as he lay helpless on the deck. And no one interfered. Leach could have killed him, but, having evidently filled the measure of his vengeance, he drew away from his prostrate foe, who was whimpering and wailing in a puppyish sort of way, and walked forward.

But these two affairs were only the opening events of the day's programme. In the afternoon Smoke and Henderson fell foul of each other, and a fusillade of shots came up from the steerage, followed by a stampede of the other four hunters for the deck. A column of thick, acrid smoke—the kind always made by black powder—was arising through the open companion-way, and down through it leaped Wolf Larsen. The sound of blows and scuffling came to our ears. Both men were wounded, and he was thrashing them both for having disobeyed his orders and crippled themselves in advance of the hunting season. In fact, they were badly wounded, and, having thrashed them, he proceeded to operate upon them in a rough surgical fashion and to dress their wounds. I served as assistant while he probed and cleansed the passages made by the bullets, and I saw the two men endure his crude surgery without anæsthetics and with no more to uphold them than a stiff tumbler of whisky.

Then, in the first dog-watch, trouble came to a head in the forecastle. It took its rise out of the tittle-tattle and tale-bearing which had been the cause of Johnson's beating, and from the noise we heard, and from the sight of the bruised men next day, it was patent that half the forecastle had soundly drubbed the other half.

The second dog-watch and the day were wound up by a fight between Johansen and the lean, Yankee-looking hunter, Latimer. It was caused by remarks of Latimer's concerning the noises made by the mate in his sleep, and though Johansen was whipped, he kept the steerage awake for the rest of the night while he blissfully slumbered and fought the fight over and over again.

As for myself, I was oppressed with nightmare. The day had been like some horrible dream. Brutality had followed brutality, and flaming passions and cold-blooded cruelty had driven men to seek one another's lives, and to strive to hurt, and maim, and destroy. My nerves were shocked. My mind itself was shocked. All my days had been passed in comparative ignorance of the animality of man. In fact, I had known life only in its intellectual phases. Brutality I had experienced, but it was the brutality of the intellect—the cutting sarcasm of Charley Furuseth, the cruel epigrams and occasional harsh witticisms of the fellows at the Bibelot, and the nasty remarks of some of the professors during my undergraduate days.

That was all. But that men should wreak their anger on others by the bruising of the flesh and the letting of blood was something strangely and fearfully new to me. Not for nothing had I been called "Sissy" Van Weyden, I thought, as I tossed restlessly on my bunk between one nightmare and another. And it seemed to me that my innocence of the realities of life had been complete indeed. I laughed bitterly to myself, and seemed to find in Wolf Larsen's forbidding philosophy a more adequate explanation of life than I found in my own.

And I was frightened when I became conscious of the trend of my thought. The continual brutality around me was degenerative in its effect. It bid fair to destroy for me all that was best and brightest in life. My reason dictated that the beating Thomas Mugridge had received was an ill thing, and yet for the life of me I could not prevent my soul joying in it. And even while I was oppressed by the enormity of my sin,—for sin it was,—I chuckled with an insane delight. I was no longer Humphrey Van Weyden. I was Hump, cabin-boy on the schooner *Ghost*. Wolf Larsen was my captain, Thomas Mugridge and the rest were my companions, and I was receiving repeated impresses from the die which had stamped them all.

CHAPTER XIII

For three days I did my own work and Thomas Mugridge's too; and I flatter myself that I did his work well. I know that it won Wolf Larsen's approval, while the sailors beamed with satisfaction during the brief time my *régime* lasted.

"The first clean bite since I come aboard," Harrison said to me at the galley door, as he returned the dinner pots and pans from the forecastle. "Somehow Tommy's grub always tastes of grease, stale grease, and I reckon he ain't changed his shirt since he left 'Frisco."

"I know he hasn't," I answered.

"And I'll bet he sleeps in it," Harrison added.

"And you won't lose," I agreed. "The same shirt, and he hasn't had it off once in all this time."

But three days was all Wolf Larsen allowed him in which to recover from the effects of the beating. On the fourth day, lame and sore, scarcely able to see, so closed were his eyes, he was haled from his bunk by the nape of the neck and set to his duty. He sniffled and wept, but Wolf Larsen was pitiless.

"And see that you serve no more slops," was his parting injunction. "No more grease and dirt, mind, and a clean shirt occasionally, or you'll get a tow over the side. Understand?"

Thomas Mugridge crawled weakly across the galley floor, and a short lurch of the *Ghost* sent him staggering. In attempting to recover himself, he reached for the iron railing which surrounded the stove and kept the pots from sliding off; but he missed the railing, and his hand, with his weight behind it, landed squarely on the hot surface. There was a sizzle and odour of burning flesh, and a sharp cry of pain.

"Oh, Gawd, Gawd, wot 'ave I done?" he wailed; sitting down in the coal-box and nursing his new hurt by rocking back and forth. "W'y 'as all this come on me? It mykes me fair sick, it does, an' I try so 'ard to go through life 'armless an' 'urtin' nobody."

The tears were running down his puffed and discoloured cheeks, and his face was drawn with pain. A savage expression flitted across it.

"Oh, 'ow I 'ate 'im! 'Ow I 'ate 'im!" he gritted out.

"Whom?" I asked; but the poor wretch was weeping again over his misfortunes. Less difficult it was to guess whom he hated than whom he did not hate. For I had come to see a malignant devil in him which impelled him to hate all the world. I sometimes thought that he hated even himself, so grotesquely had life dealt with him, and so monstrously. At such moments a great sympathy welled up within me, and I felt shame that I had ever joyed in his discomfiture or pain. Life had been unfair to him. It had played him a scurvy trick when it fashioned him into the thing he was, and it had played him scurvy tricks ever since. What chance had he to be anything else than he was? And as though answering my unspoken thought, he wailed:

"I never 'ad no chance, not 'arf a chance! 'Oo was there to send me to school, or put tommy in my 'ungry belly, or wipe my bloody nose for me, w'en I was a kiddy? 'Oo ever did anything for me, heh? 'Oo, I s'y?"

"Never mind, Tommy," I said, placing a soothing hand on his shoulder. "Cheer up. It'll all come right in the end. You've long years before you, and you can make anything you please of yourself."

"It's a lie! a bloody lie!" he shouted in my face, flinging off the hand. "It's a lie, and you know it. I'm already myde, an' myde out of leavin's an' scraps. It's all right for you, 'Ump. You was born a gentleman. You never knew wot it was to go 'ungry, to cry yerself asleep with yer little belly gnawin' an' gnawin', like a rat inside yer. It carn't come right. If I was President of the United Stytes to-morrer, 'ow would it fill my belly for one time w'en I was a kiddy and it went empty?

"'Ow could it, I s'y? I was born to sufferin' and sorrer. I've had more cruel sufferin' than any ten men, I 'ave. I've been in orspital arf my bleedin' life. I've 'ad the fever in Aspinwall, in 'Avana, in New Orleans. I near died of the scurvy and was rotten with it six months in Barbadoes. Smallpox in 'Onolulu, two broken legs in Shanghai, pnuemonia in Unalaska, three busted ribs an' my insides all twisted in 'Frisco. An' 'ere I am now. Look at me! Look at me! My ribs kicked loose from my back again. I'll be coughin' blood before eyght bells. 'Ow can it be myde up to me, I arsk? 'Oo's goin' to do it? Gawd? 'Ow Gawd must 'ave 'ated me w'en 'e signed me on for a voyage in this bloomin' world of 'is!"

This tirade against destiny went on for an hour or more, and then he buckled to his work, limping and groaning, and in his eyes a great hatred for all created things. His diagnosis was correct, however, for he was seized with occasional sicknesses, during which he vomited blood and suffered great pain. And as he said, it seemed God hated him too much to let him die, for he ultimately grew better and waxed more malignant than ever.

Several days more passed before Johnson crawled on deck and went about his work in a half-hearted way. He was still a sick man, and I more than once observed him creeping painfully aloft to a topsail, or drooping wearily as he stood at the wheel. But, still worse, it seemed that his spirit was broken. He was abject before Wolf Larsen and almost grovelled to Johansen. Not so was the conduct of Leach. He went about the deck like a tiger cub, glaring his hatred openly at Wolf Larsen and Johansen.

"I'll do for you yet, you slab-footed Swede," I heard him say to Johansen one night on deck.

The mate cursed him in the darkness, and the next moment some missile struck the galley a sharp rap. There was more cursing, and a mocking laugh, and when all was quiet I stole outside and found a heavy knife imbedded over an inch in the solid wood. A few minutes later the mate came fumbling about in search of it, but I returned it privily to Leach next day. He grinned when I handed it over, yet it was a grin that contained more sincere thanks than a multitude of the verbosities of speech common to the members of my own class.

Unlike any one else in the ship's company, I now found myself with no quarrels on my hands and in the good graces of all. The hunters possibly no more than tolerated me, though none of them disliked me; while Smoke and Henderson, convalescent under a deck awning and swinging day and night in their hammocks, assured me that I was better than any hospital nurse, and that they would not forget me at the end of the voyage when they were paid off. (As though I stood in need of their money! I, who could have bought them out, bag and baggage, and the schooner and its equipment, a score of times over!) But upon me had devolved the task of tending their wounds, and pulling them through, and I did my best by them.

Wolf Larsen underwent another bad attack of headache which lasted two days. He must have suffered severely, for he called me in and obeyed my commands like a sick child. But nothing I could do seemed to relieve him. At my suggestion, however, he gave up smoking and drinking; though why such a magnificent animal as he should have headaches at all puzzles me.

"'Tis the hand of God, I'm tellin' you," is the way Louis sees it. "'Tis a visitation for his black-hearted deeds, and there's more behind and comin', or else—"

"Or else," I prompted.

"God is noddin' and not doin' his duty, though it's me as shouldn't say it."

I was mistaken when I said that I was in the good graces of all. Not only does Thomas Mugridge continue to hate me, but he has discovered a new reason for hating me. It took me no little while to puzzle it out, but I finally discovered that it was because I was more luckily born than he—"gentleman born," he put it.

"And still no more dead men," I twitted Louis, when Smoke and Henderson, side by side, in friendly conversation, took their first exercise on deck.

Louis surveyed me with his shrewd grey eyes, and shook his head portentously. "She's a-comin', I tell you, and it'll be sheets and halyards, stand by all hands, when she begins to howl. I've had the feel iv it this long time, and I can feel it now as plainly as I feel the rigging iv a dark night. She's close, she's close."

"Who goes first?" I queried.

"Not fat old Louis, I promise you," he laughed. "For 'tis in the bones iv me I know that come this time next year I'll be gazin' in the old mother's eyes, weary with watchin' iv the sea for the five sons she gave to it."

"Wot's 'e been s'yin' to yer?" Thomas Mugridge demanded a moment later.

"That he's going home some day to see his mother," I answered diplomatically.

"I never 'ad none," was the Cockney's comment, as he gazed with lustreless, hopeless eyes into mine.

CHAPTER XIV

It has dawned upon me that I have never placed a proper valuation upon womankind. For that matter, though not amative to any considerable degree so far as I have discovered, I was never outside the atmosphere of women until now. My mother and sisters were always about me, and I was always trying to escape them; for they worried me to distraction with their solicitude for my health and with their periodic inroads on my den, when my orderly confusion, upon which I prided myself, was turned into worse confusion and less order, though it looked neat enough to the eye. I never could find anything when they had departed. But now, alas, how welcome would have been the feel of their presence, the frou-frou and swish-swish of their skirts which I had so cordially detested! I am sure, if I ever get home, that I shall never be irritable with them again. They may dose me and doctor me morning, noon, and night, and dust and sweep and put my den to rights every minute of the day, and I shall only lean back and survey it all and be thankful in that I am possessed of a mother and some several sisters.

All of which has set me wondering. Where are the mothers of these twenty and odd men on the *Ghost*? It strikes me as unnatural and unhealthful that men should be totally separated from women and herd through the world by themselves. Coarseness and savagery are the inevitable results. These men about me should have wives, and sisters, and daughters; then would they be capable of softness, and tenderness, and sympathy. As it is, not one of them is married. In years and years not one of them has been in contact with a good woman, or within the influence, or redemption, which irresistibly radiates from such a creature. There is no balance in their lives. Their masculinity, which in itself is of the brute, has been over-developed. The other and spiritual side of their natures has been dwarfed—atrophied, in fact.

They are a company of celibates, grinding harshly against one another and growing daily more calloused from the grinding. It seems to me impossible sometimes that they ever had mothers. It would appear that they are a half-brute, half-human species, a race apart, wherein there is no such thing as sex; that they are hatched out by the sun like turtle eggs, or receive life in some similar and sordid fashion; and that all their days they fester in brutality and viciousness, and in the end die as unlovely as they have lived.

Rendered curious by this new direction of ideas, I talked with Johansen last night—the first superfluous words with which he has favoured me since the voyage began. He left Sweden when he was eighteen, is now thirty-eight, and in all the intervening time has not been home once. He had met a townsman, a couple of years before, in some sailor boarding-house in Chile, so that he knew his mother to be still alive.

"She must be a pretty old woman now," he said, staring meditatively into the binnacle and then jerking a sharp glance at Harrison, who was steering a point off the course.

"When did you last write to her?"

He performed his mental arithmetic aloud. "Eighty-one; no—eighty-two, eh? no—eighty-three? Yes, eighty-three. Ten years ago. From some little port in Madagascar. I was trading.

"You see," he went on, as though addressing his neglected mother across half the girth of the earth, "each year I was going home. So what was the good to write? It was only a year. And each year something happened, and I did not go. But I am mate, now, and when I pay off at 'Frisco, maybe with five hundred dollars, I will ship myself on a windjammer round the Horn to Liverpool, which will give me more money; and then I will pay my passage from there home. Then she will not do any more work."

"But does she work? now? How old is she?"

"About seventy," he answered. And then, boastingly, "We work from the time we are born until we die, in my country. That's why we live so long. I will live to a hundred."

I shall never forget this conversation. The words were the last I ever heard him utter. Perhaps they were the last he did utter, too. For, going down into the cabin to turn in, I decided that it was too stuffy to sleep below. It was a calm night. We were out of the Trades, and the *Ghost* was forging ahead barely a knot an hour. So I tucked a blanket and pillow under my arm and went up on deck.

As I passed between Harrison and the binnacle, which was built into the top of the cabin, I noticed that he was this time fully three points off. Thinking that he was asleep, and wishing him to escape reprimand or worse, I spoke to him. But he was not asleep. His eyes were wide and staring. He seemed greatly perturbed, unable to reply to me.

"What's the matter?" I asked. "Are you sick?"

He shook his head, and with a deep sign as of awakening, caught his breath.

"You'd better get on your course, then," I chided.

He put a few spokes over, and I watched the compass-card swing slowly to N.N.W. and steady itself with slight oscillations.

I took a fresh hold on my bedclothes and was preparing to start on, when some movement caught my eye and I looked astern to the rail. A sinewy hand, dripping with water, was clutching the rail. A second hand took form in the darkness beside it. I watched, fascinated. What visitant from the gloom of the deep was I to behold? Whatever it was, I knew that it was climbing aboard by the log-line. I saw a head, the hair wet and straight, shape itself, and then the unmistakable eyes and face of Wolf Larsen. His right cheek was red with blood, which flowed from some wound in the head.

He drew himself inboard with a quick effort, and arose to his feet, glancing swiftly, as he did so, at the man at the wheel, as though to assure himself of his identity and that there was nothing to fear from him. The sea-water was streaming from him.

It made little audible gurgles which distracted me. As he stepped toward me I shrank back instinctively, for I saw that in his eyes which spelled death.

"All right, Hump," he said in a low voice. "Where's the mate?"

I shook my head.

"Johansen!" he called softly. "Johansen!"

"Where is he?" he demanded of Harrison.

The young fellow seemed to have recovered his composure, for he answered steadily enough, "I don't know, sir. I saw him go for'ard a little while ago."

"So did I go for'ard. But you will observe that I didn't come back the way I went. Can you explain it?"

"You must have been overboard, sir."

"Shall I look for him in the steerage, sir?" I asked.

Wolf Larsen shook his head. "You wouldn't find him, Hump. But you'll do. Come on. Never mind your bedding. Leave it where it is."

I followed at his heels. There was nothing stirring amidships.

"Those cursed hunters," was his comment. "Too damned fat and lazy to stand a four-hour watch."

But on the forecastle-head we found three sailors asleep. He turned them over and looked at their faces. They composed the watch on deck, and it was the ship's custom, in good weather, to let the watch sleep with the exception of the officer, the helmsman, and the look-out.

"Who's look-out?" he demanded.

"Me, sir," answered Holyoak, one of the deep-water sailors, a slight tremor in his voice. "I winked off just this very minute, sir. I'm sorry, sir. It won't happen again."

"Did you hear or see anything on deck?"

"No, sir, I—"

But Wolf Larsen had turned away with a snort of disgust, leaving the sailor rubbing his eyes with surprise at having been let of so easily.

"Softly, now," Wolf Larsen warned me in a whisper, as he doubled his body into the forecastle scuttle and prepared to descend.

I followed with a quaking heart. What was to happen I knew no more than did I know what had happened. But blood had been shed, and it was through no whim of Wolf Larsen that he had gone over the side with his scalp laid open. Besides, Johansen was missing.

It was my first descent into the forecastle, and I shall not soon forget my impression of it, caught as I stood on my feet at the bottom of the ladder. Built directly in the eyes of the schooner, it was of the shape of a triangle, along the three sides of which stood the bunks, in double-tier, twelve of them. It was no larger than a hall bedroom in Grub Street, and yet twelve men were herded into it to eat and sleep and carry on all the functions of living. My bedroom at home was not large, yet it could have contained a dozen similar forecastles, and taking into consideration the height of the ceiling, a score at least.

It smelled sour and musty, and by the dim light of the swinging sea-lamp I saw every bit of available wall-space hung deep with sea-boots, oilskins, and garments, clean and dirty, of various sorts. These swung back and forth with every roll of the vessel, giving rise to a brushing sound, as of trees against a roof or wall. Somewhere a boot thumped loudly and at irregular intervals against the wall; and, though it was a mild night on the sea, there was a continual chorus of the creaking timbers and bulkheads and of abysmal noises beneath the flooring.

The sleepers did not mind. There were eight of them,—the two watches below,—and the air was thick with the warmth and odour of their breathing, and the ear was filled with the noise of their snoring and of their sighs and half-groans, tokens plain of the rest of the animal-man. But were they sleeping? all of them? Or had they been sleeping? This was evidently Wolf Larsen's quest—to find the men who appeared to be asleep and who were not asleep or who had not been asleep very recently. And he went about it in a way that reminded me of a story out of Boccaccio.

He took the sea-lamp from its swinging frame and handed it to me. He began at the first bunks forward on the star-board side. In the top one lay Oofty-Oofty, a Kanaka and splendid seaman, so named by his mates. He was asleep on his back and breathing as placidly as a woman. One arm was under his head, the other lay on top of the blankets. Wolf Larsen put thumb and forefinger to the wrist and counted the pulse. In the midst of it the Kanaka roused. He awoke as gently as he slept. There was no movement of the body whatever. The eyes, only, moved. They flashed wide open, big and black, and stared, unblinking, into our faces. Wolf Larsen put his finger to his lips as a sign for silence, and the eyes closed again.

In the lower bunk lay Louis, grossly fat and warm and sweaty, asleep unfeignedly and sleeping laboriously. While Wolf Larsen held his wrist he stirred uneasily, bowing his body so that for a moment it rested on shoulders and heels. His lips moved, and he gave voice to this enigmatic utterance:

"A shilling's worth a quarter; but keep your lamps out for thruppenny-bits, or the publicans 'll shove 'em on you for sixpence."

Then he rolled over on his side with a heavy, sobbing sigh, saying:

"A sixpence is a tanner, and a shilling a bob; but what a pony is I don't know."

Satisfied with the honesty of his and the Kanaka's sleep, Wolf Larsen passed on to the next two bunks on the starboard side, occupied top and bottom, as we saw in the light of the sea-lamp, by Leach and Johnson.

As Wolf Larsen bent down to the lower bunk to take Johnson's pulse, I, standing erect and holding the lamp, saw Leach's head rise stealthily as he peered over the side of his bunk to see what was going on. He must have divined Wolf Larsen's trick and the sureness of detection, for the light was at once dashed from my hand and the forecastle was left in darkness. He must have leaped, also, at the same instant, straight down on Wolf Larsen.

The first sounds were those of a conflict between a bull and a wolf. I heard a great infuriated bellow go up from Wolf Larsen, and from Leach a snarling that was desperate and blood-curdling. Johnson must have joined him immediately, so that his abject and grovelling conduct on deck for the past few days had been no more than planned deception.

I was so terror-stricken by this fight in the dark that I leaned against the ladder, trembling and unable to ascend. And upon me was that old sickness at the pit of the stomach, caused always by the spectacle of physical violence. In this instance I could not see, but I could hear the impact of the blows—the soft crushing sound made by flesh striking forcibly against flesh. Then there was the crashing about of the entwined bodies, the laboured breathing, the short quick gasps of sudden pain.

CHAPTER XIV

There must have been more men in the conspiracy to murder the captain and mate, for by the sounds I knew that Leach and Johnson had been quickly reinforced by some of their mates.

"Get a knife somebody!" Leach was shouting.

"Pound him on the head! Mash his brains out!" was Johnson's cry.

But after his first bellow, Wolf Larsen made no noise. He was fighting grimly and silently for life. He was sore beset. Down at the very first, he had been unable to gain his feet, and for all of his tremendous strength I felt that there was no hope for him.

The force with which they struggled was vividly impressed on me; for I was knocked down by their surging bodies and badly bruised. But in the confusion I managed to crawl into an empty lower bunk out of the way.

"All hands! We've got him! We've got him!" I could hear Leach crying.

"Who?" demanded those who had been really asleep, and who had wakened to they knew not what.

"It's the bloody mate!" was Leach's crafty answer, strained from him in a smothered sort of way.

This was greeted with whoops of joy, and from then on Wolf Larsen had seven strong men on top of him, Louis, I believe, taking no part in it. The forecastle was like an angry hive of bees aroused by some marauder.

"What ho! below there!" I heard Latimer shout down the scuttle, too cautious to descend into the inferno of passion he could hear raging beneath him in the darkness.

"Won't somebody get a knife? Oh, won't somebody get a knife?" Leach pleaded in the first interval of comparative silence.

The number of the assailants was a cause of confusion. They blocked their own efforts, while Wolf Larsen, with but a single purpose, achieved his. This was to fight his way across the floor to the ladder. Though in total darkness, I followed his progress by its sound. No man less than a giant could have done what he did, once he had gained the foot of the ladder. Step by step, by the might of his arms, the whole pack of men striving to drag him back and down, he drew his body up from the floor till he stood erect. And then, step by step, hand and foot, he slowly struggled up the ladder.

The very last of all, I saw. For Latimer, having finally gone for a lantern, held it so that its light shone down the scuttle. Wolf Larsen was nearly to the top, though I could not see him. All that was visible was the mass of men fastened upon him. It squirmed about, like some huge many-legged spider, and swayed back and forth to the regular roll of the vessel. And still, step by step with long intervals between, the mass ascended. Once it tottered, about to fall back, but the broken hold was regained and it still went up.

"Who is it?" Latimer cried.

In the rays of the lantern I could see his perplexed face peering down.

"Larsen," I heard a muffled voice from within the mass.

Latimer reached down with his free hand. I saw a hand shoot up to clasp his. Latimer pulled, and the next couple of steps were made with a rush. Then Wolf Larsen's other hand reached up and clutched the edge of the scuttle. The mass swung clear of the ladder, the men still clinging to their escaping foe. They began to drop off, to be brushed off against the sharp edge of the scuttle, to be knocked off by the legs which were now kicking powerfully. Leach was the last to go, falling sheer back from the top of the scuttle and striking on head and shoulders upon his sprawling mates beneath. Wolf Larsen and the lantern disappeared, and we were left in darkness.

CHAPTER XV

There was a deal of cursing and groaning as the men at the bottom of the ladder crawled to their feet.

"Somebody strike a light, my thumb's out of joint," said one of the men, Parsons, a swarthy, saturnine man, boat-steerer in Standish's boat, in which Harrison was puller.

"You'll find it knockin' about by the bitts," Leach said, sitting down on the edge of the bunk in which I was concealed.

There was a fumbling and a scratching of matches, and the sea-lamp flared up, dim and smoky, and in its weird light bare-legged men moved about nursing their bruises and caring for their hurts. Oofty-Oofty laid hold of Parsons's thumb, pulling it out stoutly and snapping it back into place. I noticed at the same time that the Kanaka's knuckles were laid open clear across and to the bone. He exhibited them, exposing beautiful white teeth in a grin as he did so, and explaining that the wounds had come from striking Wolf Larsen in the mouth.

"So it was you, was it, you black beggar?" belligerently demanded one Kelly, an Irish-American and a longshoreman, making his first trip to sea, and boat-puller for Kerfoot.

As he made the demand he spat out a mouthful of blood and teeth and shoved his pugnacious face close to Oofty-Oofty. The Kanaka leaped backward to his bunk, to return with a second leap, flourishing a long knife.

"Aw, go lay down, you make me tired," Leach interfered. He was evidently, for all of his youth and inexperience, cock of the forecastle. "G'wan, you Kelly. You leave Oofty alone. How in hell did he know it was you in the dark?"

Kelly subsided with some muttering, and the Kanaka flashed his white teeth in a grateful smile. He was a beautiful creature, almost feminine in the pleasing lines of his figure, and there was a softness and dreaminess in his large eyes which seemed to contradict his well-earned reputation for strife and action.

"How did he get away?" Johnson asked.

He was sitting on the side of his bunk, the whole pose of his figure indicating utter dejection and hopelessness. He was still breathing heavily from the exertion he had made. His shirt had been ripped entirely from him in the struggle, and blood from a gash in the cheek was flowing down his naked chest, marking a red path across his white thigh and dripping to the floor.

"Because he is the devil, as I told you before," was Leach's answer; and thereat he was on his feet and raging his disappointment with tears in his eyes.

"And not one of you to get a knife!" was his unceasing lament.

But the rest of the hands had a lively fear of consequences to come and gave no heed to him.

"How'll he know which was which?" Kelly asked, and as he went on he looked murderously about him—"unless one of us peaches."

"He'll know as soon as ever he claps eyes on us," Parsons replied. "One look at you'd be enough."

"Tell him the deck flopped up and gouged yer teeth out iv yer jaw," Louis grinned. He was the only man who was not out of his bunk, and he was jubilant in that he possessed no bruises to advertise that he had had a hand in the night's work. "Just wait till he gets a glimpse iv yer mugs to-morrow, the gang iv ye," he chuckled.

"We'll say we thought it was the mate," said one. And another, "I know what I'll say—that I heered a row, jumped out of my bunk, got a jolly good crack on the jaw for my pains, and sailed in myself. Couldn't tell who or what it was in the dark and just hit'out."

"An' 'twas me you hit, of course," Kelly seconded, his face brightening for the moment.

Leach and Johnson took no part in the discussion, and it was plain to see that their mates looked upon them as men for whom the worst was inevitable, who were beyond hope and already dead. Leach stood their fears and reproaches for some time. Then he broke out:

"You make me tired! A nice lot of gazabas you are! If you talked less with yer mouth and did something with yer hands, he'd a-ben done with by now. Why couldn't one of you, just one of you, get me a knife when I sung out? You make me sick! A-beefin' and bellerin' 'round, as though he'd kill you when he gets you! You know damn well he wont. Can't afford to. No shipping masters or beach-combers over here, and he wants yer in his business, and he wants yer bad. Who's to pull or steer or sail ship if he loses yer? It's me and Johnson have to face the music. Get into yer bunks, now, and shut yer faces; I want to get some sleep."

"That's all right all right," Parsons spoke up. "Mebbe he won't do for us, but mark my words, hell 'll be an ice-box to this ship from now on."

All the while I had been apprehensive concerning my own predicament. What would happen to me when these men discovered my presence? I could never fight my way out as Wolf Larsen had done. And at this moment Latimer called down the scuttles:

"Hump! The old man wants you!"

"He ain't down here!" Parsons called back.

"Yes, he is," I said, sliding out of the bunk and striving my hardest to keep my voice steady and bold.

The sailors looked at me in consternation. Fear was strong in their faces, and the devilishness which comes of fear.

"I'm coming!" I shouted up to Latimer.

"No you don't!" Kelly cried, stepping between me and the ladder, his right hand shaped into a veritable strangler's clutch. "You damn little sneak! I'll shut yer mouth!"

CHAPTER XV

"Let him go," Leach commanded.

"Not on yer life," was the angry retort.

Leach never changed his position on the edge of the bunk. "Let him go, I say," he repeated; but this time his voice was gritty and metallic.

The Irishman wavered. I made to step by him, and he stood aside. When I had gained the ladder, I turned to the circle of brutal and malignant faces peering at me through the semi-darkness. A sudden and deep sympathy welled up in me. I remembered the Cockney's way of putting it. How God must have hated them that they should be tortured so!

"I have seen and heard nothing, believe me," I said quietly.

"I tell yer, he's all right," I could hear Leach saying as I went up the ladder. "He don't like the old man no more nor you or me."

I found Wolf Larsen in the cabin, stripped and bloody, waiting for me. He greeted me with one of his whimsical smiles.

"Come, get to work, Doctor. The signs are favourable for an extensive practice this voyage. I don't know what the *Ghost* would have been without you, and if I could only cherish such noble sentiments I would tell you her master is deeply grateful."

I knew the run of the simple medicine-chest the *Ghost* carried, and while I was heating water on the cabin stove and getting the things ready for dressing his wounds, he moved about, laughing and chatting, and examining his hurts with a calculating eye. I had never before seen him stripped, and the sight of his body quite took my breath away. It has never been my weakness to exalt the flesh—far from it; but there is enough of the artist in me to appreciate its wonder.

I must say that I was fascinated by the perfect lines of Wolf Larsen's figure, and by what I may term the terrible beauty of it. I had noted the men in the forecastle. Powerfully muscled though some of them were, there had been something wrong with all of them, an insufficient development here, an undue development there, a twist or a crook that destroyed symmetry, legs too short or too long, or too much sinew or bone exposed, or too little. Oofty-Oofty had been the only one whose lines were at all pleasing, while, in so far as they pleased, that far had they been what I should call feminine.

But Wolf Larsen was the man-type, the masculine, and almost a god in his perfectness. As he moved about or raised his arms the great muscles leapt and moved under the satiny skin. I have forgotten to say that the bronze ended with his face. His body, thanks to his Scandinavian stock, was fair as the fairest woman's. I remember his putting his hand up to feel of the wound on his head, and my watching the biceps move like a living thing under its white sheath. It was the biceps that had nearly crushed out my life once, that I had seen strike so many killing blows. I could not take my eyes from him. I stood motionless, a roll of antiseptic cotton in my hand unwinding and spilling itself down to the floor.

He noticed me, and I became conscious that I was staring at him.

"God made you well," I said.

"Did he?" he answered. "I have often thought so myself, and wondered why."

"Purpose—" I began.

"Utility," he interrupted. "This body was made for use. These muscles were made to grip, and tear, and destroy living things that get between me and life. But have you thought of the other living things? They, too, have muscles, of one kind and another, made to grip, and tear, and destroy; and when they come between me and life, I out-grip them, out-tear them, out-destroy them. Purpose does not explain that. Utility does."

"It is not beautiful," I protested.

"Life isn't, you mean," he smiled. "Yet you say I was made well. Do you see this?"

He braced his legs and feet, pressing the cabin floor with his toes in a clutching sort of way. Knots and ridges and mounds of muscles writhed and bunched under the skin.

"Feel them," he commanded.

They were hard as iron. And I observed, also, that his whole body had unconsciously drawn itself together, tense and alert; that muscles were softly crawling and shaping about the hips, along the back, and across the shoulders; that the arms were slightly lifted, their muscles contracting, the fingers crooking till the hands were like talons; and that even the eyes had changed expression and into them were coming watchfulness and measurement and a light none other than of battle.

"Stability, equilibrium," he said, relaxing on the instant and sinking his body back into repose. "Feet with which to clutch the ground, legs to stand on and to help withstand, while with arms and hands, teeth and nails, I struggle to kill and to be not killed. Purpose? Utility is the better word."

I did not argue. I had seen the mechanism of the primitive fighting beast, and I was as strongly impressed as if I had seen the engines of a great battleship or Atlantic liner.

I was surprised, considering the fierce struggle in the forecastle, at the superficiality of his hurts, and I pride myself that I dressed them dexterously. With the exception of several bad wounds, the rest were merely severe bruises and lacerations. The blow which he had received before going overboard had laid his scalp open several inches. This, under his direction, I cleansed and sewed together, having first shaved the edges of the wound. Then the calf of his leg was badly lacerated and looked as though it had been mangled by a bulldog. Some sailor, he told me, had laid hold of it by his teeth, at the beginning of the fight, and hung on and been dragged to the top of the forecastle ladder, when he was kicked loose.

"By the way, Hump, as I have remarked, you are a handy man," Wolf Larsen began, when my work was done. "As you know, we're short a mate. Hereafter you shall stand watches, receive seventy-five dollars per month, and be addressed fore and aft as Mr. Van Weyden."

"I—I don't understand navigation, you know," I gasped.

"Not necessary at all."

"I really do not care to sit in the high places," I objected. "I find life precarious enough in my present humble situation. I have no experience. Mediocrity, you see, has its compensations."

He smiled as though it were all settled.

"I won't be mate on this hell-ship!" I cried defiantly.

I saw his face grow hard and the merciless glitter come into his eyes. He walked to the door of his room, saying:

"And now, Mr. Van Weyden, good-night."

CHAPTER XV

"Good-night, Mr. Larsen," I answered weakly.

CHAPTER XVI

I cannot say that the position of mate carried with it anything more joyful than that there were no more dishes to wash. I was ignorant of the simplest duties of mate, and would have fared badly indeed, had the sailors not sympathized with me. I knew nothing of the minutiæ of ropes and rigging, of the trimming and setting of sails; but the sailors took pains to put me to rights,—Louis proving an especially good teacher,—and I had little trouble with those under me.

With the hunters it was otherwise. Familiar in varying degree with the sea, they took me as a sort of joke. In truth, it was a joke to me, that I, the veriest landsman, should be filling the office of mate; but to be taken as a joke by others was a different matter. I made no complaint, but Wolf Larsen demanded the most punctilious sea etiquette in my case,—far more than poor Johansen had ever received; and at the expense of several rows, threats, and much grumbling, he brought the hunters to time. I was "Mr. Van Weyden" fore and aft, and it was only unofficially that Wolf Larsen himself ever addressed me as "Hump."

It was amusing. Perhaps the wind would haul a few points while we were at dinner, and as I left the table he would say, "Mr. Van Weyden, will you kindly put about on the port tack." And I would go on deck, beckon Louis to me, and learn from him what was to be done. Then, a few minutes later, having digested his instructions and thoroughly mastered the manœuvre, I would proceed to issue my orders. I remember an early instance of this kind, when Wolf Larsen appeared on the scene just as I had begun to give orders. He smoked his cigar and looked on quietly till the thing was accomplished, and then paced aft by my side along the weather poop.

"Hump," he said, "I beg pardon, Mr. Van Weyden, I congratulate you. I think you can now fire your father's legs back into the grave to him. You've discovered your own and learned to stand on them. A little rope-work, sail-making, and experience with storms and such things, and by the end of the voyage you could ship on any coasting schooner."

It was during this period, between the death of Johansen and the arrival on the sealing grounds, that I passed my pleasantest hours on the *Ghost*. Wolf Larsen was quite considerate, the sailors helped me, and I was no longer in irritating contact with Thomas Mugridge. And I make free to say, as the days went by, that I found I was taking a certain secret pride in myself. Fantastic as the situation was,—a land-lubber second in command,—I was, nevertheless, carrying it off well; and during that brief time I was proud of myself, and I grew to love the heave and roll of the *Ghost* under my feet as she wallowed north and west through the tropic sea to the islet where we filled our water-casks.

But my happiness was not unalloyed. It was comparative, a period of less misery slipped in between a past of great miseries and a future of great miseries. For the *Ghost*, so far as the seamen were concerned, was a hell-ship of the worst description. They never had a moment's rest or peace. Wolf Larsen treasured against them the attempt on his life and the drubbing he had received in the forecastle; and morning, noon, and night, and all night as well, he devoted himself to making life unlivable for them.

He knew well the psychology of the little thing, and it was the little things by which he kept the crew worked up to the verge of madness. I have seen Harrison called from his bunk to put properly away a misplaced paintbrush, and the two watches below haled from their tired sleep to accompany him and see him do it. A little thing, truly, but when multiplied by the thousand ingenious devices of such a mind, the mental state of the men in the forecastle may be slightly comprehended.

Of course much grumbling went on, and little outbursts were continually occurring. Blows were struck, and there were always two or three men nursing injuries at the hands of the human beast who was their master. Concerted action was impossible in face of the heavy arsenal of weapons carried in the steerage and cabin. Leach and Johnson were the two particular victims of Wolf Larsen's diabolic temper, and the look of profound melancholy which had settled on Johnson's face and in his eyes made my heart bleed.

With Leach it was different. There was too much of the fighting beast in him. He seemed possessed by an insatiable fury which gave no time for grief. His lips had become distorted into a permanent snarl, which at mere sight of Wolf Larsen broke out in sound, horrible and menacing and, I do believe, unconsciously. I have seen him follow Wolf Larsen about with his eyes, like an animal its keeper, the while the animal-like snarl sounded deep in his throat and vibrated forth between his teeth.

I remember once, on deck, in bright day, touching him on the shoulder as preliminary to giving an order. His back was toward me, and at the first feel of my hand he leaped upright in the air and away from me, snarling and turning his head as he leaped. He had for the moment mistaken me for the man he hated.

Both he and Johnson would have killed Wolf Larsen at the slightest opportunity, but the opportunity never came. Wolf Larsen was too wise for that, and, besides, they had no adequate weapons. With their fists alone they had no chance whatever. Time and again he fought it out with Leach who fought back always, like a wildcat, tooth and nail and fist, until stretched, exhausted or unconscious, on the deck. And he was never averse to another encounter. All the devil that was in him challenged the devil in Wolf Larsen. They had but to appear on deck at the same time, when they would be at it, cursing, snarling, striking; and I have seen Leach fling himself upon Wolf Larsen without warning or provocation. Once he threw his heavy sheath-knife, missing Wolf Larsen's throat by an inch. Another time he dropped a steel marlinspike from the mizzen crosstree. It was a difficult cast to make on a rolling ship, but the sharp point of the spike, whistling seventy-five feet through the air, barely missed Wolf Larsen's head as he emerged from the cabin companion-way and drove its length two inches and over into the solid deck-planking. Still another time, he stole into the steerage, possessed himself of a loaded shot-gun, and was making a rush for the deck with it when caught by Kerfoot and disarmed.

I often wondered why Wolf Larsen did not kill him and make an end of it. But he only laughed and seemed to enjoy it. There seemed a certain spice about it, such as men must feel who take delight in making pets of ferocious animals.

"It gives a thrill to life," he explained to me, "when life is carried in one's hand. Man is a natural gambler, and life is the biggest stake he can lay. The greater the odds, the greater the thrill. Why should I deny myself the joy of exciting Leach's soul to fever-pitch? For that matter, I do him a kindness. The greatness of sensation is mutual. He is living more royally than any man for'ard, though he does not know it. For he has what they have not—purpose, something to do and be done, an all-absorbing end to strive to attain, the desire to kill me, the hope that he may kill me. Really, Hump, he is living deep and high. I doubt that he has ever lived so swiftly and keenly before, and I honestly envy him, sometimes, when I see him raging at the summit of passion and sensibility."

"Ah, but it is cowardly, cowardly!" I cried. "You have all the advantage."

"Of the two of us, you and I, who is the greater coward?" he asked seriously. "If the situation is unpleasing, you compromise with your conscience when you make yourself a party to it. If you were really great, really true to yourself, you would join forces with Leach and Johnson. But you are afraid, you are afraid. You want to live. The life that is in you cries out that it must live, no matter what the cost; so you live ignominiously, untrue to the best you dream of, sinning against your whole pitiful little code, and, if there were a hell, heading your soul straight for it. Bah! I play the braver part. I do no sin, for I am true to the promptings of the life that is in me. I am sincere with my soul at least, and that is what you are not."

There was a sting in what he said. Perhaps, after all, I was playing a cowardly part. And the more I thought about it the more it appeared that my duty to myself lay in doing what he had advised, lay in joining forces with Johnson and Leach and working for his death. Right here, I think, entered the austere conscience of my Puritan ancestry, impelling me toward lurid deeds and sanctioning even murder as right conduct. I dwelt upon the idea. It would be a most moral act to rid the world of such a monster. Humanity would be better and happier for it, life fairer and sweeter.

I pondered it long, lying sleepless in my bunk and reviewing in endless procession the facts of the situation. I talked with Johnson and Leach, during the night watches when Wolf Larsen was below. Both men had lost hope—Johnson, because of temperamental despondency; Leach, because he had beaten himself out in the vain struggle and was exhausted. But he caught my hand in a passionate grip one night, saying:

"I think yer square, Mr. Van Weyden. But stay where you are and keep yer mouth shut. Say nothin' but saw wood. We're dead men, I know it; but all the same you might be able to do us a favour some time when we need it damn bad."

It was only next day, when Wainwright Island loomed to windward, close abeam, that Wolf Larsen opened his mouth in prophecy. He had attacked Johnson, been attacked by Leach, and had just finished whipping the pair of them.

"Leach," he said, "you know I'm going to kill you some time or other, don't you?"

A snarl was the answer.

CHAPTER XVI

"And as for you, Johnson, you'll get so tired of life before I'm through with you that you'll fling yourself over the side. See if you don't."

"That's a suggestion," he added, in an aside to me. "I'll bet you a month's pay he acts upon it."

I had cherished a hope that his victims would find an opportunity to escape while filling our water-barrels, but Wolf Larsen had selected his spot well. The *Ghost* lay half-a-mile beyond the surf-line of a lonely beach. Here debauched a deep gorge, with precipitous, volcanic walls which no man could scale. And here, under his direct supervision—for he went ashore himself—Leach and Johnson filled the small casks and rolled them down to the beach. They had no chance to make a break for liberty in one of the boats.

Harrison and Kelly, however, made such an attempt. They composed one of the boats' crews, and their task was to ply between the schooner and the shore, carrying a single cask each trip. Just before dinner, starting for the beach with an empty barrel, they altered their course and bore away to the left to round the promontory which jutted into the sea between them and liberty. Beyond its foaming base lay the pretty villages of the Japanese colonists and smiling valleys which penetrated deep into the interior. Once in the fastnesses they promised, and the two men could defy Wolf Larsen.

I had observed Henderson and Smoke loitering about the deck all morning, and I now learned why they were there. Procuring their rifles, they opened fire in a leisurely manner, upon the deserters. It was a cold-blooded exhibition of marksmanship. At first their bullets zipped harmlessly along the surface of the water on either side the boat; but, as the men continued to pull lustily, they struck closer and closer.

"Now, watch me take Kelly's right oar," Smoke said, drawing a more careful aim.

I was looking through the glasses, and I saw the oar-blade shatter as he shot. Henderson duplicated it, selecting Harrison's right oar. The boat slewed around. The two remaining oars were quickly broken. The men tried to row with the splinters, and had them shot out of their hands. Kelly ripped up a bottom board and began paddling, but dropped it with a cry of pain as its splinters drove into his hands. Then they gave up, letting the boat drift till a second boat, sent from the shore by Wolf Larsen, took them in tow and brought them aboard.

Late that afternoon we hove up anchor and got away. Nothing was before us but the three or four months' hunting on the sealing grounds. The outlook was black indeed, and I went about my work with a heavy heart. An almost funereal gloom seemed to have descended upon the *Ghost*. Wolf Larsen had taken to his bunk with one of his strange, splitting headaches. Harrison stood listlessly at the wheel, half supporting himself by it, as though wearied by the weight of his flesh. The rest of the men were morose and silent. I came upon Kelly crouching to the lee of the forecastle scuttle, his head on his knees, his arms about his head, in an attitude of unutterable despondency.

Johnson I found lying full length on the forecastle head, staring at the troubled churn of the forefoot, and I remembered with horror the suggestion Wolf Larsen had made. It seemed likely to bear fruit. I tried to break in on the man's morbid thoughts by calling him away, but he smiled sadly at me and refused to obey.

Leach approached me as I returned aft.

"I want to ask a favour, Mr. Van Weyden," he said. "If it's yer luck to ever make 'Frisco once more, will you hunt up Matt McCarthy? He's my old man. He lives on the Hill, back of the Mayfair bakery, runnin' a cobbler's shop that everybody knows, and you'll have no trouble. Tell him I lived to be sorry for the trouble I brought him and the things I done, and—and just tell him 'God bless him,' for me."

I nodded my head, but said, "We'll all win back to San Francisco, Leach, and you'll be with me when I go to see Matt McCarthy."

"I'd like to believe you," he answered, shaking my hand, "but I can't. Wolf Larsen 'll do for me, I know it; and all I can hope is, he'll do it quick."

And as he left me I was aware of the same desire at my heart. Since it was to be done, let it be done with despatch. The general gloom had gathered me into its folds. The worst appeared inevitable; and as I paced the deck, hour after hour, I found myself afflicted with Wolf Larsen's repulsive ideas. What was it all about? Where was the grandeur of life that it should permit such wanton destruction of human souls? It was a cheap and sordid thing after all, this life, and the sooner over the better. Over and done with! I, too, leaned upon the rail and gazed longingly into the sea, with the certainty that sooner or later I should be sinking down, down, through the cool green depths of its oblivion.

CHAPTER XVII

Strange to say, in spite of the general foreboding, nothing of especial moment happened on the *Ghost*. We ran on to the north and west till we raised the coast of Japan and picked up with the great seal herd. Coming from no man knew where in the illimitable Pacific, it was travelling north on its annual migration to the rookeries of Bering Sea. And north we travelled with it, ravaging and destroying, flinging the naked carcasses to the shark and salting down the skins so that they might later adorn the fair shoulders of the women of the cities.

It was wanton slaughter, and all for woman's sake. No man ate of the seal meat or the oil. After a good day's killing I have seen our decks covered with hides and bodies, slippery with fat and blood, the scuppers running red; masts, ropes, and rails spattered with the sanguinary colour; and the men, like butchers plying their trade, naked and red of arm and hand, hard at work with ripping and flensing-knives, removing the skins from the pretty sea-creatures they had killed.

It was my task to tally the pelts as they came aboard from the boats, to oversee the skinning and afterward the cleansing of the decks and bringing things ship-shape again. It was not pleasant work. My soul and my stomach revolted at it; and yet, in a way, this handling and directing of many men was good for me. It developed what little executive ability I possessed, and I was aware of a toughening or hardening which I was undergoing and which could not be anything but wholesome for "Sissy" Van Weyden.

One thing I was beginning to feel, and that was that I could never again be quite the same man I had been. While my hope and faith in human life still survived Wolf Larsen's destructive criticism, he had nevertheless been a cause of change in minor matters. He had opened up for me the world of the real, of which I had known practically nothing and from which I had always shrunk. I had learned to look more closely at life as it was lived, to recognize that there were such things as facts in the world, to emerge from the realm of mind and idea and to place certain values on the concrete and objective phases of existence.

I saw more of Wolf Larsen than ever when we had gained the grounds. For when the weather was fair and we were in the midst of the herd, all hands were away in the boats, and left on board were only he and I, and Thomas Mugridge, who did not count. But there was no play about it. The six boats, spreading out fan-wise from the schooner until the first weather boat and the last lee boat were anywhere from ten to twenty miles apart, cruised along a straight course over the sea till nightfall or bad weather drove them in. It was our duty to sail the *Ghost* well to leeward of the last lee boat, so that all the boats should have fair wind to run for us in case of squalls or threatening weather.

It is no slight matter for two men, particularly when a stiff wind has sprung up, to handle a vessel like the *Ghost*, steering, keeping look-out for the boats, and setting or taking in sail; so it devolved upon me to learn, and learn quickly. Steering I picked up easily, but running aloft to the crosstrees and swinging my whole weight by my arms when I left the ratlines and climbed still higher, was more difficult. This, too, I learned, and quickly, for I felt somehow a wild desire to vindicate myself in Wolf Larsen's eyes, to prove my right to live in ways other than of the mind. Nay, the time came when I took joy in the run of the masthead and in the clinging on by my legs at that precarious height while I swept the sea with glasses in search of the boats.

I remember one beautiful day, when the boats left early and the reports of the hunters' guns grew dim and distant and died away as they scattered far and wide over the sea. There was just the faintest wind from the westward; but it breathed its last by the time we managed to get to leeward of the last lee boat. One by one—I was at the masthead and saw—the six boats disappeared over the bulge of the earth as they followed the seal into the west. We lay, scarcely rolling on the placid sea, unable to follow. Wolf Larsen was apprehensive. The barometer was down, and the sky to the east did not please him. He studied it with unceasing vigilance.

"If she comes out of there," he said, "hard and snappy, putting us to windward of the boats, it's likely there'll be empty bunks in steerage and fo'c'sle."

By eleven o'clock the sea had become glass. By midday, though we were well up in the northerly latitudes, the heat was sickening. There was no freshness in the air. It was sultry and oppressive, reminding me of what the old Californians term "earthquake weather." There was something ominous about it, and in intangible ways one was made to feel that the worst was about to come. Slowly the whole eastern sky filled with clouds that over-towered us like some black sierra of the infernal regions. So clearly could one see cañon, gorge, and precipice, and the shadows that lie therein, that one looked unconsciously for the white surf-line and bellowing caverns where the sea charges on the land. And still we rocked gently, and there was no wind.

"It's no square" Wolf Larsen said. "Old Mother Nature's going to get up on her hind legs and howl for all that's in her, and it'll keep us jumping, Hump, to pull through with half our boats. You'd better run up and loosen the topsails."

"But if it is going to howl, and there are only two of us?" I asked, a note of protest in my voice.

"Why we've got to make the best of the first of it and run down to our boats before our canvas is ripped out of us. After that I don't give a rap what happens. The sticks 'll stand it, and you and I will have to, though we've plenty cut out for us."

Still the calm continued. We ate dinner, a hurried and anxious meal for me with eighteen men abroad on the sea and beyond the bulge of the earth, and with that heaven-rolling mountain range of clouds moving slowly down upon us. Wolf Larsen did not seem affected, however; though I noticed, when we returned to the deck, a slight twitching of the nostrils, a perceptible quickness of movement. His face was stern, the lines of it had grown hard, and yet in his eyes—blue, clear blue this day—there was a strange brilliancy, a bright scintillating light. It struck me that he was joyous, in a ferocious sort of way; that he was glad there was an impending struggle; that he was thrilled and upborne with knowledge that one of the great moments of living, when the tide of life surges up in flood, was upon him.

Once, and unwitting that he did so or that I saw, he laughed aloud, mockingly and defiantly, at the advancing storm. I see him yet standing there like a pigmy out of the *Arabian Nights* before the huge front of some malignant genie. He was daring destiny, and he was unafraid.

He walked to the galley. "Cooky, by the time you've finished pots and pans you'll be wanted on deck. Stand ready for a call."

"Hump," he said, becoming cognizant of the fascinated gaze I bent upon him, "this beats whisky and is where your Omar misses. I think he only half lived after all."

The western half of the sky had by now grown murky. The sun had dimmed and faded out of sight. It was two in the afternoon, and a ghostly twilight, shot through by wandering purplish lights, had descended upon us. In this purplish light Wolf Larsen's face glowed and glowed, and to my excited fancy he appeared encircled by a halo. We lay in the midst of an unearthly quiet, while all about us were signs and omens of oncoming sound and movement. The sultry heat had become unendurable. The sweat was standing on my forehead, and I could feel it trickling down my nose. I felt as though I should faint, and reached out to the rail for support.

And then, just then, the faintest possible whisper of air passed by. It was from the east, and like a whisper it came and went. The drooping canvas was not stirred, and yet my face had felt the air and been cooled.

"Cooky," Wolf Larsen called in a low voice. Thomas Mugridge turned a pitiable scared face. "Let go that foreboom tackle and pass it across, and when she's willing let go the sheet and come in snug with the tackle. And if you make a mess of it, it will be the last you ever make. Understand?"

"Mr. Van Weyden, stand by to pass the head-sails over. Then jump for the topsails and spread them quick as God'll let you—the quicker you do it the easier you'll find it. As for Cooky, if he isn't lively bat him between the eyes."

I was aware of the compliment and pleased, in that no threat had accompanied my instructions. We were lying head to north-west, and it was his intention to jibe over all with the first puff.

"We'll have the breeze on our quarter," he explained to me. "By the last guns the boats were bearing away slightly to the south'ard."

He turned and walked aft to the wheel. I went forward and took my station at the jibs. Another whisper of wind, and another, passed by. The canvas flapped lazily.

"Thank Gawd she's not comin' all of a bunch, Mr. Van Weyden," was the Cockney's fervent ejaculation.

And I was indeed thankful, for I had by this time learned enough to know, with all our canvas spread, what disaster in such event awaited us. The whispers of wind became puffs, the sails filled, the *Ghost* moved. Wolf Larsen put the wheel hard up, to port, and we began to pay off. The wind was now dead astern, muttering and puffing stronger and stronger, and my head-sails were pounding lustily. I did not see what went on elsewhere, though I felt the sudden surge and heel of the schooner as the wind-pressures changed to the jibing of the fore- and main-sails. My hands were full with the flying-jib, jib, and staysail; and by the time this part of my task was accomplished the *Ghost* was leaping into the south-west, the wind on her quarter and all her sheets to starboard. Without pausing for breath, though my heart was beating like a trip-hammer from my exertions, I sprang to the topsails, and before the wind had become too strong we had them fairly set and were coiling down. Then I went aft for orders.

Wolf Larsen nodded approval and relinquished the wheel to me. The wind was strengthening steadily and the sea rising. For an hour I steered, each moment becoming more difficult. I had not the experience to steer at the gait we were going on a quartering course.

"Now take a run up with the glasses and raise some of the boats. We've made at least ten knots, and we're going twelve or thirteen now. The old girl knows how to walk."

I contested myself with the fore crosstrees, some seventy feet above the deck. As I searched the vacant stretch of water before me, I comprehended thoroughly the need for haste if we were to recover any of our men. Indeed, as I gazed at the heavy sea through which we were running, I doubted that there was a boat afloat. It did not seem possible that such frail craft could survive such stress of wind and water.

I could not feel the full force of the wind, for we were running with it; but from my lofty perch I looked down as though outside the *Ghost* and apart from her, and saw the shape of her outlined sharply against the foaming sea as she tore along instinct with life. Sometimes she would lift and send across some great wave, burying her starboard-rail from view, and covering her deck to the hatches with the boiling ocean. At such moments, starting from a windward roll, I would go flying through the air with dizzying swiftness, as though I clung to the end of a huge, inverted pendulum, the arc of which, between the greater rolls, must have been seventy feet or more. Once, the terror of this giddy sweep overpowered me, and for a while I clung on, hand and foot, weak and trembling, unable to search the sea for the missing boats or to behold aught of the sea but that which roared beneath and strove to overwhelm the *Ghost*.

But the thought of the men in the midst of it steadied me, and in my quest for them I forgot myself. For an hour I saw nothing but the naked, desolate sea. And then, where a vagrant shaft of sunlight struck the ocean and turned its surface to wrathful silver, I caught a small black speck thrust skyward for an instant and swallowed up. I waited patiently. Again the tiny point of black projected itself through the wrathful blaze a couple of points off our port-bow. I did not attempt to shout, but communicated the news to Wolf Larsen by waving my arm. He changed the course, and I signalled affirmation when the speck showed dead ahead.

It grew larger, and so swiftly that for the first time I fully appreciated the speed of our flight. Wolf Larsen motioned for me to come down, and when I stood beside him at the wheel gave me instructions for heaving to.

"Expect all hell to break loose," he cautioned me, "but don't mind it. Yours is to do your own work and to have Cooky stand by the fore-sheet."

I managed to make my way forward, but there was little choice of sides, for the weather-rail seemed buried as often as the lee. Having instructed Thomas Mugridge as to what he was to do, I clambered into the fore-rigging a few feet. The boat was now very close, and I could make out plainly that it was lying head to wind and sea and dragging on its mast and sail, which had been thrown overboard and made to serve as a sea-anchor. The three men were bailing. Each rolling mountain whelmed them from view, and I would wait with sickening anxiety, fearing that they would never appear again. Then, and with black suddenness, the boat would shoot clear through the foaming crest, bow pointed to the sky, and the whole length of her bottom showing, wet and dark, till she seemed on end. There would be a fleeting glimpse of the three men flinging water in frantic haste, when she would topple over and fall into the yawning valley, bow down and showing her full inside length to the stern up-reared almost directly above the bow. Each time that she reappeared was a miracle.

The *Ghost* suddenly changed her course, keeping away, and it came to me with a shock that Wolf Larsen was giving up the rescue as impossible. Then I realized that he was preparing to heave to, and dropped to the deck to be in readiness. We were now dead before the wind, the boat far away and abreast of us. I felt an abrupt easing of the schooner, a loss for the moment of all strain and pressure, coupled with a swift acceleration of speed. She was rushing around on her heel into the wind.

As she arrived at right angles to the sea, the full force of the wind (from which we had hitherto run away) caught us. I was unfortunately and ignorantly facing it. It stood up against me like a wall, filling my lungs with air which I could not expel. And as I choked and strangled, and as the *Ghost* wallowed for an instant, broadside on and rolling straight over and far into the wind, I beheld a huge sea rise far above my head. I turned aside, caught my breath, and looked again. The wave over-topped the *Ghost*, and I gazed sheer up and into it. A shaft of sunlight smote the over-curl, and I caught a glimpse of translucent, rushing green, backed by a milky smother of foam.

Then it descended, pandemonium broke loose, everything happened at once. I was struck a crushing, stunning blow, nowhere in particular and yet everywhere. My hold had been broken loose, I was under water, and the thought passed through my mind that this was the terrible thing of which I had heard, the being swept in the trough of the sea. My body struck and pounded as it was dashed helplessly along and turned over and over, and when I could hold my breath no longer, I breathed the stinging salt water into my lungs. But through it all I clung to the one idea—*I must get the jib backed over to windward.* I had no fear of death. I had no doubt but that I should come through somehow. And as this idea of fulfilling Wolf Larsen's order persisted in my dazed consciousness, I seemed to see him standing at the wheel in the midst of the wild welter, pitting his will against the will of the storm and defying it.

I brought up violently against what I took to be the rail, breathed, and breathed the sweet air again. I tried to rise, but struck my head and was knocked back on hands and knees. By some freak of the waters I had been swept clear under the forecastle-head and into the eyes. As I scrambled out on all fours, I passed over the body of Thomas Mugridge, who lay in a groaning heap. There was no time to investigate. I must get the jib backed over.

When I emerged on deck it seemed that the end of everything had come. On all sides there was a rending and crashing of wood and steel and canvas. The *Ghost* was being wrenched and torn to fragments. The foresail and fore-topsail, emptied of the wind by the manœuvre, and with no one to bring in the sheet in time, were thundering into ribbons, the heavy boom threshing and splintering from rail to rail. The air was thick with flying wreckage, detached ropes and stays were hissing and coiling like snakes, and down through it all crashed the gaff of the foresail.

The spar could not have missed me by many inches, while it spurred me to action. Perhaps the situation was not hopeless. I remembered Wolf Larsen's caution. He had expected all hell to break loose, and here it was. And where was he? I caught sight of him toiling at the main-sheet, heaving it in and flat with his tremendous muscles, the stern of the schooner lifted high in the air and his body outlined against a white surge of sea sweeping past. All this, and more,—a whole world of chaos and wreck,—in possibly fifteen seconds I had seen and heard and grasped.

I did not stop to see what had become of the small boat, but sprang to the jib-sheet. The jib itself was beginning to slap, partially filling and emptying with sharp reports; but with a turn of the sheet and the application of my whole strength each time it slapped, I slowly backed it. This I know: I did my best. I pulled till I burst open the ends of all my fingers; and while I pulled, the flying-jib and staysail split their cloths apart and thundered into nothingness.

Still I pulled, holding what I gained each time with a double turn until the next slap gave me more. Then the sheet gave with greater ease, and Wolf Larsen was beside me, heaving in alone while I was busied taking up the slack.

"Make fast!" he shouted. "And come on!"

As I followed him, I noted that in spite of rack and ruin a rough order obtained. The *Ghost* was hove to. She was still in working order, and she was still working. Though the rest of her sails were gone, the jib, backed to windward, and the mainsail hauled down flat, were themselves holding, and holding her bow to the furious sea as well.

I looked for the boat, and, while Wolf Larsen cleared the boat-tackles, saw it lift to leeward on a big sea an not a score of feet away. And, so nicely had he made his calculation, we drifted fairly down upon it, so that nothing remained to do but hook the tackles to either end and hoist it aboard. But this was not done so easily as it is written.

In the bow was Kerfoot, Oofty-Oofty in the stern, and Kelly amidships. As we drifted closer the boat would rise on a wave while we sank in the trough, till almost straight above me I could see the heads of the three men craned overside and looking down. Then, the next moment, we would lift and soar upward while they sank far down beneath us. It seemed incredible that the next surge should not crush the *Ghost* down upon the tiny eggshell.

But, at the right moment, I passed the tackle to the Kanaka, while Wolf Larsen did the same thing forward to Kerfoot. Both tackles were hooked in a trice, and the three men, deftly timing the roll, made a simultaneous leap aboard the schooner. As the *Ghost* rolled her side out of water, the boat was lifted snugly against her, and before the return roll came, we had heaved it in over the side and turned it bottom up on the deck. I noticed blood spouting from Kerfoot's left hand. In some way the third finger had been crushed to a pulp. But he gave no sign of pain, and with his single right hand helped us lash the boat in its place.

"Stand by to let that jib over, you Oofty!" Wolf Larsen commanded, the very second we had finished with the boat. "Kelly, come aft and slack off the main-sheet! You, Kerfoot, go for'ard and see what's become of Cooky! Mr. Van Weyden, run aloft again, and cut away any stray stuff on your way!"

And having commanded, he went aft with his peculiar tigerish leaps to the wheel. While I toiled up the fore-shrouds the *Ghost* slowly paid off. This time, as we went into the trough of the sea and were swept, there were no sails to carry away. And, halfway to the crosstrees and flattened against the rigging by the full force of the wind so that it would have been impossible for me to have fallen, the *Ghost* almost on her beam-ends and the masts parallel with the water, I looked, not down, but at almost right angles from the perpendicular, to the deck of the *Ghost*. But I saw, not the deck, but where the deck should have been, for it was buried beneath a wild tumbling of water. Out of this water I could see the two masts rising, and that was all. The *Ghost*, for the moment, was buried beneath the sea. As she squared off more and more, escaping from the side pressure, she righted herself and broke her deck, like a whale's back, through the ocean surface.

Then we raced, and wildly, across the wild sea, the while I hung like a fly in the crosstrees and searched for the other boats. In half-an-hour I sighted the second one, swamped and bottom up, to which were desperately clinging Jock Horner, fat Louis, and Johnson. This time I remained aloft, and Wolf Larsen succeeded in heaving to without being swept. As before, we drifted down upon it. Tackles were made fast and lines flung to the men, who scrambled aboard like monkeys. The boat itself was crushed and splintered against the schooner's side as it came inboard; but the wreck was securely lashed, for it could be patched and made whole again.

Once more the *Ghost* bore away before the storm, this time so submerging herself that for some seconds I thought she would never reappear. Even the wheel, quite a deal higher than the waist, was covered and swept again and again. At such moments I felt strangely alone with God, alone with him and watching the chaos of his wrath. And then the wheel would reappear, and Wolf Larsen's broad shoulders, his hands gripping the spokes and holding the schooner to the course of his will, himself an earth-god, dominating the storm, flinging its descending waters from him and riding it to his own ends. And oh, the marvel of it! the marvel of it! That tiny men should live and breathe and work, and drive so frail a contrivance of wood and cloth through so tremendous an elemental strife.

As before, the *Ghost* swung out of the trough, lifting her deck again out of the sea, and dashed before the howling blast. It was now half-past five, and half-an-hour later, when the last of the day lost itself in a dim and furious twilight, I sighted a third boat. It was bottom up, and there was no sign of its crew. Wolf Larsen repeated his manœuvre, holding off and then rounding up to windward and drifting down upon it. But this time he missed by forty feet, the boat passing astern.

"Number four boat!" Oofty-Oofty cried, his keen eyes reading its number in the one second when it lifted clear of the foam, and upside down.

It was Henderson's boat and with him had been lost Holyoak and Williams, another of the deep-water crowd. Lost they indubitably were; but the boat remained, and Wolf Larsen made one more reckless effort to recover it. I had come down to the deck, and I saw Horner and Kerfoot vainly protest against the attempt.

"By God, I'll not be robbed of my boat by any storm that ever blew out of hell!" he shouted, and though we four stood with our heads together that we might hear, his voice seemed faint and far, as though removed from us an immense distance.

"Mr. Van Weyden!" he cried, and I heard through the tumult as one might hear a whisper. "Stand by that jib with Johnson and Oofty! The rest of you tail aft to the mainsheet! Lively now! or I'll sail you all into Kingdom Come! Understand?"

And when he put the wheel hard over and the *Ghost's* bow swung off, there was nothing for the hunters to do but obey and make the best of a risky chance. How great the risk I realized when I was once more buried beneath the pounding seas and clinging for life to the pinrail at the foot of the foremast. My fingers were torn loose, and I swept across to the side and over the side into the sea. I could not swim, but before I could sink I was swept back again. A strong hand gripped me, and when the *Ghost* finally emerged, I found that I owed my life to Johnson. I saw him looking anxiously about him, and noted that Kelly, who had come forward at the last moment, was missing.

This time, having missed the boat, and not being in the same position as in the previous instances, Wolf Larsen was compelled to resort to a different manœuvre. Running off before the wind with everything to starboard, he came about, and returned close-hauled on the port tack.

"Grand!" Johnson shouted in my ear, as we successfully came through the attendant deluge, and I knew he referred, not to Wolf Larsen's seamanship, but to the performance of the *Ghost* herself.

It was now so dark that there was no sign of the boat; but Wolf Larsen held back through the frightful turmoil as if guided by unerring instinct. This time, though we were continually half-buried, there was no trough in which to be swept, and we drifted squarely down upon the upturned boat, badly smashing it as it was heaved inboard.

Two hours of terrible work followed, in which all hands of us—two hunters, three sailors, Wolf Larsen and I—reefed, first one and then the other, the jib and mainsail. Hove to under this short canvas, our decks were comparatively free of water, while the *Ghost* bobbed and ducked amongst the combers like a cork.

I had burst open the ends of my fingers at the very first, and during the reefing I had worked with tears of pain running down my cheeks. And when all was done, I gave up like a woman and rolled upon the deck in the agony of exhaustion.

In the meantime Thomas Mugridge, like a drowned rat, was being dragged out from under the forecastle head where he had cravenly ensconced himself. I saw him pulled aft to the cabin, and noted with a shock of surprise that the galley had disappeared. A clean space of deck showed where it had stood.

In the cabin I found all hands assembled, sailors as well, and while coffee was being cooked over the small stove we drank whisky and crunched hard-tack. Never in my life had food been so welcome. And never had hot coffee tasted so good. So violently did the *Ghost*, pitch and toss and tumble that it was impossible for even the sailors to move about without holding on, and several times, after a cry of "Now she takes it!" we were heaped upon the wall of the port cabins as though it had been the deck.

"To hell with a look-out," I heard Wolf Larsen say when we had eaten and drunk our fill. "There's nothing can be done on deck. If anything's going to run us down we couldn't get out of its way. Turn in, all hands, and get some sleep."

The sailors slipped forward, setting the side-lights as they went, while the two hunters remained to sleep in the cabin, it not being deemed advisable to open the slide to the steerage companion-way. Wolf Larsen and I, between us, cut off Kerfoot's crushed finger and sewed up the stump. Mugridge, who, during all the time he had been compelled to cook and serve coffee and keep the fire going, had complained of internal pains, now swore that he had a broken rib or two. On examination we found that he had three. But his case was deferred to next day, principally for the reason that I did not know anything about broken ribs and would first have to read it up.

"I don't think it was worth it," I said to Wolf Larsen, "a broken boat for Kelly's life."

"But Kelly didn't amount to much," was the reply. "Good-night."

After all that had passed, suffering intolerable anguish in my finger-ends, and with three boats missing, to say nothing of the wild capers the *Ghost* was cutting, I should have thought it impossible to sleep. But my eyes must have closed the instant my head touched the pillow, and in utter exhaustion I slept throughout the night, the while the *Ghost*, lonely and undirected, fought her way through the storm.

CHAPTER XVIII

The next day, while the storm was blowing itself out, Wolf Larsen and I crammed anatomy and surgery and set Mugridge's ribs. Then, when the storm broke, Wolf Larsen cruised back and forth over that portion of the ocean where we had encountered it, and somewhat more to the westward, while the boats were being repaired and new sails made and bent. Sealing schooner after sealing schooner we sighted and boarded, most of which were in search of lost boats, and most of which were carrying boats and crews they had picked up and which did not belong to them. For the thick of the fleet had been to the westward of us, and the boats, scattered far and wide, had headed in mad flight for the nearest refuge.

Two of our boats, with men all safe, we took off the *Cisco*, and, to Wolf Larsen's huge delight and my own grief, he culled Smoke, with Nilson and Leach, from the *San Diego*. So that, at the end of five days, we found ourselves short but four men—Henderson, Holyoak, Williams, and Kelly,—and were once more hunting on the flanks of the herd.

As we followed it north we began to encounter the dreaded sea-fogs. Day after day the boats lowered and were swallowed up almost ere they touched the water, while we on board pumped the horn at regular intervals and every fifteen minutes fired the bomb gun. Boats were continually being lost and found, it being the custom for a boat to hunt, on lay, with whatever schooner picked it up, until such time it was recovered by its own schooner. But Wolf Larsen, as was to be expected, being a boat short, took possession of the first stray one and compelled its men to hunt with the *Ghost*, not permitting them to return to their own schooner when we sighted it. I remember how he forced the hunter and his two men below, a riffle at their breasts, when their captain passed by at biscuit-toss and hailed us for information.

Thomas Mugridge, so strangely and pertinaciously clinging to life, was soon limping about again and performing his double duties of cook and cabin-boy. Johnson and Leach were bullied and beaten as much as ever, and they looked for their lives to end with the end of the hunting season; while the rest of the crew lived the lives of dogs and were worked like dogs by their pitiless master. As for Wolf Larsen and myself, we got along fairly well; though I could not quite rid myself of the idea that right conduct, for me, lay in killing him. He fascinated me immeasurably, and I feared him immeasurably. And yet, I could not imagine him lying prone in death. There was an endurance, as of perpetual youth, about him, which rose up and forbade the picture. I could see him only as living always, and dominating always, fighting and destroying, himself surviving.

One diversion of his, when we were in the midst of the herd and the sea was too rough to lower the boats, was to lower with two boat-pullers and a steerer and go out himself. He was a good shot, too, and brought many a skin aboard under what the hunters termed impossible hunting conditions. It seemed the breath of his nostrils, this carrying his life in his hands and struggling for it against tremendous odds.

I was learning more and more seamanship; and one clear day—a thing we rarely encountered now—I had the satisfaction of running and handling the *Ghost* and picking up the boats myself. Wolf Larsen had been smitten with one of his headaches, and I stood at the wheel from morning until evening, sailing across the ocean after the last lee boat, and heaving to and picking it and the other five up without command or suggestion from him.

Gales we encountered now and again, for it was a raw and stormy region, and, in the middle of June, a typhoon most memorable to me and most important because of the changes wrought through it upon my future. We must have been caught nearly at the centre of this circular storm, and Wolf Larsen ran out of it and to the southward, first under a double-reefed jib, and finally under bare poles. Never had I imagined so great a sea. The seas previously encountered were as ripples compared with these, which ran a half-mile from crest to crest and which upreared, I am confident, above our masthead. So great was it that Wolf Larsen himself did not dare heave to, though he was being driven far to the southward and out of the seal herd.

We must have been well in the path of the trans-Pacific steamships when the typhoon moderated, and here, to the surprise of the hunters, we found ourselves in the midst of seals—a second herd, or sort of rear-guard, they declared, and a most unusual thing. But it was "Boats over!" the boom-boom of guns, and the pitiful slaughter through the long day.

It was at this time that I was approached by Leach. I had just finished tallying the skins of the last boat aboard, when he came to my side, in the darkness, and said in a low tone:

"Can you tell me, Mr. Van Weyden, how far we are off the coast, and what the bearings of Yokohama are?"

My heart leaped with gladness, for I knew what he had in mind, and I gave him the bearings—west-north-west, and five hundred miles away.

"Thank you, sir," was all he said as he slipped back into the darkness.

Next morning No. 3 boat and Johnson and Leach were missing. The water-breakers and grub-boxes from all the other boats were likewise missing, as were the beds and sea bags of the two men. Wolf Larsen was furious. He set sail and bore away into the west-north-west, two hunters constantly at the mastheads and sweeping the sea with glasses, himself pacing the deck like an angry lion. He knew too well my sympathy for the runaways to send me aloft as look-out.

The wind was fair but fitful, and it was like looking for a needle in a haystack to raise that tiny boat out of the blue immensity. But he put the *Ghost* through her best paces so as to get between the deserters and the land. This accomplished, he cruised back and forth across what he knew must be their course.

On the morning of the third day, shortly after eight bells, a cry that the boat was sighted came down from Smoke at the masthead. All hands lined the rail. A snappy breeze was blowing from the west with the promise of more wind behind it; and there, to leeward, in the troubled silver of the rising sun, appeared and disappeared a black speck.

We squared away and ran for it. My heart was as lead. I felt myself turning sick in anticipation; and as I looked at the gleam of triumph in Wolf Larsen's eyes, his form swam before me, and I felt almost irresistibly impelled to fling myself upon him. So unnerved was I by the thought of impending violence to Leach and Johnson that my reason must have left me. I know that I slipped down into the steerage in a daze, and that I was just beginning the ascent to the deck, a loaded shot-gun in my hands, when I heard the startled cry:

"There's five men in that boat!"

I supported myself in the companion-way, weak and trembling, while the observation was being verified by the remarks of the rest of the men. Then my knees gave from under me and I sank down, myself again, but overcome by shock at knowledge of what I had so nearly done. Also, I was very thankful as I put the gun away and slipped back on deck.

No one had remarked my absence. The boat was near enough for us to make out that it was larger than any sealing boat and built on different lines. As we drew closer, the sail was taken in and the mast unstepped. Oars were shipped, and its occupants waited for us to heave to and take them aboard.

Smoke, who had descended to the deck and was now standing by my side, began to chuckle in a significant way. I looked at him inquiringly.

"Talk of a mess!" he giggled.

"What's wrong?" I demanded.

Again he chuckled. "Don't you see there, in the stern-sheets, on the bottom? May I never shoot a seal again if that ain't a woman!"

I looked closely, but was not sure until exclamations broke out on all sides. The boat contained four men, and its fifth occupant was certainly a woman. We were agog with excitement, all except Wolf Larsen, who was too evidently disappointed in that it was not his own boat with the two victims of his malice.

We ran down the flying jib, hauled the jib-sheets to wind-ward and the main-sheet flat, and came up into the wind. The oars struck the water, and with a few strokes the boat was alongside. I now caught my first fair glimpse of the woman. She was wrapped in a long ulster, for the morning was raw; and I could see nothing but her face and a mass of light brown hair escaping from under the seaman's cap on her head. The eyes were large and brown and lustrous, the mouth sweet and sensitive, and the face itself a delicate oval, though sun and exposure to briny wind had burnt the face scarlet.

She seemed to me like a being from another world. I was aware of a hungry outreaching for her, as of a starving man for bread. But then, I had not seen a woman for a very long time. I know that I was lost in a great wonder, almost a stupor,—this, then, was a woman?—so that I forgot myself and my mate's duties, and took no part in helping the new-comers aboard. For when one of the sailors lifted her into Wolf Larsen's downstretched arms, she looked up into our curious faces and smiled amusedly and sweetly, as only a woman can smile, and as I had seen no one smile for so long that I had forgotten such smiles existed.

"Mr. Van Weyden!"

CHAPTER XVIII

Wolf Larsen's voice brought me sharply back to myself.

"Will you take the lady below and see to her comfort? Make up that spare port cabin. Put Cooky to work on it. And see what you can do for that face. It's burned badly."

He turned brusquely away from us and began to question the new men. The boat was cast adrift, though one of them called it a "bloody shame" with Yokohama so near.

I found myself strangely afraid of this woman I was escorting aft. Also I was awkward. It seemed to me that I was realizing for the first time what a delicate, fragile creature a woman is; and as I caught her arm to help her down the companion stairs, I was startled by its smallness and softness. Indeed, she was a slender, delicate woman as women go, but to me she was so ethereally slender and delicate that I was quite prepared for her arm to crumble in my grasp. All this, in frankness, to show my first impression, after long denial of women in general and of Maud Brewster in particular.

"No need to go to any great trouble for me," she protested, when I had seated her in Wolf Larsen's arm-chair, which I had dragged hastily from his cabin. "The men were looking for land at any moment this morning, and the vessel should be in by night; don't you think so?"

Her simple faith in the immediate future took me aback. How could I explain to her the situation, the strange man who stalked the sea like Destiny, all that it had taken me months to learn? But I answered honestly:

"If it were any other captain except ours, I should say you would be ashore in Yokohama to-morrow. But our captain is a strange man, and I beg of you to be prepared for anything—understand?—for anything."

"I—I confess I hardly do understand," she hesitated, a perturbed but not frightened expression in her eyes. "Or is it a misconception of mine that shipwrecked people are always shown every consideration? This is such a little thing, you know. We are so close to land."

"Candidly, I do not know," I strove to reassure her. "I wished merely to prepare you for the worst, if the worst is to come. This man, this captain, is a brute, a demon, and one can never tell what will be his next fantastic act."

I was growing excited, but she interrupted me with an "Oh, I see," and her voice sounded weary. To think was patently an effort. She was clearly on the verge of physical collapse.

She asked no further questions, and I vouchsafed no remark, devoting myself to Wolf Larsen's command, which was to make her comfortable. I bustled about in quite housewifely fashion, procuring soothing lotions for her sunburn, raiding Wolf Larsen's private stores for a bottle of port I knew to be there, and directing Thomas Mugridge in the preparation of the spare state-room.

The wind was freshening rapidly, the *Ghost* heeling over more and more, and by the time the state-room was ready she was dashing through the water at a lively clip. I had quite forgotten the existence of Leach and Johnson, when suddenly, like a thunderclap, "Boat ho!" came down the open companion-way. It was Smoke's unmistakable voice, crying from the masthead. I shot a glance at the woman, but she was leaning back in the arm-chair, her eyes closed, unutterably tired. I doubted that she had heard, and I resolved to prevent her seeing the brutality I knew would follow the capture of the deserters. She was tired. Very good. She should sleep.

There were swift commands on deck, a stamping of feet and a slapping of reef-points as the *Ghost* shot into the wind and about on the other tack. As she filled away and heeled, the arm-chair began to slide across the cabin floor, and I sprang for it just in time to prevent the rescued woman from being spilled out.

Her eyes were too heavy to suggest more than a hint of the sleepy surprise that perplexed her as she looked up at me, and she half stumbled, half tottered, as I led her to her cabin. Mugridge grinned insinuatingly in my face as I shoved him out and ordered him back to his galley work; and he won his revenge by spreading glowing reports among the hunters as to what an excellent "lydy's-myde" I was proving myself to be.

She leaned heavily against me, and I do believe that she had fallen asleep again between the arm-chair and the state-room. This I discovered when she nearly fell into the bunk during a sudden lurch of the schooner. She aroused, smiled drowsily, and was off to sleep again; and asleep I left her, under a heavy pair of sailor's blankets, her head resting on a pillow I had appropriated from Wolf Larsen's bunk.

CHAPTER XIX

I came on deck to find the *Ghost* heading up close on the port tack and cutting in to windward of a familiar spritsail close-hauled on the same tack ahead of us. All hands were on deck, for they knew that something was to happen when Leach and Johnson were dragged aboard.

It was four bells. Louis came aft to relieve the wheel. There was a dampness in the air, and I noticed he had on his oilskins.

"What are we going to have?" I asked him.

"A healthy young slip of a gale from the breath iv it, sir," he answered, "with a splatter iv rain just to wet our gills an' no more."

"Too bad we sighted them," I said, as the *Ghost's* bow was flung off a point by a large sea and the boat leaped for a moment past the jibs and into our line of vision.

Louis gave a spoke and temporized. "They'd never iv made the land, sir, I'm thinkin'."

"Think not?" I queried.

"No, sir. Did you feel that?" (A puff had caught the schooner, and he was forced to put the wheel up rapidly to keep her out of the wind.) "'Tis no egg-shell'll float on this sea an hour come, an' it's a stroke iv luck for them we're here to pick 'em up."

Wolf Larsen strode aft from amidships, where he had been talking with the rescued men. The cat-like springiness in his tread was a little more pronounced than usual, and his eyes were bright and snappy.

"Three oilers and a fourth engineer," was his greeting. "But we'll make sailors out of them, or boat-pullers at any rate. Now, what of the lady?"

I know not why, but I was aware of a twinge or pang like the cut of a knife when he mentioned her. I thought it a certain silly fastidiousness on my part, but it persisted in spite of me, and I merely shrugged my shoulders in answer.

Wolf Larsen pursed his lips in a long, quizzical whistle.

"What's her name, then?" he demanded.

"I don't know," I replied. "She is asleep. She was very tired. In fact, I am waiting to hear the news from you. What vessel was it?"

"Mail steamer," he answered shortly. "*The City of Tokio*, from 'Frisco, bound for Yokohama. Disabled in that typhoon. Old tub. Opened up top and bottom like a sieve. They were adrift four days. And you don't know who or what she is, eh?—maid, wife, or widow? Well, well."

He shook his head in a bantering way, and regarded me with laughing eyes.

"Are you—" I began. It was on the verge of my tongue to ask if he were going to take the castaways into Yokohama.

"Am I what?" he asked.

"What do you intend doing with Leach and Johnson?"

He shook his head. "Really, Hump, I don't know. You see, with these additions I've about all the crew I want."

"And they've about all the escaping they want," I said. "Why not give them a change of treatment? Take them aboard, and deal gently with them. Whatever they have done they have been hounded into doing."

"By me?"

"By you," I answered steadily. "And I give you warning, Wolf Larsen, that I may forget love of my own life in the desire to kill you if you go too far in maltreating those poor wretches."

"Bravo!" he cried. "You do me proud, Hump! You've found your legs with a vengeance. You're quite an individual. You were unfortunate in having your life cast in easy places, but you're developing, and I like you the better for it."

His voice and expression changed. His face was serious. "Do you believe in promises?" he asked. "Are they sacred things?"

"Of course," I answered.

"Then here's a compact," he went on, consummate actor. "If I promise not to lay my hands upon Leach will you promise, in turn, not to attempt to kill me?"

"Oh, not that I'm afraid of you, not that I'm afraid of you," he hastened to add.

I could hardly believe my ears. What was coming over the man?

"Is it a go?" he asked impatiently.

"A go," I answered.

His hand went out to mine, and as I shook it heartily I could have sworn I saw the mocking devil shine up for a moment in his eyes.

We strolled across the poop to the lee side. The boat was close at hand now, and in desperate plight. Johnson was steering, Leach bailing. We overhauled them about two feet to their one. Wolf Larsen motioned Louis to keep off slightly, and we dashed abreast of the boat, not a score of feet to windward. The *Ghost* blanketed it. The spritsail flapped emptily and the boat righted to an even keel, causing the two men swiftly to change position. The boat lost headway, and, as we lifted on a huge surge, toppled and fell into the trough.

It was at this moment that Leach and Johnson looked up into the faces of their shipmates, who lined the rail amidships. There was no greeting. They were as dead men in their comrades' eyes, and between them was the gulf that parts the living and the dead.

The next instant they were opposite the poop, where stood Wolf Larsen and I. We were falling in the trough, they were rising on the surge. Johnson looked at me, and I could see that his face was worn and haggard. I waved my hand to him, and he answered the greeting, but with a wave that was hopeless and despairing. It was as if he were saying farewell. I did not see into the eyes of Leach, for he was looking at Wolf Larsen, the old and implacable snarl of hatred strong as ever on his face.

Then they were gone astern. The spritsail filled with the wind, suddenly, careening the frail open craft till it seemed it would surely capsize. A whitecap foamed above it and broke across in a snow-white smother. Then the boat emerged, half swamped, Leach flinging the water out and Johnson clinging to the steering-oar, his face white and anxious.

Wolf Larsen barked a short laugh in my ear and strode away to the weather side of the poop. I expected him to give orders for the *Ghost* to heave to, but she kept on her course and he made no sign. Louis stood imperturbably at the wheel, but I noticed the grouped sailors forward turning troubled faces in our direction. Still the *Ghost* tore along, till the boat dwindled to a speck, when Wolf Larsen's voice rang out in command and he went about on the starboard tack.

Back we held, two miles and more to windward of the struggling cockle-shell, when the flying jib was run down and the schooner hove to. The sealing boats are not made for windward work. Their hope lies in keeping a weather position so that they may run before the wind for the schooner when it breezes up. But in all that wild waste there was no refuge for Leach and Johnson save on the *Ghost*, and they resolutely began the windward beat. It was slow work in the heavy sea that was running. At any moment they were liable to be overwhelmed by the hissing combers. Time and again and countless times we watched the boat luff into the big whitecaps, lose headway, and be flung back like a cork.

Johnson was a splendid seaman, and he knew as much about small boats as he did about ships. At the end of an hour and a half he was nearly alongside, standing past our stern on the last leg out, aiming to fetch us on the next leg back.

"So you've changed your mind?" I heard Wolf Larsen mutter, half to himself, half to them as though they could hear. "You want to come aboard, eh? Well, then, just keep a-coming."

"Hard up with that helm!" he commanded Oofty-Oofty, the Kanaka, who had in the meantime relieved Louis at the wheel.

Command followed command. As the schooner paid off, the fore- and main-sheets were slacked away for fair wind. And before the wind we were, and leaping, when Johnson, easing his sheet at imminent peril, cut across our wake a hundred feet away. Again Wolf Larsen laughed, at the same time beckoning them with his arm to follow. It was evidently his intention to play with them,—a lesson, I took it, in lieu of a beating, though a dangerous lesson, for the frail craft stood in momentary danger of being overwhelmed.

Johnson squared away promptly and ran after us. There was nothing else for him to do. Death stalked everywhere, and it was only a matter of time when some one of those many huge seas would fall upon the boat, roll over it, and pass on.

"'Tis the fear iv death at the hearts iv them," Louis muttered in my ear, as I passed forward to see to taking in the flying jib and staysail.

"Oh, he'll heave to in a little while and pick them up," I answered cheerfully. "He's bent upon giving them a lesson, that's all."

Louis looked at me shrewdly. "Think so?" he asked.

"Surely," I answered. "Don't you?"

"I think nothing but iv my own skin, these days," was his answer. "An' 'tis with wonder I'm filled as to the workin' out iv things. A pretty mess that 'Frisco whisky got me into, an' a prettier mess that woman's got you into aft there. Ah, it's myself that knows ye for a blitherin' fool."

"What do you mean?" I demanded; for, having sped his shaft, he was turning away.

"What do I mean?" he cried. "And it's you that asks me! 'Tis not what I mean, but what the Wolf 'll mean. The Wolf, I said, the Wolf!"

"If trouble comes, will you stand by?" I asked impulsively, for he had voiced my own fear.

"Stand by? 'Tis old fat Louis I stand by, an' trouble enough it'll be. We're at the beginnin' iv things, I'm tellin' ye, the bare beginnin' iv things."

"I had not thought you so great a coward," I sneered.

He favoured me with a contemptuous stare. "If I raised never a hand for that poor fool,"—pointing astern to the tiny sail,—"d'ye think I'm hungerin' for a broken head for a woman I never laid me eyes upon before this day?"

I turned scornfully away and went aft.

"Better get in those topsails, Mr. Van Weyden," Wolf Larsen said, as I came on the poop.

I felt relief, at least as far as the two men were concerned. It was clear he did not wish to run too far away from them. I picked up hope at the thought and put the order swiftly into execution. I had scarcely opened my mouth to issue the necessary commands, when eager men were springing to halyards and downhauls, and others were racing aloft. This eagerness on their part was noted by Wolf Larsen with a grim smile.

Still we increased our lead, and when the boat had dropped astern several miles we hove to and waited. All eyes watched it coming, even Wolf Larsen's; but he was the only unperturbed man aboard. Louis, gazing fixedly, betrayed a trouble in his face he was not quite able to hide.

The boat drew closer and closer, hurling along through the seething green like a thing alive, lifting and sending and uptossing across the huge-backed breakers, or disappearing behind them only to rush into sight again and shoot skyward. It seemed impossible that it could continue to live, yet with each dizzying sweep it did achieve the impossible. A rain-squall drove past, and out of the flying wet the boat emerged, almost upon us.

"Hard up, there!" Wolf Larsen shouted, himself springing to the wheel and whirling it over.

Again the *Ghost* sprang away and raced before the wind, and for two hours Johnson and Leach pursued us. We hove to and ran away, hove to and ran away, and ever astern the struggling patch of sail tossed skyward and fell into the rushing valleys. It was a quarter of a mile away when a thick squall of rain veiled it from view. It never emerged. The wind blew the air clear again, but no patch of sail broke the troubled surface. I thought I saw, for an instant, the boat's bottom show black in a breaking crest. At the best, that was all. For Johnson and Leach the travail of existence had ceased.

The men remained grouped amidships. No one had gone below, and no one was speaking. Nor were any looks being exchanged. Each man seemed stunned—deeply contemplative, as it were, and, not quite sure, trying to realize just what had taken place. Wolf Larsen gave them little time for thought. He at once put the *Ghost* upon her course—a course which meant the seal herd and not Yokohama harbour. But the men were no longer eager as they pulled and hauled, and I heard curses amongst them, which left their lips smothered and as heavy and lifeless as were they. Not so was it with the hunters. Smoke the irrepressible related a story, and they descended into the steerage, bellowing with laughter.

As I passed to leeward of the galley on my way aft I was approached by the engineer we had rescued. His face was white, his lips were trembling.

"Good God! sir, what kind of a craft is this?" he cried.

"You have eyes, you have seen," I answered, almost brutally, what of the pain and fear at my own heart.

"Your promise?" I said to Wolf Larsen.

"I was not thinking of taking them aboard when I made that promise," he answered. "And anyway, you'll agree I've not laid my hands upon them."

"Far from it, far from it," he laughed a moment later.

I made no reply. I was incapable of speaking, my mind was too confused. I must have time to think, I knew. This woman, sleeping even now in the spare cabin, was a responsibility, which I must consider, and the only rational thought that flickered through my mind was that I must do nothing hastily if I were to be any help to her at all.

CHAPTER XX

The remainder of the day passed uneventfully. The young slip of a gale, having wetted our gills, proceeded to moderate. The fourth engineer and the three oilers, after a warm interview with Wolf Larsen, were furnished with outfits from the slop-chests, assigned places under the hunters in the various boats and watches on the vessel, and bundled forward into the forecastle. They went protestingly, but their voices were not loud. They were awed by what they had already seen of Wolf Larsen's character, while the tale of woe they speedily heard in the forecastle took the last bit of rebellion out of them.

Miss Brewster—we had learned her name from the engineer—slept on and on. At supper I requested the hunters to lower their voices, so she was not disturbed; and it was not till next morning that she made her appearance. It had been my intention to have her meals served apart, but Wolf Larsen put down his foot. Who was she that she should be too good for cabin table and cabin society? had been his demand.

But her coming to the table had something amusing in it. The hunters fell silent as clams. Jock Horner and Smoke alone were unabashed, stealing stealthy glances at her now and again, and even taking part in the conversation. The other four men glued their eyes on their plates and chewed steadily and with thoughtful precision, their ears moving and wobbling, in time with their jaws, like the ears of so many animals.

Wolf Larsen had little to say at first, doing no more than reply when he was addressed. Not that he was abashed. Far from it. This woman was a new type to him, a different breed from any he had ever known, and he was curious. He studied her, his eyes rarely leaving her face unless to follow the movements of her hands or shoulders. I studied her myself, and though it was I who maintained the conversation, I know that I was a bit shy, not quite self-possessed. His was the perfect poise, the supreme confidence in self, which nothing could shake; and he was no more timid of a woman than he was of storm and battle.

"And when shall we arrive at Yokohama?" she asked, turning to him and looking him squarely in the eyes.

There it was, the question flat. The jaws stopped working, the ears ceased wobbling, and though eyes remained glued on plates, each man listened greedily for the answer.

"In four months, possibly three if the season closes early," Wolf Larsen said.

She caught her breath and stammered, "I—I thought—I was given to understand that Yokohama was only a day's sail away. It—" Here she paused and looked about the table at the circle of unsympathetic faces staring hard at the plates. "It is not right," she concluded.

"That is a question you must settle with Mr. Van Weyden there," he replied, nodding to me with a mischievous twinkle. "Mr. Van Weyden is what you may call an authority on such things as rights. Now I, who am only a sailor, would look upon the situation somewhat differently. It may possibly be your misfortune that you have to remain with us, but it is certainly our good fortune."

He regarded her smilingly. Her eyes fell before his gaze, but she lifted them again, and defiantly, to mine. I read the unspoken question there: was it right? But I had decided that the part I was to play must be a neutral one, so I did not answer.

"What do you think?" she demanded.

"That it is unfortunate, especially if you have any engagements falling due in the course of the next several months. But, since you say that you were voyaging to Japan for your health, I can assure you that it will improve no better anywhere than aboard the *Ghost*."

I saw her eyes flash with indignation, and this time it was I who dropped mine, while I felt my face flushing under her gaze. It was cowardly, but what else could I do?

"Mr. Van Weyden speaks with the voice of authority," Wolf Larsen laughed.

I nodded my head, and she, having recovered herself, waited expectantly.

"Not that he is much to speak of now," Wolf Larsen went on, "but he has improved wonderfully. You should have seen him when he came on board. A more scrawny, pitiful specimen of humanity one could hardly conceive. Isn't that so, Kerfoot?"

Kerfoot, thus directly addressed, was startled into dropping his knife on the floor, though he managed to grunt affirmation.

"Developed himself by peeling potatoes and washing dishes. Eh, Kerfoot?"

Again that worthy grunted.

"Look at him now. True, he is not what you would term muscular, but still he has muscles, which is more than he had when he came aboard. Also, he has legs to stand on. You would not think so to look at him, but he was quite unable to stand alone at first."

The hunters were snickering, but she looked at me with a sympathy in her eyes which more than compensated for Wolf Larsen's nastiness. In truth, it had been so long since I had received sympathy that I was softened, and I became then, and gladly, her willing slave. But I was angry with Wolf Larsen. He was challenging my manhood with his slurs, challenging the very legs he claimed to be instrumental in getting for me.

"I may have learned to stand on my own legs," I retorted. "But I have yet to stamp upon others with them."

He looked at me insolently. "Your education is only half completed, then," he said dryly, and turned to her.

"We are very hospitable upon the *Ghost*. Mr. Van Weyden has discovered that. We do everything to make our guests feel at home, eh, Mr. Van Weyden?"

"Even to the peeling of potatoes and the washing of dishes," I answered, "to say nothing to wringing their necks out of very fellowship."

"I beg of you not to receive false impressions of us from Mr. Van Weyden," he interposed with mock anxiety. "You will observe, Miss Brewster, that he carries a dirk in his belt, a—ahem—a most unusual thing for a ship's officer to do. While really very estimable, Mr. Van Weyden is sometimes—how shall I say?—er—quarrelsome, and harsh measures are necessary. He is quite reasonable and fair in his calm moments, and as he is calm now he will not deny that only yesterday he threatened my life."

I was well-nigh choking, and my eyes were certainly fiery. He drew attention to me.

"Look at him now. He can scarcely control himself in your presence. He is not accustomed to the presence of ladies anyway. I shall have to arm myself before I dare go on deck with him."

He shook his head sadly, murmuring, "Too bad, too bad," while the hunters burst into guffaws of laughter.

The deep-sea voices of these men, rumbling and bellowing in the confined space, produced a wild effect. The whole setting was wild, and for the first time, regarding this strange woman and realizing how incongruous she was in it, I was aware of how much a part of it I was myself. I knew these men and their mental processes, was one of them myself, living the seal-hunting life, eating the seal-hunting fare, thinking, largely, the seal-hunting thoughts. There was for me no strangeness to it, to the rough clothes, the coarse faces, the wild laughter, and the lurching cabin walls and swaying sea-lamps.

As I buttered a piece of bread my eyes chanced to rest upon my hand. The knuckles were skinned and inflamed clear across, the fingers swollen, the nails rimmed with black. I felt the mattress-like growth of beard on my neck, knew that the sleeve of my coat was ripped, that a button was missing from the throat of the blue shirt I wore. The dirk mentioned by Wolf Larsen rested in its sheath on my hip. It was very natural that it should be there,—how natural I had not imagined until now, when I looked upon it with her eyes and knew how strange it and all that went with it must appear to her.

But she divined the mockery in Wolf Larsen's words, and again favoured me with a sympathetic glance. But there was a look of bewilderment also in her eyes. That it was mockery made the situation more puzzling to her.

"I may be taken off by some passing vessel, perhaps," she suggested.

"There will be no passing vessels, except other sealing-schooners," Wolf Larsen made answer.

"I have no clothes, nothing," she objected. "You hardly realize, sir, that I am not a man, or that I am unaccustomed to the vagrant, careless life which you and your men seem to lead."

"The sooner you get accustomed to it, the better," he said.

"I'll furnish you with cloth, needles, and thread," he added. "I hope it will not be too dreadful a hardship for you to make yourself a dress or two."

She made a wry pucker with her mouth, as though to advertise her ignorance of dressmaking. That she was frightened and bewildered, and that she was bravely striving to hide it, was quite plain to me.

CHAPTER XX

"I suppose you're like Mr. Van Weyden there, accustomed to having things done for you. Well, I think doing a few things for yourself will hardly dislocate any joints. By the way, what do you do for a living?"

She regarded him with amazement unconcealed.

"I mean no offence, believe me. People eat, therefore they must procure the wherewithal. These men here shoot seals in order to live; for the same reason I sail this schooner; and Mr. Van Weyden, for the present at any rate, earns his salty grub by assisting me. Now what do you do?"

She shrugged her shoulders.

"Do you feed yourself? Or does some one else feed you?"

"I'm afraid some one else has fed me most of my life," she laughed, trying bravely to enter into the spirit of his quizzing, though I could see a terror dawning and growing in her eyes as she watched Wolf Larsen.

"And I suppose some one else makes your bed for you?"

"I *have* made beds," she replied.

"Very often?"

She shook her head with mock ruefulness.

"Do you know what they do to poor men in the States, who, like you, do not work for their living?"

"I am very ignorant," she pleaded. "What do they do to the poor men who are like me?"

"They send them to jail. The crime of not earning a living, in their case, is called vagrancy. If I were Mr. Van Weyden, who harps eternally on questions of right and wrong, I'd ask, by what right do you live when you do nothing to deserve living?"

"But as you are not Mr. Van Weyden, I don't have to answer, do I?"

She beamed upon him through her terror-filled eyes, and the pathos of it cut me to the heart. I must in some way break in and lead the conversation into other channels.

"Have you ever earned a dollar by your own labour?" he demanded, certain of her answer, a triumphant vindictiveness in his voice.

"Yes, I have," she answered slowly, and I could have laughed aloud at his crest-fallen visage. "I remember my father giving me a dollar once, when I was a little girl, for remaining absolutely quiet for five minutes."

He smiled indulgently.

"But that was long ago," she continued. "And you would scarcely demand a little girl of nine to earn her own living."

"At present, however," she said, after another slight pause, "I earn about eighteen hundred dollars a year."

With one accord, all eyes left the plates and settled on her. A woman who earned eighteen hundred dollars a year was worth looking at. Wolf Larsen was undisguised in his admiration.

"Salary, or piece-work?" he asked.

"Piece-work," she answered promptly.

"Eighteen hundred," he calculated. "That's a hundred and fifty dollars a month. Well, Miss Brewster, there is nothing small about the *Ghost*. Consider yourself on salary during the time you remain with us."

She made no acknowledgment. She was too unused as yet to the whims of the man to accept them with equanimity.

"I forgot to inquire," he went on suavely, "as to the nature of your occupation. What commodities do you turn out? What tools and materials do you require?"

"Paper and ink," she laughed. "And, oh! also a typewriter."

"You are Maud Brewster," I said slowly and with certainty, almost as though I were charging her with a crime.

Her eyes lifted curiously to mine. "How do you know?"

"Aren't you?" I demanded.

She acknowledged her identity with a nod. It was Wolf Larsen's turn to be puzzled. The name and its magic signified nothing to him. I was proud that it did mean something to me, and for the first time in a weary while I was convincingly conscious of a superiority over him.

"I remember writing a review of a thin little volume—" I had begun carelessly, when she interrupted me.

"You!" she cried. "You are—"

She was now staring at me in wide-eyed wonder.

I nodded my identity, in turn.

"Humphrey Van Weyden," she concluded; then added with a sigh of relief, and unaware that she had glanced that relief at Wolf Larsen, "I am so glad."

"I remember the review," she went on hastily, becoming aware of the awkwardness of her remark; "that too, too flattering review."

"Not at all," I denied valiantly. "You impeach my sober judgment and make my canons of little worth. Besides, all my brother critics were with me. Didn't Lang include your 'Kiss Endured' among the four supreme sonnets by women in the English language?"

"But you called me the American Mrs. Meynell!"

"Was it not true?" I demanded.

"No, not that," she answered. "I was hurt."

"We can measure the unknown only by the known," I replied, in my finest academic manner. "As a critic I was compelled to place you. You have now become a yardstick yourself. Seven of your thin little volumes are on my shelves; and there are two thicker volumes, the essays, which, you will pardon my saying, and I know not which is flattered more, fully equal your verse. The time is not far distant when some unknown will arise in England and the critics will name her the English Maud Brewster."

"You are very kind, I am sure," she murmured; and the very conventionality of her tones and words, with the host of associations it aroused of the old life on the other side of the world, gave me a quick thrill—rich with remembrance but stinging sharp with home-sickness.

"And you are Maud Brewster," I said solemnly, gazing across at her.

"And you are Humphrey Van Weyden," she said, gazing back at me with equal solemnity and awe. "How unusual! I don't understand. We surely are not to expect some wildly romantic sea-story from your sober pen."

"No, I am not gathering material, I assure you," was my answer. "I have neither aptitude nor inclination for fiction."

"Tell me, why have you always buried yourself in California?" she next asked. "It has not been kind of you. We of the East have seen to very little of you—too little, indeed, of the Dean of American Letters, the Second."

I bowed to, and disclaimed, the compliment. "I nearly met you, once, in Philadelphia, some Browning affair or other—you were to lecture, you know. My train was four hours late."

And then we quite forgot where we were, leaving Wolf Larsen stranded and silent in the midst of our flood of gossip. The hunters left the table and went on deck, and still we talked. Wolf Larsen alone remained. Suddenly I became aware of him, leaning back from the table and listening curiously to our alien speech of a world he did not know.

I broke short off in the middle of a sentence. The present, with all its perils and anxieties, rushed upon me with stunning force. It smote Miss Brewster likewise, a vague and nameless terror rushing into her eyes as she regarded Wolf Larsen.

He rose to his feet and laughed awkwardly. The sound of it was metallic.

"Oh, don't mind me," he said, with a self-depreciatory wave of his hand. "I don't count. Go on, go on, I pray you."

But the gates of speech were closed, and we, too, rose from the table and laughed awkwardly.

CHAPTER XXI

The chagrin Wolf Larsen felt from being ignored by Maud Brewster and me in the conversation at table had to express itself in some fashion, and it fell to Thomas Mugridge to be the victim. He had not mended his ways nor his shirt, though the latter he contended he had changed. The garment itself did not bear out the assertion, nor did the accumulations of grease on stove and pot and pan attest a general cleanliness.

"I've given you warning, Cooky," Wolf Larsen said, "and now you've got to take your medicine."

Mugridge's face turned white under its sooty veneer, and when Wolf Larsen called for a rope and a couple of men, the miserable Cockney fled wildly out of the galley and dodged and ducked about the deck with the grinning crew in pursuit. Few things could have been more to their liking than to give him a tow over the side, for to the forecastle he had sent messes and concoctions of the vilest order. Conditions favoured the undertaking. The *Ghost* was slipping through the water at no more than three miles an hour, and the sea was fairly calm. But Mugridge had little stomach for a dip in it. Possibly he had seen men towed before. Besides, the water was frightfully cold, and his was anything but a rugged constitution.

As usual, the watches below and the hunters turned out for what promised sport. Mugridge seemed to be in rabid fear of the water, and he exhibited a nimbleness and speed we did not dream he possessed. Cornered in the right-angle of the poop and galley, he sprang like a cat to the top of the cabin and ran aft. But his pursuers forestalling him, he doubled back across the cabin, passed over the galley, and gained the deck by means of the steerage-scuttle. Straight forward he raced, the boat-puller Harrison at his heels and gaining on him. But Mugridge, leaping suddenly, caught the jib-boom-lift. It happened in an instant. Holding his weight by his arms, and in mid-air doubling his body at the hips, he let fly with both feet. The oncoming Harrison caught the kick squarely in the pit of the stomach, groaned involuntarily, and doubled up and sank backward to the deck.

Hand-clapping and roars of laughter from the hunters greeted the exploit, while Mugridge, eluding half of his pursuers at the foremast, ran aft and through the remainder like a runner on the football field. Straight aft he held, to the poop and along the poop to the stern. So great was his speed that as he curved past the corner of the cabin he slipped and fell. Nilson was standing at the wheel, and the Cockney's hurtling body struck his legs. Both went down together, but Mugridge alone arose. By some freak of pressures, his frail body had snapped the strong man's leg like a pipe-stem.

Parsons took the wheel, and the pursuit continued. Round and round the decks they went, Mugridge sick with fear, the sailors hallooing and shouting directions to one another, and the hunters bellowing encouragement and laughter. Mugridge went down on the fore-hatch under three men; but he emerged from the mass like an eel, bleeding at the mouth, the offending shirt ripped into tatters, and sprang for the main-rigging. Up he went, clear up, beyond the ratlines, to the very masthead.

Half-a-dozen sailors swarmed to the crosstrees after him, where they clustered and waited while two of their number, Oofty-Oofty and Black (who was Latimer's boat-steerer), continued up the thin steel stays, lifting their bodies higher and higher by means of their arms.

It was a perilous undertaking, for, at a height of over a hundred feet from the deck, holding on by their hands, they were not in the best of positions to protect themselves from Mugridge's feet. And Mugridge kicked savagely, till the Kanaka, hanging on with one hand, seized the Cockney's foot with the other. Black duplicated the performance a moment later with the other foot. Then the three writhed together in a swaying tangle, struggling, sliding, and falling into the arms of their mates on the crosstrees.

The aërial battle was over, and Thomas Mugridge, whining and gibbering, his mouth flecked with bloody foam, was brought down to deck. Wolf Larsen rove a bowline in a piece of rope and slipped it under his shoulders. Then he was carried aft and flung into the sea. Forty,—fifty,—sixty feet of line ran out, when Wolf Larsen cried "Belay!" Oofty-Oofty took a turn on a bitt, the rope tautened, and the *Ghost*, lunging onward, jerked the cook to the surface.

It was a pitiful spectacle. Though he could not drown, and was nine-lived in addition, he was suffering all the agonies of half-drowning. The *Ghost* was going very slowly, and when her stern lifted on a wave and she slipped forward she pulled the wretch to the surface and gave him a moment in which to breathe; but between each lift the stern fell, and while the bow lazily climbed the next wave the line slacked and he sank beneath.

I had forgotten the existence of Maud Brewster, and I remembered her with a start as she stepped lightly beside me. It was her first time on deck since she had come aboard. A dead silence greeted her appearance.

"What is the cause of the merriment?" she asked.

"Ask Captain Larsen," I answered composedly and coldly, though inwardly my blood was boiling at the thought that she should be witness to such brutality.

She took my advice and was turning to put it into execution, when her eyes lighted on Oofty-Oofty, immediately before her, his body instinct with alertness and grace as he held the turn of the rope.

"Are you fishing?" she asked him.

He made no reply. His eyes, fixed intently on the sea astern, suddenly flashed.

"Shark ho, sir!" he cried.

"Heave in! Lively! All hands tail on!" Wolf Larsen shouted, springing himself to the rope in advance of the quickest.

Mugridge had heard the Kanaka's warning cry and was screaming madly. I could see a black fin cutting the water and making for him with greater swiftness than he was being pulled aboard. It was an even toss whether the shark or we would get him, and it was a matter of moments. When Mugridge was directly beneath us, the stern descended the slope of a passing wave, thus giving the advantage to the shark. The fin disappeared. The belly flashed white in swift upward rush. Almost equally swift, but not quite, was Wolf Larsen. He threw his strength into one tremendous jerk. The Cockney's body left the water; so did part of the shark's. He drew up his legs, and the man-eater seemed no more than barely to touch one foot, sinking back into the water with a splash. But at the moment of contact Thomas Mugridge cried out. Then he came in like a fresh-caught fish on a line, clearing the rail generously and striking the deck in a heap, on hands and knees, and rolling over.

But a fountain of blood was gushing forth. The right foot was missing, amputated neatly at the ankle. I looked instantly to Maud Brewster. Her face was white, her eyes dilated with horror. She was gazing, not at Thomas Mugridge, but at Wolf Larsen. And he was aware of it, for he said, with one of his short laughs:

"Man-play, Miss Brewster. Somewhat rougher, I warrant, than what you have been used to, but still-man-play. The shark was not in the reckoning. It—"

But at this juncture, Mugridge, who had lifted his head and ascertained the extent of his loss, floundered over on the deck and buried his teeth in Wolf Larsen's leg. Wolf Larsen stooped, coolly, to the Cockney, and pressed with thumb and finger at the rear of the jaws and below the ears. The jaws opened with reluctance, and Wolf Larsen stepped free.

"As I was saying," he went on, as though nothing unwonted had happened, "the shark was not in the reckoning. It was—ahem—shall we say Providence?"

She gave no sign that she had heard, though the expression of her eyes changed to one of inexpressible loathing as she started to turn away. She no more than started, for she swayed and tottered, and reached her hand weakly out to mine. I caught her in time to save her from falling, and helped her to a seat on the cabin. I thought she might faint outright, but she controlled herself.

"Will you get a tourniquet, Mr. Van Weyden," Wolf Larsen called to me.

I hesitated. Her lips moved, and though they formed no words, she commanded me with her eyes, plainly as speech, to go to the help of the unfortunate man. "Please," she managed to whisper, and I could but obey.

By now I had developed such skill at surgery that Wolf Larsen, with a few words of advice, left me to my task with a couple of sailors for assistants. For his task he elected a vengeance on the shark. A heavy swivel-hook, baited with fat salt-pork, was dropped overside; and by the time I had compressed the severed veins and arteries, the sailors were singing and heaving in the offending monster. I did not see it myself, but my assistants, first one and then the other, deserted me for a few moments to run amidships and look at what was going on. The shark, a sixteen-footer, was hoisted up against the main-rigging. Its jaws were pried apart to their greatest extension, and a stout stake, sharpened at both ends, was so inserted that when the pries were removed the spread jaws were fixed upon it. This accomplished, the hook was cut out. The shark dropped back into the sea, helpless, yet with its full strength, doomed—to lingering starvation—a living death less meet for it than for the man who devised the punishment.

CHAPTER XXII

I knew what it was as she came toward me. For ten minutes I had watched her talking earnestly with the engineer, and now, with a sign for silence, I drew her out of earshot of the helmsman. Her face was white and set; her large eyes, larger than usual what of the purpose in them, looked penetratingly into mine. I felt rather timid and apprehensive, for she had come to search Humphrey Van Weyden's soul, and Humphrey Van Weyden had nothing of which to be particularly proud since his advent on the *Ghost*.

We walked to the break of the poop, where she turned and faced me. I glanced around to see that no one was within hearing distance.

"What is it?" I asked gently; but the expression of determination on her face did not relax.

"I can readily understand," she began, "that this morning's affair was largely an accident; but I have been talking with Mr. Haskins. He tells me that the day we were rescued, even while I was in the cabin, two men were drowned, deliberately drowned—murdered."

There was a query in her voice, and she faced me accusingly, as though I were guilty of the deed, or at least a party to it.

"The information is quite correct," I answered. "The two men were murdered."

"And you permitted it!" she cried.

"I was unable to prevent it, is a better way of phrasing it," I replied, still gently.

"But you tried to prevent it?" There was an emphasis on the "tried," and a pleading little note in her voice.

"Oh, but you didn't," she hurried on, divining my answer. "But why didn't you?"

I shrugged my shoulders. "You must remember, Miss Brewster, that you are a new inhabitant of this little world, and that you do not yet understand the laws which operate within it. You bring with you certain fine conceptions of humanity, manhood, conduct, and such things; but here you will find them misconceptions. I have found it so," I added, with an involuntary sigh.

She shook her head incredulously.

"What would you advise, then?" I asked. "That I should take a knife, or a gun, or an axe, and kill this man?"

She half started back.

"No, not that!"

"Then what should I do? Kill myself?"

“You speak in purely materialistic terms,” she objected. “There is such a thing as moral courage, and moral courage is never without effect.”

“Ah,” I smiled, “you advise me to kill neither him nor myself, but to let him kill me.” I held up my hand as she was about to speak. “For moral courage is a worthless asset on this little floating world. Leach, one of the men who were murdered, had moral courage to an unusual degree. So had the other man, Johnson. Not only did it not stand them in good stead, but it destroyed them. And so with me if I should exercise what little moral courage I may possess.

“You must understand, Miss Brewster, and understand clearly, that this man is a monster. He is without conscience. Nothing is sacred to him, nothing is too terrible for him to do. It was due to his whim that I was detained aboard in the first place. It is due to his whim that I am still alive. I do nothing, can do nothing, because I am a slave to this monster, as you are now a slave to him; because I desire to live, as you will desire to live; because I cannot fight and overcome him, just as you will not be able to fight and overcome him.”

She waited for me to go on.

“What remains? Mine is the role of the weak. I remain silent and suffer ignominy, as you will remain silent and suffer ignominy. And it is well. It is the best we can do if we wish to live. The battle is not always to the strong. We have not the strength with which to fight this man; we must dissimulate, and win, if win we can, by craft. If you will be advised by me, this is what you will do. I know my position is perilous, and I may say frankly that yours is even more perilous. We must stand together, without appearing to do so, in secret alliance. I shall not be able to side with you openly, and, no matter what indignities may be put upon me, you are to remain likewise silent. We must provoke no scenes with this man, nor cross his will. And we must keep smiling faces and be friendly with him no matter how repulsive it may be.”

She brushed her hand across her forehead in a puzzled way, saying, “Still I do not understand.”

“You must do as I say,” I interrupted authoritatively, for I saw Wolf Larsen’s gaze wandering toward us from where he paced up and down with Latimer amidships. “Do as I say, and ere long you will find I am right.”

“What shall I do, then?” she asked, detecting the anxious glance I had shot at the object of our conversation, and impressed, I flatter myself, with the earnestness of my manner.

“Dispense with all the moral courage you can,” I said briskly. “Don’t arouse this man’s animosity. Be quite friendly with him, talk with him, discuss literature and art with him—he is fond of such things. You will find him an interested listener and no fool. And for your own sake try to avoid witnessing, as much as you can, the brutalities of the ship. It will make it easier for you to act your part.”

“I am to lie,” she said in steady, rebellious tones, “by speech and action to lie.”

Wolf Larsen had separated from Latimer and was coming toward us. I was desperate.

“Please, please understand me,” I said hurriedly, lowering my voice. “All your experience of men and things is worthless here. You must begin over again. I know,—I can see it—you have, among other ways, been used to managing people with your eyes, letting your moral courage speak out through them, as it were. You have already managed me with your eyes, commanded me with them. But don't try it on Wolf Larsen. You could as easily control a lion, while he would make a mock of you. He would—I have always been proud of the fact that I discovered him," I said, turning the conversation as Wolf Larsen stepped on the poop and joined us. "The editors were afraid of him and the publishers would have none of him. But I knew, and his genius and my judgment were vindicated when he made that magnificent hit with his 'Forge.'"

"And it was a newspaper poem," she said glibly.

"It did happen to see the light in a newspaper," I replied, "but not because the magazine editors had been denied a glimpse at it."

"We were talking of Harris," I said to Wolf Larsen.

"Oh, yes," he acknowledged. "I remember the 'Forge.' Filled with pretty sentiments and an almighty faith in human illusions. By the way, Mr. Van Weyden, you'd better look in on Cooky. He's complaining and restless."

Thus was I bluntly dismissed from the poop, only to find Mugridge sleeping soundly from the morphine I had given him. I made no haste to return on deck, and when I did I was gratified to see Miss Brewster in animated conversation with Wolf Larsen. As I say, the sight gratified me. She was following my advice. And yet I was conscious of a slight shock or hurt in that she was able to do the thing I had begged her to do and which she had notably disliked.

CHAPTER XXIII

Brave winds, blowing fair, swiftly drove the *Ghost* northward into the seal herd. We encountered it well up to the forty-fourth parallel, in a raw and stormy sea across which the wind harried the fog-banks in eternal flight. For days at a time we could never see the sun nor take an observation; then the wind would sweep the face of the ocean clean, the waves would ripple and flash, and we would learn where we were. A day of clear weather might follow, or three days or four, and then the fog would settle down upon us, seemingly thicker than ever.

The hunting was perilous; yet the boats, lowered day after day, were swallowed up in the grey obscurity, and were seen no more till nightfall, and often not till long after, when they would creep in like sea-wraiths, one by one, out of the grey. Wainwright—the hunter whom Wolf Larsen had stolen with boat and men—took advantage of the veiled sea and escaped. He disappeared one morning in the encircling fog with his two men, and we never saw them again, though it was not many days when we learned that they had passed from schooner to schooner until they finally regained their own.

This was the thing I had set my mind upon doing, but the opportunity never offered. It was not in the mate's province to go out in the boats, and though I manœuvred cunningly for it, Wolf Larsen never granted me the privilege. Had he done so, I should have managed somehow to carry Miss Brewster away with me. As it was, the situation was approaching a stage which I was afraid to consider. I involuntarily shunned the thought of it, and yet the thought continually arose in my mind like a haunting spectre.

I had read sea-romances in my time, wherein figured, as a matter of course, the lone woman in the midst of a shipload of men; but I learned, now, that I had never comprehended the deeper significance of such a situation—the thing the writers harped upon and exploited so thoroughly. And here it was, now, and I was face to face with it. That it should be as vital as possible, it required no more than that the woman should be Maud Brewster, who now charmed me in person as she had long charmed me through her work.

No one more out of environment could be imagined. She was a delicate, ethereal creature, swaying and willowy, light and graceful of movement. It never seemed to me that she walked, or, at least, walked after the ordinary manner of mortals. Hers was an extreme lithesomeness, and she moved with a certain indefinable airiness, approaching one as down might float or as a bird on noiseless wings.

CHAPTER XXIII

She was like a bit of Dresden china, and I was continually impressed with what I may call her fragility. As at the time I caught her arm when helping her below, so at any time I was quite prepared, should stress or rough handling befall her, to see her crumble away. I have never seen body and spirit in such perfect accord. Describe her verse, as the critics have described it, as sublimated and spiritual, and you have described her body. It seemed to partake of her soul, to have analogous attributes, and to link it to life with the slenderest of chains. Indeed, she trod the earth lightly, and in her constitution there was little of the robust clay.

She was in striking contrast to Wolf Larsen. Each was nothing that the other was, everything that the other was not. I noted them walking the deck together one morning, and I likened them to the extreme ends of the human ladder of evolution—the one the culmination of all savagery, the other the finished product of the finest civilization. True, Wolf Larsen possessed intellect to an unusual degree, but it was directed solely to the exercise of his savage instincts and made him but the more formidable a savage. He was splendidly muscled, a heavy man, and though he strode with the certitude and directness of the physical man, there was nothing heavy about his stride. The jungle and the wilderness lurked in the uplift and downput of his feet. He was cat-footed, and lithe, and strong, always strong. I likened him to some great tiger, a beast of prowess and prey. He looked it, and the piercing glitter that arose at times in his eyes was the same piercing glitter I had observed in the eyes of caged leopards and other preying creatures of the wild.

But this day, as I noted them pacing up and down, I saw that it was she who terminated the walk. They came up to where I was standing by the entrance to the companion-way. Though she betrayed it by no outward sign, I felt, somehow, that she was greatly perturbed. She made some idle remark, looking at me, and laughed lightly enough; but I saw her eyes return to his, involuntarily, as though fascinated; then they fell, but not swiftly enough to veil the rush of terror that filled them.

It was in his eyes that I saw the cause of her perturbation. Ordinarily grey and cold and harsh, they were now warm and soft and golden, and all a-dance with tiny lights that dimmed and faded, or welled up till the full orbs were flooded with a glowing radiance. Perhaps it was to this that the golden colour was due; but golden his eyes were, enticing and masterful, at the same time luring and compelling, and speaking a demand and clamour of the blood which no woman, much less Maud Brewster, could misunderstand.

Her own terror rushed upon me, and in that moment of fear—the most terrible fear a man can experience—I knew that in inexpressible ways she was dear to me. The knowledge that I loved her rushed upon me with the terror, and with both emotions gripping at my heart and causing my blood at the same time to chill and to leap riotously, I felt myself drawn by a power without me and beyond me, and found my eyes returning against my will to gaze into the eyes of Wolf Larsen. But he had recovered himself. The golden colour and the dancing lights were gone. Cold and grey and glittering they were as he bowed brusquely and turned away.

"I am afraid," she whispered, with a shiver. "I am so afraid."

I, too, was afraid, and what of my discovery of how much she meant to me my mind was in a turmoil; but, I succeeded in answering quite calmly:

"All will come right, Miss Brewster. Trust me, it will come right."

She answered with a grateful little smile that sent my heart pounding, and started to descend the companion-stairs.

For a long while I remained standing where she had left me. There was imperative need to adjust myself, to consider the significance of the changed aspect of things. It had come, at last, love had come, when I least expected it and under the most forbidding conditions. Of course, my philosophy had always recognized the inevitableness of the love-call sooner or later; but long years of bookish silence had made me inattentive and unprepared.

And now it had come! Maud Brewster! My memory flashed back to that first thin little volume on my desk, and I saw before me, as though in the concrete, the row of thin little volumes on my library shelf. How I had welcomed each of them! Each year one had come from the press, and to me each was the advent of the year. They had voiced a kindred intellect and spirit, and as such I had received them into a camaraderie of the mind; but now their place was in my heart.

My heart? A revulsion of feeling came over me. I seemed to stand outside myself and to look at myself incredulously. Maud Brewster! Humphrey Van Weyden, "the cold-blooded fish," the "emotionless monster," the "analytical demon," of Charley Furuseth's christening, in love! And then, without rhyme or reason, all sceptical, my mind flew back to a small biographical note in the red-bound *Who's Who*, and I said to myself, "She was born in Cambridge, and she is twenty-seven years old." And then I said, "Twenty-seven years old and still free and fancy free?" But how did I know she was fancy free? And the pang of new-born jealousy put all incredulity to flight. There was no doubt about it. I was jealous; therefore I loved. And the woman I loved was Maud Brewster.

I, Humphrey Van Weyden, was in love! And again the doubt assailed me. Not that I was afraid of it, however, or reluctant to meet it. On the contrary, idealist that I was to the most pronounced degree, my philosophy had always recognized and guerdoned love as the greatest thing in the world, the aim and the summit of being, the most exquisite pitch of joy and happiness to which life could thrill, the thing of all things to be hailed and welcomed and taken into the heart. But now that it had come I could not believe. I could not be so fortunate. It was too good, too good to be true. Symons's lines came into my head:

"I wandered all these years among
A world of women, seeking you."

And then I had ceased seeking. It was not for me, this greatest thing in the world, I had decided. Furuseth was right; I was abnormal, an "emotionless monster," a strange bookish creature, capable of pleasuring in sensations only of the mind. And though I had been surrounded by women all my days, my appreciation of them had been æsthetic and nothing more. I had actually, at times, considered myself outside the pale, a monkish fellow denied the eternal or the passing passions I saw and understood so well in others. And now it had come! Undreamed of and unheralded, it had come. In what could have been no less than an ecstasy, I left my post at the head of the companion-way and started along the deck, murmuring to myself those beautiful lines of Mrs. Browning:

CHAPTER XXIII

"I lived with visions for my company
Instead of men and women years ago,
And found them gentle mates, nor thought to know
A sweeter music than they played to me."

But the sweeter music was playing in my ears, and I was blind and oblivious to all about me. The sharp voice of Wolf Larsen aroused me.

"What the hell are you up to?" he was demanding.

I had strayed forward where the sailors were painting, and I came to myself to find my advancing foot on the verge of overturning a paint-pot.

"Sleep-walking, sunstroke,—what?" he barked.

"No; indigestion," I retorted, and continued my walk as if nothing untoward had occurred.

CHAPTER XXIV

Among the most vivid memories of my life are those of the events on the *Ghost* which occurred during the forty hours succeeding the discovery of my love for Maud Brewster. I, who had lived my life in quiet places, only to enter at the age of thirty-five upon a course of the most irrational adventure I could have imagined, never had more incident and excitement crammed into any forty hours of my experience. Nor can I quite close my ears to a small voice of pride which tells me I did not do so badly, all things considered.

To begin with, at the midday dinner, Wolf Larsen informed the hunters that they were to eat thenceforth in the steerage. It was an unprecedented thing on sealing-schooners, where it is the custom for the hunters to rank, unofficially as officers. He gave no reason, but his motive was obvious enough. Horner and Smoke had been displaying a gallantry toward Maud Brewster, ludicrous in itself and inoffensive to her, but to him evidently distasteful.

The announcement was received with black silence, though the other four hunters glanced significantly at the two who had been the cause of their banishment. Jock Horner, quiet as was his way, gave no sign; but the blood surged darkly across Smoke's forehead, and he half opened his mouth to speak. Wolf Larsen was watching him, waiting for him, the steely glitter in his eyes; but Smoke closed his mouth again without having said anything.

"Anything to say?" the other demanded aggressively.

It was a challenge, but Smoke refused to accept it.

"About what?" he asked, so innocently that Wolf Larsen was disconcerted, while the others smiled.

"Oh, nothing," Wolf Larsen said lamely. "I just thought you might want to register a kick."

"About what?" asked the imperturbable Smoke.

Smoke's mates were now smiling broadly. His captain could have killed him, and I doubt not that blood would have flowed had not Maud Brewster been present. For that matter, it was her presence which enabled. Smoke to act as he did. He was too discreet and cautious a man to incur Wolf Larsen's anger at a time when that anger could be expressed in terms stronger than words. I was in fear that a struggle might take place, but a cry from the helmsman made it easy for the situation to save itself.

"Smoke ho!" the cry came down the open companion-way.

"How's it bear?" Wolf Larsen called up.

CHAPTER XXIV

"Dead astern, sir."

"Maybe it's a Russian," suggested Latimer.

His words brought anxiety into the faces of the other hunters. A Russian could mean but one thing—a cruiser. The hunters, never more than roughly aware of the position of the ship, nevertheless knew that we were close to the boundaries of the forbidden sea, while Wolf Larsen's record as a poacher was notorious. All eyes centred upon him.

"We're dead safe," he assured them with a laugh. "No salt mines this time, Smoke. But I'll tell you what—I'll lay odds of five to one it's the *Macedonia*."

No one accepted his offer, and he went on: "In which event, I'll lay ten to one there's trouble breezing up."

"No, thank you," Latimer spoke up. "I don't object to losing my money, but I like to get a run for it anyway. There never was a time when there wasn't trouble when you and that brother of yours got together, and I'll lay twenty to one on that."

A general smile followed, in which Wolf Larsen joined, and the dinner went on smoothly, thanks to me, for he treated me abominably the rest of the meal, sneering at me and patronizing me till I was all a-tremble with suppressed rage. Yet I knew I must control myself for Maud Brewster's sake, and I received my reward when her eyes caught mine for a fleeting second, and they said, as distinctly as if she spoke, "Be brave, be brave."

We left the table to go on deck, for a steamer was a welcome break in the monotony of the sea on which we floated, while the conviction that it was Death Larsen and the *Macedonia* added to the excitement. The stiff breeze and heavy sea which had sprung up the previous afternoon had been moderating all morning, so that it was now possible to lower the boats for an afternoon's hunt. The hunting promised to be profitable. We had sailed since daylight across a sea barren of seals, and were now running into the herd.

The smoke was still miles astern, but overhauling us rapidly, when we lowered our boats. They spread out and struck a northerly course across the ocean. Now and again we saw a sail lower, heard the reports of the shot-guns, and saw the sail go up again. The seals were thick, the wind was dying away; everything favoured a big catch. As we ran off to get our leeward position of the last lee boat, we found the ocean fairly carpeted with sleeping seals. They were all about us, thicker than I had ever seen them before, in twos and threes and bunches, stretched full length on the surface and sleeping for all the world like so many lazy young dogs.

Under the approaching smoke the hull and upper-works of a steamer were growing larger. It was the *Macedonia.* I read her name through the glasses as she passed by scarcely a mile to starboard. Wolf Larsen looked savagely at the vessel, while Maud Brewster was curious.

"Where is the trouble you were so sure was breezing up, Captain Larsen?" she asked gaily.

He glanced at her, a moment's amusement softening his features.

"What did you expect? That they'd come aboard and cut our throats?"

"Something like that," she confessed. "You understand, seal-hunters are so new and strange to me that I am quite ready to expect anything."

He nodded his head. "Quite right, quite right. Your error is that you failed to expect the worst."

"Why, what can be worse than cutting our throats?" she asked, with pretty naïve surprise.

"Cutting our purses," he answered. "Man is so made these days that his capacity for living is determined by the money he possesses."

"'Who steals my purse steals trash,'" she quoted.

"Who steals my purse steals my right to live," was the reply, "old saws to the contrary. For he steals my bread and meat and bed, and in so doing imperils my life. There are not enough soup-kitchens and bread-lines to go around, you know, and when men have nothing in their purses they usually die, and die miserably—unless they are able to fill their purses pretty speedily."

"But I fail to see that this steamer has any designs on your purse."

"Wait and you will see," he answered grimly.

We did not have long to wait. Having passed several miles beyond our line of boats, the *Macedonia* proceeded to lower her own. We knew she carried fourteen boats to our five (we were one short through the desertion of Wainwright), and she began dropping them far to leeward of our last boat, continued dropping them athwart our course, and finished dropping them far to windward of our first weather boat. The hunting, for us, was spoiled. There were no seals behind us, and ahead of us the line of fourteen boats, like a huge broom, swept the herd before it.

Our boats hunted across the two or three miles of water between them and the point where the *Macedonia's* had been dropped, and then headed for home. The wind had fallen to a whisper, the ocean was growing calmer and calmer, and this, coupled with the presence of the great herd, made a perfect hunting day—one of the two or three days to be encountered in the whole of a lucky season. An angry lot of men, boat-pullers and steerers as well as hunters, swarmed over our side. Each man felt that he had been robbed; and the boats were hoisted in amid curses, which, if curses had power, would have settled Death Larsen for all eternity—"Dead and damned for a dozen iv eternities," commented Louis, his eyes twinkling up at me as he rested from hauling taut the lashings of his boat.

"Listen to them, and find if it is hard to discover the most vital thing in their souls," said Wolf Larsen. "Faith? and love? and high ideals? The good? the beautiful? the true?"

"Their innate sense of right has been violated," Maud Brewster said, joining the conversation.

She was standing a dozen feet away, one hand resting on the main-shrouds and her body swaying gently to the slight roll of the ship. She had not raised her voice, and yet I was struck by its clear and bell-like tone. Ah, it was sweet in my ears! I scarcely dared look at her just then, for the fear of betraying myself. A boy's cap was perched on her head, and her hair, light brown and arranged in a loose and fluffy order that caught the sun, seemed an aureole about the delicate oval of her face. She was positively bewitching, and, withal, sweetly spirituelle, if not saintly. All my old-time marvel at life returned to me at sight of this splendid incarnation of it, and Wolf Larsen's cold explanation of life and its meaning was truly ridiculous and laughable.

"A sentimentalist," he sneered, "like Mr. Van Weyden. Those men are cursing because their desires have been outraged. That is all. What desires? The desires for the good grub and soft beds ashore which a handsome pay-day brings them—the women and the drink, the gorging and the beastliness which so truly expresses them, the best that is in them, their highest aspirations, their ideals, if you please. The exhibition they make of their feelings is not a touching sight, yet it shows how deeply they have been touched, how deeply their purses have been touched, for to lay hands on their purses is to lay hands on their souls."

"'You hardly behave as if your purse had been touched," she said, smilingly.

"Then it so happens that I am behaving differently, for my purse and my soul have both been touched. At the current price of skins in the London market, and based on a fair estimate of what the afternoon's catch would have been had not the *Macedonia* hogged it, the *Ghost* has lost about fifteen hundred dollars' worth of skins."

"You speak so calmly—" she began.

"But I do not feel calm; I could kill the man who robbed me," he interrupted. "Yes, yes, I know, and that man my brother—more sentiment! Bah!"

His face underwent a sudden change. His voice was less harsh and wholly sincere as he said:

"You must be happy, you sentimentalists, really and truly happy at dreaming and finding things good, and, because you find some of them good, feeling good yourself. Now, tell me, you two, do you find me good?"

"You are good to look upon—in a way," I qualified.

"There are in you all powers for good," was Maud Brewster's answer.

"There you are!" he cried at her, half angrily. "Your words are empty to me. There is nothing clear and sharp and definite about the thought you have expressed. You cannot pick it up in your two hands and look at it. In point of fact, it is not a thought. It is a feeling, a sentiment, a something based upon illusion and not a product of the intellect at all."

As he went on his voice again grew soft, and a confiding note came into it. "Do you know, I sometimes catch myself wishing that I, too, were blind to the facts of life and only knew its fancies and illusions. They're wrong, all wrong, of course, and contrary to reason; but in the face of them my reason tells me, wrong and most wrong, that to dream and live illusions gives greater delight. And after all, delight is the wage for living. Without delight, living is a worthless act. To labour at living and be unpaid is worse than to be dead. He who delights the most lives the most, and your dreams and unrealities are less disturbing to you and more gratifying than are my facts to me."

He shook his head slowly, pondering.

"I often doubt, I often doubt, the worthwhileness of reason. Dreams must be more substantial and satisfying. Emotional delight is more filling and lasting than intellectual delight; and, besides, you pay for your moments of intellectual delight by having the blues. Emotional delight is followed by no more than jaded senses which speedily recuperate. I envy you, I envy you."

He stopped abruptly, and then on his lips formed one of his strange quizzical smiles, as he added:

"It's from my brain I envy you, take notice, and not from my heart. My reason dictates it. The envy is an intellectual product. I am like a sober man looking upon drunken men, and, greatly weary, wishing he, too, were drunk."

"Or like a wise man looking upon fools and wishing he, too, were a fool," I laughed.

"Quite so," he said. "You are a blessed, bankrupt pair of fools. You have no facts in your pocketbook."

"Yet we spend as freely as you," was Maud Brewster's contribution.

"More freely, because it costs you nothing."

"And because we draw upon eternity," she retorted.

"Whether you do or think you do, it's the same thing. You spend what you haven't got, and in return you get greater value from spending what you haven't got than I get from spending what I have got, and what I have sweated to get."

"Why don't you change the basis of your coinage, then?" she queried teasingly.

He looked at her quickly, half-hopefully, and then said, all regretfully: "Too late. I'd like to, perhaps, but I can't. My pocketbook is stuffed with the old coinage, and it's a stubborn thing. I can never bring myself to recognize anything else as valid."

He ceased speaking, and his gaze wandered absently past her and became lost in the placid sea. The old primal melancholy was strong upon him. He was quivering to it. He had reasoned himself into a spell of the blues, and within few hours one could look for the devil within him to be up and stirring. I remembered Charley Furuseth, and knew this man's sadness as the penalty which the materialist ever pays for his materialism.

CHAPTER XXV

"You've been on deck, Mr. Van Weyden," Wolf Larsen said, the following morning at the breakfast-table, "How do things look?"

"Clear enough," I answered, glancing at the sunshine which streamed down the open companion-way. "Fair westerly breeze, with a promise of stiffening, if Louis predicts correctly."

He nodded his head in a pleased way. "Any signs of fog?"

"Thick banks in the north and north-west."

He nodded his head again, evincing even greater satisfaction than before.

"What of the *Macedonia*?"

"Not sighted," I answered.

I could have sworn his face fell at the intelligence, but why he should be disappointed I could not conceive.

I was soon to learn. "Smoke ho!" came the hail from on deck, and his face brightened.

"Good!" he exclaimed, and left the table at once to go on deck and into the steerage, where the hunters were taking the first breakfast of their exile.

Maud Brewster and I scarcely touched the food before us, gazing, instead, in silent anxiety at each other, and listening to Wolf Larsen's voice, which easily penetrated the cabin through the intervening bulkhead. He spoke at length, and his conclusion was greeted with a wild roar of cheers. The bulkhead was too thick for us to hear what he said; but whatever it was it affected the hunters strongly, for the cheering was followed by loud exclamations and shouts of joy.

From the sounds on deck I knew that the sailors had been routed out and were preparing to lower the boats. Maud Brewster accompanied me on deck, but I left her at the break of the poop, where she might watch the scene and not be in it. The sailors must have learned whatever project was on hand, and the vim and snap they put into their work attested their enthusiasm. The hunters came trooping on deck with shot-guns and ammunition-boxes, and, most unusual, their rifles. The latter were rarely taken in the boats, for a seal shot at long range with a rifle invariably sank before a boat could reach it. But each hunter this day had his rifle and a large supply of cartridges. I noticed they grinned with satisfaction whenever they looked at the *Macedonia's* smoke, which was rising higher and higher as she approached from the west.

The five boats went over the side with a rush, spread out like the ribs of a fan, and set a northerly course, as on the preceding afternoon, for us to follow. I watched for some time, curiously, but there seemed nothing extraordinary about their behaviour. They lowered sails, shot seals, and hoisted sails again, and continued on their way as I had always seen them do. The *Macedonia* repeated her performance of yesterday, "hogging" the sea by dropping her line of boats in advance of ours and across our course. Fourteen boats require a considerable spread of ocean for comfortable hunting, and when she had completely lapped our line she continued steaming into the north-east, dropping more boats as she went.

"What's up?" I asked Wolf Larsen, unable longer to keep my curiosity in check.

"Never mind what's up," he answered gruffly. "You won't be a thousand years in finding out, and in the meantime just pray for plenty of wind."

"Oh, well, I don't mind telling you," he said the next moment. "I'm going to give that brother of mine a taste of his own medicine. In short, I'm going to play the hog myself, and not for one day, but for the rest of the season,—if we're in luck."

"And if we're not?" I queried.

"Not to be considered," he laughed. "We simply must be in luck, or it's all up with us."

He had the wheel at the time, and I went forward to my hospital in the forecastle, where lay the two crippled men, Nilson and Thomas Mugridge. Nilson was as cheerful as could be expected, for his broken leg was knitting nicely; but the Cockney was desperately melancholy, and I was aware of a great sympathy for the unfortunate creature. And the marvel of it was that still he lived and clung to life. The brutal years had reduced his meagre body to splintered wreckage, and yet the spark of life within burned brightly as ever.

"With an artificial foot—and they make excellent ones—you will be stumping ships' galleys to the end of time," I assured him jovially.

But his answer was serious, nay, solemn. "I don't know about wot you s'y, Mr. Van W'yden, but I do know I'll never rest 'appy till I see that 'ell-'ound bloody well dead. 'E cawn't live as long as me. 'E's got no right to live, an' as the Good Word puts it, ''E shall shorely die,' an' I s'y, 'Amen, an' damn soon at that.'"

When I returned on deck I found Wolf Larsen steering mainly with one hand, while with the other hand he held the marine glasses and studied the situation of the boats, paying particular attention to the position of the *Macedonia.* The only change noticeable in our boats was that they had hauled close on the wind and were heading several points west of north. Still, I could not see the expediency of the manœuvre, for the free sea was still intercepted by the *Macedonia's* five weather boats, which, in turn, had hauled close on the wind. Thus they slowly diverged toward the west, drawing farther away from the remainder of the boats in their line. Our boats were rowing as well as sailing. Even the hunters were pulling, and with three pairs of oars in the water they rapidly overhauled what I may appropriately term the enemy.

The smoke of the *Macedonia* had dwindled to a dim blot on the north-eastern horizon. Of the steamer herself nothing was to be seen. We had been loafing along, till now, our sails shaking half the time and spilling the wind; and twice, for short periods, we had been hove to. But there was no more loafing. Sheets were trimmed, and Wolf Larsen proceeded to put the *Ghost* through her paces. We ran past our line of boats and bore down upon the first weather boat of the other line.

"Down that flying jib, Mr. Van Weyden," Wolf Larsen commanded. "And stand by to back over the jibs."

CHAPTER XXV

I ran forward and had the downhaul of the flying jib all in and fast as we slipped by the boat a hundred feet to leeward. The three men in it gazed at us suspiciously. They had been hogging the sea, and they knew Wolf Larsen, by reputation at any rate. I noted that the hunter, a huge Scandinavian sitting in the bow, held his rifle, ready to hand, across his knees. It should have been in its proper place in the rack. When they came opposite our stern, Wolf Larsen greeted them with a wave of the hand, and cried:

"Come on board and have a 'gam'!"

"To gam," among the sealing-schooners, is a substitute for the verbs "to visit," "to gossip." It expresses the garrulity of the sea, and is a pleasant break in the monotony of the life.

The *Ghost* swung around into the wind, and I finished my work forward in time to run aft and lend a hand with the mainsheet.

"You will please stay on deck, Miss Brewster," Wolf Larsen said, as he started forward to meet his guest. "And you too, Mr. Van Weyden."

The boat had lowered its sail and run alongside. The hunter, golden bearded like a sea-king, came over the rail and dropped on deck. But his hugeness could not quite overcome his apprehensiveness. Doubt and distrust showed strongly in his face. It was a transparent face, for all of its hairy shield, and advertised instant relief when he glanced from Wolf Larsen to me, noted that there was only the pair of us, and then glanced over his own two men who had joined him. Surely he had little reason to be afraid. He towered like a Goliath above Wolf Larsen. He must have measured six feet eight or nine inches in stature, and I subsequently learned his weight—240 pounds. And there was no fat about him. It was all bone and muscle.

A return of apprehension was apparent when, at the top of the companion-way, Wolf Larsen invited him below. But he reassured himself with a glance down at his host—a big man himself but dwarfed by the propinquity of the giant. So all hesitancy vanished, and the pair descended into the cabin. In the meantime, his two men, as was the wont of visiting sailors, had gone forward into the forecastle to do some visiting themselves.

Suddenly, from the cabin came a great, choking bellow, followed by all the sounds of a furious struggle. It was the leopard and the lion, and the lion made all the noise. Wolf Larsen was the leopard.

"You see the sacredness of our hospitality," I said bitterly to Maud Brewster.

She nodded her head that she heard, and I noted in her face the signs of the same sickness at sight or sound of violent struggle from which I had suffered so severely during my first weeks on the *Ghost*.

"Wouldn't it be better if you went forward, say by the steerage companion-way, until it is over?" I suggested.

She shook her head and gazed at me pitifully. She was not frightened, but appalled, rather, at the human animality of it.

"You will understand," I took advantage of the opportunity to say, "whatever part I take in what is going on and what is to come, that I am compelled to take it—if you and I are ever to get out of this scrape with our lives."

"It is not nice—for me," I added.

"I understand," she said, in a weak, far-away voice, and her eyes showed me that she did understand.

The sounds from below soon died away. Then Wolf Larsen came alone on deck. There was a slight flush under his bronze, but otherwise he bore no signs of the battle.

"Send those two men aft, Mr. Van Weyden," he said.

I obeyed, and a minute or two later they stood before him. "Hoist in your boat," he said to them. "Your hunter's decided to stay aboard awhile and doesn't want it pounding alongside."

"Hoist in your boat, I said," he repeated, this time in sharper tones as they hesitated to do his bidding.

"Who knows? you may have to sail with me for a time," he said, quite softly, with a silken threat that belied the softness, as they moved slowly to comply, "and we might as well start with a friendly understanding. Lively now! Death Larsen makes you jump better than that, and you know it!"

Their movements perceptibly quickened under his coaching, and as the boat swung inboard I was sent forward to let go the jibs. Wolf Larsen, at the wheel, directed the *Ghost* after the *Macedonia's* second weather boat.

Under way, and with nothing for the time being to do, I turned my attention to the situation of the boats. The *Macedonia's* third weather boat was being attacked by two of ours, the fourth by our remaining three; and the fifth, turn about, was taking a hand in the defence of its nearest mate. The fight had opened at long distance, and the rifles were cracking steadily. A quick, snappy sea was being kicked up by the wind, a condition which prevented fine shooting; and now and again, as we drew closer, we could see the bullets zip-zipping from wave to wave.

The boat we were pursuing had squared away and was running before the wind to escape us, and, in the course of its flight, to take part in repulsing our general boat attack.

Attending to sheets and tacks now left me little time to see what was taking place, but I happened to be on the poop when Wolf Larsen ordered the two strange sailors forward and into the forecastle. They went sullenly, but they went. He next ordered Miss Brewster below, and smiled at the instant horror that leapt into her eyes.

"You'll find nothing gruesome down there," he said, "only an unhurt man securely made fast to the ring-bolts. Bullets are liable to come aboard, and I don't want you killed, you know."

Even as he spoke, a bullet was deflected by a brass-capped spoke of the wheel between his hands and screeched off through the air to windward.

"You see," he said to her; and then to me, "Mr. Van Weyden, will you take the wheel?"

Maud Brewster had stepped inside the companion-way so that only her head was exposed. Wolf Larsen had procured a rifle and was throwing a cartridge into the barrel. I begged her with my eyes to go below, but she smiled and said:

"We may be feeble land-creatures without legs, but we can show Captain Larsen that we are at least as brave as he."

He gave her a quick look of admiration.

"I like you a hundred per cent. better for that," he said. "Books, and brains, and bravery. You are well-rounded, a blue-stocking fit to be the wife of a pirate chief. Ahem, we'll discuss that later," he smiled, as a bullet struck solidly into the cabin wall.

I saw his eyes flash golden as he spoke, and I saw the terror mount in her own.

"We are braver," I hastened to say. "At least, speaking for myself, I know I am braver than Captain Larsen."

It was I who was now favoured by a quick look. He was wondering if I were making fun of him. I put three or four spokes over to counteract a sheer toward the wind on the part of the *Ghost*, and then steadied her. Wolf Larsen was still waiting an explanation, and I pointed down to my knees.

"You will observe there," I said, "a slight trembling. It is because I am afraid, the flesh is afraid; and I am afraid in my mind because I do not wish to die. But my spirit masters the trembling flesh and the qualms of the mind. I am more than brave. I am courageous. Your flesh is not afraid. You are not afraid. On the one hand, it costs you nothing to encounter danger; on the other hand, it even gives you delight. You enjoy it. You may be unafraid, Mr. Larsen, but you must grant that the bravery is mine."

"You're right," he acknowledged at once. "I never thought of it in that way before. But is the opposite true? If you are braver than I, am I more cowardly than you?"

We both laughed at the absurdity, and he dropped down to the deck and rested his rifle across the rail. The bullets we had received had travelled nearly a mile, but by now we had cut that distance in half. He fired three careful shots. The first struck fifty feet to windward of the boat, the second alongside; and at the third the boat-steerer let loose his steering-oar and crumpled up in the bottom of the boat.

"I guess that'll fix them," Wolf Larsen said, rising to his feet. "I couldn't afford to let the hunter have it, and there is a chance the boat-puller doesn't know how to steer. In which case, the hunter cannot steer and shoot at the same time."

His reasoning was justified, for the boat rushed at once into the wind and the hunter sprang aft to take the boat-steerer's place. There was no more shooting, though the rifles were still cracking merrily from the other boats.

The hunter had managed to get the boat before the wind again, but we ran down upon it, going at least two feet to its one. A hundred yards away, I saw the boat-puller pass a rifle to the hunter. Wolf Larsen went amidships and took the coil of the throat-halyards from its pin. Then he peered over the rail with levelled rifle. Twice I saw the hunter let go the steering-oar with one hand, reach for his rifle, and hesitate. We were now alongside and foaming past.

"Here, you!" Wolf Larsen cried suddenly to the boat-puller. "Take a turn!"

At the same time he flung the coil of rope. It struck fairly, nearly knocking the man over, but he did not obey. Instead, he looked to his hunter for orders. The hunter, in turn, was in a quandary. His rifle was between his knees, but if he let go the steering-oar in order to shoot, the boat would sweep around and collide with the schooner. Also he saw Wolf Larsen's rifle bearing upon him and knew he would be shot ere he could get his rifle into play.

"Take a turn," he said quietly to the man.

The boat-puller obeyed, taking a turn around the little forward thwart and paying the line as it jerked taut. The boat sheered out with a rush, and the hunter steadied it to a parallel course some twenty feet from the side of the *Ghost*.

"Now, get that sail down and come alongside!" Wolf Larsen ordered.

He never let go his rifle, even passing down the tackles with one hand. When they were fast, bow and stern, and the two uninjured men prepared to come aboard, the hunter picked up his rifle as if to place it in a secure position.

"Drop it!" Wolf Larsen cried, and the hunter dropped it as though it were hot and had burned him.

Once aboard, the two prisoners hoisted in the boat and under Wolf Larsen's direction carried the wounded boat-steerer down into the forecastle.

"If our five boats do as well as you and I have done, we'll have a pretty full crew," Wolf Larsen said to me.

"The man you shot—he is—I hope?" Maud Brewster quavered.

"In the shoulder," he answered. "Nothing serious, Mr. Van Weyden will pull him around as good as ever in three or four weeks."

"But he won't pull those chaps around, from the look of it," he added, pointing at the *Macedonia's* third boat, for which I had been steering and which was now nearly abreast of us. "That's Horner's and Smoke's work. I told them we wanted live men, not carcasses. But the joy of shooting to hit is a most compelling thing, when once you've learned how to shoot. Ever experienced it, Mr. Van Weyden?"

I shook my head and regarded their work. It had indeed been bloody, for they had drawn off and joined our other three boats in the attack on the remaining two of the enemy. The deserted boat was in the trough of the sea, rolling drunkenly across each comber, its loose spritsail out at right angles to it and fluttering and flapping in the wind. The hunter and boat-puller were both lying awkwardly in the bottom, but the boat-steerer lay across the gunwale, half in and half out, his arms trailing in the water and his head rolling from side to side.

"Don't look, Miss Brewster, please don't look," I had begged of her, and I was glad that she had minded me and been spared the sight.

"Head right into the bunch, Mr. Van Weyden," was Wolf Larsen's command.

As we drew nearer, the firing ceased, and we saw that the fight was over. The remaining two boats had been captured by our five, and the seven were grouped together, waiting to be picked up.

"Look at that!" I cried involuntarily, pointing to the north-east.

The blot of smoke which indicated the *Macedonia's* position had reappeared.

"Yes, I've been watching it," was Wolf Larsen's calm reply. He measured the distance away to the fog-bank, and for an instant paused to feel the weight of the wind on his cheek. "We'll make it, I think; but you can depend upon it that blessed brother of mine has twigged our little game and is just a-humping for us. Ah, look at that!"

The blot of smoke had suddenly grown larger, and it was very black.

"I'll beat you out, though, brother mine," he chuckled. "I'll beat you out, and I hope you no worse than that you rack your old engines into scrap."

When we hove to, a hasty though orderly confusion reigned. The boats came aboard from every side at once. As fast as the prisoners came over the rail they were marshalled forward to the forecastle by our hunters, while our sailors hoisted in the boats, pell-mell, dropping them anywhere upon the deck and not stopping to lash them. We were already under way, all sails set and drawing, and the sheets being slacked off for a wind abeam, as the last boat lifted clear of the water and swung in the tackles.

CHAPTER XXV

There was need for haste. The *Macedonia*, belching the blackest of smoke from her funnel, was charging down upon us from out of the north-east. Neglecting the boats that remained to her, she had altered her course so as to anticipate ours. She was not running straight for us, but ahead of us. Our courses were converging like the sides of an angle, the vertex of which was at the edge of the fog-bank. It was there, or not at all, that the *Macedonia* could hope to catch us. The hope for the *Ghost* lay in that she should pass that point before the *Macedonia* arrived at it.

Wolf Larsen was steering, his eyes glistening and snapping as they dwelt upon and leaped from detail to detail of the chase. Now he studied the sea to windward for signs of the wind slackening or freshening, now the *Macedonia*; and again, his eyes roved over every sail, and he gave commands to slack a sheet here a trifle, to come in on one there a trifle, till he was drawing out of the *Ghost* the last bit of speed she possessed. All feuds and grudges were forgotten, and I was surprised at the alacrity with which the men who had so long endured his brutality sprang to execute his orders. Strange to say, the unfortunate Johnson came into my mind as we lifted and surged and heeled along, and I was aware of a regret that he was not alive and present; he had so loved the *Ghost* and delighted in her sailing powers.

"Better get your rifles, you fellows," Wolf Larsen called to our hunters; and the five men lined the lee rail, guns in hand, and waited.

The *Macedonia* was now but a mile away, the black smoke pouring from her funnel at a right angle, so madly she raced, pounding through the sea at a seventeen-knot gait—"'Sky-hooting through the brine," as Wolf Larsen quoted while gazing at her. We were not making more than nine knots, but the fog-bank was very near.

A puff of smoke broke from the *Macedonia's* deck, we heard a heavy report, and a round hole took form in the stretched canvas of our mainsail. They were shooting at us with one of the small cannon which rumour had said they carried on board. Our men, clustering amidships, waved their hats and raised a derisive cheer. Again there was a puff of smoke and a loud report, this time the cannon-ball striking not more than twenty feet astern and glancing twice from sea to sea to windward ere it sank.

But there was no rifle-firing for the reason that all their hunters were out in the boats or our prisoners. When the two vessels were half-a-mile apart, a third shot made another hole in our mainsail. Then we entered the fog. It was about us, veiling and hiding us in its dense wet gauze.

The sudden transition was startling. The moment before we had been leaping through the sunshine, the clear sky above us, the sea breaking and rolling wide to the horizon, and a ship, vomiting smoke and fire and iron missiles, rushing madly upon us. And at once, as in an instant's leap, the sun was blotted out, there was no sky, even our mastheads were lost to view, and our horizon was such as tear-blinded eyes may see. The grey mist drove by us like a rain. Every woollen filament of our garments, every hair of our heads and faces, was jewelled with a crystal globule. The shrouds were wet with moisture; it dripped from our rigging overhead; and on the underside of our booms drops of water took shape in long swaying lines, which were detached and flung to the deck in mimic showers at each surge of the schooner. I was aware of a pent, stifled feeling. As the sounds of the ship thrusting herself through the waves were hurled back upon us by the fog, so were one's thoughts. The mind recoiled from contemplation of a world beyond this wet veil which wrapped us around. This was the world, the universe itself, its bounds so near one felt impelled to reach out both arms and push them back. It was impossible, that the rest could be beyond these walls of grey. The rest was a dream, no more than the memory of a dream.

It was weird, strangely weird. I looked at Maud Brewster and knew that she was similarly affected. Then I looked at Wolf Larsen, but there was nothing subjective about his state of consciousness. His whole concern was with the immediate, objective present. He still held the wheel, and I felt that he was timing Time, reckoning the passage of the minutes with each forward lunge and leeward roll of the *Ghost*.

"Go for'ard and hard alee without any noise," he said to me in a low voice. "Clew up the topsails first. Set men at all the sheets. Let there be no rattling of blocks, no sound of voices. No noise, understand, no noise."

When all was ready, the word "hard-a-lee" was passed forward to me from man to man; and the *Ghost* heeled about on the port tack with practically no noise at all. And what little there was,—the slapping of a few reef-points and the creaking of a sheave in a block or two,—was ghostly under the hollow echoing pall in which we were swathed.

We had scarcely filled away, it seemed, when the fog thinned abruptly and we were again in the sunshine, the wide-stretching sea breaking before us to the sky-line. But the ocean was bare. No wrathful *Macedonia* broke its surface nor blackened the sky with her smoke.

Wolf Larsen at once squared away and ran down along the rim of the fog-bank. His trick was obvious. He had entered the fog to windward of the steamer, and while the steamer had blindly driven on into the fog in the chance of catching him, he had come about and out of his shelter and was now running down to re-enter to leeward. Successful in this, the old simile of the needle in the haystack would be mild indeed compared with his brother's chance of finding him. He did not run long. Jibing the fore- and main-sails and setting the topsails again, we headed back into the bank. As we entered I could have sworn I saw a vague bulk emerging to windward. I looked quickly at Wolf Larsen. Already we were ourselves buried in the fog, but he nodded his head. He, too, had seen it—the *Macedonia*, guessing his manœuvre and failing by a moment in anticipating it. There was no doubt that we had escaped unseen.

"He can't keep this up," Wolf Larsen said. "He'll have to go back for the rest of his boats. Send a man to the wheel, Mr. Van Weyden, keep this course for the present, and you might as well set the watches, for we won't do any lingering to-night."

"I'd give five hundred dollars, though," he added, "just to be aboard the *Macedonia* for five minutes, listening to my brother curse."

"And now, Mr. Van Weyden," he said to me when he had been relieved from the wheel, "we must make these new-comers welcome. Serve out plenty of whisky to the hunters and see that a few bottles slip for'ard. I'll wager every man Jack of them is over the side to-morrow, hunting for Wolf Larsen as contentedly as ever they hunted for Death Larsen."

"But won't they escape as Wainwright did?" I asked.

He laughed shrewdly. "Not as long as our old hunters have anything to say about it. I'm dividing amongst them a dollar a skin for all the skins shot by our new hunters. At least half of their enthusiasm to-day was due to that. Oh, no, there won't be any escaping if they have anything to say about it. And now you'd better get for'ard to your hospital duties. There must be a full ward waiting for you."

CHAPTER XXVI

Wolf Larsen took the distribution of the whisky off my hands, and the bottles began to make their appearance while I worked over the fresh batch of wounded men in the forecastle. I had seen whisky drunk, such as whisky-and-soda by the men of the clubs, but never as these men drank it, from pannikins and mugs, and from the bottles—great brimming drinks, each one of which was in itself a debauch. But they did not stop at one or two. They drank and drank, and ever the bottles slipped forward and they drank more.

Everybody drank; the wounded drank; Oofty-Oofty, who helped me, drank. Only Louis refrained, no more than cautiously wetting his lips with the liquor, though he joined in the revels with an abandon equal to that of most of them. It was a saturnalia. In loud voices they shouted over the day's fighting, wrangled about details, or waxed affectionate and made friends with the men whom they had fought. Prisoners and captors hiccoughed on one another's shoulders, and swore mighty oaths of respect and esteem. They wept over the miseries of the past and over the miseries yet to come under the iron rule of Wolf Larsen. And all cursed him and told terrible tales of his brutality.

It was a strange and frightful spectacle—the small, bunk-lined space, the floor and walls leaping and lurching, the dim light, the swaying shadows lengthening and foreshortening monstrously, the thick air heavy with smoke and the smell of bodies and iodoform, and the inflamed faces of the men—half-men, I should call them. I noted Oofty-Oofty, holding the end of a bandage and looking upon the scene, his velvety and luminous eyes glistening in the light like a deer's eyes, and yet I knew the barbaric devil that lurked in his breast and belied all the softness and tenderness, almost womanly, of his face and form. And I noticed the boyish face of Harrison,—a good face once, but now a demon's,—convulsed with passion as he told the new-comers of the hell-ship they were in and shrieked curses upon the head of Wolf Larsen.

Wolf Larsen it was, always Wolf Larsen, enslaver and tormentor of men, a male Circe and these his swine, suffering brutes that grovelled before him and revolted only in drunkenness and in secrecy. And was I, too, one of his swine? I thought. And Maud Brewster? No! I ground my teeth in my anger and determination till the man I was attending winced under my hand and Oofty-Oofty looked at me with curiosity. I felt endowed with a sudden strength. What of my new-found love, I was a giant. I feared nothing. I would work my will through it all, in spite of Wolf Larsen and of my own thirty-five bookish years. All would be well. I would make it well. And so, exalted, upborne by a sense of power, I turned my back on the howling inferno and climbed to the deck, where the fog drifted ghostly through the night and the air was sweet and pure and quiet.

The steerage, where were two wounded hunters, was a repetition of the forecastle, except that Wolf Larsen was not being cursed; and it was with a great relief that I again emerged on deck and went aft to the cabin. Supper was ready, and Wolf Larsen and Maud were waiting for me.

While all his ship was getting drunk as fast as it could, he remained sober. Not a drop of liquor passed his lips. He did not dare it under the circumstances, for he had only Louis and me to depend upon, and Louis was even now at the wheel. We were sailing on through the fog without a look-out and without lights. That Wolf Larsen had turned the liquor loose among his men surprised me, but he evidently knew their psychology and the best method of cementing in cordiality, what had begun in blood-shed.

His victory over Death Larsen seemed to have had a remarkable effect upon him. The previous evening he had reasoned himself into the blues, and I had been waiting momentarily for one of his characteristic outbursts. Yet nothing had occurred, and he was now in splendid trim. Possibly his success in capturing so many hunters and boats had counteracted the customary reaction. At any rate, the blues were gone, and the blue devils had not put in an appearance. So I thought at the time; but, ah me, little I knew him or knew that even then, perhaps, he was meditating an outbreak more terrible than any I had seen.

As I say, he discovered himself in splendid trim when I entered the cabin. He had had no headaches for weeks, his eyes were clear blue as the sky, his bronze was beautiful with perfect health; life swelled through his veins in full and magnificent flood. While waiting for me he had engaged Maud in animated discussion. Temptation was the topic they had hit upon, and from the few words I heard I made out that he was contending that temptation was temptation only when a man was seduced by it and fell.

"For look you," he was saying, "as I see it, a man does things because of desire. He has many desires. He may desire to escape pain, or to enjoy pleasure. But whatever he does, he does because he desires to do it."

"But suppose he desires to do two opposite things, neither of which will permit him to do the other?" Maud interrupted.

"The very thing I was coming to," he said.

"And between these two desires is just where the soul of the man is manifest," she went on. "If it is a good soul, it will desire and do the good action, and the contrary if it is a bad soul. It is the soul that decides."

"Bosh and nonsense!" he exclaimed impatiently. "It is the desire that decides. Here is a man who wants to, say, get drunk. Also, he doesn't want to get drunk. What does he do? How does he do it? He is a puppet. He is the creature of his desires, and of the two desires he obeys the strongest one, that is all. His soul hasn't anything to do with it. How can he be tempted to get drunk and refuse to get drunk? If the desire to remain sober prevails, it is because it is the strongest desire. Temptation plays no part, unless—" he paused while grasping the new thought which had come into his mind—"unless he is tempted to remain sober.

"Ha! ha!" he laughed. "What do you think of that, Mr. Van Weyden?"

CHAPTER XXVI

"That both of you are hair-splitting," I said. "The man's soul is his desires. Or, if you will, the sum of his desires is his soul. Therein you are both wrong. You lay the stress upon the desire apart from the soul, Miss Brewster lays the stress on the soul apart from the desire, and in point of fact soul and desire are the same thing.

"However," I continued, "Miss Brewster is right in contending that temptation is temptation whether the man yield or overcome. Fire is fanned by the wind until it leaps up fiercely. So is desire like fire. It is fanned, as by a wind, by sight of the thing desired, or by a new and luring description or comprehension of the thing desired. There lies the temptation. It is the wind that fans the desire until it leaps up to mastery. That's temptation. It may not fan sufficiently to make the desire overmastering, but in so far as it fans at all, that far is it temptation. And, as you say, it may tempt for good as well as for evil."

I felt proud of myself as we sat down to the table. My words had been decisive. At least they had put an end to the discussion.

But Wolf Larsen seemed voluble, prone to speech as I had never seen him before. It was as though he were bursting with pent energy which must find an outlet somehow. Almost immediately he launched into a discussion on love. As usual, his was the sheer materialistic side, and Maud's was the idealistic. For myself, beyond a word or so of suggestion or correction now and again, I took no part.

He was brilliant, but so was Maud, and for some time I lost the thread of the conversation through studying her face as she talked. It was a face that rarely displayed colour, but to-night it was flushed and vivacious. Her wit was playing keenly, and she was enjoying the tilt as much as Wolf Larsen, and he was enjoying it hugely. For some reason, though I know not why in the argument, so utterly had I lost it in the contemplation of one stray brown lock of Maud's hair, he quoted from Iseult at Tintagel, where she says:

"Blessed am I beyond women even herein,
That beyond all born women is my sin,
And perfect my transgression."

As he had read pessimism into Omar, so now he read triumph, stinging triumph and exultation, into Swinburne's lines. And he read rightly, and he read well. He had hardly ceased reading when Louis put his head into the companion-way and whispered down:

"Be easy, will ye? The fog's lifted, an' 'tis the port light iv a steamer that's crossin' our bow this blessed minute."

Wolf Larsen sprang on deck, and so swiftly that by the time we followed him he had pulled the steerage-slide over the drunken clamour and was on his way forward to close the forecastle-scuttle. The fog, though it remained, had lifted high, where it obscured the stars and made the night quite black. Directly ahead of us I could see a bright red light and a white light, and I could hear the pulsing of a steamer's engines. Beyond a doubt it was the *Macedonia*.

Wolf Larsen had returned to the poop, and we stood in a silent group, watching the lights rapidly cross our bow.

"Lucky for me he doesn't carry a searchlight," Wolf Larsen said.

"What if I should cry out loudly?" I queried in a whisper.

"It would be all up," he answered. "But have you thought upon what would immediately happen?"

Before I had time to express any desire to know, he had me by the throat with his gorilla grip, and by a faint quiver of the muscles—a hint, as it were—he suggested to me the twist that would surely have broken my neck. The next moment he had released me and we were gazing at the *Macedonia's* lights.

"What if I should cry out?" Maud asked.

"I like you too well to hurt you," he said softly—nay, there was a tenderness and a caress in his voice that made me wince.

"But don't do it, just the same, for I'd promptly break Mr. Van Weyden's neck."

"Then she has my permission to cry out," I said defiantly.

"I hardly think you'll care to sacrifice the Dean of American Letters the Second," he sneered.

We spoke no more, though we had become too used to one another for the silence to be awkward; and when the red light and the white had disappeared we returned to the cabin to finish the interrupted supper.

Again they fell to quoting, and Maud gave Dowson's "Impenitentia Ultima." She rendered it beautifully, but I watched not her, but Wolf Larsen. I was fascinated by the fascinated look he bent upon Maud. He was quite out of himself, and I noticed the unconscious movement of his lips as he shaped word for word as fast as she uttered them. He interrupted her when she gave the lines:

> *"And her eyes should be my light while the sun went out behind me,*
> *And the viols in her voice be the last sound in my ear."*

"There are viols in your voice," he said bluntly, and his eyes flashed their golden light.

I could have shouted with joy at her control. She finished the concluding stanza without faltering and then slowly guided the conversation into less perilous channels. And all the while I sat in a half-daze, the drunken riot of the steerage breaking through the bulkhead, the man I feared and the woman I loved talking on and on. The table was not cleared. The man who had taken Mugridge's place had evidently joined his comrades in the forecastle.

If ever Wolf Larsen attained the summit of living, he attained it then. From time to time I forsook my own thoughts to follow him, and I followed in amaze, mastered for the moment by his remarkable intellect, under the spell of his passion, for he was preaching the passion of revolt. It was inevitable that Milton's Lucifer should be instanced, and the keenness with which Wolf Larsen analysed and depicted the character was a revelation of his stifled genius. It reminded me of Taine, yet I knew the man had never heard of that brilliant though dangerous thinker.

"He led a lost cause, and he was not afraid of God's thunderbolts," Wolf Larsen was saying. "Hurled into hell, he was unbeaten. A third of God's angels he had led with him, and straightway he incited man to rebel against God, and gained for himself and hell the major portion of all the generations of man. Why was he beaten out of heaven? Because he was less brave than God? less proud? less aspiring? No! A thousand times no! God was more powerful, as he said, Whom thunder hath made greater. But Lucifer was a free spirit. To serve was to suffocate. He preferred suffering in freedom to all the happiness of a comfortable servility. He did not care to serve

God. He cared to serve nothing. He was no figure-head. He stood on his own legs. He was an individual."

"The first Anarchist," Maud laughed, rising and preparing to withdraw to her state-room.

"Then it is good to be an anarchist!" he cried. He, too, had risen, and he stood facing her, where she had paused at the door of her room, as he went on:

"'Here at least
We shall be free; the Almighty hath not built
Here for his envy; will not drive us hence;
Here we may reign secure; and in my choice
To reign is worth ambition, though in hell:
Better to reign in hell than serve in heaven."

It was the defiant cry of a mighty spirit. The cabin still rang with his voice, as he stood there, swaying, his bronzed face shining, his head up and dominant, and his eyes, golden and masculine, intensely masculine and insistently soft, flashing upon Maud at the door.

Again that unnamable and unmistakable terror was in her eyes, and she said, almost in a whisper, "You are Lucifer."

The door closed and she was gone. He stood staring after her for a minute, then returned to himself and to me.

"I'll relieve Louis at the wheel," he said shortly, "and call upon you to relieve at midnight. Better turn in now and get some sleep."

He pulled on a pair of mittens, put on his cap, and ascended the companion-stairs, while I followed his suggestion by going to bed. For some unknown reason, prompted mysteriously, I did not undress, but lay down fully clothed. For a time I listened to the clamour in the steerage and marvelled upon the love which had come to me; but my sleep on the *Ghost* had become most healthful and natural, and soon the songs and cries died away, my eyes closed, and my consciousness sank down into the half-death of slumber.

I knew not what had aroused me, but I found myself out of my bunk, on my feet, wide awake, my soul vibrating to the warning of danger as it might have thrilled to a trumpet call. I threw open the door. The cabin light was burning low. I saw Maud, my Maud, straining and struggling and crushed in the embrace of Wolf Larsen's arms. I could see the vain beat and flutter of her as she strove, pressing her face against his breast, to escape from him. All this I saw on the very instant of seeing and as I sprang forward.

I struck him with my fist, on the face, as he raised his head, but it was a puny blow. He roared in a ferocious, animal-like way, and gave me a shove with his hand. It was only a shove, a flirt of the wrist, yet so tremendous was his strength that I was hurled backward as from a catapult. I struck the door of the state-room which had formerly been Mugridge's, splintering and smashing the panels with the impact of my body. I struggled to my feet, with difficulty dragging myself clear of the wrecked door, unaware of any hurt whatever. I was conscious only of an overmastering rage. I think I, too, cried aloud, as I drew the knife at my hip and sprang forward a second time.

But something had happened. They were reeling apart. I was close upon him, my knife uplifted, but I withheld the blow. I was puzzled by the strangeness of it. Maud was leaning against the wall, one hand out for support; but he was staggering, his left hand pressed against his forehead and covering his eyes, and with the right he was groping about him in a dazed sort of way. It struck against the wall, and his body seemed to express a muscular and physical relief at the contact, as though he had found his bearings, his location in space as well as something against which to lean.

Then I saw red again. All my wrongs and humiliations flashed upon me with a dazzling brightness, all that I had suffered and others had suffered at his hands, all the enormity of the man's very existence. I sprang upon him, blindly, insanely, and drove the knife into his shoulder. I knew, then, that it was no more than a flesh wound,—I had felt the steel grate on his shoulder-blade,—and I raised the knife to strike at a more vital part.

But Maud had seen my first blow, and she cried, "Don't! Please don't!"

I dropped my arm for a moment, and a moment only. Again the knife was raised, and Wolf Larsen would have surely died had she not stepped between. Her arms were around me, her hair was brushing my face. My pulse rushed up in an unwonted manner, yet my rage mounted with it. She looked me bravely in the eyes.

"For my sake," she begged.

"I would kill him for your sake!" I cried, trying to free my arm without hurting her.

"Hush!" she said, and laid her fingers lightly on my lips. I could have kissed them, had I dared, even then, in my rage, the touch of them was so sweet, so very sweet. "Please, please," she pleaded, and she disarmed me by the words, as I was to discover they would ever disarm me.

I stepped back, separating from her, and replaced the knife in its sheath. I looked at Wolf Larsen. He still pressed his left hand against his forehead. It covered his eyes. His head was bowed. He seemed to have grown limp. His body was sagging at the hips, his great shoulders were drooping and shrinking forward.

"Van, Weyden!" he called hoarsely, and with a note of fright in his voice. "Oh, Van Weyden! where are you?"

I looked at Maud. She did not speak, but nodded her head.

"Here I am," I answered, stepping to his side. "What is the matter?"

"Help me to a seat," he said, in the same hoarse, frightened voice.

"I am a sick man; a very sick man, Hump," he said, as he left my sustaining grip and sank into a chair.

His head dropped forward on the table and was buried in his hands. From time to time it rocked back and forward as with pain. Once, when he half raised it, I saw the sweat standing in heavy drops on his forehead about the roots of his hair.

"I am a sick man, a very sick man," he repeated again, and yet once again.

"What is the matter?" I asked, resting my hand on his shoulder. "What can I do for you?"

But he shook my hand off with an irritated movement, and for a long time I stood by his side in silence. Maud was looking on, her face awed and frightened. What had happened to him we could not imagine.

"Hump," he said at last, "I must get into my bunk. Lend me a hand. I'll be all right in a little while. It's those damn headaches, I believe. I was afraid of them. I had a feeling—no, I don't know what I'm talking about. Help me into my bunk."

But when I got him into his bunk he again buried his face in his hands, covering his eyes, and as I turned to go I could hear him murmuring, "I am a sick man, a very sick man."

Maud looked at me inquiringly as I emerged. I shook my head, saying:

"Something has happened to him. What, I don't know. He is helpless, and frightened, I imagine, for the first time in his life. It must have occurred before he received the knife-thrust, which made only a superficial wound. You must have seen what happened."

She shook her head. "I saw nothing. It is just as mysterious to me. He suddenly released me and staggered away. But what shall we do? What shall I do?"

"If you will wait, please, until I come back," I answered.

I went on deck. Louis was at the wheel.

"You may go for'ard and turn in," I said, taking it from him.

He was quick to obey, and I found myself alone on the deck of the *Ghost*. As quietly as was possible, I clewed up the topsails, lowered the flying jib and staysail, backed the jib over, and flattened the mainsail. Then I went below to Maud. I placed my finger on my lips for silence, and entered Wolf Larsen's room. He was in the same position in which I had left him, and his head was rocking—almost writhing—from side to side.

"Anything I can do for you?" I asked.

He made no reply at first, but on my repeating the question he answered, "No, no; I'm all right. Leave me alone till morning."

But as I turned to go I noted that his head had resumed its rocking motion. Maud was waiting patiently for me, and I took notice, with a thrill of joy, of the queenly poise of her head and her glorious, calm eyes. Calm and sure they were as her spirit itself.

"Will you trust yourself to me for a journey of six hundred miles or so?" I asked.

"You mean—?" she asked, and I knew she had guessed aright.

"Yes, I mean just that," I replied. "There is nothing left for us but the open boat."

"For me, you mean," she said. "You are certainly as safe here as you have been."

"No, there is nothing left for us but the open boat," I iterated stoutly. "Will you please dress as warmly as you can, at once, and make into a bundle whatever you wish to bring with you."

"And make all haste," I added, as she turned toward her state-room.

The lazarette was directly beneath the cabin, and, opening the trap-door in the floor and carrying a candle with me, I dropped down and began overhauling the ship's stores. I selected mainly from the canned goods, and by the time I was ready, willing hands were extended from above to receive what I passed up.

We worked in silence. I helped myself also to blankets, mittens, oilskins, caps, and such things, from the slop-chest. It was no light adventure, this trusting ourselves in a small boat to so raw and stormy a sea, and it was imperative that we should guard ourselves against the cold and wet.

We worked feverishly at carrying our plunder on deck and depositing it amidships, so feverishly that Maud, whose strength was hardly a positive quantity, had to give over, exhausted, and sit on the steps at the break of the poop. This did not serve to recover her, and she lay on her back, on the hard deck, arms stretched out, and whole body relaxed. It was a trick I remembered of my sister, and I knew she would soon be herself again. I knew, also, that weapons would not come in amiss, and I re-entered Wolf Larsen's state-room to get his rifle and shot-gun. I spoke to him, but he made no answer, though his head was still rocking from side to side and he was not asleep.

"Good-bye, Lucifer," I whispered to myself as I softly closed the door.

Next to obtain was a stock of ammunition,—an easy matter, though I had to enter the steerage companion-way to do it. Here the hunters stored the ammunition-boxes they carried in the boats, and here, but a few feet from their noisy revels, I took possession of two boxes.

Next, to lower a boat. Not so simple a task for one man. Having cast off the lashings, I hoisted first on the forward tackle, then on the aft, till the boat cleared the rail, when I lowered away, one tackle and then the other, for a couple of feet, till it hung snugly, above the water, against the schooner's side. I made certain that it contained the proper equipment of oars, rowlocks, and sail. Water was a consideration, and I robbed every boat aboard of its breaker. As there were nine boats all told, it meant that we should have plenty of water, and ballast as well, though there was the chance that the boat would be overloaded, what of the generous supply of other things I was taking.

While Maud was passing me the provisions and I was storing them in the boat, a sailor came on deck from the forecastle. He stood by the weather rail for a time (we were lowering over the lee rail), and then sauntered slowly amidships, where he again paused and stood facing the wind, with his back toward us. I could hear my heart beating as I crouched low in the boat. Maud had sunk down upon the deck and was, I knew, lying motionless, her body in the shadow of the bulwark. But the man never turned, and, after stretching his arms above his head and yawning audibly, he retraced his steps to the forecastle scuttle and disappeared.

A few minutes sufficed to finish the loading, and I lowered the boat into the water. As I helped Maud over the rail and felt her form close to mine, it was all I could do to keep from crying out, "I love you! I love you!" Truly Humphrey Van Weyden was at last in love, I thought, as her fingers clung to mine while I lowered her down to the boat. I held on to the rail with one hand and supported her weight with the other, and I was proud at the moment of the feat. It was a strength I had not possessed a few months before, on the day I said good-bye to Charley Furuseth and started for San Francisco on the ill-fated *Martinez*.

As the boat ascended on a sea, her feet touched and I released her hands. I cast off the tackles and leaped after her. I had never rowed in my life, but I put out the oars and at the expense of much effort got the boat clear of the *Ghost*. Then I experimented with the sail. I had seen the boat-steerers and hunters set their spritsails many times, yet this was my first attempt. What took them possibly two minutes took me twenty, but in the end I succeeded in setting and trimming it, and with the steering-oar in my hands hauled on the wind.

"There lies Japan," I remarked, "straight before us."

"Humphrey Van Weyden," she said, "you are a brave man."

"Nay," I answered, "it is you who are a brave woman."

CHAPTER XXVI

We turned our heads, swayed by a common impulse to see the last of the *Ghost*. Her low hull lifted and rolled to windward on a sea; her canvas loomed darkly in the night; her lashed wheel creaked as the rudder kicked; then sight and sound of her faded away, and we were alone on the dark sea.

CHAPTER XXVII

Day broke, grey and chill. The boat was close-hauled on a fresh breeze and the compass indicated that we were just making the course which would bring us to Japan. Though stoutly mittened, my fingers were cold, and they pained from the grip on the steering-oar. My feet were stinging from the bite of the frost, and I hoped fervently that the sun would shine.

Before me, in the bottom of the boat, lay Maud. She, at least, was warm, for under her and over her were thick blankets. The top one I had drawn over her face to shelter it from the night, so I could see nothing but the vague shape of her, and her light-brown hair, escaped from the covering and jewelled with moisture from the air.

Long I looked at her, dwelling upon that one visible bit of her as only a man would who deemed it the most precious thing in the world. So insistent was my gaze that at last she stirred under the blankets, the top fold was thrown back and she smiled out on me, her eyes yet heavy with sleep.

"Good-morning, Mr. Van Weyden," she said. "Have you sighted land yet?"

"No," I answered, "but we are approaching it at a rate of six miles an hour."

She made a *mouè* of disappointment.

"But that is equivalent to one hundred and forty-four miles in twenty-four hours," I added reassuringly.

Her face brightened. "And how far have we to go?"

"Siberia lies off there," I said, pointing to the west. "But to the south-west, some six hundred miles, is Japan. If this wind should hold, we'll make it in five days."

"And if it storms? The boat could not live?"

She had a way of looking one in the eyes and demanding the truth, and thus she looked at me as she asked the question.

"It would have to storm very hard," I temporized.

"And if it storms very hard?"

I nodded my head. "But we may be picked up any moment by a sealing-schooner. They are plentifully distributed over this part of the ocean."

"Why, you are chilled through!" she cried. "Look! You are shivering. Don't deny it; you are. And here I have been lying warm as toast."

"I don't see that it would help matters if you, too, sat up and were chilled," I laughed.

"It will, though, when I learn to steer, which I certainly shall."

CHAPTER XXVII

She sat up and began making her simple toilet. She shook down her hair, and it fell about her in a brown cloud, hiding her face and shoulders. Dear, damp brown hair! I wanted to kiss it, to ripple it through my fingers, to bury my face in it. I gazed entranced, till the boat ran into the wind and the flapping sail warned me I was not attending to my duties. Idealist and romanticist that I was and always had been in spite of my analytical nature, yet I had failed till now in grasping much of the physical characteristics of love. The love of man and woman, I had always held, was a sublimated something related to spirit, a spiritual bond that linked and drew their souls together. The bonds of the flesh had little part in my cosmos of love. But I was learning the sweet lesson for myself that the soul transmuted itself, expressed itself, through the flesh; that the sight and sense and touch of the loved one's hair was as much breath and voice and essence of the spirit as the light that shone from the eyes and the thoughts that fell from the lips. After all, pure spirit was unknowable, a thing to be sensed and divined only; nor could it express itself in terms of itself. Jehovah was anthropomorphic because he could address himself to the Jews only in terms of their understanding; so he was conceived as in their own image, as a cloud, a pillar of fire, a tangible, physical something which the mind of the Israelites could grasp.

And so I gazed upon Maud's light-brown hair, and loved it, and learned more of love than all the poets and singers had taught me with all their songs and sonnets. She flung it back with a sudden adroit movement, and her face emerged, smiling.

"Why don't women wear their hair down always?" I asked. "It is so much more beautiful."

"If it didn't tangle so dreadfully," she laughed. "There! I've lost one of my precious hair-pins!"

I neglected the boat and had the sail spilling the wind again and again, such was my delight in following her every movement as she searched through the blankets for the pin. I was surprised, and joyfully, that she was so much the woman, and the display of each trait and mannerism that was characteristically feminine gave me keener joy. For I had been elevating her too highly in my concepts of her, removing her too far from the plane of the human, and too far from me. I had been making of her a creature goddess-like and unapproachable. So I hailed with delight the little traits that proclaimed her only woman after all, such as the toss of the head which flung back the cloud of hair, and the search for the pin. She was woman, my kind, on my plane, and the delightful intimacy of kind, of man and woman, was possible, as well as the reverence and awe in which I knew I should always hold her.

She found the pin with an adorable little cry, and I turned my attention more fully to my steering. I proceeded to experiment, lashing and wedging the steering-oar until the boat held on fairly well by the wind without my assistance. Occasionally it came up too close, or fell off too freely; but it always recovered itself and in the main behaved satisfactorily.

"And now we shall have breakfast," I said. "But first you must be more warmly clad."

I got out a heavy shirt, new from the slop-chest and made from blanket goods. I knew the kind, so thick and so close of texture that it could resist the rain and not be soaked through after hours of wetting. When she had slipped this on over her head, I exchanged the boy's cap she wore for a man's cap, large enough to cover her hair, and, when the flap was turned down, to completely cover her neck and ears. The effect was charming. Her face was of the sort that cannot but look well under all circumstances. Nothing could destroy its exquisite oval, its well-nigh classic lines, its delicately stencilled brows, its large brown eyes, clear-seeing and calm, gloriously calm.

A puff, slightly stronger than usual, struck us just then. The boat was caught as it obliquely crossed the crest of a wave. It went over suddenly, burying its gunwale level with the sea and shipping a bucketful or so of water. I was opening a can of tongue at the moment, and I sprang to the sheet and cast it off just in time. The sail flapped and fluttered, and the boat paid off. A few minutes of regulating sufficed to put it on its course again, when I returned to the preparation of breakfast.

"It does very well, it seems, though I am not versed in things nautical," she said, nodding her head with grave approval at my steering contrivance.

"But it will serve only when we are sailing by the wind," I explained. "When running more freely, with the wind astern abeam, or on the quarter, it will be necessary for me to steer."

"I must say I don't understand your technicalities," she said, "but I do your conclusion, and I don't like it. You cannot steer night and day and for ever. So I shall expect, after breakfast, to receive my first lesson. And then you shall lie down and sleep. We'll stand watches just as they do on ships."

"I don't see how I am to teach you," I made protest. "I am just learning for myself. You little thought when you trusted yourself to me that I had had no experience whatever with small boats. This is the first time I have ever been in one."

"Then we'll learn together, sir. And since you've had a night's start you shall teach me what you have learned. And now, breakfast. My! this air does give one an appetite!"

"No coffee," I said regretfully, passing her buttered sea-biscuits and a slice of canned tongue. "And there will be no tea, no soups, nothing hot, till we have made land somewhere, somehow."

After the simple breakfast, capped with a cup of cold water, Maud took her lesson in steering. In teaching her I learned quite a deal myself, though I was applying the knowledge already acquired by sailing the *Ghost* and by watching the boat-steerers sail the small boats. She was an apt pupil, and soon learned to keep the course, to luff in the puffs and to cast off the sheet in an emergency.

Having grown tired, apparently, of the task, she relinquished the oar to me. I had folded up the blankets, but she now proceeded to spread them out on the bottom. When all was arranged snugly, she said:

"Now, sir, to bed. And you shall sleep until luncheon. Till dinner-time," she corrected, remembering the arrangement on the *Ghost*.

What could I do? She insisted, and said, "Please, please," whereupon I turned the oar over to her and obeyed. I experienced a positive sensuous delight as I crawled into the bed she had made with her hands. The calm and control which were so much a part of her seemed to have been communicated to the blankets, so that I was aware of a soft dreaminess and content, and of an oval face and brown eyes framed in a fisherman's cap and tossing against a background now of grey cloud, now of grey sea, and then I was aware that I had been asleep.

I looked at my watch. It was one o'clock. I had slept seven hours! And she had been steering seven hours! When I took the steering-oar I had first to unbend her cramped fingers. Her modicum of strength had been exhausted, and she was unable even to move from her position. I was compelled to let go the sheet while I helped her to the nest of blankets and chafed her hands and arms.

"I am so tired," she said, with a quick intake of the breath and a sigh, drooping her head wearily.

But she straightened it the next moment. "Now don't scold, don't you dare scold," she cried with mock defiance.

"I hope my face does not appear angry," I answered seriously; "for I assure you I am not in the least angry."

"N-no," she considered. "It looks only reproachful."

"Then it is an honest face, for it looks what I feel. You were not fair to yourself, nor to me. How can I ever trust you again?"

She looked penitent. "I'll be good," she said, as a naughty child might say it. "I promise—"

"To obey as a sailor would obey his captain?"

"Yes," she answered. "It was stupid of me, I know."

"Then you must promise something else," I ventured.

"Readily."

"That you will not say, 'Please, please,' too often; for when you do you are sure to override my authority."

She laughed with amused appreciation. She, too, had noticed the power of the repeated "please."

"It is a good word—" I began.

"But I must not overwork it," she broke in.

But she laughed weakly, and her head drooped again. I left the oar long enough to tuck the blankets about her feet and to pull a single fold across her face. Alas! she was not strong. I looked with misgiving toward the south-west and thought of the six hundred miles of hardship before us—ay, if it were no worse than hardship. On this sea a storm might blow up at any moment and destroy us. And yet I was unafraid. I was without confidence in the future, extremely doubtful, and yet I felt no underlying fear. It must come right, it must come right, I repeated to myself, over and over again.

The wind freshened in the afternoon, raising a stiffer sea and trying the boat and me severely. But the supply of food and the nine breakers of water enabled the boat to stand up to the sea and wind, and I held on as long as I dared. Then I removed the sprit, tightly hauling down the peak of the sail, and we raced along under what sailors call a leg-of-mutton.

Late in the afternoon I sighted a steamer's smoke on the horizon to leeward, and I knew it either for a Russian cruiser, or, more likely, the *Macedonia* still seeking the *Ghost*. The sun had not shone all day, and it had been bitter cold. As night drew on, the clouds darkened and the wind freshened, so that when Maud and I ate supper it was with our mittens on and with me still steering and eating morsels between puffs.

By the time it was dark, wind and sea had become too strong for the boat, and I reluctantly took in the sail and set about making a drag or sea-anchor. I had learned of the device from the talk of the hunters, and it was a simple thing to manufacture. Furling the sail and lashing it securely about the mast, boom, sprit, and two pairs of spare oars, I threw it overboard. A line connected it with the bow, and as it floated low in the water, practically unexposed to the wind, it drifted less rapidly than the boat. In consequence it held the boat bow on to the sea and wind—the safest position in which to escape being swamped when the sea is breaking into whitecaps.

"And now?" Maud asked cheerfully, when the task was accomplished and I pulled on my mittens.

"And now we are no longer travelling toward Japan," I answered. "Our drift is to the south-east, or south-south-east, at the rate of at least two miles an hour."

"That will be only twenty-four miles," she urged, "if the wind remains high all night."

"Yes, and only one hundred and forty miles if it continues for three days and nights."

"But it won't continue," she said with easy confidence. "It will turn around and blow fair."

"The sea is the great faithless one."

"But the wind!" she retorted. "I have heard you grow eloquent over the brave trade-wind."

"I wish I had thought to bring Wolf Larsen's chronometer and sextant," I said, still gloomily. "Sailing one direction, drifting another direction, to say nothing of the set of the current in some third direction, makes a resultant which dead reckoning can never calculate. Before long we won't know where we are by five hundred miles."

Then I begged her pardon and promised I should not be disheartened any more. At her solicitation I let her take the watch till midnight,—it was then nine o'clock, but I wrapped her in blankets and put an oilskin about her before I lay down. I slept only cat-naps. The boat was leaping and pounding as it fell over the crests, I could hear the seas rushing past, and spray was continually being thrown aboard. And still, it was not a bad night, I mused—nothing to the nights I had been through on the *Ghost*; nothing, perhaps, to the nights we should go through in this cockle-shell. Its planking was three-quarters of an inch thick. Between us and the bottom of the sea was less than an inch of wood.

And yet, I aver it, and I aver it again, I was unafraid. The death which Wolf Larsen and even Thomas Mugridge had made me fear, I no longer feared. The coming of Maud Brewster into my life seemed to have transformed me. After all, I thought, it is better and finer to love than to be loved, if it makes something in life so worth while that one is not loath to die for it. I forget my own life in the love of another life; and yet, such is the paradox, I never wanted so much to live as right now when I place the least value upon my own life. I never had so much reason for living, was my concluding thought; and after that, until I dozed, I contented myself with trying to pierce the darkness to where I knew Maud crouched low in the stern-sheets, watchful of the foaming sea and ready to call me on an instant's notice.

CHAPTER XXVIII

There is no need of going into an extended recital of our suffering in the small boat during the many days we were driven and drifted, here and there, willy-nilly, across the ocean. The high wind blew from the north-west for twenty-four hours, when it fell calm, and in the night sprang up from the south-west. This was dead in our teeth, but I took in the sea-anchor and set sail, hauling a course on the wind which took us in a south-south-easterly direction. It was an even choice between this and the west-north-westerly course which the wind permitted; but the warm airs of the south fanned my desire for a warmer sea and swayed my decision.

In three hours—it was midnight, I well remember, and as dark as I had ever seen it on the sea—the wind, still blowing out of the south-west, rose furiously, and once again I was compelled to set the sea-anchor.

Day broke and found me wan-eyed and the ocean lashed white, the boat pitching, almost on end, to its drag. We were in imminent danger of being swamped by the whitecaps. As it was, spray and spume came aboard in such quantities that I bailed without cessation. The blankets were soaking. Everything was wet except Maud, and she, in oilskins, rubber boots, and sou'wester, was dry, all but her face and hands and a stray wisp of hair. She relieved me at the bailing-hole from time to time, and bravely she threw out the water and faced the storm. All things are relative. It was no more than a stiff blow, but to us, fighting for life in our frail craft, it was indeed a storm.

Cold and cheerless, the wind beating on our faces, the white seas roaring by, we struggled through the day. Night came, but neither of us slept. Day came, and still the wind beat on our faces and the white seas roared past. By the second night Maud was falling asleep from exhaustion. I covered her with oilskins and a tarpaulin. She was comparatively dry, but she was numb with the cold. I feared greatly that she might die in the night; but day broke, cold and cheerless, with the same clouded sky and beating wind and roaring seas.

I had had no sleep for forty-eight hours. I was wet and chilled to the marrow, till I felt more dead than alive. My body was stiff from exertion as well as from cold, and my aching muscles gave me the severest torture whenever I used them, and I used them continually. And all the time we were being driven off into the north-east, directly away from Japan and toward bleak Bering Sea.

And still we lived, and the boat lived, and the wind blew unabated. In fact, toward nightfall of the third day it increased a trifle and something more. The boat's bow plunged under a crest, and we came through quarter-full of water. I bailed like a madman. The liability of shipping another such sea was enormously increased by the water that weighed the boat down and robbed it of its buoyancy. And another such sea meant the end. When I had the boat empty again I was forced to take away the tarpaulin which covered Maud, in order that I might lash it down across the bow. It was well I did, for it covered the boat fully a third of the way aft, and three times, in the next several hours, it flung off the bulk of the down-rushing water when the bow shoved under the seas.

Maud's condition was pitiable. She sat crouched in the bottom of the boat, her lips blue, her face grey and plainly showing the pain she suffered. But ever her eyes looked bravely at me, and ever her lips uttered brave words.

The worst of the storm must have blown that night, though little I noticed it. I had succumbed and slept where I sat in the stern-sheets. The morning of the fourth day found the wind diminished to a gentle whisper, the sea dying down and the sun shining upon us. Oh, the blessed sun! How we bathed our poor bodies in its delicious warmth, reviving like bugs and crawling things after a storm. We smiled again, said amusing things, and waxed optimistic over our situation. Yet it was, if anything, worse than ever. We were farther from Japan than the night we left the *Ghost*. Nor could I more than roughly guess our latitude and longitude. At a calculation of a two-mile drift per hour, during the seventy and odd hours of the storm, we had been driven at least one hundred and fifty miles to the north-east. But was such calculated drift correct? For all I knew, it might have been four miles per hour instead of two. In which case we were another hundred and fifty miles to the bad.

Where we were I did not know, though there was quite a likelihood that we were in the vicinity of the *Ghost*. There were seals about us, and I was prepared to sight a sealing-schooner at any time. We did sight one, in the afternoon, when the north-west breeze had sprung up freshly once more. But the strange schooner lost itself on the sky-line and we alone occupied the circle of the sea.

Came days of fog, when even Maud's spirit drooped and there were no merry words upon her lips; days of calm, when we floated on the lonely immensity of sea, oppressed by its greatness and yet marvelling at the miracle of tiny life, for we still lived and struggled to live; days of sleet and wind and snow-squalls, when nothing could keep us warm; or days of drizzling rain, when we filled our water-breakers from the drip of the wet sail.

And ever I loved Maud with an increasing love. She was so many-sided, so many-mooded—"protean-mooded" I called her. But I called her this, and other and dearer things, in my thoughts only. Though the declaration of my love urged and trembled on my tongue a thousand times, I knew that it was no time for such a declaration. If for no other reason, it was no time, when one was protecting and trying to save a woman, to ask that woman for her love. Delicate as was the situation, not alone in this but in other ways, I flattered myself that I was able to deal delicately with it; and also I flattered myself that by look or sign I gave no advertisement of the love I felt for her. We were like good comrades, and we grew better comrades as the days went by.

One thing about her which surprised me was her lack of timidity and fear. The terrible sea, the frail boat, the storms, the suffering, the strangeness and isolation of the situation,—all that should have frightened a robust woman,—seemed to make no impression upon her who had known life only in its most sheltered and consummately artificial aspects, and who was herself all fire and dew and mist, sublimated spirit, all that was soft and tender and clinging in woman. And yet I am wrong. She *was* timid and afraid, but she possessed courage. The flesh and the qualms of the flesh she was heir to, but the flesh bore heavily only on the flesh. And she was spirit, first and always spirit, etherealized essence of life, calm as her calm eyes, and sure of permanence in the changing order of the universe.

Came days of storm, days and nights of storm, when the ocean menaced us with its roaring whiteness, and the wind smote our struggling boat with a Titan's buffets. And ever we were flung off, farther and farther, to the north-east. It was in such a storm, and the worst that we had experienced, that I cast a weary glance to leeward, not in quest of anything, but more from the weariness of facing the elemental strife, and in mute appeal, almost, to the wrathful powers to cease and let us be. What I saw I could not at first believe. Days and nights of sleeplessness and anxiety had doubtless turned my head. I looked back at Maud, to identify myself, as it were, in time and space. The sight of her dear wet cheeks, her flying hair, and her brave brown eyes convinced me that my vision was still healthy. Again I turned my face to leeward, and again I saw the jutting promontory, black and high and naked, the raging surf that broke about its base and beat its front high up with spouting fountains, the black and forbidden coast-line running toward the south-east and fringed with a tremendous scarf of white.

"Maud," I said. "Maud."

She turned her head and beheld the sight.

"It cannot be Alaska!" she cried.

"Alas, no," I answered, and asked, "Can you swim?"

She shook her head.

"Neither can I," I said. "So we must get ashore without swimming, in some opening between the rocks through which we can drive the boat and clamber out. But we must be quick, most quick—and sure."

I spoke with a confidence she knew I did not feel, for she looked at me with that unfaltering gaze of hers and said:

"I have not thanked you yet for all you have done for me but—"

She hesitated, as if in doubt how best to word her gratitude.

"Well?" I said, brutally, for I was not quite pleased with her thanking me.

"You might help me," she smiled.

"To acknowledge your obligations before you die? Not at all. We are not going to die. We shall land on that island, and we shall be snug and sheltered before the day is done."

I spoke stoutly, but I did not believe a word. Nor was I prompted to lie through fear. I felt no fear, though I was sure of death in that boiling surge amongst the rocks which was rapidly growing nearer. It was impossible to hoist sail and claw off that shore. The wind would instantly capsize the boat; the seas would swamp it the moment it fell into the trough; and, besides, the sail, lashed to the spare oars, dragged in the sea ahead of us.

As I say, I was not afraid to meet my own death, there, a few hundred yards to leeward; but I was appalled at the thought that Maud must die. My cursed imagination saw her beaten and mangled against the rocks, and it was too terrible. I strove to compel myself to think we would make the landing safely, and so I spoke, not what I believed, but what I preferred to believe.

I recoiled before contemplation of that frightful death, and for a moment I entertained the wild idea of seizing Maud in my arms and leaping overboard. Then I resolved to wait, and at the last moment, when we entered on the final stretch, to take her in my arms and proclaim my love, and, with her in my embrace, to make the desperate struggle and die.

Instinctively we drew closer together in the bottom of the boat. I felt her mittened hand come out to mine. And thus, without speech, we waited the end. We were not far off the line the wind made with the western edge of the promontory, and I watched in the hope that some set of the current or send of the sea would drift us past before we reached the surf.

"We shall go clear," I said, with a confidence which I knew deceived neither of us.

"By God, we *will* go clear!" I cried, five minutes later.

The oath left my lips in my excitement—the first, I do believe, in my life, unless "trouble it," an expletive of my youth, be accounted an oath.

"I beg your pardon," I said.

"You have convinced me of your sincerity," she said, with a faint smile. "I do know, now, that we shall go clear."

I had seen a distant headland past the extreme edge of the promontory, and as we looked we could see grow the intervening coastline of what was evidently a deep cove. At the same time there broke upon our ears a continuous and mighty bellowing. It partook of the magnitude and volume of distant thunder, and it came to us directly from leeward, rising above the crash of the surf and travelling directly in the teeth of the storm. As we passed the point the whole cove burst upon our view, a half-moon of white sandy beach upon which broke a huge surf, and which was covered with myriads of seals. It was from them that the great bellowing went up.

"A rookery!" I cried. "Now are we indeed saved. There must be men and cruisers to protect them from the seal-hunters. Possibly there is a station ashore."

But as I studied the surf which beat upon the beach, I said, "Still bad, but not so bad. And now, if the gods be truly kind, we shall drift by that next headland and come upon a perfectly sheltered beach, where we may land without wetting our feet."

And the gods were kind. The first and second headlands were directly in line with the south-west wind; but once around the second,—and we went perilously near,—we picked up the third headland, still in line with the wind and with the other two. But the cove that intervened! It penetrated deep into the land, and the tide, setting in, drifted us under the shelter of the point. Here the sea was calm, save for a heavy but smooth ground-swell, and I took in the sea-anchor and began to row. From the point the shore curved away, more and more to the south and west, until at last it disclosed a cove within the cove, a little land-locked harbour, the water level as a pond, broken only by tiny ripples where vagrant breaths and wisps of the storm hurtled down from over the frowning wall of rock that backed the beach a hundred feet inshore.

Here were no seals whatever. The boat's stern touched the hard shingle. I sprang out, extending my hand to Maud. The next moment she was beside me. As my fingers released hers, she clutched for my arm hastily. At the same moment I swayed, as about to fall to the sand. This was the startling effect of the cessation of motion. We had been so long upon the moving, rocking sea that the stable land was a shock to us.

We expected the beach to lift up this way and that, and the rocky walls to swing back and forth like the sides of a ship; and when we braced ourselves, automatically, for these various expected movements, their non-occurrence quite overcame our equilibrium.

"I really must sit down," Maud said, with a nervous laugh and a dizzy gesture, and forthwith she sat down on the sand.

I attended to making the boat secure and joined her. Thus we landed on Endeavour Island, as we came to it, land-sick from long custom of the sea.

CHAPTER XXIX

"Fool!" I cried aloud in my vexation.

I had unloaded the boat and carried its contents high up on the beach, where I had set about making a camp. There was driftwood, though not much, on the beach, and the sight of a coffee tin I had taken from the *Ghost's* larder had given me the idea of a fire.

"Blithering idiot!" I was continuing.

But Maud said, "Tut, tut," in gentle reproval, and then asked why I was a blithering idiot.

"No matches," I groaned. "Not a match did I bring. And now we shall have no hot coffee, soup, tea, or anything!"

"Wasn't it—er—Crusoe who rubbed sticks together?" she drawled.

"But I have read the personal narratives of a score of shipwrecked men who tried, and tried in vain," I answered. "I remember Winters, a newspaper fellow with an Alaskan and Siberian reputation. Met him at the Bibelot once, and he was telling us how he attempted to make a fire with a couple of sticks. It was most amusing. He told it inimitably, but it was the story of a failure. I remember his conclusion, his black eyes flashing as he said, 'Gentlemen, the South Sea Islander may do it, the Malay may do it, but take my word it's beyond the white man.'"

"Oh, well, we've managed so far without it," she said cheerfully. "And there's no reason why we cannot still manage without it."

"But think of the coffee!" I cried. "It's good coffee, too, I know. I took it from Larsen's private stores. And look at that good wood."

I confess, I wanted the coffee badly; and I learned, not long afterward, that the berry was likewise a little weakness of Maud's. Besides, we had been so long on a cold diet that we were numb inside as well as out. Anything warm would have been most gratifying. But I complained no more and set about making a tent of the sail for Maud.

I had looked upon it as a simple task, what of the oars, mast, boom, and sprit, to say nothing of plenty of lines. But as I was without experience, and as every detail was an experiment and every successful detail an invention, the day was well gone before her shelter was an accomplished fact. And then, that night, it rained, and she was flooded out and driven back into the boat.

CHAPTER XXIX

The next morning I dug a shallow ditch around the tent, and, an hour later, a sudden gust of wind, whipping over the rocky wall behind us, picked up the tent and smashed it down on the sand thirty yards away.

Maud laughed at my crestfallen expression, and I said, "As soon as the wind abates I intend going in the boat to explore the island. There must be a station somewhere, and men. And ships must visit the station. Some Government must protect all these seals. But I wish to have you comfortable before I start."

"I should like to go with you," was all she said.

"It would be better if you remained. You have had enough of hardship. It is a miracle that you have survived. And it won't be comfortable in the boat rowing and sailing in this rainy weather. What you need is rest, and I should like you to remain and get it."

Something suspiciously akin to moistness dimmed her beautiful eyes before she dropped them and partly turned away her head.

"I should prefer going with you," she said in a low voice, in which there was just a hint of appeal.

"I might be able to help you a—" her voice broke,—"a little. And if anything should happen to you, think of me left here alone."

"Oh, I intend being very careful," I answered. "And I shall not go so far but what I can get back before night. Yes, all said and done, I think it vastly better for you to remain, and sleep, and rest and do nothing."

She turned and looked me in the eyes. Her gaze was unfaltering, but soft.

"Please, please," she said, oh, so softly.

I stiffened myself to refuse, and shook my head. Still she waited and looked at me. I tried to word my refusal, but wavered. I saw the glad light spring into her eyes and knew that I had lost. It was impossible to say no after that.

The wind died down in the afternoon, and we were prepared to start the following morning. There was no way of penetrating the island from our cove, for the walls rose perpendicularly from the beach, and, on either side of the cove, rose from the deep water.

Morning broke dull and grey, but calm, and I was awake early and had the boat in readiness.

"Fool! Imbecile! Yahoo!" I shouted, when I thought it was meet to arouse Maud; but this time I shouted in merriment as I danced about the beach, bareheaded, in mock despair.

Her head appeared under the flap of the sail.

"What now?" she asked sleepily, and, withal, curiously.

"Coffee!" I cried. "What do you say to a cup of coffee? hot coffee? piping hot?"

"My!" she murmured, "you startled me, and you are cruel. Here I have been composing my soul to do without it, and here you are vexing me with your vain suggestions."

"Watch me," I said.

From under clefts among the rocks I gathered a few dry sticks and chips. These I whittled into shavings or split into kindling. From my note-book I tore out a page, and from the ammunition box took a shot-gun shell. Removing the wads from the latter with my knife, I emptied the powder on a flat rock. Next I pried the primer, or cap, from the shell, and laid it on the rock, in the midst of the scattered powder. All was ready. Maud still watched from the tent. Holding the paper in my left hand, I smashed down upon the cap with a rock held in my right. There was a puff of white smoke, a burst of flame, and the rough edge of the paper was alight.

Maud clapped her hands gleefully. "Prometheus!" she cried.

But I was too occupied to acknowledge her delight. The feeble flame must be cherished tenderly if it were to gather strength and live. I fed it, shaving by shaving, and sliver by sliver, till at last it was snapping and crackling as it laid hold of the smaller chips and sticks. To be cast away on an island had not entered into my calculations, so we were without a kettle or cooking utensils of any sort; but I made shift with the tin used for bailing the boat, and later, as we consumed our supply of canned goods, we accumulated quite an imposing array of cooking vessels.

I boiled the water, but it was Maud who made the coffee. And how good it was! My contribution was canned beef fried with crumbled sea-biscuit and water. The breakfast was a success, and we sat about the fire much longer than enterprising explorers should have done, sipping the hot black coffee and talking over our situation.

I was confident that we should find a station in some one of the coves, for I knew that the rookeries of Bering Sea were thus guarded; but Maud advanced the theory—to prepare me for disappointment, I do believe, if disappointment were to come—that we had discovered an unknown rookery. She was in very good spirits, however, and made quite merry in accepting our plight as a grave one.

"If you are right," I said, "then we must prepare to winter here. Our food will not last, but there are the seals. They go away in the fall, so I must soon begin to lay in a supply of meat. Then there will be huts to build and driftwood to gather. Also we shall try out seal fat for lighting purposes. Altogether, we'll have our hands full if we find the island uninhabited. Which we shall not, I know."

But she was right. We sailed with a beam wind along the shore, searching the coves with our glasses and landing occasionally, without finding a sign of human life. Yet we learned that we were not the first who had landed on Endeavour Island. High up on the beach of the second cove from ours, we discovered the splintered wreck of a boat—a sealer's boat, for the rowlocks were bound in sennit, a gun-rack was on the starboard side of the bow, and in white letters was faintly visible *Gazelle* No. 2. The boat had lain there for a long time, for it was half filled with sand, and the splintered wood had that weather-worn appearance due to long exposure to the elements. In the stern-sheets I found a rusty ten-gauge shot-gun and a sailor's sheath-knife broken short across and so rusted as to be almost unrecognizable.

"They got away," I said cheerfully; but I felt a sinking at the heart and seemed to divine the presence of bleached bones somewhere on that beach.

I did not wish Maud's spirits to be dampened by such a find, so I turned seaward again with our boat and skirted the north-eastern point of the island. There were no beaches on the southern shore, and by early afternoon we rounded the black promontory and completed the circumnavigation of the island. I estimated its circumference at twenty-five miles, its width as varying from two to five miles; while my most conservative calculation placed on its beaches two hundred thousand seals. The island was highest at its extreme south-western point, the headlands and backbone diminishing regularly until the north-eastern portion was only a few feet above the sea. With the exception of our little cove, the other beaches sloped gently back for a distance of half-a-mile or so, into what I might call rocky meadows, with here and there patches of moss and tundra grass. Here the seals hauled out, and the old bulls guarded their harems, while the young bulls hauled out by themselves.

This brief description is all that Endeavour Island merits. Damp and soggy where it was not sharp and rocky, buffeted by storm winds and lashed by the sea, with the air continually a-tremble with the bellowing of two hundred thousand amphibians, it was a melancholy and miserable sojourning-place. Maud, who had prepared me for disappointment, and who had been sprightly and vivacious all day, broke down as we landed in our own little cove. She strove bravely to hide it from me, but while I was kindling another fire I knew she was stifling her sobs in the blankets under the sail-tent.

It was my turn to be cheerful, and I played the part to the best of my ability, and with such success that I brought the laughter back into her dear eyes and song on her lips; for she sang to me before she went to an early bed. It was the first time I had heard her sing, and I lay by the fire, listening and transported, for she was nothing if not an artist in everything she did, and her voice, though not strong, was wonderfully sweet and expressive.

I still slept in the boat, and I lay awake long that night, gazing up at the first stars I had seen in many nights and pondering the situation. Responsibility of this sort was a new thing to me. Wolf Larsen had been quite right. I had stood on my father's legs. My lawyers and agents had taken care of my money for me. I had had no responsibilities at all. Then, on the *Ghost* I had learned to be responsible for myself. And now, for the first time in my life, I found myself responsible for some one else. And it was required of me that this should be the gravest of responsibilities, for she was the one woman in the world—the one small woman, as I loved to think of her.

CHAPTER XXX

No wonder we called it Endeavour Island. For two weeks we toiled at building a hut. Maud insisted on helping, and I could have wept over her bruised and bleeding hands. And still, I was proud of her because of it. There was something heroic about this gently-bred woman enduring our terrible hardship and with her pittance of strength bending to the tasks of a peasant woman. She gathered many of the stones which I built into the walls of the hut; also, she turned a deaf ear to my entreaties when I begged her to desist. She compromised, however, by taking upon herself the lighter labours of cooking and gathering driftwood and moss for our winter's supply.

The hut's walls rose without difficulty, and everything went smoothly until the problem of the roof confronted me. Of what use the four walls without a roof? And of what could a roof be made? There were the spare oars, very true. They would serve as roof-beams; but with what was I to cover them? Moss would never do. Tundra grass was impracticable. We needed the sail for the boat, and the tarpaulin had begun to leak.

"Winters used walrus skins on his hut," I said.

"There are the seals," she suggested.

So next day the hunting began. I did not know how to shoot, but I proceeded to learn. And when I had expended some thirty shells for three seals, I decided that the ammunition would be exhausted before I acquired the necessary knowledge. I had used eight shells for lighting fires before I hit upon the device of banking the embers with wet moss, and there remained not over a hundred shells in the box.

"We must club the seals," I announced, when convinced of my poor marksmanship. "I have heard the sealers talk about clubbing them."

"They are so pretty," she objected. "I cannot bear to think of it being done. It is so directly brutal, you know; so different from shooting them."

"That roof must go on," I answered grimly. "Winter is almost here. It is our lives against theirs. It is unfortunate we haven't plenty of ammunition, but I think, anyway, that they suffer less from being clubbed than from being all shot up. Besides, I shall do the clubbing."

"That's just it," she began eagerly, and broke off in sudden confusion.

"Of course," I began, "if you prefer—"

"But what shall I be doing?" she interrupted, with that softness I knew full well to be insistence.

"Gathering firewood and cooking dinner," I answered lightly.

CHAPTER XXX

She shook her head. "It is too dangerous for you to attempt alone."

"I know, I know," she waived my protest. "I am only a weak woman, but just my small assistance may enable you to escape disaster."

"But the clubbing?" I suggested.

"Of course, you will do that. I shall probably scream. I'll look away when—"

"The danger is most serious," I laughed.

"I shall use my judgment when to look and when not to look," she replied with a grand air.

The upshot of the affair was that she accompanied me next morning. I rowed into the adjoining cove and up to the edge of the beach. There were seals all about us in the water, and the bellowing thousands on the beach compelled us to shout at each other to make ourselves heard.

"I know men club them," I said, trying to reassure myself, and gazing doubtfully at a large bull, not thirty feet away, upreared on his fore-flippers and regarding me intently. "But the question is, How do they club them?"

"Let us gather tundra grass and thatch the roof," Maud said.

She was as frightened as I at the prospect, and we had reason to be gazing at close range at the gleaming teeth and dog-like mouths.

"I always thought they were afraid of men," I said.

"How do I know they are not afraid?" I queried a moment later, after having rowed a few more strokes along the beach. "Perhaps, if I were to step boldly ashore, they would cut for it, and I could not catch up with one." And still I hesitated.

"I heard of a man, once, who invaded the nesting grounds of wild geese," Maud said. "They killed him."

"The geese?"

"Yes, the geese. My brother told me about it when I was a little girl."

"But I know men club them," I persisted.

"I think the tundra grass will make just as good a roof," she said.

Far from her intention, her words were maddening me, driving me on. I could not play the coward before her eyes. "Here goes," I said, backing water with one oar and running the bow ashore.

I stepped out and advanced valiantly upon a long-maned bull in the midst of his wives. I was armed with the regular club with which the boat-pullers killed the wounded seals gaffed aboard by the hunters. It was only a foot and a half long, and in my superb ignorance I never dreamed that the club used ashore when raiding the rookeries measured four to five feet. The cows lumbered out of my way, and the distance between me and the bull decreased. He raised himself on his flippers with an angry movement. We were a dozen feet apart. Still I advanced steadily, looking for him to turn tail at any moment and run.

At six feet the panicky thought rushed into my mind, What if he will not run? Why, then I shall club him, came the answer. In my fear I had forgotten that I was there to get the bull instead of to make him run. And just then he gave a snort and a snarl and rushed at me. His eyes were blazing, his mouth was wide open; the teeth gleamed cruelly white. Without shame, I confess that it was I who turned and footed it. He ran awkwardly, but he ran well. He was but two paces behind when I tumbled into the boat, and as I shoved off with an oar his teeth crunched down upon the blade. The stout wood was crushed like an egg-shell. Maud and I were astounded. A moment later he had dived under the boat, seized the keel in his mouth, and was shaking the boat violently.

"My!" said Maud. "Let's go back."

I shook my head. "I can do what other men have done, and I know that other men have clubbed seals. But I think I'll leave the bulls alone next time."

"I wish you wouldn't," she said.

"Now don't say, 'Please, please,'" I cried, half angrily, I do believe.

She made no reply, and I knew my tone must have hurt her.

"I beg your pardon," I said, or shouted, rather, in order to make myself heard above the roar of the rookery. "If you say so, I'll turn and go back; but honestly, I'd rather stay."

"Now don't say that this is what you get for bringing a woman along," she said. She smiled at me whimsically, gloriously, and I knew there was no need for forgiveness.

I rowed a couple of hundred feet along the beach so as to recover my nerves, and then stepped ashore again.

"Do be cautious," she called after me.

I nodded my head and proceeded to make a flank attack on the nearest harem. All went well until I aimed a blow at an outlying cowls head and fell short. She snorted and tried to scramble away. I ran in close and struck another blow, hitting the shoulder instead of the head.

"Watch out!" I heard Maud scream.

In my excitement I had not been taking notice of other things, and I looked up to see the lord of the harem charging down upon me. Again I fled to the boat, hotly pursued; but this time Maud made no suggestion of turning back.

"It would be better, I imagine, if you let harems alone and devoted your attention to lonely and inoffensive-looking seals," was what she said. "I think I have read something about them. Dr. Jordan's book, I believe. They are the young bulls, not old enough to have harems of their own. He called them the holluschickie, or something like that. It seems to me if we find where they haul out—"

"It seems to me that your fighting instinct is aroused," I laughed.

She flushed quickly and prettily. "I'll admit I don't like defeat any more than you do, or any more than I like the idea of killing such pretty, inoffensive creatures."

"Pretty!" I sniffed. "I failed to mark anything pre-eminently pretty about those foamy-mouthed beasts that raced me."

"Your point of view," she laughed. "You lacked perspective. Now if you did not have to get so close to the subject—"

"The very thing!" I cried. "What I need is a longer club. And there's that broken oar ready to hand."

"It just comes to me," she said, "that Captain Larsen was telling me how the men raided the rookeries. They drive the seals, in small herds, a short distance inland before they kill them."

"I don't care to undertake the herding of one of those harems," I objected.

"But there are the holluschickie," she said. "The holluschickie haul out by themselves, and Dr. Jordan says that paths are left between the harems, and that as long as the holluschickie keep strictly to the path they are unmolested by the masters of the harem."

CHAPTER XXX

"There's one now," I said, pointing to a young bull in the water. "Let's watch him, and follow him if he hauls out."

He swam directly to the beach and clambered out into a small opening between two harems, the masters of which made warning noises but did not attack him. We watched him travel slowly inward, threading about among the harems along what must have been the path.

"Here goes," I said, stepping out; but I confess my heart was in my mouth as I thought of going through the heart of that monstrous herd.

"It would be wise to make the boat fast," Maud said.

She had stepped out beside me, and I regarded her with wonderment.

She nodded her head determinedly. "Yes, I'm going with you, so you may as well secure the boat and arm me with a club."

"Let's go back," I said dejectedly. "I think tundra grass, will do, after all."

"You know it won't," was her reply. "Shall I lead?"

With a shrug of the shoulders, but with the warmest admiration and pride at heart for this woman, I equipped her with the broken oar and took another for myself. It was with nervous trepidation that we made the first few rods of the journey. Once Maud screamed in terror as a cow thrust an inquisitive nose toward her foot, and several times I quickened my pace for the same reason. But, beyond warning coughs from either side, there were no signs of hostility. It was a rookery which had never been raided by the hunters, and in consequence the seals were mild-tempered and at the same time unafraid.

In the very heart of the herd the din was terrific. It was almost dizzying in its effect. I paused and smiled reassuringly at Maud, for I had recovered my equanimity sooner than she. I could see that she was still badly frightened. She came close to me and shouted:

"I'm dreadfully afraid!"

And I was not. Though the novelty had not yet worn off, the peaceful comportment of the seals had quieted my alarm. Maud was trembling.

"I'm afraid, and I'm not afraid," she chattered with shaking jaws. "It's my miserable body, not I."

"It's all right, it's all right," I reassured her, my arm passing instinctively and protectingly around her.

I shall never forget, in that moment, how instantly conscious I became of my manhood. The primitive deeps of my nature stirred. I felt myself masculine, the protector of the weak, the fighting male. And, best of all, I felt myself the protector of my loved one. She leaned against me, so light and lily-frail, and as her trembling eased away it seemed as though I became aware of prodigious strength. I felt myself a match for the most ferocious bull in the herd, and I know, had such a bull charged upon me, that I should have met it unflinchingly and quite coolly, and I know that I should have killed it.

"I am all right now," she said, looking up at me gratefully. "Let us go on."

And that the strength in me had quieted her and given her confidence, filled me with an exultant joy. The youth of the race seemed burgeoning in me, over-civilized man that I was, and I lived for myself the old hunting days and forest nights of my remote and forgotten ancestry. I had much for which to thank Wolf Larsen, was my thought as we went along the path between the jostling harems.

A quarter of a mile inland we came upon the holluschickie—sleek young bulls, living out the loneliness of their bachelorhood and gathering strength against the day when they would fight their way into the ranks of the Benedicts.

Everything now went smoothly. I seemed to know just what to do and how to do it. Shouting, making threatening gestures with my club, and even prodding the lazy ones, I quickly cut out a score of the young bachelors from their companions. Whenever one made an attempt to break back toward the water, I headed it off. Maud took an active part in the drive, and with her cries and flourishings of the broken oar was of considerable assistance. I noticed, though, that whenever one looked tired and lagged, she let it slip past. But I noticed, also, whenever one, with a show of fight, tried to break past, that her eyes glinted and showed bright, and she rapped it smartly with her club.

"My, it's exciting!" she cried, pausing from sheer weakness. "I think I'll sit down."

I drove the little herd (a dozen strong, now, what of the escapes she had permitted) a hundred yards farther on; and by the time she joined me I had finished the slaughter and was beginning to skin. An hour later we went proudly back along the path between the harems. And twice again we came down the path burdened with skins, till I thought we had enough to roof the hut. I set the sail, laid one tack out of the cove, and on the other tack made our own little inner cove.

"It's just like home-coming," Maud said, as I ran the boat ashore.

I heard her words with a responsive thrill, it was all so dearly intimate and natural, and I said:

"It seems as though I have lived this life always. The world of books and bookish folk is very vague, more like a dream memory than an actuality. I surely have hunted and forayed and fought all the days of my life. And you, too, seem a part of it. You are—" I was on the verge of saying, "my woman, my mate," but glibly changed it to—"standing the hardship well."

But her ear had caught the flaw. She recognized a flight that midmost broke. She gave me a quick look.

"Not that. You were saying—?"

"That the American Mrs. Meynell was living the life of a savage and living it quite successfully," I said easily.

"Oh," was all she replied; but I could have sworn there was a note of disappointment in her voice.

But "my woman, my mate" kept ringing in my head for the rest of the day and for many days. Yet never did it ring more loudly than that night, as I watched her draw back the blanket of moss from the coals, blow up the fire, and cook the evening meal. It must have been latent savagery stirring in me, for the old words, so bound up with the roots of the race, to grip me and thrill me. And grip and thrill they did, till I fell asleep, murmuring them to myself over and over again.

CHAPTER XXXI

"It will smell," I said, "but it will keep in the heat and keep out the rain and snow."

We were surveying the completed seal-skin roof.

"It is clumsy, but it will serve the purpose, and that is the main thing," I went on, yearning for her praise.

And she clapped her hands and declared that she was hugely pleased.

"But it is dark in here," she said the next moment, her shoulders shrinking with a little involuntary shiver.

"You might have suggested a window when the walls were going up," I said. "It was for you, and you should have seen the need of a window."

"But I never do see the obvious, you know," she laughed back. "And besides, you can knock a hole in the wall at any time."

"Quite true; I had not thought of it," I replied, wagging my head sagely. "But have you thought of ordering the window-glass? Just call up the firm,—Red, 4451, I think it is,—and tell them what size and kind of glass you wish."

"That means—" she began.

"No window."

It was a dark and evil-appearing thing, that hut, not fit for aught better than swine in a civilized land; but for us, who had known the misery of the open boat, it was a snug little habitation. Following the housewarming, which was accomplished by means of seal-oil and a wick made from cotton calking, came the hunting for our winter's meat and the building of the second hut. It was a simple affair, now, to go forth in the morning and return by noon with a boatload of seals. And then, while I worked at building the hut, Maud tried out the oil from the blubber and kept a slow fire under the frames of meat. I had heard of jerking beef on the plains, and our seal-meat, cut in thin strips and hung in the smoke, cured excellently.

The second hut was easier to erect, for I built it against the first, and only three walls were required. But it was work, hard work, all of it. Maud and I worked from dawn till dark, to the limit of our strength, so that when night came we crawled stiffly to bed and slept the animal-like sleep exhaustion. And yet Maud declared that she had never felt better or stronger in her life. I knew this was true of myself, but hers was such a lily strength that I feared she would break down. Often and often, her last-reserve force gone, I have seen her stretched flat on her back on the sand in the way she had of resting and recuperating. And then she would be up on her feet and toiling hard as ever. Where she obtained this strength was the marvel to me.

"Think of the long rest this winter," was her reply to my remonstrances. "Why, we'll be clamorous for something to do."

We held a housewarming in my hut the night it was roofed. It was the end of the third day of a fierce storm which had swung around the compass from the south-east to the north-west, and which was then blowing directly in upon us. The beaches of the outer cove were thundering with the surf, and even in our land-locked inner cove a respectable sea was breaking. No high backbone of island sheltered us from the wind, and it whistled and bellowed about the hut till at times I feared for the strength of the walls. The skin roof, stretched tightly as a drumhead, I had thought, sagged and bellied with every gust; and innumerable interstices in the walls, not so tightly stuffed with moss as Maud had supposed, disclosed themselves. Yet the seal-oil burned brightly and we were warm and comfortable.

It was a pleasant evening indeed, and we voted that as a social function on Endeavour Island it had not yet been eclipsed. Our minds were at ease. Not only had we resigned ourselves to the bitter winter, but we were prepared for it. The seals could depart on their mysterious journey into the south at any time, now, for all we cared; and the storms held no terror for us. Not only were we sure of being dry and warm and sheltered from the wind, but we had the softest and most luxurious mattresses that could be made from moss. This had been Maud's idea, and she had herself jealously gathered all the moss. This was to be my first night on the mattress, and I knew I should sleep the sweeter because she had made it.

As she rose to go she turned to me with the whimsical way she had, and said:

"Something is going to happen—is happening, for that matter. I feel it. Something is coming here, to us. It is coming now. I don't know what, but it is coming."

"Good or bad?" I asked.

She shook her head. "I don't know, but it is there, somewhere."

She pointed in the direction of the sea and wind.

"It's a lee shore," I laughed, "and I am sure I'd rather be here than arriving, a night like this."

"You are not frightened?" I asked, as I stepped to open the door for her.

Her eyes looked bravely into mine.

"And you feel well? perfectly well?"

"Never better," was her answer.

We talked a little longer before she went.

"Good-night, Maud," I said.

"Good-night, Humphrey," she said.

This use of our given names had come about quite as a matter of course, and was as unpremeditated as it was natural. In that moment I could have put my arms around her and drawn her to me. I should certainly have done so out in that world to which we belonged. As it was, the situation stopped there in the only way it could; but I was left alone in my little hut, glowing warmly through and through with a pleasant satisfaction; and I knew that a tie, or a tacit something, existed between us which had not existed before.

CHAPTER XXXII

I awoke, oppressed by a mysterious sensation. There seemed something missing in my environment. But the mystery and oppressiveness vanished after the first few seconds of waking, when I identified the missing something as the wind. I had fallen asleep in that state of nerve tension with which one meets the continuous shock of sound or movement, and I had awakened, still tense, bracing myself to meet the pressure of something which no longer bore upon me.

It was the first night I had spent under cover in several months, and I lay luxuriously for some minutes under my blankets (for once not wet with fog or spray), analysing, first, the effect produced upon me by the cessation of the wind, and next, the joy which was mine from resting on the mattress made by Maud's hands. When I had dressed and opened the door, I heard the waves still lapping on the beach, garrulously attesting the fury of the night. It was a clear day, and the sun was shining. I had slept late, and I stepped outside with sudden energy, bent upon making up lost time as befitted a dweller on Endeavour Island.

And when outside, I stopped short. I believed my eyes without question, and yet I was for the moment stunned by what they disclosed to me. There, on the beach, not fifty feet away, bow on, dismasted, was a black-hulled vessel. Masts and booms, tangled with shrouds, sheets, and rent canvas, were rubbing gently alongside. I could have rubbed my eyes as I looked. There was the home-made galley we had built, the familiar break of the poop, the low yacht-cabin scarcely rising above the rail. It was the *Ghost*.

What freak of fortune had brought it here—here of all spots? what chance of chances? I looked at the bleak, inaccessible wall at my back and know the profundity of despair. Escape was hopeless, out of the question. I thought of Maud, asleep there in the hut we had reared; I remembered her "Good-night, Humphrey"; "my woman, my mate," went ringing through my brain, but now, alas, it was a knell that sounded. Then everything went black before my eyes.

Possibly it was the fraction of a second, but I had no knowledge of how long an interval had lapsed before I was myself again. There lay the *Ghost*, bow on to the beach, her splintered bowsprit projecting over the sand, her tangled spars rubbing against her side to the lift of the crooning waves. Something must be done, must be done.

It came upon me suddenly, as strange, that nothing moved aboard. Wearied from the night of struggle and wreck, all hands were yet asleep, I thought. My next thought was that Maud and I might yet escape. If we could take to the boat and make round the point before any one awoke? I would call her and start. My hand was lifted at her door to knock, when I recollected the smallness of the island. We could never hide ourselves upon it. There was nothing for us but the wide raw ocean. I thought of our snug little huts, our supplies of meat and oil and moss and firewood, and I knew that we could never survive the wintry sea and the great storms which were to come.

So I stood, with hesitant knuckle, without her door. It was impossible, impossible. A wild thought of rushing in and killing her as she slept rose in my mind. And then, in a flash, the better solution came to me. All hands were asleep. Why not creep aboard the *Ghost*,—well I knew the way to Wolf Larsen's bunk,—and kill him in his sleep? After that—well, we would see. But with him dead there was time and space in which to prepare to do other things; and besides, whatever new situation arose, it could not possibly be worse than the present one.

My knife was at my hip. I returned to my hut for the shot-gun, made sure it was loaded, and went down to the *Ghost*. With some difficulty, and at the expense of a wetting to the waist, I climbed aboard. The forecastle scuttle was open. I paused to listen for the breathing of the men, but there was no breathing. I almost gasped as the thought came to me: What if the *Ghost* is deserted? I listened more closely. There was no sound. I cautiously descended the ladder. The place had the empty and musty feel and smell usual to a dwelling no longer inhabited. Everywhere was a thick litter of discarded and ragged garments, old sea-boots, leaky oilskins—all the worthless forecastle dunnage of a long voyage.

Abandoned hastily, was my conclusion, as I ascended to the deck. Hope was alive again in my breast, and I looked about me with greater coolness. I noted that the boats were missing. The steerage told the same tale as the forecastle. The hunters had packed their belongings with similar haste. The *Ghost* was deserted. It was Maud's and mine. I thought of the ship's stores and the lazarette beneath the cabin, and the idea came to me of surprising Maud with something nice for breakfast.

The reaction from my fear, and the knowledge that the terrible deed I had come to do was no longer necessary, made me boyish and eager. I went up the steerage companion-way two steps at a time, with nothing distinct in my mind except joy and the hope that Maud would sleep on until the surprise breakfast was quite ready for her. As I rounded the galley, a new satisfaction was mine at thought of all the splendid cooking utensils inside. I sprang up the break of the poop, and saw—Wolf Larsen. What of my impetus and the stunning surprise, I clattered three or four steps along the deck before I could stop myself. He was standing in the companion-way, only his head and shoulders visible, staring straight at me. His arms were resting on the half-open slide. He made no movement whatever—simply stood there, staring at me.

I began to tremble. The old stomach sickness clutched me. I put one hand on the edge of the house to steady myself. My lips seemed suddenly dry and I moistened them against the need of speech. Nor did I for an instant take my eyes off him. Neither of us spoke. There was something ominous in his silence, his immobility. All my old fear of him returned and by new fear was increased an hundred-fold. And still we stood, the pair of us, staring at each other.

I was aware of the demand for action, and, my old helplessness strong upon me, I was waiting for him to take the initiative. Then, as the moments went by, it came to me that the situation was analogous to the one in which I had approached the long-maned bull, my intention of clubbing obscured by fear until it became a desire to make him run. So it was at last impressed upon me that I was there, not to have Wolf Larsen take the initiative, but to take it myself.

I cocked both barrels and levelled the shot-gun at him. Had he moved, attempted to drop down the companion-way, I know I would have shot him. But he stood motionless and staring as before. And as I faced him, with levelled gun shaking in my hands, I had time to note the worn and haggard appearance of his face. It was as if some strong anxiety had wasted it. The cheeks were sunken, and there was a wearied, puckered expression on the brow. And it seemed to me that his eyes were strange, not only the expression, but the physical seeming, as though the optic nerves and supporting muscles had suffered strain and slightly twisted the eyeballs.

All this I saw, and my brain now working rapidly, I thought a thousand thoughts; and yet I could not pull the triggers. I lowered the gun and stepped to the corner of the cabin, primarily to relieve the tension on my nerves and to make a new start, and incidentally to be closer. Again I raised the gun. He was almost at arm's length. There was no hope for him. I was resolved. There was no possible chance of missing him, no matter how poor my marksmanship. And yet I wrestled with myself and could not pull the triggers.

"Well?" he demanded impatiently.

I strove vainly to force my fingers down on the triggers, and vainly I strove to say something.

"Why don't you shoot?" he asked.

I cleared my throat of a huskiness which prevented speech. "Hump," he said slowly, "you can't do it. You are not exactly afraid. You are impotent. Your conventional morality is stronger than you. You are the slave to the opinions which have credence among the people you have known and have read about. Their code has been drummed into your head from the time you lisped, and in spite of your philosophy, and of what I have taught you, it won't let you kill an unarmed, unresisting man."

"I know it," I said hoarsely.

"And you know that I would kill an unarmed man as readily as I would smoke a cigar," he went on. "You know me for what I am,—my worth in the world by your standard. You have called me snake, tiger, shark, monster, and Caliban. And yet, you little rag puppet, you little echoing mechanism, you are unable to kill me as you would a snake or a shark, because I have hands, feet, and a body shaped somewhat like yours. Bah! I had hoped better things of you, Hump."

He stepped out of the companion-way and came up to me.

"Put down that gun. I want to ask you some questions. I haven't had a chance to look around yet. What place is this? How is the *Ghost* lying? How did you get wet? Where's Maud?—I beg your pardon, Miss Brewster—or should I say, 'Mrs. Van Weyden'?"

I had backed away from him, almost weeping at my inability to shoot him, but not fool enough to put down the gun. I hoped, desperately, that he might commit some hostile act, attempt to strike me or choke me; for in such way only I knew I could be stirred to shoot.

"This is Endeavour Island," I said.

"Never heard of it," he broke in.

"At least, that's our name for it," I amended.

"Our?" he queried. "Who's our?"

"Miss Brewster and myself. And the *Ghost* is lying, as you can see for yourself, bow on to the beach."

"There are seals here," he said. "They woke me up with their barking, or I'd be sleeping yet. I heard them when I drove in last night. They were the first warning that I was on a lee shore. It's a rookery, the kind of a thing I've hunted for years. Thanks to my brother Death, I've lighted on a fortune. It's a mint. What's its bearings?"

"Haven't the least idea," I said. "But you ought to know quite closely. What were your last observations?"

He smiled inscrutably, but did not answer.

"Well, where's all hands?" I asked. "How does it come that you are alone?"

I was prepared for him again to set aside my question, and was surprised at the readiness of his reply.

"My brother got me inside forty-eight hours, and through no fault of mine. Boarded me in the night with only the watch on deck. Hunters went back on me. He gave them a bigger lay. Heard him offering it. Did it right before me. Of course the crew gave me the go-by. That was to be expected. All hands went over the side, and there I was, marooned on my own vessel. It was Death's turn, and it's all in the family anyway."

"But how did you lose the masts?" I asked.

"Walk over and examine those lanyards," he said, pointing to where the mizzen-rigging should have been.

"They have been cut with a knife!" I exclaimed.

"Not quite," he laughed. "It was a neater job. Look again."

I looked. The lanyards had been almost severed, with just enough left to hold the shrouds till some severe strain should be put upon them.

"Cooky did that," he laughed again. "I know, though I didn't spot him at it. Kind of evened up the score a bit."

"Good for Mugridge!" I cried.

"Yes, that's what I thought when everything went over the side. Only I said it on the other side of my mouth."

"But what were you doing while all this was going on?" I asked.

"My best, you may be sure, which wasn't much under the circumstances."

I turned to re-examine Thomas Mugridge's work.

"I guess I'll sit down and take the sunshine," I heard Wolf Larsen saying.

There was a hint, just a slight hint, of physical feebleness in his voice, and it was so strange that I looked quickly at him. His hand was sweeping nervously across his face, as though he were brushing away cobwebs. I was puzzled. The whole thing was so unlike the Wolf Larsen I had known.

"How are your headaches?" I asked.

"They still trouble me," was his answer. "I think I have one coming on now."

He slipped down from his sitting posture till he lay on the deck. Then he rolled over on his side, his head resting on the biceps of the under arm, the forearm shielding his eyes from the sun. I stood regarding him wonderingly.

"Now's your chance, Hump," he said.

"I don't understand," I lied, for I thoroughly understood.

"Oh, nothing," he added softly, as if he were drowsing; "only you've got me where you want me."

"No, I haven't," I retorted; "for I want you a few thousand miles away from here."

He chuckled, and thereafter spoke no more. He did not stir as I passed by him and went down into the cabin. I lifted the trap in the floor, but for some moments gazed dubiously into the darkness of the lazarette beneath. I hesitated to descend. What if his lying down were a ruse? Pretty, indeed, to be caught there like a rat. I crept softly up the companion-way and peeped at him. He was lying as I had left him. Again I went below; but before I dropped into the lazarette I took the precaution of casting down the door in advance. At least there would be no lid to the trap. But it was all needless. I regained the cabin with a store of jams, sea-biscuits, canned meats, and such things,—all I could carry,—and replaced the trap-door.

A peep at Wolf Larsen showed me that he had not moved. A bright thought struck me. I stole into his state-room and possessed myself of his revolvers. There were no other weapons, though I thoroughly ransacked the three remaining state-rooms. To make sure, I returned and went through the steerage and forecastle, and in the galley gathered up all the sharp meat and vegetable knives. Then I bethought me of the great yachtsman's knife he always carried, and I came to him and spoke to him, first softly, then loudly. He did not move. I bent over and took it from his pocket. I breathed more freely. He had no arms with which to attack me from a distance; while I, armed, could always forestall him should he attempt to grapple me with his terrible gorilla arms.

Filling a coffee-pot and frying-pan with part of my plunder, and taking some chinaware from the cabin pantry, I left Wolf Larsen lying in the sun and went ashore.

Maud was still asleep. I blew up the embers (we had not yet arranged a winter kitchen), and quite feverishly cooked the breakfast. Toward the end, I heard her moving about within the hut, making her toilet. Just as all was ready and the coffee poured, the door opened and she came forth.

"It's not fair of you," was her greeting. "You are usurping one of my prerogatives. You know you I agreed that the cooking should be mine, and—"

"But just this once," I pleaded.

"If you promise not to do it again," she smiled. "Unless, of course, you have grown tired of my poor efforts."

To my delight she never once looked toward the beach, and I maintained the banter with such success all unconsciously she sipped coffee from the china cup, ate fried evaporated potatoes, and spread marmalade on her biscuit. But it could not last. I saw the surprise that came over her. She had discovered the china plate from which she was eating. She looked over the breakfast, noting detail after detail. Then she looked at me, and her face turned slowly toward the beach.

"Humphrey!" she said.

The old unnamable terror mounted into her eyes.

"Is—he?" she quavered.

I nodded my head.

CHAPTER XXXIIII

We waited all day for Wolf Larsen to come ashore. It was an intolerable period of anxiety. Each moment one or the other of us cast expectant glances toward the *Ghost*. But he did not come. He did not even appear on deck.

"Perhaps it is his headache," I said. "I left him lying on the poop. He may lie there all night. I think I'll go and see."

Maud looked entreaty at me.

"It is all right," I assured her. "I shall take the revolvers. You know I collected every weapon on board."

"But there are his arms, his hands, his terrible, terrible hands!" she objected. And then she cried, "Oh, Humphrey, I am afraid of him! Don't go—please don't go!"

She rested her hand appealingly on mine, and sent my pulse fluttering. My heart was surely in my eyes for a moment. The dear and lovely woman! And she was so much the woman, clinging and appealing, sunshine and dew to my manhood, rooting it deeper and sending through it the sap of a new strength. I was for putting my arm around her, as when in the midst of the seal herd; but I considered, and refrained.

"I shall not take any risks," I said. "I'll merely peep over the bow and see."

She pressed my hand earnestly and let me go. But the space on deck where I had left him lying was vacant. He had evidently gone below. That night we stood alternate watches, one of us sleeping at a time; for there was no telling what Wolf Larsen might do. He was certainly capable of anything.

The next day we waited, and the next, and still he made no sign.

"These headaches of his, these attacks," Maud said, on the afternoon of the fourth day; "Perhaps he is ill, very ill. He may be dead."

"Or dying," was her afterthought when she had waited some time for me to speak.

"Better so," I answered.

"But think, Humphrey, a fellow-creature in his last lonely hour."

"Perhaps," I suggested.

"Yes, even perhaps," she acknowledged. "But we do not know. It would be terrible if he were. I could never forgive myself. We must do something."

"Perhaps," I suggested again.

I waited, smiling inwardly at the woman of her which compelled a solicitude for Wolf Larsen, of all creatures. Where was her solicitude for me, I thought,—for me whom she had been afraid to have merely peep aboard?

CHAPTER XXXIIII

She was too subtle not to follow the trend of my silence. And she was as direct as she was subtle.

"You must go aboard, Humphrey, and find out," she said. "And if you want to laugh at me, you have my consent and forgiveness."

I arose obediently and went down the beach.

"Do be careful," she called after me.

I waved my arm from the forecastle head and dropped down to the deck. Aft I walked to the cabin companion, where I contented myself with hailing below. Wolf Larsen answered, and as he started to ascend the stairs I cocked my revolver. I displayed it openly during our conversation, but he took no notice of it. He appeared the same, physically, as when last I saw him, but he was gloomy and silent. In fact, the few words we spoke could hardly be called a conversation. I did not inquire why he had not been ashore, nor did he ask why I had not come aboard. His head was all right again, he said, and so, without further parley, I left him.

Maud received my report with obvious relief, and the sight of smoke which later rose in the galley put her in a more cheerful mood. The next day, and the next, we saw the galley smoke rising, and sometimes we caught glimpses of him on the poop. But that was all. He made no attempt to come ashore. This we knew, for we still maintained our night-watches. We were waiting for him to do something, to show his hand, so to say, and his inaction puzzled and worried us.

A week of this passed by. We had no other interest than Wolf Larsen, and his presence weighed us down with an apprehension which prevented us from doing any of the little things we had planned.

But at the end of the week the smoke ceased rising from the galley, and he no longer showed himself on the poop. I could see Maud's solicitude again growing, though she timidly—and even proudly, I think—forbore a repetition of her request. After all, what censure could be put upon her? She was divinely altruistic, and she was a woman. Besides, I was myself aware of hurt at thought of this man whom I had tried to kill, dying alone with his fellow-creatures so near. He was right. The code of my group was stronger than I. The fact that he had hands, feet, and a body shaped somewhat like mine, constituted a claim which I could not ignore.

So I did not wait a second time for Maud to send me. I discovered that we stood in need of condensed milk and marmalade, and announced that I was going aboard. I could see that she wavered. She even went so far as to murmur that they were non-essentials and that my trip after them might be inexpedient. And as she had followed the trend of my silence, she now followed the trend of my speech, and she knew that I was going aboard, not because of condensed milk and marmalade, but because of her and of her anxiety, which she knew she had failed to hide.

I took off my shoes when I gained the forecastle head, and went noiselessly aft in my stocking feet. Nor did I call this time from the top of the companion-way. Cautiously descending, I found the cabin deserted. The door to his state-room was closed. At first I thought of knocking, then I remembered my ostensible errand and resolved to carry it out. Carefully avoiding noise, I lifted the trap-door in the floor and set it to one side. The slop-chest, as well as the provisions, was stored in the lazarette, and I took advantage of the opportunity to lay in a stock of underclothing.

As I emerged from the lazarette I heard sounds in Wolf Larsen's state-room. I crouched and listened. The door-knob rattled. Furtively, instinctively, I slunk back behind the table and drew and cocked my revolver. The door swung open and he came forth. Never had I seen so profound a despair as that which I saw on his face,—the face of Wolf Larsen the fighter, the strong man, the indomitable one. For all the world like a woman wringing her hands, he raised his clenched fists and groaned. One fist unclosed, and the open palm swept across his eyes as though brushing away cobwebs.

"God! God!" he groaned, and the clenched fists were raised again to the infinite despair with which his throat vibrated.

It was horrible. I was trembling all over, and I could feel the shivers running up and down my spine and the sweat standing out on my forehead. Surely there can be little in this world more awful than the spectacle of a strong man in the moment when he is utterly weak and broken.

But Wolf Larsen regained control of himself by an exertion of his remarkable will. And it was exertion. His whole frame shook with the struggle. He resembled a man on the verge of a fit. His face strove to compose itself, writhing and twisting in the effort till he broke down again. Once more the clenched fists went upward and he groaned. He caught his breath once or twice and sobbed. Then he was successful. I could have thought him the old Wolf Larsen, and yet there was in his movements a vague suggestion of weakness and indecision. He started for the companion-way, and stepped forward quite as I had been accustomed to see him do; and yet again, in his very walk, there seemed that suggestion of weakness and indecision.

I was now concerned with fear for myself. The open trap lay directly in his path, and his discovery of it would lead instantly to his discovery of me. I was angry with myself for being caught in so cowardly a position, crouching on the floor. There was yet time. I rose swiftly to my feet, and, I know, quite unconsciously assumed a defiant attitude. He took no notice of me. Nor did he notice the open trap. Before I could grasp the situation, or act, he had walked right into the trap. One foot was descending into the opening, while the other foot was just on the verge of beginning the uplift. But when the descending foot missed the solid flooring and felt vacancy beneath, it was the old Wolf Larsen and the tiger muscles that made the falling body spring across the opening, even as it fell, so that he struck on his chest and stomach, with arms outstretched, on the floor of the opposite side. The next instant he had drawn up his legs and rolled clear. But he rolled into my marmalade and underclothes and against the trap-door.

The expression on his face was one of complete comprehension. But before I could guess what he had comprehended, he had dropped the trap-door into place, closing the lazarette. Then I understood. He thought he had me inside. Also, he was blind, blind as a bat. I watched him, breathing carefully so that he should not hear me. He stepped quickly to his state-room. I saw his hand miss the door-knob by an inch, quickly fumble for it, and find it. This was my chance. I tiptoed across the cabin and to the top of the stairs. He came back, dragging a heavy sea-chest, which he deposited on top of the trap. Not content with this he fetched a second chest and placed it on top of the first. Then he gathered up the marmalade and underclothes and put them on the table. When he started up the companion-way, I retreated, silently rolling over on top of the cabin.

He shoved the slide part way back and rested his arms on it, his body still in the companion-way. His attitude was of one looking forward the length of the schooner, or staring, rather, for his eyes were fixed and unblinking. I was only five feet away and directly in what should have been his line of vision. It was uncanny. I felt myself a ghost, what of my invisibility. I waved my hand back and forth, of course without effect; but when the moving shadow fell across his face I saw at once that he was susceptible to the impression. His face became more expectant and tense as he tried to analyze and identify the impression. He knew that he had responded to something from without, that his sensibility had been touched by a changing something in his environment; but what it was he could not discover. I ceased waving my hand, so that the shadow remained stationary. He slowly moved his head back and forth under it and turned from side to side, now in the sunshine, now in the shade, feeling the shadow, as it were, testing it by sensation.

I, too, was busy, trying to reason out how he was aware of the existence of so intangible a thing as a shadow. If it were his eyeballs only that were affected, or if his optic nerve were not wholly destroyed, the explanation was simple. If otherwise, then the only conclusion I could reach was that the sensitive skin recognized the difference of temperature between shade and sunshine. Or, perhaps,—who can tell?—it was that fabled sixth sense which conveyed to him the loom and feel of an object close at hand.

Giving over his attempt to determine the shadow, he stepped on deck and started forward, walking with a swiftness and confidence which surprised me. And still there was that hint of the feebleness of the blind in his walk. I knew it now for what it was.

To my amused chagrin, he discovered my shoes on the forecastle head and brought them back with him into the galley. I watched him build the fire and set about cooking food for himself; then I stole into the cabin for my marmalade and underclothes, slipped back past the galley, and climbed down to the beach to deliver my barefoot report.

CHAPTER XXXIV

"It's too bad the *Ghost* has lost her masts. Why we could sail away in her. Don't you think we could, Humphrey?"

I sprang excitedly to my feet.

"I wonder, I wonder," I repeated, pacing up and down.

Maud's eyes were shining with anticipation as they followed me. She had such faith in me! And the thought of it was so much added power. I remembered Michelet's "To man, woman is as the earth was to her legendary son; he has but to fall down and kiss her breast and he is strong again." For the first time I knew the wonderful truth of his words. Why, I was living them. Maud was all this to me, an unfailing, source of strength and courage. I had but to look at her, or think of her, and be strong again.

"It can be done, it can be done," I was thinking and asserting aloud. "What men have done, I can do; and if they have never done this before, still I can do it."

"What? for goodness' sake," Maud demanded. "Do be merciful. What is it you can do?"

"We can do it," I amended. "Why, nothing else than put the masts back into the *Ghost* and sail away."

"Humphrey!" she exclaimed.

And I felt as proud of my conception as if it were already a fact accomplished.

"But how is it possible to be done?" she asked.

"I don't know," was my answer. "I know only that I am capable of doing anything these days."

I smiled proudly at her—too proudly, for she dropped her eyes and was for the moment silent.

"But there is Captain Larsen," she objected.

"Blind and helpless," I answered promptly, waving him aside as a straw.

"But those terrible hands of his! You know how he leaped across the opening of the lazarette."

"And you know also how I crept about and avoided him," I contended gaily.

"And lost your shoes."

"You'd hardly expect them to avoid Wolf Larsen without my feet inside of them."

We both laughed, and then went seriously to work constructing the plan whereby we were to step the masts of the *Ghost* and return to the world. I remembered hazily the physics of my school days, while the last few months had given me practical experience with mechanical purchases. I must say, though, when we walked down to the *Ghost* to inspect more closely the task before us, that the sight of the great masts lying in the water almost disheartened me. Where were we to begin? If there had been one mast standing, something high up to which to fasten blocks and tackles! But there was nothing. It reminded me of the problem of lifting oneself by one's boot-straps. I understood the mechanics of levers; but where was I to get a fulcrum?

There was the mainmast, fifteen inches in diameter at what was now the butt, still sixty-five feet in length, and weighing, I roughly calculated, at least three thousand pounds. And then came the foremast, larger in diameter, and weighing surely thirty-five hundred pounds. Where was I to begin? Maud stood silently by my side, while I evolved in my mind the contrivance known among sailors as "shears." But, though known to sailors, I invented it there on Endeavour Island. By crossing and lashing the ends of two spars, and then elevating them in the air like an inverted "V," I could get a point above the deck to which to make fast my hoisting tackle. To this hoisting tackle I could, if necessary, attach a second hoisting tackle. And then there was the windlass!

Maud saw that I had achieved a solution, and her eyes warmed sympathetically.

"What are you going to do?" she asked.

"Clear that raffle," I answered, pointing to the tangled wreckage overside.

Ah, the decisiveness, the very sound of the words, was good in my ears. "Clear that raffle!" Imagine so salty a phrase on the lips of the Humphrey Van Weyden of a few months gone!

There must have been a touch of the melodramatic in my pose and voice, for Maud smiled. Her appreciation of the ridiculous was keen, and in all things she unerringly saw and felt, where it existed, the touch of sham, the overshading, the overtone. It was this which had given poise and penetration to her own work and made her of worth to the world. The serious critic, with the sense of humour and the power of expression, must inevitably command the world's ear. And so it was that she had commanded. Her sense of humour was really the artist's instinct for proportion.

"I'm sure I've heard it before, somewhere, in books," she murmured gleefully.

I had an instinct for proportion myself, and I collapsed forthwith, descending from the dominant pose of a master of matter to a state of humble confusion which was, to say the least, very miserable.

Her hand leapt out at once to mine.

"I'm so sorry," she said.

"No need to be," I gulped. "It does me good. There's too much of the schoolboy in me. All of which is neither here nor there. What we've got to do is actually and literally to clear that raffle. If you'll come with me in the boat, we'll get to work and straighten things out."

"'When the topmen clear the raffle with their clasp-knives in their teeth,'" she quoted at me; and for the rest of the afternoon we made merry over our labour.

Her task was to hold the boat in position while I worked at the tangle. And such a tangle—halyards, sheets, guys, down-hauls, shrouds, stays, all washed about and back and forth and through, and twined and knotted by the sea. I cut no more than was necessary, and what with passing the long ropes under and around the booms and masts, of unreeving the halyards and sheets, of coiling down in the boat and uncoiling in order to pass through another knot in the bight, I was soon wet to the skin.

The sails did require some cutting, and the canvas, heavy with water, tried my strength severely; but I succeeded before nightfall in getting it all spread out on the beach to dry. We were both very tired when we knocked off for supper, and we had done good work, too, though to the eye it appeared insignificant.

Next morning, with Maud as able assistant, I went into the hold of the *Ghost* to clear the steps of the mast-butts. We had no more than begun work when the sound of my knocking and hammering brought Wolf Larsen.

"Hello below!" he cried down the open hatch.

The sound of his voice made Maud quickly draw close to me, as for protection, and she rested one hand on my arm while we parleyed.

"Hello on deck," I replied. "Good-morning to you."

"What are you doing down there?" he demanded. "Trying to scuttle my ship for me?"

"Quite the opposite; I'm repairing her," was my answer.

"But what in thunder are you repairing?" There was puzzlement in his voice.

"Why, I'm getting everything ready for re-stepping the masts," I replied easily, as though it were the simplest project imaginable.

"It seems as though you're standing on your own legs at last, Hump," we heard him say; and then for some time he was silent.

"But I say, Hump," he called down. "You can't do it."

"Oh, yes, I can," I retorted. "I'm doing it now."

"But this is my vessel, my particular property. What if I forbid you?"

"You forget," I replied. "You are no longer the biggest bit of the ferment. You were, once, and able to eat me, as you were pleased to phrase it; but there has been a diminishing, and I am now able to eat you. The yeast has grown stale."

He gave a short, disagreeable laugh. "I see you're working my philosophy back on me for all it is worth. But don't make the mistake of under-estimating me. For your own good I warn you."

"Since when have you become a philanthropist?" I queried. "Confess, now, in warning me for my own good, that you are very consistent."

He ignored my sarcasm, saying, "Suppose I clap the hatch on, now? You won't fool me as you did in the lazarette."

"Wolf Larsen," I said sternly, for the first time addressing him by this his most familiar name, "I am unable to shoot a helpless, unresisting man. You have proved that to my satisfaction as well as yours. But I warn you now, and not so much for your own good as for mine, that I shall shoot you the moment you attempt a hostile act. I can shoot you now, as I stand here; and if you are so minded, just go ahead and try to clap on the hatch."

"Nevertheless, I forbid you, I distinctly forbid your tampering with my ship."

"But, man!" I expostulated, "you advance the fact that it is your ship as though it were a moral right. You have never considered moral rights in your dealings with others. You surely do not dream that I'll consider them in dealing with you?"

I had stepped underneath the open hatchway so that I could see him. The lack of expression on his face, so different from when I had watched him unseen, was enhanced by the unblinking, staring eyes. It was not a pleasant face to look upon.

"And none so poor, not even Hump, to do him reverence," he sneered.

The sneer was wholly in his voice. His face remained expressionless as ever.

"How do you do, Miss Brewster," he said suddenly, after a pause.

I started. She had made no noise whatever, had not even moved. Could it be that some glimmer of vision remained to him? or that his vision was coming back?

"How do you do, Captain Larsen," she answered. "Pray, how did you know I was here?"

"Heard you breathing, of course. I say, Hump's improving, don't you think so?"

"I don't know," she answered, smiling at me. "I have never seen him otherwise."

"You should have seen him before, then."

"Wolf Larsen, in large doses," I murmured, "before and after taking."

"I want to tell you again, Hump," he said threateningly, "that you'd better leave things alone."

"But don't you care to escape as well as we?" I asked incredulously.

"No," was his answer. "I intend dying here."

"Well, we don't," I concluded defiantly, beginning again my knocking and hammering.

CHAPTER XXXV

Next day, the mast-steps clear and everything in readiness, we started to get the two topmasts aboard. The maintopmast was over thirty feet in length, the foretopmast nearly thirty, and it was of these that I intended making the shears. It was puzzling work. Fastening one end of a heavy tackle to the windlass, and with the other end fast to the butt of the foretopmast, I began to heave. Maud held the turn on the windlass and coiled down the slack.

We were astonished at the ease with which the spar was lifted. It was an improved crank windlass, and the purchase it gave was enormous. Of course, what it gave us in power we paid for in distance; as many times as it doubled my strength, that many times was doubled the length of rope I heaved in. The tackle dragged heavily across the rail, increasing its drag as the spar arose more and more out of the water, and the exertion on the windlass grew severe.

But when the butt of the topmast was level with the rail, everything came to a standstill.

"I might have known it," I said impatiently. "Now we have to do it all over again."

"Why not fasten the tackle part way down the mast?" Maud suggested.

"It's what I should have done at first," I answered, hugely disgusted with myself.

Slipping off a turn, I lowered the mast back into the water and fastened the tackle a third of the way down from the butt. In an hour, what of this and of rests between the heaving, I had hoisted it to the point where I could hoist no more. Eight feet of the butt was above the rail, and I was as far away as ever from getting the spar on board. I sat down and pondered the problem. It did not take long. I sprang jubilantly to my feet.

"Now I have it!" I cried. "I ought to make the tackle fast at the point of balance. And what we learn of this will serve us with everything else we have to hoist aboard."

Once again I undid all my work by lowering the mast into the water. But I miscalculated the point of balance, so that when I heaved the top of the mast came up instead of the butt. Maud looked despair, but I laughed and said it would do just as well.

Instructing her how to hold the turn and be ready to slack away at command, I laid hold of the mast with my hands and tried to balance it inboard across the rail. When I thought I had it I cried to her to slack away; but the spar righted, despite my efforts, and dropped back toward the water. Again I heaved it up to its old position, for I had now another idea. I remembered the watch-tackle—a small double and single block affair—and fetched it.

While I was rigging it between the top of the spar and the opposite rail, Wolf Larsen came on the scene. We exchanged nothing more than good-mornings, and, though he could not see, he sat on the rail out of the way and followed by the sound all that I did.

Again instructing Maud to slack away at the windlass when I gave the word, I proceeded to heave on the watch-tackle. Slowly the mast swung in until it balanced at right angles across the rail; and then I discovered to my amazement that there was no need for Maud to slack away. In fact, the very opposite was necessary. Making the watch-tackle fast, I hove on the windlass and brought in the mast, inch by inch, till its top tilted down to the deck and finally its whole length lay on the deck.

I looked at my watch. It was twelve o'clock. My back was aching sorely, and I felt extremely tired and hungry. And there on the deck was a single stick of timber to show for a whole morning's work. For the first time I thoroughly realized the extent of the task before us. But I was learning, I was learning. The afternoon would show far more accomplished. And it did; for we returned at one o'clock, rested and strengthened by a hearty dinner.

In less than an hour I had the maintopmast on deck and was constructing the shears. Lashing the two topmasts together, and making allowance for their unequal length, at the point of intersection I attached the double block of the main throat-halyards. This, with the single block and the throat-halyards themselves, gave me a hoisting tackle. To prevent the butts of the masts from slipping on the deck, I nailed down thick cleats. Everything in readiness, I made a line fast to the apex of the shears and carried it directly to the windlass. I was growing to have faith in that windlass, for it gave me power beyond all expectation. As usual, Maud held the turn while I heaved. The shears rose in the air.

Then I discovered I had forgotten guy-ropes. This necessitated my climbing the shears, which I did twice, before I finished guying it fore and aft and to either side. Twilight had set in by the time this was accomplished. Wolf Larsen, who had sat about and listened all afternoon and never opened his mouth, had taken himself off to the galley and started his supper. I felt quite stiff across the small of the back, so much so that I straightened up with an effort and with pain. I looked proudly at my work. It was beginning to show. I was wild with desire, like a child with a new toy, to hoist something with my shears.

"I wish it weren't so late," I said. "I'd like to see how it works."

"Don't be a glutton, Humphrey," Maud chided me. "Remember, to-morrow is coming, and you're so tired now that you can hardly stand."

"And you?" I said, with sudden solicitude. "You must be very tired. You have worked hard and nobly. I am proud of you, Maud."

"Not half so proud as I am of you, nor with half the reason," she answered, looking me straight in the eyes for a moment with an expression in her own and a dancing, tremulous light which I had not seen before and which gave me a pang of quick delight, I know not why, for I did not understand it. Then she dropped her eyes, to lift them again, laughing.

"If our friends could see us now," she said. "Look at us. Have you ever paused for a moment to consider our appearance?"

"Yes, I have considered yours, frequently," I answered, puzzling over what I had seen in her eyes and puzzled by her sudden change of subject.

"Mercy!" she cried. "And what do I look like, pray?"

"A scarecrow, I'm afraid," I replied. "Just glance at your draggled skirts, for instance. Look at those three-cornered tears. And such a waist! It would not require a Sherlock Holmes to deduce that you have been cooking over a camp-fire, to say nothing of trying out seal-blubber. And to cap it all, that cap! And all that is the woman who wrote 'A Kiss Endured.'"

She made me an elaborate and stately courtesy, and said, "As for you, sir—"

And yet, through the five minutes of banter which followed, there was a serious something underneath the fun which I could not but relate to the strange and fleeting expression I had caught in her eyes. What was it? Could it be that our eyes were speaking beyond the will of our speech? My eyes had spoken, I knew, until I had found the culprits out and silenced them. This had occurred several times. But had she seen the clamour in them and understood? And had her eyes so spoken to me? What else could that expression have meant—that dancing, tremulous light, and a something more which words could not describe. And yet it could not be. It was impossible. Besides, I was not skilled in the speech of eyes. I was only Humphrey Van Weyden, a bookish fellow who loved. And to love, and to wait and win love, that surely was glorious enough for me. And thus I thought, even as we chaffed each other's appearance, until we arrived ashore and there were other things to think about.

"It's a shame, after working hard all day, that we cannot have an uninterrupted night's sleep," I complained, after supper.

"But there can be no danger now? from a blind man?" she queried.

"I shall never be able to trust him," I averred, "and far less now that he is blind. The liability is that his part helplessness will make him more malignant than ever. I know what I shall do to-morrow, the first thing—run out a light anchor and kedge the schooner off the beach. And each night when we come ashore in the boat, Mr. Wolf Larsen will be left a prisoner on board. So this will be the last night we have to stand watch, and because of that it will go the easier."

We were awake early and just finishing breakfast as daylight came.

"Oh, Humphrey!" I heard Maud cry in dismay and suddenly stop.

I looked at her. She was gazing at the *Ghost*. I followed her gaze, but could see nothing unusual. She looked at me, and I looked inquiry back.

"The shears," she said, and her voice trembled.

I had forgotten their existence. I looked again, but could not see them.

"If he has—" I muttered savagely.

She put her hand sympathetically on mine, and said, "You will have to begin over again."

"Oh, believe me, my anger means nothing; I could not hurt a fly," I smiled back bitterly. "And the worst of it is, he knows it. You are right. If he has destroyed the shears, I shall do nothing except begin over again."

"But I'll stand my watch on board hereafter," I blurted out a moment later. "And if he interferes—"

"But I dare not stay ashore all night alone," Maud was saying when I came back to myself. "It would be so much nicer if he would be friendly with us and help us. We could all live comfortably aboard."

"We will," I asserted, still savagely, for the destruction of my beloved shears had hit me hard. "That is, you and I will live aboard, friendly or not with Wolf Larsen."

"It's childish," I laughed later, "for him to do such things, and for me to grow angry over them, for that matter."

But my heart smote me when we climbed aboard and looked at the havoc he had done. The shears were gone altogether. The guys had been slashed right and left. The throat-halyards which I had rigged were cut across through every part. And he knew I could not splice. A thought struck me. I ran to the windlass. It would not work. He had broken it. We looked at each other in consternation. Then I ran to the side. The masts, booms, and gaffs I had cleared were gone. He had found the lines which held them, and cast them adrift.

Tears were in Maud's eyes, and I do believe they were for me. I could have wept myself. Where now was our project of remasting the *Ghost*? He had done his work well. I sat down on the hatch-combing and rested my chin on my hands in black despair.

"He deserves to die," I cried out; "and God forgive me, I am not man enough to be his executioner."

But Maud was by my side, passing her hand soothingly through my hair as though I were a child, and saying, "There, there; it will all come right. We are in the right, and it must come right."

I remembered Michelet and leaned my head against her; and truly I became strong again. The blessed woman was an unfailing fount of power to me. What did it matter? Only a set-back, a delay. The tide could not have carried the masts far to seaward, and there had been no wind. It meant merely more work to find them and tow them back. And besides, it was a lesson. I knew what to expect. He might have waited and destroyed our work more effectually when we had more accomplished.

"Here he comes now," she whispered.

I glanced up. He was strolling leisurely along the poop on the port side.

"Take no notice of him," I whispered. "He's coming to see how we take it. Don't let him know that we know. We can deny him that satisfaction. Take off your shoes—that's right—and carry them in your hand."

And then we played hide-and-seek with the blind man. As he came up the port side we slipped past on the starboard; and from the poop we watched him turn and start aft on our track.

He must have known, somehow, that we were on board, for he said "Good-morning" very confidently, and waited, for the greeting to be returned. Then he strolled aft, and we slipped forward.

"Oh, I know you're aboard," he called out, and I could see him listen intently after he had spoken.

It reminded me of the great hoot-owl, listening, after its booming cry, for the stir of its frightened prey. But we did not fir, and we moved only when he moved. And so we dodged about the deck, hand in hand, like a couple of children chased by a wicked ogre, till Wolf Larsen, evidently in disgust, left the deck for the cabin. There was glee in our eyes, and suppressed titters in our mouths, as we put on our shoes and clambered over the side into the boat. And as I looked into Maud's clear brown eyes I forgot the evil he had done, and I knew only that I loved her, and that because of her the strength was mine to win our way back to the world.

CHAPTER XXXVI

For two days Maud and I ranged the sea and explored the beaches in search of the missing masts. But it was not till the third day that we found them, all of them, the shears included, and, of all perilous places, in the pounding surf of the grim south-western promontory. And how we worked! At the dark end of the first day we returned, exhausted, to our little cove, towing the mainmast behind us. And we had been compelled to row, in a dead calm, practically every inch of the way.

Another day of heart-breaking and dangerous toil saw us in camp with the two topmasts to the good. The day following I was desperate, and I rafted together the foremast, the fore and main booms, and the fore and main gaffs. The wind was favourable, and I had thought to tow them back under sail, but the wind baffled, then died away, and our progress with the oars was a snail's pace. And it was such dispiriting effort. To throw one's whole strength and weight on the oars and to feel the boat checked in its forward lunge by the heavy drag behind, was not exactly exhilarating.

Night began to fall, and to make matters worse, the wind sprang up ahead. Not only did all forward motion cease, but we began to drift back and out to sea. I struggled at the oars till I was played out. Poor Maud, whom I could never prevent from working to the limit of her strength, lay weakly back in the stern-sheets. I could row no more. My bruised and swollen hands could no longer close on the oar handles. My wrists and arms ached intolerably, and though I had eaten heartily of a twelve-o'clock lunch, I had worked so hard that I was faint from hunger.

I pulled in the oars and bent forward to the line which held the tow. But Maud's hand leaped out restrainingly to mine.

"What are you going to do?" she asked in a strained, tense voice.

"Cast it off," I answered, slipping a turn of the rope.

But her fingers closed on mine.

"Please don't," she begged.

"It is useless," I answered. "Here is night and the wind blowing us off the land."

"But think, Humphrey. If we cannot sail away on the *Ghost*, we may remain for years on the island—for life even. If it has never been discovered all these years, it may never be discovered."

"You forget the boat we found on the beach," I reminded her.

"It was a seal-hunting boat," she replied, "and you know perfectly well that if the men had escaped they would have been back to make their fortunes from the rookery. You know they never escaped."

CHAPTER XXXVI

I remained silent, undecided.

"Besides," she added haltingly, "it's your idea, and I want to see you succeed."

Now I could harden my heart. As soon as she put it on a flattering personal basis, generosity compelled me to deny her.

"Better years on the island than to die to-night, or to-morrow, or the next day, in the open boat. We are not prepared to brave the sea. We have no food, no water, no blankets, nothing. Why, you'd not survive the night without blankets: I know how strong you are. You are shivering now."

"It is only nervousness," she answered. "I am afraid you will cast off the masts in spite of me."

"Oh, please, please, Humphrey, don't!" she burst out, a moment later.

And so it ended, with the phrase she knew had all power over me. We shivered miserably throughout the night. Now and again I fitfully slept, but the pain of the cold always aroused me. How Maud could stand it was beyond me. I was too tired to thrash my arms about and warm myself, but I found strength time and again to chafe her hands and feet to restore the circulation. And still she pleaded with me not to cast off the masts. About three in the morning she was caught by a cold cramp, and after I had rubbed her out of that she became quite numb. I was frightened. I got out the oars and made her row, though she was so weak I thought she would faint at every stroke.

Morning broke, and we looked long in the growing light for our island. At last it showed, small and black, on the horizon, fully fifteen miles away. I scanned the sea with my glasses. Far away in the south-west I could see a dark line on the water, which grew even as I looked at it.

"Fair wind!" I cried in a husky voice I did not recognize as my own.

Maud tried to reply, but could not speak. Her lips were blue with cold, and she was hollow-eyed—but oh, how bravely her brown eyes looked at me! How piteously brave!

Again I fell to chafing her hands and to moving her arms up and down and about until she could thrash them herself. Then I compelled her to stand up, and though she would have fallen had I not supported her, I forced her to walk back and forth the several steps between the thwart and the stern-sheets, and finally to spring up and down.

"Oh, you brave, brave woman," I said, when I saw the life coming back into her face. "Did you know that you were brave?"

"I never used to be," she answered. "I was never brave till I knew you. It is you who have made me brave."

"Nor I, until I knew you," I answered.

She gave me a quick look, and again I caught that dancing, tremulous light and something more in her eyes. But it was only for the moment. Then she smiled.

"It must have been the conditions," she said; but I knew she was wrong, and I wondered if she likewise knew. Then the wind came, fair and fresh, and the boat was soon labouring through a heavy sea toward the island. At half-past three in the afternoon we passed the south-western promontory. Not only were we hungry, but we were now suffering from thirst. Our lips were dry and cracked, nor could we longer moisten them with our tongues. Then the wind slowly died down. By night it was dead calm and I was toiling once more at the oars—but weakly, most weakly. At two in the morning the boat's bow touched the beach of our own inner cove and I staggered out to make the painter fast. Maud could not stand, nor had I strength to carry her. I fell in the sand with her, and, when I had recovered, contented myself with putting my hands under her shoulders and dragging her up the beach to the hut.

The next day we did no work. In fact, we slept till three in the afternoon, or at least I did, for I awoke to find Maud cooking dinner. Her power of recuperation was wonderful. There was something tenacious about that lily-frail body of hers, a clutch on existence which one could not reconcile with its patent weakness.

"You know I was travelling to Japan for my health," she said, as we lingered at the fire after dinner and delighted in the movelessness of loafing. "I was not very strong. I never was. The doctors recommended a sea voyage, and I chose the longest."

"You little knew what you were choosing," I laughed.

"But I shall be a different women for the experience, as well as a stronger woman," she answered; "and, I hope a better woman. At least I shall understand a great deal more life."

Then, as the short day waned, we fell to discussing Wolf Larsen's blindness. It was inexplicable. And that it was grave, I instanced his statement that he intended to stay and die on Endeavour Island. When he, strong man that he was, loving life as he did, accepted his death, it was plain that he was troubled by something more than mere blindness. There had been his terrific headaches, and we were agreed that it was some sort of brain break-down, and that in his attacks he endured pain beyond our comprehension.

I noticed as we talked over his condition, that Maud's sympathy went out to him more and more; yet I could not but love her for it, so sweetly womanly was it. Besides, there was no false sentiment about her feeling. She was agreed that the most rigorous treatment was necessary if we were to escape, though she recoiled at the suggestion that I might some time be compelled to take his life to save my own—"our own," she put it.

In the morning we had breakfast and were at work by daylight. I found a light kedge anchor in the fore-hold, where such things were kept; and with a deal of exertion got it on deck and into the boat. With a long running-line coiled down in the stem, I rowed well out into our little cove and dropped the anchor into the water. There was no wind, the tide was high, and the schooner floated. Casting off the shore-lines, I kedged her out by main strength (the windlass being broken), till she rode nearly up and down to the small anchor—too small to hold her in any breeze. So I lowered the big starboard anchor, giving plenty of slack; and by afternoon I was at work on the windlass.

Three days I worked on that windlass. Least of all things was I a mechanic, and in that time I accomplished what an ordinary machinist would have done in as many hours. I had to learn my tools to begin with, and every simple mechanical principle which such a man would have at his finger ends I had likewise to learn. And at the end of three days I had a windlass which worked clumsily. It never gave the satisfaction the old windlass had given, but it worked and made my work possible.

In half a day I got the two topmasts aboard and the shears rigged and guyed as before. And that night I slept on board and on deck beside my work. Maud, who refused to stay alone ashore, slept in the forecastle. Wolf Larsen had sat about, listening to my repairing the windlass and talking with Maud and me upon indifferent subjects. No reference was made on either side to the destruction of the shears; nor did he say anything further about my leaving his ship alone. But still I had feared him, blind and helpless and listening, always listening, and I never let his strong arms get within reach of me while I worked.

On this night, sleeping under my beloved shears, I was aroused by his footsteps on the deck. It was a starlight night, and I could see the bulk of him dimly as he moved about. I rolled out of my blankets and crept noiselessly after him in my stocking feet. He had armed himself with a draw-knife from the tool-locker, and with this he prepared to cut across the throat-halyards I had again rigged to the shears. He felt the halyards with his hands and discovered that I had not made them fast. This would not do for a draw-knife, so he laid hold of the running part, hove taut, and made fast. Then he prepared to saw across with the draw-knife.

"I wouldn't, if I were you," I said quietly.

He heard the click of my pistol and laughed.

"Hello, Hump," he said. "I knew you were here all the time. You can't fool my ears."

"That's a lie, Wolf Larsen," I said, just as quietly as before. "However, I am aching for a chance to kill you, so go ahead and cut."

"You have the chance always," he sneered.

"Go ahead and cut," I threatened ominously.

"I'd rather disappoint you," he laughed, and turned on his heel and went aft.

"Something must be done, Humphrey," Maud said, next morning, when I had told her of the night's occurrence. "If he has liberty, he may do anything. He may sink the vessel, or set fire to it. There is no telling what he may do. We must make him a prisoner."

"But how?" I asked, with a helpless shrug. "I dare not come within reach of his arms, and he knows that so long as his resistance is passive I cannot shoot him."

"There must be some way," she contended. "Let me think."

"There is one way," I said grimly.

She waited.

I picked up a seal-club.

"It won't kill him," I said. "And before he could recover I'd have him bound hard and fast."

She shook her head with a shudder. "No, not that. There must be some less brutal way. Let us wait."

But we did not have to wait long, and the problem solved itself. In the morning, after several trials, I found the point of balance in the foremast and attached my hoisting tackle a few feet above it. Maud held the turn on the windlass and coiled down while I heaved. Had the windlass been in order it would not have been so difficult; as it was, I was compelled to apply all my weight and strength to every inch of the heaving. I had to rest frequently. In truth, my spells of resting were longer than those of working. Maud even contrived, at times when all my efforts could not budge the windlass, to hold the turn with one hand and with the other to throw the weight of her slim body to my assistance.

At the end of an hour the single and double blocks came together at the top of the shears. I could hoist no more. And yet the mast was not swung entirely inboard. The butt rested against the outside of the port rail, while the top of the mast overhung the water far beyond the starboard rail. My shears were too short. All my work had been for nothing. But I no longer despaired in the old way. I was acquiring more confidence in myself and more confidence in the possibilities of windlasses, shears, and hoisting tackles. There was a way in which it could be done, and it remained for me to find that way.

While I was considering the problem, Wolf Larsen came on deck. We noticed something strange about him at once. The indecisiveness, or feebleness, of his movements was more pronounced. His walk was actually tottery as he came down the port side of the cabin. At the break of the poop he reeled, raised one hand to his eyes with the familiar brushing gesture, and fell down the steps—still on his feet—to the main deck, across which he staggered, falling and flinging out his arms for support. He regained his balance by the steerage companion-way and stood there dizzily for a space, when he suddenly crumpled up and collapsed, his legs bending under him as he sank to the deck.

"One of his attacks," I whispered to Maud.

She nodded her head; and I could see sympathy warm in eyes.

We went up to him, but he seemed unconscious, breathing spasmodically. She took charge of him, lifting his head to keep the blood out of it and despatching me to the cabin for a pillow. I also brought blankets, and we made him comfortable. I took his pulse. It beat steadily and strong, and was quite normal. This puzzled me. I became suspicious.

"What if he should be feigning this?" I asked, still holding his wrist.

Maud shook her head, and there was reproof in her eyes. But just then the wrist I held leaped from my hand, and the hand clasped like a steel trap about my wrist. I cried aloud in awful fear, a wild inarticulate cry; and I caught one glimpse of his face, malignant and triumphant, as his other hand compassed my body and I was drawn down to him in a terrible grip.

My wrist was released, but his other arm, passed around my back, held both my arms so that I could not move. His free hand went to my throat, and in that moment I knew the bitterest foretaste of death earned by one's own idiocy. Why had I trusted myself within reach of those terrible arms? I could feel other hands at my throat. They were Maud's hands, striving vainly to tear loose the hand that was throttling me. She gave it up, and I heard her scream in a way that cut me to the soul, for it was a woman's scream of fear and heart-breaking despair. I had heard it before, during the sinking of the *Martinez*.

My face was against his chest and I could not see, but I heard Maud turn and run swiftly away along the deck. Everything was happening quickly. I had not yet had a glimmering of unconsciousness, and it seemed that an interminable period of time was lapsing before I heard her feet flying back. And just then I felt the whole man sink under me. The breath was leaving his lungs and his chest was collapsing under my weight. Whether it was merely the expelled breath, or his consciousness of his growing impotence, I know not, but his throat vibrated with a deep groan. The hand at my throat relaxed. I breathed. It fluttered and tightened again. But even his tremendous will could not overcome the dissolution that assailed it. That will of his was breaking down. He was fainting.

Maud's footsteps were very near as his hand fluttered for the last time and my throat was released. I rolled off and over to the deck on my back, gasping and blinking in the sunshine. Maud was pale but composed,—my eyes had gone instantly to her face,—and she was looking at me with mingled alarm and relief. A heavy seal-club in her hand caught my eyes, and at that moment she followed my gaze down to it. The club dropped from her hand as though it had suddenly stung her, and at the same moment my heart surged with a great joy. Truly she was my woman, my mate-woman, fighting with me and for me as the mate of a caveman would have fought, all the primitive in her aroused, forgetful of her culture, hard under the softening civilization of the only life she had ever known.

"Dear woman!" I cried, scrambling to my feet.

The next moment she was in my arms, weeping convulsively on my shoulder while I clasped her close. I looked down at the brown glory of her hair, glinting gems in the sunshine far more precious to me than those in the treasure-chests of kings. And I bent my head and kissed her hair softly, so softly that she did not know.

Then sober thought came to me. After all, she was only a woman, crying her relief, now that the danger was past, in the arms of her protector or of the one who had been endangered. Had I been father or brother, the situation would have been in nowise different. Besides, time and place were not meet, and I wished to earn a better right to declare my love. So once again I softly kissed her hair as I felt her receding from my clasp.

"It was a real attack this time," I said: "another shock like the one that made him blind. He feigned at first, and in doing so brought it on."

Maud was already rearranging his pillow.

"No," I said, "not yet. Now that I have him helpless, helpless he shall remain. From this day we live in the cabin. Wolf Larsen shall live in the steerage."

I caught him under the shoulders and dragged him to the companion-way. At my direction Maud fetched a rope. Placing this under his shoulders, I balanced him across the threshold and lowered him down the steps to the floor. I could not lift him directly into a bunk, but with Maud's help I lifted first his shoulders and head, then his body, balanced him across the edge, and rolled him into a lower bunk.

But this was not to be all. I recollected the handcuffs in his state-room, which he preferred to use on sailors instead of the ancient and clumsy ship irons. So, when we left him, he lay handcuffed hand and foot. For the first time in many days I breathed freely. I felt strangely light as I came on deck, as though a weight had been lifted off my shoulders. I felt, also, that Maud and I had drawn more closely together. And I wondered if she, too, felt it, as we walked along the deck side by side to where the stalled foremast hung in the shears.

CHAPTER XXXVII

At once we moved aboard the *Ghost*, occupying our old state-rooms and cooking in the galley. The imprisonment of Wolf Larsen had happened most opportunely, for what must have been the Indian summer of this high latitude was gone and drizzling stormy weather had set in. We were very comfortable, and the inadequate shears, with the foremast suspended from them, gave a business-like air to the schooner and a promise of departure.

And now that we had Wolf Larsen in irons, how little did we need it! Like his first attack, his second had been accompanied by serious disablement. Maud made the discovery in the afternoon while trying to give him nourishment. He had shown signs of consciousness, and she had spoken to him, eliciting no response. He was lying on his left side at the time, and in evident pain. With a restless movement he rolled his head around, clearing his left ear from the pillow against which it had been pressed. At once he heard and answered her, and at once she came to me.

Pressing the pillow against his left ear, I asked him if he heard me, but he gave no sign. Removing the pillow and, repeating the question he answered promptly that he did.

"Do you know you are deaf in the right ear?" I asked.

"Yes," he answered in a low, strong voice, "and worse than that. My whole right side is affected. It seems asleep. I cannot move arm or leg."

"Feigning again?" I demanded angrily.

He shook his head, his stern mouth shaping the strangest, twisted smile. It was indeed a twisted smile, for it was on the left side only, the facial muscles of the right side moving not at all.

"That was the last play of the Wolf," he said. "I am paralysed. I shall never walk again. Oh, only on the other side," he added, as though divining the suspicious glance I flung at his left leg, the knee of which had just then drawn up, and elevated the blankets.

"It's unfortunate," he continued. "I'd liked to have done for you first, Hump. And I thought I had that much left in me."

"But why?" I asked; partly in horror, partly out of curiosity.

Again his stern mouth framed the twisted smile, as he said:

"Oh, just to be alive, to be living and doing, to be the biggest bit of the ferment to the end, to eat you. But to die this way."

He shrugged his shoulders, or attempted to shrug them, rather, for the left shoulder alone moved. Like the smile, the shrug was twisted.

"But how can you account for it?" I asked. "Where is the seat of your trouble?"

"The brain," he said at once. "It was those cursed headaches brought it on."

"Symptoms," I said.

He nodded his head. "There is no accounting for it. I was never sick in my life. Something's gone wrong with my brain. A cancer, a tumour, or something of that nature,—a thing that devours and destroys. It's attacking my nerve-centres, eating them up, bit by bit, cell by cell—from the pain."

"The motor-centres, too," I suggested.

"So it would seem; and the curse of it is that I must lie here, conscious, mentally unimpaired, knowing that the lines are going down, breaking bit by bit communication with the world. I cannot see, hearing and feeling are leaving me, at this rate I shall soon cease to speak; yet all the time I shall be here, alive, active, and powerless."

"When you say *you* are here, I'd suggest the likelihood of the soul," I said.

"Bosh!" was his retort. "It simply means that in the attack on my brain the higher psychical centres are untouched. I can remember, I can think and reason. When that goes, I go. I am not. The soul?"

He broke out in mocking laughter, then turned his left ear to the pillow as a sign that he wished no further conversation.

Maud and I went about our work oppressed by the fearful fate which had overtaken him,—how fearful we were yet fully to realize. There was the awfulness of retribution about it. Our thoughts were deep and solemn, and we spoke to each other scarcely above whispers.

"You might remove the handcuffs," he said that night, as we stood in consultation over him. "It's dead safe. I'm a paralytic now. The next thing to watch out for is bed sores."

He smiled his twisted smile, and Maud, her eyes wide with horror, was compelled to turn away her head.

"Do you know that your smile is crooked?" I asked him; for I knew that she must attend him, and I wished to save her as much as possible.

"Then I shall smile no more," he said calmly. "I thought something was wrong. My right cheek has been numb all day. Yes, and I've had warnings of this for the last three days; by spells, my right side seemed going to sleep, sometimes arm or hand, sometimes leg or foot."

"So my smile is crooked?" he queried a short while after. "Well, consider henceforth that I smile internally, with my soul, if you please, my soul. Consider that I am smiling now."

And for the space of several minutes he lay there, quiet, indulging his grotesque fancy.

The man of him was not changed. It was the old, indomitable, terrible Wolf Larsen, imprisoned somewhere within that flesh which had once been so invincible and splendid. Now it bound him with insentient fetters, walling his soul in darkness and silence, blocking it from the world which to him had been a riot of action. No more would he conjugate the verb "to do in every mood and tense." "To be" was all that remained to him—to be, as he had defined death, without movement; to will, but not to execute; to think and reason and in the spirit of him to be as alive as ever, but in the flesh to be dead, quite dead.

And yet, though I even removed the handcuffs, we could not adjust ourselves to his condition. Our minds revolted. To us he was full of potentiality. We knew not what to expect of him next, what fearful thing, rising above the flesh, he might break out and do. Our experience warranted this state of mind, and we went about our work with anxiety always upon us.

I had solved the problem which had arisen through the shortness of the shears. By means of the watch-tackle (I had made a new one), I heaved the butt of the foremast across the rail and then lowered it to the deck. Next, by means of the shears, I hoisted the main boom on board. Its forty feet of length would supply the height necessary properly to swing the mast. By means of a secondary tackle I had attached to the shears, I swung the boom to a nearly perpendicular position, then lowered the butt to the deck, where, to prevent slipping, I spiked great cleats around it. The single block of my original shears-tackle I had attached to the end of the boom. Thus, by carrying this tackle to the windlass, I could raise and lower the end of the boom at will, the butt always remaining stationary, and, by means of guys, I could swing the boom from side to side. To the end of the boom I had likewise rigged a hoisting tackle; and when the whole arrangement was completed I could not but be startled by the power and latitude it gave me.

Of course, two days' work was required for the accomplishment of this part of my task, and it was not till the morning of the third day that I swung the foremast from the deck and proceeded to square its butt to fit the step. Here I was especially awkward. I sawed and chopped and chiselled the weathered wood till it had the appearance of having been gnawed by some gigantic mouse. But it fitted.

"It will work, I know it will work," I cried.

"Do you know Dr. Jordan's final test of truth?" Maud asked.

I shook my head and paused in the act of dislodging the shavings which had drifted down my neck.

"Can we make it work? Can we trust our lives to it? is the test."

"He is a favourite of yours," I said.

"When I dismantled my old Pantheon and cast out Napoleon and Cæsar and their fellows, I straightway erected a new Pantheon," she answered gravely, "and the first I installed as Dr. Jordan."

"A modern hero."

"And a greater because modern," she added. "How can the Old World heroes compare with ours?"

I shook my head. We were too much alike in many things for argument. Our points of view and outlook on life at least were very alike.

"For a pair of critics we agree famously," I laughed.

"And as shipwright and able assistant," she laughed back.

But there was little time for laughter in those days, what of our heavy work and of the awfulness of Wolf Larsen's living death.

He had received another stroke. He had lost his voice, or he was losing it. He had only intermittent use of it. As he phrased it, the wires were like the stock market, now up, now down. Occasionally the wires were up and he spoke as well as ever, though slowly and heavily. Then speech would suddenly desert him, in the middle of a sentence perhaps, and for hours, sometimes, we would wait for the connection to be re-established. He complained of great pain in his head, and it was during this period that he arranged a system of communication against the time when speech should leave him altogether—one pressure of the hand for "yes," two for "no." It was well that it was arranged, for by evening his voice had gone from him. By hand pressures, after that, he answered our questions, and when he wished to speak he scrawled his thoughts with his left hand, quite legibly, on a sheet of paper.

The fierce winter had now descended upon us. Gale followed gale, with snow and sleet and rain. The seals had started on their great southern migration, and the rookery was practically deserted. I worked feverishly. In spite of the bad weather, and of the wind which especially hindered me, I was on deck from daylight till dark and making substantial progress.

I profited by my lesson learned through raising the shears and then climbing them to attach the guys. To the top of the foremast, which was just lifted conveniently from the deck, I attached the rigging, stays and throat and peak halyards. As usual, I had underrated the amount of work involved in this portion of the task, and two long days were necessary to complete it. And there was so much yet to be done—the sails, for instance, which practically had to be made over.

While I toiled at rigging the foremast, Maud sewed on canvas, ready always to drop everything and come to my assistance when more hands than two were required. The canvas was heavy and hard, and she sewed with the regular sailor's palm and three-cornered sail-needle. Her hands were soon sadly blistered, but she struggled bravely on, and in addition doing the cooking and taking care of the sick man.

"A fig for superstition," I said on Friday morning. "That mast goes in to-day."

Everything was ready for the attempt. Carrying the boom-tackle to the windlass, I hoisted the mast nearly clear of the deck. Making this tackle fast, I took to the windlass the shears-tackle (which was connected with the end of the boom), and with a few turns had the mast perpendicular and clear.

Maud clapped her hands the instant she was relieved from holding the turn, crying:

"It works! It works! We'll trust our lives to it!"

Then she assumed a rueful expression.

"It's not over the hole," she add. "Will you have to begin all over?"

I smiled in superior fashion, and, slacking off on one of the boom-guys and taking in on the other, swung the mast perfectly in the centre of the deck. Still it was not over the hole. Again the rueful expression came on her face, and again I smiled in a superior way. Slacking away on the boom-tackle and hoisting an equivalent amount on the shears-tackle, I brought the butt of the mast into position directly over the hole in the deck. Then I gave Maud careful instructions for lowering away and went into the hold to the step on the schooner's bottom.

I called to her, and the mast moved easily and accurately. Straight toward the square hole of the step the square butt descended; but as it descended it slowly twisted so that square would not fit into square. But I had not even a moment's indecision. Calling to Maud to cease lowering, I went on deck and made the watch-tackle fast to the mast with a rolling hitch. I left Maud to pull on it while I went below. By the light of the lantern I saw the butt twist slowly around till its sides coincided with the sides of the step. Maud made fast and returned to the windlass. Slowly the butt descended the several intervening inches, at the same time slightly twisting again. Again Maud rectified the twist with the watch-tackle, and again she lowered away from the windlass. Square fitted into square. The mast was stepped.

I raised a shout, and she ran down to see. In the yellow lantern light we peered at what we had accomplished. We looked at each other, and our hands felt their way and clasped. The eyes of both of us, I think, were moist with the joy of success.

"It was done so easily after all," I remarked. "All the work was in the preparation."

"And all the wonder in the completion," Maud added. "I can scarcely bring myself to realize that that great mast is really up and in; that you have lifted it from the water, swung it through the air, and deposited it here where it belongs. It is a Titan's task."

"And they made themselves many inventions," I began merrily, then paused to sniff the air.

I looked hastily at the lantern. It was not smoking. Again I sniffed.

"Something is burning," Maud said, with sudden conviction.

We sprang together for the ladder, but I raced past her to the deck. A dense volume of smoke was pouring out of the steerage companion-way.

"The Wolf is not yet dead," I muttered to myself as I sprang down through the smoke.

It was so thick in the confined space that I was compelled to feel my way; and so potent was the spell of Wolf Larsen on my imagination, I was quite prepared for the helpless giant to grip my neck in a strangle hold. I hesitated, the desire to race back and up the steps to the deck almost overpowering me. Then I recollected Maud. The vision of her, as I had last seen her, in the lantern light of the schooner's hold, her brown eyes warm and moist with joy, flashed before me, and I knew that I could not go back.

I was choking and suffocating by the time I reached Wolf Larsen's bunk. I reached my hand and felt for his. He was lying motionless, but moved slightly at the touch of my hand. I felt over and under his blankets. There was no warmth, no sign of fire. Yet that smoke which blinded me and made me cough and gasp must have a source. I lost my head temporarily and dashed frantically about the steerage. A collision with the table partially knocked the wind from my body and brought me to myself. I reasoned that a helpless man could start a fire only near to where he lay.

I returned to Wolf Larsen's bunk. There I encountered Maud. How long she had been there in that suffocating atmosphere I could not guess.

"Go up on deck!" I commanded peremptorily.

"But, Humphrey—" she began to protest in a queer, husky voice.

"Please! please!" I shouted at her harshly.

She drew away obediently, and then I thought, What if she cannot find the steps? I started after her, to stop at the foot of the companion-way. Perhaps she had gone up. As I stood there, hesitant, I heard her cry softly:

"Oh, Humphrey, I am lost."

I found her fumbling at the wall of the after bulkhead, and, half leading her, half carrying her, I took her up the companion-way. The pure air was like nectar. Maud was only faint and dizzy, and I left her lying on the deck when I took my second plunge below.

CHAPTER XXXVII

The source of the smoke must be very close to Wolf Larsen—my mind was made up to this, and I went straight to his bunk. As I felt about among his blankets, something hot fell on the back of my hand. It burned me, and I jerked my hand away. Then I understood. Through the cracks in the bottom of the upper bunk he had set fire to the mattress. He still retained sufficient use of his left arm to do this. The damp straw of the mattress, fired from beneath and denied air, had been smouldering all the while.

As I dragged the mattress out of the bunk it seemed to disintegrate in mid-air, at the same time bursting into flames. I beat out the burning remnants of straw in the bunk, then made a dash for the deck for fresh air.

Several buckets of water sufficed to put out the burning mattress in the middle of the steerage floor; and ten minutes later, when the smoke had fairly cleared, I allowed Maud to come below. Wolf Larsen was unconscious, but it was a matter of minutes for the fresh air to restore him. We were working over him, however, when he signed for paper and pencil.

"Pray do not interrupt me," he wrote. "I am smiling."

"I am still a bit of the ferment, you see," he wrote a little later.

"I am glad you are as small a bit as you are," I said.

"Thank you," he wrote. "But just think of how much smaller I shall be before I die."

"And yet I am all here, Hump," he wrote with a final flourish. "I can think more clearly than ever in my life before. Nothing to disturb me. Concentration is perfect. I am all here and more than here."

It was like a message from the night of the grave; for this man's body had become his mausoleum. And there, in so strange sepulchre, his spirit fluttered and lived. It would flutter and live till the last line of communication was broken, and after that who was to say how much longer it might continue to flutter and live?

CHAPTER XXXVIII

"I think my left side is going," Wolf Larsen wrote, the morning after his attempt to fire the ship. "The numbness is growing. I can hardly move my hand. You will have to speak louder. The last lines are going down."

"Are you in pain?" I asked.

I was compelled to repeat my question loudly before he answered:

"Not all the time."

The left hand stumbled slowly and painfully across the paper, and it was with extreme difficulty that we deciphered the scrawl. It was like a "spirit message," such as are delivered at séances of spiritualists for a dollar admission.

"But I am still here, all here," the hand scrawled more slowly and painfully than ever.

The pencil dropped, and we had to replace it in the hand.

"When there is no pain I have perfect peace and quiet. I have never thought so clearly. I can ponder life and death like a Hindoo sage."

"And immortality?" Maud queried loudly in the ear.

Three times the hand essayed to write but fumbled hopelessly. The pencil fell. In vain we tried to replace it. The fingers could not close on it. Then Maud pressed and held the fingers about the pencil with her own hand and the hand wrote, in large letters, and so slowly that the minutes ticked off to each letter:

"B-O-S-H."

It was Wolf Larsen's last word, "bosh," sceptical and invincible to the end. The arm and hand relaxed. The trunk of the body moved slightly. Then there was no movement. Maud released the hand. The fingers spread slightly, falling apart of their own weight, and the pencil rolled away.

"Do you still hear?" I shouted, holding the fingers and waiting for the single pressure which would signify "Yes." There was no response. The hand was dead.

"I noticed the lips slightly move," Maud said.

I repeated the question. The lips moved. She placed the tips of her fingers on them. Again I repeated the question. "Yes," Maud announced. We looked at each other expectantly.

"What good is it?" I asked. "What can we say now?"

"Oh, ask him—"

She hesitated.

"Ask him something that requires no for an answer," I suggested. "Then we will know for certainty."

"Are you hungry?" she cried.

The lips moved under her fingers, and she answered, "Yes."

"Will you have some beef?" was her next query.

"No," she announced.

"Beef-tea?"

"Yes, he will have some beef-tea," she said, quietly, looking up at me. "Until his hearing goes we shall be able to communicate with him. And after that—"

She looked at me queerly. I saw her lips trembling and the tears swimming up in her eyes. She swayed toward me and I caught her in my arms.

"Oh, Humphrey," she sobbed, "when will it all end? I am so tired, so tired."

She buried her head on my shoulder, her frail form shaken with a storm of weeping. She was like a feather in my arms, so slender, so ethereal. "She has broken down at last," I thought. "What can I do without her help?"

But I soothed and comforted her, till she pulled herself bravely together and recuperated mentally as quickly as she was wont to do physically.

"I ought to be ashamed of myself," she said. Then added, with the whimsical smile I adored, "but I am only one, small woman."

That phrase, the "one small woman," startled me like an electric shock. It was my own phrase, my pet, secret phrase, my love phrase for her.

"Where did you get that phrase?" I demanded, with an abruptness that in turn startled her.

"What phrase?" she asked.

"One small woman."

"Is it yours?" she asked.

"Yes," I answered. "Mine. I made it."

"Then you must have talked in your sleep," she smiled.

The dancing, tremulous light was in her eyes. Mine, I knew, were speaking beyond the will of my speech. I leaned toward her. Without volition I leaned toward her, as a tree is swayed by the wind. Ah, we were very close together in that moment. But she shook her head, as one might shake off sleep or a dream, saying:

"I have known it all my life. It was my father's name for my mother."

"It is my phrase too," I said stubbornly.

"For your mother?"

"No," I answered, and she questioned no further, though I could have sworn her eyes retained for some time a mocking, teasing expression.

With the foremast in, the work now went on apace. Almost before I knew it, and without one serious hitch, I had the mainmast stepped. A derrick-boom, rigged to the foremast, had accomplished this; and several days more found all stays and shrouds in place, and everything set up taut. Topsails would be a nuisance and a danger for a crew of two, so I heaved the topmasts on deck and lashed them fast.

Several more days were consumed in finishing the sails and putting them on. There were only three—the jib, foresail, and mainsail; and, patched, shortened, and distorted, they were a ridiculously ill-fitting suit for so trim a craft as the *Ghost*.

"But they'll work!" Maud cried jubilantly. "We'll make them work, and trust our lives to them!"

Certainly, among my many new trades, I shone least as a sail-maker. I could sail them better than make them, and I had no doubt of my power to bring the schooner to some northern port of Japan. In fact, I had crammed navigation from text-books aboard; and besides, there was Wolf Larsen's star-scale, so simple a device that a child could work it.

As for its inventor, beyond an increasing deafness and the movement of the lips growing fainter and fainter, there had been little change in his condition for a week. But on the day we finished bending the schooner's sails, he heard his last, and the last movement of his lips died away—but not before I had asked him, "Are you all there?" and the lips had answered, "Yes."

The last line was down. Somewhere within that tomb of the flesh still dwelt the soul of the man. Walled by the living clay, that fierce intelligence we had known burned on; but it burned on in silence and darkness. And it was disembodied. To that intelligence there could be no objective knowledge of a body. It knew no body. The very world was not. It knew only itself and the vastness and profundity of the quiet and the dark.

CHAPTER XXXIX

The day came for our departure. There was no longer anything to detain us on Endeavour Island. The *Ghost's* stumpy masts were in place, her crazy sails bent. All my handiwork was strong, none of it beautiful; but I knew that it would work, and I felt myself a man of power as I looked at it.

"I did it! I did it! With my own hands I did it!" I wanted to cry aloud.

But Maud and I had a way of voicing each other's thoughts, and she said, as we prepared to hoist the mainsail:

"To think, Humphrey, you did it all with your own hands?"

"But there were two other hands," I answered. "Two small hands, and don't say that was a phrase, also, of your father."

She laughed and shook her head, and held her hands up for inspection.

"I can never get them clean again," she wailed, "nor soften the weather-beat."

"Then dirt and weather-beat shall be your guerdon of honour," I said, holding them in mine; and, spite of my resolutions, I would have kissed the two dear hands had she not swiftly withdrawn them.

Our comradeship was becoming tremulous, I had mastered my love long and well, but now it was mastering me. Wilfully had it disobeyed and won my eyes to speech, and now it was winning my tongue—ay, and my lips, for they were mad this moment to kiss the two small hands which had toiled so faithfully and hard. And I, too, was mad. There was a cry in my being like bugles calling me to her. And there was a wind blowing upon me which I could not resist, swaying the very body of me till I leaned toward her, all unconscious that I leaned. And she knew it. She could not but know it as she swiftly drew away her hands, and yet, could not forbear one quick searching look before she turned away her eyes.

By means of deck-tackles I had arranged to carry the halyards forward to the windlass; and now I hoisted the mainsail, peak and throat, at the same time. It was a clumsy way, but it did not take long, and soon the foresail as well was up and fluttering.

"We can never get that anchor up in this narrow place, once it has left the bottom," I said. "We should be on the rocks first."

"What can you do?" she asked.

"Slip it," was my answer. "And when I do, you must do your first work on the windlass. I shall have to run at once to the wheel, and at the same time you must be hoisting the jib."

This manœuvre of getting under way I had studied and worked out a score of times; and, with the jib-halyard to the windlass, I knew Maud was capable of hoisting that most necessary sail. A brisk wind was blowing into the cove, and though the water was calm, rapid work was required to get us safely out.

When I knocked the shackle-bolt loose, the chain roared out through the hawse-hole and into the sea. I raced aft, putting the wheel up. The *Ghost* seemed to start into life as she heeled to the first fill of her sails. The jib was rising. As it filled, the *Ghost's* bow swung off and I had to put the wheel down a few spokes and steady her.

I had devised an automatic jib-sheet which passed the jib across of itself, so there was no need for Maud to attend to that; but she was still hoisting the jib when I put the wheel hard down. It was a moment of anxiety, for the *Ghost* was rushing directly upon the beach, a stone's throw distant. But she swung obediently on her heel into the wind. There was a great fluttering and flapping of canvas and reef-points, most welcome to my ears, then she filled away on the other tack.

Maud had finished her task and come aft, where she stood beside me, a small cap perched on her wind-blown hair, her cheeks flushed from exertion, her eyes wide and bright with the excitement, her nostrils quivering to the rush and bite of the fresh salt air. Her brown eyes were like a startled deer's. There was a wild, keen look in them I had never seen before, and her lips parted and her breath suspended as the *Ghost*, charging upon the wall of rock at the entrance to the inner cove, swept into the wind and filled away into safe water.

My first mate's berth on the sealing grounds stood me in good stead, and I cleared the inner cove and laid a long tack along the shore of the outer cove. Once again about, and the *Ghost* headed out to open sea. She had now caught the bosom-breathing of the ocean, and was herself a-breath with the rhythm of it as she smoothly mounted and slipped down each broad-backed wave. The day had been dull and overcast, but the sun now burst through the clouds, a welcome omen, and shone upon the curving beach where together we had dared the lords of the harem and slain the holluschickie. All Endeavour Island brightened under the sun. Even the grim south-western promontory showed less grim, and here and there, where the sea-spray wet its surface, high lights flashed and dazzled in the sun.

"I shall always think of it with pride," I said to Maud.

She threw her head back in a queenly way but said, "Dear, dear Endeavour Island! I shall always love it."

"And I," I said quickly.

It seemed our eyes must meet in a great understanding, and yet, loath, they struggled away and did not meet.

There was a silence I might almost call awkward, till I broke it, saying:

"See those black clouds to windward. You remember, I told you last night the barometer was falling."

"And the sun is gone," she said, her eyes still fixed upon our island, where we had proved our mastery over matter and attained to the truest comradeship that may fall to man and woman.

"And it's slack off the sheets for Japan!" I cried gaily. "A fair wind and a flowing sheet, you know, or however it goes."

Lashing the wheel I ran forward, eased the fore and mainsheets, took in on the boom-tackles and trimmed everything for the quartering breeze which was ours. It was a fresh breeze, very fresh, but I resolved to run as long as I dared. Unfortunately, when running free, it is impossible to lash the wheel, so I faced an all-night watch. Maud insisted on relieving me, but proved that she had not the strength to steer in a heavy sea, even if she could have gained the wisdom on such short notice. She appeared quite heart-broken over the discovery, but recovered her spirits by coiling down tackles and halyards and all stray ropes. Then there were meals to be cooked in the galley, beds to make, Wolf Larsen to be attended upon, and she finished the day with a grand house-cleaning attack upon the cabin and steerage.

All night I steered, without relief, the wind slowly and steadily increasing and the sea rising. At five in the morning Maud brought me hot coffee and biscuits she had baked, and at seven a substantial and piping hot breakfast put new lift into me.

Throughout the day, and as slowly and steadily as ever, the wind increased. It impressed one with its sullen determination to blow, and blow harder, and keep on blowing. And still the *Ghost* foamed along, racing off the miles till I was certain she was making at least eleven knots. It was too good to lose, but by nightfall I was exhausted. Though in splendid physical trim, a thirty-six-hour trick at the wheel was the limit of my endurance. Besides, Maud begged me to heave to, and I knew, if the wind and sea increased at the same rate during the night, that it would soon be impossible to heave to. So, as twilight deepened, gladly and at the same time reluctantly, I brought the *Ghost* up on the wind.

But I had not reckoned upon the colossal task the reefing of three sails meant for one man. While running away from the wind I had not appreciated its force, but when we ceased to run I learned to my sorrow, and well-nigh to my despair, how fiercely it was really blowing. The wind balked my every effort, ripping the canvas out of my hands and in an instant undoing what I had gained by ten minutes of severest struggle. At eight o'clock I had succeeded only in putting the second reef into the foresail. At eleven o'clock I was no farther along. Blood dripped from every finger-end, while the nails were broken to the quick. From pain and sheer exhaustion I wept in the darkness, secretly, so that Maud should not know.

Then, in desperation, I abandoned the attempt to reef the mainsail and resolved to try the experiment of heaving to under the close-reefed foresail. Three hours more were required to gasket the mainsail and jib, and at two in the morning, nearly dead, the life almost buffeted and worked out of me, I had barely sufficient consciousness to know the experiment was a success. The close-reefed foresail worked. The *Ghost* clung on close to the wind and betrayed no inclination to fall off broadside to the trough.

I was famished, but Maud tried vainly to get me to eat. I dozed with my mouth full of food. I would fall asleep in the act of carrying food to my mouth and waken in torment to find the act yet uncompleted. So sleepily helpless was I that she was compelled to hold me in my chair to prevent my being flung to the floor by the violent pitching of the schooner.

Of the passage from the galley to the cabin I knew nothing. It was a sleep-walker Maud guided and supported. In fact, I was aware of nothing till I awoke, how long after I could not imagine, in my bunk with my boots off. It was dark. I was stiff and lame, and cried out with pain when the bed-clothes touched my poor finger-ends.

Morning had evidently not come, so I closed my eyes and went to sleep again. I did not know it, but I had slept the clock around and it was night again.

Once more I woke, troubled because I could sleep no better. I struck a match and looked at my watch. It marked midnight. And I had not left the deck until three! I should have been puzzled had I not guessed the solution. No wonder I was sleeping brokenly. I had slept twenty-one hours. I listened for a while to the behaviour of the *Ghost*, to the pounding of the seas and the muffled roar of the wind on deck, and then turned over on my ride and slept peacefully until morning.

When I arose at seven I saw no sign of Maud and concluded she was in the galley preparing breakfast. On deck I found the *Ghost* doing splendidly under her patch of canvas. But in the galley, though a fire was burning and water boiling, I found no Maud.

I discovered her in the steerage, by Wolf Larsen's bunk. I looked at him, the man who had been hurled down from the topmost pitch of life to be buried alive and be worse than dead. There seemed a relaxation of his expressionless face which was new. Maud looked at me and I understood.

"His life flickered out in the storm," I said.

"But he still lives," she answered, infinite faith in her voice.

"He had too great strength."

"Yes," she said, "but now it no longer shackles him. He is a free spirit."

"He is a free spirit surely," I answered; and, taking her hand, I led her on deck.

The storm broke that night, which is to say that it diminished as slowly as it had arisen. After breakfast next morning, when I had hoisted Wolf Larsen's body on deck ready for burial, it was still blowing heavily and a large sea was running. The deck was continually awash with the sea which came inboard over the rail and through the scuppers. The wind smote the schooner with a sudden gust, and she heeled over till her lee rail was buried, the roar in her rigging rising in pitch to a shriek. We stood in the water to our knees as I bared my head.

"I remember only one part of the service," I said, "and that is, 'And the body shall be cast into the sea.'"

Maud looked at me, surprised and shocked; but the spirit of something I had seen before was strong upon me, impelling me to give service to Wolf Larsen as Wolf Larsen had once given service to another man. I lifted the end of the hatch cover and the canvas-shrouded body slipped feet first into the sea. The weight of iron dragged it down. It was gone.

"Good-bye, Lucifer, proud spirit," Maud whispered, so low that it was drowned by the shouting of the wind; but I saw the movement of her lips and knew.

As we clung to the lee rail and worked our way aft, I happened to glance to leeward. The *Ghost*, at the moment, was uptossed on a sea, and I caught a clear view of a small steamship two or three miles away, rolling and pitching, head on to the sea, as it steamed toward us. It was painted black, and from the talk of the hunters of their poaching exploits I recognized it as a United States revenue cutter. I pointed it out to Maud and hurriedly led her aft to the safety of the poop.

I started to rush below to the flag-locker, then remembered that in rigging the *Ghost*. I had forgotten to make provision for a flag-halyard.

"We need no distress signal," Maud said. "They have only to see us."

"We are saved," I said, soberly and solemnly. And then, in an exuberance of joy, "I hardly know whether to be glad or not."

I looked at her. Our eyes were not loath to meet. We leaned toward each other, and before I knew it my arms were about her.

"Need I?" I asked.

And she answered, "There is no need, though the telling of it would be sweet, so sweet."

Her lips met the press of mine, and, by what strange trick of the imagination I know not, the scene in the cabin of the *Ghost* flashed upon me, when she had pressed her fingers lightly on my lips and said, "Hush, hush."

"My woman, my one small woman," I said, my free hand petting her shoulder in the way all lovers know though never learn in school.

"My man," she said, looking at me for an instant with tremulous lids which fluttered down and veiled her eyes as she snuggled her head against my breast with a happy little sigh.

I looked toward the cutter. It was very close. A boat was being lowered.

"One kiss, dear love," I whispered. "One kiss more before they come."

"And rescue us from ourselves," she completed, with a most adorable smile, whimsical as I had never seen it, for it was whimsical with love.

THE END

THE IRON HEEL

"At first, this Earth, a stage so gloomed with woe
 You almost sicken at the shifting of the scenes.
And yet be patient. Our Playwright may show
 In some fifth act what this Wild Drama means."

FOREWORD

It cannot be said that the Everhard Manuscript is an important historical document. To the historian it bristles with errors—not errors of fact, but errors of interpretation. Looking back across the seven centuries that have lapsed since Avis Everhard completed her manuscript, events, and the bearings of events, that were confused and veiled to her, are clear to us. She lacked perspective. She was too close to the events she writes about. Nay, she was merged in the events she has described.

Nevertheless, as a personal document, the Everhard Manuscript is of inestimable value. But here again enter error of perspective, and vitiation due to the bias of love. Yet we smile, indeed, and forgive Avis Everhard for the heroic lines upon which she modelled her husband. We know to-day that he was not so colossal, and that he loomed among the events of his times less largely than the Manuscript would lead us to believe.

We know that Ernest Everhard was an exceptionally strong man, but not so exceptional as his wife thought him to be. He was, after all, but one of a large number of heroes who, throughout the world, devoted their lives to the Revolution; though it must be conceded that he did unusual work, especially in his elaboration and interpretation of working-class philosophy. "Proletarian science" and "proletarian philosophy" were his phrases for it, and therein he shows the provincialism of his mind—a defect, however, that was due to the times and that none in that day could escape.

But to return to the Manuscript. Especially valuable is it in communicating to us the FEEL of those terrible times. Nowhere do we find more vividly portrayed the psychology of the persons that lived in that turbulent period embraced between the years 1912 and 1932—their mistakes and ignorance, their doubts and fears and misapprehensions, their ethical delusions, their violent passions, their inconceivable sordidness and selfishness. These are the things that are so hard for us of this enlightened age to understand. History tells us that these things were, and biology and psychology tell us why they were; but history and biology and psychology do not make these things alive. We accept them as facts, but we are left without sympathetic comprehension of them.

This sympathy comes to us, however, as we peruse the Everhard Manuscript. We enter into the minds of the actors in that long-ago world-drama, and for the time being their mental processes are our mental processes. Not alone do we understand Avis Everhard's love for her hero-husband, but we feel, as he felt, in those first days, the vague and terrible loom of the Oligarchy. The Iron Heel (well named) we feel descending upon and crushing mankind.

And in passing we note that that historic phrase, the Iron Heel, originated in Ernest Everhard's mind. This, we may say, is the one moot question that this new-found document clears up. Previous to this, the earliest-known use of the phrase occurred in the pamphlet, "Ye Slaves," written by George Milford and published in December, 1912. This George Milford was an obscure agitator about whom nothing is known, save the one additional bit of information gained from the Manuscript, which mentions that he was shot in the Chicago Commune. Evidently he had heard Ernest Everhard make use of the phrase in some public speech, most probably when he was running for Congress in the fall of 1912. From the Manuscript we learn that Everhard used the phrase at a private dinner in the spring of 1912. This is, without discussion, the earliest-known occasion on which the Oligarchy was so designated.

The rise of the Oligarchy will always remain a cause of secret wonder to the historian and the philosopher. Other great historical events have their place in social evolution. They were inevitable. Their coming could have been predicted with the same certitude that astronomers to-day predict the outcome of the movements of stars. Without these other great historical events, social evolution could not have proceeded. Primitive communism, chattel slavery, serf slavery, and wage slavery were necessary stepping-stones in the evolution of society. But it were ridiculous to assert that the Iron Heel was a necessary stepping-stone. Rather, to-day, is it adjudged a step aside, or a step backward, to the social tyrannies that made the early world a hell, but that were as necessary as the Iron Heel was unnecessary.

Black as Feudalism was, yet the coming of it was inevitable. What else than Feudalism could have followed upon the breakdown of that great centralized governmental machine known as the Roman Empire? Not so, however, with the Iron Heel. In the orderly procedure of social evolution there was no place for it. It was not necessary, and it was not inevitable. It must always remain the great curiosity of history—a whim, a fantasy, an apparition, a thing unexpected and undreamed; and it should serve as a warning to those rash political theorists of to-day who speak with certitude of social processes.

Capitalism was adjudged by the sociologists of the time to be the culmination of bourgeois rule, the ripened fruit of the bourgeois revolution. And we of to-day can but applaud that judgment. Following upon Capitalism, it was held, even by such intellectual and antagonistic giants as Herbert Spencer, that Socialism would come. Out of the decay of self-seeking capitalism, it was held, would arise that flower of the ages, the Brotherhood of Man. Instead of which, appalling alike to us who look back and to those that lived at the time, capitalism, rotten-ripe, sent forth that monstrous offshoot, the Oligarchy.

Too late did the socialist movement of the early twentieth century divine the coming of the Oligarchy. Even as it was divined, the Oligarchy was there—a fact established in blood, a stupendous and awful reality. Nor even then, as the Everhard Manuscript well shows, was any permanence attributed to the Iron Heel. Its overthrow was a matter of a few short years, was the judgment of the revolutionists. It is true, they realized that the Peasant Revolt was unplanned, and that the First Revolt was premature; but they little realized that the Second Revolt, planned and mature, was doomed to equal futility and more terrible punishment.

FOREWORD

It is apparent that Avis Everhard completed the Manuscript during the last days of preparation for the Second Revolt; hence the fact that there is no mention of the disastrous outcome of the Second Revolt. It is quite clear that she intended the Manuscript for immediate publication, as soon as the Iron Heel was overthrown, so that her husband, so recently dead, should receive full credit for all that he had ventured and accomplished. Then came the frightful crushing of the Second Revolt, and it is probable that in the moment of danger, ere she fled or was captured by the Mercenaries, she hid the Manuscript in the hollow oak at Wake Robin Lodge.

Of Avis Everhard there is no further record. Undoubtedly she was executed by the Mercenaries; and, as is well known, no record of such executions was kept by the Iron Heel. But little did she realize, even then, as she hid the Manuscript and prepared to flee, how terrible had been the breakdown of the Second Revolt. Little did she realize that the tortuous and distorted evolution of the next three centuries would compel a Third Revolt and a Fourth Revolt, and many Revolts, all drowned in seas of blood, ere the world-movement of labor should come into its own. And little did she dream that for seven long centuries the tribute of her love to Ernest Everhard would repose undisturbed in the heart of the ancient oak of Wake Robin Lodge.

ANTHONY MEREDITH

Ardis,
November 27, 419 B.O.M.

CHAPTER I - MY EAGLE

The soft summer wind stirs the redwoods, and Wild-Water ripples sweet cadences over its mossy stones. There are butterflies in the sunshine, and from everywhere arises the drowsy hum of bees. It is so quiet and peaceful, and I sit here, and ponder, and am restless. It is the quiet that makes me restless. It seems unreal. All the world is quiet, but it is the quiet before the storm. I strain my ears, and all my senses, for some betrayal of that impending storm. Oh, that it may not be premature! That it may not be premature![1]

Small wonder that I am restless. I think, and think, and I cannot cease from thinking. I have been in the thick of life so long that I am oppressed by the peace and quiet, and I cannot forbear from dwelling upon that mad maelstrom of death and destruction so soon to burst forth. In my ears are the cries of the stricken; and I can see, as I have seen in the past[2], all the marring and mangling of the sweet, beautiful flesh, and the souls torn with violence from proud bodies and hurled to God. Thus do we poor humans attain our ends, striving through carnage and destruction to bring lasting peace and happiness upon the earth.

And then I am lonely. When I do not think of what is to come, I think of what has been and is no more—my Eagle, beating with tireless wings the void, soaring toward what was ever his sun, the flaming ideal of human freedom. I cannot sit idly by and wait the great event that is his making, though he is not here to see. He devoted all the years of his manhood to it, and for it he gave his life. It is his handiwork. He made it[3].

And so it is, in this anxious time of waiting, that I shall write of my husband. There is much light that I alone of all persons living can throw upon his character, and

---

[1] The Second Revolt was largely the work of Ernest Everhard, though he cooperated, of course, with the European leaders. The capture and secret execution of Everhard was the great event of the spring of 1932 A.D. Yet so thoroughly had he prepared for the revolt, that his fellow-conspirators were able, with little confusion or delay, to carry out his plans. It was after Everhard's execution that his wife went to Wake Robin Lodge, a small bungalow in the Sonoma Hills of California.

[2] Without doubt she here refers to the Chicago Commune.

[3] With all respect to Avis Everhard, it must be pointed out that Everhard was but one of many able leaders who planned the Second Revolt. And we to-day, looking back across the centuries, can safely say that even had he lived, the Second Revolt would not have been less calamitous in its outcome than it was.

so noble a character cannot be blazoned forth too brightly. His was a great soul, and, when my love grows unselfish, my chiefest regret is that he is not here to witness to-morrow's dawn. We cannot fail. He has built too stoutly and too surely for that. Woe to the Iron Heel! Soon shall it be thrust back from off prostrate humanity. When the word goes forth, the labor hosts of all the world shall rise. There has been nothing like it in the history of the world. The solidarity of labor is assured, and for the first time will there be an international revolution wide as the world is wide[1].

You see, I am full of what is impending. I have lived it day and night utterly and for so long that it is ever present in my mind. For that matter, I cannot think of my husband without thinking of it. He was the soul of it, and how can I possibly separate the two in thought?

As I have said, there is much light that I alone can throw upon his character. It is well known that he toiled hard for liberty and suffered sore. How hard he toiled and how greatly he suffered, I well know; for I have been with him during these twenty anxious years and I know his patience, his untiring effort, his infinite devotion to the Cause for which, only two months gone, he laid down his life.

I shall try to write simply and to tell here how Ernest Everhard entered my life—how I first met him, how he grew until I became a part of him, and the tremendous changes he wrought in my life. In this way may you look at him through my eyes and learn him as I learned him—in all save the things too secret and sweet for me to tell.

It was in February, 1912, that I first met him, when, as a guest of my father's[2] at dinner, he came to our house in Berkeley. I cannot say that my very first impression of him was favorable. He was one of many at dinner, and in the drawing-room where we gathered and waited for all to arrive, he made a rather incongruous appearance. It was "preacher's night," as my father privately called it, and Ernest was certainly out of place in the midst of the churchmen.

In the first place, his clothes did not fit him. He wore a ready-made suit of dark cloth that was ill adjusted to his body. In fact, no ready-made suit of clothes ever could fit his body. And on this night, as always, the cloth bulged with his muscles, while the coat between the shoulders, what of the heavy shoulder-development, was a

---

[1] The Second Revolt was truly international. It was a colossal plan—too colossal to be wrought by the genius of one man alone. Labor, in all the oligarchies of the world, was prepared to rise at the signal. Germany, Italy, France, and all Australasia were labor countries—socialist states. They were ready to lend aid to the revolution. Gallantly they did; and it was for this reason, when the Second Revolt was crushed, that they, too, were crushed by the united oligarchies of the world, their socialist governments being replaced by oligarchical governments.

[2] John Cunningham, Avis Everhard's father, was a professor at the State University at Berkeley, California. His chosen field was physics, and in addition he did much original research and was greatly distinguished as a scientist. His chief contribution to science was his studies of the electron and his monumental work on the "Identification of Matter and Energy," wherein he established, beyond cavil and for all time, that the ultimate unit of matter and the ultimate unit of force were identical. This idea had been earlier advanced, but not demonstrated, by Sir Oliver Lodge and other students in the new field of radio-activity.

maze of wrinkles. His neck was the neck of a prize-fighter,[1] thick and strong. So this was the social philosopher and ex-horseshoer my father had discovered, was my thought. And he certainly looked it with those bulging muscles and that bull-throat. Immediately I classified him—a sort of prodigy, I thought, a Blind Tom[2] of the working class.

And then, when he shook hands with me! His handshake was firm and strong, but he looked at me boldly with his black eyes—too boldly, I thought. You see, I was a creature of environment, and at that time had strong class instincts. Such boldness on the part of a man of my own class would have been almost unforgivable. I know that I could not avoid dropping my eyes, and I was quite relieved when I passed him on and turned to greet Bishop Morehouse—a favorite of mine, a sweet and serious man of middle age, Christ-like in appearance and goodness, and a scholar as well.

But this boldness that I took to be presumption was a vital clew to the nature of Ernest Everhard. He was simple, direct, afraid of nothing, and he refused to waste time on conventional mannerisms. "You pleased me," he explained long afterward; "and why should I not fill my eyes with that which pleases me?" I have said that he was afraid of nothing. He was a natural aristocrat—and this in spite of the fact that he was in the camp of the non-aristocrats. He was a superman, a blond beast such as Nietzsche[3] has described, and in addition he was aflame with democracy.

In the interest of meeting the other guests, and what of my unfavorable impression, I forgot all about the working-class philosopher, though once or twice at table I noticed him—especially the twinkle in his eye as he listened to the talk first of one minister and then of another. He has humor, I thought, and I almost forgave him his clothes. But the time went by, and the dinner went by, and he never opened his mouth to speak, while the ministers talked interminably about the working class and its relation to the church, and what the church had done and was doing for it. I noticed that my father was annoyed because Ernest did not talk. Once father took advantage of a lull and asked him to say something; but Ernest shrugged his shoulders and with an "I have nothing to say" went on eating salted almonds.

But father was not to be denied. After a while he said:

"We have with us a member of the working class. I am sure that he can present things from a new point of view that will be interesting and refreshing. I refer to Mr. Everhard."

The others betrayed a well-mannered interest, and urged Ernest for a statement of his views. Their attitude toward him was so broadly tolerant and kindly that it was really patronizing. And I saw that Ernest noted it and was amused. He looked slowly about him, and I saw the glint of laughter in his eyes.

---

[1] In that day it was the custom of men to compete for purses of money. They fought with their hands. When one was beaten into insensibility or killed, the survivor took the money.

[2] This obscure reference applies to a blind negro musician who took the world by storm in the latter half of the nineteenth century of the Christian Era.

[3] Friederich Nietzsche, the mad philosopher of the nineteenth century of the Christian Era, who caught wild glimpses of truth, but who, before he was done, reasoned himself around the great circle of human thought and off into madness.

"I am not versed in the courtesies of ecclesiastical controversy," he began, and then hesitated with modesty and indecision.

"Go on," they urged, and Dr. Hammerfield said: "We do not mind the truth that is in any man. If it is sincere," he amended.

"Then you separate sincerity from truth?" Ernest laughed quickly.

Dr. Hammerfield gasped, and managed to answer, "The best of us may be mistaken, young man, the best of us."

Ernest's manner changed on the instant. He became another man.

"All right, then," he answered; "and let me begin by saying that you are all mistaken. You know nothing, and worse than nothing, about the working class. Your sociology is as vicious and worthless as is your method of thinking."

It was not so much what he said as how he said it. I roused at the first sound of his voice. It was as bold as his eyes. It was a clarion-call that thrilled me. And the whole table was aroused, shaken alive from monotony and drowsiness.

"What is so dreadfully vicious and worthless in our method of thinking, young man?" Dr. Hammerfield demanded, and already there was something unpleasant in his voice and manner of utterance.

"You are metaphysicians. You can prove anything by metaphysics; and having done so, every metaphysician can prove every other metaphysician wrong—to his own satisfaction. You are anarchists in the realm of thought. And you are mad cosmos-makers. Each of you dwells in a cosmos of his own making, created out of his own fancies and desires. You do not know the real world in which you live, and your thinking has no place in the real world except in so far as it is phenomena of mental aberration.

"Do you know what I was reminded of as I sat at table and listened to you talk and talk? You reminded me for all the world of the scholastics of the Middle Ages who gravely and learnedly debated the absorbing question of how many angels could dance on the point of a needle. Why, my dear sirs, you are as remote from the intellectual life of the twentieth century as an Indian medicine-man making incantation in the primeval forest ten thousand years ago."

As Ernest talked he seemed in a fine passion; his face glowed, his eyes snapped and flashed, and his chin and jaw were eloquent with aggressiveness. But it was only a way he had. It always aroused people. His smashing, sledge-hammer manner of attack invariably made them forget themselves. And they were forgetting themselves now. Bishop Morehouse was leaning forward and listening intently. Exasperation and anger were flushing the face of Dr. Hammerfield. And others were exasperated, too, and some were smiling in an amused and superior way. As for myself, I found it most enjoyable. I glanced at father, and I was afraid he was going to giggle at the effect of this human bombshell he had been guilty of launching amongst us.

"Your terms are rather vague," Dr. Hammerfield interrupted. "Just precisely what do you mean when you call us metaphysicians?"

"I call you metaphysicians because you reason metaphysically," Ernest went on. "Your method of reasoning is the opposite to that of science. There is no validity to your conclusions. You can prove everything and nothing, and no two of you can agree upon anything. Each of you goes into his own consciousness to explain himself and the universe. As well may you lift yourselves by your own bootstraps as to explain consciousness by consciousness."

"I do not understand," Bishop Morehouse said. "It seems to me that all things of the mind are metaphysical. That most exact and convincing of all sciences, mathematics, is sheerly metaphysical. Each and every thought-process of the scientific reasoner is metaphysical. Surely you will agree with me?"

"As you say, you do not understand," Ernest replied. "The metaphysician reasons deductively out of his own subjectivity. The scientist reasons inductively from the facts of experience. The metaphysician reasons from theory to facts, the scientist reasons from facts to theory. The metaphysician explains the universe by himself, the scientist explains himself by the universe."

"Thank God we are not scientists," Dr. Hammerfield murmured complacently.

"What are you then?" Ernest demanded.

"Philosophers."

"There you go," Ernest laughed. "You have left the real and solid earth and are up in the air with a word for a flying machine. Pray come down to earth and tell me precisely what you do mean by philosophy."

"Philosophy is—" (Dr. Hammerfield paused and cleared his throat)—"something that cannot be defined comprehensively except to such minds and temperaments as are philosophical. The narrow scientist with his nose in a test-tube cannot understand philosophy."

Ernest ignored the thrust. It was always his way to turn the point back upon an opponent, and he did it now, with a beaming brotherliness of face and utterance.

"Then you will undoubtedly understand the definition I shall now make of philosophy. But before I make it, I shall challenge you to point out error in it or to remain a silent metaphysician. Philosophy is merely the widest science of all. Its reasoning method is the same as that of any particular science and of all particular sciences. And by that same method of reasoning, the inductive method, philosophy fuses all particular sciences into one great science. As Spencer says, the data of any particular science are partially unified knowledge. Philosophy unifies the knowledge that is contributed by all the sciences. Philosophy is the science of science, the master science, if you please. How do you like my definition?"

"Very creditable, very creditable," Dr. Hammerfield muttered lamely.

But Ernest was merciless.

"Remember," he warned, "my definition is fatal to metaphysics. If you do not now point out a flaw in my definition, you are disqualified later on from advancing metaphysical arguments. You must go through life seeking that flaw and remaining metaphysically silent until you have found it."

Ernest waited. The silence was painful. Dr. Hammerfield was pained. He was also puzzled. Ernest's sledge-hammer attack disconcerted him. He was not used to the simple and direct method of controversy. He looked appealingly around the table, but no one answered for him. I caught father grinning into his napkin.

"There is another way of disqualifying the metaphysicians," Ernest said, when he had rendered Dr. Hammerfield's discomfiture complete. "Judge them by their works. What have they done for mankind beyond the spinning of airy fancies and the mistaking of their own shadows for gods? They have added to the gayety of mankind, I grant; but what tangible good have they wrought for mankind? They philosophized, if you will pardon my misuse of the word, about the heart as the seat of the emotions, while the scientists were formulating the circulation of the blood. They declaimed about famine and pestilence as being scourges of God, while the scientists were building granaries and draining cities. They builded gods in their own shapes and out of their own desires, while the scientists were building roads and bridges. They were describing the earth as the centre of the universe, while the scientists were discovering America and probing space for the stars and the laws of the stars. In short, the metaphysicians have done nothing, absolutely nothing, for mankind. Step by step, before the advance of science, they have been driven back. As fast as the ascertained facts of science have overthrown their subjective explanations of things, they have made new subjective explanations of things, including explanations of the latest ascertained facts. And this, I doubt not, they will go on doing to the end of time. Gentlemen, a metaphysician is a medicine man. The difference between you and the Eskimo who makes a fur-clad blubber-eating god is merely a difference of several thousand years of ascertained facts. That is all."

"Yet the thought of Aristotle ruled Europe for twelve centuries," Dr. Ballingford announced pompously. "And Aristotle was a metaphysician."

Dr. Ballingford glanced around the table and was rewarded by nods and smiles of approval.

"Your illustration is most unfortunate," Ernest replied. "You refer to a very dark period in human history. In fact, we call that period the Dark Ages. A period wherein science was raped by the metaphysicians, wherein physics became a search for the Philosopher's Stone, wherein chemistry became alchemy, and astronomy became astrology. Sorry the domination of Aristotle's thought!"

Dr. Ballingford looked pained, then he brightened up and said:

"Granted this horrible picture you have drawn, yet you must confess that metaphysics was inherently potent in so far as it drew humanity out of this dark period and on into the illumination of the succeeding centuries."

"Metaphysics had nothing to do with it," Ernest retorted.

"What?" Dr. Hammerfield cried. "It was not the thinking and the speculation that led to the voyages of discovery?"

"Ah, my dear sir," Ernest smiled, "I thought you were disqualified. You have not yet picked out the flaw in my definition of philosophy. You are now on an unsubstantial basis. But it is the way of the metaphysicians, and I forgive you. No, I repeat, metaphysics had nothing to do with it. Bread and butter, silks and jewels, dollars and cents, and, incidentally, the closing up of the overland trade-routes to India, were the things that caused the voyages of discovery. With the fall of Constantinople, in 1453, the Turks blocked the way of the caravans to India. The traders of Europe had to find another route. Here was the original cause for the voyages of discovery. Columbus sailed to find a new route to the Indies. It is so stated in all the history books. Incidentally, new facts were learned about the nature, size, and form of the earth, and the Ptolemaic system went glimmering."

Dr. Hammerfield snorted.

"You do not agree with me?" Ernest queried. "Then wherein am I wrong?"

"I can only reaffirm my position," Dr. Hammerfield retorted tartly. "It is too long a story to enter into now."

"No story is too long for the scientist," Ernest said sweetly. "That is why the scientist gets to places. That is why he got to America."

I shall not describe the whole evening, though it is a joy to me to recall every moment, every detail, of those first hours of my coming to know Ernest Everhard.

Battle royal raged, and the ministers grew red-faced and excited, especially at the moments when Ernest called them romantic philosophers, shadow-projectors, and similar things. And always he checked them back to facts. "The fact, man, the irrefragable fact!" he would proclaim triumphantly, when he had brought one of them a cropper. He bristled with facts. He tripped them up with facts, ambuscaded them with facts, bombarded them with broadsides of facts.

"You seem to worship at the shrine of fact," Dr. Hammerfield taunted him.

"There is no God but Fact, and Mr. Everhard is its prophet," Dr. Ballingford paraphrased.

Ernest smilingly acquiesced.

"I'm like the man from Texas," he said. And, on being solicited, he explained. "You see, the man from Missouri always says, 'You've got to show me.' But the man from Texas says, 'You've got to put it in my hand.' From which it is apparent that he is no metaphysician."

Another time, when Ernest had just said that the metaphysical philosophers could never stand the test of truth, Dr. Hammerfield suddenly demanded:

"What is the test of truth, young man? Will you kindly explain what has so long puzzled wiser heads than yours?"

"Certainly," Ernest answered. His cocksureness irritated them. "The wise heads have puzzled so sorely over truth because they went up into the air after it. Had they remained on the solid earth, they would have found it easily enough—ay, they would have found that they themselves were precisely testing truth with every practical act and thought of their lives."

"The test, the test," Dr. Hammerfield repeated impatiently. "Never mind the preamble. Give us that which we have sought so long—the test of truth. Give it us, and we will be as gods."

There was an impolite and sneering scepticism in his words and manner that secretly pleased most of them at the table, though it seemed to bother Bishop Morehouse.

"Dr. Jordan[1] has stated it very clearly," Ernest said. "His test of truth is: 'Will it work? Will you trust your life to it?'"

"Pish!" Dr. Hammerfield sneered. "You have not taken Bishop Berkeley[2] into account. He has never been answered."

"The noblest metaphysician of them all," Ernest laughed. "But your example is unfortunate. As Berkeley himself attested, his metaphysics didn't work."

Dr. Hammerfield was angry, righteously angry. It was as though he had caught Ernest in a theft or a lie.

---

[1] A noted educator of the late nineteenth and early twentieth centuries of the Christian Era. He was president of the Stanford University, a private benefaction of the times.

[2] An idealistic monist who long puzzled the philosophers of that time with his denial of the existence of matter, but whose clever argument was finally demolished when the new empiric facts of science were philosophically generalized.

"Young man," he trumpeted, "that statement is on a par with all you have uttered to-night. It is a base and unwarranted assumption."

"I am quite crushed," Ernest murmured meekly. "Only I don't know what hit me. You'll have to put it in my hand, Doctor."

"I will, I will," Dr. Hammerfield spluttered. "How do you know? You do not know that Bishop Berkeley attested that his metaphysics did not work. You have no proof. Young man, they have always worked."

"I take it as proof that Berkeley's metaphysics did not work, because—" Ernest paused calmly for a moment. "Because Berkeley made an invariable practice of going through doors instead of walls. Because he trusted his life to solid bread and butter and roast beef. Because he shaved himself with a razor that worked when it removed the hair from his face."

"But those are actual things!" Dr. Hammerfield cried. "Metaphysics is of the mind."

"And they work—in the mind?" Ernest queried softly.

The other nodded.

"And even a multitude of angels can dance on the point of a needle—in the mind," Ernest went on reflectively. "And a blubber-eating, fur-clad god can exist and work—in the mind; and there are no proofs to the contrary—in the mind. I suppose, Doctor, you live in the mind?"

"My mind to me a kingdom is," was the answer.

"That's another way of saying that you live up in the air. But you come back to earth at meal-time, I am sure, or when an earthquake happens along. Or, tell me, Doctor, do you have no apprehension in an earthquake that that incorporeal body of yours will be hit by an immaterial brick?"

Instantly, and quite unconsciously, Dr. Hammerfield's hand shot up to his head, where a scar disappeared under the hair. It happened that Ernest had blundered on an apposite illustration. Dr. Hammerfield had been nearly killed in the Great Earthquake[1] by a falling chimney. Everybody broke out into roars of laughter.

"Well?" Ernest asked, when the merriment had subsided. "Proofs to the contrary?"

And in the silence he asked again, "Well?" Then he added, "Still well, but not so well, that argument of yours."

But Dr. Hammerfield was temporarily crushed, and the battle raged on in new directions. On point after point, Ernest challenged the ministers. When they affirmed that they knew the working class, he told them fundamental truths about the working class that they did not know, and challenged them for disproofs. He gave them facts, always facts, checked their excursions into the air, and brought them back to the solid earth and its facts.

How the scene comes back to me! I can hear him now, with that war-note in his voice, flaying them with his facts, each fact a lash that stung and stung again. And he

[1] The Great Earthquake of 1906 A.D. that destroyed San Francisco.

was merciless. He took no quarter,[1] and gave none. I can never forget the flaying he gave them at the end:

"You have repeatedly confessed to-night, by direct avowal or ignorant statement, that you do not know the working class. But you are not to be blamed for this. How can you know anything about the working class? You do not live in the same locality with the working class. You herd with the capitalist class in another locality. And why not? It is the capitalist class that pays you, that feeds you, that puts the very clothes on your backs that you are wearing to-night. And in return you preach to your employers the brands of metaphysics that are especially acceptable to them; and the especially acceptable brands are acceptable because they do not menace the established order of society."

Here there was a stir of dissent around the table.

"Oh, I am not challenging your sincerity," Ernest continued. "You are sincere. You preach what you believe. There lies your strength and your value—to the capitalist class. But should you change your belief to something that menaces the established order, your preaching would be unacceptable to your employers, and you would be discharged. Every little while some one or another of you is so discharged.[2] Am I not right?"

This time there was no dissent. They sat dumbly acquiescent, with the exception of Dr. Hammerfield, who said:

"It is when their thinking is wrong that they are asked to resign."

"Which is another way of saying when their thinking is unacceptable," Ernest answered, and then went on. "So I say to you, go ahead and preach and earn your pay, but for goodness' sake leave the working class alone. You belong in the enemy's camp. You have nothing in common with the working class. Your hands are soft with the work others have performed for you. Your stomachs are round with the plenitude of eating." (Here Dr. Ballingford winced, and every eye glanced at his prodigious girth. It was said he had not seen his own feet in years.) "And your minds are filled with doctrines that are buttresses of the established order. You are as much mercenaries (sincere mercenaries, I grant) as were the men of the Swiss Guard.[3] Be true to your salt and your hire; guard, with your preaching, the interests of your employers; but do not come down to the working class and serve as false leaders. You cannot honestly be in the two camps at once. The working class has done without you. Believe me, the working class will continue to do without you. And, furthermore, the working class can do better without you than with you."

---

[1] This figure arises from the customs of the times. When, among men fighting to the death in their wild-animal way, a beaten man threw down his weapons, it was at the option of the victor to slay him or spare him.

[2] During this period there were many ministers cast out of the church for preaching unacceptable doctrine. Especially were they cast out when their preaching became tainted with socialism.

[3] The hired foreign palace guards of Louis XVI, a king of France that was beheaded by his people.

CHAPTER II - CHALLENGES.

After the guests had gone, father threw himself into a chair and gave vent to roars of Gargantuan laughter. Not since the death of my mother had I known him to laugh so heartily.

"I'll wager Dr. Hammerfield was never up against anything like it in his life," he laughed. "'The courtesies of ecclesiastical controversy!' Did you notice how he began like a lamb—Everhard, I mean, and how quickly he became a roaring lion? He has a splendidly disciplined mind. He would have made a good scientist if his energies had been directed that way."

I need scarcely say that I was deeply interested in Ernest Everhard. It was not alone what he had said and how he had said it, but it was the man himself. I had never met a man like him. I suppose that was why, in spite of my twenty-four years, I had not married. I liked him; I had to confess it to myself. And my like for him was founded on things beyond intellect and argument. Regardless of his bulging muscles and prize-fighter's throat, he impressed me as an ingenuous boy. I felt that under the guise of an intellectual swashbuckler was a delicate and sensitive spirit. I sensed this, in ways I knew not, save that they were my woman's intuitions.

There was something in that clarion-call of his that went to my heart. It still rang in my ears, and I felt that I should like to hear it again—and to see again that glint of laughter in his eyes that belied the impassioned seriousness of his face. And there were further reaches of vague and indeterminate feelings that stirred in me. I almost loved him then, though I am confident, had I never seen him again, that the vague feelings would have passed away and that I should easily have forgotten him.

But I was not destined never to see him again. My father's new-born interest in sociology and the dinner parties he gave would not permit. Father was not a sociologist. His marriage with my mother had been very happy, and in the researches of his own science, physics, he had been very happy. But when mother died, his own work could not fill the emptiness. At first, in a mild way, he had dabbled in philosophy; then, becoming interested, he had drifted on into economics and sociology. He had a strong sense of justice, and he soon became fired with a passion to redress wrong. It was with gratitude that I hailed these signs of a new interest in life, though I little dreamed what the outcome would be. With the enthusiasm of a boy he plunged excitedly into these new pursuits, regardless of whither they led him.

He had been used always to the laboratory, and so it was that he turned the dining room into a sociological laboratory. Here came to dinner all sorts and conditions of men,—scientists, politicians, bankers, merchants, professors, labor leaders, socialists, and anarchists. He stirred them to discussion, and analyzed their thoughts of life and society.

He had met Ernest shortly prior to the "preacher's night." And after the guests were gone, I learned how he had met him, passing down a street at night and stopping to listen to a man on a soap-box who was addressing a crowd of workingmen. The man on the box was Ernest. Not that he was a mere soap-box orator. He stood high in the councils of the socialist party, was one of the leaders, and was the acknowledged leader in the philosophy of socialism. But he had a certain clear way of stating the abstruse in simple language, was a born expositor and teacher, and was not above the soap-box as a means of interpreting economics to the workingmen.

My father stopped to listen, became interested, effected a meeting, and, after quite an acquaintance, invited him to the ministers' dinner. It was after the dinner that father told me what little he knew about him. He had been born in the working class, though he was a descendant of the old line of Everhards that for over two hundred years had lived in America.[1] At ten years of age he had gone to work in the mills, and later he served his apprenticeship and became a horseshoer. He was self-educated, had taught himself German and French, and at that time was earning a meagre living by translating scientific and philosophical works for a struggling socialist publishing house in Chicago. Also, his earnings were added to by the royalties from the small sales of his own economic and philosophic works.

This much I learned of him before I went to bed, and I lay long awake, listening in memory to the sound of his voice. I grew frightened at my thoughts. He was so unlike the men of my own class, so alien and so strong. His masterfulness delighted me and terrified me, for my fancies wantonly roved until I found myself considering him as a lover, as a husband. I had always heard that the strength of men was an irresistible attraction to women; but he was too strong. "No! no!" I cried out. "It is impossible, absurd!" And on the morrow I awoke to find in myself a longing to see him again. I wanted to see him mastering men in discussion, the war-note in his voice; to see him, in all his certitude and strength, shattering their complacency, shaking them out of their ruts of thinking. What if he did swashbuckle? To use his own phrase, "it worked," it produced effects. And, besides, his swashbuckling was a fine thing to see. It stirred one like the onset of battle.

Several days passed during which I read Ernest's books, borrowed from my father. His written word was as his spoken word, clear and convincing. It was its absolute simplicity that convinced even while one continued to doubt. He had the gift of lucidity. He was the perfect expositor. Yet, in spite of his style, there was much that I did not like. He laid too great stress on what he called the class struggle, the antagonism between labor and capital, the conflict of interest.

Father reported with glee Dr. Hammerfield's judgment of Ernest, which was to the effect that he was "an insolent young puppy, made bumptious by a little and very inadequate learning." Also, Dr. Hammerfield declined to meet Ernest again.

---

[1] The distinction between being native born and foreign born was sharp and invidious in those days.

CHAPTER II - CHALLENGES.

But Bishop Morehouse turned out to have become interested in Ernest, and was anxious for another meeting. "A strong young man," he said; "and very much alive, very much alive. But he is too sure, too sure."

Ernest came one afternoon with father. The Bishop had already arrived, and we were having tea on the veranda. Ernest's continued presence in Berkeley, by the way, was accounted for by the fact that he was taking special courses in biology at the university, and also that he was hard at work on a new book entitled "Philosophy and Revolution." [1]

The veranda seemed suddenly to have become small when Ernest arrived. Not that he was so very large—he stood only five feet nine inches; but that he seemed to radiate an atmosphere of largeness. As he stopped to meet me, he betrayed a certain slight awkwardness that was strangely at variance with his bold-looking eyes and his firm, sure hand that clasped for a moment in greeting. And in that moment his eyes were just as steady and sure. There seemed a question in them this time, and as before he looked at me over long.

"I have been reading your 'Working-class Philosophy,'" I said, and his eyes lighted in a pleased way.

"Of course," he answered, "you took into consideration the audience to which it was addressed."

"I did, and it is because I did that I have a quarrel with you," I challenged.

"I, too, have a quarrel with you, Mr. Everhard," Bishop Morehouse said.

Ernest shrugged his shoulders whimsically and accepted a cup of tea.

The Bishop bowed and gave me precedence.

"You foment class hatred," I said. "I consider it wrong and criminal to appeal to all that is narrow and brutal in the working class. Class hatred is anti-social, and, it seems to me, anti-socialistic."

"Not guilty," he answered. "Class hatred is neither in the text nor in the spirit of anything I have every written."

"Oh!" I cried reproachfully, and reached for his book and opened it.

He sipped his tea and smiled at me while I ran over the pages.

"Page one hundred and thirty-two," I read aloud: "'The class struggle, therefore, presents itself in the present stage of social development between the wage-paying and the wage-paid classes.'"

I looked at him triumphantly.

"No mention there of class hatred," he smiled back.

"But," I answered, "you say 'class struggle.'"

"A different thing from class hatred," he replied. "And, believe me, we foment no hatred. We say that the class struggle is a law of social development. We are not responsible for it. We do not make the class struggle. We merely explain it, as Newton explained gravitation. We explain the nature of the conflict of interest that produces the class struggle."

"But there should be no conflict of interest!" I cried.

---

[1] This book continued to be secretly printed throughout the three centuries of the Iron Heel. There are several copies of various editions in the National Library of Ardis.

"I agree with you heartily," he answered. "That is what we socialists are trying to bring about,—the abolition of the conflict of interest. Pardon me. Let me read an extract." He took his book and turned back several pages. "Page one hundred and twenty-six: 'The cycle of class struggles which began with the dissolution of rude, tribal communism and the rise of private property will end with the passing of private property in the means of social existence.'"

"But I disagree with you," the Bishop interposed, his pale, ascetic face betraying by a faint glow the intensity of his feelings. "Your premise is wrong. There is no such thing as a conflict of interest between labor and capital—or, rather, there ought not to be."

"Thank you," Ernest said gravely. "By that last statement you have given me back my premise."

"But why should there be a conflict?" the Bishop demanded warmly.

Ernest shrugged his shoulders. "Because we are so made, I guess."

"But we are not so made!" cried the other.

"Are you discussing the ideal man?" Ernest asked, "—unselfish and godlike, and so few in numbers as to be practically non-existent, or are you discussing the common and ordinary average man?"

"The common and ordinary man," was the answer.

"Who is weak and fallible, prone to error?"

Bishop Morehouse nodded.

"And petty and selfish?"

Again he nodded.

"Watch out!" Ernest warned. "I said 'selfish.'"

"The average man IS selfish," the Bishop affirmed valiantly.

"Wants all he can get?"

"Wants all he can get—true but deplorable."

"Then I've got you." Ernest's jaw snapped like a trap. "Let me show you. Here is a man who works on the street railways."

"He couldn't work if it weren't for capital," the Bishop interrupted.

"True, and you will grant that capital would perish if there were no labor to earn the dividends."

The Bishop was silent.

"Won't you?" Ernest insisted.

The Bishop nodded.

"Then our statements cancel each other," Ernest said in a matter-of-fact tone, "and we are where we were. Now to begin again. The workingmen on the street railway furnish the labor. The stockholders furnish the capital. By the joint effort of the workingmen and the capital, money is earned.[1] They divide between them this money that is earned. Capital's share is called 'dividends.' Labor's share is called 'wages.'"

"Very good," the Bishop interposed. "And there is no reason that the division should not be amicable."

---

[1] In those days, groups of predatory individuals controlled all the means of transportation, and for the use of same levied toll upon the public.

"You have already forgotten what we had agreed upon," Ernest replied. "We agreed that the average man is selfish. He is the man that is. You have gone up in the air and are arranging a division between the kind of men that ought to be but are not. But to return to the earth, the workingman, being selfish, wants all he can get in the division. The capitalist, being selfish, wants all he can get in the division. When there is only so much of the same thing, and when two men want all they can get of the same thing, there is a conflict of interest between labor and capital. And it is an irreconcilable conflict. As long as workingmen and capitalists exist, they will continue to quarrel over the division. If you were in San Francisco this afternoon, you'd have to walk. There isn't a street car running."

"Another strike?"[1] the Bishop queried with alarm.

"Yes, they're quarrelling over the division of the earnings of the street railways."

Bishop Morehouse became excited.

"It is wrong!" he cried. "It is so short-sighted on the part of the workingmen. How can they hope to keep our sympathy—"

"When we are compelled to walk," Ernest said slyly.

But Bishop Morehouse ignored him and went on:

"Their outlook is too narrow. Men should be men, not brutes. There will be violence and murder now, and sorrowing widows and orphans. Capital and labor should be friends. They should work hand in hand and to their mutual benefit."

"Ah, now you are up in the air again," Ernest remarked dryly. "Come back to earth. Remember, we agreed that the average man is selfish."

"But he ought not to be!" the Bishop cried.

"And there I agree with you," was Ernest's rejoinder. "He ought not to be selfish, but he will continue to be selfish as long as he lives in a social system that is based on pig-ethics."

The Bishop was aghast, and my father chuckled.

"Yes, pig-ethics," Ernest went on remorselessly. "That is the meaning of the capitalist system. And that is what your church is standing for, what you are preaching for every time you get up in the pulpit. Pig-ethics! There is no other name for it."

Bishop Morehouse turned appealingly to my father, but he laughed and nodded his head.

"I'm afraid Mr. Everhard is right," he said. "LAISSEZ-FAIRE, the let-alone policy of each for himself and devil take the hindmost. As Mr. Everhard said the other night, the function you churchmen perform is to maintain the established order of society, and society is established on that foundation."

"But that is not the teaching of Christ!" cried the Bishop.

"The Church is not teaching Christ these days," Ernest put in quickly. "That is why the workingmen will have nothing to do with the Church. The Church condones

---

[1] These quarrels were very common in those irrational and anarchic times. Sometimes the laborers refused to work. Sometimes the capitalists refused to let the laborers work. In the violence and turbulence of such disagreements much property was destroyed and many lives lost. All this is inconceivable to us—as inconceivable as another custom of that time, namely, the habit the men of the lower classes had of breaking the furniture when they quarrelled with their wives.

the frightful brutality and savagery with which the capitalist class treats the working class."

"The Church does not condone it," the Bishop objected.

"The Church does not protest against it," Ernest replied. "And in so far as the Church does not protest, it condones, for remember the Church is supported by the capitalist class."

"I had not looked at it in that light," the Bishop said naively. "You must be wrong. I know that there is much that is sad and wicked in this world. I know that the Church has lost the—what you call the proletariat." [1]

"You never had the proletariat," Ernest cried. "The proletariat has grown up outside the Church and without the Church."

"I do not follow you," the Bishop said faintly.

"Then let me explain. With the introduction of machinery and the factory system in the latter part of the eighteenth century, the great mass of the working people was separated from the land. The old system of labor was broken down. The working people were driven from their villages and herded in factory towns. The mothers and children were put to work at the new machines. Family life ceased. The conditions were frightful. It is a tale of blood."

"I know, I know," Bishop Morehouse interrupted with an agonized expression on his face. "It was terrible. But it occurred a century and a half ago."

"And there, a century and a half ago, originated the modern proletariat," Ernest continued. "And the Church ignored it. While a slaughter-house was made of the nation by the capitalist, the Church was dumb. It did not protest, as to-day it does not protest. As Austin Lewis[2] says, speaking of that time, those to whom the command 'Feed my lambs' had been given, saw those lambs sold into slavery and worked to death without a protest.[3] The Church was dumb, then, and before I go on I want you either flatly to agree with me or flatly to disagree with me. Was the Church dumb then?"

Bishop Morehouse hesitated. Like Dr. Hammerfield, he was unused to this fierce "infighting," as Ernest called it.

"The history of the eighteenth century is written," Ernest prompted. "If the Church was not dumb, it will be found not dumb in the books."

"I am afraid the Church was dumb," the Bishop confessed.

"And the Church is dumb to-day."

"There I disagree," said the Bishop.

---

[1] Proletariat: Derived originally from the Latin PROLETARII, the name given in the census of Servius Tullius to those who were of value to the state only as the rearers of offspring (PROLES); in other words, they were of no importance either for wealth, or position, or exceptional ability.

[2] Candidate for Governor of California on the Socialist ticket in the fall election of 1906 Christian Era. An Englishman by birth, a writer of many books on political economy and philosophy, and one of the Socialist leaders of the times.

[3] There is no more horrible page in history than the treatment of the child and women slaves in the English factories in the latter half of the eighteenth century of the Christian Era. In such industrial hells arose some of the proudest fortunes of that day.

CHAPTER II - CHALLENGES.

Ernest paused, looked at him searchingly, and accepted the challenge.

"All right," he said. "Let us see. In Chicago there are women who toil all the week for ninety cents. Has the Church protested?"

"This is news to me," was the answer. "Ninety cents per week! It is horrible!"

"Has the Church protested?" Ernest insisted.

"The Church does not know." The Bishop was struggling hard.

"Yet the command to the Church was, 'Feed my lambs,'" Ernest sneered. And then, the next moment, "Pardon my sneer, Bishop. But can you wonder that we lose patience with you? When have you protested to your capitalistic congregations at the working of children in the Southern cotton mills?[1] Children, six and seven years of age, working every night at twelve-hour shifts? They never see the blessed sunshine. They die like flies. The dividends are paid out of their blood. And out of the dividends magnificent churches are builded in New England, wherein your kind preaches pleasant platitudes to the sleek, full-bellied recipients of those dividends."

"I did not know," the Bishop murmured faintly. His face was pale, and he seemed suffering from nausea.

"Then you have not protested?"

The Bishop shook his head.

"Then the Church is dumb to-day, as it was in the eighteenth century?"

---

[1] Everhard might have drawn a better illustration from the Southern Church's outspoken defence of chattel slavery prior to what is known as the "War of the Rebellion." Several such illustrations, culled from the documents of the times, are here appended. In 1835 A.D., the General Assembly of the Presbyterian Church resolved that: "slavery is recognized in both the Old and the New Testaments, and is not condemned by the authority of God." The Charleston Baptist Association issued the following, in an address, in 1835 A.D.: "The right of masters to dispose of the time of their slaves has been distinctly recognized by the Creator of all things, who is surely at liberty to vest the right of property over any object whomsoever He pleases." The Rev. E. D. Simon, Doctor of Divinity and professor in the Randolph-Macon Methodist College of Virginia, wrote: "Extracts from Holy Writ unequivocally assert the right of property in slaves, together with the usual incidents to that right. The right to buy and sell is clearly stated. Upon the whole, then, whether we consult the Jewish policy instituted by God himself, or the uniform opinion and practice of mankind in all ages, or the injunctions of the New Testament and the moral law, we are brought to the conclusion that slavery is not immoral. Having established the point that the first African slaves were legally brought into bondage, the right to detain their children in bondage follows as an indispensable consequence. Thus we see that the slavery that exists in America was founded in right."

It is not at all remarkable that this same note should have been struck by the Church a generation or so later in relation to the defence of capitalistic property. In the great museum at Asgard there is a book entitled "Essays in Application," written by Henry van Dyke. The book was published in 1905 of the Christian Era. From what we can make out, Van Dyke must have been a churchman. The book is a good example of what Everhard would have called bourgeois thinking. Note the similarity between the utterance of the Charleston Baptist Association quoted above, and the following utterance of Van Dyke seventy years later: "The Bible teaches that God owns the world. He distributes to every man according to His own good pleasure, conformably to general laws."

The Bishop was silent, and for once Ernest forbore to press the point.

"And do not forget, whenever a churchman does protest, that he is discharged."

"I hardly think that is fair," was the objection.

"Will you protest?" Ernest demanded.

"Show me evils, such as you mention, in our own community, and I will protest."

"I'll show you," Ernest said quietly. "I am at your disposal. I will take you on a journey through hell."

"And I shall protest." The Bishop straightened himself in his chair, and over his gentle face spread the harshness of the warrior. "The Church shall not be dumb!"

"You will be discharged," was the warning.

"I shall prove the contrary," was the retort. "I shall prove, if what you say is so, that the Church has erred through ignorance. And, furthermore, I hold that whatever is horrible in industrial society is due to the ignorance of the capitalist class. It will mend all that is wrong as soon as it receives the message. And this message it shall be the duty of the Church to deliver."

Ernest laughed. He laughed brutally, and I was driven to the Bishop's defence.

"Remember," I said, "you see but one side of the shield. There is much good in us, though you give us credit for no good at all. Bishop Morehouse is right. The industrial wrong, terrible as you say it is, is due to ignorance. The divisions of society have become too widely separated."

"The wild Indian is not so brutal and savage as the capitalist class," he answered; and in that moment I hated him.

"You do not know us," I answered. "We are not brutal and savage."

"Prove it," he challenged.

"How can I prove it . . . to you?" I was growing angry.

He shook his head. "I do not ask you to prove it to me. I ask you to prove it to yourself."

"I know," I said.

"You know nothing," was his rude reply.

"There, there, children," father said soothingly.

"I don't care—" I began indignantly, but Ernest interrupted.

"I understand you have money, or your father has, which is the same thing—money invested in the Sierra Mills."

"What has that to do with it?" I cried.

"Nothing much," he began slowly, "except that the gown you wear is stained with blood. The food you eat is a bloody stew. The blood of little children and of strong men is dripping from your very roof-beams. I can close my eyes, now, and hear it drip, drop, drip, drop, all about me."

And suiting the action to the words, he closed his eyes and leaned back in his chair. I burst into tears of mortification and hurt vanity. I had never been so brutally treated in my life. Both the Bishop and my father were embarrassed and perturbed. They tried to lead the conversation away into easier channels; but Ernest opened his eyes, looked at me, and waved them aside. His mouth was stern, and his eyes too; and in the latter there was no glint of laughter. What he was about to say, what terrible castigation he was going to give me, I never knew; for at that moment a man, passing along the sidewalk, stopped and glanced in at us. He was a large man, poorly dressed, and on his back was a great load of rattan and bamboo stands, chairs, and screens. He looked at the house as if debating whether or not he should come in and try to sell some of his wares.

"That man's name is Jackson," Ernest said.

"With that strong body of his he should be at work, and not peddling,"[1] I answered curtly.

"Notice the sleeve of his left arm," Ernest said gently.

I looked, and saw that the sleeve was empty.

"It was some of the blood from that arm that I heard dripping from your roof-beams," Ernest said with continued gentleness. "He lost his arm in the Sierra Mills, and like a broken-down horse you turned him out on the highway to die. When I say 'you,' I mean the superintendent and the officials that you and the other stockholders pay to manage the mills for you. It was an accident. It was caused by his trying to save the company a few dollars. The toothed drum of the picker caught his arm. He might have let the small flint that he saw in the teeth go through. It would have smashed out a double row of spikes. But he reached for the flint, and his arm was picked and clawed to shreds from the finger tips to the shoulder. It was at night. The mills were working overtime. They paid a fat dividend that quarter. Jackson had been working many hours, and his muscles had lost their resiliency and snap. They made his movements a bit slow. That was why the machine caught him. He had a wife and three children."

"And what did the company do for him?" I asked.

"Nothing. Oh, yes, they did do something. They successfully fought the damage suit he brought when he came out of hospital. The company employs very efficient lawyers, you know."

"You have not told the whole story," I said with conviction. "Or else you do not know the whole story. Maybe the man was insolent."

"Insolent! Ha! ha!" His laughter was Mephistophelian. "Great God! Insolent! And with his arm chewed off! Nevertheless he was a meek and lowly servant, and there is no record of his having been insolent."

"But the courts," I urged. "The case would not have been decided against him had there been no more to the affair than you have mentioned."

"Colonel Ingram is leading counsel for the company. He is a shrewd lawyer." Ernest looked at me intently for a moment, then went on. "I'll tell you what you do, Miss Cunningham. You investigate Jackson's case."

"I had already determined to," I said coldly.

"All right," he beamed good-naturedly, "and I'll tell you where to find him. But I tremble for you when I think of all you are to prove by Jackson's arm."

And so it came about that both the Bishop and I accepted Ernest's challenges. They went away together, leaving me smarting with a sense of injustice that had been done me and my class. The man was a beast. I hated him, then, and consoled myself

---

[1] In that day there were many thousands of these poor merchants called PEDLERS. They carried their whole stock in trade from door to door. It was a most wasteful expenditure of energy. Distribution was as confused and irrational as the whole general system of society.

with the thought that his behavior was what was to be expected from a man of the working class.

CHAPTER III - JACKSON'S ARM.

Little did I dream the fateful part Jackson's arm was to play in my life. Jackson himself did not impress me when I hunted him out. I found him in a crazy, ramshackle[1] house down near the bay on the edge of the marsh. Pools of stagnant water stood around the house, their surfaces covered with a green and putrid-looking scum, while the stench that arose from them was intolerable.

I found Jackson the meek and lowly man he had been described. He was making some sort of rattan-work, and he toiled on stolidly while I talked with him. But in spite of his meekness and lowliness, I fancied I caught the first note of a nascent bitterness in him when he said:

"They might a-given me a job as watchman,[2] anyway."

I got little out of him. He struck me as stupid, and yet the deftness with which he worked with his one hand seemed to belie his stupidity. This suggested an idea to me.

"How did you happen to get your arm caught in the machine?" I asked.

He looked at me in a slow and pondering way, and shook his head. "I don't know. It just happened."

"Carelessness?" I prompted.

"No," he answered, "I ain't for callin' it that. I was workin' overtime, an' I guess I was tired out some. I worked seventeen years in them mills, an' I've took notice that most of the accidents happens just before whistle-blow.[3] I'm willin' to bet that more accidents happens in the hour before whistle-blow than in all the rest of the day. A

---

[1] An adjective descriptive of ruined and dilapidated houses in which great numbers of the working people found shelter in those days. They invariably paid rent, and, considering the value of such houses, enormous rent, to the landlords.

[2] In those days thievery was incredibly prevalent. Everybody stole property from everybody else. The lords of society stole legally or else legalized their stealing, while the poorer classes stole illegally. Nothing was safe unless guarded. Enormous numbers of men were employed as watchmen to protect property. The houses of the well-to-do were a combination of safe deposit vault and fortress. The appropriation of the personal belongings of others by our own children of to-day is looked upon as a rudimentary survival of the theft-characteristic that in those early times was universal.

[3] The laborers were called to work and dismissed by savage, screaming, nerve-racking steam-whistles.

man ain't so quick after workin' steady for hours. I've seen too many of 'em cut up an' gouged an' chawed not to know."

"Many of them?" I queried.

"Hundreds an' hundreds, an' children, too."

With the exception of the terrible details, Jackson's story of his accident was the same as that I had already heard. When I asked him if he had broken some rule of working the machinery, he shook his head.

"I chucked off the belt with my right hand," he said, "an' made a reach for the flint with my left. I didn't stop to see if the belt was off. I thought my right hand had done it—only it didn't. I reached quick, and the belt wasn't all the way off. And then my arm was chewed off."

"It must have been painful," I said sympathetically.

"The crunchin' of the bones wasn't nice," was his answer.

His mind was rather hazy concerning the damage suit. Only one thing was clear to him, and that was that he had not got any damages. He had a feeling that the testimony of the foremen and the superintendent had brought about the adverse decision of the court. Their testimony, as he put it, "wasn't what it ought to have ben." And to them I resolved to go.

One thing was plain, Jackson's situation was wretched. His wife was in ill health, and he was unable to earn, by his rattan-work and peddling, sufficient food for the family. He was back in his rent, and the oldest boy, a lad of eleven, had started to work in the mills.

"They might a-given me that watchman's job," were his last words as I went away.

By the time I had seen the lawyer who had handled Jackson's case, and the two foremen and the superintendent at the mills who had testified, I began to feel that there was something after all in Ernest's contention.

He was a weak and inefficient-looking man, the lawyer, and at sight of him I did not wonder that Jackson's case had been lost. My first thought was that it had served Jackson right for getting such a lawyer. But the next moment two of Ernest's statements came flashing into my consciousness: "The company employs very efficient lawyers" and "Colonel Ingram is a shrewd lawyer." I did some rapid thinking. It dawned upon me that of course the company could afford finer legal talent than could a workingman like Jackson. But this was merely a minor detail. There was some very good reason, I was sure, why Jackson's case had gone against him.

"Why did you lose the case?" I asked.

The lawyer was perplexed and worried for a moment, and I found it in my heart to pity the wretched little creature. Then he began to whine. I do believe his whine was congenital. He was a man beaten at birth. He whined about the testimony. The witnesses had given only the evidence that helped the other side. Not one word could he get out of them that would have helped Jackson. They knew which side their bread was buttered on. Jackson was a fool. He had been brow-beaten and confused by Colonel Ingram. Colonel Ingram was brilliant at cross-examination. He had made Jackson answer damaging questions.

"How could his answers be damaging if he had the right on his side?" I demanded.

"What's right got to do with it?" he demanded back. "You see all those books." He moved his hand over the array of volumes on the walls of his tiny office. "All my reading and studying of them has taught me that law is one thing and right is another thing. Ask any lawyer. You go to Sunday-school to learn what is right. But you go to those books to learn . . . law."

"Do you mean to tell me that Jackson had the right on his side and yet was beaten?" I queried tentatively. "Do you mean to tell me that there is no justice in Judge Caldwell's court?"

The little lawyer glared at me a moment, and then the belligerence faded out of his face.

"I hadn't a fair chance," he began whining again. "They made a fool out of Jackson and out of me, too. What chance had I? Colonel Ingram is a great lawyer. If he wasn't great, would he have charge of the law business of the Sierra Mills, of the Erston Land Syndicate, of the Berkeley Consolidated, of the Oakland, San Leandro, and Pleasanton Electric? He's a corporation lawyer, and corporation lawyers are not paid for being fools.[1] What do you think the Sierra Mills alone give him twenty thousand dollars a year for? Because he's worth twenty thousand dollars a year to them, that's what for. I'm not worth that much. If I was, I wouldn't be on the outside, starving and taking cases like Jackson's. What do you think I'd have got if I'd won Jackson's case?"

"You'd have robbed him, most probably," I answered.

"Of course I would," he cried angrily. "I've got to live, haven't I?" [2]

"He has a wife and children," I chided.

"So have I a wife and children," he retorted. "And there's not a soul in this world except myself that cares whether they starve or not."

His face suddenly softened, and he opened his watch and showed me a small photograph of a woman and two little girls pasted inside the case.

"There they are. Look at them. We've had a hard time, a hard time. I had hoped to send them away to the country if I'd won Jackson's case. They're not healthy here, but I can't afford to send them away."

When I started to leave, he dropped back into his whine.

"I hadn't the ghost of a chance. Colonel Ingram and Judge Caldwell are pretty friendly. I'm not saying that if I'd got the right kind of testimony out of their witnesses on cross-examination, that friendship would have decided the case. And yet I must say that Judge Caldwell did a whole lot to prevent my getting that very testimony. Why, Judge Caldwell and Colonel Ingram belong to the same lodge and the same club. They live in the same neighborhood—one I can't afford. And their wives are

---

[1] The function of the corporation lawyer was to serve, by corrupt methods, the money-grabbing propensities of the corporations. It is on record that Theodore Roosevelt, at that time President of the United States, said in 1905 A.D., in his address at Harvard Commencement: "We all know that, as things actually are, many of the most influential and most highly remunerated members of the Bar in every centre of wealth, make it their special task to work out bold and ingenious schemes by which their wealthy clients, individual or corporate, can evade the laws which were made to regulate, in the interests of the public, the uses of great wealth."

[2] A typical illustration of the internecine strife that permeated all society. Men preyed upon one another like ravening wolves. The big wolves ate the little wolves, and in the social pack Jackson was one of the least of the little wolves.

always in and out of each other's houses. They're always having whist parties and such things back and forth."

"And yet you think Jackson had the right of it?" I asked, pausing for the moment on the threshold.

"I don't think; I know it," was his answer. "And at first I thought he had some show, too. But I didn't tell my wife. I didn't want to disappoint her. She had her heart set on a trip to the country hard enough as it was."

"Why did you not call attention to the fact that Jackson was trying to save the machinery from being injured?" I asked Peter Donnelly, one of the foremen who had testified at the trial.

He pondered a long time before replying. Then he cast an anxious look about him and said:

"Because I've a good wife an' three of the sweetest children ye ever laid eyes on, that's why."

"I do not understand," I said.

"In other words, because it wouldn't a-ben healthy," he answered.

"You mean—" I began.

But he interrupted passionately.

"I mean what I said. It's long years I've worked in the mills. I began as a little lad on the spindles. I worked up ever since. It's by hard work I got to my present exalted position. I'm a foreman, if you please. An' I doubt me if there's a man in the mills that'd put out a hand to drag me from drownin'. I used to belong to the union. But I've stayed by the company through two strikes. They called me 'scab.' There's not a man among 'em to-day to take a drink with me if I asked him. D'ye see the scars on me head where I was struck with flying bricks? There ain't a child at the spindles but what would curse me name. Me only friend is the company. It's not me duty, but me bread an' butter an' the life of me children to stand by the mills. That's why."

"Was Jackson to blame?" I asked.

"He should a-got the damages. He was a good worker an' never made trouble."

"Then you were not at liberty to tell the whole truth, as you had sworn to do?"

He shook his head.

"The truth, the whole truth, and nothing but the truth?" I said solemnly.

Again his face became impassioned, and he lifted it, not to me, but to heaven.

"I'd let me soul an' body burn in everlastin' hell for them children of mine," was his answer.

Henry Dallas, the superintendent, was a vulpine-faced creature who regarded me insolently and refused to talk. Not a word could I get from him concerning the trial and his testimony. But with the other foreman I had better luck. James Smith was a hard-faced man, and my heart sank as I encountered him. He, too, gave me the impression that he was not a free agent, as we talked I began to see that he was mentally superior to the average of his kind. He agreed with Peter Donnelly that Jackson should have got damages, and he went farther and called the action heartless and cold-blooded that had turned the worker adrift after he had been made helpless by the accident. Also, he explained that there were many accidents in the mills, and that the company's policy was to fight to the bitter end all consequent damage suits.

"It means hundreds of thousands a year to the stockholders," he said; and as he spoke I remembered the last dividend that had been paid my father, and the pretty gown for me and the books for him that had been bought out of that dividend. I remembered Ernest's charge that my gown was stained with blood, and my flesh began to crawl underneath my garments.

"When you testified at the trial, you didn't point out that Jackson received his accident through trying to save the machinery from damage?" I said.

"No, I did not," was the answer, and his mouth set bitterly. "I testified to the effect that Jackson injured himself by neglect and carelessness, and that the company was not in any way to blame or liable."

"Was it carelessness?" I asked.

"Call it that, or anything you want to call it. The fact is, a man gets tired after he's been working for hours."

I was becoming interested in the man. He certainly was of a superior kind.

"You are better educated than most workingmen," I said.

"I went through high school," he replied. "I worked my way through doing janitor-work. I wanted to go through the university. But my father died, and I came to work in the mills.

"I wanted to become a naturalist," he explained shyly, as though confessing a weakness. "I love animals. But I came to work in the mills. When I was promoted to foreman I got married, then the family came, and . . . well, I wasn't my own boss any more."

"What do you mean by that?" I asked.

"I was explaining why I testified at the trial the way I did—why I followed instructions."

"Whose instructions?"

"Colonel Ingram. He outlined the evidence I was to give."

"And it lost Jackson's case for him."

He nodded, and the blood began to rise darkly in his face.

"And Jackson had a wife and two children dependent on him."

"I know," he said quietly, though his face was growing darker.

"Tell me," I went on, "was it easy to make yourself over from what you were, say in high school, to the man you must have become to do such a thing at the trial?"

The suddenness of his outburst startled and frightened me. He ripped[1] out a savage oath, and clenched his fist as though about to strike me.

"I beg your pardon," he said the next moment. "No, it was not easy. And now I guess you can go away. You've got all you wanted out of me. But let me tell you this before you go. It won't do you any good to repeat anything I've said. I'll deny it, and there are no witnesses. I'll deny every word of it; and if I have to, I'll do it under oath on the witness stand."

After my interview with Smith I went to my father's office in the Chemistry Building and there encountered Ernest. It was quite unexpected, but he met me with his bold eyes and firm hand-clasp, and with that curious blend of his awkwardness and

---

[1] It is interesting to note the virilities of language that were common speech in that day, as indicative of the life, 'red of claw and fang,' that was then lived. Reference is here made, of course, not to the oath of Smith, but to the verb ripped used by Avis Everhard.

ease. It was as though our last stormy meeting was forgotten; but I was not in the mood to have it forgotten.

"I have been looking up Jackson's case," I said abruptly.

He was all interested attention, and waited for me to go on, though I could see in his eyes the certitude that my convictions had been shaken.

"He seems to have been badly treated," I confessed. "I—I—think some of his blood is dripping from our roof-beams."

"Of course," he answered. "If Jackson and all his fellows were treated mercifully, the dividends would not be so large."

"I shall never be able to take pleasure in pretty gowns again," I added.

I felt humble and contrite, and was aware of a sweet feeling that Ernest was a sort of father confessor. Then, as ever after, his strength appealed to me. It seemed to radiate a promise of peace and protection.

"Nor will you be able to take pleasure in sackcloth," he said gravely. "There are the jute mills, you know, and the same thing goes on there. It goes on everywhere. Our boasted civilization is based upon blood, soaked in blood, and neither you nor I nor any of us can escape the scarlet stain. The men you talked with—who were they?"

I told him all that had taken place.

"And not one of them was a free agent," he said. "They were all tied to the merciless industrial machine. And the pathos of it and the tragedy is that they are tied by their heartstrings. Their children—always the young life that it is their instinct to protect. This instinct is stronger than any ethic they possess. My father! He lied, he stole, he did all sorts of dishonorable things to put bread into my mouth and into the mouths of my brothers and sisters. He was a slave to the industrial machine, and it stamped his life out, worked him to death."

"But you," I interjected. "You are surely a free agent."

"Not wholly," he replied. "I am not tied by my heartstrings. I am often thankful that I have no children, and I dearly love children. Yet if I married I should not dare to have any."

"That surely is bad doctrine," I cried.

"I know it is," he said sadly. "But it is expedient doctrine. I am a revolutionist, and it is a perilous vocation."

I laughed incredulously.

"If I tried to enter your father's house at night to steal his dividends from the Sierra Mills, what would he do?"

"He sleeps with a revolver on the stand by the bed," I answered. "He would most probably shoot you."

"And if I and a few others should lead a million and a half of men[1] into the houses of all the well-to-do, there would be a great deal of shooting, wouldn't there?"

"Yes, but you are not doing that," I objected.

---

[1] This reference is to the socialist vote cast in the United States in 1910. The rise of this vote clearly indicates the swift growth of the party of revolution. Its voting strength in the United States in 1888 was 2068; in 1902, 127,713; in 1904, 435,040; in 1908, 1,108,427; and in 1910, 1,688,211.

"It is precisely what I am doing. And we intend to take, not the mere wealth in the houses, but all the sources of that wealth, all the mines, and railroads, and factories, and banks, and stores. That is the revolution. It is truly perilous. There will be more shooting, I am afraid, than even I dream of. But as I was saying, no one to-day is a free agent. We are all caught up in the wheels and cogs of the industrial machine. You found that you were, and that the men you talked with were. Talk with more of them. Go and see Colonel Ingram. Look up the reporters that kept Jackson's case out of the papers, and the editors that run the papers. You will find them all slaves of the machine."

A little later in our conversation I asked him a simple little question about the liability of workingmen to accidents, and received a statistical lecture in return.

"It is all in the books," he said. "The figures have been gathered, and it has been proved conclusively that accidents rarely occur in the first hours of the morning work, but that they increase rapidly in the succeeding hours as the workers grow tired and slower in both their muscular and mental processes.

"Why, do you know that your father has three times as many chances for safety of life and limb than has a working-man? He has. The insurance[1] companies know. They will charge him four dollars and twenty cents a year on a thousand-dollar accident policy, and for the same policy they will charge a laborer fifteen dollars."

"And you?" I asked; and in the moment of asking I was aware of a solicitude that was something more than slight.

"Oh, as a revolutionist, I have about eight chances to the workingman's one of being injured or killed," he answered carelessly. "The insurance companies charge the highly trained chemists that handle explosives eight times what they charge the workingmen. I don't think they'd insure me at all. Why did you ask?"

My eyes fluttered, and I could feel the blood warm in my face. It was not that he had caught me in my solicitude, but that I had caught myself, and in his presence.

Just then my father came in and began making preparations to depart with me. Ernest returned some books he had borrowed, and went away first. But just as he was going, he turned and said:

"Oh, by the way, while you are ruining your own peace of mind and I am ruining the Bishop's, you'd better look up Mrs. Wickson and Mrs. Pertonwaithe. Their husbands, you know, are the two principal stockholders in the Mills. Like all the rest of humanity, those two women are tied to the machine, but they are so tied that they sit on top of it."

---

[1] In the terrible wolf-struggle of those centuries, no man was permanently safe, no matter how much wealth he amassed. Out of fear for the welfare of their families, men devised the scheme of insurance. To us, in this intelligent age, such a device is laughably absurd and primitive. But in that age insurance was a very serious matter. The amusing part of it is that the funds of the insurance companies were frequently plundered and wasted by the very officials who were intrusted with the management of them.

CHAPTER IV - SLAVES OF THE MACHINE

The more I thought of Jackson's arm, the more shaken I was. I was confronted by the concrete. For the first time I was seeing life. My university life, and study and culture, had not been real. I had learned nothing but theories of life and society that looked all very well on the printed page, but now I had seen life itself. Jackson's arm was a fact of life. "The fact, man, the irrefragable fact!" of Ernest's was ringing in my consciousness.

It seemed monstrous, impossible, that our whole society was based upon blood. And yet there was Jackson. I could not get away from him. Constantly my thought swung back to him as the compass to the Pole. He had been monstrously treated. His blood had not been paid for in order that a larger dividend might be paid. And I knew a score of happy complacent families that had received those dividends and by that much had profited by Jackson's blood. If one man could be so monstrously treated and society move on its way unheeding, might not many men be so monstrously treated? I remembered Ernest's women of Chicago who toiled for ninety cents a week, and the child slaves of the Southern cotton mills he had described. And I could see their wan white hands, from which the blood had been pressed, at work upon the cloth out of which had been made my gown. And then I thought of the Sierra Mills and the dividends that had been paid, and I saw the blood of Jackson upon my gown as well. Jackson I could not escape. Always my meditations led me back to him.

Down in the depths of me I had a feeling that I stood on the edge of a precipice. It was as though I were about to see a new and awful revelation of life. And not I alone. My whole world was turning over. There was my father. I could see the effect Ernest was beginning to have on him. And then there was the Bishop. When I had last seen him he had looked a sick man. He was at high nervous tension, and in his eyes there was unspeakable horror. From the little I learned I knew that Ernest had been keeping his promise of taking him through hell. But what scenes of hell the Bishop's eyes had seen, I knew not, for he seemed too stunned to speak about them.

Once, the feeling strong upon me that my little world and all the world was turning over, I thought of Ernest as the cause of it; and also I thought, "We were so happy and peaceful before he came!" And the next moment I was aware that the thought was a treason against truth, and Ernest rose before me transfigured, the apostle of truth, with shining brows and the fearlessness of one of Gods own angels, battling for the truth and the right, and battling for the succor of the poor and lonely and oppressed. And then there arose before me another figure, the Christ! He, too, had taken the part of the lowly and oppressed, and against all the established power of priest and pharisee. And I remembered his end upon the cross, and my heart contracted with a pang as I thought of Ernest. Was he, too, destined for a cross?—he, with his clarion call and war-noted voice, and all the fine man's vigor of him!

And in that moment I knew that I loved him, and that I was melting with desire to comfort him. I thought of his life. A sordid, harsh, and meagre life it must have been. And I thought of his father, who had lied and stolen for him and been worked to death. And he himself had gone into the mills when he was ten! All my heart seemed bursting with desire to fold my arms around him, and to rest his head on my breast—his head that must be weary with so many thoughts; and to give him rest—just rest—and easement and forgetfulness for a tender space.

I met Colonel Ingram at a church reception. Him I knew well and had known well for many years. I trapped him behind large palms and rubber plants, though he did not know he was trapped. He met me with the conventional gayety and gallantry. He was ever a graceful man, diplomatic, tactful, and considerate. And as for appearance, he was the most distinguished-looking man in our society. Beside him even the venerable head of the university looked tawdry and small.

And yet I found Colonel Ingram situated the same as the unlettered mechanics. He was not a free agent. He, too, was bound upon the wheel. I shall never forget the change in him when I mentioned Jackson's case. His smiling good nature vanished like a ghost. A sudden, frightful expression distorted his well-bred face. I felt the same alarm that I had felt when James Smith broke out. But Colonel Ingram did not curse. That was the slight difference that was left between the workingman and him. He was famed as a wit, but he had no wit now. And, unconsciously, this way and that he glanced for avenues of escape. But he was trapped amid the palms and rubber trees.

Oh, he was sick of the sound of Jackson's name. Why had I brought the matter up? He did not relish my joke. It was poor taste on my part, and very inconsiderate. Did I not know that in his profession personal feelings did not count? He left his personal feelings at home when he went down to the office. At the office he had only professional feelings.

"Should Jackson have received damages?" I asked.

"Certainly," he answered. "That is, personally, I have a feeling that he should. But that has nothing to do with the legal aspects of the case."

He was getting his scattered wits slightly in hand.

"Tell me, has right anything to do with the law?" I asked.

"You have used the wrong initial consonant," he smiled in answer.

"Might?" I queried; and he nodded his head. "And yet we are supposed to get justice by means of the law?"

"That is the paradox of it," he countered. "We do get justice."

"You are speaking professionally now, are you not?" I asked.

Colonel Ingram blushed, actually blushed, and again he looked anxiously about him for a way of escape. But I blocked his path and did not offer to move.

"Tell me," I said, "when one surrenders his personal feelings to his professional feelings, may not the action be defined as a sort of spiritual mayhem?"

I did not get an answer. Colonel Ingram had ingloriously bolted, overturning a palm in his flight.

Next I tried the newspapers. I wrote a quiet, restrained, dispassionate account of Jackson's case. I made no charges against the men with whom I had talked, nor, for that matter, did I even mention them. I gave the actual facts of the case, the long years Jackson had worked in the mills, his effort to save the machinery from damage and the consequent accident, and his own present wretched and starving condition. The three local newspapers rejected my communication, likewise did the two weeklies.

I got hold of Percy Layton. He was a graduate of the university, had gone in for journalism, and was then serving his apprenticeship as reporter on the most influential of the three newspapers. He smiled when I asked him the reason the newspapers suppressed all mention of Jackson or his case.

"Editorial policy," he said. "We have nothing to do with that. It's up to the editors."

"But why is it policy?" I asked.

"We're all solid with the corporations," he answered. "If you paid advertising rates, you couldn't get any such matter into the papers. A man who tried to smuggle it in would lose his job. You couldn't get it in if you paid ten times the regular advertising rates."

"How about your own policy?" I questioned. "It would seem your function is to twist truth at the command of your employers, who, in turn, obey the behests of the corporations."

"I haven't anything to do with that." He looked uncomfortable for the moment, then brightened as he saw his way out. "I, myself, do not write untruthful things. I keep square all right with my own conscience. Of course, there's lots that's repugnant in the course of the day's work. But then, you see, that's all part of the day's work," he wound up boyishly.

"Yet you expect to sit at an editor's desk some day and conduct a policy."

"I'll be case-hardened by that time," was his reply.

"Since you are not yet case-hardened, tell me what you think right now about the general editorial policy."

"I don't think," he answered quickly. "One can't kick over the ropes if he's going to succeed in journalism. I've learned that much, at any rate."

And he nodded his young head sagely.

"But the right?" I persisted.

"You don't understand the game. Of course it's all right, because it comes out all right, don't you see?"

"Delightfully vague," I murmured; but my heart was aching for the youth of him, and I felt that I must either scream or burst into tears.

I was beginning to see through the appearances of the society in which I had always lived, and to find the frightful realities that were beneath. There seemed a tacit conspiracy against Jackson, and I was aware of a thrill of sympathy for the whining lawyer who had ingloriously fought his case. But this tacit conspiracy grew large. Not alone was it aimed against Jackson. It was aimed against every workingman who was maimed in the mills. And if against every man in the mills, why not against every man in all the other mills and factories? In fact, was it not true of all the industries?

And if this was so, then society was a lie. I shrank back from my own conclusions. It was too terrible and awful to be true. But there was Jackson, and Jackson's arm, and the blood that stained my gown and dripped from my own roof-beams. And there were many Jacksons—hundreds of them in the mills alone, as Jackson himself had said. Jackson I could not escape.

I saw Mr. Wickson and Mr. Pertonwaithe, the two men who held most of the stock in the Sierra Mills. But I could not shake them as I had shaken the mechanics in their employ. I discovered that they had an ethic superior to that of the rest of society. It was what I may call the aristocratic ethic or the master ethic.[1] They talked in large ways of policy, and they identified policy and right. And to me they talked in fatherly ways, patronizing my youth and inexperience. They were the most hopeless of all I had encountered in my quest. They believed absolutely that their conduct was right. There was no question about it, no discussion. They were convinced that they were the saviours of society, and that it was they who made happiness for the many. And they drew pathetic pictures of what would be the sufferings of the working class were it not for the employment that they, and they alone, by their wisdom, provided for it.

Fresh from these two masters, I met Ernest and related my experience. He looked at me with a pleased expression, and said:

"Really, this is fine. You are beginning to dig truth for yourself. It is your own empirical generalization, and it is correct. No man in the industrial machine is a free-will agent, except the large capitalist, and he isn't, if you'll pardon the Irishism.[2] You see, the masters are quite sure that they are right in what they are doing. That is the crowning absurdity of the whole situation. They are so tied by their human nature that they can't do a thing unless they think it is right. They must have a sanction for their acts.

"When they want to do a thing, in business of course, they must wait till there arises in their brains, somehow, a religious, or ethical, or scientific, or philosophic, concept that the thing is right. And then they go ahead and do it, unwitting that one of the weaknesses of the human mind is that the wish is parent to the thought. No matter what they want to do, the sanction always comes. They are superficial casuists. They are Jesuitical. They even see their way to doing wrong that right may come of it. One of the pleasant and axiomatic fictions they have created is that they are superior to the rest of mankind in wisdom and efficiency. Therefrom comes their sanction to manage the bread and butter of the rest of mankind. They have even resurrected the theory of the divine right of kings—commercial kings in their case.[3]

"The weakness in their position lies in that they are merely business men. They are not philosophers. They are not biologists nor sociologists. If they were, of course all would be well. A business man who was also a biologist and a sociologist would know, approximately, the right thing to do for humanity. But, outside the realm of

---

[1] Before Avis Everhard was born, John Stuart Mill, in his essay, ON LIBERTY, wrote: "Wherever there is an ascendant class, a large portion of the morality emanates from its class interests and its class feelings of superiority."

[2] Verbal contradictions, called BULLS, were long an amiable weakness of the ancient Irish.

[3] The newspapers, in 1902 of that era, credited the president of the Anthracite Coal Trust, George F. Baer, with the enunciation of the following principle: "The rights and interests of the laboring man will be protected by the Christian men to whom God in His infinite wisdom has given the property interests of the country."

business, these men are stupid. They know only business. They do not know mankind nor society, and yet they set themselves up as arbiters of the fates of the hungry millions and all the other millions thrown in. History, some day, will have an excruciating laugh at their expense."

I was not surprised when I had my talk out with Mrs. Wickson and Mrs. Pertonwaithe. They were society women.[1] Their homes were palaces. They had many homes scattered over the country, in the mountains, on lakes, and by the sea. They were tended by armies of servants, and their social activities were bewildering. They patronized the university and the churches, and the pastors especially bowed at their knees in meek subservience.[2] They were powers, these two women, what of the money that was theirs. The power of subsidization of thought was theirs to a remarkable degree, as I was soon to learn under Ernest's tuition.

They aped their husbands, and talked in the same large ways about policy, and the duties and responsibilities of the rich. They were swayed by the same ethic that dominated their husbands—the ethic of their class; and they uttered glib phrases that their own ears did not understand.

Also, they grew irritated when I told them of the deplorable condition of Jackson's family, and when I wondered that they had made no voluntary provision for the man. I was told that they thanked no one for instructing them in their social duties. When I asked them flatly to assist Jackson, they as flatly refused. The astounding thing about it was that they refused in almost identically the same language, and this in face of the fact that I interviewed them separately and that one did not know that I had seen or was going to see the other. Their common reply was that they were glad of the opportunity to make it perfectly plain that no premium would ever be put on carelessness by them; nor would they, by paying for accident, tempt the poor to hurt themselves in the machinery.[3]

And they were sincere, these two women. They were drunk with conviction of the superiority of their class and of themselves. They had a sanction, in their own class-ethic, for every act they performed. As I drove away from Mrs. Pertonwaithe's great house, I looked back at it, and I remembered Ernest's expression that they were bound to the machine, but that they were so bound that they sat on top of it.

---

[1] SOCIETY is here used in a restricted sense, a common usage of the times to denote the gilded drones that did no labor, but only glutted themselves at the honey-vats of the workers. Neither the business men nor the laborers had time or opportunity for SOCIETY. SOCIETY was the creation of the idle rich who toiled not and who in this way played.

[2] "Bring on your tainted money," was the expressed sentiment of the Church during this period.

[3] In the files of the OUTLOOK, a critical weekly of the period, in the number dated August 18, 1906, is related the circumstance of a workingman losing his arm, the details of which are quite similar to those of Jackson's case as related by Avis Everhard.

CHAPTER V - THE PHILOMATHS

Ernest was often at the house. Nor was it my father, merely, nor the controversial dinners, that drew him there. Even at that time I flattered myself that I played some part in causing his visits, and it was not long before I learned the correctness of my surmise. For never was there such a lover as Ernest Everhard. His gaze and his handclasp grew firmer and steadier, if that were possible; and the question that had grown from the first in his eyes, grew only the more imperative.

My impression of him, the first time I saw him, had been unfavorable. Then I had found myself attracted toward him. Next came my repulsion, when he so savagely attacked my class and me. After that, as I saw that he had not maligned my class, and that the harsh and bitter things he said about it were justified, I had drawn closer to him again. He became my oracle. For me he tore the sham from the face of society and gave me glimpses of reality that were as unpleasant as they were undeniably true.

As I have said, there was never such a lover as he. No girl could live in a university town till she was twenty-four and not have love experiences. I had been made love to by beardless sophomores and gray professors, and by the athletes and the football giants. But not one of them made love to me as Ernest did. His arms were around me before I knew. His lips were on mine before I could protest or resist. Before his earnestness conventional maiden dignity was ridiculous. He swept me off my feet by the splendid invincible rush of him. He did not propose. He put his arms around me and kissed me and took it for granted that we should be married. There was no discussion about it. The only discussion—and that arose afterward—was when we should be married.

It was unprecedented. It was unreal. Yet, in accordance with Ernest's test of truth, it worked. I trusted my life to it. And fortunate was the trust. Yet during those first days of our love, fear of the future came often to me when I thought of the violence and impetuosity of his love-making. Yet such fears were groundless. No woman was ever blessed with a gentler, tenderer husband. This gentleness and violence on his part was a curious blend similar to the one in his carriage of awkwardness and ease. That slight awkwardness! He never got over it, and it was delicious. His behavior in our drawing-room reminded me of a careful bull in a china shop.[1]

---

[1] In those days it was still the custom to fill the living rooms with bric-a-brac. They had not discovered simplicity of living. Such rooms were museums, entailing endless labor to

It was at this time that vanished my last doubt of the completeness of my love for him (a subconscious doubt, at most). It was at the Philomath Club—a wonderful night of battle, wherein Ernest bearded the masters in their lair. Now the Philomath Club was the most select on the Pacific Coast. It was the creation of Miss Brentwood, an enormously wealthy old maid; and it was her husband, and family, and toy. Its members were the wealthiest in the community, and the strongest-minded of the wealthy, with, of course, a sprinkling of scholars to give it intellectual tone.

The Philomath had no club house. It was not that kind of a club. Once a month its members gathered at some one of their private houses to listen to a lecture. The lecturers were usually, though not always, hired. If a chemist in New York made a new discovery in say radium, all his expenses across the continent were paid, and as well he received a princely fee for his time. The same with a returning explorer from the polar regions, or the latest literary or artistic success. No visitors were allowed, while it was the Philomath's policy to permit none of its discussions to get into the papers. Thus great statesmen—and there had been such occasions—were able fully to speak their minds.

I spread before me a wrinkled letter, written to me by Ernest twenty years ago, and from it I copy the following:

"Your father is a member of the Philomath, so you are able to come. Therefore come next Tuesday night. I promise you that you will have the time of your life. In your recent encounters, you failed to shake the masters. If you come, I'll shake them for you. I'll make them snarl like wolves. You merely questioned their morality. When their morality is questioned, they grow only the more complacent and superior. But I shall menace their money-bags. That will shake them to the roots of their primitive natures. If you can come, you will see the cave-man, in evening dress, snarling and snapping over a bone. I promise you a great caterwauling and an illuminating insight into the nature of the beast.

"They've invited me in order to tear me to pieces. This is the idea of Miss Brentwood. She clumsily hinted as much when she invited me. She's given them that kind of fun before. They delight in getting trustful-souled gentle reformers before them. Miss Brentwood thinks I am as mild as a kitten and as good-natured and stolid as the family cow. I'll not deny that I helped to give her that impression. She was very tentative at first, until she divined my harmlessness. I am to receive a handsome fee—two hundred and fifty dollars—as befits the man who, though a radical, once ran for governor. Also, I am to wear evening dress. This is compulsory. I never was so apparelled in my life. I suppose I'll have to hire one somewhere. But I'd do more than that to get a chance at the Philomaths."

Of all places, the Club gathered that night at the Pertonwaithe house. Extra chairs had been brought into the great drawing-room, and in all there must have been two hundred Philomaths that sat down to hear Ernest. They were truly lords of society. I amused myself with running over in my mind the sum of the fortunes represented, and it ran well into the hundreds of millions. And the possessors were not of the idle

---

keep clean. The dust-demon was the lord of the household. There were a myriad devices for catching dust, and only a few devices for getting rid of it.

rich. They were men of affairs who took most active parts in industrial and political life.

We were all seated when Miss Brentwood brought Ernest in. They moved at once to the head of the room, from where he was to speak. He was in evening dress, and, what of his broad shoulders and kingly head, he looked magnificent. And then there was that faint and unmistakable touch of awkwardness in his movements. I almost think I could have loved him for that alone. And as I looked at him I was aware of a great joy. I felt again the pulse of his palm on mine, the touch of his lips; and such pride was mine that I felt I must rise up and cry out to the assembled company: "He is mine! He has held me in his arms, and I, mere I, have filled that mind of his to the exclusion of all his multitudinous and kingly thoughts!"

At the head of the room, Miss Brentwood introduced him to Colonel Van Gilbert, and I knew that the latter was to preside. Colonel Van Gilbert was a great corporation lawyer. In addition, he was immensely wealthy. The smallest fee he would deign to notice was a hundred thousand dollars. He was a master of law. The law was a puppet with which he played. He moulded it like clay, twisted and distorted it like a Chinese puzzle into any design he chose. In appearance and rhetoric he was old-fashioned, but in imagination and knowledge and resource he was as young as the latest statute. His first prominence had come when he broke the Shardwell will.[1] His fee for this one act was five hundred thousand dollars. From then on he had risen like a rocket. He was often called the greatest lawyer in the country—corporation lawyer, of course; and no classification of the three greatest lawyers in the United States could have excluded him.

He arose and began, in a few well-chosen phrases that carried an undertone of faint irony, to introduce Ernest. Colonel Van Gilbert was subtly facetious in his introduction of the social reformer and member of the working class, and the audience smiled. It made me angry, and I glanced at Ernest. The sight of him made me doubly angry. He did not seem to resent the delicate slurs. Worse than that, he did not seem to be aware of them. There he sat, gentle, and stolid, and somnolent. He really looked stupid. And for a moment the thought rose in my mind, What if he were overawed by this imposing array of power and brains? Then I smiled. He couldn't fool me. But he fooled the others, just as he had fooled Miss Brentwood. She occupied a chair right up to the front, and several times she turned her head toward one or another of her CONFRERES and smiled her appreciation of the remarks.

Colonel Van Gilbert done, Ernest arose and began to speak. He began in a low voice, haltingly and modestly, and with an air of evident embarrassment. He spoke of

---

[1] This breaking of wills was a peculiar feature of the period. With the accumulation of vast fortunes, the problem of disposing of these fortunes after death was a vexing one to the accumulators. Will-making and will-breaking became complementary trades, like armor-making and gun-making. The shrewdest will-making lawyers were called in to make wills that could not be broken. But these wills were always broken, and very often by the very lawyers that had drawn them up. Nevertheless the delusion persisted in the wealthy class that an absolutely unbreakable will could be cast; and so, through the generations, clients and lawyers pursued the illusion. It was a pursuit like unto that of the Universal Solvent of the mediaeval alchemists.

his birth in the working class, and of the sordidness and wretchedness of his environment, where flesh and spirit were alike starved and tormented. He described his ambitions and ideals, and his conception of the paradise wherein lived the people of the upper classes. As he said:

"Up above me, I knew, were unselfishnesses of the spirit, clean and noble thinking, keen intellectual living. I knew all this because I read 'Seaside Library'[1] novels, in which, with the exception of the villains and adventuresses, all men and women thought beautiful thoughts, spoke a beautiful tongue, and performed glorious deeds. In short, as I accepted the rising of the sun, I accepted that up above me was all that was fine and noble and gracious, all that gave decency and dignity to life, all that made life worth living and that remunerated one for his travail and misery."

He went on and traced his life in the mills, the learning of the horseshoeing trade, and his meeting with the socialists. Among them, he said, he had found keen intellects and brilliant wits, ministers of the Gospel who had been broken because their Christianity was too wide for any congregation of mammon-worshippers, and professors who had been broken on the wheel of university subservience to the ruling class. The socialists were revolutionists, he said, struggling to overthrow the irrational society of the present and out of the material to build the rational society of the future. Much more he said that would take too long to write, but I shall never forget how he described the life among the revolutionists. All halting utterance vanished. His voice grew strong and confident, and it glowed as he glowed, and as the thoughts glowed that poured out from him. He said:

"Amongst the revolutionists I found, also, warm faith in the human, ardent idealism, sweetnesses of unselfishness, renunciation, and martyrdom—all the splendid, stinging things of the spirit. Here life was clean, noble, and alive. I was in touch with great souls who exalted flesh and spirit over dollars and cents, and to whom the thin wail of the starved slum child meant more than all the pomp and circumstance of commercial expansion and world empire. All about me were nobleness of purpose and heroism of effort, and my days and nights were sunshine and starshine, all fire and dew, with before my eyes, ever burning and blazing, the Holy Grail, Christ's own Grail, the warm human, long-suffering and maltreated but to be rescued and saved at the last."

As before I had seen him transfigured, so now he stood transfigured before me. His brows were bright with the divine that was in him, and brighter yet shone his eyes from the midst of the radiance that seemed to envelop him as a mantle. But the others did not see this radiance, and I assumed that it was due to the tears of joy and love that dimmed my vision. At any rate, Mr. Wickson, who sat behind me, was unaffected, for I heard him sneer aloud, "Utopian."[2]

---

[1] A curious and amazing literature that served to make the working class utterly misapprehend the nature of the leisure class.

[2] The people of that age were phrase slaves. The abjectness of their servitude is incomprehensible to us. There was a magic in words greater than the conjurer's art. So befuddled and chaotic were their minds that the utterance of a single word could negative the generalizations of a lifetime of serious research and thought. Such a word was the adjective UTOPIAN. The mere utterance of it could damn any scheme, no matter how

CHAPTER V - THE PHILOMATHS

Ernest went on to his rise in society, till at last he came in touch with members of the upper classes, and rubbed shoulders with the men who sat in the high places. Then came his disillusionment, and this disillusionment he described in terms that did not flatter his audience. He was surprised at the commonness of the clay. Life proved not to be fine and gracious. He was appalled by the selfishness he encountered, and what had surprised him even more than that was the absence of intellectual life. Fresh from his revolutionists, he was shocked by the intellectual stupidity of the master class. And then, in spite of their magnificent churches and well-paid preachers, he had found the masters, men and women, grossly material. It was true that they prattled sweet little ideals and dear little moralities, but in spite of their prattle the dominant key of the life they lived was materialistic. And they were without real morality—for instance, that which Christ had preached but which was no longer preached.

"I met men," he said, "who invoked the name of the Prince of Peace in their diatribes against war, and who put rifles in the hands of Pinkertons[1] with which to shoot down strikers in their own factories. I met men incoherent with indignation at the brutality of prize-fighting, and who, at the same time, were parties to the adulteration of food that killed each year more babes than even red-handed Herod had killed.

"This delicate, aristocratic-featured gentleman was a dummy director and a tool of corporations that secretly robbed widows and orphans. This gentleman, who collected fine editions and was a patron of literature, paid blackmail to a heavy-jowled, black-browed boss of a municipal machine. This editor, who published patent medicine advertisements, called me a scoundrelly demagogue because I dared him to print in his paper the truth about patent medicines.[2] This man, talking soberly and earnestly about the beauties of idealism and the goodness of God, had just betrayed his comrades in a business deal. This man, a pillar of the church and heavy contributor to foreign missions, worked his shop girls ten hours a day on a starvation wage and thereby directly encouraged prostitution. This man, who endowed chairs in universities and erected magnificent chapels, perjured himself in courts of law over dollars and cents. This railroad magnate broke his word as a citizen, as a gentleman, and as a Christian, when he granted a secret rebate, and he granted many secret rebates. This senator was the tool and the slave, the little puppet, of a brutal uneducated machine boss;[3] so was this governor and this supreme court judge; and all three rode on railroad passes; and, al-

---

sanely conceived, of economic amelioration or regeneration. Vast populations grew frenzied over such phrases as "an honest dollar" and "a full dinner pail." The coinage of such phrases was considered strokes of genius.

[1] Originally, they were private detectives; but they quickly became hired fighting men of the capitalists, and ultimately developed into the Mercenaries of the Oligarchy.

[2] PATENT MEDICINES were patent lies, but, like the charms and indulgences of the Middle Ages, they deceived the people. The only difference lay in that the patent medicines were more harmful and more costly.

[3] Even as late as 1912, A.D., the great mass of the people still persisted in the belief that they ruled the country by virtue of their ballots. In reality, the country was ruled by what were called POLITICAL MACHINES. At first the machine bosses charged the master capitalists extortionate tolls for legislation; but in a short time the master capitalists found it cheaper to own the political machines themselves and to hire the machine bosses.

so, this sleek capitalist owned the machine, the machine boss, and the railroads that issued the passes.

"And so it was, instead of in paradise, that I found myself in the arid desert of commercialism. I found nothing but stupidity, except for business. I found none clean, noble, and alive, though I found many who were alive—with rottenness. What I did find was monstrous selfishness and heartlessness, and a gross, gluttonous, practised, and practical materialism."

Much more Ernest told them of themselves and of his disillusionment. Intellectually they had bored him; morally and spiritually they had sickened him; so that he was glad to go back to his revolutionists, who were clean, noble, and alive, and all that the capitalists were not.

"And now," he said, "let me tell you about that revolution."

But first I must say that his terrible diatribe had not touched them. I looked about me at their faces and saw that they remained complacently superior to what he had charged. And I remembered what he had told me: that no indictment of their morality could shake them. However, I could see that the boldness of his language had affected Miss Brentwood. She was looking worried and apprehensive.

Ernest began by describing the army of revolution, and as he gave the figures of its strength (the votes cast in the various countries), the assemblage began to grow restless. Concern showed in their faces, and I noticed a tightening of lips. At last the gage of battle had been thrown down. He described the international organization of the socialists that united the million and a half in the United States with the twenty-three millions and a half in the rest of the world.

"Such an army of revolution," he said, "twenty-five millions strong, is a thing to make rulers and ruling classes pause and consider. The cry of this army is: 'No quarter! We want all that you possess. We will be content with nothing less than all that you possess. We want in our hands the reins of power and the destiny of mankind. Here are our hands. They are strong hands. We are going to take your governments, your palaces, and all your purpled ease away from you, and in that day you shall work for your bread even as the peasant in the field or the starved and runty clerk in your metropolises. Here are our hands. They are strong hands!'"

And as he spoke he extended from his splendid shoulders his two great arms, and the horseshoer's hands were clutching the air like eagle's talons. He was the spirit of regnant labor as he stood there, his hands outreaching to rend and crush his audience. I was aware of a faintly perceptible shrinking on the part of the listeners before this figure of revolution, concrete, potential, and menacing. That is, the women shrank, and fear was in their faces. Not so with the men. They were of the active rich, and not the idle, and they were fighters. A low, throaty rumble arose, lingered on the air a moment, and ceased. It was the forerunner of the snarl, and I was to hear it many times that night—the token of the brute in man, the earnest of his primitive passions. And they were unconscious that they had made this sound. It was the growl of the pack, mouthed by the pack, and mouthed in all unconsciousness. And in that moment, as I saw the harshness form in their faces and saw the fight-light flashing in their eyes, I realized that not easily would they let their lordship of the world be wrested from them.

Ernest proceeded with his attack. He accounted for the existence of the million and a half of revolutionists in the United States by charging the capitalist class with having mismanaged society. He sketched the economic condition of the cave-man and of the savage peoples of to-day, pointing out that they possessed neither tools nor machines, and possessed only a natural efficiency of one in producing power. Then he traced the development of machinery and social organization so that to-day the producing power of civilized man was a thousand times greater than that of the savage.

"Five men," he said, "can produce bread for a thousand. One man can produce cotton cloth for two hundred and fifty people, woollens for three hundred, and boots and shoes for a thousand. One would conclude from this that under a capable management of society modern civilized man would be a great deal better off than the cave-man. But is he? Let us see. In the United States to-day there are fifteen million[1] people living in poverty; and by poverty is meant that condition in life in which, through lack of food and adequate shelter, the mere standard of working efficiency cannot be maintained. In the United States to-day, in spite of all your so-called labor legislation, there are three millions of child laborers.[2] In twelve years their numbers have been doubled. And in passing I will ask you managers of society why you did not make public the census figures of 1910? And I will answer for you, that you were afraid. The figures of misery would have precipitated the revolution that even now is gathering.

"But to return to my indictment. If modern man's producing power is a thousand times greater than that of the cave-man, why then, in the United States to-day, are there fifteen million people who are not properly sheltered and properly fed? Why then, in the United States to-day, are there three million child laborers? It is a true indictment. The capitalist class has mismanaged. In face of the facts that modern man lives more wretchedly than the cave-man, and that his producing power is a thousand times greater than that of the cave-man, no other conclusion is possible than that the capitalist class has mismanaged, that you have mismanaged, my masters, that you have criminally and selfishly mismanaged. And on this count you cannot answer me here to-night, face to face, any more than can your whole class answer the million and a half of revolutionists in the United States. You cannot answer. I challenge you to answer. And furthermore, I dare to say to you now that when I have finished you will not answer. On that point you will be tongue-tied, though you will talk wordily enough about other things.

"You have failed in your management. You have made a shambles of civilization. You have been blind and greedy. You have risen up (as you to-day rise up), shamelessly, in our legislative halls, and declared that profits were impossible without the toil of children and babes. Don't take my word for it. It is all in the records against you. You have lulled your conscience to sleep with prattle of sweet ideals and dear moralities. You are fat with power and possession, drunken with success; and you have no more hope against us than have the drones, clustered about the honey-vats, when the worker-bees spring upon them to end their rotund existence. You have failed in your management of society, and your management is to be taken away from

---

[1] Robert Hunter, in 1906, in a book entitled "Poverty," pointed out that at that time there were ten millions in the United States living in poverty.

[2] In the United States Census of 1900 (the last census the figures of which were made public), the number of child laborers was placed at 1,752,187.

you. A million and a half of the men of the working class say that they are going to get the rest of the working class to join with them and take the management away from you. This is the revolution, my masters. Stop it if you can."

For an appreciable lapse of time Ernest's voice continued to ring through the great room. Then arose the throaty rumble I had heard before, and a dozen men were on their feet clamoring for recognition from Colonel Van Gilbert. I noticed Miss Brentwood's shoulders moving convulsively, and for the moment I was angry, for I thought that she was laughing at Ernest. And then I discovered that it was not laughter, but hysteria. She was appalled by what she had done in bringing this firebrand before her blessed Philomath Club.

Colonel Van Gilbert did not notice the dozen men, with passion-wrought faces, who strove to get permission from him to speak. His own face was passion-wrought. He sprang to his feet, waving his arms, and for a moment could utter only incoherent sounds. Then speech poured from him. But it was not the speech of a one-hundred-thousand-dollar lawyer, nor was the rhetoric old-fashioned.

"Fallacy upon fallacy!" he cried. "Never in all my life have I heard so many fallacies uttered in one short hour. And besides, young man, I must tell you that you have said nothing new. I learned all that at college before you were born. Jean Jacques Rousseau enunciated your socialistic theory nearly two centuries ago. A return to the soil, forsooth! Reversion! Our biology teaches the absurdity of it. It has been truly said that a little learning is a dangerous thing, and you have exemplified it to-night with your madcap theories. Fallacy upon fallacy! I was never so nauseated in my life with overplus of fallacy. That for your immature generalizations and childish reasonings!"

He snapped his fingers contemptuously and proceeded to sit down. There were lip-exclamations of approval on the part of the women, and hoarser notes of confirmation came from the men. As for the dozen men who were clamoring for the floor, half of them began speaking at once. The confusion and babel was indescribable. Never had Mrs. Pertonwaithe's spacious walls beheld such a spectacle. These, then, were the cool captains of industry and lords of society, these snarling, growling savages in evening clothes. Truly Ernest had shaken them when he stretched out his hands for their moneybags, his hands that had appeared in their eyes as the hands of the fifteen hundred thousand revolutionists.

But Ernest never lost his head in a situation. Before Colonel Van Gilbert had succeeded in sitting down, Ernest was on his feet and had sprung forward.

"One at a time!" he roared at them.

The sound arose from his great lungs and dominated the human tempest. By sheer compulsion of personality he commanded silence.

"One at a time," he repeated softly. "Let me answer Colonel Van Gilbert. After that the rest of you can come at me—but one at a time, remember. No mass-plays here. This is not a football field.

"As for you," he went on, turning toward Colonel Van Gilbert, "you have replied to nothing I have said. You have merely made a few excited and dogmatic assertions about my mental caliber. That may serve you in your business, but you can't talk to me like that. I am not a workingman, cap in hand, asking you to increase my wages or to protect me from the machine at which I work. You cannot be dogmatic with truth when you deal with me. Save that for dealing with your wage-slaves. They will not dare reply to you because you hold their bread and butter, their lives, in your hands.

"As for this return to nature that you say you learned at college before I was born, permit me to point out that on the face of it you cannot have learned anything since. Socialism has no more to do with the state of nature than has differential calculus with a Bible class. I have called your class stupid when outside the realm of business. You, sir, have brilliantly exemplified my statement."

This terrible castigation of her hundred-thousand-dollar lawyer was too much for Miss Brentwood's nerves. Her hysteria became violent, and she was helped, weeping and laughing, out of the room. It was just as well, for there was worse to follow.

"Don't take my word for it," Ernest continued, when the interruption had been led away. "Your own authorities with one unanimous voice will prove you stupid. Your own hired purveyors of knowledge will tell you that you are wrong. Go to your meekest little assistant instructor of sociology and ask him what is the difference between Rousseau's theory of the return to nature and the theory of socialism; ask your greatest orthodox bourgeois political economists and sociologists; question through the pages of every text-book written on the subject and stored on the shelves of your subsidized libraries; and from one and all the answer will be that there is nothing congruous between the return to nature and socialism. On the other hand, the unanimous affirmative answer will be that the return to nature and socialism are diametrically opposed to each other. As I say, don't take my word for it. The record of your stupidity is there in the books, your own books that you never read. And so far as your stupidity is concerned, you are but the exemplar of your class.

"You know law and business, Colonel Van Gilbert. You know how to serve corporations and increase dividends by twisting the law. Very good. Stick to it. You are quite a figure. You are a very good lawyer, but you are a poor historian, you know nothing of sociology, and your biology is contemporaneous with Pliny."

Here Colonel Van Gilbert writhed in his chair. There was perfect quiet in the room. Everybody sat fascinated—paralyzed, I may say. Such fearful treatment of the great Colonel Van Gilbert was unheard of, undreamed of, impossible to believe—the great Colonel Van Gilbert before whom judges trembled when he arose in court. But Ernest never gave quarter to an enemy.

"This is, of course, no reflection on you," Ernest said. "Every man to his trade. Only you stick to your trade, and I'll stick to mine. You have specialized. When it comes to a knowledge of the law, of how best to evade the law or make new law for the benefit of thieving corporations, I am down in the dirt at your feet. But when it comes to sociology—my trade—you are down in the dirt at my feet. Remember that. Remember, also, that your law is the stuff of a day, and that you are not versatile in the stuff of more than a day. Therefore your dogmatic assertions and rash generalizations on things historical and sociological are not worth the breath you waste on them."

Ernest paused for a moment and regarded him thoughtfully, noting his face dark and twisted with anger, his panting chest, his writhing body, and his slim white hands nervously clenching and unclenching.

"But it seems you have breath to use, and I'll give you a chance to use it. I indicted your class. Show me that my indictment is wrong. I pointed out to you the wretchedness of modern man—three million child slaves in the United States, without whose labor profits would not be possible, and fifteen million under-fed, ill-clothed, and worse-housed people. I pointed out that modern man's producing power through social organization and the use of machinery was a thousand times greater than that of the cave-man. And I stated that from these two facts no other conclusion was possible than that the capitalist class had mismanaged. This was my indictment, and I specifically and at length challenged you to answer it. Nay, I did more. I prophesied that you would not answer. It remains for your breath to smash my prophecy. You called my speech fallacy. Show the fallacy, Colonel Van Gilbert. Answer the indictment that I and my fifteen hundred thousand comrades have brought against your class and you."

Colonel Van Gilbert quite forgot that he was presiding, and that in courtesy he should permit the other clamorers to speak. He was on his feet, flinging his arms, his rhetoric, and his control to the winds, alternately abusing Ernest for his youth and demagoguery, and savagely attacking the working class, elaborating its inefficiency and worthlessness.

"For a lawyer, you are the hardest man to keep to a point I ever saw," Ernest began his answer to the tirade. "My youth has nothing to do with what I have enunciated. Nor has the worthlessness of the working class. I charged the capitalist class with having mismanaged society. You have not answered. You have made no attempt to answer. Why? Is it because you have no answer? You are the champion of this whole audience. Every one here, except me, is hanging on your lips for that answer. They are hanging on your lips for that answer because they have no answer themselves. As for me, as I said before, I know that you not only cannot answer, but that you will not attempt an answer."

"This is intolerable!" Colonel Van Gilbert cried out. "This is insult!"

"That you should not answer is intolerable," Ernest replied gravely. "No man can be intellectually insulted. Insult, in its very nature, is emotional. Recover yourself. Give me an intellectual answer to my intellectual charge that the capitalist class has mismanaged society."

Colonel Van Gilbert remained silent, a sullen, superior expression on his face, such as will appear on the face of a man who will not bandy words with a ruffian.

"Do not be downcast," Ernest said. "Take consolation in the fact that no member of your class has ever yet answered that charge." He turned to the other men who were anxious to speak. "And now it's your chance. Fire away, and do not forget that I here challenge you to give the answer that Colonel Van Gilbert has failed to give."

It would be impossible for me to write all that was said in the discussion. I never realized before how many words could be spoken in three short hours. At any rate, it was glorious. The more his opponents grew excited, the more Ernest deliberately excited them. He had an encyclopaedic command of the field of knowledge, and by a word or a phrase, by delicate rapier thrusts, he punctured them. He named the points of their illogic. This was a false syllogism, that conclusion had no connection with the premise, while that next premise was an impostor because it had cunningly hidden in it the conclusion that was being attempted to be proved. This was an error, that was an assumption, and the next was an assertion contrary to ascertained truth as printed in all the text-books.

And so it went. Sometimes he exchanged the rapier for the club and went smashing amongst their thoughts right and left. And always he demanded facts and refused to discuss theories. And his facts made for them a Waterloo. When they attacked the working class, he always retorted, "The pot calling the kettle black; that is no answer to the charge that your own face is dirty." And to one and all he said: "Why have you not answered the charge that your class has mismanaged? You have talked about other things and things concerning other things, but you have not answered. Is it because you have no answer?"

It was at the end of the discussion that Mr. Wickson spoke. He was the only one that was cool, and Ernest treated him with a respect he had not accorded the others.

"No answer is necessary," Mr. Wickson said with slow deliberation. "I have followed the whole discussion with amazement and disgust. I am disgusted with you gentlemen, members of my class. You have behaved like foolish little schoolboys, what with intruding ethics and the thunder of the common politician into such a discussion. You have been outgeneralled and outclassed. You have been very wordy, and all you have done is buzz. You have buzzed like gnats about a bear. Gentlemen, there stands the bear" (he pointed at Ernest), "and your buzzing has only tickled his ears.

"Believe me, the situation is serious. That bear reached out his paws tonight to crush us. He has said there are a million and a half of revolutionists in the United States. That is a fact. He has said that it is their intention to take away from us our governments, our palaces, and all our purpled ease. That, also, is a fact. A change, a great change, is coming in society; but, haply, it may not be the change the bear anticipates. The bear has said that he will crush us. What if we crush the bear?"

The throat-rumble arose in the great room, and man nodded to man with indorsement and certitude. Their faces were set hard. They were fighters, that was certain.

"But not by buzzing will we crush the bear," Mr. Wickson went on coldly and dispassionately. "We will hunt the bear. We will not reply to the bear in words. Our reply shall be couched in terms of lead. We are in power. Nobody will deny it. By virtue of that power we shall remain in power."

He turned suddenly upon Ernest. The moment was dramatic.

"This, then, is our answer. We have no words to waste on you. When you reach out your vaunted strong hands for our palaces and purpled ease, we will show you what strength is. In roar of shell and shrapnel and in whine of machine-guns will our answer be couched.[1] We will grind you revolutionists down under our heel, and we shall walk upon your faces. The world is ours, we are its lords, and ours it shall remain. As for the host of labor, it has been in the dirt since history began, and I read history aright. And in the dirt it shall remain so long as I and mine and those that come after us have the power. There is the word. It is the king of words—Power. Not God, not Mammon, but Power. Pour it over your tongue till it tingles with it. Power."

"I am answered," Ernest said quietly. "It is the only answer that could be given. Power. It is what we of the working class preach. We know, and well we know by bitter experience, that no appeal for the right, for justice, for humanity, can ever touch you. Your hearts are hard as your heels with which you tread upon the faces of the

[1] To show the tenor of thought, the following definition is quoted from "The Cynic's Word Book" (1906 A.D.), written by one Ambrose Bierce, an avowed and confirmed misanthrope of the period: "Grapeshot, n. An argument which the future is preparing in answer to the demands of American Socialism."

poor. So we have preached power. By the power of our ballots on election day will we take your government away from you—"

"What if you do get a majority, a sweeping majority, on election day?" Mr. Wickson broke in to demand. "Suppose we refuse to turn the government over to you after you have captured it at the ballot-box?"

"That, also, have we considered," Ernest replied. "And we shall give you an answer in terms of lead. Power you have proclaimed the king of words. Very good. Power it shall be. And in the day that we sweep to victory at the ballot-box, and you refuse to turn over to us the government we have constitutionally and peacefully captured, and you demand what we are going to do about it—in that day, I say, we shall answer you; and in roar of shell and shrapnel and in whine of machine-guns shall our answer be couched.

"You cannot escape us. It is true that you have read history aright. It is true that labor has from the beginning of history been in the dirt. And it is equally true that so long as you and yours and those that come after you have power, that labor shall remain in the dirt. I agree with you. I agree with all that you have said. Power will be the arbiter, as it always has been the arbiter. It is a struggle of classes. Just as your class dragged down the old feudal nobility, so shall it be dragged down by my class, the working class. If you will read your biology and your sociology as clearly as you do your history, you will see that this end I have described is inevitable. It does not matter whether it is in one year, ten, or a thousand—your class shall be dragged down. And it shall be done by power. We of the labor hosts have conned that word over till our minds are all a-tingle with it. Power. It is a kingly word."

And so ended the night with the Philomaths.

CHAPTER VI - ADUMBRATIONS

It was about this time that the warnings of coming events began to fall about us thick and fast. Ernest had already questioned father's policy of having socialists and labor leaders at his house, and of openly attending socialist meetings; and father had only laughed at him for his pains. As for myself, I was learning much from this contact with the working-class leaders and thinkers. I was seeing the other side of the shield. I was delighted with the unselfishness and high idealism I encountered, though I was appalled by the vast philosophic and scientific literature of socialism that was opened up to me. I was learning fast, but I learned not fast enough to realize then the peril of our position.

There were warnings, but I did not heed them. For instance, Mrs. Pertonwaithe and Mrs. Wickson exercised tremendous social power in the university town, and from them emanated the sentiment that I was a too-forward and self-assertive young woman with a mischievous penchant for officiousness and interference in other persons' affairs. This I thought no more than natural, considering the part I had played in investigating the case of Jackson's arm. But the effect of such a sentiment, enunciated by two such powerful social arbiters, I underestimated.

True, I noticed a certain aloofness on the part of my general friends, but this I ascribed to the disapproval that was prevalent in my circles of my intended marriage with Ernest. It was not till some time afterward that Ernest pointed out to me clearly that this general attitude of my class was something more than spontaneous, that behind it were the hidden springs of an organized conduct. "You have given shelter to an enemy of your class," he said. "And not alone shelter, for you have given your love, yourself. This is treason to your class. Think not that you will escape being penalized."

But it was before this that father returned one afternoon. Ernest was with me, and we could see that father was angry—philosophically angry. He was rarely really angry; but a certain measure of controlled anger he allowed himself. He called it a tonic. And we could see that he was tonic-angry when he entered the room.

"What do you think?" he demanded. "I had luncheon with Wilcox."

Wilcox was the superannuated president of the university, whose withered mind was stored with generalizations that were young in 1870, and which he had since failed to revise.

"I was invited," father announced. "I was sent for."

He paused, and we waited.

"Oh, it was done very nicely, I'll allow; but I was reprimanded. I! And by that old fossil!"

"I'll wager I know what you were reprimanded for," Ernest said.

"Not in three guesses," father laughed.

"One guess will do," Ernest retorted. "And it won't be a guess. It will be a deduction. You were reprimanded for your private life."

"The very thing!" father cried. "How did you guess?"

"I knew it was coming. I warned you before about it."

"Yes, you did," father meditated. "But I couldn't believe it. At any rate, it is only so much more clinching evidence for my book."

"It is nothing to what will come," Ernest went on, "if you persist in your policy of having these socialists and radicals of all sorts at your house, myself included."

"Just what old Wilcox said. And of all unwarranted things! He said it was in poor taste, utterly profitless, anyway, and not in harmony with university traditions and policy. He said much more of the same vague sort, and I couldn't pin him down to anything specific. I made it pretty awkward for him, and he could only go on repeating himself and telling me how much he honored me, and all the world honored me, as a scientist. It wasn't an agreeable task for him. I could see he didn't like it."

"He was not a free agent," Ernest said. "The leg-bar[1] is not always worn graciously."

"Yes. I got that much out of him. He said the university needed ever so much more money this year than the state was willing to furnish; and that it must come from wealthy personages who could not but be offended by the swerving of the university from its high ideal of the passionless pursuit of passionless intelligence. When I tried to pin him down to what my home life had to do with swerving the university from its high ideal, he offered me a two years' vacation, on full pay, in Europe, for recreation and research. Of course I couldn't accept it under the circumstances."

"It would have been far better if you had," Ernest said gravely.

"It was a bribe," father protested; and Ernest nodded.

"Also, the beggar said that there was talk, tea-table gossip and so forth, about my daughter being seen in public with so notorious a character as you, and that it was not in keeping with university tone and dignity. Not that he personally objected—oh, no; but that there was talk and that I would understand."

Ernest considered this announcement for a moment, and then said, and his face was very grave, withal there was a sombre wrath in it:

"There is more behind this than a mere university ideal. Somebody has put pressure on President Wilcox."

"Do you think so?" father asked, and his face showed that he was interested rather than frightened.

"I wish I could convey to you the conception that is dimly forming in my own mind," Ernest said. "Never in the history of the world was society in so terrific flux as it is right now. The swift changes in our industrial system are causing equally swift changes in our religious, political, and social structures. An unseen and fearful revolu-

[1] LEG-BAR—the African slaves were so manacled; also criminals. It was not until the coming of the Brotherhood of Man that the leg-bar passed out of use.

tion is taking place in the fibre and structure of society. One can only dimly feel these things. But they are in the air, now, to-day. One can feel the loom of them—things vast, vague, and terrible. My mind recoils from contemplation of what they may crystallize into. You heard Wickson talk the other night. Behind what he said were the same nameless, formless things that I feel. He spoke out of a superconscious apprehension of them."

"You mean . . . ?" father began, then paused.

"I mean that there is a shadow of something colossal and menacing that even now is beginning to fall across the land. Call it the shadow of an oligarchy, if you will; it is the nearest I dare approximate it. What its nature may be I refuse to imagine.[1] But what I wanted to say was this: You are in a perilous position—a peril that my own fear enhances because I am not able even to measure it. Take my advice and accept the vacation."

"But it would be cowardly," was the protest.

"Not at all. You are an old man. You have done your work in the world, and a great work. Leave the present battle to youth and strength. We young fellows have our work yet to do. Avis will stand by my side in what is to come. She will be your representative in the battle-front."

"But they can't hurt me," father objected. "Thank God I am independent. Oh, I assure you, I know the frightful persecution they can wage on a professor who is economically dependent on his university. But I am independent. I have not been a professor for the sake of my salary. I can get along very comfortably on my own income, and the salary is all they can take away from me."

"But you do not realize," Ernest answered. "If all that I fear be so, your private income, your principal itself, can be taken from you just as easily as your salary."

Father was silent for a few minutes. He was thinking deeply, and I could see the lines of decision forming in his face. At last he spoke.

"I shall not take the vacation." He paused again. "I shall go on with my book.[2] You may be wrong, but whether you are wrong or right, I shall stand by my guns."

---

[1] Though, like Everhard, they did not dream of the nature of it, there were men, even before his time, who caught glimpses of the shadow. John C. Calhoun said: "A power has risen up in the government greater than the people themselves, consisting of many and various and powerful interests, combined into one mass, and held together by the cohesive power of the vast surplus in the banks." And that great humanist, Abraham Lincoln, said, just before his assassination: "I see in the near future a crisis approaching that unnerves me and causes me to tremble for the safety of my country. . . . Corporations have been enthroned, an era of corruption in high places will follow, and the money-power of the country will endeavor to prolong its reign by working upon the prejudices of the people until the wealth is aggregated in a few hands and the Republic is destroyed."

[2] This book, "Economics and Education," was published in that year. Three copies of it are extant; two at Ardis, and one at Asgard. It dealt, in elaborate detail, with one factor in the persistence of the established, namely, the capitalistic bias of the universities and common schools. It was a logical and crushing indictment of the whole system of education that developed in the minds of the students only such ideas as were favorable to the

"All right," Ernest said. "You are travelling the same path that Bishop Morehouse is, and toward a similar smash-up. You'll both be proletarians before you're done with it."

The conversation turned upon the Bishop, and we got Ernest to explain what he had been doing with him.

"He is soul-sick from the journey through hell I have given him. I took him through the homes of a few of our factory workers. I showed him the human wrecks cast aside by the industrial machine, and he listened to their life stories. I took him through the slums of San Francisco, and in drunkenness, prostitution, and criminality he learned a deeper cause than innate depravity. He is very sick, and, worse than that, he has got out of hand. He is too ethical. He has been too severely touched. And, as usual, he is unpractical. He is up in the air with all kinds of ethical delusions and plans for mission work among the cultured. He feels it is his bounden duty to resurrect the ancient spirit of the Church and to deliver its message to the masters. He is overwrought. Sooner or later he is going to break out, and then there's going to be a smash-up. What form it will take I can't even guess. He is a pure, exalted soul, but he is so unpractical. He's beyond me. I can't keep his feet on the earth. And through the air he is rushing on to his Gethsemane. And after this his crucifixion. Such high souls are made for crucifixion."

"And you?" I asked; and beneath my smile was the seriousness of the anxiety of love.

"Not I," he laughed back. "I may be executed, or assassinated, but I shall never be crucified. I am planted too solidly and stolidly upon the earth."

"But why should you bring about the crucifixion of the Bishop?" I asked. "You will not deny that you are the cause of it."

"Why should I leave one comfortable soul in comfort when there are millions in travail and misery?" he demanded back.

"Then why did you advise father to accept the vacation?"

"Because I am not a pure, exalted soul," was the answer. "Because I am solid and stolid and selfish. Because I love you and, like Ruth of old, thy people are my people. As for the Bishop, he has no daughter. Besides, no matter how small the good, nevertheless his little inadequate wail will be productive of some good in the revolution, and every little bit counts."

I could not agree with Ernest. I knew well the noble nature of Bishop Morehouse, and I could not conceive that his voice raised for righteousness would be no more than a little inadequate wail. But I did not yet have the harsh facts of life at my fingers' ends as Ernest had. He saw clearly the futility of the Bishop's great soul, as coming events were soon to show as clearly to me.

It was shortly after this day that Ernest told me, as a good story, the offer he had received from the government, namely, an appointment as United States Commissioner of Labor. I was overjoyed. The salary was comparatively large, and would make safe our marriage. And then it surely was congenial work for Ernest, and, fur-

---

capitalistic regime, to the exclusion of all ideas that were inimical and subversive. The book created a furor, and was promptly suppressed by the Oligarchy.

thermore, my jealous pride in him made me hail the proffered appointment as a recognition of his abilities.

Then I noticed the twinkle in his eyes. He was laughing at me.

"You are not going to . . . to decline?" I quavered.

"It is a bribe," he said. "Behind it is the fine hand of Wickson, and behind him the hands of greater men than he. It is an old trick, old as the class struggle is old—stealing the captains from the army of labor. Poor betrayed labor! If you but knew how many of its leaders have been bought out in similar ways in the past. It is cheaper, so much cheaper, to buy a general than to fight him and his whole army. There was—but I'll not call any names. I'm bitter enough over it as it is. Dear heart, I am a captain of labor. I could not sell out. If for no other reason, the memory of my poor old father and the way he was worked to death would prevent."

The tears were in his eyes, this great, strong hero of mine. He never could forgive the way his father had been malformed—the sordid lies and the petty thefts he had been compelled to, in order to put food in his children's mouths.

"My father was a good man," Ernest once said to me. "The soul of him was good, and yet it was twisted, and maimed, and blunted by the savagery of his life. He was made into a broken-down beast by his masters, the arch-beasts. He should be alive today, like your father. He had a strong constitution. But he was caught in the machine and worked to death—for profit. Think of it. For profit—his life blood transmuted into a wine-supper, or a jewelled gewgaw, or some similar sense-orgy of the parasitic and idle rich, his masters, the arch-beasts."

CHAPTER VII - THE BISHOP'S VISION

"The Bishop is out of hand," Ernest wrote me. "He is clear up in the air. Tonight he is going to begin putting to rights this very miserable world of ours. He is going to deliver his message. He has told me so, and I cannot dissuade him. To-night he is chairman of the I.P.H.,[1] and he will embody his message in his introductory remarks.

"May I bring you to hear him? Of course, he is foredoomed to futility. It will break your heart—it will break his; but for you it will be an excellent object lesson. You know, dear heart, how proud I am because you love me. And because of that I want you to know my fullest value, I want to redeem, in your eyes, some small measure of my unworthiness. And so it is that my pride desires that you shall know my thinking is correct and right. My views are harsh; the futility of so noble a soul as the Bishop will show you the compulsion for such harshness. So come to-night. Sad though this night's happening will be, I feel that it will but draw you more closely to me."

The I.P.H. held its convention that night in San Francisco.[2] This convention had been called to consider public immorality and the remedy for it. Bishop Morehouse presided. He was very nervous as he sat on the platform, and I could see the high tension he was under. By his side were Bishop Dickinson; H. H. Jones, the head of the ethical department in the University of California; Mrs. W. W. Hurd, the great charity organizer; Philip Ward, the equally great philanthropist; and several lesser luminaries in the field of morality and charity. Bishop Morehouse arose and abruptly began:

"I was in my brougham, driving through the streets. It was night-time. Now and then I looked through the carriage windows, and suddenly my eyes seemed to be opened, and I saw things as they really are. At first I covered my eyes with my hands to shut out the awful sight, and then, in the darkness, the question came to me: What is to be done? What is to be done? A little later the question came to me in another way: What would the Master do? And with the question a great light seemed to fill the place, and I saw my duty sun-clear, as Saul saw his on the way to Damascus.

"I stopped the carriage, got out, and, after a few minutes' conversation, persuaded two of the public women to get into the brougham with me. If Jesus was right, then these two unfortunates were my sisters, and the only hope of their purification was in my affection and tenderness.

---

[1] There is no clew to the name of the organization for which these initials stand.

[2] It took but a few minutes to cross by ferry from Berkeley to San Francisco. These, and the other bay cities, practically composed one community.

"I live in one of the loveliest localities of San Francisco. The house in which I live cost a hundred thousand dollars, and its furnishings, books, and works of art cost as much more. The house is a mansion. No, it is a palace, wherein there are many servants. I never knew what palaces were good for. I had thought they were to live in. But now I know. I took the two women of the street to my palace, and they are going to stay with me. I hope to fill every room in my palace with such sisters as they."

The audience had been growing more and more restless and unsettled, and the faces of those that sat on the platform had been betraying greater and greater dismay and consternation. And at this point Bishop Dickinson arose, and with an expression of disgust on his face, fled from the platform and the hall. But Bishop Morehouse, oblivious to all, his eyes filled with his vision, continued:

"Oh, sisters and brothers, in this act of mine I find the solution of all my difficulties. I didn't know what broughams were made for, but now I know. They are made to carry the weak, the sick, and the aged; they are made to show honor to those who have lost the sense even of shame.

"I did not know what palaces were made for, but now I have found a use for them. The palaces of the Church should be hospitals and nurseries for those who have fallen by the wayside and are perishing."

He made a long pause, plainly overcome by the thought that was in him, and nervous how best to express it.

"I am not fit, dear brethren, to tell you anything about morality. I have lived in shame and hypocrisies too long to be able to help others; but my action with those women, sisters of mine, shows me that the better way is easy to find. To those who believe in Jesus and his gospel there can be no other relation between man and man than the relation of affection. Love alone is stronger than sin—stronger than death. I therefore say to the rich among you that it is their duty to do what I have done and am doing. Let each one of you who is prosperous take into his house some thief and treat him as his brother, some unfortunate and treat her as his sister, and San Francisco will need no police force and no magistrates; the prisons will be turned into hospitals, and the criminal will disappear with his crime.

"We must give ourselves and not our money alone. We must do as Christ did; that is the message of the Church today. We have wandered far from the Master's teaching. We are consumed in our own flesh-pots. We have put mammon in the place of Christ. I have here a poem that tells the whole story. I should like to read it to you. It was written by an erring soul who yet saw clearly.[1] It must not be mistaken for an attack upon the Catholic Church. It is an attack upon all churches, upon the pomp and splendor of all churches that have wandered from the Master's path and hedged themselves in from his lambs. Here it is:

"The silver trumpets rang across the Dome;
The people knelt upon the ground with awe;
And borne upon the necks of men I saw,
Like some great God, the Holy Lord of Rome.

---

[1] Oscar Wilde, one of the lords of language of the nineteenth century of the Christian Era.

"Priest-like, he wore a robe more white than foam,
And, king-like, swathed himself in royal red,
Three crowns of gold rose high upon his head;
In splendor and in light the Pope passed home.

"My heart stole back across wide wastes of years
To One who wandered by a lonely sea;
And sought in vain for any place of rest:
'Foxes have holes, and every bird its nest,
I, only I, must wander wearily,
And bruise my feet, and drink wine salt with tears.'"

The audience was agitated, but unresponsive. Yet Bishop Morehouse was not aware of it. He held steadily on his way.

"And so I say to the rich among you, and to all the rich, that bitterly you oppress the Master's lambs. You have hardened your hearts. You have closed your ears to the voices that are crying in the land—the voices of pain and sorrow that you will not hear but that some day will be heard. And so I say—"

But at this point H. H. Jones and Philip Ward, who had already risen from their chairs, led the Bishop off the platform, while the audience sat breathless and shocked.

Ernest laughed harshly and savagely when he had gained the street. His laughter jarred upon me. My heart seemed ready to burst with suppressed tears.

"He has delivered his message," Ernest cried. "The manhood and the deep-hidden, tender nature of their Bishop burst out, and his Christian audience, that loved him, concluded that he was crazy! Did you see them leading him so solicitously from the platform? There must have been laughter in hell at the spectacle."

"Nevertheless, it will make a great impression, what the Bishop did and said to-night," I said.

"Think so?" Ernest queried mockingly.

"It will make a sensation," I asserted. "Didn't you see the reporters scribbling like mad while he was speaking?"

"Not a line of which will appear in to-morrow's papers."

"I can't believe it," I cried.

"Just wait and see," was the answer. "Not a line, not a thought that he uttered. The daily press? The daily suppressage!"

"But the reporters," I objected. "I saw them."

"Not a word that he uttered will see print. You have forgotten the editors. They draw their salaries for the policy they maintain. Their policy is to print nothing that is a vital menace to the established. The Bishop's utterance was a violent assault upon the established morality. It was heresy. They led him from the platform to prevent him from uttering more heresy. The newspapers will purge his heresy in the oblivion of silence. The press of the United States? It is a parasitic growth that battens on the capitalist class. Its function is to serve the established by moulding public opinion, and right well it serves it.

"Let me prophesy. To-morrow's papers will merely mention that the Bishop is in poor health, that he has been working too hard, and that he broke down last night. The next mention, some days hence, will be to the effect that he is suffering from nervous prostration and has been given a vacation by his grateful flock. After that, one of two things will happen: either the Bishop will see the error of his way and return from his vacation a well man in whose eyes there are no more visions, or else he will persist in his madness, and then you may expect to see in the papers, couched pathetically and tenderly, the announcement of his insanity. After that he will be left to gibber his visions to padded walls."

"Now there you go too far!" I cried out.

"In the eyes of society it will truly be insanity," he replied. "What honest man, who is not insane, would take lost women and thieves into his house to dwell with him sisterly and brotherly? True, Christ died between two thieves, but that is another story. Insanity? The mental processes of the man with whom one disagrees, are always wrong. Therefore the mind of the man is wrong. Where is the line between wrong mind and insane mind? It is inconceivable that any sane man can radically disagree with one's most sane conclusions.

"There is a good example of it in this evening's paper. Mary McKenna lives south of Market Street. She is a poor but honest woman. She is also patriotic. But she has erroneous ideas concerning the American flag and the protection it is supposed to symbolize. And here's what happened to her. Her husband had an accident and was laid up in hospital three months. In spite of taking in washing, she got behind in her rent. Yesterday they evicted her. But first, she hoisted an American flag, and from under its folds she announced that by virtue of its protection they could not turn her out on to the cold street. What was done? She was arrested and arraigned for insanity. To-day she was examined by the regular insanity experts. She was found insane. She was consigned to the Napa Asylum."

"But that is far-fetched," I objected. "Suppose I should disagree with everybody about the literary style of a book. They wouldn't send me to an asylum for that."

"Very true," he replied. "But such divergence of opinion would constitute no menace to society. Therein lies the difference. The divergence of opinion on the parts of Mary McKenna and the Bishop do menace society. What if all the poor people should refuse to pay rent and shelter themselves under the American flag? Landlordism would go crumbling. The Bishop's views are just as perilous to society. Ergo, to the asylum with him."

But still I refused to believe.

"Wait and see," Ernest said, and I waited.

Next morning I sent out for all the papers. So far Ernest was right. Not a word that Bishop Morehouse had uttered was in print. Mention was made in one or two of the papers that he had been overcome by his feelings. Yet the platitudes of the speakers that followed him were reported at length.

Several days later the brief announcement was made that he had gone away on a vacation to recover from the effects of overwork. So far so good, but there had been no hint of insanity, nor even of nervous collapse. Little did I dream the terrible road the Bishop was destined to travel—the Gethsemane and crucifixion that Ernest had pondered about.

CHAPTER VIII - THE MACHINE BREAKERS

It was just before Ernest ran for Congress, on the socialist ticket, that father gave what he privately called his "Profit and Loss" dinner. Ernest called it the dinner of the Machine Breakers. In point of fact, it was merely a dinner for business men—small business men, of course. I doubt if one of them was interested in any business the total capitalization of which exceeded a couple of hundred thousand dollars. They were truly representative middle-class business men.

There was Owen, of Silverberg, Owen & Company—a large grocery firm with several branch stores. We bought our groceries from them. There were both partners of the big drug firm of Kowalt & Washburn, and Mr. Asmunsen, the owner of a large granite quarry in Contra Costa County. And there were many similar men, owners or part-owners in small factories, small businesses and small industries—small capitalists, in short.

They were shrewd-faced, interesting men, and they talked with simplicity and clearness. Their unanimous complaint was against the corporations and trusts. Their creed was, "Bust the Trusts." All oppression originated in the trusts, and one and all told the same tale of woe. They advocated government ownership of such trusts as the railroads and telegraphs, and excessive income taxes, graduated with ferocity, to destroy large accumulations. Likewise they advocated, as a cure for local ills, municipal ownership of such public utilities as water, gas, telephones, and street railways.

Especially interesting was Mr. Asmunsen's narrative of his tribulations as a quarry owner. He confessed that he never made any profits out of his quarry, and this, in spite of the enormous volume of business that had been caused by the destruction of San Francisco by the big earthquake. For six years the rebuilding of San Francisco had been going on, and his business had quadrupled and octupled, and yet he was no better off.

"The railroad knows my business just a little bit better than I do," he said. "It knows my operating expenses to a cent, and it knows the terms of my contracts. How it knows these things I can only guess. It must have spies in my employ, and it must have access to the parties to all my contracts. For look you, when I place a big contract, the terms of which favor me a goodly profit, the freight rate from my quarry to market is promptly raised. No explanation is made. The railroad gets my profit. Under such circumstances I have never succeeded in getting the railroad to reconsider its raise. On the other hand, when there have been accidents, increased expenses of operating, or contracts with less profitable terms, I have always succeeded in getting the railroad to lower its rate. What is the result? Large or small, the railroad always gets my profits."

"What remains to you over and above," Ernest interrupted to ask, "would roughly be the equivalent of your salary as a manager did the railroad own the quarry."

"The very thing," Mr. Asmunsen replied. "Only a short time ago I had my books gone through for the past ten years. I discovered that for those ten years my gain was just equivalent to a manager's salary. The railroad might just as well have owned my quarry and hired me to run it."

"But with this difference," Ernest laughed; "the railroad would have had to assume all the risk which you so obligingly assumed for it."

"Very true," Mr. Asmunsen answered sadly.

Having let them have they say, Ernest began asking questions right and left. He began with Mr. Owen.

"You started a branch store here in Berkeley about six months ago?"

"Yes," Mr. Owen answered.

"And since then I've noticed that three little corner groceries have gone out of business. Was your branch store the cause of it?"

Mr. Owen affirmed with a complacent smile. "They had no chance against us."

"Why not?"

"We had greater capital. With a large business there is always less waste and greater efficiency."

"And your branch store absorbed the profits of the three small ones. I see. But tell me, what became of the owners of the three stores?"

"One is driving a delivery wagon for us. I don't know what happened to the other two."

Ernest turned abruptly on Mr. Kowalt.

"You sell a great deal at cut-rates.[1] What have become of the owners of the small drug stores that you forced to the wall?"

"One of them, Mr. Haasfurther, has charge now of our prescription department," was the answer.

"And you absorbed the profits they had been making?"

"Surely. That is what we are in business for."

"And you?" Ernest said suddenly to Mr. Asmunsen. "You are disgusted because the railroad has absorbed your profits?"

Mr. Asmunsen nodded.

"What you want is to make profits yourself?"

Again Mr. Asmunsen nodded.

"Out of others?"

There was no answer.

"Out of others?" Ernest insisted.

"That is the way profits are made," Mr. Asmunsen replied curtly.

---

[1] A lowering of selling price to cost, and even to less than cost. Thus, a large company could sell at a loss for a longer period than a small company, and so drive the small company out of business. A common device of competition.

"Then the business game is to make profits out of others, and to prevent others from making profits out of you. That's it, isn't it?"

Ernest had to repeat his question before Mr. Asmunsen gave an answer, and then he said:

"Yes, that's it, except that we do not object to the others making profits so long as they are not extortionate."

"By extortionate you mean large; yet you do not object to making large profits yourself? . . . Surely not?"

And Mr. Asmunsen amiably confessed to the weakness. There was one other man who was quizzed by Ernest at this juncture, a Mr. Calvin, who had once been a great dairy-owner.

"Some time ago you were fighting the Milk Trust," Ernest said to him; "and now you are in Grange politics.[1] How did it happen?"

"Oh, I haven't quit the fight," Mr. Calvin answered, and he looked belligerent enough. "I'm fighting the Trust on the only field where it is possible to fight—the political field. Let me show you. A few years ago we dairymen had everything our own way."

"But you competed among yourselves?" Ernest interrupted.

"Yes, that was what kept the profits down. We did try to organize, but independent dairymen always broke through us. Then came the Milk Trust."

"Financed by surplus capital from Standard Oil,"[2] Ernest said.

"Yes," Mr. Calvin acknowledged. "But we did not know it at the time. Its agents approached us with a club. "Come in and be fat," was their proposition, "or stay out and starve." Most of us came in. Those that didn't, starved. Oh, it paid us . . . at first. Milk was raised a cent a quart. One-quarter of this cent came to us. Three-quarters of it went to the Trust. Then milk was raised another cent, only we didn't get any of that cent. Our complaints were useless. The Trust was in control. We discovered that we were pawns. Finally, the additional quarter of a cent was denied us. Then the Trust began to squeeze us out. What could we do? We were squeezed out. There were no dairymen, only a Milk Trust."

"But with milk two cents higher, I should think you could have competed," Ernest suggested slyly.

"So we thought. We tried it." Mr. Calvin paused a moment. "It broke us. The Trust could put milk upon the market more cheaply than we. It could sell still at a slight profit when we were selling at actual loss. I dropped fifty thousand dollars in that venture. Most of us went bankrupt.[3] The dairymen were wiped out of existence."

"So the Trust took your profits away from you," Ernest said, "and you've gone into politics in order to legislate the Trust out of existence and get the profits back?"

---

[1] Many efforts were made during this period to organize the perishing farmer class into a political party, the aim of which was destroy the trusts and corporations by drastic legislation. All such attempts ended in failure.

[2] The first successful great trust—almost a generation in advance of the rest.

[3] Bankruptcy—a peculiar institution that enabled an individual, who had failed in competitive industry, to forego paying his debts. The effect was to ameliorate the too savage conditions of the fang-and-claw social struggle.

Mr. Calvin's face lighted up. "That is precisely what I say in my speeches to the farmers. That's our whole idea in a nutshell."

"And yet the Trust produces milk more cheaply than could the independent dairymen?" Ernest queried.

"Why shouldn't it, with the splendid organization and new machinery its large capital makes possible?"

"There is no discussion," Ernest answered. "It certainly should, and, furthermore, it does."

Mr. Calvin here launched out into a political speech in exposition of his views. He was warmly followed by a number of the others, and the cry of all was to destroy the trusts.

"Poor simple folk," Ernest said to me in an undertone. "They see clearly as far as they see, but they see only to the ends of their noses."

A little later he got the floor again, and in his characteristic way controlled it for the rest of the evening.

"I have listened carefully to all of you," he began, "and I see plainly that you play the business game in the orthodox fashion. Life sums itself up to you in profits. You have a firm and abiding belief that you were created for the sole purpose of making profits. Only there is a hitch. In the midst of your own profit-making along comes the trust and takes your profits away from you. This is a dilemma that interferes somehow with the aim of creation, and the only way out, as it seems to you, is to destroy that which takes from you your profits.

"I have listened carefully, and there is only one name that will epitomize you. I shall call you that name. You are machine-breakers. Do you know what a machine-breaker is? Let me tell you. In the eighteenth century, in England, men and women wove cloth on hand-looms in their own cottages. It was a slow, clumsy, and costly way of weaving cloth, this cottage system of manufacture. Along came the steam-engine and labor-saving machinery. A thousand looms assembled in a large factory, and driven by a central engine wove cloth vastly more cheaply than could the cottage weavers on their hand-looms. Here in the factory was combination, and before it competition faded away. The men and women who had worked the hand-looms for themselves now went into the factories and worked the machine-looms, not for themselves, but for the capitalist owners. Furthermore, little children went to work on the machine-looms, at lower wages, and displaced the men. This made hard times for the men. Their standard of living fell. They starved. And they said it was all the fault of the machines. Therefore, they proceeded to break the machines. They did not succeed, and they were very stupid.

"Yet you have not learned their lesson. Here are you, a century and a half later, trying to break machines. By your own confession the trust machines do the work more efficiently and more cheaply than you can. That is why you cannot compete with them. And yet you would break those machines. You are even more stupid than the stupid workmen of England. And while you maunder about restoring competition, the trusts go on destroying you.

"One and all you tell the same story,—the passing away of competition and the coming on of combination. You, Mr. Owen, destroyed competition here in Berkeley when your branch store drove the three small groceries out of business. Your combination was more effective. Yet you feel the pressure of other combinations on you, the trust combinations, and you cry out. It is because you are not a trust. If you were a grocery trust for the whole United States, you would be singing another song. And the song would be, 'Blessed are the trusts.' And yet again, not only is your small combination not a trust, but you are aware yourself of its lack of strength. You are beginning to divine your own end. You feel yourself and your branch stores a pawn in the game. You see the powerful interests rising and growing more powerful day by day; you feel their mailed hands descending upon your profits and taking a pinch here and a pinch there—the railroad trust, the oil trust, the steel trust, the coal trust; and you know that in the end they will destroy you, take away from you the last per cent of your little profits.

"You, sir, are a poor gamester. When you squeezed out the three small groceries here in Berkeley by virtue of your superior combination, you swelled out your chest, talked about efficiency and enterprise, and sent your wife to Europe on the profits you had gained by eating up the three small groceries. It is dog eat dog, and you ate them up. But, on the other hand, you are being eaten up in turn by the bigger dogs, wherefore you squeal. And what I say to you is true of all of you at this table. You are all squealing. You are all playing the losing game, and you are all squealing about it.

"But when you squeal you don't state the situation flatly, as I have stated it. You don't say that you like to squeeze profits out of others, and that you are making all the row because others are squeezing your profits out of you. No, you are too cunning for that. You say something else. You make small-capitalist political speeches such as Mr. Calvin made. What did he say? Here are a few of his phrases I caught: 'Our original principles are all right,' 'What this country requires is a return to fundamental American methods—free opportunity for all,' 'The spirit of liberty in which this nation was born,' 'Let us return to the principles of our forefathers.'

"When he says 'free opportunity for all,' he means free opportunity to squeeze profits, which freedom of opportunity is now denied him by the great trusts. And the absurd thing about it is that you have repeated these phrases so often that you believe them. You want opportunity to plunder your fellow-men in your own small way, but you hypnotize yourselves into thinking you want freedom. You are piggish and acquisitive, but the magic of your phrases leads you to believe that you are patriotic. Your desire for profits, which is sheer selfishness, you metamorphose into altruistic solicitude for suffering humanity. Come on now, right here amongst ourselves, and be honest for once. Look the matter in the face and state it in direct terms."

There were flushed and angry faces at the table, and withal a measure of awe. They were a little frightened at this smooth-faced young fellow, and the swing and smash of his words, and his dreadful trait of calling a spade a spade. Mr. Calvin promptly replied.

"And why not?" he demanded. "Why can we not return to ways of our fathers when this republic was founded? You have spoken much truth, Mr. Everhard, unpalatable though it has been. But here amongst ourselves let us speak out. Let us throw off all disguise and accept the truth as Mr. Everhard has flatly stated it. It is true that we smaller capitalists are after profits, and that the trusts are taking our profits away from us. It is true that we want to destroy the trusts in order that our profits may remain to us. And why can we not do it? Why not? I say, why not?"

"Ah, now we come to the gist of the matter," Ernest said with a pleased expression. "I'll try to tell you why not, though the telling will be rather hard. You see, you fellows have studied business, in a small way, but you have not studied social evolution at all. You are in the midst of a transition stage now in economic evolution, but you do not understand it, and that's what causes all the confusion. Why cannot you return? Because you can't. You can no more make water run up hill than can you cause the tide of economic evolution to flow back in its channel along the way it came. Joshua made the sun stand still upon Gibeon, but you would outdo Joshua. You would make the sun go backward in the sky. You would have time retrace its steps from noon to morning.

"In the face of labor-saving machinery, of organized production, of the increased efficiency of combination, you would set the economic sun back a whole generation or so to the time when there were no great capitalists, no great machinery, no railroads—a time when a host of little capitalists warred with each other in economic anarchy, and when production was primitive, wasteful, unorganized, and costly. Believe me, Joshua's task was easier, and he had Jehovah to help him. But God has forsaken you small capitalists. The sun of the small capitalists is setting. It will never rise again. Nor is it in your power even to make it stand still. You are perishing, and you are doomed to perish utterly from the face of society.

"This is the fiat of evolution. It is the word of God. Combination is stronger than competition. Primitive man was a puny creature hiding in the crevices of the rocks. He combined and made war upon his carnivorous enemies. They were competitive beasts. Primitive man was a combinative beast, and because of it he rose to primacy over all the animals. And man has been achieving greater and greater combinations ever since. It is combination versus competition, a thousand centuries long struggle, in which competition has always been worsted. Whoso enlists on the side of competition perishes."

"But the trusts themselves arose out of competition," Mr. Calvin interrupted.

"Very true," Ernest answered. "And the trusts themselves destroyed competition. That, by your own word, is why you are no longer in the dairy business."

The first laughter of the evening went around the table, and even Mr. Calvin joined in the laugh against himself.

"And now, while we are on the trusts," Ernest went on, "let us settle a few things. I shall make certain statements, and if you disagree with them, speak up. Silence will mean agreement. Is it not true that a machine-loom will weave more cloth and weave more cheaply than a hand-loom?" He paused, but nobody spoke up. "Is it not then highly irrational to break the machine-loom and go back to the clumsy and more costly hand-loom method of weaving?" Heads nodded in acquiescence. "Is it not true that that known as a trust produces more efficiently and cheaply than can a thousand competing small concerns?" Still no one objected. "Then is it not irrational to destroy that cheap and efficient combination?"

No one answered for a long time. Then Mr. Kowalt spoke.

"What are we to do, then?" he demanded. "To destroy the trusts is the only way we can see to escape their domination."

Ernest was all fire and aliveness on the instant.

"I'll show you another way!" he cried. "Let us not destroy those wonderful machines that produce efficiently and cheaply. Let us control them. Let us profit by their efficiency and cheapness. Let us run them for ourselves. Let us oust the present owners of the wonderful machines, and let us own the wonderful machines ourselves.

That, gentlemen, is socialism, a greater combination than the trusts, a greater economic and social combination than any that has as yet appeared on the planet. It is in line with evolution. We meet combination with greater combination. It is the winning side. Come on over with us socialists and play on the winning side."

Here arose dissent. There was a shaking of heads, and mutterings arose.

"All right, then, you prefer to be anachronisms," Ernest laughed. "You prefer to play atavistic roles. You are doomed to perish as all atavisms perish. Have you ever asked what will happen to you when greater combinations than even the present trusts arise? Have you ever considered where you will stand when the great trusts themselves combine into the combination of combinations—into the social, economic, and political trust?"

He turned abruptly and irrelevantly upon Mr. Calvin.

"Tell me," Ernest said, "if this is not true. You are compelled to form a new political party because the old parties are in the hands of the trusts. The chief obstacle to your Grange propaganda is the trusts. Behind every obstacle you encounter, every blow that smites you, every defeat that you receive, is the hand of the trusts. Is this not so? Tell me."

Mr. Calvin sat in uncomfortable silence.

"Go ahead," Ernest encouraged.

"It is true," Mr. Calvin confessed. "We captured the state legislature of Oregon and put through splendid protective legislation, and it was vetoed by the governor, who was a creature of the trusts. We elected a governor of Colorado, and the legislature refused to permit him to take office. Twice we have passed a national income tax, and each time the supreme court smashed it as unconstitutional. The courts are in the hands of the trusts. We, the people, do not pay our judges sufficiently. But there will come a time—"

"When the combination of the trusts will control all legislation, when the combination of the trusts will itself be the government," Ernest interrupted.

"Never! never!" were the cries that arose. Everybody was excited and belligerent.

"Tell me," Ernest demanded, "what will you do when such a time comes?"

"We will rise in our strength!" Mr. Asmunsen cried, and many voices backed his decision.

"That will be civil war," Ernest warned them.

"So be it, civil war," was Mr. Asmunsen's answer, with the cries of all the men at the table behind him. "We have not forgotten the deeds of our forefathers. For our liberties we are ready to fight and die."

Ernest smiled.

"Do not forget," he said, "that we had tacitly agreed that liberty in your case, gentlemen, means liberty to squeeze profits out of others."

The table was angry, now, fighting angry; but Ernest controlled the tumult and made himself heard.

"One more question. When you rise in your strength, remember, the reason for your rising will be that the government is in the hands of the trusts. Therefore, against your strength the government will turn the regular army, the navy, the militia, the police—in short, the whole organized war machinery of the United States. Where will your strength be then?"

Dismay sat on their faces, and before they could recover, Ernest struck again.

"Do you remember, not so long ago, when our regular army was only fifty thousand? Year by year it has been increased until to-day it is three hundred thousand."

Again he struck.

"Nor is that all. While you diligently pursued that favorite phantom of yours, called profits, and moralized about that favorite fetich of yours, called competition, even greater and more direful things have been accomplished by combination. There is the militia."

"It is our strength!" cried Mr. Kowalt. "With it we would repel the invasion of the regular army."

"You would go into the militia yourself," was Ernest's retort, "and be sent to Maine, or Florida, or the Philippines, or anywhere else, to drown in blood your own comrades civil-warring for their liberties. While from Kansas, or Wisconsin, or any other state, your own comrades would go into the militia and come here to California to drown in blood your own civil-warring."

Now they were really shocked, and they sat wordless, until Mr. Owen murmured:

"We would not go into the militia. That would settle it. We would not be so foolish."

Ernest laughed outright.

"You do not understand the combination that has been effected. You could not help yourself. You would be drafted into the militia."

"There is such a thing as civil law," Mr. Owen insisted.

"Not when the government suspends civil law. In that day when you speak of rising in your strength, your strength would be turned against yourself. Into the militia you would go, willy-nilly. Habeas corpus, I heard some one mutter just now. Instead of habeas corpus you would get post mortems. If you refused to go into the militia, or to obey after you were in, you would be tried by drumhead court martial and shot down like dogs. It is the law."

"It is not the law!" Mr. Calvin asserted positively. "There is no such law. Young man, you have dreamed all this. Why, you spoke of sending the militia to the Philippines. That is unconstitutional. The Constitution especially states that the militia cannot be sent out of the country."

"What's the Constitution got to do with it?" Ernest demanded. "The courts interpret the Constitution, and the courts, as Mr. Asmunsen agreed, are the creatures of the trusts. Besides, it is as I have said, the law. It has been the law for years, for nine years, gentlemen."

"That we can be drafted into the militia?" Mr. Calvin asked incredulously. "That they can shoot us by drumhead court martial if we refuse?"

"Yes," Ernest answered, "precisely that."

"How is it that we have never heard of this law?" my father asked, and I could see that it was likewise new to him.

"For two reasons," Ernest said. "First, there has been no need to enforce it. If there had, you'd have heard of it soon enough. And secondly, the law was rushed through Congress and the Senate secretly, with practically no discussion. Of course, the newspapers made no mention of it. But we socialists knew about it. We published it in our papers. But you never read our papers."

"I still insist you are dreaming," Mr. Calvin said stubbornly. "The country would never have permitted it."

"But the country did permit it," Ernest replied. "And as for my dreaming—" he put his hand in his pocket and drew out a small pamphlet—"tell me if this looks like dream-stuff."

He opened it and began to read:

"'Section One, be it enacted, and so forth and so forth, that the militia shall consist of every able-bodied male citizen of the respective states, territories, and District of Columbia, who is more than eighteen and less than forty-five years of age.'

"'Section Seven, that any officer or enlisted man'—remember Section One, gentlemen, you are all enlisted men—'that any enlisted man of the militia who shall refuse or neglect to present himself to such mustering officer upon being called forth as herein prescribed, shall be subject to trial by court martial, and shall be punished as such court martial shall direct.'

"'Section Eight, that courts martial, for the trial of officers or men of the militia, shall be composed of militia officers only.'

"'Section Nine, that the militia, when called into the actual service of the United States, shall be subject to the same rules and articles of war as the regular troops of the United States.'

"There you are gentlemen, American citizens, and fellow-militiamen. Nine years ago we socialists thought that law was aimed against labor. But it would seem that it was aimed against you, too. Congressman Wiley, in the brief discussion that was permitted, said that the bill 'provided for a reserve force to take the mob by the throat'—you're the mob, gentlemen—'and protect at all hazards life, liberty, and property.' And in the time to come, when you rise in your strength, remember that you will be rising against the property of the trusts, and the liberty of the trusts, according to the law, to squeeze you. Your teeth are pulled, gentlemen. Your claws are trimmed. In the day you rise in your strength, toothless and clawless, you will be as harmless as any army of clams."

"I don't believe it!" Kowalt cried. "There is no such law. It is a canard got up by you socialists."

"This bill was introduced in the House of Representatives on July 30, 1902," was the reply. "It was introduced by Representative Dick of Ohio. It was rushed through. It was passed unanimously by the Senate on January 14, 1903. And just seven days afterward was approved by the President of the United States."[1]

---

[1] Everhard was right in the essential particulars, though his date of the introduction of the bill is in error. The bill was introduced on June 30, and not on July 30. The Congressional Record is here in Ardis, and a reference to it shows mention of the bill on the following dates: June 30, December 9, 15, 16, and 17, 1902, and January 7 and 14, 1903. The ignorance evidenced by the business men at the dinner was nothing unusual. Very few people knew of the existence of this law. E. Untermann, a revolutionist, in July, 1903, published a pamphlet at Girard, Kansas, on the "Militia Bill." This pamphlet had a small circulation among workingmen; but already had the segregation of classes proceeded so far, that the members of the middle class never heard of the pamphlet at all, and so remained in ignorance of the law.

CHAPTER IX - THE MATHEMATICS OF A DREAM

In the midst of the consternation his revelation had produced, Ernest began again to speak.

"You have said, a dozen of you to-night, that socialism is impossible. You have asserted the impossible, now let me demonstrate the inevitable. Not only is it inevitable that you small capitalists shall pass away, but it is inevitable that the large capitalists, and the trusts also, shall pass away. Remember, the tide of evolution never flows backward. It flows on and on, and it flows from competition to combination, and from little combination to large combination, and from large combination to colossal combination, and it flows on to socialism, which is the most colossal combination of all.

"You tell me that I dream. Very good. I'll give you the mathematics of my dream; and here, in advance, I challenge you to show that my mathematics are wrong. I shall develop the inevitability of the breakdown of the capitalist system, and I shall demonstrate mathematically why it must break down. Here goes, and bear with me if at first I seem irrelevant.

"Let us, first of all, investigate a particular industrial process, and whenever I state something with which you disagree, please interrupt me. Here is a shoe factory. This factory takes leather and makes it into shoes. Here is one hundred dollars' worth of leather. It goes through the factory and comes out in the form of shoes, worth, let us say, two hundred dollars. What has happened? One hundred dollars has been added to the value of the leather. How was it added? Let us see.

"Capital and labor added this value of one hundred dollars. Capital furnished the factory, the machines, and paid all the expenses. Labor furnished labor. By the joint effort of capital and labor one hundred dollars of value was added. Are you all agreed so far?"

Heads nodded around the table in affirmation.

"Labor and capital having produced this one hundred dollars, now proceed to divide it. The statistics of this division are fractional; so let us, for the sake of convenience, make them roughly approximate. Capital takes fifty dollars as its share, and labor gets in wages fifty dollars as its share. We will not enter into the squabbling over the division.[1] No matter how much squabbling takes place, in one percentage or another the division is arranged. And take notice here, that what is true of this particular industrial process is true of all industrial processes. Am I right?"

Again the whole table agreed with Ernest.

"Now, suppose labor, having received its fifty dollars, wanted to buy back shoes. It could only buy back fifty dollars' worth. That's clear, isn't it?

"And now we shift from this particular process to the sum total of all industrial processes in the United States, which includes the leather itself, raw material, transportation, selling, everything. We will say, for the sake of round figures, that the total production of wealth in the United States is one year is four billion dollars. Then labor has received in wages, during the same period, two billion dollars. Four billion dollars has been produced. How much of this can labor buy back? Two billions. There is no discussion of this, I am sure. For that matter, my percentages are mild. Because of a thousand capitalistic devices, labor cannot buy back even half of the total product.

"But to return. We will say labor buys back two billions. Then it stands to reason that labor can consume only two billions. There are still two billions to be accounted for, which labor cannot buy back and consume."

"Labor does not consume its two billions, even," Mr. Kowalt spoke up. "If it did, it would not have any deposits in the savings banks."

"Labor's deposits in the savings banks are only a sort of reserve fund that is consumed as fast as it accumulates. These deposits are saved for old age, for sickness and accident, and for funeral expenses. The savings bank deposit is simply a piece of the loaf put back on the shelf to be eaten next day. No, labor consumes all of the total product that its wages will buy back.

"Two billions are left to capital. After it has paid its expenses, does it consume the remainder? Does capital consume all of its two billions?"

Ernest stopped and put the question point blank to a number of the men. They shook their heads.

"I don't know," one of them frankly said.

"Of course you do," Ernest went on. "Stop and think a moment. If capital consumed its share, the sum total of capital could not increase. It would remain constant. If you will look at the economic history of the United States, you will see that the sum total of capital has continually increased. Therefore capital does not consume its share. Do you remember when England owned so much of our railroad bonds? As the years went by, we bought back those bonds. What does that mean? That part of capital's unconsumed share bought back the bonds. What is the meaning of the fact that to-day the capitalists of the United States own hundreds and hundreds of millions of dollars of Mexican bonds, Russian bonds, Italian bonds, Grecian bonds? The meaning is that those hundreds and hundreds of millions were part of capital's share which cap-

---

[1] Everhard here clearly develops the cause of all the labor troubles of that time. In the division of the joint-product, capital wanted all it could get, and labor wanted all it could get. This quarrel over the division was irreconcilable. So long as the system of capitalistic production existed, labor and capital continued to quarrel over the division of the joint-product. It is a ludicrous spectacle to us, but we must not forget that we have seven centuries' advantage over those that lived in that time.

ital did not consume. Furthermore, from the very beginning of the capitalist system, capital has never consumed all of its share.

"And now we come to the point. Four billion dollars of wealth is produced in one year in the United States. Labor buys back and consumes two billions. Capital does not consume the remaining two billions. There is a large balance left over unconsumed. What is done with this balance? What can be done with it? Labor cannot consume any of it, for labor has already spent all its wages. Capital will not consume this balance, because, already, according to its nature, it has consumed all it can. And still remains the balance. What can be done with it? What is done with it?"

"It is sold abroad," Mr. Kowalt volunteered.

"The very thing," Ernest agreed. "Because of this balance arises our need for a foreign market. This is sold abroad. It has to be sold abroad. There is no other way of getting rid of it. And that unconsumed surplus, sold abroad, becomes what we call our favorable balance of trade. Are we all agreed so far?"

"Surely it is a waste of time to elaborate these A B C's of commerce," Mr. Calvin said tartly. "We all understand them."

"And it is by these A B C's I have so carefully elaborated that I shall confound you," Ernest retorted. "There's the beauty of it. And I'm going to confound you with them right now. Here goes.

"The United States is a capitalist country that has developed its resources. According to its capitalist system of industry, it has an unconsumed surplus that must be got rid of, and that must be got rid of abroad.[1] What is true of the United States is true of every other capitalist country with developed resources. Every one of such countries has an unconsumed surplus. Don't forget that they have already traded with one another, and that these surpluses yet remain. Labor in all these countries has spent it wages, and cannot buy any of the surpluses. Capital in all these countries has already consumed all it is able according to its nature. And still remain the surpluses. They cannot dispose of these surpluses to one another. How are they going to get rid of them?"

"Sell them to countries with undeveloped resources," Mr. Kowalt suggested.

"The very thing. You see, my argument is so clear and simple that in your own minds you carry it on for me. And now for the next step. Suppose the United States disposes of its surplus to a country with undeveloped resources like, say, Brazil. Remember this surplus is over and above trade, which articles of trade have been consumed. What, then, does the United States get in return from Brazil?"

"Gold," said Mr. Kowalt.

---

[1] Theodore Roosevelt, President of the United States a few years prior to this time, made the following public declaration: "A more liberal and extensive reciprocity in the purchase and sale of commodities is necessary, so that the overproduction of the United States can be satisfactorily disposed of to foreign countries." Of course, this overproduction he mentions was the profits of the capitalist system over and beyond the consuming power of the capitalists. It was at this time that Senator Mark Hanna said: "The production of wealth in the United States is one-third larger annually than its consumption." Also a fellow-Senator, Chauncey Depew, said: "The American people produce annually two billions more wealth than they consume."

"But there is only so much gold, and not much of it, in the world," Ernest objected.

"Gold in the form of securities and bonds and so forth," Mr. Kowalt amended.

"Now you've struck it," Ernest said. "From Brazil the United States, in return for her surplus, gets bonds and securities. And what does that mean? It means that the United States is coming to own railroads in Brazil, factories, mines, and lands in Brazil. And what is the meaning of that in turn?"

Mr. Kowalt pondered and shook his head.

"I'll tell you," Ernest continued. "It means that the resources of Brazil are being developed. And now, the next point. When Brazil, under the capitalist system, has developed her resources, she will herself have an unconsumed surplus. Can she get rid of this surplus to the United States? No, because the United States has herself a surplus. Can the United States do what she previously did—get rid of her surplus to Brazil? No, for Brazil now has a surplus, too.

"What happens? The United States and Brazil must both seek out other countries with undeveloped resources, in order to unload the surpluses on them. But by the very process of unloading the surpluses, the resources of those countries are in turn developed. Soon they have surpluses, and are seeking other countries on which to unload. Now, gentlemen, follow me. The planet is only so large. There are only so many countries in the world. What will happen when every country in the world, down to the smallest and last, with a surplus in its hands, stands confronting every other country with surpluses in their hands?"

He paused and regarded his listeners. The bepuzzlement in their faces was delicious. Also, there was awe in their faces. Out of abstractions Ernest had conjured a vision and made them see it. They were seeing it then, as they sat there, and they were frightened by it.

"We started with A B C, Mr. Calvin," Ernest said slyly. "I have now given you the rest of the alphabet. It is very simple. That is the beauty of it. You surely have the answer forthcoming. What, then, when every country in the world has an unconsumed surplus? Where will your capitalist system be then?"

But Mr. Calvin shook a troubled head. He was obviously questing back through Ernest's reasoning in search of an error.

"Let me briefly go over the ground with you again," Ernest said. "We began with a particular industrial process, the shoe factory. We found that the division of the joint product that took place there was similar to the division that took place in the sum total of all industrial processes. We found that labor could buy back with its wages only so much of the product, and that capital did not consume all of the remainder of the product. We found that when labor had consumed to the full extent of its wages, and when capital had consumed all it wanted, there was still left an unconsumed surplus. We agreed that this surplus could only be disposed of abroad. We agreed, also, that the effect of unloading this surplus on another country would be to develop the resources of that country, and that in a short time that country would have an unconsumed surplus. We extended this process to all the countries on the planet, till every country was producing every year, and every day, an unconsumed surplus, which it could dispose of to no other country. And now I ask you again, what are we going to do with those surpluses?"

Still no one answered.

"Mr. Calvin?" Ernest queried.

"It beats me," Mr. Calvin confessed.

"I never dreamed of such a thing," Mr. Asmunsen said. "And yet it does seem clear as print."

It was the first time I had ever heard Karl Marx's[1] doctrine of surplus value elaborated, and Ernest had done it so simply that I, too, sat puzzled and dumbfounded.

"I'll tell you a way to get rid of the surplus," Ernest said. "Throw it into the sea. Throw every year hundreds of millions of dollars' worth of shoes and wheat and clothing and all the commodities of commerce into the sea. Won't that fix it?"

"It will certainly fix it," Mr. Calvin answered. "But it is absurd for you to talk that way."

Ernest was upon him like a flash.

"Is it a bit more absurd than what you advocate, you machine-breaker, returning to the antediluvian ways of your forefathers? What do you propose in order to get rid of the surplus? You would escape the problem of the surplus by not producing any surplus. And how do you propose to avoid producing a surplus? By returning to a primitive method of production, so confused and disorderly and irrational, so wasteful and costly, that it will be impossible to produce a surplus."

Mr. Calvin swallowed. The point had been driven home. He swallowed again and cleared his throat.

"You are right," he said. "I stand convicted. It is absurd. But we've got to do something. It is a case of life and death for us of the middle class. We refuse to perish. We elect to be absurd and to return to the truly crude and wasteful methods of our forefathers. We will put back industry to its pre-trust stage. We will break the machines. And what are you going to do about it?"

"But you can't break the machines," Ernest replied. "You cannot make the tide of evolution flow backward. Opposed to you are two great forces, each of which is more powerful than you of the middle class. The large capitalists, the trusts, in short, will not let you turn back. They don't want the machines destroyed. And greater than the trusts, and more powerful, is labor. It will not let you destroy the machines. The ownership of the world, along with the machines, lies between the trusts and labor. That is the battle alignment. Neither side wants the destruction of the machines. But each side wants to possess the machines. In this battle the middle class has no place. The middle class is a pygmy between two giants. Don't you see, you poor perishing middle class, you are caught between the upper and nether millstones, and even now has the grinding begun.

"I have demonstrated to you mathematically the inevitable breakdown of the capitalist system. When every country stands with an unconsumed and unsalable surplus on its hands, the capitalist system will break down under the terrific structure of profits that it itself has reared. And in that day there won't be any destruction of the machines. The struggle then will be for the ownership of the machines. If labor wins,

---

[1] Karl Marx—the great intellectual hero of Socialism. A German Jew of the nineteenth century. A contemporary of John Stuart Mill. It seems incredible to us that whole generations should have elapsed after the enunciation of Marx's economic discoveries, in which time he was sneered at by the world's accepted thinkers and scholars. Because of his discoveries he was banished from his native country, and he died an exile in England.

your way will be easy. The United States, and the whole world for that matter, will enter upon a new and tremendous era. Instead of being crushed by the machines, life will be made fairer, and happier, and nobler by them. You of the destroyed middle class, along with labor—there will be nothing but labor then; so you, and all the rest of labor, will participate in the equitable distribution of the products of the wonderful machines. And we, all of us, will make new and more wonderful machines. And there won't be any unconsumed surplus, because there won't be any profits."

"But suppose the trusts win in this battle over the ownership of the machines and the world?" Mr. Kowalt asked.

"Then," Ernest answered, "you, and labor, and all of us, will be crushed under the iron heel of a despotism as relentless and terrible as any despotism that has blackened the pages of the history of man. That will be a good name for that despotism, the Iron Heel."[1]

There was a long pause, and every man at the table meditated in ways unwonted and profound.

"But this socialism of yours is a dream," Mr. Calvin said; and repeated, "a dream."

"I'll show you something that isn't a dream, then," Ernest answered. "And that something I shall call the Oligarchy. You call it the Plutocracy. We both mean the same thing, the large capitalists or the trusts. Let us see where the power lies today. And in order to do so, let us apportion society into its class divisions.

"There are three big classes in society. First comes the Plutocracy, which is composed of wealthy bankers, railway magnates, corporation directors, and trust magnates. Second, is the middle class, your class, gentlemen, which is composed of farmers, merchants, small manufacturers, and professional men. And third and last comes my class, the proletariat, which is composed of the wage-workers.[2]

"You cannot but grant that the ownership of wealth constitutes essential power in the United States to-day. How is this wealth owned by these three classes? Here are the figures. The Plutocracy owns sixty-seven billions of wealth. Of the total number of persons engaged in occupations in the United States, only nine-tenths of one per cent are from the Plutocracy, yet the Plutocracy owns seventy per cent of the total wealth. The middle class owns twenty-four billions. Twenty-nine per cent of those in occupations are from the middle class, and they own twenty-five per cent of the total wealth. Remains the proletariat. It owns four billions. Of all persons in occupations, seventy per cent come from the proletariat; and the proletariat owns four per cent of the total wealth. Where does the power lie, gentlemen?"

"From your own figures, we of the middle class are more powerful than labor," Mr. Asmunsen remarked.

"Calling us weak does not make you stronger in the face of the strength of the Plutocracy," Ernest retorted. "And furthermore, I'm not done with you. There is a greater strength than wealth, and it is greater because it cannot be taken away. Our strength,

---

[1] The earliest known use of that name to designate the Oligarchy.

[2] This division of society made by Everhard is in accordance with that made by Lucien Sanial, one of the statistical authorities of that time. His calculation of the membership of these divisions by occupation, from the United States Census of 1900, is as follows: Plutocratic class, 250,251; Middle class, 8,429,845; and Proletariat class, 20,393,137.

the strength of the proletariat, is in our muscles, in our hands to cast ballots, in our fingers to pull triggers. This strength we cannot be stripped of. It is the primitive strength, it is the strength that is to life germane, it is the strength that is stronger than wealth, and that wealth cannot take away.

"But your strength is detachable. It can be taken away from you. Even now the Plutocracy is taking it away from you. In the end it will take it all away from you. And then you will cease to be the middle class. You will descend to us. You will become proletarians. And the beauty of it is that you will then add to our strength. We will hail you brothers, and we will fight shoulder to shoulder in the cause of humanity.

"You see, labor has nothing concrete of which to be despoiled. Its share of the wealth of the country consists of clothes and household furniture, with here and there, in very rare cases, an unencumbered home. But you have the concrete wealth, twenty-four billions of it, and the Plutocracy will take it away from you. Of course, there is the large likelihood that the proletariat will take it away first. Don't you see your position, gentlemen? The middle class is a wobbly little lamb between a lion and a tiger. If one doesn't get you, the other will. And if the Plutocracy gets you first, why it's only a matter of time when the Proletariat gets the Plutocracy.

"Even your present wealth is not a true measure of your power. The strength of your wealth at this moment is only an empty shell. That is why you are crying out your feeble little battle-cry, 'Return to the ways of our fathers.' You are aware of your impotency. You know that your strength is an empty shell. And I'll show you the emptiness of it.

"What power have the farmers? Over fifty per cent are thralls by virtue of the fact that they are merely tenants or are mortgaged. And all of them are thralls by virtue of the fact that the trusts already own or control (which is the same thing only better)—own and control all the means of marketing the crops, such as cold storage, railroads, elevators, and steamship lines. And, furthermore, the trusts control the markets. In all this the farmers are without power. As regards their political and governmental power, I'll take that up later, along with the political and governmental power of the whole middle class.

"Day by day the trusts squeeze out the farmers as they squeezed out Mr. Calvin and the rest of the dairymen. And day by day are the merchants squeezed out in the same way. Do you remember how, in six months, the Tobacco Trust squeezed out over four hundred cigar stores in New York City alone? Where are the old-time owners of the coal fields? You know today, without my telling you, that the Railroad Trust owns or controls the entire anthracite and bituminous coal fields. Doesn't the Standard Oil Trust[1] own a score of the ocean lines? And does it not also control copper, to say nothing of running a smelter trust as a little side enterprise? There are ten thousand cities in the United States to-night lighted by the companies owned or controlled by Standard Oil, and in as many cities all the electric transportation,—urban, suburban, and interurban,—is in the hands of Standard Oil. The small capitalists who

---

[1] Standard Oil and Rockefeller—see upcoming footnote: "Rockefeller began as a member . . ."

were in these thousands of enterprises are gone. You know that. It's the same way that you are going.

"The small manufacturer is like the farmer; and small manufacturers and farmers to-day are reduced, to all intents and purposes, to feudal tenure. For that matter, the professional men and the artists are at this present moment villeins in everything but name, while the politicians are henchmen. Why do you, Mr. Calvin, work all your nights and days to organize the farmers, along with the rest of the middle class, into a new political party? Because the politicians of the old parties will have nothing to do with your atavistic ideas; and with your atavistic ideas, they will have nothing to do because they are what I said they are, henchmen, retainers of the Plutocracy.

"I spoke of the professional men and the artists as villeins. What else are they? One and all, the professors, the preachers, and the editors, hold their jobs by serving the Plutocracy, and their service consists of propagating only such ideas as are either harmless to or commendatory of the Plutocracy. Whenever they propagate ideas that menace the Plutocracy, they lose their jobs, in which case, if they have not provided for the rainy day, they descend into the proletariat and either perish or become working-class agitators. And don't forget that it is the press, the pulpit, and the university that mould public opinion, set the thought-pace of the nation. As for the artists, they merely pander to the little less than ignoble tastes of the Plutocracy.

"But after all, wealth in itself is not the real power; it is the means to power, and power is governmental. Who controls the government to-day? The proletariat with its twenty millions engaged in occupations? Even you laugh at the idea. Does the middle class, with its eight million occupied members? No more than the proletariat. Who, then, controls the government? The Plutocracy, with its paltry quarter of a million of occupied members. But this quarter of a million does not control the government, though it renders yeoman service. It is the brain of the Plutocracy that controls the government, and this brain consists of seven[1] small and powerful groups of men. And do not forget that these groups are working to-day practically in unison.

"Let me point out the power of but one of them, the railroad group. It employs forty thousand lawyers to defeat the people in the courts. It issues countless thousands of free passes to judges, bankers, editors, ministers, university men, members of state legislatures, and of Congress. It maintains luxurious lobbies[2] at every state capital, and at the national capital; and in all the cities and towns of the land it employs an

---

[1] Even as late as 1907, it was considered that eleven groups dominated the country, but this number was reduced by the amalgamation of the five railroad groups into a supreme combination of all the railroads. These five groups so amalgamated, along with their financial and political allies, were (1) James J. Hill with his control of the Northwest; (2) the Pennsylvania railway group, Schiff financial manager, with big banking firms of Philadelphia and New York; (3) Harriman, with Frick for counsel and Odell as political lieutenant, controlling the central continental, Southwestern and Southern Pacific Coast lines of transportation; (4) the Gould family railway interests; and (5) Moore, Reid, and Leeds, known as the "Rock Island crowd." These strong oligarchs arose out of the conflict of competition and travelled the inevitable road toward combination.

[2] Lobby—a peculiar institution for bribing, bulldozing, and corrupting the legislators who were supposed to represent the people's interests.

immense army of pettifoggers and small politicians whose business is to attend primaries, pack conventions, get on juries, bribe judges, and in every way to work for its interests. [1]

"Gentlemen, I have merely sketched the power of one of the seven groups that constitute the brain of the Plutocracy.[2] Your twenty-four billions of wealth does not

---

[1] A decade before this speech of Everhard's, the New York Board of Trade issued a report from which the following is quoted: "The railroads control absolutely the legislatures of a majority of the states of the Union; they make and unmake United States Senators, congressmen, and governors, and are practically dictators of the governmental policy of the United States."

[2] Rockefeller began as a member of the proletariat, and through thrift and cunning succeeded in developing the first perfect trust, namely that known as Standard Oil. We cannot forbear giving the following remarkable page from the history of the times, to show how the need for reinvestment of the Standard Oil surplus crushed out small capitalists and hastened the breakdown of the capitalist system. David Graham Phillips was a radical writer of the period, and the quotation, by him, is taken from a copy of the Saturday Evening Post, dated October 4, 1902 A.D. This is the only copy of this publication that has come down to us, and yet, from its appearance and content, we cannot but conclude that it was one of the popular periodicals with a large circulation. The quotation here follows:

"About ten years ago Rockefeller's income was given as thirty millions by an excellent authority. He had reached the limit of profitable investment of profits in the oil industry. Here, then, were these enormous sums in cash pouring in—more than $2,000,000 a month for John Davison Rockefeller alone. The problem of reinvestment became more serious. It became a nightmare. The oil income was swelling, swelling, and the number of sound investments limited, even more limited than it is now. It was through no special eagerness for more gains that the Rockefellers began to branch out from oil into other things. They were forced, swept on by this inrolling tide of wealth which their monopoly magnet irresistibly attracted. They developed a staff of investment seekers and investigators. It is said that the chief of this staff has a salary of $125,000 a year.

"The first conspicuous excursion and incursion of the Rockefellers was into the railway field. By 1895 they controlled one-fifth of the railway mileage of the country. What do they own or, through dominant ownership, control to-day? They are powerful in all the great railways of New York, north, east, and west, except one, where their share is only a few millions. They are in most of the great railways radiating from Chicago. They dominate in several of the systems that extend to the Pacific. It is their votes that make Mr. Morgan so potent, though, it may be added, they need his brains more than he needs their votes— at present, and the combination of the two constitutes in large measure the 'community of interest.'

"But railways could not alone absorb rapidly enough those mighty floods of gold. Presently John D. Rockefeller's $2,500,000 a month had increased to four, to five, to six millions a month, to $75,000,000 a year. Illuminating oil was becoming all profit. The reinvestments of income were adding their mite of many annual millions.

"The Rockefellers went into gas and electricity when those industries had developed to the safe investment stage. And now a large part of the American people must begin to enrich the Rockefellers as soon as the sun goes down, no matter what form of illuminant they use. They went into farm mortgages. It is said that when prosperity a few years ago ena-

give you twenty-five cents' worth of governmental power. It is an empty shell, and soon even the empty shell will be taken away from you. The Plutocracy has all power in its hands to-day. It to-day makes the laws, for it owns the Senate, Congress, the courts, and the state legislatures. And not only that. Behind law must be force to execute the law. To-day the Plutocracy makes the law, and to enforce the law it has at its beck and call the, police, the army, the navy, and, lastly, the militia, which is you, and me, and all of us."

---

bled the farmers to rid themselves of their mortgages, John D. Rockefeller was moved almost to tears; eight millions which he had thought taken care of for years to come at a good interest were suddenly dumped upon his doorstep and there set up a-squawking for a new home. This unexpected addition to his worriments in finding places for the progeny of his petroleum and their progeny and their progeny's progeny was too much for the equanimity of a man without a digestion. . . .

"The Rockefellers went into mines—iron and coal and copper and lead; into other industrial companies; into street railways, into national, state, and municipal bonds; into steamships and steamboats and telegraphy; into real estate, into skyscrapers and residences and hotels and business blocks; into life insurance, into banking. There was soon literally no field of industry where their millions were not at work. . . .

"The Rockefeller bank—the National City Bank—is by itself far and away the biggest bank in the United States. It is exceeded in the world only by the Bank of England and the Bank of France. The deposits average more than one hundred millions a day; and it dominates the call loan market on Wall Street and the stock market. But it is not alone; it is the head of the Rockefeller chain of banks, which includes fourteen banks and trust companies in New York City, and banks of great strength and influence in every large money center in the country.

"John D. Rockefeller owns Standard Oil stock worth between four and five hundred millions at the market quotations. He has a hundred millions in the steel trust, almost as much in a single western railway system, half as much in a second, and so on and on and on until the mind wearies of the cataloguing. His income last year was about $100,000,000— it is doubtful if the incomes of all the Rothschilds together make a greater sum. And it is going up by leaps and bounds."

Little discussion took place after this, and the dinner soon broke up. All were quiet and subdued, and leave-taking was done with low voices. It seemed almost that they were scared by the vision of the times they had seen.

"The situation is, indeed, serious," Mr. Calvin said to Ernest. "I have little quarrel with the way you have depicted it. Only I disagree with you about the doom of the middle class. We shall survive, and we shall overthrow the trusts."

"And return to the ways of your fathers," Ernest finished for him.

"Even so," Mr. Calvin answered gravely. "I know it's a sort of machine-breaking, and that it is absurd. But then life seems absurd to-day, what of the machinations of the Plutocracy. And at any rate, our sort of machine-breaking is at least practical and possible, which your dream is not. Your socialistic dream is . . . well, a dream. We cannot follow you."

"I only wish you fellows knew a little something about evolution and sociology," Ernest said wistfully, as they shook hands. "We would be saved so much trouble if you did."

CHAPTER X - THE VORTEX

Following like thunder claps upon the Business Men's dinner, occurred event after event of terrifying moment; and I, little I, who had lived so placidly all my days in the quiet university town, found myself and my personal affairs drawn into the vortex of the great world-affairs. Whether it was my love for Ernest, or the clear sight he had given me of the society in which I lived, that made me a revolutionist, I know not; but a revolutionist I became, and I was plunged into a whirl of happenings that would have been inconceivable three short months before.

The crisis in my own fortunes came simultaneously with great crises in society. First of all, father was discharged from the university. Oh, he was not technically discharged. His resignation was demanded, that was all. This, in itself, did not amount to much. Father, in fact, was delighted. He was especially delighted because his discharge had been precipitated by the publication of his book, "Economics and Education." It clinched his argument, he contended. What better evidence could be advanced to prove that education was dominated by the capitalist class?

But this proof never got anywhere. Nobody knew he had been forced to resign from the university. He was so eminent a scientist that such an announcement, coupled with the reason for his enforced resignation, would have created somewhat of a furor all over the world. The newspapers showered him with praise and honor, and commended him for having given up the drudgery of the lecture room in order to devote his whole time to scientific research.

At first father laughed. Then he became angry—tonic angry. Then came the suppression of his book. This suppression was performed secretly, so secretly that at first we could not comprehend. The publication of the book had immediately caused a bit of excitement in the country. Father had been politely abused in the capitalist press, the tone of the abuse being to the effect that it was a pity so great a scientist should leave his field and invade the realm of sociology, about which he knew nothing and wherein he had promptly become lost. This lasted for a week, while father chuckled and said the book had touched a sore spot on capitalism. And then, abruptly, the newspapers and the critical magazines ceased saying anything about the book at all. Also, and with equal suddenness, the book disappeared from the market. Not a copy was obtainable from any bookseller. Father wrote to the publishers and was informed that the plates had been accidentally injured. An unsatisfactory correspondence followed. Driven finally to an unequivocal stand, the publishers stated that they could not see their way to putting the book into type again, but that they were willing to relinquish their rights in it.

"And you won't find another publishing house in the country to touch it," Ernest said. "And if I were you, I'd hunt cover right now. You've merely got a foretaste of the Iron Heel."

But father was nothing if not a scientist. He never believed in jumping to conclusions. A laboratory experiment was no experiment if it were not carried through in all its details. So he patiently went the round of the publishing houses. They gave a multitude of excuses, but not one house would consider the book.

When father became convinced that the book had actually been suppressed, he tried to get the fact into the newspapers; but his communications were ignored. At a political meeting of the socialists, where many reporters were present, father saw his chance. He arose and related the history of the suppression of the book. He laughed next day when he read the newspapers, and then he grew angry to a degree that eliminated all tonic qualities. The papers made no mention of the book, but they misreported him beautifully. They twisted his words and phrases away from the context, and turned his subdued and controlled remarks into a howling anarchistic speech. It was done artfully. One instance, in particular, I remember. He had used the phrase "social revolution." The reporter merely dropped out "social." This was sent out all over the country in an Associated Press despatch, and from all over the country arose a cry of alarm. Father was branded as a nihilist and an anarchist, and in one cartoon that was copied widely he was portrayed waving a red flag at the head of a mob of long-haired, wild-eyed men who bore in their hands torches, knives, and dynamite bombs.

He was assailed terribly in the press, in long and abusive editorials, for his anarchy, and hints were made of mental breakdown on his part. This behavior, on the part of the capitalist press, was nothing new, Ernest told us. It was the custom, he said, to send reporters to all the socialist meetings for the express purpose of misreporting and distorting what was said, in order to frighten the middle class away from any possible affiliation with the proletariat. And repeatedly Ernest warned father to cease fighting and to take to cover.

The socialist press of the country took up the fight, however, and throughout the reading portion of the working class it was known that the book had been suppressed. But this knowledge stopped with the working class. Next, the "Appeal to Reason," a big socialist publishing house, arranged with father to bring out the book. Father was jubilant, but Ernest was alarmed.

"I tell you we are on the verge of the unknown," he insisted. "Big things are happening secretly all around us. We can feel them. We do not know what they are, but they are there. The whole fabric of society is a-tremble with them. Don't ask me. I don't know myself. But out of this flux of society something is about to crystallize. It is crystallizing now. The suppression of the book is a precipitation. How many books have been suppressed? We haven't the least idea. We are in the dark. We have no way of learning. Watch out next for the suppression of the socialist press and socialist publishing houses. I'm afraid it's coming. We are going to be throttled."

Ernest had his hand on the pulse of events even more closely than the rest of the socialists, and within two days the first blow was struck. The Appeal to Reason was a weekly, and its regular circulation amongst the proletariat was seven hundred and fifty thousand. Also, it very frequently got out special editions of from two to five millions. These great editions were paid for and distributed by the small army of voluntary workers who had marshalled around the Appeal. The first blow was aimed at these special editions, and it was a crushing one. By an arbitrary ruling of the Post Office, these editions were decided to be not the regular circulation of the paper, and for that reason were denied admission to the mails.

A week later the Post Office Department ruled that the paper was seditious, and barred it entirely from the mails. This was a fearful blow to the socialist propaganda. The Appeal was desperate. It devised a plan of reaching its subscribers through the express companies, but they declined to handle it. This was the end of the Appeal. But not quite. It prepared to go on with its book publishing. Twenty thousand copies of father's book were in the bindery, and the presses were turning off more. And then, without warning, a mob arose one night, and, under a waving American flag, singing patriotic songs, set fire to the great plant of the Appeal and totally destroyed it.

Now Girard, Kansas, was a quiet, peaceable town. There had never been any labor troubles there. The Appeal paid union wages; and, in fact, was the backbone of the town, giving employment to hundreds of men and women. It was not the citizens of Girard that composed the mob. This mob had risen up out of the earth apparently, and to all intents and purposes, its work done, it had gone back into the earth. Ernest saw in the affair the most sinister import.

"The Black Hundreds[1] are being organized in the United States," he said. "This is the beginning. There will be more of it. The Iron Heel is getting bold."

And so perished father's book. We were to see much of the Black Hundreds as the days went by. Week by week more of the socialist papers were barred from the mails, and in a number of instances the Black Hundreds destroyed the socialist presses. Of course, the newspapers of the land lived up to the reactionary policy of the ruling class, and the destroyed socialist press was misrepresented and vilified, while the Black Hundreds were represented as true patriots and saviours of society. So convincing was all this misrepresentation that even sincere ministers in the pulpit praised the Black Hundreds while regretting the necessity of violence.

History was making fast. The fall elections were soon to occur, and Ernest was nominated by the socialist party to run for Congress. His chance for election was most favorable. The street-car strike in San Francisco had been broken. And following upon it the teamsters' strike had been broken. These two defeats had been very disastrous to organized labor. The whole Water Front Federation, along with its allies in the structural trades, had backed up the teamsters, and all had smashed down ingloriously. It had been a bloody strike. The police had broken countless heads with their riot clubs; and the death list had been augmented by the turning loose of a machine-gun on the strikers from the barns of the Marsden Special Delivery Company.

In consequence, the men were sullen and vindictive. They wanted blood, and revenge. Beaten on their chosen field, they were ripe to seek revenge by means of

---

[1] The Black Hundreds were reactionary mobs organized by the perishing Autocracy in the Russian Revolution. These reactionary groups attacked the revolutionary groups, and also, at needed moments, rioted and destroyed property so as to afford the Autocracy the pretext of calling out the Cossacks.

political action. They still maintained their labor organization, and this gave them strength in the political struggle that was on. Ernest's chance for election grew stronger and stronger. Day by day unions and more unions voted their support to the socialists, until even Ernest laughed when the Undertakers' Assistants and the Chicken Pickers fell into line. Labor became mulish. While it packed the socialist meetings with mad enthusiasm, it was impervious to the wiles of the old-party politicians. The old-party orators were usually greeted with empty halls, though occasionally they encountered full halls where they were so roughly handled that more than once it was necessary to call out the police reserves.

History was making fast. The air was vibrant with things happening and impending. The country was on the verge of hard times,[1] caused by a series of prosperous years wherein the difficulty of disposing abroad of the unconsumed surplus had become increasingly difficult. Industries were working short time; many great factories were standing idle against the time when the surplus should be gone; and wages were being cut right and left.

Also, the great machinist strike had been broken. Two hundred thousand machinists, along with their five hundred thousand allies in the metalworking trades, had been defeated in as bloody a strike as had ever marred the United States. Pitched battles had been fought with the small armies of armed strike-breakers[2] put in the field by the employers' associations; the Black Hundreds, appearing in scores of wide-scattered places, had destroyed property; and, in consequence, a hundred thousand regular soldiers of the United States has been called out to put a frightful end to the whole affair. A number of the labor leaders had been executed; many others had been sentenced to prison, while thousands of the rank and file of the strikers had been herded into bull-pens[3] and abominably treated by the soldiers.

The years of prosperity were now to be paid for. All markets were glutted; all markets were falling; and amidst the general crumble of prices the price of labor crumbled fastest of all. The land was convulsed with industrial dissensions. Labor was striking here, there, and everywhere; and where it was not striking, it was being

---

[1] Under the capitalist regime these periods of hard times were as inevitable as they were absurd. Prosperity always brought calamity. This, of course, was due to the excess of unconsumed profits that was piled up.

[2] Strike-breakers—these were, in purpose and practice and everything except name, the private soldiers of the capitalists. They were thoroughly organized and well armed, and they were held in readiness to be hurled in special trains to any part of the country where labor went on strike or was locked out by the employers. Only those curious times could have given rise to the amazing spectacle of one, Farley, a notorious commander of strike-breakers, who, in 1906, swept across the United States in special trains from New York to San Francisco with an army of twenty-five hundred men, fully armed and equipped, to break a strike of the San Francisco street-car men. Such an act was in direct violation of the laws of the land. The fact that this act, and thousands of similar acts, went unpunished, goes to show how completely the judiciary was the creature of the Plutocracy.

[3] Bull-pen—in a miners' strike in Idaho, in the latter part of the nineteenth century, it happened that many of the strikers were confined in a bull-pen by the troops. The practice and the name continued in the twentieth century.

turned out by the capitalists. The papers were filled with tales of violence and blood. And through it all the Black Hundreds played their part. Riot, arson, and wanton destruction of property was their function, and well they performed it. The whole regular army was in the field, called there by the actions of the Black Hundreds.[1] All cities and towns were like armed camps, and laborers were shot down like dogs. Out of the vast army of the unemployed the strike-breakers were recruited; and when the strike-breakers were worsted by the labor unions, the troops always appeared and crushed the unions. Then there was the militia. As yet, it was not necessary to have recourse to the secret militia law. Only the regularly organized militia was out, and it was out everywhere. And in this time of terror, the regular army was increased an additional hundred thousand by the government.

Never had labor received such an all-around beating. The great captains of industry, the oligarchs, had for the first time thrown their full weight into the breach the struggling employers' associations had made. These associations were practically middle-class affairs, and now, compelled by hard times and crashing markets, and aided by the great captains of industry, they gave organized labor an awful and decisive defeat. It was an all-powerful alliance, but it was an alliance of the lion and the lamb, as the middle class was soon to learn.

Labor was bloody and sullen, but crushed. Yet its defeat did not put an end to the hard times. The banks, themselves constituting one of the most important forces of the Oligarchy, continued to call in credits. The Wall Street[2] group turned the stock market into a maelstrom where the values of all the land crumbled away almost to nothingness. And out of all the rack and ruin rose the form of the nascent Oligarchy, imperturbable, indifferent, and sure. Its serenity and certitude was terrifying. Not only did it use its own vast power, but it used all the power of the United States Treasury to carry out its plans.

The captains of industry had turned upon the middle class. The employers' associations, that had helped the captains of industry to tear and rend labor, were now torn and rent by their quondam allies. Amidst the crashing of the middle men, the small business men and manufacturers, the trusts stood firm. Nay, the trusts did more than stand firm. They were active. They sowed wind, and wind, and ever more wind; for

---

[1] The name only, and not the idea, was imported from Russia. The Black Hundreds were a development out of the secret agents of the capitalists, and their use arose in the labor struggles of the nineteenth century. There is no discussion of this. No less an authority of the times than Carroll D. Wright, United States Commissioner of Labor, is responsible for the statement. From his book, entitled "The Battles of Labor," is quoted the declaration that "in some of the great historic strikes the employers themselves have instigated acts of violence;" that manufacturers have deliberately provoked strikes in order to get rid of surplus stock; and that freight cars have been burned by employers' agents during railroad strikes in order to increase disorder. It was out of these secret agents of the employers that the Black Hundreds arose; and it was they, in turn, that later became that terrible weapon of the Oligarchy, the agents- provocateurs.

[2] Wall Street—so named from a street in ancient New York, where was situated the stock exchange, and where the irrational organization of society permitted underhanded manipulation of all the industries of the country.

they alone knew how to reap the whirlwind and make a profit out of it. And such profits! Colossal profits! Strong enough themselves to weather the storm that was largely their own brewing, they turned loose and plundered the wrecks that floated about them. Values were pitifully and inconceivably shrunken, and the trusts added hugely to their holdings, even extending their enterprises into many new fields—and always at the expense of the middle class.

Thus the summer of 1912 witnessed the virtual death-thrust to the middle class. Even Ernest was astounded at the quickness with which it had been done. He shook his head ominously and looked forward without hope to the fall elections.

"It's no use," he said. "We are beaten. The Iron Heel is here. I had hoped for a peaceable victory at the ballot-box. I was wrong. Wickson was right. We shall be robbed of our few remaining liberties; the Iron Heel will walk upon our faces; nothing remains but a bloody revolution of the working class. Of course we will win, but I shudder to think of it."

And from then on Ernest pinned his faith in revolution. In this he was in advance of his party. His fellow-socialists could not agree with him. They still insisted that victory could be gained through the elections. It was not that they were stunned. They were too cool-headed and courageous for that. They were merely incredulous, that was all. Ernest could not get them seriously to fear the coming of the Oligarchy. They were stirred by him, but they were too sure of their own strength. There was no room in their theoretical social evolution for an oligarchy, therefore the Oligarchy could not be.

"We'll send you to Congress and it will be all right," they told him at one of our secret meetings.

"And when they take me out of Congress," Ernest replied coldly, "and put me against a wall, and blow my brains out—what then?"

"Then we'll rise in our might," a dozen voices answered at once.

"Then you'll welter in your gore," was his retort. "I've heard that song sung by the middle class, and where is it now in its might?"

CHAPTER XI - THE GREAT ADVENTURE

Mr. Wickson did not send for father. They met by chance on the ferry-boat to San Francisco, so that the warning he gave father was not premeditated. Had they not met accidentally, there would not have been any warning. Not that the outcome would have been different, however. Father came of stout old Mayflower[1] stock, and the blood was imperative in him.

"Ernest was right," he told me, as soon as he had returned home. "Ernest is a very remarkable young man, and I'd rather see you his wife than the wife of Rockefeller himself or the King of England."

"What's the matter?" I asked in alarm.

"The Oligarchy is about to tread upon our faces—yours and mine. Wickson as much as told me so. He was very kind—for an oligarch. He offered to reinstate me in the university. What do you think of that? He, Wickson, a sordid money-grabber, has the power to determine whether I shall or shall not teach in the university of the state. But he offered me even better than that—offered to make me president of some great college of physical sciences that is being planned—the Oligarchy must get rid of its surplus somehow, you see.

"'Do you remember what I told that socialist lover of your daughter's?' he said. 'I told him that we would walk upon the faces of the working class. And so we shall. As for you, I have for you a deep respect as a scientist; but if you throw your fortunes in with the working class—well, watch out for your face, that is all.' And then he turned and left me."

"It means we'll have to marry earlier than you planned," was Ernest's comment when we told him.

I could not follow his reasoning, but I was soon to learn it. It was at this time that the quarterly dividend of the Sierra Mills was paid—or, rather, should have been paid, for father did not receive his. After waiting several days, father wrote to the secretary. Promptly came the reply that there was no record on the books of father's owning any stock, and a polite request for more explicit information.

---

[1] One of the first ships that carried colonies to America, after the discovery of the New World. Descendants of these original colonists were for a while inordinately proud of their genealogy; but in time the blood became so widely diffused that it ran in the veins practically of all Americans.

"I'll make it explicit enough, confound him," father declared, and departed for the bank to get the stock in question from his safe-deposit box.

"Ernest is a very remarkable man," he said when he got back and while I was helping him off with his overcoat. "I repeat, my daughter, that young man of yours is a very remarkable young man."

I had learned, whenever he praised Ernest in such fashion, to expect disaster.

"They have already walked upon my face," father explained. "There was no stock. The box was empty. You and Ernest will have to get married pretty quickly."

Father insisted on laboratory methods. He brought the Sierra Mills into court, but he could not bring the books of the Sierra Mills into court. He did not control the courts, and the Sierra Mills did. That explained it all. He was thoroughly beaten by the law, and the bare-faced robbery held good.

It is almost laughable now, when I look back on it, the way father was beaten. He met Wickson accidentally on the street in San Francisco, and he told Wickson that he was a damned scoundrel. And then father was arrested for attempted assault, fined in the police court, and bound over to keep the peace. It was all so ridiculous that when he got home he had to laugh himself. But what a furor was raised in the local papers! There was grave talk about the bacillus of violence that infected all men who embraced socialism; and father, with his long and peaceful life, was instanced as a shining example of how the bacillus of violence worked. Also, it was asserted by more than one paper that father's mind had weakened under the strain of scientific study, and confinement in a state asylum for the insane was suggested. Nor was this merely talk. It was an imminent peril. But father was wise enough to see it. He had the Bishop's experience to lesson from, and he lessoned well. He kept quiet no matter what injustice was perpetrated on him, and really, I think, surprised his enemies.

There was the matter of the house—our home. A mortgage was foreclosed on it, and we had to give up possession. Of course there wasn't any mortgage, and never had been any mortgage. The ground had been bought outright, and the house had been paid for when it was built. And house and lot had always been free and unencumbered. Nevertheless there was the mortgage, properly and legally drawn up and signed, with a record of the payments of interest through a number of years. Father made no outcry. As he had been robbed of his money, so was he now robbed of his home. And he had no recourse. The machinery of society was in the hands of those who were bent on breaking him. He was a philosopher at heart, and he was no longer even angry.

"I am doomed to be broken," he said to me; "but that is no reason that I should not try to be shattered as little as possible. These old bones of mine are fragile, and I've learned my lesson. God knows I don't want to spend my last days in an insane asylum."

Which reminds me of Bishop Morehouse, whom I have neglected for many pages. But first let me tell of my marriage. In the play of events, my marriage sinks into insignificance, I know, so I shall barely mention it.

"Now we shall become real proletarians," father said, when we were driven from our home. "I have often envied that young man of yours for his actual knowledge of the proletariat. Now I shall see and learn for myself."

Father must have had strong in him the blood of adventure. He looked upon our catastrophe in the light of an adventure. No anger nor bitterness possessed him. He was too philosophic and simple to be vindictive, and he lived too much in the world of mind to miss the creature comforts we were giving up. So it was, when we moved to San Francisco into four wretched rooms in the slum south of Market Street, that he embarked upon the adventure with the joy and enthusiasm of a child—combined with the clear sight and mental grasp of an extraordinary intellect. He really never crystallized mentally. He had no false sense of values. Conventional or habitual values meant nothing to him. The only values he recognized were mathematical and scientific facts. My father was a great man. He had the mind and the soul that only great men have. In ways he was even greater than Ernest, than whom I have known none greater.

Even I found some relief in our change of living. If nothing else, I was escaping from the organized ostracism that had been our increasing portion in the university town ever since the enmity of the nascent Oligarchy had been incurred. And the change was to me likewise adventure, and the greatest of all, for it was love-adventure. The change in our fortunes had hastened my marriage, and it was as a wife that I came to live in the four rooms on Pell Street, in the San Francisco slum.

And this out of all remains: I made Ernest happy. I came into his stormy life, not as a new perturbing force, but as one that made toward peace and repose. I gave him rest. It was the guerdon of my love for him. It was the one infallible token that I had not failed. To bring forgetfulness, or the light of gladness, into those poor tired eyes of his—what greater joy could have blessed me than that?

Those dear tired eyes. He toiled as few men ever toiled, and all his lifetime he toiled for others. That was the measure of his manhood. He was a humanist and a lover. And he, with his incarnate spirit of battle, his gladiator body and his eagle spirit—he was as gentle and tender to me as a poet. He was a poet. A singer in deeds. And all his life he sang the song of man. And he did it out of sheer love of man, and for man he gave his life and was crucified.

And all this he did with no hope of future reward. In his conception of things there was no future life. He, who fairly burnt with immortality, denied himself immortality—such was the paradox of him. He, so warm in spirit, was dominated by that cold and forbidding philosophy, materialistic monism. I used to refute him by telling him that I measured his immortality by the wings of his soul, and that I should have to live endless aeons in order to achieve the full measurement. Whereat he would laugh, and his arms would leap out to me, and he would call me his sweet metaphysician; and the tiredness would pass out of his eyes, and into them would flood the happy love-light that was in itself a new and sufficient advertisement of his immortality.

Also, he used to call me his dualist, and he would explain how Kant, by means of pure reason, had abolished reason, in order to worship God. And he drew the parallel and included me guilty of a similar act. And when I pleaded guilty, but defended the act as highly rational, he but pressed me closer and laughed as only one of God's own lovers could laugh. I was wont to deny that heredity and environment could explain his own originality and genius, any more than could the cold groping finger of science catch and analyze and classify that elusive essence that lurked in the constitution of life itself.

I held that space was an apparition of God, and that soul was a projection of the character of God; and when he called me his sweet metaphysician, I called him my immortal materialist. And so we loved and were happy; and I forgave him his materialism because of his tremendous work in the world, performed without thought of soul-gain thereby, and because of his so exceeding modesty of spirit that prevented him from having pride and regal consciousness of himself and his soul.

But he had pride. How could he have been an eagle and not have pride? His contention was that it was finer for a finite mortal speck of life to feel Godlike, than for a god to feel godlike; and so it was that he exalted what he deemed his mortality. He was fond of quoting a fragment from a certain poem. He had never seen the whole poem, and he had tried vainly to learn its authorship. I here give the fragment, not alone because he loved it, but because it epitomized the paradox that he was in the spirit of him, and his conception of his spirit. For how can a man, with thrilling, and burning, and exaltation, recite the following and still be mere mortal earth, a bit of fugitive force, an evanescent form? Here it is:

"Joy upon joy and gain upon gain
Are the destined rights of my birth,
And I shout the praise of my endless days
To the echoing edge of the earth.
Though I suffer all deaths that a man can die
To the uttermost end of time,
I have deep-drained this, my cup of bliss,
In every age and clime—

"The froth of Pride, the tang of Power,
The sweet of Womanhood!
I drain the lees upon my knees,
For oh, the draught is good;
I drink to Life, I drink to Death,
And smack my lips with song,
For when I die, another 'I' shall pass the cup along.

"The man you drove from Eden's grove
Was I, my Lord, was I,
And I shall be there when the earth and the air
Are rent from sea to sky;
For it is my world, my gorgeous world,
The world of my dearest woes,
From the first faint cry of the newborn
To the rack of the woman's throes.

"Packed with the pulse of an unborn race,
Torn with a world's desire,
The surging flood of my wild young blood
Would quench the judgment fire.
I am Man, Man, Man, from the tingling flesh
To the dust of my earthly goal,
From the nestling gloom of the pregnant womb
To the sheen of my naked soul.

Bone of my bone and flesh of my flesh
The whole world leaps to my will,
And the unslaked thirst of an Eden cursed
Shall harrow the earth for its fill.
Almighty God, when I drain life's glass
Of all its rainbow gleams,
The hapless plight of eternal night
Shall be none too long for my dreams.

"The man you drove from Eden's grove
Was I, my Lord, was I,
And I shall be there when the earth and the air
Are rent from sea to sky;
For it is my world, my gorgeous world,
The world of my dear delight,
From the brightest gleam of the Arctic stream
To the dusk of my own love-night."

Ernest always overworked. His wonderful constitution kept him up; but even that constitution could not keep the tired look out of his eyes. His dear, tired eyes! He never slept more than four and one-half hours a night; yet he never found time to do all the work he wanted to do. He never ceased from his activities as a propagandist, and was always scheduled long in advance for lectures to workingmen's organizations. Then there was the campaign. He did a man's full work in that alone. With the suppression of the socialist publishing houses, his meagre royalties ceased, and he was hard-put to make a living; for he had to make a living in addition to all his other labor. He did a great deal of translating for the magazines on scientific and philosophic subjects; and, coming home late at night, worn out from the strain of the campaign, he would plunge into his translating and toil on well into the morning hours. And in addition to everything, there was his studying. To the day of his death he kept up his studies, and he studied prodigiously.

And yet he found time in which to love me and make me happy. But this was accomplished only through my merging my life completely into his. I learned shorthand and typewriting, and became his secretary. He insisted that I succeeded in cutting his work in half; and so it was that I schooled myself to understand his work. Our interests became mutual, and we worked together and played together.

And then there were our sweet stolen moments in the midst of our work—just a word, or caress, or flash of love-light; and our moments were sweeter for being stolen. For we lived on the heights, where the air was keen and sparkling, where the toil was for humanity, and where sordidness and selfishness never entered. We loved love, and our love was never smirched by anything less than the best. And this out of all remains: I did not fail. I gave him rest—he who worked so hard for others, my dear, tired-eyed mortalist.

CHAPTER XII - THE BISHOP

It was after my marriage that I chanced upon Bishop Morehouse. But I must give the events in their proper sequence. After his outbreak at the I. P. H. Convention, the Bishop, being a gentle soul, had yielded to the friendly pressure brought to bear upon him, and had gone away on a vacation. But he returned more fixed than ever in his determination to preach the message of the Church. To the consternation of his congregation, his first sermon was quite similar to the address he had given before the Convention. Again he said, and at length and with distressing detail, that the Church had wandered away from the Master's teaching, and that Mammon had been instated in the place of Christ.

And the result was, willy-nilly, that he was led away to a private sanitarium for mental disease, while in the newspapers appeared pathetic accounts of his mental breakdown and of the saintliness of his character. He was held a prisoner in the sanitarium. I called repeatedly, but was denied access to him; and I was terribly impressed by the tragedy of a sane, normal, saintly man being crushed by the brutal will of society. For the Bishop was sane, and pure, and noble. As Ernest said, all that was the matter with him was that he had incorrect notions of biology and sociology, and because of his incorrect notions he had not gone about it in the right way to rectify matters.

What terrified me was the Bishop's helplessness. If he persisted in the truth as he saw it, he was doomed to an insane ward. And he could do nothing. His money, his position, his culture, could not save him. His views were perilous to society, and society could not conceive that such perilous views could be the product of a sane mind. Or, at least, it seems to me that such was society's attitude.

But the Bishop, in spite of the gentleness and purity of his spirit, was possessed of guile. He apprehended clearly his danger. He saw himself caught in the web, and he tried to escape from it. Denied help from his friends, such as father and Ernest and I could have given, he was left to battle for himself alone. And in the enforced solitude of the sanitarium he recovered. He became again sane. His eyes ceased to see visions; his brain was purged of the fancy that it was the duty of society to feed the Master's lambs.

As I say, he became well, quite well, and the newspapers and the church people hailed his return with joy. I went once to his church. The sermon was of the same order as the ones he had preached long before his eyes had seen visions. I was disappointed, shocked. Had society then beaten him into submission? Was he a coward? Had he been bulldozed into recanting? Or had the strain been too great for him, and had he meekly surrendered to the juggernaut of the established?

I called upon him in his beautiful home. He was woefully changed. He was thinner, and there were lines on his face which I had never seen before. He was manifestly distressed by my coming. He plucked nervously at his sleeve as we talked; and his eyes were restless, fluttering here, there, and everywhere, and refusing to meet mine. His mind seemed preoccupied, and there were strange pauses in his conversation, abrupt changes of topic, and an inconsecutiveness that was bewildering. Could this, then, be the firm-poised, Christ-like man I had known, with pure, limpid eyes and a gaze steady and unfaltering as his soul? He had been man-handled; he had been cowed into subjection. His spirit was too gentle. It had not been mighty enough to face the organized wolf-pack of society.

I felt sad, unutterably sad. He talked ambiguously, and was so apprehensive of what I might say that I had not the heart to catechise him. He spoke in a far-away manner of his illness, and we talked disjointedly about the church, the alterations in the organ, and about petty charities; and he saw me depart with such evident relief that I should have laughed had not my heart been so full of tears.

The poor little hero! If I had only known! He was battling like a giant, and I did not guess it. Alone, all alone, in the midst of millions of his fellow-men, he was fighting his fight. Torn by his horror of the asylum and his fidelity to truth and the right, he clung steadfastly to truth and the right; but so alone was he that he did not dare to trust even me. He had learned his lesson well—too well.

But I was soon to know. One day the Bishop disappeared. He had told nobody that he was going away; and as the days went by and he did not reappear, there was much gossip to the effect that he had committed suicide while temporarily deranged. But this idea was dispelled when it was learned that he had sold all his possessions,—his city mansion, his country house at Menlo Park, his paintings, and collections, and even his cherished library. It was patent that he had made a clean and secret sweep of everything before he disappeared.

This happened during the time when calamity had overtaken us in our own affairs; and it was not till we were well settled in our new home that we had opportunity really to wonder and speculate about the Bishop's doings. And then, everything was suddenly made clear. Early one evening, while it was yet twilight, I had run across the street and into the butcher-shop to get some chops for Ernest's supper. We called the last meal of the day "supper" in our new environment.

Just at the moment I came out of the butcher-shop, a man emerged from the corner grocery that stood alongside. A queer sense familiarity made me look again. But the man had turned and was walking rapidly away. There was something about the slope of the shoulders and the fringe of silver hair between coat collar and slouch hat that aroused vague memories. Instead of crossing the street, I hurried after the man. I quickened my pace, trying not to think the thoughts that formed unbidden in my brain. No, it was impossible. It could not be—not in those faded overalls, too long in the legs and frayed at the bottoms.

I paused, laughed at myself, and almost abandoned the chase. But the haunting familiarity of those shoulders and that silver hair! Again I hurried on. As I passed him, I shot a keen look at his face; then I whirled around abruptly and confronted—the Bishop.

He halted with equal abruptness, and gasped. A large paper bag in his right hand fell to the sidewalk. It burst, and about his feet and mine bounced and rolled a flood of potatoes. He looked at me with surprise and alarm, then he seemed to wilt away; the shoulders drooped with dejection, and he uttered a deep sigh.

I held out my hand. He shook it, but his hand felt clammy. He cleared his throat in embarrassment, and I could see the sweat starting out on his forehead. It was evident that he was badly frightened.

"The potatoes," he murmured faintly. "They are precious."

Between us we picked them up and replaced them in the broken bag, which he now held carefully in the hollow of his arm. I tried to tell him my gladness at meeting him and that he must come right home with me.

"Father will be rejoiced to see you," I said. "We live only a stone's throw away.

"I can't," he said, "I must be going. Good-by."

He looked apprehensively about him, as though dreading discovery, and made an attempt to walk on.

"Tell me where you live, and I shall call later," he said, when he saw that I walked beside him and that it was my intention to stick to him now that he was found.

"No," I answered firmly. "You must come now."

He looked at the potatoes spilling on his arm, and at the small parcels on his other arm.

"Really, it is impossible," he said. "Forgive me for my rudeness. If you only knew."

He looked as if he were going to break down, but the next moment he had himself in control.

"Besides, this food," he went on. "It is a sad case. It is terrible. She is an old woman. I must take it to her at once. She is suffering from want of it. I must go at once. You understand. Then I will return. I promise you."

"Let me go with you," I volunteered. "Is it far?"

He sighed again, and surrendered.

"Only two blocks," he said. "Let us hasten."

Under the Bishop's guidance I learned something of my own neighborhood. I had not dreamed such wretchedness and misery existed in it. Of course, this was because I did not concern myself with charity. I had become convinced that Ernest was right when he sneered at charity as a poulticing of an ulcer. Remove the ulcer, was his remedy; give to the worker his product; pension as soldiers those who grow honorably old in their toil, and there will be no need for charity. Convinced of this, I toiled with him at the revolution, and did not exhaust my energy in alleviating the social ills that continuously arose from the injustice of the system.

I followed the Bishop into a small room, ten by twelve, in a rear tenement. And there we found a little old German woman—sixty-four years old, the Bishop said. She was surprised at seeing me, but she nodded a pleasant greeting and went on sewing on the pair of men's trousers in her lap. Beside her, on the floor, was a pile of trousers. The Bishop discovered there was neither coal nor kindling, and went out to buy some.

I took up a pair of trousers and examined her work.

"Six cents, lady," she said, nodding her head gently while she went on stitching. She stitched slowly, but never did she cease from stitching. She seemed mastered by the verb "to stitch."

"For all that work?" I asked. "Is that what they pay? How long does it take you?"

"Yes," she answered, "that is what they pay. Six cents for finishing. Two hours' sewing on each pair."

"But the boss doesn't know that," she added quickly, betraying a fear of getting him into trouble. "I'm slow. I've got the rheumatism in my hands. Girls work much faster. They finish in half that time. The boss is kind. He lets me take the work home, now that I am old and the noise of the machine bothers my head. If it wasn't for his kindness, I'd starve.

"Yes, those who work in the shop get eight cents. But what can you do? There is not enough work for the young. The old have no chance. Often one pair is all I can get. Sometimes, like to-day, I am given eight pair to finish before night."

I asked her the hours she worked, and she said it depended on the season.

"In the summer, when there is a rush order, I work from five in the morning to nine at night. But in the winter it is too cold. The hands do not early get over the stiffness. Then you must work later—till after midnight sometimes.

"Yes, it has been a bad summer. The hard times. God must be angry. This is the first work the boss has given me in a week. It is true, one cannot eat much when there is no work. I am used to it. I have sewed all my life, in the old country and here in San Francisco—thirty-three years.

"If you are sure of the rent, it is all right. The houseman is very kind, but he must have his rent. It is fair. He only charges three dollars for this room. That is cheap. But it is not easy for you to find all of three dollars every month."

She ceased talking, and, nodding her head, went on stitching.

"You have to be very careful as to how you spend your earnings," I suggested.

She nodded emphatically.

"After the rent it's not so bad. Of course you can't buy meat. And there is no milk for the coffee. But always there is one meal a day, and often two."

She said this last proudly. There was a smack of success in her words. But as she stitched on in silence, I noticed the sadness in her pleasant eyes and the droop of her mouth. The look in her eyes became far away. She rubbed the dimness hastily out of them; it interfered with her stitching.

"No, it is not the hunger that makes the heart ache," she explained. "You get used to being hungry. It is for my child that I cry. It was the machine that killed her. It is true she worked hard, but I cannot understand. She was strong. And she was young—only forty; and she worked only thirty years. She began young, it is true; but my man died. The boiler exploded down at the works. And what were we to do? She was ten, but she was very strong. But the machine killed her. Yes, it did. It killed her, and she was the fastest worker in the shop. I have thought about it often, and I know. That is why I cannot work in the shop. The machine bothers my head. Always I hear it saying, 'I did it, I did it.' And it says that all day long. And then I think of my daughter, and I cannot work."

The moistness was in her old eyes again, and she had to wipe it away before she could go on stitching.

I heard the Bishop stumbling up the stairs, and I opened the door. What a spectacle he was. On his back he carried half a sack of coal, with kindling on top. Some of the coal dust had coated his face, and the sweat from his exertions was running in streaks. He dropped his burden in the corner by the stove and wiped his face on a coarse bandana handkerchief. I could scarcely accept the verdict of my senses. The Bishop, black as a coal-heaver, in a workingman's cheap cotton shirt (one button was missing from the throat), and in overalls! That was the most incongruous of all—the overalls, frayed at the bottoms, dragged down at the heels, and held up by a narrow leather belt around the hips such as laborers wear.

Though the Bishop was warm, the poor swollen hands of the old woman were already cramping with the cold; and before we left her, the Bishop had built the fire, while I had peeled the potatoes and put them on to boil. I was to learn, as time went by, that there were many cases similar to hers, and many worse, hidden away in the monstrous depths of the tenements in my neighborhood.

We got back to find Ernest alarmed by my absence. After the first surprise of greeting was over, the Bishop leaned back in his chair, stretched out his overall-covered legs, and actually sighed a comfortable sigh. We were the first of his old friends he had met since his disappearance, he told us; and during the intervening weeks he must have suffered greatly from loneliness. He told us much, though he told us more of the joy he had experienced in doing the Master's bidding.

"For truly now," he said, "I am feeding his lambs. And I have learned a great lesson. The soul cannot be ministered to till the stomach is appeased. His lambs must be fed bread and butter and potatoes and meat; after that, and only after that, are their spirits ready for more refined nourishment."

He ate heartily of the supper I cooked. Never had he had such an appetite at our table in the old days. We spoke of it, and he said that he had never been so healthy in his life.

"I walk always now," he said, and a blush was on his cheek at the thought of the time when he rode in his carriage, as though it were a sin not lightly to be laid.

"My health is better for it," he added hastily. "And I am very happy—indeed, most happy. At last I am a consecrated spirit."

And yet there was in his face a permanent pain, the pain of the world that he was now taking to himself. He was seeing life in the raw, and it was a different life from what he had known within the printed books of his library.

"And you are responsible for all this, young man," he said directly to Ernest.

Ernest was embarrassed and awkward.

"I—I warned you," he faltered.

"No, you misunderstand," the Bishop answered. "I speak not in reproach, but in gratitude. I have you to thank for showing me my path. You led me from theories about life to life itself. You pulled aside the veils from the social shams. You were light in my darkness, but now I, too, see the light. And I am very happy, only . . ." he hesitated painfully, and in his eyes fear leaped large. "Only the persecution. I harm no one. Why will they not let me alone? But it is not that. It is the nature of the persecution. I shouldn't mind if they cut my flesh with stripes, or burned me at the stake, or crucified me head—downward. But it is the asylum that frightens me. Think of it! Of me—in an asylum for the insane! It is revolting. I saw some of the cases at the sanitarium. They were violent. My blood chills when I think of it. And to be imprisoned for the rest of my life amid scenes of screaming madness! No! no! Not that! Not that!"

It was pitiful. His hands shook, his whole body quivered and shrank away from the picture he had conjured. But the next moment he was calm.

"Forgive me," he said simply. "It is my wretched nerves. And if the Master's work leads there, so be it. Who am I to complain?"

I felt like crying aloud as I looked at him: "Great Bishop! O hero! God's hero!"

As the evening wore on we learned more of his doings.

"I sold my house—my houses, rather," he said, "all my other possessions. I knew I must do it secretly, else they would have taken everything away from me. That would have been terrible. I often marvel these days at the immense quantity of potatoes two or three hundred thousand dollars will buy, or bread, or meat, or coal and kindling." He turned to Ernest. "You are right, young man. Labor is dreadfully underpaid. I never did a bit of work in my life, except to appeal aesthetically to Pharisees—I thought I was preaching the message—and yet I was worth half a million dollars. I never knew what half a million dollars meant until I realized how much potatoes and bread and butter and meat it could buy. And then I realized something more. I realized that all those potatoes and that bread and butter and meat were mine, and that I had not worked to make them. Then it was clear to me, some one else had worked and made them and been robbed of them. And when I came down amongst the poor I found those who had been robbed and who were hungry and wretched because they had been robbed."

We drew him back to his narrative.

"The money? I have it deposited in many different banks under different names. It can never be taken away from me, because it can never be found. And it is so good, that money. It buys so much food. I never knew before what money was good for."

"I wish we could get some of it for the propaganda," Ernest said wistfully. "It would do immense good."

"Do you think so?" the Bishop said. "I do not have much faith in politics. In fact, I am afraid I do not understand politics."

Ernest was delicate in such matters. He did not repeat his suggestion, though he knew only too well the sore straits the Socialist Party was in through lack of money.

"I sleep in cheap lodging houses," the Bishop went on. "But I am afraid, and never stay long in one place. Also, I rent two rooms in workingmen's houses in different quarters of the city. It is a great extravagance, I know, but it is necessary. I make up for it in part by doing my own cooking, though sometimes I get something to eat in cheap coffee-houses. And I have made a discovery. Tamales[1] are very good when the air grows chilly late at night. Only they are so expensive. But I have discovered a place where I can get three for ten cents. They are not so good as the others, but they are very warming.

"And so I have at last found my work in the world, thanks to you, young man. It is the Master's work." He looked at me, and his eyes twinkled. "You caught me feeding his lambs, you know. And of course you will all keep my secret."

He spoke carelessly enough, but there was real fear behind the speech. He promised to call upon us again. But a week later we read in the newspaper of the sad case of Bishop Morehouse, who had been committed to the Napa Asylum and for whom there were still hopes held out. In vain we tried to see him, to have his case reconsid-

---

[1] A Mexican dish, referred to occasionally in the literature of the times. It is supposed that it was warmly seasoned. No recipe of it has come down to us.

ered or investigated. Nor could we learn anything about him except the reiterated statements that slight hopes were still held for his recovery.

"Christ told the rich young man to sell all he had," Ernest said bitterly. "The Bishop obeyed Christ's injunction and got locked up in a madhouse. Times have changed since Christ's day. A rich man to-day who gives all he has to the poor is crazy. There is no discussion. Society has spoken."

CHAPTER XIII - THE GENERAL STRIKE

Of course Ernest was elected to Congress in the great socialist landslide that took place in the fall of 1912. One great factor that helped to swell the socialist vote was the destruction of Hearst.[1] This the Plutocracy found an easy task. It cost Hearst eighteen million dollars a year to run his various papers, and this sum, and more, he got back from the middle class in payment for advertising. The source of his financial strength lay wholly in the middle class. The trusts did not advertise.[2] To destroy Hearst, all that was necessary was to take away from him his advertising.

The whole middle class had not yet been exterminated. The sturdy skeleton of it remained; but it was without power. The small manufacturers and small business men who still survived were at the complete mercy of the Plutocracy. They had no economic nor political souls of their own. When the fiat of the Plutocracy went forth, they withdrew their advertisements from the Hearst papers.

Hearst made a gallant fight. He brought his papers out at a loss of a million and a half each month. He continued to publish the advertisements for which he no longer received pay. Again the fiat of the Plutocracy went forth, and the small business men and manufacturers swamped him with a flood of notices that he must discontinue running their old advertisements. Hearst persisted. Injunctions were served on him. Still he persisted. He received six months' imprisonment for contempt of court in disobeying the injunctions, while he was bankrupted by countless damage suits. He had no chance. The Plutocracy had passed sentence on him. The courts were in the hands of the Plutocracy to carry the sentence out. And with Hearst crashed also to destruction the Democratic Party that he had so recently captured.

---

[1] William Randolph Hearst—a young California millionaire who became the most powerful newspaper owner in the country. His newspapers were published in all the large cities, and they appealed to the perishing middle class and to the proletariat. So large was his following that he managed to take possession of the empty shell of the old Democratic Party. He occupied an anomalous position, preaching an emasculated socialism combined with a nondescript sort of petty bourgeois capitalism. It was oil and water, and there was no hope for him, though for a short period he was a source of serious apprehension to the Plutocrats.

[2] The cost of advertising was amazing in those helter- skelter times. Only the small capitalists competed, and therefore they did the advertising. There being no competition where there was a trust, there was no need for the trusts to advertise.

With the destruction of Hearst and the Democratic Party, there were only two paths for his following to take. One was into the Socialist Party; the other was into the Republican Party. Then it was that we socialists reaped the fruit of Hearst's pseudo-socialistic preaching; for the great Majority of his followers came over to us.

The expropriation of the farmers that took place at this time would also have swelled our vote had it not been for the brief and futile rise of the Grange Party. Ernest and the socialist leaders fought fiercely to capture the farmers; but the destruction of the socialist press and publishing houses constituted too great a handicap, while the mouth-to-mouth propaganda had not yet been perfected. So it was that politicians like Mr. Calvin, who were themselves farmers long since expropriated, captured the farmers and threw their political strength away in a vain campaign.

"The poor farmers," Ernest once laughed savagely; "the trusts have them both coming and going."

And that was really the situation. The seven great trusts, working together, had pooled their enormous surpluses and made a farm trust. The railroads, controlling rates, and the bankers and stock exchange gamesters, controlling prices, had long since bled the farmers into indebtedness. The bankers, and all the trusts for that matter, had likewise long since loaned colossal amounts of money to the farmers. The farmers were in the net. All that remained to be done was the drawing in of the net. This the farm trust proceeded to do.

The hard times of 1912 had already caused a frightful slump in the farm markets. Prices were now deliberately pressed down to bankruptcy, while the railroads, with extortionate rates, broke the back of the farmer-camel. Thus the farmers were compelled to borrow more and more, while they were prevented from paying back old loans. Then ensued the great foreclosing of mortgages and enforced collection of notes. The farmers simply surrendered the land to the farm trust. There was nothing else for them to do. And having surrendered the land, the farmers next went to work for the farm trust, becoming managers, superintendents, foremen, and common laborers. They worked for wages. They became villeins, in short—serfs bound to the soil by a living wage. They could not leave their masters, for their masters composed the Plutocracy. They could not go to the cities, for there, also, the Plutocracy was in control. They had but one alternative,—to leave the soil and become vagrants, in brief, to starve. And even there they were frustrated, for stringent vagrancy laws were passed and rigidly enforced.

Of course, here and there, farmers, and even whole communities of farmers, escaped expropriation by virtue of exceptional conditions. But they were merely strays and did not count, and they were gathered in anyway during the following year.[1]

---

[1] The destruction of the Roman yeomanry proceeded far less rapidly than the destruction of the American farmers and small capitalists. There was momentum in the twentieth century, while there was practically none in ancient Rome.

Numbers of the farmers, impelled by an insane lust for the soil, and willing to show what beasts they could become, tried to escape expropriation by withdrawing from any and all market-dealing. They sold nothing. They bought nothing. Among themselves a primitive barter began to spring up. Their privation and hardships were terrible, but they persisted. It became quite a movement, in fact. The manner in which they were beaten was unique

CHAPTER XIII - THE GENERAL STRIKE

Thus it was that in the fall of 1912 the socialist leaders, with the exception of Ernest, decided that the end of capitalism had come. What of the hard times and the consequent vast army of the unemployed; what of the destruction of the farmers and the middle class; and what of the decisive defeat administered all along the line to the labor unions; the socialists were really justified in believing that the end of capitalism had come and in themselves throwing down the gauntlet to the Plutocracy.

Alas, how we underestimated the strength of the enemy! Everywhere the socialists proclaimed their coming victory at the ballot-box, while, in unmistakable terms, they stated the situation. The Plutocracy accepted the challenge. It was the Plutocracy, weighing and balancing, that defeated us by dividing our strength. It was the Plutocracy, through its secret agents, that raised the cry that socialism was sacrilegious and atheistic; it was the Plutocracy that whipped the churches, and especially the Catholic Church, into line, and robbed us of a portion of the labor vote. And it was the Plutocracy, through its secret agents of course, that encouraged the Grange Party and even spread it to the cities into the ranks of the dying middle class.

Nevertheless the socialist landslide occurred. But, instead of a sweeping victory with chief executive officers and majorities in all legislative bodies, we found ourselves in the minority. It is true, we elected fifty Congressmen; but when they took their seats in the spring of 1913, they found themselves without power of any sort. Yet they were more fortunate than the Grangers, who captured a dozen state governments, and who, in the spring, were not permitted to take possession of the captured offices. The incumbents refused to retire, and the courts were in the hands of the Oligarchy. But this is too far in advance of events. I have yet to tell of the stirring times of the winter of 1912.

The hard times at home had caused an immense decrease in consumption. Labor, out of work, had no wages with which to buy. The result was that the Plutocracy found a greater surplus than ever on its hands. This surplus it was compelled to dispose of abroad, and, what of its colossal plans, it needed money. Because of its strenuous efforts to dispose of the surplus in the world market, the Plutocracy clashed with Germany. Economic clashes were usually succeeded by wars, and this particular clash was no exception. The great German war-lord prepared, and so did the United States prepare.

The war-cloud hovered dark and ominous. The stage was set for a world-catastrophe, for in all the world were hard times, labor troubles, perishing middle classes, armies of unemployed, clashes of economic interests in the world-market, and mutterings and rumblings of the socialist revolution.[1]

---

and logical and simple. The Plutocracy, by virtue of its possession of the government, raised their taxes. It was the weak joint in their armor. Neither buying nor selling, they had no money, and in the end their land was sold to pay the taxes.

[1] For a long time these mutterings and rumblings had been heard. As far back as 1906 A.D., Lord Avebury, an Englishman, uttered the following in the House of Lords: "The unrest in Europe, the spread of socialism, and the ominous rise of Anarchism, are warnings to the governments and the ruling classes that the condition of the working classes in Europe is becoming intolerable, and that if a revolution is to be avoided some steps must be taken to increase wages, reduce the hours of labor, and lower the prices of the neces-

The Oligarchy wanted the war with Germany. And it wanted the war for a dozen reasons. In the juggling of events such a war would cause, in the reshuffling of the international cards and the making of new treaties and alliances, the Oligarchy had much to gain. And, furthermore, the war would consume many national surpluses, reduce the armies of unemployed that menaced all countries, and give the Oligarchy a breathing space in which to perfect its plans and carry them out. Such a war would virtually put the Oligarchy in possession of the world-market. Also, such a war would create a large standing army that need never be disbanded, while in the minds of the people would be substituted the issue, "America versus Germany," in place of "Socialism versus Oligarchy."

And truly the war would have done all these things had it not been for the socialists. A secret meeting of the Western leaders was held in our four tiny rooms in Pell Street. Here was first considered the stand the socialists were to take. It was not the first time we had put our foot down upon war,[1] but it was the first time we had done so in the United States. After our secret meeting we got in touch with the national organization, and soon our code cables were passing back and forth across the Atlantic between us and the International Bureau.

The German socialists were ready to act with us. There were over five million of them, many of them in the standing army, and, in addition, they were on friendly terms with the labor unions. In both countries the socialists came out in bold declaration against the war and threatened the general strike. And in the meantime they made preparation for the general strike. Furthermore, the revolutionary parties in all countries gave public utterance to the socialist principle of international peace that must be preserved at all hazards, even to the extent of revolt and revolution at home.

The general strike was the one great victory we American socialists won. On the 4th of December the American minister was withdrawn from the German capital.

---

saries of life." The Wall Street Journal, a stock gamesters' publication, in commenting upon Lord Avebury's speech, said: "These words were spoken by an aristocrat and a member of the most conservative body in all Europe. That gives them all the more significance. They contain more valuable political economy than is to be found in most of the books. They sound a note of warning. Take heed, gentlemen of the war and navy departments!"

At the same time, Sydney Brooks, writing in America, in Harper's Weekly, said: "You will not hear the socialists mentioned in Washington. Why should you? The politicians are always the last people in this country to see what is going on under their noses. They will jeer at me when I prophesy, and prophesy with the utmost confidence, that at the next presidential election the socialists will poll over a million votes."

[1] It was at the very beginning of the twentieth century A.D., that the international organization of the socialists finally formulated their long-maturing policy on war. Epitomized their doctrine was: "Why should the workingmen of one country fight with the workingmen of another country for the benefit of their capitalist masters?"

On May 21, 1905 A.D., when war threatened between Austria and Italy, the socialists of Italy, Austria, and Hungary held a conference at Trieste, and threatened a general strike of the workingmen of both countries in case war was declared. This was repeated the following year, when the "Morocco Affair" threatened to involve France, Germany, and England.

That night a German fleet made a dash on Honolulu, sinking three American cruisers and a revenue cutter, and bombarding the city. Next day both Germany and the United States declared war, and within an hour the socialists called the general strike in both countries.

For the first time the German war-lord faced the men of his empire who made his empire go. Without them he could not run his empire. The novelty of the situation lay in that their revolt was passive. They did not fight. They did nothing. And by doing nothing they tied their war-lord's hands. He would have asked for nothing better than an opportunity to loose his war-dogs on his rebellious proletariat. But this was denied him. He could not loose his war-dogs. Neither could he mobilize his army to go forth to war, nor could he punish his recalcitrant subjects. Not a wheel moved in his empire. Not a train ran, not a telegraphic message went over the wires, for the telegraphers and railroad men had ceased work along with the rest of the population.

And as it was in Germany, so it was in the United States. At last organized labor had learned its lesson. Beaten decisively on its own chosen field, it had abandoned that field and come over to the political field of the socialists; for the general strike was a political strike. Besides, organized labor had been so badly beaten that it did not care. It joined in the general strike out of sheer desperation. The workers threw down their tools and left their tasks by the millions. Especially notable were the machinists. Their heads were bloody, their organization had apparently been destroyed, yet out they came, along with their allies in the metal-working trades.

Even the common laborers and all unorganized labor ceased work. The strike had tied everything up so that nobody could work. Besides, the women proved to be the strongest promoters of the strike. They set their faces against the war. They did not want their men to go forth to die. Then, also, the idea of the general strike caught the mood of the people. It struck their sense of humor. The idea was infectious. The children struck in all the schools, and such teachers as came, went home again from deserted class rooms. The general strike took the form of a great national picnic. And the idea of the solidarity of labor, so evidenced, appealed to the imagination of all. And, finally, there was no danger to be incurred by the colossal frolic. When everybody was guilty, how was anybody to be punished?

The United States was paralyzed. No one knew what was happening. There were no newspapers, no letters, no despatches. Every community was as completely isolated as though ten thousand miles of primeval wilderness stretched between it and the rest of the world. For that matter, the world had ceased to exist. And for a week this state of affairs was maintained.

In San Francisco we did not know what was happening even across the bay in Oakland or Berkeley. The effect on one's sensibilities was weird, depressing. It seemed as though some great cosmic thing lay dead. The pulse of the land had ceased to beat. Of a truth the nation had died. There were no wagons rumbling on the streets, no factory whistles, no hum of electricity in the air, no passing of street cars, no cries of news-boys—nothing but persons who at rare intervals went by like furtive ghosts, themselves oppressed and made unreal by the silence.

And during that week of silence the Oligarchy was taught its lesson. And well it learned the lesson. The general strike was a warning. It should never occur again. The Oligarchy would see to that.

At the end of the week, as had been prearranged, the telegraphers of Germany and the United States returned to their posts. Through them the socialist leaders of both countries presented their ultimatum to the rulers. The war should be called off, or the general strike would continue. It did not take long to come to an understanding. The war was declared off, and the populations of both countries returned to their tasks.

It was this renewal of peace that brought about the alliance between Germany and the United States. In reality, this was an alliance between the Emperor and the Oligarchy, for the purpose of meeting their common foe, the revolutionary proletariat of both countries. And it was this alliance that the Oligarchy afterward so treacherously broke when the German socialists rose and drove the war-lord from his throne. It was the very thing the Oligarchy had played for—the destruction of its great rival in the world-market. With the German Emperor out of the way, Germany would have no surplus to sell abroad. By the very nature of the socialist state, the German population would consume all that it produced. Of course, it would trade abroad certain things it produced for things it did not produce; but this would be quite different from an unconsumable surplus.

"I'll wager the Oligarchy finds justification," Ernest said, when its treachery to the German Emperor became known. "As usual, the Oligarchy will believe it has done right."

And sure enough. The Oligarchy's public defence for the act was that it had done it for the sake of the American people whose interests it was looking out for. It had flung its hated rival out of the world-market and enabled us to dispose of our surplus in that market.

"And the howling folly of it is that we are so helpless that such idiots really are managing our interests," was Ernest's comment. "They have enabled us to sell more abroad, which means that we'll be compelled to consume less at home."

CHAPTER XIV - THE BEGINNING OF THE END

As early as January, 1913, Ernest saw the true trend of affairs, but he could not get his brother leaders to see the vision of the Iron Heel that had arisen in his brain. They were too confident. Events were rushing too rapidly to culmination. A crisis had come in world affairs. The American Oligarchy was practically in possession of the world-market, and scores of countries were flung out of that market with unconsumable and unsalable surpluses on their hands. For such countries nothing remained but reorganization. They could not continue their method of producing surpluses. The capitalistic system, so far as they were concerned, had hopelessly broken down.

The reorganization of these countries took the form of revolution. It was a time of confusion and violence. Everywhere institutions and governments were crashing. Everywhere, with the exception of two or three countries, the erstwhile capitalist masters fought bitterly for their possessions. But the governments were taken away from them by the militant proletariat. At last was being realized Karl Marx's classic: "The knell of private capitalist property sounds. The expropriators are expropriated." And as fast as capitalistic governments crashed, cooperative commonwealths arose in their place.

"Why does the United States lag behind?"; "Get busy, you American revolutionists!"; "What's the matter with America?"—were the messages sent to us by our successful comrades in other lands. But we could not keep up. The Oligarchy stood in the way. Its bulk, like that of some huge monster, blocked our path.

"Wait till we take office in the spring," we answered. "Then you'll see."

Behind this lay our secret. We had won over the Grangers, and in the spring a dozen states would pass into their hands by virtue of the elections of the preceding fall. At once would be instituted a dozen cooperative commonwealth states. After that, the rest would be easy.

"But what if the Grangers fail to get possession?" Ernest demanded. And his comrades called him a calamity howler.

But this failure to get possession was not the chief danger that Ernest had in mind. What he foresaw was the defection of the great labor unions and the rise of the castes.

"Ghent has taught the oligarchs how to do it," Ernest said. "I'll wager they've made a text-book out of his 'Benevolent Feudalism.'"[1]

Never shall I forget the night when, after a hot discussion with half a dozen labor leaders, Ernest turned to me and said quietly: "That settles it. The Iron Heel has won. The end is in sight."

This little conference in our home was unofficial; but Ernest, like the rest of his comrades, was working for assurances from the labor leaders that they would call out their men in the next general strike. O'Connor, the president of the Association of Machinists, had been foremost of the six leaders present in refusing to give such assurance.

"You have seen that you were beaten soundly at your old tactics of strike and boycott," Ernest urged.

O'Connor and the others nodded their heads.

"And you saw what a general strike would do," Ernest went on. "We stopped the war with Germany. Never was there so fine a display of the solidarity and the power of labor. Labor can and will rule the world. If you continue to stand with us, we'll put an end to the reign of capitalism. It is your only hope. And what is more, you know it. There is no other way out. No matter what you do under your old tactics, you are doomed to defeat, if for no other reason because the masters control the courts."[2]

"You run ahead too fast," O'Connor answered. "You don't know all the ways out. There is another way out. We know what we're about. We're sick of strikes. They've got us beaten that way to a frazzle. But I don't think we'll ever need to call our men out again."

"What is your way out?" Ernest demanded bluntly.

---

[1] "Our Benevolent Feudalism," a book published in 1902 A.D., by W. J. Ghent. It has always been insisted that Ghent put the idea of the Oligarchy into the minds of the great capitalists. This belief persists throughout the literature of the three centuries of the Iron Heel, and even in the literature of the first century of the Brotherhood of Man. To-day we know better, but our knowledge does not overcome the fact that Ghent remains the most abused innocent man in all history.

[2] As a sample of the decisions of the courts adverse to labor, the following instances are given. In the coal- mining regions the employment of children was notorious. In 1905 A.D., labor succeeded in getting a law passed in Pennsylvania providing that proof of the age of the child and of certain educational qualifications must accompany the oath of the parent. This was promptly declared unconstitutional by the Luzerne County Court, on the ground that it violated the Fourteenth Amendment in that it discriminated between individuals of the same class—namely, children above fourteen years of age and children below. The state court sustained the decision. The New York Court of Special Sessions, in 1905 A.D., declared unconstitutional the law prohibiting minors and women from working in factories after nine o'clock at night, the ground taken being that such a law was "class legislation." Again, the bakers of that time were terribly overworked. The New York Legislature passed a law restricting work in bakeries to ten hours a day. In 1906 A.D., the Supreme Court of the United States declared this law to be unconstitutional. In part the decision read: "There is no reasonable ground for interfering with the liberty of persons or the right of free contract by determining the hours of labor in the occupation of a baker."

O'Connor laughed and shook his head. "I can tell you this much: We've not been asleep. And we're not dreaming now."

"There's nothing to be afraid of, or ashamed of, I hope," Ernest challenged.

"I guess we know our business best," was the retort.

"It's a dark business, from the way you hide it," Ernest said with growing anger.

"We've paid for our experience in sweat and blood, and we've earned all that's coming to us," was the reply. "Charity begins at home."

"If you're afraid to tell me your way out, I'll tell it to you." Ernest's blood was up. "You're going in for grab-sharing. You've made terms with the enemy, that's what you've done. You've sold out the cause of labor, of all labor. You are leaving the battle-field like cowards."

"I'm not saying anything," O'Connor answered sullenly. "Only I guess we know what's best for us a little bit better than you do."

"And you don't care a cent for what is best for the rest of labor. You kick it into the ditch."

"I'm not saying anything," O'Connor replied, "except that I'm president of the Machinists' Association, and it's my business to consider the interests of the men I represent, that's all."

And then, when the labor leaders had left, Ernest, with the calmness of defeat, outlined to me the course of events to come.

"The socialists used to foretell with joy," he said, "the coming of the day when organized labor, defeated on the industrial field, would come over on to the political field. Well, the Iron Heel has defeated the labor unions on the industrial field and driven them over to the political field; and instead of this being joyful for us, it will be a source of grief. The Iron Heel learned its lesson. We showed it our power in the general strike. It has taken steps to prevent another general strike."

"But how?" I asked.

"Simply by subsidizing the great unions. They won't join in the next general strike. Therefore it won't be a general strike."

"But the Iron Heel can't maintain so costly a programme forever," I objected.

"Oh, it hasn't subsidized all of the unions. That's not necessary. Here is what is going to happen. Wages are going to be advanced and hours shortened in the railroad unions, the iron and steel workers unions, and the engineer and machinist unions. In these unions more favorable conditions will continue to prevail. Membership in these unions will become like seats in Paradise."

"Still I don't see," I objected. "What is to become of the other unions? There are far more unions outside of this combination than in it."

"The other unions will be ground out of existence—all of them. For, don't you see, the railway men, machinists and engineers, iron and steel workers, do all of the vitally essential work in our machine civilization. Assured of their faithfulness, the Iron Heel can snap its fingers at all the rest of labor. Iron, steel, coal, machinery, and transportation constitute the backbone of the whole industrial fabric."

"But coal?" I queried. "There are nearly a million coal miners."

They are practically unskilled labor. They will not count. Their wages will go down and their hours will increase. They will be slaves like all the rest of us, and they will become about the most bestial of all of us. They will be compelled to work, just as the farmers are compelled to work now for the masters who robbed them of their land. And the same with all the other unions outside the combination. Watch them wobble and go to pieces, and their members become slaves driven to toil by empty stomachs and the law of the land.

"Do you know what will happen to Farley[1] and his strike-breakers? I'll tell you. Strike-breaking as an occupation will cease. There won't be any more strikes. In place of strikes will be slave revolts. Farley and his gang will be promoted to slave-driving. Oh, it won't be called that; it will be called enforcing the law of the land that compels the laborers to work. It simply prolongs the fight, this treachery of the big unions. Heaven only knows now where and when the Revolution will triumph."

"But with such a powerful combination as the Oligarchy and the big unions, is there any reason to believe that the Revolution will ever triumph?" I queried. "May not the combination endure forever?"

He shook his head. "One of our generalizations is that every system founded upon class and caste contains within itself the germs of its own decay. When a system is founded upon class, how can caste be prevented? The Iron Heel will not be able to prevent it, and in the end caste will destroy the Iron Heel. The oligarchs have already developed caste among themselves; but wait until the favored unions develop caste. The Iron Heel will use all its power to prevent it, but it will fail.

"In the favored unions are the flower of the American workingmen. They are strong, efficient men. They have become members of those unions through competition for place. Every fit workman in the United States will be possessed by the ambition to become a member of the favored unions. The Oligarchy will encourage such ambition and the consequent competition. Thus will the strong men, who might else be revolutionists, be won away and their strength used to bolster the Oligarchy.

"On the other hand, the labor castes, the members of the favored unions, will strive to make their organizations into close corporations. And they will succeed. Membership in the labor castes will become hereditary. Sons will succeed fathers, and there will be no inflow of new strength from that eternal reservoir of strength, the common people. This will mean deterioration of the labor castes, and in the end they will become weaker and weaker. At the same time, as an institution, they will become temporarily all-powerful. They will be like the guards of the palace in old Rome, and there will be palace revolutions whereby the labor castes will seize the reins of power. And there will be counter-palace revolutions of the oligarchs, and sometimes the one, and sometimes the other, will be in power. And through it all the inevitable caste-weakening will go on, so that in the end the common people will come into their own."

This foreshadowing of a slow social evolution was made when Ernest was first depressed by the defection of the great unions. I never agreed with him in it, and I disagree now, as I write these lines, more heartily than ever; for even now, though Ernest is gone, we are on the verge of the revolt that will sweep all oligarchies away. Yet I have here given Ernest's prophecy because it was his prophecy. In spite of his

---

[1] James Farley—a notorious strike-breaker of the period. A man more courageous than ethical, and of undeniable ability. He rose high under the rule of the Iron Heel and finally was translated into the oligarch class. He was assassinated in 1932 by Sarah Jenkins, whose husband, thirty years before, had been killed by Farley's strike-breakers.

belief in it, he worked like a giant against it, and he, more than any man, has made possible the revolt that even now waits the signal to burst forth.[1]

"But if the Oligarchy persists," I asked him that evening, "what will become of the great surpluses that will fall to its share every year?"

"The surpluses will have to be expended somehow," he answered; "and trust the oligarchs to find a way. Magnificent roads will be built. There will be great achievements in science, and especially in art. When the oligarchs have completely mastered the people, they will have time to spare for other things. They will become worshippers of beauty. They will become art-lovers. And under their direction and generously rewarded, will toil the artists. The result will be great art; for no longer, as up to yesterday, will the artists pander to the bourgeois taste of the middle class. It will be great art, I tell you, and wonder cities will arise that will make tawdry and cheap the cities of old time. And in these cities will the oligarchs dwell and worship beauty.[2]

> "Thus will the surplus be constantly expended while labor does the work. The building of these great works and cities will give a starvation ration to millions of common laborers, for the enormous bulk of the surplus will compel an equally enormous expenditure, and the oligarchs will build for a thousand years—ay, for ten thousand years. They will build as the Egyptians and the Babylonians never dreamed of building; and when the oligarchs have passed away, their great roads and their wonder cities will remain for the brotherhood of labor to tread upon and dwell within.[3]

"These things the oligarchs will do because they cannot help doing them. These great works will be the form their expenditure of the surplus will take, and in the same way that the ruling classes of Egypt of long ago expended the surplus they robbed from the people by the building of temples and pyramids. Under the oligarchs will flourish, not a priest class, but an artist class. And in place of the merchant class of bourgeoisie will be the labor castes. And beneath will be the abyss, wherein will fester and starve and rot, and ever renew itself, the common people, the great bulk of the population. And in the end, who knows in what day, the common people will rise up out of the abyss; the labor castes and the Oligarchy will crumble away; and then, at

---

[1] Everhard's social foresight was remarkable. As clearly as in the light of past events, he saw the defection of the favored unions, the rise and the slow decay of the labor castes, and the struggle between the decaying oligarchs and labor castes for control of the great governmental machine.

[2] We cannot but marvel at Everhard's foresight. Before ever the thought of wonder cities like Ardis and Asgard entered the minds of the oligarchs, Everhard saw those cities and the inevitable necessity for their creation.

[3] And since that day of prophecy, have passed away the three centuries of the Iron Heel and the four centuries of the Brotherhood of Man, and to-day we tread the roads and dwell in the cities that the oligarchs built. It is true, we are even now building still more wonderful wonder cities, but the wonder cities of the oligarchs endure, and I write these lines in Ardis, one of the most wonderful of them all.

last, after the travail of the centuries, will it be the day of the common man. I had thought to see that day; but now I know that I shall never see it."

He paused and looked at me, and added:

"Social evolution is exasperatingly slow, isn't it, sweetheart?"

My arms were about him, and his head was on my breast.

"Sing me to sleep," he murmured whimsically. "I have had a visioning, and I wish to forget."

CHAPTER XV - LAST DAYS

It was near the end of January, 1913, that the changed attitude of the Oligarchy toward the favored unions was made public. The newspapers published information of an unprecedented rise in wages and shortening of hours for the railroad employees, the iron and steel workers, and the engineers and machinists. But the whole truth was not told. The oligarchs did not dare permit the telling of the whole truth. In reality, the wages had been raised much higher, and the privileges were correspondingly greater. All this was secret, but secrets will out. Members of the favored unions told their wives, and the wives gossiped, and soon all the labor world knew what had happened.

It was merely the logical development of what in the nineteenth century had been known as grab-sharing. In the industrial warfare of that time, profit-sharing had been tried. That is, the capitalists had striven to placate the workers by interesting them financially in their work. But profit-sharing, as a system, was ridiculous and impossible. Profit-sharing could be successful only in isolated cases in the midst of a system of industrial strife; for if all labor and all capital shared profits, the same conditions would obtain as did obtain when there was no profit-sharing.

So, out of the unpractical idea of profit-sharing, arose the practical idea of grab-sharing. "Give us more pay and charge it to the public," was the slogan of the strong unions.[1] And here and there this selfish policy worked successfully. In charging it to the public, it was charged to the great mass of unorganized labor and of weakly organized labor. These workers actually paid the increased wages of their stronger brothers who were members of unions that were labor monopolies. This idea, as I say, was merely carried to its logical conclusion, on a large scale, by the combination of the oligarchs and the favored unions.

---

[1] All the railroad unions entered into this combination with the oligarchs, and it is of interest to note that the first definite application of the policy of profit-grabbing was made by a railroad union in the nineteenth century A.D., namely, the Brotherhood of Locomotive Engineers. P. M. Arthur was for twenty years Grand Chief of the Brotherhood. After the strike on the Pennsylvania Railroad in 1877, he broached a scheme to have the Locomotive Engineers make terms with the railroads and to "go it alone" so far as the rest of the labor unions were concerned. This scheme was eminently successful. It was as successful as it was selfish, and out of it was coined the word "arthurization," to denote grab-sharing on the part of labor unions. This word "arthurization" has long puzzled the etymologists, but its derivation, I hope, is now made clear.

As soon as the secret of the defection of the favored unions leaked out, there were rumblings and mutterings in the labor world. Next, the favored unions withdrew from the international organizations and broke off all affiliations. Then came trouble and violence. The members of the favored unions were branded as traitors, and in saloons and brothels, on the streets and at work, and, in fact, everywhere, they were assaulted by the comrades they had so treacherously deserted.

Countless heads were broken, and there were many killed. No member of the favored unions was safe. They gathered together in bands in order to go to work or to return from work. They walked always in the middle of the street. On the sidewalk they were liable to have their skulls crushed by bricks and cobblestones thrown from windows and house-tops. They were permitted to carry weapons, and the authorities aided them in every way. Their persecutors were sentenced to long terms in prison, where they were harshly treated; while no man, not a member of the favored unions, was permitted to carry weapons. Violation of this law was made a high misdemeanor and punished accordingly.

Outraged labor continued to wreak vengeance on the traitors. Caste lines formed automatically. The children of the traitors were persecuted by the children of the workers who had been betrayed, until it was impossible for the former to play on the streets or to attend the public schools. Also, the wives and families of the traitors were ostracized, while the corner groceryman who sold provisions to them was boycotted.

As a result, driven back upon themselves from every side, the traitors and their families became clannish. Finding it impossible to dwell in safety in the midst of the betrayed proletariat, they moved into new localities inhabited by themselves alone. In this they were favored by the oligarchs. Good dwellings, modern and sanitary, were built for them, surrounded by spacious yards, and separated here and there by parks and playgrounds. Their children attended schools especially built for them, and in these schools manual training and applied science were specialized upon. Thus, and unavoidably, at the very beginning, out of this segregation arose caste. The members of the favored unions became the aristocracy of labor. They were set apart from the rest of labor. They were better housed, better clothed, better fed, better treated. They were grab-sharing with a vengeance.

In the meantime, the rest of the working class was more harshly treated. Many little privileges were taken away from it, while its wages and its standard of living steadily sank down. Incidentally, its public schools deteriorated, and education slowly ceased to be compulsory. The increase in the younger generation of children who could not read nor write was perilous.

The capture of the world-market by the United States had disrupted the rest of the world. Institutions and governments were everywhere crashing or transforming. Germany, Italy, France, Australia, and New Zealand were busy forming cooperative commonwealths. The British Empire was falling apart. England's hands were full. In India revolt was in full swing. The cry in all Asia was, "Asia for the Asiatics!" And behind this cry was Japan, ever urging and aiding the yellow and brown races against the white. And while Japan dreamed of continental empire and strove to realize the dream, she suppressed her own proletarian revolution. It was a simple war of the castes, Coolie versus Samurai, and the coolie socialists were executed by tens of thousands. Forty thousand were killed in the street-fighting of Tokio and in the futile assault on the Mikado's palace. Kobe was a shambles; the slaughter of the cotton operatives by machine-guns became classic as the most terrific execution ever achieved by modern war machines. Most savage of all was the Japanese Oligarchy that arose. Japan dominated the East, and took to herself the whole Asiatic portion of the world-market, with the exception of India.

England managed to crush her own proletarian revolution and to hold on to India, though she was brought to the verge of exhaustion. Also, she was compelled to let her great colonies slip away from her. So it was that the socialists succeeded in making Australia and New Zealand into cooperative commonwealths. And it was for the same reason that Canada was lost to the mother country. But Canada crushed her own socialist revolution, being aided in this by the Iron Heel. At the same time, the Iron Heel helped Mexico and Cuba to put down revolt. The result was that the Iron Heel was firmly established in the New World. It had welded into one compact political mass the whole of North America from the Panama Canal to the Arctic Ocean.

And England, at the sacrifice of her great colonies, had succeeded only in retaining India. But this was no more than temporary. The struggle with Japan and the rest of Asia for India was merely delayed. England was destined shortly to lose India, while behind that event loomed the struggle between a united Asia and the world.

And while all the world was torn with conflict, we of the United States were not placid and peaceful. The defection of the great unions had prevented our proletarian revolt, but violence was everywhere. In addition to the labor troubles, and the discontent of the farmers and of the remnant of the middle class, a religious revival had blazed up. An offshoot of the Seventh Day Adventists sprang into sudden prominence, proclaiming the end of the world.

"Confusion thrice confounded!" Ernest cried. "How can we hope for solidarity with all these cross purposes and conflicts?"

And truly the religious revival assumed formidable proportions. The people, what of their wretchedness, and of their disappointment in all things earthly, were ripe and eager for a heaven where industrial tyrants entered no more than camels passed through needle-eyes. Wild-eyed itinerant preachers swarmed over the land; and despite the prohibition of the civil authorities, and the persecution for disobedience, the flames of religious frenzy were fanned by countless camp-meetings.

It was the last days, they claimed, the beginning of the end of the world. The four winds had been loosed. God had stirred the nations to strife. It was a time of visions and miracles, while seers and prophetesses were legion. The people ceased work by hundreds of thousands and fled to the mountains, there to await the imminent coming of God and the rising of the hundred and forty and four thousand to heaven. But in the meantime God did not come, and they starved to death in great numbers. In their desperation they ravaged the farms for food, and the consequent tumult and anarchy in the country districts but increased the woes of the poor expropriated farmers.

Also, the farms and warehouses were the property of the Iron Heel. Armies of troops were put into the field, and the fanatics were herded back at the bayonet point to their tasks in the cities. There they broke out in ever recurring mobs and riots. Their leaders were executed for sedition or confined in madhouses. Those who were executed went to their deaths with all the gladness of martyrs. It was a time of madness. The unrest spread. In the swamps and deserts and waste places, from Florida to Alaska, the small groups of Indians that survived were dancing ghost dances and waiting the coming of a Messiah of their own.

And through it all, with a serenity and certitude that was terrifying, continued to rise the form of that monster of the ages, the Oligarchy. With iron hand and iron heel it mastered the surging millions, out of confusion brought order, out of the very chaos wrought its own foundation and structure.

"Just wait till we get in," the Grangers said—Calvin said it to us in our Pell Street quarters. "Look at the states we've captured. With you socialists to back us, we'll make them sing another song when we take office."

"The millions of the discontented and the impoverished are ours," the socialists said. "The Grangers have come over to us, the farmers, the middle class, and the laborers. The capitalist system will fall to pieces. In another month we send fifty men to Congress. Two years hence every office will be ours, from the President down to the local dog-catcher."

To all of which Ernest would shake his head and say:

"How many rifles have you got? Do you know where you can get plenty of lead? When it comes to powder, chemical mixtures are better than mechanical mixtures, you take my word."

CHAPTER XVI - THE END

When it came time for Ernest and me to go to Washington, father did not accompany us. He had become enamoured of proletarian life. He looked upon our slum neighborhood as a great sociological laboratory, and he had embarked upon an apparently endless orgy of investigation. He chummed with the laborers, and was an intimate in scores of homes. Also, he worked at odd jobs, and the work was play as well as learned investigation, for he delighted in it and was always returning home with copious notes and bubbling over with new adventures. He was the perfect scientist.

There was no need for his working at all, because Ernest managed to earn enough from his translating to take care of the three of us. But father insisted on pursuing his favorite phantom, and a protean phantom it was, judging from the jobs he worked at. I shall never forget the evening he brought home his street pedler's outfit of shoe-laces and suspenders, nor the time I went into the little corner grocery to make some purchase and had him wait on me. After that I was not surprised when he tended bar for a week in the saloon across the street. He worked as a night watchman, hawked potatoes on the street, pasted labels in a cannery warehouse, was utility man in a paper-box factory, and water-carrier for a street railway construction gang, and even joined the Dishwashers' Union just before it fell to pieces.

I think the Bishop's example, so far as wearing apparel was concerned, must have fascinated father, for he wore the cheap cotton shirt of the laborer and the overalls with the narrow strap about the hips. Yet one habit remained to him from the old life; he always dressed for dinner, or supper, rather.

I could be happy anywhere with Ernest; and father's happiness in our changed circumstances rounded out my own happiness.

"When I was a boy," father said, "I was very curious. I wanted to know why things were and how they came to pass. That was why I became a physicist. The life in me to-day is just as curious as it was in my boyhood, and it's the being curious that makes life worth living."

Sometimes he ventured north of Market Street into the shopping and theatre district, where he sold papers, ran errands, and opened cabs. There, one day, closing a cab, he encountered Mr. Wickson. In high glee father described the incident to us that evening.

"Wickson looked at me sharply when I closed the door on him, and muttered, 'Well, I'll be damned.' Just like that he said it, 'Well, I'll be damned.' His face turned red and he was so confused that he forgot to tip me. But he must have recovered himself quickly, for the cab hadn't gone fifty feet before it turned around and came back. He leaned out of the door.

"'Look here, Professor,' he said, 'this is too much. What can I do for you?'

"'I closed the cab door for you,' I answered. 'According to common custom you might give me a dime.'

"'Bother that!' he snorted. 'I mean something substantial.'

"He was certainly serious—a twinge of ossified conscience or something; and so I considered with grave deliberation for a moment.

"His face was quite expectant when I began my answer, but you should have seen it when I finished.

"'You might give me back my home,' I said, 'and my stock in the Sierra Mills.'"

Father paused.

"What did he say?" I questioned eagerly.

"What could he say? He said nothing. But I said. 'I hope you are happy.' He looked at me curiously. 'Tell me, are you happy?'" I asked.

"He ordered the cabman to drive on, and went away swearing horribly. And he didn't give me the dime, much less the home and stock; so you see, my dear, your father's street-arab career is beset with disappointments."

And so it was that father kept on at our Pell Street quarters, while Ernest and I went to Washington. Except for the final consummation, the old order had passed away, and the final consummation was nearer than I dreamed. Contrary to our expectation, no obstacles were raised to prevent the socialist Congressmen from taking their seats. Everything went smoothly, and I laughed at Ernest when he looked upon the very smoothness as something ominous.

We found our socialist comrades confident, optimistic of their strength and of the things they would accomplish. A few Grangers who had been elected to Congress increased our strength, and an elaborate programme of what was to be done was prepared by the united forces. In all of which Ernest joined loyally and energetically, though he could not forbear, now and again, from saying, apropos of nothing in particular, "When it comes to powder, chemical mixtures are better than mechanical mixtures, you take my word."

The trouble arose first with the Grangers in the various states they had captured at the last election. There were a dozen of these states, but the Grangers who had been elected were not permitted to take office. The incumbents refused to get out. It was very simple. They merely charged illegality in the elections and wrapped up the whole situation in the interminable red tape of the law. The Grangers were powerless. The courts were in the hands of their enemies.

This was the moment of danger. If the cheated Grangers became violent, all was lost. How we socialists worked to hold them back! There were days and nights when Ernest never closed his eyes in sleep. The big leaders of the Grangers saw the peril and were with us to a man. But it was all of no avail. The Oligarchy wanted violence, and it set its agents-provocateurs to work. Without discussion, it was the agents-provocateurs who caused the Peasant Revolt.

In a dozen states the revolt flared up. The expropriated farmers took forcible possession of the state governments. Of course this was unconstitutional, and of course the United States put its soldiers into the field. Everywhere the agents-provocateurs urged the people on. These emissaries of the Iron Heel disguised themselves as artisans, farmers, and farm laborers. In Sacramento, the capital of California, the Grangers had succeeded in maintaining order. Thousands of secret agents were rushed to the devoted city. In mobs composed wholly of themselves, they fired and looted buildings and factories. They worked the people up until they joined them in the pillage. Liquor in large quantities was distributed among the slum classes further to inflame their minds. And then, when all was ready, appeared upon the scene the soldiers of the United States, who were, in reality, the soldiers of the Iron Heel. Eleven thousand men, women, and children were shot down on the streets of Sacramento or murdered in their houses. The national government took possession of the state government, and all was over for California.

And as with California, so elsewhere. Every Granger state was ravaged with violence and washed in blood. First, disorder was precipitated by the secret agents and the Black Hundreds, then the troops were called out. Rioting and mob-rule reigned throughout the rural districts. Day and night the smoke of burning farms, warehouses, villages, and cities filled the sky. Dynamite appeared. Railroad bridges and tunnels were blown up and trains were wrecked. The poor farmers were shot and hanged in great numbers. Reprisals were bitter, and many plutocrats and army officers were murdered. Blood and vengeance were in men's hearts. The regular troops fought the farmers as savagely as had they been Indians. And the regular troops had cause. Twenty-eight hundred of them had been annihilated in a tremendous series of dynamite explosions in Oregon, and in a similar manner, a number of train loads, at different times and places, had been destroyed. So it was that the regular troops fought for their lives as well as did the farmers.

As for the militia, the militia law of 1903 was put into effect, and the workers of one state were compelled, under pain of death, to shoot down their comrade-workers in other states. Of course, the militia law did not work smoothly at first. Many militia officers were murdered, and many militiamen were executed by drumhead court martial. Ernest's prophecy was strikingly fulfilled in the cases of Mr. Kowalt and Mr. Asmunsen. Both were eligible for the militia, and both were drafted to serve in the punitive expedition that was despatched from California against the farmers of Missouri. Mr. Kowalt and Mr. Asmunsen refused to serve. They were given short shrift. Drumhead court martial was their portion, and military execution their end. They were shot with their backs to the firing squad.

Many young men fled into the mountains to escape serving in the militia. There they became outlaws, and it was not until more peaceful times that they received their punishment. It was drastic. The government issued a proclamation for all law-abiding citizens to come in from the mountains for a period of three months. When the proclaimed date arrived, half a million soldiers were sent into the mountainous districts everywhere. There was no investigation, no trial. Wherever a man was encountered, he was shot down on the spot. The troops operated on the basis that no man not an outlaw remained in the mountains. Some bands, in strong positions, fought gallantly, but in the end every deserter from the militia met death.

A more immediate lesson, however, was impressed on the minds of the people by the punishment meted out to the Kansas militia. The great Kansas Mutiny occurred at the very beginning of military operations against the Grangers. Six thousand of the militia mutinied. They had been for several weeks very turbulent and sullen, and for that reason had been kept in camp. Their open mutiny, however, was without doubt precipitated by the agents-provocateurs.

On the night of the 22d of April they arose and murdered their officers, only a small remnant of the latter escaping. This was beyond the scheme of the Iron Heel, for the agents-provocateurs had done their work too well. But everything was grist to the Iron Heel. It had prepared for the outbreak, and the killing of so many officers gave it justification for what followed. As by magic, forty thousand soldiers of the regular army surrounded the malcontents. It was a trap. The wretched militiamen found that their machine-guns had been tampered with, and that the cartridges from the captured magazines did not fit their rifles. They hoisted the white flag of surrender, but it was ignored. There were no survivors. The entire six thousand were annihilated. Common shell and shrapnel were thrown in upon them from a distance, and, when, in their desperation, they charged the encircling lines, they were mowed down by the machine-guns. I talked with an eye-witness, and he said that the nearest any militiaman approached the machine-guns was a hundred and fifty yards. The earth was carpeted with the slain, and a final charge of cavalry, with trampling of horses' hoofs, revolvers, and sabres, crushed the wounded into the ground.

Simultaneously with the destruction of the Grangers came the revolt of the coal miners. It was the expiring effort of organized labor. Three-quarters of a million of miners went out on strike. But they were too widely scattered over the country to advantage from their own strength. They were segregated in their own districts and beaten into submission. This was the first great slave-drive. Pocock[1] won his spurs as a slave-driver and earned the undying hatred of the proletariat. Countless attempts were made upon his life, but he seemed to bear a charmed existence. It was he who was responsible for the introduction of the Russian passport system among the miners, and the denial of their right of removal from one part of the country to another.

In the meantime, the socialists held firm. While the Grangers expired in flame and blood, and organized labor was disrupted, the socialists held their peace and perfected their secret organization. In vain the Grangers pleaded with us. We rightly contended that any revolt on our part was virtually suicide for the whole Revolution. The Iron Heel, at first dubious about dealing with the entire proletariat at one time, had found the work easier than it had expected, and would have asked nothing better than an uprising on our part. But we avoided the issue, in spite of the fact that agents-provocateurs swarmed in our midst. In those early days, the agents of the Iron Heel

---

[1] Albert Pocock, another of the notorious strike-breakers of earlier years, who, to the day of his death, successfully held all the coal-miners of the country to their task. He was succeeded by his son, Lewis Pocock, and for five generations this remarkable line of slave-drivers handled the coal mines. The elder Pocock, known as Pocock I., has been described as follows: "A long, lean head, semicircled by a fringe of brown and gray hair, with big cheek-bones and a heavy chin, . . . a pale face, lustreless gray eyes, a metallic voice, and a languid manner." He was born of humble parents, and began his career as a bartender. He next became a private detective for a street railway corporation, and by successive steps developed into a professional strikebreaker. Pocock V., the last of the line, was blown up in a pump-house by a bomb during a petty revolt of the miners in the Indian Territory. This occurred in 2073 A.D.

were clumsy in their methods. They had much to learn and in the meantime our Fighting Groups weeded them out. It was bitter, bloody work, but we were fighting for life and for the Revolution, and we had to fight the enemy with its own weapons. Yet we were fair. No agent of the Iron Heel was executed without a trial. We may have made mistakes, but if so, very rarely. The bravest, and the most combative and self-sacrificing of our comrades went into the Fighting Groups. Once, after ten years had passed, Ernest made a calculation from figures furnished by the chiefs of the Fighting Groups, and his conclusion was that the average life of a man or woman after becoming a member was five years. The comrades of the Fighting Groups were heroes all, and the peculiar thing about it was that they were opposed to the taking of life. They violated their own natures, yet they loved liberty and knew of no sacrifice too great to make for the Cause.[1]

---

[1] These Fighting groups were modelled somewhat after the Fighting Organization of the Russian Revolution, and, despite the unceasing efforts of the Iron Heel, these groups persisted throughout the three centuries of its existence. Composed of men and women actuated by lofty purpose and unafraid to die, the Fighting Groups exercised tremendous influence and tempered the savage brutality of the rulers. Not alone was their work confined to unseen warfare with the secret agents of the Oligarchy. The oligarchs themselves were compelled to listen to the decrees of the Groups, and often, when they disobeyed, were punished by death—and likewise with the subordinates of the oligarchs, with the officers of the army and the leaders of the labor castes.

Stern justice was meted out by these organized avengers, but most remarkable was their passionless and judicial procedure. There were no snap judgments. When a man was captured he was given fair trial and opportunity for defence. Of necessity, many men were tried and condemned by proxy, as in the case of General Lampton. This occurred in 2138 A.D. Possibly the most bloodthirsty and malignant of all the mercenaries that ever served the Iron Heel, he was informed by the Fighting Groups that they had tried him, found him guilty, and condemned him to death—and this, after three warnings for him to cease from his ferocious treatment of the proletariat. After his condemnation he surrounded himself with a myriad protective devices. Years passed, and in vain the Fighting Groups strove to execute their decree. Comrade after comrade, men and women, failed in their attempts, and were cruelly executed by the Oligarchy. It was the case of General Lampton that revived crucifixion as a legal method of execution. But in the end the condemned man found his executioner in the form of a slender girl of seventeen, Madeline Provence, who, to accomplish her purpose, served two years in his palace as a seamstress to the household. She died in solitary confinement after horrible and prolonged torture; but to-day she stands in imperishable bronze in the Pantheon of Brotherhood in the wonder city of Serles.

We, who by personal experience know nothing of bloodshed, must not judge harshly the heroes of the Fighting Groups. They gave up their lives for humanity, no sacrifice was too great for them to accomplish, while inexorable necessity compelled them to bloody expression in an age of blood. The Fighting Groups constituted the one thorn in the side of the Iron Heel that the Iron Heel could never remove. Everhard was the father of this curious army, and its accomplishments and successful persistence for three hundred years bear witness to the wisdom with which he organized and the solid foundation he laid for the succeeding generations to build upon. In some respects, despite his great economic

The task we set ourselves was threefold. First, the weeding out from our circles of the secret agents of the Oligarchy. Second, the organizing of the Fighting Groups, and outside of them, of the general secret organization of the Revolution. And third, the introduction of our own secret agents into every branch of the Oligarchy—into the labor castes and especially among the telegraphers and secretaries and clerks, into the army, the agents-provocateurs, and the slave-drivers. It was slow work, and perilous, and often were our efforts rewarded with costly failures.

The Iron Heel had triumphed in open warfare, but we held our own in the new warfare, strange and awful and subterranean, that we instituted. All was unseen, much was unguessed; the blind fought the blind; and yet through it all was order, purpose, control. We permeated the entire organization of the Iron Heel with our agents, while our own organization was permeated with the agents of the Iron Heel. It was warfare dark and devious, replete with intrigue and conspiracy, plot and counterplot. And behind all, ever menacing, was death, violent and terrible. Men and women disappeared, our nearest and dearest comrades. We saw them to-day. To-morrow they were gone; we never saw them again, and we knew that they had died.

There was no trust, no confidence anywhere. The man who plotted beside us, for all we knew, might be an agent of the Iron Heel. We mined the organization of the Iron Heel with our secret agents, and the Iron Heel countermined with its secret agents inside its own organization. And it was the same with our organization. And despite the absence of confidence and trust we were compelled to base our every effort on confidence and trust. Often were we betrayed. Men were weak. The Iron Heel could offer money, leisure, the joys and pleasures that waited in the repose of the wonder cities. We could offer nothing but the satisfaction of being faithful to a noble ideal. As for the rest, the wages of those who were loyal were unceasing peril, torture, and death.

Men were weak, I say, and because of their weakness we were compelled to make the only other reward that was within our power. It was the reward of death. Out of necessity we had to punish our traitors. For every man who betrayed us, from one to a dozen faithful avengers were loosed upon his heels. We might fail to carry out our decrees against our enemies, such as the Pococks, for instance; but the one thing we could not afford to fail in was the punishment of our own traitors. Comrades turned traitor by permission, in order to win to the wonder cities and there execute our sentences on the real traitors. In fact, so terrible did we make ourselves, that it became a greater peril to betray us than to remain loyal to us.

The Revolution took on largely the character of religion. We worshipped at the shrine of the Revolution, which was the shrine of liberty. It was the divine flashing through us. Men and women devoted their lives to the Cause, and new-born babes were sealed to it as of old they had been sealed to the service of God. We were lovers of Humanity.

---

and sociological contributions, and his work as a general leader in the Revolution, his organization of the Fighting Groups must be regarded as his greatest achievement.

CHAPTER XVII - THE SCARLET LIVERY

With the destruction of the Granger states, the Grangers in Congress disappeared. They were being tried for high treason, and their places were taken by the creatures of the Iron Heel. The socialists were in a pitiful minority, and they knew that their end was near. Congress and the Senate were empty pretences, farces. Public questions were gravely debated and passed upon according to the old forms, while in reality all that was done was to give the stamp of constitutional procedure to the mandates of the Oligarchy.

Ernest was in the thick of the fight when the end came. It was in the debate on the bill to assist the unemployed. The hard times of the preceding year had thrust great masses of the proletariat beneath the starvation line, and the continued and wide-reaching disorder had but sunk them deeper. Millions of people were starving, while the oligarchs and their supporters were surfeiting on the surplus.[1] We called these wretched people the people of the abyss,[2] and it was to alleviate their awful suffering that the socialists had introduced the unemployed bill. But this was not to the fancy of the Iron Heel. In its own way it was preparing to set these millions to work, but the way was not our way, wherefore it had issued its orders that our bill should be voted down. Ernest and his fellows knew that their effort was futile, but they were tired of the suspense. They wanted something to happen. They were accomplishing nothing, and the best they hoped for was the putting of an end to the legislative farce in which

---

[1] The same conditions obtained in the nineteenth century A.D. under British rule in India. The natives died of starvation by the million, while their rulers robbed them of the fruits of their toil and expended it on magnificent pageants and mumbo-jumbo fooleries. Perforce, in this enlightened age, we have much to blush for in the acts of our ancestors. Our only consolation is philosophic. We must accept the capitalistic stage in social evolution as about on a par with the earlier monkey stage. The human had to pass through those stages in its rise from the mire and slime of low organic life. It was inevitable that much of the mire and slime should cling and be not easily shaken off.

[2] The people of the abyss—this phrase was struck out by the genius of H. G. Wells in the late nineteenth century A.D. Wells was a sociological seer, sane and normal as well as warm human. Many fragments of his work have come down to us, while two of his greatest achievements, "Anticipations" and "Mankind in the Making," have come down intact. Before the oligarchs, and before Everhard, Wells speculated upon the building of the wonder cities, though in his writings they are referred to as "pleasure cities."

they were unwilling players. They knew not what end would come, but they never anticipated a more disastrous end than the one that did come.

I sat in the gallery that day. We all knew that something terrible was imminent. It was in the air, and its presence was made visible by the armed soldiers drawn up in lines in the corridors, and by the officers grouped in the entrances to the House itself. The Oligarchy was about to strike. Ernest was speaking. He was describing the sufferings of the unemployed, as if with the wild idea of in some way touching their hearts and consciences; but the Republican and Democratic members sneered and jeered at him, and there was uproar and confusion. Ernest abruptly changed front.

"I know nothing that I may say can influence you," he said. "You have no souls to be influenced. You are spineless, flaccid things. You pompously call yourselves Republicans and Democrats. There is no Republican Party. There is no Democratic Party. There are no Republicans nor Democrats in this House. You are lick-spittlers and panderers, the creatures of the Plutocracy. You talk verbosely in antiquated terminology of your love of liberty, and all the while you wear the scarlet livery of the Iron Heel."

Here the shouting and the cries of "Order! order!" drowned his voice, and he stood disdainfully till the din had somewhat subsided. He waved his hand to include all of them, turned to his own comrades, and said:

"Listen to the bellowing of the well-fed beasts."

Pandemonium broke out again. The Speaker rapped for order and glanced expectantly at the officers in the doorways. There were cries of "Sedition!" and a great, rotund New York member began shouting "Anarchist!" at Ernest. And Ernest was not pleasant to look at. Every fighting fibre of him was quivering, and his face was the face of a fighting animal, withal he was cool and collected.

"Remember," he said, in a voice that made itself heard above the din, "that as you show mercy now to the proletariat, some day will that same proletariat show mercy to you."

The cries of "Sedition!" and "Anarchist!" redoubled.

"I know that you will not vote for this bill," Ernest went on. "You have received the command from your masters to vote against it. And yet you call me anarchist. You, who have destroyed the government of the people, and who shamelessly flaunt your scarlet shame in public places, call me anarchist. I do not believe in hell-fire and brimstone; but in moments like this I regret my unbelief. Nay, in moments like this I almost do believe. Surely there must be a hell, for in no less place could it be possible for you to receive punishment adequate to your crimes. So long as you exist, there is a vital need for hell-fire in the Cosmos."

There was movement in the doorways. Ernest, the Speaker, all the members turned to see.

"Why do you not call your soldiers in, Mr. Speaker, and bid them do their work?" Ernest demanded. "They should carry out your plan with expedition."

"There are other plans afoot," was the retort. "That is why the soldiers are present."

"Our plans, I suppose," Ernest sneered. "Assassination or something kindred."

But at the word "assassination" the uproar broke out again. Ernest could not make himself heard, but he remained on his feet waiting for a lull. And then it happened. From my place in the gallery I saw nothing except the flash of the explosion. The roar of it filled my ears and I saw Ernest reeling and falling in a swirl of smoke, and the soldiers rushing up all the aisles. His comrades were on their feet, wild with anger, capable of any violence. But Ernest steadied himself for a moment, and waved his arms for silence.

"It is a plot!" his voice rang out in warning to his comrades. "Do nothing, or you will be destroyed."

Then he slowly sank down, and the soldiers reached him. The next moment soldiers were clearing the galleries and I saw no more.

Though he was my husband, I was not permitted to get to him. When I announced who I was, I was promptly placed under arrest. And at the same time were arrested all socialist Congressmen in Washington, including the unfortunate Simpson, who lay ill with typhoid fever in his hotel.

The trial was prompt and brief. The men were foredoomed. The wonder was that Ernest was not executed. This was a blunder on the part of the Oligarchy, and a costly one. But the Oligarchy was too confident in those days. It was drunk with success, and little did it dream that that small handful of heroes had within them the power to rock it to its foundations. To-morrow, when the Great Revolt breaks out and all the world resounds with the tramp, tramp of the millions, the Oligarchy, will realize, and too late, how mightily that band of heroes has grown.[1]

As a revolutionist myself, as one on the inside who knew the hopes and fears and secret plans of the revolutionists, I am fitted to answer, as very few are, the charge that they were guilty of exploding the bomb in Congress. And I can say flatly, without qualification or doubt of any sort, that the socialists, in Congress and out, had no hand in the affair. Who threw the bomb we do not know, but the one thing we are absolutely sure of is that we did not throw it.

On the other hand, there is evidence to show that the Iron Heel was responsible for the act. Of course, we cannot prove this. Our conclusion is merely presumptive. But here are such facts as we do know. It had been reported to the Speaker of the House, by secret-service agents of the government, that the Socialist Congressmen were about to resort to terroristic tactics, and that they had decided upon the day when their

---

[1] Avis Everhard took for granted that her narrative would be read in her own day, and so omits to mention the outcome of the trial for high treason. Many other similar disconcerting omissions will be noticed in the Manuscript. Fifty-two socialist Congressmen were tried, and all were found guilty. Strange to relate, not one received the death sentence. Everhard and eleven others, among whom were Theodore Donnelson and Matthew Kent, received life imprisonment. The remaining forty received sentences varying from thirty to forty-five years; while Arthur Simpson, referred to in the Manuscript as being ill of typhoid fever at the time of the explosion, received only fifteen years. It is the tradition that he died of starvation in solitary confinement, and this harsh treatment is explained as having been caused by his uncompromising stubbornness and his fiery and tactless hatred for all men that served the despotism. He died in Cabanas in Cuba, where three of his comrades were also confined. The fifty- two socialist Congressmen were confined in military fortresses scattered all over the United States. Thus, Du Bois and Woods were held in Porto Rico, while Everhard and Merryweather were placed in Alcatraz, an island in San Francisco Bay that had already seen long service as a military prison.

tactics would go into effect. This day was the very day of the explosion. Wherefore the Capitol had been packed with troops in anticipation. Since we knew nothing about the bomb, and since a bomb actually was exploded, and since the authorities had prepared in advance for the explosion, it is only fair to conclude that the Iron Heel did know. Furthermore, we charge that the Iron Heel was guilty of the outrage, and that the Iron Heel planned and perpetrated the outrage for the purpose of foisting the guilt on our shoulders and so bringing about our destruction.

From the Speaker the warning leaked out to all the creatures in the House that wore the scarlet livery. They knew, while Ernest was speaking, that some violent act was to be committed. And to do them justice, they honestly believed that the act was to be committed by the socialists. At the trial, and still with honest belief, several testified to having seen Ernest prepare to throw the bomb, and that it exploded prematurely. Of course they saw nothing of the sort. In the fevered imagination of fear they thought they saw, that was all.

As Ernest said at the trial: "Does it stand to reason, if I were going to throw a bomb, that I should elect to throw a feeble little squib like the one that was thrown? There wasn't enough powder in it. It made a lot of smoke, but hurt no one except me. It exploded right at my feet, and yet it did not kill me. Believe me, when I get to throwing bombs, I'll do damage. There'll be more than smoke in my petards."

In return it was argued by the prosecution that the weakness of the bomb was a blunder on the part of the socialists, just as its premature explosion, caused by Ernest's losing his nerve and dropping it, was a blunder. And to clinch the argument, there were the several Congressmen who testified to having seen Ernest fumble and drop the bomb.

As for ourselves, not one of us knew how the bomb was thrown. Ernest told me that the fraction of an instant before it exploded he both heard and saw it strike at his feet. He testified to this at the trial, but no one believed him. Besides, the whole thing, in popular slang, was "cooked up." The Iron Heel had made up its mind to destroy us, and there was no withstanding it.

There is a saying that truth will out. I have come to doubt that saying. Nineteen years have elapsed, and despite our untiring efforts, we have failed to find the man who really did throw the bomb. Undoubtedly he was some emissary of the Iron Heel, but he has escaped detection. We have never got the slightest clew to his identity. And now, at this late date, nothing remains but for the affair to take its place among the mysteries of history.[1]

---

[1] Avis Everhard would have had to live for many generations ere she could have seen the clearing up of this particular mystery. A little less than a hundred years ago, and a little more than six hundred years after the death, the confession of Pervaise was discovered in the secret archives of the Vatican. It is perhaps well to tell a little something about this obscure document, which, in the main, is of interest to the historian only.

Pervaise was an American, of French descent, who in 1913 A.D., was lying in the Tombs Prison, New York City, awaiting trial for murder. From his confession we learn that he was not a criminal. He was warm-blooded, passionate, emotional. In an insane fit of jealousy he killed his wife—a very common act in those times. Pervaise was mastered by the fear of death, all of which is recounted at length in his confession. To escape death he would have done anything, and the police agents prepared him by assuring him that he could not possibly escape conviction of murder in the first degree when his trial came off. In those days, murder in the first degree was a capital offense. The guilty man or woman was placed in a specially constructed death-chair, and, under the supervision of competent physicians, was destroyed by a current of electricity. This was called electrocution, and it was very popular during that period. Anaesthesia, as a mode of compulsory death, was not introduced until later.

This man, good at heart but with a ferocious animalism close at the surface of his being, lying in jail and expectant of nothing less than death, was prevailed upon by the agents of the Iron Heel to throw the bomb in the House of Representatives. In his confession he states explicitly that he was informed that the bomb was to be a feeble thing and that no lives would be lost. This is directly in line with the fact that the bomb was lightly charged, and that its explosion at Everhard's feet was not deadly.

Pervaise was smuggled into one of the galleries ostensibly closed for repairs. He was to select the moment for the throwing of the bomb, and he naively confesses that in his interest in Everhard's tirade and the general commotion raised thereby, he nearly forgot his mission.

Not only was he released from prison in reward for his deed, but he was granted an income for life. This he did not long enjoy. In 1914 A.D., in September, he was stricken with rheumatism of the heart and lived for three days. It was then that he sent for the Catholic priest, Father Peter Durban, and to him made confession. So important did it seem to the priest, that he had the confession taken down in writing and sworn to. What happened after this we can only surmise. The document was certainly important enough to find its way to Rome. Powerful influences must have been brought to bear, hence its suppression. For centuries no hint of its existence reached the world. It was not until in the last century that Lorbia, the brilliant Italian scholar, stumbled upon it quite by chance during his researches in the Vatican.

There is to-day no doubt whatever that the Iron Heel was responsible for the bomb that exploded in the House of Representatives in 1913 A.D. Even though the Pervaise confession had never come to light, no reasonable doubt could obtain; for the act in question, that sent fifty-two Congressmen to prison, was on a par with countless other acts committed by the oligarchs, and, before them, by the capitalists.

There is the classic instance of the ferocious and wanton judicial murder of the innocent and so-called Haymarket Anarchists in Chicago in the penultimate decade of the nineteenth century A.D. In a category by itself is the deliberate burning and destruction of capitalist property by the capitalists themselves. For such destruction of property innocent men were frequently punished—"railroaded" in the parlance of the times.

In the labor troubles of the first decade of the twentieth century A.D., between the capitalists and the Western Federation of Miners, similar but more bloody tactics were employed. The railroad station at Independence was blown up by the agents of the capitalists. Thirteen men were killed, and many more were wounded. And then the capitalists, controlling the legislative and judicial machinery of the state of Colorado, charged the miners with the crime and came very near to convicting them. Romaines, one of the tools in this affair, like Pervaise, was lying in jail in another state, Kansas, awaiting trial, when he was approached by the agents of the capitalists. But, unlike Pervaise the confession of Romaines was made public in his own time.

Then, during this same period, there was the case of Moyer and Haywood, two strong, fearless leaders of labor. One was president and the other was secretary of the Western Federation of Miners. The ex-governor of Idaho had been mysteriously murdered. The crime, at the time, was openly charged to the mine owners by the socialists and miners. Nevertheless, in violation of the national and state constitutions, and by means of conspiracy on the parts of the governors of Idaho and Colorado, Moyer and Haywood were kidnapped, thrown into jail, and charged with the murder. It was this instance that provoked from Eugene V. Debs, national leader of the American socialists at the time, the following words: "The labor leaders that cannot be bribed nor bullied, must be ambushed and murdered. The only crime of Moyer and Haywood is that they have been unswervingly true to the working class. The capitalists have stolen our country, debauched our politics, defiled our judiciary, and ridden over us rough-shod, and now they propose to murder those who will not abjectly surrender to their brutal dominion. The governors of Colorado and Idaho are but executing the mandates of their masters, the Plutocracy. The issue is the Workers versus the Plutocracy. If they strike the first violent blow, we will strike the last."

CHAPTER XVIII - IN THE SHADOW OF SONOMA

Of myself, during this period, there is not much to say. For six months I was kept in prison, though charged with no crime. I was a suspect—a word of fear that all revolutionists were soon to come to know. But our own nascent secret service was beginning to work. By the end of my second month in prison, one of the jailers made himself known as a revolutionist in touch with the organization. Several weeks later, Joseph Parkhurst, the prison doctor who had just been appointed, proved himself to be a member of one of the Fighting Groups.

Thus, throughout the organization of the Oligarchy, our own organization, weblike and spidery, was insinuating itself. And so I was kept in touch with all that was happening in the world without. And furthermore, every one of our imprisoned leaders was in contact with brave comrades who masqueraded in the livery of the Iron Heel. Though Ernest lay in prison three thousand miles away, on the Pacific Coast, I was in unbroken communication with him, and our letters passed regularly back and forth.

The leaders, in prison and out, were able to discuss and direct the campaign. It would have been possible, within a few months, to have effected the escape of some of them; but since imprisonment proved no bar to our activities, it was decided to avoid anything premature. Fifty-two Congressmen were in prison, and fully three hundred more of our leaders. It was planned that they should be delivered simultaneously. If part of them escaped, the vigilance of the oligarchs might be aroused so as to prevent the escape of the remainder. On the other hand, it was held that a simultaneous jail-delivery all over the land would have immense psychological influence on the proletariat. It would show our strength and give confidence.

So it was arranged, when I was released at the end of six months, that I was to disappear and prepare a secure hiding-place for Ernest. To disappear was in itself no easy thing. No sooner did I get my freedom than my footsteps began to be dogged by the spies of the Iron Heel. It was necessary that they should be thrown off the track, and that I should win to California. It is laughable, the way this was accomplished.

Already the passport system, modelled on the Russian, was developing. I dared not cross the continent in my own character. It was necessary that I should be completely lost if ever I was to see Ernest again, for by trailing me after he escaped, he would be caught once more. Again, I could not disguise myself as a proletarian and travel. There remained the disguise of a member of the Oligarchy. While the arch-oligarchs were no more than a handful, there were myriads of lesser ones of the type, say, of Mr. Wickson—men, worth a few millions, who were adherents of the arch-oligarchs. The wives and daughters of these lesser oligarchs were legion, and it was decided that I should assume the disguise of such a one. A few years later this would have been impossible, because the passport system was to become so perfect that no man, woman, nor child in all the land was unregistered and unaccounted for in his or her movements.

When the time was ripe, the spies were thrown off my track. An hour later Avis Everhard was no more. At that time one Felice Van Verdighan, accompanied by two maids and a lap-dog, with another maid for the lap-dog,[1] entered a drawing-room on a Pullman,[2] and a few minutes later was speeding west.

The three maids who accompanied me were revolutionists. Two were members of the Fighting Groups, and the third, Grace Holbrook, entered a group the following year, and six months later was executed by the Iron Heel. She it was who waited upon the dog. Of the other two, Bertha Stole disappeared twelve years later, while Anna Roylston still lives and plays an increasingly important part in the Revolution.[3]

Without adventure we crossed the United States to California. When the train stopped at Sixteenth Street Station, in Oakland, we alighted, and there Felice Van Verdighan, with her two maids, her lap-dog, and her lap-dog's maid, disappeared forever. The maids, guided by trusty comrades, were led away. Other comrades took charge of me. Within half an hour after leaving the train I was on board a small fishing boat and out on the waters of San Francisco Bay. The winds baffled, and we drifted aimlessly the greater part of the night. But I saw the lights of Alcatraz where Ernest lay, and found comfort in the thought of nearness to him. By dawn, what with the rowing of the fishermen, we made the Marin Islands. Here we lay in hiding all day, and on the following night, swept on by a flood tide and a fresh wind, we crossed San Pablo Bay in two hours and ran up Petaluma Creek.

Here horses were ready and another comrade, and without delay we were away through the starlight. To the north I could see the loom of Sonoma Mountain, toward which we rode. We left the old town of Sonoma to the right and rode up a canyon that lay between outlying buttresses of the mountain. The wagon-road became a wood-road, the wood-road became a cow-path, and the cow-path dwindled away and ceased

---

[1] This ridiculous picture well illustrates the heartless conduct of the masters. While people starved, lap-dogs were waited upon by maids. This was a serious masquerade on the part of Avis Everhard. Life and death and the Cause were in the issue; therefore the picture must be accepted as a true picture. It affords a striking commentary of the times.

[2] Pullman—the designation of the more luxurious railway cars of the period and so named from the inventor.

[3] Despite continual and almost inconceivable hazards, Anna Roylston lived to the royal age of ninety-one. As the Pococks defied the executioners of the Fighting Groups, so she defied the executioners of the Iron Heel. She bore a charmed life and prospered amid dangers and alarms. She herself was an executioner for the Fighting Groups, and, known as the Red Virgin, she became one of the inspired figures of the Revolution. When she was an old woman of sixty-nine she shot "Bloody" Halcliffe down in the midst of his armed escort and got away unscathed. In the end she died peaceably of old age in a secret refuge of the revolutionists in the Ozark mountains.

among the upland pastures. Straight over Sonoma Mountain we rode. It was the safest route. There was no one to mark our passing.

Dawn caught us on the northern brow, and in the gray light we dropped down through chaparral into redwood canyons deep and warm with the breath of passing summer. It was old country to me that I knew and loved, and soon I became the guide. The hiding-place was mine. I had selected it. We let down the bars and crossed an upland meadow. Next, we went over a low, oak-covered ridge and descended into a smaller meadow. Again we climbed a ridge, this time riding under red-limbed madronos and manzanitas of deeper red. The first rays of the sun streamed upon our backs as we climbed. A flight of quail thrummed off through the thickets. A big jackrabbit crossed our path, leaping swiftly and silently like a deer. And then a deer, a many-pronged buck, the sun flashing red-gold from neck and shoulders, cleared the crest of the ridge before us and was gone.

We followed in his wake a space, then dropped down a zigzag trail that he disdained into a group of noble redwoods that stood about a pool of water murky with minerals from the mountain side. I knew every inch of the way. Once a writer friend of mine had owned the ranch; but he, too, had become a revolutionist, though more disastrously than I, for he was already dead and gone, and none knew where nor how. He alone, in the days he had lived, knew the secret of the hiding-place for which I was bound. He had bought the ranch for beauty, and paid a round price for it, much to the disgust of the local farmers. He used to tell with great glee how they were wont to shake their heads mournfully at the price, to accomplish ponderously a bit of mental arithmetic, and then to say, "But you can't make six per cent on it."

But he was dead now, nor did the ranch descend to his children. Of all men, it was now the property of Mr. Wickson, who owned the whole eastern and northern slopes of Sonoma Mountain, running from the Spreckels estate to the divide of Bennett Valley. Out of it he had made a magnificent deer-park, where, over thousands of acres of sweet slopes and glades and canyons, the deer ran almost in primitive wildness. The people who had owned the soil had been driven away. A state home for the feeble-minded had also been demolished to make room for the deer.

To cap it all, Wickson's hunting lodge was a quarter of a mile from my hiding-place. This, instead of being a danger, was an added security. We were sheltered under the very aegis of one of the minor oligarchs. Suspicion, by the nature of the situation, was turned aside. The last place in the world the spies of the Iron Heel would dream of looking for me, and for Ernest when he joined me, was Wickson's deer-park.

We tied our horses among the redwoods at the pool. From a cache behind a hollow rotting log my companion brought out a variety of things,—a fifty-pound sack of flour, tinned foods of all sorts, cooking utensils, blankets, a canvas tarpaulin, books and writing material, a great bundle of letters, a five-gallon can of kerosene, an oil stove, and, last and most important, a large coil of stout rope. So large was the supply of things that a number of trips would be necessary to carry them to the refuge.

But the refuge was very near. Taking the rope and leading the way, I passed through a glade of tangled vines and bushes that ran between two wooded knolls. The glade ended abruptly at the steep bank of a stream. It was a little stream, rising from springs, and the hottest summer never dried it up. On every hand were tall wooded knolls, a group of them, with all the seeming of having been flung there from some careless Titan's hand. There was no bed-rock in them. They rose from their bases hundreds of feet, and they were composed of red volcanic earth, the famous wine-soil of Sonoma. Through these the tiny stream had cut its deep and precipitous channel.

It was quite a scramble down to the stream bed, and, once on the bed, we went down stream perhaps for a hundred feet. And then we came to the great hole. There was no warning of the existence of the hole, nor was it a hole in the common sense of the word. One crawled through tight-locked briers and branches, and found oneself on the very edge, peering out and down through a green screen. A couple of hundred feet in length and width, it was half of that in depth. Possibly because of some fault that had occurred when the knolls were flung together, and certainly helped by freakish erosion, the hole had been scooped out in the course of centuries by the wash of water. Nowhere did the raw earth appear. All was garmented by vegetation, from tiny maiden-hair and gold-back ferns to mighty redwood and Douglas spruces. These great trees even sprang out from the walls of the hole. Some leaned over at angles as great as forty-five degrees, though the majority towered straight up from the soft and almost perpendicular earth walls.

It was a perfect hiding-place. No one ever came there, not even the village boys of Glen Ellen. Had this hole existed in the bed of a canyon a mile long, or several miles long, it would have been well known. But this was no canyon. From beginning to end the length of the stream was no more than five hundred yards. Three hundred yards above the hole the stream took its rise in a spring at the foot of a flat meadow. A hundred yards below the hole the stream ran out into open country, joining the main stream and flowing across rolling and grass-covered land.

My companion took a turn of the rope around a tree, and with me fast on the other end lowered away. In no time I was on the bottom. And in but a short while he had carried all the articles from the cache and lowered them down to me. He hauled the rope up and hid it, and before he went away called down to me a cheerful parting.

Before I go on I want to say a word for this comrade, John Carlson, a humble figure of the Revolution, one of the countless faithful ones in the ranks. He worked for Wickson, in the stables near the hunting lodge. In fact, it was on Wickson's horses that we had ridden over Sonoma Mountain. For nearly twenty years now John Carlson has been custodian of the refuge. No thought of disloyalty, I am sure, has ever entered his mind during all that time. To betray his trust would have been in his mind a thing undreamed. He was phlegmatic, stolid to such a degree that one could not but wonder how the Revolution had any meaning to him at all. And yet love of freedom glowed sombrely and steadily in his dim soul. In ways it was indeed good that he was not flighty and imaginative. He never lost his head. He could obey orders, and he was neither curious nor garrulous. Once I asked how it was that he was a revolutionist.

"When I was a young man I was a soldier," was his answer. "It was in Germany. There all young men must be in the army. So I was in the army. There was another soldier there, a young man, too. His father was what you call an agitator, and his father was in jail for lese majesty—what you call speaking the truth about the Emperor. And the young man, the son, talked with me much about people, and work, and the robbery of the people by the capitalists. He made me see things in new ways, and I became a socialist. His talk was very true and good, and I have never forgotten. When I came to the United States I hunted up the socialists. I became a member of a section—that was in the day of the S. L. P. Then later, when the split came, I joined the local of the S. P. I was working in a livery stable in San Francisco then. That was before the Earthquake. I have paid my dues for twenty-two years. I am yet a member, and I yet pay my dues, though it is very secret now. I will always pay my dues, and when the cooperative commonwealth comes, I will be glad."

Left to myself, I proceeded to cook breakfast on the oil stove and to prepare my home. Often, in the early morning, or in the evening after dark, Carlson would steal down to the refuge and work for a couple of hours. At first my home was the tarpaulin. Later, a small tent was put up. And still later, when we became assured of the perfect security of the place, a small house was erected. This house was completely hidden from any chance eye that might peer down from the edge of the hole. The lush vegetation of that sheltered spot make a natural shield. Also, the house was built against the perpendicular wall; and in the wall itself, shored by strong timbers, well drained and ventilated, we excavated two small rooms. Oh, believe me, we had many comforts. When Biedenbach, the German terrorist, hid with us some time later, he installed a smoke-consuming device that enabled us to sit by crackling wood fires on winter nights.

And here I must say a word for that gentle-souled terrorist, than whom there is no comrade in the Revolution more fearfully misunderstood. Comrade Biedenbach did not betray the Cause. Nor was he executed by the comrades as is commonly supposed. This canard was circulated by the creatures of the Oligarchy. Comrade Biedenbach was absent-minded, forgetful. He was shot by one of our lookouts at the cave-refuge at Carmel, through failure on his part to remember the secret signals. It was all a sad mistake. And that he betrayed his Fighting Group is an absolute lie. No truer, more loyal man ever labored for the Cause.[1]

For nineteen years now the refuge that I selected had been almost continuously occupied, and in all that time, with one exception, it has never been discovered by an outsider. And yet it was only a quarter of a mile from Wickson's hunting-lodge, and a short mile from the village of Glen Ellen. I was able, always, to hear the morning and evening trains arrive and depart, and I used to set my watch by the whistle at the brickyards.[2]

---

[1] Search as we may through all the material of those times that has come down to us, we can find no clew to the Biedenbach here referred to. No mention is made of him anywhere save in the Everhard Manuscript.

[2] If the curious traveller will turn south from Glen Ellen, he will find himself on a boulevard that is identical with the old country road seven centuries ago. A quarter of a mile from Glen Ellen, after the second bridge is passed, to the right will be noticed a barranca that runs like a scar across the rolling land toward a group of wooded knolls. The barranca is the site of the ancient right of way that in the time of private property in land ran across the holding of one Chauvet, a French pioneer of California who came from his native country in the fabled days of gold. The wooded knolls are the same knolls referred to by Avis Everhard.

The Great Earthquake of 2368 A.D. broke off the side of one of these knolls and toppled it into the hole where the Everhards made their refuge. Since the finding of the Manuscript excavations have been made, and the house, the two cave rooms, and all the accumulated rubbish of long occupancy have been brought to light. Many valuable relics have been found, among which, curious to relate, is the smoke-consuming device of Biedenbach's mentioned in the narrative. Students interested in such matters should read the brochure of Arnold Bentham soon to be published.

A mile northwest from the wooded knolls brings one to the site of Wake Robin Lodge at the junction of Wild-Water and Sonoma Creeks. It may be noticed, in passing, that Wild-Water was originally called Graham Creek and was so named on the early local maps. But the later name sticks. It was at Wake Robin Lodge that Avis Everhard later lived for short periods, when, disguised as an agent-provocateur of the Iron Heel, she was enabled to play with impunity her part among men and events. The official permission to occupy Wake Robin Lodge is still on the records, signed by no less a man than Wickson, the minor oligarch of the Manuscript.

CHAPTER XIX - TRANSFORMATION

"You must make yourself over again," Ernest wrote to me. "You must cease to be. You must become another woman—and not merely in the clothes you wear, but inside your skin under the clothes. You must make yourself over again so that even I would not know you—your voice, your gestures, your mannerisms, your carriage, your walk, everything."

This command I obeyed. Every day I practised for hours in burying forever the old Avis Everhard beneath the skin of another woman whom I may call my other self. It was only by long practice that such results could be obtained. In the mere detail of voice intonation I practised almost perpetually till the voice of my new self became fixed, automatic. It was this automatic assumption of a role that was considered imperative. One must become so adept as to deceive oneself. It was like learning a new language, say the French. At first speech in French is self-conscious, a matter of the will. The student thinks in English and then transmutes into French, or reads in French but transmutes into English before he can understand. Then later, becoming firmly grounded, automatic, the student reads, writes, and THINKS in French, without any recourse to English at all.

And so with our disguises. It was necessary for us to practise until our assumed roles became real; until to be our original selves would require a watchful and strong exercise of will. Of course, at first, much was mere blundering experiment. We were creating a new art, and we had much to discover. But the work was going on everywhere; masters in the art were developing, and a fund of tricks and expedients was being accumulated. This fund became a sort of text-book that was passed on, a part of the curriculum, as it were, of the school of Revolution.[1]

It was at this time that my father disappeared. His letters, which had come to me regularly, ceased. He no longer appeared at our Pell Street quarters. Our comrades sought him everywhere. Through our secret service we ransacked every prison in the

---

[1] Disguise did become a veritable art during that period. The revolutionists maintained schools of acting in all their refuges. They scorned accessories, such as wigs and beards, false eyebrows, and such aids of the theatrical actors. The game of revolution was a game of life and death, and mere accessories were traps. Disguise had to be fundamental, intrinsic, part and parcel of one's being, second nature. The Red Virgin is reported to have been one of the most adept in the art, to which must be ascribed her long and successful career.

land. But he was lost as completely as if the earth had swallowed him up, and to this day no clew to his end has been discovered.[1]

Six lonely months I spent in the refuge, but they were not idle months. Our organization went on apace, and there were mountains of work always waiting to be done. Ernest and his fellow-leaders, from their prisons, decided what should be done; and it remained for us on the outside to do it. There was the organization of the mouth-to-mouth propaganda; the organization, with all its ramifications, of our spy system; the establishment of our secret printing-presses; and the establishment of our underground railways, which meant the knitting together of all our myriads of places of refuge, and the formation of new refuges where links were missing in the chains we ran over all the land.

So I say, the work was never done. At the end of six months my loneliness was broken by the arrival of two comrades. They were young girls, brave souls and passionate lovers of liberty: Lora Peterson, who disappeared in 1922, and Kate Bierce, who later married Du Bois,[2] and who is still with us with eyes lifted to to-morrow's sun, that heralds in the new age.

The two girls arrived in a flurry of excitement, danger, and sudden death. In the crew of the fishing boat that conveyed them across San Pablo Bay was a spy. A creature of the Iron Heel, he had successfully masqueraded as a revolutionist and penetrated deep into the secrets of our organization. Without doubt he was on my trail, for we had long since learned that my disappearance had been cause of deep concern to the secret service of the Oligarchy. Luckily, as the outcome proved, he had not divulged his discoveries to any one. He had evidently delayed reporting, preferring to wait until he had brought things to a successful conclusion by discovering my hiding-place and capturing me. His information died with him. Under some pretext, after the girls had landed at Petaluma Creek and taken to the horses, he managed to get away from the boat.

Part way up Sonoma Mountain, John Carlson let the girls go on, leading his horse, while he went back on foot. His suspicions had been aroused. He captured the spy, and as to what then happened, Carlson gave us a fair idea.

"I fixed him," was Carlson's unimaginative way of describing the affair. "I fixed him," he repeated, while a sombre light burnt in his eyes, and his huge, toil-distorted hands opened and closed eloquently. "He made no noise. I hid him, and tonight I will go back and bury him deep."

During that period I used to marvel at my own metamorphosis. At times it seemed impossible, either that I had ever lived a placid, peaceful life in a college town, or else that I had become a revolutionist inured to scenes of violence and death. One or the other could not be. One was real, the other was a dream, but which was which? Was

---

[1] Disappearance was one of the horrors of the time. As a motif, in song and story, it constantly crops up. It was an inevitable concomitant of the subterranean warfare that raged through those three centuries. This phenomenon was almost as common in the oligarch class and the labor castes, as it was in the ranks of the revolutionists. Without warning, without trace, men and women, and even children, disappeared and were seen no more, their end shrouded in mystery.

[2] Du Bois, the present librarian of Ardis, is a lineal descendant of this revolutionary pair.

this present life of a revolutionist, hiding in a hole, a nightmare? or was I a revolutionist who had somewhere, somehow, dreamed that in some former existence I have lived in Berkeley and never known of life more violent than teas and dances, debating societies, and lectures rooms? But then I suppose this was a common experience of all of us who had rallied under the red banner of the brotherhood of man.

I often remembered figures from that other life, and, curiously enough, they appeared and disappeared, now and again, in my new life. There was Bishop Morehouse. In vain we searched for him after our organization had developed. He had been transferred from asylum to asylum. We traced him from the state hospital for the insane at Napa to the one in Stockton, and from there to the one in the Santa Clara Valley called Agnews, and there the trail ceased. There was no record of his death. In some way he must have escaped. Little did I dream of the awful manner in which I was to see him once again—the fleeting glimpse of him in the whirlwind carnage of the Chicago Commune.

Jackson, who had lost his arm in the Sierra Mills and who had been the cause of my own conversion into a revolutionist, I never saw again; but we all knew what he did before he died. He never joined the revolutionists. Embittered by his fate, brooding over his wrongs, he became an anarchist—not a philosophic anarchist, but a mere animal, mad with hate and lust for revenge. And well he revenged himself. Evading the guards, in the nighttime while all were asleep, he blew the Pertonwaithe palace into atoms. Not a soul escaped, not even the guards. And in prison, while awaiting trial, he suffocated himself under his blankets.

Dr. Hammerfield and Dr. Ballingford achieved quite different fates from that of Jackson. They have been faithful to their salt, and they have been correspondingly rewarded with ecclesiastical palaces wherein they dwell at peace with the world. Both are apologists for the Oligarchy. Both have grown very fat. "Dr. Hammerfield," as Ernest once said, "has succeeded in modifying his metaphysics so as to give God's sanction to the Iron Heel, and also to include much worship of beauty and to reduce to an invisible wraith the gaseous vertebrate described by Haeckel—the difference between Dr. Hammerfield and Dr. Ballingford being that the latter has made the God of the oligarchs a little more gaseous and a little less vertebrate."

Peter Donnelly, the scab foreman at the Sierra Mills whom I encountered while investigating the case of Jackson, was a surprise to all of us. In 1918 I was present at a meeting of the 'Frisco Reds. Of all our Fighting Groups this one was the most formidable, ferocious, and merciless. It was really not a part of our organization. Its members were fanatics, madmen. We dared not encourage such a spirit. On the other hand, though they did not belong to us, we remained on friendly terms with them. It was a matter of vital importance that brought me there that night. I, alone in the midst of a score of men, was the only person unmasked. After the business that brought me there was transacted, I was led away by one of them. In a dark passage this guide struck a match, and, holding it close to his face, slipped back his mask. For a moment I gazed upon the passion-wrought features of Peter Donnelly. Then the match went out.

"I just wanted you to know it was me," he said in the darkness. "D'you remember Dallas, the superintendent?"

I nodded at recollection of the vulpine-face superintendent of the Sierra Mills.

"Well, I got him first," Donnelly said with pride. "'Twas after that I joined the Reds."

"But how comes it that you are here?" I queried. "Your wife and children?"

"Dead," he answered. "That's why. No," he went on hastily, "'tis not revenge for them. They died easily in their beds—sickness, you see, one time and another. They tied my arms while they lived. And now that they're gone, 'tis revenge for my blasted manhood I'm after. I was once Peter Donnelly, the scab foreman. But to-night I'm Number 27 of the 'Frisco Reds. Come on now, and I'll get you out of this."

More I heard of him afterward. In his own way he had told the truth when he said all were dead. But one lived, Timothy, and him his father considered dead because he had taken service with the Iron Heel in the Mercenaries.[1] A member of the 'Frisco Reds pledged himself to twelve annual executions. The penalty for failure was death. A member who failed to complete his number committed suicide. These executions were not haphazard. This group of madmen met frequently and passed wholesale judgments upon offending members and servitors of the Oligarchy. The executions were afterward apportioned by lot.

In fact, the business that brought me there the night of my visit was such a trial. One of our own comrades, who for years had successfully maintained himself in a clerical position in the local bureau of the secret service of the Iron Heel, had fallen under the ban of the 'Frisco Reds and was being tried. Of course he was not present, and of course his judges did not know that he was one of our men. My mission had been to testify to his identity and loyalty. It may be wondered how we came to know of the affair at all. The explanation is simple. One of our secret agents was a member of the 'Frisco Reds. It was necessary for us to keep an eye on friend as well as foe, and this group of madmen was not too unimportant to escape our surveillance.

But to return to Peter Donnelly and his son. All went well with Donnelly until, in the following year, he found among the sheaf of executions that fell to him the name of Timothy Donnelly. Then it was that that clannishness, which was his to so extraordinary a degree, asserted itself. To save his son, he betrayed his comrades. In this he was partially blocked, but a dozen of the 'Frisco Reds were executed, and the group was well-nigh destroyed. In retaliation, the survivors meted out to Donnelly the death he had earned by his treason.

Nor did Timothy Donnelly long survive. The 'Frisco Reds pledged themselves to his execution. Every effort was made by the Oligarchy to save him. He was transferred from one part of the country to another. Three of the Reds lost their lives in vain efforts to get him. The Group was composed only of men. In the end they fell back on a woman, one of our comrades, and none other than Anna Roylston. Our Inner Circle forbade her, but she had ever a will of her own and disdained discipline. Furthermore, she was a genius and lovable, and we could never discipline her any-

---

[1] In addition to the labor castes, there arose another caste, the military. A standing army of professional soldiers was created, officered by members of the Oligarchy and known as the Mercenaries. This institution took the place of the militia, which had proved impracticable under the new regime. Outside the regular secret service of the Iron Heel, there was further established a secret service of the Mercenaries, this latter forming a connecting link between the police and the military.

way. She is in a class by herself and not amenable to the ordinary standards of the revolutionists.

Despite our refusal to grant permission to do the deed, she went on with it. Now Anna Roylston was a fascinating woman. All she had to do was to beckon a man to her. She broke the hearts of scores of our young comrades, and scores of others she captured, and by their heart-strings led into our organization. Yet she steadfastly refused to marry. She dearly loved children, but she held that a child of her own would claim her from the Cause, and that it was the Cause to which her life was devoted.

It was an easy task for Anna Roylston to win Timothy Donnelly. Her conscience did not trouble her, for at that very time occurred the Nashville Massacre, when the Mercenaries, Donnelly in command, literally murdered eight hundred weavers of that city. But she did not kill Donnelly. She turned him over, a prisoner, to the 'Frisco Reds. This happened only last year, and now she had been renamed. The revolutionists everywhere are calling her the "Red Virgin."[1]

Colonel Ingram and Colonel Van Gilbert are two more familiar figures that I was later to encounter. Colonel Ingram rose high in the Oligarchy and became Minister to Germany. He was cordially detested by the proletariat of both countries. It was in Berlin that I met him, where, as an accredited international spy of the Iron Heel, I was received by him and afforded much assistance. Incidentally, I may state that in my dual role I managed a few important things for the Revolution.

Colonel Van Gilbert became known as "Snarling" Van Gilbert. His important part was played in drafting the new code after the Chicago Commune. But before that, as trial judge, he had earned sentence of death by his fiendish malignancy. I was one of those that tried him and passed sentence upon him. Anna Roylston carried out the execution.

Still another figure arises out of the old life—Jackson's lawyer. Least of all would I have expected again to meet this man, Joseph Hurd. It was a strange meeting. Late at night, two years after the Chicago Commune, Ernest and I arrived together at the Benton Harbor refuge. This was in Michigan, across the lake from Chicago. We arrived just at the conclusion of the trial of a spy. Sentence of death had been passed, and he was being led away. Such was the scene as we came upon it. The next moment the wretched man had wrenched free from his captors and flung himself at my feet, his arms clutching me about the knees in a vicelike grip as he prayed in a frenzy for mercy. As he turned his agonized face up to me, I recognized him as Joseph Hurd. Of all the terrible things I have witnessed, never have I been so unnerved as by this frantic creature's pleading for life. He was mad for life. It was pitiable. He refused to let go of me, despite the hands of a dozen comrades. And when at last he was dragged

---

[1] It was not until the Second Revolt was crushed, that the 'Frisco Reds flourished again. And for two generations the Group flourished. Then an agent of the Iron Heel managed to become a member, penetrated all its secrets, and brought about its total annihilation. This occurred in 2002 A.D. The members were executed one at a time, at intervals of three weeks, and their bodies exposed in the labor-ghetto of San Francisco.

shrieking away, I sank down fainting upon the floor. It is far easier to see brave men die than to hear a coward beg for life.[1]

---

[1] The Benton Harbor refuge was a catacomb, the entrance of which was cunningly contrived by way of a well. It has been maintained in a fair state of preservation, and the curious visitor may to-day tread its labyrinths to the assembly hall, where, without doubt, occurred the scene described by Avis Everhard. Farther on are the cells where the prisoners were confined, and the death chamber where the executions took place. Beyond is the cemetery—long, winding galleries hewn out of the solid rock, with recesses on either hand, wherein, tier above tier, lie the revolutionists just as they were laid away by their comrades long years agone.

CHAPTER XX - A LOST OLIGARCH

But in remembering the old life I have run ahead of my story into the new life. The wholesale jail delivery did not occur until well along into 1915. Complicated as it was, it was carried through without a hitch, and as a very creditable achievement it cheered us on in our work. From Cuba to California, out of scores of jails, military prisons, and fortresses, in a single night, we delivered fifty-one of our fifty-two Congressmen, and in addition over three hundred other leaders. There was not a single instance of miscarriage. Not only did they escape, but every one of them won to the refuges as planned. The one comrade Congressman we did not get was Arthur Simpson, and he had already died in Cabanas after cruel tortures.

The eighteen months that followed was perhaps the happiest of my life with Ernest. During that time we were never apart. Later, when we went back into the world, we were separated much. Not more impatiently do I await the flame of to-morrow's revolt than did I that night await the coming of Ernest. I had not seen him for so long, and the thought of a possible hitch or error in our plans that would keep him still in his island prison almost drove me mad. The hours passed like ages. I was all alone. Biedenbach, and three young men who had been living in the refuge, were out and over the mountain, heavily armed and prepared for anything. The refuges all over the land were quite empty, I imagine, of comrades that night.

Just as the sky paled with the first warning of dawn, I heard the signal from above and gave the answer. In the darkness I almost embraced Biedenbach, who came down first; but the next moment I was in Ernest's arms. And in that moment, so complete had been my transformation, I discovered it was only by an effort of will that I could be the old Avis Everhard, with the old mannerisms and smiles, phrases and intonations of voice. It was by strong effort only that I was able to maintain my old identity; I could not allow myself to forget for an instant, so automatically imperative had become the new personality I had created.

Once inside the little cabin, I saw Ernest's face in the light. With the exception of the prison pallor, there was no change in him—at least, not much. He was my same lover-husband and hero. And yet there was a certain ascetic lengthening of the lines of his face. But he could well stand it, for it seemed to add a certain nobility of refinement to the riotous excess of life that had always marked his features. He might have been a trifle graver than of yore, but the glint of laughter still was in his eyes. He was twenty pounds lighter, but in splendid physical condition. He had kept up exercise during the whole period of confinement, and his muscles were like iron. In truth, he was in better condition than when he had entered prison. Hours passed before his head touched pillow and I had soothed him off to sleep. But there was no sleep for me. I was too happy, and the fatigue of jail-breaking and riding horseback had not been mine.

While Ernest slept, I changed my dress, arranged my hair differently, and came back to my new automatic self. Then, when Biedenbach and the other comrades awoke, with their aid I concocted a little conspiracy. All was ready, and we were in the cave-room that served for kitchen and dining room when Ernest opened the door and entered. At that moment Biedenbach addressed me as Mary, and I turned and answered him. Then I glanced at Ernest with curious interest, such as any young comrade might betray on seeing for the first time so noted a hero of the Revolution. But Ernest's glance took me in and questioned impatiently past and around the room. The next moment I was being introduced to him as Mary Holmes.

To complete the deception, an extra plate was laid, and when we sat down to table one chair was not occupied. I could have cried with joy as I noted Ernest's increasing uneasiness and impatience. Finally he could stand it no longer.

"Where's my wife?" he demanded bluntly.

"She is still asleep," I answered.

It was the crucial moment. But my voice was a strange voice, and in it he recognized nothing familiar. The meal went on. I talked a great deal, and enthusiastically, as a hero-worshipper might talk, and it was obvious that he was my hero. I rose to a climax of enthusiasm and worship, and, before he could guess my intention, threw my arms around his neck and kissed him on the lips. He held me from him at arm's length and stared about in annoyance and perplexity. The four men greeted him with roars of laughter, and explanations were made. At first he was sceptical. He scrutinized me keenly and was half convinced, then shook his head and would not believe. It was not until I became the old Avis Everhard and whispered secrets in his ear that none knew but he and Avis Everhard, that he accepted me as his really, truly wife.

It was later in the day that he took me in his arms, manifesting great embarrassment and claiming polygamous emotions.

"You are my Avis," he said, "and you are also some one else. You are two women, and therefore you are my harem. At any rate, we are safe now. If the United States becomes too hot for us, why I have qualified for citizenship in Turkey."[1]

Life became for me very happy in the refuge. It is true, we worked hard and for long hours; but we worked together. We had each other for eighteen precious months, and we were not lonely, for there was always a coming and going of leaders and comrades—strange voices from the under-world of intrigue and revolution, bringing stranger tales of strife and war from all our battle-line. And there was much fun and delight. We were not mere gloomy conspirators. We toiled hard and suffered greatly, filled the gaps in our ranks and went on, and through all the labour and the play and interplay of life and death we found time to laugh and love. There were artists, scientists, scholars, musicians, and poets among us; and in that hole in the ground culture was higher and finer than in the palaces of wonder-cities of the oligarchs. In truth,

---

[1] At that time polygamy was still practised in Turkey.

many of our comrades toiled at making beautiful those same palaces and wonder-cities.[1]

Nor were we confined to the refuge itself. Often at night we rode over the mountains for exercise, and we rode on Wickson's horses. If only he knew how many revolutionists his horses have carried! We even went on picnics to isolated spots we knew, where we remained all day, going before daylight and returning after dark. Also, we used Wickson's cream and butter,[2] and Ernest was not above shooting Wickson's quail and rabbits, and, on occasion, his young bucks.

Indeed, it was a safe refuge. I have said that it was discovered only once, and this brings me to the clearing up of the mystery of the disappearance of young Wickson. Now that he is dead, I am free to speak. There was a nook on the bottom of the great hole where the sun shone for several hours and which was hidden from above. Here we had carried many loads of gravel from the creek-bed, so that it was dry and warm, a pleasant basking place; and here, one afternoon, I was drowsing, half asleep, over a volume of Mendenhall.[3] I was so comfortable and secure that even his flaming lyrics failed to stir me.

I was aroused by a clod of earth striking at my feet. Then from above, I heard a sound of scrambling. The next moment a young man, with a final slide down the crumbling wall, alighted at my feet. It was Philip Wickson, though I did not know him at the time. He looked at me coolly and uttered a low whistle of surprise.

"Well," he said; and the next moment, cap in hand, he was saying, "I beg your pardon. I did not expect to find any one here."

I was not so cool. I was still a tyro so far as concerned knowing how to behave in desperate circumstances. Later on, when I was an international spy, I should have been less clumsy, I am sure. As it was, I scrambled to my feet and cried out the danger call.

"Why did you do that?" he asked, looking at me searchingly.

It was evident that he had no suspicion of our presence when making the descent. I recognized this with relief.

"For what purpose do you think I did it?" I countered. I was indeed clumsy in those days.

"I don't know," he answered, shaking his head. "Unless you've got friends about. Anyway, you've got some explanations to make. I don't like the look of it. You are trespassing. This is my father's land, and—"

---

[1] This is not braggadocio on the part of Avis Everhard. The flower of the artistic and intellectual world were revolutionists. With the exception of a few of the musicians and singers, and of a few of the oligarchs, all the great creators of the period whose names have come down to us, were revolutionists.

[2] Even as late as that period, cream and butter were still crudely extracted from cow's milk. The laboratory preparation of foods had not yet begun.

[3] In all the extant literature and documents of that period, continual reference is made to the poems of Rudolph Mendenhall. By his comrades he was called "The Flame." He was undoubtedly a great genius; yet, beyond weird and haunting fragments of his verse, quoted in the writings of others, nothing of his has come down to us. He was executed by the Iron Heel in 1928 A.D.

But at that moment, Biedenbach, every polite and gentle, said from behind him in a low voice, "Hands up, my young sir."

Young Wickson put his hands up first, then turned to confront Biedenbach, who held a thirty-thirty automatic rifle on him. Wickson was imperturbable.

"Oh, ho," he said, "a nest of revolutionists—and quite a hornet's nest it would seem. Well, you won't abide here long, I can tell you."

"Maybe you'll abide here long enough to reconsider that statement," Biedenbach said quietly. "And in the meanwhile I must ask you to come inside with me."

"Inside?" The young man was genuinely astonished. "Have you a catacomb here? I have heard of such things."

"Come and see," Biedenbach answered with his adorable accent.

"But it is unlawful," was the protest.

"Yes, by your law," the terrorist replied significantly. "But by our law, believe me, it is quite lawful. You must accustom yourself to the fact that you are in another world than the one of oppression and brutality in which you have lived."

"There is room for argument there," Wickson muttered.

"Then stay with us and discuss it."

The young fellow laughed and followed his captor into the house. He was led into the inner cave-room, and one of the young comrades left to guard him, while we discussed the situation in the kitchen.

Biedenbach, with tears in his eyes, held that Wickson must die, and was quite relieved when we outvoted him and his horrible proposition. On the other hand, we could not dream of allowing the young oligarch to depart.

"I'll tell you what to do," Ernest said. "We'll keep him and give him an education."

"I bespeak the privilege, then, of enlightening him in jurisprudence," Biedenbach cried.

And so a decision was laughingly reached. We would keep Philip Wickson a prisoner and educate him in our ethics and sociology. But in the meantime there was work to be done. All trace of the young oligarch must be obliterated. There were the marks he had left when descending the crumbling wall of the hole. This task fell to Biedenbach, and, slung on a rope from above, he toiled cunningly for the rest of the day till no sign remained. Back up the canyon from the lip of the hole all marks were likewise removed. Then, at twilight, came John Carlson, who demanded Wickson's shoes.

The young man did not want to give up his shoes, and even offered to fight for them, till he felt the horseshoer's strength in Ernest's hands. Carlson afterward reported several blisters and much grievous loss of skin due to the smallness of the shoes, but he succeeded in doing gallant work with them. Back from the lip of the hole, where ended the young man's obliterated trial, Carlson put on the shoes and walked away to the left. He walked for miles, around knolls, over ridges and through canyons, and finally covered the trail in the running water of a creek-bed. Here he removed the shoes, and, still hiding trail for a distance, at last put on his own shoes. A week later Wickson got back his shoes.

That night the hounds were out, and there was little sleep in the refuge. Next day, time and again, the baying hounds came down the canyon, plunged off to the left on the trail Carlson had made for them, and were lost to ear in the farther canyons high up the mountain. And all the time our men waited in the refuge, weapons in hand—

automatic revolvers and rifles, to say nothing of half a dozen infernal machines of Biedenbach's manufacture. A more surprised party of rescuers could not be imagined, had they ventured down into our hiding-place.

I have now given the true disappearance of Philip Wickson, one-time oligarch, and, later, comrade in the Revolution. For we converted him in the end. His mind was fresh and plastic, and by nature he was very ethical. Several months later we rode him, on one of his father's horses, over Sonoma Mountains to Petaluma Creek and embarked him in a small fishing-launch. By easy stages we smuggled him along our underground railway to the Carmel refuge.

There he remained eight months, at the end of which time, for two reasons, he was loath to leave us. One reason was that he had fallen in love with Anna Roylston, and the other was that he had become one of us. It was not until he became convinced of the hopelessness of his love affair that he acceded to our wishes and went back to his father. Ostensibly an oligarch until his death, he was in reality one of the most valuable of our agents. Often and often has the Iron Heel been dumbfounded by the miscarriage of its plans and operations against us. If it but knew the number of its own members who are our agents, it would understand. Young Wickson never wavered in his loyalty to the Cause. In truth, his very death was incurred by his devotion to duty. In the great storm of 1927, while attending a meeting of our leaders, he contracted the pneumonia of which he died.[1]

[1] The case of this young man was not unusual. Many young men of the Oligarchy, impelled by sense of right conduct, or their imaginations captured by the glory of the Revolution, ethically or romantically devoted their lives to it. In similar way, many sons of the Russian nobility played their parts in the earlier and protracted revolution in that country.

CHAPTER XXI - THE ROARING ABYSMAL BEAST

During the long period of our stay in the refuge, we were kept closely in touch with what was happening in the world without, and we were learning thoroughly the strength of the Oligarchy with which we were at war. Out of the flux of transition the new institutions were forming more definitely and taking on the appearance and attributes of permanence. The oligarchs had succeeded in devising a governmental machine, as intricate as it was vast, that worked—and this despite all our efforts to clog and hamper.

This was a surprise to many of the revolutionists. They had not conceived it possible. Nevertheless the work of the country went on. The men toiled in the mines and fields—perforce they were no more than slaves. As for the vital industries, everything prospered. The members of the great labor castes were contented and worked on merrily. For the first time in their lives they knew industrial peace. No more were they worried by slack times, strike and lockout, and the union label. They lived in more comfortable homes and in delightful cities of their own—delightful compared with the slums and ghettos in which they had formerly dwelt. They had better food to eat, less hours of labor, more holidays, and a greater amount and variety of interests and pleasures. And for their less fortunate brothers and sisters, the unfavored laborers, the driven people of the abyss, they cared nothing. An age of selfishness was dawning upon mankind. And yet this is not altogether true. The labor castes were honeycombed by our agents—men whose eyes saw, beyond the belly-need, the radiant figure of liberty and brotherhood.

Another great institution that had taken form and was working smoothly was the Mercenaries. This body of soldiers had been evolved out of the old regular army and was now a million strong, to say nothing of the colonial forces. The Mercenaries constituted a race apart. They dwelt in cities of their own which were practically self-governed, and they were granted many privileges. By them a large portion of the perplexing surplus was consumed. They were losing all touch and sympathy with the rest of the people, and, in fact, were developing their own class morality and consciousness. And yet we had thousands of our agents among them.[1]

---

[1] The Mercenaries, in the last days of the Iron Heel, played an important role. They constituted the balance of power in the struggles between the labor castes and the oligarchs,

CHAPTER XXI - THE ROARING ABYSMAL BEAST

The oligarchs themselves were going through a remarkable and, it must be confessed, unexpected development. As a class, they disciplined themselves. Every member had his work to do in the world, and this work he was compelled to do. There were no more idle-rich young men. Their strength was used to give united strength to the Oligarchy. They served as leaders of troops and as lieutenants and captains of industry. They found careers in applied science, and many of them became great engineers. They went into the multitudinous divisions of the government, took service in the colonial possessions, and by tens of thousands went into the various secret services. They were, I may say, apprenticed to education, to art, to the church, to science, to literature; and in those fields they served the important function of moulding the thought-processes of the nation in the direction of the perpetuity of the Oligarchy.

They were taught, and later they in turn taught, that what they were doing was right. They assimilated the aristocratic idea from the moment they began, as children, to receive impressions of the world. The aristocratic idea was woven into the making of them until it became bone of them and flesh of them. They looked upon themselves as wild-animal trainers, rulers of beasts. From beneath their feet rose always the subterranean rumbles of revolt. Violent death ever stalked in their midst; bomb and knife and bullet were looked upon as so many fangs of the roaring abysmal beast they must dominate if humanity were to persist. They were the saviours of humanity, and they regarded themselves as heroic and sacrificing laborers for the highest good.

They, as a class, believed that they alone maintained civilization. It was their belief that if ever they weakened, the great beast would ingulf them and everything of beauty and wonder and joy and good in its cavernous and slime-dripping maw. Without them, anarchy would reign and humanity would drop backward into the primitive night out of which it had so painfully emerged. The horrid picture of anarchy was held always before their child's eyes until they, in turn, obsessed by this cultivated fear, held the picture of anarchy before the eyes of the children that followed them. This was the beast to be stamped upon, and the highest duty of the aristocrat was to stamp upon it. In short, they alone, by their unremitting toil and sacrifice, stood between weak humanity and the all-devouring beast; and they believed it, firmly believed it.

I cannot lay too great stress upon this high ethical righteousness of the whole oligarch class. This has been the strength of the Iron Heel, and too many of the comrades have been slow or loath to realize it. Many of them have ascribed the strength of the Iron Heel to its system of reward and punishment. This is a mistake. Heaven and hell may be the prime factors of zeal in the religion of a fanatic; but for the great majority of the religious, heaven and hell are incidental to right and wrong. Love of the right, desire for the right, unhappiness with anything less than the right—in short, right conduct, is the prime factor of religion. And so with the Oligarchy. Prisons, banishment and degradation, honors and palaces and wonder-cities, are all incidental. The great driving force of the oligarchs is the belief that they are doing right. Never mind the exceptions, and never mind the oppression and injustice in which the Iron Heel

---

and now to one side and now to the other, threw their strength according to the play of intrigue and conspiracy.

was conceived. All is granted. The point is that the strength of the Oligarchy today lies in its satisfied conception of its own righteousness.[1]

For that matter, the strength of the Revolution, during these frightful twenty years, has resided in nothing else than the sense of righteousness. In no other way can be explained our sacrifices and martyrdoms. For no other reason did Rudolph Mendenhall flame out his soul for the Cause and sing his wild swan-song that last night of life. For no other reason did Hurlbert die under torture, refusing to the last to betray his comrades. For no other reason has Anna Roylston refused blessed motherhood. For no other reason has John Carlson been the faithful and unrewarded custodian of the Glen Ellen Refuge. It does not matter, young or old, man or woman, high or low, genius or clod, go where one will among the comrades of the Revolution, the motor-force will be found to be a great and abiding desire for the right.

But I have run away from my narrative. Ernest and I well understood, before we left the refuge, how the strength of the Iron Heel was developing. The labor castes, the Mercenaries, and the great hordes of secret agents and police of various sorts were all pledged to the Oligarchy. In the main, and ignoring the loss of liberty, they were better off than they had been. On the other hand, the great helpless mass of the population, the people of the abyss, was sinking into a brutish apathy of content with misery. Whenever strong proletarians asserted their strength in the midst of the mass, they were drawn away from the mass by the oligarchs and given better conditions by being made members of the labor castes or of the Mercenaries. Thus discontent was lulled and the proletariat robbed of its natural leaders.

The condition of the people of the abyss was pitiable. Common school education, so far as they were concerned, had ceased. They lived like beasts in great squalid labor-ghettos, festering in misery and degradation. All their old liberties were gone. They were labor-slaves. Choice of work was denied them. Likewise was denied them the right to move from place to place, or the right to bear or possess arms. They were not land serfs like the farmers. They were machine-serfs and labor-serfs. When unusual needs arose for them, such as the building of the great highways and air-lines, of canals, tunnels, subways, and fortifications, levies were made on the labor-ghettos, and tens of thousands of serfs, willy-nilly, were transported to the scene of operations. Great armies of them are toiling now at the building of Ardis, housed in wretched barracks where family life cannot exist, and where decency is displaced by dull bestiality. In all truth, there in the labor-ghettos is the roaring abysmal beast the oligarchs fear so dreadfully—but it is the beast of their own making. In it they will not let the ape and tiger die.

---

[1] Out of the ethical incoherency and inconsistency of capitalism, the oligarchs emerged with a new ethics, coherent and definite, sharp and severe as steel, the most absurd and unscientific and at the same time the most potent ever possessed by any tyrant class. The oligarchs believed their ethics, in spite of the fact that biology and evolution gave them the lie; and, because of their faith, for three centuries they were able to hold back the mighty tide of human progress—a spectacle, profound, tremendous, puzzling to the metaphysical moralist, and one that to the materialist is the cause of many doubts and reconsiderations.

And just now the word has gone forth that new levies are being imposed for the building of Asgard, the projected wonder-city that will far exceed Ardis when the latter is completed.[1] We of the Revolution will go on with that great work, but it will not be done by the miserable serfs. The walls and towers and shafts of that fair city will arise to the sound of singing, and into its beauty and wonder will be woven, not sighs and groans, but music and laughter.

Ernest was madly impatient to be out in the world and doing, for our ill-fated First Revolt, that had miscarried in the Chicago Commune, was ripening fast. Yet he possessed his soul with patience, and during this time of his torment, when Hadly, who had been brought for the purpose from Illinois, made him over into another man[2] he revolved great plans in his head for the organization of the learned proletariat, and for the maintenance of at least the rudiments of education amongst the people of the abyss—all this of course in the event of the First Revolt being a failure.

It was not until January, 1917, that we left the refuge. All had been arranged. We took our place at once as agents-provocateurs in the scheme of the Iron Heel. I was supposed to be Ernest's sister. By oligarchs and comrades on the inside who were high in authority, place had been made for us, we were in possession of all necessary documents, and our pasts were accounted for. With help on the inside, this was not difficult, for in that shadow-world of secret service identity was nebulous. Like ghosts the agents came and went, obeying commands, fulfilling duties, following clews, making their reports often to officers they never saw or cooperating with other agents they had never seen before and would never see again.

---

[1] Ardis was completed in 1942 A.D., Asgard was not completed until 1984 A.D. It was fifty-two years in the building, during which time a permanent army of half a million serfs was employed. At times these numbers swelled to over a million—without any account being taken of the hundreds of thousands of the labor castes and the artists.

[2] Among the Revolutionists were many surgeons, and in vivisection they attained marvellous proficiency. In Avis Everhard's words, they could literally make a man over. To them the elimination of scars and disfigurements was a trivial detail. They changed the features with such microscopic care that no traces were left of their handiwork. The nose was a favorite organ to work upon. Skin-grafting and hair-transplanting were among their commonest devices. The changes in expression they accomplished were wizard-like. Eyes and eyebrows, lips, mouths, and ears, were radically altered. By cunning operations on tongue, throat, larynx, and nasal cavities a man's whole enunciation and manner of speech could be changed. Desperate times give need for desperate remedies, and the surgeons of the Revolution rose to the need. Among other things, they could increase an adult's stature by as much as four or five inches and decrease it by one or two inches. What they did is to-day a lost art. We have no need for it.

CHAPTER XXII - THE CHICAGO COMMUNE

As agents-provocateurs, not alone were we able to travel a great deal, but our very work threw us in contact with the proletariat and with our comrades, the revolutionists. Thus we were in both camps at the same time, ostensibly serving the Iron Heel and secretly working with all our might for the Cause. There were many of us in the various secret services of the Oligarchy, and despite the shakings-up and reorganizations the secret services have undergone, they have never been able to weed all of us out.

Ernest had largely planned the First Revolt, and the date set had been somewhere early in the spring of 1918. In the fall of 1917 we were not ready; much remained to be done, and when the Revolt was precipitated, of course it was doomed to failure. The plot of necessity was frightfully intricate, and anything premature was sure to destroy it. This the Iron Heel foresaw and laid its schemes accordingly.

We had planned to strike our first blow at the nervous system of the Oligarchy. The latter had remembered the general strike, and had guarded against the defection of the telegraphers by installing wireless stations, in the control of the Mercenaries. We, in turn, had countered this move. When the signal was given, from every refuge, all over the land, and from the cities, and towns, and barracks, devoted comrades were to go forth and blow up the wireless stations. Thus at the first shock would the Iron Heel be brought to earth and lie practically dismembered.

At the same moment, other comrades were to blow up the bridges and tunnels and disrupt the whole network of railroads. Still further, other groups of comrades, at the signal, were to seize the officers of the Mercenaries and the police, as well as all Oligarchs of unusual ability or who held executive positions. Thus would the leaders of the enemy be removed from the field of the local battles that would inevitably be fought all over the land.

Many things were to occur simultaneously when the signal went forth. The Canadian and Mexican patriots, who were far stronger than the Iron Heel dreamed, were to duplicate our tactics. Then there were comrades (these were the women, for the men would be busy elsewhere) who were to post the proclamations from our secret presses. Those of us in the higher employ of the Iron Heel were to proceed immediately to make confusion and anarchy in all our departments. Inside the Mercenaries were thousands of our comrades. Their work was to blow up the magazines and to destroy the delicate mechanism of all the war machinery. In the cities of the Mercenaries and of the labor castes similar programmes of disruption were to be carried out.

In short, a sudden, colossal, stunning blow was to be struck. Before the paralyzed Oligarchy could recover itself, its end would have come. It would have meant terrible times and great loss of life, but no revolutionist hesitates at such things. Why, we even depended much, in our plan, on the unorganized people of the abyss. They were to be loosed on the palaces and cities of the masters. Never mind the destruction of life and property. Let the abysmal brute roar and the police and Mercenaries slay. The abysmal brute would roar anyway, and the police and Mercenaries would slay anyway. It would merely mean that various dangers to us were harmlessly destroying one another. In the meantime we would be doing our own work, largely unhampered, and gaining control of all the machinery of society.

Such was our plan, every detail of which had to be worked out in secret, and, as the day drew near, communicated to more and more comrades. This was the danger point, the stretching of the conspiracy. But that danger-point was never reached. Through its spy-system the Iron Heel got wind of the Revolt and prepared to teach us another of its bloody lessons. Chicago was the devoted city selected for the instruction, and well were we instructed.

Chicago[1] was the ripest of all—Chicago which of old time was the city of blood and which was to earn anew its name. There the revolutionary spirit was strong. Too many bitter strikes had been curbed there in the days of capitalism for the workers to forget and forgive. Even the labor castes of the city were alive with revolt. Too many heads had been broken in the early strikes. Despite their changed and favorable conditions, their hatred for the master class had not died. This spirit had infected the Mercenaries, of which three regiments in particular were ready to come over to us en masse.

Chicago had always been the storm-centre of the conflict between labor and capital, a city of street-battles and violent death, with a class-conscious capitalist organization and a class-conscious workman organization, where, in the old days, the very school-teachers were formed into labor unions and affiliated with the hod-carriers and brick-layers in the American Federation of Labor. And Chicago became the storm-centre of the premature First Revolt.

The trouble was precipitated by the Iron Heel. It was cleverly done. The whole population, including the favored labor castes, was given a course of outrageous treatment. Promises and agreements were broken, and most drastic punishments visited upon even petty offenders. The people of the abyss were tormented out of their apathy. In fact, the Iron Heel was preparing to make the abysmal beast roar. And hand in hand with this, in all precautionary measures in Chicago, the Iron Heel was incon-

---

[1] Chicago was the industrial inferno of the nineteenth century A.D. A curious anecdote has come down to us of John Burns, a great English labor leader and one time member of the British Cabinet. In Chicago, while on a visit to the United States, he was asked by a newspaper reporter for his opinion of that city. "Chicago," he answered, "is a pocket edition of hell." Some time later, as he was going aboard his steamer to sail to England, he was approached by another reporter, who wanted to know if he had changed his opinion of Chicago. "Yes, I have," was his reply. "My present opinion is that hell is a pocket edition of Chicago."

ceivably careless. Discipline was relaxed among the Mercenaries that remained, while many regiments had been withdrawn and sent to various parts of the country.

It did not take long to carry out this programme—only several weeks. We of the Revolution caught vague rumors of the state of affairs, but had nothing definite enough for an understanding. In fact, we thought it was a spontaneous spirit of revolt that would require careful curbing on our part, and never dreamed that it was deliberately manufactured—and it had been manufactured so secretly, from the very innermost circle of the Iron Heel, that we had got no inkling. The counter-plot was an able achievement, and ably carried out.

I was in New York when I received the order to proceed immediately to Chicago. The man who gave me the order was one of the oligarchs, I could tell that by his speech, though I did not know his name nor see his face. His instructions were too clear for me to make a mistake. Plainly I read between the lines that our plot had been discovered, that we had been countermined. The explosion was ready for the flash of powder, and countless agents of the Iron Heel, including me, either on the ground or being sent there, were to supply that flash. I flatter myself that I maintained my composure under the keen eye of the oligarch, but my heart was beating madly. I could almost have shrieked and flown at his throat with my naked hands before his final, cold-blooded instructions were given.

Once out of his presence, I calculated the time. I had just the moments to spare, if I were lucky, to get in touch with some local leader before catching my train. Guarding against being trailed, I made a rush of it for the Emergency Hospital. Luck was with me, and I gained access at once to comrade Galvin, the surgeon-in-chief. I started to gasp out my information, but he stopped me.

"I already know," he said quietly, though his Irish eyes were flashing. "I knew what you had come for. I got the word fifteen minutes ago, and I have already passed it along. Everything shall be done here to keep the comrades quiet. Chicago is to be sacrificed, but it shall be Chicago alone."

"Have you tried to get word to Chicago?" I asked.

He shook his head. "No telegraphic communication. Chicago is shut off. It's going to be hell there."

He paused a moment, and I saw his white hands clinch. Then he burst out:

"By God! I wish I were going to be there!"

"There is yet a chance to stop it," I said, "if nothing happens to the train and I can get there in time. Or if some of the other secret-service comrades who have learned the truth can get there in time."

"You on the inside were caught napping this time," he said.

I nodded my head humbly.

"It was very secret," I answered. "Only the inner chiefs could have known up to to-day. We haven't yet penetrated that far, so we couldn't escape being kept in the dark. If only Ernest were here. Maybe he is in Chicago now, and all is well."

Dr. Galvin shook his head. "The last news I heard of him was that he had been sent to Boston or New Haven. This secret service for the enemy must hamper him a lot, but it's better than lying in a refuge."

I started to go, and Galvin wrung my hand.

"Keep a stout heart," were his parting words. "What if the First Revolt is lost? There will be a second, and we will be wiser then. Good-by and good luck. I don't know whether I'll ever see you again. It's going to be hell there, but I'd give ten years of my life for your chance to be in it."

The Twentieth Century[1] left New York at six in the evening, and was supposed to arrive at Chicago at seven next morning. But it lost time that night. We were running behind another train. Among the travellers in my Pullman was comrade Hartman, like myself in the secret service of the Iron Heel. He it was who told me of the train that immediately preceded us. It was an exact duplicate of our train, though it contained no passengers. The idea was that the empty train should receive the disaster were an attempt made to blow up the Twentieth Century. For that matter there were very few people on the train—only a baker's dozen in our car.

"There must be some big men on board," Hartman concluded. "I noticed a private car on the rear."

Night had fallen when we made our first change of engine, and I walked down the platform for a breath of fresh air and to see what I could see. Through the windows of the private car I caught a glimpse of three men whom I recognized. Hartman was right. One of the men was General Altendorff; and the other two were Mason and Vanderbold, the brains of the inner circle of the Oligarchy's secret service.

It was a quiet moonlight night, but I tossed restlessly and could not sleep. At five in the morning I dressed and abandoned my bed.

I asked the maid in the dressing-room how late the train was, and she told me two hours. She was a mulatto woman, and I noticed that her face was haggard, with great circles under the eyes, while the eyes themselves were wide with some haunting fear.

"What is the matter?" I asked.

"Nothing, miss; I didn't sleep well, I guess," was her reply.

I looked at her closely, and tried her with one of our signals. She responded, and I made sure of her.

"Something terrible is going to happen in Chicago," she said. "There's that fake[2] train in front of us. That and the troop-trains have made us late."

"Troop-trains?" I queried.

She nodded her head. "The line is thick with them. We've been passing them all night. And they're all heading for Chicago. And bringing them over the air-line—that means business.

"I've a lover in Chicago," she added apologetically. "He's one of us, and he's in the Mercenaries, and I'm afraid for him."

Poor girl. Her lover was in one of the three disloyal regiments.

Hartman and I had breakfast together in the dining car, and I forced myself to eat. The sky had clouded, and the train rushed on like a sullen thunderbolt through the gray pall of advancing day. The very negroes that waited on us knew that something terrible was impending. Oppression sat heavily upon them; the lightness of their natures had ebbed out of them; they were slack and absent-minded in their service, and they whispered gloomily to one another in the far end of the car next to the kitchen. Hartman was hopeless over the situation.

---

[1] This was reputed to be the fastest train in the world then. It was quite a famous train.

[2] False.

"What can we do?" he demanded for the twentieth time, with a helpless shrug of the shoulders.

He pointed out of the window. "See, all is ready. You can depend upon it that they're holding them like this, thirty or forty miles outside the city, on every road."

He had reference to troop-trains on the side-track. The soldiers were cooking their breakfasts over fires built on the ground beside the track, and they looked up curiously at us as we thundered past without slackening our terrific speed.

All was quiet as we entered Chicago. It was evident nothing had happened yet. In the suburbs the morning papers came on board the train. There was nothing in them, and yet there was much in them for those skilled in reading between the lines that it was intended the ordinary reader should read into the text. The fine hand of the Iron Heel was apparent in every column. Glimmerings of weakness in the armor of the Oligarchy were given. Of course, there was nothing definite. It was intended that the reader should feel his way to these glimmerings. It was cleverly done. As fiction, those morning papers of October 27th were masterpieces.

The local news was missing. This in itself was a masterstroke. It shrouded Chicago in mystery, and it suggested to the average Chicago reader that the Oligarchy did not dare give the local news. Hints that were untrue, of course, were given of insubordination all over the land, crudely disguised with complacent references to punitive measures to be taken. There were reports of numerous wireless stations that had been blown up, with heavy rewards offered for the detection of the perpetrators. Of course no wireless stations had been blown up. Many similar outrages, that dovetailed with the plot of the revolutionists, were given. The impression to be made on the minds of the Chicago comrades was that the general Revolt was beginning, albeit with a confusing miscarriage in many details. It was impossible for one uninformed to escape the vague yet certain feeling that all the land was ripe for the revolt that had already begun to break out.

It was reported that the defection of the Mercenaries in California had become so serious that half a dozen regiments had been disbanded and broken, and that their members with their families had been driven from their own city and on into the labor-ghettos. And the California Mercenaries were in reality the most faithful of all to their salt! But how was Chicago, shut off from the rest of the world, to know? Then there was a ragged telegram describing an outbreak of the populace in New York City, in which the labor castes were joining, concluding with the statement (intended to be accepted as a bluff[1]) that the troops had the situation in hand.

And as the oligarchs had done with the morning papers, so had they done in a thousand other ways. These we learned afterward, as, for example, the secret messages of the oligarchs, sent with the express purpose of leaking to the ears of the revolutionists, that had come over the wires, now and again, during the first part of the night.

"I guess the Iron Heel won't need our services," Hartman remarked, putting down the paper he had been reading, when the train pulled into the central depot. "They wasted their time sending us here. Their plans have evidently prospered better than they expected. Hell will break loose any second now."

---

[1] A lie.

He turned and looked down the train as we alighted.

"I thought so," he muttered. "They dropped that private car when the papers came aboard."

Hartman was hopelessly depressed. I tried to cheer him up, but he ignored my effort and suddenly began talking very hurriedly, in a low voice, as we passed through the station. At first I could not understand.

"I have not been sure," he was saying, "and I have told no one. I have been working on it for weeks, and I cannot make sure. Watch out for Knowlton. I suspect him. He knows the secrets of a score of our refuges. He carries the lives of hundreds of us in his hands, and I think he is a traitor. It's more a feeling on my part than anything else. But I thought I marked a change in him a short while back. There is the danger that he has sold us out, or is going to sell us out. I am almost sure of it. I wouldn't whisper my suspicions to a soul, but, somehow, I don't think I'll leave Chicago alive. Keep your eye on Knowlton. Trap him. Find out. I don't know anything more. It is only an intuition, and so far I have failed to find the slightest clew." We were just stepping out upon the sidewalk. "Remember," Hartman concluded earnestly. "Keep your eyes upon Knowlton."

And Hartman was right. Before a month went by Knowlton paid for his treason with his life. He was formally executed by the comrades in Milwaukee.

All was quiet on the streets—too quiet. Chicago lay dead. There was no roar and rumble of traffic. There were not even cabs on the streets. The surface cars and the elevated were not running. Only occasionally, on the sidewalks, were there stray pedestrians, and these pedestrians did not loiter. They went their ways with great haste and definiteness, withal there was a curious indecision in their movements, as though they expected the buildings to topple over on them or the sidewalks to sink under their feet or fly up in the air. A few gamins, however, were around, in their eyes a suppressed eagerness in anticipation of wonderful and exciting things to happen.

From somewhere, far to the south, the dull sound of an explosion came to our ears. That was all. Then quiet again, though the gamins had startled and listened, like young deer, at the sound. The doorways to all the buildings were closed; the shutters to the shops were up. But there were many police and watchmen in evidence, and now and again automobile patrols of the Mercenaries slipped swiftly past.

Hartman and I agreed that it was useless to report ourselves to the local chiefs of the secret service. Our failure so to report would be excused, we knew, in the light of subsequent events. So we headed for the great labor-ghetto on the South Side in the hope of getting in contact with some of the comrades. Too late! We knew it. But we could not stand still and do nothing in those ghastly, silent streets. Where was Ernest? I was wondering. What was happening in the cities of the labor castes and Mercenaries? In the fortresses?

As if in answer, a great screaming roar went up, dim with distance, punctuated with detonation after detonation.

"It's the fortresses," Hartman said. "God pity those three regiments!"

At a crossing we noticed, in the direction of the stockyards, a gigantic pillar of smoke. At the next crossing several similar smoke pillars were rising skyward in the direction of the West Side. Over the city of the Mercenaries we saw a great captive war-balloon that burst even as we looked at it, and fell in flaming wreckage toward the earth. There was no clew to that tragedy of the air. We could not determine whether the balloon had been manned by comrades or enemies. A vague sound came to our ears, like the bubbling of a gigantic caldron a long way off, and Hartman said it was machine-guns and automatic rifles.

And still we walked in immediate quietude. Nothing was happening where we were. The police and the automobile patrols went by, and once half a dozen fire-engines, returning evidently from some conflagration. A question was called to the fireman by an officer in an automobile, and we heard one shout in reply: "No water! They've blown up the mains!"

"We've smashed the water supply," Hartman cried excitedly to me. "If we can do all this in a premature, isolated, abortive attempt, what can't we do in a concerted, ripened effort all over the land?"

The automobile containing the officer who had asked the question darted on. Suddenly there was a deafening roar. The machine, with its human freight, lifted in an upburst of smoke, and sank down a mass of wreckage and death.

Hartman was jubilant. "Well done! well done!" he was repeating, over and over, in a whisper. "The proletariat gets its lesson to-day, but it gives one, too."

Police were running for the spot. Also, another patrol machine had halted. As for myself, I was in a daze. The suddenness of it was stunning. How had it happened? I knew not how, and yet I had been looking directly at it. So dazed was I for the moment that I was scarcely aware of the fact that we were being held up by the police. I abruptly saw that a policeman was in the act of shooting Hartman. But Hartman was cool and was giving the proper passwords. I saw the levelled revolver hesitate, then sink down, and heard the disgusted grunt of the policeman. He was very angry, and was cursing the whole secret service. It was always in the way, he was averring, while Hartman was talking back to him and with fitting secret-service pride explaining to him the clumsiness of the police.

The next moment I knew how it had happened. There was quite a group about the wreck, and two men were just lifting up the wounded officer to carry him to the other machine. A panic seized all of them, and they scattered in every direction, running in blind terror, the wounded officer, roughly dropped, being left behind. The cursing policeman alongside of me also ran, and Hartman and I ran, too, we knew not why, obsessed with the same blind terror to get away from that particular spot.

Nothing really happened then, but everything was explained. The flying men were sheepishly coming back, but all the while their eyes were raised apprehensively to the many-windowed, lofty buildings that towered like the sheer walls of a canyon on each side of the street. From one of those countless windows the bomb had been thrown, but which window? There had been no second bomb, only a fear of one.

Thereafter we looked with speculative comprehension at the windows. Any of them contained possible death. Each building was a possible ambuscade. This was warfare in that modern jungle, a great city. Every street was a canyon, every building a mountain. We had not changed much from primitive man, despite the war automobiles that were sliding by.

Turning a corner, we came upon a woman. She was lying on the pavement, in a pool of blood. Hartman bent over and examined her. As for myself, I turned deathly sick. I was to see many dead that day, but the total carnage was not to affect me as did this first forlorn body lying there at my feet abandoned on the pavement. "Shot in the breast," was Hartman's report. Clasped in the hollow of her arm, as a child might be clasped, was a bundle of printed matter. Even in death she seemed loath to part with that which had caused her death; for when Hartman had succeeded in withdrawing the bundle, we found that it consisted of large printed sheets, the proclamations of the revolutionists.

"A comrade," I said.

But Hartman only cursed the Iron Heel, and we passed on. Often we were halted by the police and patrols, but our passwords enabled us to proceed. No more bombs fell from the windows, the last pedestrians seemed to have vanished from the streets, and our immediate quietude grew more profound; though the gigantic caldron continued to bubble in the distance, dull roars of explosions came to us from all directions, and the smoke-pillars were towering more ominously in the heavens.

CHAPTER XXIII - THE PEOPLE OF THE ABYSS

Suddenly a change came over the face of things. A tingle of excitement ran along the air. Automobiles fled past, two, three, a dozen, and from them warnings were shouted to us. One of the machines swerved wildly at high speed half a block down, and the next moment, already left well behind it, the pavement was torn into a great hole by a bursting bomb. We saw the police disappearing down the cross-streets on the run, and knew that something terrible was coming. We could hear the rising roar of it.

"Our brave comrades are coming," Hartman said.

We could see the front of their column filling the street from gutter to gutter, as the last war-automobile fled past. The machine stopped for a moment just abreast of us. A soldier leaped from it, carrying something carefully in his hands. This, with the same care, he deposited in the gutter. Then he leaped back to his seat and the machine dashed on, took the turn at the corner, and was gone from sight. Hartman ran to the gutter and stooped over the object.

"Keep back," he warned me.

I could see he was working rapidly with his hands. When he returned to me the sweat was heavy on his forehead.

"I disconnected it," he said, "and just in the nick of time. The soldier was clumsy. He intended it for our comrades, but he didn't give it enough time. It would have exploded prematurely. Now it won't explode at all."

Everything was happening rapidly now. Across the street and half a block down, high up in a building, I could see heads peering out. I had just pointed them out to Hartman, when a sheet of flame and smoke ran along that portion of the face of the building where the heads had appeared, and the air was shaken by the explosion. In places the stone facing of the building was torn away, exposing the iron construction beneath. The next moment similar sheets of flame and smoke smote the front of the building across the street opposite it. Between the explosions we could hear the rattle of the automatic pistols and rifles. For several minutes this mid-air battle continued, then died out. It was patent that our comrades were in one building, that Mercenaries were in the other, and that they were fighting across the street. But we could not tell which was which—which building contained our comrades and which the Mercenaries.

By this time the column on the street was almost on us. As the front of it passed under the warring buildings, both went into action again—one building dropping bombs into the street, being attacked from across the street, and in return replying to that attack. Thus we learned which building was held by our comrades, and they did good work, saving those in the street from the bombs of the enemy.

Hartman gripped my arm and dragged me into a wide entrance.

"They're not our comrades," he shouted in my ear.

The inner doors to the entrance were locked and bolted. We could not escape. The next moment the front of the column went by. It was not a column, but a mob, an awful river that filled the street, the people of the abyss, mad with drink and wrong, up at last and roaring for the blood of their masters. I had seen the people of the abyss before, gone through its ghettos, and thought I knew it; but I found that I was now looking on it for the first time. Dumb apathy had vanished. It was now dynamic—a fascinating spectacle of dread. It surged past my vision in concrete waves of wrath, snarling and growling, carnivorous, drunk with whiskey from pillaged warehouses, drunk with hatred, drunk with lust for blood—men, women, and children, in rags and tatters, dim ferocious intelligences with all the godlike blotted from their features and all the fiendlike stamped in, apes and tigers, anaemic consumptives and great hairy beasts of burden, wan faces from which vampire society had sucked the juice of life, bloated forms swollen with physical grossness and corruption, withered hags and death's-heads bearded like patriarchs, festering youth and festering age, faces of fiends, crooked, twisted, misshapen monsters blasted with the ravages of disease and all the horrors of chronic innutrition—the refuse and the scum of life, a raging, screaming, screeching, demoniacal horde.

And why not? The people of the abyss had nothing to lose but the misery and pain of living. And to gain?—nothing, save one final, awful glut of vengeance. And as I looked the thought came to me that in that rushing stream of human lava were men, comrades and heroes, whose mission had been to rouse the abysmal beast and to keep the enemy occupied in coping with it.

And now a strange thing happened to me. A transformation came over me. The fear of death, for myself and for others, left me. I was strangely exalted, another being in another life. Nothing mattered. The Cause for this one time was lost, but the Cause would be here to-morrow, the same Cause, ever fresh and ever burning. And thereafter, in the orgy of horror that raged through the succeeding hours, I was able to take a calm interest. Death meant nothing, life meant nothing. I was an interested spectator of events, and, sometimes swept on by the rush, was myself a curious participant. For my mind had leaped to a star-cool altitude and grasped a passionless transvaluation of values. Had it not done this, I know that I should have died.

Half a mile of the mob had swept by when we were discovered. A woman in fantastic rags, with cheeks cavernously hollow and with narrow black eyes like burning gimlets, caught a glimpse of Hartman and me. She let out a shrill shriek and bore in upon us. A section of the mob tore itself loose and surged in after her. I can see her now, as I write these lines, a leap in advance, her gray hair flying in thin tangled strings, the blood dripping down her forehead from some wound in the scalp, in her right hand a hatchet, her left hand, lean and wrinkled, a yellow talon, gripping the air convulsively. Hartman sprang in front of me. This was no time for explanations. We were well dressed, and that was enough. His fist shot out, striking the woman between her burning eyes. The impact of the blow drove her backward, but she struck the wall of her on-coming fellows and bounced forward again, dazed and helpless, the brandished hatchet falling feebly on Hartman's shoulder.

The next moment I knew not what was happening. I was overborne by the crowd. The confined space was filled with shrieks and yells and curses. Blows were falling on me. Hands were ripping and tearing at my flesh and garments. I felt that I was being torn to pieces. I was being borne down, suffocated. Some strong hand gripped my shoulder in the thick of the press and was dragging fiercely at me. Between pain and pressure I fainted. Hartman never came out of that entrance. He had shielded me and received the first brunt of the attack. This had saved me, for the jam had quickly become too dense for anything more than the mad gripping and tearing of hands.

I came to in the midst of wild movement. All about me was the same movement. I had been caught up in a monstrous flood that was sweeping me I knew not whither. Fresh air was on my cheek and biting sweetly in my lungs. Faint and dizzy, I was vaguely aware of a strong arm around my body under the arms, and half-lifting me and dragging me along. Feebly my own limbs were helping me. In front of me I could see the moving back of a man's coat. It had been slit from top to bottom along the centre seam, and it pulsed rhythmically, the slit opening and closing regularly with every leap of the wearer. This phenomenon fascinated me for a time, while my senses were coming back to me. Next I became aware of stinging cheeks and nose, and could feel blood dripping on my face. My hat was gone. My hair was down and flying, and from the stinging of the scalp I managed to recollect a hand in the press of the entrance that had torn at my hair. My chest and arms were bruised and aching in a score of places.

My brain grew clearer, and I turned as I ran and looked at the man who was holding me up. He it was who had dragged me out and saved me. He noticed my movement.

"It's all right!" he shouted hoarsely. "I knew you on the instant."

I failed to recognize him, but before I could speak I trod upon something that was alive and that squirmed under my foot. I was swept on by those behind and could not look down and see, and yet I knew that it was a woman who had fallen and who was being trampled into the pavement by thousands of successive feet.

"It's all right," he repeated. "I'm Garthwaite."

He was bearded and gaunt and dirty, but I succeeded in remembering him as the stalwart youth that had spent several months in our Glen Ellen refuge three years before. He passed me the signals of the Iron Heel's secret service, in token that he, too, was in its employ.

"I'll get you out of this as soon as I can get a chance," he assured me. "But watch your footing. On your life don't stumble and go down."

All things happened abruptly on that day, and with an abruptness that was sickening the mob checked itself. I came in violent collision with a large woman in front of me (the man with the split coat had vanished), while those behind collided against me. A devilish pandemonium reigned,—shrieks, curses, and cries of death, while above all rose the churning rattle of machine-guns and the put-a-put, put-a-put of rifles. At first I could make out nothing. People were falling about me right and left. The woman in front doubled up and went down, her hands on her abdomen in a frenzied clutch. A man was quivering against my legs in a death-struggle.

It came to me that we were at the head of the column. Half a mile of it had disappeared—where or how I never learned. To this day I do not know what became of that half-mile of humanity—whether it was blotted out by some frightful bolt of war, whether it was scattered and destroyed piecemeal, or whether it escaped. But there we were, at the head of the column instead of in its middle, and we were being swept out of life by a torrent of shrieking lead.

As soon as death had thinned the jam, Garthwaite, still grasping my arm, led a rush of survivors into the wide entrance of an office building. Here, at the rear, against the doors, we were pressed by a panting, gasping mass of creatures. For some time we remained in this position without a change in the situation.

"I did it beautifully," Garthwaite was lamenting to me. "Ran you right into a trap. We had a gambler's chance in the street, but in here there is no chance at all. It's all over but the shouting. Vive la Revolution!"

Then, what he expected, began. The Mercenaries were killing without quarter. At first, the surge back upon us was crushing, but as the killing continued the pressure was eased. The dead and dying went down and made room. Garthwaite put his mouth to my ear and shouted, but in the frightful din I could not catch what he said. He did not wait. He seized me and threw me down. Next he dragged a dying woman over on top of me, and, with much squeezing and shoving, crawled in beside me and partly over me. A mound of dead and dying began to pile up over us, and over this mound, pawing and moaning, crept those that still survived. But these, too, soon ceased, and a semi-silence settled down, broken by groans and sobs and sounds of strangulation.

I should have been crushed had it not been for Garthwaite. As it was, it seemed inconceivable that I could bear the weight I did and live. And yet, outside of pain, the only feeling I possessed was one of curiosity. How was it going to end? What would death be like? Thus did I receive my red baptism in that Chicago shambles. Prior to that, death to me had been a theory; but ever afterward death has been a simple fact that does not matter, it is so easy.

But the Mercenaries were not content with what they had done. They invaded the entrance, killing the wounded and searching out the unhurt that, like ourselves, were playing dead. I remember one man they dragged out of a heap, who pleaded abjectly until a revolver shot cut him short. Then there was a woman who charged from a heap, snarling and shooting. She fired six shots before they got her, though what damage she did we could not know. We could follow these tragedies only by the sound. Every little while flurries like this occurred, each flurry culminating in the revolver shot that put an end to it. In the intervals we could hear the soldiers talking and swearing as they rummaged among the carcasses, urged on by their officers to hurry up.

At last they went to work on our heap, and we could feel the pressure diminish as they dragged away the dead and wounded. Garthwaite began uttering aloud the signals. At first he was not heard. Then he raised his voice.

"Listen to that," we heard a soldier say. And next the sharp voice of an officer. "Hold on there! Careful as you go!"

Oh, that first breath of air as we were dragged out! Garthwaite did the talking at first, but I was compelled to undergo a brief examination to prove service with the Iron Heel.

"Agents-provocateurs all right," was the officer's conclusion. He was a beardless young fellow, a cadet, evidently, of some great oligarch family.

"It's a hell of a job," Garthwaite grumbled. "I'm going to try and resign and get into the army. You fellows have a snap."

"You've earned it," was the young officer's answer. "I've got some pull, and I'll see if it can be managed. I can tell them how I found you."

He took Garthwaite's name and number, then turned to me.

"And you?"

"Oh, I'm going to be married," I answered lightly, "and then I'll be out of it all."

And so we talked, while the killing of the wounded went on. It is all a dream, now, as I look back on it; but at the time it was the most natural thing in the world. Garthwaite and the young officer fell into an animated conversation over the difference between so-called modern warfare and the present street-fighting and sky-scraper fighting that was taking place all over the city. I followed them intently, fixing up my hair at the same time and pinning together my torn skirts. And all the time the killing of the wounded went on. Sometimes the revolver shots drowned the voices of Garthwaite and the officer, and they were compelled to repeat what they had been saying.

I lived through three days of the Chicago Commune, and the vastness of it and of the slaughter may be imagined when I say that in all that time I saw practically nothing outside the killing of the people of the abyss and the mid-air fighting between sky-scrapers. I really saw nothing of the heroic work done by the comrades. I could hear the explosions of their mines and bombs, and see the smoke of their conflagrations, and that was all. The mid-air part of one great deed I saw, however, and that was the balloon attacks made by our comrades on the fortresses. That was on the second day. The three disloyal regiments had been destroyed in the fortresses to the last man. The fortresses were crowded with Mercenaries, the wind blew in the right direction, and up went our balloons from one of the office buildings in the city.

Now Biedenbach, after he left Glen Ellen, had invented a most powerful explosive—"expedite" he called it. This was the weapon the balloons used. They were only hot-air balloons, clumsily and hastily made, but they did the work. I saw it all from the top of an office building. The first balloon missed the fortresses completely and disappeared into the country; but we learned about it afterward. Burton and O'Sullivan were in it. As they were descending they swept across a railroad directly over a troop-train that was heading at full speed for Chicago. They dropped their whole supply of expedite upon the locomotive. The resulting wreck tied the line up for days. And the best of it was that, released from the weight of expedite, the balloon shot up into the air and did not come down for half a dozen miles, both heroes escaping unharmed.

The second balloon was a failure. Its flight was lame. It floated too low and was shot full of holes before it could reach the fortresses. Herford and Guinness were in it, and they were blown to pieces along with the field into which they fell. Biedenbach was in despair—we heard all about it afterward—and he went up alone in the third balloon. He, too, made a low flight, but he was in luck, for they failed seriously to puncture his balloon. I can see it now as I did then, from the lofty top of the building—that inflated bag drifting along the air, and that tiny speck of a man clinging on beneath. I could not see the fortress, but those on the roof with me said he was directly over it. I did not see the expedite fall when he cut it loose. But I did see the balloon suddenly leap up into the sky. An appreciable time after that the great column of the explosion towered in the air, and after that, in turn, I heard the roar of it. Biedenbach the gentle had destroyed a fortress. Two other balloons followed at the same time. One was blown to pieces in the air, the expedite exploding, and the shock of it disrupted the second balloon, which fell prettily into the remaining fortress. It couldn't have been better planned, though the two comrades in it sacrificed their lives.

But to return to the people of the abyss. My experiences were confined to them. They raged and slaughtered and destroyed all over the city proper, and were in turn destroyed; but never once did they succeed in reaching the city of the oligarchs over on the west side. The oligarchs had protected themselves well. No matter what destruction was wreaked in the heart of the city, they, and their womenkind and children, were to escape hurt. I am told that their children played in the parks during those terrible days and that their favorite game was an imitation of their elders stamping upon the proletariat.

But the Mercenaries found it no easy task to cope with the people of the abyss and at the same time fight with the comrades. Chicago was true to her traditions, and though a generation of revolutionists was wiped out, it took along with it pretty close to a generation of its enemies. Of course, the Iron Heel kept the figures secret, but, at a very conservative estimate, at least one hundred and thirty thousand Mercenaries were slain. But the comrades had no chance. Instead of the whole country being hand in hand in revolt, they were all alone, and the total strength of the Oligarchy could have been directed against them if necessary. As it was, hour after hour, day after day, in endless train-loads, by hundreds of thousands, the Mercenaries were hurled into Chicago.

And there were so many of the people of the abyss! Tiring of the slaughter, a great herding movement was begun by the soldiers, the intent of which was to drive the street mobs, like cattle, into Lake Michigan. It was at the beginning of this movement that Garthwaite and I had encountered the young officer. This herding movement was practically a failure, thanks to the splendid work of the comrades. Instead of the great host the Mercenaries had hoped to gather together, they succeeded in driving no more than forty thousand of the wretches into the lake. Time and again, when a mob of them was well in hand and being driven along the streets to the water, the comrades would create a diversion, and the mob would escape through the consequent hole torn in the encircling net.

Garthwaite and I saw an example of this shortly after meeting with the young officer. The mob of which we had been a part, and which had been put in retreat, was prevented from escaping to the south and east by strong bodies of troops. The troops we had fallen in with had held it back on the west. The only outlet was north, and north it went toward the lake, driven on from east and west and south by machine-gun fire and automatics. Whether it divined that it was being driven toward the lake, or whether it was merely a blind squirm of the monster, I do not know; but at any rate the mob took a cross street to the west, turned down the next street, and came back upon its track, heading south toward the great ghetto.

Garthwaite and I at that time were trying to make our way westward to get out of the territory of street-fighting, and we were caught right in the thick of it again. As we came to the corner we saw the howling mob bearing down upon us. Garthwaite seized my arm and we were just starting to run, when he dragged me back from in front of the wheels of half a dozen war automobiles, equipped with machine-guns, that were rushing for the spot. Behind them came the soldiers with their automatic rifles. By the time they took position, the mob was upon them, and it looked as though they would be overwhelmed before they could get into action.

Here and there a soldier was discharging his rifle, but this scattered fire had no effect in checking the mob. On it came, bellowing with brute rage. It seemed the machine-guns could not get started. The automobiles on which they were mounted blocked the street, compelling the soldiers to find positions in, between, and on the sidewalks. More and more soldiers were arriving, and in the jam we were unable to get away. Garthwaite held me by the arm, and we pressed close against the front of a building.

The mob was no more than twenty-five feet away when the machine-guns opened up; but before that flaming sheet of death nothing could live. The mob came on, but it could not advance. It piled up in a heap, a mound, a huge and growing wave of dead and dying. Those behind urged on, and the column, from gutter to gutter, telescoped upon itself. Wounded creatures, men and women, were vomited over the top of that awful wave and fell squirming down the face of it till they threshed about under the automobiles and against the legs of the soldiers. The latter bayoneted the struggling wretches, though one I saw who gained his feet and flew at a soldier's throat with his teeth. Together they went down, soldier and slave, into the welter.

The firing ceased. The work was done. The mob had been stopped in its wild attempt to break through. Orders were being given to clear the wheels of the war-machines. They could not advance over that wave of dead, and the idea was to run them down the cross street. The soldiers were dragging the bodies away from the wheels when it happened. We learned afterward how it happened. A block distant a hundred of our comrades had been holding a building. Across roofs and through buildings they made their way, till they found themselves looking down upon the close-packed soldiers. Then it was counter-massacre.

Without warning, a shower of bombs fell from the top of the building. The automobiles were blown to fragments, along with many soldiers. We, with the survivors, swept back in mad retreat. Half a block down another building opened fire on us. As the soldiers had carpeted the street with dead slaves, so, in turn, did they themselves become carpet. Garthwaite and I bore charmed lives. As we had done before, so again we sought shelter in an entrance. But he was not to be caught napping this time. As the roar of the bombs died away, he began peering out.

"The mob's coming back!" he called to me. "We've got to get out of this!"

We fled, hand in hand, down the bloody pavement, slipping and sliding, and making for the corner. Down the cross street we could see a few soldiers still running. Nothing was happening to them. The way was clear. So we paused a moment and looked back. The mob came on slowly. It was busy arming itself with the rifles of the slain and killing the wounded. We saw the end of the young officer who had rescued us. He painfully lifted himself on his elbow and turned loose with his automatic pistol.

"There goes my chance of promotion," Garthwaite laughed, as a woman bore down on the wounded man, brandishing a butcher's cleaver. "Come on. It's the wrong direction, but we'll get out somehow."

And we fled eastward through the quiet streets, prepared at every cross street for anything to happen. To the south a monster conflagration was filling the sky, and we knew that the great ghetto was burning. At last I sank down on the sidewalk. I was exhausted and could go no farther. I was bruised and sore and aching in every limb; yet I could not escape smiling at Garthwaite, who was rolling a cigarette and saying:

"I know I'm making a mess of rescuing you, but I can't get head nor tail of the situation. It's all a mess. Every time we try to break out, something happens and we're turned back. We're only a couple of blocks now from where I got you out of that entrance. Friend and foe are all mixed up. It's chaos. You can't tell who is in those darned buildings. Try to find out, and you get a bomb on your head. Try to go peaceably on your way, and you run into a mob and are killed by machine-guns, or you run into the Mercenaries and are killed by your own comrades from a roof. And on the top of it all the mob comes along and kills you, too."

He shook his head dolefully, lighted his cigarette, and sat down beside me.

"And I'm that hungry," he added, "I could eat cobblestones."

The next moment he was on his feet again and out in the street prying up a cobblestone. He came back with it and assaulted the window of a store behind us.

"It's ground floor and no good," he explained as he helped me through the hole he had made; "but it's the best we can do. You get a nap and I'll reconnoitre. I'll finish this rescue all right, but I want time, time, lots of it—and something to eat."

It was a harness store we found ourselves in, and he fixed me up a couch of horse blankets in the private office well to the rear. To add to my wretchedness a splitting headache was coming on, and I was only too glad to close my eyes and try to sleep.

"I'll be back," were his parting words. "I don't hope to get an auto, but I'll surely bring some grub,[1] anyway."

And that was the last I saw of Garthwaite for three years. Instead of coming back, he was carried away to a hospital with a bullet through his lungs and another through the fleshy part of his neck.

---

[1] Food.

CHAPTER XXIV - NIGHTMARE

I had not closed my eyes the night before on the Twentieth Century, and what of that and of my exhaustion I slept soundly. When I first awoke, it was night. Garthwaite had not returned. I had lost my watch and had no idea of the time. As I lay with my eyes closed, I heard the same dull sound of distant explosions. The inferno was still raging. I crept through the store to the front. The reflection from the sky of vast conflagrations made the street almost as light as day. One could have read the finest print with ease. From several blocks away came the crackle of small hand-bombs and the churning of machine-guns, and from a long way off came a long series of heavy explosions. I crept back to my horse blankets and slept again.

When next I awoke, a sickly yellow light was filtering in on me. It was dawn of the second day. I crept to the front of the store. A smoke pall, shot through with lurid gleams, filled the sky. Down the opposite side of the street tottered a wretched slave. One hand he held tightly against his side, and behind him he left a bloody trail. His eyes roved everywhere, and they were filled with apprehension and dread. Once he looked straight across at me, and in his face was all the dumb pathos of the wounded and hunted animal. He saw me, but there was no kinship between us, and with him, at least, no sympathy of understanding; for he cowered perceptibly and dragged himself on. He could expect no aid in all God's world. He was a helot in the great hunt of helots that the masters were making. All he could hope for, all he sought, was some hole to crawl away in and hide like any animal. The sharp clang of a passing ambulance at the corner gave him a start. Ambulances were not for such as he. With a groan of pain he threw himself into a doorway. A minute later he was out again and desperately hobbling on.

I went back to my horse blankets and waited an hour for Garthwaite. My headache had not gone away. On the contrary, it was increasing. It was by an effort of will only that I was able to open my eyes and look at objects. And with the opening of my eyes and the looking came intolerable torment. Also, a great pulse was beating in my brain. Weak and reeling, I went out through the broken window and down the street, seeking to escape, instinctively and gropingly, from the awful shambles. And thereafter I lived nightmare. My memory of what happened in the succeeding hours is the memory one would have of nightmare. Many events are focussed sharply on my brain, but between these indelible pictures I retain are intervals of unconsciousness. What occurred in those intervals I know not, and never shall know.

CHAPTER XXIV - NIGHTMARE

I remember stumbling at the corner over the legs of a man. It was the poor hunted wretch that had dragged himself past my hiding-place. How distinctly do I remember his poor, pitiful, gnarled hands as he lay there on the pavement—hands that were more hoof and claw than hands, all twisted and distorted by the toil of all his days, with on the palms a horny growth of callous a half inch thick. And as I picked myself up and started on, I looked into the face of the thing and saw that it still lived; for the eyes, dimly intelligent, were looking at me and seeing me.

After that came a kindly blank. I knew nothing, saw nothing, merely tottered on in my quest for safety. My next nightmare vision was a quiet street of the dead. I came upon it abruptly, as a wanderer in the country would come upon a flowing stream. Only this stream I gazed upon did not flow. It was congealed in death. From pavement to pavement, and covering the sidewalks, it lay there, spread out quite evenly, with only here and there a lump or mound of bodies to break the surface. Poor driven people of the abyss, hunted helots—they lay there as the rabbits in California after a drive.[1] Up the street and down I looked. There was no movement, no sound. The quiet buildings looked down upon the scene from their many windows. And once, and once only, I saw an arm that moved in that dead stream. I swear I saw it move, with a strange writhing gesture of agony, and with it lifted a head, gory with nameless horror, that gibbered at me and then lay down again and moved no more.

I remember another street, with quiet buildings on either side, and the panic that smote me into consciousness as again I saw the people of the abyss, but this time in a stream that flowed and came on. And then I saw there was nothing to fear. The stream moved slowly, while from it arose groans and lamentations, cursings, babblings of senility, hysteria, and insanity; for these were the very young and the very old, the feeble and the sick, the helpless and the hopeless, all the wreckage of the ghetto. The burning of the great ghetto on the South Side had driven them forth into the inferno of the street-fighting, and whither they wended and whatever became of them I did not know and never learned.[2]

I have faint memories of breaking a window and hiding in some shop to escape a street mob that was pursued by soldiers. Also, a bomb burst near me, once, in some still street, where, look as I would, up and down, I could see no human being. But my next sharp recollection begins with the crack of a rifle and an abrupt becoming aware that I am being fired at by a soldier in an automobile. The shot missed, and the next moment I was screaming and motioning the signals. My memory of riding in the automobile is very hazy, though this ride, in turn, is broken by one vivid picture. The crack of the rifle of the soldier sitting beside me made me open my eyes, and I saw George Milford, whom I had known in the Pell Street days, sinking slowly down to

---

[1] In those days, so sparsely populated was the land that wild animals often became pests. In California the custom of rabbit-driving obtained. On a given day all the farmers in a locality would assemble and sweep across the country in converging lines, driving the rabbits by scores of thousands into a prepared enclosure, where they were clubbed to death by men and boys.

[2] It was long a question of debate, whether the burning of the South Side ghetto was accidental, or whether it was done by the Mercenaries; but it is definitely settled now that the ghetto was fired by the Mercenaries under orders from their chiefs.

the sidewalk. Even as he sank the soldier fired again, and Milford doubled in, then flung his body out, and fell sprawling. The soldier chuckled, and the automobile sped on.

The next I knew after that I was awakened out of a sound sleep by a man who walked up and down close beside me. His face was drawn and strained, and the sweat rolled down his nose from his forehead. One hand was clutched tightly against his chest by the other hand, and blood dripped down upon the floor as he walked. He wore the uniform of the Mercenaries. From without, as through thick walls, came the muffled roar of bursting bombs. I was in some building that was locked in combat with some other building.

A surgeon came in to dress the wounded soldier, and I learned that it was two in the afternoon. My headache was no better, and the surgeon paused from his work long enough to give me a powerful drug that would depress the heart and bring relief. I slept again, and the next I knew I was on top of the building. The immediate fighting had ceased, and I was watching the balloon attack on the fortresses. Some one had an arm around me and I was leaning close against him. It came to me quite as a matter of course that this was Ernest, and I found myself wondering how he had got his hair and eyebrows so badly singed.

It was by the merest chance that we had found each other in that terrible city. He had had no idea that I had left New York, and, coming through the room where I lay asleep, could not at first believe that it was I. Little more I saw of the Chicago Commune. After watching the balloon attack, Ernest took me down into the heart of the building, where I slept the afternoon out and the night. The third day we spent in the building, and on the fourth, Ernest having got permission and an automobile from the authorities, we left Chicago.

My headache was gone, but, body and soul, I was very tired. I lay back against Ernest in the automobile, and with apathetic eyes watched the soldiers trying to get the machine out of the city. Fighting was still going on, but only in isolated localities. Here and there whole districts were still in possession of the comrades, but such districts were surrounded and guarded by heavy bodies of troops. In a hundred segregated traps were the comrades thus held while the work of subjugating them went on. Subjugation meant death, for no quarter was given, and they fought heroically to the last man.[1]

Whenever we approached such localities, the guards turned us back and sent us around. Once, the only way past two strong positions of the comrades was through a burnt section that lay between. From either side we could hear the rattle and roar of war, while the automobile picked its way through smoking ruins and tottering walls. Often the streets were blocked by mountains of debris that compelled us to go around. We were in a labyrinth of ruin, and our progress was slow.

---

[1] Numbers of the buildings held out over a week, while one held out eleven days. Each building had to be stormed like a fort, and the Mercenaries fought their way upward floor by floor. It was deadly fighting. Quarter was neither given nor taken, and in the fighting the revolutionists had the advantage of being above. While the revolutionists were wiped out, the loss was not one-sided. The proud Chicago proletariat lived up to its ancient boast. For as many of itself as were killed, it killed that many of the enemy.

The stockyards (ghetto, plant, and everything) were smouldering ruins. Far off to the right a wide smoke haze dimmed the sky,—the town of Pullman, the soldier chauffeur told us, or what had been the town of Pullman, for it was utterly destroyed. He had driven the machine out there, with despatches, on the afternoon of the third day. Some of the heaviest fighting had occurred there, he said, many of the streets being rendered impassable by the heaps of the dead.

Swinging around the shattered walls of a building, in the stockyards district, the automobile was stopped by a wave of dead. It was for all the world like a wave tossed up by the sea. It was patent to us what had happened. As the mob charged past the corner, it had been swept, at right angles and point-blank range, by the machine-guns drawn up on the cross street. But disaster had come to the soldiers. A chance bomb must have exploded among them, for the mob, checked until its dead and dying formed the wave, had white-capped and flung forward its foam of living, fighting slaves. Soldiers and slaves lay together, torn and mangled, around and over the wreckage of the automobiles and guns.

Ernest sprang out. A familiar pair of shoulders in a cotton shirt and a familiar fringe of white hair had caught his eye. I did not watch him, and it was not until he was back beside me and we were speeding on that he said:

"It was Bishop Morehouse."

Soon we were in the green country, and I took one last glance back at the smoke-filled sky. Faint and far came the low thud of an explosion. Then I turned my face against Ernest's breast and wept softly for the Cause that was lost. Ernest's arm about me was eloquent with love.

"For this time lost, dear heart," he said, "but not forever. We have learned. To-morrow the Cause will rise again, strong with wisdom and discipline."

The automobile drew up at a railroad station. Here we would catch a train to New York. As we waited on the platform, three trains thundered past, bound west to Chicago. They were crowded with ragged, unskilled laborers, people of the abyss.

"Slave-levies for the rebuilding of Chicago," Ernest said. "You see, the Chicago slaves are all killed."

CHAPTER XXV - THE TERRORISTS

It was not until Ernest and I were back in New York, and after weeks had elapsed, that we were able to comprehend thoroughly the full sweep of the disaster that had befallen the Cause. The situation was bitter and bloody. In many places, scattered over the country, slave revolts and massacres had occurred. The roll of the martyrs increased mightily. Countless executions took place everywhere. The mountains and waste regions were filled with outlaws and refugees who were being hunted down mercilessly. Our own refuges were packed with comrades who had prices on their heads. Through information furnished by its spies, scores of our refuges were raided by the soldiers of the Iron Heel.

Many of the comrades were disheartened, and they retaliated with terroristic tactics. The set-back to their hopes made them despairing and desperate. Many terrorist organizations unaffiliated with us sprang into existence and caused us much trouble.[1] These misguided people sacrificed their own lives wantonly, very often made our own plans go astray, and retarded our organization.

And through it all moved the Iron Heel, impassive and deliberate, shaking up the whole fabric of the social structure in its search for the comrades, combing out the Mercenaries, the labor castes, and all its secret services, punishing without mercy and

---

[1] The annals of this short-lived era of despair make bloody reading. Revenge was the ruling motive, and the members of the terroristic organizations were careless of their own lives and hopeless about the future. The Danites, taking their name from the avenging angels of the Mormon mythology, sprang up in the mountains of the Great West and spread over the Pacific Coast from Panama to Alaska. The Valkyries were women. They were the most terrible of all. No woman was eligible for membership who had not lost near relatives at the hands of the Oligarchy. They were guilty of torturing their prisoners to death. Another famous organization of women was The Widows of War. A companion organization to the Valkyries was the Berserkers. These men placed no value whatever upon their own lives, and it was they who totally destroyed the great Mercenary city of Bellona along with its population of over a hundred thousand souls. The Bedlamites and the Helldamites were twin slave organizations, while a new religious sect that did not flourish long was called The Wrath of God. Among others, to show the whimsicality of their deadly seriousness, may be mentioned the following: The Bleeding Hearts, Sons of the Morning, the Morning Stars, The Flamingoes, The Triple Triangles, The Three Bars, The Rubonics, The Vindicators, The Comanches, and the Erebusites.

without malice, suffering in silence all retaliations that were made upon it, and filling the gaps in its fighting line as fast as they appeared. And hand in hand with this, Ernest and the other leaders were hard at work reorganizing the forces of the Revolution. The magnitude of the task may be understood when it is taken into.[1]

---

[1] This is the end of the Everhard Manuscript. It breaks off abruptly in the middle of a sentence. She must have received warning of the coming of the Mercenaries, for she had time safely to hide the Manuscript before she fled or was captured. It is to be regretted that she did not live to complete her narrative, for then, undoubtedly, would have been cleared away the mystery that has shrouded for seven centuries the execution of Ernest Everhard.

MARTIN EDEN

CHAPTER I

The one opened the door with a latch-key and went in, followed by a young fellow who awkwardly removed his cap. He wore rough clothes that smacked of the sea, and he was manifestly out of place in the spacious hall in which he found himself. He did not know what to do with his cap, and was stuffing it into his coat pocket when the other took it from him. The act was done quietly and naturally, and the awkward young fellow appreciated it. "He understands," was his thought. "He'll see me through all right."

He walked at the other's heels with a swing to his shoulders, and his legs spread unwittingly, as if the level floors were tilting up and sinking down to the heave and lunge of the sea. The wide rooms seemed too narrow for his rolling gait, and to himself he was in terror lest his broad shoulders should collide with the doorways or sweep the bric-a-brac from the low mantel. He recoiled from side to side between the various objects and multiplied the hazards that in reality lodged only in his mind. Between a grand piano and a centre-table piled high with books was space for a half a dozen to walk abreast, yet he essayed it with trepidation. His heavy arms hung loosely at his sides. He did not know what to do with those arms and hands, and when, to his excited vision, one arm seemed liable to brush against the books on the table, he lurched away like a frightened horse, barely missing the piano stool. He watched the easy walk of the other in front of him, and for the first time realized that his walk was different from that of other men. He experienced a momentary pang of shame that he should walk so uncouthly. The sweat burst through the skin of his forehead in tiny beads, and he paused and mopped his bronzed face with his handkerchief.

"Hold on, Arthur, my boy," he said, attempting to mask his anxiety with facetious utterance. "This is too much all at once for yours truly. Give me a chance to get my nerve. You know I didn't want to come, an' I guess your fam'ly ain't hankerin' to see me neither."

"That's all right," was the reassuring answer. "You mustn't be frightened at us. We're just homely people—Hello, there's a letter for me."

He stepped back to the table, tore open the envelope, and began to read, giving the stranger an opportunity to recover himself. And the stranger understood and appreciated. His was the gift of sympathy, understanding; and beneath his alarmed exterior that sympathetic process went on. He mopped his forehead dry and glanced about him with a controlled face, though in the eyes there was an expression such as wild animals betray when they fear the trap. He was surrounded by the unknown, apprehensive of what might happen, ignorant of what he should do, aware that he walked and bore himself awkwardly, fearful that every attribute and power of him was similarly afflicted. He was keenly sensitive, hopelessly self-conscious, and the amused glance that the other stole privily at him over the top of the letter burned into him like a dagger-thrust. He saw the glance, but he gave no sign, for among the things he had learned was discipline. Also, that dagger-thrust went to his pride. He cursed himself for having come, and at the same time resolved that, happen what would, having come, he would carry it through. The lines of his face hardened, and into his eyes came a fighting light. He looked about more unconcernedly, sharply observant, every detail of the pretty interior registering itself on his brain. His eyes were wide apart; nothing in their field of vision escaped; and as they drank in the beauty before them the fighting light died out and a warm glow took its place. He was responsive to beauty, and here was cause to respond.

An oil painting caught and held him. A heavy surf thundered and burst over an outjutting rock; lowering storm-clouds covered the sky; and, outside the line of surf, a pilot-schooner, close-hauled, heeled over till every detail of her deck was visible, was surging along against a stormy sunset sky. There was beauty, and it drew him irresistibly. He forgot his awkward walk and came closer to the painting, very close. The beauty faded out of the canvas. His face expressed his bepuzzlement. He stared at what seemed a careless daub of paint, then stepped away. Immediately all the beauty flashed back into the canvas. "A trick picture," was his thought, as he dismissed it, though in the midst of the multitudinous impressions he was receiving he found time to feel a prod of indignation that so much beauty should be sacrificed to make a trick. He did not know painting. He had been brought up on chromos and lithographs that were always definite and sharp, near or far. He had seen oil paintings, it was true, in the show windows of shops, but the glass of the windows had prevented his eager eyes from approaching too near.

He glanced around at his friend reading the letter and saw the books on the table. Into his eyes leaped a wistfulness and a yearning as promptly as the yearning leaps into the eyes of a starving man at sight of food. An impulsive stride, with one lurch to right and left of the shoulders, brought him to the table, where he began affectionately handling the books. He glanced at the titles and the authors' names, read fragments of text, caressing the volumes with his eyes and hands, and, once, recognized a book he had read. For the rest, they were strange books and strange authors. He chanced upon a volume of Swinburne and began reading steadily, forgetful of where he was, his face glowing. Twice he closed the book on his forefinger to look at the name of the author. Swinburne! he would remember that name. That fellow had eyes, and he had certainly seen color and flashing light. But who was Swinburne? Was he dead a hundred years or so, like most of the poets? Or was he alive still, and writing? He turned to the title-page . . . yes, he had written other books; well, he would go to the free library the first thing in the morning and try to get hold of some of Swinburne's stuff. He went back to the text and lost himself. He did not notice that a young woman had entered the room. The first he knew was when he heard Arthur's voice saying:-

"Ruth, this is Mr. Eden."

The book was closed on his forefinger, and before he turned he was thrilling to the first new impression, which was not of the girl, but of her brother's words. Under that muscled body of his he was a mass of quivering sensibilities. At the slightest impact of the outside world upon his consciousness, his thoughts, sympathies, and emotions leapt and played like lambent flame. He was extraordinarily receptive and responsive, while his imagination, pitched high, was ever at work establishing relations of likeness and difference. "Mr. Eden," was what he had thrilled to—he who had been called "Eden," or "Martin Eden," or just "Martin," all his life. And "*Mister*!" It was certainly going some, was his internal comment. His mind seemed to turn, on the instant, into a vast camera obscura, and he saw arrayed around his consciousness endless pictures from his life, of stoke-holes and forecastles, camps and beaches, jails and boozing-kens, fever-hospitals and slum streets, wherein the thread of association was the fashion in which he had been addressed in those various situations.

And then he turned and saw the girl. The phantasmagoria of his brain vanished at sight of her. She was a pale, ethereal creature, with wide, spiritual blue eyes and a wealth of golden hair. He did not know how she was dressed, except that the dress was as wonderful as she. He likened her to a pale gold flower upon a slender stem. No, she was a spirit, a divinity, a goddess; such sublimated beauty was not of the earth. Or perhaps the books were right, and there were many such as she in the upper walks of life. She might well be sung by that chap, Swinburne. Perhaps he had had somebody like her in mind when he painted that girl, Iseult, in the book there on the table. All this plethora of sight, and feeling, and thought occurred on the instant. There was no pause of the realities wherein he moved. He saw her hand coming out to his, and she looked him straight in the eyes as she shook hands, frankly, like a man. The women he had known did not shake hands that way. For that matter, most of them did not shake hands at all. A flood of associations, visions of various ways he had made the acquaintance of women, rushed into his mind and threatened to swamp it. But he shook them aside and looked at her. Never had he seen such a woman. The women he had known! Immediately, beside her, on either hand, ranged the women he had known. For an eternal second he stood in the midst of a portrait gallery, wherein she occupied the central place, while about her were limned many women, all to be weighed and measured by a fleeting glance, herself the unit of weight and measure. He saw the weak and sickly faces of the girls of the factories, and the simpering, boisterous girls from the south of Market. There were women of the cattle camps, and swarthy cigarette-smoking women of Old Mexico. These, in turn, were crowded out by Japanese women, doll-like, stepping mincingly on wooden clogs; by Eurasians, delicate featured, stamped with degeneracy; by full-bodied South-Sea-Island women, flower-crowned and brown-skinned. All these were blotted out by a grotesque and terrible nightmare brood—frowsy, shuffling creatures from the pavements of Whitechapel, gin-bloated hags of the stews, and all the vast hell's following of harpies, vile-mouthed and filthy, that under the guise of monstrous female form prey upon sailors, the scrapings of the ports, the scum and slime of the human pit.

"Won't you sit down, Mr. Eden?" the girl was saying. "I have been looking forward to meeting you ever since Arthur told us. It was brave of you—"

He waved his hand deprecatingly and muttered that it was nothing at all, what he had done, and that any fellow would have done it. She noticed that the hand he waved was covered with fresh abrasions, in the process of healing, and a glance at the other loose-hanging hand showed it to be in the same condition. Also, with quick, critical eye, she noted a scar on his cheek, another that peeped out from under the hair of the forehead, and a third that ran down and disappeared under the starched collar. She repressed a smile at sight of the red line that marked the chafe of the collar against the bronzed neck. He was evidently unused to stiff collars. Likewise her feminine eye took in the clothes he wore, the cheap and unaesthetic cut, the wrinkling of the coat across the shoulders, and the series of wrinkles in the sleeves that advertised bulging biceps muscles.

While he waved his hand and muttered that he had done nothing at all, he was obeying her behest by trying to get into a chair. He found time to admire the ease with which she sat down, then lurched toward a chair facing her, overwhelmed with consciousness of the awkward figure he was cutting. This was a new experience for him. All his life, up to then, he had been unaware of being either graceful or awkward. Such thoughts of self had never entered his mind. He sat down gingerly on the edge of the chair, greatly worried by his hands. They were in the way wherever he put them. Arthur was leaving the room, and Martin Eden followed his exit with longing eyes. He felt lost, alone there in the room with that pale spirit of a woman. There was no bar-keeper upon whom to call for drinks, no small boy to send around the corner for a can of beer and by means of that social fluid start the amenities of friendship flowing.

"You have such a scar on your neck, Mr. Eden," the girl was saying. "How did it happen? I am sure it must have been some adventure."

"A Mexican with a knife, miss," he answered, moistening his parched lips and clearing hip throat. "It was just a fight. After I got the knife away, he tried to bite off my nose."

Baldly as he had stated it, in his eyes was a rich vision of that hot, starry night at Salina Cruz, the white strip of beach, the lights of the sugar steamers in the harbor, the voices of the drunken sailors in the distance, the jostling stevedores, the flaming passion in the Mexican's face, the glint of the beast-eyes in the starlight, the sting of the steel in his neck, and the rush of blood, the crowd and the cries, the two bodies, his and the Mexican's, locked together, rolling over and over and tearing up the sand, and from away off somewhere the mellow tinkling of a guitar. Such was the picture, and he thrilled to the memory of it, wondering if the man could paint it who had painted the pilot-schooner on the wall. The white beach, the stars, and the lights of the sugar steamers would look great, he thought, and midway on the sand the dark group of figures that surrounded the fighters. The knife occupied a place in the picture, he decided, and would show well, with a sort of gleam, in the light of the stars. But of all this no hint had crept into his speech. "He tried to bite off my nose," he concluded.

"Oh," the girl said, in a faint, far voice, and he noticed the shock in her sensitive face.

He felt a shock himself, and a blush of embarrassment shone faintly on his sunburned cheeks, though to him it burned as hotly as when his cheeks had been exposed to the open furnace-door in the fire-room. Such sordid things as stabbing affrays were evidently not fit subjects for conversation with a lady. People in the books, in her walk of life, did not talk about such things—perhaps they did not know about them, either.

CHAPTER I

There was a brief pause in the conversation they were trying to get started. Then she asked tentatively about the scar on his cheek. Even as she asked, he realized that she was making an effort to talk his talk, and he resolved to get away from it and talk hers.

"It was just an accident," he said, putting his hand to his cheek. "One night, in a calm, with a heavy sea running, the main-boom-lift carried away, an' next the tackle. The lift was wire, an' it was threshin' around like a snake. The whole watch was tryin' to grab it, an' I rushed in an' got swatted."

"Oh," she said, this time with an accent of comprehension, though secretly his speech had been so much Greek to her and she was wondering what a *lift* was and what *swatted* meant.

"This man Swineburne," he began, attempting to put his plan into execution and pronouncing the *i* long.

"Who?"

"Swineburne," he repeated, with the same mispronunciation. "The poet."

"Swinburne," she corrected.

"Yes, that's the chap," he stammered, his cheeks hot again. "How long since he died?"

"Why, I haven't heard that he was dead." She looked at him curiously. "Where did you make his acquaintance?"

"I never clapped eyes on him," was the reply. "But I read some of his poetry out of that book there on the table just before you come in. How do you like his poetry?"

And thereat she began to talk quickly and easily upon the subject he had suggested. He felt better, and settled back slightly from the edge of the chair, holding tightly to its arms with his hands, as if it might get away from him and buck him to the floor. He had succeeded in making her talk her talk, and while she rattled on, he strove to follow her, marvelling at all the knowledge that was stowed away in that pretty head of hers, and drinking in the pale beauty of her face. Follow her he did, though bothered by unfamiliar words that fell glibly from her lips and by critical phrases and thought-processes that were foreign to his mind, but that nevertheless stimulated his mind and set it tingling. Here was intellectual life, he thought, and here was beauty, warm and wonderful as he had never dreamed it could be. He forgot himself and stared at her with hungry eyes. Here was something to live for, to win to, to fight for—ay, and die for. The books were true. There were such women in the world. She was one of them. She lent wings to his imagination, and great, luminous canvases spread themselves before him whereon loomed vague, gigantic figures of love and romance, and of heroic deeds for woman's sake—for a pale woman, a flower of gold. And through the swaying, palpitant vision, as through a fairy mirage, he stared at the real woman, sitting there and talking of literature and art. He listened as well, but he stared, unconscious of the fixity of his gaze or of the fact that all that was essentially masculine in his nature was shining in his eyes. But she, who knew little of the world of men, being a woman, was keenly aware of his burning eyes. She had never had men look at her in such fashion, and it embarrassed her. She stumbled and halted in her utterance. The thread of argument slipped from her. He frightened her, and at the same time it was strangely pleasant to be so looked upon. Her training warned her of peril and of wrong, subtle, mysterious, luring; while her instincts rang clarion-voiced through her being, impelling her to hurdle caste and place and gain to this traveller from another world, to this uncouth young fellow with lacerated hands and a line of raw red caused by the unaccustomed linen at his throat, who, all too evidently, was soiled and tainted by ungracious existence. She was clean, and her cleanness revolted; but she was woman, and she was just beginning to learn the paradox of woman.

"As I was saying—what was I saying?" She broke off abruptly and laughed merrily at her predicament.

"You was saying that this man Swinburne failed bein' a great poet because—an' that was as far as you got, miss," he prompted, while to himself he seemed suddenly hungry, and delicious little thrills crawled up and down his spine at the sound of her laughter. Like silver, he thought to himself, like tinkling silver bells; and on the instant, and for an instant, he was transported to a far land, where under pink cherry blossoms, he smoked a cigarette and listened to the bells of the peaked pagoda calling straw-sandalled devotees to worship.

"Yes, thank you," she said. "Swinburne fails, when all is said, because he is, well, indelicate. There are many of his poems that should never be read. Every line of the really great poets is filled with beautiful truth, and calls to all that is high and noble in the human. Not a line of the great poets can be spared without impoverishing the world by that much."

"I thought it was great," he said hesitatingly, "the little I read. I had no idea he was such a—a scoundrel. I guess that crops out in his other books."

"There are many lines that could be spared from the book you were reading," she said, her voice primly firm and dogmatic.

"I must 'a' missed 'em," he announced. "What I read was the real goods. It was all lighted up an' shining, an' it shun right into me an' lighted me up inside, like the sun or a searchlight. That's the way it landed on me, but I guess I ain't up much on poetry, miss."

He broke off lamely. He was confused, painfully conscious of his inarticulateness. He had felt the bigness and glow of life in what he had read, but his speech was inadequate. He could not express what he felt, and to himself he likened himself to a sailor, in a strange ship, on a dark night, groping about in the unfamiliar running rigging. Well, he decided, it was up to him to get acquainted in this new world. He had never seen anything that he couldn't get the hang of when he wanted to and it was about time for him to want to learn to talk the things that were inside of him so that she could understand. *She* was bulking large on his horizon.

"Now Longfellow—" she was saying.

"Yes, I've read 'm," he broke in impulsively, spurred on to exhibit and make the most of his little store of book knowledge, desirous of showing her that he was not wholly a stupid clod. "'The Psalm of Life,' 'Excelsior,' an' . . . I guess that's all."

She nodded her head and smiled, and he felt, somehow, that her smile was tolerant, pitifully tolerant. He was a fool to attempt to make a pretence that way. That Longfellow chap most likely had written countless books of poetry.

"Excuse me, miss, for buttin' in that way. I guess the real facts is that I don't know nothin' much about such things. It ain't in my class. But I'm goin' to make it in my class."

It sounded like a threat. His voice was determined, his eyes were flashing, the lines of his face had grown harsh. And to her it seemed that the angle of his jaw had changed; its pitch had become unpleasantly aggressive. At the same time a wave of intense virility seemed to surge out from him and impinge upon her.

"I think you could make it in—in your class," she finished with a laugh. "You are very strong."

Her gaze rested for a moment on the muscular neck, heavy corded, almost bull-like, bronzed by the sun, spilling over with rugged health and strength. And though he sat there, blushing and humble, again she felt drawn to him. She was surprised by a wanton thought that rushed into her mind. It seemed to her that if she could lay her two hands upon that neck that all its strength and vigor would flow out to her. She was shocked by this thought. It seemed to reveal to her an undreamed depravity in her nature. Besides, strength to her was a gross and brutish thing. Her ideal of masculine beauty had always been slender gracefulness. Yet the thought still persisted. It bewildered her that she should desire to place her hands on that sunburned neck. In truth, she was far from robust, and the need of her body and mind was for strength. But she did not know it. She knew only that no man had ever affected her before as this one had, who shocked her from moment to moment with his awful grammar.

"Yes, I ain't no invalid," he said. "When it comes down to hard-pan, I can digest scrap-iron. But just now I've got dyspepsia. Most of what you was sayin' I can't digest. Never trained that way, you see. I like books and poetry, and what time I've had I've read 'em, but I've never thought about 'em the way you have. That's why I can't talk about 'em. I'm like a navigator adrift on a strange sea without chart or compass. Now I want to get my bearin's. Mebbe you can put me right. How did you learn all this you've ben talkin'?"

"By going to school, I fancy, and by studying," she answered.

"I went to school when I was a kid," he began to object.

"Yes; but I mean high school, and lectures, and the university."

"You've gone to the university?" he demanded in frank amazement. He felt that she had become remoter from him by at least a million miles.

"I'm going there now. I'm taking special courses in English."

He did not know what "English" meant, but he made a mental note of that item of ignorance and passed on.

"How long would I have to study before I could go to the university?" he asked.

She beamed encouragement upon his desire for knowledge, and said: "That depends upon how much studying you have already done. You have never attended high school? Of course not. But did you finish grammar school?"

"I had two years to run, when I left," he answered. "But I was always honorably promoted at school."

The next moment, angry with himself for the boast, he had gripped the arms of the chair so savagely that every finger-end was stinging. At the same moment he became aware that a woman was entering the room. He saw the girl leave her chair and trip swiftly across the floor to the newcomer. They kissed each other, and, with arms around each other's waists, they advanced toward him. That must be her mother, he thought. She was a tall, blond woman, slender, and stately, and beautiful. Her gown was what he might expect in such a house. His eyes delighted in the graceful lines of it. She and her dress together reminded him of women on the stage. Then he remembered seeing similar grand ladies and gowns entering the London theatres while he stood and watched and the policemen shoved him back into the drizzle beyond the awning. Next his mind leaped to the Grand Hotel at Yokohama, where, too, from the sidewalk, he had seen grand ladies. Then the city and the harbor of Yokohama, in a thousand pictures, began flashing before his eyes. But he swiftly dismissed the kaleidoscope of memory, oppressed by the urgent need of the present. He knew that he must stand up to be introduced, and he struggled painfully to his feet, where he stood with trousers bagging at the knees, his arms loose-hanging and ludicrous, his face set hard for the impending ordeal.

CHAPTER II

The process of getting into the dining room was a nightmare to him. Between halts and stumbles, jerks and lurches, locomotion had at times seemed impossible. But at last he had made it, and was seated alongside of Her. The array of knives and forks frightened him. They bristled with unknown perils, and he gazed at them, fascinated, till their dazzle became a background across which moved a succession of forecastle pictures, wherein he and his mates sat eating salt beef with sheath-knives and fingers, or scooping thick pea-soup out of pannikins by means of battered iron spoons. The stench of bad beef was in his nostrils, while in his ears, to the accompaniment of creaking timbers and groaning bulkheads, echoed the loud mouth-noises of the eaters. He watched them eating, and decided that they ate like pigs. Well, he would be careful here. He would make no noise. He would keep his mind upon it all the time.

He glanced around the table. Opposite him was Arthur, and Arthur's brother, Norman. They were her brothers, he reminded himself, and his heart warmed toward them. How they loved each other, the members of this family! There flashed into his mind the picture of her mother, of the kiss of greeting, and of the pair of them walking toward him with arms entwined. Not in his world were such displays of affection between parents and children made. It was a revelation of the heights of existence that were attained in the world above. It was the finest thing yet that he had seen in this small glimpse of that world. He was moved deeply by appreciation of it, and his heart was melting with sympathetic tenderness. He had starved for love all his life. His nature craved love. It was an organic demand of his being. Yet he had gone without, and hardened himself in the process. He had not known that he needed love. Nor did he know it now. He merely saw it in operation, and thrilled to it, and thought it fine, and high, and splendid.

He was glad that Mr. Morse was not there. It was difficult enough getting acquainted with her, and her mother, and her brother, Norman. Arthur he already knew somewhat. The father would have been too much for him, he felt sure. It seemed to him that he had never worked so hard in his life. The severest toil was child's play compared with this. Tiny nodules of moisture stood out on his forehead, and his shirt was wet with sweat from the exertion of doing so many unaccustomed things at once. He had to eat as he had never eaten before, to handle strange tools, to glance surreptitiously about and learn how to accomplish each new thing, to receive the flood of impressions that was pouring in upon him and being mentally annotated and classified; to be conscious of a yearning for her that perturbed him in the form of a dull, aching restlessness; to feel the prod of desire to win to the walk in life whereon she trod, and to have his mind ever and again straying off in speculation and vague plans of how to reach to her. Also, when his secret glance went across to Norman opposite him, or to any one else, to ascertain just what knife or fork was to be used in any particular occasion, that person's features were seized upon by his mind, which automatically strove to appraise them and to divine what they were—all in relation to her. Then he had to talk, to hear what was said to him and what was said back and forth, and to answer, when it was necessary, with a tongue prone to looseness of speech that required a constant curb. And to add confusion to confusion, there was the servant, an unceasing menace, that appeared noiselessly at his shoulder, a dire Sphinx that propounded puzzles and conundrums demanding instantaneous solution. He was oppressed throughout the meal by the thought of finger-bowls. Irrelevantly, insistently, scores of times, he wondered when they would come on and what they looked like. He had heard of such things, and now, sooner or later, somewhere in the next few minutes, he would see them, sit at table with exalted beings who used them—ay, and he would use them himself. And most important of all, far down and yet always at the surface of his thought, was the problem of how he should comport himself toward these persons. What should his attitude be? He wrestled continually and anxiously with the problem. There were cowardly suggestions that he should make believe, assume a part; and there were still more cowardly suggestions that warned him he would fail in such course, that his nature was not fitted to live up to it, and that he would make a fool of himself.

It was during the first part of the dinner, struggling to decide upon his attitude, that he was very quiet. He did not know that his quietness was giving the lie to Arthur's words of the day before, when that brother of hers had announced that he was going to bring a wild man home to dinner and for them not to be alarmed, because they would find him an interesting wild man. Martin Eden could not have found it in him, just then, to believe that her brother could be guilty of such treachery—especially when he had been the means of getting this particular brother out of an unpleasant row. So he sat at table, perturbed by his own unfitness and at the same time charmed by all that went on about him. For the first time he realized that eating was something more than a utilitarian function. He was unaware of what he ate. It was merely food. He was feasting his love of beauty at this table where eating was an aesthetic function. It was an intellectual function, too. His mind was stirred. He heard words spoken that were meaningless to him, and other words that he had seen only in books and that no man or woman he had known was of large enough mental caliber to pronounce. When he heard such words dropping carelessly from the lips of the members of this marvellous family, her family, he thrilled with delight. The romance, and beauty, and high vigor of the books were coming true. He was in that rare and blissful state wherein a man sees his dreams stalk out from the crannies of fantasy and become fact.

Never had he been at such an altitude of living, and he kept himself in the background, listening, observing, and pleasuring, replying in reticent monosyllables, saying, "Yes, miss," and "No, miss," to her, and "Yes, ma'am," and "No, ma'am," to her mother. He curbed the impulse, arising out of his sea-training, to say "Yes, sir," and "No, sir," to her brothers. He felt that it would be inappropriate and a confession of inferiority on his part—which would never do if he was to win to her. Also, it was a dictate of his pride. "By God!" he cried to himself, once; "I'm just as good as them, and if they do know lots that I don't, I could learn 'm a few myself, all the same!" And the next moment, when she or her mother addressed him as "Mr. Eden," his aggressive pride was forgotten, and he was glowing and warm with delight. He was a civilized man, that was what he was, shoulder to shoulder, at dinner, with people he had read about in books. He was in the books himself, adventuring through the printed pages of bound volumes.

But while he belied Arthur's description, and appeared a gentle lamb rather than a wild man, he was racking his brains for a course of action. He was no gentle lamb, and the part of second fiddle would never do for the high-pitched dominance of his nature. He talked only when he had to, and then his speech was like his walk to the table, filled with jerks and halts as he groped in his polyglot vocabulary for words, debating over words he knew were fit but which he feared he could not pronounce, rejecting other words he knew would not be understood or would be raw and harsh. But all the time he was oppressed by the consciousness that this carefulness of diction was making a booby of him, preventing him from expressing what he had in him. Also, his love of freedom chafed against the restriction in much the same way his neck chafed against the starched fetter of a collar. Besides, he was confident that he could not keep it up. He was by nature powerful of thought and sensibility, and the creative spirit was restive and urgent. He was swiftly mastered by the concept or sensation in him that struggled in birth-throes to receive expression and form, and then he forgot himself and where he was, and the old words—the tools of speech he knew—slipped out.

Once, he declined something from the servant who interrupted and pestered at his shoulder, and he said, shortly and emphatically, "Pew!"

On the instant those at the table were keyed up and expectant, the servant was smugly pleased, and he was wallowing in mortification. But he recovered himself quickly.

"It's the Kanaka for 'finish,'" he explained, "and it just come out naturally. It's spelt p-a-u."

He caught her curious and speculative eyes fixed on his hands, and, being in explanatory mood, he said:-

"I just come down the Coast on one of the Pacific mail steamers. She was behind time, an' around the Puget Sound ports we worked like niggers, storing cargo-mixed freight, if you know what that means. That's how the skin got knocked off."

"Oh, it wasn't that," she hastened to explain, in turn. "Your hands seemed too small for your body."

His cheeks were hot. He took it as an exposure of another of his deficiencies.

"Yes," he said depreciatingly. "They ain't big enough to stand the strain. I can hit like a mule with my arms and shoulders. They are too strong, an' when I smash a man on the jaw the hands get smashed, too."

He was not happy at what he had said. He was filled with disgust at himself. He had loosed the guard upon his tongue and talked about things that were not nice.

"It was brave of you to help Arthur the way you did—and you a stranger," she said tactfully, aware of his discomfiture though not of the reason for it.

He, in turn, realized what she had done, and in the consequent warm surge of gratefulness that overwhelmed him forgot his loose-worded tongue.

"It wasn't nothin' at all," he said. "Any guy 'ud do it for another. That bunch of hoodlums was lookin' for trouble, an' Arthur wasn't botherin' 'em none. They butted in on 'm, an' then I butted in on them an' poked a few. That's where some of the skin off my hands went, along with some of the teeth of the gang. I wouldn't 'a' missed it for anything. When I seen—"

He paused, open-mouthed, on the verge of the pit of his own depravity and utter worthlessness to breathe the same air she did. And while Arthur took up the tale, for the twentieth time, of his adventure with the drunken hoodlums on the ferry-boat and of how Martin Eden had rushed in and rescued him, that individual, with frowning brows, meditated upon the fool he had made of himself, and wrestled more determinedly with the problem of how he should conduct himself toward these people. He certainly had not succeeded so far. He wasn't of their tribe, and he couldn't talk their lingo, was the way he put it to himself. He couldn't fake being their kind. The masquerade would fail, and besides, masquerade was foreign to his nature. There was no room in him for sham or artifice. Whatever happened, he must be real. He couldn't talk their talk just yet, though in time he would. Upon that he was resolved. But in the meantime, talk he must, and it must be his own talk, toned down, of course, so as to be comprehensible to them and so as not to shook them too much. And furthermore, he wouldn't claim, not even by tacit acceptance, to be familiar with anything that was unfamiliar. In pursuance of this decision, when the two brothers, talking university shop, had used "trig" several times, Martin Eden demanded:-

"What is *trig*?"

"Trignometry," Norman said; "a higher form of math."

"And what is math?" was the next question, which, somehow, brought the laugh on Norman.

"Mathematics, arithmetic," was the answer.

Martin Eden nodded. He had caught a glimpse of the apparently illimitable vistas of knowledge. What he saw took on tangibility. His abnormal power of vision made abstractions take on concrete form. In the alchemy of his brain, trigonometry and mathematics and the whole field of knowledge which they betokened were transmuted into so much landscape. The vistas he saw were vistas of green foliage and forest glades, all softly luminous or shot through with flashing lights. In the distance, detail was veiled and blurred by a purple haze, but behind this purple haze, he knew, was the glamour of the unknown, the lure of romance. It was like wine to him. Here was adventure, something to do with head and hand, a world to conquer—and straightway from the back of his consciousness rushed the thought, *conquering, to win to her, that lily-pale spirit sitting beside him.*

The glimmering vision was rent asunder and dissipated by Arthur, who, all evening, had been trying to draw his wild man out. Martin Eden remembered his decision. For the first time he became himself, consciously and deliberately at first, but soon lost in the joy of creating in making life as he knew it appear before his listeners' eyes. He had been a member of the crew of the smuggling schooner *Halcyon* when she was captured by a revenue cutter. He saw with wide eyes, and he could tell what he saw. He brought the pulsing sea before them, and the men and the ships upon the sea. He communicated his power of vision, till they saw with his eyes what he had seen. He selected from the vast mass of detail with an artist's touch, drawing pictures of life that glowed and burned with light and color, injecting movement so that his listeners surged along with him on the flood of rough eloquence, enthusiasm, and power. At times he shocked them with the vividness of the narrative and his terms of speech, but beauty always followed fast upon the heels of violence, and tragedy was relieved by humor, by interpretations of the strange twists and quirks of sailors' minds.

And while he talked, the girl looked at him with startled eyes. His fire warmed her. She wondered if she had been cold all her days. She wanted to lean toward this burning, blazing man that was like a volcano spouting forth strength, robustness, and health. She felt that she must lean toward him, and resisted by an effort. Then, too, there was the counter impulse to shrink away from him. She was repelled by those lacerated hands, grimed by toil so that the very dirt of life was ingrained in the flesh itself, by that red chafe of the collar and those bulging muscles. His roughness frightened her; each roughness of speech was an insult to her ear, each rough phase of his life an insult to her soul. And ever and again would come the draw of him, till she thought he must be evil to have such power over her. All that was most firmly established in her mind was rocking. His romance and adventure were battering at the conventions. Before his facile perils and ready laugh, life was no longer an affair of serious effort and restraint, but a toy, to be played with and turned topsy-turvy, carelessly to be lived and pleasured in, and carelessly to be flung aside. "Therefore, play!" was the cry that rang through her. "Lean toward him, if so you will, and place your two hands upon his neck!" She wanted to cry out at the recklessness of the thought, and in vain she appraised her own cleanness and culture and balanced all that she was against what he was not. She glanced about her and saw the others gazing at him with rapt attention; and she would have despaired had not she seen horror in her mother's eyes—fascinated horror, it was true, but none the less horror. This man from outer darkness was evil. Her mother saw it, and her mother was right. She would trust her mother's judgment in this as she had always trusted it in all things. The fire of him was no longer warm, and the fear of him was no longer poignant.

Later, at the piano, she played for him, and at him, aggressively, with the vague intent of emphasizing the impassableness of the gulf that separated them. Her music was a club that she swung brutally upon his head; and though it stunned him and crushed him down, it incited him. He gazed upon her in awe. In his mind, as in her own, the gulf widened; but faster than it widened, towered his ambition to win across it. But he was too complicated a plexus of sensibilities to sit staring at a gulf a whole evening, especially when there was music. He was remarkably susceptible to music. It was like strong drink, firing him to audacities of feeling,—a drug that laid hold of his imagination and went cloud-soaring through the sky. It banished sordid fact, flooded his mind with beauty, loosed romance and to its heels added wings. He did not understand the music she played. It was different from the dance-hall piano-banging and blatant brass bands he had heard. But he had caught hints of such music from the books, and he accepted her playing largely on faith, patiently waiting, at first, for the lifting measures of pronounced and simple rhythm, puzzled because those measures were not long continued. Just as he caught the swing of them and started, his imagination attuned in flight, always they vanished away in a chaotic scramble of sounds that was meaningless to him, and that dropped his imagination, an inert weight, back to earth.

Once, it entered his mind that there was a deliberate rebuff in all this. He caught her spirit of antagonism and strove to divine the message that her hands pronounced upon the keys. Then he dismissed the thought as unworthy and impossible, and yielded himself more freely to the music. The old delightful condition began to be induced. His feet were no longer clay, and his flesh became spirit; before his eyes and behind his eyes shone a great glory; and then the scene before him vanished and he was away, rocking over the world that was to him a very dear world. The known and the unknown were commingled in the dream-pageant that thronged his vision. He entered strange ports of sun-washed lands, and trod market-places among barbaric peoples that no man had ever seen. The scent of the spice islands was in his nostrils as he had known it on warm, breathless nights at sea, or he beat up against the south-east trades through long tropic days, sinking palm-tufted coral islets in the turquoise sea behind and lifting palm-tufted coral islets in the turquoise sea ahead. Swift as thought the pictures came and went. One instant he was astride a broncho and flying through the fairy-colored Painted Desert country; the next instant he was gazing down through shimmering heat into the whited sepulchre of Death Valley, or pulling an oar on a freezing ocean where great ice islands towered and glistened in the sun. He lay on a coral beach where the cocoanuts grew down to the mellow-sounding surf. The hulk of an ancient wreck burned with blue fires, in the light of which danced the *hula* dancers to the barbaric love-calls of the singers, who chanted to tinkling *ukuleles* and rumbling tom-toms. It was a sensuous, tropic night. In the background a volcano crater was silhouetted against the stars. Overhead drifted a pale crescent moon, and the Southern Cross burned low in the sky.

He was a harp; all life that he had known and that was his consciousness was the strings; and the flood of music was a wind that poured against those strings and set them vibrating with memories and dreams. He did not merely feel. Sensation invested itself in form and color and radiance, and what his imagination dared, it objectified in some sublimated and magic way. Past, present, and future mingled; and he went on oscillating across the broad, warm world, through high adventure and noble deeds to Her—ay, and with her, winning her, his arm about her, and carrying her on in flight through the empery of his mind.

And she, glancing at him across her shoulder, saw something of all this in his face. It was a transfigured face, with great shining eyes that gazed beyond the veil of sound and saw behind it the leap and pulse of life and the gigantic phantoms of the spirit. She was startled. The raw, stumbling lout was gone. The ill-fitting clothes, battered hands, and sunburned face remained; but these seemed the prison-bars through which she saw a great soul looking forth, inarticulate and dumb because of those feeble lips that would not give it speech. Only for a flashing moment did she see this, then she saw the lout returned, and she laughed at the whim of her fancy. But the impression of that fleeting glimpse lingered, and when the time came for him to beat a stumbling retreat and go, she lent him the volume of Swinburne, and another of Browning—she was studying Browning in one of her English courses. He seemed such a boy, as he stood blushing and stammering his thanks, that a wave of pity, maternal in its prompting, welled up in her. She did not remember the lout, nor the imprisoned soul, nor the man who had stared at her in all masculineness and delighted and frightened her. She saw before her only a boy, who was shaking her hand with a hand so calloused that it felt like a nutmeg-grater and rasped her skin, and who was saying jerkily:-

"The greatest time of my life. You see, I ain't used to things. . . " He looked about him helplessly. "To people and houses like this. It's all new to me, and I like it."

"I hope you'll call again," she said, as he was saying good night to her brothers.

He pulled on his cap, lurched desperately through the doorway, and was gone.

"Well, what do you think of him?" Arthur demanded.

"He is most interesting, a whiff of ozone," she answered. "How old is he?"

"Twenty—almost twenty-one. I asked him this afternoon. I didn't think he was that young."

And I am three years older, was the thought in her mind as she kissed her brothers goodnight.

CHAPTER III

As Martin Eden went down the steps, his hand dropped into his coat pocket. It came out with a brown rice paper and a pinch of Mexican tobacco, which were deftly rolled together into a cigarette. He drew the first whiff of smoke deep into his lungs and expelled it in a long and lingering exhalation. "By God!" he said aloud, in a voice of awe and wonder. "By God!" he repeated. And yet again he murmured, "By God!" Then his hand went to his collar, which he ripped out of the shirt and stuffed into his pocket. A cold drizzle was falling, but he bared his head to it and unbuttoned his vest, swinging along in splendid unconcern. He was only dimly aware that it was raining. He was in an ecstasy, dreaming dreams and reconstructing the scenes just past.

He had met the woman at last—the woman that he had thought little about, not being given to thinking about women, but whom he had expected, in a remote way, he would sometime meet. He had sat next to her at table. He had felt her hand in his, he had looked into her eyes and caught a vision of a beautiful spirit;—but no more beautiful than the eyes through which it shone, nor than the flesh that gave it expression and form. He did not think of her flesh as flesh,—which was new to him; for of the women he had known that was the only way he thought. Her flesh was somehow different. He did not conceive of her body as a body, subject to the ills and frailties of bodies. Her body was more than the garb of her spirit. It was an emanation of her spirit, a pure and gracious crystallization of her divine essence. This feeling of the divine startled him. It shocked him from his dreams to sober thought. No word, no clew, no hint, of the divine had ever reached him before. He had never believed in the divine. He had always been irreligious, scoffing good-naturedly at the sky-pilots and their immortality of the soul. There was no life beyond, he had contended; it was here and now, then darkness everlasting. But what he had seen in her eyes was soul—immortal soul that could never die. No man he had known, nor any woman, had given him the message of immortality. But she had. She had whispered it to him the first moment she looked at him. Her face shimmered before his eyes as he walked along,—pale and serious, sweet and sensitive, smiling with pity and tenderness as only a spirit could smile, and pure as he had never dreamed purity could be. Her purity smote him like a blow. It startled him. He had known good and bad; but purity, as an attribute of existence, had never entered his mind. And now, in her, he conceived purity to be the superlative of goodness and of cleanness, the sum of which constituted eternal life.

CHAPTER III

And promptly urged his ambition to grasp at eternal life. He was not fit to carry water for her—he knew that; it was a miracle of luck and a fantastic stroke that had enabled him to see her and be with her and talk with her that night. It was accidental. There was no merit in it. He did not deserve such fortune. His mood was essentially religious. He was humble and meek, filled with self-disparagement and abasement. In such frame of mind sinners come to the penitent form. He was convicted of sin. But as the meek and lowly at the penitent form catch splendid glimpses of their future lordly existence, so did he catch similar glimpses of the state he would gain to by possessing her. But this possession of her was dim and nebulous and totally different from possession as he had known it. Ambition soared on mad wings, and he saw himself climbing the heights with her, sharing thoughts with her, pleasuring in beautiful and noble things with her. It was a soul-possession he dreamed, refined beyond any grossness, a free comradeship of spirit that he could not put into definite thought. He did not think it. For that matter, he did not think at all. Sensation usurped reason, and he was quivering and palpitant with emotions he had never known, drifting deliciously on a sea of sensibility where feeling itself was exalted and spiritualized and carried beyond the summits of life.

He staggered along like a drunken man, murmuring fervently aloud: "By God! By God!"

A policeman on a street corner eyed him suspiciously, then noted his sailor roll.

"Where did you get it?" the policeman demanded.

Martin Eden came back to earth. His was a fluid organism, swiftly adjustable, capable of flowing into and filling all sorts of nooks and crannies. With the policeman's hail he was immediately his ordinary self, grasping the situation clearly.

"It's a beaut, ain't it?" he laughed back. "I didn't know I was talkin' out loud."

"You'll be singing next," was the policeman's diagnosis.

"No, I won't. Gimme a match an' I'll catch the next car home."

He lighted his cigarette, said good night, and went on. "Now wouldn't that rattle you?" he ejaculated under his breath. "That copper thought I was drunk." He smiled to himself and meditated. "I guess I was," he added; "but I didn't think a woman's face'd do it."

He caught a Telegraph Avenue car that was going to Berkeley. It was crowded with youths and young men who were singing songs and ever and again barking out college yells. He studied them curiously. They were university boys. They went to the same university that she did, were in her class socially, could know her, could see her every day if they wanted to. He wondered that they did not want to, that they had been out having a good time instead of being with her that evening, talking with her, sitting around her in a worshipful and adoring circle. His thoughts wandered on. He noticed one with narrow-slitted eyes and a loose-lipped mouth. That fellow was vicious, he decided. On shipboard he would be a sneak, a whiner, a tattler. He, Martin Eden, was a better man than that fellow. The thought cheered him. It seemed to draw him nearer to Her. He began comparing himself with the students. He grew conscious of the muscled mechanism of his body and felt confident that he was physically their master. But their heads were filled with knowledge that enabled them to talk her talk,—the thought depressed him. But what was a brain for? he demanded passionately. What they had done, he could do. They had been studying about life from the books while he had been busy living life. His brain was just as full of knowledge as theirs, though it was a different kind of knowledge. How many of them could tie a lanyard knot, or take a wheel or a lookout? His life spread out before him in a series of pictures of danger and daring, hardship and toil. He remembered his failures and scrapes in the process of learning. He was that much to the good, anyway. Later on they would have to begin living life and going through the mill as he had gone. Very well. While they were busy with that, he could be learning the other side of life from the books.

As the car crossed the zone of scattered dwellings that separated Oakland from Berkeley, he kept a lookout for a familiar, two-story building along the front of which ran the proud sign, HIGGINBOTHAM'S CASH STORE. Martin Eden got off at this corner. He stared up for a moment at the sign. It carried a message to him beyond its mere wording. A personality of smallness and egotism and petty underhandedness seemed to emanate from the letters themselves. Bernard Higginbotham had married his sister, and he knew him well. He let himself in with a latch-key and climbed the stairs to the second floor. Here lived his brother-in-law. The grocery was below. There was a smell of stale vegetables in the air. As he groped his way across the hall he stumbled over a toy-cart, left there by one of his numerous nephews and nieces, and brought up against a door with a resounding bang. "The pincher," was his thought; "too miserly to burn two cents' worth of gas and save his boarders' necks."

He fumbled for the knob and entered a lighted room, where sat his sister and Bernard Higginbotham. She was patching a pair of his trousers, while his lean body was distributed over two chairs, his feet dangling in dilapidated carpet-slippers over the edge of the second chair. He glanced across the top of the paper he was reading, showing a pair of dark, insincere, sharp-staring eyes. Martin Eden never looked at him without experiencing a sense of repulsion. What his sister had seen in the man was beyond him. The other affected him as so much vermin, and always aroused in him an impulse to crush him under his foot. "Some day I'll beat the face off of him," was the way he often consoled himself for enduring the man's existence. The eyes, weasel-like and cruel, were looking at him complainingly.

"Well," Martin demanded. "Out with it."

"I had that door painted only last week," Mr. Higginbotham half whined, half bullied; "and you know what union wages are. You should be more careful."

Martin had intended to reply, but he was struck by the hopelessness of it. He gazed across the monstrous sordidness of soul to a chromo on the wall. It surprised him. He had always liked it, but it seemed that now he was seeing it for the first time. It was cheap, that was what it was, like everything else in this house. His mind went back to the house he had just left, and he saw, first, the paintings, and next, Her, looking at him with melting sweetness as she shook his hand at leaving. He forgot where he was and Bernard Higginbotham's existence, till that gentleman demanded:-

"Seen a ghost?"

Martin came back and looked at the beady eyes, sneering, truculent, cowardly, and there leaped into his vision, as on a screen, the same eyes when their owner was making a sale in the store below—subservient eyes, smug, and oily, and flattering.

"Yes," Martin answered. "I seen a ghost. Good night. Good night, Gertrude."

He started to leave the room, tripping over a loose seam in the slatternly carpet.

"Don't bang the door," Mr. Higginbotham cautioned him.

CHAPTER III

He felt the blood crawl in his veins, but controlled himself and closed the door softly behind him.

Mr. Higginbotham looked at his wife exultantly.

"He's ben drinkin'," he proclaimed in a hoarse whisper. "I told you he would."

She nodded her head resignedly.

"His eyes was pretty shiny," she confessed; "and he didn't have no collar, though he went away with one. But mebbe he didn't have more'n a couple of glasses."

"He couldn't stand up straight," asserted her husband. "I watched him. He couldn't walk across the floor without stumblin'. You heard 'm yourself almost fall down in the hall."

"I think it was over Alice's cart," she said. "He couldn't see it in the dark."

Mr. Higginbotham's voice and wrath began to rise. All day he effaced himself in the store, reserving for the evening, with his family, the privilege of being himself.

"I tell you that precious brother of yours was drunk."

His voice was cold, sharp, and final, his lips stamping the enunciation of each word like the die of a machine. His wife sighed and remained silent. She was a large, stout woman, always dressed slatternly and always tired from the burdens of her flesh, her work, and her husband.

"He's got it in him, I tell you, from his father," Mr. Higginbotham went on accusingly. "An' he'll croak in the gutter the same way. You know that."

She nodded, sighed, and went on stitching. They were agreed that Martin had come home drunk. They did not have it in their souls to know beauty, or they would have known that those shining eyes and that glowing face betokened youth's first vision of love.

"Settin' a fine example to the children," Mr. Higginbotham snorted, suddenly, in the silence for which his wife was responsible and which he resented. Sometimes he almost wished she would oppose him more. "If he does it again, he's got to get out. Understand! I won't put up with his shinanigan—debotchin' innocent children with his boozing." Mr. Higginbotham liked the word, which was a new one in his vocabulary, recently gleaned from a newspaper column. "That's what it is, debotchin'—there ain't no other name for it."

Still his wife sighed, shook her head sorrowfully, and stitched on. Mr. Higginbotham resumed the newspaper.

"Has he paid last week's board?" he shot across the top of the newspaper.

She nodded, then added, "He still has some money."

"When is he goin' to sea again?"

"When his pay-day's spent, I guess," she answered. "He was over to San Francisco yesterday looking for a ship. But he's got money, yet, an' he's particular about the kind of ship he signs for."

"It's not for a deck-swab like him to put on airs," Mr. Higginbotham snorted. "Particular! Him!"

"He said something about a schooner that's gettin' ready to go off to some outlandish place to look for buried treasure, that he'd sail on her if his money held out."

"If he only wanted to steady down, I'd give him a job drivin' the wagon," her husband said, but with no trace of benevolence in his voice. "Tom's quit."

His wife looked alarm and interrogation.

"Quit to-night. Is goin' to work for Carruthers. They paid 'm more'n I could afford."

"I told you you'd lose 'm," she cried out. "He was worth more'n you was giving him."

"Now look here, old woman," Higginbotham bullied, "for the thousandth time I've told you to keep your nose out of the business. I won't tell you again."

"I don't care," she sniffled. "Tom was a good boy." Her husband glared at her. This was unqualified defiance.

"If that brother of yours was worth his salt, he could take the wagon," he snorted.

"He pays his board, just the same," was the retort. "An' he's my brother, an' so long as he don't owe you money you've got no right to be jumping on him all the time. I've got some feelings, if I have been married to you for seven years."

"Did you tell 'm you'd charge him for gas if he goes on readin' in bed?" he demanded.

Mrs. Higginbotham made no reply. Her revolt faded away, her spirit wilting down into her tired flesh. Her husband was triumphant. He had her. His eyes snapped vindictively, while his ears joyed in the sniffles she emitted. He extracted great happiness from squelching her, and she squelched easily these days, though it had been different in the first years of their married life, before the brood of children and his incessant nagging had sapped her energy.

"Well, you tell 'm to-morrow, that's all," he said. "An' I just want to tell you, before I forget it, that you'd better send for Marian to-morrow to take care of the children. With Tom quit, I'll have to be out on the wagon, an' you can make up your mind to it to be down below waitin' on the counter."

"But to-morrow's wash day," she objected weakly.

"Get up early, then, an' do it first. I won't start out till ten o'clock."

He crinkled the paper viciously and resumed his reading.

CHAPTER IV

Martin Eden, with blood still crawling from contact with his brother-in-law, felt his way along the unlighted back hall and entered his room, a tiny cubbyhole with space for a bed, a wash-stand, and one chair. Mr. Higginbotham was too thrifty to keep a servant when his wife could do the work. Besides, the servant's room enabled them to take in two boarders instead of one. Martin placed the Swinburne and Browning on the chair, took off his coat, and sat down on the bed. A screeching of asthmatic springs greeted the weight of his body, but he did not notice them. He started to take off his shoes, but fell to staring at the white plaster wall opposite him, broken by long streaks of dirty brown where rain had leaked through the roof. On this befouled background visions began to flow and burn. He forgot his shoes and stared long, till his lips began to move and he murmured, "Ruth."

"Ruth." He had not thought a simple sound could be so beautiful. It delighted his ear, and he grew intoxicated with the repetition of it. "Ruth." It was a talisman, a magic word to conjure with. Each time he murmured it, her face shimmered before him, suffusing the foul wall with a golden radiance. This radiance did not stop at the wall. It extended on into infinity, and through its golden depths his soul went questing after hers. The best that was in him was out in splendid flood. The very thought of her ennobled and purified him, made him better, and made him want to be better. This was new to him. He had never known women who had made him better. They had always had the counter effect of making him beastly. He did not know that many of them had done their best, bad as it was. Never having been conscious of himself, he did not know that he had that in his being that drew love from women and which had been the cause of their reaching out for his youth. Though they had often bothered him, he had never bothered about them; and he would never have dreamed that there were women who had been better because of him. Always in sublime carelessness had he lived, till now, and now it seemed to him that they had always reached out and dragged at him with vile hands. This was not just to them, nor to himself. But he, who for the first time was becoming conscious of himself, was in no condition to judge, and he burned with shame as he stared at the vision of his infamy.

He got up abruptly and tried to see himself in the dirty looking-glass over the wash-stand. He passed a towel over it and looked again, long and carefully. It was the first time he had ever really seen himself. His eyes were made for seeing, but up to that moment they had been filled with the ever changing panorama of the world, at which he had been too busy gazing, ever to gaze at himself. He saw the head and face of a young fellow of twenty, but, being unused to such appraisement, he did not know how to value it. Above a square-domed forehead he saw a mop of brown hair, nut-brown, with a wave to it and hints of curls that were a delight to any woman, making hands tingle to stroke it and fingers tingle to pass caresses through it. But he passed it by as without merit, in Her eyes, and dwelt long and thoughtfully on the high, square forehead,—striving to penetrate it and learn the quality of its content. What kind of a brain lay behind there? was his insistent interrogation. What was it capable of? How far would it take him? Would it take him to her?

He wondered if there was soul in those steel-gray eyes that were often quite blue of color and that were strong with the briny airs of the sun-washed deep. He wondered, also, how his eyes looked to her. He tried to imagine himself she, gazing into those eyes of his, but failed in the jugglery. He could successfully put himself inside other men's minds, but they had to be men whose ways of life he knew. He did not know her way of life. She was wonder and mystery, and how could he guess one thought of hers? Well, they were honest eyes, he concluded, and in them was neither smallness nor meanness. The brown sunburn of his face surprised him. He had not dreamed he was so black. He rolled up his shirt-sleeve and compared the white underside if the arm with his face. Yes, he was a white man, after all. But the arms were sunburned, too. He twisted his arm, rolled the biceps over with his other hand, and gazed underneath where he was least touched by the sun. It was very white. He laughed at his bronzed face in the glass at the thought that it was once as white as the underside of his arm; nor did he dream that in the world there were few pale spirits of women who could boast fairer or smoother skins than he—fairer than where he had escaped the ravages of the sun.

His might have been a cherub's mouth, had not the full, sensuous lips a trick, under stress, of drawing firmly across the teeth. At times, so tightly did they draw, the mouth became stern and harsh, even ascetic. They were the lips of a fighter and of a lover. They could taste the sweetness of life with relish, and they could put the sweetness aside and command life. The chin and jaw, strong and just hinting of square aggressiveness, helped the lips to command life. Strength balanced sensuousness and had upon it a tonic effect, compelling him to love beauty that was healthy and making him vibrate to sensations that were wholesome. And between the lips were teeth that had never known nor needed the dentist's care. They were white and strong and regular, he decided, as he looked at them. But as he looked, he began to be troubled. Somewhere, stored away in the recesses of his mind and vaguely remembered, was the impression that there were people who washed their teeth every day. They were the people from up above—people in her class. She must wash her teeth every day, too. What would she think if she learned that he had never washed his teeth in all the days of his life? He resolved to get a tooth-brush and form the habit. He would begin at once, to-morrow. It was not by mere achievement that he could hope to win to her. He must make a personal reform in all things, even to tooth-washing and neck-gear, though a starched collar affected him as a renunciation of freedom.

He held up his hand, rubbing the ball of the thumb over the calloused palm and gazing at the dirt that was ingrained in the flesh itself and which no brush could scrub away. How different was her palm! He thrilled deliciously at the remembrance. Like a rose-petal, he thought; cool and soft as a snowflake. He had never thought that a mere woman's hand could be so sweetly soft. He caught himself imagining the wonder of a caress from such a hand, and flushed guiltily. It was too gross a thought for her. In ways it seemed to impugn her high spirituality. She was a pale, slender spirit, exalted far beyond the flesh; but nevertheless the softness of her palm persisted in his thoughts. He was used to the harsh callousness of factory girls and working women. Well he knew why their hands were rough; but this hand of hers . . . It was soft because she had never used it to work with. The gulf yawned between her and him at the awesome thought of a person who did not have to work for a living. He suddenly saw the aristocracy of the people who did not labor. It towered before him on the wall, a figure in brass, arrogant and powerful. He had worked himself; his first memories seemed connected with work, and all his family had worked. There was Gertrude. When her hands were not hard from the endless housework, they were swollen and red like boiled beef, what of the washing. And there was his sister Marian. She had worked in the cannery the preceding summer, and her slim, pretty hands were all scarred with the tomato-knives. Besides, the tips of two of her fingers had been left in the cutting machine at the paper-box factory the preceding winter. He remembered the hard palms of his mother as she lay in her coffin. And his father had worked to the last fading gasp; the horned growth on his hands must have been half an inch thick when he died. But Her hands were soft, and her mother's hands, and her brothers'. This last came to him as a surprise; it was tremendously indicative of the highness of their caste, of the enormous distance that stretched between her and him.

He sat back on the bed with a bitter laugh, and finished taking off his shoes. He was a fool; he had been made drunken by a woman's face and by a woman's soft, white hands. And then, suddenly, before his eyes, on the foul plaster-wall appeared a vision. He stood in front of a gloomy tenement house. It was night-time, in the East End of London, and before him stood Margey, a little factory girl of fifteen. He had seen her home after the bean-feast. She lived in that gloomy tenement, a place not fit for swine. His hand was going out to hers as he said good night. She had put her lips up to be kissed, but he wasn't going to kiss her. Somehow he was afraid of her. And then her hand closed on his and pressed feverishly. He felt her callouses grind and grate on his, and a great wave of pity welled over him. He saw her yearning, hungry eyes, and her ill-fed female form which had been rushed from childhood into a frightened and ferocious maturity; then he put his arms about her in large tolerance and stooped and kissed her on the lips. Her glad little cry rang in his ears, and he felt her clinging to him like a cat. Poor little starveling! He continued to stare at the vision of what had happened in the long ago. His flesh was crawling as it had crawled that night when she clung to him, and his heart was warm with pity. It was a gray scene, greasy gray, and the rain drizzled greasily on the pavement stones. And then a radiant glory shone on the wall, and up through the other vision, displacing it, glimmered Her pale face under its crown of golden hair, remote and inaccessible as a star.

He took the Browning and the Swinburne from the chair and kissed them. Just the same, she told me to call again, he thought. He took another look at himself in the glass, and said aloud, with great solemnity:-

"Martin Eden, the first thing to-morrow you go to the free library an' read up on etiquette. Understand!"

He turned off the gas, and the springs shrieked under his body.

"But you've got to quit cussin', Martin, old boy; you've got to quit cussin'," he said aloud.

Then he dozed off to sleep and to dream dreams that for madness and audacity rivalled those of poppy-eaters.

CHAPTER V

He awoke next morning from rosy scenes of dream to a steamy atmosphere that smelled of soapsuds and dirty clothes, and that was vibrant with the jar and jangle of tormented life. As he came out of his room he heard the slosh of water, a sharp exclamation, and a resounding smack as his sister visited her irritation upon one of her numerous progeny. The squall of the child went through him like a knife. He was aware that the whole thing, the very air he breathed, was repulsive and mean. How different, he thought, from the atmosphere of beauty and repose of the house wherein Ruth dwelt. There it was all spiritual. Here it was all material, and meanly material.

"Come here, Alfred," he called to the crying child, at the same time thrusting his hand into his trousers pocket, where he carried his money loose in the same large way that he lived life in general. He put a quarter in the youngster's hand and held him in his arms a moment, soothing his sobs. "Now run along and get some candy, and don't forget to give some to your brothers and sisters. Be sure and get the kind that lasts longest."

His sister lifted a flushed face from the wash-tub and looked at him.

"A nickel'd ha' ben enough," she said. "It's just like you, no idea of the value of money. The child'll eat himself sick."

"That's all right, sis," he answered jovially. "My money'll take care of itself. If you weren't so busy, I'd kiss you good morning."

He wanted to be affectionate to this sister, who was good, and who, in her way, he knew, loved him. But, somehow, she grew less herself as the years went by, and more and more baffling. It was the hard work, the many children, and the nagging of her husband, he decided, that had changed her. It came to him, in a flash of fancy, that her nature seemed taking on the attributes of stale vegetables, smelly soapsuds, and of the greasy dimes, nickels, and quarters she took in over the counter of the store.

"Go along an' get your breakfast," she said roughly, though secretly pleased. Of all her wandering brood of brothers he had always been her favorite. "I declare I *will* kiss you," she said, with a sudden stir at her heart.

With thumb and forefinger she swept the dripping suds first from one arm and then from the other. He put his arms round her massive waist and kissed her wet steamy lips. The tears welled into her eyes—not so much from strength of feeling as from the weakness of chronic overwork. She shoved him away from her, but not before he caught a glimpse of her moist eyes.

"You'll find breakfast in the oven," she said hurriedly. "Jim ought to be up now. I had to get up early for the washing. Now get along with you and get out of the house early. It won't be nice to-day, what of Tom quittin' an' nobody but Bernard to drive the wagon."

Martin went into the kitchen with a sinking heart, the image of her red face and slatternly form eating its way like acid into his brain. She might love him if she only had some time, he concluded. But she was worked to death. Bernard Higginbotham was a brute to work her so hard. But he could not help but feel, on the other hand, that there had not been anything beautiful in that kiss. It was true, it was an unusual kiss. For years she had kissed him only when he returned from voyages or departed on voyages. But this kiss had tasted soapsuds, and the lips, he had noticed, were flabby. There had been no quick, vigorous lip-pressure such as should accompany any kiss. Hers was the kiss of a tired woman who had been tired so long that she had forgotten how to kiss. He remembered her as a girl, before her marriage, when she would dance with the best, all night, after a hard day's work at the laundry, and think nothing of leaving the dance to go to another day's hard work. And then he thought of Ruth and the cool sweetness that must reside in her lips as it resided in all about her. Her kiss would be like her hand-shake or the way she looked at one, firm and frank. In imagination he dared to think of her lips on his, and so vividly did he imagine that he went dizzy at the thought and seemed to rift through clouds of rose-petals, filling his brain with their perfume.

In the kitchen he found Jim, the other boarder, eating mush very languidly, with a sick, far-away look in his eyes. Jim was a plumber's apprentice whose weak chin and hedonistic temperament, coupled with a certain nervous stupidity, promised to take him nowhere in the race for bread and butter.

"Why don't you eat?" he demanded, as Martin dipped dolefully into the cold, half-cooked oatmeal mush. "Was you drunk again last night?"

Martin shook his head. He was oppressed by the utter squalidness of it all. Ruth Morse seemed farther removed than ever.

"I was," Jim went on with a boastful, nervous giggle. "I was loaded right to the neck. Oh, she was a daisy. Billy brought me home."

Martin nodded that he heard,—it was a habit of nature with him to pay heed to whoever talked to him,—and poured a cup of lukewarm coffee.

"Goin' to the Lotus Club dance to-night?" Jim demanded. "They're goin' to have beer, an' if that Temescal bunch comes, there'll be a rough-house. I don't care, though. I'm takin' my lady friend just the same. Cripes, but I've got a taste in my mouth!"

He made a wry face and attempted to wash the taste away with coffee.

"D'ye know Julia?"

Martin shook his head.

"She's my lady friend," Jim explained, "and she's a peach. I'd introduce you to her, only you'd win her. I don't see what the girls see in you, honest I don't; but the way you win them away from the fellers is sickenin'."

"I never got any away from you," Martin answered uninterestedly. The breakfast had to be got through somehow.

"Yes, you did, too," the other asserted warmly. "There was Maggie."

CHAPTER V

"Never had anything to do with her. Never danced with her except that one night."

"Yes, an' that's just what did it," Jim cried out. "You just danced with her an' looked at her, an' it was all off. Of course you didn't mean nothin' by it, but it settled me for keeps. Wouldn't look at me again. Always askin' about you. She'd have made fast dates enough with you if you'd wanted to."

"But I didn't want to."

"Wasn't necessary. I was left at the pole." Jim looked at him admiringly. "How d'ye do it, anyway, Mart?"

"By not carin' about 'em," was the answer.

"You mean makin' b'lieve you don't care about them?" Jim queried eagerly.

Martin considered for a moment, then answered, "Perhaps that will do, but with me I guess it's different. I never have cared—much. If you can put it on, it's all right, most likely."

"You should 'a' ben up at Riley's barn last night," Jim announced inconsequently. "A lot of the fellers put on the gloves. There was a peach from West Oakland. They called 'm 'The Rat.' Slick as silk. No one could touch 'm. We was all wishin' you was there. Where was you anyway?"

"Down in Oakland," Martin replied.

"To the show?"

Martin shoved his plate away and got up.

"Comin' to the dance to-night?" the other called after him.

"No, I think not," he answered.

He went downstairs and out into the street, breathing great breaths of air. He had been suffocating in that atmosphere, while the apprentice's chatter had driven him frantic. There had been times when it was all he could do to refrain from reaching over and mopping Jim's face in the mush-plate. The more he had chattered, the more remote had Ruth seemed to him. How could he, herding with such cattle, ever become worthy of her? He was appalled at the problem confronting him, weighted down by the incubus of his working-class station. Everything reached out to hold him down—his sister, his sister's house and family, Jim the apprentice, everybody he knew, every tie of life. Existence did not taste good in his mouth. Up to then he had accepted existence, as he had lived it with all about him, as a good thing. He had never questioned it, except when he read books; but then, they were only books, fairy stories of a fairer and impossible world. But now he had seen that world, possible and real, with a flower of a woman called Ruth in the midmost centre of it; and thenceforth he must know bitter tastes, and longings sharp as pain, and hopelessness that tantalized because it fed on hope.

He had debated between the Berkeley Free Library and the Oakland Free Library, and decided upon the latter because Ruth lived in Oakland. Who could tell?—a library was a most likely place for her, and he might see her there. He did not know the way of libraries, and he wandered through endless rows of fiction, till the delicate-featured French-looking girl who seemed in charge, told him that the reference department was upstairs. He did not know enough to ask the man at the desk, and began his adventures in the philosophy alcove. He had heard of book philosophy, but had not imagined there had been so much written about it. The high, bulging shelves of heavy tomes humbled him and at the same time stimulated him. Here was work for the vigor of his brain. He found books on trigonometry in the mathematics section, and ran the pages, and stared at the meaningless formulas and figures. He could read English, but he saw there an alien speech. Norman and Arthur knew that speech. He had heard them talking it. And they were her brothers. He left the alcove in despair. From every side the books seemed to press upon him and crush him.

He had never dreamed that the fund of human knowledge bulked so big. He was frightened. How could his brain ever master it all? Later, he remembered that there were other men, many men, who had mastered it; and he breathed a great oath, passionately, under his breath, swearing that his brain could do what theirs had done.

And so he wandered on, alternating between depression and elation as he stared at the shelves packed with wisdom. In one miscellaneous section he came upon a "Norrie's Epitome." He turned the pages reverently. In a way, it spoke a kindred speech. Both he and it were of the sea. Then he found a "Bowditch" and books by Lecky and Marshall. There it was; he would teach himself navigation. He would quit drinking, work up, and become a captain. Ruth seemed very near to him in that moment. As a captain, he could marry her (if she would have him). And if she wouldn't, well—he would live a good life among men, because of Her, and he would quit drinking anyway. Then he remembered the underwriters and the owners, the two masters a captain must serve, either of which could and would break him and whose interests were diametrically opposed. He cast his eyes about the room and closed the lids down on a vision of ten thousand books. No; no more of the sea for him. There was power in all that wealth of books, and if he would do great things, he must do them on the land. Besides, captains were not allowed to take their wives to sea with them.

Noon came, and afternoon. He forgot to eat, and sought on for the books on etiquette; for, in addition to career, his mind was vexed by a simple and very concrete problem: *When you meet a young lady and she asks you to call, how soon can you call*? was the way he worded it to himself. But when he found the right shelf, he sought vainly for the answer. He was appalled at the vast edifice of etiquette, and lost himself in the mazes of visiting-card conduct between persons in polite society. He abandoned his search. He had not found what he wanted, though he had found that it would take all of a man's time to be polite, and that he would have to live a preliminary life in which to learn how to be polite.

"Did you find what you wanted?" the man at the desk asked him as he was leaving.

"Yes, sir," he answered. "You have a fine library here."

The man nodded. "We should be glad to see you here often. Are you a sailor?"

"Yes, sir," he answered. "And I'll come again."

Now, how did he know that? he asked himself as he went down the stairs.

And for the first block along the street he walked very stiff and straight and awkwardly, until he forgot himself in his thoughts, whereupon his rolling gait gracefully returned to him.

CHAPTER VI

A terrible restlessness that was akin to hunger afflicted Martin Eden. He was famished for a sight of the girl whose slender hands had gripped his life with a giant's grasp. He could not steel himself to call upon her. He was afraid that he might call too soon, and so be guilty of an awful breach of that awful thing called etiquette. He spent long hours in the Oakland and Berkeley libraries, and made out application blanks for membership for himself, his sisters Gertrude and Marian, and Jim, the latter's consent being obtained at the expense of several glasses of beer. With four cards permitting him to draw books, he burned the gas late in the servant's room, and was charged fifty cents a week for it by Mr. Higginbotham.

The many books he read but served to whet his unrest. Every page of every book was a peep-hole into the realm of knowledge. His hunger fed upon what he read, and increased. Also, he did not know where to begin, and continually suffered from lack of preparation. The commonest references, that he could see plainly every reader was expected to know, he did not know. And the same was true of the poetry he read which maddened him with delight. He read more of Swinburne than was contained in the volume Ruth had lent him; and "Dolores" he understood thoroughly. But surely Ruth did not understand it, he concluded. How could she, living the refined life she did? Then he chanced upon Kipling's poems, and was swept away by the lilt and swing and glamour with which familiar things had been invested. He was amazed at the man's sympathy with life and at his incisive psychology. *Psychology* was a new word in Martin's vocabulary. He had bought a dictionary, which deed had decreased his supply of money and brought nearer the day on which he must sail in search of more. Also, it incensed Mr. Higginbotham, who would have preferred the money taking the form of board.

He dared not go near Ruth's neighborhood in the daytime, but night found him lurking like a thief around the Morse home, stealing glimpses at the windows and loving the very walls that sheltered her. Several times he barely escaped being caught by her brothers, and once he trailed Mr. Morse down town and studied his face in the lighted streets, longing all the while for some quick danger of death to threaten so that he might spring in and save her father. On another night, his vigil was rewarded by a glimpse of Ruth through a second-story window. He saw only her head and shoulders, and her arms raised as she fixed her hair before a mirror. It was only for a moment, but it was a long moment to him, during which his blood turned to wine and sang through his veins. Then she pulled down the shade. But it was her room—he had learned that; and thereafter he strayed there often, hiding under a dark tree on the opposite side of the street and smoking countless cigarettes. One afternoon he saw her mother coming out of a bank, and received another proof of the enormous distance that separated Ruth from him. She was of the class that dealt with banks. He had never been inside a bank in his life, and he had an idea that such institutions were frequented only by the very rich and the very powerful.

In one way, he had undergone a moral revolution. Her cleanness and purity had reacted upon him, and he felt in his being a crying need to be clean. He must be that if he were ever to be worthy of breathing the same air with her. He washed his teeth, and scrubbed his hands with a kitchen scrub-brush till he saw a nail-brush in a drug-store window and divined its use. While purchasing it, the clerk glanced at his nails, suggested a nail-file, and so he became possessed of an additional toilet-tool. He ran across a book in the library on the care of the body, and promptly developed a penchant for a cold-water bath every morning, much to the amazement of Jim, and to the bewilderment of Mr. Higginbotham, who was not in sympathy with such high-fangled notions and who seriously debated whether or not he should charge Martin extra for the water. Another stride was in the direction of creased trousers. Now that Martin was aroused in such matters, he swiftly noted the difference between the baggy knees of the trousers worn by the working class and the straight line from knee to foot of those worn by the men above the working class. Also, he learned the reason why, and invaded his sister's kitchen in search of irons and ironing-board. He had misadventures at first, hopelessly burning one pair and buying another, which expenditure again brought nearer the day on which he must put to sea.

But the reform went deeper than mere outward appearance. He still smoked, but he drank no more. Up to that time, drinking had seemed to him the proper thing for men to do, and he had prided himself on his strong head which enabled him to drink most men under the table. Whenever he encountered a chance shipmate, and there were many in San Francisco, he treated them and was treated in turn, as of old, but he ordered for himself root beer or ginger ale and good-naturedly endured their chaffing. And as they waxed maudlin he studied them, watching the beast rise and master them and thanking God that he was no longer as they. They had their limitations to forget, and when they were drunk, their dim, stupid spirits were even as gods, and each ruled in his heaven of intoxicated desire. With Martin the need for strong drink had vanished. He was drunken in new and more profound ways—with Ruth, who had fired him with love and with a glimpse of higher and eternal life; with books, that had set a myriad maggots of desire gnawing in his brain; and with the sense of personal cleanliness he was achieving, that gave him even more superb health than what he had enjoyed and that made his whole body sing with physical well-being.

One night he went to the theatre, on the blind chance that he might see her there, and from the second balcony he did see her. He saw her come down the aisle, with Arthur and a strange young man with a football mop of hair and eyeglasses, the sight of whom spurred him to instant apprehension and jealousy. He saw her take her seat in the orchestra circle, and little else than her did he see that night—a pair of slender white shoulders and a mass of pale gold hair, dim with distance. But there were others who saw, and now and again, glancing at those about him, he noted two young girls who looked back from the row in front, a dozen seats along, and who smiled at him with bold eyes. He had always been easy-going. It was not in his nature to give rebuff. In the old days he would have smiled back, and gone further and encouraged smiling. But now it was different. He did smile back, then looked away, and looked no more deliberately. But several times, forgetting the existence of the two girls, his eyes caught their smiles. He could not re-thumb himself in a day, nor could he violate the intrinsic kindliness of his nature; so, at such moments, he smiled at the girls in warm human friendliness. It was nothing new to him. He knew they were reaching out their woman's hands to him. But it was different now. Far down there in the orchestra circle was the one woman in all the world, so different, so terrifically different, from these two girls of his class, that he could feel for them only pity and sorrow. He had it in his heart to wish that they could possess, in some small measure, her goodness and glory. And not for the world could he hurt them because of their outreaching. He was not flattered by it; he even felt a slight shame at his lowliness that permitted it. He knew, did he belong in Ruth's class, that there would be no overtures from these girls; and with each glance of theirs he felt the fingers of his own class clutching at him to hold him down.

He left his seat before the curtain went down on the last act, intent on seeing Her as she passed out. There were always numbers of men who stood on the sidewalk outside, and he could pull his cap down over his eyes and screen himself behind some one's shoulder so that she should not see him. He emerged from the theatre with the first of the crowd; but scarcely had he taken his position on the edge of the sidewalk when the two girls appeared. They were looking for him, he knew; and for the moment he could have cursed that in him which drew women. Their casual edging across the sidewalk to the curb, as they drew near, apprised him of discovery. They slowed down, and were in the thick of the crown as they came up with him. One of them brushed against him and apparently for the first time noticed him. She was a slender, dark girl, with black, defiant eyes. But they smiled at him, and he smiled back.

"Hello," he said.

It was automatic; he had said it so often before under similar circumstances of first meetings. Besides, he could do no less. There was that large tolerance and sympathy in his nature that would permit him to do no less. The black-eyed girl smiled gratification and greeting, and showed signs of stopping, while her companion, arm linked in arm, giggled and likewise showed signs of halting. He thought quickly. It would never do for Her to come out and see him talking there with them. Quite naturally, as a matter of course, he swung in along-side the dark-eyed one and walked with her. There was no awkwardness on his part, no numb tongue. He was at home here, and he held his own royally in the badinage, bristling with slang and sharpness, that was always the preliminary to getting acquainted in these swift-moving affairs. At the corner where the main stream of people flowed onward, he started to edge out into the cross street. But the girl with the black eyes caught his arm, following him and dragging her companion after her, as she cried:

"Hold on, Bill! What's yer rush? You're not goin' to shake us so sudden as all that?"

He halted with a laugh, and turned, facing them. Across their shoulders he could see the moving throng passing under the street lamps. Where he stood it was not so light, and, unseen, he would be able to see Her as she passed by. She would certainly pass by, for that way led home.

"What's her name?" he asked of the giggling girl, nodding at the dark-eyed one.

"You ask her," was the convulsed response.

"Well, what is it?" he demanded, turning squarely on the girl in question.

"You ain't told me yours, yet," she retorted.

"You never asked it," he smiled. "Besides, you guessed the first rattle. It's Bill, all right, all right."

"Aw, go 'long with you." She looked him in the eyes, her own sharply passionate and inviting. "What is it, honest?"

Again she looked. All the centuries of woman since sex began were eloquent in her eyes. And he measured her in a careless way, and knew, bold now, that she would begin to retreat, coyly and delicately, as he pursued, ever ready to reverse the game should he turn fainthearted. And, too, he was human, and could feel the draw of her, while his ego could not but appreciate the flattery of her kindness. Oh, he knew it all, and knew them well, from A to Z. Good, as goodness might be measured in their particular class, hard-working for meagre wages and scorning the sale of self for easier ways, nervously desirous for some small pinch of happiness in the desert of existence, and facing a future that was a gamble between the ugliness of unending toil and the black pit of more terrible wretchedness, the way whereto being briefer though better paid.

"Bill," he answered, nodding his head. "Sure, Pete, Bill an' no other."

"No joshin'?" she queried.

"It ain't Bill at all," the other broke in.

"How do you know?" he demanded. "You never laid eyes on me before."

"No need to, to know you're lyin'," was the retort.

"Straight, Bill, what is it?" the first girl asked.

"Bill'll do," he confessed.

She reached out to his arm and shook him playfully. "I knew you was lyin', but you look good to me just the same."

He captured the hand that invited, and felt on the palm familiar markings and distortions.

"When'd you chuck the cannery?" he asked.

"How'd yeh know?" and, "My, ain't cheh a mind-reader!" the girls chorussed.

And while he exchanged the stupidities of stupid minds with them, before his inner sight towered the book-shelves of the library, filled with the wisdom of the ages. He smiled bitterly at the incongruity of it, and was assailed by doubts. But between inner vision and outward pleasantry he found time to watch the theatre crowd streaming by. And then he saw Her, under the lights, between her brother and the strange young man with glasses, and his heart seemed to stand still. He had waited long for this moment. He had time to note the light, fluffy something that hid her queenly head, the tasteful lines of her wrapped figure, the gracefulness of her carriage and of the hand that caught up her skirts; and then she was gone and he was left staring at the two girls of the cannery, at their tawdry attempts at prettiness of dress, their tragic efforts to be clean and trim, the cheap cloth, the cheap ribbons, and the cheap rings on the fingers. He felt a tug at his arm, and heard a voice saying:-

"Wake up, Bill! What's the matter with you?"

"What was you sayin'?" he asked.

"Oh, nothin'," the dark girl answered, with a toss of her head. "I was only remarkin'—"

"What?"

"Well, I was whisperin' it'd be a good idea if you could dig up a gentleman friend—for her" (indicating her companion), "and then, we could go off an' have ice-cream soda somewhere, or coffee, or anything."

He was afflicted by a sudden spiritual nausea. The transition from Ruth to this had been too abrupt. Ranged side by side with the bold, defiant eyes of the girl before him, he saw Ruth's clear, luminous eyes, like a saint's, gazing at him out of unplumbed depths of purity. And, somehow, he felt within him a stir of power. He was better than this. Life meant more to him than it meant to these two girls whose thoughts did not go beyond ice-cream and a gentleman friend. He remembered that he had led always a secret life in his thoughts. These thoughts he had tried to share, but never had he found a woman capable of understanding—nor a man. He had tried, at times, but had only puzzled his listeners. And as his thoughts had been beyond them, so, he argued now, he must be beyond them. He felt power move in him, and clenched his fists. If life meant more to him, then it was for him to demand more from life, but he could not demand it from such companionship as this. Those bold black eyes had nothing to offer. He knew the thoughts behind them—of ice-cream and of something else. But those saint's eyes alongside—they offered all he knew and more than he could guess. They offered books and painting, beauty and repose, and all the fine elegance of higher existence. Behind those black eyes he knew every thought process. It was like clockwork. He could watch every wheel go around. Their bid was low pleasure, narrow as the grave, that palled, and the grave was at the end of it. But the bid of the saint's eyes was mystery, and wonder unthinkable, and eternal life. He had caught glimpses of the soul in them, and glimpses of his own soul, too.

"There's only one thing wrong with the programme," he said aloud. "I've got a date already."

The girl's eyes blazed her disappointment.

"To sit up with a sick friend, I suppose?" she sneered.

"No, a real, honest date with—" he faltered, "with a girl."

"You're not stringin' me?" she asked earnestly.

He looked her in the eyes and answered: "It's straight, all right. But why can't we meet some other time? You ain't told me your name yet. An' where d'ye live?"

"Lizzie," she replied, softening toward him, her hand pressing his arm, while her body leaned against his. "Lizzie Connolly. And I live at Fifth an' Market."

He talked on a few minutes before saying good night. He did not go home immediately; and under the tree where he kept his vigils he looked up at a window and murmured: "That date was with you, Ruth. I kept it for you."

CHAPTER VII

A week of heavy reading had passed since the evening he first met Ruth Morse, and still he dared not call. Time and again he nerved himself up to call, but under the doubts that assailed him his determination died away. He did not know the proper time to call, nor was there any one to tell him, and he was afraid of committing himself to an irretrievable blunder. Having shaken himself free from his old companions and old ways of life, and having no new companions, nothing remained for him but to read, and the long hours he devoted to it would have ruined a dozen pairs of ordinary eyes. But his eyes were strong, and they were backed by a body superbly strong. Furthermore, his mind was fallow. It had lain fallow all his life so far as the abstract thought of the books was concerned, and it was ripe for the sowing. It had never been jaded by study, and it bit hold of the knowledge in the books with sharp teeth that would not let go.

It seemed to him, by the end of the week, that he had lived centuries, so far behind were the old life and outlook. But he was baffled by lack of preparation. He attempted to read books that required years of preliminary specialization. One day he would read a book of antiquated philosophy, and the next day one that was ultra-modern, so that his head would be whirling with the conflict and contradiction of ideas. It was the same with the economists. On the one shelf at the library he found Karl Marx, Ricardo, Adam Smith, and Mill, and the abstruse formulas of the one gave no clew that the ideas of another were obsolete. He was bewildered, and yet he wanted to know. He had become interested, in a day, in economics, industry, and politics. Passing through the City Hall Park, he had noticed a group of men, in the centre of which were half a dozen, with flushed faces and raised voices, earnestly carrying on a discussion. He joined the listeners, and heard a new, alien tongue in the mouths of the philosophers of the people. One was a tramp, another was a labor agitator, a third was a law-school student, and the remainder was composed of wordy workingmen. For the first time he heard of socialism, anarchism, and single tax, and learned that there were warring social philosophies. He heard hundreds of technical words that were new to him, belonging to fields of thought that his meagre reading had never touched upon. Because of this he could not follow the arguments closely, and he could only guess at and surmise the ideas wrapped up in such strange expressions. Then there was a black-eyed restaurant waiter who was a theosophist, a union baker who was an agnostic, an old man who baffled all of them with the strange philosophy that *what is is right*, and another old man who discoursed interminably about the cosmos and the father-atom and the mother-atom.

Martin Eden's head was in a state of addlement when he went away after several hours, and he hurried to the library to look up the definitions of a dozen unusual words. And when he left the library, he carried under his arm four volumes: Madam Blavatsky's "Secret Doctrine," "Progress and Poverty," "The Quintessence of Socialism," and, "Warfare of Religion and Science." Unfortunately, he began on the "Secret Doctrine." Every line bristled with many-syllabled words he did not understand. He sat up in bed, and the dictionary was in front of him more often than the book. He looked up so many new words that when they recurred, he had forgotten their meaning and had to look them up again. He devised the plan of writing the definitions in a note-book, and filled page after page with them. And still he could not understand. He read until three in the morning, and his brain was in a turmoil, but not one essential thought in the text had he grasped. He looked up, and it seemed that the room was lifting, heeling, and plunging like a ship upon the sea. Then he hurled the "Secret Doctrine" and many curses across the room, turned off the gas, and composed himself to sleep. Nor did he have much better luck with the other three books. It was not that his brain was weak or incapable; it could think these thoughts were it not for lack of training in thinking and lack of the thought-tools with which to think. He guessed this, and for a while entertained the idea of reading nothing but the dictionary until he had mastered every word in it.

Poetry, however, was his solace, and he read much of it, finding his greatest joy in the simpler poets, who were more understandable. He loved beauty, and there he found beauty. Poetry, like music, stirred him profoundly, and, though he did not know it, he was preparing his mind for the heavier work that was to come. The pages of his mind were blank, and, without effort, much he read and liked, stanza by stanza, was impressed upon those pages, so that he was soon able to extract great joy from chanting aloud or under his breath the music and the beauty of the printed words he had read. Then he stumbled upon Gayley's "Classic Myths" and Bulfinch's "Age of Fable," side by side on a library shelf. It was illumination, a great light in the darkness of his ignorance, and he read poetry more avidly than ever.

The man at the desk in the library had seen Martin there so often that he had become quite cordial, always greeting him with a smile and a nod when he entered. It was because of this that Martin did a daring thing. Drawing out some books at the desk, and while the man was stamping the cards, Martin blurted out:-

"Say, there's something I'd like to ask you."

The man smiled and paid attention.

"When you meet a young lady an' she asks you to call, how soon can you call?"

Martin felt his shirt press and cling to his shoulders, what of the sweat of the effort.

"Why I'd say any time," the man answered.

"Yes, but this is different," Martin objected. "She—I—well, you see, it's this way: maybe she won't be there. She goes to the university."

"Then call again."

"What I said ain't what I meant," Martin confessed falteringly, while he made up his mind to throw himself wholly upon the other's mercy. "I'm just a rough sort of a fellow, an' I ain't never seen anything of society. This girl is all that I ain't, an' I ain't anything that she is. You don't think I'm playin' the fool, do you?" he demanded abruptly.

"No, no; not at all, I assure you," the other protested. "Your request is not exactly in the scope of the reference department, but I shall be only too pleased to assist you."

Martin looked at him admiringly.

"If I could tear it off that way, I'd be all right," he said.

"I beg pardon?"

"I mean if I could talk easy that way, an' polite, an' all the rest."

"Oh," said the other, with comprehension.

"What is the best time to call? The afternoon?—not too close to meal-time? Or the evening? Or Sunday?"

"I'll tell you," the librarian said with a brightening face. "You call her up on the telephone and find out."

"I'll do it," he said, picking up his books and starting away.

He turned back and asked:-

"When you're speakin' to a young lady—say, for instance, Miss Lizzie Smith—do you say 'Miss Lizzie'? or 'Miss Smith'?"

"Say 'Miss Smith,'" the librarian stated authoritatively. "Say 'Miss Smith' always—until you come to know her better."

So it was that Martin Eden solved the problem.

"Come down any time; I'll be at home all afternoon," was Ruth's reply over the telephone to his stammered request as to when he could return the borrowed books.

She met him at the door herself, and her woman's eyes took in immediately the creased trousers and the certain slight but indefinable change in him for the better. Also, she was struck by his face. It was almost violent, this health of his, and it seemed to rush out of him and at her in waves of force. She felt the urge again of the desire to lean toward him for warmth, and marvelled again at the effect his presence produced upon her. And he, in turn, knew again the swimming sensation of bliss when he felt the contact of her hand in greeting. The difference between them lay in that she was cool and self-possessed while his face flushed to the roots of the hair. He stumbled with his old awkwardness after her, and his shoulders swung and lurched perilously.

Once they were seated in the living-room, he began to get on easily—more easily by far than he had expected. She made it easy for him; and the gracious spirit with which she did it made him love her more madly than ever. They talked first of the borrowed books, of the Swinburne he was devoted to, and of the Browning he did not understand; and she led the conversation on from subject to subject, while she pondered the problem of how she could be of help to him. She had thought of this often since their first meeting. She wanted to help him. He made a call upon her pity and tenderness that no one had ever made before, and the pity was not so much derogatory of him as maternal in her. Her pity could not be of the common sort, when the man who drew it was so much man as to shock her with maidenly fears and set her mind and pulse thrilling with strange thoughts and feelings. The old fascination of his neck was there, and there was sweetness in the thought of laying her hands upon it. It seemed still a wanton impulse, but she had grown more used to it. She did not dream that in such guise new-born love would epitomize itself. Nor did she dream that the feeling he excited in her was love. She thought she was merely interested in him as an unusual type possessing various potential excellencies, and she even felt philanthropic about it.

She did not know she desired him; but with him it was different. He knew that he loved her, and he desired her as he had never before desired anything in his life. He had loved poetry for beauty's sake; but since he met her the gates to the vast field of love-poetry had been opened wide. She had given him understanding even more than Bulfinch and Gayley. There was a line that a week before he would not have favored with a second thought—"God's own mad lover dying on a kiss"; but now it was ever insistent in his mind. He marvelled at the wonder of it and the truth; and as he gazed upon her he knew that he could die gladly upon a kiss. He felt himself God's own mad lover, and no accolade of knighthood could have given him greater pride. And at last he knew the meaning of life and why he had been born.

As he gazed at her and listened, his thoughts grew daring. He reviewed all the wild delight of the pressure of her hand in his at the door, and longed for it again. His gaze wandered often toward her lips, and he yearned for them hungrily. But there was nothing gross or earthly about this yearning. It gave him exquisite delight to watch every movement and play of those lips as they enunciated the words she spoke; yet they were not ordinary lips such as all men and women had. Their substance was not mere human clay. They were lips of pure spirit, and his desire for them seemed absolutely different from the desire that had led him to other women's lips. He could kiss her lips, rest his own physical lips upon them, but it would be with the lofty and awful fervor with which one would kiss the robe of God. He was not conscious of this transvaluation of values that had taken place in him, and was unaware that the light that shone in his eyes when he looked at her was quite the same light that shines in all men's eyes when the desire of love is upon them. He did not dream how ardent and masculine his gaze was, nor that the warm flame of it was affecting the alchemy of her spirit. Her penetrative virginity exalted and disguised his own emotions, elevating his thoughts to a star-cool chastity, and he would have been startled to learn that there was that shining out of his eyes, like warm waves, that flowed through her and kindled a kindred warmth. She was subtly perturbed by it, and more than once, though she knew not why, it disrupted her train of thought with its delicious intrusion and compelled her to grope for the remainder of ideas partly uttered. Speech was always easy with her, and these interruptions would have puzzled her had she not decided that it was because he was a remarkable type. She was very sensitive to impressions, and it was not strange, after all, that this aura of a traveller from another world should so affect her.

The problem in the background of her consciousness was how to help him, and she turned the conversation in that direction; but it was Martin who came to the point first.

"I wonder if I can get some advice from you," he began, and received an acquiescence of willingness that made his heart bound. "You remember the other time I was here I said I couldn't talk about books an' things because I didn't know how? Well, I've ben doin' a lot of thinkin' ever since. I've ben to the library a whole lot, but most of the books I've tackled have ben over my head. Mebbe I'd better begin at the beginnin'. I ain't never had no advantages. I've worked pretty hard ever since I was a kid, an' since I've ben to the library, lookin' with new eyes at books—an' lookin' at new books, too—I've just about concluded that I ain't ben reading the right kind.

You know the books you find in cattle-camps an' fo'c's'ls ain't the same you've got in this house, for instance. Well, that's the sort of readin' matter I've ben accustomed to. And yet—an' I ain't just makin' a brag of it—I've ben different from the people I've herded with. Not that I'm any better than the sailors an' cow-punchers I travelled with,—I was cow-punchin' for a short time, you know,—but I always liked books, read everything I could lay hands on, an'—well, I guess I think differently from most of 'em.

"Now, to come to what I'm drivin' at. I was never inside a house like this. When I come a week ago, an' saw all this, an' you, an' your mother, an' brothers, an' everything—well, I liked it. I'd heard about such things an' read about such things in some of the books, an' when I looked around at your house, why, the books come true. But the thing I'm after is I liked it. I wanted it. I want it now. I want to breathe air like you get in this house—air that is filled with books, and pictures, and beautiful things, where people talk in low voices an' are clean, an' their thoughts are clean. The air I always breathed was mixed up with grub an' house-rent an' scrappin' an booze an' that's all they talked about, too. Why, when you was crossin' the room to kiss your mother, I thought it was the most beautiful thing I ever seen. I've seen a whole lot of life, an' somehow I've seen a whole lot more of it than most of them that was with me. I like to see, an' I want to see more, an' I want to see it different.

"But I ain't got to the point yet. Here it is. I want to make my way to the kind of life you have in this house. There's more in life than booze, an' hard work, an' knockin' about. Now, how am I goin' to get it? Where do I take hold an' begin? I'm willin' to work my passage, you know, an' I can make most men sick when it comes to hard work. Once I get started, I'll work night an' day. Mebbe you think it's funny, me askin' you about all this. I know you're the last person in the world I ought to ask, but I don't know anybody else I could ask—unless it's Arthur. Mebbe I ought to ask him. If I was—"

His voice died away. His firmly planned intention had come to a halt on the verge of the horrible probability that he should have asked Arthur and that he had made a fool of himself. Ruth did not speak immediately. She was too absorbed in striving to reconcile the stumbling, uncouth speech and its simplicity of thought with what she saw in his face. She had never looked in eyes that expressed greater power. Here was a man who could do anything, was the message she read there, and it accorded ill with the weakness of his spoken thought. And for that matter so complex and quick was her own mind that she did not have a just appreciation of simplicity. And yet she had caught an impression of power in the very groping of this mind. It had seemed to her like a giant writhing and straining at the bonds that held him down. Her face was all sympathy when she did speak.

"What you need, you realize yourself, and it is education. You should go back and finish grammar school, and then go through to high school and university."

"But that takes money," he interrupted.

"Oh!" she cried. "I had not thought of that. But then you have relatives, somebody who could assist you?"

He shook his head.

"My father and mother are dead. I've two sisters, one married, an' the other'll get married soon, I suppose. Then I've a string of brothers,—I'm the youngest,—but they never helped nobody. They've just knocked around over the world, lookin' out for number one. The oldest died in India. Two are in South Africa now, an' another's on a whaling voyage, an' one's travellin' with a circus—he does trapeze work. An' I guess I'm just like them. I've taken care of myself since I was eleven—that's when my mother died. I've got to study by myself, I guess, an' what I want to know is where to begin."

"I should say the first thing of all would be to get a grammar. Your grammar is—" She had intended saying "awful," but she amended it to "is not particularly good."

He flushed and sweated.

"I know I must talk a lot of slang an' words you don't understand. But then they're the only words I know—how to speak. I've got other words in my mind, picked 'em up from books, but I can't pronounce 'em, so I don't use 'em."

"It isn't what you say, so much as how you say it. You don't mind my being frank, do you? I don't want to hurt you."

"No, no," he cried, while he secretly blessed her for her kindness. "Fire away. I've got to know, an' I'd sooner know from you than anybody else."

"Well, then, you say, 'You was'; it should be, 'You were.' You say 'I seen' for 'I saw.' You use the double negative—"

"What's the double negative?" he demanded; then added humbly, "You see, I don't even understand your explanations."

"I'm afraid I didn't explain that," she smiled. "A double negative is—let me see—well, you say, 'never helped nobody.' 'Never' is a negative. 'Nobody' is another negative. It is a rule that two negatives make a positive. 'Never helped nobody' means that, not helping nobody, they must have helped somebody."

"That's pretty clear," he said. "I never thought of it before. But it don't mean they *must* have helped somebody, does it? Seems to me that 'never helped nobody' just naturally fails to say whether or not they helped somebody. I never thought of it before, and I'll never say it again."

She was pleased and surprised with the quickness and surety of his mind. As soon as he had got the clew he not only understood but corrected her error.

"You'll find it all in the grammar," she went on. "There's something else I noticed in your speech. You say 'don't' when you shouldn't. 'Don't' is a contraction and stands for two words. Do you know them?"

He thought a moment, then answered, "'Do not.'"

She nodded her head, and said, "And you use 'don't' when you mean 'does not.'"

He was puzzled over this, and did not get it so quickly.

"Give me an illustration," he asked.

"Well—" She puckered her brows and pursed up her mouth as she thought, while he looked on and decided that her expression was most adorable. "'It don't do to be hasty.' Change 'don't' to 'do not,' and it reads, 'It do not do to be hasty,' which is perfectly absurd."

He turned it over in his mind and considered.

"Doesn't it jar on your ear?" she suggested.

"Can't say that it does," he replied judicially.

"Why didn't you say, 'Can't say that it do'?" she queried.

"That sounds wrong," he said slowly. "As for the other I can't make up my mind. I guess my ear ain't had the trainin' yours has."

"There is no such word as 'ain't,'" she said, prettily emphatic.

Martin flushed again.

"And you say 'ben' for 'been,'" she continued; "'come' for 'came'; and the way you chop your endings is something dreadful."

"How do you mean?" He leaned forward, feeling that he ought to get down on his knees before so marvellous a mind. "How do I chop?"

"You don't complete the endings. 'A-n-d' spells 'and.' You pronounce it 'an'.' 'I-n-g' spells 'ing.' Sometimes you pronounce it 'ing' and sometimes you leave off the 'g.' And then you slur by dropping initial letters and diphthongs. 'T-h-e-m' spells 'them.' You pronounce it—oh, well, it is not necessary to go over all of them. What you need is the grammar. I'll get one and show you how to begin."

As she arose, there shot through his mind something that he had read in the etiquette books, and he stood up awkwardly, worrying as to whether he was doing the right thing, and fearing that she might take it as a sign that he was about to go.

"By the way, Mr. Eden," she called back, as she was leaving the room. "What is *booze*? You used it several times, you know."

"Oh, booze," he laughed. "It's slang. It means whiskey an' beer—anything that will make you drunk."

"And another thing," she laughed back. "Don't use 'you' when you are impersonal. 'You' is very personal, and your use of it just now was not precisely what you meant."

"I don't just see that."

"Why, you said just now, to me, 'whiskey and beer—anything that will make you drunk'—make me drunk, don't you see?"

"Well, it would, wouldn't it?"

"Yes, of course," she smiled. "But it would be nicer not to bring me into it. Substitute 'one' for 'you' and see how much better it sounds."

When she returned with the grammar, she drew a chair near his—he wondered if he should have helped her with the chair—and sat down beside him. She turned the pages of the grammar, and their heads were inclined toward each other. He could hardly follow her outlining of the work he must do, so amazed was he by her delightful propinquity. But when she began to lay down the importance of conjugation, he forgot all about her. He had never heard of conjugation, and was fascinated by the glimpse he was catching into the tie-ribs of language. He leaned closer to the page, and her hair touched his cheek. He had fainted but once in his life, and he thought he was going to faint again. He could scarcely breathe, and his heart was pounding the blood up into his throat and suffocating him. Never had she seemed so accessible as now. For the moment the great gulf that separated them was bridged. But there was no diminution in the loftiness of his feeling for her. She had not descended to him. It was he who had been caught up into the clouds and carried to her. His reverence for her, in that moment, was of the same order as religious awe and fervor. It seemed to him that he had intruded upon the holy of holies, and slowly and carefully he moved his head aside from the contact which thrilled him like an electric shock and of which she had not been aware.

CHAPTER VIII

Several weeks went by, during which Martin Eden studied his grammar, reviewed the books on etiquette, and read voraciously the books that caught his fancy. Of his own class he saw nothing. The girls of the Lotus Club wondered what had become of him and worried Jim with questions, and some of the fellows who put on the glove at Riley's were glad that Martin came no more. He made another discovery of treasure-trove in the library. As the grammar had shown him the tie-ribs of language, so that book showed him the tie-ribs of poetry, and he began to learn metre and construction and form, beneath the beauty he loved finding the why and wherefore of that beauty. Another modern book he found treated poetry as a representative art, treated it exhaustively, with copious illustrations from the best in literature. Never had he read fiction with so keen zest as he studied these books. And his fresh mind, untaxed for twenty years and impelled by maturity of desire, gripped hold of what he read with a virility unusual to the student mind.

When he looked back now from his vantage-ground, the old world he had known, the world of land and sea and ships, of sailor-men and harpy-women, seemed a very small world; and yet it blended in with this new world and expanded. His mind made for unity, and he was surprised when at first he began to see points of contact between the two worlds. And he was ennobled, as well, by the loftiness of thought and beauty he found in the books. This led him to believe more firmly than ever that up above him, in society like Ruth and her family, all men and women thought these thoughts and lived them. Down below where he lived was the ignoble, and he wanted to purge himself of the ignoble that had soiled all his days, and to rise to that sublimated realm where dwelt the upper classes. All his childhood and youth had been troubled by a vague unrest; he had never known what he wanted, but he had wanted something that he had hunted vainly for until he met Ruth. And now his unrest had become sharp and painful, and he knew at last, clearly and definitely, that it was beauty, and intellect, and love that he must have.

During those several weeks he saw Ruth half a dozen times, and each time was an added inspiration. She helped him with his English, corrected his pronunciation, and started him on arithmetic. But their intercourse was not all devoted to elementary study. He had seen too much of life, and his mind was too matured, to be wholly content with fractions, cube root, parsing, and analysis; and there were times when their conversation turned on other themes—the last poetry he had read, the latest poet she had studied. And when she read aloud to him her favorite passages, he ascended to the topmost heaven of delight. Never, in all the women he had heard speak, had he heard a voice like hers. The least sound of it was a stimulus to his love, and he thrilled and throbbed with every word she uttered. It was the quality of it, the repose, and the musical modulation—the soft, rich, indefinable product of culture and a gentle soul. As he listened to her, there rang in the ears of his memory the harsh cries of barbarian women and of hags, and, in lesser degrees of harshness, the strident voices of working women and of the girls of his own class. Then the chemistry of vision would begin to work, and they would troop in review across his mind, each, by contrast, multiplying Ruth's glories. Then, too, his bliss was heightened by the knowledge that her mind was comprehending what she read and was quivering with appreciation of the beauty of the written thought. She read to him much from "The Princess," and often he saw her eyes swimming with tears, so finely was her aesthetic nature strung. At such moments her own emotions elevated him till he was as a god, and, as he gazed at her and listened, he seemed gazing on the face of life and reading its deepest secrets. And then, becoming aware of the heights of exquisite sensibility he attained, he decided that this was love and that love was the greatest thing in the world. And in review would pass along the corridors of memory all previous thrills and burnings he had known,—the drunkenness of wine, the caresses of women, the rough play and give and take of physical contests,—and they seemed trivial and mean compared with this sublime ardor he now enjoyed.

The situation was obscured to Ruth. She had never had any experiences of the heart. Her only experiences in such matters were of the books, where the facts of ordinary day were translated by fancy into a fairy realm of unreality; and she little knew that this rough sailor was creeping into her heart and storing there pent forces that would some day burst forth and surge through her in waves of fire. She did not know the actual fire of love. Her knowledge of love was purely theoretical, and she conceived of it as lambent flame, gentle as the fall of dew or the ripple of quiet water, and cool as the velvet-dark of summer nights. Her idea of love was more that of placid affection, serving the loved one softly in an atmosphere, flower-scented and dim-lighted, of ethereal calm. She did not dream of the volcanic convulsions of love, its scorching heat and sterile wastes of parched ashes. She knew neither her own potencies, nor the potencies of the world; and the deeps of life were to her seas of illusion. The conjugal affection of her father and mother constituted her ideal of love-affinity, and she looked forward some day to emerging, without shock or friction, into that same quiet sweetness of existence with a loved one.

So it was that she looked upon Martin Eden as a novelty, a strange individual, and she identified with novelty and strangeness the effects he produced upon her. It was only natural. In similar ways she had experienced unusual feelings when she looked at wild animals in the menagerie, or when she witnessed a storm of wind, or shuddered at the bright-ribbed lightning. There was something cosmic in such things, and there was something cosmic in him. He came to her breathing of large airs and great spaces. The blaze of tropic suns was in his face, and in his swelling, resilient muscles was the primordial vigor of life. He was marred and scarred by that mysterious world of rough men and rougher deeds, the outposts of which began beyond her horizon. He was untamed, wild, and in secret ways her vanity was touched by the fact that he came so mildly to her hand. Likewise she was stirred by the common impulse to tame the wild thing. It was an unconscious impulse, and farthest from her thoughts that her desire was to re-thumb the clay of him into a likeness of her father's image, which image she believed to be the finest in the world. Nor was there any way, out of her inexperience, for her to know that the cosmic feel she caught of him was that most cosmic of things, love, which with equal power drew men and women together across the world, compelled stags to kill each other in the rutting season, and drove even the elements irresistibly to unite.

His swift development was a source of surprise and interest. She detected unguessed finenesses in him that seemed to bud, day by day, like flowers in congenial soil. She read Browning aloud to him, and was often puzzled by the strange interpretations he gave to mooted passages. It was beyond her to realize that, out of his experience of men and women and life, his interpretations were far more frequently correct than hers. His conceptions seemed naive to her, though she was often fired by his daring flights of comprehension, whose orbit-path was so wide among the stars that she could not follow and could only sit and thrill to the impact of unguessed power. Then she played to him—no longer at him—and probed him with music that sank to depths beyond her plumb-line. His nature opened to music as a flower to the sun, and the transition was quick from his working-class rag-time and jingles to her classical display pieces that she knew nearly by heart. Yet he betrayed a democratic fondness for Wagner, and the "Tannhäuser" overture, when she had given him the clew to it, claimed him as nothing else she played. In an immediate way it personified his life. All his past was the *Venusburg* motif, while her he identified somehow with the *Pilgrim's Chorus* motif; and from the exalted state this elevated him to, he swept onward and upward into that vast shadow-realm of spirit-groping, where good and evil war eternally.

Sometimes he questioned, and induced in her mind temporary doubts as to the correctness of her own definitions and conceptions of music. But her singing he did not question. It was too wholly her, and he sat always amazed at the divine melody of her pure soprano voice. And he could not help but contrast it with the weak pipings and shrill quaverings of factory girls, ill-nourished and untrained, and with the raucous shriekings from gin-cracked throats of the women of the seaport towns. She enjoyed singing and playing to him. In truth, it was the first time she had ever had a human soul to play with, and the plastic clay of him was a delight to mould; for she thought she was moulding it, and her intentions were good. Besides, it was pleasant to be with him. He did not repel her. That first repulsion had been really a fear of her undiscovered self, and the fear had gone to sleep. Though she did not know it, she had a feeling in him of proprietary right. Also, he had a tonic effect upon her. She was studying hard at the university, and it seemed to strengthen her to emerge from the dusty books and have the fresh sea-breeze of his personality blow upon her. Strength! Strength was what she needed, and he gave it to her in generous measure. To come into the same room with him, or to meet him at the door, was to take heart of life. And when he had gone, she would return to her books with a keener zest and fresh store of energy.

She knew her Browning, but it had never sunk into her that it was an awkward thing to play with souls. As her interest in Martin increased, the remodelling of his life became a passion with her.

"There is Mr. Butler," she said one afternoon, when grammar and arithmetic and poetry had been put aside.

"He had comparatively no advantages at first. His father had been a bank cashier, but he lingered for years, dying of consumption in Arizona, so that when he was dead, Mr. Butler, Charles Butler he was called, found himself alone in the world. His father had come from Australia, you know, and so he had no relatives in California. He went to work in a printing-office,—I have heard him tell of it many times,—and he got three dollars a week, at first. His income to-day is at least thirty thousand a year. How did he do it? He was honest, and faithful, and industrious, and economical. He denied himself the enjoyments that most boys indulge in. He made it a point to save so much every week, no matter what he had to do without in order to save it. Of course, he was soon earning more than three dollars a week, and as his wages increased he saved more and more.

"He worked in the daytime, and at night he went to night school. He had his eyes fixed always on the future. Later on he went to night high school. When he was only seventeen, he was earning excellent wages at setting type, but he was ambitious. He wanted a career, not a livelihood, and he was content to make immediate sacrifices for his ultimate again. He decided upon the law, and he entered father's office as an office boy—think of that!—and got only four dollars a week. But he had learned how to be economical, and out of that four dollars he went on saving money."

She paused for breath, and to note how Martin was receiving it. His face was lighted up with interest in the youthful struggles of Mr. Butler; but there was a frown upon his face as well.

"I'd say they was pretty hard lines for a young fellow," he remarked. "Four dollars a week! How could he live on it? You can bet he didn't have any frills. Why, I pay five dollars a week for board now, an' there's nothin' excitin' about it, you can lay to that. He must have lived like a dog. The food he ate—"

"He cooked for himself," she interrupted, "on a little kerosene stove."

"The food he ate must have been worse than what a sailor gets on the worst-feedin' deep-water ships, than which there ain't much that can be possibly worse."

"But think of him now!" she cried enthusiastically. "Think of what his income affords him. His early denials are paid for a thousand-fold."

Martin looked at her sharply.

"There's one thing I'll bet you," he said, "and it is that Mr. Butler is nothin' gay-hearted now in his fat days. He fed himself like that for years an' years, on a boy's stomach, an' I bet his stomach's none too good now for it."

Her eyes dropped before his searching gaze.

"I'll bet he's got dyspepsia right now!" Martin challenged.

"Yes, he has," she confessed; "but—"

"An' I bet," Martin dashed on, "that he's solemn an' serious as an old owl, an' doesn't care a rap for a good time, for all his thirty thousand a year. An' I'll bet he's not particularly joyful at seein' others have a good time. Ain't I right?"

She nodded her head in agreement, and hastened to explain:-

"But he is not that type of man. By nature he is sober and serious. He always was that."

"You can bet he was," Martin proclaimed. "Three dollars a week, an' four dollars a week, an' a young boy cookin' for himself on an oil-burner an' layin' up money, workin' all day an' studyin' all night, just workin' an' never playin', never havin' a good time, an' never learnin' how to have a good time—of course his thirty thousand came along too late."

His sympathetic imagination was flashing upon his inner sight all the thousands of details of the boy's existence and of his narrow spiritual development into a thirty-thousand-dollar-a-year man. With the swiftness and wide-reaching of multitudinous thought Charles Butler's whole life was telescoped upon his vision.

"Do you know," he added, "I feel sorry for Mr. Butler. He was too young to know better, but he robbed himself of life for the sake of thirty thousand a year that's clean wasted upon him. Why, thirty thousand, lump sum, wouldn't buy for him right now what ten cents he was layin' up would have bought him, when he was a kid, in the way of candy an' peanuts or a seat in nigger heaven."

It was just such uniqueness of points of view that startled Ruth. Not only were they new to her, and contrary to her own beliefs, but she always felt in them germs of truth that threatened to unseat or modify her own convictions. Had she been fourteen instead of twenty-four, she might have been changed by them; but she was twenty-four, conservative by nature and upbringing, and already crystallized into the cranny of life where she had been born and formed. It was true, his bizarre judgments troubled her in the moments they were uttered, but she ascribed them to his novelty of type and strangeness of living, and they were soon forgotten. Nevertheless, while she disapproved of them, the strength of their utterance, and the flashing of eyes and earnestness of face that accompanied them, always thrilled her and drew her toward him. She would never have guessed that this man who had come from beyond her horizon, was, in such moments, flashing on beyond her horizon with wider and deeper concepts. Her own limits were the limits of her horizon; but limited minds can recognize limitations only in others. And so she felt that her outlook was very wide indeed, and that where his conflicted with hers marked his limitations; and she dreamed of helping him to see as she saw, of widening his horizon until it was identified with hers.

"But I have not finished my story," she said. "He worked, so father says, as no other office boy he ever had. Mr. Butler was always eager to work. He never was late, and he was usually at the office a few minutes before his regular time. And yet he saved his time. Every spare moment was devoted to study. He studied book-keeping and type-writing, and he paid for lessons in shorthand by dictating at night to a court reporter who needed practice. He quickly became a clerk, and he made himself invaluable. Father appreciated him and saw that he was bound to rise. It was on father's suggestion that he went to law college. He became a lawyer, and hardly was he back in the office when father took him in as junior partner. He is a great man. He refused the United States Senate several times, and father says he could become a justice of the Supreme Court any time a vacancy occurs, if he wants to. Such a life is an inspiration to all of us. It shows us that a man with will may rise superior to his environment."

"He is a great man," Martin said sincerely.

But it seemed to him there was something in the recital that jarred upon his sense of beauty and life. He could not find an adequate motive in Mr. Butler's life of pinching and privation. Had he done it for love of a woman, or for attainment of beauty, Martin would have understood. God's own mad lover should do anything for the kiss, but not for thirty thousand dollars a year. He was dissatisfied with Mr. Butler's career. There was something paltry about it, after all. Thirty thousand a year was all right, but dyspepsia and inability to be humanly happy robbed such princely income of all its value.

Much of this he strove to express to Ruth, and shocked her and made it clear that more remodelling was necessary. Hers was that common insularity of mind that makes human creatures believe that their color, creed, and politics are best and right and that other human creatures scattered over the world are less fortunately placed than they. It was the same insularity of mind that made the ancient Jew thank God he was not born a woman, and sent the modern missionary god-substituting to the ends of the earth; and it made Ruth desire to shape this man from other crannies of life into the likeness of the men who lived in her particular cranny of life.

CHAPTER IX

Back from sea Martin Eden came, homing for California with a lover's desire. His store of money exhausted, he had shipped before the mast on the treasure-hunting schooner; and the Solomon Islands, after eight months of failure to find treasure, had witnessed the breaking up of the expedition. The men had been paid off in Australia, and Martin had immediately shipped on a deep-water vessel for San Francisco. Not alone had those eight months earned him enough money to stay on land for many weeks, but they had enabled him to do a great deal of studying and reading.

His was the student's mind, and behind his ability to learn was the indomitability of his nature and his love for Ruth. The grammar he had taken along he went through again and again until his unjaded brain had mastered it. He noticed the bad grammar used by his shipmates, and made a point of mentally correcting and reconstructing their crudities of speech. To his great joy he discovered that his ear was becoming sensitive and that he was developing grammatical nerves. A double negative jarred him like a discord, and often, from lack of practice, it was from his own lips that the jar came. His tongue refused to learn new tricks in a day.

After he had been through the grammar repeatedly, he took up the dictionary and added twenty words a day to his vocabulary. He found that this was no light task, and at wheel or lookout he steadily went over and over his lengthening list of pronunciations and definitions, while he invariably memorized himself to sleep. "Never did anything," "if I were," and "those things," were phrases, with many variations, that he repeated under his breath in order to accustom his tongue to the language spoken by Ruth. "And" and "ing," with the "d" and "g" pronounced emphatically, he went over thousands of times; and to his surprise he noticed that he was beginning to speak cleaner and more correct English than the officers themselves and the gentleman-adventurers in the cabin who had financed the expedition.

The captain was a fishy-eyed Norwegian who somehow had fallen into possession of a complete Shakespeare, which he never read, and Martin had washed his clothes for him and in return been permitted access to the precious volumes. For a time, so steeped was he in the plays and in the many favorite passages that impressed themselves almost without effort on his brain, that all the world seemed to shape itself into forms of Elizabethan tragedy or comedy and his very thoughts were in blank verse. It trained his ear and gave him a fine appreciation for noble English; withal it introduced into his mind much that was archaic and obsolete.

The eight months had been well spent, and, in addition to what he had learned of right speaking and high thinking, he had learned much of himself. Along with his humbleness because he knew so little, there arose a conviction of power. He felt a sharp gradation between himself and his shipmates, and was wise enough to realize that the difference lay in potentiality rather than achievement. What he could do,—they could do; but within him he felt a confused ferment working that told him there was more in him than he had done. He was tortured by the exquisite beauty of the world, and wished that Ruth were there to share it with him. He decided that he would describe to her many of the bits of South Sea beauty. The creative spirit in him flamed up at the thought and urged that he recreate this beauty for a wider audience than Ruth. And then, in splendor and glory, came the great idea. He would write. He would be one of the eyes through which the world saw, one of the ears through which it heard, one of the hearts through which it felt. He would write—everything—poetry and prose, fiction and description, and plays like Shakespeare. There was career and the way to win to Ruth. The men of literature were the world's giants, and he conceived them to be far finer than the Mr. Butlers who earned thirty thousand a year and could be Supreme Court justices if they wanted to.

Once the idea had germinated, it mastered him, and the return voyage to San Francisco was like a dream. He was drunken with unguessed power and felt that he could do anything. In the midst of the great and lonely sea he gained perspective. Clearly, and for the first lime, he saw Ruth and her world. It was all visualized in his mind as a concrete thing which he could take up in his two hands and turn around and about and examine. There was much that was dim and nebulous in that world, but he saw it as a whole and not in detail, and he saw, also, the way to master it. To write! The thought was fire in him. He would begin as soon as he got back. The first thing he would do would be to describe the voyage of the treasure-hunters. He would sell it to some San Francisco newspaper. He would not tell Ruth anything about it, and she would be surprised and pleased when she saw his name in print. While he wrote, he could go on studying. There were twenty-four hours in each day. He was invincible. He knew how to work, and the citadels would go down before him. He would not have to go to sea again—as a sailor; and for the instant he caught a vision of a steam yacht. There were other writers who possessed steam yachts. Of course, he cautioned himself, it would be slow succeeding at first, and for a time he would be content to earn enough money by his writing to enable him to go on studying. And then, after some time,—a very indeterminate time,—when he had learned and prepared himself, he would write the great things and his name would be on all men's lips. But greater than that, infinitely greater and greatest of all, he would have proved himself worthy of Ruth. Fame was all very well, but it was for Ruth that his splendid dream arose. He was not a fame-monger, but merely one of God's mad lovers.

Arrived in Oakland, with his snug pay-day in his pocket, he took up his old room at Bernard Higginbotham's and set to work. He did not even let Ruth know he was back. He would go and see her when he finished the article on the treasure-hunters. It was not so difficult to abstain from seeing her, because of the violent heat of creative fever that burned in him. Besides, the very article he was writing would bring her nearer to him. He did not know how long an article he should write, but he counted the words in a double-page article in the Sunday supplement of the *San Francisco Examiner*, and guided himself by that. Three days, at white heat, completed his narrative; but when he had copied it carefully, in a large scrawl that was easy to read, he learned from a rhetoric he picked up in the library that there were such things as paragraphs and quotation marks. He had never thought of such things before; and he promptly set to work writing the article over, referring continually to the pages of the rhetoric and learning more in a day about composition than the average schoolboy in a year. When he had copied the article a second time and rolled it up carefully, he read in a newspaper an item on hints to beginners, and discovered the iron law that manuscripts should never be rolled and that they should be written on one side of the paper. He had violated the law on both counts. Also, he learned from the item that first-class papers paid a minimum of ten dollars a column. So, while he copied the manuscript a third time, he consoled himself by multiplying ten columns by ten dollars. The product was always the same, one hundred dollars, and he decided that that was better than seafaring. If it hadn't been for his blunders, he would have finished the article in three days. One hundred dollars in three days! It would have taken him three months and longer on the sea to earn a similar amount. A man was a fool to go to sea when he could write, he concluded, though the money in itself meant nothing to him. Its value was in the liberty it would get him, the presentable garments it would buy him, all of which would bring him nearer, swiftly nearer, to the slender, pale girl who had turned his life back upon itself and given him inspiration.

He mailed the manuscript in a flat envelope, and addressed it to the editor of the *San Francisco Examiner*. He had an idea that anything accepted by a paper was published immediately, and as he had sent the manuscript in on Friday he expected it to come out on the following Sunday. He conceived that it would be fine to let that event apprise Ruth of his return. Then, Sunday afternoon, he would call and see her. In the meantime he was occupied by another idea, which he prided himself upon as being a particularly sane, careful, and modest idea. He would write an adventure story for boys and sell it to *The Youth's Companion*. He went to the free reading-room and looked through the files of *The Youth's Companion*. Serial stories, he found, were usually published in that weekly in five instalments of about three thousand words each. He discovered several serials that ran to seven instalments, and decided to write one of that length.

He had been on a whaling voyage in the Arctic, once—a voyage that was to have been for three years and which had terminated in shipwreck at the end of six months. While his imagination was fanciful, even fantastic at times, he had a basic love of reality that compelled him to write about the things he knew. He knew whaling, and out of the real materials of his knowledge he proceeded to manufacture the fictitious adventures of the two boys he intended to use as joint heroes. It was easy work, he decided on Saturday evening. He had completed on that day the first instalment of three thousand words—much to the amusement of Jim, and to the open derision of Mr. Higginbotham, who sneered throughout meal-time at the "litery" person they had discovered in the family.

Martin contented himself by picturing his brother-in-law's surprise on Sunday morning when he opened his *Examiner* and saw the article on the treasure-hunters. Early that morning he was out himself to the front door, nervously racing through the many-sheeted newspaper. He went through it a second time, very carefully, then folded it up and left it where he had found it. He was glad he had not told any one about his article. On second thought he concluded that he had been wrong about the speed with which things found their way into newspaper columns. Besides, there had not been any news value in his article, and most likely the editor would write to him about it first.

After breakfast he went on with his serial. The words flowed from his pen, though he broke off from the writing frequently to look up definitions in the dictionary or to refer to the rhetoric. He often read or re-read a chapter at a time, during such pauses; and he consoled himself that while he was not writing the great things he felt to be in him, he was learning composition, at any rate, and training himself to shape up and express his thoughts. He toiled on till dark, when he went out to the reading-room and explored magazines and weeklies until the place closed at ten o'clock. This was his programme for a week. Each day he did three thousand words, and each evening he puzzled his way through the magazines, taking note of the stories, articles, and poems that editors saw fit to publish. One thing was certain: What these multitudinous writers did he could do, and only give him time and he would do what they could not do. He was cheered to read in *Book News*, in a paragraph on the payment of magazine writers, not that Rudyard Kipling received a dollar per word, but that the minimum rate paid by first-class magazines was two cents a word. *The Youth's Companion* was certainly first class, and at that rate the three thousand words he had written that day would bring him sixty dollars—two months' wages on the sea!

On Friday night he finished the serial, twenty-one thousand words long. At two cents a word, he calculated, that would bring him four hundred and twenty dollars. Not a bad week's work. It was more money than he had ever possessed at one time. He did not know how he could spend it all. He had tapped a gold mine. Where this came from he could always get more. He planned to buy some more clothes, to subscribe to many magazines, and to buy dozens of reference books that at present he was compelled to go to the library to consult. And still there was a large portion of the four hundred and twenty dollars unspent. This worried him until the thought came to him of hiring a servant for Gertrude and of buying a bicycle for Marion.

He mailed the bulky manuscript to *The Youth's Companion*, and on Saturday afternoon, after having planned an article on pearl-diving, he went to see Ruth. He had telephoned, and she went herself to greet him at the door. The old familiar blaze of health rushed out from him and struck her like a blow. It seemed to enter into her body and course through her veins in a liquid glow, and to set her quivering with its imparted strength. He flushed warmly as he took her hand and looked into her blue eyes, but the fresh bronze of eight months of sun hid the flush, though it did not protect the neck from the gnawing chafe of the stiff collar. She noted the red line of it with amusement which quickly vanished as she glanced at his clothes. They really fitted him,—it was his first made-to-order suit,—and he seemed slimmer and better modelled. In addition, his cloth cap had been replaced by a soft hat, which she commanded him to put on and then complimented him on his appearance. She did not remember when she had felt so happy. This change in him was her handiwork, and she was proud of it and fired with ambition further to help him.

But the most radical change of all, and the one that pleased her most, was the change in his speech. Not only did he speak more correctly, but he spoke more easily, and there were many new words in his vocabulary. When he grew excited or enthusiastic, however, he dropped back into the old slurring and the dropping of final consonants. Also, there was an awkward hesitancy, at times, as he essayed the new words he had learned. On the other hand, along with his ease of expression, he displayed a lightness and facetiousness of thought that delighted her. It was his old spirit of humor and badinage that had made him a favorite in his own class, but which he had hitherto been unable to use in her presence through lack of words and training. He was just beginning to orientate himself and to feel that he was not wholly an intruder. But he was very tentative, fastidiously so, letting Ruth set the pace of sprightliness and fancy, keeping up with her but never daring to go beyond her.

He told her of what he had been doing, and of his plan to write for a livelihood and of going on with his studies. But he was disappointed at her lack of approval. She did not think much of his plan.

"You see," she said frankly, "writing must be a trade, like anything else. Not that I know anything about it, of course. I only bring common judgment to bear. You couldn't hope to be a blacksmith without spending three years at learning the trade—or is it five years! Now writers are so much better paid than blacksmiths that there must be ever so many more men who would like to write, who—try to write."

"But then, may not I be peculiarly constituted to write?" he queried, secretly exulting at the language he had used, his swift imagination throwing the whole scene and atmosphere upon a vast screen along with a thousand other scenes from his life—scenes that were rough and raw, gross and bestial.

The whole composite vision was achieved with the speed of light, producing no pause in the conversation, nor interrupting his calm train of thought. On the screen of his imagination he saw himself and this sweet and beautiful girl, facing each other and conversing in good English, in a room of books and paintings and tone and culture, and all illuminated by a bright light of steadfast brilliance; while ranged about and fading away to the remote edges of the screen were antithetical scenes, each scene a picture, and he the onlooker, free to look at will upon what he wished. He saw these other scenes through drifting vapors and swirls of sullen fog dissolving before shafts of red and garish light. He saw cowboys at the bar, drinking fierce whiskey, the air filled with obscenity and ribald language, and he saw himself with them drinking and cursing with the wildest, or sitting at table with them, under smoking kerosene lamps, while the chips clicked and clattered and the cards were dealt around. He saw himself, stripped to the waist, with naked fists, fighting his great fight with Liverpool Red in the forecastle of the *Susquehanna*; and he saw the bloody deck of the *John Rogers*, that gray morning of attempted mutiny, the mate kicking in death-throes on the main-hatch, the revolver in the old man's hand spitting fire and smoke, the men with passion-wrenched faces, of brutes screaming vile blasphemies and falling about him—and then he returned to the central scene, calm and clean in the steadfast light, where Ruth sat and talked with him amid books and paintings; and he saw the grand piano upon which she would later play to him; and he heard the echoes of his own selected and correct words, "But then, may I not be peculiarly constituted to write?"

"But no matter how peculiarly constituted a man may be for blacksmithing," she was laughing, "I never heard of one becoming a blacksmith without first serving his apprenticeship."

"What would you advise?" he asked. "And don't forget that I feel in me this capacity to write—I can't explain it; I just know that it is in me."

"You must get a thorough education," was the answer, "whether or not you ultimately become a writer. This education is indispensable for whatever career you select, and it must not be slipshod or sketchy. You should go to high school."

"Yes—" he began; but she interrupted with an afterthought:-

"Of course, you could go on with your writing, too."

"I would have to," he said grimly.

"Why?" She looked at him, prettily puzzled, for she did not quite like the persistence with which he clung to his notion.

"Because, without writing there wouldn't be any high school. I must live and buy books and clothes, you know."

"I'd forgotten that," she laughed. "Why weren't you born with an income?"

"I'd rather have good health and imagination," he answered. "I can make good on the income, but the other things have to be made good for—" He almost said "you," then amended his sentence to, "have to be made good for one."

"Don't say 'make good,'" she cried, sweetly petulant. "It's slang, and it's horrid."

He flushed, and stammered, "That's right, and I only wish you'd correct me every time."

"I—I'd like to," she said haltingly. "You have so much in you that is good that I want to see you perfect."

He was clay in her hands immediately, as passionately desirous of being moulded by her as she was desirous of shaping him into the image of her ideal of man. And when she pointed out the opportuneness of the time, that the entrance examinations to high school began on the following Monday, he promptly volunteered that he would take them.

Then she played and sang to him, while he gazed with hungry yearning at her, drinking in her loveliness and marvelling that there should not be a hundred suitors listening there and longing for her as he listened and longed.

CHAPTER X

He stopped to dinner that evening, and, much to Ruth's satisfaction, made a favorable impression on her father. They talked about the sea as a career, a subject which Martin had at his finger-ends, and Mr. Morse remarked afterward that he seemed a very clear-headed young man. In his avoidance of slang and his search after right words, Martin was compelled to talk slowly, which enabled him to find the best thoughts that were in him. He was more at ease than that first night at dinner, nearly a year before, and his shyness and modesty even commended him to Mrs. Morse, who was pleased at his manifest improvement.

"He is the first man that ever drew passing notice from Ruth," she told her husband. "She has been so singularly backward where men are concerned that I have been worried greatly."

Mr. Morse looked at his wife curiously.

"You mean to use this young sailor to wake her up?" he questioned.

"I mean that she is not to die an old maid if I can help it," was the answer. "If this young Eden can arouse her interest in mankind in general, it will be a good thing."

"A very good thing," he commented. "But suppose,—and we must suppose, sometimes, my dear,—suppose he arouses her interest too particularly in him?"

"Impossible," Mrs. Morse laughed. "She is three years older than he, and, besides, it is impossible. Nothing will ever come of it. Trust that to me."

And so Martin's rôle was arranged for him, while he, led on by Arthur and Norman, was meditating an extravagance. They were going out for a ride into the hills Sunday morning on their wheels, which did not interest Martin until he learned that Ruth, too, rode a wheel and was going along. He did not ride, nor own a wheel, but if Ruth rode, it was up to him to begin, was his decision; and when he said good night, he stopped in at a cyclery on his way home and spent forty dollars for a wheel. It was more than a month's hard-earned wages, and it reduced his stock of money amazingly; but when he added the hundred dollars he was to receive from the *Examiner* to the four hundred and twenty dollars that was the least *The Youth's Companion* could pay him, he felt that he had reduced the perplexity the unwonted amount of money had caused him. Nor did he mind, in the course of learning to ride the wheel home, the fact that he ruined his suit of clothes. He caught the tailor by telephone that night from Mr. Higginbotham's store and ordered another suit. Then he carried the wheel up the narrow stairway that clung like a fire-escape to the rear wall of the building, and when he had moved his bed out from the wall, found there was just space enough in the small room for himself and the wheel.

Sunday he had intended to devote to studying for the high school examination, but the pearl-diving article lured him away, and he spent the day in the white-hot fever of re-creating the beauty and romance that burned in him. The fact that the *Examiner* of that morning had failed to publish his treasure-hunting article did not dash his spirits. He was at too great a height for that, and having been deaf to a twice-repeated summons, he went without the heavy Sunday dinner with which Mr. Higginbotham invariably graced his table. To Mr. Higginbotham such a dinner was advertisement of his worldly achievement and prosperity, and he honored it by delivering platitudinous sermonettes upon American institutions and the opportunity said institutions gave to any hard-working man to rise—the rise, in his case, which he pointed out unfailingly, being from a grocer's clerk to the ownership of Higginbotham's Cash Store.

Martin Eden looked with a sigh at his unfinished "Pearl-diving" on Monday morning, and took the car down to Oakland to the high school. And when, days later, he applied for the results of his examinations, he learned that he had failed in everything save grammar.

"Your grammar is excellent," Professor Hilton informed him, staring at him through heavy spectacles; "but you know nothing, positively nothing, in the other branches, and your United States history is abominable—there is no other word for it, abominable. I should advise you—"

Professor Hilton paused and glared at him, unsympathetic and unimaginative as one of his own test-tubes. He was professor of physics in the high school, possessor of a large family, a meagre salary, and a select fund of parrot-learned knowledge.

"Yes, sir," Martin said humbly, wishing somehow that the man at the desk in the library was in Professor Hilton's place just then.

"And I should advise you to go back to the grammar school for at least two years. Good day."

Martin was not deeply affected by his failure, though he was surprised at Ruth's shocked expression when he told her Professor Hilton's advice. Her disappointment was so evident that he was sorry he had failed, but chiefly so for her sake.

"You see I was right," she said. "You know far more than any of the students entering high school, and yet you can't pass the examinations. It is because what education you have is fragmentary, sketchy. You need the discipline of study, such as only skilled teachers can give you. You must be thoroughly grounded. Professor Hilton is right, and if I were you, I'd go to night school. A year and a half of it might enable you to catch up that additional six months. Besides, that would leave you your days in which to write, or, if you could not make your living by your pen, you would have your days in which to work in some position."

But if my days are taken up with work and my nights with school, when am I going to see you?—was Martin's first thought, though he refrained from uttering it. Instead, he said:-

"It seems so babyish for me to be going to night school. But I wouldn't mind that if I thought it would pay. But I don't think it will pay. I can do the work quicker than they can teach me. It would be a loss of time—" he thought of her and his desire to have her—"and I can't afford the time. I haven't the time to spare, in fact."

"There is so much that is necessary." She looked at him gently, and he was a brute to oppose her. "Physics and chemistry—you can't do them without laboratory study; and you'll find algebra and geometry almost hopeless with instruction. You need the skilled teachers, the specialists in the art of imparting knowledge."

He was silent for a minute, casting about for the least vainglorious way in which to express himself.

"Please don't think I'm bragging," he began. "I don't intend it that way at all. But I have a feeling that I am what I may call a natural student. I can study by myself. I take to it kindly, like a duck to water. You see yourself what I did with grammar. And I've learned much of other things—you would never dream how much. And I'm only getting started. Wait till I get—" He hesitated and assured himself of the pronunciation before he said "momentum. I'm getting my first real feel of things now. I'm beginning to size up the situation—"

"Please don't say 'size up,'" she interrupted.

"To get a line on things," he hastily amended.

"That doesn't mean anything in correct English," she objected.

He floundered for a fresh start.

"What I'm driving at is that I'm beginning to get the lay of the land."

Out of pity she forebore, and he went on.

"Knowledge seems to me like a chart-room. Whenever I go into the library, I am impressed that way. The part played by teachers is to teach the student the contents of the chart-room in a systematic way. The teachers are guides to the chart-room, that's all. It's not something that they have in their own heads. They don't make it up, don't create it. It's all in the chart-room and they know their way about in it, and it's their business to show the place to strangers who might else get lost. Now I don't get lost easily. I have the bump of location. I usually know where I'm at—What's wrong now?"

"Don't say 'where I'm at.'"

"That's right," he said gratefully, "where I am. But where am I at—I mean, where am I? Oh, yes, in the chart-room. Well, some people—"

"Persons," she corrected.

"Some persons need guides, most persons do; but I think I can get along without them. I've spent a lot of time in the chart-room now, and I'm on the edge of knowing my way about, what charts I want to refer to, what coasts I want to explore. And from the way I line it up, I'll explore a whole lot more quickly by myself. The speed of a fleet, you know, is the speed of the slowest ship, and the speed of the teachers is affected the same way. They can't go any faster than the ruck of their scholars, and I can set a faster pace for myself than they set for a whole schoolroom."

"'He travels the fastest who travels alone,'" she quoted at him.

But I'd travel faster with you just the same, was what he wanted to blurt out, as he caught a vision of a world without end of sunlit spaces and starry voids through which he drifted with her, his arm around her, her pale gold hair blowing about his face. In the same instant he was aware of the pitiful inadequacy of speech. God! If he could so frame words that she could see what he then saw! And he felt the stir in him, like a throe of yearning pain, of the desire to paint these visions that flashed unsummoned on the mirror of his mind. Ah, that was it! He caught at the hem of the secret. It was the very thing that the great writers and master-poets did. That was why they were giants. They knew how to express what they thought, and felt, and saw. Dogs asleep in the sun often whined and barked, but they were unable to tell what they saw that made them whine and bark. He had often wondered what it was. And that was all he was, a dog asleep in the sun. He saw noble and beautiful visions, but he could only whine and bark at Ruth. But he would cease sleeping in the sun. He would stand up, with open eyes, and he would struggle and toil and learn until, with eyes unblinded and tongue untied, he could share with her his visioned wealth. Other men had discovered the trick of expression, of making words obedient servitors, and of making combinations of words mean more than the sum of their separate meanings. He was stirred profoundly by the passing glimpse at the secret, and he was again caught up in the vision of sunlit spaces and starry voids—until it came to him that it was very quiet, and he saw Ruth regarding him with an amused expression and a smile in her eyes.

"I have had a great visioning," he said, and at the sound of his words in his own ears his heart gave a leap. Where had those words come from? They had adequately expressed the pause his vision had put in the conversation. It was a miracle. Never had he so loftily framed a lofty thought. But never had he attempted to frame lofty thoughts in words. That was it. That explained it. He had never tried. But Swinburne had, and Tennyson, and Kipling, and all the other poets. His mind flashed on to his "Pearl-diving." He had never dared the big things, the spirit of the beauty that was a fire in him. That article would be a different thing when he was done with it. He was appalled by the vastness of the beauty that rightfully belonged in it, and again his mind flashed and dared, and he demanded of himself why he could not chant that beauty in noble verse as the great poets did. And there was all the mysterious delight and spiritual wonder of his love for Ruth. Why could he not chant that, too, as the poets did? They had sung of love. So would he. By God!—

And in his frightened ears he heard his exclamation echoing. Carried away, he had breathed it aloud. The blood surged into his face, wave upon wave, mastering the bronze of it till the blush of shame flaunted itself from collar-rim to the roots of his hair.

"I—I—beg your pardon," he stammered. "I was thinking."

"It sounded as if you were praying," she said bravely, but she felt herself inside to be withering and shrinking. It was the first time she had heard an oath from the lips of a man she knew, and she was shocked, not merely as a matter of principle and training, but shocked in spirit by this rough blast of life in the garden of her sheltered maidenhood.

But she forgave, and with surprise at the ease of her forgiveness. Somehow it was not so difficult to forgive him anything. He had not had a chance to be as other men, and he was trying so hard, and succeeding, too. It never entered her head that there could be any other reason for her being kindly disposed toward him. She was tenderly disposed toward him, but she did not know it. She had no way of knowing it. The placid poise of twenty-four years without a single love affair did not fit her with a keen perception of her own feelings, and she who had never warmed to actual love was unaware that she was warming now.

CHAPTER XI

Martin went back to his pearl-diving article, which would have been finished sooner if it had not been broken in upon so frequently by his attempts to write poetry. His poems were love poems, inspired by Ruth, but they were never completed. Not in a day could he learn to chant in noble verse. Rhyme and metre and structure were serious enough in themselves, but there was, over and beyond them, an intangible and evasive something that he caught in all great poetry, but which he could not catch and imprison in his own. It was the elusive spirit of poetry itself that he sensed and sought after but could not capture. It seemed a glow to him, a warm and trailing vapor, ever beyond his reaching, though sometimes he was rewarded by catching at shreds of it and weaving them into phrases that echoed in his brain with haunting notes or drifted across his vision in misty wafture of unseen beauty. It was baffling. He ached with desire to express and could but gibber prosaically as everybody gibbered. He read his fragments aloud. The metre marched along on perfect feet, and the rhyme pounded a longer and equally faultless rhythm, but the glow and high exaltation that he felt within were lacking. He could not understand, and time and again, in despair, defeated and depressed, he returned to his article. Prose was certainly an easier medium.

Following the "Pearl-diving," he wrote an article on the sea as a career, another on turtle-catching, and a third on the northeast trades. Then he tried, as an experiment, a short story, and before he broke his stride he had finished six short stories and despatched them to various magazines. He wrote prolifically, intensely, from morning till night, and late at night, except when he broke off to go to the reading-room, draw books from the library, or to call on Ruth. He was profoundly happy. Life was pitched high. He was in a fever that never broke. The joy of creation that is supposed to belong to the gods was his. All the life about him—the odors of stale vegetables and soapsuds, the slatternly form of his sister, and the jeering face of Mr. Higginbotham—was a dream. The real world was in his mind, and the stories he wrote were so many pieces of reality out of his mind.

The days were too short. There was so much he wanted to study. He cut his sleep down to five hours and found that he could get along upon it. He tried four hours and a half, and regretfully came back to five. He could joyfully have spent all his waking hours upon any one of his pursuits. It was with regret that he ceased from writing to study, that he ceased from study to go to the library, that he tore himself away from that chart-room of knowledge or from the magazines in the reading-room that were filled with the secrets of writers who succeeded in selling their wares. It was like severing heart strings, when he was with Ruth, to stand up and go; and he scorched through the dark streets so as to get home to his books at the least possible expense of time. And hardest of all was it to shut up the algebra or physics, put note-book and pencil aside, and close his tired eyes in sleep. He hated the thought of ceasing to live, even for so short a time, and his sole consolation was that the alarm clock was set five hours ahead. He would lose only five hours anyway, and then the jangling bell would jerk him out of unconsciousness and he would have before him another glorious day of nineteen hours.

In the meantime the weeks were passing, his money was ebbing low, and there was no money coming in. A month after he had mailed it, the adventure serial for boys was returned to him by *The Youth's Companion.* The rejection slip was so tactfully worded that he felt kindly toward the editor. But he did not feel so kindly toward the editor of the *San Francisco Examiner.* After waiting two whole weeks, Martin had written to him. A week later he wrote again. At the end of the month, he went over to San Francisco and personally called upon the editor. But he did not meet that exalted personage, thanks to a Cerberus of an office boy, of tender years and red hair, who guarded the portals. At the end of the fifth week the manuscript came back to him, by mail, without comment. There was no rejection slip, no explanation, nothing. In the same way his other articles were tied up with the other leading San Francisco papers. When he recovered them, he sent them to the magazines in the East, from which they were returned more promptly, accompanied always by the printed rejection slips.

The short stories were returned in similar fashion. He read them over and over, and liked them so much that he could not puzzle out the cause of their rejection, until, one day, he read in a newspaper that manuscripts should always be typewritten. That explained it. Of course editors were so busy that they could not afford the time and strain of reading handwriting. Martin rented a typewriter and spent a day mastering the machine. Each day he typed what he composed, and he typed his earlier manuscripts as fast as they were returned him. He was surprised when the typed ones began to come back. His jaw seemed to become squarer, his chin more aggressive, and he bundled the manuscripts off to new editors.

The thought came to him that he was not a good judge of his own work. He tried it out on Gertrude. He read his stories aloud to her. Her eyes glistened, and she looked at him proudly as she said:-

"Ain't it grand, you writin' those sort of things."

"Yes, yes," he demanded impatiently. "But the story—how did you like it?"

"Just grand," was the reply. "Just grand, an' thrilling, too. I was all worked up."

He could see that her mind was not clear. The perplexity was strong in her good-natured face. So he waited.

"But, say, Mart," after a long pause, "how did it end? Did that young man who spoke so highfalutin' get her?"

And, after he had explained the end, which he thought he had made artistically obvious, she would say:-

"That's what I wanted to know. Why didn't you write that way in the story?"

One thing he learned, after he had read her a number of stories, namely, that she liked happy endings.

CHAPTER XI

"That story was perfectly grand," she announced, straightening up from the wash-tub with a tired sigh and wiping the sweat from her forehead with a red, steamy hand; "but it makes me sad. I want to cry. There is too many sad things in the world any-way. It makes me happy to think about happy things. Now if he'd married her, and—You don't mind, Mart?" she queried apprehensively. "I just happen to feel that way, because I'm tired, I guess. But the story was grand just the same, perfectly grand. Where are you goin' to sell it?"

"That's a horse of another color," he laughed.

"But if you *did* sell it, what do you think you'd get for it?"

"Oh, a hundred dollars. That would be the least, the way prices go."

"My! I do hope you'll sell it!"

"Easy money, eh?" Then he added proudly: "I wrote it in two days. That's fifty dollars a day."

He longed to read his stories to Ruth, but did not dare. He would wait till some were published, he decided, then she would understand what he had been working for. In the meantime he toiled on. Never had the spirit of adventure lured him more strongly than on this amazing exploration of the realm of mind. He bought the text-books on physics and chemistry, and, along with his algebra, worked out problems and demonstrations. He took the laboratory proofs on faith, and his intense power of vision enabled him to see the reactions of chemicals more understandingly than the average student saw them in the laboratory. Martin wandered on through the heavy pages, overwhelmed by the clews he was getting to the nature of things. He had accepted the world as the world, but now he was comprehending the organization of it, the play and interplay of force and matter. Spontaneous explanations of old matters were continually arising in his mind. Levers and purchases fascinated him, and his mind roved backward to hand-spikes and blocks and tackles at sea. The theory of navigation, which enabled the ships to travel unerringly their courses over the pathless ocean, was made clear to him. The mysteries of storm, and rain, and tide were revealed, and the reason for the existence of trade-winds made him wonder whether he had written his article on the northeast trade too soon. At any rate he knew he could write it better now. One afternoon he went out with Arthur to the University of California, and, with bated breath and a feeling of religious awe, went through the laboratories, saw demonstrations, and listened to a physics professor lecturing to his classes.

But he did not neglect his writing. A stream of short stories flowed from his pen, and he branched out into the easier forms of verse—the kind he saw printed in the magazines—though he lost his head and wasted two weeks on a tragedy in blank verse, the swift rejection of which, by half a dozen magazines, dumfounded him. Then he discovered Henley and wrote a series of sea-poems on the model of "Hospital Sketches." They were simple poems, of light and color, and romance and adventure. "Sea Lyrics," he called them, and he judged them to be the best work he had yet done. There were thirty, and he completed them in a month, doing one a day after having done his regular day's work on fiction, which day's work was the equivalent to a week's work of the average successful writer. The toil meant nothing to him. It was not toil. He was finding speech, and all the beauty and wonder that had been pent for years behind his inarticulate lips was now pouring forth in a wild and virile flood.

He showed the "Sea Lyrics" to no one, not even to the editors. He had become distrustful of editors. But it was not distrust that prevented him from submitting the "Lyrics." They were so beautiful to him that he was impelled to save them to share with Ruth in some glorious, far-off time when he would dare to read to her what he had written. Against that time he kept them with him, reading them aloud, going over them until he knew them by heart.

He lived every moment of his waking hours, and he lived in his sleep, his subjective mind rioting through his five hours of surcease and combining the thoughts and events of the day into grotesque and impossible marvels. In reality, he never rested, and a weaker body or a less firmly poised brain would have been prostrated in a general break-down. His late afternoon calls on Ruth were rarer now, for June was approaching, when she would take her degree and finish with the university. Bachelor of Arts!—when he thought of her degree, it seemed she fled beyond him faster than he could pursue.

One afternoon a week she gave to him, and arriving late, he usually stayed for dinner and for music afterward. Those were his red-letter days. The atmosphere of the house, in such contrast with that in which he lived, and the mere nearness to her, sent him forth each time with a firmer grip on his resolve to climb the heights. In spite of the beauty in him, and the aching desire to create, it was for her that he struggled. He was a lover first and always. All other things he subordinated to love.

Greater than his adventure in the world of thought was his love-adventure. The world itself was not so amazing because of the atoms and molecules that composed it according to the propulsions of irresistible force; what made it amazing was the fact that Ruth lived in it. She was the most amazing thing he had ever known, or dreamed, or guessed.

But he was oppressed always by her remoteness. She was so far from him, and he did not know how to approach her. He had been a success with girls and women in his own class; but he had never loved any of them, while he did love her, and besides, she was not merely of another class. His very love elevated her above all classes. She was a being apart, so far apart that he did not know how to draw near to her as a lover should draw near. It was true, as he acquired knowledge and language, that he was drawing nearer, talking her speech, discovering ideas and delights in common; but this did not satisfy his lover's yearning. His lover's imagination had made her holy, too holy, too spiritualized, to have any kinship with him in the flesh. It was his own love that thrust her from him and made her seem impossible for him. Love itself denied him the one thing that it desired.

And then, one day, without warning, the gulf between them was bridged for a moment, and thereafter, though the gulf remained, it was ever narrower. They had been eating cherries—great, luscious, black cherries with a juice of the color of dark wine. And later, as she read aloud to him from "The Princess," he chanced to notice the stain of the cherries on her lips. For the moment her divinity was shattered. She was clay, after all, mere clay, subject to the common law of clay as his clay was subject, or anybody's clay. Her lips were flesh like his, and cherries dyed them as cherries dyed his. And if so with her lips, then was it so with all of her. She was woman, all woman, just like any woman. It came upon him abruptly. It was a revelation that stunned him. It was as if he had seen the sun fall out of the sky, or had seen worshipped purity polluted.

CHAPTER XI

Then he realized the significance of it, and his heart began pounding and challenging him to play the lover with this woman who was not a spirit from other worlds but a mere woman with lips a cherry could stain. He trembled at the audacity of his thought; but all his soul was singing, and reason, in a triumphant paean, assured him he was right. Something of this change in him must have reached her, for she paused from her reading, looked up at him, and smiled. His eyes dropped from her blue eyes to her lips, and the sight of the stain maddened him. His arms all but flashed out to her and around her, in the way of his old careless life. She seemed to lean toward him, to wait, and all his will fought to hold him back.

"You were not following a word," she pouted.

Then she laughed at him, delighting in his confusion, and as he looked into her frank eyes and knew that she had divined nothing of what he felt, he became abashed. He had indeed in thought dared too far. Of all the women he had known there was no woman who would not have guessed—save her. And she had not guessed. There was the difference. She was different. He was appalled by his own grossness, awed by her clear innocence, and he gazed again at her across the gulf. The bridge had broken down.

But still the incident had brought him nearer. The memory of it persisted, and in the moments when he was most cast down, he dwelt upon it eagerly. The gulf was never again so wide. He had accomplished a distance vastly greater than a bachelorship of arts, or a dozen bachelorships. She was pure, it was true, as he had never dreamed of purity; but cherries stained her lips. She was subject to the laws of the universe just as inexorably as he was. She had to eat to live, and when she got her feet wet, she caught cold. But that was not the point. If she could feel hunger and thirst, and heat and cold, then could she feel love—and love for a man. Well, he was a man. And why could he not be the man? "It's up to me to make good," he would murmur fervently. "I will be *the* man. I will make myself *the* man. I will make good."

CHAPTER XII

Early one evening, struggling with a sonnet that twisted all awry the beauty and thought that trailed in glow and vapor through his brain, Martin was called to the telephone.

"It's a lady's voice, a fine lady's," Mr. Higginbotham, who had called him, jeered.

Martin went to the telephone in the corner of the room, and felt a wave of warmth rush through him as he heard Ruth's voice. In his battle with the sonnet he had forgotten her existence, and at the sound of her voice his love for her smote him like a sudden blow. And such a voice!—delicate and sweet, like a strain of music heard far off and faint, or, better, like a bell of silver, a perfect tone, crystal-pure. No mere woman had a voice like that. There was something celestial about it, and it came from other worlds. He could scarcely hear what it said, so ravished was he, though he controlled his face, for he knew that Mr. Higginbotham's ferret eyes were fixed upon him.

It was not much that Ruth wanted to say—merely that Norman had been going to take her to a lecture that night, but that he had a headache, and she was so disappointed, and she had the tickets, and that if he had no other engagement, would he be good enough to take her?

Would he! He fought to suppress the eagerness in his voice. It was amazing. He had always seen her in her own house. And he had never dared to ask her to go anywhere with him. Quite irrelevantly, still at the telephone and talking with her, he felt an overpowering desire to die for her, and visions of heroic sacrifice shaped and dissolved in his whirling brain. He loved her so much, so terribly, so hopelessly. In that moment of mad happiness that she should go out with him, go to a lecture with him—with him, Martin Eden—she soared so far above him that there seemed nothing else for him to do than die for her. It was the only fit way in which he could express the tremendous and lofty emotion he felt for her. It was the sublime abnegation of true love that comes to all lovers, and it came to him there, at the telephone, in a whirlwind of fire and glory; and to die for her, he felt, was to have lived and loved well. And he was only twenty-one, and he had never been in love before.

His hand trembled as he hung up the receiver, and he was weak from the organ which had stirred him. His eyes were shining like an angel's, and his face was transfigured, purged of all earthly dross, and pure and holy.

"Makin' dates outside, eh?" his brother-in-law sneered. "You know what that means. You'll be in the police court yet."

CHAPTER XII

But Martin could not come down from the height. Not even the bestiality of the allusion could bring him back to earth. Anger and hurt were beneath him. He had seen a great vision and was as a god, and he could feel only profound and awful pity for this maggot of a man. He did not look at him, and though his eyes passed over him, he did not see him; and as in a dream he passed out of the room to dress. It was not until he had reached his own room and was tying his necktie that he became aware of a sound that lingered unpleasantly in his ears. On investigating this sound he identified it as the final snort of Bernard Higginbotham, which somehow had not penetrated to his brain before.

As Ruth's front door closed behind them and he came down the steps with her, he found himself greatly perturbed. It was not unalloyed bliss, taking her to the lecture. He did not know what he ought to do. He had seen, on the streets, with persons of her class, that the women took the men's arms. But then, again, he had seen them when they didn't; and he wondered if it was only in the evening that arms were taken, or only between husbands and wives and relatives.

Just before he reached the sidewalk, he remembered Minnie. Minnie had always been a stickler. She had called him down the second time she walked out with him, because he had gone along on the inside, and she had laid the law down to him that a gentleman always walked on the outside—when he was with a lady. And Minnie had made a practice of kicking his heels, whenever they crossed from one side of the street to the other, to remind him to get over on the outside. He wondered where she had got that item of etiquette, and whether it had filtered down from above and was all right.

It wouldn't do any harm to try it, he decided, by the time they had reached the sidewalk; and he swung behind Ruth and took up his station on the outside. Then the other problem presented itself. Should he offer her his arm? He had never offered anybody his arm in his life. The girls he had known never took the fellows' arms. For the first several times they walked freely, side by side, and after that it was arms around the waists, and heads against the fellows' shoulders where the streets were unlighted. But this was different. She wasn't that kind of a girl. He must do something.

He crooked the arm next to her—crooked it very slightly and with secret tentativeness, not invitingly, but just casually, as though he was accustomed to walk that way. And then the wonderful thing happened. He felt her hand upon his arm. Delicious thrills ran through him at the contact, and for a few sweet moments it seemed that he had left the solid earth and was flying with her through the air. But he was soon back again, perturbed by a new complication. They were crossing the street. This would put him on the inside. He should be on the outside. Should he therefore drop her arm and change over? And if he did so, would he have to repeat the manoeuvre the next time? And the next? There was something wrong about it, and he resolved not to caper about and play the fool. Yet he was not satisfied with his conclusion, and when he found himself on the inside, he talked quickly and earnestly, making a show of being carried away by what he was saying, so that, in case he was wrong in not changing sides, his enthusiasm would seem the cause for his carelessness.

As they crossed Broadway, he came face to face with a new problem. In the blaze of the electric lights, he saw Lizzie Connolly and her giggly friend. Only for an instant he hesitated, then his hand went up and his hat came off. He could not be disloyal to his kind, and it was to more than Lizzie Connolly that his hat was lifted. She nodded and looked at him boldly, not with soft and gentle eyes like Ruth's, but with eyes that were handsome and hard, and that swept on past him to Ruth and itemized her face and dress and station. And he was aware that Ruth looked, too, with quick eyes that were timid and mild as a dove's, but which saw, in a look that was a flutter on and past, the working-class girl in her cheap finery and under the strange hat that all working-class girls were wearing just then.

"What a pretty girl!" Ruth said a moment later.

Martin could have blessed her, though he said:-

"I don't know. I guess it's all a matter of personal taste, but she doesn't strike me as being particularly pretty."

"Why, there isn't one woman in ten thousand with features as regular as hers. They are splendid. Her face is as clear-cut as a cameo. And her eyes are beautiful."

"Do you think so?" Martin queried absently, for to him there was only one beautiful woman in the world, and she was beside him, her hand upon his arm.

"Do I think so? If that girl had proper opportunity to dress, Mr. Eden, and if she were taught how to carry herself, you would be fairly dazzled by her, and so would all men."

"She would have to be taught how to speak," he commented, "or else most of the men wouldn't understand her. I'm sure you couldn't understand a quarter of what she said if she just spoke naturally."

"Nonsense! You are as bad as Arthur when you try to make your point."

"You forget how I talked when you first met me. I have learned a new language since then. Before that time I talked as that girl talks. Now I can manage to make myself understood sufficiently in your language to explain that you do not know that other girl's language. And do you know why she carries herself the way she does? I think about such things now, though I never used to think about them, and I am beginning to understand—much."

"But why does she?"

"She has worked long hours for years at machines. When one's body is young, it is very pliable, and hard work will mould it like putty according to the nature of the work. I can tell at a glance the trades of many workingmen I meet on the street. Look at me. Why am I rolling all about the shop? Because of the years I put in on the sea. If I'd put in the same years cow-punching, with my body young and pliable, I wouldn't be rolling now, but I'd be bow-legged. And so with that girl. You noticed that her eyes were what I might call hard. She has never been sheltered. She has had to take care of herself, and a young girl can't take care of herself and keep her eyes soft and gentle like—like yours, for example."

"I think you are right," Ruth said in a low voice. "And it is too bad. She is such a pretty girl."

He looked at her and saw her eyes luminous with pity. And then he remembered that he loved her and was lost in amazement at his fortune that permitted him to love her and to take her on his arm to a lecture.

Who are you, Martin Eden? he demanded of himself in the looking-glass, that night when he got back to his room. He gazed at himself long and curiously. Who are you? What are you? Where do you belong? You belong by rights to girls like

Lizzie Connolly. You belong with the legions of toil, with all that is low, and vulgar, and unbeautiful. You belong with the oxen and the drudges, in dirty surroundings among smells and stenches. There are the stale vegetables now. Those potatoes are rotting. Smell them, damn you, smell them. And yet you dare to open the books, to listen to beautiful music, to learn to love beautiful paintings, to speak good English, to think thoughts that none of your own kind thinks, to tear yourself away from the oxen and the Lizzie Connollys and to love a pale spirit of a woman who is a million miles beyond you and who lives in the stars! Who are you? and what are you? damn you! And are you going to make good?

He shook his fist at himself in the glass, and sat down on the edge of the bed to dream for a space with wide eyes. Then he got out note-book and algebra and lost himself in quadratic equations, while the hours slipped by, and the stars dimmed, and the gray of dawn flooded against his window.

CHAPTER XIII

It was the knot of wordy socialists and working-class philosophers that held forth in the City Hall Park on warm afternoons that was responsible for the great discovery. Once or twice in the month, while riding through the park on his way to the library, Martin dismounted from his wheel and listened to the arguments, and each time he tore himself away reluctantly. The tone of discussion was much lower than at Mr. Morse's table. The men were not grave and dignified. They lost their tempers easily and called one another names, while oaths and obscene allusions were frequent on their lips. Once or twice he had seen them come to blows. And yet, he knew not why, there seemed something vital about the stuff of these men's thoughts. Their logomachy was far more stimulating to his intellect than the reserved and quiet dogmatism of Mr. Morse. These men, who slaughtered English, gesticulated like lunatics, and fought one another's ideas with primitive anger, seemed somehow to be more alive than Mr. Morse and his crony, Mr. Butler.

Martin had heard Herbert Spencer quoted several times in the park, but one afternoon a disciple of Spencer's appeared, a seedy tramp with a dirty coat buttoned tightly at the throat to conceal the absence of a shirt. Battle royal was waged, amid the smoking of many cigarettes and the expectoration of much tobacco-juice, wherein the tramp successfully held his own, even when a socialist workman sneered, "There is no god but the Unknowable, and Herbert Spencer is his prophet." Martin was puzzled as to what the discussion was about, but when he rode on to the library he carried with him a new-born interest in Herbert Spencer, and because of the frequency with which the tramp had mentioned "First Principles," Martin drew out that volume.

So the great discovery began. Once before he had tried Spencer, and choosing the "Principles of Psychology" to begin with, he had failed as abjectly as he had failed with Madam Blavatsky. There had been no understanding the book, and he had returned it unread. But this night, after algebra and physics, and an attempt at a sonnet, he got into bed and opened "First Principles." Morning found him still reading. It was impossible for him to sleep. Nor did he write that day. He lay on the bed till his body grew tired, when he tried the hard floor, reading on his back, the book held in the air above him, or changing from side to side. He slept that night, and did his writing next morning, and then the book tempted him and he fell, reading all afternoon, oblivious to everything and oblivious to the fact that that was the afternoon Ruth gave to him. His first consciousness of the immediate world about him was when Bernard

Higginbotham jerked open the door and demanded to know if he thought they were running a restaurant.

Martin Eden had been mastered by curiosity all his days. He wanted to know, and it was this desire that had sent him adventuring over the world. But he was now learning from Spencer that he never had known, and that he never could have known had he continued his sailing and wandering forever. He had merely skimmed over the surface of things, observing detached phenomena, accumulating fragments of facts, making superficial little generalizations—and all and everything quite unrelated in a capricious and disorderly world of whim and chance. The mechanism of the flight of birds he had watched and reasoned about with understanding; but it had never entered his head to try to explain the process whereby birds, as organic flying mechanisms, had been developed. He had never dreamed there was such a process. That birds should have come to be, was unguessed. They always had been. They just happened.

And as it was with birds, so had it been with everything. His ignorant and unprepared attempts at philosophy had been fruitless. The medieval metaphysics of Kant had given him the key to nothing, and had served the sole purpose of making him doubt his own intellectual powers. In similar manner his attempt to study evolution had been confined to a hopelessly technical volume by Romanes. He had understood nothing, and the only idea he had gathered was that evolution was a dry-as-dust theory, of a lot of little men possessed of huge and unintelligible vocabularies. And now he learned that evolution was no mere theory but an accepted process of development; that scientists no longer disagreed about it, their only differences being over the method of evolution.

And here was the man Spencer, organizing all knowledge for him, reducing everything to unity, elaborating ultimate realities, and presenting to his startled gaze a universe so concrete of realization that it was like the model of a ship such as sailors make and put into glass bottles. There was no caprice, no chance. All was law. It was in obedience to law that the bird flew, and it was in obedience to the same law that fermenting slime had writhed and squirmed and put out legs and wings and become a bird.

Martin had ascended from pitch to pitch of intellectual living, and here he was at a higher pitch than ever. All the hidden things were laying their secrets bare. He was drunken with comprehension. At night, asleep, he lived with the gods in colossal nightmare; and awake, in the day, he went around like a somnambulist, with absent stare, gazing upon the world he had just discovered. At table he failed to hear the conversation about petty and ignoble things, his eager mind seeking out and following cause and effect in everything before him. In the meat on the platter he saw the shining sun and traced its energy back through all its transformations to its source a hundred million miles away, or traced its energy ahead to the moving muscles in his arms that enabled him to cut the meat, and to the brain wherewith he willed the muscles to move to cut the meat, until, with inward gaze, he saw the same sun shining in his brain. He was entranced by illumination, and did not hear the "Bughouse," whispered by Jim, nor see the anxiety on his sister's face, nor notice the rotary motion of Bernard Higginbotham's finger, whereby he imparted the suggestion of wheels revolving in his brother-in-law's head.

What, in a way, most profoundly impressed Martin, was the correlation of knowledge—of all knowledge. He had been curious to know things, and whatever he acquired he had filed away in separate memory compartments in his brain. Thus, on the subject of sailing he had an immense store. On the subject of woman he had a fairly large store. But these two subjects had been unrelated. Between the two memory compartments there had been no connection. That, in the fabric of knowledge, there should be any connection whatever between a woman with hysterics and a schooner carrying a weather-helm or heaving to in a gale, would have struck him as ridiculous and impossible. But Herbert Spencer had shown him not only that it was not ridiculous, but that it was impossible for there to be no connection. All things were related to all other things from the farthermost star in the wastes of space to the myriads of atoms in the grain of sand under one's foot. This new concept was a perpetual amazement to Martin, and he found himself engaged continually in tracing the relationship between all things under the sun and on the other side of the sun. He drew up lists of the most incongruous things and was unhappy until he succeeded in establishing kinship between them all—kinship between love, poetry, earthquake, fire, rattlesnakes, rainbows, precious gems, monstrosities, sunsets, the roaring of lions, illuminating gas, cannibalism, beauty, murder, lovers, fulcrums, and tobacco. Thus, he unified the universe and held it up and looked at it, or wandered through its byways and alleys and jungles, not as a terrified traveller in the thick of mysteries seeking an unknown goal, but observing and charting and becoming familiar with all there was to know. And the more he knew, the more passionately he admired the universe, and life, and his own life in the midst of it all.

"You fool!" he cried at his image in the looking-glass. "You wanted to write, and you tried to write, and you had nothing in you to write about. What did you have in you?—some childish notions, a few half-baked sentiments, a lot of undigested beauty, a great black mass of ignorance, a heart filled to bursting with love, and an ambition as big as your love and as futile as your ignorance. And you wanted to write! Why, you're just on the edge of beginning to get something in you to write about. You wanted to create beauty, but how could you when you knew nothing about the nature of beauty? You wanted to write about life when you knew nothing of the essential characteristics of life. You wanted to write about the world and the scheme of existence when the world was a Chinese puzzle to you and all that you could have written would have been about what you did not know of the scheme of existence. But cheer up, Martin, my boy. You'll write yet. You know a little, a very little, and you're on the right road now to know more. Some day, if you're lucky, you may come pretty close to knowing all that may be known. Then you will write."

He brought his great discovery to Ruth, sharing with her all his joy and wonder in it. But she did not seem to be so enthusiastic over it. She tacitly accepted it and, in a way, seemed aware of it from her own studies. It did not stir her deeply, as it did him, and he would have been surprised had he not reasoned it out that it was not new and fresh to her as it was to him. Arthur and Norman, he found, believed in evolution and had read Spencer, though it did not seem to have made any vital impression upon them, while the young fellow with the glasses and the mop of hair, Will Olney, sneered disagreeably at Spencer and repeated the epigram, "There is no god but the Unknowable, and Herbert Spencer is his prophet."

But Martin forgave him the sneer, for he had begun to discover that Olney was not in love with Ruth. Later, he was dumfounded to learn from various little happenings not only that Olney did not care for Ruth, but that he had a positive dislike for her.

CHAPTER XIII

Martin could not understand this. It was a bit of phenomena that he could not correlate with all the rest of the phenomena in the universe. But nevertheless he felt sorry for the young fellow because of the great lack in his nature that prevented him from a proper appreciation of Ruth's fineness and beauty. They rode out into the hills several Sundays on their wheels, and Martin had ample opportunity to observe the armed truce that existed between Ruth and Olney. The latter chummed with Norman, throwing Arthur and Martin into company with Ruth, for which Martin was duly grateful.

Those Sundays were great days for Martin, greatest because he was with Ruth, and great, also, because they were putting him more on a par with the young men of her class. In spite of their long years of disciplined education, he was finding himself their intellectual equal, and the hours spent with them in conversation was so much practice for him in the use of the grammar he had studied so hard. He had abandoned the etiquette books, falling back upon observation to show him the right things to do. Except when carried away by his enthusiasm, he was always on guard, keenly watchful of their actions and learning their little courtesies and refinements of conduct.

The fact that Spencer was very little read was for some time a source of surprise to Martin. "Herbert Spencer," said the man at the desk in the library, "oh, yes, a great mind." But the man did not seem to know anything of the content of that great mind. One evening, at dinner, when Mr. Butler was there, Martin turned the conversation upon Spencer. Mr. Morse bitterly arraigned the English philosopher's agnosticism, but confessed that he had not read "First Principles"; while Mr. Butler stated that he had no patience with Spencer, had never read a line of him, and had managed to get along quite well without him. Doubts arose in Martin's mind, and had he been less strongly individual he would have accepted the general opinion and given Herbert Spencer up. As it was, he found Spencer's explanation of things convincing; and, as he phrased it to himself, to give up Spencer would be equivalent to a navigator throwing the compass and chronometer overboard. So Martin went on into a thorough study of evolution, mastering more and more the subject himself, and being convinced by the corroborative testimony of a thousand independent writers. The more he studied, the more vistas he caught of fields of knowledge yet unexplored, and the regret that days were only twenty-four hours long became a chronic complaint with him.

One day, because the days were so short, he decided to give up algebra and geometry. Trigonometry he had not even attempted. Then he cut chemistry from his study-list, retaining only physics.

"I am not a specialist," he said, in defence, to Ruth. "Nor am I going to try to be a specialist. There are too many special fields for any one man, in a whole lifetime, to master a tithe of them. I must pursue general knowledge. When I need the work of specialists, I shall refer to their books."

"But that is not like having the knowledge yourself," she protested.

"But it is unnecessary to have it. We profit from the work of the specialists. That's what they are for. When I came in, I noticed the chimney-sweeps at work. They're specialists, and when they get done, you will enjoy clean chimneys without knowing anything about the construction of chimneys."

"That's far-fetched, I am afraid."

She looked at him curiously, and he felt a reproach in her gaze and manner. But he was convinced of the rightness of his position.

"All thinkers on general subjects, the greatest minds in the world, in fact, rely on the specialists. Herbert Spencer did that. He generalized upon the findings of thousands of investigators. He would have had to live a thousand lives in order to do it all himself. And so with Darwin. He took advantage of all that had been learned by the florists and cattle-breeders."

"You're right, Martin," Olney said. "You know what you're after, and Ruth doesn't. She doesn't know what she is after for herself even."

"—Oh, yes," Olney rushed on, heading off her objection, "I know you call it general culture. But it doesn't matter what you study if you want general culture. You can study French, or you can study German, or cut them both out and study Esperanto, you'll get the culture tone just the same. You can study Greek or Latin, too, for the same purpose, though it will never be any use to you. It will be culture, though. Why, Ruth studied Saxon, became clever in it,—that was two years ago,—and all that she remembers of it now is 'Whan that sweet Aprile with his schowers soote'—isn't that the way it goes?"

"But it's given you the culture tone just the same," he laughed, again heading her off. "I know. We were in the same classes."

"But you speak of culture as if it should be a means to something," Ruth cried out. Her eyes were flashing, and in her cheeks were two spots of color. "Culture is the end in itself."

"But that is not what Martin wants."

"How do you know?"

"What do you want, Martin?" Olney demanded, turning squarely upon him.

Martin felt very uncomfortable, and looked entreaty at Ruth.

"Yes, what do you want?" Ruth asked. "That will settle it."

"Yes, of course, I want culture," Martin faltered. "I love beauty, and culture will give me a finer and keener appreciation of beauty."

She nodded her head and looked triumph.

"Rot, and you know it," was Olney's comment. "Martin's after career, not culture. It just happens that culture, in his case, is incidental to career. If he wanted to be a chemist, culture would be unnecessary. Martin wants to write, but he's afraid to say so because it will put you in the wrong."

"And why does Martin want to write?" he went on. "Because he isn't rolling in wealth. Why do you fill your head with Saxon and general culture? Because you don't have to make your way in the world. Your father sees to that. He buys your clothes for you, and all the rest. What rotten good is our education, yours and mine and Arthur's and Norman's? We're soaked in general culture, and if our daddies went broke to-day, we'd be falling down to-morrow on teachers' examinations. The best job you could get, Ruth, would be a country school or music teacher in a girls' boarding-school."

"And pray what would you do?" she asked.

"Not a blessed thing. I could earn a dollar and a half a day, common labor, and I might get in as instructor in Hanley's cramming joint—I say might, mind you, and I might be chucked out at the end of the week for sheer inability."

Martin followed the discussion closely, and while he was convinced that Olney was right, he resented the rather cavalier treatment he accorded Ruth. A new conception of love formed in his mind as he listened. Reason had nothing to do with love. It mattered not whether the woman he loved reasoned correctly or incorrectly. Love was above reason. If it just happened that she did not fully appreciate his necessity for a career, that did not make her a bit less lovable. She was all lovable, and what she thought had nothing to do with her lovableness.

"What's that?" he replied to a question from Olney that broke in upon his train of thought.

"I was saying that I hoped you wouldn't be fool enough to tackle Latin."

"But Latin is more than culture," Ruth broke in. "It is equipment."

"Well, are you going to tackle it?" Olney persisted.

Martin was sore beset. He could see that Ruth was hanging eagerly upon his answer.

"I am afraid I won't have time," he said finally. "I'd like to, but I won't have time."

"You see, Martin's not seeking culture," Olney exulted. "He's trying to get somewhere, to do something."

"Oh, but it's mental training. It's mind discipline. It's what makes disciplined minds." Ruth looked expectantly at Martin, as if waiting for him to change his judgment. "You know, the foot-ball players have to train before the big game. And that is what Latin does for the thinker. It trains."

"Rot and bosh! That's what they told us when we were kids. But there is one thing they didn't tell us then. They let us find it out for ourselves afterwards." Olney paused for effect, then added, "And what they didn't tell us was that every gentleman should have studied Latin, but that no gentleman should know Latin."

"Now that's unfair," Ruth cried. "I knew you were turning the conversation just in order to get off something."

"It's clever all right," was the retort, "but it's fair, too. The only men who know their Latin are the apothecaries, the lawyers, and the Latin professors. And if Martin wants to be one of them, I miss my guess. But what's all that got to do with Herbert Spencer anyway? Martin's just discovered Spencer, and he's wild over him. Why? Because Spencer is taking him somewhere. Spencer couldn't take me anywhere, nor you. We haven't got anywhere to go. You'll get married some day, and I'll have nothing to do but keep track of the lawyers and business agents who will take care of the money my father's going to leave me."

Onley got up to go, but turned at the door and delivered a parting shot.

"You leave Martin alone, Ruth. He knows what's best for himself. Look at what he's done already. He makes me sick sometimes, sick and ashamed of myself. He knows more now about the world, and life, and man's place, and all the rest, than Arthur, or Norman, or I, or you, too, for that matter, and in spite of all our Latin, and French, and Saxon, and culture."

"But Ruth is my teacher," Martin answered chivalrously. "She is responsible for what little I have learned."

"Rats!" Olney looked at Ruth, and his expression was malicious. "I suppose you'll be telling me next that you read Spencer on her recommendation—only you didn't. And she doesn't know anything more about Darwin and evolution than I do about King Solomon's mines. What's that jawbreaker definition about something or other, of Spencer's, that you sprang on us the other day—that indefinite, incoherent homogeneity thing? Spring it on her, and see if she understands a word of it. That isn't culture, you see. Well, tra la, and if you tackle Latin, Martin, I won't have any respect for you."

And all the while, interested in the discussion, Martin had been aware of an irk in it as well. It was about studies and lessons, dealing with the rudiments of knowledge, and the schoolboyish tone of it conflicted with the big things that were stirring in him—with the grip upon life that was even then crooking his fingers like eagle's talons, with the cosmic thrills that made him ache, and with the inchoate consciousness of mastery of it all. He likened himself to a poet, wrecked on the shores of a strange land, filled with power of beauty, stumbling and stammering and vainly trying to sing in the rough, barbaric tongue of his brethren in the new land. And so with him. He was alive, painfully alive, to the great universal things, and yet he was compelled to potter and grope among schoolboy topics and debate whether or not he should study Latin.

"What in hell has Latin to do with it?" he demanded before his mirror that night. "I wish dead people would stay dead. Why should I and the beauty in me be ruled by the dead? Beauty is alive and everlasting. Languages come and go. They are the dust of the dead."

And his next thought was that he had been phrasing his ideas very well, and he went to bed wondering why he could not talk in similar fashion when he was with Ruth. He was only a schoolboy, with a schoolboy's tongue, when he was in her presence.

"Give me time," he said aloud. "Only give me time."

Time! Time! Time! was his unending plaint.

CHAPTER XIV

It was not because of Olney, but in spite of Ruth, and his love for Ruth, that he finally decided not to take up Latin. His money meant time. There was so much that was more important than Latin, so many studies that clamored with imperious voices. And he must write. He must earn money. He had had no acceptances. Twoscore of manuscripts were travelling the endless round of the magazines. How did the others do it? He spent long hours in the free reading-room, going over what others had written, studying their work eagerly and critically, comparing it with his own, and wondering, wondering, about the secret trick they had discovered which enabled them to sell their work.

He was amazed at the immense amount of printed stuff that was dead. No light, no life, no color, was shot through it. There was no breath of life in it, and yet it sold, at two cents a word, twenty dollars a thousand—the newspaper clipping had said so. He was puzzled by countless short stories, written lightly and cleverly he confessed, but without vitality or reality. Life was so strange and wonderful, filled with an immensity of problems, of dreams, and of heroic toils, and yet these stories dealt only with the commonplaces of life. He felt the stress and strain of life, its fevers and sweats and wild insurgences—surely this was the stuff to write about! He wanted to glorify the leaders of forlorn hopes, the mad lovers, the giants that fought under stress and strain, amid terror and tragedy, making life crackle with the strength of their endeavor. And yet the magazine short stories seemed intent on glorifying the Mr. Butlers, the sordid dollar-chasers, and the commonplace little love affairs of commonplace little men and women. Was it because the editors of the magazines were commonplace? he demanded. Or were they afraid of life, these writers and editors and readers?

But his chief trouble was that he did not know any editors or writers. And not merely did he not know any writers, but he did not know anybody who had ever attempted to write. There was nobody to tell him, to hint to him, to give him the least word of advice. He began to doubt that editors were real men. They seemed cogs in a machine. That was what it was, a machine. He poured his soul into stories, articles, and poems, and intrusted them to the machine. He folded them just so, put the proper stamps inside the long envelope along with the manuscript, sealed the envelope, put more stamps outside, and dropped it into the mail-box. It travelled across the continent, and after a certain lapse of time the postman returned him the manuscript in another long envelope, on the outside of which were the stamps he had enclosed.

There was no human editor at the other end, but a mere cunning arrangement of cogs that changed the manuscript from one envelope to another and stuck on the stamps. It was like the slot machines wherein one dropped pennies, and, with a metallic whirl of machinery had delivered to him a stick of chewing-gum or a tablet of chocolate. It depended upon which slot one dropped the penny in, whether he got chocolate or gum. And so with the editorial machine. One slot brought checks and the other brought rejection slips. So far he had found only the latter slot.

It was the rejection slips that completed the horrible machinelikeness of the process. These slips were printed in stereotyped forms and he had received hundreds of them—as many as a dozen or more on each of his earlier manuscripts. If he had received one line, one personal line, along with one rejection of all his rejections, he would have been cheered. But not one editor had given that proof of existence. And he could conclude only that there were no warm human men at the other end, only mere cogs, well oiled and running beautifully in the machine.

He was a good fighter, whole-souled and stubborn, and he would have been content to continue feeding the machine for years; but he was bleeding to death, and not years but weeks would determine the fight. Each week his board bill brought him nearer destruction, while the postage on forty manuscripts bled him almost as severely. He no longer bought books, and he economized in petty ways and sought to delay the inevitable end; though he did not know how to economize, and brought the end nearer by a week when he gave his sister Marian five dollars for a dress.

He struggled in the dark, without advice, without encouragement, and in the teeth of discouragement. Even Gertrude was beginning to look askance. At first she had tolerated with sisterly fondness what she conceived to be his foolishness; but now, out of sisterly solicitude, she grew anxious. To her it seemed that his foolishness was becoming a madness. Martin knew this and suffered more keenly from it than from the open and nagging contempt of Bernard Higginbotham. Martin had faith in himself, but he was alone in this faith. Not even Ruth had faith. She had wanted him to devote himself to study, and, though she had not openly disapproved of his writing, she had never approved.

He had never offered to show her his work. A fastidious delicacy had prevented him. Besides, she had been studying heavily at the university, and he felt averse to robbing her of her time. But when she had taken her degree, she asked him herself to let her see something of what he had been doing. Martin was elated and diffident. Here was a judge. She was a bachelor of arts. She had studied literature under skilled instructors. Perhaps the editors were capable judges, too. But she would be different from them. She would not hand him a stereotyped rejection slip, nor would she inform him that lack of preference for his work did not necessarily imply lack of merit in his work. She would talk, a warm human being, in her quick, bright way, and, most important of all, she would catch glimpses of the real Martin Eden. In his work she would discern what his heart and soul were like, and she would come to understand something, a little something, of the stuff of his dreams and the strength of his power.

Martin gathered together a number of carbon copies of his short stories, hesitated a moment, then added his "Sea Lyrics." They mounted their wheels on a late June afternoon and rode for the hills. It was the second time he had been out with her alone, and as they rode along through the balmy warmth, just chilled by she sea-breeze to refreshing coolness, he was profoundly impressed by the fact that it was a very beautiful and well-ordered world and that it was good to be alive and to love. They left their wheels by the roadside and climbed to the brown top of an open knoll where the sunburnt grass breathed a harvest breath of dry sweetness and content.

"Its work is done," Martin said, as they seated themselves, she upon his coat, and he sprawling close to the warm earth. He sniffed the sweetness of the tawny grass, which entered his brain and set his thoughts whirling on from the particular to the universal. "It has achieved its reason for existence," he went on, patting the dry grass affectionately. "It quickened with ambition under the dreary downpour of last winter, fought the violent early spring, flowered, and lured the insects and the bees, scattered its seeds, squared itself with its duty and the world, and—"

"Why do you always look at things with such dreadfully practical eyes?" she interrupted.

"Because I've been studying evolution, I guess. It's only recently that I got my eyesight, if the truth were told."

"But it seems to me you lose sight of beauty by being so practical, that you destroy beauty like the boys who catch butterflies and rub the down off their beautiful wings."

He shook his head.

"Beauty has significance, but I never knew its significance before. I just accepted beauty as something meaningless, as something that was just beautiful without rhyme or reason. I did not know anything about beauty. But now I know, or, rather, am just beginning to know. This grass is more beautiful to me now that I know why it is grass, and all the hidden chemistry of sun and rain and earth that makes it become grass. Why, there is romance in the life-history of any grass, yes, and adventure, too. The very thought of it stirs me. When I think of the play of force and matter, and all the tremendous struggle of it, I feel as if I could write an epic on the grass.

"How well you talk," she said absently, and he noted that she was looking at him in a searching way.

He was all confusion and embarrassment on the instant, the blood flushing red on his neck and brow.

"I hope I am learning to talk," he stammered. "There seems to be so much in me I want to say. But it is all so big. I can't find ways to say what is really in me. Sometimes it seems to me that all the world, all life, everything, had taken up residence inside of me and was clamoring for me to be the spokesman. I feel—oh, I can't describe it—I feel the bigness of it, but when I speak, I babble like a little child. It is a great task to transmute feeling and sensation into speech, written or spoken, that will, in turn, in him who reads or listens, transmute itself back into the selfsame feeling and sensation. It is a lordly task. See, I bury my face in the grass, and the breath I draw in through my nostrils sets me quivering with a thousand thoughts and fancies. It is a breath of the universe I have breathed. I know song and laughter, and success and pain, and struggle and death; and I see visions that arise in my brain somehow out of the scent of the grass, and I would like to tell them to you, to the world. But how can I? My tongue is tied. I have tried, by the spoken word, just now, to describe to you the effect on me of the scent of the grass. But I have not succeeded. I have no more than hinted in awkward speech. My words seem gibberish to me. And yet I am stifled with desire to tell. Oh!—" he threw up his hands with a despairing gesture—"it is impossible! It is not understandable! It is incommunicable!"

"But you do talk well," she insisted. "Just think how you have improved in the short time I have known you. Mr. Butler is a noted public speaker. He is always asked by the State Committee to go out on stump during campaign. Yet you talked just as well as he the other night at dinner. Only he was more controlled. You get too excited; but you will get over that with practice. Why, you would make a good public speaker. You can go far—if you want to. You are masterly. You can lead men, I am sure, and there is no reason why you should not succeed at anything you set your hand to, just as you have succeeded with grammar. You would make a good lawyer. You should shine in politics. There is nothing to prevent you from making as great a success as Mr. Butler has made. And minus the dyspepsia," she added with a smile.

They talked on; she, in her gently persistent way, returning always to the need of thorough grounding in education and to the advantages of Latin as part of the foundation for any career. She drew her ideal of the successful man, and it was largely in her father's image, with a few unmistakable lines and touches of color from the image of Mr. Butler. He listened eagerly, with receptive ears, lying on his back and looking up and joying in each movement of her lips as she talked. But his brain was not receptive. There was nothing alluring in the pictures she drew, and he was aware of a dull pain of disappointment and of a sharper ache of love for her. In all she said there was no mention of his writing, and the manuscripts he had brought to read lay neglected on the ground.

At last, in a pause, he glanced at the sun, measured its height above the horizon, and suggested his manuscripts by picking them up.

"I had forgotten," she said quickly. "And I am so anxious to hear."

He read to her a story, one that he flattered himself was among his very best. He called it "The Wine of Life," and the wine of it, that had stolen into his brain when he wrote it, stole into his brain now as he read it. There was a certain magic in the original conception, and he had adorned it with more magic of phrase and touch. All the old fire and passion with which he had written it were reborn in him, and he was swayed and swept away so that he was blind and deaf to the faults of it. But it was not so with Ruth. Her trained ear detected the weaknesses and exaggerations, the overemphasis of the tyro, and she was instantly aware each time the sentence-rhythm tripped and faltered. She scarcely noted the rhythm otherwise, except when it became too pompous, at which moments she was disagreeably impressed with its amateurishness. That was her final judgment on the story as a whole—amateurish, though she did not tell him so. Instead, when he had done, she pointed out the minor flaws and said that she liked the story.

But he was disappointed. Her criticism was just. He acknowledged that, but he had a feeling that he was not sharing his work with her for the purpose of schoolroom correction. The details did not matter. They could take care of themselves. He could mend them, he could learn to mend them. Out of life he had captured something big and attempted to imprison it in the story. It was the big thing out of life he had read to her, not sentence-structure and semicolons. He wanted her to feel with him this big thing that was his, that he had seen with his own eyes, grappled with his own brain, and placed there on the page with his own hands in printed words. Well, he had failed, was his secret decision. Perhaps the editors were right. He had felt the big thing, but he had failed to transmute it. He concealed his disappointment, and joined so easily with her in her criticism that she did not realize that deep down in him was running a strong undercurrent of disagreement.

"This next thing I've called 'The Pot'," he said, unfolding the manuscript. "It has been refused by four or five magazines now, but still I think it is good. In fact, I don't know what to think of it, except that I've caught something there. Maybe it won't affect you as it does me. It's a short thing—only two thousand words."

"How dreadful!" she cried, when he had finished. "It is horrible, unutterably horrible!"

He noted her pale face, her eyes wide and tense, and her clenched hands, with secret satisfaction. He had succeeded. He had communicated the stuff of fancy and feeling from out of his brain. It had struck home. No matter whether she liked it or not, it had gripped her and mastered her, made her sit there and listen and forget details.

"It is life," he said, "and life is not always beautiful. And yet, perhaps because I am strangely made, I find something beautiful there. It seems to me that the beauty is tenfold enhanced because it is there—"

"But why couldn't the poor woman—" she broke in disconnectedly. Then she left the revolt of her thought unexpressed to cry out: "Oh! It is degrading! It is not nice! It is nasty!"

For the moment it seemed to him that his heart stood still. *Nasty*! He had never dreamed it. He had not meant it. The whole sketch stood before him in letters of fire, and in such blaze of illumination he sought vainly for nastiness. Then his heart began to beat again. He was not guilty.

"Why didn't you select a nice subject?" she was saying. "We know there are nasty things in the world, but that is no reason—"

She talked on in her indignant strain, but he was not following her. He was smiling to himself as he looked up into her virginal face, so innocent, so penetratingly innocent, that its purity seemed always to enter into him, driving out of him all dross and bathing him in some ethereal effulgence that was as cool and soft and velvety as starshine. *We know there are nasty things in the world*! He cuddled to him the notion of her knowing, and chuckled over it as a love joke. The next moment, in a flashing vision of multitudinous detail, he sighted the whole sea of life's nastiness that he had known and voyaged over and through, and he forgave her for not understanding the story. It was through no fault of hers that she could not understand. He thanked God that she had been born and sheltered to such innocence. But he knew life, its foulness as well as its fairness, its greatness in spite of the slime that infested it, and by God he was going to have his say on it to the world. Saints in heaven—how could they be anything but fair and pure? No praise to them. But saints in slime—ah, that was the everlasting wonder! That was what made life worth while. To see moral grandeur rising out of cesspools of iniquity; to rise himself and first glimpse beauty, faint and far, through mud-dripping eyes; to see out of weakness, and frailty, and viciousness, and all abysmal brutishness, arising strength, and truth, and high spiritual endowment—

He caught a stray sequence of sentences she was uttering.

"The tone of it all is low. And there is so much that is high. Take 'In Memoriam.'"

He was impelled to suggest "Locksley Hall," and would have done so, had not his vision gripped him again and left him staring at her, the female of his kind, who, out of the primordial ferment, creeping and crawling up the vast ladder of life for a thousand thousand centuries, had emerged on the topmost rung, having become one Ruth, pure, and fair, and divine, and with power to make him know love, and to aspire toward purity, and to desire to taste divinity—him, Martin Eden, who, too, had come up in some amazing fashion from out of the ruck and the mire and the countless mistakes and abortions of unending creation. There was the romance, and the wonder, and the glory. There was the stuff to write, if he could only find speech. Saints in heaven!—They were only saints and could not help themselves. But he was a man.

"You have strength," he could hear her saying, "but it is untutored strength."

"Like a bull in a china shop," he suggested, and won a smile.

"And you must develop discrimination. You must consult taste, and fineness, and tone."

"I dare too much," he muttered.

She smiled approbation, and settled herself to listen to another story.

"I don't know what you'll make of this," he said apologetically. "It's a funny thing. I'm afraid I got beyond my depth in it, but my intentions were good. Don't bother about the little features of it. Just see if you catch the feel of the big thing in it. It is big, and it is true, though the chance is large that I have failed to make it intelligible."

He read, and as he read he watched her. At last he had reached her, he thought. She sat without movement, her eyes steadfast upon him, scarcely breathing, caught up and out of herself, he thought, by the witchery of the thing he had created. He had entitled the story "Adventure," and it was the apotheosis of adventure—not of the adventure of the storybooks, but of real adventure, the savage taskmaster, awful of punishment and awful of reward, faithless and whimsical, demanding terrible patience and heartbreaking days and nights of toil, offering the blazing sunlight glory or dark death at the end of thirst and famine or of the long drag and monstrous delirium of rotting fever, through blood and sweat and stinging insects leading up by long chains of petty and ignoble contacts to royal culminations and lordly achievements.

It was this, all of it, and more, that he had put into his story, and it was this, he believed, that warmed her as she sat and listened. Her eyes were wide, color was in her pale cheeks, and before he finished it seemed to him that she was almost panting. Truly, she was warmed; but she was warmed, not by the story, but by him. She did not think much of the story; it was Martin's intensity of power, the old excess of strength that seemed to pour from his body and on and over her. The paradox of it was that it was the story itself that was freighted with his power, that was the channel, for the time being, through which his strength poured out to her. She was aware only of the strength, and not of the medium, and when she seemed most carried away by what he had written, in reality she had been carried away by something quite foreign to it—by a thought, terrible and perilous, that had formed itself unsummoned in her brain. She had caught herself wondering what marriage was like, and the becoming conscious of the waywardness and ardor of the thought had terrified her. It was unmaidenly. It was not like her. She had never been tormented by womanhood, and she had lived in a dreamland of Tennysonian poesy, dense even to the full significance of that delicate master's delicate allusions to the grossnesses that intrude upon the relations of queens and knights. She had been asleep, always, and now life was thundering imperatively at all her doors. Mentally she was in a panic to shoot the bolts and drop the bars into place, while wanton instincts urged her to throw wide her portals and bid the deliciously strange visitor to enter in.

Martin waited with satisfaction for her verdict. He had no doubt of what it would be, and he was astounded when he heard her say:

"It is beautiful."

"It is beautiful," she repeated, with emphasis, after a pause.

Of course it was beautiful; but there was something more than mere beauty in it, something more stingingly splendid which had made beauty its handmaiden. He sprawled silently on the ground, watching the grisly form of a great doubt rising before him. He had failed. He was inarticulate. He had seen one of the greatest things in the world, and he had not expressed it.

"What did you think of the—" He hesitated, abashed at his first attempt to use a strange word. "Of the *motif*?" he asked.

"It was confused," she answered. "That is my only criticism in the large way. I followed the story, but there seemed so much else. It is too wordy. You clog the action by introducing so much extraneous material."

"That was the major *motif*," he hurriedly explained, "the big underrunning *motif*, the cosmic and universal thing. I tried to make it keep time with the story itself, which was only superficial after all. I was on the right scent, but I guess I did it badly. I did not succeed in suggesting what I was driving at. But I'll learn in time."

She did not follow him. She was a bachelor of arts, but he had gone beyond her limitations. This she did not comprehend, attributing her incomprehension to his incoherence.

"You were too voluble," she said. "But it was beautiful, in places."

He heard her voice as from far off, for he was debating whether he would read her the "Sea Lyrics." He lay in dull despair, while she watched him searchingly, pondering again upon unsummoned and wayward thoughts of marriage.

"You want to be famous?" she asked abruptly.

"Yes, a little bit," he confessed. "That is part of the adventure. It is not the being famous, but the process of becoming so, that counts. And after all, to be famous would be, for me, only a means to something else. I want to be famous very much, for that matter, and for that reason."

"For your sake," he wanted to add, and might have added had she proved enthusiastic over what he had read to her.

But she was too busy in her mind, carving out a career for him that would at least be possible, to ask what the ultimate something was which he had hinted at. There was no career for him in literature. Of that she was convinced. He had proved it today, with his amateurish and sophomoric productions. He could talk well, but he was incapable of expressing himself in a literary way. She compared Tennyson, and Browning, and her favorite prose masters with him, and to his hopeless discredit. Yet she did not tell him her whole mind. Her strange interest in him led her to temporize. His desire to write was, after all, a little weakness which he would grow out of in time. Then he would devote himself to the more serious affairs of life. And he would succeed, too. She knew that. He was so strong that he could not fail—if only he would drop writing.

"I wish you would show me all you write, Mr. Eden," she said.

He flushed with pleasure. She was interested, that much was sure. And at least she had not given him a rejection slip. She had called certain portions of his work beautiful, and that was the first encouragement he had ever received from any one.

"I will," he said passionately. "And I promise you, Miss Morse, that I will make good. I have come far, I know that; and I have far to go, and I will cover it if I have to do it on my hands and knees." He held up a bunch of manuscript. "Here are the 'Sea Lyrics.' When you get home, I'll turn them over to you to read at your leisure. And you must be sure to tell me just what you think of them. What I need, you know, above all things, is criticism. And do, please, be frank with me."

"I will be perfectly frank," she promised, with an uneasy conviction that she had not been frank with him and with a doubt if she could be quite frank with him the next time.

CHAPTER XV

"The first battle, fought and finished," Martin said to the looking-glass ten days later. "But there will be a second battle, and a third battle, and battles to the end of time, unless—"

He had not finished the sentence, but looked about the mean little room and let his eyes dwell sadly upon a heap of returned manuscripts, still in their long envelopes, which lay in a corner on the floor. He had no stamps with which to continue them on their travels, and for a week they had been piling up. More of them would come in on the morrow, and on the next day, and the next, till they were all in. And he would be unable to start them out again. He was a month's rent behind on the typewriter, which he could not pay, having barely enough for the week's board which was due and for the employment office fees.

He sat down and regarded the table thoughtfully. There were ink stains upon it, and he suddenly discovered that he was fond of it.

"Dear old table," he said, "I've spent some happy hours with you, and you've been a pretty good friend when all is said and done. You never turned me down, never passed me out a reward-of-unmerit rejection slip, never complained about working overtime."

He dropped his arms upon the table and buried his face in them. His throat was aching, and he wanted to cry. It reminded him of his first fight, when he was six years old, when he punched away with the tears running down his cheeks while the other boy, two years his elder, had beaten and pounded him into exhaustion. He saw the ring of boys, howling like barbarians as he went down at last, writhing in the throes of nausea, the blood streaming from his nose and the tears from his bruised eyes.

"Poor little shaver," he murmured. "And you're just as badly licked now. You're beaten to a pulp. You're down and out."

But the vision of that first fight still lingered under his eyelids, and as he watched he saw it dissolve and reshape into the series of fights which had followed. Six months later Cheese-Face (that was the boy) had whipped him again. But he had blacked Cheese-Face's eye that time. That was going some. He saw them all, fight after fight, himself always whipped and Cheese-Face exulting over him. But he had never run away. He felt strengthened by the memory of that. He had always stayed and taken his medicine. Cheese-Face had been a little fiend at fighting, and had never once shown mercy to him. But he had stayed! He had stayed with it!

Next, he saw a narrow alley, between ramshackle frame buildings. The end of the alley was blocked by a one-story brick building, out of which issued the rhythmic thunder of the presses, running off the first edition of the *Enquirer*. He was eleven, and Cheese-Face was thirteen, and they both carried the *Enquirer*. That was why they were there, waiting for their papers. And, of course, Cheese-Face had picked on him again, and there was another fight that was indeterminate, because at quarter to four the door of the press-room was thrown open and the gang of boys crowded in to fold their papers.

"I'll lick you to-morrow," he heard Cheese-Face promise; and he heard his own voice, piping and trembling with unshed tears, agreeing to be there on the morrow.

And he had come there the next day, hurrying from school to be there first, and beating Cheese-Face by two minutes. The other boys said he was all right, and gave him advice, pointing out his faults as a scrapper and promising him victory if he carried out their instructions. The same boys gave Cheese-Face advice, too. How they had enjoyed the fight! He paused in his recollections long enough to envy them the spectacle he and Cheese-Face had put up. Then the fight was on, and it went on, without rounds, for thirty minutes, until the press-room door was opened.

He watched the youthful apparition of himself, day after day, hurrying from school to the *Enquirer* alley. He could not walk very fast. He was stiff and lame from the incessant fighting. His forearms were black and blue from wrist to elbow, what of the countless blows he had warded off, and here and there the tortured flesh was beginning to fester. His head and arms and shoulders ached, the small of his back ached,—he ached all over, and his brain was heavy and dazed. He did not play at school. Nor did he study. Even to sit still all day at his desk, as he did, was a torment. It seemed centuries since he had begun the round of daily fights, and time stretched away into a nightmare and infinite future of daily fights. Why couldn't Cheese-Face be licked? he often thought; that would put him, Martin, out of his misery. It never entered his head to cease fighting, to allow Cheese-Face to whip him.

And so he dragged himself to the *Enquirer* alley, sick in body and soul, but learning the long patience, to confront his eternal enemy, Cheese-Face, who was just as sick as he, and just a bit willing to quit if it were not for the gang of newsboys that looked on and made pride painful and necessary. One afternoon, after twenty minutes of desperate efforts to annihilate each other according to set rules that did not permit kicking, striking below the belt, nor hitting when one was down, Cheese-Face, panting for breath and reeling, offered to call it quits. And Martin, head on arms, thrilled at the picture he caught of himself, at that moment in the afternoon of long ago, when he reeled and panted and choked with the blood that ran into his mouth and down his throat from his cut lips; when he tottered toward Cheese-Face, spitting out a mouthful of blood so that he could speak, crying out that he would never quit, though Cheese-Face could give in if he wanted to. And Cheese-Face did not give in, and the fight went on.

The next day and the next, days without end, witnessed the afternoon fight. When he put up his arms, each day, to begin, they pained exquisitely, and the first few blows, struck and received, racked his soul; after that things grew numb, and he fought on blindly, seeing as in a dream, dancing and wavering, the large features and burning, animal-like eyes of Cheese-Face. He concentrated upon that face; all else about him was a whirling void. There was nothing else in the world but that face, and he would never know rest, blessed rest, until he had beaten that face into a pulp with his bleeding knuckles, or until the bleeding knuckles that somehow belonged to that face had beaten him into a pulp. And then, one way or the other, he would have rest. But to quit,—for him, Martin, to quit,—that was impossible!

Came the day when he dragged himself into the *Enquirer* alley, and there was no Cheese-Face. Nor did Cheese-Face come. The boys congratulated him, and told him that he had licked Cheese-Face. But Martin was not satisfied. He had not licked Cheese-Face, nor had Cheese-Face licked him. The problem had not been solved. It was not until afterward that they learned that Cheese-Face's father had died suddenly that very day.

Martin skipped on through the years to the night in the nigger heaven at the Auditorium. He was seventeen and just back from sea. A row started. Somebody was bullying somebody, and Martin interfered, to be confronted by Cheese-Face's blazing eyes.

"I'll fix you after de show," his ancient enemy hissed.

Martin nodded. The nigger-heaven bouncer was making his way toward the disturbance.

"I'll meet you outside, after the last act," Martin whispered, the while his face showed undivided interest in the buck-and-wing dancing on the stage.

The bouncer glared and went away.

"Got a gang?" he asked Cheese-Face, at the end of the act.

"Sure."

"Then I got to get one," Martin announced.

Between the acts he mustered his following—three fellows he knew from the nail works, a railroad fireman, and half a dozen of the Boo Gang, along with as many more from the dread Eighteen-and-Market Gang.

When the theatre let out, the two gangs strung along inconspicuously on opposite sides of the street. When they came to a quiet corner, they united and held a council of war.

"Eighth Street Bridge is the place," said a red-headed fellow belonging to Cheese-Face's Gang. "You kin fight in the middle, under the electric light, an' whichever way the bulls come in we kin sneak the other way."

"That's agreeable to me," Martin said, after consulting with the leaders of his own gang.

The Eighth Street Bridge, crossing an arm of San Antonio Estuary, was the length of three city blocks. In the middle of the bridge, and at each end, were electric lights. No policeman could pass those end-lights unseen. It was the safe place for the battle that revived itself under Martin's eyelids. He saw the two gangs, aggressive and sullen, rigidly keeping apart from each other and backing their respective champions; and he saw himself and Cheese-Face stripping. A short distance away lookouts were set, their task being to watch the lighted ends of the bridge. A member of the Boo Gang held Martin's coat, and shirt, and cap, ready to race with them into safety in case the police interfered. Martin watched himself go into the centre, facing Cheese-Face, and he heard himself say, as he held up his hand warningly:-

"They ain't no hand-shakin' in this. Understand? They ain't nothin' but scrap. No throwin' up the sponge. This is a grudge-fight an' it's to a finish. Understand? Somebody's goin' to get licked."

Cheese-Face wanted to demur,—Martin could see that,—but Cheese-Face's old perilous pride was touched before the two gangs.

"Aw, come on," he replied. "Wot's the good of chewin' de rag about it? I'm wit' cheh to de finish."

Then they fell upon each other, like young bulls, in all the glory of youth, with naked fists, with hatred, with desire to hurt, to maim, to destroy. All the painful, thousand years' gains of man in his upward climb through creation were lost. Only the electric light remained, a milestone on the path of the great human adventure. Martin and Cheese-Face were two savages, of the stone age, of the squatting place and the tree refuge. They sank lower and lower into the muddy abyss, back into the dregs of the raw beginnings of life, striving blindly and chemically, as atoms strive, as the star-dust if the heavens strives, colliding, recoiling, and colliding again and eternally again.

"God! We are animals! Brute-beasts!" Martin muttered aloud, as he watched the progress of the fight. It was to him, with his splendid power of vision, like gazing into a kinetoscope. He was both onlooker and participant. His long months of culture and refinement shuddered at the sight; then the present was blotted out of his consciousness and the ghosts of the past possessed him, and he was Martin Eden, just returned from sea and fighting Cheese-Face on the Eighth Street Bridge. He suffered and toiled and sweated and bled, and exulted when his naked knuckles smashed home.

They were twin whirlwinds of hatred, revolving about each other monstrously. The time passed, and the two hostile gangs became very quiet. They had never witnessed such intensity of ferocity, and they were awed by it. The two fighters were greater brutes than they. The first splendid velvet edge of youth and condition wore off, and they fought more cautiously and deliberately. There had been no advantage gained either way. "It's anybody's fight," Martin heard some one saying. Then he followed up a feint, right and left, was fiercely countered, and felt his cheek laid open to the bone. No bare knuckle had done that. He heard mutters of amazement at the ghastly damage wrought, and was drenched with his own blood. But he gave no sign. He became immensely wary, for he was wise with knowledge of the low cunning and foul vileness of his kind. He watched and waited, until he feigned a wild rush, which he stopped midway, for he had seen the glint of metal.

"Hold up yer hand!" he screamed. "Them's brass knuckles, an' you hit me with 'em!"

Both gangs surged forward, growling and snarling. In a second there would be a free-for-all fight, and he would be robbed of his vengeance. He was beside himself.

"You guys keep out!" he screamed hoarsely. "Understand? Say, d'ye understand?"

They shrank away from him. They were brutes, but he was the arch-brute, a thing of terror that towered over them and dominated them.

"This is my scrap, an' they ain't goin' to be no buttin' in. Gimme them knuckles."

Cheese-Face, sobered and a bit frightened, surrendered the foul weapon.

"You passed 'em to him, you red-head sneakin' in behind the push there," Martin went on, as he tossed the knuckles into the water. "I seen you, an' I was wonderin' what you was up to. If you try anything like that again, I'll beat cheh to death. Understand?"

CHAPTER XV

They fought on, through exhaustion and beyond, to exhaustion immeasurable and inconceivable, until the crowd of brutes, its blood-lust sated, terrified by what it saw, begged them impartially to cease. And Cheese-Face, ready to drop and die, or to stay on his legs and die, a grisly monster out of whose features all likeness to Cheese-Face had been beaten, wavered and hesitated; but Martin sprang in and smashed him again and again.

Next, after a seeming century or so, with Cheese-Face weakening fast, in a mix-up of blows there was a loud snap, and Martin's right arm dropped to his side. It was a broken bone. Everybody heard it and knew; and Cheese-Face knew, rushing like a tiger in the other's extremity and raining blow on blow. Martin's gang surged forward to interfere. Dazed by the rapid succession of blows, Martin warned them back with vile and earnest curses sobbed out and groaned in ultimate desolation and despair.

He punched on, with his left hand only, and as he punched, doggedly, only half-conscious, as from a remote distance he heard murmurs of fear in the gangs, and one who said with shaking voice: "This ain't a scrap, fellows. It's murder, an' we ought to stop it."

But no one stopped it, and he was glad, punching on wearily and endlessly with his one arm, battering away at a bloody something before him that was not a face but a horror, an oscillating, hideous, gibbering, nameless thing that persisted before his wavering vision and would not go away. And he punched on and on, slower and slower, as the last shreds of vitality oozed from him, through centuries and aeons and enormous lapses of time, until, in a dim way, he became aware that the nameless thing was sinking, slowly sinking down to the rough board-planking of the bridge. And the next moment he was standing over it, staggering and swaying on shaky legs, clutching at the air for support, and saying in a voice he did not recognize:-

"D'ye want any more? Say, d'ye want any more?"

He was still saying it, over and over,—demanding, entreating, threatening, to know if it wanted any more,—when he felt the fellows of his gang laying hands on him, patting him on the back and trying to put his coat on him. And then came a sudden rush of blackness and oblivion.

The tin alarm-clock on the table ticked on, but Martin Eden, his face buried on his arms, did not hear it. He heard nothing. He did not think. So absolutely had he relived life that he had fainted just as he fainted years before on the Eighth Street Bridge. For a full minute the blackness and the blankness endured. Then, like one from the dead, he sprang upright, eyes flaming, sweat pouring down his face, shouting:-

"I licked you, Cheese-Face! It took me eleven years, but I licked you!"

His knees were trembling under him, he felt faint, and he staggered back to the bed, sinking down and sitting on the edge of it. He was still in the clutch of the past. He looked about the room, perplexed, alarmed, wondering where he was, until he caught sight of the pile of manuscripts in the corner. Then the wheels of memory slipped ahead through four years of time, and he was aware of the present, of the books he had opened and the universe he had won from their pages, of his dreams and ambitions, and of his love for a pale wraith of a girl, sensitive and sheltered and ethereal, who would die of horror did she witness but one moment of what he had just lived through—one moment of all the muck of life through which he had waded.

He arose to his feet and confronted himself in the looking-glass.

"And so you arise from the mud, Martin Eden," he said solemnly. "And you cleanse your eyes in a great brightness, and thrust your shoulders among the stars, doing what all life has done, letting the 'ape and tiger die' and wresting highest heritage from all powers that be."

He looked more closely at himself and laughed.

"A bit of hysteria and melodrama, eh?" he queried. "Well, never mind. You licked Cheese-Face, and you'll lick the editors if it takes twice eleven years to do it in. You can't stop here. You've got to go on. It's to a finish, you know."

CHAPTER XVI

The alarm-clock went off, jerking Martin out of sleep with a suddenness that would have given headache to one with less splendid constitution. Though he slept soundly, he awoke instantly, like a cat, and he awoke eagerly, glad that the five hours of unconsciousness were gone. He hated the oblivion of sleep. There was too much to do, too much of life to live. He grudged every moment of life sleep robbed him of, and before the clock had ceased its clattering he was head and ears in the washbasin and thrilling to the cold bite of the water.

But he did not follow his regular programme. There was no unfinished story waiting his hand, no new story demanding articulation. He had studied late, and it was nearly time for breakfast. He tried to read a chapter in Fiske, but his brain was restless and he closed the book. To-day witnessed the beginning of the new battle, wherein for some time there would be no writing. He was aware of a sadness akin to that with which one leaves home and family. He looked at the manuscripts in the corner. That was it. He was going away from them, his pitiful, dishonored children that were welcome nowhere. He went over and began to rummage among them, reading snatches here and there, his favorite portions. "The Pot" he honored with reading aloud, as he did "Adventure." "Joy," his latest-born, completed the day before and tossed into the corner for lack of stamps, won his keenest approbation.

"I can't understand," he murmured. "Or maybe it's the editors who can't understand. There's nothing wrong with that. They publish worse every month. Everything they publish is worse—nearly everything, anyway."

After breakfast he put the type-writer in its case and carried it down into Oakland.

"I owe a month on it," he told the clerk in the store. "But you tell the manager I'm going to work and that I'll be in in a month or so and straighten up."

He crossed on the ferry to San Francisco and made his way to an employment office. "Any kind of work, no trade," he told the agent; and was interrupted by a newcomer, dressed rather foppishly, as some workingmen dress who have instincts for finer things. The agent shook his head despondently.

"Nothin' doin' eh?" said the other. "Well, I got to get somebody to-day."

He turned and stared at Martin, and Martin, staring back, noted the puffed and discolored face, handsome and weak, and knew that he had been making a night of it.

"Lookin' for a job?" the other queried. "What can you do?"

"Hard labor, sailorizing, run a type-writer, no shorthand, can sit on a horse, willing to do anything and tackle anything," was the answer.

The other nodded.

"Sounds good to me. My name's Dawson, Joe Dawson, an' I'm tryin' to scare up a laundryman."

"Too much for me." Martin caught an amusing glimpse of himself ironing fluffy white things that women wear. But he had taken a liking to the other, and he added: "I might do the plain washing. I learned that much at sea." Joe Dawson thought visibly for a moment.

"Look here, let's get together an' frame it up. Willin' to listen?"

Martin nodded.

"This is a small laundry, up country, belongs to Shelly Hot Springs,—hotel, you know. Two men do the work, boss and assistant. I'm the boss. You don't work for me, but you work under me. Think you'd be willin' to learn?"

Martin paused to think. The prospect was alluring. A few months of it, and he would have time to himself for study. He could work hard and study hard.

"Good grub an' a room to yourself," Joe said.

That settled it. A room to himself where he could burn the midnight oil unmolested.

"But work like hell," the other added.

Martin caressed his swelling shoulder-muscles significantly. "That came from hard work."

"Then let's get to it." Joe held his hand to his head for a moment. "Gee, but it's a stem-winder. Can hardly see. I went down the line last night—everything—everything. Here's the frame-up. The wages for two is a hundred and board. I've ben drawin' down sixty, the second man forty. But he knew the biz. You're green. If I break you in, I'll be doing plenty of your work at first. Suppose you begin at thirty, an' work up to the forty. I'll play fair. Just as soon as you can do your share you get the forty."

"I'll go you," Martin announced, stretching out his hand, which the other shook. "Any advance?—for rail-road ticket and extras?"

"I blew it in," was Joe's sad answer, with another reach at his aching head. "All I got is a return ticket."

"And I'm broke—when I pay my board."

"Jump it," Joe advised.

"Can't. Owe it to my sister."

Joe whistled a long, perplexed whistle, and racked his brains to little purpose.

"I've got the price of the drinks," he said desperately. "Come on, an' mebbe we'll cook up something."

Martin declined.

"Water-wagon?"

This time Martin nodded, and Joe lamented, "Wish I was."

"But I somehow just can't," he said in extenuation. "After I've ben workin' like hell all week I just got to booze up. If I didn't, I'd cut my throat or burn up the premises. But I'm glad you're on the wagon. Stay with it."

Martin knew of the enormous gulf between him and this man—the gulf the books had made; but he found no difficulty in crossing back over that gulf. He had lived all his life in the working-class world, and the *camaraderie* of labor was second nature with him. He solved the difficulty of transportation that was too much for the other's aching head. He would send his trunk up to Shelly Hot Springs on Joe's ticket. As for himself, there was his wheel. It was seventy miles, and he could ride it on Sunday and be ready for work Monday morning. In the meantime he would go home and pack up. There was no one to say good-by to. Ruth and her whole family were spending the long summer in the Sierras, at Lake Tahoe.

He arrived at Shelly Hot Springs, tired and dusty, on Sunday night. Joe greeted him exuberantly. With a wet towel bound about his aching brow, he had been at work all day.

"Part of last week's washin' mounted up, me bein' away to get you," he explained. "Your box arrived all right. It's in your room. But it's a hell of a thing to call a trunk. An' what's in it? Gold bricks?"

Joe sat on the bed while Martin unpacked. The box was a packing-case for breakfast food, and Mr. Higginbotham had charged him half a dollar for it. Two rope handles, nailed on by Martin, had technically transformed it into a trunk eligible for the baggage-car. Joe watched, with bulging eyes, a few shirts and several changes of underclothes come out of the box, followed by books, and more books.

"Books clean to the bottom?" he asked.

Martin nodded, and went on arranging the books on a kitchen table which served in the room in place of a wash-stand.

"Gee!" Joe exploded, then waited in silence for the deduction to arise in his brain. At last it came.

"Say, you don't care for the girls—much?" he queried.

"No," was the answer. "I used to chase a lot before I tackled the books. But since then there's no time."

"And there won't be any time here. All you can do is work an' sleep."

Martin thought of his five hours' sleep a night, and smiled. The room was situated over the laundry and was in the same building with the engine that pumped water, made electricity, and ran the laundry machinery. The engineer, who occupied the adjoining room, dropped in to meet the new hand and helped Martin rig up an electric bulb, on an extension wire, so that it travelled along a stretched cord from over the table to the bed.

The next morning, at quarter-past six, Martin was routed out for a quarter-to-seven breakfast. There happened to be a bath-tub for the servants in the laundry building, and he electrified Joe by taking a cold bath.

"Gee, but you're a hummer!" Joe announced, as they sat down to breakfast in a corner of the hotel kitchen.

With them was the engineer, the gardener, and the assistant gardener, and two or three men from the stable. They ate hurriedly and gloomily, with but little conversation, and as Martin ate and listened he realized how far he had travelled from their status. Their small mental caliber was depressing to him, and he was anxious to get away from them. So he bolted his breakfast, a sickly, sloppy affair, as rapidly as they, and heaved a sigh of relief when he passed out through the kitchen door.

It was a perfectly appointed, small steam laundry, wherein the most modern machinery did everything that was possible for machinery to do. Martin, after a few instructions, sorted the great heaps of soiled clothes, while Joe started the masher and made up fresh supplies of soft-soap, compounded of biting chemicals that compelled him to swathe his mouth and nostrils and eyes in bath-towels till he resembled a mummy. Finished the sorting, Martin lent a hand in wringing the clothes. This was done by dumping them into a spinning receptacle that went at a rate of a few thousand revolutions a minute, tearing the matter from the clothes by centrifugal force. Then Martin began to alternate between the dryer and the wringer, between times "shaking out" socks and stockings. By the afternoon, one feeding and one, stacking up, they were running socks and stockings through the mangle while the irons were heating. Then it was hot irons and underclothes till six o'clock, at which time Joe shook his head dubiously.

"Way behind," he said. "Got to work after supper." And after supper they worked until ten o'clock, under the blazing electric lights, until the last piece of under-clothing was ironed and folded away in the distributing room. It was a hot California night, and though the windows were thrown wide, the room, with its red-hot ironing-stove, was a furnace. Martin and Joe, down to undershirts, bare armed, sweated and panted for air.

"Like trimming cargo in the tropics," Martin said, when they went upstairs.

"You'll do," Joe answered. "You take hold like a good fellow. If you keep up the pace, you'll be on thirty dollars only one month. The second month you'll be gettin' your forty. But don't tell me you never ironed before. I know better."

"Never ironed a rag in my life, honestly, until to-day," Martin protested.

He was surprised at his weariness when he act into his room, forgetful of the fact that he had been on his feet and working without let up for fourteen hours. He set the alarm clock at six, and measured back five hours to one o'clock. He could read until then. Slipping off his shoes, to ease his swollen feet, he sat down at the table with his books. He opened Fiske, where he had left off to read. But he found trouble began to read it through a second time. Then he awoke, in pain from his stiffened muscles and chilled by the mountain wind that had begun to blow in through the window. He looked at the clock. It marked two. He had been asleep four hours. He pulled off his clothes and crawled into bed, where he was asleep the moment after his head touched the pillow.

Tuesday was a day of similar unremitting toil. The speed with which Joe worked won Martin's admiration. Joe was a dozen of demons for work. He was keyed up to concert pitch, and there was never a moment in the long day when he was not fighting for moments. He concentrated himself upon his work and upon how to save time, pointing out to Martin where he did in five motions what could be done in three, or in three motions what could be done in two. "Elimination of waste motion," Martin phrased it as he watched and patterned after. He was a good workman himself, quick and deft, and it had always been a point of pride with him that no man should do any of his work for him or outwork him. As a result, he concentrated with a similar singleness of purpose, greedily snapping up the hints and suggestions thrown out by his working mate. He "rubbed out" collars and cuffs, rubbing the starch out from between the double thicknesses of linen so that there would be no blisters when it came to the ironing, and doing it at a pace that elicited Joe's praise.

There was never an interval when something was not at hand to be done. Joe waited for nothing, waited on nothing, and went on the jump from task to task. They starched two hundred white shirts, with a single gathering movement seizing a shirt so that the wristbands, neckband, yoke, and bosom protruded beyond the circling right hand. At the same moment the left hand held up the body of the shirt so that it would not enter the starch, and at the moment the right hand dipped into the starch—starch so hot that, in order to wring it out, their hands had to thrust, and thrust continually, into a bucket of cold water. And that night they worked till half-past ten, dipping "fancy starch"—all the frilled and airy, delicate wear of ladies.

"Me for the tropics and no clothes," Martin laughed.

"And me out of a job," Joe answered seriously. "I don't know nothin' but laundrying."

"And you know it well."

"I ought to. Began in the Contra Costa in Oakland when I was eleven, shakin' out for the mangle. That was eighteen years ago, an' I've never done a tap of anything else. But this job is the fiercest I ever had. Ought to be one more man on it at least. We work to-morrow night. Always run the mangle Wednesday nights—collars an' cuffs."

Martin set his alarm, drew up to the table, and opened Fiske. He did not finish the first paragraph. The lines blurred and ran together and his head nodded. He walked up and down, batting his head savagely with his fists, but he could not conquer the numbness of sleep. He propped the book before him, and propped his eyelids with his fingers, and fell asleep with his eyes wide open. Then he surrendered, and, scarcely conscious of what he did, got off his clothes and into bed. He slept seven hours of heavy, animal-like sleep, and awoke by the alarm, feeling that he had not had enough.

"Doin' much readin'?" Joe asked.

Martin shook his head.

"Never mind. We got to run the mangle to-night, but Thursday we'll knock off at six. That'll give you a chance."

Martin washed woollens that day, by hand, in a large barrel, with strong soft-soap, by means of a hub from a wagon wheel, mounted on a plunger-pole that was attached to a spring-pole overhead.

"My invention," Joe said proudly. "Beats a washboard an' your knuckles, and, besides, it saves at least fifteen minutes in the week, an' fifteen minutes ain't to be sneezed at in this shebang."

Running the collars and cuffs through the mangle was also Joe's idea. That night, while they toiled on under the electric lights, he explained it.

"Something no laundry ever does, except this one. An' I got to do it if I'm goin' to get done Saturday afternoon at three o'clock. But I know how, an' that's the difference. Got to have right heat, right pressure, and run 'em through three times. Look at that!" He held a cuff aloft. "Couldn't do it better by hand or on a tiler."

Thursday, Joe was in a rage. A bundle of extra "fancy starch" had come in.

"I'm goin' to quit," he announced. "I won't stand for it. I'm goin' to quit it cold. What's the good of me workin' like a slave all week, a-savin' minutes, an' them a-comin' an' ringin' in fancy-starch extras on me? This is a free country, an' I'm to tell that fat Dutchman what I think of him. An' I won't tell 'm in French. Plain United States is good enough for me. Him a-ringin' in fancy starch extras!"

"We got to work to-night," he said the next moment, reversing his judgment and surrendering to fate.

And Martin did no reading that night. He had seen no daily paper all week, and, strangely to him, felt no desire to see one. He was not interested in the news. He was too tired and jaded to be interested in anything, though he planned to leave Saturday afternoon, if they finished at three, and ride on his wheel to Oakland. It was seventy miles, and the same distance back on Sunday afternoon would leave him anything but rested for the second week's work. It would have been easier to go on the train, but the round trip was two dollars and a half, and he was intent on saving money.

CHAPTER XVII

Martin learned to do many things. In the course of the first week, in one afternoon, he and Joe accounted for the two hundred white shirts. Joe ran the tiler, a machine wherein a hot iron was hooked on a steel string which furnished the pressure. By this means he ironed the yoke, wristbands, and neckband, setting the latter at right angles to the shirt, and put the glossy finish on the bosom. As fast as he finished them, he flung the shirts on a rack between him and Martin, who caught them up and "backed" them. This task consisted of ironing all the unstarched portions of the shirts.

It was exhausting work, carried on, hour after hour, at top speed. Out on the broad verandas of the hotel, men and women, in cool white, sipped iced drinks and kept their circulation down. But in the laundry the air was sizzling. The huge stove roared red hot and white hot, while the irons, moving over the damp cloth, sent up clouds of steam. The heat of these irons was different from that used by housewives. An iron that stood the ordinary test of a wet finger was too cold for Joe and Martin, and such test was useless. They went wholly by holding the irons close to their cheeks, gauging the heat by some secret mental process that Martin admired but could not understand. When the fresh irons proved too hot, they hooked them on iron rods and dipped them into cold water. This again required a precise and subtle judgment. A fraction of a second too long in the water and the fine and silken edge of the proper heat was lost, and Martin found time to marvel at the accuracy he developed—an automatic accuracy, founded upon criteria that were machine-like and unerring.

But there was little time in which to marvel. All Martin's consciousness was concentrated in the work. Ceaselessly active, head and hand, an intelligent machine, all that constituted him a man was devoted to furnishing that intelligence. There was no room in his brain for the universe and its mighty problems. All the broad and spacious corridors of his mind were closed and hermetically sealed. The echoing chamber of his soul was a narrow room, a conning tower, whence were directed his arm and shoulder muscles, his ten nimble fingers, and the swift-moving iron along its steaming path in broad, sweeping strokes, just so many strokes and no more, just so far with each stroke and not a fraction of an inch farther, rushing along interminable sleeves, sides, backs, and tails, and tossing the finished shirts, without rumpling, upon the receiving frame. And even as his hurrying soul tossed, it was reaching for another shirt. This went on, hour after hour, while outside all the world swooned under the overhead California sun. But there was no swooning in that superheated room. The cool guests on the verandas needed clean linen.

The sweat poured from Martin. He drank enormous quantities of water, but so great was the heat of the day and of his exertions, that the water sluiced through the interstices of his flesh and out at all his pores. Always, at sea, except at rare intervals, the work he performed had given him ample opportunity to commune with himself. The master of the ship had been lord of Martin's time; but here the manager of the hotel was lord of Martin's thoughts as well. He had no thoughts save for the nerve-racking, body-destroying toil. Outside of that it was impossible to think. He did not know that he loved Ruth. She did not even exist, for his driven soul had no time to remember her. It was only when he crawled to bed at night, or to breakfast in the morning, that she asserted herself to him in fleeting memories.

"This is hell, ain't it?" Joe remarked once.

Martin nodded, but felt a rasp of irritation. The statement had been obvious and unnecessary. They did not talk while they worked. Conversation threw them out of their stride, as it did this time, compelling Martin to miss a stroke of his iron and to make two extra motions before he caught his stride again.

On Friday morning the washer ran. Twice a week they had to put through hotel linen,—the sheets, pillow-slips, spreads, table-cloths, and napkins. This finished, they buckled down to "fancy starch." It was slow work, fastidious and delicate, and Martin did not learn it so readily. Besides, he could not take chances. Mistakes were disastrous.

"See that," Joe said, holding up a filmy corset-cover that he could have crumpled from view in one hand. "Scorch that an' it's twenty dollars out of your wages."

So Martin did not scorch that, and eased down on his muscular tension, though nervous tension rose higher than ever, and he listened sympathetically to the other's blasphemies as he toiled and suffered over the beautiful things that women wear when they do not have to do their own laundrying. "Fancy starch" was Martin's nightmare, and it was Joe's, too. It was "fancy starch" that robbed them of their hard-won minutes. They toiled at it all day. At seven in the evening they broke off to run the hotel linen through the mangle. At ten o'clock, while the hotel guests slept, the two laundrymen sweated on at "fancy starch" till midnight, till one, till two. At half-past two they knocked off.

Saturday morning it was "fancy starch," and odds and ends, and at three in the afternoon the week's work was done.

"You ain't a-goin' to ride them seventy miles into Oakland on top of this?" Joe demanded, as they sat on the stairs and took a triumphant smoke.

"Got to," was the answer.

"What are you goin' for?—a girl?"

"No; to save two and a half on the railroad ticket. I want to renew some books at the library."

"Why don't you send 'em down an' up by express? That'll cost only a quarter each way."

Martin considered it.

"An' take a rest to-morrow," the other urged. "You need it. I know I do. I'm plumb tuckered out."

CHAPTER XVII

He looked it. Indomitable, never resting, fighting for seconds and minutes all week, circumventing delays and crushing down obstacles, a fount of resistless energy, a high-driven human motor, a demon for work, now that he had accomplished the week's task he was in a state of collapse. He was worn and haggard, and his handsome face drooped in lean exhaustion. He pulled his cigarette spiritlessly, and his voice was peculiarly dead and monotonous. All the snap and fire had gone out of him. His triumph seemed a sorry one.

"An' next week we got to do it all over again," he said sadly. "An' what's the good of it all, hey? Sometimes I wish I was a hobo. They don't work, an' they get their livin'. Gee! I wish I had a glass of beer; but I can't get up the gumption to go down to the village an' get it. You'll stay over, an' send your books dawn by express, or else you're a damn fool."

"But what can I do here all day Sunday?" Martin asked.

"Rest. You don't know how tired you are. Why, I'm that tired Sunday I can't even read the papers. I was sick once—typhoid. In the hospital two months an' a half. Didn't do a tap of work all that time. It was beautiful."

"It was beautiful," he repeated dreamily, a minute later.

Martin took a bath, after which he found that the head laundryman had disappeared. Most likely he had gone for a glass of beer Martin decided, but the half-mile walk down to the village to find out seemed a long journey to him. He lay on his bed with his shoes off, trying to make up his mind. He did not reach out for a book. He was too tired to feel sleepy, and he lay, scarcely thinking, in a semi-stupor of weariness, until it was time for supper. Joe did not appear for that function, and when Martin heard the gardener remark that most likely he was ripping the slats off the bar, Martin understood. He went to bed immediately afterward, and in the morning decided that he was greatly rested. Joe being still absent, Martin procured a Sunday paper and lay down in a shady nook under the trees. The morning passed, he knew not how. He did not sleep, nobody disturbed him, and he did not finish the paper. He came back to it in the afternoon, after dinner, and fell asleep over it.

So passed Sunday, and Monday morning he was hard at work, sorting clothes, while Joe, a towel bound tightly around his head, with groans and blasphemies, was running the washer and mixing soft-soap.

"I simply can't help it," he explained. "I got to drink when Saturday night comes around."

Another week passed, a great battle that continued under the electric lights each night and that culminated on Saturday afternoon at three o'clock, when Joe tasted his moment of wilted triumph and then drifted down to the village to forget. Martin's Sunday was the same as before. He slept in the shade of the trees, toiled aimlessly through the newspaper, and spent long hours lying on his back, doing nothing, thinking nothing. He was too dazed to think, though he was aware that he did not like himself. He was self-repelled, as though he had undergone some degradation or was intrinsically foul. All that was god-like in him was blotted out. The spur of ambition was blunted; he had no vitality with which to feel the prod of it. He was dead. His soul seemed dead. He was a beast, a work-beast. He saw no beauty in the sunshine sifting down through the green leaves, nor did the azure vault of the sky whisper as of old and hint of cosmic vastness and secrets trembling to disclosure. Life was intolerably dull and stupid, and its taste was bad in his mouth. A black screen was drawn across his mirror of inner vision, and fancy lay in a darkened sick-room where entered no ray of light. He envied Joe, down in the village, rampant, tearing the slats off the bar, his brain gnawing with maggots, exulting in maudlin ways over maudlin things, fantastically and gloriously drunk and forgetful of Monday morning and the week of deadening toil to come.

A third week went by, and Martin loathed himself, and loathed life. He was oppressed by a sense of failure. There was reason for the editors refusing his stuff. He could see that clearly now, and laugh at himself and the dreams he had dreamed. Ruth returned his "Sea Lyrics" by mail. He read her letter apathetically. She did her best to say how much she liked them and that they were beautiful. But she could not lie, and she could not disguise the truth from herself. She knew they were failures, and he read her disapproval in every perfunctory and unenthusiastic line of her letter. And she was right. He was firmly convinced of it as he read the poems over. Beauty and wonder had departed from him, and as he read the poems he caught himself puzzling as to what he had had in mind when he wrote them. His audacities of phrase struck him as grotesque, his felicities of expression were monstrosities, and everything was absurd, unreal, and impossible. He would have burned the "Sea Lyrics" on the spot, had his will been strong enough to set them aflame. There was the engine-room, but the exertion of carrying them to the furnace was not worth while. All his exertion was used in washing other persons' clothes. He did not have any left for private affairs.

He resolved that when Sunday came he would pull himself together and answer Ruth's letter. But Saturday afternoon, after work was finished and he had taken a bath, the desire to forget overpowered him. "I guess I'll go down and see how Joe's getting on," was the way he put it to himself; and in the same moment he knew that he lied. But he did not have the energy to consider the lie. If he had had the energy, he would have refused to consider the lie, because he wanted to forget. He started for the village slowly and casually, increasing his pace in spite of himself as he neared the saloon.

"I thought you was on the water-wagon," was Joe's greeting.

Martin did not deign to offer excuses, but called for whiskey, filling his own glass brimming before he passed the bottle.

"Don't take all night about it," he said roughly.

The other was dawdling with the bottle, and Martin refused to wait for him, tossing the glass off in a gulp and refilling it.

"Now, I can wait for you," he said grimly; "but hurry up."

Joe hurried, and they drank together.

"The work did it, eh?" Joe queried.

Martin refused to discuss the matter.

"It's fair hell, I know," the other went on, "but I kind of hate to see you come off the wagon, Mart. Well, here's how!"

Martin drank on silently, biting out his orders and invitations and awing the barkeeper, an effeminate country youngster with watery blue eyes and hair parted in the middle.

"It's something scandalous the way they work us poor devils," Joe was remarking. "If I didn't bowl up, I'd break loose an' burn down the shebang. My bowlin' up is all that saves 'em, I can tell you that."

CHAPTER XVII

But Martin made no answer. A few more drinks, and in his brain he felt the maggots of intoxication beginning to crawl. Ah, it was living, the first breath of life he had breathed in three weeks. His dreams came back to him. Fancy came out of the darkened room and lured him on, a thing of flaming brightness. His mirror of vision was silver-clear, a flashing, dazzling palimpsest of imagery. Wonder and beauty walked with him, hand in hand, and all power was his. He tried to tell it to Joe, but Joe had visions of his own, infallible schemes whereby he would escape the slavery of laundry-work and become himself the owner of a great steam laundry.

"I tell yeh, Mart, they won't be no kids workin' in my laundry—not on yer life. An' they won't be no workin' a livin' soul after six P.M. You hear me talk! They'll be machinery enough an' hands enough to do it all in decent workin' hours, an' Mart, s'help me, I'll make yeh superintendent of the shebang—the whole of it, all of it. Now here's the scheme. I get on the water-wagon an' save my money for two years—save an' then—"

But Martin turned away, leaving him to tell it to the barkeeper, until that worthy was called away to furnish drinks to two farmers who, coming in, accepted Martin's invitation. Martin dispensed royal largess, inviting everybody up, farm-hands, a stableman, and the gardener's assistant from the hotel, the barkeeper, and the furtive hobo who slid in like a shadow and like a shadow hovered at the end of the bar.

CHAPTER XVIII

Monday morning, Joe groaned over the first truck load of clothes to the washer.

"I say," he began.

"Don't talk to me," Martin snarled.

"I'm sorry, Joe," he said at noon, when they knocked off for dinner.

Tears came into the other's eyes.

"That's all right, old man," he said. "We're in hell, an' we can't help ourselves. An', you know, I kind of like you a whole lot. That's what made it—hurt. I cottoned to you from the first."

Martin shook his hand.

"Let's quit," Joe suggested. "Let's chuck it, an' go hoboin'. I ain't never tried it, but it must be dead easy. An' nothin' to do. Just think of it, nothin' to do. I was sick once, typhoid, in the hospital, an' it was beautiful. I wish I'd get sick again."

The week dragged on. The hotel was full, and extra "fancy starch" poured in upon them. They performed prodigies of valor. They fought late each night under the electric lights, bolted their meals, and even got in a half hour's work before breakfast. Martin no longer took his cold baths. Every moment was drive, drive, drive, and Joe was the masterful shepherd of moments, herding them carefully, never losing one, counting them over like a miser counting gold, working on in a frenzy, toil-mad, a feverish machine, aided ably by that other machine that thought of itself as once having been one Martin Eden, a man.

But it was only at rare moments that Martin was able to think. The house of thought was closed, its windows boarded up, and he was its shadowy caretaker. He was a shadow. Joe was right. They were both shadows, and this was the unending limbo of toil. Or was it a dream? Sometimes, in the steaming, sizzling heat, as he swung the heavy irons back and forth over the white garments, it came to him that it was a dream. In a short while, or maybe after a thousand years or so, he would awake, in his little room with the ink-stained table, and take up his writing where he had left off the day before. Or maybe that was a dream, too, and the awakening would be the changing of the watches, when he would drop down out of his bunk in the lurching forecastle and go up on deck, under the tropic stars, and take the wheel and feel the cool tradewind blowing through his flesh.

Came Saturday and its hollow victory at three o'clock.

"Guess I'll go down an' get a glass of beer," Joe said, in the queer, monotonous tones that marked his week-end collapse.

CHAPTER XVIII

Martin seemed suddenly to wake up. He opened the kit bag and oiled his wheel, putting graphite on the chain and adjusting the bearings. Joe was halfway down to the saloon when Martin passed by, bending low over the handle-bars, his legs driving the ninety-six gear with rhythmic strength, his face set for seventy miles of road and grade and dust. He slept in Oakland that night, and on Sunday covered the seventy miles back. And on Monday morning, weary, he began the new week's work, but he had kept sober.

A fifth week passed, and a sixth, during which he lived and toiled as a machine, with just a spark of something more in him, just a glimmering bit of soul, that compelled him, at each week-end, to scorch off the hundred and forty miles. But this was not rest. It was super-machinelike, and it helped to crush out the glimmering bit of soul that was all that was left him from former life. At the end of the seventh week, without intending it, too weak to resist, he drifted down to the village with Joe and drowned life and found life until Monday morning.

Again, at the week-ends, he ground out the one hundred and forty miles, obliterating the numbness of too great exertion by the numbness of still greater exertion. At the end of three months he went down a third time to the village with Joe. He forgot, and lived again, and, living, he saw, in clear illumination, the beast he was making of himself—not by the drink, but by the work. The drink was an effect, not a cause. It followed inevitably upon the work, as the night follows upon the day. Not by becoming a toil-beast could he win to the heights, was the message the whiskey whispered to him, and he nodded approbation. The whiskey was wise. It told secrets on itself.

He called for paper and pencil, and for drinks all around, and while they drank his very good health, he clung to the bar and scribbled.

"A telegram, Joe," he said. "Read it."

Joe read it with a drunken, quizzical leer. But what he read seemed to sober him. He looked at the other reproachfully, tears oozing into his eyes and down his cheeks.

"You ain't goin' back on me, Mart?" he queried hopelessly.

Martin nodded, and called one of the loungers to him to take the message to the telegraph office.

"Hold on," Joe muttered thickly. "Lemme think."

He held on to the bar, his legs wobbling under him, Martin's arm around him and supporting him, while he thought.

"Make that two laundrymen," he said abruptly. "Here, lemme fix it."

"What are you quitting for?" Martin demanded.

"Same reason as you."

"But I'm going to sea. You can't do that."

"Nope," was the answer, "but I can hobo all right, all right."

Martin looked at him searchingly for a moment, then cried:-

"By God, I think you're right! Better a hobo than a beast of toil. Why, man, you'll live. And that's more than you ever did before."

"I was in hospital, once," Joe corrected. "It was beautiful. Typhoid—did I tell you?"

While Martin changed the telegram to "two laundrymen," Joe went on:-

"I never wanted to drink when I was in hospital. Funny, ain't it? But when I've ben workin' like a slave all week, I just got to bowl up. Ever noticed that cooks drink like hell?—an' bakers, too? It's the work. They've sure got to. Here, lemme pay half of that telegram."

"I'll shake you for it," Martin offered.

"Come on, everybody drink," Joe called, as they rattled the dice and rolled them out on the damp bar.

Monday morning Joe was wild with anticipation. He did not mind his aching head, nor did he take interest in his work. Whole herds of moments stole away and were lost while their careless shepherd gazed out of the window at the sunshine and the trees.

"Just look at it!" he cried. "An' it's all mine! It's free. I can lie down under them trees an' sleep for a thousan' years if I want to. Aw, come on, Mart, let's chuck it. What's the good of waitin' another moment. That's the land of nothin' to do out there, an' I got a ticket for it—an' it ain't no return ticket, b'gosh!"

A few minutes later, filling the truck with soiled clothes for the washer, Joe spied the hotel manager's shirt. He knew its mark, and with a sudden glorious consciousness of freedom he threw it on the floor and stamped on it.

"I wish you was in it, you pig-headed Dutchman!" he shouted. "In it, an' right there where I've got you! Take that! an' that! an' that! damn you! Hold me back, somebody! Hold me back!"

Martin laughed and held him to his work. On Tuesday night the new laundrymen arrived, and the rest of the week was spent breaking them into the routine. Joe sat around and explained his system, but he did no more work.

"Not a tap," he announced. "Not a tap. They can fire me if they want to, but if they do, I'll quit. No more work in mine, thank you kindly. Me for the freight cars an' the shade under the trees. Go to it, you slaves! That's right. Slave an' sweat! Slave an' sweat! An' when you're dead, you'll rot the same as me, an' what's it matter how you live?—eh? Tell me that—what's it matter in the long run?"

On Saturday they drew their pay and came to the parting of the ways.

"They ain't no use in me askin' you to change your mind an' hit the road with me?" Joe asked hopelessly:

Martin shook his head. He was standing by his wheel, ready to start. They shook hands, and Joe held on to his for a moment, as he said:-

"I'm goin' to see you again, Mart, before you an' me die. That's straight dope. I feel it in my bones. Good-by, Mart, an' be good. I like you like hell, you know."

He stood, a forlorn figure, in the middle of the road, watching until Martin turned a bend and was gone from sight.

"He's a good Indian, that boy," he muttered. "A good Indian."

Then he plodded down the road himself, to the water tank, where half a dozen empties lay on a side-track waiting for the up freight.

CHAPTER XIX

Ruth and her family were home again, and Martin, returned to Oakland, saw much of her. Having gained her degree, she was doing no more studying; and he, having worked all vitality out of his mind and body, was doing no writing. This gave them time for each other that they had never had before, and their intimacy ripened fast.

At first, Martin had done nothing but rest. He had slept a great deal, and spent long hours musing and thinking and doing nothing. He was like one recovering from some terrible bout if hardship. The first signs of reawakening came when he discovered more than languid interest in the daily paper. Then he began to read again—light novels, and poetry; and after several days more he was head over heels in his long-neglected Fiske. His splendid body and health made new vitality, and he possessed all the resiliency and rebound of youth.

Ruth showed her disappointment plainly when he announced that he was going to sea for another voyage as soon as he was well rested.

"Why do you want to do that?" she asked.

"Money," was the answer. "I'll have to lay in a supply for my next attack on the editors. Money is the sinews of war, in my case—money and patience."

"But if all you wanted was money, why didn't you stay in the laundry?"

"Because the laundry was making a beast of me. Too much work of that sort drives to drink."

She stared at him with horror in her eyes.

"Do you mean—?" she quavered.

It would have been easy for him to get out of it; but his natural impulse was for frankness, and he remembered his old resolve to be frank, no matter what happened.

"Yes," he answered. "Just that. Several times."

She shivered and drew away from him.

"No man that I have ever known did that—ever did that."

"Then they never worked in the laundry at Shelly Hot Springs," he laughed bitterly. "Toil is a good thing. It is necessary for human health, so all the preachers say, and Heaven knows I've never been afraid of it. But there is such a thing as too much of a good thing, and the laundry up there is one of them. And that's why I'm going to sea one more voyage. It will be my last, I think, for when I come back, I shall break into the magazines. I am certain of it."

She was silent, unsympathetic, and he watched her moodily, realizing how impossible it was for her to understand what he had been through.

"Some day I shall write it up—'The Degradation of Toil' or the 'Psychology of Drink in the Working-class,' or something like that for a title."

Never, since the first meeting, had they seemed so far apart as that day. His confession, told in frankness, with the spirit of revolt behind, had repelled her. But she was more shocked by the repulsion itself than by the cause of it. It pointed out to her how near she had drawn to him, and once accepted, it paved the way for greater intimacy. Pity, too, was aroused, and innocent, idealistic thoughts of reform. She would save this raw young man who had come so far. She would save him from the curse of his early environment, and she would save him from himself in spite of himself. And all this affected her as a very noble state of consciousness; nor did she dream that behind it and underlying it were the jealousy and desire of love.

They rode on their wheels much in the delightful fall weather, and out in the hills they read poetry aloud, now one and now the other, noble, uplifting poetry that turned one's thoughts to higher things. Renunciation, sacrifice, patience, industry, and high endeavor were the principles she thus indirectly preached—such abstractions being objectified in her mind by her father, and Mr. Butler, and by Andrew Carnegie, who, from a poor immigrant boy had arisen to be the book-giver of the world. All of which was appreciated and enjoyed by Martin. He followed her mental processes more clearly now, and her soul was no longer the sealed wonder it had been. He was on terms of intellectual equality with her. But the points of disagreement did not affect his love. His love was more ardent than ever, for he loved her for what she was, and even her physical frailty was an added charm in his eyes. He read of sickly Elizabeth Barrett, who for years had not placed her feet upon the ground, until that day of flame when she eloped with Browning and stood upright, upon the earth, under the open sky; and what Browning had done for her, Martin decided he could do for Ruth. But first, she must love him. The rest would be easy. He would give her strength and health. And he caught glimpses of their life, in the years to come, wherein, against a background of work and comfort and general well-being, he saw himself and Ruth reading and discussing poetry, she propped amid a multitude of cushions on the ground while she read aloud to him. This was the key to the life they would live. And always he saw that particular picture. Sometimes it was she who leaned against him while he read, one arm about her, her head upon his shoulder. Sometimes they pored together over the printed pages of beauty. Then, too, she loved nature, and with generous imagination he changed the scene of their reading—sometimes they read in closed-in valleys with precipitous walls, or in high mountain meadows, and, again, down by the gray sand-dunes with a wreath of billows at their feet, or afar on some volcanic tropic isle where waterfalls descended and became mist, reaching the sea in vapor veils that swayed and shivered to every vagrant wisp of wind. But always, in the foreground, lords of beauty and eternally reading and sharing, lay he and Ruth, and always in the background that was beyond the background of nature, dim and hazy, were work and success and money earned that made them free of the world and all its treasures.

"I should recommend my little girl to be careful," her mother warned her one day.

"I know what you mean. But it is impossible. He if; not—"

Ruth was blushing, but it was the blush of maidenhood called upon for the first time to discuss the sacred things of life with a mother held equally sacred.

"Your kind." Her mother finished the sentence for her.

CHAPTER XIX

Ruth nodded.

"I did not want to say it, but he is not. He is rough, brutal, strong—too strong. He has not—"

She hesitated and could not go on. It was a new experience, talking over such matters with her mother. And again her mother completed her thought for her.

"He has not lived a clean life, is what you wanted to say."

Again Ruth nodded, and again a blush mantled her face.

"It is just that," she said. "It has not been his fault, but he has played much with—"

"With pitch?"

"Yes, with pitch. And he frightens me. Sometimes I am positively in terror of him, when he talks in that free and easy way of the things he has done—as if they did not matter. They do matter, don't they?"

They sat with their arms twined around each other, and in the pause her mother patted her hand and waited for her to go on.

"But I am interested in him dreadfully," she continued. "In a way he is my protégé. Then, too, he is my first boy friend—but not exactly friend; rather protégé and friend combined. Sometimes, too, when he frightens me, it seems that he is a bulldog I have taken for a plaything, like some of the 'frat' girls, and he is tugging hard, and showing his teeth, and threatening to break loose."

Again her mother waited.

"He interests me, I suppose, like the bulldog. And there is much good in him, too; but there is much in him that I would not like in—in the other way. You see, I have been thinking. He swears, he smokes, he drinks, he has fought with his fists (he has told me so, and he likes it; he says so). He is all that a man should not be—a man I would want for my—" her voice sank very low—"husband. Then he is too strong. My prince must be tall, and slender, and dark—a graceful, bewitching prince. No, there is no danger of my failing in love with Martin Eden. It would be the worst fate that could befall me."

"But it is not that that I spoke about," her mother equivocated. "Have you thought about him? He is so ineligible in every way, you know, and suppose he should come to love you?"

"But he does—already," she cried.

"It was to be expected," Mrs. Morse said gently. "How could it be otherwise with any one who knew you?"

"Olney hates me!" she exclaimed passionately. "And I hate Olney. I feel always like a cat when he is around. I feel that I must be nasty to him, and even when I don't happen to feel that way, why, he's nasty to me, anyway. But I am happy with Martin Eden. No one ever loved me before—no man, I mean, in that way. And it is sweet to be loved—that way. You know what I mean, mother dear. It is sweet to feel that you are really and truly a woman." She buried her face in her mother's lap, sobbing. "You think I am dreadful, I know, but I am honest, and I tell you just how I feel."

Mrs. Morse was strangely sad and happy. Her child-daughter, who was a bachelor of arts, was gone; but in her place was a woman-daughter. The experiment had succeeded. The strange void in Ruth's nature had been filled, and filled without danger or penalty. This rough sailor-fellow had been the instrument, and, though Ruth did not love him, he had made her conscious of her womanhood.

"His hand trembles," Ruth was confessing, her face, for shame's sake, still buried. "It is most amusing and ridiculous, but I feel sorry for him, too. And when his hands are too trembly, and his eyes too shiny, why, I lecture him about his life and the wrong way he is going about it to mend it. But he worships me, I know. His eyes and his hands do not lie. And it makes me feel grown-up, the thought of it, the very thought of it; and I feel that I am possessed of something that is by rights my own—that makes me like the other girls—and—and young women. And, then, too, I knew that I was not like them before, and I knew that it worried you. You thought you did not let me know that dear worry of yours, but I did, and I wanted to—'to make good,' as Martin Eden says."

It was a holy hour for mother and daughter, and their eyes were wet as they talked on in the twilight, Ruth all white innocence and frankness, her mother sympathetic, receptive, yet calmly explaining and guiding.

"He is four years younger than you," she said. "He has no place in the world. He has neither position nor salary. He is impractical. Loving you, he should, in the name of common sense, be doing something that would give him the right to marry, instead of paltering around with those stories of his and with childish dreams. Martin Eden, I am afraid, will never grow up. He does not take to responsibility and a man's work in the world like your father did, or like all our friends, Mr. Butler for one. Martin Eden, I am afraid, will never be a money-earner. And this world is so ordered that money is necessary to happiness—oh, no, not these swollen fortunes, but enough of money to permit of common comfort and decency. He—he has never spoken?"

"He has not breathed a word. He has not attempted to; but if he did, I would not let him, because, you see, I do not love him."

"I am glad of that. I should not care to see my daughter, my one daughter, who is so clean and pure, love a man like him. There are noble men in the world who are clean and true and manly. Wait for them. You will find one some day, and you will love him and be loved by him, and you will be happy with him as your father and I have been happy with each other. And there is one thing you must always carry in mind—"

"Yes, mother."

Mrs. Morse's voice was low and sweet as she said, "And that is the children."

"I—have thought about them," Ruth confessed, remembering the wanton thoughts that had vexed her in the past, her face again red with maiden shame that she should be telling such things.

"And it is that, the children, that makes Mr. Eden impossible," Mrs. Morse went on incisively. "Their heritage must be clean, and he is, I am afraid, not clean. Your father has told me of sailors' lives, and—and you understand."

Ruth pressed her mother's hand in assent, feeling that she really did understand, though her conception was of something vague, remote, and terrible that was beyond the scope of imagination.

"You know I do nothing without telling you," she began. "—Only, sometimes you must ask me, like this time. I wanted to tell you, but I did not know how. It is false modesty, I know it is that, but you can make it easy for me. Sometimes, like this time, you must ask me, you must give me a chance."

"Why, mother, you are a woman, too!" she cried exultantly, as they stood up, catching her mother's hands and standing erect, facing her in the twilight, conscious of a strangely sweet equality between them. "I should never have thought of you in that way if we had not had this talk. I had to learn that I was a woman to know that you were one, too."

"We are women together," her mother said, drawing her to her and kissing her. "We are women together," she repeated, as they went out of the room, their arms around each other's waists, their hearts swelling with a new sense of companionship.

"Our little girl has become a woman," Mrs. Morse said proudly to her husband an hour later.

"That means," he said, after a long look at his wife, "that means she is in love."

"No, but that she is loved," was the smiling rejoinder. "The experiment has succeeded. She is awakened at last."

"Then we'll have to get rid of him." Mr. Morse spoke briskly, in matter-of-fact, businesslike tones.

But his wife shook her head. "It will not be necessary. Ruth says he is going to sea in a few days. When he comes back, she will not be here. We will send her to Aunt Clara's. And, besides, a year in the East, with the change in climate, people, ideas, and everything, is just the thing she needs."

CHAPTER XX

The desire to write was stirring in Martin once more. Stories and poems were springing into spontaneous creation in his brain, and he made notes of them against the future time when he would give them expression. But he did not write. This was his little vacation; he had resolved to devote it to rest and love, and in both matters he prospered. He was soon spilling over with vitality, and each day he saw Ruth, at the moment of meeting, she experienced the old shock of his strength and health.

"Be careful," her mother warned her once again. "I am afraid you are seeing too much of Martin Eden."

But Ruth laughed from security. She was sure of herself, and in a few days he would be off to sea. Then, by the time he returned, she would be away on her visit East. There was a magic, however, in the strength and health of Martin. He, too, had been told of her contemplated Eastern trip, and he felt the need for haste. Yet he did not know how to make love to a girl like Ruth. Then, too, he was handicapped by the possession of a great fund of experience with girls and women who had been absolutely different from her. They had known about love and life and flirtation, while she knew nothing about such things. Her prodigious innocence appalled him, freezing on his lips all ardors of speech, and convincing him, in spite of himself, of his own unworthiness. Also he was handicapped in another way. He had himself never been in love before. He had liked women in that turgid past of his, and been fascinated by some of them, but he had not known what it was to love them. He had whistled in a masterful, careless way, and they had come to him. They had been diversions, incidents, part of the game men play, but a small part at most. And now, and for the first time, he was a suppliant, tender and timid and doubting. He did not know the way of love, nor its speech, while he was frightened at his loved one's clear innocence.

In the course of getting acquainted with a varied world, whirling on through the ever changing phases of it, he had learned a rule of conduct which was to the effect that when one played a strange game, he should let the other fellow play first. This had stood him in good stead a thousand times and trained him as an observer as well. He knew how to watch the thing that was strange, and to wait for a weakness, for a place of entrance, to divulge itself. It was like sparring for an opening in fist-fighting. And when such an opening came, he knew by long experience to play for it and to play hard.

CHAPTER XX

So he waited with Ruth and watched, desiring to speak his love but not daring. He was afraid of shocking her, and he was not sure of himself. Had he but known it, he was following the right course with her. Love came into the world before articulate speech, and in its own early youth it had learned ways and means that it had never forgotten. It was in this old, primitive way that Martin wooed Ruth. He did not know he was doing it at first, though later he divined it. The touch of his hand on hers was vastly more potent than any word he could utter, the impact of his strength on her imagination was more alluring than the printed poems and spoken passions of a thousand generations of lovers. Whatever his tongue could express would have appealed, in part, to her judgment; but the touch of hand, the fleeting contact, made its way directly to her instinct. Her judgment was as young as she, but her instincts were as old as the race and older. They had been young when love was young, and they were wiser than convention and opinion and all the new-born things. So her judgment did not act. There was no call upon it, and she did not realize the strength of the appeal Martin made from moment to moment to her love-nature. That he loved her, on the other hand, was as clear as day, and she consciously delighted in beholding his love-manifestations—the glowing eyes with their tender lights, the trembling hands, and the never failing swarthy flush that flooded darkly under his sunburn. She even went farther, in a timid way inciting him, but doing it so delicately that he never suspected, and doing it half-consciously, so that she scarcely suspected herself. She thrilled with these proofs of her power that proclaimed her a woman, and she took an Eve-like delight in tormenting him and playing upon him.

Tongue-tied by inexperience and by excess of ardor, wooing unwittingly and awkwardly, Martin continued his approach by contact. The touch of his hand was pleasant to her, and something deliciously more than pleasant. Martin did not know it, but he did know that it was not distasteful to her. Not that they touched hands often, save at meeting and parting; but that in handling the bicycles, in strapping on the books of verse they carried into the hills, and in conning the pages of books side by side, there were opportunities for hand to stray against hand. And there were opportunities, too, for her hair to brush his cheek, and for shoulder to touch shoulder, as they leaned together over the beauty of the books. She smiled to herself at vagrant impulses which arose from nowhere and suggested that she rumple his hair; while he desired greatly, when they tired of reading, to rest his head in her lap and dream with closed eyes about the future that was to be theirs. On Sunday picnics at Shellmound Park and Schuetzen Park, in the past, he had rested his head on many laps, and, usually, he had slept soundly and selfishly while the girls shaded his face from the sun and looked down and loved him and wondered at his lordly carelessness of their love. To rest his head in a girl's lap had been the easiest thing in the world until now, and now he found Ruth's lap inaccessible and impossible. Yet it was right here, in his reticence, that the strength of his wooing lay. It was because of this reticence that he never alarmed her. Herself fastidious and timid, she never awakened to the perilous trend of their intercourse. Subtly and unaware she grew toward him and closer to him, while he, sensing the growing closeness, longed to dare but was afraid.

Once he dared, one afternoon, when he found her in the darkened living room with a blinding headache.

"Nothing can do it any good," she had answered his inquiries. "And besides, I don't take headache powders. Doctor Hall won't permit me."

"I can cure it, I think, and without drugs," was Martin's answer. "I am not sure, of course, but I'd like to try. It's simply massage. I learned the trick first from the Japanese. They are a race of masseurs, you know. Then I learned it all over again with variations from the Hawaiians. They call it *lomi-lomi*. It can accomplish most of the things drugs accomplish and a few things that drugs can't."

Scarcely had his hands touched her head when she sighed deeply.

"That is so good," she said.

She spoke once again, half an hour later, when she asked, "Aren't you tired?"

The question was perfunctory, and she knew what the answer would be. Then she lost herself in drowsy contemplation of the soothing balm of his strength: Life poured from the ends of his fingers, driving the pain before it, or so it seemed to her, until with the easement of pain, she fell asleep and he stole away.

She called him up by telephone that evening to thank him.

"I slept until dinner," she said. "You cured me completely, Mr. Eden, and I don't know how to thank you."

He was warm, and bungling of speech, and very happy, as he replied to her, and there was dancing in his mind, throughout the telephone conversation, the memory of Browning and of sickly Elizabeth Barrett. What had been done could be done again, and he, Martin Eden, could do it and would do it for Ruth Morse. He went back to his room and to the volume of Spencer's "Sociology" lying open on the bed. But he could not read. Love tormented him and overrode his will, so that, despite all determination, he found himself at the little ink-stained table. The sonnet he composed that night was the first of a love-cycle of fifty sonnets which was completed within two months. He had the "Love-sonnets from the Portuguese" in mind as he wrote, and he wrote under the best conditions for great work, at a climacteric of living, in the throes of his own sweet love-madness.

The many hours he was not with Ruth he devoted to the "Love-cycle," to reading at home, or to the public reading-rooms, where he got more closely in touch with the magazines of the day and the nature of their policy and content. The hours he spent with Ruth were maddening alike in promise and in inconclusiveness. It was a week after he cured her headache that a moonlight sail on Lake Merritt was proposed by Norman and seconded by Arthur and Olney. Martin was the only one capable of handling a boat, and he was pressed into service. Ruth sat near him in the stern, while the three young fellows lounged amidships, deep in a wordy wrangle over "frat" affairs.

The moon had not yet risen, and Ruth, gazing into the starry vault of the sky and exchanging no speech with Martin, experienced a sudden feeling of loneliness. She glanced at him. A puff of wind was heeling the boat over till the deck was awash, and he, one hand on tiller and the other on main-sheet, was luffing slightly, at the same time peering ahead to make out the near-lying north shore. He was unaware of her gaze, and she watched him intently, speculating fancifully about the strange warp of soul that led him, a young man with signal powers, to fritter away his time on the writing of stories and poems foredoomed to mediocrity and failure.

Her eyes wandered along the strong throat, dimly seen in the starlight, and over the firm-poised head, and the old desire to lay her hands upon his neck came back to her. The strength she abhorred attracted her. Her feeling of loneliness became more pronounced, and she felt tired. Her position on the heeling boat irked her, and she remembered the headache he had cured and the soothing rest that resided in him. He was sitting beside her, quite beside her, and the boat seemed to tilt her toward him. Then arose in her the impulse to lean against him, to rest herself against his strength—a vague, half-formed impulse, which, even as she considered it, mastered her and made her lean toward him. Or was it the heeling of the boat? She did not know. She never knew. She knew only that she was leaning against him and that the easement and soothing rest were very good. Perhaps it had been the boat's fault, but she made no effort to retrieve it. She leaned lightly against his shoulder, but she leaned, and she continued to lean when he shifted his position to make it more comfortable for her.

It was a madness, but she refused to consider the madness. She was no longer herself but a woman, with a woman's clinging need; and though she leaned ever so lightly, the need seemed satisfied. She was no longer tired. Martin did not speak. Had he, the spell would have been broken. But his reticence of love prolonged it. He was dazed and dizzy. He could not understand what was happening. It was too wonderful to be anything but a delirium. He conquered a mad desire to let go sheet and tiller and to clasp her in his arms. His intuition told him it was the wrong thing to do, and he was glad that sheet and tiller kept his hands occupied and fended off temptation. But he luffed the boat less delicately, spilling the wind shamelessly from the sail so as to prolong the tack to the north shore. The shore would compel him to go about, and the contact would be broken. He sailed with skill, stopping way on the boat without exciting the notice of the wranglers, and mentally forgiving his hardest voyages in that they had made this marvellous night possible, giving him mastery over sea and boat and wind so that he could sail with her beside him, her dear weight against him on his shoulder.

When the first light of the rising moon touched the sail, illuminating the boat with pearly radiance, Ruth moved away from him. And, even as she moved, she felt him move away. The impulse to avoid detection was mutual. The episode was tacitly and secretly intimate. She sat apart from him with burning cheeks, while the full force of it came home to her. She had been guilty of something she would not have her brothers see, nor Olney see. Why had she done it? She had never done anything like it in her life, and yet she had been moonlight-sailing with young men before. She had never desired to do anything like it. She was overcome with shame and with the mystery of her own burgeoning womanhood. She stole a glance at Martin, who was busy putting the boat about on the other tack, and she could have hated him for having made her do an immodest and shameful thing. And he, of all men! Perhaps her mother was right, and she was seeing too much of him. It would never happen again, she resolved, and she would see less of him in the future. She entertained a wild idea of explaining to him the first time they were alone together, of lying to him, of mentioning casually the attack of faintness that had overpowered her just before the moon came up. Then she remembered how they had drawn mutually away before the revealing moon, and she knew he would know it for a lie.

In the days that swiftly followed she was no longer herself but a strange, puzzling creature, wilful over judgment and scornful of self-analysis, refusing to peer into the future or to think about herself and whither she was drifting. She was in a fever of tingling mystery, alternately frightened and charmed, and in constant bewilderment. She had one idea firmly fixed, however, which insured her security. She would not let Martin speak his love. As long as she did this, all would be well. In a few days he would be off to sea. And even if he did speak, all would be well. It could not be otherwise, for she did not love him. Of course, it would be a painful half hour for him, and an embarrassing half hour for her, because it would be her first proposal. She thrilled deliciously at the thought. She was really a woman, with a man ripe to ask for her in marriage. It was a lure to all that was fundamental in her sex. The fabric of her life, of all that constituted her, quivered and grew tremulous. The thought fluttered in her mind like a flame-attracted moth. She went so far as to imagine Martin proposing, herself putting the words into his mouth; and she rehearsed her refusal, tempering it with kindness and exhorting him to true and noble manhood. And especially he must stop smoking cigarettes. She would make a point of that. But no, she must not let him speak at all. She could stop him, and she had told her mother that she would. All flushed and burning, she regretfully dismissed the conjured situation. Her first proposal would have to be deferred to a more propitious time and a more eligible suitor.

CHAPTER XXI

Came a beautiful fall day, warm and languid, palpitant with the hush of the changing season, a California Indian summer day, with hazy sun and wandering wisps of breeze that did not stir the slumber of the air. Filmy purple mists, that were not vapors but fabrics woven of color, hid in the recesses of the hills. San Francisco lay like a blur of smoke upon her heights. The intervening bay was a dull sheen of molten metal, whereon sailing craft lay motionless or drifted with the lazy tide. Far Tamalpais, barely seen in the silver haze, bulked hugely by the Golden Gate, the latter a pale gold pathway under the westering sun. Beyond, the Pacific, dim and vast, was raising on its sky-line tumbled cloud-masses that swept landward, giving warning of the first blustering breath of winter.

The erasure of summer was at hand. Yet summer lingered, fading and fainting among her hills, deepening the purple of her valleys, spinning a shroud of haze from waning powers and sated raptures, dying with the calm content of having lived and lived well. And among the hills, on their favorite knoll, Martin and Ruth sat side by side, their heads bent over the same pages, he reading aloud from the love-sonnets of the woman who had loved Browning as it is given to few men to be loved.

But the reading languished. The spell of passing beauty all about them was too strong. The golden year was dying as it had lived, a beautiful and unrepentant voluptuary, and reminiscent rapture and content freighted heavily the air. It entered into them, dreamy and languorous, weakening the fibres of resolution, suffusing the face of morality, or of judgment, with haze and purple mist. Martin felt tender and melting, and from time to time warm glows passed over him. His head was very near to hers, and when wandering phantoms of breeze stirred her hair so that it touched his face, the printed pages swam before his eyes.

"I don't believe you know a word of what you are reading," she said once when he had lost his place.

He looked at her with burning eyes, and was on the verge of becoming awkward, when a retort came to his lips.

"I don't believe you know either. What was the last sonnet about?"

"I don't know," she laughed frankly. "I've already forgotten. Don't let us read any more. The day is too beautiful."

"It will be our last in the hills for some time," he announced gravely. "There's a storm gathering out there on the sea-rim."

The book slipped from his hands to the ground, and they sat idly and silently, gazing out over the dreamy bay with eyes that dreamed and did not see. Ruth glanced sidewise at his neck. She did not lean toward him. She was drawn by some force outside of herself and stronger than gravitation, strong as destiny. It was only an inch to lean, and it was accomplished without volition on her part. Her shoulder touched his as lightly as a butterfly touches a flower, and just as lightly was the counter-pressure. She felt his shoulder press hers, and a tremor run through him. Then was the time for her to draw back. But she had become an automaton. Her actions had passed beyond the control of her will—she never thought of control or will in the delicious madness that was upon her. His arm began to steal behind her and around her. She waited its slow progress in a torment of delight. She waited, she knew not for what, panting, with dry, burning lips, a leaping pulse, and a fever of expectancy in all her blood. The girdling arm lifted higher and drew her toward him, drew her slowly and caressingly. She could wait no longer. With a tired sigh, and with an impulsive movement all her own, unpremeditated, spasmodic, she rested her head upon his breast. His head bent over swiftly, and, as his lips approached, hers flew to meet them.

This must be love, she thought, in the one rational moment that was vouchsafed her. If it was not love, it was too shameful. It could be nothing else than love. She loved the man whose arms were around her and whose lips were pressed to hers. She pressed more, tightly to him, with a snuggling movement of her body. And a moment later, tearing herself half out of his embrace, suddenly and exultantly she reached up and placed both hands upon Martin Eden's sunburnt neck. So exquisite was the pang of love and desire fulfilled that she uttered a low moan, relaxed her hands, and lay half-swooning in his arms.

Not a word had been spoken, and not a word was spoken for a long time. Twice he bent and kissed her, and each time her lips met his shyly and her body made its happy, nestling movement. She clung to him, unable to release herself, and he sat, half supporting her in his arms, as he gazed with unseeing eyes at the blur of the great city across the bay. For once there were no visions in his brain. Only colors and lights and glows pulsed there, warm as the day and warm as his love. He bent over her. She was speaking.

"When did you love me?" she whispered.

"From the first, the very first, the first moment I laid eye on you. I was mad for love of you then, and in all the time that has passed since then I have only grown the madder. I am maddest, now, dear. I am almost a lunatic, my head is so turned with joy."

"I am glad I am a woman, Martin—dear," she said, after a long sigh.

He crushed her in his arms again and again, and then asked:-

"And you? When did you first know?"

"Oh, I knew it all the time, almost, from the first."

"And I have been as blind as a bat!" he cried, a ring of vexation in his voice. "I never dreamed it until just how, when I—when I kissed you."

"I didn't mean that." She drew herself partly away and looked at him. "I meant I knew you loved almost from the first."

"And you?" he demanded.

CHAPTER XXI

"It came to me suddenly." She was speaking very slowly, her eyes warm and fluttery and melting, a soft flush on her cheeks that did not go away. "I never knew until just now when—you put your arms around me. And I never expected to marry you, Martin, not until just now. How did you make me love you?"

"I don't know," he laughed, "unless just by loving you, for I loved you hard enough to melt the heart of a stone, much less the heart of the living, breathing woman you are."

"This is so different from what I thought love would be," she announced irrelevantly.

"What did you think it would be like?"

"I didn't think it would be like this." She was looking into his eyes at the moment, but her own dropped as she continued, "You see, I didn't know what this was like."

He offered to draw her toward him again, but it was no more than a tentative muscular movement of the girdling arm, for he feared that he might be greedy. Then he felt her body yielding, and once again she was close in his arms and lips were pressed on lips.

"What will my people say?" she queried, with sudden apprehension, in one of the pauses.

"I don't know. We can find out very easily any time we are so minded."

"But if mamma objects? I am sure I am afraid to tell her."

"Let me tell her," he volunteered valiantly. "I think your mother does not like me, but I can win her around. A fellow who can win you can win anything. And if we don't—"

"Yes?"

"Why, we'll have each other. But there's no danger not winning your mother to our marriage. She loves you too well."

"I should not like to break her heart," Ruth said pensively.

He felt like assuring her that mothers' hearts were not so easily broken, but instead he said, "And love is the greatest thing in the world."

"Do you know, Martin, you sometimes frighten me. I am frightened now, when I think of you and of what you have been. You must be very, very good to me. Remember, after all, that I am only a child. I never loved before."

"Nor I. We are both children together. And we are fortunate above most, for we have found our first love in each other."

"But that is impossible!" she cried, withdrawing herself from his arms with a swift, passionate movement. "Impossible for you. You have been a sailor, and sailors, I have heard, are—are—"

Her voice faltered and died away.

"Are addicted to having a wife in every port?" he suggested. "Is that what you mean?"

"Yes," she answered in a low voice.

"But that is not love." He spoke authoritatively. "I have been in many ports, but I never knew a passing touch of love until I saw you that first night. Do you know, when I said good night and went away, I was almost arrested."

"Arrested?"

"Yes. The policeman thought I was drunk; and I was, too—with love for you."

"But you said we were children, and I said it was impossible, for you, and we have strayed away from the point."

"I said that I never loved anybody but you," he replied. "You are my first, my very first."

"And yet you have been a sailor," she objected.

"But that doesn't prevent me from loving you the first."

"And there have been women—other women—oh!"

And to Martin Eden's supreme surprise, she burst into a storm of tears that took more kisses than one and many caresses to drive away. And all the while there was running through his head Kipling's line: "*And the Colonel's lady and Judy O'Grady are sisters under their skins*." It was true, he decided; though the novels he had read had led him to believe otherwise. His idea, for which the novels were responsible, had been that only formal proposals obtained in the upper classes. It was all right enough, down whence he had come, for youths and maidens to win each other by contact; but for the exalted personages up above on the heights to make love in similar fashion had seemed unthinkable. Yet the novels were wrong. Here was a proof of it. The same pressures and caresses, unaccompanied by speech, that were efficacious with the girls of the working-class, were equally efficacious with the girls above the working-class. They were all of the same flesh, after all, sisters under their skins; and he might have known as much himself had he remembered his Spencer. As he held Ruth in his arms and soothed her, he took great consolation in the thought that the Colonel's lady and Judy O'Grady were pretty much alike under their skins. It brought Ruth closer to him, made her possible. Her dear flesh was as anybody's flesh, as his flesh. There was no bar to their marriage. Class difference was the only difference, and class was extrinsic. It could be shaken off. A slave, he had read, had risen to the Roman purple. That being so, then he could rise to Ruth. Under her purity, and saintliness, and culture, and ethereal beauty of soul, she was, in things fundamentally human, just like Lizzie Connolly and all Lizzie Connollys. All that was possible of them was possible of her. She could love, and hate, maybe have hysterics; and she could certainly be jealous, as she was jealous now, uttering her last sobs in his arms.

"Besides, I am older than you," she remarked suddenly, opening her eyes and looking up at him, "three years older."

"Hush, you are only a child, and I am forty years older than you, in experience," was his answer.

In truth, they were children together, so far as love was concerned, and they were as naive and immature in the expression of their love as a pair of children, and this despite the fact that she was crammed with a university education and that his head was full of scientific philosophy and the hard facts of life.

They sat on through the passing glory of the day, talking as lovers are prone to talk, marvelling at the wonder of love and at destiny that had flung them so strangely together, and dogmatically believing that they loved to a degree never attained by lovers before. And they returned insistently, again and again, to a rehearsal of their first impressions of each other and to hopeless attempts to analyze just precisely what they felt for each other and how much there was of it.

The cloud-masses on the western horizon received the descending sun, and the circle of the sky turned to rose, while the zenith glowed with the same warm color.

CHAPTER XXI

The rosy light was all about them, flooding over them, as she sang, "Good-by, Sweet Day." She sang softly, leaning in the cradle of his arm, her hands in his, their hearts in each other's hands.

CHAPTER XXII

Mrs. Morse did not require a mother's intuition to read the advertisement in Ruth's face when she returned home. The flush that would not leave the cheeks told the simple story, and more eloquently did the eyes, large and bright, reflecting an unmistakable inward glory.

"What has happened?" Mrs. Morse asked, having bided her time till Ruth had gone to bed.

"You know?" Ruth queried, with trembling lips.

For reply, her mother's arm went around her, and a hand was softly caressing her hair.

"He did not speak," she blurted out. "I did not intend that it should happen, and I would never have let him speak—only he didn't speak."

"But if he did not speak, then nothing could have happened, could it?"

"But it did, just the same."

"In the name of goodness, child, what are you babbling about?" Mrs. Morse was bewildered. "I don't think I know what happened, after all. What did happen?"

Ruth looked at her mother in surprise.

"I thought you knew. Why, we're engaged, Martin and I."

Mrs. Morse laughed with incredulous vexation.

"No, he didn't speak," Ruth explained. "He just loved me, that was all. I was as surprised as you are. He didn't say a word. He just put his arm around me. And—and I was not myself. And he kissed me, and I kissed him. I couldn't help it. I just had to. And then I knew I loved him."

She paused, waiting with expectancy the benediction of her mother's kiss, but Mrs. Morse was coldly silent.

"It is a dreadful accident, I know," Ruth recommenced with a sinking voice. "And I don't know how you will ever forgive me. But I couldn't help it. I did not dream that I loved him until that moment. And you must tell father for me."

"Would it not be better not to tell your father? Let me see Martin Eden, and talk with him, and explain. He will understand and release you."

"No! no!" Ruth cried, starting up. "I do not want to be released. I love him, and love is very sweet. I am going to marry him—of course, if you will let me."

"We have other plans for you, Ruth, dear, your father and I—oh, no, no; no man picked out for you, or anything like that. Our plans go no farther than your marrying some man in your own station in life, a good and honorable gentleman, whom you will select yourself, when you love him."

"But I love Martin already," was the plaintive protest.

"We would not influence your choice in any way; but you are our daughter, and we could not bear to see you make a marriage such as this. He has nothing but roughness and coarseness to offer you in exchange for all that is refined and delicate in you. He is no match for you in any way. He could not support you. We have no foolish ideas about wealth, but comfort is another matter, and our daughter should at least marry a man who can give her that—and not a penniless adventurer, a sailor, a cowboy, a smuggler, and Heaven knows what else, who, in addition to everything, is hare-brained and irresponsible."

Ruth was silent. Every word she recognized as true.

"He wastes his time over his writing, trying to accomplish what geniuses and rare men with college educations sometimes accomplish. A man thinking of marriage should be preparing for marriage. But not he. As I have said, and I know you agree with me, he is irresponsible. And why should he not be? It is the way of sailors. He has never learned to be economical or temperate. The spendthrift years have marked him. It is not his fault, of course, but that does not alter his nature. And have you thought of the years of licentiousness he inevitably has lived? Have you thought of that, daughter? You know what marriage means."

Ruth shuddered and clung close to her mother.

"I have thought." Ruth waited a long time for the thought to frame itself. "And it is terrible. It sickens me to think of it. I told you it was a dreadful accident, my loving him; but I can't help myself. Could you help loving father? Then it is the same with me. There is something in me, in him—I never knew it was there until to-day—but it is there, and it makes me love him. I never thought to love him, but, you see, I do," she concluded, a certain faint triumph in her voice.

They talked long, and to little purpose, in conclusion agreeing to wait an indeterminate time without doing anything.

The same conclusion was reached, a little later that night, between Mrs. Morse and her husband, after she had made due confession of the miscarriage of her plans.

"It could hardly have come otherwise," was Mr. Morse's judgment. "This sailor-fellow has been the only man she was in touch with. Sooner or later she was going to awaken anyway; and she did awaken, and lo! here was this sailor-fellow, the only accessible man at the moment, and of course she promptly loved him, or thought she did, which amounts to the same thing."

Mrs. Morse took it upon herself to work slowly and indirectly upon Ruth, rather than to combat her. There would be plenty of time for this, for Martin was not in position to marry.

"Let her see all she wants of him," was Mr. Morse's advice. "The more she knows him, the less she'll love him, I wager. And give her plenty of contrast. Make a point of having young people at the house. Young women and young men, all sorts of young men, clever men, men who have done something or who are doing things, men of her own class, gentlemen. She can gauge him by them. They will show him up for what he is. And after all, he is a mere boy of twenty-one. Ruth is no more than a child. It is calf love with the pair of them, and they will grow out of it."

So the matter rested. Within the family it was accepted that Ruth and Martin were engaged, but no announcement was made. The family did not think it would ever be necessary. Also, it was tacitly understood that it was to be a long engagement. They did not ask Martin to go to work, nor to cease writing. They did not intend to encourage him to mend himself. And he aided and abetted them in their unfriendly designs, for going to work was farthest from his thoughts.

"I wonder if you'll like what I have done!" he said to Ruth several days later. "I've decided that boarding with my sister is too expensive, and I am going to board myself. I've rented a little room out in North Oakland, retired neighborhood and all the rest, you know, and I've bought an oil-burner on which to cook."

Ruth was overjoyed. The oil-burner especially pleased her.

"That was the way Mr. Butler began his start," she said.

Martin frowned inwardly at the citation of that worthy gentleman, and went on: "I put stamps on all my manuscripts and started them off to the editors again. Then to-day I moved in, and to-morrow I start to work."

"A position!" she cried, betraying the gladness of her surprise in all her body, nestling closer to him, pressing his hand, smiling. "And you never told me! What is it?"

He shook his head.

"I meant that I was going to work at my writing." Her face fell, and he went on hastily. "Don't misjudge me. I am not going in this time with any iridescent ideas. It is to be a cold, prosaic, matter-of-fact business proposition. It is better than going to sea again, and I shall earn more money than any position in Oakland can bring an unskilled man."

"You see, this vacation I have taken has given me perspective. I haven't been working the life out of my body, and I haven't been writing, at least not for publication. All I've done has been to love you and to think. I've read some, too, but it has been part of my thinking, and I have read principally magazines. I have generalized about myself, and the world, my place in it, and my chance to win to a place that will be fit for you. Also, I've been reading Spencer's 'Philosophy of Style,' and found out a lot of what was the matter with me—or my writing, rather; and for that matter with most of the writing that is published every month in the magazines."

"But the upshot of it all—of my thinking and reading and loving—is that I am going to move to Grub Street. I shall leave masterpieces alone and do hack-work—jokes, paragraphs, feature articles, humorous verse, and society verse—all the rot for which there seems so much demand. Then there are the newspaper syndicates, and the newspaper short-story syndicates, and the syndicates for the Sunday supplements. I can go ahead and hammer out the stuff they want, and earn the equivalent of a good salary by it. There are free-lances, you know, who earn as much as four or five hundred a month. I don't care to become as they; but I'll earn a good living, and have plenty of time to myself, which I wouldn't have in any position."

"Then, I'll have my spare time for study and for real work. In between the grind I'll try my hand at masterpieces, and I'll study and prepare myself for the writing of masterpieces. Why, I am amazed at the distance I have come already. When I first tried to write, I had nothing to write about except a few paltry experiences which I neither understood nor appreciated. But I had no thoughts. I really didn't. I didn't even have the words with which to think. My experiences were so many meaningless pictures. But as I began to add to my knowledge, and to my vocabulary, I saw something more in my experiences than mere pictures. I retained the pictures and I found their interpretation. That was when I began to do good work, when I wrote 'Adventure,' 'Joy,' 'The Pot,' 'The Wine of Life,' 'The Jostling Street,' the 'Love-cycle,' and the 'Sea Lyrics.' I shall write more like them, and better; but I shall do it in my spare time. My feet are on the solid earth, now. Hack-work and income first, masterpieces afterward. Just to show you, I wrote half a dozen jokes last night for the comic weeklies; and just as I was going to bed, the thought struck me to try my hand at a triolet—a humorous one; and inside an hour I had written four. They ought to be worth a dollar apiece. Four dollars right there for a few afterthoughts on the way to bed."

"Of course it's all valueless, just so much dull and sordid plodding; but it is no more dull and sordid than keeping books at sixty dollars a month, adding up endless columns of meaningless figures until one dies. And furthermore, the hack-work keeps me in touch with things literary and gives me time to try bigger things."

"But what good are these bigger-things, these masterpieces?" Ruth demanded. "You can't sell them."

"Oh, yes, I can," he began; but she interrupted.

"All those you named, and which you say yourself are good—you have not sold any of them. We can't get married on masterpieces that won't sell."

"Then we'll get married on triolets that will sell," he asserted stoutly, putting his arm around her and drawing a very unresponsive sweetheart toward him.

"Listen to this," he went on in attempted gayety. "It's not art, but it's a dollar.

"He came in
When I was out,
To borrow some tin
Was why he came in,
And he went without;
So I was in
And he was out."

The merry lilt with which he had invested the jingle was at variance with the dejection that came into his face as he finished. He had drawn no smile from Ruth. She was looking at him in an earnest and troubled way.

"It may be a dollar," she said, "but it is a jester's dollar, the fee of a clown. Don't you see, Martin, the whole thing is lowering. I want the man I love and honor to be something finer and higher than a perpetrator of jokes and doggerel."

"You want him to be like—say Mr. Butler?" he suggested.

"I know you don't like Mr. Butler," she began.

"Mr. Butler's all right," he interrupted. "It's only his indigestion I find fault with. But to save me I can't see any difference between writing jokes or comic verse and running a type-writer, taking dictation, or keeping sets of books. It is all a means to an end. Your theory is for me to begin with keeping books in order to become a successful lawyer or man of business. Mine is to begin with hack-work and develop into an able author."

"There is a difference," she insisted.

"What is it?"

"Why, your good work, what you yourself call good, you can't sell. You have tried, you know that,—but the editors won't buy it."

"Give me time, dear," he pleaded. "The hack-work is only makeshift, and I don't take it seriously. Give me two years. I shall succeed in that time, and the editors will be glad to buy my good work. I know what I am saying; I have faith in myself. I know what I have in me; I know what literature is, now; I know the average rot that is poured'out by a lot of little men; and I know that at the end of two years I shall be on the highroad to success. As for business, I shall never succeed at it. I am not in sympathy with it. It strikes me as dull, and stupid, and mercenary, and tricky. Anyway I am not adapted for it. I'd never get beyond a clerkship, and how could you and I be happy on the paltry earnings of a clerk? I want the best of everything in the world for you, and the only time when I won't want it will be when there is something better. And I'm going to get it, going to get all of it. The income of a successful author makes Mr. Butler look cheap. A 'best-seller' will earn anywhere between fifty and a hundred thousand dollars—sometimes more and sometimes less; but, as a rule, pretty close to those figures."

She remained silent; her disappointment was apparent.

"Well?" he asked.

"I had hoped and planned otherwise. I had thought, and I still think, that the best thing for you would be to study shorthand—you already know type-writing—and go into father's office. You have a good mind, and I am confident you would succeed as a lawyer."

CHAPTER XXIII

That Ruth had little faith in his power as a writer, did not alter her nor diminish her in Martin's eyes. In the breathing spell of the vacation he had taken, he had spent many hours in self-analysis, and thereby learned much of himself. He had discovered that he loved beauty more than fame, and that what desire he had for fame was largely for Ruth's sake. It was for this reason that his desire for fame was strong. He wanted to be great in the world's eyes; "to make good," as he expressed it, in order that the woman he loved should be proud of him and deem him worthy.

As for himself, he loved beauty passionately, and the joy of serving her was to him sufficient wage. And more than beauty he loved Ruth. He considered love the finest thing in the world. It was love that had worked the revolution in him, changing him from an uncouth sailor to a student and an artist; therefore, to him, the finest and greatest of the three, greater than learning and artistry, was love. Already he had discovered that his brain went beyond Ruth's, just as it went beyond the brains of her brothers, or the brain of her father. In spite of every advantage of university training, and in the face of her bachelorship of arts, his power of intellect overshadowed hers, and his year or so of self-study and equipment gave him a mastery of the affairs of the world and art and life that she could never hope to possess.

All this he realized, but it did not affect his love for her, nor her love for him. Love was too fine and noble, and he was too loyal a lover for him to besmirch love with criticism. What did love have to do with Ruth's divergent views on art, right conduct, the French Revolution, or equal suffrage? They were mental processes, but love was beyond reason; it was superrational. He could not belittle love. He worshipped it. Love lay on the mountain-tops beyond the valley-land of reason. It was a sublimates condition of existence, the topmost peak of living, and it came rarely. Thanks to the school of scientific philosophers he favored, he knew the biological significance of love; but by a refined process of the same scientific reasoning he reached the conclusion that the human organism achieved its highest purpose in love, that love must not be questioned, but must be accepted as the highest guerdon of life. Thus, he considered the lover blessed over all creatures, and it was a delight to him to think of "God's own mad lover," rising above the things of earth, above wealth and judgment, public opinion and applause, rising above life itself and "dying on a kiss."

Much of this Martin had already reasoned out, and some of it he reasoned out later. In the meantime he worked, taking no recreation except when he went to see Ruth, and living like a Spartan. He paid two dollars and a half a month rent for the small room he got from his Portuguese landlady, Maria Silva, a virago and a widow, hard working and harsher tempered, rearing her large brood of children somehow, and drowning her sorrow and fatigue at irregular intervals in a gallon of the thin, sour wine that she bought from the corner grocery and saloon for fifteen cents. From detesting her and her foul tongue at first, Martin grew to admire her as he observed the brave fight she made. There were but four rooms in the little house—three, when Martin's was subtracted. One of these, the parlor, gay with an ingrain carpet and dolorous with a funeral card and a death-picture of one of her numerous departed babes, was kept strictly for company. The blinds were always down, and her barefooted tribe was never permitted to enter the sacred precinct save on state occasions. She cooked, and all ate, in the kitchen, where she likewise washed, starched, and ironed clothes on all days of the week except Sunday; for her income came largely from taking in washing from her more prosperous neighbors. Remained the bedroom, small as the one occupied by Martin, into which she and her seven little ones crowded and slept. It was an everlasting miracle to Martin how it was accomplished, and from her side of the thin partition he heard nightly every detail of the going to bed, the squalls and squabbles, the soft chattering, and the sleepy, twittering noises as of birds. Another source of income to Maria were her cows, two of them, which she milked night and morning and which gained a surreptitious livelihood from vacant lots and the grass that grew on either side the public side walks, attended always by one or more of her ragged boys, whose watchful guardianship consisted chiefly in keeping their eyes out for the poundmen.

In his own small room Martin lived, slept, studied, wrote, and kept house. Before the one window, looking out on the tiny front porch, was the kitchen table that served as desk, library, and type-writing stand. The bed, against the rear wall, occupied two-thirds of the total space of the room. The table was flanked on one side by a gaudy bureau, manufactured for profit and not for service, the thin veneer of which was shed day by day. This bureau stood in the corner, and in the opposite corner, on the table's other flank, was the kitchen—the oil-stove on a dry-goods box, inside of which were dishes and cooking utensils, a shelf on the wall for provisions, and a bucket of water on the floor. Martin had to carry his water from the kitchen sink, there being no tap in his room. On days when there was much steam to his cooking, the harvest of veneer from the bureau was unusually generous. Over the bed, hoisted by a tackle to the ceiling, was his bicycle. At first he had tried to keep it in the basement; but the tribe of Silva, loosening the bearings and puncturing the tires, had driven him out. Next he attempted the tiny front porch, until a howling southeaster drenched the wheel a night-long. Then he had retreated with it to his room and slung it aloft.

A small closet contained his clothes and the books he had accumulated and for which there was no room on the table or under the table. Hand in hand with reading, he had developed the habit of making notes, and so copiously did he make them that there would have been no existence for him in the confined quarters had he not rigged several clothes-lines across the room on which the notes were hung. Even so, he was crowded until navigating the room was a difficult task. He could not open the door without first closing the closet door, and *vice versa.* It was impossible for him anywhere to traverse the room in a straight line. To go from the door to the head of the bed was a zigzag course that he was never quite able to accomplish in the dark without collisions. Having settled the difficulty of the conflicting doors, he had to steer sharply to the right to avoid the kitchen. Next, he sheered to the left, to escape the foot of the bed; but this sheer, if too generous, brought him against the corner of the table. With a sudden twitch and lurch, he terminated the sheer and bore off to the right along a sort of canal, one bank of which was the bed, the other the table. When the one chair in the room was at its usual place before the table, the canal was unnavigable. When the chair was not in use, it reposed on top of the bed, though sometimes he sat on the chair when cooking, reading a book while the water boiled, and even becoming skilful enough to manage a paragraph or two while steak was frying. Also, so small was the little corner that constituted the kitchen, he was able, sitting down, to reach anything he needed. In fact, it was expedient to cook sitting down; standing up, he was too often in his own way.

In conjunction with a perfect stomach that could digest anything, he possessed knowledge of the various foods that were at the same time nutritious and cheap. Pea-soup was a common article in his diet, as well as potatoes and beans, the latter large and brown and cooked in Mexican style. Rice, cooked as American housewives never cook it and can never learn to cook it, appeared on Martin's table at least once a day. Dried fruits were less expensive than fresh, and he had usually a pot of them, cooked and ready at hand, for they took the place of butter on his bread. Occasionally he graced his table with a piece of round-steak, or with a soup-bone. Coffee, without cream or milk, he had twice a day, in the evening substituting tea; but both coffee and tea were excellently cooked.

There was need for him to be economical. His vacation had consumed nearly all he had earned in the laundry, and he was so far from his market that weeks must elapse before he could hope for the first returns from his hack-work. Except at such times as he saw Ruth, or dropped in to see his sister Gertude, he lived a recluse, in each day accomplishing at least three days' labor of ordinary men. He slept a scant five hours, and only one with a constitution of iron could have held himself down, as Martin did, day after day, to nineteen consecutive hours of toil. He never lost a moment. On the looking-glass were lists of definitions and pronunciations; when shaving, or dressing, or combing his hair, he conned these lists over. Similar lists were on the wall over the oil-stove, and they were similarly conned while he was engaged in cooking or in washing the dishes. New lists continually displaced the old ones. Every strange or partly familiar word encountered in his reading was immediately jotted down, and later, when a sufficient number had been accumulated, were typed and pinned to the wall or looking-glass. He even carried them in his pockets, and reviewed them at odd moments on the street, or while waiting in butcher shop or grocery to be served.

He went farther in the matter. Reading the works of men who had arrived, he noted every result achieved by them, and worked out the tricks by which they had been achieved—the tricks of narrative, of exposition, of style, the points of view, the contrasts, the epigrams; and of all these he made lists for study. He did not ape. He sought principles. He drew up lists of effective and fetching mannerisms, till out of many such, culled from many writers, he was able to induce the general principle of mannerism, and, thus equipped, to cast about for new and original ones of his own, and to weigh and measure and appraise them properly. In similar manner he collected lists of strong phrases, the phrases of living language, phrases that bit like acid and scorched like flame, or that glowed and were mellow and luscious in the midst of the arid desert of common speech. He sought always for the principle that lay behind and beneath. He wanted to know how the thing was done; after that he could do it for himself. He was not content with the fair face of beauty. He dissected beauty in his crowded little bedroom laboratory, where cooking smells alternated with the outer bedlam of the Silva tribe; and, having dissected and learned the anatomy of beauty, he was nearer being able to create beauty itself.

He was so made that he could work only with understanding. He could not work blindly, in the dark, ignorant of what he was producing and trusting to chance and the star of his genius that the effect produced should be right and fine. He had no patience with chance effects. He wanted to know why and how. His was deliberate creative genius, and, before he began a story or poem, the thing itself was already alive in his brain, with the end in sight and the means of realizing that end in his conscious possession. Otherwise the effort was doomed to failure. On the other hand, he appreciated the chance effects in words and phrases that came lightly and easily into his brain, and that later stood all tests of beauty and power and developed tremendous and incommunicable connotations. Before such he bowed down and marvelled, knowing that they were beyond the deliberate creation of any man. And no matter how much he dissected beauty in search of the principles that underlie beauty and make beauty possible, he was aware, always, of the innermost mystery of beauty to which he did not penetrate and to which no man had ever penetrated. He knew full well, from his Spencer, that man can never attain ultimate knowledge of anything, and that the mystery of beauty was no less than that of life—nay, more that the fibres of beauty and life were intertwisted, and that he himself was but a bit of the same nonunderstandable fabric, twisted of sunshine and star-dust and wonder.

In fact, it was when filled with these thoughts that he wrote his essay entitled "Star-dust," in which he had his fling, not at the principles of criticism, but at the principal critics. It was brilliant, deep, philosophical, and deliciously touched with laughter. Also it was promptly rejected by the magazines as often as it was submitted. But having cleared his mind of it, he went serenely on his way. It was a habit he developed, of incubating and maturing his thought upon a subject, and of then rushing into the type-writer with it. That it did not see print was a matter a small moment with him. The writing of it was the culminating act of a long mental process, the drawing together of scattered threads of thought and the final generalizing upon all the data with which his mind was burdened. To write such an article was the conscious effort by which he freed his mind and made it ready for fresh material and problems. It was in a way akin to that common habit of men and women troubled by real or fancied grievances, who periodically and volubly break their long-suffering silence and "have their say" till the last word is said.

CHAPTER XXIV

The weeks passed. Martin ran out of money, and publishers' checks were far away as ever. All his important manuscripts had come back and been started out again, and his hack-work fared no better. His little kitchen was no longer graced with a variety of foods. Caught in the pinch with a part sack of rice and a few pounds of dried apricots, rice and apricots was his menu three times a day for five days hand-running. Then he startled to realize on his credit. The Portuguese grocer, to whom he had hitherto paid cash, called a halt when Martin's bill reached the magnificent total of three dollars and eighty-five cents.

"For you see," said the grocer, "you no catcha da work, I losa da mon'."

And Martin could reply nothing. There was no way of explaining. It was not true business principle to allow credit to a strong-bodied young fellow of the working-class who was too lazy to work.

"You catcha da job, I let you have mora da grub," the grocer assured Martin. "No job, no grub. Thata da business." And then, to show that it was purely business foresight and not prejudice, "Hava da drink on da house—good friends justa da same."

So Martin drank, in his easy way, to show that he was good friends with the house, and then went supperless to bed.

The fruit store, where Martin had bought his vegetables, was run by an American whose business principles were so weak that he let Martin run a bill of five dollars before stopping his credit. The baker stopped at two dollars, and the butcher at four dollars. Martin added his debts and found that he was possessed of a total credit in all the world of fourteen dollars and eighty-five cents. He was up with his type-writer rent, but he estimated that he could get two months' credit on that, which would be eight dollars. When that occurred, he would have exhausted all possible credit.

The last purchase from the fruit store had been a sack of potatoes, and for a week he had potatoes, and nothing but potatoes, three times a day. An occasional dinner at Ruth's helped to keep strength in his body, though he found it tantalizing enough to refuse further helping when his appetite was raging at sight of so much food spread before it. Now and again, though afflicted with secret shame, he dropped in at his sister's at meal-time and ate as much as he dared—more than he dared at the Morse table.

Day by day he worked on, and day by day the postman delivered to him rejected manuscripts. He had no money for stamps, so the manuscripts accumulated in a heap under the table. Came a day when for forty hours he had not tasted food. He could not hope for a meal at Ruth's, for she was away to San Rafael on a two weeks' visit; and for very shame's sake he could not go to his sister's. To cap misfortune, the postman, in his afternoon round, brought him five returned manuscripts. Then it was that Martin wore his overcoat down into Oakland, and came back without it, but with five dollars tinkling in his pocket. He paid a dollar each on account to the four tradesmen, and in his kitchen fried steak and onions, made coffee, and stewed a large pot of prunes. And having dined, he sat down at his table-desk and completed before midnight an essay which he entitled "The Dignity of Usury." Having typed it out, he flung it under the table, for there had been nothing left from the five dollars with which to buy stamps.

Later on he pawned his watch, and still later his wheel, reducing the amount available for food by putting stamps on all his manuscripts and sending them out. He was disappointed with his hack-work. Nobody cared to buy. He compared it with what he found in the newspapers, weeklies, and cheap magazines, and decided that his was better, far better, than the average; yet it would not sell. Then he discovered that most of the newspapers printed a great deal of what was called "plate" stuff, and he got the address of the association that furnished it. His own work that he sent in was returned, along with a stereotyped slip informing him that the staff supplied all the copy that was needed.

In one of the great juvenile periodicals he noted whole columns of incident and anecdote. Here was a chance. His paragraphs were returned, and though he tried repeatedly he never succeeded in placing one. Later on, when it no longer mattered, he learned that the associate editors and sub-editors augmented their salaries by supplying those paragraphs themselves. The comic weeklies returned his jokes and humorous verse, and the light society verse he wrote for the large magazines found no abiding-place. Then there was the newspaper storiette. He knew that he could write better ones than were published. Managing to obtain the addresses of two newspaper syndicates, he deluged them with storiettes. When he had written twenty and failed to place one of them, he ceased. And yet, from day to day, he read storiettes in the dailies and weeklies, scores and scores of storiettes, not one of which would compare with his. In his despondency, he concluded that he had no judgment whatever, that he was hypnotized by what he wrote, and that he was a self-deluded pretender.

The inhuman editorial machine ran smoothly as ever. He folded the stamps in with his manuscript, dropped it into the letter-box, and from three weeks to a month afterward the postman came up the steps and handed him the manuscript. Surely there were no live, warm editors at the other end. It was all wheels and cogs and oil-cups—a clever mechanism operated by automatons. He reached stages of despair wherein he doubted if editors existed at all. He had never received a sign of the existence of one, and from absence of judgment in rejecting all he wrote it seemed plausible that editors were myths, manufactured and maintained by office boys, typesetters, and pressmen.

The hours he spent with Ruth were the only happy ones he had, and they were not all happy. He was afflicted always with a gnawing restlessness, more tantalizing than in the old days before he possessed her love; for now that he did possess her love, the possession of her was far away as ever. He had asked for two years; time was flying, and he was achieving nothing. Again, he was always conscious of the fact that she did not approve what he was doing. She did not say so directly. Yet indirectly she let him understand it as clearly and definitely as she could have spoken it. It was not resentment with her, but disapproval; though less sweet-natured women might have resented where she was no more than disappointed. Her disappointment lay in that this man she had taken to mould, refused to be moulded. To a certain extent she had found his clay plastic, then it had developed stubbornness, declining to be shaped in the image of her father or of Mr. Butler.

What was great and strong in him, she missed, or, worse yet, misunderstood. This man, whose clay was so plastic that he could live in any number of pigeonholes of human existence, she thought wilful and most obstinate because she could not shape him to live in her pigeonhole, which was the only one she knew. She could not follow the flights of his mind, and when his brain got beyond her, she deemed him erratic. Nobody else's brain ever got beyond her. She could always follow her father and mother, her brothers and Olney; wherefore, when she could not follow Martin, she believed the fault lay with him. It was the old tragedy of insularity trying to serve as mentor to the universal.

"You worship at the shrine of the established," he told her once, in a discussion they had over Praps and Vanderwater. "I grant that as authorities to quote they are most excellent—the two foremost literary critics in the United States. Every school teacher in the land looks up to Vanderwater as the Dean of American criticism. Yet I read his stuff, and it seems to me the perfection of the felicitous expression of the inane. Why, he is no more than a ponderous bromide, thanks to Gelett Burgess. And Praps is no better. His 'Hemlock Mosses,' for instance is beautifully written. Not a comma is out of place; and the tone—ah!—is lofty, so lofty. He is the best-paid critic in the United States. Though, Heaven forbid! he's not a critic at all. They do criticism better in England.

"But the point is, they sound the popular note, and they sound it so beautifully and morally and contentedly. Their reviews remind me of a British Sunday. They are the popular mouthpieces. They back up your professors of English, and your professors of English back them up. And there isn't an original idea in any of their skulls. They know only the established,—in fact, they are the established. They are weak minded, and the established impresses itself upon them as easily as the name of the brewery is impressed on a beer bottle. And their function is to catch all the young fellows attending the university, to drive out of their minds any glimmering originality that may chance to be there, and to put upon them the stamp of the established."

"I think I am nearer the truth," she replied, "when I stand by the established, than you are, raging around like an iconoclastic South Sea Islander."

"It was the missionary who did the image breaking," he laughed. "And unfortunately, all the missionaries are off among the heathen, so there are none left at home to break those old images, Mr. Vanderwater and Mr. Praps."

"And the college professors, as well," she added.

He shook his head emphatically. "No; the science professors should live. They're really great. But it would be a good deed to break the heads of nine-tenths of the English professors—little, microscopic-minded parrots!"

Which was rather severe on the professors, but which to Ruth was blasphemy. She could not help but measure the professors, neat, scholarly, in fitting clothes, speaking in well-modulated voices, breathing of culture and refinement, with this almost indescribable young fellow whom somehow she loved, whose clothes never would fit him, whose heavy muscles told of damning toil, who grew excited when he talked, substituting abuse for calm statement and passionate utterance for cool self-possession. They at least earned good salaries and were—yes, she compelled herself to face it—were gentlemen; while he could not earn a penny, and he was not as they.

She did not weigh Martin's words nor judge his argument by them. Her conclusion that his argument was wrong was reached—unconsciously, it is true—by a comparison of externals. They, the professors, were right in their literary judgments because they were successes. Martin's literary judgments were wrong because he could not sell his wares. To use his own phrase, they made good, and he did not make good. And besides, it did not seem reasonable that he should be right—he who had stood, so short a time before, in that same living room, blushing and awkward, acknowledging his introduction, looking fearfully about him at the bric-a-brac his swinging shoulders threatened to break, asking how long since Swinburne died, and boastfully announcing that he had read "Excelsior" and the "Psalm of Life."

Unwittingly, Ruth herself proved his point that she worshipped the established. Martin followed the processes of her thoughts, but forbore to go farther. He did not love her for what she thought of Praps and Vanderwater and English professors, and he was coming to realize, with increasing conviction, that he possessed brain-areas and stretches of knowledge which she could never comprehend nor know existed.

In music she thought him unreasonable, and in the matter of opera not only unreasonable but wilfully perverse.

"How did you like it?" she asked him one night, on the way home from the opera.

It was a night when he had taken her at the expense of a month's rigid economizing on food. After vainly waiting for him to speak about it, herself still tremulous and stirred by what she had just seen and heard, she had asked the question.

"I liked the overture," was his answer. "It was splendid."

"Yes, but the opera itself?"

"That was splendid too; that is, the orchestra was, though I'd have enjoyed it more if those jumping-jacks had kept quiet or gone off the stage."

Ruth was aghast.

"You don't mean Tetralani or Barillo?" she queried.

"All of them—the whole kit and crew."

"But they are great artists," she protested.

"They spoiled the music just the same, with their antics and unrealities."

"But don't you like Barillo's voice?" Ruth asked. "He is next to Caruso, they say."

"Of course I liked him, and I liked Tetralani even better. Her voice is exquisite—or at least I think so."

"But, but—" Ruth stammered. "I don't know what you mean, then. You admire their voices, yet say they spoiled the music."

"Precisely that. I'd give anything to hear them in concert, and I'd give even a bit more not to hear them when the orchestra is playing. I'm afraid I am a hopeless realist. Great singers are not great actors. To hear Barillo sing a love passage with the voice of an angel, and to hear Tetralani reply like another angel, and to hear it all accompanied by a perfect orgy of glowing and colorful music—is ravishing, most ravishing. I do not admit it. I assert it. But the whole effect is spoiled when I look at them—at Tetralani, five feet ten in her stocking feet and weighing a hundred and ninety pounds, and at Barillo, a scant five feet four, greasy-featured, with the chest of a squat, undersized blacksmith, and at the pair of them, attitudinizing, clasping their breasts, flinging their arms in the air like demented creatures in an asylum; and when I am expected to accept all this as the faithful illusion of a love-scene between a slender and beautiful princess and a handsome, romantic, young prince—why, I can't accept it, that's all. It's rot; it's absurd; it's unreal. That's what's the matter with it. It's not real. Don't tell me that anybody in this world ever made love that way. Why, if I'd made love to you in such fashion, you'd have boxed my ears."

"But you misunderstand," Ruth protested. "Every form of art has its limitations." (She was busy recalling a lecture she had heard at the university on the conventions of the arts.) "In painting there are only two dimensions to the canvas, yet you accept the illusion of three dimensions which the art of a painter enables him to throw into the canvas. In writing, again, the author must be omnipotent. You accept as perfectly legitimate the author's account of the secret thoughts of the heroine, and yet all the time you know that the heroine was alone when thinking these thoughts, and that neither the author nor any one else was capable of hearing them. And so with the stage, with sculpture, with opera, with every art form. Certain irreconcilable things must be accepted."

"Yes, I understood that," Martin answered. "All the arts have their conventions." (Ruth was surprised at his use of the word. It was as if he had studied at the university himself, instead of being ill-equipped from browsing at haphazard through the books in the library.) "But even the conventions must be real. Trees, painted on flat cardboard and stuck up on each side of the stage, we accept as a forest. It is a real enough convention. But, on the other hand, we would not accept a sea scene as a forest. We can't do it. It violates our senses. Nor would you, or, rather, should you, accept the ravings and writhings and agonized contortions of those two lunatics to-night as a convincing portrayal of love."

"But you don't hold yourself superior to all the judges of music?" she protested.

"No, no, not for a moment. I merely maintain my right as an individual. I have just been telling you what I think, in order to explain why the elephantine gambols of Madame Tetralani spoil the orchestra for me. The world's judges of music may all be right. But I am I, and I won't subordinate my taste to the unanimous judgment of mankind. If I don't like a thing, I don't like it, that's all; and there is no reason under the sun why I should ape a liking for it just because the majority of my fellow-creatures like it, or make believe they like it. I can't follow the fashions in the things I like or dislike."

"But music, you know, is a matter of training," Ruth argued; "and opera is even more a matter of training. May it not be—"

"That I am not trained in opera?" he dashed in.

She nodded.

"The very thing," he agreed. "And I consider I am fortunate in not having been caught when I was young. If I had, I could have wept sentimental tears to-night, and the clownish antics of that precious pair would have but enhanced the beauty of their voices and the beauty of the accompanying orchestra. You are right. It's mostly a matter of training. And I am too old, now. I must have the real or nothing. An illusion that won't convince is a palpable lie, and that's what grand opera is to me when little Barillo throws a fit, clutches mighty Tetralani in his arms (also in a fit), and tells her how passionately he adores her."

Again Ruth measured his thoughts by comparison of externals and in accordance with her belief in the established. Who was he that he should be right and all the cultured world wrong? His words and thoughts made no impression upon her. She was too firmly intrenched in the established to have any sympathy with revolutionary ideas. She had always been used to music, and she had enjoyed opera ever since she was a child, and all her world had enjoyed it, too. Then by what right did Martin Eden emerge, as he had so recently emerged, from his rag-time and working-class songs, and pass judgment on the world's music? She was vexed with him, and as she walked beside him she had a vague feeling of outrage. At the best, in her most charitable frame of mind, she considered the statement of his views to be a caprice, an erratic and uncalled-for prank. But when he took her in his arms at the door and kissed her good night in tender lover-fashion, she forgot everything in the outrush of her own love to him. And later, on a sleepless pillow, she puzzled, as she had often puzzled of late, as to how it was that she loved so strange a man, and loved him despite the disapproval of her people.

And next day Martin Eden cast hack-work aside, and at white heat hammered out an essay to which he gave the title, "The Philosophy of Illusion." A stamp started it on its travels, but it was destined to receive many stamps and to be started on many travels in the months that followed.

CHAPTER XXV

Maria Silva was poor, and all the ways of poverty were clear to her. Poverty, to Ruth, was a word signifying a not-nice condition of existence. That was her total knowledge on the subject. She knew Martin was poor, and his condition she associated in her mind with the boyhood of Abraham Lincoln, of Mr. Butler, and of other men who had become successes. Also, while aware that poverty was anything but delectable, she had a comfortable middle-class feeling that poverty was salutary, that it was a sharp spur that urged on to success all men who were not degraded and hopeless drudges. So that her knowledge that Martin was so poor that he had pawned his watch and overcoat did not disturb her. She even considered it the hopeful side of the situation, believing that sooner or later it would arouse him and compel him to abandon his writing.

Ruth never read hunger in Martin's face, which had grown lean and had enlarged the slight hollows in the cheeks. In fact, she marked the change in his face with satisfaction. It seemed to refine him, to remove from him much of the dross of flesh and the too animal-like vigor that lured her while she detested it. Sometimes, when with her, she noted an unusual brightness in his eyes, and she admired it, for it made him appear more the poet and the scholar—the things he would have liked to be and which she would have liked him to be. But Maria Silva read a different tale in the hollow cheeks and the burning eyes, and she noted the changes in them from day to day, by them following the ebb and flow of his fortunes. She saw him leave the house with his overcoat and return without it, though the day was chill and raw, and promptly she saw his cheeks fill out slightly and the fire of hunger leave his eyes. In the same way she had seen his wheel and watch go, and after each event she had seen his vigor bloom again.

Likewise she watched his toils, and knew the measure of the midnight oil he burned. Work! She knew that he outdid her, though his work was of a different order. And she was surprised to behold that the less food he had, the harder he worked. On occasion, in a casual sort of way, when she thought hunger pinched hardest, she would send him in a loaf of new baking, awkwardly covering the act with banter to the effect that it was better than he could bake. And again, she would send one of her toddlers in to him with a great pitcher of hot soup, debating inwardly the while whether she was justified in taking it from the mouths of her own flesh and blood. Nor was Martin ungrateful, knowing as he did the lives of the poor, and that if ever in the world there was charity, this was it.

On a day when she had filled her brood with what was left in the house, Maria invested her last fifteen cents in a gallon of cheap wine. Martin, coming into her kitchen to fetch water, was invited to sit down and drink. He drank her very-good health, and in return she drank his. Then she drank to prosperity in his undertakings, and he drank to the hope that James Grant would show up and pay her for his washing. James Grant was a journeymen carpenter who did not always pay his bills and who owed Maria three dollars.

Both Maria and Martin drank the sour new wine on empty stomachs, and it went swiftly to their heads. Utterly differentiated creatures that they were, they were lonely in their misery, and though the misery was tacitly ignored, it was the bond that drew them together. Maria was amazed to learn that he had been in the Azores, where she had lived until she was eleven. She was doubly amazed that he had been in the Hawaiian Islands, whither she had migrated from the Azores with her people. But her amazement passed all bounds when he told her he had been on Maui, the particular island whereon she had attained womanhood and married. Kahului, where she had first met her husband,—he, Martin, had been there twice! Yes, she remembered the sugar steamers, and he had been on them—well, well, it was a small world. And Wailuku! That place, too! Did he know the head-luna of the plantation? Yes, and had had a couple of drinks with him.

And so they reminiscenced and drowned their hunger in the raw, sour wine. To Martin the future did not seem so dim. Success trembled just before him. He was on the verge of clasping it. Then he studied the deep-lined face of the toil-worn woman before him, remembered her soups and loaves of new baking, and felt spring up in him the warmest gratitude and philanthropy.

"Maria," he exclaimed suddenly. "What would you like to have?"

She looked at him, bepuzzled.

"What would you like to have now, right now, if you could get it?"

"Shoe alla da roun' for da childs—seven pairs da shoe."

"You shall have them," he announced, while she nodded her head gravely. "But I mean a big wish, something big that you want."

Her eyes sparkled good-naturedly. He was choosing to make fun with her, Maria, with whom few made fun these days.

"Think hard," he cautioned, just as she was opening her mouth to speak.

"Alla right," she answered. "I thinka da hard. I lika da house, dis house—all mine, no paya da rent, seven dollar da month."

"You shall have it," he granted, "and in a short time. Now wish the great wish. Make believe I am God, and I say to you anything you want you can have. Then you wish that thing, and I listen."

Maria considered solemnly for a space.

"You no 'fraid?" she asked warningly.

"No, no," he laughed, "I'm not afraid. Go ahead."

"Most verra big," she warned again.

"All right. Fire away."

"Well, den—" She drew a big breath like a child, as she voiced to the uttermost all she cared to demand of life. "I lika da have one milka ranch—good milka ranch. Plenty cow, plenty land, plenty grass. I lika da have near San Le-an; my sister liva dere. I sella da milk in Oakland. I maka da plentee mon. Joe an' Nick no runna da cow. Dey go-a to school. Bimeby maka da good engineer, worka da railroad. Yes, I lika da milka ranch."

She paused and regarded Martin with twinkling eyes.

"You shall have it," he answered promptly.

She nodded her head and touched her lips courteously to the wine-glass and to the giver of the gift she knew would never be given. His heart was right, and in her own heart she appreciated his intention as much as if the gift had gone with it.

"No, Maria," he went on; "Nick and Joe won't have to peddle milk, and all the kids can go to school and wear shoes the whole year round. It will be a first-class milk ranch—everything complete. There will be a house to live in and a stable for the horses, and cow-barns, of course. There will be chickens, pigs, vegetables, fruit trees, and everything like that; and there will be enough cows to pay for a hired man or two. Then you won't have anything to do but take care of the children. For that matter, if you find a good man, you can marry and take it easy while he runs the ranch."

And from such largess, dispensed from his future, Martin turned and took his one good suit of clothes to the pawnshop. His plight was desperate for him to do this, for it cut him off from Ruth. He had no second-best suit that was presentable, and though he could go to the butcher and the baker, and even on occasion to his sister's, it was beyond all daring to dream of entering the Morse home so disreputably apparelled.

He toiled on, miserable and well-nigh hopeless. It began to appear to him that the second battle was lost and that he would have to go to work. In doing this he would satisfy everybody—the grocer, his sister, Ruth, and even Maria, to whom he owed a month's room rent. He was two months behind with his type-writer, and the agency was clamoring for payment or for the return of the machine. In desperation, all but ready to surrender, to make a truce with fate until he could get a fresh start, he took the civil service examinations for the Railway Mail. To his surprise, he passed first. The job was assured, though when the call would come to enter upon his duties nobody knew.

It was at this time, at the lowest ebb, that the smooth-running editorial machine broke down. A cog must have slipped or an oil-cup run dry, for the postman brought him one morning a short, thin envelope. Martin glanced at the upper left-hand corner and read the name and address of the *Transcontinental Monthly*. His heart gave a great leap, and he suddenly felt faint, the sinking feeling accompanied by a strange trembling of the knees. He staggered into his room and sat down on the bed, the envelope still unopened, and in that moment came understanding to him how people suddenly fall dead upon receipt of extraordinarily good news.

Of course this was good news. There was no manuscript in that thin envelope, therefore it was an acceptance. He knew the story in the hands of the *Transcontinental*. It was "The Ring of Bells," one of his horror stories, and it was an even five thousand words. And, since first-class magazines always paid on acceptance, there was a check inside. Two cents a word—twenty dollars a thousand; the check must be a hundred dollars. One hundred dollars! As he tore the envelope open, every item of all his debts surged in his brain—$3.85 to the grocer; butcher $4.00 flat; baker, $2.00; fruit store, $5.00; total, $14.85. Then there was room rent, $2.50; another month in advance, $2.50; two months' type-writer, $8.00; a month in advance, $4.00; total, $31.85. And finally to be added, his pledges, plus interest, with the pawnbroker—watch, $5.50; overcoat, $5.50; wheel, $7.75; suit of clothes, $5.50 (60 % interest, but what did it matter?)—grand total, $56.10. He saw, as if visible in the air before him, in illuminated figures, the whole sum, and the subtraction that followed and that gave a remainder of $43.90. When he had squared every debt, redeemed every pledge, he would still have jingling in his pockets a princely $43.90. And on top of that he would have a month's rent paid in advance on the type-writer and on the room.

By this time he had drawn the single sheet of type-written letter out and spread it open. There was no check. He peered into the envelope, held it to the light, but could not trust his eyes, and in trembling haste tore the envelope apart. There was no check. He read the letter, skimming it line by line, dashing through the editor's praise of his story to the meat of the letter, the statement why the check had not been sent. He found no such statement, but he did find that which made him suddenly wilt. The letter slid from his hand. His eyes went lack-lustre, and he lay back on the pillow, pulling the blanket about him and up to his chin.

Five dollars for "The Ring of Bells"—five dollars for five thousand words! Instead of two cents a word, ten words for a cent! And the editor had praised it, too. And he would receive the check when the story was published. Then it was all poppycock, two cents a word for minimum rate and payment upon acceptance. It was a lie, and it had led him astray. He would never have attempted to write had he known that. He would have gone to work—to work for Ruth. He went back to the day he first attempted to write, and was appalled at the enormous waste of time—and all for ten words for a cent. And the other high rewards of writers, that he had read about, must be lies, too. His second-hand ideas of authorship were wrong, for here was the proof of it.

The *Transcontinental* sold for twenty-five cents, and its dignified and artistic cover proclaimed it as among the first-class magazines. It was a staid, respectable magazine, and it had been published continuously since long before he was born. Why, on the outside cover were printed every month the words of one of the world's great writers, words proclaiming the inspired mission of the *Transcontinental* by a star of literature whose first coruscations had appeared inside those self-same covers. And the high and lofty, heaven-inspired *Transcontinental* paid five dollars for five thousand words! The great writer had recently died in a foreign land—in dire poverty, Martin remembered, which was not to be wondered at, considering the magnificent pay authors receive.

Well, he had taken the bait, the newspaper lies about writers and their pay, and he had wasted two years over it. But he would disgorge the bait now. Not another line would he ever write. He would do what Ruth wanted him to do, what everybody wanted him to do—get a job. The thought of going to work reminded him of Joe—Joe, tramping through the land of nothing-to-do. Martin heaved a great sigh of envy. The reaction of nineteen hours a day for many days was strong upon him. But then, Joe was not in love, had none of the responsibilities of love, and he could afford to loaf through the land of nothing-to-do. He, Martin, had something to work for, and go to work he would. He would start out early next morning to hunt a job. And he would let Ruth know, too, that he had mended his ways and was willing to go into her father's office.

Five dollars for five thousand words, ten words for a cent, the market price for art. The disappointment of it, the lie of it, the infamy of it, were uppermost in his thoughts; and under his closed eyelids, in fiery figures, burned the "$3.85" he owed the grocer. He shivered, and was aware of an aching in his bones. The small of his back ached especially. His head ached, the top of it ached, the back of it ached, the brains inside of it ached and seemed to be swelling, while the ache over his brows was intolerable. And beneath the brows, planted under his lids, was the merciless "$3.85." He opened his eyes to escape it, but the white light of the room seemed to sear the balls and forced him to close his eyes, when the "$3.85" confronted him again.

Five dollars for five thousand words, ten words for a cent—that particular thought took up its residence in his brain, and he could no more escape it than he could the "$3.85" under his eyelids. A change seemed to come over the latter, and he watched curiously, till "$2.00" burned in its stead. Ah, he thought, that was the baker. The next sum that appeared was "$2.50." It puzzled him, and he pondered it as if life and death hung on the solution. He owed somebody two dollars and a half, that was certain, but who was it? To find it was the task set him by an imperious and malignant universe, and he wandered through the endless corridors of his mind, opening all manner of lumber rooms and chambers stored with odds and ends of memories and knowledge as he vainly sought the answer. After several centuries it came to him, easily, without effort, that it was Maria. With a great relief he turned his soul to the screen of torment under his lids. He had solved the problem; now he could rest. But no, the "$2.50" faded away, and in its place burned "$8.00." Who was that? He must go the dreary round of his mind again and find out.

How long he was gone on this quest he did not know, but after what seemed an enormous lapse of time, he was called back to himself by a knock at the door, and by Maria's asking if he was sick. He replied in a muffled voice he did not recognize, saying that he was merely taking a nap. He was surprised when he noted the darkness of night in the room. He had received the letter at two in the afternoon, and he realized that he was sick.

Then the "$8.00" began to smoulder under his lids again, and he returned himself to servitude. But he grew cunning. There was no need for him to wander through his mind. He had been a fool. He pulled a lever and made his mind revolve about him, a monstrous wheel of fortune, a merry-go-round of memory, a revolving sphere of wisdom. Faster and faster it revolved, until its vortex sucked him in and he was flung whirling through black chaos.

Quite naturally he found himself at a mangle, feeding starched cuffs. But as he fed he noticed figures printed in the cuffs. It was a new way of marking linen, he thought, until, looking closer, he saw "$3.85" on one of the cuffs. Then it came to him that it was the grocer's bill, and that these were his bills flying around on the drum of the mangle. A crafty idea came to him. He would throw the bills on the floor and so escape paying them. No sooner thought than done, and he crumpled the cuffs spitefully as he flung them upon an unusually dirty floor. Ever the heap grew, and though each bill was duplicated a thousand times, he found only one for two dollars and a half, which was what he owed Maria. That meant that Maria would not press for payment, and he resolved generously that it would be the only one he would pay; so he began searching through the cast-out heap for hers. He sought it desperately, for ages, and was still searching when the manager of the hotel entered, the fat Dutchman. His face blazed with wrath, and he shouted in stentorian tones that echoed down the universe, "I shall deduct the cost of those cuffs from your wages!" The pile of cuffs grew into a mountain, and Martin knew that he was doomed to toil for a thousand years to pay for them. Well, there was nothing left to do but kill the manager and burn down the laundry. But the big Dutchman frustrated him, seizing him by the nape of the neck and dancing him up and down. He danced him over the ironing tables, the stove, and the mangles, and out into the wash-room and over the wringer and washer. Martin was danced until his teeth rattled and his head ached, and he marvelled that the Dutchman was so strong.

And then he found himself before the mangle, this time receiving the cuffs an editor of a magazine was feeding from the other side. Each cuff was a check, and Martin went over them anxiously, in a fever of expectation, but they were all blanks. He stood there and received the blanks for a million years or so, never letting one go by for fear it might be filled out. At last he found it. With trembling fingers he held it to the light. It was for five dollars. "Ha! Ha!" laughed the editor across the mangle. "Well, then, I shall kill you," Martin said. He went out into the wash-room to get the axe, and found Joe starching manuscripts. He tried to make him desist, then swung the axe for him. But the weapon remained poised in mid-air, for Martin found himself back in the ironing room in the midst of a snow-storm. No, it was not snow that was falling, but checks of large denomination, the smallest not less than a thousand dollars. He began to collect them and sort them out, in packages of a hundred, tying each package securely with twine.

He looked up from his task and saw Joe standing before him juggling flat-irons, starched shirts, and manuscripts. Now and again he reached out and added a bundle of checks to the flying miscellany that soared through the roof and out of sight in a tremendous circle. Martin struck at him, but he seized the axe and added it to the flying circle. Then he plucked Martin and added him. Martin went up through the roof, clutching at manuscripts, so that by the time he came down he had a large armful. But no sooner down than up again, and a second and a third time and countless times he flew around the circle. From far off he could hear a childish treble singing: "Waltz me around again, Willie, around, around, around."

He recovered the axe in the midst of the Milky Way of checks, starched shirts, and manuscripts, and prepared, when he came down, to kill Joe. But he did not come down. Instead, at two in the morning, Maria, having heard his groans through the thin partition, came into his room, to put hot flat-irons against his body and damp cloths upon his aching eyes.

CHAPTER XXVI

Martin Eden did not go out to hunt for a job in the morning. It was late afternoon before he came out of his delirium and gazed with aching eyes about the room. Mary, one of the tribe of Silva, eight years old, keeping watch, raised a screech at sight of his returning consciousness. Maria hurried into the room from the kitchen. She put her work-calloused hand upon his hot forehead and felt his pulse.

"You lika da eat?" she asked.

He shook his head. Eating was farthest from his desire, and he wondered that he should ever have been hungry in his life.

"I'm sick, Maria," he said weakly. "What is it? Do you know?"

"Grip," she answered. "Two or three days you alla da right. Better you no eat now. Bimeby plenty can eat, to-morrow can eat maybe."

Martin was not used to sickness, and when Maria and her little girl left him, he essayed to get up and dress. By a supreme exertion of will, with rearing brain and eyes that ached so that he could not keep them open, he managed to get out of bed, only to be left stranded by his senses upon the table. Half an hour later he managed to regain the bed, where he was content to lie with closed eyes and analyze his various pains and weaknesses. Maria came in several times to change the cold cloths on his forehead. Otherwise she left him in peace, too wise to vex him with chatter. This moved him to gratitude, and he murmured to himself, "Maria, you getta da milka ranch, all righta, all right."

Then he remembered his long-buried past of yesterday.

It seemed a life-time since he had received that letter from the *Transcontinental*, a life-time since it was all over and done with and a new page turned. He had shot his bolt, and shot it hard, and now he was down on his back. If he hadn't starved himself, he wouldn't have been caught by La Grippe. He had been run down, and he had not had the strength to throw off the germ of disease which had invaded his system. This was what resulted.

"What does it profit a man to write a whole library and lose his own life?" he demanded aloud. "This is no place for me. No more literature in mine. Me for the counting-house and ledger, the monthly salary, and the little home with Ruth."

Two days later, having eaten an egg and two slices of toast and drunk a cup of tea, he asked for his mail, but found his eyes still hurt too much to permit him to read.

"You read for me, Maria," he said. "Never mind the big, long letters. Throw them under the table. Read me the small letters."

"No can," was the answer. "Teresa, she go to school, she can."

So Teresa Silva, aged nine, opened his letters and read them to him. He listened absently to a long dun from the type-writer people, his mind busy with ways and means of finding a job. Suddenly he was shocked back to himself.

"'We offer you forty dollars for all serial rights in your story,'" Teresa slowly spelled out, "'provided you allow us to make the alterations suggested.'"

"What magazine is that?" Martin shouted. "Here, give it to me!"

He could see to read, now, and he was unaware of the pain of the action. It was the *White Mouse* that was offering him forty dollars, and the story was "The Whirlpool," another of his early horror stories. He read the letter through again and again. The editor told him plainly that he had not handled the idea properly, but that it was the idea they were buying because it was original. If they could cut the story down one-third, they would take it and send him forty dollars on receipt of his answer.

He called for pen and ink, and told the editor he could cut the story down three-thirds if he wanted to, and to send the forty dollars right along.

The letter despatched to the letter-box by Teresa, Martin lay back and thought. It wasn't a lie, after all. The *White Mouse* paid on acceptance. There were three thousand words in "The Whirlpool." Cut down a third, there would be two thousand. At forty dollars that would be two cents a word. Pay on acceptance and two cents a word—the newspapers had told the truth. And he had thought the *White Mouse* a third-rater! It was evident that he did not know the magazines. He had deemed the *Transcontinental* a first-rater, and it paid a cent for ten words. He had classed the *White Mouse* as of no account, and it paid twenty times as much as the *Transcontinental* and also had paid on acceptance.

Well, there was one thing certain: when he got well, he would not go out looking for a job. There were more stories in his head as good as "The Whirlpool," and at forty dollars apiece he could earn far more than in any job or position. Just when he thought the battle lost, it was won. He had proved for his career. The way was clear. Beginning with the *White Mouse* he would add magazine after magazine to his growing list of patrons. Hack-work could be put aside. For that matter, it had been wasted time, for it had not brought him a dollar. He would devote himself to work, good work, and he would pour out the best that was in him. He wished Ruth was there to share in his joy, and when he went over the letters left lying on his bed, he found one from her. It was sweetly reproachful, wondering what had kept him away for so dreadful a length of time. He reread the letter adoringly, dwelling over her handwriting, loving each stroke of her pen, and in the end kissing her signature.

And when he answered, he told her recklessly that he had not been to see her because his best clothes were in pawn. He told her that he had been sick, but was once more nearly well, and that inside ten days or two weeks (as soon as a letter could travel to New York City and return) he would redeem his clothes and be with her.

But Ruth did not care to wait ten days or two weeks. Besides, her lover was sick. The next afternoon, accompanied by Arthur, she arrived in the Morse carriage, to the unqualified delight of the Silva tribe and of all the urchins on the street, and to the consternation of Maria. She boxed the ears of the Silvas who crowded about the visitors on the tiny front porch, and in more than usual atrocious English tried to apologize for her appearance. Sleeves rolled up from soap-flecked arms and a wet gunny-sack around her waist told of the task at which she had been caught. So flustered was she by two such grand young people asking for her lodger, that she forgot to invite them to sit down in the little parlor. To enter Martin's room, they passed through the kitchen, warm and moist and steamy from the big washing in progress. Maria, in her excitement, jammed the bedroom and bedroom-closet doors together, and for five minutes, through the partly open door, clouds of steam, smelling of soap-suds and dirt, poured into the sick chamber.

Ruth succeeded in veering right and left and right again, and in running the narrow passage between table and bed to Martin's side; but Arthur veered too wide and fetched up with clatter and bang of pots and pans in the corner where Martin did his cooking. Arthur did not linger long. Ruth occupied the only chair, and having done his duty, he went outside and stood by the gate, the centre of seven marvelling Silvas, who watched him as they would have watched a curiosity in a side-show. All about the carriage were gathered the children from a dozen blocks, waiting and eager for some tragic and terrible dénouement. Carriages were seen on their street only for weddings and funerals. Here was neither marriage nor death: therefore, it was something transcending experience and well worth waiting for.

Martin had been wild to see Ruth. His was essentially a love-nature, and he possessed more than the average man's need for sympathy. He was starving for sympathy, which, with him, meant intelligent understanding; and he had yet to learn that Ruth's sympathy was largely sentimental and tactful, and that it proceeded from gentleness of nature rather than from understanding of the objects of her sympathy. So it was while Martin held her hand and gladly talked, that her love for him prompted her to press his hand in return, and that her eyes were moist and luminous at sight of his helplessness and of the marks suffering had stamped upon his face.

But while he told her of his two acceptances, of his despair when he received the one from the *Transcontinental*, and of the corresponding delight with which he received the one from the *White Mouse*, she did not follow him. She heard the words he uttered and understood their literal import, but she was not with him in his despair and his delight. She could not get out of herself. She was not interested in selling stories to magazines. What was important to her was matrimony. She was not aware of it, however, any more than she was aware that her desire that Martin take a position was the instinctive and preparative impulse of motherhood. She would have blushed had she been told as much in plain, set terms, and next, she might have grown indignant and asserted that her sole interest lay in the man she loved and her desire for him to make the best of himself. So, while Martin poured out his heart to her, elated with the first success his chosen work in the world had received, she paid heed to his bare words only, gazing now and again about the room, shocked by what she saw.

For the first time Ruth gazed upon the sordid face of poverty. Starving lovers had always seemed romantic to her,—but she had had no idea how starving lovers lived. She had never dreamed it could be like this. Ever her gaze shifted from the room to him and back again. The steamy smell of dirty clothes, which had entered with her from the kitchen, was sickening. Martin must be soaked with it, Ruth concluded, if that awful woman washed frequently. Such was the contagiousness of degradation. When she looked at Martin, she seemed to see the smirch left upon him by his surroundings. She had never seen him unshaven, and the three days' growth of beard on his face was repulsive to her. Not alone did it give him the same dark and murky aspect of the Silva house, inside and out, but it seemed to emphasize that animal-like strength of his which she detested. And here he was, being confirmed in his madness by the two acceptances he took such pride in telling her about. A little longer and he would have surrendered and gone to work. Now he would continue on in this horrible house, writing and starving for a few more months.

"What is that smell?" she asked suddenly.

"Some of Maria's washing smells, I imagine," was the answer. "I am growing quite accustomed to them."

"No, no; not that. It is something else. A stale, sickish smell."

Martin sampled the air before replying.

"I can't smell anything else, except stale tobacco smoke," he announced.

"That's it. It is terrible. Why do you smoke so much, Martin?"

"I don't know, except that I smoke more than usual when I am lonely. And then, too, it's such a long-standing habit. I learned when I was only a youngster."

"It is not a nice habit, you know," she reproved. "It smells to heaven."

"That's the fault of the tobacco. I can afford only the cheapest. But wait until I get that forty-dollar check. I'll use a brand that is not offensive even to the angels. But that wasn't so bad, was it, two acceptances in three days? That forty-five dollars will pay about all my debts."

"For two years' work?" she queried.

"No, for less than a week's work. Please pass me that book over on the far corner of the table, the account book with the gray cover." He opened it and began turning over the pages rapidly. "Yes, I was right. Four days for 'The Ring of Bells,' two days for 'The Whirlpool.' That's forty-five dollars for a week's work, one hundred and eighty dollars a month. That beats any salary I can command. And, besides, I'm just beginning. A thousand dollars a month is not too much to buy for you all I want you to have. A salary of five hundred a month would be too small. That forty-five dollars is just a starter. Wait till I get my stride. Then watch my smoke."

Ruth misunderstood his slang, and reverted to cigarettes.

"You smoke more than enough as it is, and the brand of tobacco will make no difference. It is the smoking itself that is not nice, no matter what the brand may be. You are a chimney, a living volcano, a perambulating smoke-stack, and you are a perfect disgrace, Martin dear, you know you are."

She leaned toward him, entreaty in her eyes, and as he looked at her delicate face and into her pure, limpid eyes, as of old he was struck with his own unworthiness.

"I wish you wouldn't smoke any more," she whispered. "Please, for—my sake."

"All right, I won't," he cried. "I'll do anything you ask, dear love, anything; you know that."

A great temptation assailed her. In an insistent way she had caught glimpses of the large, easy-going side of his nature, and she felt sure, if she asked him to cease attempting to write, that he would grant her wish. In the swift instant that elapsed, the words trembled on her lips. But she did not utter them. She was not quite brave enough; she did not quite dare. Instead, she leaned toward him to meet him, and in his arms murmured:-

"You know, it is really not for my sake, Martin, but for your own. I am sure smoking hurts you; and besides, it is not good to be a slave to anything, to a drug least of all."

"I shall always be your slave," he smiled.

"In which case, I shall begin issuing my commands."

She looked at him mischievously, though deep down she was already regretting that she had not preferred her largest request.

"I live but to obey, your majesty."

"Well, then, my first commandment is, Thou shalt not omit to shave every day. Look how you have scratched my cheek."

And so it ended in caresses and love-laughter. But she had made one point, and she could not expect to make more than one at a time. She felt a woman's pride in that she had made him stop smoking. Another time she would persuade him to take a position, for had he not said he would do anything she asked?

She left his side to explore the room, examining the clothes-lines of notes overhead, learning the mystery of the tackle used for suspending his wheel under the ceiling, and being saddened by the heap of manuscripts under the table which represented to her just so much wasted time. The oil-stove won her admiration, but on investigating the food shelves she found them empty.

"Why, you haven't anything to eat, you poor dear," she said with tender compassion. "You must be starving."

"I store my food in Maria's safe and in her pantry," he lied. "It keeps better there. No danger of my starving. Look at that."

She had come back to his side, and she saw him double his arm at the elbow, the biceps crawling under his shirt-sleeve and swelling into a knot of muscle, heavy and hard. The sight repelled her. Sentimentally, she disliked it. But her pulse, her blood, every fibre of her, loved it and yearned for it, and, in the old, inexplicable way, she leaned toward him, not away from him. And in the moment that followed, when he crushed her in his arms, the brain of her, concerned with the superficial aspects of life, was in revolt; while the heart of her, the woman of her, concerned with life itself, exulted triumphantly. It was in moments like this that she felt to the uttermost the greatness of her love for Martin, for it was almost a swoon of delight to her to feel his strong arms about her, holding her tightly, hurting her with the grip of their fervor. At such moments she found justification for her treason to her standards, for her violation of her own high ideals, and, most of all, for her tacit disobedience to her mother and father. They did not want her to marry this man. It shocked them that she should love him. It shocked her, too, sometimes, when she was apart from him, a cool and reasoning creature. With him, she loved him—in truth, at times a vexed and worried love; but love it was, a love that was stronger than she.

"This La Grippe is nothing," he was saying. "It hurts a bit, and gives one a nasty headache, but it doesn't compare with break-bone fever."

"Have you had that, too?" she queried absently, intent on the heaven-sent justification she was finding in his arms.

And so, with absent queries, she led him on, till suddenly his words startled her.

He had had the fever in a secret colony of thirty lepers on one of the Hawaiian Islands.

"But why did you go there?" she demanded.

Such royal carelessness of body seemed criminal.

"Because I didn't know," he answered. "I never dreamed of lepers. When I deserted the schooner and landed on the beach, I headed inland for some place of hiding. For three days I lived off guavas, *ohia*-apples, and bananas, all of which grew wild in the jungle. On the fourth day I found the trail—a mere foot-trail. It led inland, and it led up. It was the way I wanted to go, and it showed signs of recent travel. At one place it ran along the crest of a ridge that was no more than a knife-edge. The trail wasn't three feet wide on the crest, and on either side the ridge fell away in precipices hundreds of feet deep. One man, with plenty of ammunition, could have held it against a hundred thousand.

"It was the only way in to the hiding-place. Three hours after I found the trail I was there, in a little mountain valley, a pocket in the midst of lava peaks. The whole place was terraced for taro-patches, fruit trees grew there, and there were eight or ten grass huts. But as soon as I saw the inhabitants I knew what I'd struck. One sight of them was enough."

"What did you do?" Ruth demanded breathlessly, listening, like any Desdemona, appalled and fascinated.

"Nothing for me to do. Their leader was a kind old fellow, pretty far gone, but he ruled like a king. He had discovered the little valley and founded the settlement—all of which was against the law. But he had guns, plenty of ammunition, and those Kanakas, trained to the shooting of wild cattle and wild pig, were dead shots. No, there wasn't any running away for Martin Eden. He stayed—for three months."

"But how did you escape?"

"I'd have been there yet, if it hadn't been for a girl there, a half-Chinese, quarter-white, and quarter-Hawaiian. She was a beauty, poor thing, and well educated. Her mother, in Honolulu, was worth a million or so. Well, this girl got me away at last. Her mother financed the settlement, you see, so the girl wasn't afraid of being punished for letting me go. But she made me swear, first, never to reveal the hiding-place; and I never have. This is the first time I have even mentioned it. The girl had just the first signs of leprosy. The fingers of her right hand were slightly twisted, and there was a small spot on her arm. That was all. I guess she is dead, now."

"But weren't you frightened? And weren't you glad to get away without catching that dreadful disease?"

"Well," he confessed, "I was a bit shivery at first; but I got used to it. I used to feel sorry for that poor girl, though. That made me forget to be afraid. She was such a beauty, in spirit as well as in appearance, and she was only slightly touched; yet she was doomed to lie there, living the life of a primitive savage and rotting slowly away. Leprosy is far more terrible than you can imagine it."

"Poor thing," Ruth murmured softly. "It's a wonder she let you get away."

"How do you mean?" Martin asked unwittingly.

"Because she must have loved you," Ruth said, still softly. "Candidly, now, didn't she?"

Martin's sunburn had been bleached by his work in the laundry and by the indoor life he was living, while the hunger and the sickness had made his face even pale; and across this pallor flowed the slow wave of a blush. He was opening his mouth to speak, but Ruth shut him off.

"Never mind, don't answer; it's not necessary," she laughed.

But it seemed to him there was something metallic in her laughter, and that the light in her eyes was cold. On the spur of the moment it reminded him of a gale he had once experienced in the North Pacific. And for the moment the apparition of the gale rose before his eyes—a gale at night, with a clear sky and under a full moon, the huge seas glinting coldly in the moonlight. Next, he saw the girl in the leper refuge and remembered it was for love of him that she had let him go.

"She was noble," he said simply. "She gave me life."

That was all of the incident, but he heard Ruth muffle a dry sob in her throat, and noticed that she turned her face away to gaze out of the window. When she turned it back to him, it was composed, and there was no hint of the gale in her eyes.

"I'm such a silly," she said plaintively. "But I can't help it. I do so love you, Martin, I do, I do. I shall grow more catholic in time, but at present I can't help being jealous of those ghosts of the past, and you know your past is full of ghosts."

"It must be," she silenced his protest. "It could not be otherwise. And there's poor Arthur motioning me to come. He's tired waiting. And now good-by, dear."

"There's some kind of a mixture, put up by the druggists, that helps men to stop the use of tobacco," she called back from the door, "and I am going to send you some."

The door closed, but opened again.

"I do, I do," she whispered to him; and this time she was really gone.

Maria, with worshipful eyes that none the less were keen to note the texture of Ruth's garments and the cut of them (a cut unknown that produced an effect mysteriously beautiful), saw her to the carriage. The crowd of disappointed urchins stared till the carriage disappeared from view, then transferred their stare to Maria, who had abruptly become the most important person on the street. But it was one of her progeny who blasted Maria's reputation by announcing that the grand visitors had been for her lodger. After that Maria dropped back into her old obscurity and Martin began to notice the respectful manner in which he was regarded by the small fry of the neighborhood. As for Maria, Martin rose in her estimation a full hundred per cent, and had the Portuguese grocer witnessed that afternoon carriage-call he would have allowed Martin an additional three-dollars-and-eighty-five-cents' worth of credit.

CHAPTER XXVII

The sun of Martin's good fortune rose. The day after Ruth's visit, he received a check for three dollars from a New York scandal weekly in payment for three of his triolets. Two days later a newspaper published in Chicago accepted his "Treasure Hunters," promising to pay ten dollars for it on publication. The price was small, but it was the first article he had written, his very first attempt to express his thought on the printed page. To cap everything, the adventure serial for boys, his second attempt, was accepted before the end of the week by a juvenile monthly calling itself *Youth and Age*. It was true the serial was twenty-one thousand words, and they offered to pay him sixteen dollars on publication, which was something like seventy-five cents a thousand words; but it was equally true that it was the second thing he had attempted to write and that he was himself thoroughly aware of its clumsy worthlessness.

But even his earliest efforts were not marked with the clumsiness of mediocrity. What characterized them was the clumsiness of too great strength—the clumsiness which the tyro betrays when he crushes butterflies with battering rams and hammers out vignettes with a war-club. So it was that Martin was glad to sell his early efforts for songs. He knew them for what they were, and it had not taken him long to acquire this knowledge. What he pinned his faith to was his later work. He had striven to be something more than a mere writer of magazine fiction. He had sought to equip himself with the tools of artistry. On the other hand, he had not sacrificed strength. His conscious aim had been to increase his strength by avoiding excess of strength. Nor had he departed from his love of reality. His work was realism, though he had endeavored to fuse with it the fancies and beauties of imagination. What he sought was an impassioned realism, shot through with human aspiration and faith. What he wanted was life as it was, with all its spirit-groping and soul-reaching left in.

He had discovered, in the course of his reading, two schools of fiction. One treated of man as a god, ignoring his earthly origin; the other treated of man as a clod, ignoring his heaven-sent dreams and divine possibilities. Both the god and the clod schools erred, in Martin's estimation, and erred through too great singleness of sight and purpose. There was a compromise that approximated the truth, though it flattered not the school of god, while it challenged the brute-savageness of the school of clod. It was his story, "Adventure," which had dragged with Ruth, that Martin believed had achieved his ideal of the true in fiction; and it was in an essay, "God and Clod," that he had expressed his views on the whole general subject.

CHAPTER XXVII

But "Adventure," and all that he deemed his best work, still went begging among the editors. His early work counted for nothing in his eyes except for the money it brought, and his horror stories, two of which he had sold, he did not consider high work nor his best work. To him they were frankly imaginative and fantastic, though invested with all the glamour of the real, wherein lay their power. This investiture of the grotesque and impossible with reality, he looked upon as a trick—a skilful trick at best. Great literature could not reside in such a field. Their artistry was high, but he denied the worthwhileness of artistry when divorced from humanness. The trick had been to fling over the face of his artistry a mask of humanness, and this he had done in the half-dozen or so stories of the horror brand he had written before he emerged upon the high peaks of "Adventure," "Joy," "The Pot," and "The Wine of Life."

The three dollars he received for the triolets he used to eke out a precarious existence against the arrival of the *White Mouse* check. He cashed the first check with the suspicious Portuguese grocer, paying a dollar on account and dividing the remaining two dollars between the baker and the fruit store. Martin was not yet rich enough to afford meat, and he was on slim allowance when the *White Mouse* check arrived. He was divided on the cashing of it. He had never been in a bank in his life, much less been in one on business, and he had a naive and childlike desire to walk into one of the big banks down in Oakland and fling down his indorsed check for forty dollars. On the other hand, practical common sense ruled that he should cash it with his grocer and thereby make an impression that would later result in an increase of credit. Reluctantly Martin yielded to the claims of the grocer, paying his bill with him in full, and receiving in change a pocketful of jingling coin. Also, he paid the other tradesmen in full, redeemed his suit and his bicycle, paid one month's rent on the typewriter, and paid Maria the overdue month for his room and a month in advance. This left him in his pocket, for emergencies, a balance of nearly three dollars.

In itself, this small sum seemed a fortune. Immediately on recovering his clothes he had gone to see Ruth, and on the way he could not refrain from jingling the little handful of silver in his pocket. He had been so long without money that, like a rescued starving man who cannot let the unconsumed food out of his sight, Martin could not keep his hand off the silver. He was not mean, nor avaricious, but the money meant more than so many dollars and cents. It stood for success, and the eagles stamped upon the coins were to him so many winged victories.

It came to him insensibly that it was a very good world. It certainly appeared more beautiful to him. For weeks it had been a very dull and sombre world; but now, with nearly all debts paid, three dollars jingling in his pocket, and in his mind the consciousness of success, the sun shone bright and warm, and even a rain-squall that soaked unprepared pedestrians seemed a merry happening to him. When he starved, his thoughts had dwelt often upon the thousands he knew were starving the world over; but now that he was feasted full, the fact of the thousands starving was no longer pregnant in his brain. He forgot about them, and, being in love, remembered the countless lovers in the world. Without deliberately thinking about it, *motifs* for love-lyrics began to agitate his brain. Swept away by the creative impulse, he got off the electric car, without vexation, two blocks beyond his crossing.

He found a number of persons in the Morse home. Ruth's two girl-cousins were visiting her from San Rafael, and Mrs. Morse, under pretext of entertaining them, was pursuing her plan of surrounding Ruth with young people. The campaign had begun during Martin's enforced absence, and was already in full swing. She was making a point of having at the house men who were doing things. Thus, in addition to the cousins Dorothy and Florence, Martin encountered two university professors, one of Latin, the other of English; a young army officer just back from the Philippines, one-time school-mate of Ruth's; a young fellow named Melville, private secretary to Joseph Perkins, head of the San Francisco Trust Company; and finally of the men, a live bank cashier, Charles Hapgood, a youngish man of thirty-five, graduate of Stanford University, member of the Nile Club and the Unity Club, and a conservative speaker for the Republican Party during campaigns—in short, a rising young man in every way. Among the women was one who painted portraits, another who was a professional musician, and still another who possessed the degree of Doctor of Sociology and who was locally famous for her social settlement work in the slums of San Francisco. But the women did not count for much in Mrs. Morse's plan. At the best, they were necessary accessories. The men who did things must be drawn to the house somehow.

"Don't get excited when you talk," Ruth admonished Martin, before the ordeal of introduction began.

He bore himself a bit stiffly at first, oppressed by a sense of his own awkwardness, especially of his shoulders, which were up to their old trick of threatening destruction to furniture and ornaments. Also, he was rendered self-conscious by the company. He had never before been in contact with such exalted beings nor with so many of them. Melville, the bank cashier, fascinated him, and he resolved to investigate him at the first opportunity. For underneath Martin's awe lurked his assertive ego, and he felt the urge to measure himself with these men and women and to find out what they had learned from the books and life which he had not learned.

Ruth's eyes roved to him frequently to see how he was getting on, and she was surprised and gladdened by the ease with which he got acquainted with her cousins. He certainly did not grow excited, while being seated removed from him the worry of his shoulders. Ruth knew them for clever girls, superficially brilliant, and she could scarcely understand their praise of Martin later that night at going to bed. But he, on the other hand, a wit in his own class, a gay quizzer and laughter-maker at dances and Sunday picnics, had found the making of fun and the breaking of good-natured lances simple enough in this environment. And on this evening success stood at his back, patting him on the shoulder and telling him that he was making good, so that he could afford to laugh and make laughter and remain unabashed.

Later, Ruth's anxiety found justification. Martin and Professor Caldwell had got together in a conspicuous corner, and though Martin no longer wove the air with his hands, to Ruth's critical eye he permitted his own eyes to flash and glitter too frequently, talked too rapidly and warmly, grew too intense, and allowed his aroused blood to redden his cheeks too much. He lacked decorum and control, and was in decided contrast to the young professor of English with whom he talked.

But Martin was not concerned with appearances! He had been swift to note the other's trained mind and to appreciate his command of knowledge. Furthermore, Professor Caldwell did not realize Martin's concept of the average English professor. Martin wanted him to talk shop, and, though he seemed averse at first, succeeded in making him do it. For Martin did not see why a man should not talk shop.

CHAPTER XXVII

"It's absurd and unfair," he had told Ruth weeks before, "this objection to talking shop. For what reason under the sun do men and women come together if not for the exchange of the best that is in them? And the best that is in them is what they are interested in, the thing by which they make their living, the thing they've specialized on and sat up days and nights over, and even dreamed about. Imagine Mr. Butler living up to social etiquette and enunciating his views on Paul Verlaine or the German drama or the novels of D'Annunzio. We'd be bored to death. I, for one, if I must listen to Mr. Butler, prefer to hear him talk about his law. It's the best that is in him, and life is so short that I want the best of every man and woman I meet."

"But," Ruth had objected, "there are the topics of general interest to all."

"There, you mistake," he had rushed on. "All persons in society, all cliques in society—or, rather, nearly all persons and cliques—ape their betters. Now, who are the best betters? The idlers, the wealthy idlers. They do not know, as a rule, the things known by the persons who are doing something in the world. To listen to conversation about such things would mean to be bored, wherefore the idlers decree that such things are shop and must not be talked about. Likewise they decree the things that are not shop and which may be talked about, and those things are the latest operas, latest novels, cards, billiards, cocktails, automobiles, horse shows, trout fishing, tuna-fishing, big-game shooting, yacht sailing, and so forth—and mark you, these are the things the idlers know. In all truth, they constitute the shop-talk of the idlers. And the funniest part of it is that many of the clever people, and all the would-be clever people, allow the idlers so to impose upon them. As for me, I want the best a man's got in him, call it shop vulgarity or anything you please."

And Ruth had not understood. This attack of his on the established had seemed to her just so much wilfulness of opinion.

So Martin contaminated Professor Caldwell with his own earnestness, challenging him to speak his mind. As Ruth paused beside them she heard Martin saying:-

"You surely don't pronounce such heresies in the University of California?"

Professor Caldwell shrugged his shoulders. "The honest taxpayer and the politician, you know. Sacramento gives us our appropriations and therefore we kowtow to Sacramento, and to the Board of Regents, and to the party press, or to the press of both parties."

"Yes, that's clear; but how about you?" Martin urged. "You must be a fish out of the water."

"Few like me, I imagine, in the university pond. Sometimes I am fairly sure I am out of water, and that I should belong in Paris, in Grub Street, in a hermit's cave, or in some sadly wild Bohemian crowd, drinking claret,—dago-red they call it in San Francisco,—dining in cheap restaurants in the Latin Quarter, and expressing vociferously radical views upon all creation. Really, I am frequently almost sure that I was cut out to be a radical. But then, there are so many questions on which I am not sure. I grow timid when I am face to face with my human frailty, which ever prevents me from grasping all the factors in any problem—human, vital problems, you know."

And as he talked on, Martin became aware that to his own lips had come the "Song of the Trade Wind":-

"I am strongest at noon,
But under the moon
I stiffen the bunt of the sail."

He was almost humming the words, and it dawned upon him that the other reminded him of the trade wind, of the Northeast Trade, steady, and cool, and strong. He was equable, he was to be relied upon, and withal there was a certain bafflement about him. Martin had the feeling that he never spoke his full mind, just as he had often had the feeling that the trades never blew their strongest but always held reserves of strength that were never used. Martin's trick of visioning was active as ever. His brain was a most accessible storehouse of remembered fact and fancy, and its contents seemed ever ordered and spread for his inspection. Whatever occurred in the instant present, Martin's mind immediately presented associated antithesis or similitude which ordinarily expressed themselves to him in vision. It was sheerly automatic, and his visioning was an unfailing accompaniment to the living present. Just as Ruth's face, in a momentary jealousy had called before his eyes a forgotten moonlight gale, and as Professor Caldwell made him see again the Northeast Trade herding the white billows across the purple sea, so, from moment to moment, not disconcerting but rather identifying and classifying, new memory-visions rose before him, or spread under his eyelids, or were thrown upon the screen of his consciousness. These visions came out of the actions and sensations of the past, out of things and events and books of yesterday and last week—a countless host of apparitions that, waking or sleeping, forever thronged his mind.

So it was, as he listened to Professor Caldwell's easy flow of speech—the conversation of a clever, cultured man—that Martin kept seeing himself down all his past. He saw himself when he had been quite the hoodlum, wearing a "stiff-rim" Stetson hat and a square-cut, double-breasted coat, with a certain swagger to the shoulders and possessing the ideal of being as tough as the police permitted. He did not disguise it to himself, nor attempt to palliate it. At one time in his life he had been just a common hoodlum, the leader of a gang that worried the police and terrorized honest, working-class householders. But his ideals had changed. He glanced about him at the well-bred, well-dressed men and women, and breathed into his lungs the atmosphere of culture and refinement, and at the same moment the ghost of his early youth, in stiff-rim and square-cut, with swagger and toughness, stalked across the room. This figure, of the corner hoodlum, he saw merge into himself, sitting and talking with an actual university professor.

For, after all, he had never found his permanent abiding place. He had fitted in wherever he found himself, been a favorite always and everywhere by virtue of holding his own at work and at play and by his willingness and ability to fight for his rights and command respect. But he had never taken root. He had fitted in sufficiently to satisfy his fellows but not to satisfy himself. He had been perturbed always by a feeling of unrest, had heard always the call of something from beyond, and had wandered on through life seeking it until he found books and art and love. And here he was, in the midst of all this, the only one of all the comrades he had adventured with who could have made themselves eligible for the inside of the Morse home.

But such thoughts and visions did not prevent him from following Professor Caldwell closely. And as he followed, comprehendingly and critically, he noted the unbroken field of the other's knowledge. As for himself, from moment to moment the conversation showed him gaps and open stretches, whole subjects with which he was unfamiliar. Nevertheless, thanks to his Spencer, he saw that he possessed the outlines of the field of knowledge. It was a matter only of time, when he would fill in the outline. Then watch out, he thought—'ware shoal, everybody! He felt like sitting at the feet of the professor, worshipful and absorbent; but, as he listened, he began to discern a weakness in the other's judgments—a weakness so stray and elusive that he might not have caught it had it not been ever present. And when he did catch it, he leapt to equality at once.

Ruth came up to them a second time, just as Martin began to speak.

"I'll tell you where you are wrong, or, rather, what weakens your judgments," he said. "You lack biology. It has no place in your scheme of things.—Oh, I mean the real interpretative biology, from the ground up, from the laboratory and the test-tube and the vitalized inorganic right on up to the widest aesthetic and sociological generalizations."

Ruth was appalled. She had sat two lecture courses under Professor Caldwell and looked up to him as the living repository of all knowledge.

"I scarcely follow you," he said dubiously.

Martin was not so sure but what he had followed him.

"Then I'll try to explain," he said. "I remember reading in Egyptian history something to the effect that understanding could not be had of Egyptian art without first studying the land question."

"Quite right," the professor nodded.

"And it seems to me," Martin continued, "that knowledge of the land question, in turn, of all questions, for that matter, cannot be had without previous knowledge of the stuff and the constitution of life. How can we understand laws and institutions, religions and customs, without understanding, not merely the nature of the creatures that made them, but the nature of the stuff out of which the creatures are made? Is literature less human than the architecture and sculpture of Egypt? Is there one thing in the known universe that is not subject to the law of evolution?—Oh, I know there is an elaborate evolution of the various arts laid down, but it seems to me to be too mechanical. The human himself is left out. The evolution of the tool, of the harp, of music and song and dance, are all beautifully elaborated; but how about the evolution of the human himself, the development of the basic and intrinsic parts that were in him before he made his first tool or gibbered his first chant? It is that which you do not consider, and which I call biology. It is biology in its largest aspects.

"I know I express myself incoherently, but I've tried to hammer out the idea. It came to me as you were talking, so I was not primed and ready to deliver it. You spoke yourself of the human frailty that prevented one from taking all the factors into consideration. And you, in turn,—or so it seems to me,—leave out the biological factor, the very stuff out of which has been spun the fabric of all the arts, the warp and the woof of all human actions and achievements."

To Ruth's amazement, Martin was not immediately crushed, and that the professor replied in the way he did struck her as forbearance for Martin's youth. Professor Caldwell sat for a full minute, silent and fingering his watch chain.

"Do you know," he said at last, "I've had that same criticism passed on me once before—by a very great man, a scientist and evolutionist, Joseph Le Conte. But he is dead, and I thought to remain undetected; and now you come along and expose me. Seriously, though—and this is confession—I think there is something in your contention—a great deal, in fact. I am too classical, not enough up-to-date in the interpretative branches of science, and I can only plead the disadvantages of my education and a temperamental slothfulness that prevents me from doing the work. I wonder if you'll believe that I've never been inside a physics or chemistry laboratory? It is true, nevertheless. Le Conte was right, and so are you, Mr. Eden, at least to an extent—how much I do not know."

Ruth drew Martin away with her on a pretext; when she had got him aside, whispering:-

"You shouldn't have monopolized Professor Caldwell that way. There may be others who want to talk with him."

"My mistake," Martin admitted contritely. "But I'd got him stirred up, and he was so interesting that I did not think. Do you know, he is the brightest, the most intellectual, man I have ever talked with. And I'll tell you something else. I once thought that everybody who went to universities, or who sat in the high places in society, was just as brilliant and intelligent as he."

"He's an exception," she answered.

"I should say so. Whom do you want me to talk to now?—Oh, say, bring me up against that cashier-fellow."

Martin talked for fifteen minutes with him, nor could Ruth have wished better behavior on her lover's part. Not once did his eyes flash nor his cheeks flush, while the calmness and poise with which he talked surprised her. But in Martin's estimation the whole tribe of bank cashiers fell a few hundred per cent, and for the rest of the evening he labored under the impression that bank cashiers and talkers of platitudes were synonymous phrases. The army officer he found good-natured and simple, a healthy, wholesome young fellow, content to occupy the place in life into which birth and luck had flung him. On learning that he had completed two years in the university, Martin was puzzled to know where he had stored it away. Nevertheless Martin liked him better than the platitudinous bank cashier.

"I really don't object to platitudes," he told Ruth later; "but what worries me into nervousness is the pompous, smugly complacent, superior certitude with which they are uttered and the time taken to do it. Why, I could give that man the whole history of the Reformation in the time he took to tell me that the Union-Labor Party had fused with the Democrats. Do you know, he skins his words as a professional poker-player skins the cards that are dealt out to him. Some day I'll show you what I mean."

"I'm sorry you don't like him," was her reply. "He's a favorite of Mr. Butler's. Mr. Butler says he is safe and honest—calls him the Rock, Peter, and says that upon him any banking institution can well be built."

"I don't doubt it—from the little I saw of him and the less I heard from him; but I don't think so much of banks as I did. You don't mind my speaking my mind this way, dear?"

"No, no; it is most interesting."

"Yes," Martin went on heartily, "I'm no more than a barbarian getting my first impressions of civilization. Such impressions must be entertainingly novel to the civilized person."

"What did you think of my cousins?" Ruth queried.

"I liked them better than the other women. There's plenty of fun in them along with paucity of pretence."

"Then you did like the other women?"

He shook his head.

"That social-settlement woman is no more than a sociological poll-parrot. I swear, if you winnowed her out between the stars, like Tomlinson, there would be found in her not one original thought. As for the portrait-painter, she was a positive bore. She'd make a good wife for the cashier. And the musician woman! I don't care how nimble her fingers are, how perfect her technique, how wonderful her expression—the fact is, she knows nothing about music."

"She plays beautifully," Ruth protested.

"Yes, she's undoubtedly gymnastic in the externals of music, but the intrinsic spirit of music is unguessed by her. I asked her what music meant to her—you know I'm always curious to know that particular thing; and she did not know what it meant to her, except that she adored it, that it was the greatest of the arts, and that it meant more than life to her."

"You were making them talk shop," Ruth charged him.

"I confess it. And if they were failures on shop, imagine my sufferings if they had discoursed on other subjects. Why, I used to think that up here, where all the advantages of culture were enjoyed—" He paused for a moment, and watched the youthful shade of himself, in stiff-rim and square-cut, enter the door and swagger across the room. "As I was saying, up here I thought all men and women were brilliant and radiant. But now, from what little I've seen of them, they strike me as a pack of ninnies, most of them, and ninety percent of the remainder as bores. Now there's Professor Caldwell—he's different. He's a man, every inch of him and every atom of his gray matter."

Ruth's face brightened.

"Tell me about him," she urged. "Not what is large and brilliant—I know those qualities; but whatever you feel is adverse. I am most curious to know."

"Perhaps I'll get myself in a pickle." Martin debated humorously for a moment. "Suppose you tell me first. Or maybe you find in him nothing less than the best."

"I attended two lecture courses under him, and I have known him for two years; that is why I am anxious for your first impression."

"Bad impression, you mean? Well, here goes. He is all the fine things you think about him, I guess. At least, he is the finest specimen of intellectual man I have met; but he is a man with a secret shame."

"Oh, no, no!" he hastened to cry. "Nothing paltry nor vulgar. What I mean is that he strikes me as a man who has gone to the bottom of things, and is so afraid of what he saw that he makes believe to himself that he never saw it. Perhaps that's not the clearest way to express it. Here's another way. A man who has found the path to the hidden temple but has not followed it; who has, perhaps, caught glimpses of the temple and striven afterward to convince himself that it was only a mirage of foliage. Yet another way. A man who could have done things but who placed no value on the doing, and who, all the time, in his innermost heart, is regretting that he has not done them; who has secretly laughed at the rewards for doing, and yet, still more secretly, has yearned for the rewards and for the joy of doing."

"I don't read him that way," she said. "And for that matter, I don't see just what you mean."

"It is only a vague feeling on my part," Martin temporized. "I have no reason for it. It is only a feeling, and most likely it is wrong. You certainly should know him better than I."

From the evening at Ruth's Martin brought away with him strange confusions and conflicting feelings. He was disappointed in his goal, in the persons he had climbed to be with. On the other hand, he was encouraged with his success. The climb had been easier than he expected. He was superior to the climb, and (he did not, with false modesty, hide it from himself) he was superior to the beings among whom he had climbed—with the exception, of course, of Professor Caldwell. About life and the books he knew more than they, and he wondered into what nooks and crannies they had cast aside their educations. He did not know that he was himself possessed of unusual brain vigor; nor did he know that the persons who were given to probing the depths and to thinking ultimate thoughts were not to be found in the drawing rooms of the world's Morses; nor did he dream that such persons were as lonely eagles sailing solitary in the azure sky far above the earth and its swarming freight of gregarious life.

CHAPTER XXVIII

But success had lost Martin's address, and her messengers no longer came to his door. For twenty-five days, working Sundays and holidays, he toiled on "The Shame of the Sun," a long essay of some thirty thousand words. It was a deliberate attack on the mysticism of the Maeterlinck school—an attack from the citadel of positive science upon the wonder-dreamers, but an attack nevertheless that retained much of beauty and wonder of the sort compatible with ascertained fact. It was a little later that he followed up the attack with two short essays, "The Wonder-Dreamers" and "The Yardstick of the Ego." And on essays, long and short, he began to pay the travelling expenses from magazine to magazine.

During the twenty-five days spent on "The Shame of the Sun," he sold hack-work to the extent of six dollars and fifty cents. A joke had brought in fifty cents, and a second one, sold to a high-grade comic weekly, had fetched a dollar. Then two humorous poems had earned two dollars and three dollars respectively. As a result, having exhausted his credit with the tradesmen (though he had increased his credit with the grocer to five dollars), his wheel and suit of clothes went back to the pawnbroker. The type-writer people were again clamoring for money, insistently pointing out that according to the agreement rent was to be paid strictly in advance.

Encouraged by his several small sales, Martin went back to hack-work. Perhaps there was a living in it, after all. Stored away under his table were the twenty storiettes which had been rejected by the newspaper short-story syndicate. He read them over in order to find out how not to write newspaper storiettes, and so doing, reasoned out the perfect formula. He found that the newspaper storiette should never be tragic, should never end unhappily, and should never contain beauty of language, subtlety of thought, nor real delicacy of sentiment. Sentiment it must contain, plenty of it, pure and noble, of the sort that in his own early youth had brought his applause from "nigger heaven"—the "For-God-my-country-and-the-Czar" and "I-may-be-poor-but-I-am-honest" brand of sentiment.

Having learned such precautions, Martin consulted "The Duchess" for tone, and proceeded to mix according to formula. The formula consists of three parts: (1) a pair of lovers are jarred apart; (2) by some deed or event they are reunited; (3) marriage bells. The third part was an unvarying quantity, but the first and second parts could be varied an infinite number of times. Thus, the pair of lovers could be jarred apart by misunderstood motives, by accident of fate, by jealous rivals, by irate parents, by crafty guardians, by scheming relatives, and so forth and so forth; they could be reunited by a brave deed of the man lover, by a similar deed of the woman lover, by change of heart in one lover or the other, by forced confession of crafty guardian, scheming relative, or jealous rival, by voluntary confession of same, by discovery of some unguessed secret, by lover storming girl's heart, by lover making long and noble self-sacrifice, and so on, endlessly. It was very fetching to make the girl propose in the course of being reunited, and Martin discovered, bit by bit, other decidedly piquant and fetching ruses. But marriage bells at the end was the one thing he could take no liberties with; though the heavens rolled up as a scroll and the stars fell, the wedding bells must go on ringing just the same. In quantity, the formula prescribed twelve hundred words minimum dose, fifteen hundred words maximum dose.

Before he got very far along in the art of the storiette, Martin worked out half a dozen stock forms, which he always consulted when constructing storiettes. These forms were like the cunning tables used by mathematicians, which may be entered from top, bottom, right, and left, which entrances consist of scores of lines and dozens of columns, and from which may be drawn, without reasoning or thinking, thousands of different conclusions, all unchallengably precise and true. Thus, in the course of half an hour with his forms, Martin could frame up a dozen or so storiettes, which he put aside and filled in at his convenience. He found that he could fill one in, after a day of serious work, in the hour before going to bed. As he later confessed to Ruth, he could almost do it in his sleep. The real work was in constructing the frames, and that was merely mechanical.

He had no doubt whatever of the efficacy of his formula, and for once he knew the editorial mind when he said positively to himself that the first two he sent off would bring checks. And checks they brought, for four dollars each, at the end of twelve days.

In the meantime he was making fresh and alarming discoveries concerning the magazines. Though the *Transcontinental* had published "The Ring of Bells," no check was forthcoming. Martin needed it, and he wrote for it. An evasive answer and a request for more of his work was all he received. He had gone hungry two days waiting for the reply, and it was then that he put his wheel back in pawn. He wrote regularly, twice a week, to the *Transcontinental* for his five dollars, though it was only semi-occasionally that he elicited a reply. He did not know that the *Transcontinental* had been staggering along precariously for years, that it was a fourth-rater, or tenth-rater, without standing, with a crazy circulation that partly rested on petty bullying and partly on patriotic appealing, and with advertisements that were scarcely more than charitable donations. Nor did he know that the *Transcontinental* was the sole livelihood of the editor and the business manager, and that they could wring their livelihood out of it only by moving to escape paying rent and by never paying any bill they could evade. Nor could he have guessed that the particular five dollars that belonged to him had been appropriated by the business manager for the painting of his house in Alameda, which painting he performed himself, on week-day afternoons, because he could not afford to pay union wages and because the first scab he had employed had had a ladder jerked out from under him and been sent to the hospital with a broken collar-bone.

The ten dollars for which Martin had sold "Treasure Hunters" to the Chicago newspaper did not come to hand. The article had been published, as he had ascertained at the file in the Central Reading-room, but no word could he get from the editor. His letters were ignored. To satisfy himself that they had been received, he registered several of them. It was nothing less than robbery, he concluded—a cold-blooded steal; while he starved, he was pilfered of his merchandise, of his goods, the sale of which was the sole way of getting bread to eat.

Youth and Age was a weekly, and it had published two-thirds of his twenty-one-thousand-word serial when it went out of business. With it went all hopes of getting his sixteen dollars.

To cap the situation, "The Pot," which he looked upon as one of the best things he had written, was lost to him. In despair, casting about frantically among the magazines, he had sent it to *The Billow*, a society weekly in San Francisco. His chief reason for submitting it to that publication was that, having only to travel across the bay from Oakland, a quick decision could be reached. Two weeks later he was overjoyed to see, in the latest number on the news-stand, his story printed in full, illustrated, and in the place of honor. He went home with leaping pulse, wondering how much they would pay him for one of the best things he had done. Also, the celerity with which it had been accepted and published was a pleasant thought to him. That the editor had not informed him of the acceptance made the surprise more complete. After waiting a week, two weeks, and half a week longer, desperation conquered diffidence, and he wrote to the editor of *The Billow*, suggesting that possibly through some negligence of the business manager his little account had been overlooked.

Even if it isn't more than five dollars, Martin thought to himself, it will buy enough beans and pea-soup to enable me to write half a dozen like it, and possibly as good.

Back came a cool letter from the editor that at least elicited Martin's admiration.

"We thank you," it ran, "for your excellent contribution. All of us in the office enjoyed it immensely, and, as you see, it was given the place of honor and immediate publication. We earnestly hope that you liked the illustrations.

"On rereading your letter it seems to us that you are laboring under the misapprehension that we pay for unsolicited manuscripts. This is not our custom, and of course yours was unsolicited. We assumed, naturally, when we received your story, that you understood the situation. We can only deeply regret this unfortunate misunderstanding, and assure you of our unfailing regard. Again, thanking you for your kind contribution, and hoping to receive more from you in the near future, we remain, etc."

There was also a postscript to the effect that though *The Billow* carried no free-list, it took great pleasure in sending him a complimentary subscription for the ensuing year.

After that experience, Martin typed at the top of the first sheet of all his manuscripts: "Submitted at your usual rate."

Some day, he consoled himself, they will be submitted at *my* usual rate.

He discovered in himself, at this period, a passion for perfection, under the sway of which he rewrote and polished "The Jostling Street," "The Wine of Life," "Joy," the "Sea Lyrics," and others of his earlier work. As of old, nineteen hours of labor a day was all too little to suit him. He wrote prodigiously, and he read prodigiously, forgetting in his toil the pangs caused by giving up his tobacco. Ruth's promised cure for the habit, flamboyantly labelled, he stowed away in the most inaccessible corner of his bureau. Especially during his stretches of famine he suffered from lack of the weed; but no matter how often he mastered the craving, it remained with him as strong as ever. He regarded it as the biggest thing he had ever achieved. Ruth's point of view was that he was doing no more than was right. She brought him the anti-tobacco remedy, purchased out of her glove money, and in a few days forgot all about it.

His machine-made storiettes, though he hated them and derided them, were successful. By means of them he redeemed all his pledges, paid most of his bills, and bought a new set of tires for his wheel. The storiettes at least kept the pot a-boiling and gave him time for ambitious work; while the one thing that upheld him was the forty dollars he had received from *The White Mouse*. He anchored his faith to that, and was confident that the really first-class magazines would pay an unknown writer at least an equal rate, if not a better one. But the thing was, how to get into the first-class magazines. His best stories, essays, and poems went begging among them, and yet, each month, he read reams of dull, prosy, inartistic stuff between all their various covers. If only one editor, he sometimes thought, would descend from his high seat of pride to write me one cheering line! No matter if my work is unusual, no matter if it is unfit, for prudential reasons, for their pages, surely there must be some sparks in it, somewhere, a few, to warm them to some sort of appreciation. And thereupon he would get out one or another of his manuscripts, such as "Adventure," and read it over and over in a vain attempt to vindicate the editorial silence.

As the sweet California spring came on, his period of plenty came to an end. For several weeks he had been worried by a strange silence on the part of the newspaper storiette syndicate. Then, one day, came back to him through the mail ten of his immaculate machine-made storiettes. They were accompanied by a brief letter to the effect that the syndicate was overstocked, and that some months would elapse before it would be in the market again for manuscripts. Martin had even been extravagant on the strength of those ten storiettes. Toward the last the syndicate had been paying him five dollars each for them and accepting every one he sent. So he had looked upon the ten as good as sold, and he had lived accordingly, on a basis of fifty dollars in the bank. So it was that he entered abruptly upon a lean period, wherein he continued selling his earlier efforts to publications that would not pay and submitting his later work to magazines that would not buy. Also, he resumed his trips to the pawn-broker down in Oakland. A few jokes and snatches of humorous verse, sold to the New York weeklies, made existence barely possible for him. It was at this time that he wrote letters of inquiry to the several great monthly and quarterly reviews, and learned in reply that they rarely considered unsolicited articles, and that most of their contents were written upon order by well-known specialists who were authorities in their various fields.

CHAPTER XXIX

It was a hard summer for Martin. Manuscript readers and editors were away on vacation, and publications that ordinarily returned a decision in three weeks now retained his manuscript for three months or more. The consolation he drew from it was that a saving in postage was effected by the deadlock. Only the robber-publications seemed to remain actively in business, and to them Martin disposed of all his early efforts, such as "Pearl-diving," "The Sea as a Career," "Turtle-catching," and "The Northeast Trades." For these manuscripts he never received a penny. It is true, after six months' correspondence, he effected a compromise, whereby he received a safety razor for "Turtle-catching," and that *The Acropolis*, having agreed to give him five dollars cash and five yearly subscriptions: for "The Northeast Trades," fulfilled the second part of the agreement.

For a sonnet on Stevenson he managed to wring two dollars out of a Boston editor who was running a magazine with a Matthew Arnold taste and a penny-dreadful purse. "The Peri and the Pearl," a clever skit of a poem of two hundred lines, just finished, white hot from his brain, won the heart of the editor of a San Francisco magazine published in the interest of a great railroad. When the editor wrote, offering him payment in transportation, Martin wrote back to inquire if the transportation was transferable. It was not, and so, being prevented from peddling it, he asked for the return of the poem. Back it came, with the editor's regrets, and Martin sent it to San Francisco again, this time to *The Hornet*, a pretentious monthly that had been fanned into a constellation of the first magnitude by the brilliant journalist who founded it. But *The Hornet's* light had begun to dim long before Martin was born. The editor promised Martin fifteen dollars for the poem, but, when it was published, seemed to forget about it. Several of his letters being ignored, Martin indicted an angry one which drew a reply. It was written by a new editor, who coolly informed Martin that he declined to be held responsible for the old editor's mistakes, and that he did not think much of "The Peri and the Pearl" anyway.

But *The Globe*, a Chicago magazine, gave Martin the most cruel treatment of all. He had refrained from offering his "Sea Lyrics" for publication, until driven to it by starvation. After having been rejected by a dozen magazines, they had come to rest in *The Globe* office. There were thirty poems in the collection, and he was to receive a dollar apiece for them. The first month four were published, and he promptly received a cheek for four dollars; but when he looked over the magazine, he was appalled at the slaughter. In some cases the titles had been altered: "Finis," for instance, being changed to "The Finish," and "The Song of the Outer Reef" to "The Song of the Coral Reef." In one case, an absolutely different title, a misappropriate title, was substituted. In place of his own, "Medusa Lights," the editor had printed, "The Backward Track." But the slaughter in the body of the poems was terrifying. Martin groaned and sweated and thrust his hands through his hair. Phrases, lines, and stanzas were cut out, interchanged, or juggled about in the most incomprehensible manner. Sometimes lines and stanzas not his own were substituted for his. He could not believe that a sane editor could be guilty of such maltreatment, and his favorite hypothesis was that his poems must have been doctored by the office boy or the stenographer. Martin wrote immediately, begging the editor to cease publishing the lyrics and to return them to him.

He wrote again and again, begging, entreating, threatening, but his letters were ignored. Month by month the slaughter went on till the thirty poems were published, and month by month he received a check for those which had appeared in the current number.

Despite these various misadventures, the memory of the *White Mouse* forty-dollar check sustained him, though he was driven more and more to hack-work. He discovered a bread-and-butter field in the agricultural weeklies and trade journals, though among the religious weeklies he found he could easily starve. At his lowest ebb, when his black suit was in pawn, he made a ten-strike—or so it seemed to him—in a prize contest arranged by the County Committee of the Republican Party. There were three branches of the contest, and he entered them all, laughing at himself bitterly the while in that he was driven to such straits to live. His poem won the first prize of ten dollars, his campaign song the second prize of five dollars, his essay on the principles of the Republican Party the first prize of twenty-five dollars. Which was very gratifying to him until he tried to collect. Something had gone wrong in the County Committee, and, though a rich banker and a state senator were members of it, the money was not forthcoming. While this affair was hanging fire, he proved that he understood the principles of the Democratic Party by winning the first prize for his essay in a similar contest. And, moreover, he received the money, twenty-five dollars. But the forty dollars won in the first contest he never received.

Driven to shifts in order to see Ruth, and deciding that the long walk from north Oakland to her house and back again consumed too much time, he kept his black suit in pawn in place of his bicycle. The latter gave him exercise, saved him hours of time for work, and enabled him to see Ruth just the same. A pair of knee duck trousers and an old sweater made him a presentable wheel costume, so that he could go with Ruth on afternoon rides. Besides, he no longer had opportunity to see much of her in her own home, where Mrs. Morse was thoroughly prosecuting her campaign of entertainment. The exalted beings he met there, and to whom he had looked up but a short time before, now bored him. They were no longer exalted. He was nervous and irritable, what of his hard times, disappointments, and close application to work, and the conversation of such people was maddening. He was not unduly egotistic. He measured the narrowness of their minds by the minds of the thinkers in the books he read. At Ruth's home he never met a large mind, with the exception of Professor Caldwell, and Caldwell he had met there only once. As for the rest, they were numskulls, ninnies, superficial, dogmatic, and ignorant. It was their ignorance that astounded him. What was the matter with them? What had they done with their educations? They had had access to the same books he had. How did it happen that they had drawn nothing from them?

He knew that the great minds, the deep and rational thinkers, existed. He had his proofs from the books, the books that had educated him beyond the Morse standard. And he knew that higher intellects than those of the Morse circle were to be found in the world. He read English society novels, wherein he caught glimpses of men and women talking politics and philosophy. And he read of salons in great cities, even in the United States, where art and intellect congregated. Foolishly, in the past, he had conceived that all well-groomed persons above the working class were persons with power of intellect and vigor of beauty. Culture and collars had gone together, to him, and he had been deceived into believing that college educations and mastery were the same things.

Well, he would fight his way on and up higher. And he would take Ruth with him. Her he dearly loved, and he was confident that she would shine anywhere. As it was clear to him that he had been handicapped by his early environment, so now he perceived that she was similarly handicapped. She had not had a chance to expand. The books on her father's shelves, the paintings on the walls, the music on the piano—all was just so much meretricious display. To real literature, real painting, real music, the Morses and their kind, were dead. And bigger than such things was life, of which they were densely, hopelessly ignorant. In spite of their Unitarian proclivities and their masks of conservative broadmindedness, they were two generations behind interpretative science: their mental processes were mediaeval, while their thinking on the ultimate data of existence and of the universe struck him as the same metaphysical method that was as young as the youngest race, as old as the cave-man, and older—the same that moved the first Pleistocene ape-man to fear the dark; that moved the first hasty Hebrew savage to incarnate Eve from Adam's rib; that moved Descartes to build an idealistic system of the universe out of the projections of his own puny ego; and that moved the famous British ecclesiastic to denounce evolution in satire so scathing as to win immediate applause and leave his name a notorious scrawl on the page of history.

So Martin thought, and he thought further, till it dawned upon him that the difference between these lawyers, officers, business men, and bank cashiers he had met and the members of the working class he had known was on a par with the difference in the food they ate, clothes they wore, neighborhoods in which they lived. Certainly, in all of them was lacking the something more which he found in himself and in the books. The Morses had shown him the best their social position could produce, and he was not impressed by it. A pauper himself, a slave to the money-lender, he knew himself the superior of those he met at the Morses'; and, when his one decent suit of clothes was out of pawn, he moved among them a lord of life, quivering with a sense of outrage akin to what a prince would suffer if condemned to live with goat-herds.

"You hate and fear the socialists," he remarked to Mr. Morse, one evening at dinner; "but why? You know neither them nor their doctrines."

The conversation had been swung in that direction by Mrs. Morse, who had been invidiously singing the praises of Mr. Hapgood. The cashier was Martin's black beast, and his temper was a trifle short where the talker of platitudes was concerned.

"Yes," he had said, "Charley Hapgood is what they call a rising young man—somebody told me as much. And it is true. He'll make the Governor's Chair before he dies, and, who knows? maybe the United States Senate."

"What makes you think so?" Mrs. Morse had inquired.

"I've heard him make a campaign speech. It was so cleverly stupid and unoriginal, and also so convincing, that the leaders cannot help but regard him as safe and sure, while his platitudes are so much like the platitudes of the average voter that—oh, well, you know you flatter any man by dressing up his own thoughts for him and presenting them to him."

"I actually think you are jealous of Mr. Hapgood," Ruth had chimed in.

"Heaven forbid!"

The look of horror on Martin's face stirred Mrs. Morse to belligerence.

"You surely don't mean to say that Mr. Hapgood is stupid?" she demanded icily.

"No more than the average Republican," was the retort, "or average Democrat, either. They are all stupid when they are not crafty, and very few of them are crafty. The only wise Republicans are the millionnaires and their conscious henchmen. They know which side their bread is buttered on, and they know why."

"I am a Republican," Mr. Morse put in lightly. "Pray, how do you classify me?"

"Oh, you are an unconscious henchman."

"Henchman?"

"Why, yes. You do corporation work. You have no working-class nor criminal practice. You don't depend upon wife-beaters and pickpockets for your income. You get your livelihood from the masters of society, and whoever feeds a man is that man's master. Yes, you are a henchman. You are interested in advancing the interests of the aggregations of capital you serve."

Mr. Morse's face was a trifle red.

"I confess, sir," he said, "that you talk like a scoundrelly socialist."

Then it was that Martin made his remark:

"You hate and fear the socialists; but why? You know neither them nor their doctrines."

"Your doctrine certainly sounds like socialism," Mr. Morse replied, while Ruth gazed anxiously from one to the other, and Mrs. Morse beamed happily at the opportunity afforded of rousing her liege lord's antagonism.

"Because I say Republicans are stupid, and hold that liberty, equality, and fraternity are exploded bubbles, does not make me a socialist," Martin said with a smile. "Because I question Jefferson and the unscientific Frenchmen who informed his mind, does not make me a socialist. Believe me, Mr. Morse, you are far nearer socialism than I who am its avowed enemy."

"Now you please to be facetious," was all the other could say.

"Not at all. I speak in all seriousness. You still believe in equality, and yet you do the work of the corporations, and the corporations, from day to day, are busily engaged in burying equality. And you call me a socialist because I deny equality, because I affirm just what you live up to. The Republicans are foes to equality, though most of them fight the battle against equality with the very word itself the slogan on their lips. In the name of equality they destroy equality. That was why I called them stupid. As for myself, I am an individualist. I believe the race is to the swift, the battle to the strong. Such is the lesson I have learned from biology, or at least think I have learned. As I said, I am an individualist, and individualism is the hereditary and eternal foe of socialism."

"But you frequent socialist meetings," Mr. Morse challenged.

"Certainly, just as spies frequent hostile camps. How else are you to learn about the enemy? Besides, I enjoy myself at their meetings. They are good fighters, and, right or wrong, they have read the books. Any one of them knows far more about sociology and all the other ologies than the average captain of industry. Yes, I have been to half a dozen of their meetings, but that doesn't make me a socialist any more than hearing Charley Hapgood orate made me a Republican."

"I can't help it," Mr. Morse said feebly, "but I still believe you incline that way."

Bless me, Martin thought to himself, he doesn't know what I was talking about. He hasn't understood a word of it. What did he do with his education, anyway?

Thus, in his development, Martin found himself face to face with economic morality, or the morality of class; and soon it became to him a grisly monster. Personally, he was an intellectual moralist, and more offending to him than platitudinous pomposity was the morality of those about him, which was a curious hotchpotch of the economic, the metaphysical, the sentimental, and the imitative.

A sample of this curious messy mixture he encountered nearer home. His sister Marian had been keeping company with an industrious young mechanic, of German extraction, who, after thoroughly learning the trade, had set up for himself in a bicycle-repair shop. Also, having got the agency for a low-grade make of wheel, he was prosperous. Marian had called on Martin in his room a short time before to announce her engagement, during which visit she had playfully inspected Martin's palm and told his fortune. On her next visit she brought Hermann von Schmidt along with her. Martin did the honors and congratulated both of them in language so easy and graceful as to affect disagreeably the peasant-mind of his sister's lover. This bad impression was further heightened by Martin's reading aloud the half-dozen stanzas of verse with which he had commemorated Marian's previous visit. It was a bit of society verse, airy and delicate, which he had named "The Palmist." He was surprised, when he finished reading it, to note no enjoyment in his sister's face. Instead, her eyes were fixed anxiously upon her betrothed, and Martin, following her gaze, saw spread on that worthy's asymmetrical features nothing but black and sullen disapproval. The incident passed over, they made an early departure, and Martin forgot all about it, though for the moment he had been puzzled that any woman, even of the working class, should not have been flattered and delighted by having poetry written about her.

Several evenings later Marian again visited him, this time alone. Nor did she waste time in coming to the point, upbraiding him sorrowfully for what he had done.

"Why, Marian," he chided, "you talk as though you were ashamed of your relatives, or of your brother at any rate."

"And I am, too," she blurted out.

Martin was bewildered by the tears of mortification he saw in her eyes. The mood, whatever it was, was genuine.

"But, Marian, why should your Hermann be jealous of my writing poetry about my own sister?"

"He ain't jealous," she sobbed. "He says it was indecent, ob—obscene."

Martin emitted a long, low whistle of incredulity, then proceeded to resurrect and read a carbon copy of "The Palmist."

"I can't see it," he said finally, proffering the manuscript to her. "Read it yourself and show me whatever strikes you as obscene—that was the word, wasn't it?"

"He says so, and he ought to know," was the answer, with a wave aside of the manuscript, accompanied by a look of loathing. "And he says you've got to tear it up. He says he won't have no wife of his with such things written about her which anybody can read. He says it's a disgrace, an' he won't stand for it."

"Now, look here, Marian, this is nothing but nonsense," Martin began; then abruptly changed his mind.

He saw before him an unhappy girl, knew the futility of attempting to convince her husband or her, and, though the whole situation was absurd and preposterous, he resolved to surrender.

"All right," he announced, tearing the manuscript into half a dozen pieces and throwing it into the waste-basket.

He contented himself with the knowledge that even then the original type-written manuscript was reposing in the office of a New York magazine. Marian and her husband would never know, and neither himself nor they nor the world would lose if the pretty, harmless poem ever were published.

Marian, starting to reach into the waste-basket, refrained.

"Can I?" she pleaded.

He nodded his head, regarding her thoughtfully as she gathered the torn pieces of manuscript and tucked them into the pocket of her jacket—ocular evidence of the success of her mission. She reminded him of Lizzie Connolly, though there was less of fire and gorgeous flaunting life in her than in that other girl of the working class whom he had seen twice. But they were on a par, the pair of them, in dress and carriage, and he smiled with inward amusement at the caprice of his fancy which suggested the appearance of either of them in Mrs. Morse's drawing-room. The amusement faded, and he was aware of a great loneliness. This sister of his and the Morse drawing-room were milestones of the road he had travelled. And he had left them behind. He glanced affectionately about him at his few books. They were all the comrades left to him.

"Hello, what's that?" he demanded in startled surprise.

Marian repeated her question.

"Why don't I go to work?" He broke into a laugh that was only half-hearted. "That Hermann of yours has been talking to you."

She shook her head.

"Don't lie," he commanded, and the nod of her head affirmed his charge.

"Well, you tell that Hermann of yours to mind his own business; that when I write poetry about the girl he's keeping company with it's his business, but that outside of that he's got no say so. Understand?

"So you don't think I'll succeed as a writer, eh?" he went on. "You think I'm no good?—that I've fallen down and am a disgrace to the family?"

"I think it would be much better if you got a job," she said firmly, and he saw she was sincere. "Hermann says—"

"Damn Hermann!" he broke out good-naturedly. "What I want to know is when you're going to get married. Also, you find out from your Hermann if he will deign to permit you to accept a wedding present from me."

He mused over the incident after she had gone, and once or twice broke out into laughter that was bitter as he saw his sister and her betrothed, all the members of his own class and the members of Ruth's class, directing their narrow little lives by narrow little formulas—herd-creatures, flocking together and patterning their lives by one another's opinions, failing of being individuals and of really living life because of the childlike formulas by which they were enslaved. He summoned them before him in apparitional procession: Bernard Higginbotham arm in arm with Mr. Butler, Hermann von Schmidt cheek by jowl with Charley Hapgood, and one by one and in pairs he judged them and dismissed them—judged them by the standards of intellect and morality he had learned from the books. Vainly he asked: Where are the great souls, the great men and women? He found them not among the careless, gross, and stupid intelligences that answered the call of vision to his narrow room. He felt a loathing for them such as Circe must have felt for her swine. When he had dismissed the last one and thought himself alone, a late-comer entered, unexpected and unsummoned. Martin watched him and saw the stiff-rim, the square-cut, double-breasted coat and the swaggering shoulders, of the youthful hoodlum who had once been he.

"You were like all the rest, young fellow," Martin sneered. "Your morality and your knowledge were just the same as theirs. You did not think and act for yourself. Your opinions, like your clothes, were ready made; your acts were shaped by popular approval. You were cock of your gang because others acclaimed you the real thing. You fought and ruled the gang, not because you liked to,—you know you really despised it,—but because the other fellows patted you on the shoulder. You licked Cheese-Face because you wouldn't give in, and you wouldn't give in partly because you were an abysmal brute and for the rest because you believed what every one about you believed, that the measure of manhood was the carnivorous ferocity displayed in injuring and marring fellow-creatures' anatomies. Why, you whelp, you even won other fellows' girls away from them, not because you wanted the girls, but because in the marrow of those about you, those who set your moral pace, was the instinct of the wild stallion and the bull-seal. Well, the years have passed, and what do you think about it now?"

As if in reply, the vision underwent a swift metamorphosis. The stiff-rim and the square-cut vanished, being replaced by milder garments; the toughness went out of the face, the hardness out of the eyes; and, the face, chastened and refined, was irradiated from an inner life of communion with beauty and knowledge. The apparition was very like his present self, and, as he regarded it, he noted the student-lamp by which it was illuminated, and the book over which it pored. He glanced at the title and read, "The Science of AEsthetics." Next, he entered into the apparition, trimmed the student-lamp, and himself went on reading "The Science of AEsthetics."

CHAPTER XXX

On a beautiful fall day, a day of similar Indian summer to that which had seen their love declared the year before, Martin read his "Love-cycle" to Ruth. It was in the afternoon, and, as before, they had ridden out to their favorite knoll in the hills. Now and again she had interrupted his reading with exclamations of pleasure, and now, as he laid the last sheet of manuscript with its fellows, he waited her judgment.

She delayed to speak, and at last she spoke haltingly, hesitating to frame in words the harshness of her thought.

"I think they are beautiful, very beautiful," she said; "but you can't sell them, can you? You see what I mean," she said, almost pleaded. "This writing of yours is not practical. Something is the matter—maybe it is with the market—that prevents you from earning a living by it. And please, dear, don't misunderstand me. I am flattered, and made proud, and all that—I could not be a true woman were it otherwise—that you should write these poems to me. But they do not make our marriage possible. Don't you see, Martin? Don't think me mercenary. It is love, the thought of our future, with which I am burdened. A whole year has gone by since we learned we loved each other, and our wedding day is no nearer. Don't think me immodest in thus talking about our wedding, for really I have my heart, all that I am, at stake. Why don't you try to get work on a newspaper, if you are so bound up in your writing? Why not become a reporter?—for a while, at least?"

"It would spoil my style," was his answer, in a low, monotonous voice. "You have no idea how I've worked for style."

"But those storiettes," she argued. "You called them hack-work. You wrote many of them. Didn't they spoil your style?"

"No, the cases are different. The storiettes were ground out, jaded, at the end of a long day of application to style. But a reporter's work is all hack from morning till night, is the one paramount thing of life. And it is a whirlwind life, the life of the moment, with neither past nor future, and certainly without thought of any style but reportorial style, and that certainly is not literature. To become a reporter now, just as my style is taking form, crystallizing, would be to commit literary suicide. As it is, every storiette, every word of every storiette, was a violation of myself, of my self-respect, of my respect for beauty. I tell you it was sickening. I was guilty of sin. And I was secretly glad when the markets failed, even if my clothes did go into pawn. But the joy of writing the 'Love-cycle'! The creative joy in its noblest form! That was compensation for everything."

CHAPTER XXX

Martin did not know that Ruth was unsympathetic concerning the creative joy. She used the phrase—it was on her lips he had first heard it. She had read about it, studied about it, in the university in the course of earning her Bachelorship of Arts; but she was not original, not creative, and all manifestations of culture on her part were but harpings of the harpings of others.

"May not the editor have been right in his revision of your 'Sea Lyrics'?" she questioned. "Remember, an editor must have proved qualifications or else he would not be an editor."

"That's in line with the persistence of the established," he rejoined, his heat against the editor-folk getting the better of him. "What is, is not only right, but is the best possible. The existence of anything is sufficient vindication of its fitness to exist—to exist, mark you, as the average person unconsciously believes, not merely in present conditions, but in all conditions. It is their ignorance, of course, that makes them believe such rot—their ignorance, which is nothing more nor less than the henidical mental process described by Weininger. They think they think, and such thinkless creatures are the arbiters of the lives of the few who really think."

He paused, overcome by the consciousness that he had been talking over Ruth's head.

"I'm sure I don't know who this Weininger is," she retorted. "And you are so dreadfully general that I fail to follow you. What I was speaking of was the qualification of editors—"

"And I'll tell you," he interrupted. "The chief qualification of ninety-nine per cent of all editors is failure. They have failed as writers. Don't think they prefer the drudgery of the desk and the slavery to their circulation and to the business manager to the joy of writing. They have tried to write, and they have failed. And right there is the cursed paradox of it. Every portal to success in literature is guarded by those watch-dogs, the failures in literature. The editors, sub-editors, associate editors, most of them, and the manuscript-readers for the magazines and book-publishers, most of them, nearly all of them, are men who wanted to write and who have failed. And yet they, of all creatures under the sun the most unfit, are the very creatures who decide what shall and what shall not find its way into print—they, who have proved themselves not original, who have demonstrated that they lack the divine fire, sit in judgment upon originality and genius. And after them come the reviewers, just so many more failures. Don't tell me that they have not dreamed the dream and attempted to write poetry or fiction; for they have, and they have failed. Why, the average review is more nauseating than cod-liver oil. But you know my opinion on the reviewers and the alleged critics. There are great critics, but they are as rare as comets. If I fail as a writer, I shall have proved for the career of editorship. There's bread and butter and jam, at any rate."

Ruth's mind was quick, and her disapproval of her lover's views was buttressed by the contradiction she found in his contention.

"But, Martin, if that be so, if all the doors are closed as you have shown so conclusively, how is it possible that any of the great writers ever arrived?"

"They arrived by achieving the impossible," he answered. "They did such blazing, glorious work as to burn to ashes those that opposed them. They arrived by course of miracle, by winning a thousand-to-one wager against them. They arrived because they were Carlyle's battle-scarred giants who will not be kept down. And that is what I must do; I must achieve the impossible."

"But if you fail? You must consider me as well, Martin."

"If I fail?" He regarded her for a moment as though the thought she had uttered was unthinkable. Then intelligence illumined his eyes. "If I fail, I shall become an editor, and you will be an editor's wife."

She frowned at his facetiousness—a pretty, adorable frown that made him put his arm around her and kiss it away.

"There, that's enough," she urged, by an effort of will withdrawing herself from the fascination of his strength. "I have talked with father and mother. I never before asserted myself so against them. I demanded to be heard. I was very undutiful. They are against you, you know; but I assured them over and over of my abiding love for you, and at last father agreed that if you wanted to, you could begin right away in his office. And then, of his own accord, he said he would pay you enough at the start so that we could get married and have a little cottage somewhere. Which I think was very fine of him—don't you?"

Martin, with the dull pain of despair at his heart, mechanically reaching for the tobacco and paper (which he no longer carried) to roll a cigarette, muttered something inarticulate, and Ruth went on.

"Frankly, though, and don't let it hurt you—I tell you, to show you precisely how you stand with him—he doesn't like your radical views, and he thinks you are lazy. Of course I know you are not. I know you work hard."

How hard, even she did not know, was the thought in Martin's mind.

"Well, then," he said, "how about my views? Do you think they are so radical?"

He held her eyes and waited the answer.

"I think them, well, very disconcerting," she replied.

The question was answered for him, and so oppressed was he by the grayness of life that he forgot the tentative proposition she had made for him to go to work. And she, having gone as far as she dared, was willing to wait the answer till she should bring the question up again.

She had not long to wait. Martin had a question of his own to propound to her. He wanted to ascertain the measure of her faith in him, and within the week each was answered. Martin precipitated it by reading to her his "The Shame of the Sun."

"Why don't you become a reporter?" she asked when he had finished. "You love writing so, and I am sure you would succeed. You could rise in journalism and make a name for yourself. There are a number of great special correspondents. Their salaries are large, and their field is the world. They are sent everywhere, to the heart of Africa, like Stanley, or to interview the Pope, or to explore unknown Thibet."

"Then you don't like my essay?" he rejoined. "You believe that I have some show in journalism but none in literature?"

"No, no; I do like it. It reads well. But I am afraid it's over the heads of your readers. At least it is over mine. It sounds beautiful, but I don't understand it. Your scientific slang is beyond me. You are an extremist, you know, dear, and what may be intelligible to you may not be intelligible to the rest of us."

"I imagine it's the philosophic slang that bothers you," was all he could say.

He was flaming from the fresh reading of the ripest thought he had expressed, and her verdict stunned him.

"No matter how poorly it is done," he persisted, "don't you see anything in it?—in the thought of it, I mean?"

She shook her head.

"No, it is so different from anything I have read. I read Maeterlinck and understand him—"

"His mysticism, you understand that?" Martin flashed out.

"Yes, but this of yours, which is supposed to be an attack upon him, I don't understand. Of course, if originality counts—"

He stopped her with an impatient gesture that was not followed by speech. He became suddenly aware that she was speaking and that she had been speaking for some time.

"After all, your writing has been a toy to you," she was saying. "Surely you have played with it long enough. It is time to take up life seriously—*our* life, Martin. Hitherto you have lived solely your own."

"You want me to go to work?" he asked.

"Yes. Father has offered—"

"I understand all that," he broke in; "but what I want to know is whether or not you have lost faith in me?"

She pressed his hand mutely, her eyes dim.

"In your writing, dear," she admitted in a half-whisper.

"You've read lots of my stuff," he went on brutally. "What do you think of it? Is it utterly hopeless? How does it compare with other men's work?"

"But they sell theirs, and you—don't."

"That doesn't answer my question. Do you think that literature is not at all my vocation?"

"Then I will answer." She steeled herself to do it. "I don't think you were made to write. Forgive me, dear. You compel me to say it; and you know I know more about literature than you do."

"Yes, you are a Bachelor of Arts," he said meditatively; "and you ought to know."

"But there is more to be said," he continued, after a pause painful to both. "I know what I have in me. No one knows that so well as I. I know I shall succeed. I will not be kept down. I am afire with what I have to say in verse, and fiction, and essay. I do not ask you to have faith in that, though. I do not ask you to have faith in me, nor in my writing. What I do ask of you is to love me and have faith in love."

"A year ago I believed for two years. One of those years is yet to run. And I do believe, upon my honor and my soul, that before that year is run I shall have succeeded. You remember what you told me long ago, that I must serve my apprenticeship to writing. Well, I have served it. I have crammed it and telescoped it. With you at the end awaiting me, I have never shirked. Do you know, I have forgotten what it is to fall peacefully asleep. A few million years ago I knew what it was to sleep my fill and to awake naturally from very glut of sleep. I am awakened always now by an alarm clock. If I fall asleep early or late, I set the alarm accordingly; and this, and the putting out of the lamp, are my last conscious actions."

"When I begin to feel drowsy, I change the heavy book I am reading for a lighter one. And when I doze over that, I beat my head with my knuckles in order to drive sleep away. Somewhere I read of a man who was afraid to sleep. Kipling wrote the story. This man arranged a spur so that when unconsciousness came, his naked body pressed against the iron teeth. Well, I've done the same. I look at the time, and I resolve that not until midnight, or not until one o'clock, or two o'clock, or three o'clock, shall the spur be removed. And so it rowels me awake until the appointed time. That spur has been my bed-mate for months. I have grown so desperate that five and a half hours of sleep is an extravagance. I sleep four hours now. I am starved for sleep. There are times when I am light-headed from want of sleep, times when death, with its rest and sleep, is a positive lure to me, times when I am haunted by Longfellow's lines:

"'The sea is still and deep;
All things within its bosom sleep;
A single step and all is o'er,
A plunge, a bubble, and no more.'

"Of course, this is sheer nonsense. It comes from nervousness, from an overwrought mind. But the point is: Why have I done this? For you. To shorten my apprenticeship. To compel Success to hasten. And my apprenticeship is now served. I know my equipment. I swear that I learn more each month than the average college man learns in a year. I know it, I tell you. But were my need for you to understand not so desperate I should not tell you. It is not boasting. I measure the results by the books. Your brothers, to-day, are ignorant barbarians compared with me and the knowledge I have wrung from the books in the hours they were sleeping. Long ago I wanted to be famous. I care very little for fame now. What I want is you; I am more hungry for you than for food, or clothing, or recognition. I have a dream of laying my head on your breast and sleeping an aeon or so, and the dream will come true ere another year is gone."

His power beat against her, wave upon wave; and in the moment his will opposed hers most she felt herself most strongly drawn toward him. The strength that had always poured out from him to her was now flowering in his impassioned voice, his flashing eyes, and the vigor of life and intellect surging in him. And in that moment, and for the moment, she was aware of a rift that showed in her certitude—a rift through which she caught sight of the real Martin Eden, splendid and invincible; and as animal-trainers have their moments of doubt, so she, for the instant, seemed to doubt her power to tame this wild spirit of a man.

"And another thing," he swept on. "You love me. But why do you love me? The thing in me that compels me to write is the very thing that draws your love. You love me because I am somehow different from the men you have known and might have loved. I was not made for the desk and counting-house, for petty business squabbling, and legal jangling. Make me do such things, make me like those other men, doing the work they do, breathing the air they breathe, developing the point of view they have developed, and you have destroyed the difference, destroyed me, destroyed the thing you love. My desire to write is the most vital thing in me. Had I been a mere clod, neither would I have desired to write, nor would you have desired me for a husband."

"But you forget," she interrupted, the quick surface of her mind glimpsing a parallel. "There have been eccentric inventors, starving their families while they sought such chimeras as perpetual motion. Doubtless their wives loved them, and suffered with them and for them, not because of but in spite of their infatuation for perpetual motion."

"True," was the reply. "But there have been inventors who were not eccentric and who starved while they sought to invent practical things; and sometimes, it is recorded, they succeeded. Certainly I do not seek any impossibilities—"

"You have called it 'achieving the impossible,'" she interpolated.

"I spoke figuratively. I seek to do what men have done before me—to write and to live by my writing."

Her silence spurred him on.

"To you, then, my goal is as much a chimera as perpetual motion?" he demanded.

He read her answer in the pressure of her hand on his—the pitying mother-hand for the hurt child. And to her, just then, he was the hurt child, the infatuated man striving to achieve the impossible.

Toward the close of their talk she warned him again of the antagonism of her father and mother.

"But you love me?" he asked.

"I do! I do!" she cried.

"And I love you, not them, and nothing they do can hurt me." Triumph sounded in his voice. "For I have faith in your love, not fear of their enmity. All things may go astray in this world, but not love. Love cannot go wrong unless it be a weakling that faints and stumbles by the way."

CHAPTER XXXI

Martin had encountered his sister Gertrude by chance on Broadway—as it proved, a most propitious yet disconcerting chance. Waiting on the corner for a car, she had seen him first, and noted the eager, hungry lines of his face and the desperate, worried look of his eyes. In truth, he was desperate and worried. He had just come from a fruitless interview with the pawnbroker, from whom he had tried to wring an additional loan on his wheel. The muddy fall weather having come on, Martin had pledged his wheel some time since and retained his black suit.

"There's the black suit," the pawnbroker, who knew his every asset, had answered. "You needn't tell me you've gone and pledged it with that Jew, Lipka. Because if you have—"

The man had looked the threat, and Martin hastened to cry:-

"No, no; I've got it. But I want to wear it on a matter of business."

"All right," the mollified usurer had replied. "And I want it on a matter of business before I can let you have any more money. You don't think I'm in it for my health?"

"But it's a forty-dollar wheel, in good condition," Martin had argued. "And you've only let me have seven dollars on it. No, not even seven. Six and a quarter; you took the interest in advance."

"If you want some more, bring the suit," had been the reply that sent Martin out of the stuffy little den, so desperate at heart as to reflect it in his face and touch his sister to pity.

Scarcely had they met when the Telegraph Avenue car came along and stopped to take on a crowd of afternoon shoppers. Mrs. Higginbotham divined from the grip on her arm as he helped her on, that he was not going to follow her. She turned on the step and looked down upon him. His haggard face smote her to the heart again.

"Ain't you comin'?" she asked

The next moment she had descended to his side.

"I'm walking—exercise, you know," he explained.

"Then I'll go along for a few blocks," she announced. "Mebbe it'll do me good. I ain't ben feelin' any too spry these last few days."

Martin glanced at her and verified her statement in her general slovenly appearance, in the unhealthy fat, in the drooping shoulders, the tired face with the sagging lines, and in the heavy fall of her feet, without elasticity—a very caricature of the walk that belongs to a free and happy body.

CHAPTER XXXI

"You'd better stop here," he said, though she had already come to a halt at the first corner, "and take the next car."

"My goodness!—if I ain't all tired a'ready!" she panted. "But I'm just as able to walk as you in them soles. They're that thin they'll bu'st long before you git out to North Oakland."

"I've a better pair at home," was the answer.

"Come out to dinner to-morrow," she invited irrelevantly. "Mr. Higginbotham won't be there. He's goin' to San Leandro on business."

Martin shook his head, but he had failed to keep back the wolfish, hungry look that leapt into his eyes at the suggestion of dinner.

"You haven't a penny, Mart, and that's why you're walkin'. Exercise!" She tried to sniff contemptuously, but succeeded in producing only a sniffle. "Here, lemme see."

And, fumbling in her satchel, she pressed a five-dollar piece into his hand. "I guess I forgot your last birthday, Mart," she mumbled lamely.

Martin's hand instinctively closed on the piece of gold. In the same instant he knew he ought not to accept, and found himself struggling in the throes of indecision. That bit of gold meant food, life, and light in his body and brain, power to go on writing, and—who was to say?—maybe to write something that would bring in many pieces of gold. Clear on his vision burned the manuscripts of two essays he had just completed. He saw them under the table on top of the heap of returned manuscripts for which he had no stamps, and he saw their titles, just as he had typed them—"The High Priests of Mystery," and "The Cradle of Beauty." He had never submitted them anywhere. They were as good as anything he had done in that line. If only he had stamps for them! Then the certitude of his ultimate success rose up in him, an able ally of hunger, and with a quick movement he slipped the coin into his pocket.

"I'll pay you back, Gertrude, a hundred times over," he gulped out, his throat painfully contracted and in his eyes a swift hint of moisture.

"Mark my words!" he cried with abrupt positiveness. "Before the year is out I'll put an even hundred of those little yellow-boys into your hand. I don't ask you to believe me. All you have to do is wait and see."

Nor did she believe. Her incredulity made her uncomfortable, and failing of other expedient, she said:-

"I know you're hungry, Mart. It's sticking out all over you. Come in to meals any time. I'll send one of the children to tell you when Mr. Higginbotham ain't to be there. An' Mart—"

He waited, though he knew in his secret heart what she was about to say, so visible was her thought process to him.

"Don't you think it's about time you got a job?"

"You don't think I'll win out?" he asked.

She shook her head.

"Nobody has faith in me, Gertrude, except myself." His voice was passionately rebellious. "I've done good work already, plenty of it, and sooner or later it will sell."

"How do you know it is good?"

"Because—" He faltered as the whole vast field of literature and the history of literature stirred in his brain and pointed the futility of his attempting to convey to her the reasons for his faith. "Well, because it's better than ninety-nine per cent of what is published in the magazines."

"I wish't you'd listen to reason," she answered feebly, but with unwavering belief in the correctness of her diagnosis of what was ailing him. "I wish't you'd listen to reason," she repeated, "an' come to dinner to-morrow."

After Martin had helped her on the car, he hurried to the post-office and invested three of the five dollars in stamps; and when, later in the day, on the way to the Morse home, he stopped in at the post-office to weigh a large number of long, bulky envelopes, he affixed to them all the stamps save three of the two-cent denomination.

It proved a momentous night for Martin, for after dinner he met Russ Brissenden. How he chanced to come there, whose friend he was or what acquaintance brought him, Martin did not know. Nor had he the curiosity to inquire about him of Ruth. In short, Brissenden struck Martin as anaemic and feather-brained, and was promptly dismissed from his mind. An hour later he decided that Brissenden was a boor as well, what of the way he prowled about from one room to another, staring at the pictures or poking his nose into books and magazines he picked up from the table or drew from the shelves. Though a stranger in the house he finally isolated himself in the midst of the company, huddling into a capacious Morris chair and reading steadily from a thin volume he had drawn from his pocket. As he read, he abstractedly ran his fingers, with a caressing movement, through his hair. Martin noticed him no more that evening, except once when he observed him chaffing with great apparent success with several of the young women.

It chanced that when Martin was leaving, he overtook Brissenden already half down the walk to the street.

"Hello, is that you?" Martin said.

The other replied with an ungracious grunt, but swung alongside. Martin made no further attempt at conversation, and for several blocks unbroken silence lay upon them.

"Pompous old ass!"

The suddenness and the virulence of the exclamation startled Martin. He felt amused, and at the same time was aware of a growing dislike for the other.

"What do you go to such a place for?" was abruptly flung at him after another block of silence.

"Why do you?" Martin countered.

"Bless me, I don't know," came back. "At least this is my first indiscretion. There are twenty-four hours in each day, and I must spend them somehow. Come and have a drink."

"All right," Martin answered.

The next moment he was nonplussed by the readiness of his acceptance. At home was several hours' hack-work waiting for him before he went to bed, and after he went to bed there was a volume of Weismann waiting for him, to say nothing of Herbert Spencer's Autobiography, which was as replete for him with romance as any thrilling novel. Why should he waste any time with this man he did not like? was his thought. And yet, it was not so much the man nor the drink as was it what was associated with the drink—the bright lights, the mirrors and dazzling array of glasses, the warm and glowing faces and the resonant hum of the voices of men. That was it, it was the voices of men, optimistic men, men who breathed success and spent their money for drinks like men. He was lonely, that was what was the matter with him; that was why he had snapped at the invitation as a bonita strikes at a white rag on a hook. Not since with Joe, at Shelly Hot Springs, with the one exception of the wine he took with the Portuguese grocer, had Martin had a drink at a public bar. Mental exhaustion did not produce a craving for liquor such as physical exhaustion did, and he had felt no need for it. But just now he felt desire for the drink, or, rather, for the atmosphere wherein drinks were dispensed and disposed of. Such a place was the Grotto, where Brissenden and he lounged in capacious leather chairs and drank Scotch and soda.

They talked. They talked about many things, and now Brissenden and now Martin took turn in ordering Scotch and soda. Martin, who was extremely strong-headed, marvelled at the other's capacity for liquor, and ever and anon broke off to marvel at the other's conversation. He was not long in assuming that Brissenden knew everything, and in deciding that here was the second intellectual man he had met. But he noted that Brissenden had what Professor Caldwell lacked—namely, fire, the flashing insight and perception, the flaming uncontrol of genius. Living language flowed from him. His thin lips, like the dies of a machine, stamped out phrases that cut and stung; or again, pursing caressingly about the inchoate sound they articulated, the thin lips shaped soft and velvety things, mellow phrases of glow and glory, of haunting beauty, reverberant of the mystery and inscrutableness of life; and yet again the thin lips were like a bugle, from which rang the crash and tumult of cosmic strife, phrases that sounded clear as silver, that were luminous as starry spaces, that epitomized the final word of science and yet said something more—the poet's word, the transcendental truth, elusive and without words which could express, and which none the less found expression in the subtle and all but ungraspable connotations of common words. He, by some wonder of vision, saw beyond the farthest outpost of empiricism, where was no language for narration, and yet, by some golden miracle of speech, investing known words with unknown significances, he conveyed to Martin's consciousness messages that were incommunicable to ordinary souls.

Martin forgot his first impression of dislike. Here was the best the books had to offer coming true. Here was an intelligence, a living man for him to look up to. "I am down in the dirt at your feet," Martin repeated to himself again and again.

"You've studied biology," he said aloud, in significant allusion.

To his surprise Brissenden shook his head.

"But you are stating truths that are substantiated only by biology," Martin insisted, and was rewarded by a blank stare. "Your conclusions are in line with the books which you must have read."

"I am glad to hear it," was the answer. "That my smattering of knowledge should enable me to short-cut my way to truth is most reassuring. As for myself, I never bother to find out if I am right or not. It is all valueless anyway. Man can never know the ultimate verities."

"You are a disciple of Spencer!" Martin cried triumphantly.

"I haven't read him since adolescence, and all I read then was his 'Education.'"

"I wish I could gather knowledge as carelessly," Martin broke out half an hour later. He had been closely analyzing Brissenden's mental equipment. "You are a sheer dogmatist, and that's what makes it so marvellous. You state dogmatically the latest facts which science has been able to establish only by *à posteriori* reasoning. You jump at correct conclusions. You certainly short-cut with a vengeance. You feel your way with the speed of light, by some hyperrational process, to truth."

"Yes, that was what used to bother Father Joseph, and Brother Dutton," Brissenden replied. "Oh, no," he added; "I am not anything. It was a lucky trick of fate that sent me to a Catholic college for my education. Where did you pick up what you know?"

And while Martin told him, he was busy studying Brissenden, ranging from a long, lean, aristocratic face and drooping shoulders to the overcoat on a neighboring chair, its pockets sagged and bulged by the freightage of many books. Brissenden's face and long, slender hands were browned by the sun—excessively browned, Martin thought. This sunburn bothered Martin. It was patent that Brissenden was no outdoor man. Then how had he been ravaged by the sun? Something morbid and significant attached to that sunburn, was Martin's thought as he returned to a study of the face, narrow, with high cheek-bones and cavernous hollows, and graced with as delicate and fine an aquiline nose as Martin had ever seen. There was nothing remarkable about the size of the eyes. They were neither large nor small, while their color was a nondescript brown; but in them smouldered a fire, or, rather, lurked an expression dual and strangely contradictory. Defiant, indomitable, even harsh to excess, they at the same time aroused pity. Martin found himself pitying him he knew not why, though he was soon to learn.

"Oh, I'm a lunger," Brissenden announced, offhand, a little later, having already stated that he came from Arizona. "I've been down there a couple of years living on the climate."

"Aren't you afraid to venture it up in this climate?"

"Afraid?"

There was no special emphasis of his repetition of Martin's word. But Martin saw in that ascetic face the advertisement that there was nothing of which it was afraid. The eyes had narrowed till they were eagle-like, and Martin almost caught his breath as he noted the eagle beak with its dilated nostrils, defiant, assertive, aggressive. Magnificent, was what he commented to himself, his blood thrilling at the sight. Aloud, he quoted:-

"'Under the bludgeoning of Chance
My head is bloody but unbowed.'"

"You like Henley," Brissenden said, his expression changing swiftly to large graciousness and tenderness. "Of course, I couldn't have expected anything else of you. Ah, Henley! A brave soul. He stands out among contemporary rhymesters—magazine rhymesters—as a gladiator stands out in the midst of a band of eunuchs."

"You don't like the magazines," Martin softly impeached.

"Do you?" was snarled back at him so savagely as to startle him.

"I—I write, or, rather, try to write, for the magazines," Martin faltered.

"That's better," was the mollified rejoinder. "You try to write, but you don't succeed. I respect and admire your failure. I know what you write. I can see it with half an eye, and there's one ingredient in it that shuts it out of the magazines. It's guts, and magazines have no use for that particular commodity. What they want is wish-wash and slush, and God knows they get it, but not from you."

"I'm not above hack-work," Martin contended.

"On the contrary—" Brissenden paused and ran an insolent eye over Martin's objective poverty, passing from the well-worn tie and the saw-edged collar to the shiny sleeves of the coat and on to the slight fray of one cuff, winding up and dwelling upon Martin's sunken cheeks. "On the contrary, hack-work is above you, so far above you that you can never hope to rise to it. Why, man, I could insult you by asking you to have something to eat."

Martin felt the heat in his face of the involuntary blood, and Brissenden laughed triumphantly.

"A full man is not insulted by such an invitation," he concluded.

"You are a devil," Martin cried irritably.

"Anyway, I didn't ask you."

"You didn't dare."

"Oh, I don't know about that. I invite you now."

Brissenden half rose from his chair as he spoke, as if with the intention of departing to the restaurant forthwith.

Martin's fists were tight-clenched, and his blood was drumming in his temples.

"Bosco! He eats 'em alive! Eats 'em alive!" Brissenden exclaimed, imitating the *spieler* of a locally famous snake-eater.

"I could certainly eat you alive," Martin said, in turn running insolent eyes over the other's disease-ravaged frame.

"Only I'm not worthy of it?"

"On the contrary," Martin considered, "because the incident is not worthy." He broke into a laugh, hearty and wholesome. "I confess you made a fool of me, Brissenden. That I am hungry and you are aware of it are only ordinary phenomena, and there's no disgrace. You see, I laugh at the conventional little moralities of the herd; then you drift by, say a sharp, true word, and immediately I am the slave of the same little moralities."

"You were insulted," Brissenden affirmed.

"I certainly was, a moment ago. The prejudice of early youth, you know. I learned such things then, and they cheapen what I have since learned. They are the skeletons in my particular closet."

"But you've got the door shut on them now?"

"I certainly have."

"Sure?"

"Sure."

"Then let's go and get something to eat."

"I'll go you," Martin answered, attempting to pay for the current Scotch and soda with the last change from his two dollars and seeing the waiter bullied by Brissenden into putting that change back on the table.

Martin pocketed it with a grimace, and felt for a moment the kindly weight of Brissenden's hand upon his shoulder.

CHAPTER XXXII

Promptly, the next afternoon, Maria was excited by Martin's second visitor. But she did not lose her head this time, for she seated Brissenden in her parlor's grandeur of respectability.

"Hope you don't mind my coming?" Brissenden began.

"No, no, not at all," Martin answered, shaking hands and waving him to the solitary chair, himself taking to the bed. "But how did you know where I lived?"

"Called up the Morses. Miss Morse answered the 'phone. And here I am." He tugged at his coat pocket and flung a thin volume on the table. "There's a book, by a poet. Read it and keep it." And then, in reply to Martin's protest: "What have I to do with books? I had another hemorrhage this morning. Got any whiskey? No, of course not. Wait a minute."

He was off and away. Martin watched his long figure go down the outside steps, and, on turning to close the gate, noted with a pang the shoulders, which had once been broad, drawn in now over, the collapsed ruin of the chest. Martin got two tumblers, and fell to reading the book of verse, Henry Vaughn Marlow's latest collection.

"No Scotch," Brissenden announced on his return. "The beggar sells nothing but American whiskey. But here's a quart of it."

"I'll send one of the youngsters for lemons, and we'll make a toddy," Martin offered.

"I wonder what a book like that will earn Marlow?" he went on, holding up the volume in question.

"Possibly fifty dollars," came the answer. "Though he's lucky if he pulls even on it, or if he can inveigle a publisher to risk bringing it out."

"Then one can't make a living out of poetry?"

Martin's tone and face alike showed his dejection.

"Certainly not. What fool expects to? Out of rhyming, yes. There's Bruce, and Virginia Spring, and Sedgwick. They do very nicely. But poetry—do you know how Vaughn Marlow makes his living?—teaching in a boys' cramming-joint down in Pennsylvania, and of all private little hells such a billet is the limit. I wouldn't trade places with him if he had fifty years of life before him. And yet his work stands out from the ruck of the contemporary versifiers as a balas ruby among carrots. And the reviews he gets! Damn them, all of them, the crass manikins!"

CHAPTER XXXII

"Too much is written by the men who can't write about the men who do write," Martin concurred. "Why, I was appalled at the quantities of rubbish written about Stevenson and his work."

"Ghouls and harpies!" Brissenden snapped out with clicking teeth. "Yes, I know the spawn—complacently pecking at him for his Father Damien letter, analyzing him, weighing him—"

"Measuring him by the yardstick of their own miserable egos," Martin broke in.

"Yes, that's it, a good phrase,—mouthing and besliming the True, and Beautiful, and Good, and finally patting him on the back and saying, 'Good dog, Fido.' Faugh! 'The little chattering daws of men,' Richard Realf called them the night he died."

"Pecking at star-dust," Martin took up the strain warmly; "at the meteoric flight of the master-men. I once wrote a squib on them—the critics, or the reviewers, rather."

"Let's see it," Brissenden begged eagerly.

So Martin unearthed a carbon copy of "Star-dust," and during the reading of it Brissenden chuckled, rubbed his hands, and forgot to sip his toddy.

"Strikes me you're a bit of star-dust yourself, flung into a world of cowled gnomes who cannot see," was his comment at the end of it. "Of course it was snapped up by the first magazine?"

Martin ran over the pages of his manuscript book. "It has been refused by twenty-seven of them."

Brissenden essayed a long and hearty laugh, but broke down in a fit of coughing.

"Say, you needn't tell me you haven't tackled poetry," he gasped. "Let me see some of it."

"Don't read it now," Martin pleaded. "I want to talk with you. I'll make up a bundle and you can take it home."

Brissenden departed with the "Love-cycle," and "The Peri and the Pearl," returning next day to greet Martin with:-

"I want more."

Not only did he assure Martin that he was a poet, but Martin learned that Brissenden also was one. He was swept off his feet by the other's work, and astounded that no attempt had been made to publish it.

"A plague on all their houses!" was Brissenden's answer to Martin's volunteering to market his work for him. "Love Beauty for its own sake," was his counsel, "and leave the magazines alone. Back to your ships and your sea—that's my advice to you, Martin Eden. What do you want in these sick and rotten cities of men? You are cutting your throat every day you waste in them trying to prostitute beauty to the needs of magazinedom. What was it you quoted me the other day?—Oh, yes, 'Man, the latest of the ephemera.' Well, what do you, the latest of the ephemera, want with fame? If you got it, it would be poison to you. You are too simple, too elemental, and too rational, by my faith, to prosper on such pap. I hope you never do sell a line to the magazines. Beauty is the only master to serve. Serve her and damn the multitude! Success! What in hell's success if it isn't right there in your Stevenson sonnet, which outranks Henley's 'Apparition,' in that 'Love-cycle,' in those sea-poems?

"It is not in what you succeed in doing that you get your joy, but in the doing of it. You can't tell me. I know it. You know it. Beauty hurts you. It is an everlasting pain in you, a wound that does not heal, a knife of flame. Why should you palter with magazines? Let beauty be your end. Why should you mint beauty into gold? Anyway, you can't; so there's no use in my getting excited over it. You can read the magazines for a thousand years and you won't find the value of one line of Keats. Leave fame and coin alone, sign away on a ship to-morrow, and go back to your sea."

"Not for fame, but for love," Martin laughed. "Love seems to have no place in your Cosmos; in mine, Beauty is the handmaiden of Love."

Brissenden looked at him pityingly and admiringly. "You are so young, Martin boy, so young. You will flutter high, but your wings are of the finest gauze, dusted with the fairest pigments. Do not scorch them. But of course you have scorched them already. It required some glorified petticoat to account for that 'Love-cycle,' and that's the shame of it."

"It glorifies love as well as the petticoat," Martin laughed.

"The philosophy of madness," was the retort. "So have I assured myself when wandering in hasheesh dreams. But beware. These bourgeois cities will kill you. Look at that den of traitors where I met you. Dry rot is no name for it. One can't keep his sanity in such an atmosphere. It's degrading. There's not one of them who is not degrading, man and woman, all of them animated stomachs guided by the high intellectual and artistic impulses of clams—"

He broke off suddenly and regarded Martin. Then, with a flash of divination, he saw the situation. The expression on his face turned to wondering horror.

"And you wrote that tremendous 'Love-cycle' to her—that pale, shrivelled, female thing!"

The next instant Martin's right hand had shot to a throttling clutch on his throat, and he was being shaken till his teeth rattled. But Martin, looking into his eyes, saw no fear there,—naught but a curious and mocking devil. Martin remembered himself, and flung Brissenden, by the neck, sidelong upon the bed, at the same moment releasing his hold.

Brissenden panted and gasped painfully for a moment, then began to chuckle.

"You had made me eternally your debtor had you shaken out the flame," he said.

"My nerves are on a hair-trigger these days," Martin apologized. "Hope I didn't hurt you. Here, let me mix a fresh toddy."

"Ah, you young Greek!" Brissenden went on. "I wonder if you take just pride in that body of yours. You are devilish strong. You are a young panther, a lion cub. Well, well, it is you who must pay for that strength."

"What do you mean?" Martin asked curiously, passing aim a glass. "Here, down this and be good."

"Because—" Brissenden sipped his toddy and smiled appreciation of it. "Because of the women. They will worry you until you die, as they have already worried you, or else I was born yesterday. Now there's no use in your choking me; I'm going to have my say. This is undoubtedly your calf love; but for Beauty's sake show better taste next time. What under heaven do you want with a daughter of the bourgeoisie? Leave them alone. Pick out some great, wanton flame of a woman, who laughs at life and jeers at death and loves one while she may. There are such women, and they will love you just as readily as any pusillanimous product of bourgeois sheltered life."

"Pusillanimous?" Martin protested.

"Just so, pusillanimous; prattling out little moralities that have been prattled into them, and afraid to live life. They will love you, Martin, but they will love their little moralities more. What you want is the magnificent abandon of life, the great free souls, the blazing butterflies and not the little gray moths. Oh, you will grow tired of them, too, of all the female things, if you are unlucky enough to live. But you won't live. You won't go back to your ships and sea; therefore, you'll hang around these pest-holes of cities until your bones are rotten, and then you'll die."

"You can lecture me, but you can't make me talk back," Martin said. "After all, you have but the wisdom of your temperament, and the wisdom of my temperament is just as unimpeachable as yours."

They disagreed about love, and the magazines, and many things, but they liked each other, and on Martin's part it was no less than a profound liking. Day after day they were together, if for no more than the hour Brissenden spent in Martin's stuffy room. Brissenden never arrived without his quart of whiskey, and when they dined together down-town, he drank Scotch and soda throughout the meal. He invariably paid the way for both, and it was through him that Martin learned the refinements of food, drank his first champagne, and made acquaintance with Rhenish wines.

But Brissenden was always an enigma. With the face of an ascetic, he was, in all the failing blood of him, a frank voluptuary. He was unafraid to die, bitter and cynical of all the ways of living; and yet, dying, he loved life, to the last atom of it. He was possessed by a madness to live, to thrill, "to squirm my little space in the cosmic dust whence I came," as he phrased it once himself. He had tampered with drugs and done many strange things in quest of new thrills, new sensations. As he told Martin, he had once gone three days without water, had done so voluntarily, in order to experience the exquisite delight of such a thirst assuaged. Who or what he was, Martin never learned. He was a man without a past, whose future was the imminent grave and whose present was a bitter fever of living.

CHAPTER XXXIII

Martin was steadily losing his battle. Economize as he would, the earnings from hack-work did not balance expenses. Thanksgiving found him with his black suit in pawn and unable to accept the Morses' invitation to dinner. Ruth was not made happy by his reason for not coming, and the corresponding effect on him was one of desperation. He told her that he would come, after all; that he would go over to San Francisco, to the *Transcontinental* office, collect the five dollars due him, and with it redeem his suit of clothes.

In the morning he borrowed ten cents from Maria. He would have borrowed it, by preference, from Brissenden, but that erratic individual had disappeared. Two weeks had passed since Martin had seen him, and he vainly cudgelled his brains for some cause of offence. The ten cents carried Martin across the ferry to San Francisco, and as he walked up Market Street he speculated upon his predicament in case he failed to collect the money. There would then be no way for him to return to Oakland, and he knew no one in San Francisco from whom to borrow another ten cents.

The door to the *Transcontinental* office was ajar, and Martin, in the act of opening it, was brought to a sudden pause by a loud voice from within, which exclaimed:- "But that is not the question, Mr. Ford." (Ford, Martin knew, from his correspondence, to be the editor's name.) "The question is, are you prepared to pay?—cash, and cash down, I mean? I am not interested in the prospects of the *Transcontinental* and what you expect to make it next year. What I want is to be paid for what I do. And I tell you, right now, the Christmas *Transcontinental* don't go to press till I have the money in my hand. Good day. When you get the money, come and see me."

The door jerked open, and the man flung past Martin, with an angry countenance and went down the corridor, muttering curses and clenching his fists. Martin decided not to enter immediately, and lingered in the hallways for a quarter of an hour. Then he shoved the door open and walked in. It was a new experience, the first time he had been inside an editorial office. Cards evidently were not necessary in that office, for the boy carried word to an inner room that there was a man who wanted to see Mr. Ford. Returning, the boy beckoned him from halfway across the room and led him to the private office, the editorial sanctum. Martin's first impression was of the disorder and cluttered confusion of the room. Next he noticed a bewhiskered, youthful-looking man, sitting at a roll-top desk, who regarded him curiously. Martin marvelled at the calm repose of his face. It was evident that the squabble with the printer had not affected his equanimity.

CHAPTER XXXIII

"I—I am Martin Eden," Martin began the conversation. ("And I want my five dollars," was what he would have liked to say.)

But this was his first editor, and under the circumstances he did not desire to scare him too abruptly. To his surprise, Mr. Ford leaped into the air with a "You don't say so!" and the next moment, with both hands, was shaking Martin's hand effusively.

"Can't say how glad I am to see you, Mr. Eden. Often wondered what you were like."

Here he held Martin off at arm's length and ran his beaming eyes over Martin's second-best suit, which was also his worst suit, and which was ragged and past repair, though the trousers showed the careful crease he had put in with Maria's flat-irons.

"I confess, though, I conceived you to be a much older man than you are. Your story, you know, showed such breadth, and vigor, such maturity and depth of thought. A masterpiece, that story—I knew it when I had read the first half-dozen lines. Let me tell you how I first read it. But no; first let me introduce you to the staff."

Still talking, Mr. Ford led him into the general office, where he introduced him to the associate editor, Mr. White, a slender, frail little man whose hand seemed strangely cold, as if he were suffering from a chill, and whose whiskers were sparse and silky.

"And Mr. Ends, Mr. Eden. Mr. Ends is our business manager, you know."

Martin found himself shaking hands with a cranky-eyed, bald-headed man, whose face looked youthful enough from what little could be seen of it, for most of it was covered by a snow-white beard, carefully trimmed—by his wife, who did it on Sundays, at which times she also shaved the back of his neck.

The three men surrounded Martin, all talking admiringly and at once, until it seemed to him that they were talking against time for a wager.

"We often wondered why you didn't call," Mr. White was saying.

"I didn't have the carfare, and I live across the Bay," Martin answered bluntly, with the idea of showing them his imperative need for the money.

Surely, he thought to himself, my glad rags in themselves are eloquent advertisement of my need. Time and again, whenever opportunity offered, he hinted about the purpose of his business. But his admirers' ears were deaf. They sang his praises, told him what they had thought of his story at first sight, what they subsequently thought, what their wives and families thought; but not one hint did they breathe of intention to pay him for it.

"Did I tell you how I first read your story?" Mr. Ford said. "Of course I didn't. I was coming west from New York, and when the train stopped at Ogden, the train-boy on the new run brought aboard the current number of the *Transcontinental*."

My God! Martin thought; you can travel in a Pullman while I starve for the paltry five dollars you owe me. A wave of anger rushed over him. The wrong done him by the *Transcontinental* loomed colossal, for strong upon him were all the dreary months of vain yearning, of hunger and privation, and his present hunger awoke and gnawed at him, reminding him that he had eaten nothing since the day before, and little enough then. For the moment he saw red. These creatures were not even robbers. They were sneak-thieves. By lies and broken promises they had tricked him out of his story. Well, he would show them. And a great resolve surged into his will to the effect that he would not leave the office until he got his money. He remembered, if he did not get it, that there was no way for him to go back to Oakland. He controlled himself with an effort, but not before the wolfish expression of his face had awed and perturbed them.

They became more voluble than ever. Mr. Ford started anew to tell how he had first read "The Ring of Bells," and Mr. Ends at the same time was striving to repeat his niece's appreciation of "The Ring of Bells," said niece being a school-teacher in Alameda.

"I'll tell you what I came for," Martin said finally. "To be paid for that story all of you like so well. Five dollars, I believe, is what you promised me would be paid on publication."

Mr. Ford, with an expression on his mobile features of mediate and happy acquiescence, started to reach for his pocket, then turned suddenly to Mr. Ends, and said that he had left his money home. That Mr. Ends resented this, was patent; and Martin saw the twitch of his arm as if to protect his trousers pocket. Martin knew that the money was there.

"I am sorry," said Mr. Ends, "but I paid the printer not an hour ago, and he took my ready change. It was careless of me to be so short; but the bill was not yet due, and the printer's request, as a favor, to make an immediate advance, was quite unexpected."

Both men looked expectantly at Mr. White, but that gentleman laughed and shrugged his shoulders. His conscience was clean at any rate. He had come into the *Transcontinental* to learn magazine-literature, instead of which he had principally learned finance. The *Transcontinental* owed him four months' salary, and he knew that the printer must be appeased before the associate editor.

"It's rather absurd, Mr. Eden, to have caught us in this shape," Mr. Ford preambled airily. "All carelessness, I assure you. But I'll tell you what we'll do. We'll mail you a check the first thing in the morning. You have Mr. Eden's address, haven't you, Mr. Ends?"

Yes, Mr. Ends had the address, and the check would be mailed the first thing in the morning. Martin's knowledge of banks and checks was hazy, but he could see no reason why they should not give him the check on this day just as well as on the next.

"Then it is understood, Mr. Eden, that we'll mail you the check to-morrow?" Mr. Ford said.

"I need the money to-day," Martin answered stolidly.

"The unfortunate circumstances—if you had chanced here any other day," Mr. Ford began suavely, only to be interrupted by Mr. Ends, whose cranky eyes justified themselves in his shortness of temper.

"Mr. Ford has already explained the situation," he said with asperity. "And so have I. The check will be mailed—"

"I also have explained," Martin broke in, "and I have explained that I want the money to-day."

He had felt his pulse quicken a trifle at the business manager's brusqueness, and upon him he kept an alert eye, for it was in that gentleman's trousers pocket that he divined the *Transcontinental's* ready cash was reposing.

"It is too bad—" Mr. Ford began.

But at that moment, with an impatient movement, Mr. Ends turned as if about to leave the room. At the same instant Martin sprang for him, clutching him by the throat with one hand in such fashion that Mr. Ends' snow-white beard, still maintaining its immaculate trimness, pointed ceilingward at an angle of forty-five degrees. To the horror of Mr. White and Mr. Ford, they saw their business manager shaken like an Astrakhan rug.

"Dig up, you venerable discourager of rising young talent!" Martin exhorted. "Dig up, or I'll shake it out of you, even if it's all in nickels." Then, to the two affrighted onlookers: "Keep away! If you interfere, somebody's liable to get hurt."

Mr. Ends was choking, and it was not until the grip on his throat was eased that he was able to signify his acquiescence in the digging-up programme. All together, after repeated digs, its trousers pocket yielded four dollars and fifteen cents.

"Inside out with it," Martin commanded.

An additional ten cents fell out. Martin counted the result of his raid a second time to make sure.

"You next!" he shouted at Mr. Ford. "I want seventy-five cents more."

Mr. Ford did not wait, but ransacked his pockets, with the result of sixty cents.

"Sure that is all?" Martin demanded menacingly, possessing himself of it. "What have you got in your vest pockets?"

In token of his good faith, Mr. Ford turned two of his pockets inside out. A strip of cardboard fell to the floor from one of them. He recovered it and was in the act of returning it, when Martin cried:-

"What's that?—A ferry ticket? Here, give it to me. It's worth ten cents. I'll credit you with it. I've now got four dollars and ninety-five cents, including the ticket. Five cents is still due me."

He looked fiercely at Mr. White, and found that fragile creature in the act of handing him a nickel.

"Thank you," Martin said, addressing them collectively. "I wish you a good day."

"Robber!" Mr. Ends snarled after him.

"Sneak-thief!" Martin retorted, slamming the door as he passed out.

Martin was elated—so elated that when he recollected that *The Hornet* owed him fifteen dollars for "The Peri and the Pearl," he decided forthwith to go and collect it. But *The Hornet* was run by a set of clean-shaven, strapping young men, frank buccaneers who robbed everything and everybody, not excepting one another. After some breakage of the office furniture, the editor (an ex-college athlete), ably assisted by the business manager, an advertising agent, and the porter, succeeded in removing Martin from the office and in accelerating, by initial impulse, his descent of the first flight of stairs.

"Come again, Mr. Eden; glad to see you any time," they laughed down at him from the landing above.

Martin grinned as he picked himself up.

"Phew!" he murmured back. "The *Transcontinental* crowd were nanny-goats, but you fellows are a lot of prize-fighters."

More laughter greeted this.

"I must say, Mr. Eden," the editor of *The Hornet* called down, "that for a poet you can go some yourself. Where did you learn that right cross—if I may ask?"

"Where you learned that half-Nelson," Martin answered. "Anyway, you're going to have a black eye."

"I hope your neck doesn't stiffen up," the editor wished solicitously: "What do you say we all go out and have a drink on it—not the neck, of course, but the little rough-house?"

"I'll go you if I lose," Martin accepted.

And robbers and robbed drank together, amicably agreeing that the battle was to the strong, and that the fifteen dollars for "The Peri and the Pearl" belonged by right to *The Hornet's* editorial staff.

CHAPTER XXXIV

Arthur remained at the gate while Ruth climbed Maria's front steps. She heard the rapid click of the type-writer, and when Martin let her in, found him on the last page of a manuscript. She had come to make certain whether or not he would be at their table for Thanksgiving dinner; but before she could broach the subject Martin plunged into the one with which he was full.

"Here, let me read you this," he cried, separating the carbon copies and running the pages of manuscript into shape. "It's my latest, and different from anything I've done. It is so altogether different that I am almost afraid of it, and yet I've a sneaking idea it is good. You be judge. It's an Hawaiian story. I've called it 'Wiki-wiki.'"

His face was bright with the creative glow, though she shivered in the cold room and had been struck by the coldness of his hands at greeting. She listened closely while he read, and though he from time to time had seen only disapprobation in her face, at the close he asked:-

"Frankly, what do you think of it?"

"I—I don't know," she, answered. "Will it—do you think it will sell?"

"I'm afraid not," was the confession. "It's too strong for the magazines. But it's true, on my word it's true."

"But why do you persist in writing such things when you know they won't sell?" she went on inexorably. "The reason for your writing is to make a living, isn't it?"

"Yes, that's right; but the miserable story got away with me. I couldn't help writing it. It demanded to be written."

"But that character, that Wiki-Wiki, why do you make him talk so roughly? Surely it will offend your readers, and surely that is why the editors are justified in refusing your work."

"Because the real Wiki-Wiki would have talked that way."

"But it is not good taste."

"It is life," he replied bluntly. "It is real. It is true. And I must write life as I see it."

She made no answer, and for an awkward moment they sat silent. It was because he loved her that he did not quite understand her, and she could not understand him because he was so large that he bulked beyond her horizon.

"Well, I've collected from the *Transcontinental*," he said in an effort to shift the conversation to a more comfortable subject. The picture of the bewhiskered trio, as he had last seen them, mulcted of four dollars and ninety cents and a ferry ticket, made him chuckle.

"Then you'll come!" she cried joyously. "That was what I came to find out."

"Come?" he muttered absently. "Where?"

"Why, to dinner to-morrow. You know you said you'd recover your suit if you got that money."

"I forgot all about it," he said humbly. "You see, this morning the poundman got Maria's two cows and the baby calf, and—well, it happened that Maria didn't have any money, and so I had to recover her cows for her. That's where the *Transcontinental* fiver went—'The Ring of Bells' went into the poundman's pocket."

"Then you won't come?"

He looked down at his clothing.

"I can't."

Tears of disappointment and reproach glistened in her blue eyes, but she said nothing.

"Next Thanksgiving you'll have dinner with me in Delmonico's," he said cheerily; "or in London, or Paris, or anywhere you wish. I know it."

"I saw in the paper a few days ago," she announced abruptly, "that there had been several local appointments to the Railway Mail. You passed first, didn't you?"

He was compelled to admit that the call had come for him, but that he had declined it. "I was so sure—I am so sure—of myself," he concluded. "A year from now I'll be earning more than a dozen men in the Railway Mail. You wait and see."

"Oh," was all she said, when he finished. She stood up, pulling at her gloves. "I must go, Martin. Arthur is waiting for me."

He took her in his arms and kissed her, but she proved a passive sweetheart. There was no tenseness in her body, her arms did not go around him, and her lips met his without their wonted pressure.

She was angry with him, he concluded, as he returned from the gate. But why? It was unfortunate that the poundman had gobbled Maria's cows. But it was only a stroke of fate. Nobody could be blamed for it. Nor did it enter his head that he could have done aught otherwise than what he had done. Well, yes, he was to blame a little, was his next thought, for having refused the call to the Railway Mail. And she had not liked "Wiki-Wiki."

He turned at the head of the steps to meet the letter-carrier on his afternoon round. The ever recurrent fever of expectancy assailed Martin as he took the bundle of long envelopes. One was not long. It was short and thin, and outside was printed the address of *The New York Outview*. He paused in the act of tearing the envelope open. It could not be an acceptance. He had no manuscripts with that publication. Perhaps—his heart almost stood still at the—wild thought—perhaps they were ordering an article from him; but the next instant he dismissed the surmise as hopelessly impossible.

It was a short, formal letter, signed by the office editor, merely informing him that an anonymous letter which they had received was enclosed, and that he could rest assured the *Outview's* staff never under any circumstances gave consideration to anonymous correspondence.

The enclosed letter Martin found to be crudely printed by hand. It was a hotchpotch of illiterate abuse of Martin, and of assertion that the "so-called Martin Eden" who was selling stories to magazines was no writer at all, and that in reality he was stealing stories from old magazines, typing them, and sending them out as his own. The envelope was postmarked "San Leandro." Martin did not require a second thought to discover the author. Higginbotham's grammar, Higginbotham's colloquialisms, Higginbotham's mental quirks and processes, were apparent throughout. Martin saw in every line, not the fine Italian hand, but the coarse grocer's fist, of his brother-in-law.

But why? he vainly questioned. What injury had he done Bernard Higginbotham? The thing was so unreasonable, so wanton. There was no explaining it. In the course of the week a dozen similar letters were forwarded to Martin by the editors of various Eastern magazines. The editors were behaving handsomely, Martin concluded. He was wholly unknown to them, yet some of them had even been sympathetic. It was evident that they detested anonymity. He saw that the malicious attempt to hurt him had failed. In fact, if anything came of it, it was bound to be good, for at least his name had been called to the attention of a number of editors. Sometime, perhaps, reading a submitted manuscript of his, they might remember him as the fellow about whom they had received an anonymous letter. And who was to say that such a remembrance might not sway the balance of their judgment just a trifle in his favor?

It was about this time that Martin took a great slump in Maria's estimation. He found her in the kitchen one morning groaning with pain, tears of weakness running down her cheeks, vainly endeavoring to put through a large ironing. He promptly diagnosed her affliction as La Grippe, dosed her with hot whiskey (the remnants in the bottles for which Brissenden was responsible), and ordered her to bed. But Maria was refractory. The ironing had to be done, she protested, and delivered that night, or else there would be no food on the morrow for the seven small and hungry Silvas.

To her astonishment (and it was something that she never ceased from relating to her dying day), she saw Martin Eden seize an iron from the stove and throw a fancy shirt-waist on the ironing-board. It was Kate Flanagan's best Sunday waist, than whom there was no more exacting and fastidiously dressed woman in Maria's world. Also, Miss Flanagan had sent special instruction that said waist must be delivered by that night. As every one knew, she was keeping company with John Collins, the blacksmith, and, as Maria knew privily, Miss Flanagan and Mr. Collins were going next day to Golden Gate Park. Vain was Maria's attempt to rescue the garment. Martin guided her tottering footsteps to a chair, from where she watched him with bulging eyes. In a quarter of the time it would have taken her she saw the shirt-waist safely ironed, and ironed as well as she could have done it, as Martin made her grant.

"I could work faster," he explained, "if your irons were only hotter."

To her, the irons he swung were much hotter than she ever dared to use.

"Your sprinkling is all wrong," he complained next. "Here, let me teach you how to sprinkle. Pressure is what's wanted. Sprinkle under pressure if you want to iron fast."

He procured a packing-case from the woodpile in the cellar, fitted a cover to it, and raided the scrap-iron the Silva tribe was collecting for the junkman. With fresh-sprinkled garments in the box, covered with the board and pressed by the iron, the device was complete and in operation.

"Now you watch me, Maria," he said, stripping off to his undershirt and gripping an iron that was what he called "really hot."

"An' when he feenish da iron' he washa da wools," as she described it afterward. "He say, 'Maria, you are da greata fool. I showa you how to washa da wools,' an' he shows me, too. Ten minutes he maka da machine—one barrel, one wheel-hub, two poles, justa like dat."

Martin had learned the contrivance from Joe at the Shelly Hot Springs. The old wheel-hub, fixed on the end of the upright pole, constituted the plunger. Making this, in turn, fast to the spring-pole attached to the kitchen rafters, so that the hub played upon the woollens in the barrel, he was able, with one hand, thoroughly to pound them.

"No more Maria washa da wools," her story always ended. "I maka da kids worka da pole an' da hub an' da barrel. Him da smarta man, Mister Eden."

Nevertheless, by his masterly operation and improvement of her kitchen-laundry he fell an immense distance in her regard. The glamour of romance with which her imagination had invested him faded away in the cold light of fact that he was an ex-laundryman. All his books, and his grand friends who visited him in carriages or with countless bottles of whiskey, went for naught. He was, after all, a mere workingman, a member of her own class and caste. He was more human and approachable, but, he was no longer mystery.

Martin's alienation from his family continued. Following upon Mr. Higginbotham's unprovoked attack, Mr. Hermann von Schmidt showed his hand. The fortunate sale of several storiettes, some humorous verse, and a few jokes gave Martin a temporary splurge of prosperity. Not only did he partially pay up his bills, but he had sufficient balance left to redeem his black suit and wheel. The latter, by virtue of a twisted crank-hanger, required repairing, and, as a matter of friendliness with his future brother-in-law, he sent it to Von Schmidt's shop.

The afternoon of the same day Martin was pleased by the wheel being delivered by a small boy. Von Schmidt was also inclined to be friendly, was Martin's conclusion from this unusual favor. Repaired wheels usually had to be called for. But when he examined the wheel, he discovered no repairs had been made. A little later in the day he telephoned his sister's betrothed, and learned that that person didn't want anything to do with him in "any shape, manner, or form."

"Hermann von Schmidt," Martin answered cheerfully, "I've a good mind to come over and punch that Dutch nose of yours."

"You come to my shop," came the reply, "an' I'll send for the police. An' I'll put you through, too. Oh, I know you, but you can't make no rough-house with me. I don't want nothin' to do with the likes of you. You're a loafer, that's what, an' I ain't asleep. You ain't goin' to do no spongin' off me just because I'm marryin' your sister. Why don't you go to work an' earn an honest livin', eh? Answer me that."

Martin's philosophy asserted itself, dissipating his anger, and he hung up the receiver with a long whistle of incredulous amusement. But after the amusement came the reaction, and he was oppressed by his loneliness. Nobody understood him, nobody seemed to have any use for him, except Brissenden, and Brissenden had disappeared, God alone knew where.

Twilight was falling as Martin left the fruit store and turned homeward, his marketing on his arm. At the corner an electric car had stopped, and at sight of a lean, familiar figure alighting, his heart leapt with joy. It was Brissenden, and in the fleeting glimpse, ere the car started up, Martin noted the overcoat pockets, one bulging with books, the other bulging with a quart bottle of whiskey.

CHAPTER XXXV

Brissenden gave no explanation of his long absence, nor did Martin pry into it. He was content to see his friend's cadaverous face opposite him through the steam rising from a tumbler of toddy.

"I, too, have not been idle," Brissenden proclaimed, after hearing Martin's account of the work he had accomplished.

He pulled a manuscript from his inside coat pocket and passed it to Martin, who looked at the title and glanced up curiously.

"Yes, that's it," Brissenden laughed. "Pretty good title, eh? 'Ephemera'—it is the one word. And you're responsible for it, what of your *man*, who is always the erected, the vitalized inorganic, the latest of the ephemera, the creature of temperature strutting his little space on the thermometer. It got into my head and I had to write it to get rid of it. Tell me what you think of it."

Martin's face, flushed at first, paled as he read on. It was perfect art. Form triumphed over substance, if triumph it could be called where the last conceivable atom of substance had found expression in so perfect construction as to make Martin's head swim with delight, to put passionate tears into his eyes, and to send chills creeping up and down his back. It was a long poem of six or seven hundred lines, and it was a fantastic, amazing, unearthly thing. It was terrific, impossible; and yet there it was, scrawled in black ink across the sheets of paper. It dealt with man and his soul-gropings in their ultimate terms, plumbing the abysses of space for the testimony of remotest suns and rainbow spectrums. It was a mad orgy of imagination, wassailing in the skull of a dying man who half sobbed under his breath and was quick with the wild flutter of fading heart-beats. The poem swung in majestic rhythm to the cool tumult of interstellar conflict, to the onset of starry hosts, to the impact of cold suns and the flaming up of nebular in the darkened void; and through it all, unceasing and faint, like a silver shuttle, ran the frail, piping voice of man, a querulous chirp amid the screaming of planets and the crash of systems.

"There is nothing like it in literature," Martin said, when at last he was able to speak. "It's wonderful!—wonderful! It has gone to my head. I am drunken with it. That great, infinitesimal question—I can't shake it out of my thoughts. That questing, eternal, ever recurring, thin little wailing voice of man is still ringing in my ears. It is like the dead-march of a gnat amid the trumpeting of elephants and the roaring of lions. It is insatiable with microscopic desire. I now I'm making a fool of myself, but the thing has obsessed me. You are—I don't know what you are—you are wonderful, that's all. But how do you do it? How do you do it?"

Martin paused from his rhapsody, only to break out afresh.

"I shall never write again. I am a dauber in clay. You have shown me the work of the real artificer-artisan. Genius! This is something more than genius. It transcends genius. It is truth gone mad. It is true, man, every line of it. I wonder if you realize that, you dogmatist. Science cannot give you the lie. It is the truth of the sneer, stamped out from the black iron of the Cosmos and interwoven with mighty rhythms of sound into a fabric of splendor and beauty. And now I won't say another word. I am overwhelmed, crushed. Yes, I will, too. Let me market it for you."

Brissenden grinned. "There's not a magazine in Christendom that would dare to publish it—you know that."

"I know nothing of the sort. I know there's not a magazine in Christendom that wouldn't jump at it. They don't get things like that every day. That's no mere poem of the year. It's the poem of the century."

"I'd like to take you up on the proposition."

"Now don't get cynical," Martin exhorted. "The magazine editors are not wholly fatuous. I know that. And I'll close with you on the bet. I'll wager anything you want that 'Ephemera' is accepted either on the first or second offering."

"There's just one thing that prevents me from taking you." Brissenden waited a moment. "The thing is big—the biggest I've ever done. I know that. It's my swan song. I am almighty proud of it. I worship it. It's better than whiskey. It is what I dreamed of—the great and perfect thing—when I was a simple young man, with sweet illusions and clean ideals. And I've got it, now, in my last grasp, and I'll not have it pawed over and soiled by a lot of swine. No, I won't take the bet. It's mine. I made it, and I've shared it with you."

"But think of the rest of the world," Martin protested. "The function of beauty is joy-making."

"It's my beauty."

"Don't be selfish."

"I'm not selfish." Brissenden grinned soberly in the way he had when pleased by the thing his thin lips were about to shape. "I'm as unselfish as a famished hog."

In vain Martin strove to shake him from his decision. Martin told him that his hatred of the magazines was rabid, fanatical, and that his conduct was a thousand times more despicable than that of the youth who burned the temple of Diana at Ephesus. Under the storm of denunciation Brissenden complacently sipped his toddy and affirmed that everything the other said was quite true, with the exception of the magazine editors. His hatred of them knew no bounds, and he excelled Martin in denunciation when he turned upon them.

"I wish you'd type it for me," he said. "You know how a thousand times better than any stenographer. And now I want to give you some advice." He drew a bulky manuscript from his outside coat pocket. "Here's your 'Shame of the Sun.' I've read it not once, but twice and three times—the highest compliment I can pay you. After what you've said about 'Ephemera' I must be silent. But this I will say: when 'The Shame of the Sun' is published, it will make a hit. It will start a controversy that will be worth thousands to you just in advertising."

Martin laughed. "I suppose your next advice will be to submit it to the magazines."

"By all means no—that is, if you want to see it in print. Offer it to the first-class houses. Some publisher's reader may be mad enough or drunk enough to report favorably on it. You've read the books. The meat of them has been transmuted in the alembic of Martin Eden's mind and poured into 'The Shame of the Sun,' and one day Martin Eden will be famous, and not the least of his fame will rest upon that work. So you must get a publisher for it—the sooner the better."

Brissenden went home late that night; and just as he mounted the first step of the car, he swung suddenly back on Martin and thrust into his hand a small, tightly crumpled wad of paper.

"Here, take this," he said. "I was out to the races to-day, and I had the right dope."

The bell clanged and the car pulled out, leaving Martin wondering as to the nature of the crinkly, greasy wad he clutched in his hand. Back in his room he unrolled it and found a hundred-dollar bill.

He did not scruple to use it. He knew his friend had always plenty of money, and he knew also, with profound certitude, that his success would enable him to repay it. In the morning he paid every bill, gave Maria three months' advance on the room, and redeemed every pledge at the pawnshop. Next he bought Marian's wedding present, and simpler presents, suitable to Christmas, for Ruth and Gertrude. And finally, on the balance remaining to him, he herded the whole Silva tribe down into Oakland. He was a winter late in redeeming his promise, but redeemed it was, for the last, least Silva got a pair of shoes, as well as Maria herself. Also, there were horns, and dolls, and toys of various sorts, and parcels and bundles of candies and nuts that filled the arms of all the Silvas to overflowing.

It was with this extraordinary procession trooping at his and Maria's heels into a confectioner's in quest if the biggest candy-cane ever made, that he encountered Ruth and her mother. Mrs. Morse was shocked. Even Ruth was hurt, for she had some regard for appearances, and her lover, cheek by jowl with Maria, at the head of that army of Portuguese ragamuffins, was not a pretty sight. But it was not that which hurt so much as what she took to be his lack of pride and self-respect. Further, and keenest of all, she read into the incident the impossibility of his living down his working-class origin. There was stigma enough in the fact of it, but shamelessly to flaunt it in the face of the world—her world—was going too far. Though her engagement to Martin had been kept secret, their long intimacy had not been unproductive of gossip; and in the shop, glancing covertly at her lover and his following, had been several of her acquaintances. She lacked the easy largeness of Martin and could not rise superior to her environment. She had been hurt to the quick, and her sensitive nature was quivering with the shame of it. So it was, when Martin arrived later in the day, that he kept her present in his breast-pocket, deferring the giving of it to a more propitious occasion. Ruth in tears—passionate, angry tears—was a revelation to him. The spectacle of her suffering convinced him that he had been a brute, yet in the soul of him he could not see how nor why. It never entered his head to be ashamed of those he knew, and to take the Silvas out to a Christmas treat could in no way, so it seemed to him, show lack of consideration for Ruth. On the other hand, he did see Ruth's point of view, after she had explained it; and he looked upon it as a feminine weakness, such as afflicted all women and the best of women.

CHAPTER XXXVI

"Come on,—I'll show you the real dirt," Brissenden said to him, one evening in January.

They had dined together in San Francisco, and were at the Ferry Building, returning to Oakland, when the whim came to him to show Martin the "real dirt." He turned and fled across the water-front, a meagre shadow in a flapping overcoat, with Martin straining to keep up with him. At a wholesale liquor store he bought two gallon-demijohns of old port, and with one in each hand boarded a Mission Street car, Martin at his heels burdened with several quart-bottles of whiskey.

If Ruth could see me now, was his thought, while he wondered as to what constituted the real dirt.

"Maybe nobody will be there," Brissenden said, when they dismounted and plunged off to the right into the heart of the working-class ghetto, south of Market Street. "In which case you'll miss what you've been looking for so long."

"And what the deuce is that?" Martin asked.

"Men, intelligent men, and not the gibbering nonentities I found you consorting with in that trader's den. You read the books and you found yourself all alone. Well, I'm going to show you to-night some other men who've read the books, so that you won't be lonely any more."

"Not that I bother my head about their everlasting discussions," he said at the end of a block. "I'm not interested in book philosophy. But you'll find these fellows intelligences and not bourgeois swine. But watch out, they'll talk an arm off of you on any subject under the sun."

"Hope Norton's there," he panted a little later, resisting Martin's effort to relieve him of the two demijohns. "Norton's an idealist—a Harvard man. Prodigious memory. Idealism led him to philosophic anarchy, and his family threw him off. Father's a railroad president and many times millionnaire, but the son's starving in 'Frisco, editing an anarchist sheet for twenty-five a month."

Martin was little acquainted in San Francisco, and not at all south of Market; so he had no idea of where he was being led.

"Go ahead," he said; "tell me about them beforehand. What do they do for a living? How do they happen to be here?"

"Hope Hamilton's there." Brissenden paused and rested his hands. "Strawn-Hamilton's his name—hyphenated, you know—comes of old Southern stock. He's a tramp—laziest man I ever knew, though he's clerking, or trying to, in a socialist coöperative store for six dollars a week. But he's a confirmed hobo. Tramped into town. I've seen him sit all day on a bench and never a bite pass his lips, and in the evening, when I invited him to dinner—restaurant two blocks away—have him say, 'Too much trouble, old man. Buy me a package of cigarettes instead.' He was a Spencerian like you till Kreis turned him to materialistic monism. I'll start him on monism if I can. Norton's another monist—only he affirms naught but spirit. He can give Kreis and Hamilton all they want, too."

"Who is Kreis?" Martin asked.

"His rooms we're going to. One time professor—fired from university—usual story. A mind like a steel trap. Makes his living any old way. I know he's been a street fakir when he was down. Unscrupulous. Rob a corpse of a shroud—anything. Difference between him—and the bourgeoisie is that he robs without illusion. He'll talk Nietzsche, or Schopenhauer, or Kant, or anything, but the only thing in this world, not excepting Mary, that he really cares for, is his monism. Haeckel is his little tin god. The only way to insult him is to take a slap at Haeckel."

"Here's the hang-out." Brissenden rested his demijohn at the upstairs entrance, preliminary to the climb. It was the usual two-story corner building, with a saloon and grocery underneath. "The gang lives here—got the whole upstairs to themselves. But Kreis is the only one who has two rooms. Come on."

No lights burned in the upper hall, but Brissenden threaded the utter blackness like a familiar ghost. He stopped to speak to Martin.

"There's one fellow—Stevens—a theosophist. Makes a pretty tangle when he gets going. Just now he's dish-washer in a restaurant. Likes a good cigar. I've seen him eat in a ten-cent hash-house and pay fifty cents for the cigar he smoked afterward. I've got a couple in my pocket for him, if he shows up."

"And there's another fellow—Parry—an Australian, a statistician and a sporting encyclopaedia. Ask him the grain output of Paraguay for 1903, or the English importation of sheetings into China for 1890, or at what weight Jimmy Britt fought Battling Nelson, or who was welter-weight champion of the United States in '68, and you'll get the correct answer with the automatic celerity of a slot-machine. And there's Andy, a stone-mason, has ideas on everything, a good chess-player; and another fellow, Harry, a baker, red hot socialist and strong union man. By the way, you remember Cooks' and Waiters' strike—Hamilton was the chap who organized that union and precipitated the strike—planned it all out in advance, right here in Kreis's rooms. Did it just for the fun of it, but was too lazy to stay by the union. Yet he could have risen high if he wanted to. There's no end to the possibilities in that man—if he weren't so insuperably lazy."

Brissenden advanced through the darkness till a thread of light marked the threshold of a door. A knock and an answer opened it, and Martin found himself shaking hands with Kreis, a handsome brunette man, with dazzling white teeth, a drooping black mustache, and large, flashing black eyes. Mary, a matronly young blonde, was washing dishes in the little back room that served for kitchen and dining room. The front room served as bedchamber and living room. Overhead was the week's washing, hanging in festoons so low that Martin did not see at first the two men talking in a corner. They hailed Brissenden and his demijohns with acclamation, and, on being introduced, Martin learned they were Andy and Parry. He joined them and listened attentively to the description of a prize-fight Parry had seen the night before; while

Brissenden, in his glory, plunged into the manufacture of a toddy and the serving of wine and whiskey-and-sodas. At his command, "Bring in the clan," Andy departed to go the round of the rooms for the lodgers.

"We're lucky that most of them are here," Brissenden whispered to Martin. "There's Norton and Hamilton; come on and meet them. Stevens isn't around, I hear. I'm going to get them started on monism if I can. Wait till they get a few jolts in them and they'll warm up."

At first the conversation was desultory. Nevertheless Martin could not fail to appreciate the keen play of their minds. They were men with opinions, though the opinions often clashed, and, though they were witty and clever, they were not superficial. He swiftly saw, no matter upon what they talked, that each man applied the correlation of knowledge and had also a deep-seated and unified conception of society and the Cosmos. Nobody manufactured their opinions for them; they were all rebels of one variety or another, and their lips were strangers to platitudes. Never had Martin, at the Morses', heard so amazing a range of topics discussed. There seemed no limit save time to the things they were alive to. The talk wandered from Mrs. Humphry Ward's new book to Shaw's latest play, through the future of the drama to reminiscences of Mansfield. They appreciated or sneered at the morning editorials, jumped from labor conditions in New Zealand to Henry James and Brander Matthews, passed on to the German designs in the Far East and the economic aspect of the Yellow Peril, wrangled over the German elections and Bebel's last speech, and settled down to local politics, the latest plans and scandals in the union labor party administration, and the wires that were pulled to bring about the Coast Seamen's strike. Martin was struck by the inside knowledge they possessed. They knew what was never printed in the newspapers—the wires and strings and the hidden hands that made the puppets dance. To Martin's surprise, the girl, Mary, joined in the conversation, displaying an intelligence he had never encountered in the few women he had met. They talked together on Swinburne and Rossetti, after which she led him beyond his depth into the by-paths of French literature. His revenge came when she defended Maeterlinck and he brought into action the carefully-thought-out thesis of "The Shame of the Sun."

Several other men had dropped in, and the air was thick with tobacco smoke, when Brissenden waved the red flag.

"Here's fresh meat for your axe, Kreis," he said; "a rose-white youth with the ardor of a lover for Herbert Spencer. Make a Haeckelite of him—if you can."

Kreis seemed to wake up and flash like some metallic, magnetic thing, while Norton looked at Martin sympathetically, with a sweet, girlish smile, as much as to say that he would be amply protected.

Kreis began directly on Martin, but step by step Norton interfered, until he and Kreis were off and away in a personal battle. Martin listened and fain would have rubbed his eyes. It was impossible that this should be, much less in the labor ghetto south of Market. The books were alive in these men. They talked with fire and enthusiasm, the intellectual stimulant stirring them as he had seen drink and anger stir other men. What he heard was no longer the philosophy of the dry, printed word, written by half-mythical demigods like Kant and Spencer. It was living philosophy, with warm, red blood, incarnated in these two men till its very features worked with excitement. Now and again other men joined in, and all followed the discussion with cigarettes going out in their hands and with alert, intent faces.

Idealism had never attracted Martin, but the exposition it now received at the hands of Norton was a revelation. The logical plausibility of it, that made an appeal to his intellect, seemed missed by Kreis and Hamilton, who sneered at Norton as a metaphysician, and who, in turn, sneered back at them as metaphysicians. *Phenomenon* and *noumenon* were bandied back and forth. They charged him with attempting to explain consciousness by itself. He charged them with word-jugglery, with reasoning from words to theory instead of from facts to theory. At this they were aghast. It was the cardinal tenet of their mode of reasoning to start with facts and to give names to the facts.

When Norton wandered into the intricacies of Kant, Kreis reminded him that all good little German philosophies when they died went to Oxford. A little later Norton reminded them of Hamilton's Law of Parsimony, the application of which they immediately claimed for every reasoning process of theirs. And Martin hugged his knees and exulted in it all. But Norton was no Spencerian, and he, too, strove for Martin's philosophic soul, talking as much at him as to his two opponents.

"You know Berkeley has never been answered," he said, looking directly at Martin. "Herbert Spencer came the nearest, which was not very near. Even the stanchest of Spencer's followers will not go farther. I was reading an essay of Saleeby's the other day, and the best Saleeby could say was that Herbert Spencer *nearly* succeeded in answering Berkeley."

"You know what Hume said?" Hamilton asked. Norton nodded, but Hamilton gave it for the benefit of the rest. "He said that Berkeley's arguments admit of no answer and produce no conviction."

"In his, Hume's, mind," was the reply. "And Hume's mind was the same as yours, with this difference: he was wise enough to admit there was no answering Berkeley."

Norton was sensitive and excitable, though he never lost his head, while Kreis and Hamilton were like a pair of cold-blooded savages, seeking out tender places to prod and poke. As the evening grew late, Norton, smarting under the repeated charges of being a metaphysician, clutching his chair to keep from jumping to his feet, his gray eyes snapping and his girlish face grown harsh and sure, made a grand attack upon their position.

"All right, you Haeckelites, I may reason like a medicine man, but, pray, how do you reason? You have nothing to stand on, you unscientific dogmatists with your positive science which you are always lugging about into places it has no right to be. Long before the school of materialistic monism arose, the ground was removed so that there could be no foundation. Locke was the man, John Locke. Two hundred years ago—more than that, even in his 'Essay concerning the Human Understanding,' he proved the non-existence of innate ideas. The best of it is that that is precisely what you claim. To-night, again and again, you have asserted the non-existence of innate ideas.

"And what does that mean? It means that you can never know ultimate reality. Your brains are empty when you are born. Appearances, or phenomena, are all the content your minds can receive from your five senses. Then noumena, which are not in your minds when you are born, have no way of getting in—"

"I deny—" Kreis started to interrupt.

"You wait till I'm done," Norton shouted. "You can know only that much of the play and interplay of force and matter as impinges in one way or another on our senses. You see, I am willing to admit, for the sake of the argument, that matter exists; and what I am about to do is to efface you by your own argument. I can't do it any other way, for you are both congenitally unable to understand a philosophic abstraction."

"And now, what do you know of matter, according to your own positive science? You know it only by its phenomena, its appearances. You are aware only of its changes, or of such changes in it as cause changes in your consciousness. Positive science deals only with phenomena, yet you are foolish enough to strive to be ontologists and to deal with noumena. Yet, by the very definition of positive science, science is concerned only with appearances. As somebody has said, phenomenal knowledge cannot transcend phenomena."

"You cannot answer Berkeley, even if you have annihilated Kant, and yet, perforce, you assume that Berkeley is wrong when you affirm that science proves the non-existence of God, or, as much to the point, the existence of matter.—You know I granted the reality of matter only in order to make myself intelligible to your understanding. Be positive scientists, if you please; but ontology has no place in positive science, so leave it alone. Spencer is right in his agnosticism, but if Spencer—"

But it was time to catch the last ferry-boat for Oakland, and Brissenden and Martin slipped out, leaving Norton still talking and Kreis and Hamilton waiting to pounce on him like a pair of hounds as soon as he finished.

"You have given me a glimpse of fairyland," Martin said on the ferry-boat. "It makes life worth while to meet people like that. My mind is all worked up. I never appreciated idealism before. Yet I can't accept it. I know that I shall always be a realist. I am so made, I guess. But I'd like to have made a reply to Kreis and Hamilton, and I think I'd have had a word or two for Norton. I didn't see that Spencer was damaged any. I'm as excited as a child on its first visit to the circus. I see I must read up some more. I'm going to get hold of Saleeby. I still think Spencer is unassailable, and next time I'm going to take a hand myself."

But Brissenden, breathing painfully, had dropped off to sleep, his chin buried in a scarf and resting on his sunken chest, his body wrapped in the long overcoat and shaking to the vibration of the propellers.

CHAPTER XXXVII

The first thing Martin did next morning was to go counter both to Brissenden's advice and command. "The Shame of the Sun" he wrapped and mailed to *The Acropolis*. He believed he could find magazine publication for it, and he felt that recognition by the magazines would commend him to the book-publishing houses. "Ephemera" he likewise wrapped and mailed to a magazine. Despite Brissenden's prejudice against the magazines, which was a pronounced mania with him, Martin decided that the great poem should see print. He did not intend, however, to publish it without the other's permission. His plan was to get it accepted by one of the high magazines, and, thus armed, again to wrestle with Brissenden for consent.

Martin began, that morning, a story which he had sketched out a number of weeks before and which ever since had been worrying him with its insistent clamor to be created. Apparently it was to be a rattling sea story, a tale of twentieth-century adventure and romance, handling real characters, in a real world, under real conditions. But beneath the swing and go of the story was to be something else—something that the superficial reader would never discern and which, on the other hand, would not diminish in any way the interest and enjoyment for such a reader. It was this, and not the mere story, that impelled Martin to write it. For that matter, it was always the great, universal motif that suggested plots to him. After having found such a motif, he cast about for the particular persons and particular location in time and space wherewith and wherein to utter the universal thing. "Overdue" was the title he had decided for it, and its length he believed would not be more than sixty thousand words—a bagatelle for him with his splendid vigor of production. On this first day he took hold of it with conscious delight in the mastery of his tools. He no longer worried for fear that the sharp, cutting edges should slip and mar his work. The long months of intense application and study had brought their reward. He could now devote himself with sure hand to the larger phases of the thing he shaped; and as he worked, hour after hour, he felt, as never before, the sure and cosmic grasp with which he held life and the affairs of life. "Overdue" would tell a story that would be true of its particular characters and its particular events; but it would tell, too, he was confident, great vital things that would be true of all time, and all sea, and all life—thanks to Herbert Spencer, he thought, leaning back for a moment from the table. Ay, thanks to Herbert Spencer and to the master-key of life, evolution, which Spencer had placed in his hands.

CHAPTER XXXVII

He was conscious that it was great stuff he was writing. "It will go! It will go!" was the refrain that kept, sounding in his ears. Of course it would go. At last he was turning out the thing at which the magazines would jump. The whole story worked out before him in lightning flashes. He broke off from it long enough to write a paragraph in his note-book. This would be the last paragraph in "Overdue"; but so thoroughly was the whole book already composed in his brain that he could write, weeks before he had arrived at the end, the end itself. He compared the tale, as yet unwritten, with the tales of the sea-writers, and he felt it to be immeasurably superior. "There's only one man who could touch it," he murmured aloud, "and that's Conrad. And it ought to make even him sit up and shake hands with me, and say, 'Well done, Martin, my boy.'"

He toiled on all day, recollecting, at the last moment, that he was to have dinner at the Morses'. Thanks to Brissenden, his black suit was out of pawn and he was again eligible for dinner parties. Down town he stopped off long enough to run into the library and search for Saleeby's books. He drew out "The Cycle of Life," and on the car turned to the essay Norton had mentioned on Spencer. As Martin read, he grew angry. His face flushed, his jaw set, and unconsciously his hand clenched, unclenched, and clenched again as if he were taking fresh grips upon some hateful thing out of which he was squeezing the life. When he left the car, he strode along the sidewalk as a wrathful man will stride, and he rang the Morse bell with such viciousness that it roused him to consciousness of his condition, so that he entered in good nature, smiling with amusement at himself. No sooner, however, was he inside than a great depression descended upon him. He fell from the height where he had been upborne all day on the wings of inspiration. "Bourgeois," "trader's den"—Brissenden's epithets repeated themselves in his mind. But what of that? he demanded angrily. He was marrying Ruth, not her family.

It seemed to him that he had never seen Ruth more beautiful, more spiritual and ethereal and at the same time more healthy. There was color in her cheeks, and her eyes drew him again and again—the eyes in which he had first read immortality. He had forgotten immortality of late, and the trend of his scientific reading had been away from it; but here, in Ruth's eyes, he read an argument without words that transcended all worded arguments. He saw that in her eyes before which all discussion fled away, for he saw love there. And in his own eyes was love; and love was unanswerable. Such was his passionate doctrine.

The half hour he had with her, before they went in to dinner, left him supremely happy and supremely satisfied with life. Nevertheless, at table, the inevitable reaction and exhaustion consequent upon the hard day seized hold of him. He was aware that his eyes were tired and that he was irritable. He remembered it was at this table, at which he now sneered and was so often bored, that he had first eaten with civilized beings in what he had imagined was an atmosphere of high culture and refinement. He caught a glimpse of that pathetic figure of him, so long ago, a self-conscious savage, sprouting sweat at every pore in an agony of apprehension, puzzled by the bewildering minutiae of eating-implements, tortured by the ogre of a servant, striving at a leap to live at such dizzy social altitude, and deciding in the end to be frankly himself, pretending no knowledge and no polish he did not possess.

He glanced at Ruth for reassurance, much in the same manner that a passenger, with sudden panic thought of possible shipwreck, will strive to locate the life preservers. Well, that much had come out of it—love and Ruth. All the rest had failed to stand the test of the books. But Ruth and love had stood the test; for them he found a biological sanction. Love was the most exalted expression of life. Nature had been busy designing him, as she had been busy with all normal men, for the purpose of loving. She had spent ten thousand centuries—ay, a hundred thousand and a million centuries—upon the task, and he was the best she could do. She had made love the strongest thing in him, increased its power a myriad per cent with her gift of imagination, and sent him forth into the ephemera to thrill and melt and mate. His hand sought Ruth's hand beside him hidden by the table, and a warm pressure was given and received. She looked at him a swift instant, and her eyes were radiant and melting. So were his in the thrill that pervaded him; nor did he realize how much that was radiant and melting in her eyes had been aroused by what she had seen in his.

Across the table from him, cater-cornered, at Mr. Morse's right, sat Judge Blount, a local superior court judge. Martin had met him a number of times and had failed to like him. He and Ruth's father were discussing labor union politics, the local situation, and socialism, and Mr. Morse was endeavoring to twit Martin on the latter topic. At last Judge Blount looked across the table with benignant and fatherly pity. Martin smiled to himself.

"You'll grow out of it, young man," he said soothingly. "Time is the best cure for such youthful distempers." He turned to Mr. Morse. "I do not believe discussion is good in such cases. It makes the patient obstinate."

"That is true," the other assented gravely. "But it is well to warn the patient occasionally of his condition."

Martin laughed merrily, but it was with an effort. The day had been too long, the day's effort too intense, and he was deep in the throes of the reaction.

"Undoubtedly you are both excellent doctors," he said; "but if you care a whit for the opinion of the patient, let him tell you that you are poor diagnosticians. In fact, you are both suffering from the disease you think you find in me. As for me, I am immune. The socialist philosophy that riots half-baked in your veins has passed me by."

"Clever, clever," murmured the judge. "An excellent ruse in controversy, to reverse positions."

"Out of your mouth." Martin's eyes were sparkling, but he kept control of himself. "You see, Judge, I've heard your campaign speeches. By some henidical process—henidical, by the way is a favorite word of mine which nobody understands—by some henidical process you persuade yourself that you believe in the competitive system and the survival of the strong, and at the same time you indorse with might and main all sorts of measures to shear the strength from the strong."

"My young man—"

"Remember, I've heard your campaign speeches," Martin warned. "It's on record, your position on interstate commerce regulation, on regulation of the railway trust and Standard Oil, on the conservation of the forests, on a thousand and one restrictive measures that are nothing else than socialistic."

"Do you mean to tell me that you do not believe in regulating these various outrageous exercises of power?"

"That's not the point. I mean to tell you that you are a poor diagnostician. I mean to tell you that I am not suffering from the microbe of socialism. I mean to tell you that it is you who are suffering from the emasculating ravages of that same microbe. As for me, I am an inveterate opponent of socialism just as I am an inveterate opponent of your own mongrel democracy that is nothing else than pseudo-socialism masquerading under a garb of words that will not stand the test of the dictionary."

"I am a reactionary—so complete a reactionary that my position is incomprehensible to you who live in a veiled lie of social organization and whose sight is not keen enough to pierce the veil. You make believe that you believe in the survival of the strong and the rule of the strong. I believe. That is the difference. When I was a trifle younger,—a few months younger,—I believed the same thing. You see, the ideas of you and yours had impressed me. But merchants and traders are cowardly rulers at best; they grunt and grub all their days in the trough of money-getting, and I have swung back to aristocracy, if you please. I am the only individualist in this room. I look to the state for nothing. I look only to the strong man, the man on horseback, to save the state from its own rotten futility."

"Nietzsche was right. I won't take the time to tell you who Nietzsche was, but he was right. The world belongs to the strong—to the strong who are noble as well and who do not wallow in the swine-trough of trade and exchange. The world belongs to the true nobleman, to the great blond beasts, to the noncompromisers, to the 'yes-sayers.' And they will eat you up, you socialists—who are afraid of socialism and who think yourselves individualists. Your slave-morality of the meek and lowly will never save you.—Oh, it's all Greek, I know, and I won't bother you any more with it. But remember one thing. There aren't half a dozen individualists in Oakland, but Martin Eden is one of them."

He signified that he was done with the discussion, and turned to Ruth.

"I'm wrought up to-day," he said in an undertone. "All I want to do is to love, not talk."

He ignored Mr. Morse, who said:-

"I am unconvinced. All socialists are Jesuits. That is the way to tell them."

"We'll make a good Republican out of you yet," said Judge Blount.

"The man on horseback will arrive before that time," Martin retorted with good humor, and returned to Ruth.

But Mr. Morse was not content. He did not like the laziness and the disinclination for sober, legitimate work of this prospective son-in-law of his, for whose ideas he had no respect and of whose nature he had no understanding. So he turned the conversation to Herbert Spencer. Judge Blount ably seconded him, and Martin, whose ears had pricked at the first mention of the philosopher's name, listened to the judge enunciate a grave and complacent diatribe against Spencer. From time to time Mr. Morse glanced at Martin, as much as to say, "There, my boy, you see."

"Chattering daws," Martin muttered under his breath, and went on talking with Ruth and Arthur.

But the long day and the "real dirt" of the night before were telling upon him; and, besides, still in his burnt mind was what had made him angry when he read it on the car.

"What is the matter?" Ruth asked suddenly alarmed by the effort he was making to contain himself.

"There is no god but the Unknowable, and Herbert Spencer is its prophet," Judge Blount was saying at that moment.

Martin turned upon him.

"A cheap judgment," he remarked quietly. "I heard it first in the City Hall Park, on the lips of a workingman who ought to have known better. I have heard it often since, and each time the clap-trap of it nauseates me. You ought to be ashamed of yourself. To hear that great and noble man's name upon your lips is like finding a dew-drop in a cesspool. You are disgusting."

It was like a thunderbolt. Judge Blount glared at him with apoplectic countenance, and silence reigned. Mr. Morse was secretly pleased. He could see that his daughter was shocked. It was what he wanted to do—to bring out the innate ruffianism of this man he did not like.

Ruth's hand sought Martin's beseechingly under the table, but his blood was up. He was inflamed by the intellectual pretence and fraud of those who sat in the high places. A Superior Court Judge! It was only several years before that he had looked up from the mire at such glorious entities and deemed them gods.

Judge Blount recovered himself and attempted to go on, addressing himself to Martin with an assumption of politeness that the latter understood was for the benefit of the ladies. Even this added to his anger. Was there no honesty in the world?

"You can't discuss Spencer with me," he cried. "You do not know any more about Spencer than do his own countrymen. But it is no fault of yours, I grant. It is just a phase of the contemptible ignorance of the times. I ran across a sample of it on my way here this evening. I was reading an essay by Saleeby on Spencer. You should read it. It is accessible to all men. You can buy it in any book-store or draw it from the public library. You would feel ashamed of your paucity of abuse and ignorance of that noble man compared with what Saleeby has collected on the subject. It is a record of shame that would shame your shame."

"'The philosopher of the half-educated,' he was called by an academic Philosopher who was not worthy to pollute the atmosphere he breathed. I don't think you have read ten pages of Spencer, but there have been critics, assumably more intelligent than you, who have read no more than you of Spencer, who publicly challenged his followers to adduce one single idea from all his writings—from Herbert Spencer's writings, the man who has impressed the stamp of his genius over the whole field of scientific research and modern thought; the father of psychology; the man who revolutionized pedagogy, so that to-day the child of the French peasant is taught the three R's according to principles laid down by him. And the little gnats of men sting his memory when they get their very bread and butter from the technical application of his ideas. What little of worth resides in their brains is largely due to him. It is certain that had he never lived, most of what is correct in their parrot-learned knowledge would be absent."

"And yet a man like Principal Fairbanks of Oxford—a man who sits in an even higher place than you, Judge Blount—has said that Spencer will be dismissed by posterity as a poet and dreamer rather than a thinker. Yappers and blatherskites, the whole brood of them! '"First Principles" is not wholly destitute of a certain literary power,' said one of them. And others of them have said that he was an industrious plodder rather than an original thinker. Yappers and blatherskites! Yappers and blatherskites!"

Martin ceased abruptly, in a dead silence. Everybody in Ruth's family looked up to Judge Blount as a man of power and achievement, and they were horrified at Martin's outbreak. The remainder of the dinner passed like a funeral, the judge and Mr. Morse confining their talk to each other, and the rest of the conversation being extremely desultory. Then afterward, when Ruth and Martin were alone, there was a scene.

"You are unbearable," she wept.

But his anger still smouldered, and he kept muttering, "The beasts! The beasts!"

When she averred he had insulted the judge, he retorted:-

"By telling the truth about him?"

"I don't care whether it was true or not," she insisted. "There are certain bounds of decency, and you had no license to insult anybody."

"Then where did Judge Blount get the license to assault truth?" Martin demanded. "Surely to assault truth is a more serious misdemeanor than to insult a pygmy personality such as the judge's. He did worse than that. He blackened the name of a great, noble man who is dead. Oh, the beasts! The beasts!"

His complex anger flamed afresh, and Ruth was in terror of him. Never had she seen him so angry, and it was all mystified and unreasonable to her comprehension. And yet, through her very terror ran the fibres of fascination that had drawn and that still drew her to him—that had compelled her to lean towards him, and, in that mad, culminating moment, lay her hands upon his neck. She was hurt and outraged by what had taken place, and yet she lay in his arms and quivered while he went on muttering, "The beasts! The beasts!" And she still lay there when he said: "I'll not bother your table again, dear. They do not like me, and it is wrong of me to thrust my objectionable presence upon them. Besides, they are just as objectionable to me. Faugh! They are sickening. And to think of it, I dreamed in my innocence that the persons who sat in the high places, who lived in fine houses and had educations and bank accounts, were worth while!"

CHAPTER XXXVIII

"Come on, let's go down to the local."

So spoke Brissenden, faint from a hemorrhage of half an hour before—the second hemorrhage in three days. The perennial whiskey glass was in his hands, and he drained it with shaking fingers.

"What do I want with socialism?" Martin demanded.

"Outsiders are allowed five-minute speeches," the sick man urged. "Get up and spout. Tell them why you don't want socialism. Tell them what you think about them and their ghetto ethics. Slam Nietzsche into them and get walloped for your pains. Make a scrap of it. It will do them good. Discussion is what they want, and what you want, too. You see, I'd like to see you a socialist before I'm gone. It will give you a sanction for your existence. It is the one thing that will save you in the time of disappointment that is coming to you."

"I never can puzzle out why you, of all men, are a socialist," Martin pondered. "You detest the crowd so. Surely there is nothing in the canaille to recommend it to your aesthetic soul." He pointed an accusing finger at the whiskey glass which the other was refilling. "Socialism doesn't seem to save you."

"I'm very sick," was the answer. "With you it is different. You have health and much to live for, and you must be handcuffed to life somehow. As for me, you wonder why I am a socialist. I'll tell you. It is because Socialism is inevitable; because the present rotten and irrational system cannot endure; because the day is past for your man on horseback. The slaves won't stand for it. They are too many, and willy-nilly they'll drag down the would-be equestrian before ever he gets astride. You can't get away from them, and you'll have to swallow the whole slave-morality. It's not a nice mess, I'll allow. But it's been a-brewing and swallow it you must. You are antediluvian anyway, with your Nietzsche ideas. The past is past, and the man who says history repeats itself is a liar. Of course I don't like the crowd, but what's a poor chap to do? We can't have the man on horseback, and anything is preferable to the timid swine that now rule. But come on, anyway. I'm loaded to the guards now, and if I sit here any longer, I'll get drunk. And you know the doctor says—damn the doctor! I'll fool him yet."

It was Sunday night, and they found the small hall packed by the Oakland socialists, chiefly members of the working class. The speaker, a clever Jew, won Martin's admiration at the same time that he aroused his antagonism. The man's stooped and narrow shoulders and weazened chest proclaimed him the true child of the crowded ghetto, and strong on Martin was the age-long struggle of the feeble, wretched slaves against the lordly handful of men who had ruled over them and would rule over them to the end of time. To Martin this withered wisp of a creature was a symbol. He was the figure that stood forth representative of the whole miserable mass of weaklings and inefficients who perished according to biological law on the ragged confines of life. They were the unfit. In spite of their cunning philosophy and of their antlike proclivities for coöperation, Nature rejected them for the exceptional man. Out of the plentiful spawn of life she flung from her prolific hand she selected only the best. It was by the same method that men, aping her, bred race-horses and cucumbers. Doubtless, a creator of a Cosmos could have devised a better method; but creatures of this particular Cosmos must put up with this particular method. Of course, they could squirm as they perished, as the socialists squirmed, as the speaker on the platform and the perspiring crowd were squirming even now as they counselled together for some new device with which to minimize the penalties of living and outwit the Cosmos.

So Martin thought, and so he spoke when Brissenden urged him to give them hell. He obeyed the mandate, walking up to the platform, as was the custom, and addressing the chairman. He began in a low voice, haltingly, forming into order the ideas which had surged in his brain while the Jew was speaking. In such meetings five minutes was the time allotted to each speaker; but when Martin's five minutes were up, he was in full stride, his attack upon their doctrines but half completed. He had caught their interest, and the audience urged the chairman by acclamation to extend Martin's time. They appreciated him as a foeman worthy of their intellect, and they listened intently, following every word. He spoke with fire and conviction, mincing no words in his attack upon the slaves and their morality and tactics and frankly alluding to his hearers as the slaves in question. He quoted Spencer and Malthus, and enunciated the biological law of development.

"And so," he concluded, in a swift résumé, "no state composed of the slave-types can endure. The old law of development still holds. In the struggle for existence, as I have shown, the strong and the progeny of the strong tend to survive, while the weak and the progeny of the weak are crushed and tend to perish. The result is that the strong and the progeny of the strong survive, and, so long as the struggle obtains, the strength of each generation increases. That is development. But you slaves—it is too bad to be slaves, I grant—but you slaves dream of a society where the law of development will be annulled, where no weaklings and inefficients will perish, where every inefficient will have as much as he wants to eat as many times a day as he desires, and where all will marry and have progeny—the weak as well as the strong. What will be the result? No longer will the strength and life-value of each generation increase. On the contrary, it will diminish. There is the Nemesis of your slave philosophy. Your society of slaves—of, by, and for, slaves—must inevitably weaken and go to pieces as the life which composes it weakens and goes to pieces.

"Remember, I am enunciating biology and not sentimental ethics. No state of slaves can stand—"

"How about the United States?" a man yelled from the audience.

"And how about it?" Martin retorted. "The thirteen colonies threw off their rulers and formed the Republic so-called. The slaves were their own masters. There were no more masters of the sword. But you couldn't get along without masters of some sort, and there arose a new set of masters—not the great, virile, noble men, but the shrewd and spidery traders and money-lenders. And they enslaved you over again—but not frankly, as the true, noble men would do with weight of their own right arms, but secretly, by spidery machinations and by wheedling and cajolery and lies. They have purchased your slave judges, they have debauched your slave legislatures, and they have forced to worse horrors than chattel slavery your slave boys and girls. Two million of your children are toiling to-day in this trader-oligarchy of the United States. Ten millions of you slaves are not properly sheltered nor properly fed."

"But to return. I have shown that no society of slaves can endure, because, in its very nature, such society must annul the law of development. No sooner can a slave society be organized than deterioration sets in. It is easy for you to talk of annulling the law of development, but where is the new law of development that will maintain your strength? Formulate it. Is it already formulated? Then state it."

Martin took his seat amidst an uproar of voices. A score of men were on their feet clamoring for recognition from the chair. And one by one, encouraged by vociferous applause, speaking with fire and enthusiasm and excited gestures, they replied to the attack. It was a wild night—but it was wild intellectually, a battle of ideas. Some strayed from the point, but most of the speakers replied directly to Martin. They shook him with lines of thought that were new to him; and gave him insights, not into new biological laws, but into new applications of the old laws. They were too earnest to be always polite, and more than once the chairman rapped and pounded for order.

It chanced that a cub reporter sat in the audience, detailed there on a day dull of news and impressed by the urgent need of journalism for sensation. He was not a bright cub reporter. He was merely facile and glib. He was too dense to follow the discussion. In fact, he had a comfortable feeling that he was vastly superior to these wordy maniacs of the working class. Also, he had a great respect for those who sat in the high places and dictated the policies of nations and newspapers. Further, he had an ideal, namely, of achieving that excellence of the perfect reporter who is able to make something—even a great deal—out of nothing.

He did not know what all the talk was about. It was not necessary. Words like *revolution* gave him his cue. Like a paleontologist, able to reconstruct an entire skeleton from one fossil bone, he was able to reconstruct a whole speech from the one word *revolution*. He did it that night, and he did it well; and since Martin had made the biggest stir, he put it all into his mouth and made him the arch-anarch of the show, transforming his reactionary individualism into the most lurid, red-shirt socialist utterance. The cub reporter was an artist, and it was a large brush with which he laid on the local color—wild-eyed long-haired men, neurasthenia and degenerate types of men, voices shaken with passion, clenched fists raised on high, and all projected against a background of oaths, yells, and the throaty rumbling of angry men.

CHAPTER XXXIX

Over the coffee, in his little room, Martin read next morning's paper. It was a novel experience to find himself head-lined, on the first page at that; and he was surprised to learn that he was the most notorious leader of the Oakland socialists. He ran over the violent speech the cub reporter had constructed for him, and, though at first he was angered by the fabrication, in the end he tossed the paper aside with a laugh.

"Either the man was drunk or criminally malicious," he said that afternoon, from his perch on the bed, when Brissenden had arrived and dropped limply into the one chair.

"But what do you care?" Brissenden asked. "Surely you don't desire the approval of the bourgeois swine that read the newspapers?"

Martin thought for a while, then said:-

"No, I really don't care for their approval, not a whit. On the other hand, it's very likely to make my relations with Ruth's family a trifle awkward. Her father always contended I was a socialist, and this miserable stuff will clinch his belief. Not that I care for his opinion—but what's the odds? I want to read you what I've been doing to-day. It's 'Overdue,' of course, and I'm just about halfway through."

He was reading aloud when Maria thrust open the door and ushered in a young man in a natty suit who glanced briskly about him, noting the oil-burner and the kitchen in the corner before his gaze wandered on to Martin.

"Sit down," Brissenden said.

Martin made room for the young man on the bed and waited for him to broach his business.

"I heard you speak last night, Mr. Eden, and I've come to interview you," he began.

Brissenden burst out in a hearty laugh.

"A brother socialist?" the reporter asked, with a quick glance at Brissenden that appraised the color-value of that cadaverous and dying man.

"And he wrote that report," Martin said softly. "Why, he is only a boy!"

"Why don't you poke him?" Brissenden asked. "I'd give a thousand dollars to have my lungs back for five minutes."

The cub reporter was a trifle perplexed by this talking over him and around him and at him. But he had been commended for his brilliant description of the socialist meeting and had further been detailed to get a personal interview with Martin Eden, the leader of the organized menace to society.

"You do not object to having your picture taken, Mr. Eden?" he said. "I've a staff photographer outside, you see, and he says it will be better to take you right away before the sun gets lower. Then we can have the interview afterward."

"A photographer," Brissenden said meditatively. "Poke him, Martin! Poke him!"

"I guess I'm getting old," was the answer. "I know I ought, but I really haven't the heart. It doesn't seem to matter."

"For his mother's sake," Brissenden urged.

"It's worth considering," Martin replied; "but it doesn't seem worth while enough to rouse sufficient energy in me. You see, it does take energy to give a fellow a poking. Besides, what does it matter?"

"That's right—that's the way to take it," the cub announced airily, though he had already begun to glance anxiously at the door.

"But it wasn't true, not a word of what he wrote," Martin went on, confining his attention to Brissenden.

"It was just in a general way a description, you understand," the cub ventured, "and besides, it's good advertising. That's what counts. It was a favor to you."

"It's good advertising, Martin, old boy," Brissenden repeated solemnly.

"And it was a favor to me—think of that!" was Martin's contribution.

"Let me see—where were you born, Mr. Eden?" the cub asked, assuming an air of expectant attention.

"He doesn't take notes," said Brissenden. "He remembers it all."

"That is sufficient for me." The cub was trying not to look worried. "No decent reporter needs to bother with notes."

"That was sufficient—for last night." But Brissenden was not a disciple of quietism, and he changed his attitude abruptly. "Martin, if you don't poke him, I'll do it myself, if I fall dead on the floor the next moment."

"How will a spanking do?" Martin asked.

Brissenden considered judicially, and nodded his head.

The next instant Martin was seated on the edge of the bed with the cub face downward across his knees.

"Now don't bite," Martin warned, "or else I'll have to punch your face. It would be a pity, for it is such a pretty face."

His uplifted hand descended, and thereafter rose and fell in a swift and steady rhythm. The cub struggled and cursed and squirmed, but did not offer to bite. Brissenden looked on gravely, though once he grew excited and gripped the whiskey bottle, pleading, "Here, just let me swat him once."

"Sorry my hand played out," Martin said, when at last he desisted. "It is quite numb."

He uprighted the cub and perched him on the bed.

"I'll have you arrested for this," he snarled, tears of boyish indignation running down his flushed cheeks. "I'll make you sweat for this. You'll see."

"The pretty thing," Martin remarked. "He doesn't realize that he has entered upon the downward path. It is not honest, it is not square, it is not manly, to tell lies about one's fellow-creatures the way he has done, and he doesn't know it."

"He has to come to us to be told," Brissenden filled in a pause.

"Yes, to me whom he has maligned and injured. My grocery will undoubtedly refuse me credit now. The worst of it is that the poor boy will keep on this way until he deteriorates into a first-class newspaper man and also a first-class scoundrel."

"But there is yet time," quoth Brissenden. "Who knows but what you may prove the humble instrument to save him. Why didn't you let me swat him just once? I'd like to have had a hand in it."

"I'll have you arrested, the pair of you, you b-b-big brutes," sobbed the erring soul.

"No, his mouth is too pretty and too weak." Martin shook his head lugubriously. "I'm afraid I've numbed my hand in vain. The young man cannot reform. He will become eventually a very great and successful newspaper man. He has no conscience. That alone will make him great."

With that the cub passed out the door in trepidation to the last for fear that Brissenden would hit him in the back with the bottle he still clutched.

In the next morning's paper Martin learned a great deal more about himself that was new to him. "We are the sworn enemies of society," he found himself quoted as saying in a column interview. "No, we are not anarchists but socialists." When the reporter pointed out to him that there seemed little difference between the two schools, Martin had shrugged his shoulders in silent affirmation. His face was described as bilaterally asymmetrical, and various other signs of degeneration were described. Especially notable were his thuglike hands and the fiery gleams in his blood-shot eyes.

He learned, also, that he spoke nightly to the workmen in the City Hall Park, and that among the anarchists and agitators that there inflamed the minds of the people he drew the largest audiences and made the most revolutionary speeches. The cub painted a high-light picture of his poor little room, its oil-stove and the one chair, and of the death's-head tramp who kept him company and who looked as if he had just emerged from twenty years of solitary confinement in some fortress dungeon.

The cub had been industrious. He had scurried around and nosed out Martin's family history, and procured a photograph of Higginbotham's Cash Store with Bernard Higginbotham himself standing out in front. That gentleman was depicted as an intelligent, dignified businessman who had no patience with his brother-in-law's socialistic views, and no patience with the brother-in-law, either, whom he was quoted as characterizing as a lazy good-for-nothing who wouldn't take a job when it was offered to him and who would go to jail yet. Hermann Von Schmidt, Marian's husband, had likewise been interviewed. He had called Martin the black sheep of the family and repudiated him. "He tried to sponge off of me, but I put a stop to that good and quick," Von Schmidt had said to the reporter. "He knows better than to come bumming around here. A man who won't work is no good, take that from me."

This time Martin was genuinely angry. Brissenden looked upon the affair as a good joke, but he could not console Martin, who knew that it would be no easy task to explain to Ruth. As for her father, he knew that he must be overjoyed with what had happened and that he would make the most of it to break off the engagement. How much he would make of it he was soon to realize. The afternoon mail brought a letter from Ruth. Martin opened it with a premonition of disaster, and read it standing at the open door when he had received it from the postman. As he read, mechanically his hand sought his pocket for the tobacco and brown paper of his old cigarette days.

He was not aware that the pocket was empty or that he had even reached for the materials with which to roll a cigarette.

It was not a passionate letter. There were no touches of anger in it. But all the way through, from the first sentence to the last, was sounded the note of hurt and disappointment. She had expected better of him. She had thought he had got over his youthful wildness, that her love for him had been sufficiently worth while to enable him to live seriously and decently. And now her father and mother had taken a firm stand and commanded that the engagement be broken. That they were justified in this she could not but admit. Their relation could never be a happy one. It had been unfortunate from the first. But one regret she voiced in the whole letter, and it was a bitter one to Martin. "If only you had settled down to some position and attempted to make something of yourself," she wrote. "But it was not to be. Your past life had been too wild and irregular. I can understand that you are not to be blamed. You could act only according to your nature and your early training. So I do not blame you, Martin. Please remember that. It was simply a mistake. As father and mother have contended, we were not made for each other, and we should both be happy because it was discovered not too late." . . "There is no use trying to see me," she said toward the last. "It would be an unhappy meeting for both of us, as well as for my mother. I feel, as it is, that I have caused her great pain and worry. I shall have to do much living to atone for it."

He read it through to the end, carefully, a second time, then sat down and replied. He outlined the remarks he had uttered at the socialist meeting, pointing out that they were in all ways the converse of what the newspaper had put in his mouth. Toward the end of the letter he was God's own lover pleading passionately for love. "Please answer," he said, "and in your answer you have to tell me but one thing. Do you love me? That is all—the answer to that one question."

But no answer came the next day, nor the next. "Overdue" lay untouched upon the table, and each day the heap of returned manuscripts under the table grew larger. For the first time Martin's glorious sleep was interrupted by insomnia, and he tossed through long, restless nights. Three times he called at the Morse home, but was turned away by the servant who answered the bell. Brissenden lay sick in his hotel, too feeble to stir out, and, though Martin was with him often, he did not worry him with his troubles.

For Martin's troubles were many. The aftermath of the cub reporter's deed was even wider than Martin had anticipated. The Portuguese grocer refused him further credit, while the greengrocer, who was an American and proud of it, had called him a traitor to his country and refused further dealings with him—carrying his patriotism to such a degree that he cancelled Martin's account and forbade him ever to attempt to pay it. The talk in the neighborhood reflected the same feeling, and indignation against Martin ran high. No one would have anything to do with a socialist traitor. Poor Maria was dubious and frightened, but she remained loyal. The children of the neighborhood recovered from the awe of the grand carriage which once had visited Martin, and from safe distances they called him "hobo" and "bum." The Silva tribe, however, stanchly defended him, fighting more than one pitched battle for his honor, and black eyes and bloody noses became quite the order of the day and added to Maria's perplexities and troubles.

CHAPTER XXXIX

Once, Martin met Gertrude on the street, down in Oakland, and learned what he knew could not be otherwise—that Bernard Higginbotham was furious with him for having dragged the family into public disgrace, and that he had forbidden him the house.

"Why don't you go away, Martin?" Gertrude had begged. "Go away and get a job somewhere and steady down. Afterwards, when this all blows over, you can come back."

Martin shook his head, but gave no explanations. How could he explain? He was appalled at the awful intellectual chasm that yawned between him and his people. He could never cross it and explain to them his position,—the Nietzschean position, in regard to socialism. There were not words enough in the English language, nor in any language, to make his attitude and conduct intelligible to them. Their highest concept of right conduct, in his case, was to get a job. That was their first word and their last. It constituted their whole lexicon of ideas. Get a job! Go to work! Poor, stupid slaves, he thought, while his sister talked. Small wonder the world belonged to the strong. The slaves were obsessed by their own slavery. A job was to them a golden fetich before which they fell down and worshipped.

He shook his head again, when Gertrude offered him money, though he knew that within the day he would have to make a trip to the pawnbroker.

"Don't come near Bernard now," she admonished him. "After a few months, when he is cooled down, if you want to, you can get the job of drivin' delivery-wagon for him. Any time you want me, just send for me an' I'll come. Don't forget."

She went away weeping audibly, and he felt a pang of sorrow shoot through him at sight of her heavy body and uncouth gait. As he watched her go, the Nietzschean edifice seemed to shake and totter. The slave-class in the abstract was all very well, but it was not wholly satisfactory when it was brought home to his own family. And yet, if there was ever a slave trampled by the strong, that slave was his sister Gertrude. He grinned savagely at the paradox. A fine Nietzsche-man he was, to allow his intellectual concepts to be shaken by the first sentiment or emotion that strayed along—ay, to be shaken by the slave-morality itself, for that was what his pity for his sister really was. The true noble men were above pity and compassion. Pity and compassion had been generated in the subterranean barracoons of the slaves and were no more than the agony and sweat of the crowded miserables and weaklings.

CHAPTER XL

"Overdue" still continued to lie forgotten on the table. Every manuscript that he had had out now lay under the table. Only one manuscript he kept going, and that was Brissenden's "Ephemera." His bicycle and black suit were again in pawn, and the type-writer people were once more worrying about the rent. But such things no longer bothered him. He was seeking a new orientation, and until that was found his life must stand still.

After several weeks, what he had been waiting for happened. He met Ruth on the street. It was true, she was accompanied by her brother, Norman, and it was true that they tried to ignore him and that Norman attempted to wave him aside.

"If you interfere with my sister, I'll call an officer," Norman threatened. "She does not wish to speak with you, and your insistence is insult."

"If you persist, you'll have to call that officer, and then you'll get your name in the papers," Martin answered grimly. "And now, get out of my way and get the officer if you want to. I'm going to talk with Ruth."

"I want to have it from your own lips," he said to her.

She was pale and trembling, but she held up and looked inquiringly.

"The question I asked in my letter," he prompted.

Norman made an impatient movement, but Martin checked him with a swift look.

She shook her head.

"Is all this of your own free will?" he demanded.

"It is." She spoke in a low, firm voice and with deliberation. "It is of my own free will. You have disgraced me so that I am ashamed to meet my friends. They are all talking about me, I know. That is all I can tell you. You have made me very unhappy, and I never wish to see you again."

"Friends! Gossip! Newspaper misreports! Surely such things are not stronger than love! I can only believe that you never loved me."

A blush drove the pallor from her face.

"After what has passed?" she said faintly. "Martin, you do not know what you are saying. I am not common."

"You see, she doesn't want to have anything to do with you," Norman blurted out, starting on with her.

Martin stood aside and let them pass, fumbling unconsciously in his coat pocket for the tobacco and brown papers that were not there.

It was a long walk to North Oakland, but it was not until he went up the steps and entered his room that he knew he had walked it. He found himself sitting on the edge of the bed and staring about him like an awakened somnambulist. He noticed "Overdue" lying on the table and drew up his chair and reached for his pen. There was in his nature a logical compulsion toward completeness. Here was something undone. It had been deferred against the completion of something else. Now that something else had been finished, and he would apply himself to this task until it was finished. What he would do next he did not know. All that he did know was that a climacteric in his life had been attained. A period had been reached, and he was rounding it off in workman-like fashion. He was not curious about the future. He would soon enough find out what it held in store for him. Whatever it was, it did not matter. Nothing seemed to matter.

For five days he toiled on at "Overdue," going nowhere, seeing nobody, and eating meagrely. On the morning of the sixth day the postman brought him a thin letter from the editor of *The Parthenon.* A glance told him that "Ephemera" was accepted. "We have submitted the poem to Mr. Cartwright Bruce," the editor went on to say, "and he has reported so favorably upon it that we cannot let it go. As an earnest of our pleasure in publishing the poem, let me tell you that we have set it for the August number, our July number being already made up. Kindly extend our pleasure and our thanks to Mr. Brissenden. Please send by return mail his photograph and biographical data. If our honorarium is unsatisfactory, kindly telegraph us at once and state what you consider a fair price."

Since the honorarium they had offered was three hundred and fifty dollars, Martin thought it not worth while to telegraph. Then, too, there was Brissenden's consent to be gained. Well, he had been right, after all. Here was one magazine editor who knew real poetry when he saw it. And the price was splendid, even though it was for the poem of a century. As for Cartwright Bruce, Martin knew that he was the one critic for whose opinions Brissenden had any respect.

Martin rode down town on an electric car, and as he watched the houses and cross-streets slipping by he was aware of a regret that he was not more elated over his friend's success and over his own signal victory. The one critic in the United States had pronounced favorably on the poem, while his own contention that good stuff could find its way into the magazines had proved correct. But enthusiasm had lost its spring in him, and he found that he was more anxious to see Brissenden than he was to carry the good news. The acceptance of *The Parthenon* had recalled to him that during his five days' devotion to "Overdue" he had not heard from Brissenden nor even thought about him. For the first time Martin realized the daze he had been in, and he felt shame for having forgotten his friend. But even the shame did not burn very sharply. He was numb to emotions of any sort save the artistic ones concerned in the writing of "Overdue." So far as other affairs were concerned, he had been in a trance. For that matter, he was still in a trance. All this life through which the electric car whirred seemed remote and unreal, and he would have experienced little interest and less shook if the great stone steeple of the church he passed had suddenly crumbled to mortar-dust upon his head.

At the hotel he hurried up to Brissenden's room, and hurried down again. The room was empty. All luggage was gone.

"Did Mr. Brissenden leave any address?" he asked the clerk, who looked at him curiously for a moment.

"Haven't you heard?" he asked.

Martin shook his head.

"Why, the papers were full of it. He was found dead in bed. Suicide. Shot himself through the head."

"Is he buried yet?" Martin seemed to hear his voice, like some one else's voice, from a long way off, asking the question.

"No. The body was shipped East after the inquest. Lawyers engaged by his people saw to the arrangements."

"They were quick about it, I must say," Martin commented.

"Oh, I don't know. It happened five days ago."

"Five days ago?"

"Yes, five days ago."

"Oh," Martin said as he turned and went out.

At the corner he stepped into the Western Union and sent a telegram to *The Parthenon*, advising them to proceed with the publication of the poem. He had in his pocket but five cents with which to pay his carfare home, so he sent the message collect.

Once in his room, he resumed his writing. The days and nights came and went, and he sat at his table and wrote on. He went nowhere, save to the pawnbroker, took no exercise, and ate methodically when he was hungry and had something to cook, and just as methodically went without when he had nothing to cook. Composed as the story was, in advance, chapter by chapter, he nevertheless saw and developed an opening that increased the power of it, though it necessitated twenty thousand additional words. It was not that there was any vital need that the thing should be well done, but that his artistic canons compelled him to do it well. He worked on in the daze, strangely detached from the world around him, feeling like a familiar ghost among these literary trappings of his former life. He remembered that some one had said that a ghost was the spirit of a man who was dead and who did not have sense enough to know it; and he paused for the moment to wonder if he were really dead did unaware of it.

Came the day when "Overdue" was finished. The agent of the type-writer firm had come for the machine, and he sat on the bed while Martin, on the one chair, typed the last pages of the final chapter. "Finis," he wrote, in capitals, at the end, and to him it was indeed finis. He watched the type-writer carried out the door with a feeling of relief, then went over and lay down on the bed. He was faint from hunger. Food had not passed his lips in thirty-six hours, but he did not think about it. He lay on his back, with closed eyes, and did not think at all, while the daze or stupor slowly welled up, saturating his consciousness. Half in delirium, he began muttering aloud the lines of an anonymous poem Brissenden had been fond of quoting to him. Maria, listening anxiously outside his door, was perturbed by his monotonous utterance. The words in themselves were not significant to her, but the fact that he was saying them was. "I have done," was the burden of the poem.

> "'I have done—
> Put by the lute.
> Song and singing soon are over
> As the airy shades that hover
> In among the purple clover.

I have done—
Put by the lute.
Once I sang as early thrushes
Sing among the dewy bushes;
Now I'm mute.
I am like a weary linnet,
For my throat has no song in it;
I have had my singing minute.
I have done.
Put by the lute.'"

Maria could stand it no longer, and hurried away to the stove, where she filled a quart-bowl with soup, putting into it the lion's share of chopped meat and vegetables which her ladle scraped from the bottom of the pot. Martin roused himself and sat up and began to eat, between spoonfuls reassuring Maria that he had not been talking in his sleep and that he did not have any fever.

After she left him he sat drearily, with drooping shoulders, on the edge of the bed, gazing about him with lack-lustre eyes that saw nothing until the torn wrapper of a magazine, which had come in the morning's mail and which lay unopened, shot a gleam of light into his darkened brain. It is *The Parthenon*, he thought, the August *Parthenon*, and it must contain "Ephemera." If only Brissenden were here to see!

He was turning the pages of the magazine, when suddenly he stopped. "Ephemera" had been featured, with gorgeous head-piece and Beardsley-like margin decorations. On one side of the head-piece was Brissenden's photograph, on the other side was the photograph of Sir John Value, the British Ambassador. A preliminary editorial note quoted Sir John Value as saying that there were no poets in America, and the publication of "Ephemera" was *The Parthenon's*. "There, take that, Sir John Value!" Cartwright Bruce was described as the greatest critic in America, and he was quoted as saying that "Ephemera" was the greatest poem ever written in America. And finally, the editor's foreword ended with: "We have not yet made up our minds entirely as to the merits of "Ephemera"; perhaps we shall never be able to do so. But we have read it often, wondering at the words and their arrangement, wondering where Mr. Brissenden got them, and how he could fasten them together." Then followed the poem.

"Pretty good thing you died, Briss, old man," Martin murmured, letting the magazine slip between his knees to the floor.

The cheapness and vulgarity of it was nauseating, and Martin noted apathetically that he was not nauseated very much. He wished he could get angry, but did not have energy enough to try. He was too numb. His blood was too congealed to accelerate to the swift tidal flow of indignation. After all, what did it matter? It was on a par with all the rest that Brissenden had condemned in bourgeois society.

"Poor Briss," Martin communed; "he would never have forgiven me."

Rousing himself with an effort, he possessed himself of a box which had once contained type-writer paper. Going through its contents, he drew forth eleven poems which his friend had written. These he tore lengthwise and crosswise and dropped into the waste basket. He did it languidly, and, when he had finished, sat on the edge of the bed staring blankly before him.

How long he sat there he did not know, until, suddenly, across his sightless vision he saw form a long horizontal line of white. It was curious. But as he watched it grow in definiteness he saw that it was a coral reef smoking in the white Pacific surges. Next, in the line of breakers he made out a small canoe, an outrigger canoe. In the stern he saw a young bronzed god in scarlet hip-cloth dipping a flashing paddle. He recognized him. He was Moti, the youngest son of Tati, the chief, and this was Tahiti, and beyond that smoking reef lay the sweet land of Papara and the chief's grass house by the river's mouth. It was the end of the day, and Moti was coming home from the fishing. He was waiting for the rush of a big breaker whereon to jump the reef. Then he saw himself, sitting forward in the canoe as he had often sat in the past, dipping a paddle that waited Moti's word to dig in like mad when the turquoise wall of the great breaker rose behind them. Next, he was no longer an onlooker but was himself in the canoe, Moti was crying out, they were both thrusting hard with their paddles, racing on the steep face of the flying turquoise. Under the bow the water was hissing as from a steam jet, the air was filled with driven spray, there was a rush and rumble and long-echoing roar, and the canoe floated on the placid water of the lagoon. Moti laughed and shook the salt water from his eyes, and together they paddled in to the pounded-coral beach where Tati's grass walls through the cocoanut-palms showed golden in the setting sun.

The picture faded, and before his eyes stretched the disorder of his squalid room. He strove in vain to see Tahiti again. He knew there was singing among the trees and that the maidens were dancing in the moonlight, but he could not see them. He could see only the littered writing-table, the empty space where the type-writer had stood, and the unwashed window-pane. He closed his eyes with a groan, and slept.

CHAPTER XLI

He slept heavily all night, and did not stir until aroused by the postman on his morning round. Martin felt tired and passive, and went through his letters aimlessly. One thin envelope, from a robber magazine, contained for twenty-two dollars. He had been dunning for it for a year and a half. He noted its amount apathetically. The old-time thrill at receiving a publisher's check was gone. Unlike his earlier checks, this one was not pregnant with promise of great things to come. To him it was a check for twenty-two dollars, that was all, and it would buy him something to eat.

Another check was in the same mail, sent from a New York weekly in payment for some humorous verse which had been accepted months before. It was for ten dollars. An idea came to him, which he calmly considered. He did not know what he was going to do, and he felt in no hurry to do anything. In the meantime he must live. Also he owed numerous debts. Would it not be a paying investment to put stamps on the huge pile of manuscripts under the table and start them on their travels again? One or two of them might be accepted. That would help him to live. He decided on the investment, and, after he had cashed the checks at the bank down in Oakland, he bought ten dollars' worth of postage stamps. The thought of going home to cook breakfast in his stuffy little room was repulsive to him. For the first time he refused to consider his debts. He knew that in his room he could manufacture a substantial breakfast at a cost of from fifteen to twenty cents. But, instead, he went into the Forum Café and ordered a breakfast that cost two dollars. He tipped the waiter a quarter, and spent fifty cents for a package of Egyptian cigarettes. It was the first time he had smoked since Ruth had asked him to stop. But he could see now no reason why he should not, and besides, he wanted to smoke. And what did the money matter? For five cents he could have bought a package of Durham and brown papers and rolled forty cigarettes—but what of it? Money had no meaning to him now except what it would immediately buy. He was chartless and rudderless, and he had no port to make, while drifting involved the least living, and it was living that hurt.

The days slipped along, and he slept eight hours regularly every night. Though now, while waiting for more checks, he ate in the Japanese restaurants where meals were served for ten cents, his wasted body filled out, as did the hollows in his cheeks. He no longer abused himself with short sleep, overwork, and overstudy. He wrote nothing, and the books were closed. He walked much, out in the hills, and loafed long hours in the quiet parks. He had no friends nor acquaintances, nor did he make any. He had no inclination. He was waiting for some impulse, from he knew not where, to put his stopped life into motion again. In the meantime his life remained run down, planless, and empty and idle.

Once he made a trip to San Francisco to look up the "real dirt." But at the last moment, as he stepped into the upstairs entrance, he recoiled and turned and fled through the swarming ghetto. He was frightened at the thought of hearing philosophy discussed, and he fled furtively, for fear that some one of the "real dirt" might chance along and recognize him.

Sometimes he glanced over the magazines and newspapers to see how "Ephemera" was being maltreated. It had made a hit. But what a hit! Everybody had read it, and everybody was discussing whether or not it was really poetry. The local papers had taken it up, and daily there appeared columns of learned criticisms, facetious editorials, and serious letters from subscribers. Helen Della Delmar (proclaimed with a flourish of trumpets and rolling of tomtoms to be the greatest woman poet in the United States) denied Brissenden a seat beside her on Pegasus and wrote voluminous letters to the public, proving that he was no poet.

The Parthenon came out in its next number patting itself on the back for the stir it had made, sneering at Sir John Value, and exploiting Brissenden's death with ruthless commercialism. A newspaper with a sworn circulation of half a million published an original and spontaneous poem by Helen Della Delmar, in which she gibed and sneered at Brissenden. Also, she was guilty of a second poem, in which she parodied him.

Martin had many times to be glad that Brissenden was dead. He had hated the crowd so, and here all that was finest and most sacred of him had been thrown to the crowd. Daily the vivisection of Beauty went on. Every nincompoop in the land rushed into free print, floating their wizened little egos into the public eye on the surge of Brissenden's greatness. Quoth one paper: "We have received a letter from a gentleman who wrote a poem just like it, only better, some time ago." Another paper, in deadly seriousness, reproving Helen Della Delmar for her parody, said: "But unquestionably Miss Delmar wrote it in a moment of badinage and not quite with the respect that one great poet should show to another and perhaps to the greatest. However, whether Miss Delmar be jealous or not of the man who invented 'Ephemera,' it is certain that she, like thousands of others, is fascinated by his work, and that the day may come when she will try to write lines like his."

Ministers began to preach sermons against "Ephemera," and one, who too stoutly stood for much of its content, was expelled for heresy. The great poem contributed to the gayety of the world. The comic verse-writers and the cartoonists took hold of it with screaming laughter, and in the personal columns of society weeklies jokes were perpetrated on it to the effect that Charley Frensham told Archie Jennings, in confidence, that five lines of "Ephemera" would drive a man to beat a cripple, and that ten lines would send him to the bottom of the river.

Martin did not laugh; nor did he grit his teeth in anger. The effect produced upon him was one of great sadness. In the crash of his whole world, with love on the pinnacle, the crash of magazinedom and the dear public was a small crash indeed. Brissenden had been wholly right in his judgment of the magazines, and he, Martin, had spent arduous and futile years in order to find it out for himself. The magazines were all Brissenden had said they were and more. Well, he was done, he solaced himself. He had hitched his wagon to a star and been landed in a pestiferous marsh.

CHAPTER XLI

The visions of Tahiti—clean, sweet Tahiti—were coming to him more frequently. And there were the low Paumotus, and the high Marquesas; he saw himself often, now, on board trading schooners or frail little cutters, slipping out at dawn through the reef at Papeete and beginning the long beat through the pearl-atolls to Nukahiva and the Bay of Taiohae, where Tamari, he knew, would kill a pig in honor of his coming, and where Tamari's flower-garlanded daughters would seize his hands and with song and laughter garland him with flowers. The South Seas were calling, and he knew that sooner or later he would answer the call.

In the meantime he drifted, resting and recuperating after the long traverse he had made through the realm of knowledge. When *The Parthenon* check of three hundred and fifty dollars was forwarded to him, he turned it over to the local lawyer who had attended to Brissenden's affairs for his family. Martin took a receipt for the check, and at the same time gave a note for the hundred dollars Brissenden had let him have.

The time was not long when Martin ceased patronizing the Japanese restaurants. At the very moment when he had abandoned the fight, the tide turned. But it had turned too late. Without a thrill he opened a thick envelope from *The Millennium*, scanned the face of a check that represented three hundred dollars, and noted that it was the payment on acceptance for "Adventure." Every debt he owed in the world, including the pawnshop, with its usurious interest, amounted to less than a hundred dollars. And when he had paid everything, and lifted the hundred-dollar note with Brissenden's lawyer, he still had over a hundred dollars in pocket. He ordered a suit of clothes from the tailor and ate his meals in the best cafés in town. He still slept in his little room at Maria's, but the sight of his new clothes caused the neighborhood children to cease from calling him "hobo" and "tramp" from the roofs of woodsheds and over back fences.

"Wiki-Wiki," his Hawaiian short story, was bought by *Warren's Monthly* for two hundred and fifty dollars. *The Northern Review* took his essay, "The Cradle of Beauty," and *Mackintosh's Magazine* took "The Palmist"—the poem he had written to Marian. The editors and readers were back from their summer vacations, and manuscripts were being handled quickly. But Martin could not puzzle out what strange whim animated them to this general acceptance of the things they had persistently rejected for two years. Nothing of his had been published. He was not known anywhere outside of Oakland, and in Oakland, with the few who thought they knew him, he was notorious as a red-shirt and a socialist. So there was no explaining this sudden acceptability of his wares. It was sheer jugglery of fate.

After it had been refused by a number of magazines, he had taken Brissenden's rejected advice and started, "The Shame of the Sun" on the round of publishers. After several refusals, Singletree, Darnley & Co. accepted it, promising fall publication. When Martin asked for an advance on royalties, they wrote that such was not their custom, that books of that nature rarely paid for themselves, and that they doubted if his book would sell a thousand copies. Martin figured what the book would earn him on such a sale. Retailed at a dollar, on a royalty of fifteen per cent, it would bring him one hundred and fifty dollars. He decided that if he had it to do over again he would confine himself to fiction. "Adventure," one-fourth as long, had brought him twice as much from *The Millennium*. That newspaper paragraph he had read so long ago had been true, after all. The first-class magazines did not pay on acceptance, and they paid well. Not two cents a word, but four cents a word, had *The Millennium* paid him. And, furthermore, they bought good stuff, too, for were they not buying his? This last thought he accompanied with a grin.

He wrote to Singletree, Darnley & Co., offering to sell out his rights in "The Shame of the Sun" for a hundred dollars, but they did not care to take the risk. In the meantime he was not in need of money, for several of his later stories had been accepted and paid for. He actually opened a bank account, where, without a debt in the world, he had several hundred dollars to his credit. "Overdue," after having been declined by a number of magazines, came to rest at the Meredith-Lowell Company. Martin remembered the five dollars Gertrude had given him, and his resolve to return it to her a hundred times over; so he wrote for an advance on royalties of five hundred dollars. To his surprise a check for that amount, accompanied by a contract, came by return mail. He cashed the check into five-dollar gold pieces and telephoned Gertrude that he wanted to see her.

She arrived at the house panting and short of breath from the haste she had made. Apprehensive of trouble, she had stuffed the few dollars she possessed into her hand-satchel; and so sure was she that disaster had overtaken her brother, that she stumbled forward, sobbing, into his arms, at the same time thrusting the satchel mutely at him.

"I'd have come myself," he said. "But I didn't want a row with Mr. Higginbotham, and that is what would have surely happened."

"He'll be all right after a time," she assured him, while she wondered what the trouble was that Martin was in. "But you'd best get a job first an' steady down. Bernard does like to see a man at honest work. That stuff in the newspapers broke 'm all up. I never saw 'm so mad before."

"I'm not going to get a job," Martin said with a smile. "And you can tell him so from me. I don't need a job, and there's the proof of it."

He emptied the hundred gold pieces into her lap in a glinting, tinkling stream.

"You remember that fiver you gave me the time I didn't have carfare? Well, there it is, with ninety-nine brothers of different ages but all of the same size."

If Gertrude had been frightened when she arrived, she was now in a panic of fear. Her fear was such that it was certitude. She was not suspicious. She was convinced. She looked at Martin in horror, and her heavy limbs shrank under the golden stream as though it were burning her.

"It's yours," he laughed.

She burst into tears, and began to moan, "My poor boy, my poor boy!"

He was puzzled for a moment. Then he divined the cause of her agitation and handed her the Meredith-Lowell letter which had accompanied the check. She stumbled through it, pausing now and again to wipe her eyes, and when she had finished, said:-

"An' does it mean that you come by the money honestly?"

"More honestly than if I'd won it in a lottery. I earned it."

Slowly faith came back to her, and she reread the letter carefully. It took him long to explain to her the nature of the transaction which had put the money into his possession, and longer still to get her to understand that the money was really hers and that he did not need it.

"I'll put it in the bank for you," she said finally.

"You'll do nothing of the sort. It's yours, to do with as you please, and if you won't take it, I'll give it to Maria. She'll know what to do with it. I'd suggest, though, that you hire a servant and take a good long rest."

"I'm goin' to tell Bernard all about it," she announced, when she was leaving.

Martin winced, then grinned.

"Yes, do," he said. "And then, maybe, he'll invite me to dinner again."

"Yes, he will—I'm sure he will!" she exclaimed fervently, as she drew him to her and kissed and hugged him.

CHAPTER XLII

One day Martin became aware that he was lonely. He was healthy and strong, and had nothing to do. The cessation from writing and studying, the death of Brissenden, and the estrangement from Ruth had made a big hole in his life; and his life refused to be pinned down to good living in cafés and the smoking of Egyptian cigarettes. It was true the South Seas were calling to him, but he had a feeling that the game was not yet played out in the United States. Two books were soon to be published, and he had more books that might find publication. Money could be made out of them, and he would wait and take a sackful of it into the South Seas. He knew a valley and a bay in the Marquesas that he could buy for a thousand Chili dollars. The valley ran from the horseshoe, land-locked bay to the tops of the dizzy, cloud-capped peaks and contained perhaps ten thousand acres. It was filled with tropical fruits, wild chickens, and wild pigs, with an occasional herd of wild cattle, while high up among the peaks were herds of wild goats harried by packs of wild dogs. The whole place was wild. Not a human lived in it. And he could buy it and the bay for a thousand Chili dollars.

The bay, as he remembered it, was magnificent, with water deep enough to accommodate the largest vessel afloat, and so safe that the South Pacific Directory recommended it to the best careening place for ships for hundreds of miles around. He would buy a schooner—one of those yacht-like, coppered crafts that sailed like witches—and go trading copra and pearling among the islands. He would make the valley and the bay his headquarters. He would build a patriarchal grass house like Tati's, and have it and the valley and the schooner filled with dark-skinned servitors. He would entertain there the factor of Taiohae, captains of wandering traders, and all the best of the South Pacific riffraff. He would keep open house and entertain like a prince. And he would forget the books he had opened and the world that had proved an illusion.

To do all this he must wait in California to fill the sack with money. Already it was beginning to flow in. If one of the books made a strike, it might enable him to sell the whole heap of manuscripts. Also he could collect the stories and the poems into books, and make sure of the valley and the bay and the schooner. He would never write again. Upon that he was resolved. But in the meantime, awaiting the publication of the books, he must do something more than live dazed and stupid in the sort of uncaring trance into which he had fallen.

He noted, one Sunday morning, that the Bricklayers' Picnic took place that day at Shell Mound Park, and to Shell Mound Park he went. He had been to the working-class picnics too often in his earlier life not to know what they were like, and as he entered the park he experienced a recrudescence of all the old sensations. After all, they were his kind, these working people. He had been born among them, he had lived among them, and though he had strayed for a time, it was well to come back among them.

"If it ain't Mart!" he heard some one say, and the next moment a hearty hand was on his shoulder. "Where you ben all the time? Off to sea? Come on an' have a drink."

It was the old crowd in which he found himself—the old crowd, with here and there a gap, and here and there a new face. The fellows were not bricklayers, but, as in the old days, they attended all Sunday picnics for the dancing, and the fighting, and the fun. Martin drank with them, and began to feel really human once more. He was a fool to have ever left them, he thought; and he was very certain that his sum of happiness would have been greater had he remained with them and let alone the books and the people who sat in the high places. Yet the beer seemed not so good as of yore. It didn't taste as it used to taste. Brissenden had spoiled him for steam beer, he concluded, and wondered if, after all, the books had spoiled him for companionship with these friends of his youth. He resolved that he would not be so spoiled, and he went on to the dancing pavilion. Jimmy, the plumber, he met there, in the company of a tall, blond girl who promptly forsook him for Martin.

"Gee, it's like old times," Jimmy explained to the gang that gave him the laugh as Martin and the blonde whirled away in a waltz. "An' I don't give a rap. I'm too damned glad to see 'm back. Watch 'm waltz, eh? It's like silk. Who'd blame any girl?"

But Martin restored the blonde to Jimmy, and the three of them, with half a dozen friends, watched the revolving couples and laughed and joked with one another. Everybody was glad to see Martin back. No book of his been published; he carried no fictitious value in their eyes. They liked him for himself. He felt like a prince returned from excile, and his lonely heart burgeoned in the geniality in which it bathed. He made a mad day of it, and was at his best. Also, he had money in his pockets, and, as in the old days when he returned from sea with a pay-day, he made the money fly.

Once, on the dancing-floor, he saw Lizzie Connolly go by in the arms of a young workingman; and, later, when he made the round of the pavilion, he came upon her sitting by a refreshment table. Surprise and greetings over, he led her away into the grounds, where they could talk without shouting down the music. From the instant he spoke to her, she was his. He knew it. She showed it in the proud humility of her eyes, in every caressing movement of her proudly carried body, and in the way she hung upon his speech. She was not the young girl as he had known her. She was a woman, now, and Martin noted that her wild, defiant beauty had improved, losing none of its wildness, while the defiance and the fire seemed more in control. "A beauty, a perfect beauty," he murmured admiringly under his breath. And he knew she was his, that all he had to do was to say "Come," and she would go with him over the world wherever he led.

Even as the thought flashed through his brain he received a heavy blow on the side of his head that nearly knocked him down. It was a man's fist, directed by a man so angry and in such haste that the fist had missed the jaw for which it was aimed. Martin turned as he staggered, and saw the fist coming at him in a wild swing. Quite as a matter of course he ducked, and the fist flew harmlessly past, pivoting the man who had driven it. Martin hooked with his left, landing on the pivoting man with the weight of his body behind the blow. The man went to the ground sidewise, leaped to his feet, and made a mad rush. Martin saw his passion-distorted face and wondered what could be the cause of the fellow's anger. But while he wondered, he shot in a straight left, the weight of his body behind the blow. The man went over backward and fell in a crumpled heap. Jimmy and others of the gang were running toward them.

Martin was thrilling all over. This was the old days with a vengeance, with their dancing, and their fighting, and their fun. While he kept a wary eye on his antagonist, he glanced at Lizzie. Usually the girls screamed when the fellows got to scrapping, but she had not screamed. She was looking on with bated breath, leaning slightly forward, so keen was her interest, one hand pressed to her breast, her cheek flushed, and in her eyes a great and amazed admiration.

The man had gained his feet and was struggling to escape the restraining arms that were laid on him.

"She was waitin' for me to come back!" he was proclaiming to all and sundry. "She was waitin' for me to come back, an' then that fresh guy comes buttin' in. Let go o' me, I tell yeh. I'm goin' to fix 'm."

"What's eatin' yer?" Jimmy was demanding, as he helped hold the young fellow back. "That guy's Mart Eden. He's nifty with his mits, lemme tell you that, an' he'll eat you alive if you monkey with 'm."

"He can't steal her on me that way," the other interjected.

"He licked the Flyin' Dutchman, an' you know *him*," Jimmy went on expostulating. "An' he did it in five rounds. You couldn't last a minute against him. See?"

This information seemed to have a mollifying effect, and the irate young man favored Martin with a measuring stare.

"He don't look it," he sneered; but the sneer was without passion.

"That's what the Flyin' Dutchman thought," Jimmy assured him. "Come on, now, let's get outa this. There's lots of other girls. Come on."

The young fellow allowed himself to be led away toward the pavilion, and the gang followed after him.

"Who is he?" Martin asked Lizzie. "And what's it all about, anyway?"

Already the zest of combat, which of old had been so keen and lasting, had died down, and he discovered that he was self-analytical, too much so to live, single heart and single hand, so primitive an existence.

Lizzie tossed her head.

"Oh, he's nobody," she said. "He's just ben keepin' company with me."

"I had to, you see," she explained after a pause. "I was gettin' pretty lonesome. But I never forgot." Her voice sank lower, and she looked straight before her. "I'd throw 'm down for you any time."

Martin looking at her averted face, knowing that all he had to do was to reach out his hand and pluck her, fell to pondering whether, after all, there was any real worth in refined, grammatical English, and, so, forgot to reply to her.

"You put it all over him," she said tentatively, with a laugh.

"He's a husky young fellow, though," he admitted generously. "If they hadn't taken him away, he might have given me my hands full."

CHAPTER XLII

"Who was that lady friend I seen you with that night?" she asked abruptly.

"Oh, just a lady friend," was his answer.

"It was a long time ago," she murmured contemplatively. "It seems like a thousand years."

But Martin went no further into the matter. He led the conversation off into other channels. They had lunch in the restaurant, where he ordered wine and expensive delicacies and afterward he danced with her and with no one but her, till she was tired. He was a good dancer, and she whirled around and around with him in a heaven of delight, her head against his shoulder, wishing that it could last forever. Later in the afternoon they strayed off among the trees, where, in the good old fashion, she sat down while he sprawled on his back, his head in her lap. He lay and dozed, while she fondled his hair, looked down on his closed eyes, and loved him without reserve. Looking up suddenly, he read the tender advertisement in her face. Her eyes fluttered down, then they opened and looked into his with soft defiance.

"I've kept straight all these years," she said, her voice so low that it was almost a whisper.

In his heart Martin knew that it was the miraculous truth. And at his heart pleaded a great temptation. It was in his power to make her happy. Denied happiness himself, why should he deny happiness to her? He could marry her and take her down with him to dwell in the grass-walled castle in the Marquesas. The desire to do it was strong, but stronger still was the imperative command of his nature not to do it. In spite of himself he was still faithful to Love. The old days of license and easy living were gone. He could not bring them back, nor could he go back to them. He was changed—how changed he had not realized until now.

"I am not a marrying man, Lizzie," he said lightly.

The hand caressing his hair paused perceptibly, then went on with the same gentle stroke. He noticed her face harden, but it was with the hardness of resolution, for still the soft color was in her cheeks and she was all glowing and melting.

"I did not mean that—" she began, then faltered. "Or anyway I don't care."

"I don't care," she repeated. "I'm proud to be your friend. I'd do anything for you. I'm made that way, I guess."

Martin sat up. He took her hand in his. He did it deliberately, with warmth but without passion; and such warmth chilled her.

"Don't let's talk about it," she said.

"You are a great and noble woman," he said. "And it is I who should be proud to know you. And I am, I am. You are a ray of light to me in a very dark world, and I've got to be straight with you, just as straight as you have been."

"I don't care whether you're straight with me or not. You could do anything with me. You could throw me in the dirt an' walk on me. An' you're the only man in the world that can," she added with a defiant flash. "I ain't taken care of myself ever since I was a kid for nothin'."

"And it's just because of that that I'm not going to," he said gently. "You are so big and generous that you challenge me to equal generousness. I'm not marrying, and I'm not—well, loving without marrying, though I've done my share of that in the past. I'm sorry I came here to-day and met you. But it can't be helped now, and I never expected it would turn out this way."

"But look here, Lizzie. I can't begin to tell you how much I like you. I do more than like you. I admire and respect you. You are magnificent, and you are magnificently good. But what's the use of words? Yet there's something I'd like to do. You've had a hard life; let me make it easy for you." (A joyous light welled into her eyes, then faded out again.) "I'm pretty sure of getting hold of some money soon—lots of it."

In that moment he abandoned the idea of the valley and the bay, the grass-walled castle and the trim, white schooner. After all, what did it matter? He could go away, as he had done so often, before the mast, on any ship bound anywhere.

"I'd like to turn it over to you. There must be something you want—to go to school or business college. You might like to study and be a stenographer. I could fix it for you. Or maybe your father and mother are living—I could set them up in a grocery store or something. Anything you want, just name it, and I can fix it for you."

She made no reply, but sat, gazing straight before her, dry-eyed and motionless, but with an ache in the throat which Martin divined so strongly that it made his own throat ache. He regretted that he had spoken. It seemed so tawdry what he had offered her—mere money—compared with what she offered him. He offered her an extraneous thing with which he could part without a pang, while she offered him herself, along with disgrace and shame, and sin, and all her hopes of heaven.

"Don't let's talk about it," she said with a catch in her voice that she changed to a cough. She stood up. "Come on, let's go home. I'm all tired out."

The day was done, and the merrymakers had nearly all departed. But as Martin and Lizzie emerged from the trees they found the gang waiting for them. Martin knew immediately the meaning of it. Trouble was brewing. The gang was his bodyguard. They passed out through the gates of the park with, straggling in the rear, a second gang, the friends that Lizzie's young man had collected to avenge the loss of his lady. Several constables and special police officers, anticipating trouble, trailed along to prevent it, and herded the two gangs separately aboard the train for San Francisco. Martin told Jimmy that he would get off at Sixteenth Street Station and catch the electric car into Oakland. Lizzie was very quiet and without interest in what was impending. The train pulled in to Sixteenth Street Station, and the waiting electric car could be seen, the conductor of which was impatiently clanging the gong.

"There she is," Jimmy counselled. "Make a run for it, an' we'll hold 'em back. Now you go! Hit her up!"

The hostile gang was temporarily disconcerted by the manoeuvre, then it dashed from the train in pursuit. The staid and sober Oakland folk who sat upon the car scarcely noted the young fellow and the girl who ran for it and found a seat in front on the outside. They did not connect the couple with Jimmy, who sprang on the steps, crying to the motorman:-

"Slam on the juice, old man, and beat it outa here!"

The next moment Jimmy whirled about, and the passengers saw him land his fist on the face of a running man who was trying to board the car. But fists were landing on faces the whole length of the car. Thus, Jimmy and his gang, strung out on the long, lower steps, met the attacking gang. The car started with a great clanging of its gong, and, as Jimmy's gang drove off the last assailants, they, too, jumped off to finish the job. The car dashed on, leaving the flurry of combat far behind, and its dumfounded passengers never dreamed that the quiet young man and the pretty working-girl sitting in the corner on the outside seat had been the cause of the row.

Martin had enjoyed the fight, with a recrudescence of the old fighting thrills. But they quickly died away, and he was oppressed by a great sadness. He felt very old—centuries older than those careless, care-free young companions of his others days. He had travelled far, too far to go back. Their mode of life, which had once been his, was now distasteful to him. He was disappointed in it all. He had developed into an alien. As the steam beer had tasted raw, so their companionship seemed raw to him. He was too far removed. Too many thousands of opened books yawned between them and him. He had exiled himself. He had travelled in the vast realm of intellect until he could no longer return home. On the other hand, he was human, and his gregarious need for companionship remained unsatisfied. He had found no new home. As the gang could not understand him, as his own family could not understand him, as the bourgeoisie could not understand him, so this girl beside him, whom he honored high, could not understand him nor the honor he paid her. His sadness was not untouched with bitterness as he thought it over.

"Make it up with him," he advised Lizzie, at parting, as they stood in front of the workingman's shack in which she lived, near Sixth and Market. He referred to the young fellow whose place he had usurped that day.

"I can't—now," she said.

"Oh, go on," he said jovially. "All you have to do is whistle and he'll come running."

"I didn't mean that," she said simply.

And he knew what she had meant.

She leaned toward him as he was about to say good night. But she leaned not imperatively, not seductively, but wistfully and humbly. He was touched to the heart. His large tolerance rose up in him. He put his arms around her, and kissed her, and knew that upon his own lips rested as true a kiss as man ever received.

"My God!" she sobbed. "I could die for you. I could die for you."

She tore herself from him suddenly and ran up the steps. He felt a quick moisture in his eyes.

"Martin Eden," he communed. "You're not a brute, and you're a damn poor Nietzscheman. You'd marry her if you could and fill her quivering heart full with happiness. But you can't, you can't. And it's a damn shame."

"'A poor old tramp explains his poor old ulcers,'" he muttered, remembering his Henly. "'Life is, I think, a blunder and a shame.' It is—a blunder and a shame."

CHAPTER XLIII

"The Shame of the Sun" was published in October. As Martin cut the cords of the express package and the half-dozen complimentary copies from the publishers spilled out on the table, a heavy sadness fell upon him. He thought of the wild delight that would have been his had this happened a few short months before, and he contrasted that delight that should have been with his present uncaring coldness. His book, his first book, and his pulse had not gone up a fraction of a beat, and he was only sad. It meant little to him now. The most it meant was that it might bring some money, and little enough did he care for money.

He carried a copy out into the kitchen and presented it to Maria.

"I did it," he explained, in order to clear up her bewilderment. "I wrote it in the room there, and I guess some few quarts of your vegetable soup went into the making of it. Keep it. It's yours. Just to remember me by, you know."

He was not bragging, not showing off. His sole motive was to make her happy, to make her proud of him, to justify her long faith in him. She put the book in the front room on top of the family Bible. A sacred thing was this book her lodger had made, a fetich of friendship. It softened the blow of his having been a laundryman, and though she could not understand a line of it, she knew that every line of it was great. She was a simple, practical, hard-working woman, but she possessed faith in large endowment.

Just as emotionlessly as he had received "The Shame of the Sun" did he read the reviews of it that came in weekly from the clipping bureau. The book was making a hit, that was evident. It meant more gold in the money sack. He could fix up Lizzie, redeem all his promises, and still have enough left to build his grass-walled castle.

Singletree, Darnley & Co. had cautiously brought out an edition of fifteen hundred copies, but the first reviews had started a second edition of twice the size through the presses; and ere this was delivered a third edition of five thousand had been ordered. A London firm made arrangements by cable for an English edition, and hot-footed upon this came the news of French, German, and Scandinavian translations in progress. The attack upon the Maeterlinck school could not have been made at a more opportune moment. A fierce controversy was precipitated. Saleeby and Haeckel indorsed and defended "The Shame of the Sun," for once finding themselves on the same side of a question. Crookes and Wallace ranged up on the opposing side, while Sir Oliver Lodge attempted to formulate a compromise that would jibe with his particular cosmic theories. Maeterlinck's followers rallied around the standard of mysticism. Chesterton set the whole world laughing with a series of alleged non-partisan essays on the subject, and the whole affair, controversy and controversialists, was well-nigh swept into the pit by a thundering broadside from George Bernard Shaw. Needless to say the arena was crowded with hosts of lesser lights, and the dust and sweat and din became terrific.

"It is a most marvellous happening," Singletree, Darnley & Co. wrote Martin, "a critical philosophic essay selling like a novel. You could not have chosen your subject better, and all contributory factors have been unwarrantedly propitious. We need scarcely to assure you that we are making hay while the sun shines. Over forty thousand copies have already been sold in the United States and Canada, and a new edition of twenty thousand is on the presses. We are overworked, trying to supply the demand. Nevertheless we have helped to create that demand. We have already spent five thousand dollars in advertising. The book is bound to be a record-breaker."

"Please find herewith a contract in duplicate for your next book which we have taken the liberty of forwarding to you. You will please note that we have increased your royalties to twenty per cent, which is about as high as a conservative publishing house dares go. If our offer is agreeable to you, please fill in the proper blank space with the title of your book. We make no stipulations concerning its nature. Any book on any subject. If you have one already written, so much the better. Now is the time to strike. The iron could not be hotter."

"On receipt of signed contract we shall be pleased to make you an advance on royalties of five thousand dollars. You see, we have faith in you, and we are going in on this thing big. We should like, also, to discuss with you the drawing up of a contract for a term of years, say ten, during which we shall have the exclusive right of publishing in book-form all that you produce. But more of this anon."

Martin laid down the letter and worked a problem in mental arithmetic, finding the product of fifteen cents times sixty thousand to be nine thousand dollars. He signed the new contract, inserting "The Smoke of Joy" in the blank space, and mailed it back to the publishers along with the twenty storiettes he had written in the days before he discovered the formula for the newspaper storiette. And promptly as the United States mail could deliver and return, came Singletree, Darnley & Co.'s check for five thousand dollars.

"I want you to come down town with me, Maria, this afternoon about two o'clock," Martin said, the morning the check arrived. "Or, better, meet me at Fourteenth and Broadway at two o'clock. I'll be looking out for you."

At the appointed time she was there; but *shoes* was the only clew to the mystery her mind had been capable of evolving, and she suffered a distinct shock of disappointment when Martin walked her right by a shoe-store and dived into a real estate office. What happened thereupon resided forever after in her memory as a dream. Fine gentlemen smiled at her benevolently as they talked with Martin and one another; a type-writer clicked; signatures were affixed to an imposing document; her own landlord was there, too, and affixed his signature; and when all was over and she was outside on the sidewalk, her landlord spoke to her, saying, "Well, Maria, you won't have to pay me no seven dollars and a half this month."

Maria was too stunned for speech.

"Or next month, or the next, or the next," her landlord said.

She thanked him incoherently, as if for a favor. And it was not until she had returned home to North Oakland and conferred with her own kind, and had the Portuguese grocer investigate, that she really knew that she was the owner of the little house in which she had lived and for which she had paid rent so long.

"Why don't you trade with me no more?" the Portuguese grocer asked Martin that evening, stepping out to hail him when he got off the car; and Martin explained that he wasn't doing his own cooking any more, and then went in and had a drink of wine on the house. He noted it was the best wine the grocer had in stock.

"Maria," Martin announced that night, "I'm going to leave you. And you're going to leave here yourself soon. Then you can rent the house and be a landlord yourself. You've a brother in San Leandro or Haywards, and he's in the milk business. I want you to send all your washing back unwashed—understand?—unwashed, and to go out to San Leandro to-morrow, or Haywards, or wherever it is, and see that brother of yours. Tell him to come to see me. I'll be stopping at the Metropole down in Oakland. He'll know a good milk-ranch when he sees one."

And so it was that Maria became a landlord and the sole owner of a dairy, with two hired men to do the work for her and a bank account that steadily increased despite the fact that her whole brood wore shoes and went to school. Few persons ever meet the fairy princes they dream about; but Maria, who worked hard and whose head was hard, never dreaming about fairy princes, entertained hers in the guise of an ex-laundryman.

In the meantime the world had begun to ask: "Who is this Martin Eden?" He had declined to give any biographical data to his publishers, but the newspapers were not to be denied. Oakland was his own town, and the reporters nosed out scores of individuals who could supply information. All that he was and was not, all that he had done and most of what he had not done, was spread out for the delectation of the public, accompanied by snapshots and photographs—the latter procured from the local photographer who had once taken Martin's picture and who promptly copyrighted it and put it on the market. At first, so great was his disgust with the magazines and all bourgeois society, Martin fought against publicity; but in the end, because it was easier than not to, he surrendered. He found that he could not refuse himself to the special writers who travelled long distances to see him. Then again, each day was so many hours long, and, since he no longer was occupied with writing and studying, those hours had to be occupied somehow; so he yielded to what was to him a whim, permitted interviews, gave his opinions on literature and philosophy, and even accepted invitations of the bourgeoisie. He had settled down into a strange and comfortable state of mind. He no longer cared. He forgave everybody, even the cub reporter who had painted him red and to whom he now granted a full page with specially posed photographs.

He saw Lizzie occasionally, and it was patent that she regretted the greatness that had come to him. It widened the space between them. Perhaps it was with the hope of narrowing it that she yielded to his persuasions to go to night school and business college and to have herself gowned by a wonderful dressmaker who charged outrageous prices. She improved visibly from day to day, until Martin wondered if he was doing right, for he knew that all her compliance and endeavor was for his sake. She was trying to make herself of worth in his eyes—of the sort of worth he seemed to value. Yet he gave her no hope, treating her in brotherly fashion and rarely seeing her.

"Overdue" was rushed upon the market by the Meredith-Lowell Company in the height of his popularity, and being fiction, in point of sales it made even a bigger strike than "The Shame of the Sun." Week after week his was the credit of the unprecedented performance of having two books at the head of the list of best-sellers. Not only did the story take with the fiction-readers, but those who read "The Shame of the Sun" with avidity were likewise attracted to the sea-story by the cosmic grasp of mastery with which he had handled it. First he had attacked the literature of mysticism, and had done it exceeding well; and, next, he had successfully supplied the very literature he had exposited, thus proving himself to be that rare genius, a critic and a creator in one.

Money poured in on him, fame poured in on him; he flashed, comet-like, through the world of literature, and he was more amused than interested by the stir he was making. One thing was puzzling him, a little thing that would have puzzled the world had it known. But the world would have puzzled over his bepuzzlement rather than over the little thing that to him loomed gigantic. Judge Blount invited him to dinner. That was the little thing, or the beginning of the little thing, that was soon to become the big thing. He had insulted Judge Blount, treated him abominably, and Judge Blount, meeting him on the street, invited him to dinner. Martin bethought himself of the numerous occasions on which he had met Judge Blount at the Morses' and when Judge Blount had not invited him to dinner. Why had he not invited him to dinner then? he asked himself. He had not changed. He was the same Martin Eden. What made the difference? The fact that the stuff he had written had appeared inside the covers of books? But it was work performed. It was not something he had done since. It was achievement accomplished at the very time Judge Blount was sharing this general view and sneering at his Spencer and his intellect. Therefore it was not for any real value, but for a purely fictitious value that Judge Blount invited him to dinner.

Martin grinned and accepted the invitation, marvelling the while at his complacence. And at the dinner, where, with their womankind, were half a dozen of those that sat in high places, and where Martin found himself quite the lion, Judge Blount, warmly seconded by Judge Hanwell, urged privately that Martin should permit his name to be put up for the Styx—the ultra-select club to which belonged, not the mere men of wealth, but the men of attainment. And Martin declined, and was more puzzled than ever.

He was kept busy disposing of his heap of manuscripts. He was overwhelmed by requests from editors. It had been discovered that he was a stylist, with meat under his style. *The Northern Review*, after publishing "The Cradle of Beauty," had written him for half a dozen similar essays, which would have been supplied out of the heap, had not *Burton's Magazine*, in a speculative mood, offered him five hundred dollars each for five essays. He wrote back that he would supply the demand, but at a thousand dollars an essay. He remembered that all these manuscripts had been refused by the very magazines that were now clamoring for them. And their refusals had been cold-blooded, automatic, stereotyped. They had made him sweat, and now he intended to make them sweat. *Burton's Magazine* paid his price for five essays, and the remaining four, at the same rate, were snapped up by *Mackintosh's Monthly, The*

Northern Review being too poor to stand the pace. Thus went out to the world "The High Priests of Mystery," "The Wonder-Dreamers," "The Yardstick of the Ego," "Philosophy of Illusion," "God and Clod," "Art and Biology," "Critics and Test-tubes," "Star-dust," and "The Dignity of Usury,"—to raise storms and rumblings and mutterings that were many a day in dying down.

Editors wrote to him telling him to name his own terms, which he did, but it was always for work performed. He refused resolutely to pledge himself to any new thing. The thought of again setting pen to paper maddened him. He had seen Brissenden torn to pieces by the crowd, and despite the fact that him the crowd acclaimed, he could not get over the shock nor gather any respect for the crowd. His very popularity seemed a disgrace and a treason to Brissenden. It made him wince, but he made up his mind to go on and fill the money-bag.

He received letters from editors like the following: "About a year ago we were unfortunate enough to refuse your collection of love-poems. We were greatly impressed by them at the time, but certain arrangements already entered into prevented our taking them. If you still have them, and if you will be kind enough to forward them, we shall be glad to publish the entire collection on your own terms. We are also prepared to make a most advantageous offer for bringing them out in book-form."

Martin recollected his blank-verse tragedy, and sent it instead. He read it over before mailing, and was particularly impressed by its sophomoric amateurishness and general worthlessness. But he sent it; and it was published, to the everlasting regret of the editor. The public was indignant and incredulous. It was too far a cry from Martin Eden's high standard to that serious bosh. It was asserted that he had never written it, that the magazine had faked it very clumsily, or that Martin Eden was emulating the elder Dumas and at the height of success was hiring his writing done for him. But when he explained that the tragedy was an early effort of his literary childhood, and that the magazine had refused to be happy unless it got it, a great laugh went up at the magazine's expense and a change in the editorship followed. The tragedy was never brought out in book-form, though Martin pocketed the advance royalties that had been paid.

Coleman's Weekly sent Martin a lengthy telegram, costing nearly three hundred dollars, offering him a thousand dollars an article for twenty articles. He was to travel over the United States, with all expenses paid, and select whatever topics interested him. The body of the telegram was devoted to hypothetical topics in order to show him the freedom of range that was to be his. The only restriction placed upon him was that he must confine himself to the United States. Martin sent his inability to accept and his regrets by wire "collect."

"Wiki-Wiki," published in *Warren's Monthly*, was an instantaneous success. It was brought out forward in a wide-margined, beautifully decorated volume that struck the holiday trade and sold like wildfire. The critics were unanimous in the belief that it would take its place with those two classics by two great writers, "The Bottle Imp" and "The Magic Skin."

The public, however, received the "Smoke of Joy" collection rather dubiously and coldly. The audacity and unconventionality of the storiettes was a shock to bourgeois morality and prejudice; but when Paris went mad over the immediate translation that was made, the American and English reading public followed suit and bought so many copies that Martin compelled the conservative house of Singletree, Darnley &

Co. to pay a flat royalty of twenty-five per cent for a third book, and thirty per cent flat for a fourth. These two volumes comprised all the short stories he had written and which had received, or were receiving, serial publication. "The Ring of Bells" and his horror stories constituted one collection; the other collection was composed of "Adventure," "The Pot," "The Wine of Life," "The Whirlpool," "The Jostling Street," and four other stories. The Lowell-Meredith Company captured the collection of all his essays, and the Maxmillian Company got his "Sea Lyrics" and the "Love-cycle," the latter receiving serial publication in the *Ladies' Home Companion* after the payment of an extortionate price.

Martin heaved a sigh of relief when he had disposed of the last manuscript. The grass-walled castle and the white, coppered schooner were very near to him. Well, at any rate he had discovered Brissenden's contention that nothing of merit found its way into the magazines. His own success demonstrated that Brissenden had been wrong.

And yet, somehow, he had a feeling that Brissenden had been right, after all. "The Shame of the Sun" had been the cause of his success more than the stuff he had written. That stuff had been merely incidental. It had been rejected right and left by the magazines. The publication of "The Shame of the Sun" had started a controversy and precipitated the landslide in his favor. Had there been no "Shame of the Sun" there would have been no landslide, and had there been no miracle in the go of "The Shame of the Sun" there would have been no landslide. Singletree, Darnley & Co. attested that miracle. They had brought out a first edition of fifteen hundred copies and been dubious of selling it. They were experienced publishers and no one had been more astounded than they at the success which had followed. To them it had been in truth a miracle. They never got over it, and every letter they wrote him reflected their reverent awe of that first mysterious happening. They did not attempt to explain it. There was no explaining it. It had happened. In the face of all experience to the contrary, it had happened.

So it was, reasoning thus, that Martin questioned the validity of his popularity. It was the bourgeoisie that bought his books and poured its gold into his money-sack, and from what little he knew of the bourgeoisie it was not clear to him how it could possibly appreciate or comprehend what he had written. His intrinsic beauty and power meant nothing to the hundreds of thousands who were acclaiming him and buying his books. He was the fad of the hour, the adventurer who had stormed Parnassus while the gods nodded. The hundreds of thousands read him and acclaimed him with the same brute non-understanding with which they had flung themselves on Brissenden's "Ephemera" and torn it to pieces—a wolf-rabble that fawned on him instead of fanging him. Fawn or fang, it was all a matter of chance. One thing he knew with absolute certitude: "Ephemera" was infinitely greater than anything he had done. It was infinitely greater than anything he had in him. It was a poem of centuries. Then the tribute the mob paid him was a sorry tribute indeed, for that same mob had wallowed "Ephemera" into the mire. He sighed heavily and with satisfaction. He was glad the last manuscript was sold and that he would soon be done with it all.

CHAPTER XLIV

Mr. Morse met Martin in the office of the Hotel Metropole. Whether he had happened there just casually, intent on other affairs, or whether he had come there for the direct purpose of inviting him to dinner, Martin never could quite make up his mind, though he inclined toward the second hypothesis. At any rate, invited to dinner he was by Mr. Morse—Ruth's father, who had forbidden him the house and broken off the engagement.

Martin was not angry. He was not even on his dignity. He tolerated Mr. Morse, wondering the while how it felt to eat such humble pie. He did not decline the invitation. Instead, he put it off with vagueness and indefiniteness and inquired after the family, particularly after Mrs. Morse and Ruth. He spoke her name without hesitancy, naturally, though secretly surprised that he had had no inward quiver, no old, familiar increase of pulse and warm surge of blood.

He had many invitations to dinner, some of which he accepted. Persons got themselves introduced to him in order to invite him to dinner. And he went on puzzling over the little thing that was becoming a great thing. Bernard Higginbotham invited him to dinner. He puzzled the harder. He remembered the days of his desperate starvation when no one invited him to dinner. That was the time he needed dinners, and went weak and faint for lack of them and lost weight from sheer famine. That was the paradox of it. When he wanted dinners, no one gave them to him, and now that he could buy a hundred thousand dinners and was losing his appetite, dinners were thrust upon him right and left. But why? There was no justice in it, no merit on his part. He was no different. All the work he had done was even at that time work performed. Mr. and Mrs. Morse had condemned him for an idler and a shirk and through Ruth had urged that he take a clerk's position in an office. Furthermore, they had been aware of his work performed. Manuscript after manuscript of his had been turned over to them by Ruth. They had read them. It was the very same work that had put his name in all the papers, and, it was his name being in all the papers that led them to invite him.

One thing was certain: the Morses had not cared to have him for himself or for his work. Therefore they could not want him now for himself or for his work, but for the fame that was his, because he was somebody amongst men, and—why not?—because he had a hundred thousand dollars or so. That was the way bourgeois society valued a man, and who was he to expect it otherwise? But he was proud. He disdained such valuation. He desired to be valued for himself, or for his work, which, after all, was an expression of himself. That was the way Lizzie valued him. The work, with her, did not even count. She valued him, himself. That was the way Jimmy, the plumber, and all the old gang valued him. That had been proved often enough in the days when he ran with them; it had been proved that Sunday at Shell Mound Park. His work could go hang. What they liked, and were willing to scrap for, was just Mart Eden, one of the bunch and a pretty good guy.

Then there was Ruth. She had liked him for himself, that was indisputable. And yet, much as she had liked him she had liked the bourgeois standard of valuation more. She had opposed his writing, and principally, it seemed to him, because it did not earn money. That had been her criticism of his "Love-cycle." She, too, had urged him to get a job. It was true, she refined it to "position," but it meant the same thing, and in his own mind the old nomenclature stuck. He had read her all that he wrote—poems, stories, essays—"Wiki-Wiki," "The Shame of the Sun," everything. And she had always and consistently urged him to get a job, to go to work—good God!—as if he hadn't been working, robbing sleep, exhausting life, in order to be worthy of her.

So the little thing grew bigger. He was healthy and normal, ate regularly, slept long hours, and yet the growing little thing was becoming an obsession. *Work performed.* The phrase haunted his brain. He sat opposite Bernard Higginbotham at a heavy Sunday dinner over Higginbotham's Cash Store, and it was all he could do to restrain himself from shouting out:-

"It was work performed! And now you feed me, when then you let me starve, forbade me your house, and damned me because I wouldn't get a job. And the work was already done, all done. And now, when I speak, you check the thought unuttered on your lips and hang on my lips and pay respectful attention to whatever I choose to say. I tell you your party is rotten and filled with grafters, and instead of flying into a rage you hum and haw and admit there is a great deal in what I say. And why? Because I'm famous; because I've a lot of money. Not because I'm Martin Eden, a pretty good fellow and not particularly a fool. I could tell you the moon is made of green cheese and you would subscribe to the notion, at least you would not repudiate it, because I've got dollars, mountains of them. And it was all done long ago; it was work performed, I tell you, when you spat upon me as the dirt under your feet."

But Martin did not shout out. The thought gnawed in his brain, an unceasing torment, while he smiled and succeeded in being tolerant. As he grew silent, Bernard Higginbotham got the reins and did the talking. He was a success himself, and proud of it. He was self-made. No one had helped him. He owed no man. He was fulfilling his duty as a citizen and bringing up a large family. And there was Higginbotham's Cash Store, that monument of his own industry and ability. He loved Higginbotham's Cash Store as some men loved their wives. He opened up his heart to Martin, showed with what keenness and with what enormous planning he had made the store. And he had plans for it, ambitious plans. The neighborhood was growing up fast. The store was really too small. If he had more room, he would be able to put in a score of labor-saving and money-saving improvements. And he would do it yet. He was straining every effort for the day when he could buy the adjoining lot and put up another two-story frame building. The upstairs he could rent, and the whole ground-floor of both buildings would be Higginbotham's Cash Store. His eyes glistened when he spoke of the new sign that would stretch clear across both buildings.

Martin forgot to listen. The refrain of "Work performed," in his own brain, was drowning the other's clatter. The refrain maddened him, and he tried to escape from it.

"How much did you say it would cost?" he asked suddenly.

His brother-in-law paused in the middle of an expatiation on the business opportunities of the neighborhood. He hadn't said how much it would cost. But he knew. He had figured it out a score of times.

"At the way lumber is now," he said, "four thousand could do it."

"Including the sign?"

"I didn't count on that. It'd just have to come, onc't the buildin' was there."

"And the ground?"

"Three thousand more."

He leaned forward, licking his lips, nervously spreading and closing his fingers, while he watched Martin write a check. When it was passed over to him, he glanced at the amount-seven thousand dollars.

"I—I can't afford to pay more than six per cent," he said huskily.

Martin wanted to laugh, but, instead, demanded:-

"How much would that be?"

"Lemme see. Six per cent—six times seven—four hundred an' twenty."

"That would be thirty-five dollars a month, wouldn't it?"

Higginbotham nodded.

"Then, if you've no objection, well arrange it this way." Martin glanced at Gertrude. "You can have the principal to keep for yourself, if you'll use the thirty-five dollars a month for cooking and washing and scrubbing. The seven thousand is yours if you'll guarantee that Gertrude does no more drudgery. Is it a go?"

Mr. Higginbotham swallowed hard. That his wife should do no more housework was an affront to his thrifty soul. The magnificent present was the coating of a pill, a bitter pill. That his wife should not work! It gagged him.

"All right, then," Martin said. "I'll pay the thirty-five a month, and—"

He reached across the table for the check. But Bernard Higginbotham got his hand on it first, crying:

"I accept! I accept!"

When Martin got on the electric car, he was very sick and tired. He looked up at the assertive sign.

"The swine," he groaned. "The swine, the swine."

When *Mackintosh's Magazine* published "The Palmist," featuring it with decorations by Berthier and with two pictures by Wenn, Hermann von Schmidt forgot that he had called the verses obscene. He announced that his wife had inspired the poem, saw to it that the news reached the ears of a reporter, and submitted to an interview by a staff writer who was accompanied by a staff photographer and a staff artist. The result was a full page in a Sunday supplement, filled with photographs and idealized drawings of Marian, with many intimate details of Martin Eden and his family, and with the full text of "The Palmist" in large type, and republished by special permission of *Mackintosh's Magazine*. It caused quite a stir in the neighborhood, and good housewives were proud to have the acquaintances of the great writer's sister, while those who had not made haste to cultivate it. Hermann von Schmidt chuckled in his little repair shop and decided to order a new lathe. "Better than advertising," he told Marian, "and it costs nothing."

"We'd better have him to dinner," she suggested.

And to dinner Martin came, making himself agreeable with the fat wholesale butcher and his fatter wife—important folk, they, likely to be of use to a rising young man like Hermann Von Schmidt. No less a bait, however, had been required to draw them to his house than his great brother-in-law. Another man at table who had swallowed the same bait was the superintendent of the Pacific Coast agencies for the Asa Bicycle Company. Him Von Schmidt desired to please and propitiate because from him could be obtained the Oakland agency for the bicycle. So Hermann von Schmidt found it a goodly asset to have Martin for a brother-in-law, but in his heart of hearts he couldn't understand where it all came in. In the silent watches of the night, while his wife slept, he had floundered through Martin's books and poems, and decided that the world was a fool to buy them.

And in his heart of hearts Martin understood the situation only too well, as he leaned back and gloated at Von Schmidt's head, in fancy punching it well-nigh off of him, sending blow after blow home just right—the chuckle-headed Dutchman! One thing he did like about him, however. Poor as he was, and determined to rise as he was, he nevertheless hired one servant to take the heavy work off of Marian's hands. Martin talked with the superintendent of the Asa agencies, and after dinner he drew him aside with Hermann, whom he backed financially for the best bicycle store with fittings in Oakland. He went further, and in a private talk with Hermann told him to keep his eyes open for an automobile agency and garage, for there was no reason that he should not be able to run both establishments successfully.

With tears in her eyes and her arms around his neck, Marian, at parting, told Martin how much she loved him and always had loved him. It was true, there was a perceptible halt midway in her assertion, which she glossed over with more tears and kisses and incoherent stammerings, and which Martin inferred to be her appeal for forgiveness for the time she had lacked faith in him and insisted on his getting a job.

"He can't never keep his money, that's sure," Hermann von Schmidt confided to his wife. "He got mad when I spoke of interest, an' he said damn the principal and if I mentioned it again, he'd punch my Dutch head off. That's what he said—my Dutch head. But he's all right, even if he ain't no business man. He's given me my chance, an' he's all right."

Invitations to dinner poured in on Martin; and the more they poured, the more he puzzled. He sat, the guest of honor, at an Arden Club banquet, with men of note whom he had heard about and read about all his life; and they told him how, when they had read "The Ring of Bells" in the *Transcontinental*, and "The Peri and the Pearl" in *The Hornet*, they had immediately picked him for a winner. My God! and I was hungry and in rags, he thought to himself. Why didn't you give me a dinner then? Then was the time. It was work performed. If you are feeding me now for work performed, why did you not feed me then when I needed it? Not one word in "The Ring of Bells," nor in "The Peri and the Pearl" has been changed. No; you're not feeding me now for work performed. You are feeding me because everybody else is feeding me and because it is an honor to feed me. You are feeding me now because you are herd animals; because you are part of the mob; because the one blind, automatic thought in the mob-mind just now is to feed me. And where does Martin Eden and the work Martin Eden performed come in in all this? he asked himself plaintively, then arose to respond cleverly and wittily to a clever and witty toast.

So it went. Wherever he happened to be—at the Press Club, at the Redwood Club, at pink teas and literary gatherings—always were remembered "The Ring of Bells" and "The Peri and the Pearl" when they were first published. And always was Martin's maddening and unuttered demand: Why didn't you feed me then? It was work performed. "The Ring of Bells" and "The Peri and the Pearl" are not changed one iota. They were just as artistic, just as worth while, then as now. But you are not feeding me for their sake, nor for the sake of anything else I have written. You're feeding me because it is the style of feeding just now, because the whole mob is crazy with the idea of feeding Martin Eden.

And often, at such times, he would abruptly see slouch in among the company a young hoodlum in square-cut coat and under a stiff-rim Stetson hat. It happened to him at the Gallina Society in Oakland one afternoon. As he rose from his chair and stepped forward across the platform, he saw stalk through the wide door at the rear of the great room the young hoodlum with the square-cut coat and stiff-rim hat. Five hundred fashionably gowned women turned their heads, so intent and steadfast was Martin's gaze, to see what he was seeing. But they saw only the empty centre aisle. He saw the young tough lurching down that aisle and wondered if he would remove the stiff-rim which never yet had he seen him without. Straight down the aisle he came, and up the platform. Martin could have wept over that youthful shade of himself, when he thought of all that lay before him. Across the platform he swaggered, right up to Martin, and into the foreground of Martin's consciousness disappeared. The five hundred women applauded softly with gloved hands, seeking to encourage the bashful great man who was their guest. And Martin shook the vision from his brain, smiled, and began to speak.

The Superintendent of Schools, good old man, stopped Martin on the street and remembered him, recalling seances in his office when Martin was expelled from school for fighting.

"I read your 'Ring of Bells' in one of the magazines quite a time ago," he said. "It was as good as Poe. Splendid, I said at the time, splendid!"

Yes, and twice in the months that followed you passed me on the street and did not know me, Martin almost said aloud. Each time I was hungry and heading for the pawnbroker. Yet it was work performed. You did not know me then. Why do you know me now?

"I was remarking to my wife only the other day," the other was saying, "wouldn't it be a good idea to have you out to dinner some time? And she quite agreed with me. Yes, she quite agreed with me."

"Dinner?" Martin said so sharply that it was almost a snarl.

"Why, yes, yes, dinner, you know—just pot luck with us, with your old superintendent, you rascal," he uttered nervously, poking Martin in an attempt at jocular fellowship.

Martin went down the street in a daze. He stopped at the corner and looked about him vacantly.

"Well, I'll be damned!" he murmured at last. "The old fellow was afraid of me."

CHAPTER XLV

Kreis came to Martin one day—Kreis, of the "real dirt"; and Martin turned to him with relief, to receive the glowing details of a scheme sufficiently wild-catty to interest him as a fictionist rather than an investor. Kreis paused long enough in the midst of his exposition to tell him that in most of his "Shame of the Sun" he had been a chump.

"But I didn't come here to spout philosophy," Kreis went on. "What I want to know is whether or not you will put a thousand dollars in on this deal?"

"No, I'm not chump enough for that, at any rate," Martin answered. "But I'll tell you what I will do. You gave me the greatest night of my life. You gave me what money cannot buy. Now I've got money, and it means nothing to me. I'd like to turn over to you a thousand dollars of what I don't value for what you gave me that night and which was beyond price. You need the money. I've got more than I need. You want it. You came for it. There's no use scheming it out of me. Take it."

Kreis betrayed no surprise. He folded the check away in his pocket.

"At that rate I'd like the contract of providing you with many such nights," he said.

"Too late." Martin shook his head. "That night was the one night for me. I was in paradise. It's commonplace with you, I know. But it wasn't to me. I shall never live at such a pitch again. I'm done with philosophy. I want never to hear another word of it."

"The first dollar I ever made in my life out of my philosophy," Kreis remarked, as he paused in the doorway. "And then the market broke."

Mrs. Morse drove by Martin on the street one day, and smiled and nodded. He smiled back and lifted his hat. The episode did not affect him. A month before it might have disgusted him, or made him curious and set him to speculating about her state of consciousness at that moment. But now it was not provocative of a second thought. He forgot about it the next moment. He forgot about it as he would have forgotten the Central Bank Building or the City Hall after having walked past them. Yet his mind was preternaturally active. His thoughts went ever around and around in a circle. The centre of that circle was "work performed"; it ate at his brain like a deathless maggot. He awoke to it in the morning. It tormented his dreams at night. Every affair of life around him that penetrated through his senses immediately related itself to "work performed." He drove along the path of relentless logic to the conclusion that he was nobody, nothing. Mart Eden, the hoodlum, and Mart Eden, the sailor, had been real, had been he; but Martin Eden! the famous writer, did not exist. Martin Eden, the famous writer, was a vapor that had arisen in the mob-mind and by the mob-mind had been thrust into the corporeal being of Mart Eden, the hoodlum and sailor. But it couldn't fool him. He was not that sun-myth that the mob was worshipping and sacrificing dinners to. He knew better.

He read the magazines about himself, and pored over portraits of himself published therein until he was unable to associate his identity with those portraits. He was the fellow who had lived and thrilled and loved; who had been easy-going and tolerant of the frailties of life; who had served in the forecastle, wandered in strange lands, and led his gang in the old fighting days. He was the fellow who had been stunned at first by the thousands of books in the free library, and who had afterward learned his way among them and mastered them; he was the fellow who had burned the midnight oil and bedded with a spur and written books himself. But the one thing he was not was that colossal appetite that all the mob was bent upon feeding.

There were things, however, in the magazines that amused him. All the magazines were claiming him. *Warren's Monthly* advertised to its subscribers that it was always on the quest after new writers, and that, among others, it had introduced Martin Eden to the reading public. *The White Mouse* claimed him; so did *The Northern Review* and *Mackintosh's Magazine*, until silenced by *The Globe*, which pointed triumphantly to its files where the mangled "Sea Lyrics" lay buried. *Youth and Age*, which had come to life again after having escaped paying its bills, put in a prior claim, which nobody but farmers' children ever read. The *Transcontinental* made a dignified and convincing statement of how it first discovered Martin Eden, which was warmly disputed by *The Hornet*, with the exhibit of "The Peri and the Pearl." The modest claim of Singletree, Darnley & Co. was lost in the din. Besides, that publishing firm did not own a magazine wherewith to make its claim less modest.

The newspapers calculated Martin's royalties. In some way the magnificent offers certain magazines had made him leaked out, and Oakland ministers called upon him in a friendly way, while professional begging letters began to clutter his mail. But worse than all this were the women. His photographs were published broadcast, and special writers exploited his strong, bronzed face, his scars, his heavy shoulders, his clear, quiet eyes, and the slight hollows in his cheeks like an ascetic's. At this last he remembered his wild youth and smiled. Often, among the women he met, he would see now one, now another, looking at him, appraising him, selecting him. He laughed to himself. He remembered Brissenden's warning and laughed again. The women would never destroy him, that much was certain. He had gone past that stage.

Once, walking with Lizzie toward night school, she caught a glance directed toward him by a well-gowned, handsome woman of the bourgeoisie. The glance was a trifle too long, a shade too considerative. Lizzie knew it for what it was, and her body tensed angrily. Martin noticed, noticed the cause of it, told her how used he was becoming to it and that he did not care anyway.

"You ought to care," she answered with blazing eyes. "You're sick. That's what's the matter."

"Never healthier in my life. I weigh five pounds more than I ever did."

"It ain't your body. It's your head. Something's wrong with your think-machine. Even I can see that, an' I ain't nobody."

He walked on beside her, reflecting.

CHAPTER XLV

"I'd give anything to see you get over it," she broke out impulsively. "You ought to care when women look at you that way, a man like you. It's not natural. It's all right enough for sissy-boys. But you ain't made that way. So help me, I'd be willing an' glad if the right woman came along an' made you care."

When he left Lizzie at night school, he returned to the Metropole.

Once in his rooms, he dropped into a Morris chair and sat staring straight before him. He did not doze. Nor did he think. His mind was a blank, save for the intervals when unsummoned memory pictures took form and color and radiance just under his eyelids. He saw these pictures, but he was scarcely conscious of them—no more so than if they had been dreams. Yet he was not asleep. Once, he roused himself and glanced at his watch. It was just eight o'clock. He had nothing to do, and it was too early for bed. Then his mind went blank again, and the pictures began to form and vanish under his eyelids. There was nothing distinctive about the pictures. They were always masses of leaves and shrub-like branches shot through with hot sunshine.

A knock at the door aroused him. He was not asleep, and his mind immediately connected the knock with a telegram, or letter, or perhaps one of the servants bringing back clean clothes from the laundry. He was thinking about Joe and wondering where he was, as he said, "Come in."

He was still thinking about Joe, and did not turn toward the door. He heard it close softly. There was a long silence. He forgot that there had been a knock at the door, and was still staring blankly before him when he heard a woman's sob. It was involuntary, spasmodic, checked, and stifled—he noted that as he turned about. The next instant he was on his feet.

"Ruth!" he said, amazed and bewildered.

Her face was white and strained. She stood just inside the door, one hand against it for support, the other pressed to her side. She extended both hands toward him piteously, and started forward to meet him. As he caught her hands and led her to the Morris chair he noticed how cold they were. He drew up another chair and sat down on the broad arm of it. He was too confused to speak. In his own mind his affair with Ruth was closed and sealed. He felt much in the same way that he would have felt had the Shelly Hot Springs Laundry suddenly invaded the Hotel Metropole with a whole week's washing ready for him to pitch into. Several times he was about to speak, and each time he hesitated.

"No one knows I am here," Ruth said in a faint voice, with an appealing smile.

"What did you say?"

He was surprised at the sound of his own voice.

She repeated her words.

"Oh," he said, then wondered what more he could possibly say.

"I saw you come in, and I waited a few minutes."

"Oh," he said again.

He had never been so tongue-tied in his life. Positively he did not have an idea in his head. He felt stupid and awkward, but for the life of him he could think of nothing to say. It would have been easier had the intrusion been the Shelly Hot Springs laundry. He could have rolled up his sleeves and gone to work.

"And then you came in," he said finally.

She nodded, with a slightly arch expression, and loosened the scarf at her throat.

"I saw you first from across the street when you were with that girl."

"Oh, yes," he said simply. "I took her down to night school."

"Well, aren't you glad to see me?" she said at the end of another silence.

"Yes, yes." He spoke hastily. "But wasn't it rash of you to come here?"

"I slipped in. Nobody knows I am here. I wanted to see you. I came to tell you I have been very foolish. I came because I could no longer stay away, because my heart compelled me to come, because—because I wanted to come."

She came forward, out of her chair and over to him. She rested her hand on his shoulder a moment, breathing quickly, and then slipped into his arms. And in his large, easy way, desirous of not inflicting hurt, knowing that to repulse this proffer of herself was to inflict the most grievous hurt a woman could receive, he folded his arms around her and held her close. But there was no warmth in the embrace, no caress in the contact. She had come into his arms, and he held her, that was all. She nestled against him, and then, with a change of position, her hands crept up and rested upon his neck. But his flesh was not fire beneath those hands, and he felt awkward and uncomfortable.

"What makes you tremble so?" he asked. "Is it a chill? Shall I light the grate?"

He made a movement to disengage himself, but she clung more closely to him, shivering violently.

"It is merely nervousness," she said with chattering teeth. "I'll control myself in a minute. There, I am better already."

Slowly her shivering died away. He continued to hold her, but he was no longer puzzled. He knew now for what she had come.

"My mother wanted me to marry Charley Hapgood," she announced.

"Charley Hapgood, that fellow who speaks always in platitudes?" Martin groaned. Then he added, "And now, I suppose, your mother wants you to marry me."

He did not put it in the form of a question. He stated it as a certitude, and before his eyes began to dance the rows of figures of his royalties.

"She will not object, I know that much," Ruth said.

"She considers me quite eligible?"

Ruth nodded.

"And yet I am not a bit more eligible now than I was when she broke our engagement," he meditated. "I haven't changed any. I'm the same Martin Eden, though for that matter I'm a bit worse—I smoke now. Don't you smell my breath?"

In reply she pressed her open fingers against his lips, placed them graciously and playfully, and in expectancy of the kiss that of old had always been a consequence. But there was no caressing answer of Martin's lips. He waited until the fingers were removed and then went on.

"I am not changed. I haven't got a job. I'm not looking for a job. Furthermore, I am not going to look for a job. And I still believe that Herbert Spencer is a great and noble man and that Judge Blount is an unmitigated ass. I had dinner with him the other night, so I ought to know."

"But you didn't accept father's invitation," she chided.

"So you know about that? Who sent him? Your mother?"

She remained silent.

"Then she did send him. I thought so. And now I suppose she has sent you."

"No one knows that I am here," she protested. "Do you think my mother would permit this?"

"She'd permit you to marry me, that's certain."

She gave a sharp cry. "Oh, Martin, don't be cruel. You have not kissed me once. You are as unresponsive as a stone. And think what I have dared to do." She looked about her with a shiver, though half the look was curiosity. "Just think of where I am."

"*I could die for you! I could die for you*!"—Lizzie's words were ringing in his ears.

"Why didn't you dare it before?" he asked harshly. "When I hadn't a job? When I was starving? When I was just as I am now, as a man, as an artist, the same Martin Eden? That's the question I've been propounding to myself for many a day—not concerning you merely, but concerning everybody. You see I have not changed, though my sudden apparent appreciation in value compels me constantly to reassure myself on that point. I've got the same flesh on my bones, the same ten fingers and toes. I am the same. I have not developed any new strength nor virtue. My brain is the same old brain. I haven't made even one new generalization on literature or philosophy. I am personally of the same value that I was when nobody wanted me. And what is puzzling me is why they want me now. Surely they don't want me for myself, for myself is the same old self they did not want. Then they must want me for something else, for something that is outside of me, for something that is not I! Shall I tell you what that something is? It is for the recognition I have received. That recognition is not I. It resides in the minds of others. Then again for the money I have earned and am earning. But that money is not I. It resides in banks and in the pockets of Tom, Dick, and Harry. And is it for that, for the recognition and the money, that you now want me?"

"You are breaking my heart," she sobbed. "You know I love you, that I am here because I love you."

"I am afraid you don't see my point," he said gently. "What I mean is: if you love me, how does it happen that you love me now so much more than you did when your love was weak enough to deny me?"

"Forget and forgive," she cried passionately. "I loved you all the time, remember that, and I am here, now, in your arms."

"I'm afraid I am a shrewd merchant, peering into the scales, trying to weigh your love and find out what manner of thing it is."

She withdrew herself from his arms, sat upright, and looked at him long and searchingly. She was about to speak, then faltered and changed her mind.

"You see, it appears this way to me," he went on. "When I was all that I am now, nobody out of my own class seemed to care for me. When my books were all written, no one who had read the manuscripts seemed to care for them. In point of fact, because of the stuff I had written they seemed to care even less for me. In writing the stuff it seemed that I had committed acts that were, to say the least, derogatory. 'Get a job,' everybody said."

She made a movement of dissent.

"Yes, yes," he said; "except in your case you told me to get a position. The homely word *job*, like much that I have written, offends you. It is brutal. But I assure you it was no less brutal to me when everybody I knew recommended it to me as they would recommend right conduct to an immoral creature. But to return. The publication of what I had written, and the public notice I received, wrought a change in the fibre of your love. Martin Eden, with his work all performed, you would not marry. Your love for him was not strong enough to enable you to marry him. But your love is now strong enough, and I cannot avoid the conclusion that its strength arises from the publication and the public notice. In your case I do not mention royalties, though I am certain that they apply to the change wrought in your mother and father. Of course, all this is not flattering to me. But worst of all, it makes me question love, sacred love. Is love so gross a thing that it must feed upon publication and public notice? It would seem so. I have sat and thought upon it till my head went around."

"Poor, dear head." She reached up a hand and passed the fingers soothingly through his hair. "Let it go around no more. Let us begin anew, now. I loved you all the time. I know that I was weak in yielding to my mother's will. I should not have done so. Yet I have heard you speak so often with broad charity of the fallibility and frailty of humankind. Extend that charity to me. I acted mistakenly. Forgive me."

"Oh, I do forgive," he said impatiently. "It is easy to forgive where there is really nothing to forgive. Nothing that you have done requires forgiveness. One acts according to one's lights, and more than that one cannot do. As well might I ask you to forgive me for my not getting a job."

"I meant well," she protested. "You know that I could not have loved you and not meant well."

"True; but you would have destroyed me out of your well-meaning."

"Yes, yes," he shut off her attempted objection. "You would have destroyed my writing and my career. Realism is imperative to my nature, and the bourgeois spirit hates realism. The bourgeoisie is cowardly. It is afraid of life. And all your effort was to make me afraid of life. You would have formalized me. You would have compressed me into a two-by-four pigeonhole of life, where all life's values are unreal, and false, and vulgar." He felt her stir protestingly. "Vulgarity—a hearty vulgarity, I'll admit—is the basis of bourgeois refinement and culture. As I say, you wanted to formalize me, to make me over into one of your own class, with your class-ideals, class-values, and class-prejudices." He shook his head sadly. "And you do not understand, even now, what I am saying. My words do not mean to you what I endeavor to make them mean. What I say is so much fantasy to you. Yet to me it is vital reality. At the best you are a trifle puzzled and amused that this raw boy, crawling up out of the mire of the abyss, should pass judgment upon your class and call it vulgar."

She leaned her head wearily against his shoulder, and her body shivered with recurrent nervousness. He waited for a time for her to speak, and then went on.

"And now you want to renew our love. You want us to be married. You want me. And yet, listen—if my books had not been noticed, I'd nevertheless have been just what I am now. And you would have stayed away. It is all those damned books—"

"Don't swear," she interrupted.

Her reproof startled him. He broke into a harsh laugh.

"That's it," he said, "at a high moment, when what seems your life's happiness is at stake, you are afraid of life in the same old way—afraid of life and a healthy oath."

She was stung by his words into realization of the puerility of her act, and yet she felt that he had magnified it unduly and was consequently resentful. They sat in silence for a long time, she thinking desperately and he pondering upon his love which had departed. He knew, now, that he had not really loved her. It was an idealized Ruth he had loved, an ethereal creature of his own creating, the bright and luminous spirit of his love-poems. The real bourgeois Ruth, with all the bourgeois failings and with the hopeless cramp of the bourgeois psychology in her mind, he had never loved.

She suddenly began to speak.

"I know that much you have said is so. I have been afraid of life. I did not love you well enough. I have learned to love better. I love you for what you are, for what you were, for the ways even by which you have become. I love you for the ways wherein you differ from what you call my class, for your beliefs which I do not understand but which I know I can come to understand. I shall devote myself to understanding them. And even your smoking and your swearing—they are part of you and I will love you for them, too. I can still learn. In the last ten minutes I have learned much. That I have dared to come here is a token of what I have already learned. Oh, Martin!—"

She was sobbing and nestling close against him.

For the first time his arms folded her gently and with sympathy, and she acknowledged it with a happy movement and a brightening face.

"It is too late," he said. He remembered Lizzie's words. "I am a sick man—oh, not my body. It is my soul, my brain. I seem to have lost all values. I care for nothing. If you had been this way a few months ago, it would have been different. It is too late, now."

"It is not too late," she cried. "I will show you. I will prove to you that my love has grown, that it is greater to me than my class and all that is dearest to me. All that is dearest to the bourgeoisie I will flout. I am no longer afraid of life. I will leave my father and mother, and let my name become a by-word with my friends. I will come to you here and now, in free love if you will, and I will be proud and glad to be with you. If I have been a traitor to love, I will now, for love's sake, be a traitor to all that made that earlier treason."

She stood before him, with shining eyes.

"I am waiting, Martin," she whispered, "waiting for you to accept me. Look at me."

It was splendid, he thought, looking at her. She had redeemed herself for all that she had lacked, rising up at last, true woman, superior to the iron rule of bourgeois convention. It was splendid, magnificent, desperate. And yet, what was the matter with him? He was not thrilled nor stirred by what she had done. It was splendid and magnificent only intellectually. In what should have been a moment of fire, he coldly appraised her. His heart was untouched. He was unaware of any desire for her. Again he remembered Lizzie's words.

"I am sick, very sick," he said with a despairing gesture. "How sick I did not know till now. Something has gone out of me. I have always been unafraid of life, but I never dreamed of being sated with life. Life has so filled me that I am empty of any desire for anything. If there were room, I should want you, now. You see how sick I am."

He leaned his head back and closed his eyes; and like a child, crying, that forgets its grief in watching the sunlight percolate through the tear-dimmed films over the pupils, so Martin forgot his sickness, the presence of Ruth, everything, in watching the masses of vegetation, shot through hotly with sunshine that took form and blazed against this background of his eyelids. It was not restful, that green foliage. The sunlight was too raw and glaring. It hurt him to look at it, and yet he looked, he knew not why.

He was brought back to himself by the rattle of the door-knob. Ruth was at the door.

"How shall I get out?" she questioned tearfully. "I am afraid."

"Oh, forgive me," he cried, springing to his feet. "I'm not myself, you know. I forgot you were here." He put his hand to his head. "You see, I'm not just right. I'll take you home. We can go out by the servants' entrance. No one will see us. Pull down that veil and everything will be all right."

She clung to his arm through the dim-lighted passages and down the narrow stairs.

"I am safe now," she said, when they emerged on the sidewalk, at the same time starting to take her hand from his arm.

"No, no, I'll see you home," he answered.

"No, please don't," she objected. "It is unnecessary."

Again she started to remove her hand. He felt a momentary curiosity. Now that she was out of danger she was afraid. She was in almost a panic to be quit of him. He could see no reason for it and attributed it to her nervousness. So he restrained her withdrawing hand and started to walk on with her. Halfway down the block, he saw a man in a long overcoat shrink back into a doorway. He shot a glance in as he passed by, and, despite the high turned-up collar, he was certain that he recognized Ruth's brother, Norman.

During the walk Ruth and Martin held little conversation. She was stunned. He was apathetic. Once, he mentioned that he was going away, back to the South Seas, and, once, she asked him to forgive her having come to him. And that was all. The parting at her door was conventional. They shook hands, said good night, and he lifted his hat. The door swung shut, and he lighted a cigarette and turned back for his hotel. When he came to the doorway into which he had seen Norman shrink, he stopped and looked in in a speculative humor.

"She lied," he said aloud. "She made believe to me that she had dared greatly, and all the while she knew the brother that brought her was waiting to take her back." He burst into laughter. "Oh, these bourgeois! When I was broke, I was not fit to be seen with his sister. When I have a bank account, he brings her to me."

As he swung on his heel to go on, a tramp, going in the same direction, begged him over his shoulder.

"Say, mister, can you give me a quarter to get a bed?" were the words.

But it was the voice that made Martin turn around. The next instant he had Joe by the hand.

"D'ye remember that time we parted at the Hot Springs?" the other was saying. "I said then we'd meet again. I felt it in my bones. An' here we are."

"You're looking good," Martin said admiringly, "and you've put on weight."

"I sure have." Joe's face was beaming. "I never knew what it was to live till I hit hoboin'. I'm thirty pounds heavier an' feel tiptop all the time. Why, I was worked to skin an' bone in them old days. Hoboin' sure agrees with me."

"But you're looking for a bed just the same," Martin chided, "and it's a cold night."

"Huh? Lookin' for a bed?" Joe shot a hand into his hip pocket and brought it out filled with small change. "That beats hard graft," he exulted. "You just looked good; that's why I battered you."

Martin laughed and gave in.

"You've several full-sized drunks right there," he insinuated.

Joe slid the money back into his pocket.

"Not in mine," he announced. "No gettin' oryide for me, though there ain't nothin' to stop me except I don't want to. I've ben drunk once since I seen you last, an' then it was unexpected, bein' on an empty stomach. When I work like a beast, I drink like a beast. When I live like a man, I drink like a man—a jolt now an' again when I feel like it, an' that's all."

Martin arranged to meet him next day, and went on to the hotel. He paused in the office to look up steamer sailings. The *Mariposa* sailed for Tahiti in five days.

"Telephone over to-morrow and reserve a stateroom for me," he told the clerk. "No deck-stateroom, but down below, on the weather-side,—the port-side, remember that, the port-side. You'd better write it down."

Once in his room he got into bed and slipped off to sleep as gently as a child. The occurrences of the evening had made no impression on him. His mind was dead to impressions. The glow of warmth with which he met Joe had been most fleeting. The succeeding minute he had been bothered by the ex-laundryman's presence and by the compulsion of conversation. That in five more days he sailed for his loved South Seas meant nothing to him. So he closed his eyes and slept normally and comfortably for eight uninterrupted hours. He was not restless. He did not change his position, nor did he dream. Sleep had become to him oblivion, and each day that he awoke, he awoke with regret. Life worried and bored him, and time was a vexation.

CHAPTER XLVI

"Say, Joe," was his greeting to his old-time working-mate next morning, "there's a Frenchman out on Twenty-eighth Street. He's made a pot of money, and he's going back to France. It's a dandy, well-appointed, small steam laundry. There's a start for you if you want to settle down. Here, take this; buy some clothes with it and be at this man's office by ten o'clock. He looked up the laundry for me, and he'll take you out and show you around. If you like it, and think it is worth the price—twelve thousand—let me know and it is yours. Now run along. I'm busy. I'll see you later."

"Now look here, Mart," the other said slowly, with kindling anger, "I come here this mornin' to see you. Savve? I didn't come here to get no laundry. I come a here for a talk for old friends' sake, and you shove a laundry at me. I tell you, what you can do. You can take that laundry an' go to hell."

He was out of the room when Martin caught him and whirled him around.

"Now look here, Joe," he said; "if you act that way, I'll punch your head. An for old friends' sake I'll punch it hard. Savve?—you will, will you?"

Joe had clinched and attempted to throw him, and he was twisting and writhing out of the advantage of the other's hold. They reeled about the room, locked in each other's arms, and came down with a crash across the splintered wreckage of a wicker chair. Joe was underneath, with arms spread out and held and with Martin's knee on his chest. He was panting and gasping for breath when Martin released him.

"Now we'll talk a moment," Martin said. "You can't get fresh with me. I want that laundry business finished first of all. Then you can come back and we'll talk for old sake's sake. I told you I was busy. Look at that."

A servant had just come in with the morning mail, a great mass of letters and magazines.

"How can I wade through that and talk with you? You go and fix up that laundry, and then we'll get together."

"All right," Joe admitted reluctantly. "I thought you was turnin' me down, but I guess I was mistaken. But you can't lick me, Mart, in a stand-up fight. I've got the reach on you."

"We'll put on the gloves sometime and see," Martin said with a smile.

"Sure; as soon as I get that laundry going." Joe extended his arm. "You see that reach? It'll make you go a few."

Martin heaved a sigh of relief when the door closed behind the laundryman. He was becoming anti-social. Daily he found it a severer strain to be decent with people.

Their presence perturbed him, and the effort of conversation irritated him. They made him restless, and no sooner was he in contact with them than he was casting about for excuses to get rid of them.

He did not proceed to attack his mail, and for a half hour he lolled in his chair, doing nothing, while no more than vague, half-formed thoughts occasionally filtered through his intelligence, or rather, at wide intervals, themselves constituted the flickering of his intelligence.

He roused himself and began glancing through his mail. There were a dozen requests for autographs—he knew them at sight; there were professional begging letters; and there were letters from cranks, ranging from the man with a working model of perpetual motion, and the man who demonstrated that the surface of the earth was the inside of a hollow sphere, to the man seeking financial aid to purchase the Peninsula of Lower California for the purpose of communist colonization. There were letters from women seeking to know him, and over one such he smiled, for enclosed was her receipt for pew-rent, sent as evidence of her good faith and as proof of her respectability.

Editors and publishers contributed to the daily heap of letters, the former on their knees for his manuscripts, the latter on their knees for his books—his poor disdained manuscripts that had kept all he possessed in pawn for so many dreary months in order to find them in postage. There were unexpected checks for English serial rights and for advance payments on foreign translations. His English agent announced the sale of German translation rights in three of his books, and informed him that Swedish editions, from which he could expect nothing because Sweden was not a party to the Berne Convention, were already on the market. Then there was a nominal request for his permission for a Russian translation, that country being likewise outside the Berne Convention.

He turned to the huge bundle of clippings which had come in from his press bureau, and read about himself and his vogue, which had become a furore. All his creative output had been flung to the public in one magnificent sweep. That seemed to account for it. He had taken the public off its feet, the way Kipling had, that time when he lay near to death and all the mob, animated by a mob-mind thought, began suddenly to read him. Martin remembered how that same world-mob, having read him and acclaimed him and not understood him in the least, had, abruptly, a few months later, flung itself upon him and torn him to pieces. Martin grinned at the thought. Who was he that he should not be similarly treated in a few more months? Well, he would fool the mob. He would be away, in the South Seas, building his grass house, trading for pearls and copra, jumping reefs in frail outriggers, catching sharks and bonitas, hunting wild goats among the cliffs of the valley that lay next to the valley of Taiohae.

In the moment of that thought the desperateness of his situation dawned upon him. He saw, cleared eyed, that he was in the Valley of the Shadow. All the life that was in him was fading, fainting, making toward death.

He realized how much he slept, and how much he desired to sleep. Of old, he had hated sleep. It had robbed him of precious moments of living. Four hours of sleep in the twenty-four had meant being robbed of four hours of life. How he had grudged sleep! Now it was life he grudged. Life was not good; its taste in his mouth was without tang, and bitter. This was his peril. Life that did not yearn toward life was in fair way toward ceasing. Some remote instinct for preservation stirred in him, and he knew he must get away. He glanced about the room, and the thought of packing was burdensome. Perhaps it would be better to leave that to the last. In the meantime he might be getting an outfit.

He put on his hat and went out, stopping in at a gun-store, where he spent the remainder of the morning buying automatic rifles, ammunition, and fishing tackle. Fashions changed in trading, and he knew he would have to wait till he reached Tahiti before ordering his trade-goods. They could come up from Australia, anyway. This solution was a source of pleasure. He had avoided doing something, and the doing of anything just now was unpleasant. He went back to the hotel gladly, with a feeling of satisfaction in that the comfortable Morris chair was waiting for him; and he groaned inwardly, on entering his room, at sight of Joe in the Morris chair.

Joe was delighted with the laundry. Everything was settled, and he would enter into possession next day. Martin lay on the bed, with closed eyes, while the other talked on. Martin's thoughts were far away—so far away that he was rarely aware that he was thinking. It was only by an effort that he occasionally responded. And yet this was Joe, whom he had always liked. But Joe was too keen with life. The boisterous impact of it on Martin's jaded mind was a hurt. It was an aching probe to his tired sensitiveness. When Joe reminded him that sometime in the future they were going to put on the gloves together, he could almost have screamed.

"Remember, Joe, you're to run the laundry according to those old rules you used to lay down at Shelly Hot Springs," he said. "No overworking. No working at night. And no children at the mangles. No children anywhere. And a fair wage."

Joe nodded and pulled out a note-book.

"Look at here. I was workin' out them rules before breakfast this A.M. What d'ye think of them?"

He read them aloud, and Martin approved, worrying at the same time as to when Joe would take himself off.

It was late afternoon when he awoke. Slowly the fact of life came back to him. He glanced about the room. Joe had evidently stolen away after he had dozed off. That was considerate of Joe, he thought. Then he closed his eyes and slept again.

In the days that followed Joe was too busy organizing and taking hold of the laundry to bother him much; and it was not until the day before sailing that the newspapers made the announcement that he had taken passage on the *Mariposa*. Once, when the instinct of preservation fluttered, he went to a doctor and underwent a searching physical examination. Nothing could be found the matter with him. His heart and lungs were pronounced magnificent. Every organ, so far as the doctor could know, was normal and was working normally.

"There is nothing the matter with you, Mr. Eden," he said, "positively nothing the matter with you. You are in the pink of condition. Candidly, I envy you your health. It is superb. Look at that chest. There, and in your stomach, lies the secret of your remarkable constitution. Physically, you are a man in a thousand—in ten thousand. Barring accidents, you should live to be a hundred."

And Martin knew that Lizzie's diagnosis had been correct. Physically he was all right. It was his "think-machine" that had gone wrong, and there was no cure for that except to get away to the South Seas. The trouble was that now, on the verge of departure, he had no desire to go. The South Seas charmed him no more than did bourgeois civilization. There was no zest in the thought of departure, while the act of departure appalled him as a weariness of the flesh. He would have felt better if he were already on board and gone.

The last day was a sore trial. Having read of his sailing in the morning papers, Bernard Higginbotham, Gertrude, and all the family came to say good-by, as did Hermann von Schmidt and Marian. Then there was business to be transacted, bills to be paid, and everlasting reporters to be endured. He said good-by to Lizzie Connolly, abruptly, at the entrance to night school, and hurried away. At the hotel he found Joe, too busy all day with the laundry to have come to him earlier. It was the last straw, but Martin gripped the arms of his chair and talked and listened for half an hour.

"You know, Joe," he said, "that you are not tied down to that laundry. There are no strings on it. You can sell it any time and blow the money. Any time you get sick of it and want to hit the road, just pull out. Do what will make you the happiest."

Joe shook his head.

"No more road in mine, thank you kindly. Hoboin's all right, exceptin' for one thing—the girls. I can't help it, but I'm a ladies' man. I can't get along without 'em, and you've got to get along without 'em when you're hoboin'. The times I've passed by houses where dances an' parties was goin' on, an' heard the women laugh, an' saw their white dresses and smiling faces through the windows—Gee! I tell you them moments was plain hell. I like dancin' an' picnics, an' walking in the moonlight, an' all the rest too well. Me for the laundry, and a good front, with big iron dollars clinkin' in my jeans. I seen a girl already, just yesterday, and, d'ye know, I'm feelin' already I'd just as soon marry her as not. I've ben whistlin' all day at the thought of it. She's a beaut, with the kindest eyes and softest voice you ever heard. Me for her, you can stack on that. Say, why don't you get married with all this money to burn? You could get the finest girl in the land."

Martin shook his head with a smile, but in his secret heart he was wondering why any man wanted to marry. It seemed an amazing and incomprehensible thing.

From the deck of the *Mariposa*, at the sailing hour, he saw Lizzie Connolly hiding in the skirts of the crowd on the wharf. Take her with you, came the thought. It is easy to be kind. She will be supremely happy. It was almost a temptation one moment, and the succeeding moment it became a terror. He was in a panic at the thought of it. His tired soul cried out in protest. He turned away from the rail with a groan, muttering, "Man, you are too sick, you are too sick."

He fled to his stateroom, where he lurked until the steamer was clear of the dock. In the dining saloon, at luncheon, he found himself in the place of honor, at the captain's right; and he was not long in discovering that he was the great man on board. But no more unsatisfactory great man ever sailed on a ship. He spent the afternoon in a deck-chair, with closed eyes, dozing brokenly most of the time, and in the evening went early to bed.

After the second day, recovered from seasickness, the full passenger list was in evidence, and the more he saw of the passengers the more he disliked them. Yet he knew that he did them injustice. They were good and kindly people, he forced himself to acknowledge, and in the moment of acknowledgment he qualified—good and kindly like all the bourgeoisie, with all the psychological cramp and intellectual futility of their kind, they bored him when they talked with him, their little superficial minds were so filled with emptiness; while the boisterous high spirits and the excessive energy of the younger people shocked him. They were never quiet, ceaselessly playing deck-quoits, tossing rings, promenading, or rushing to the rail with loud cries to watch the leaping porpoises and the first schools of flying fish.

He slept much. After breakfast he sought his deck-chair with a magazine he never finished. The printed pages tired him. He puzzled that men found so much to write about, and, puzzling, dozed in his chair. When the gong awoke him for luncheon, he was irritated that he must awaken. There was no satisfaction in being awake.

Once, he tried to arouse himself from his lethargy, and went forward into the forecastle with the sailors. But the breed of sailors seemed to have changed since the days he had lived in the forecastle. He could find no kinship with these stolid-faced, ox-minded bestial creatures. He was in despair. Up above nobody had wanted Martin Eden for his own sake, and he could not go back to those of his own class who had wanted him in the past. He did not want them. He could not stand them any more than he could stand the stupid first-cabin passengers and the riotous young people.

Life was to him like strong, white light that hurts the tired eyes of a sick person. During every conscious moment life blazed in a raw glare around him and upon him. It hurt. It hurt intolerably. It was the first time in his life that Martin had travelled first class. On ships at sea he had always been in the forecastle, the steerage, or in the black depths of the coal-hold, passing coal. In those days, climbing up the iron ladders out the pit of stifling heat, he had often caught glimpses of the passengers, in cool white, doing nothing but enjoy themselves, under awnings spread to keep the sun and wind away from them, with subservient stewards taking care of their every want and whim, and it had seemed to him that the realm in which they moved and had their being was nothing else than paradise. Well, here he was, the great man on board, in the midmost centre of it, sitting at the captain's right hand, and yet vainly harking back to forecastle and stoke-hole in quest of the Paradise he had lost. He had found no new one, and now he could not find the old one.

He strove to stir himself and find something to interest him. He ventured the petty officers' mess, and was glad to get away. He talked with a quartermaster off duty, an intelligent man who promptly prodded him with the socialist propaganda and forced into his hands a bunch of leaflets and pamphlets. He listened to the man expounding the slave-morality, and as he listened, he thought languidly of his own Nietzsche philosophy. But what was it worth, after all? He remembered one of Nietzsche's mad utterances wherein that madman had doubted truth. And who was to say? Perhaps Nietzsche had been right. Perhaps there was no truth in anything, no truth in truth—no such thing as truth. But his mind wearied quickly, and he was content to go back to his chair and doze.

Miserable as he was on the steamer, a new misery came upon him. What when the steamer reached Tahiti? He would have to go ashore. He would have to order his trade-goods, to find a passage on a schooner to the Marquesas, to do a thousand and one things that were awful to contemplate. Whenever he steeled himself deliberately to think, he could see the desperate peril in which he stood. In all truth, he was in the Valley of the Shadow, and his danger lay in that he was not afraid. If he were only afraid, he would make toward life. Being unafraid, he was drifting deeper into the shadow. He found no delight in the old familiar things of life. The *Mariposa* was now in the northeast trades, and this wine of wind, surging against him, irritated him.

He had his chair moved to escape the embrace of this lusty comrade of old days and nights.

The day the *Mariposa* entered the doldrums, Martin was more miserable than ever. He could no longer sleep. He was soaked with sleep, and perforce he must now stay awake and endure the white glare of life. He moved about restlessly. The air was sticky and humid, and the rain-squalls were unrefreshing. He ached with life. He walked around the deck until that hurt too much, then sat in his chair until he was compelled to walk again. He forced himself at last to finish the magazine, and from the steamer library he culled several volumes of poetry. But they could not hold him, and once more he took to walking.

He stayed late on deck, after dinner, but that did not help him, for when he went below, he could not sleep. This surcease from life had failed him. It was too much. He turned on the electric light and tried to read. One of the volumes was a Swinburne. He lay in bed, glancing through its pages, until suddenly he became aware that he was reading with interest. He finished the stanza, attempted to read on, then came back to it. He rested the book face downward on his breast and fell to thinking. That was it. The very thing. Strange that it had never come to him before. That was the meaning of it all; he had been drifting that way all the time, and now Swinburne showed him that it was the happy way out. He wanted rest, and here was rest awaiting him. He glanced at the open port-hole. Yes, it was large enough. For the first time in weeks he felt happy. At last he had discovered the cure of his ill. He picked up the book and read the stanza slowly aloud:-

"'From too much love of living,
From hope and fear set free,
We thank with brief thanksgiving
Whatever gods may be
That no life lives forever;
That dead men rise up never;
That even the weariest river
Winds somewhere safe to sea.'"

He looked again at the open port. Swinburne had furnished the key. Life was ill, or, rather, it had become ill—an unbearable thing. "That dead men rise up never!" That line stirred him with a profound feeling of gratitude. It was the one beneficent thing in the universe. When life became an aching weariness, death was ready to soothe away to everlasting sleep. But what was he waiting for? It was time to go.

He arose and thrust his head out the port-hole, looking down into the milky wash. The *Mariposa* was deeply loaded, and, hanging by his hands, his feet would be in the water. He could slip in noiselessly. No one would hear. A smother of spray dashed up, wetting his face. It tasted salt on his lips, and the taste was good. He wondered if he ought to write a swan-song, but laughed the thought away. There was no time. He was too impatient to be gone.

Turning off the light in his room so that it might not betray him, he went out the port-hole feet first. His shoulders stuck, and he forced himself back so as to try it with one arm down by his side. A roll of the steamer aided him, and he was through, hanging by his hands. When his feet touched the sea, he let go. He was in a milky froth of water. The side of the *Mariposa* rushed past him like a dark wall, broken here and there by lighted ports. She was certainly making time. Almost before he knew it, he was astern, swimming gently on the foam-crackling surface.

A bonita struck at his white body, and he laughed aloud. It had taken a piece out, and the sting of it reminded him of why he was there. In the work to do he had forgotten the purpose of it. The lights of the *Mariposa* were growing dim in the distance, and there he was, swimming confidently, as though it were his intention to make for the nearest land a thousand miles or so away.

It was the automatic instinct to live. He ceased swimming, but the moment he felt the water rising above his mouth the hands struck out sharply with a lifting movement. The will to live, was his thought, and the thought was accompanied by a sneer. Well, he had will,—ay, will strong enough that with one last exertion it could destroy itself and cease to be.

He changed his position to a vertical one. He glanced up at the quiet stars, at the same time emptying his lungs of air. With swift, vigorous propulsion of hands and feet, he lifted his shoulders and half his chest out of water. This was to gain impetus for the descent. Then he let himself go and sank without movement, a white statue, into the sea. He breathed in the water deeply, deliberately, after the manner of a man taking an anaesthetic. When he strangled, quite involuntarily his arms and legs clawed the water and drove him up to the surface and into the clear sight of the stars.

The will to live, he thought disdainfully, vainly endeavoring not to breathe the air into his bursting lungs. Well, he would have to try a new way. He filled his lungs with air, filled them full. This supply would take him far down. He turned over and went down head first, swimming with all his strength and all his will. Deeper and deeper he went. His eyes were open, and he watched the ghostly, phosphorescent trails of the darting bonita. As he swam, he hoped that they would not strike at him, for it might snap the tension of his will. But they did not strike, and he found time to be grateful for this last kindness of life.

Down, down, he swam till his arms and leg grew tired and hardly moved. He knew that he was deep. The pressure on his ear-drums was a pain, and there was a buzzing in his head. His endurance was faltering, but he compelled his arms and legs to drive him deeper until his will snapped and the air drove from his lungs in a great explosive rush. The bubbles rubbed and bounded like tiny balloons against his cheeks and eyes as they took their upward flight. Then came pain and strangulation. This hurt was not death, was the thought that oscillated through his reeling consciousness. Death did not hurt. It was life, the pangs of life, this awful, suffocating feeling; it was the last blow life could deal him.

His wilful hands and feet began to beat and churn about, spasmodically and feebly. But he had fooled them and the will to live that made them beat and churn. He was too deep down. They could never bring him to the surface. He seemed floating languidly in a sea of dreamy vision. Colors and radiances surrounded him and bathed him and pervaded him. What was that? It seemed a lighthouse; but it was inside his brain—a flashing, bright white light. It flashed swifter and swifter. There was a long rumble of sound, and it seemed to him that he was falling down a vast and interminable stairway. And somewhere at the bottom he fell into darkness. That much he knew. He had fallen into darkness. And at the instant he knew, he ceased to know.

THE VALLEY OF THE MOON

BOOK I

CHAPTER 1

"You hear me, Saxon? Come on along. What if it is the Bricklayers? I'll have gentlemen friends there, and so'll you. The Al Vista band'll be along, an' you know it plays heavenly. An' you just love dancin'—-"

Twenty feet away, a stout, elderly woman interrupted the girl's persuasions. The elderly woman's back was turned, and the back-loose, bulging, and misshapen—began a convulsive heaving.

"Gawd!" she cried out. "O Gawd!"

She flung wild glances, like those of an entrapped animal, up and down the big whitewashed room that panted with heat and that was thickly humid with the steam that sizzled from the damp cloth under the irons of the many ironers. From the girls and women near her, all swinging irons steadily but at high pace, came quick glances, and labor efficiency suffered to the extent of a score of suspended or inadequate movements. The elderly woman's cry had caused a tremor of money-loss to pass among the piece-work ironers of fancy starch.

She gripped herself and her iron with a visible effort, and dabbed futilely at the frail, frilled garment on the board under her hand.

"I thought she'd got'em again—didn't you?" the girl said.

"It's a shame, a women of her age, and... condition," Saxon answered, as she frilled a lace ruffle with a hot fluting-iron. Her movements were delicate, safe, and swift, and though her face was wan with fatigue and exhausting heat, there was no slackening in her pace.

"An' her with seven, an' two of 'em in reform school," the girl at the next board sniffed sympathetic agreement. "But you just got to come to Weasel Park to-morrow, Saxon. The Bricklayers' is always lively—tugs-of-war, fat-man races, real Irish jiggin', an'... an' everything. An' The floor of the pavilion's swell."

But the elderly woman brought another interruption. She dropped her iron on the shirtwaist, clutched at the board, fumbled it, caved in at the knees and hips, and like a half-empty sack collapsed on the floor, her long shriek rising in the pent room to the acrid smell of scorching cloth. The women at the boards near to her scrambled, first, to the hot iron to save the cloth, and then to her, while the forewoman hurried belligerently down the aisle. The women farther away continued unsteadily at their work, losing movements to the extent of a minute's set-back to the totality of the efficiency of the fancy-starch room.

"Enough to kill a dog," the girl muttered, thumping her iron down on its rest with reckless determination. "Workin' girls' life ain't what it's cracked up. Me to quit—that's what I'm comin' to."

"Mary!" Saxon uttered the other's name with a reproach so profound that she was compelled to rest her own iron for emphasis and so lose a dozen movements.

Mary flashed a half-frightened look across.

"I didn't mean it, Saxon," she whimpered. "Honest, I didn't. I wouldn't never go that way. But I leave it to you, if a day like this don't get on anybody's nerves. Listen to that!"

The stricken woman, on her back, drumming her heels on the floor, was shrieking persistently and monotonously, like a mechanical siren. Two women, clutching her under the arms, were dragging her down the aisle. She drummed and shrieked the length of it. The door opened, and a vast, muffled roar of machinery burst in; and in the roar of it the drumming and the shrieking were drowned ere the door swung shut. Remained of the episode only the scorch of cloth drifting ominously through the air.

"It's sickenin'," said Mary.

And thereafter, for a long time, the many irons rose and fell, the pace of the room in no wise diminished; while the forewoman strode the aisles with a threatening eye for incipient breakdown and hysteria. Occasionally an ironer lost the stride for an instant, gasped or sighed, then caught it up again with weary determination. The long summer day waned, but not the heat, and under the raw flare of electric light the work went on.

By nine o'clock the first women began to go home. The mountain of fancy starch had been demolished—all save the few remnants, here and there, on the boards, where the ironers still labored.

Saxon finished ahead of Mary, at whose board she paused on the way out.

"Saturday night an' another week gone," Mary said mournfully, her young cheeks pallid and hollowed, her black eyes blue-shadowed and tired. "What d'you think you've made, Saxon?"

"Twelve and a quarter," was the answer, just touched with pride "And I'd a-made more if it wasn't for that fake bunch of starchers."

"My! I got to pass it to you," Mary congratulated. "You're a sure fierce hustler—just eat it up. Me—I've only ten an' a half, an' for a hard week... See you on the nine-forty. Sure now. We can just fool around until the dancin' begins. A lot of my gentlemen friends'll be there in the afternoon."

Two blocks from the laundry, where an arc-light showed a gang of toughs on the corner, Saxon quickened her pace. Unconsciously her face set and hardened as she passed. She did not catch the words of the muttered comment, but the rough laughter it raised made her guess and warmed her checks with resentful blood. Three blocks more, turning once to left and once to right, she walked on through the night that was already growing cool. On either side were workingmen's houses, of weathered wood, the ancient paint grimed with the dust of years, conspicuous only for cheapness and ugliness.

Dark it was, but she made no mistake, the familiar sag and screeching reproach of the front gate welcome under her hand. She went along the narrow walk to the rear, avoided the missing step without thinking about it, and entered the kitchen, where a solitary gas-jet flickered. She turned it up to the best of its flame. It was a small room, not disorderly, because of lack of furnishings to disorder it. The plaster, discolored by the steam of many wash-days, was crisscrossed with cracks from the big earthquake of the previous spring. The floor was ridged, wide-cracked, and uneven, and in front of the stove it was worn through and repaired with a five-gallon oil-can hammered flat and double. A sink, a dirty roller-towel, several chairs, and a wooden table completed the picture.

An apple-core crunched under her foot as she drew a chair to the table. On the frayed oilcloth, a supper waited. She attempted the cold beans, thick with grease, but gave them up, and buttered a slice of bread.

The rickety house shook to a heavy, prideless tread, and through the inner door came Sarah, middle-aged, lop-breasted, hair-tousled, her face lined with care and fat petulance.

"Huh, it's you," she grunted a greeting. "I just couldn't keep things warm. Such a day! I near died of the heat. An' little Henry cut his lip awful. The doctor had to put four stitches in it."

Sarah came over and stood mountainously by the table.

"What's the matter with them beans?" she challenged.

"Nothing, only..." Saxon caught her breath and avoided the threatened outburst. "Only I'm not hungry. It's been so hot all day. It was terrible in the laundry."

Recklessly she took a mouthful of the cold tea that had been steeped so long that it was like acid in her mouth, and recklessly, under the eye of her sister-in-law, she swallowed it and the rest of the cupful. She wiped her mouth on her handkerchief and got up.

"I guess I'll go to bed."

"Wonder you ain't out to a dance," Sarah sniffed. "Funny, ain't it, you come home so dead tired every night, an' yet any night in the week you can get out an' dance unearthly hours."

Saxon started to speak, suppressed herself with tightened lips, then lost control and blazed out. "Wasn't you ever young?"

Without waiting for reply, she turned to her bedroom, which opened directly off the kitchen. It was a small room, eight by twelve, and the earthquake had left its marks upon the plaster. A bed and chair of cheap pine and a very ancient chest of drawers constituted the furniture. Saxon had known this chest of drawers all her life. The vision of it was woven into her earliest recollections. She knew it had crossed the plains with her people in a prairie schooner. It was of solid mahogany. One end was cracked and dented from the capsize of the wagon in Rock Canyon. A bullet-hole, plugged, in the face of the top drawer, told of the fight with the Indians at Little Meadow. Of these happenings her mother had told her; also had she told that the chest had come with the family originally from England in a day even earlier than the day on which George Washington was born.

Above the chest of drawers, on the wall, hung a small looking-glass. Thrust under the molding were photographs of young men and women, and of picnic groups wherein the young men, with hats rakishly on the backs of their heads, encircled the girls with their arms. Farther along on the wall were a colored calendar and numerous colored advertisements and sketches torn out of magazines. Most of these sketches were of horses. From the gas-fixture hung a tangled bunch of well-scribbled dance programs.

Saxon started to take off her hat, but suddenly sat down on the bed. She sobbed softly, with considered repression, but the weak-latched door swung noiselessly open, and she was startled by her sister-in-law's voice.

"NOW what's the matter with you? If you didn't like them beans—"

"No, no," Saxon explained hurriedly. "I'm just tired, that's all, and my feet hurt. I wasn't hungry, Sarah. I'm just beat out."

"If you took care of this house," came the retort, "an' cooked an' baked, an' washed, an' put up with what I put up, you'd have something to be beat out about. You've got a snap, you have. But just wait." Sarah broke off to cackle gloatingly. "Just wait, that's all, an' you'll be fool enough to get married some day, like me, an' then you'll get yours—an' it'll be brats, an' brats, an' brats, an' no more dancin', an' silk stockin's, an' three pairs of shoes at one time. You've got a cinch-nobody to think of but your own precious self—an' a lot of young hoodlums makin' eyes at you an' tellin' you how beautiful your eyes are. Huh! Some fine day you'll tie up to one of 'em, an' then, mebbe, on occasion, you'll wear black eyes for a change."

"Don't say that, Sarah," Saxon protested. "My brother never laid hands on you. You know that."

"No more he didn't. He never had the gumption. Just the same, he's better stock than that tough crowd you run with, if he can't make a livin' an' keep his wife in three pairs of shoes. Just the same he's oodles better'n your bunch of hoodlums that no decent woman'd wipe her one pair of shoes on. How you've missed trouble this long is beyond me. Mebbe the younger generation is wiser in such thins—I don't know. But I do know that a young woman that has three pairs of shoes ain't thinkin' of anything but her own enjoyment, an' she's goin' to get hers, I can tell her that much. When I was a girl there wasn't such doin's. My mother'd taken the hide off me if I done the things you do. An' she was right, just as everything in the world is wrong now. Look at your brother, a-runnin' around to socialist meetin's, an' chewin' hot air, an' diggin' up extra strike dues to the union that means so much bread out of the mouths of his children, instead of makin' good with his bosses. Why, the dues he pays would keep me in seventeen pairs of shoes if I was nannygoat enough to want 'em. Some day, mark my words, he'll get his time, an' then what'll we do? What'll I do, with five mouths to feed an' nothin' comin' in?"

She stopped, out of breath but seething with the tirade yet to come.

"Oh, Sarah, please won't you shut the door?" Saxon pleaded.

The door slammed violently, and Saxon, ere she fell to crying again, could hear her sister-in-law lumbering about the kitchen and talking loudly to herself.

CHAPTER II

Each bought her own ticket at the entrance to Weasel Park. And each, as she laid her half-dollar down, was distinctly aware of how many pieces of fancy starch were represented by the coin. It was too early for the crowd, but bricklayers and their families, laden with huge lunch-baskets and armfuls of babies, were already going in—a healthy, husky race of workmen, well-paid and robustly fed. And with them, here and there, undisguised by their decent American clothing, smaller in bulk and stature, weazened not alone by age but by the pinch of lean years and early hardship, were grandfathers and mothers who had patently first seen the light of day on old Irish soil. Their faces showed content and pride as they limped along with this lusty progeny of theirs that had fed on better food.

Not with these did Mary and Saxon belong. They knew them not, had no acquaintances among them. It did not matter whether the festival were Irish, German, or Slavonian; whether the picnic was the Bricklayers', the Brewers', or the Butchers'. They, the girls, were of the dancing crowd that swelled by a certain constant percentage the gate receipts of all the picnics.

They strolled about among the booths where peanuts were grinding and popcorn was roasting in preparation for the day, and went on and inspected the dance floor of the pavilion. Saxon, clinging to an imaginary partner, essayed a few steps of the dip-waltz. Mary clapped her hands.

"My!" she cried. "You're just swell! An' them stockin's is peaches."

Saxon smiled with appreciation, pointed out her foot, velvet-slippered with high Cuban heels, and slightly lifted the tight black skirt, exposing a trim ankle and delicate swell of calf, the white flesh gleaming through the thinnest and flimsiest of fifty-cent black silk stockings. She was slender, not tall, yet the due round lines of womanhood were hers. On her white shirtwaist was a pleated jabot of cheap lace, caught with a large novelty pin of imitation coral. Over the shirtwaist was a natty jacket, elbow-sleeved, and to the elbows she wore gloves of imitation suede. The one essentially natural touch about her appearance was the few curls, strangers to curling-irons, that escaped from under the little naughty hat of black velvet pulled low over the eyes.

Mary's dark eyes flashed with joy at the sight, and with a swift little run she caught the other girl in her arms and kissed her in a breast-crushing embrace. She released her, blushing at her own extravagance.

"You look good to me," she cried, in extenuation. "If I was a man I couldn't keep my hands off you. I'd eat you, I sure would."

They went out of the pavilion hand in hand, and on through the sunshine they strolled, swinging hands gaily, reacting exuberantly from the week of deadening toil. They hung over the railing of the bear-pit, shivering at the huge and lonely denizen, and passed quickly on to ten minutes of laughter at the monkey cage. Crossing the grounds, they looked down into the little race track on the bed of a natural amphitheater where the early afternoon games were to take place. After that they explored the woods, threaded by countless paths, ever opening out in new surprises of green-painted rustic tables and benches in leafy nooks, many of which were already pre-empted by family parties. On a grassy slope, tree-surrounded, they spread a newspaper and sat down on the short grass already tawny-dry under the California sun. Half were they minded to do this because of the grateful indolence after six days of insistent motion, half in conservation for the hours of dancing to come.

"Bert Wanhope'll be sure to come," Mary chattered. "An' he said he was going to bring Billy Roberts—'Big Bill,' all the fellows call him. He's just a big boy, but he's awfully tough. He's a prizefighter, an' all the girls run after him. I'm afraid of him. He ain't quick in talkin'. He's more like that big bear we saw. Brr-rf! Brr-rf!—bite your head off, just like that. He ain't really a prize-fighter. He's a teamster—belongs to the union. Drives for Coberly and Morrison. But sometimes he fights in the clubs. Most of the fellows are scared of him. He's got a bad temper, an' he'd just as soon hit a fellow as eat, just like that. You won't like him, but he's a swell dancer. He's heavy, you know, an' he just slides and glides around. You wanta have a dance with'm anyway. He's a good spender, too. Never pinches. But my!—he's got one temper."

The talk wandered on, a monologue on Mary's part, that centered always on Bert Wanhope.

"You and he are pretty thick," Saxon ventured.

"I'd marry'm to-morrow," Mary flashed out impulsively. Then her face went bleakly forlorn, hard almost in its helpless pathos. "Only, he never asks me. He's..." Her pause was broken by sudden passion. "You watch out for him, Saxon, if he ever comes foolin' around you. He's no good. Just the same, I'd marry him to-morrow. He'll never get me any other way." Her mouth opened, but instead of speaking she drew a long sigh. "It's a funny world, ain't it?" she added. "More like a scream. And all the stars are worlds, too. I wonder where God hides. Bert Wanhope says there ain't no God. But he's just terrible. He says the most terrible things. I believe in God. Don't you? What do you think about God, Saxon?"

Saxon shrugged her shoulders and laughed.

"But if we do wrong we get ours, don't we?" Mary persisted. "That's what they all say, except Bert. He says he don't care what he does, he'll never get his, because when he dies he's dead, an' when he's dead he'd like to see any one put anything across on him that'd wake him up. Ain't he terrible, though? But it's all so funny. Sometimes I get scared when I think God's keepin' an eye on me all the time. Do you think he knows what I'm sayin' now? What do you think he looks like, anyway?"

"I don't know," Saxon answered. "He's just a funny proposition."

"Oh!" the other gasped.

"He IS, just the same, from what all people say of him," Saxon went on stoutly. "My brother thinks he looks like Abraham Lincoln. Sarah thinks he has whiskers."

CHAPTER II

"An' I never think of him with his hair parted," Mary confessed, daring the thought and shivering with apprehension. "He just couldn't have his hair parted. THAT'D be funny."

"You know that little, wrinkly Mexican that sells wire puzzles?" Saxon queried. "Well, God somehow always reminds me of him."

Mary laughed outright.

"Now that IS funny. I never thought of him like that How do you make it out?"

"Well, just like the little Mexican, he seems to spend his time peddling puzzles. He passes a puzzle out to everybody, and they spend all their lives tryin' to work it out They all get stuck. I can't work mine out. I don't know where to start. And look at the puzzle he passed Sarah. And she's part of Tom's puzzle, and she only makes his worse. And they all, an' everybody I know—you, too—are part of my puzzle."

"Mebbe the puzzles is all right," Mary considered. "But God don't look like that yellow little Greaser. THAT I won't fall for. God don't look like anybody. Don't you remember on the wall at the Salvation Army it says 'God is a spirit'?"

"That's another one of his puzzles, I guess, because nobody knows what a spirit looks like."

"That's right, too." Mary shuddered with reminiscent fear. "Whenever I try to think of God as a spirit, I can see Hen Miller all wrapped up in a sheet an' runnin' us girls. We didn't know, an' it scared the life out of us. Little Maggie Murphy fainted dead away, and Beatrice Peralta fell an' scratched her face horrible. When I think of a spirit all I can see is a white sheet runnin' in the dark. Just the same, God don't look like a Mexican, an' he don't wear his hair parted."

A strain of music from the dancing pavilion brought both girls scrambling to their feet.

"We can get a couple of dances in before we eat," Mary proposed. "An' then it'll be afternoon an' all the fellows 'll be here. Most of them are pinchers—that's why they don't come early, so as to get out of taking the girls to dinner. But Bert's free with his money, an' so is Billy. If we can beat the other girls to it, they'll take us to the restaurant. Come on, hurry, Saxon."

There were few couples on the floor when they arrived at the pavilion, and the two girls essayed the first waltz together.

"There's Bert now," Saxon whispered, as they came around the second time.

"Don't take any notice of them," Mary whispered back. "We'll just keep on goin'. They needn't think we're chasin' after them."

But Saxon noted the heightened color in the other's cheek, and felt her quicker breathing.

"Did you see that other one?" Mary asked, as she backed Saxon in a long slide across the far end of the pavilion. "That was Billy Roberts. Bert said he'd come. He'll take you to dinner, and Bert'll take me. It's goin' to be a swell day, you'll see. My! I only wish the music'll hold out till we can get back to the other end."

Down the floor they danced, on man-trapping and dinner-getting intent, two fresh young things that undeniably danced well and that were delightfully surprised when the music stranded them perilously near to their desire.

Bert and Mary addressed each other by their given names, but to Saxon Bert was "Mr. Wanhope," though he called her by her first name. The only introduction was of Saxon and Billy Roberts. Mary carried it off with a flurry of nervous carelessness.

"Mr. Robert—Miss Brown. She's my best friend. Her first name's Saxon. Ain't it a scream of a name?"

"Sounds good to me," Billy retorted, hat off and hand extended. "Pleased to meet you, Miss Brown."

As their hands clasped and she felt the teamster callouses on his palm, her quick eyes saw a score of things. About all that he saw was her eyes, and then it was with a vague impression that they were blue. Not till later in the day did he realize that they were gray. She, on the contrary, saw his eyes as they really were—deep blue, wide, and handsome in a sullen-boyish way. She saw that they were straight-looking, and she liked them, as she had liked the glimpse she had caught of his hand, and as she liked the contact of his hand itself. Then, too, but not sharply, she had perceived the short, square-set nose, the rosiness of cheek, and the firm, short upper lip, ere delight centered her flash of gaze on the well-modeled, large clean mouth where red lips smiled clear of the white, enviable teeth. A BOY, A GREAT BIG MAN-BOY, was her thought; and, as they smiled at each other and their hands slipped apart, she was startled by a glimpse of his hair—short and crisp and sandy, hinting almost of palest gold save that it was too flaxen to hint of gold at all.

So blond was he that she was reminded of stage-types she had seen, such as Ole Olson and Yon Yonson; but there resemblance ceased. It was a matter of color only, for the eyes were dark-lashed and -browed, and were cloudy with temperament rather than staring a child-gaze of wonder, and the suit of smooth brown cloth had been made by a tailor. Saxon appraised the suit on the instant, and her secret judgment was NOT A CENT LESS THAN FIFTY DOLLARS. Further, he had none of the awkwardness of the Scandinavian immigrant. On the contrary, he was one of those rare individuals that radiate muscular grace through the ungraceful man-garments of civilization. Every movement was supple, slow, and apparently considered. This she did not see nor analyze. She saw only a clothed man with grace of carriage and movement. She felt, rather than perceived, the calm and certitude of all the muscular play of him, and she felt, too, the promise of easement and rest that was especially grateful and craved-for by one who had incessantly, for six days and at top-speed, ironed fancy starch. As the touch of his hand had been good, so, to her, this subtler feel of all of him, body and mind, was good.

As he took her program and skirmished and joked after the way of young men, she realized the immediacy of delight she had taken in him. Never in her life had she been so affected by any man. She wondered to herself: IS THIS THE MAN?

He danced beautifully. The joy was hers that good dancers take when they have found a good dancer for a partner. The grace of those slow-moving, certain muscles of his accorded perfectly with the rhythm of the music. There was never doubt, never a betrayal of indecision. She glanced at Bert, dancing "tough" with Mary, caroming down the long floor with more than one collision with the increasing couples. Graceful himself in his slender, tall, lean-stomached way, Bert was accounted a good dancer; yet Saxon did not remember ever having danced with him with keen pleasure. Just a hit of a jerk spoiled his dancing—a jerk that did not occur, usually, but that always impended. There was something spasmodic in his mind. He was too quick, or he continually threatened to be too quick. He always seemed just on the verge of overrunning the time. It was disquieting. He made for unrest.

CHAPTER II

"You're a dream of a dancer," Billy Roberts was saying. "I've heard lots of the fellows talk about your dancing."

"I love it," she answered.

But from the way she said it he sensed her reluctance to speak, and danced on in silence, while she warmed with the appreciation of a woman for gentle consideration. Gentle consideration was a thing rarely encountered in the life she lived. IS THIS THE MAN? She remembered Mary's "I'd marry him to-morrow," and caught herself speculating on marrying Billy Roberts by the next day—if he asked her.

With eyes that dreamily desired to close, she moved on in the arms of this masterful, guiding pressure. A PRIZE-FIGHTER! She experienced a thrill of wickedness as she thought of what Sarah would say could she see her now. Only he wasn't a prize-fighter, but a teamster.

Came an abrupt lengthening of step, the guiding pressure grew more compelling, and she was caught up and carried along, though her velvet-shod feet never left the floor. Then came the sudden control down to the shorter step again, and she felt herself being held slightly from him so that he might look into her face and laugh with her in joy at the exploit. At the end, as the band slowed in the last bars, they, too, slowed, their dance fading with the music in a lengthening glide that ceased with the last lingering tone.

"We're sure cut out for each other when it comes to dancin'," he said, as they made their way to rejoin the other couple.

"It was a dream," she replied.

So low was her voice that he bent to hear, and saw the flush in her cheeks that seemed communicated to her eyes, which were softly warm and sensuous. He took the program from her and gravely and gigantically wrote his name across all the length of it.

"An' now it's no good," he dared. "Ain't no need for it."

He tore it across and tossed it aside.

"Me for you, Saxon, for the next," was Bert's greeting, as they came up. "You take Mary for the next whirl, Bill."

"Nothin' doin', Bo," was the retort. "Me an' Saxon's framed up to last the day."

"Watch out for him, Saxon," Mary warned facetiously. "He's liable to get a crush on you."

"I guess I know a good thing when I see it," Billy responded gallantly.

"And so do I," Saxon aided and abetted.

"I'd 'a' known you if I'd seen you in the dark," Billy added.

Mary regarded them with mock alarm, and Bert said good-naturedly:

"All I got to say is you ain't wastin' any time gettin' together. Just the same, if' you can spare a few minutes from each other after a couple more whirls, Mary an' me'd be complimented to have your presence at dinner."

"Just like that," chimed Mary.

"Quit your kiddin'," Billy laughed back, turning his head to look into Saxon's eyes. "Don't listen to 'em. They're grouched because they got to dance together. Bert's a rotten dancer, and Mary ain't so much. Come on, there she goes. See you after two more dances."

CHAPTER III

They had dinner in the open-air, tree-walled dining-room, and Saxon noted that it was Billy who paid the reckoning for the four. They knew many of the young men and women at the other tables, and greetings and fun flew back and forth. Bert was very possessive with Mary, almost roughly so, resting his hand on hers, catching and holding it, and, once, forcibly slipping off her two rings and refusing to return them for a long while. At times, when he put his arm around her waist, Mary promptly disengaged it; and at other times, with elaborate obliviousness that deceived no one, she allowed it to remain.

And Saxon, talking little but studying Billy Roberts very intently, was satisfied that there would be an utter difference in the way he would do such things... if ever he would do them. Anyway, he'd never paw a girl as Bert and lots of the other fellows did. She measured the breadth of Billy's heavy shoulders.

"Why do they call you 'Big' Bill?" she asked. "You're not so very tall."

"Nope," he agreed. "I'm only five feet eight an' three-quarters. I guess it must be my weight."

"He fights at a hundred an' eighty," Bert interjected.

"Oh, out it," Billy said quickly, a cloud-rift of displeasure showing in his eyes. "I ain't a fighter. I ain't fought in six months. I've quit it. It don't pay."

"Yon got two hundred the night you put the Frisco Slasher to the bad," Bert urged proudly.

"Cut it. Cut it now.—Say, Saxon, you ain't so big yourself, are you? But you're built just right if anybody should ask you. You're round an' slender at the same time. I bet I can guess your weight."

"Everybody guesses over it," she warned, while inwardly she was puzzled that she should at the same time be glad and regretful that he did not fight any more.

"Not me," he was saying. "I'm a wooz at weight-guessin'. Just you watch me." He regarded her critically, and it was patent that warm approval played its little rivalry with the judgment of his gaze. "Wait a minute."

He reached over to her and felt her arm at the biceps. The pressure of the encircling fingers was firm and honest, and Saxon thrilled to it. There was magic in this man-boy. She would have known only irritation had Bert or any other man felt her arm. But this man! IS HE THE MAN? she was questioning, when he voiced his conclusion.

CHAPTER III

"Your clothes don't weigh more'n seven pounds. And seven from—hum—say one hundred an' twenty-three—one hundred an' sixteen is your stripped weight."

But at the penultimate word, Mary cried out with sharp reproof:

"Why, Billy Roberts, people don't talk about such things."

He looked at her with slow-growing, uncomprehending surprise.

"What things?" he demanded finally.

"There you go again! You ought to be ashamed of yourself. Look! You've got Saxon blushing!"

"I am not," Saxon denied indignantly.

"An' if you keep on, Mary, you'll have me blushing," Billy growled. "I guess I know what's right an' what ain't. It ain't what a guy says, but what he thinks. An' I'm thinkin' right, an' Saxon knows it. An' she an' I ain't thinkin' what you're thinkin' at all."

"Oh! Oh!" Mary cried. "You're gettin' worse an' worse. I never think such things."

"Whoa, Mary! Backup!" Bert checked her peremptorily. "You're in the wrong stall. Billy never makes mistakes like that."

"But he needn't be so raw," she persisted.

"Come on, Mary, an' be good, an' cut that stuff," was Billy's dismissal of her, as he turned to Saxon. "How near did I come to it?"

"One hundred and twenty-two," she answered, looking deliberately at Mary. "One twenty two with my clothes."

Billy burst into hearty laughter, in which Bert joined.

"I don't care," Mary protested, "You're terrible, both of you—an' you, too, Saxon. I'd never a-thought it of you."

"Listen to me, kid," Bert began soothingly, as his arm slipped around her waist.

But in the false excitement she had worked herself into, Mary rudely repulsed the arm, and then, fearing that she had wounded her lover's feelings, she took advantage of the teasing and banter to recover her good humor. His arm was permitted to return, and with heads bent together, they talked in whispers.

Billy discreetly began to make conversation with Saxon.

"Say, you know, your name is a funny one. I never heard it tagged on anybody before. But it's all right. I like it."

"My mother gave it to me. She was educated, and knew all kinds of words. She was always reading books, almost until she died. And she wrote lots and lots. I've got some of her poetry published in a San Jose newspaper long ago. The Saxons were a race of people—she told me all about them when I was a little girl. They were wild, like Indians, only they were white. And they had blue eyes, and yellow hair, and they were awful fighters."

As she talked, Billy followed her solemnly, his eyes steadily turned on hers.

"Never heard of them," he confessed. "Did they live anywhere around here?"

She laughed.

"No. They lived in England. They were the first English, and you know the Americans came from the English. We're Saxons, you an' me, an' Mary, an' Bert, and all the Americans that are real Americans, you know, and not Dagoes and Japs and such."

"My folks lived in America a long time," Billy said slowly, digesting the information she had given and relating himself to it. "Anyway, my mother's folks did. They crossed to Maine hundreds of years ago."

"My father was 'State of Maine," she broke in, with a little gurgle of joy. "And my mother was horn in Ohio, or where Ohio is now. She used to call it the Great Western Reserve. What was your father?"

"Don't know." Billy shrugged his shoulders. "He didn't know himself. Nobody ever knew, though he was American, all right, all right."

"His name's regular old American," Saxon suggested. "There's a big English general right now whose name is Roberts. I've read it in the papers."

"But Roberts wasn't my father's name. He never knew what his name was. Roberts was the name of a gold-miner who adopted him. You see, it was this way. When they was Indian-fightin' up there with the Modoc Indians, a lot of the miners an' settlers took a hand. Roberts was captain of one outfit, and once, after a fight, they took a lot of prisoners—squaws, an' kids an' babies. An' one of the kids was my father. They figured he was about five years old. He didn't know nothin' but Indian."

Saxon clapped her hands, and her eyes sparkled: "He'd been captured on an Indian raid!"

"That's the way they figured it," Billy nodded. "They recollected a wagon-train of Oregon settlers that'd been killed by the Modocs four years before. Roberts adopted him, and that's why I don't know his real name. But you can bank on it, he crossed the plains just the same."

"So did my father," Saxon said proudly.

"An' my mother, too," Billy added, pride touching his own voice. "Anyway, she came pretty close to crossin' the plains, because she was born in a wagon on the River Platte on the way out."

"My mother, too," said Saxon. "She was eight years old, an' she walked most of the way after the oxen began to give out."

Billy thrust out his hand.

"Put her there, kid," he said. "We're just like old friends, what with the same kind of folks behind us."

With shining eyes, Saxon extended her hand to his, and gravely they shook.

"Isn't it wonderful?" she murmured. "We're both old American stock. And if you aren't a Saxon there never was one—your hair, your eyes, your skin, everything. And you're a fighter, too."

"I guess all our old folks was fighters when it comes to that. It come natural to 'em, an' dog-gone it, they just had to fight or they'd never come through."

"What are you two talkin' about?" Mary broke in upon them.

"They're thicker'n mush in no time," Bert girded. "You'd think they'd known each other a week already."

"Oh, we knew each other longer than that," Saxon returned. "Before ever we were born our folks were walkin' across the plains together."

"When your folks was waitin' for the railroad to be built an' all the Indians killed off before they dasted to start for California," was Billy's way of proclaiming the new alliance. "We're the real goods, Saxon an'n me, if anybody should ride up on a buzz-wagon an' ask you."

"Oh, I don't know," Mary boasted with quiet petulance. "My father stayed behind to fight in the Civil War. He was a drummer-boy. That's why he didn't come to California until afterward."

"And my father went back to fight in the Civil War," Saxon said.

"And mine, too," said Billy.

They looked at each other gleefully. Again they had found a new contact.

"Well, they're all dead, ain't they?" was Bert's saturnine comment. "There ain't no difference dyin' in battle or in the poorhouse. The thing is they're deado. I wouldn't care a rap if my father'd been hanged. It's all the same in a thousand years. This braggin' about folks makes me tired. Besides, my father couldn't a-fought. He wasn't born till two years after the war. Just the same, two of my uncles were killed at Gettysburg. Guess we done our share."

"Just like that," Mary applauded.

Bert's arm went around her waist again.

"We're here, ain't we?" he said. "An' that's what counts. The dead are dead, an' you can bet your sweet life they just keep on stayin' dead."

Mary put her hand over his mouth and began to chide him for his awfulness, whereupon he kissed the palm of her hand and put his head closer to hers.

The merry clatter of dishes was increasing as the dining-room filled up. Here and there voices were raised in snatches of song. There were shrill squeals and screams and bursts of heavier male laughter as the everlasting skirmishing between the young men and girls played on. Among some of the men the signs of drink were already manifest. At a near table girls were calling out to Billy. And Saxon, the sense of temporary possession already strong on her, noted with jealous eyes that he was a favorite and desired object to them.

"Ain't they awful?" Mary voiced her disapproval. "They got a nerve. I know who they are. No respectable girl 'd have a thing to do with them. Listen to that!"

"Oh, you Bill, you," one of them, a buxom young brunette, was calling. "Hope you ain't forgotten me, Bill."

"Oh, you chicken," he called back gallantly.

Saxon flattered herself that he showed vexation, and she conceived an immense dislike for the brunette.

"Goin' to dance?" the latter called.

"Mebbe," he answered, and turned abruptly to Saxon. "Say, we old Americans oughta stick together, don't you think? They ain't many of us left. The country's fillin' up with all kinds of foreigners."

He talked on steadily, in a low, confidential voice, head close to hers, as advertisement to the other girl that he was occupied.

From the next table on the opposite side, a young man had singled out Saxon. His dress was tough. His companions, male and female, were tough. His face was inflamed, his eyes touched with wildness.

"Hey, you!" he called. "You with the velvet slippers. Me for you."

The girl beside him put her arm around his neck and tried to hush him, and through the mufflement of her embrace they could hear him gurgling:

"I tell you she's some goods. Watch me go across an' win her from them cheap skates."

"Butchertown hoodlums," Mary sniffed.

Saxon's eyes encountered the eyes of the girl, who glared hatred across at her. And in Billy's eyes she saw moody anger smouldering. The eyes were more sullen, more handsome than ever, and clouds and veils and lights and shadowe shifted and deepened in the blue of them until they gave her a sense of unfathomable depth. He had stopped talking, and he made no effort to talk.

"Don't start a rough house, Bill," Bert cautioned. "They're from across the hay an' they don't know you, that's all."

Bert stood up suddenly, stepped over to the other table, whispered briefly, and came back. Every face at the table was turned on Billy. The offender arose brokenly, shook off the detaining hand of his girl, and came over. He was a large man, with a hard, malignant face and bitter eyes. Also, he was a subdued man.

"You're Big Bill Roberts," he said thickly, clinging to the table as he reeled. "I take my hat off to you. I apologize. I admire your taste in skirts, an' take it from me that's a compliment; but I did'nt know who you was. If I'd knowed you was Bill Roberts there wouldn't been a peep from my fly-trap. D'ye get me? I apologize. Will you shake hands?"

Gruffly, Billy said, "It's all right—forget it, sport;" and sullenly he shook hands and with a slow, massive movement thrust the other back toward his own table.

Saxon was glowing. Here was a man, a protector, something to lean against, of whom even the Butchertown toughs were afraid as soon as his name was mentioned.

CHAPTER IV

After dinner there were two dances in the pavilion, and then the band led the way to the race track for the games. The dancers followed, and all through the grounds the picnic parties left their tables to join in. Five thousand packed the grassy slopes of the amphitheater and swarmed inside the race track. Here, first of the events, the men were lining up for a tug of war. The contest was between the Oakland Bricklayers and the San Francisco Bricklayers, and the picked braves, huge and heavy, were taking their positions along the rope. They kicked heel-holds in the soft earth, rubbed their hands with the soil from underfoot, and laughed and joked with the crowd that surged about them.

The judges and watchers struggled vainly to keep back this crowd of relatives and friends. The Celtic blood was up, and the Celtic faction spirit ran high. The air was filled with cries of cheer, advice, warning, and threat. Many elected to leave the side of their own team and go to the side of the other team with the intention of circumventing foul play. There were as many women as men among the jostling supporters. The dust from the trampling, scuffling feet rose in the air, and Mary gasped and coughed and begged Bert to take her away. But he, the imp in him elated with the prospect of trouble, insisted on urging in closer. Saxon clung to Billy, who slowly and methodically elbowed and shouldered a way for her.

"No place for a girl," he grumbled, looking down at her with a masked expression of absent-mindedness, while his elbow powerfully crushed on the ribs of a big Irishman who gave room. "Things'll break loose when they start pullin'. They's been too much drink, an' you know what the Micks are for a rough house."

Saxon was very much out of place among these large-bodied men and women. She seemed very small and childlike, delicate and fragile, a creature from another race. Only Billy's skilled bulk and muscle saved her. He was continually glancing from face to face of the women and always returning to study her face, nor was she unaware of the contrast he was making.

Some excitement occurred a score of feet away from them, and to the sound of exclamations and blows a surge ran through the crowd. A large man, wedged sidewise in the jam, was shoved against Saxon, crushing her closely against Billy, who reached across to the man's shoulder with a massive thrust that was not so slow as usual. An involuntary grunt came from the victim, who turned his head, showing sun-reddened blond skin and unmistakable angry Irish eyes.

"What's eatin' yeh?" he snarled.

"Get off your foot; you're standin' on it," was Billy's contemptuous reply, emphasized by an increase of thrust.

The Irishman grunted again and made a frantic struggle to twist his body around, but the wedging bodies on either side held him in a vise.

"I'll break yer ugly face for yeh in a minute," he announced in wrath-thick tones.

Then his own face underwent transformation. The snarl left the lips, and the angry eyes grew genial.

"An' sure an' it's yerself," he said. "I didn't know it was yeh a-shovin'. I seen yeh lick the Terrible Swede, if yeh WAS robbed on the decision."

"No, you didn't, Bo," Billy answered pleasantly. "You saw me take a good beatin' that night. The decision was all right."

The Irishman was now beaming. He had endeavored to pay a compliment with a lie, and the prompt repudiation of the lie served only to increase his hero-worship.

"Sure, an' a bad beatin' it was," he acknowledged, "but yeh showed the grit of a bunch of wildcats. Soon as I can get me arm free I'm goin' to shake yeh by the hand an' help yeh aise yer young lady."

Frustrated in the struggle to get the crowd back, the referee fired his revolver in the air, and the tug-of-war was on. Pandemonium broke loose. Saxon, protected by the two big men, was near enough to the front to see much that ensued. The men on the rope pulled and strained till their faces were red with effort and their joints crackled. The rope was new, and, as their hands slipped, their wives and daughters sprang in, scooping up the earth in double handfuls and pouring it on the rope and the hands of their men to give them better grip.

A stout, middle-aged woman, carried beyond herself by the passion of the contest, seized the rope and pulled beside her husband, encouraged him with loud cries. A watcher from the opposing team dragged her screaming away and was dropped like a steer by an ear-blow from a partisan from the woman's team. He, in turn, went down, and brawny women joined with their men in the battle. Vainly the judges and watchers begged, pleaded, yelled, and swung with their fists. Men, as well as women, were springing in to the rope and pulling. No longer was it team against team, but all Oakland against all San Francisco, festooned with a free-for-all fight. Hands overlaid hands two and three deep in the struggle to grasp the rope. And hands that found no holds, doubled into bunches of knuckles that impacted on the jaws of the watchers who strove to tear hand-holds from the rope.

Bert yelped with joy, while Mary clung to him, mad with fear. Close to the rope the fighters were going down and being trampled. The dust arose in clouds, while from beyond, all around, unable to get into the battle, could be heard the shrill and impotent rage-screams and rage-yells of women and men.

"Dirty work, dirty work," Billy muttered over and over; and, though he saw much that occurred, assisted by the friendly Irishman he was coolly and safely working Saxon back out of the melee.

At last the break came. The losing team, accompanied by its host of volunteers, was dragged in a rush over the ground and disappeared under the avalanche of battling forms of the onlookers.

Leaving Saxon under the protection of the Irishman in an outer eddy of calm, Billy plunged back into the mix-up. Several minutes later he emerged with the missing couple—Bert bleeding from a blow on the ear, but hilarious, and Mary rumpled and hysterical.

"This ain't sport," she kept repeating. "It's a shame, a dirty shame."

"We got to get outa this," Billy said. "The fun's only commenced."

"Aw, wait," Bert begged. "It's worth eight dollars. It's cheap at any price. I ain't seen so many black eyes and bloody noses in a month of Sundays."

"Well, go on back an' enjoy yourself," Billy commended. "I'll take the girls up there on the side hill where we can look on. But I won't give much for your good looks if some of them Micks lands on you."

The trouble was over in an amazingly short time, for from the judges' stand beside the track the announcer was bellowing the start of the boys' foot-race; and Bert, disappointed, joined Billy and the two girls on the hillside looking down upon the track.

There were boys' races and girls' races, races of young women and old women, of fat men and fat women, sack races and three-legged races, and the contestants strove around the small track through a Bedlam of cheering supporters. The tug-of-war was already forgotten, and good nature reigned again.

Five young men toed the mark, crouching with fingertips to the ground and waiting the starter's revolver-shot. Three were in their stocking-feet, and the remaining two wore spiked running-shoes.

"Young men's race," Bert read from the program. "An' only one prize—twenty-five dollars. See the red-head with the spikes—the one next to the outside. San Francisco's set on him winning. He's their crack, an' there's a lot of bets up."

"Who's goin' to win?" Mary deferred to Billy's superior athletic knowledge.

"How can I tell!" he answered. "I never saw any of 'em before. But they all look good to me. May the best one win, that's all."

The revolver was fired, and the five runners were off and away. Three were outdistanced at the start. Redhead led, with a black-haired young man at his shoulder, and it was plain that the race lay between these two. Halfway around, the black-haired one took the lead in a spurt that was intended to last to the finish. Ten feet he gained, nor could Red-head cut it down an inch.

"The boy's a streak," Billy commented. "He ain't tryin' his hardest, an' Red-head's just bustin' himself."

Still ten feet in the lead, the black-haired one breasted the tape in a hubbub of cheers. Yet yells of disapproval could be distinguished. Bert hugged himself with joy.

"Mm-mm," he gloated. "Ain't Frisco sore? Watch out for fireworks now. See! He's bein' challenged. The judges ain't payin' him the money. An' he's got a gang behind him. Oh! Oh! Oh! Ain't had so much fun since my old woman broke her leg!"

"Why don't they pay him, Billy?" Saxon asked. "He won."

"The Frisco bunch is challengin' him for a professional," Billy elucidated. "That's what they're all beefin' about. But it ain't right. They all ran for that money, so they're all professional."

The crowd surged and argued and roared in front of the judges' stand. The stand was a rickety, two-story affair, the second story open at the front, and here the judges could be seen debating as heatedly as the crowd beneath them.

"There she starts!" Bert cried. "Oh, you rough-house!"

The black-haired racer, backed by a dozen supporters, was climbing the outside stairs to the judges.

"The purse-holder's his friend," Billy said. "See, he's paid him, an' some of the judges is willin' an' some are beefin'. An' now that other gang's going up—they're Redhead's." He turned to Saxon with a reassuring smile. "We're well out of it this time. There's goin' to be rough stuff down there in a minute."

"The judges are tryin' to make him give the money back," Bert explained. "An' if he don't the other gang'll take it away from him. See! They're reachin' for it now."

High above his head, the winner held the roll of paper containing the twenty-five silver dollars. His gang, around him, was shouldering back those who tried to seize the money. No blows had been struck yet, but the struggle increased until the frail structure shook and swayed. From the crowd beneath the winner was variously addressed: "Give it back, you dog!" "Hang on to it, Tim!" "You won fair, Timmy!" "Give it back, you dirty robber!" Abuse unprintable as well as friendly advice was hurled at him.

The struggle grew more violent. Tim's supporters strove to hold him off the floor so that his hand would still be above the grasping hands that shot up. Once, for an instant, his arm was jerked down. Again it went up. But evidently the paper had broken, and with a last desperate effort, before he went down, Tim flung the coin out in a silvery shower upon the heads of the crowd beneath. Then ensued a weary period of arguing and quarreling.

"I wish they'd finish, so as we could get back to the dancin'," Mary complained. "This ain't no fun."

Slowly and painfully the judges' stand was cleared, and an announcer, stepping to the front of the stand, spread his arms appealing for silence. The angry clamor died down.

"The judges have decided," he shouted, "that this day of good fellowship an' brotherhood—"

"Hear! Hear!" Many of the cooler heads applauded. "That's the stuff!" "No fightin'!" "No hard feelin's!"

"An' therefore," the announcer became audible again, "the judges have decided to put up another purse of twenty-five dollars an' run the race over again!"

"An' Tim?" bellowed scores of throats. "What about Tim?" "He's been robbed!" "The judges is rotten!"

Again the announcer stilled the tumult with his arm appeal.

"The judges have decided, for the sake of good feelin', that Timothy McManus will also run. If he wins, the money's his."

"Now wouldn't that jar you?" Billy grumbled disgustedly. "If Tim's eligible now, he was eligible the first time. An' if he was eligible the first time, then the money was his."

"Red-head'll bust himself wide open this time," Bert jubilated.

"An' so will Tim," Billy rejoined. "You can bet he's mad clean through, and he'll let out the links he was holdin' in last time."

Another quarter of an hour was spent in clearing the track of the excited crowd, and this time only Tim and Red-head toed the mark. The other three young men had abandoned the contest.

The leap of Tim, at the report of the revolver, put him a clean yard in the lead.

"I guess he's professional, all right, all right," Billy remarked. "An' just look at him go!"

CHAPTER IV

Half-way around, Tim led by fifty feet, and, running swiftly, maintaining the same lead, he came down the homestretch an easy winner. When directly beneath the group on the hillside, the incredible and unthinkable happened. Standing close to the inside edge of the track was a dapper young man with a light switch cane. He was distinctly out of place in such a gathering, for upon him was no ear-mark of the working class. Afterward, Bert was of the opinion that he looked like a swell dancing master, while Billy called him "the dude."

So far as Timothy McManus was concerned, the dapper young man was destiny; for as Tim passed him, the young man, with utmost deliberation, thrust his cane between Tim's flying legs. Tim sailed through the air in a headlong pitch, struck spread-eagled on his face, and plowed along in a cloud of dust.

There was an instant of vast and gasping silence. The young man, too, seemed petrified by the ghastliness of his deed. It took an appreciable interval of time for him, as well as for the onlookers, to realize what he had done. They recovered first, and from a thousand throats the wild Irish yell went up. Red-head won the race without a cheer. The storm center had shifted to the young man with the cane. After the yell, he had one moment of indecision; then he turned and darted up the track.

"Go it, sport!" Bert cheered, waving his hat in the air. "You're the goods for me! Who'd a-thought it? Who'd a-thought it? Say!—wouldn't it, now? Just wouldn't it?"

"Phew! He's a streak himself," Billy admired. "But what did he do it for? He's no bricklayer."

Like a frightened rabbit, the mad roar at his heels, the young man tore up the track to an open space on the hillside, up which he clawed and disappeared among the trees. Behind him toiled a hundred vengeful runners.

"It's too bad he's missing the rest of it," Billy said. "Look at 'em goin' to it."

Bert was beside himself. He leaped up and down and cried continuously.

"Look at 'em! Look at 'em! Look at 'em!"

The Oakland faction was outraged. Twice had its favorite runner been jobbed out of the race. This last was only another vile trick of the Frisco faction. So Oakland doubled its brawny fists and swung into San Francisco for blood. And San Francisco, consciously innocent, was no less willing to join issues. To be charged with such a crime was no less monstrous than the crime itself. Besides, for too many tedious hours had the Irish heroically suppressed themselves. Five thousands of them exploded into joyous battle. The women joined with them. The whole amphitheater was filled with the conflict. There were rallies, retreats, charges, and counter-charges. Weaker groups were forced fighting up the hillsides. Other groups, bested, fled among the trees to carry on guerrilla warfare, emerging in sudden dashes to overwhelm isolated enemies. Half a dozen special policemen, hired by the Weasel Park management, received an impartial trouncing from both sides.

"Nobody's the friend of a policeman," Bert chortled, dabbing his handkerchief to his injured ear, which still bled.

The bushes crackled behind him, and he sprang aside to let the locked forms of two men go by, rolling over and over down the hill, each striking when uppermost, and followed by a screaming woman who rained blows on the one who was patently not of her clan.

The judges, in the second story of the stand, valiantly withstood a fierce assault until the frail structure toppled to the ground in splinters.

"What's that woman doing?" Saxon asked, calling attention to an elderly woman beneath them on the track, who had sat down and was pulling from her foot an elastic-sided shoe of generous dimensions.

"Goin' swimming," Bert chuckled, as the stocking followed.

They watched, fascinated. The shoe was pulled on again over the bare foot. Then the woman slipped a rock the size of her fist into the stocking, and, brandishing this ancient and horrible weapon, lumbered into the nearest fray.

"Oh!—Oh!—Oh!" Bert screamed, with every blow she struck "Hey, old flannel-mouth! Watch out! You'll get yours in a second. Oh! Oh! A peach! Did you see it? Hurray for the old lady! Look at her tearin' into 'em! Watch out, old girl!... Ah-h-h."

His voice died away regretfully, as the one with the stocking, whose hair had been clutched from behind by another Amazon, was whirled about in a dizzy semicircle.

Vainly Mary clung to his arm, shaking him back and forth and remonstrating.

"Can't you be sensible?" she cried. "It's awful! I tell you it's awful!"

But Bert was irrepressible.

"Go it, old girl!" he encouraged. "You win! Me for you every time! Now's your chance! Swat! Oh! My! A peach! A peach!"

"It's the biggest rough-house I ever saw," Billy confided to Saxon. "It sure takes the Micks to mix it. But what did that dude wanta do it for? That's what gets me. He wasn't a bricklayer—not even a workingman—just a regular sissy dude that didn't know a livin' soul in the grounds. But if he wanted to raise a rough-house he certainly done it. Look at 'em. They're fightin' everywhere."

He broke into sudden laughter, so hearty that the tears came into his eyes.

"What is it?" Saxon asked, anxious not to miss anything.

"It's that dude," Billy explained between gusts. "What did he wanta do it for? That's what gets my goat. What'd he wanta do it for?"

There was more crashing in the brush, and two women erupted upon the scene, one in flight, the other pursuing. Almost ere they could realize it, the little group found itself merged in the astounding conflict that covered, if not the face of creation, at least all the visible landscape of Weasel Park.

The fleeing woman stumbled in rounding the end of a picnic bench, and would have been caught had she not seized Mary's arm to recover balance, and then flung Mary full into the arms of the woman who pursued. This woman, largely built, middle-aged, and too irate to comprehend, clutched Mary's hair by one hand and lifted the other to smack her. Before the blow could fall, Billy had seized both the woman's wrists.

"Come on, old girl, cut it out," he said appeasingly. "You're in wrong. She ain't done nothin'."

Then the woman did a strange thing. Making no resistance, but maintaining her hold on the girl's hair, she stood still and calmly began to scream. The scream was hideously compounded of fright and fear. Yet in her face was neither fright nor fear. She regarded Billy coolly and appraisingly, as if to see how he took it—her scream merely the cry to the clan for help.

"Aw, shut up, you battleax!" Bert vociferated, trying to drag her off by the shoulders.

CHAPTER IV

The result was that The four rocked back and forth, while the woman calmly went on screaming. The scream became touched with triumph as more crashing was heard in the brush.

Saxon saw Billy's slow eyes glint suddenly to the hardness of steel, and at the same time she saw him put pressure on his wrist-holds. The woman released her grip on Mary and was shoved back and free. Then the first man of the rescue was upon them. He did not pause to inquire into the merits of the affair. It was sufficient that he saw the woman reeling away from Billy and screaming with pain that was largely feigned.

"It's all a mistake," Billy cried hurriedly. "We apologize, sport—"

The Irishman swung ponderously. Billy ducked, cutting his apology short, and as the sledge-like fist passed over his head, he drove his left to the other's jaw. The big Irishman toppled over sidewise and sprawled on the edge of the slope. Half-scrambled back to his feet and out of balance, he was caught by Bert's fist, and this time went clawing down the slope that was slippery with short, dry grass. Bert was redoubtable. "That for you, old girl—my compliments," was his cry, as he shoved the woman over the edge on to the treacherous slope. Three more men were emerging from the brush.

In the meantime, Billy had put Saxon in behind the protection of the picnic table. Mary, who was hysterical, had evinced a desire to cling to him, and he had sent her sliding across the top of the table to Saxon.

"Come on, you flannel-mouths!" Bert yelled at the newcomers, himself swept away by passion, his black eyes flashing wildly, his dark face inflamed by the too-ready blood. "Come on, you cheap skates! Talk about Gettysburg. We'll show you all the Americans ain't dead yet!"

"Shut your trap—we don't want a scrap with the girls here," Billy growled harshly, holding his position in front of the table. He turned to the three rescuers, who were bewildered by the lack of anything visible to rescue. "Go on, sports. We don't want a row. You're in wrong. They ain't nothin' doin' in the fight line. We don't wanta fight—d'ye get me?"

They still hesitated, and Billy might have succeeded in avoiding trouble had not the man who had gone down the bank chosen that unfortunate moment to reappear, crawling groggily on hands and knees and showing a bleeding face. Again Bert reached him and sent him downslope, and the other three, with wild yells, sprang in on Billy, who punched, shifted position, ducked and punched, and shifted again ere he struck the third time. His blows were clean end hard, scientifically delivered, with the weight of his body behind.

Saxon, looking on, saw his eyes and learned more about him. She was frightened, but clear-seeing, and she was startled by the disappearance of all depth of light and shadow in his eyes. They showed surface only—a hard, bright surface, almost glazed, devoid of all expression save deadly seriousness. Bert's eyes showed madness. The eyes of the Irishmen were angry and serious, and yet not all serious. There was a wayward gleam in them, as if they enjoyed the fracas. But in Billy's eyes was no enjoyment. It was as if he had certain work to do and had doggedly settled down to do it.

Scarcely more expression did she note in the face, though there was nothing in common between it and the one she had seen all day. The boyishness had vanished.

This face was mature in a terrifying, ageless way. There was no anger in it, nor was it even pitiless. It seemed to have glazed as hard and passionlessly as his eyes. Something came to her of her wonderful mother's tales of the ancient Saxons, and he seemed to her one of those Saxons, and she caught a glimpse, on the well of her consciousness, of a long, dark boat, with a prow like the beak of a bird of prey, and of huge, half-naked men, wing-helmeted, and one of their faces, it seemed to her, was his face. She did not reason this. She felt it, and visioned it as by an unthinkable clairvoyance, and gasped, for the flurry of war was over. It had lasted only seconds, Bert was dancing on the edge of the slippery slope and mocking the vanquished who had slid impotently to the bottom. But Billy took charge.

"Come on, you girls," he commanded. "Get onto yourself, Bert. We got to get onta this. We can't fight an army."

He led the retreat, holding Saxon's arm, and Bert, giggling and jubilant, brought up the rear with an indignant Mary who protested vainly in his unheeding ears.

For a hundred yards they ran and twisted through the trees, and then, no signs of pursuit appearing, they slowed down to a dignified saunter. Bert, the trouble-seeker, pricked his ears to the muffled sound of blows and sobs, and stepped aside to investigate.

"Oh! look what I've found!" he called.

They joined him on the edge of a dry ditch and looked down. In the bottom were two men, strays from the fight, grappled together and still fighting. They were weeping out of sheer fatigue and helplessness, and the blows they only occasionally struck were open-handed and ineffectual.

"Hey, you, sport—throw sand in his eyes," Bert counseled. "That's it, blind him an' he's your'n."

"Stop that!" Billy shouted at the man, who was following instructions, "Or I'll come down there an' beat you up myself. It's all over—d'ye get me? It's all over an' everybody's friends. Shake an' make up. The drinks are on both of you. That's right—here, gimme your hand an' I'll pull you out."

They left them shaking hands and brushing each other's clothes.

"It soon will be over," Billy grinned to Saxon. "I know 'em. Fight's fun with them. An' this big scrap's made the days howlin' success. What did I tell you!—look over at that table there."

A group of disheveled men and women, still breathing heavily, were shaking hands all around.

"Come on, let's dance," Mary pleaded, urging them in the direction of the pavilion.

All over the park the warring bricklayers were shaking hands and making up, while the open-air bars were crowded with the drinkers.

Saxon walked very close to Billy. She was proud of him. He could fight, and he could avoid trouble. In all that had occurred he had striven to avoid trouble. And, also, consideration for her and Mary had been uppermost in his mind.

"You are brave," she said to him.

"It's like takin' candy from a baby," he disclaimed. "They only rough-house. They don't know boxin'. They're wide open, an' all you gotta do is hit 'em. It ain't real fightin', you know." With a troubled, boyish look in his eyes, he stared at his bruised knuckles. "An' I'll have to drive team to-morrow with 'em," he lamented. "Which ain't fun, I'm tellin' you, when they stiffen up."

CHAPTER V

At eight o'clock the Al Vista band played "Home, Sweet Home," and, following the hurried rush through the twilight to the picnic train, the four managed to get double seats facing each other. When the aisles and platforms were packed by the hilarious crowd, the train pulled out for the short run from the suburbs into Oakland. All the car was singing a score of songs at once, and Bert, his head pillowed on Mary's breast with her arms around him, started "On the Banks of the Wabash." And he sang the song through, undeterred by the bedlam of two general fights, one on the adjacent platform, the other at the opposite end of the car, both of which were finally subdued by special policemen to the screams of women and the crash of glass.

Billy sang a lugubrious song of many stanzas about a cowboy, the refrain of which was, "Bury me out on the lone pr-rairie."

"That's one you never heard before; my father used to sing it," he told Saxon, who was glad that it was ended.

She had discovered the first flaw in him. He was tonedeaf. Not once had he been on the key.

"I don't sing often," he added.

"You bet your sweet life he don't," Bert exclaimed. "His friends'd kill him if he did."

"They all make fun of my singin'," he complained to Saxon. "Honest, now, do you find it as rotten as all that?"

"It's... it's maybe flat a bit," she admitted reluctantly.

"It don't sound flat to me," he protested. "It's a regular josh on me. I'll bet Bert put you up to it. You sing something now, Saxon. I bet you sing good. I can tell it from lookin' at you."

She began "When the Harvest Days Are Over." Bert and Mary joined in; but when Billy attempted to add his voice he was dissuaded by a shin-kick from Bert. Saxon sang in a clear, true soprano, thin but sweet, and she was aware that she was singing to Billy.

"Now THAT is singing what is," he proclaimed, when she had finished. "Sing it again. Aw, go on. You do it just right. It's great."

His hand slipped to hers and gathered it in, and as she sang again she felt the tide of his strength flood warmingly through her.

"Look at 'em holdin' hands," Bert jeered. "Just a-holdin' hands like they was afraid. Look at Mary an' me. Come on an' kick in, you cold-feets. Get together. If you don't, it'll look suspicious. I got my suspicions already. You're framin' somethin' up."

There was no mistaking his innuendo, and Saxon felt her cheeks flaming.

"Get onto yourself, Bert," Billy reproved.

"Shut up!" Mary added the weight of her indignation. "You're awfully raw, Bert Wanhope, an' I won't have anything more to do with you—there!"

She withdrew her arms and shoved him away, only to receive him forgivingly half a dozen seconds afterward.

"Come on, the four of us," Bert went on irrepressibly. "The night's young. Let's make a time of it—Pabst's Cafe first, and then some. What you say, Bill? What you say, Saxon? Mary's game."

Saxon waited and wondered, half sick with apprehension of this man beside her whom she had known so short a time.

"Nope," he said slowly. "I gotta get up to a hard day's work to-morrow, and I guess the girls has got to, too."

Saxon forgave him his tone-deafness. Here was the kind of man she always had known existed. It was for some such man that she had waited. She was twenty-two, and her first marriage offer had come when she was sixteen. The last had occurred only the month before, from the foreman of the washing-room, and he had been good and kind, but not young. But this one beside her—he was strong and kind and good, and YOUNG. She was too young herself not to desire youth. There would have been rest from fancy starch with the foreman, but there would have been no warmth. But this man beside her.... She caught herself on the verge involuntarily of pressing his hand that held hers.

"No, Bert, don't tease he's right," Mary was saying. "We've got to get some sleep. It's fancy starch to-morrow, and all day on our feet."

It came to Saxon with a chill pang that she was surely older than Billy. She stole glances at the smoothness of his face, and the essential boyishness of him, so much desired, shocked her. Of course he would marry some girl years younger than himself, than herself. How old was he? Could it be that he was too young for her? As he seemed to grow inaccessible, she was drawn toward him more compellingly. He was so strong, so gentle. She lived over the events of the day. There was no flaw there. He had considered her and Mary, always. And he had torn the program up and danced only with her. Surely he had liked her, or he would not have done it.

She slightly moved her hand in his and felt the harsh contact of his teamster callouses. The sensation was exquisite. He, too, moved his hand, to accommodate the shift of hers, and she waited fearfully. She did not want him to prove like other men, and she could have hated him had he dared to take advantage of that slight movement of her fingers and put his arm around her. He did not, and she flamed toward him. There was fineness in him. He was neither rattle-brained, like Bert, nor coarse like other men she had encountered. For she had had experiences, not nice, and she had been made to suffer by the lack of what was termed chivalry, though she, in turn, lacked that word to describe what she divined and desired.

And he was a prizefighter. The thought of it almost made her gasp. Yet he answered not at all to her conception of a prizefighter. But, then, he wasn't a prizefighter. He had said he was not. She resolved to ask him about it some time if...

if he took her out again. Yet there was little doubt of that, for when a man danced with one girl a whole day he did not drop her immediately. Almost she hoped that he was a prizefighter. There was a delicious tickle of wickedness about it. Prizefighters were such terrible and mysterious men. In so far as they were out of the ordinary and were not mere common workingmen such as carpenters and laundrymen, they represented romance. Power also they represented. They did not work for bosses, but spectacularly and magnificently, with their own might, grappled with the great world and wrung splendid living from its reluctant hands. Some of them even owned automobiles and traveled with a retinue of trainers and servants. Perhaps it had been only Billy's modesty that made him say he had quit fighting. And yet, there were the callouses on his hands. That showed he had quit.

CHAPTER VI

They said good-bye at the gate. Billy betrayed awkwardness that was sweet to Saxon. He was not one of the take-it-for-granted young men. There was a pause, while she feigned desire to go into the house, yet waited in secret eagerness for the words she wanted him to say.

"When am I goin' to see you again?" he asked, holding her hand in his.

She laughed consentingly.

"I live 'way up in East Oakland," he explained. "You know there's where the stable is, an' most of our teaming is done in that section, so I don't knock around down this way much. But, say—" His hand tightened on hers. "We just gotta dance together some more. I'll tell you, the Orindore Club has its dance Wednesday. If you haven't a date—have you?"

"No," she said.

"Then Wednesday. What time'll I come for you?"

And when they had arranged the details, and he had agreed that she should dance some of the dances with the other fellows, and said good night again, his hand closed more tightly on hers and drew her toward him. She resisted slightly, but honestly. It was the custom, but she felt she ought not for fear he might misunderstand. And yet she wanted to kiss him as she had never wanted to kiss a man. When it came, her face upturned to his, she realized that on his part it was an honest kiss. There hinted nothing behind it. Rugged and kind as himself, it was virginal almost, and betrayed no long practice in the art of saying good-bye. All men were not brutes after all, was her thought.

"Good night," she murmured; the gate screeched under her hand; and she hurried along the narrow walk that led around to the corner of the house.

"Wednesday," he celled softly.

"Wednesday," she answered.

But in the shadow of the narrow alley between the two houses she stood still and pleasured in the ring of his foot falls down the cement sidewalk. Not until they had quite died away did she go on. She crept up the back stairs and across the kitchen to her room, registering her thanksgiving that Sarah was asleep.

She lighted the gas, and, as she removed the little velvet hat, she felt her lips still tingling with the kiss. Yet it had meant nothing. It was the way of the young men. They all did it. But their good-night kisses had never tingled, while this one tingled in her brain as wall as on her lip. What was it? What did it mean? With a sudden impulse she looked at herself in the glass. The eyes were happy and bright. The color that tinted her cheeks so easily was in them and glowing. It was a pretty reflection, and she smiled, partly in joy, partly in appreciation, and the smile grew at sight of the even rows of strong white teeth. Why shouldn't Billy like that face? was her unvoiced query. Other men had liked it. Other men did like it. Even the other girls admitted she was a good-looker. Charley Long certainly liked it from the way he made life miserable for her.

She glanced aside to the rim of the looking-glass where his photograph was wedged, shuddered, and made a moue of distaste. There was cruelty in those eyes, and brutishness. He was a brute. For a year, now, he had bullied her. Other fellows were afraid to go with her. He warned them off. She had been forced into almost slavery to his attentions. She remembered the young bookkeeper at the laundry—not a workingman, but a soft-handed, soft-voiced gentleman—whom Charley had beaten up at the corner because he had been bold enough to come to take her to the theater. And she had been helpless. For his own sake she had never dared accept another invitation to go out with him.

And now, Wednesday night, she was going with Billy. Billy! Her heart leaped. There would be trouble, but Billy would save her from him. She'd like to see him try and beat Billy up.

With a quick movement, she jerked the photograph from its niche and threw it face down upon the chest of drawers. It fell beside a small square case of dark and tarnished leather. With a feeling as of profanation she again seized the offending photograph and flung it across the room into a corner. At the same time she picked up the leather case. Springing it open, she gazed at the daguerreotype of a worn little woman with steady gray eyes and a hopeful, pathetic mouth. Opposite, on the velvet lining, done in gold lettering, was, CARLTON FROM DAISY. She read it reverently, for it represented the father she had never known, and the mother she had so little known, though she could never forget that those wise sad eyes were gray.

Despite lack of conventional religion, Saxon's nature was deeply religious. Her thoughts of God were vague and nebulous, and there she was frankly puzzled. She could not vision God. Here, in the daguerreotype, was the concrete; much she had grasped from it, and always there seemed an infinite more to grasp. She did not go to church. This was her high altar and holy of holies. She came to it in trouble, in loneliness, for counsel, divination, end comfort. In so far as she found herself different from the girls of her acquaintance, she quested here to try to identify her characteristics in the pictured face. Her mother had been different from other women, too. This, forsooth, meant to her what God meant to others. To this she strove to be true, and not to hurt nor vex. And how little she really knew of her mother, and of how much was conjecture and surmise, she was unaware; for it was through many years she had erected this mother-myth.

Yet was it all myth? She resented the doubt with quick jealousy, and, opening the bottom drawer of the chest, drew forth a battered portfolio. Out rolled manuscripts, faded and worn, and arose a faint far scent of sweet-kept age. The writing was delicate and curled, with the quaint fineness of half a century before. She read a stanza to herself:

"Sweet as a wind-lute's airy strains Your gentle muse has learned to sing, And California's boundless plains Prolong the soft notes echoing."

She wondered, for the thousandth time, what a windlute was; yet much of beauty, much of beyondness, she sensed of this dimly remembered beautiful mother of hers. She communed a while, then unrolled a second manuscript. "To C. B.," it read. To Carlton Brown, she knew, to her father, a love-poem from her mother. Saxon pondered the opening lines:

"I have stolen away from the crowd in the groves, Where the nude statues stand, and the leaves point and shiver At ivy-crowned Bacchus, the Queen of the Loves, Pandora and Psyche, struck voiceless forever."

This, too, was beyond her. But she breathed the beauty of it. Bacchus, and Pandora and Psyche—talismans to conjure with! But alas! the necromancy was her mother's. Strange, meaningless words that meant so much! Her marvelous mother had known their meaning. Saxon spelled the three words aloud, letter by letter, for she did not dare their pronunciation; and in her consciousness glimmered august connotations, profound and unthinkable. Her mind stumbled and halted on the star-bright and dazzling boundaries of a world beyond her world in which her mother had roamed at will. Again and again, solemnly, she went over the four lines. They were radiance and light to the world, haunted with phantoms of pain and unrest, in which she had her being. There, hidden among those cryptic singing lines, was the clue. If she could only grasp it, all would be made clear. Of this she was sublimely confident. She would understand Sarah's sharp tongue, her unhappy brother, the cruelty of Charley Long, the justness of the bookkeeper's beating, the day-long, month-long, year-long toil at the ironing-board.

She skipped a stanza that she knew was hopelessly beyond her, and tried again:

"The dusk of the greenhouse is luminous yet
With quivers of opal and tremors of gold;
For the sun is at rest, and the light from the west,
Like delicate wine that is mellow and old,

"Flushes faintly the brow of a naiad that stands In the spray of a fountain, whose seed-amethysts Tremble lightly a moment on bosom and hands, Then dip in their basin from bosom and wrists."

"It's beautiful, just beautiful," she sighed. And then, appalled at the length of all the poem, at the volume of the mystery, she rolled the manuscript and put it away. Again she dipped in the drawer, seeking the clue among the cherished fragments of her mother's hidden soul.

This time it was a small package, wrapped in tissue paper and tied with ribbon. She opened it carefully, with the deep gravity and circumstance of a priest before an altar. Appeared a little red-satin Spanish girdle, whale-boned like a tiny corset, pointed, the pioneer finery of a frontier woman who had crossed the plains. It was handmade after the California-Spanish model of forgotten days. The very whalebone had been home-shaped of the raw material from the whaleships traded for in hides and tallow. The black lace trimming her mother had made. The triple edging of black velvet strips—her mother's hands had sewn the stitches.

Saxon dreamed over it in a maze of incoherent thought. This was concrete. This she understood. This she worshiped as man-created gods have been worshiped on less tangible evidence of their sojourn on earth.

CHAPTER VI

Twenty-two inches it measured around. She knew it out of many verifications. She stood up and put it about her waist. This was part of the ritual. It almost met. In places it did meet. Without her dress it would meet everywhere as it had met on her mother. Closest of all, this survival of old California-Ventura days brought Saxon in touch. Hers was her mother's form. Physically, she was like her mother. Her grit, her ability to turn off work that was such an amazement to others, were her mother's. Just so had her mother been an amazement to her generation—her mother, the toy-like creature, the smallest and the youngest of the strapping pioneer brood, who nevertheless had mothered the brood. Always it had been her wisdom that was sought, even by the brothers and sisters a dozen years her senior. Daisy, it was, who had put her tiny foot down and commanded the removal from the fever flatlands of Colusa to the healthy mountains of Ventura; who had backed the savage old Indian-fighter of a father into a corner and fought the entire family that Vila might marry the man of her choice; who had flown in the face of the family and of community morality and demanded the divorce of Laura from her criminally weak husband; and who on the other hand, had held the branches of the family together when only misunderstanding and weak humanness threatened to drive them apart.

The peacemaker and the warrior! All the old tales trooped before Saxon's eyes. They were sharp with detail, for she had visioned them many times, though their content was of things she had never seen. So far as details were concerned, they were her own creation, for she had never seen an ox, a wild Indian, nor a prairie schooner. Yet, palpitating and real, shimmering in the sun-flashed dust of ten thousand hoofs, she saw pass, from East to West, across a continent, the great hegira of the land-hungry Anglo-Saxon. It was part and fiber of her. She had been nursed on its traditions and its facts from the lips of those who had taken part. Clearly she saw the long wagon-train, the lean, gaunt men who walked before, the youths goading the lowing oxen that fell and were goaded to their feet to fall again. And through it all, a flying shuttle, weaving the golden dazzling thread of personality, moved the form of her little, indomitable mother, eight years old, and nine ere the great traverse was ended, a necromancer and a law-giver, willing her way, and the way and the willing always good and right.

Saxon saw Punch, the little, rough-coated Skye-terrier with the honest eyes (who had plodded for weary months), gone lame and abandoned; she saw Daisy, the chit of a child, hide Punch in the wagon. She saw the savage old worried father discover the added burden of the several pounds to the dying oxen. She saw his wrath, as he held Punch by the scruff of the neck. And she saw Daisy, between the muzzle of the long-barreled rifle and the little dog. And she saw Daisy thereafter, through days of alkali and heat, walking, stumbling, in the dust of the wagons, the little sick dog, like a baby, in her arms.

But most vivid of all, Saxon saw the fight at Little Meadow—and Daisy, dressed as for a gala day, in white, a ribbon sash about her waist, ribbons and a round-comb in her hair, in her hands small water-pails, step forth into the sunshine on the flower-grown open ground from the wagon circle, wheels interlocked, where the wounded screamed their delirium and babbled of flowing fountains, and go on, through the sunshine and the wonder-inhibition of the bullet-dealing Indians, a hundred yards to the waterhole and back again.

Saxon kissed the little, red satin Spanish girdle passionately, and wrapped it up in haste, with dewy eyes, abandoning the mystery and godhead of mother and all the strange enigma of living.

In bed, she projected against her closed eyelids the few rich scenes of her mother that her child-memory retained. It was her favorite way of wooing sleep. She had done it all her life—sunk into the death-blackness of sleep with her mother limned to the last on her fading consciousness. But this mother was not the Daisy of the plains nor of the daguerreotype. They had been before Saxon's time. This that she saw nightly was an older mother, broken with insomnia and brave with sorrow, who crept, always crept, a pale, frail creature, gentle and unfaltering, dying from lack of sleep, living by will, and by will refraining from going mad, who, nevertheless, could not will sleep, and whom not even the whole tribe of doctors could make sleep. Crept—always she crept, about the house, from weary bed to weary chair and back again through long days and weeks of torment, never complaining, though her unfailing smile was twisted with pain, and the wise gray eyes, still wise and gray, were grown unutterably larger and profoundly deep.

But on this night Saxon did not win to sleep quickly; the little creeping mother came and went; and in the intervals the face of Billy, with the cloud-drifted, sullen, handsome eyes, burned against her eyelids. And once again, as sleep welled up to smother her, she put to herself the question IS THIS THE MAN?

CHAPTER VII

Tun work in the ironing-room slipped off, but the three days until Wednesday night were very long. She hummed over the fancy starch that flew under the iron at an astounding rate.

"I can't see how you do it," Mary admired. "You'll make thirteen or fourteen this week at that rate."

Saxon laughed, and in the steam from the iron she saw dancing golden letters that spelled WEDNESDAY.

"What do you think of Billy?" Mary asked.

"I like him," was the frank answer.

"Well, don't let it go farther than that."

"I will if I want to," Saxon retorted gaily.

"Better not," came the warning. "You'll only make trouble for yourself. He ain't marryin'. Many a girl's found that out. They just throw themselves at his head, too."

"I'm not going to throw myself at him, or any other man."

"Just thought I'd tell you," Mary concluded. "A word to the wise."

Saxon had become grave.

"He's not... not..." she began, than looked the significance of the question she could not complete.

"Oh, nothin' like that—though there's nothin' to stop him. He's straight, all right, all right. But he just won't fall for anything in skirts. He dances, an' runs around, an' has a good time, an' beyond that—nitsky. A lot of 'em's got fooled on him. I bet you there's a dozen girls in love with him right now. An' he just goes on turnin' 'em down. There was Lily Sanderson—you know her. You seen her at that Slavonic picnic last summer at Shellmound—that tall, nice-lookin' blonde that was with Butch Willows?"

"Yes, I remember her," Saxon sald. "What about her?"

"Well, she'd been runnin' with Butch Willows pretty steady, an' just because she could dance, Billy dances a lot with her. Butch ain't afraid of nothin'. He wades right in for a showdown, an' nails Billy outside, before everybody, an' reads the riot act. An' Billy listens in that slow, sleepy way of his, an' Butch gets hotter an' hotter, an' everybody expects a scrap.

"An' then Billy says to Butch, 'Are you done?' 'Yes,' Butch says; 'I've said my say, an' what are you goin' to do about it?' An' Billy says—an' what d'ye think he said, with everybody lookin' on an' Butch with blood in his eye? Well, he said, 'I guess nothin', Butch.' Just like that. Butch was that surprised you could knocked him over with a feather. 'An' never dance with her no more?' he says. 'Not if you say I can't, Butch,' Billy says. Just like that.

"Well, you know, any other man to take water the way he did from Butch—why, everybody'd despise him. But not Billy. You see, he can afford to. He's got a rep as a fighter, an' when he just stood back 'an' let Butch have his way, everybody knew he wasn't scared, or backin' down, or anything. He didn't care a rap for Lily Sanderson, that was all, an' anybody could see she was just crazy after him."

The telling of this episode caused Saxon no little worry. Hers was the average woman's pride, but in the matter of man-conquering prowess she was not unduly conceited. Billy had enjoyed her dancing, and she wondered if that were all. If Charley Long bullied up to him would he let her go as he had let Lily Sanderson go? He was not a marrying man; nor could Saxon blind her eyes to the fact that he was eminently marriageable. No wonder the girls ran after him. And he was a man-subduer as well as a woman-subduer. Men liked him. Bert Wanhope seemed actually to love him. She remembered the Butchertown tough in the dining-room at Weasel Park who had come over to the table to apologize, and the Irishman at the tug-of-war who had abandoned all thought of fighting with him the moment he learned his identity.

A very much spoiled young man was a thought that flitted frequently through Saxon's mind; and each time she condemned it as ungenerous. He was gentle in that tantalizing slow way of his. Despite his strength, he did not walk rough-shod over others. There was the affair with Lily Sanderson. Saxon analysed it again and again. He had not cared for the girl, and he had immediately stepped from between her and Butch. It was just the thing that Bert, out of sheer wickedness and love of trouble, would not have done. There would have been a fight, hard feelings, Butch turned into an enemy, and nothing profited to Lily. But Billy had done the right thing—done it slowly and imperturbably and with the least hurt to everybody. All of which made him more desirable to Saxon and less possible.

She bought another pair of silk stockings that she had hesitated at for weeks, and on Tuesday night sewed and drowsed wearily over a new shirtwaist and earned complaint from Sarah concerning her extravagant use of gas.

Wednesday night, at the Orindore dance, was not all undiluted pleasure. It was shameless the way the girls made up to Billy, and, at times, Saxon found his easy consideration for them almost irritating. Yet she was compelled to acknowledge to herself that he hurt none of the other fellows' feelings in the way the girls hurt hers. They all but asked him outright to dance with them, and little of their open pursuit of him escaped her eyes. She resolved that she would not be guilty of throwing herself at him, and withheld dance after dance, and yet was secretly and thrillingly aware that she was pursuing the right tactics. She deliberately demonstrated that she was desirable to other men, as he involuntarily demonstrated his own desirableness to the women.

Her happiness came when he coolly overrode her objections and insisted on two dances more than she had allotted him. And she was pleased, as well as angered, when she chanced to overhear two of the strapping young cannery girls. "The way that little sawed-off is monopolizin' him," said one. And the other: "You'd think she might have the good taste to run after somebody of her own age." "Cradle-snatcher," was the final sting that sent the angry blood into Saxon's cheeks as the two girls moved away, unaware that they had been overheard.

CHAPTER VII

Billy saw her home, kissed her at the gate, and got her consent to go with him to the dance at Germania Hall on Friday night.

"I wasn't thinkin' of goin'," he sald. "But if you'll say the word... Bert's goin' to be there."

Next day, at the ironing boards, Mary told her that she and Bert were dated for Germania Hall.

"Are you goin'?" Mary asked.

Saxon nodded.

"Billy Roberts?"

The nod was repeated, and Mary, with suspended iron, gave her a long and curions look.

"Say, an' what if Charley Long butts in?"

Saxon shrugged her shoulders.

They ironed swiftly and silently for a quarter of an hour.

"Well," Mary decided, "if he does butt in maybe he'll get his. I'd like to see him get it—the big stiff! It all depends how Billy feels—about you, I mean."

"I'm no Lily Sanderson," Saxon answered indignantly. "I'll never give Billy Roberts a chance to turn me down."

"You will, if Charley Long butts in. Take it from me, Saxon, he ain't no gentleman. Look what he done to Mr. Moody. That was a awful beatin'. An' Mr. Moody only a quiet little man that wouldn't harm a fly. Well, he won't find Billy Roberts a sissy by a long shot."

That night, outside the laundry entrance, Saxon found Charley Long waiting. As he stepped forward to greet her and walk alongside, she felt the sickening palpitation that he had so thoroughly taught her to know. The blood ebbed from her face with the apprehension and fear his appearance caused. She was afraid of the rough bulk of the man; of the heavy brown eyes, dominant and confident; of the big blacksmith-hands and the thick strong fingers with the hair-pads on the back to every first joint. He was unlovely to the eye, and he was unlovely to all her finer sensibilities. It was not his strength itself, but the quality of it and the misuse of it, that affronted her. The beating he had given the gentle Mr. Moody had meant half-hours of horror to her afterward. Always did the memory of it come to her accompanied by a shudder. And yet, without shock, she had seen Billy fight at Weasel Park in the same primitive man-animal way. But it had been different. She recognized, but could not analyze, the difference. She was aware only of the brutishness of this man's hands and mind.

"You're lookin' white an' all beat to a frazzle," he was saying. "Why don't you cut the work? You got to some time, anyway. You can't lose me, kid."

"I wish I could," she replied.

He laughed with harsh joviality. "Nothin' to it, Saxon. You're just cut out to be Mrs. Long, an' you're sure goin' to be."

"I wish I was as certain about all things as you are," she said with mild sarcasm that missed.

"Take it from me," he went on, "there's just one thing you can be certain of—an' that is that I am certain." He was pleased with the cleverness of his idea and laughed approvingly. "When I go after anything I get it, an' if anything gets in between it gets hurt. D'ye get that? It's me for you, an' that's all there is to it, so you might as well make up your mind and go to workin' in my home instead of the laundry. Why, it's a snap. There wouldn't be much to do. I make good money, an' you wouldn't want for anything. You know, I just washed up from work an' skinned over here to tell it to you once more, so you wouldn't forget. I ain't ate yet, an' that shows how much I think of you."

"You'd better go and eat then," she advised, though she knew the futility of attempting to get rid of him.

She scarcely heard what he said. It had come upon her suddenly that she was very tired and very small and very weak alongside this colossus of a man. Would he dog her always? she asked despairingly, and seemed to glimpse a vision of all her future life stretched out before her, with always the form and face of the burly blacksmith pursuing her.

"Come on, kid, an' kick in," he continued. "It's the good old summer time, an' that's the time to get married."

"But I'm not going to marry you," she protested. "I've told you a thousand times already."

"Aw, forget it. You want to get them ideas out of your think-box. Of course, you're goin' to marry me. It's a pipe. An' I'll tell you another pipe. You an' me's goin' acrost to Frisco Friday night. There's goin' to be big doin's with the Horseshoers."

"Only I'm not," she contradicted.

"Oh, yes you are," he asserted with absolute assurance. "We'll catch the last boat back, an' you'll have one fine time. An' I'll put you next to some of the good dancers. Oh, I ain't a pincher, an' I know you like dancin'."

"But I tell you I can't," she reiterated.

He shot a glance of suspicion at her from under the black thatch of brows that met above his nose and were as one brow.

"Why can't you?"

"A date," she said.

"Who's the bloke?"

"None of your business, Charley Long. I've got a date, that's all."

"I'll make it my business. Remember that lah-de-dah bookkeeper rummy? Well, just keep on rememberin' him an' what he got."

"I wish you'd leave me alone," she pleaded resentfully. "Can't you be kind just for once?"

The blacksmith laughed unpleasantly.

"If any rummy thinks he can butt in on you an' me, he'll learn different, an' I'm the little boy that'll learn 'm.—Friday night, eh? Where?"

"I won't tell you."

"Where?" he repeated.

Her lips were drawn in tight silence, and in her cheeks were little angry spots of blood.

"Huh!—As if I couldn't guess! Germania Hall. Well, I'll be there, an' I'll take you home afterward. D'ye get that? An' you'd better tell the rummy to beat it unless you want to see'm get his face hurt."

Saxon, hurt as a prideful woman can be hurt by cavalier treatment, was tempted to cry out the name and prowess of her new-found protector. And then came fear. This was a big man, and Billy was only a boy. That was the way he affected her. She remembered her first impression of his hands and glanced quickly at the hands of the man beside her. They seemed twice as large as Billy's, and the mats of hair seemed to advertise a terrible strength. No, Billy could not fight this big brute. He must not. And then to Saxon came a wicked little hope that by the mysterious and unthinkable ability that prizefighters possessed, Billy might be able to whip this bully and rid her of him. With the next glance doubt came again, for her eye dwelt on the blacksmith's broad shoulders, the cloth of the coat muscle-wrinkled and the sleeves bulging above the biceps.

"If you lay a hand on anybody I'm going with again—-" she began.

"Why, they'll get hurt, of course," Long grinned. "And they'll deserve it, too. Any rummy that comes between a fellow an' his girl ought to get hurt."

"But I'm not your girl, and all your saying so doesn't make it so."

"That's right, get mad," he approved. "I like you for that, too. You've got spunk an' fight. I like to see it. It's what a man needs in his wife—and not these fat cows of women. They're the dead ones. Now you're a live one, all wool, a yard long and a yard wide."

She stopped before the house and put her hand on the gate.

"Good-bye," she said. "I'm going in."

"Come on out afterward for a run to Idora Park," he suggested.

"No, I'm not feeling good, and I'm going straight to bed as soon as I eat supper."

"Huh!" he sneered. "Gettin' in shape for the fling to-morrow night, eh?"

With an impatient movement she opened the gate and stepped inside.

"I've given it to you straight," he went on. "If you don't go with me to-morrow night somebody'll get hurt."

"I hope it will be you," she cried vindictively.

He laughed as he threw his head back, stretched his big chest, and half-lifted his heavy arms. The action reminded her disgustingly of a great ape she had once seen in a circus.

"Well, good-bye," he said. "See you to-morrow night at Germania Hall."

"I haven't told you it was Germania Hall."

"And you haven't told me it wasn't. All the same, I'll be there. And I'll take you home, too. Be sure an' keep plenty of round dances open fer me. That's right. Get mad. It makes you look fine."

CHAPTER VIII

The music stopped at the end of the waltz, leaving Billy and Saxon at the big entrance doorway of the ballroom. Her hand rested lightly on his arm, and they were promenading on to find seats, when Charley Long, evidently just arrived, thrust his way in front of them.

"So you're the buttinsky, eh?" he demanded, his face malignant with passion and menace.

"Who?—me?" Billy queried gently. "Some mistake, sport. I never butt in."

"You're goin' to get your head beaten off if you don't make yourself scarce pretty lively."

"I wouldn't want that to happen for the world," Billy drawled. "Come on, Saxon. This neighborhood's unhealthy for us."

He started to go on with her, but Long thrust in front again.

"You're too fresh to keep, young fellow," he snarled. "You need saltin' down. D'ye get me?"

Billy scratched his head, on his face exaggerated puzzlement.

"No, I don't get you," he said. "Now just what was it you said?"

But the big blacksmith turned contemptuously away from him to Saxon.

"Come here, you. Let's see your program."

"Do you want to dance with him?" Billy asked.

She shook her head.

"Sorry, sport, nothin' doin'," Billy said, again making to start on.

For the third time the blacksmith blocked the way.

"Get off your foot," said Billy. "You're standin' on it."

Long all but sprang upon him, his hands clenched, one arm just starting back for the punch while at the same instant shoulders and chest were coming forward. But he restrained himself at sight of Billy's unstartled body and cold and cloudy ayes. He had made no move of mind or muscle. It was as if he were unaware of the threatened attack. All of which constituted a new thing in Long's experience.

"Maybe you don't know who I am," he bullied.

"Yep, I do," Billy answered airily. "You're a record-breaker at rough-housin'." (Here Long's face showed pleasure.) "You ought to have the Police Gazette diamond belt for rough-bousin' baby buggies'. I guess there ain't a one you're afraid to tackle."

"Leave 'm alone, Charley," advised one of the young men who had crowded about them. "He's Bill Roberts, the fighter. You know'm. Big Bill."

"I don't care if he's Jim Jeffries. He can't butt in on me this way."

Nevertheless it was noticeable, even to Saxon, that the fire had gone out of his fierceness. Billy's name seemed to have a quieting effect on obstreperous males.

"Do you know him?" Billy asked her.

She signified yes with her eyes, though it seemed she must cry out a thousand things against this man who so steadfastly persecuted her. Billy turned to the blacksmith.

"Look here, sport, you don't want trouble with me. I've got your number. Besides, what do we want to fight for? Hasn't she got a say so in the matter?"

"No, she hasn't. This is my affair an' yourn."

Billy shook his head slowly. "No; you're in wrong. I think she has a say in the matter."

"Well, say it then," Long snarled at Saxon, "who're you goin' to go with?—me or him? Let's get it settled."

For reply, Saxon reached her free hand over to the hand that rested on Billy's arm.

"Nuff said," was Billy's remark.

Long glared at Saxon, then transferred the glare to her protector.

"I've a good mind to mix it with you anyway," Long gritted through his teeth.

Saxon was elated as they started to move away. Lily Sanderson's fate had not been hers, and her wonderful man-boy, without the threat of a blow, slow of speech and imperturbable, had conquered the big blacksmith.

"He's forced himself upon me all the time," she whispered to Billy. "He's tried to run me, and beaten up every man that came near me. I never want to see him again."

Billy halted immediately. Long, who was reluctantly moving to get out of the way, also halted.

"She says she don't want anything more to do with you," Billy said to him. "An' what she says goes. If I get a whisper any time that you've been botherin' her, I'll attend to your case. D'ye get that?"

Long glowered and remained silent.

"D'ye get that?" Billy repeated, more imperatively.

A growl of assent came from the blacksmith

"All right, then. See you remember it. An' now get outa the way or I'll walk over you."

Long slunk back, muttering inarticulate threats, and Saxon moved on as in a dream. Charley Long had taken water. He had been afraid of this smooth-skinned, blue-eyed boy. She was quit of him—something no other man had dared attempt for her. And Billy had liked her better than Lily Sanderson.

Twice Saxon tried to tell Billy the details of her acquaintance with Long, but each time was put off.

"I don't care a rap about it," Billy said the second time. "You're here, ain't you?"

But she insisted, and when, worked up and angry by the recital, she had finished, he patted her hand soothingly.

"It's all right, Saxon," he said. "He's just a big stiff. I took his measure as soon as I looked at him. He won't bother you again. I know his kind. He's a dog. Roughhouse? He couldn't rough-house a milk wagon."

"But how do you do it?" she asked breathlessly. "Why are men so afraid of you? You're just wonderful."

He smiled in an embarrassed way and changed the subject.

"Say," he said, "I like your teeth. They're so white an' regular, an' not big, an' not dinky little baby's teeth either. They're ... they're just right, an' they fit you. I never seen such fine teeth on a girl yet. D'ye know, honest, they kind of make me hungry when I look at 'em. They're good enough to eat."

At midnight, leaving the insatiable Bert and Mary still dancing, Billy and Saxon started for home. It was on his suggestion that they left early, and he felt called upon to explain.

"It's one thing the fightin' game's taught me," he said. "To take care of myself. A fellow can't work all day and dance all night and keep in condition. It's the same way with drinkin'—an' not that I'm a little tin angel. I know what it is. I've been soused to the guards an' all the rest of it. I like my beer—big schooners of it; but I don't drink all I want of it. I've tried, but it don't pay. Take that big stiff to-night that butted in on us. He ought to had my number. He's a dog anyway, but besides he had beer bloat. I sized that up the first rattle, an' that's the difference about who takes the other fellow's number. Condition, that's what it is."

"But he is so big," Saxon protested. "Why, his fists are twice as big as yours."

"That don't mean anything. What counts is what's behind the fists. He'd turn loose like a buckin' bronco. If I couldn't drop him at the start, all I'd do is to keep away, smother up, an' wait. An' all of a sudden he'd blow up—go all to pieces, you know, wind, heart, everything, and then I'd have him where I wanted him. And the point is he knows it, too."

"You're the first prizefighter I ever knew," Saxon said, after a pause.

"I'm not any more," he disclaimed hastily. "That's one thing the fightin' game taught me—to leave it alone. It don't pay. A fellow trains as fine as silk—till he's all silk, his skin, everything, and he's fit to live for a hundred years; an' then he climbs through the ropes for a hard twenty rounds with some tough customer that's just as good as he is, and in those twenty rounds he frazzles out all his silk an' blows in a year of his life. Yes, sometimes he blows in five years of it, or cuts it in half, or uses up all of it. I've watched 'em. I've seen fellows strong as bulls fight a hard battle and die inside the year of consumption, or kidney disease, or anything else. Now what's the good of it? Money can't buy what they throw away. That's why I quit the game and went back to drivin' team. I got my silk, an' I'm goin' to keep it, that's all."

"It must make you feel proud to know you are the master of other men," she said softly, aware herself of pride in the strength and skill of him.

"It does," he admitted frankly. "I'm glad I went into the game—just as glad as I am that I pulled out of it.... Yep, it's taught me a lot—to keep my eyes open an' my head cool. Oh, I've got a temper, a peach of a temper. I get scared of myself sometimes. I used to be always breakin' loose. But the fightin' taught me to keep down the steam an' not do things I'd be sorry for afterward."

"Why, you're the sweetest, easiest tempered man I know," she interjected.

"Don't you believe it. Just watch me, and sometime you'll see me break out that bad that I won't know what I'm doin' myself. Oh, I'm a holy terror when I get started!"

This tacit promise of continued acquaintance gave Saxon a little joy-thrill.

"Say," he said, as they neared her neighborhood, "what are you doin' next Sunday?"

"Nothing. No plans at all."

CHAPTER VIII

"Well, suppose you an' me go buggy-riding all day out in the hills?"

She did not answer immediately, and for the moment she was seeing the nightmare vision of her last buggy-ride; of her fear and her leap from the buggy; and of the long miles and the stumbling through the darkness in thin-soled shoes that bruised her feet on every rock. And then it came to her with a great swell of joy that this man beside her was not such a man.

"I love horses," she said. "I almost love them better than I do dancing, only I don't know anything about them. My father rode a great roan war-horse. He was a captain of cavalry, you know. I never saw him, but somehow I always can see him on that big horse, with a sash around his waist and his sword at his side. My brother George has the sword now, but Tom—he's the brother I live with says it is mine because it wasn't his father's. You see, they're only my half-brothers. I was the only child by my mother's second marriage. That was her real marriage—her love-marriage, I mean."

Saxon ceased abruptly, embarrassed by her own garrulity; and yet the impulse was strong to tell this young man all about herself, and it seemed to her that these far memories were a large part of her.

"Go on an' tell me about it," Billy urged. "I like to hear about the old people of the old days. My people was along in there, too, an' somehow I think it was a better world to live in than now. Things was more sensible and natural. I don't exactly say what I mean. But it's like this: I don't understand life to-day. There's the labor unions an' employers' associations, an' strikes', an' hard times, an' huntin' for jobs, an' all the rest. Things wasn't like that in the old days. Everybody farmed, an' shot their meat, an' got enough to eat, an' took care of their old folks. But now it's all a mix-up that I can't understand. Mebbe I'm a fool, I don't know. But, anyway, go ahead an' tell us about your mother."

"Well, you see, when she was only a young woman she and Captain Brown fell in love. He was a soldier then, before the war. And he was ordered East for the war when she was away nursing her sister Laura. And then came the news that he was killed at Shiloh. And she married a man who had loved her for years and years. He was a boy in the same wagon-train coming across the plains. She liked him, but she didn't love him. And afterward came the news that my father wasn't killed after all. So it made her very sad, but it did not spoil her life. She was a good mother end a good wife and all that, but she was always sad, and sweet, and gentle, and I think her voice was the most beautiful in the world."

"She was game, all right," Billy approved.

"And my father never married. He loved her all the time. I've got a lovely poem home that she wrote to him. It's just wonderful, and it sings like music. Well, long, long afterward her husband died, and then she and my father made their love marriage. They didn't get married until 1882, and she was pretty well along."

More she told him, as they stood by the gate, and Saxon tried to think that the good-bye kiss was a trifle longer than just ordinary.

"How about nine o'clock?" he queried across the gate. "Don't bother about lunch or anything. I'll fix all that up. You just be ready at nine."

CHAPTER IX

Sunday morning Saxon was beforehand in getting ready, and on her return to the kitchen from her second journey to peep through the front windows, Sarah began her customary attack.

"It's a shame an' a disgrace the way some people can afford silk stockings," she began. "Look at me, a-toilin' and a-stewin' day an' night, and I never get silk stockings—nor shoes, three pairs of them all at one time. But there's a just God in heaven, and there'll be some mighty big surprises for some when the end comes and folks get passed out what's comin' to them."

Tom, smoking his pipe and cuddling his youngest-born on his knees, dropped an eyelid surreptitiously on his cheek in token that Sarah was in a tantrum. Saxon devoted herself to tying a ribbon in the hair of one of the little girls. Sarah lumbered heavily about the kitchen, washing and putting away the breakfast dishes. She straightened her back from the sink with a groan and glared at Saxon with fresh hostility.

"You ain't sayin' anything, eh? An' why don't you? Because I guess you still got some natural shame in you a-runnin' with a prizefighter. Oh, I've heard about your goings-on with Bill Roberts. A nice specimen he is. But just you wait till Charley Long gets his hands on him, that's all."

"Oh, I don't know," Tom intervened. "Bill Roberts is a pretty good boy from what I hear."

Saxon smiled with superior knowledge, and Sarah, catching her, was infuriated.

"Why don't you marry Charley Long? He's crazy for you, and he ain't a drinkin' man."

"I guess he gets outside his share of beer," Saxon retorted.

"That's right," her brother supplemented. "An' I know for a fact that he keeps a keg in the house all the time as well."

"Maybe you've been guzzling from it," Sarah snapped.

"Maybe I have," Tom said, wiping his mouth reminiscently with the back of his hand.

"Well, he can afford to keep a keg in the house if he wants to," she returned to the attack, which now was directed at her husband as well. "He pays his bills, and he certainly makes good money—better than most men, anyway."

"An' he hasn't a wife an' children to watch out for," Tom said.

"Nor everlastin' dues to unions that don't do him no good."

CHAPTER IX

"Oh, yes, he has," Tom urged genially. "Blamed little he'd work in that shop, or any other shop in Oakland, if he didn't keep in good standing with the Blacksmiths. You don't understand labor conditions, Sarah. The unions have got to stick, if the men aren't to starve to death."

"Oh, of course not," Sarah sniffed. "I don't understand anything. I ain't got a mind. I'm a fool, an' you tell me so right before the children." She turned savagely on her eldest, who startled and shrank away. "Willie, your mother is a fool. Do you get that? Your father says she's a fool—says it right before her face and yourn. She's just a plain fool. Next he'll be sayin' she's crazy an' puttin' her away in the asylum. An' how will you like that, Willie? How will you like to see your mother in a straitjacket an' a padded cell, shut out from the light of the sun an' beaten like a nigger before the war, Willie, beaten an' clubbed like a regular black nigger? That's the kind of a father you've got, Willie. Think of it, Willie, in a padded cell, the mother that bore you, with the lunatics screechin' an' screamin' all around, an' the quick-lime eatin' into the dead bodies of them that's beaten to death by the cruel wardens—"

She continued tirelessly, painting with pessimistic strokes the growing black future her husband was meditating for her, while the boy, fearful of some vague, incomprehensible catastrophe, began to weep silently, with a pendulous, trembling underlip. Saxon, for the moment, lost control of herself.

"Oh, for heaven's sake, can't we be together five minutes without quarreling?" she blazed.

Sarah broke off from asylum conjurations and turned upon her sister-in-law.

"Who's quarreling? Can't I open my head without bein' jumped on by the two of you?"

Saxon shrugged her shoulders despairingly, and Sarah swung about on her husband.

"Seein' you love your sister so much better than your wife, why did you want to marry me, that's borne your children for you, an' slaved for you, an' toiled for you, an' worked her fingernails off for you, with no thanks, an 'insultin' me before the children, an' sayin' I'm crazy to their faces. An' what have you ever did for me? That's what I want to know—me, that's cooked for you, an' washed your stinkin' clothes, and fixed your socks, an' sat up nights with your brats when they was ailin'. Look at that!"

She thrust out a shapeless, swollen foot, encased in a monstrous, untended shoe, the dry, raw leather of which showed white on the edges of bulging cracks.

"Look at that! That's what I say. Look at that!" Her voice was persistently rising and at the same time growing throaty. "The only shoes I got. Me. Your wife. Ain't you ashamed? Where are my three pairs? Look at that stockin'."

Speech failed her, and she sat down suddenly on a chair at the table, glaring unutterable malevolence and misery. She arose with the abrupt stiffness of an automaton, poured herself a cup of cold coffee, and in the same jerky way sat down again. As if too hot for her lips, she filled her saucer with the greasy-looking, nondescript fluid, and continued her set glare, her breast rising and falling with staccato, mechanical movement.

"Now, Sarah, be c'am, be c'am," Tom pleaded anxiously.

In response, slowly, with utmost deliberation, as if the destiny of empires rested on the certitude of her act, she turned the saucer of coffee upside down on the table. She lifted her right hand, slowly, hugely, and in the same slow, huge way landed the open palm with a sounding slap on Tom's astounded cheek. Immediately thereafter she raised her voice in the shrill, hoarse, monotonous madness of hysteria, sat down on the floor, and rocked back and forth in the throes of an abysmal grief.

Willie's silent weeping turned to noise, and the two little girls, with the fresh ribbons in their hair, joined him. Tom's face was drawn and white, though the smitten cheek still blazed, and Saxon wanted to put her arms comfortingly around him, yet dared not. He bent over his wife.

"Sarah, you ain't feelin' well. Let me put you to bed, and I'll finish tidying up."

"Don't touch me!—don't touch me!" she screamed, jerking violently away from him.

"Take the children out in the yard, Tom, for a walk, anything—get them away," Saxon said. She was sick, and white, and trembling. "Go, Tom, please, please. There's your hat. I'll take care of her. I know just how."

Left to herself, Saxon worked with frantic haste, assuming the calm she did not possess, but which she must impart to the screaming bedlamite upon the floor. The light frame house leaked the noise hideously, and Saxon knew that the houses on either side were hearing, and the street itself and the houses across the street. Her fear was that Billy should arrive in the midst of it. Further, she was incensed, violated. Every fiber rebelled, almost in a nausea; yet she maintained cool control and stroked Sarah's forehead and hair with slow, soothing movements. Soon, with one arm around her, she managed to win the first diminution in the strident, atrocious, unceasing screamı A few minutes later, sobbing heavily, the elder woman lay in bed, across her forehead and eyes a wet-pack of towel for easement of the headache she and Saxon tacitly accepted as substitute for the brain-storm.

When a clatter of hoofs came down the street and stopped, Saxon was able to slip to the front door and wave her hand to Billy. In the kitchen she found Tom waiting in sad anxiousness.

"It's all right," she said. "Billy Roberts has come, and I've got to go. You go in and sit beside her for a while, and maybe she'll go to sleep. But don't rush her. Let her have her own way. If she'll let you take her hand, why do it. Try it, anyway. But first of all, as an opener and just as a matter of course, start wetting the towel over her eyes."

He was a kindly, easy-going man; but, after the way of a large percentage of the Western stock, he was undemonstrative. He nodded, turned toward the door to obey, and paused irresolutely. The look he gave back to Saxon was almost dog-like in gratitude and all-brotherly in love. She felt it, and in spirit leapt toward it.

"It's all right—everything's all right," she cried hastily.

Tom shook his head.

"No, it ain't. It's a shame, a blamed shame, that's what it is." He shrugged his shoulders. "Oh, I don't care for myself. But it's for you. You got your life before you yet, little kid sister. You'll get old, and all that means, fast enough. But it's a bad start for a day off. The thing for you to do is to forget all this, and skin out with your fellow, an' have a good time." In the open door, his hand on the knob to close it after him, he halted a second time. A spasm contracted his brow. "Hell! Think of it! Sarah and I used to go buggy-riding once on a time. And I guess she had her three pairs of shoes, too. Can you beat it?"

CHAPTER IX

In her bedroom Saxon completed her dressing, for an instant stepping upon a chair so as to glimpse critically in the small wall-mirror the hang of her ready-made linen skirt. This, and the jacket, she had altered to fit, and she had double-stitched the seams to achieve the coveted tailored effect. Still on the chair, all in the moment of quick clear-seeing, she drew the skirt tightly back and raised it. The sight was good to her, nor did she under-appraise the lines of the slender ankle above the low tan tie nor did she under-appraise the delicate yet mature swell of calf outlined in the fresh brown of a new cotton stocking. Down from the chair, she pinned on a firm sailor hat of white straw with a brown ribbon around the crown that matched her ribbon belt. She rubbed her cheeks quickly and fiercely to bring back the color Sarah had driven out of them, and delayed a moment longer to put on her tan lisle-thread gloves. Once, in the fashion-page of a Sunday supplement, she had read that no lady ever put on her gloves after she left the door.

With a resolute self-grip, as she crossed the parlor and passed the door to Sarah's bedroom, through the thin wood of which came elephantine moanings and low slub-berings, she steeled herself to keep the color in her cheeks and the brightness in her eyes. And so well did she succeed that Billy never dreamed that the radiant, live young thing, tripping lightly down the steps to him, had just come from a bout with soul-sickening hysteria and madness.

To her, in the bright sun, Billy's blondness was startling. His cheeks, smooth as a girl's, were touched with color. The blue eyes seemed more cloudily blue than usual, and the crisp, sandy hair hinted more than ever of the pale straw-gold that was not there. Never had she seen him quite so royally young. As he smiled to greet her, with a slow white flash of teeth from between red lips, she caught again the promise of easement and rest. Fresh from the shattering chaos of her sister-in-law's mind, Billy's tremendous calm was especially satisfying, and Saxon mentally laughed to scorn the terrible temper he had charged to himself.

She had been buggy-riding before, but always behind one horse, jaded, and livery, in a top-buggy, heavy and dingy, such as livery stables rent because of sturdy un-breakableness. But here stood two horses, head-tossing and restless, shouting in every high-light glint of their satin, golden-sorrel coats that they had never been rented out in all their glorious young lives. Between them was a pole inconceivably slender, on them were harnesses preposterously string-like and fragile. And Billy belonged here, by elemental right, a part of them and of it, a master-part and a component, along with the spidery-delicate, narrow-boxed, wide- and yellow-wheeled, rubber-tired rig, effi-cient and capable, as different as he was different from the other man who had taken her out behind stolid, lumbering horses. He held the reins in one hand, yet, with low, steady voice, confident and assuring, held the nervous young animals more by the will and the spirit of him.

It was no time for lingering. With the quick glance and fore-knowledge of a wom-an, Saxon saw, not merely the curious children clustering about, but the peering of adult faces from open doors and windows, and past window-shades lifted up or held aside. With his free hand, Billy drew back the linen robe and helped her to a place beside him. The high-backed, luxuriously upholstered seat of brown leather gave her a sense of great comfort; yet even greater, it seemed to her, was the nearness and comfort of the man himself and of his body.

"How d'ye like 'em?" he asked, changing the reins to both hands and chirruping the horses, which went out with a jerk in an immediacy of action that was new to her. "They're the boss's, you know. Couldn't rent animals like them. He lets me take them out for exercise sometimes. If they ain't exercised regular they're a handful.—Look at King, there, prancin'. Some style, eh? Some style! The other one's the real goods, though. Prince is his name. Got to have some bit on him to hold'm.—Ah! Would you?—Did you see'm, Saxon? Some horse! Some horse!"

From behind came the admiring cheer of the neighborhood children, and Saxon, with a sigh of content, knew that the happy day had at last begun.

CHAPTER X

"I don't know horses," Saxon said. "I've never been on one's back, and the only ones I've tried to drive were single, and lame, or almost falling down, or something. But I'm not afraid of horses. I just love them. I was born loving them, I guess."

Billy threw an admiring, appreciative glance at her.

"That's the stuff. That's what I like in a woman—grit. Some of the girls I've had out—well, take it from me, they made me sick. Oh, I'm hep to 'em. Nervous, an' trembly, an' screechy, an' wabbly. I reckon they come out on my account an' not for the ponies. But me for the brave kid that likes the ponies. You're the real goods, Saxon, honest to God you are. Why, I can talk like a streak with you. The rest of 'em make me sick. I'm like a clam. They don't know nothin', an' they're that scared all the time—well, I guess you get me"

"You have to be born to love horses, maybe," she answered. "Maybe it's because I always think of my father on his roan war-horse that makes me love horses. But, anyway, I do. When I was a little girl I was drawing horses all the time. My mother always encouraged me. I've a scrapbook mostly filled with horses I drew when I was little. Do you know, Billy, sometimes I dream I actually own a horse, all my own. And lots of times I dream I'm on a horse's back, or driving him."

"I'll let you drive 'em, after a while, when they've worked their edge off. They're pullin' now.—There, put your hands in front of mine—take hold tight. Feel that? Sure you feel it. An' you ain't feelin' it all by a long shot. I don't dast slack, you bein' such a lightweight."

Her eyes sparkled as she felt the apportioned pull of the mouths of the beautiful, live things; and he, looking at her, sparkled with her in her delight.

"What's the good of a woman if she can't keep up with a man?" he broke out enthusiastically.

"People that like the same things always get along best together," she answered, with a triteness that concealed the joy that was hers at being so spontaneously in touch with him.

"Why, Saxon, I've fought battles, good ones, frazzlin' my silk away to beat the band before whisky-soaked, smokin' audiences of rotten fight-fans, that just made me sick clean through. An' them, that couldn't take just one stiff jolt or hook to jaw or stomach, a-cheerin' me an' yellin' for blood. Blood, mind you! An' them without the blood of a shrimp in their bodies. Why, honest, now, I'd sooner fight before an audience of one—you for instance, or anybody I liked. It'd do me proud. But them sickenin', sap-headed stiffs, with the grit of rabbits and the silk of mangy ky-yi's, a-cheerin' me—ME! Can you blame me for quittin' the dirty game?—Why, I'd sooner fight before broke-down old plugs of work-horses that's candidates for chicken-meat, than before them rotten bunches of stiffs with nothin' thicker'n water in their veins, an' Contra Costa water at that when the rains is heavy on the hills."

"I... I didn't know prizefighting was like that," she faltered, as she released her hold on the lines and sank back again beside him.

"It ain't the fightin', it's the fight-crowds," he defended with instant jealousy. "Of course, fightin' hurts a young fellow because it frazzles the silk outa him an' all that. But it's the low-lifers in the audience that gets me. Why the good things they say to me, the praise an' that, is insulting. Do you get me? It makes me cheap. Think of it—booze-guzzlin' stiffs that 'd be afraid to mix it with a sick cat, not fit to hold the coat of any decent man, think of them a-standin' up on their hind legs an' yellin' an' cheerin' me—ME!"

"Ha! ha! What d'ye think of that? Ain't he a rogue?"

A big bulldog, sliding obliquely and silently across the street, unconcerned with the team he was avoiding, had passed so close that Prince, baring his teeth like a stallion, plunged his head down against reins and check in an effort to seize the dog.

"Now he's some fighter, that Prince. An' he's natural. He didn't make that reach just for some low-lifer to yell'm on. He just done it outa pure cussedness and himself. That's clean. That's right. Because it's natural. But them fight-fans! Honest to God, Saxon...."

And Saxon, glimpsing him sidewise, as he watched the horses and their way on the Sunday morning streets, checking them back suddenly and swerving to avoid two boys coasting across street on a toy wagon, saw in him deeps and intensities, all the magic connotations of temperament, the glimmer and hint of rages profound, bleaknesses as cold and far as the stars, savagery as keen as a wolf's and clean as a stallion's, wrath as implacable as a destroying angel's, and youth that was fire and life beyond time and place. She was awed and fascinated, with the hunger of woman bridging the vastness to him, daring to love him with arms and breast that ached to him, murmuring to herself and through all the halls of her soul, "You dear, you dear."

"Honest to God, Saxon," he took up the broken thread, "they's times when I've hated them, when I wanted to jump over the ropes and wade into them, knock-down and drag-out, an' show'm what fightin' was. Take that night with Billy Murphy. Billy Murphy!—if you only knew him. My friend. As clean an' game a boy as ever jumped inside the ropes to take the decision. Him! We went to the Durant School together. We grew up chums. His fight was my fight. My trouble was his trouble. We both took to the fightin' game. They matched us. Not the first time. Twice we'd fought draws. Once the decision was his; once it was mine. The fifth fight of two lovin' men that just loved each other. He's three years older'n me. He's a wife and two or three kids, an' I know them, too. And he's my friend. Get it?

"I'm ten pounds heavier—but with heavyweights that 'a all right. He can't time an' distance as good as me, an' I can keep set better, too. But he's cleverer an' quicker. I never was quick like him. We both can take punishment, an' we're both two-handed, a wallop in all our fists. I know the kick of his, an' he knows my kick, an' we're both real respectful. And we're even-matched. Two draws, and a decision to each. Honest, I ain't any kind of a hunch who's gain' to win, we're that even.

CHAPTER X

"Now, the fight.—You ain't squeamish, are you?"

"No, no," she cried. "I'd just love to hear—you are so wonderful."

He took the praise with a clear, unwavering look, and without hint of acknowledgment.

"We go along—six rounds—seven rounds—eight rounds; an' honors even. I've been timin' his rushes an' straight-leftin' him, an' meetin' his duck with a wicked little right upper-cut, an' he's shaken me on the jaw an' walloped my ears till my head's all singin' an' buzzin'. An' everything lovely with both of us, with a noise like a draw decision in sight. Twenty rounds is the distance, you know.

"An' then his bad luck comes. We're just mixin' into a clinch that ain't arrived yet, when he shoots a short hook to my head—his left, an' a real hay-maker if it reaches my jaw. I make a forward duck, not quick enough, an' he lands bingo on the side of my head. Honest to God, Saxon, it's that heavy I see some stars. But it don't hurt an' ain't serious, that high up where the bone's thick. An' right there he finishes himself, for his bad thumb, which I've known since he first got it as a kid fightin' in the sandlot at Watts Tract—he smashes that thumb right there, on my hard head, back into the socket with an out-twist, an' all the old cords that'd never got strong gets theirs again. I didn't mean it. A dirty trick, fair in the game, though, to make a guy smash his hand on your head. But not between friends. I couldn't a-done that to Bill Murphy for a million dollars. It was a accident, just because I was slow, because I was born slow.

"The hurt of it! Honest, Saxon, you don't know what hurt is till you've got a old hurt like that hurt again. What can Billy Murphy do but slow down? He's got to. He ain't fightin' two-handed any more. He knows it; I know it; The referee knows it; but nobody else. He goes on a-moving that left of his like it's all right. But it ain't. It's hurtin' him like a knife dug into him. He don't dast strike a real blow with that left of his. But it hurts, anyway. Just to move it or not move it hurts, an' every little dab-feint that I'm too wise to guard, knowin' there's no weight behind, why them little dab-touches on that poor thumb goes right to the heart of him, an' hurts worse than a thousand boils or a thousand knockouts—just hurts all over again, an' worse, each time an' touch.

"Now suppose he an' me was boxin' for fun, out in the back yard, an' he hurts his thumb that way, why we'd have the gloves off in a jiffy an' I'd be putting cold compresses on that poor thumb of his an' bandagin' it that tight to keep the inflammation down. But no. This is a fight for fight-fans that's paid their admission for blood, an' blood they're goin' to get. They ain't men. They're wolves.

"He has to go easy, now, an' I ain't a-forcin' him none. I'm all shot to pieces. I don't know what to do. So I slow down, an' the fans get hep to it. 'Why don't you fight?' they begin to yell; 'Fake! Fake!' 'Why don't you kiss'm?' 'Lovin' cup for yours, Bill Roberts!' an' that sort of bunk.

"'Fight!' says The referee to me, low an' savage. 'Fight, or I'll disqualify you—you, Bill, I mean you.' An' this to me, with a touch on the shoulder 'so they's no mistakin'.

"It ain't pretty. It ain't right. D'ye know what we was fightin' for? A hundred bucks. Think of it! An' the game is we got to do our best to put our man down for the count because of the fans has bet on us. Sweet, ain't it? Well, that's my last fight. It finishes me deado. Never again for yours truly.

"'Quit,' I says to Billy Murphy in a clinch; 'for the love of God, Bill, quit.' An' he says back, in a whisper, 'I can't, Bill—you know that.'

"An' then the referee drags us apart, an' a lot of the fans begins to hoot an' boo.

"'Now kick in, damn you, Bill Roberts, an' finish'm' the referee says to me, an' I tell'm to go to hell as Bill an' me flop into the next clinch, not hittin', an' Bill touches his thumb again, an' I see the pain shoot across his face. Game? That good boy's the limit. An' to look into the eyes of a brave man that's sick with pain, an' love 'm, an' see love in them eyes of his, an' then have to go on givin' 'm pain—call that sport? I can't see it. But the crowd's got its money on us. We don't count. We've sold ourselves for a hundred bucks, an' we gotta deliver the goods.

"Let me tell you, Saxon, honest to God, that was one of the times I wanted to go through the ropes an' drop them fans a-yellin' for blood an' show 'em what blood is.

"'For God's sake finish me, Bill,' Bill says to me in that clinch; 'put her over an' I'll fall for it, but I can't lay down.'

"D'ye want to know? I cry there, right in the ring, in that clinch. The weeps for me. 'I can't do it, Bill,' I whisper back, hangin' onto'm like a brother an' the referee ragin' an' draggin' at us to get us apart, an' all the wolves in the house snarlin'.

"'You got 'm!' the audience is yellin'. 'Go in an' finish 'm!' 'The hay for him, Bill; put her across to the jaw an' see 'm fall!'

"'You got to, Bill, or you're a dog,' Bill says, lookin' love at me in his eyes as the referee's grip untangles us clear.

"An' them wolves of fans yellin': 'Fake! Fake! Fake!' like that, an' keepin' it up.

"Well, I done it. They's only that way out. I done it. By God, I done it. I had to. I feint for 'm, draw his left, duck to the right past it, takin' it across my shoulder, an come up with my right to his jaw. An' he knows the trick. He's hep. He's beaten me to it an' blocked it with his shoulder a thousan' times. But this time he don't. He keeps himself wide open on purpose. Blim! It lands. He's dead in the air, an' he goes down sideways, strikin' his face first on the rosin-canvas an' then layin' dead, his head twisted under 'm till you'd a-thought his neck was broke. ME—I did that for a hundred bucks an' a bunch of stiffs I'd be ashamed to wipe my feet on. An' then I pick Bill up in my arms an' carry'm to his corner, an' help bring'm around. Well, they ain't no kick comin'. They pay their money an' they get their blood, an' a knockout. An' a better man than them, that I love, layin' there dead to the world with a skinned face on the mat."

For a moment he was still, gazing straight before him at the horses, his face hard and angry. He sighed, looked at Saxon, and smiled.

"An' I quit the game right there. An' Billy Murphy's laughed at me for it. He still follows it. A side-line, you know, because he works at a good trade. But once in a while, when the house needs paintin', or the doctor bills are up, or his oldest kid wants a bicycle, he jumps out an' makes fifty or a hundred bucks before some of the clubs. I want you to meet him when it comes handy. He's some boy I'm tellin' you. But it did make me sick that night."

Again the harshness and anger were in his face, and Saxon amazed herself by doing unconsciously what women higher in the social scale have done with deliberate sincerity. Her hand went out impulsively to his holding the lines, resting on top of it for a moment with quick, firm pressure. Her reward was a smile from lips and eyes, as his face turned toward her.

"Gee!" he exclaimed. "I never talk a streak like this to anybody. I just hold my hush an' keep my thinks to myself. But, somehow, I guess it's funny, I kind of have a feelin' I want to make good with you. An' that's why I'm tellin' you my thinks. Anybody can dance."

The way led uptown, past the City Hall and the Fourteenth Street skyscrapers, and out Broadway to Mountain View. Turning to the right at the cemetery, they climbed the Piedmont Heights to Blair Park and plunged into the green coolness of Jack Hayes Canyon. Saxon could not suppress her surprise and joy at the quickness with which they covered the ground.

"They are beautiful," she said. "I never dreamed I'd ever ride behind horses like them. I'm afraid I'll wake up now and find it's a dream. You know, I dream horses all the time. I'd give anything to own one some time."

"It's funny, ain't it?" Billy answered. "I like horses that way. The boss says I'm a wooz at horses. An' I know he's a dub. He don't know the first thing. An' yet he owns two hundred big heavy draughts besides this light drivin' pair, an' I don't own one."

"Yet God makes the horses," Saxon said.

"It's a sure thing the boss don't. Then how does he have so many?—two hundred of 'em, I'm tellin' you. He thinks he likes horses. Honest to God, Saxon, he don't like all his horses as much as I like the last hair on the last tail of the scrubbiest of the bunch. Yet they're his. Wouldn't it jar you?"

"Wouldn't it?" Saxon laughed appreciatively. "I just love fancy shirtwaists, an' I spent my life ironing some of the beautifullest I've ever seen. It's funny, an' it isn't fair."

Billy gritted his teeth in another of his rages.

"An' the way some of them women gets their shirtwaists. It makes me sick, thinkin' of you ironin' 'em. You know what I mean, Saxon. They ain't no use wastin' words over it. You know. I know. Everybody knows. An' it's a hell of a world if men an' women sometimes can't talk to each other about such things." His manner was almost apologetic yet it was defiantly and assertively right. "I never talk this way to other girls. They'd think I'm workin up to designs on 'em. They make me sick the way they're always lookin' for them designs. But you're different I can talk to you that way. I know I've got to. It's the square thing. You're like Billy Murphy, or any other man a man can talk to."

She sighed with a great happiness, and looked at him with unconscious, love-shining eyes.

"It's the same way with me," she said. "The fellows I've run with I've never dared let talk about such things, because I knew they'd take advantage of it. Why, all the time, with them, I've a feeling that we're cheating and lying to each other, playing a game like at a masquerade ball." She paused for a moment, hesitant and debating, then went on in a queer low voice. "I haven't been asleep. I've seen... and heard. I've had my chances, when I was that tired of the laundry I'd have done almost anything. I could have got those fancy shirtwaists... an' all the rest... and maybe a horse to ride. There was a bank cashier... married, too, if you please. He talked to me straight out. I didn't count, you know. I wasn't a girl, with a girl's feelings, or anything. I was nobody. It was just like a business talk. I learned about men from him. He told me what he'd do. He..."

Her voice died away in sadness, and in the silence she could hear Billy grit his teeth.

"You can't tell me," he cried. "I know. It's a dirty world—an unfair, lousy world. I can't make it out. They's no squareness in it.—Women, with the best that's in 'em, bought an' sold like horses. I don't understand women that way. I don't understand men that way. I can't see how a man gets anything but cheated when he buys such things. It's funny, ain't it? Take my boss an' his horses. He owns women, too. He might a-owned you, just because he's got the price. An', Saxon, you was made for fancy shirtwaists an' all that, but, honest to God, I can't see you payin' for them that way. It'd be a crime—"

He broke off abruptly and reined in the horses. Around a sharp turn, speeding down the grade upon them, had appeared an automobile. With slamming of brakes it was brought to a stop, while the faces of the occupants took new lease of interest of life and stared at the young man and woman in the light rig that barred the way. Billy held up his hand.

"Take the outside, sport," he said to the chauffeur.

"Nothin' doin', kiddo," came the answer, as the chauffeur measured with hard, wise eyes the crumbling edge of the road and the downfall of the outside bank.

"Then we camp," Billy announced cheerfully. "I know the rules of the road. These animals ain't automobile broke altogether, an' if you think I'm goin' to have 'em shy off the grade you got another guess comin'."

A confusion of injured protestation arose from those that sat in the car.

"You needn't be a road-hog because you're a Rube," said the chauffeur. "We ain't a-goin' to hurt your horses. Pull out so we can pass. If you don't..."

"That'll do you, sport," was Billy's retort. "You can't talk that way to yours truly. I got your number an' your tag, my son. You're standin' on your foot. Back up the grade an' get off of it. Stop on the outside at the first psssin'-place an' we'll pass you. You've got the juice. Throw on the reverse."

After a nervous consultation, the chauffeur obeyed, and the car backed up the hill and out of sight around the turn.

"Them cheap skates," Billy sneered to Saxon, "with a couple of gallons of gasoline an' the price of a machine a-thinkin' they own the roads your folks an' my folks made."

"Talkin' all night about it?" came the chauffeur's voice from around the bend. "Get a move on. You can pass."

"Get off your foot," Billy retorted contemptuously. "I'm a-comin' when I'm ready to come, an' if you ain't given room enough I'll go clean over you an' your load of chicken meat."

He slightly slacked the reins on the restless, head-tossing animals, and without need of chirrup they took the weight of the light vehicle and passed up the hill and apprehensively on the inside of the purring machine.

"Where was we?" Billy queried, as the clear road showed in front. "Yep, take my boss. Why should he own two hundred horses, an' women, an' the rest, an' you an' me own nothin'?"

"You own your silk, Billy," she said softly.

"An' you yours. Yet we sell it to 'em like it was cloth across the counter at so much a yard. I guess you're hep to what a few more years in the laundry'll do to you. Take me. I'm sellin' my silk slow every day I work. See that little finger?" He shifted the reins to one hand for a moment and held up the free hand for inspection. "I can't straighten it like the others, an' it's growin'. I never put it out fightin'. The teamin's done it. That's silk gone across the counter, that's all. Ever see a old four-horse teamster's hands? They look like claws they're that crippled an' twisted."

"Things weren't like that in the old days when our folks crossed the plains," she answered. "They might a-got their fingers twisted, but they owned the best goin' in the way of horses and such."

"Sure. They worked for themselves. They twisted their fingers for themselves. But I'm twistin' my fingers for my boss. Why, d'ye know, Saxon, his hands is soft as a woman's that's never done any work. Yet he owns the horses an' the stables, an' never does a tap of work, an' I manage to scratch my meal-ticket an' my clothes. It's got my goat the way things is run. An' who runs 'em that way? That's what I want to know. Times has changed. Who changed 'em?"

"God didn't."

"You bet your life he didn't. An' that's another thing that gets me. Who's God anyway? If he's runnin' things—an' what good is he if he ain't?—then why does he let my boss, an' men like that cashier you mentioned, why does he let them own the horses, an' buy the women, the nice little girls that oughta be lovin' their own husbands, an' havin' children they're not ashamed of, an' just bein' happy accordin' to their nature?"

CHAPTER XI

The horses, resting frequently and lathered by the work, had climbed the steep grade of the old road to Moraga Valley, and on the divide of the Contra Costa hills the way descended sharply through the green and sunny stillness of Redwood Canyon.

"Say, ain't it swell?" Billy queried, with a wave of his hand indicating the circled tree-groups, the trickle of unseen water, and the summer hum of bees.

"I love it'" Saxon affirmed. "It makes me want to live in the country, and I never have."

"Me, too, Saxon. I've never lived in the country in my life—an' all my folks was country folks."

"No cities then. Everybody lived in the country."

"I guess you're right," he nodded. "They just had to live in the country."

There was no brake on the light carriage, and Billy became absorbed in managing his team down the steep, winding road. Saxon leaned back, eyes closed, with a feeling of ineffable rest. Time and again he shot glances at her closed eyes.

"What's the matter?" he asked finally, in mild alarm. "You ain't sick?"

"It's so beautiful I'm afraid to look," she answered. "It's so brave it hurts."

"BRAVE?—now that's funny."

"Isn't it? But it just makes me feel that way. It's brave. Now the houses and streets and things in the city aren't brave. But this is. I don't know why. It just is."

"By golly, I think you're right," he exclaimed. "It strikes me that way, now you speak of it. They ain't no games or tricks here, no cheatin' an' no lyin'. Them trees just stand up natural an' strong an' clean like young boys their first time in the ring before they've learned its rottenness an' how to double-cross an' lay down to the bettin' odds an' the fight-fans. Yep; it is brave. Say, Saxon, you see things, don't you?" His pause was almost wistful, and he looked at her and studied her with a caressing softness that ran through her in resurgent thrills. "D'ye know, I'd just like you to see me fight some time—a real fight, with something doin' every moment. I'd be proud to death to do it for you. An' I'd sure fight some with you lookin' on an' understandin'. That'd be a fight what is, take it from me. An' that's funny, too. I never wanted to fight before a woman in my life. They squeal and screech an' don't understand. But you'd understand. It's dead open an' shut you would."

A little later, swinging along the flat of the valley, through the little clearings of the farmers and the ripe grain-stretches golden in the sunshine, Billy turned to Saxon again.

CHAPTER XI

"Say, you've ben in love with fellows, lots of times. Tell me about it. What's it like?"

She shook her head slowly.

"I only thought I was in love—and not many times, either—"

"Many times!" he cried.

"Not really ever," she assured him, secretly exultant at his unconscious jealousy. "I never was really in love. If I had been I'd be married now. You see, I couldn't see anything else to it but to marry a man if I loved him."

"But suppose he didn't love you?"

"Oh, I don't know," she smiled, half with facetiousness and half with certainty and pride. "I think I could make him love me."

"I guess you sure could," Billy proclaimed enthusiastically.

"The trouble is," she went on, "the men that loved me I never cared for that way.—Oh, look!"

A cottontail rabbit had scuttled across the road, and a tiny dust cloud lingered like smoke, marking the way of his flight. At the next turn a dozen quail exploded into the air from under the noses of the horses. Billy and Saxon exclaimed in mutual delight.

"Gee," he muttered, "I almost wisht I'd ben born a farmer. Folks wasn't made to live in cities."

"Not our kind, at least," she agreed. Followed a pause and a long sigh. "It's all so beautiful. It would be a dream just to live all your life in it. I'd like to be an Indian squaw sometimes."

Several times Billy checked himself on the verge of speech.

"About those fellows you thought you was in love with," he said finally. "You ain't told me, yet."

"You want to know?" she asked. "They didn't amount to anything."

"Of course I want to know. Go ahead. Fire away."

"Well, first there was Al Stanley—"

"What did he do for a livin'?" Billy demanded, almost as with authority.

"He was a gambler."

Billy's face abruptly stiffened, and she could see his eyes cloudy with doubt in the quick glance he flung at her.

"Oh, it was all right," she laughed. "I was only eight years old. You see, I'm beginning at the beginning. It was after my mother died and when I was adopted by Cady. He kept a hotel and saloon. It was down in Los Angeles. Just a small hotel. Workingmen, just common laborers, mostly, and some railroad men, stopped at it, and I guess Al Stanley got his share of their wages. He was so handsome and so quiet and soft-spoken. And he had the nicest eyes and the softest, cleanest hands. I can see them now. He played with me sometimes, in the afternoon, and gave me candy and little presents. He used to sleep most of the day. I didn't know why, then. I thought he was a fairy prince in disguise. And then he got killed, right in the bar-room, but first he killed the man that killed him. So that was the end of that love affair.

"Next was after the asylum, when I was thirteen and living with my brother—I've lived with him ever since. He was a boy that drove a bakery wagon. Almost every morning, on the way to school, I used to pass him. He would come driving down Wood Street and turn in on Twelfth. Maybe it was because he drove a horse that attracted me. Anyway, I must have loved him for a couple of months. Then he lost his job, or something, for another boy drove the wagon. And we'd never even spoken to each other.

"Then there was a bookkeeper when I was sixteen. I seem to run to bookkeepers. It was a bookkeeper at the laundry that Charley Long beat up. This other one was when I was working in Hickmeyer's Cannery. He had soft hands, too. But I quickly got all I wanted of him. He was... well, anyway, he had ideas like your boss. And I never really did love him, truly and honest, Billy. I felt from the first that he wasn't just right. And when I was working in the paper-box factory I thought I loved a clerk in Kahn's Emporium—you know, on Eleventh and Washington. He was all right. That was the trouble with him. He was too much all right. He didn't have any life in him, any go. He wanted to marry me, though. But somehow I couldn't see it. That shows I didn't love him. He was narrow-chested and skinny, and his hands were always cold and fishy. But my! he could dress—just like he came out of a bandbox. He said he was going to drown himself, and all kinds of things, but I broke with him just the same.

"And after that... well, there isn't any after that. I must have got particular, I guess, but I didn't see anybody I could love. It seemed more like a game with the men I met, or a fight. And we never fought fair on either side. Seemed as if we always had cards up our sleeves. We weren't honest or outspoken, but instead it seemed as if we were trying to take advantage of each other. Charley Long was honest, though. And so was that bank cashier. And even they made me have the fight feeling harder than ever. All of them always made me feel I had to take care of myself. They wouldn't. That was sure."

She stopped and looked with interest at the clean profile of his face as he watched and guided the homes. He looked at her inquiringly, and her eyes laughed lazily into his as she stretched her arms.

"That's all," she concluded. "I've told you everything, which I've never done before to any one. And it's your turn now."

"Not much of a turn, Saxon. I've never cared for girls—that is, not enough to want to marry 'em. I always liked men better—fellows like Billy Murphy. Besides, I guess I was too interested in trainin' an' fightin' to bother with women much. Why, Saxon, honest, while I ain't ben altogether good—you understand what I mean—just the same I ain't never talked love to a girl in my life. They was no call to."

"The girls have loved you just the same," she teased, while in her heart was a curious elation at his virginal confession.

He devoted himself to the horses.

"Lots of them," she urged.

Still he did not reply.

"Now, haven't they?"

"Well, it wasn't my fault," he said slowly. "If they wanted to look sideways at me it was up to them. And it was up to me to sidestep if I wanted to, wasn't it? You've no idea, Saxon, how a prizefighter is run after. Why, sometimes it's seemed to me that girls an' women ain't got an ounce of natural shame in their make-up. Oh, I was never afraid of them, believe muh, but I didn't hanker after 'em. A man's a fool that'd let them kind get his goat.

"Maybe you haven't got love in you," she challenged.

"Maybe I haven't," was his discouraging reply. "Anyway, I don't see myself lovin' a girl that runs after me. It's all right for Charley-boys, but a man that is a man don't like bein' chased by women."

"My mother always said that love was the greatest thing in the world," Saxon argued. "She wrote poems about it, too. Some of them were published in the San Jose Mercury."

"What do you think about it?"

"Oh, I don't know," she baffled, meeting his eyes with another lazy smile. "All I know is it's pretty good to be alive a day like this."

"On a trip like this—you bet it is," he added promptly.

At one o'clock Billy turned off the road and drove into an open space among the trees.

"Here's where we eat," he announced. "I thought it'd be better to have a lunch by ourselves than atop at one of these roadside dinner counters. An' now, just to make everything safe an' comfortable, I'm goin' to unharness the horses. We got lots of time. You can get the lunch basket out an' spread it on the lap-robe."

As Saxon unpacked she basket she was appalled at his extravagance. She spread an amazing array of ham and chicken sandwiches, crab salad, hard-boiled eggs, pickled pigs' feet, ripe olives and dill pickles, Swiss cheese, salted almonds, oranges and bananas, and several pint bottles of beer. It was the quantity as well as the variety that bothered her. It had the appearance of a reckless attempt to buy out a whole delicatessen shop.

"You oughtn't to blow yourself that way," she reproved him as he sat down beside her. "Why it's enough for half a dozen bricklayers."

"It's all right, isn't it?"

"Yes," she acknowledged. "But that's the trouble. It's too much so."

"Then it's all right," he concluded. "I always believe in havin' plenty. Have some beer to wash the dust away before we begin? Watch out for the glasses. I gotta return them."

Later, the meal finished, he lay on his back, smoking a cigarette, and questioned her about her earlier history. She had been telling him of her life in her brother's house, where she paid four dollars and a half a week board. At fifteen she had graduated from grammar school and gone to work in the jute mills for four dollars a week, three of which she had paid to Sarah.

"How about that saloonkeeper?" Billy asked. "How come it he adopted you?"

She shrugged her shoulders. "I don't know, except that all my relatives were hard up. It seemed they just couldn't get on. They managed to scratch a lean living for themselves, and that was all. Cady—he was the saloonkeeper—had been a soldier in my father's company, and he always swore by Captain Kit, which was their nickname for him. My father had kept the surgeons from amputating his leg in the war, and he never forgot it. He was making money in the hotel and saloon, and I found out afterward he helped out a lot to pay the doctors and to bury my mother alongside of father. I was to go to Uncle Will—that was my mother's wish; but there had been fighting up in the Ventura Mountains where his ranch was, and men had been killed. It was about fences and cattlemen or something, and anyway he was in jail a long time, and when he got his freedom the lawyers had got his ranch. He was an old man, then, and broken, and his wife took sick, and he got a job as night watchman for forty dollars a month. So he couldn't do anything for me, and Cady adopted me.

"Cady was a good man, if he did run a saloon. His wife was a big, handsome-looking woman. I don't think she was all right... and I've heard so since. But she was good to me. I don't care what they say about her, or what she was. She was awful good to me. After he died, she went altogether bad, and so I went into the orphan asylum. It wasn't any too good there, and I had three years of it. And then Tom had married and settled down to steady work, and he took me out to live with him. And—well, I've been working pretty steady ever since."

She gazed sadly away across the fields until her eyes came to rest on a fence bright-splashed with poppies at its base. Billy, who from his supine position had been looking up at her, studying and pleasuring in the pointed oval of her woman's face, reached his hand out slowly as he murmured:

"You poor little kid."

His hand closed sympathetically on her bare forearm, and as she looked down to greet his eyes she saw in them surprise and delight.

"Say, ain't your skin cool though," he said. "Now me, I'm always warm. Feel my hand."

It was warmly moist, and she noted microscopic beads of sweat on his forehead and clean-shaven upper lip.

"My, but you are sweaty."

She bent to him and with her handkerchief dabbed his lip and forehead dry, then dried his palms.

"I breathe through my skin, I guess," he explained. "The wise guys in the trainin' camps and gyms say it's a good sign for health. But somehow I'm sweatin' more than usual now. Funny, ain't it?"

She had been forced to unclasp his hand from her arm in order to dry it, and when she finished, it returned to its old position.

"But, say, ain't your skin cool," he repeated with renewed wonder. "Soft as velvet, too, an' smooth as silk. It feels great."

Gently explorative, he slid his hand from wrist to elbow and came to rest half way back. Tired and languid from the morning in the sun, she found herself thrilling to his touch and half-dreamily deciding that here was a man she could love, hands and all.

"Now I've taken the cool all out of that spot." He did not look up to her, and she could see the roguish smile that curled on his lips. "So I guess I'll try another."

He shifted his hand along her arm with soft sensuousness, and she, looking down at his lips, remembered the long tingling they had given hers the first time they had met.

"Go on and talk," he urged, after a delicious five minutes of silence. "I like to watch your lips talking. It's funny, but every move they make looks like a tickly kiss."

Greatly she wanted to stay where she was. Instead, she said:

"If I talk, you won't like what I say."

"Go on," he insisted. "You can't say anything I won't like."

"Well, there's some poppies over there by the fence I want to pick. And then it's time for us to be going."

CHAPTER XI

"I lose," he laughed. "But you made twenty-five tickle kisses just the same. I counted 'em. I'll tell you what: you sing 'When the Harvest Days Are Over,' and let me have your other cool arm while you're doin' it, and then we'll go."

She sang looking down into his eyes, which ware centered, not on hers, but on her lips. When she finished, she slipped his hands from her arms and got up. He was about to start for the horses, when she held her jacket out to him. Despite the independence natural to a girl who earned her own living, she had an innate love of the little services and finenesses; and, also, she remembered from her childhood the talk by the pioneer women of the courtesy and attendance of the caballeros of the Spanish-California days.

Sunset greeted them when, after a wide circle to the east and south, they cleared the divide of the Contra Costa hills and began dropping down the long grade that led past Redwood Peak to Fruitvale. Beneath them stretched the flatlands to the bay, checkerboarded into fields and broken by the towns of Elmhurst, San Leandro, and Haywards. The smoke of Oakland filled the western sky with haze and murk, while beyond, across the bay, they could see the first winking lights of San Francisco.

Darkness was on them, and Billy had become curiously silent. For half an hour he had given no recognition of her existence save once, when the chill evening wind caused him to tuck the robe tightly about her and himself. Half a dozen times Saxon found herself on the verge of the remark, "What's on your mind?" but each time let it remain unuttered. She sat very close to him. The warmth of their bodies intermingled, and she was aware of a great restfulness and content.

"Say, Saxon," he began abruptly. "It's no use my holdin' it in any longer. It's ben in my mouth all day, ever since lunch. What's the matter with you an' me gettin' married?"

She knew, very quietly and very gladly, that he meant it. Instinctively she was impelled to hold off, to make him woo her, to make herself more desirably valuable ere she yielded. Further, her woman's sensitiveness and pride were offended. She had never dreamed of so forthright and bald a proposal from the man to whom she would give herself. The simplicity and directness of Billy's proposal constituted almost a hurt. On the other hand she wanted him so much—how much she had not realized until now, when he had so unexpectedly made himself accessible.

"Well you gotta say something, Saxon. Hand it to me, good or bad; but anyway hand it to me. An' just take into consideration that I love you. Why, I love you like the very devil, Saxon. I must, because I'm askin' you to marry me, an' I never asked any girl that before."

Another silence fell, and Saxon found herself dwelling on the warmth, tingling now, under the lap-robe. When she realized whither her thoughts led, she blushed guiltily in the darkness.

"How old are you, Billy?" she questioned, with a suddenness and irrelevance as disconcerting as his first words had been.

"Twenty-two," he answered.

"I am twenty-four."

"As if I didn't know. When you left the orphan asylum and how old you were, how long you worked in the jute mills, the cannery, the paper-box factory, the laundry—maybe you think I can't do addition. I knew how old you was, even to your birthday."

"That doesn't change the fact that I'm two years older."

"What of it? If it counted for anything, I wouldn't be lovin' you, would I? Your mother was dead right. Love's the big stuff. It's what counts. Don't you see? I just love you, an' I gotta have you. It's natural, I guess; and I've always found with horses, dogs, and other folks, that what's natural is right. There's no gettin' away from it, Saxon; I gotta have you, an' I'm just hopin' hard you gotta have me. Maybe my hands ain't soft like bookkeepers' an' clerks, but they can work for you, an' fight like Sam Hill for you, and, Saxon, they can love you."

The old sex antagonism which she had always experienced with men seemed to have vanished. She had no sense of being on the defensive. This was no game. It was what she had been looking for and dreaming about. Before Billy she was defenseless, and there was an all-satisfaction in the knowledge. She could deny him nothing. Not even if he proved to be like the others. And out of the greatness of the thought rose a greater thought—he would not so prove himself.

She did not speak. Instead, in a glow of spirit and flesh, she reached out to his left hand and gently tried to remove it from the rein. He did not understand; but when she persisted he shifted the rein to his right and let her have her will with the other hand. Her head bent over it, and she kissed the teamster callouses.

For the moment he was stunned.

"You mean it?" he stammered.

For reply, she kissed the hand again and murmured:

"I love your hands, Billy. To me they are the most beautiful hands in the world, and it would take hours of talking to tell you all they mean to me."

"Whoa!" he called to the horses.

He pulled them in to a standstill, soothed them with his voice, and made the reins fast around the whip. Then he turned to her with arms around her and lips to lips.

"Oh, Billy, I'll make you a good wife," she sobbed, when the kiss was broken.

He kissed her wet eyes and found her lips again.

"Now you know what I was thinkin' and why I was sweatin' when we was eatin' lunch. Just seemed I couldn't hold in much longer from tellin' you. Why, you know, you looked good to me from the first moment I spotted you."

"And I think I loved you from that first day, too, Billy. And I was so proud of you all that day, you were so kind and gentle, and so strong, and the way the men all respected you and the girls all wanted you, and the way you fought those three Irishmen when I was behind the picnic table. I couldn't love or marry a man I wasn't proud of, and I'm so proud of you, so proud."

"Not half as much as I am right now of myself," he answered, "for having won you. It's too good to be true. Maybe the alarm clock'll go off and wake me up in a couple of minutes. Well, anyway, if it does, I'm goin' to make the best of them two minutes first. Watch out I don't eat you, I'm that hungry for you."

He smothered her in an embrace, holding her so tightly to him that it almost hurt. After what was to her an age-long period of bliss, his arms relaxed and he seemed to make an effort to draw himself together.

"An' the clock ain't gone off yet," he whispered against her cheek. "And it's a dark night, an' there's Fruitvale right ahead, an' if there ain't King and Prince standin' still in the middle of the road. I never thought the time'd come when I wouldn't want to take the ribbons on a fine pair of horses. But this is that time. I just can't let go of you, and I've gotta some time to-night. It hurts worse'n poison, but here goes."

CHAPTER XI

He restored her to herself, tucked the disarranged robe about her, and chirruped to the impatient team.

Half an hour later he called "Whoa!"

"I know I'm awake now, but I don't know but maybe I dreamed all the rest, and I just want to make sure."

And again be made the reins fast and took her in his arms.

CHAPTER XII

The days flew by for Saxon. She worked on steadily at the laundry, even doing more overtime than usual, and all her free waking hours were devoted to preparations for the great change and to Billy. He had proved himself God's own impetuous lover by insisting on getting married the next day after the proposal, and then by resolutely refusing to compromise on more than a week's delay.

"Why wait?" he demanded. "We're not gettin' any younger so far as I can notice, an' think of all we lose every day we wait."

In the end, he gave in to a month, which was well, for in two weeks he was transferred, with half a dozen other drivers, to work from the big stables of Corberly and Morrison in West Oakland. House-hunting in the other end of town ceased, and on Pine Street, between Fifth and Fourth, and in immediate proximity to the great Southern Pacific railroad yards, Billy and Saxon rented a neat cottage of four small rooms for ten dollars a month.

"Dog-cheap is what I call it, when I think of the small rooms I've ben soaked for," was Billy's judgment. "Look at the one I got now, not as big as the smallest here, an' me payin' six dollars a month for it."

"But it's furnished," Saxon reminded him. "You see, that makes a difference."

But Billy didn't see.

"I ain't much of a scholar, Saxon, but I know simple arithmetic; I've soaked my watch when I was hard up, and I can calculate interest. How much do you figure it will cost to furnish the house, carpets on the floor, linoleum on the kitchen, and all?"

"We can do it nicely for three hundred dollars," she answered. "I've been thinking it over and I'm sure we can do it for that."

"Three hundred," he muttered, wrinkling his brows with concentration. "Three hundred, say at six per cent.—that'd be six cents on the dollar, sixty cents on ten dollars, six dollars on the hundred, on three hundred eighteen dollars. Say—I'm a bear at multiplyin' by ten. Now divide eighteen by twelve, that'd be a dollar an' a half a month interest." He stopped, satisfied that he had proved his contention. Then his face quickened with a fresh thought. "Hold on! That ain't all. That'd be the interest on the furniture for four rooms. Divide by four. What's a dollar an' a half divided by four?"

"Four into fifteen, three times and three to carry," Saxon recited glibly. "Four into thirty is seven, twenty-eight, two to carry; and two-fourths is one-half. There you are."

CHAPTER XII

"Gee! You're the real bear at figures." He hesitated. "I didn't follow you. How much did you say it was?"

"Thirty-seven and a half cents."

"Ah, ha! Now we'll see how much I've ben gouged for my one room. Ten dollars a month for four rooms is two an' a half for one. Add thirty-seven an' a half cents interest on furniture, an' that makes two dollars an' eighty-seven an' a half cents. Subtract from six dollars...."

"Three dollars and twelve and a half cents," she supplied quickly.

"There we are! Three dollars an' twelve an' a half cents I'm jiggered out of on the room I'm rentin'. Say! Bein' married is like savin' money, ain't it?"

"But furniture wears out, Billy."

"By golly, I never thought of that. It ought to be figured, too. Anyway, we've got a snap here, and next Saturday afternoon you've gotta get off from the laundry so as we can go an' buy our furniture. I saw Salinger's last night. I give'm fifty down, and the rest installment plan, ten dollars a month. In twenty-five months the furniture's ourn. An' remember, Saxon, you wanta buy everything you want, no matter how much it costs. No scrimpin' on what's for you an' me. Get me?"

She nodded, with no betrayal on her face of the myriad secret economies that filled her mind. A hint of moisture glistened in her eyes.

"You're so good to me, Billy," she murmured, as she came to him and was met inside his arms.

"So you've gone an' done it," Mary commented, one morning in the laundry. They had not been at work ten minutes ere her eye had glimpsed the topaz ring on the third finger of Saxon's left hand. "Who's the lucky one? Charley Long or Billy Roberts?"

"Billy," was the answer.

"Huh! Takin' a young boy to raise, eh?"

Saxon showed that the stab had gone home, and Mary was all contrition.

"Can't you take a josh? I'm glad to death at the news. Billy's a awful good man, and I'm glad to see you get him. There ain't many like him knockin' 'round, an' they ain't to be had for the askin'. An' you're both lucky. You was just made for each other, an' you'll make him a better wife than any girl I know. When is it to be?"

Going home from the laundry a few days later, Saxon encountered Charley Long. He blocked the sidewalk, and compelled speech with her.

"So you're runnin' with a prizefighter," he sneered. "A blind man can see your finish."

For the first time she was unafraid of this big-bodied, black-browed men with the hairy-matted hands and fingers. She held up her left hand.

"See that? It's something, with all your strength, that you could never put on my finger. Billy Roberts put it on inside a week. He got your number, Charley Long, and at the same time he got me."

"Skiddoo for you," Long retorted. "Twenty-three's your number."

"He's not like you," Saxon went on. "He's a man, every bit of him, a fine, clean man."

Long laughed hoarsely.

"He's got your goat all right."

"And yours," she flashed back.

"I could tell you things about him. Saxon, straight, he ain't no good. If I was to tell you—"

"You'd better get out of my way," she interrupted, "or I'll tell him, and you know what you'll get, you great big bully."

Long shuffled uneasily, then reluctantly stepped aside.

"You're a caution," he said, half admiringly.

"So's Billy Roberts," she laughed, and continued on her way. After half a dozen steps she stopped. "Say," she called.

The big blacksmith turned toward her with eagerness.

"About a block back," she said, "I saw a man with hip disease. You might go and beat him up."

Of one extravagance Saxon was guilty in the course of the brief engagement period. A full day's wages she spent in the purchase of half a dozen cabinet photographs of herself. Billy had insisted that life was unendurable could he not look upon her semblance the last thing when he went to bed at night and the first thing when he got up in the morning. In return, his photographs, one conventional and one in the stripped fighting costume of the ring, ornamented her looking glass. It was while gazing at the latter that she was reminded of her wonderful mother's tales of the ancient Saxons and sea-foragers of the English coasts. From the chest of drawers that had crossed the plains she drew forth another of her several precious heirloom—a scrapbook of her mother's in which was pasted much of the fugitive newspaper verse of pioneer California days. Also, there were copies of paintings and old wood engravings from the magazines of a generation and more before.

Saxon ran the pages with familiar fingers and stopped at the picture she was seeking. Between bold headlands of rock and under a gray cloud-blown sky, a dozen boats, long and lean and dark, beaked like monstrous birds, were landing on a foam-whitened beach of sand. The men in the boats, half naked, huge-muscled and fair-haired, wore winged helmets. In their hands were swords and spears, and they were leaping, waist-deep, into the sea-wash and wading ashore. Opposed to them, contesting the landing, were skin-clad savages, unlike Indians, however, who clustered on the beach or waded into the water to their knees. The first blows were being struck, and here and there the bodies of the dead and wounded rolled in the surf. One fair-haired invader lay across the gunwale of a boat, the manner of his death told by the arrow that transfixed his breast. In the air, leaping past him into the water, sword in hand, was Billy. There was no mistaking it. The striking blondness, the face, the eyes, the mouth were the same. The very expression on the face was what had been on Billy's the day of the picnic when he faced the three wild Irishmen.

Somewhere out of the ruck of those warring races had emerged Billy's ancestors, and hers, was her afterthought, as she closed the book and put it back in the drawer. And some of those ancestors had made this ancient and battered chest of drawers which had crossed the salt ocean and the plains and been pierced by a bullet in the fight with the Indians at Little Meadow. Almost, it seemed, she could visualize the women who had kept their pretties and their family homespun in its drawers—the women of those wandering generations who were grandmothers and greater great grandmothers of her own mother. Well, she sighed, it was a good stock to be born of, a hard-working, hard-fighting stock. She fell to wondering what her life would have been like had she been born a Chinese woman, or an Italian woman like those she saw, head-shawled or bareheaded, squat, ungainly and swarthy, who carried great loads of driftwood on their heads up from the beach. Then she laughed at her foolishness, remembered Billy and the four-roomed cottage on Pine Street, and went to bed with her mind filled for the hundredth time with the details of the furniture.

CHAPTER XIII

"Our cattle were all played out," Saxon was saying, "and winter was so near that we couldn't dare try to cross the Great American Desert, so our train stopped in Salt Lake City that winter. The Mormons hadn't got bad yet, and they were good to us."

"You talk as though you were there," Bert commented.

"My mother was," Saxon answered proudly. "She was nine years old that winter."

They were seated around the table in the kitchen of the little Pine Street cottage, making a cold lunch of sandwiches, tamales, and bottled beer. It being Sunday, the four were free from work, and they had come early, to work harder than on any week day, washing walls and windows, scrubbing floors, laying carpets and linoleum, hanging curtains, setting up the stove, putting the kitchen utensils and dishes away, and placing the furniture.

"Go on with the story, Saxon," Mary begged. "I'm just dyin' to hear. And Bert, you just shut up and listen."

"Well, that winter was when Del Hancock showed up. He was Kentucky born, but he'd been in the West for years. He was a scout, like Kit Carson, and he knew him well. Many's a time Kit Carson and he slept under the same blankets. They were together to California and Oregon with General Fremont. Well, Del Hancock was passing on his way through Salt Lake, going I don't know where to raise a company of Rocky Mountain trappers to go after beaver some new place he knew about. Ha was a handsome man. He wore his hair long like in pictures, and had a silk sash around his waist he'd learned to wear in California from the Spanish, and two revolvers in his belt. Any woman 'd fall in love with him first sight. Well, he saw Sadie, who was my mother's oldest sister, and I guess she looked good to him, for he stopped right there in Salt Lake and didn't go a step. He was a great Indian fighter, too, and I heard my Aunt Villa say, when I was a little girl, that he had the blackest, brightest eyes, and that the way he looked was like an eagle. He'd fought duels, too, the way they did in those days, and he wasn't afraid of anything.

"Sadie was a beauty, and she flirted with him and drove him crazy. Maybe she wasn't sure of her own mind, I don't know. But I do know that she didn't give in as easy as I did to Billy. Finally, he couldn't stand it any more. Ha rode up that night on horseback, wild as could be. 'Sadie,' he said, 'if you don't promise to marry me to-morrow, I'll shoot myself to-night right back of the corral.' And he'd have done it, too, and Sadie knew it, and said she would. Didn't they make love fast in those days?"

CHAPTER XIII

"Oh, I don't know," Mary sniffed. "A week after you first laid eyes on Billy you was engaged. Did Billy say he was going to shoot himself back of the laundry if you turned him down?"

"I didn't give him a chance," Saxon confessed. "Anyway Del Hancock and Aunt Sadie got married next day. And they were very happy afterward, only she died. And after that he was killed, with General Custer and all the rest, by the Indians. He was an old man by then, but I guess he got his share of Indians before they got him. Men like him always died fighting, and they took their dead with them. I used to know Al Stanley when I was a little girl. He was a gambler, but he was game. A railroad man shot him in the back when he was sitting at a table. That shot killed him, too. He died in about two seconds. But before he died he'd pulled his gun and put three bullets into the man that killed him."

"I don't like fightin'," Mary protested. "It makes me nervous. Bert gives me the willies the way he's always lookin' for trouble. There ain't no sense in it."

"And I wouldn't give a snap of my fingers for a man without fighting spirit," Saxon answered. "Why, we wouldn't be here to-day if it wasn't for the fighting spirit of our people before us."

"You've got the real goods of a fighter in Billy," Bert assured her; "a yard long and a yard wide and genuine A Number One, long-fleeced wool. Billy's a Mohegan with a scalp-lock, that's what he is. And when he gets his mad up it's a case of get out from under or something will fall on you—hard."

"Just like that," Mary added.

Billy, who had taken no part in the conversation, got up, glanced into the bedroom off the kitchen, went into the parlor and the bedroom off the parlor, then returned and stood gazing with puzzled brows into the kitchen bedroom.

"What's eatin' you, old man," Bert queried. "You look as though you'd lost something or was markin' a three-way ticket. What you got on your chest? Cough it up."

"Why, I'm just thinkin' where in Sam Hill's the bed an' stuff for the back bedroom."

"There isn't any," Saxon explained. "We didn't order any."

"Then I'll see about it to-morrow."

"What d'ye want another bed for?" asked Bert. "Ain't one bed enough for the two of you?"

"You shut up, Bert!" Mary cried. "Don't get raw."

"Whoa, Mary!" Bert grinned. "Back up. You're in the wrong stall as usual."

"We don't need that room," Saxon was saying to Billy. "And so I didn't plan any furniture. That money went to buy better carpets and a better stove."

Billy came over to her, lifted her from the chair, and seated himself with her on his knees.

"That's right, little girl. I'm glad you did. The best for us every time. And to-morrow night I want you to run up with me to Salinger's an' pick out a good bedroom set an' carpet for that room. And it must be good. Nothin' snide."

"It will cost fifty dollars," she objected.

"That's right," he nodded. "Make it cost fifty dollars and not a cent less. We're goin' to have the best. And what's the good of an empty room? It'd make the house look cheap. Why, I go around now, seein' this little nest just as it grows an' softens, day by day, from the day we paid the cash money down an' nailed the keys. Why, almost every moment I'm drivin' the horses, all day long, I just keep on seein' this nest. And when we're married, I'll go on seein' it. And I want to see it complete. If that room'd he bare-floored an' empty, I'd see nothin' but it and its bare floor all day long. I'd be cheated. The house'd be a lie. Look at them curtains you put up in it, Saxon. That's to make believe to the neighbors that it's furnished. Saxon, them curtains are lyin' about that room, makin' a noise for every one to hear that that room's furnished. Nitsky for us. I'm goin' to see that them curtains tell the truth."

"You might rent it," Bert suggested. "You're close to the railroad yards, and it's only two blocks to a restaurant."

"Not on your life. I ain't marryin' Saxon to take in lodgers. If I can't take care of her, d'ye know what I'll do? Go down to Long Wharf, say 'Here goes nothin',' an' jump into the bay with a stone tied to my neck. Ain't I right, Saxon?"

It was contrary to her prudent judgment, but it fanned her pride. She threw her arms around her lover's neck, and said, ere she kissed him:

"You're the boss, Billy. What you say goes, and always will go."

"Listen to that!" Bert gibed to Mary. "That's the stuff. Saxon's onto her job."

"I guess we'll talk things over together first before ever I do anything," Billy was saying to Saxon.

"Listen to that," Mary triumphed. "You bet the man that marries me'll have to talk things over first."

"Billy's only givin' her hot air," Bert plagued. "They all do it before they're married."

Mary sniffed contemptuously.

"I'll bet Saxon leads him around by the nose. And I'm goin' to say, loud an' strong, that I'll lead the man around by the nose that marries me."

"Not if you love him," Saxon interposed.

"All the more reason," Mary pursued.

Bert assumed an expression and attitude of mournful dejection.

"Now you see why me an' Mary don't get married," he said. "I'm some big Indian myself, an' I'll be everlastingly jiggerooed if I put up for a wigwam I can't be boss of."

"And I'm no squaw," Mary retaliated, "an' I wouldn't marry a big buck Indian if all the rest of the men in the world was dead."

"Well this big buck Indian ain't asked you yet."

"He knows what he'd get if he did."

"And after that maybe he'll think twice before he does ask you."

Saxon, intent on diverting the conversation into pleasanter channels, clapped her hands as if with sudden recollection.

"Oh! I forgot! I want to show you something." From her purse she drew a slender ring of plain gold and passed it around. "My mother's wedding ring. I've worn it around my neck always, like a locket. I cried for it so in the orphan asylum that the matron gave it back for me to wear. And now, just to think, after next Tuesday I'll be wearing it on my finger. Look, Billy, see the engraving on the inside."

"C to D, 1879," he read.

"Carlton to Daisy—Carlton was my father's first name. And now, Billy, you've got to get it engraved for you and me."

Mary was all eagerness and delight.

"Oh, it's fine," she cried. "W to S, 1907."

CHAPTER XIII

Billy considered a moment.

"No, that wouldn't be right, because I'm not giving it to Saxon."

"I'll tell you what," Saxon said. "W and S."

"Nope." Billy shook his head. "S and W, because you come first with me."

"If I come first with you, you come first with us. Billy, dear, I insist on W and S."

"You see," Mary said to Bert. "Having her own way and leading him by the nose already."

Saxon acknowledged the sting.

"Anyway you want, Billy," she surrendered. His arms tightened about her.

"We'll talk it over first, I guess."

CHAPTER XIV

Sarah was conservative. Worse, she had crystallized at the end of her love-time with the coming of her first child. After that she was as set in her ways as plaster in a mold. Her mold was the prejudices and notions of her girlhood and the house she lived in. So habitual was she that any change in the customary round assumed the proportions of a revolution. Tom had gone through many of these revolutions, three of them when he moved house. Then his stamina broke, and he never moved house again.

So it was that Saxon had held back the announcement of her approaching marriage until it was unavoidable. She expected a scene, and she got it.

"A prizefighter, a hoodlum, a plug-ugly," Sarah sneered, after she had exhausted herself of all calamitous forecasts of her own future and the future of her children in the absence of Saxon's weekly four dollars and a half. "I don't know what your mother'd thought if she lived to see the day when you took up with a tough like Bill Roberts. Bill! Why, your mother was too refined to associate with a man that was called Bill. And all I can say is you can say good-bye to silk stockings and your three pair of shoes. It won't be long before you'll think yourself lucky to go sloppin' around in Congress gaiters and cotton stockin's two pair for a quarter."

"Oh, I'm not afraid of Billy not being able to keep me in all kinds of shoes," Saxon retorted with a proud toss of her head.

"You don't know what you're talkin' about." Sarah paused to laugh in mirthless discordance. "Watch for the babies to come. They come faster than wages raise these days."

"But we're not going to have any babies... that is, at first. Not until after the furniture is all paid for anyway."

"Wise in your generation, eh? In my days girls were more modest than to know anything about disgraceful subjects."

"As babies?" Saxon queried, with a touch of gentle malice.

"Yes, as babies."

"The first I knew that babies were disgraceful. Why, Sarah, you, with your five, how disgraceful you have been. Billy and I have decided not to be half as disgraceful. We're only going to have two—a boy and a girl."

Tom chuckled, but held the peace by hiding his face in his coffee cup. Sarah, though checked by this flank attack, was herself an old hand in the art. So temporary was the setback that she scarcely paused ere hurling her assault from a new angle.

CHAPTER XIV

"An' marryin' so quick, all of a sudden, eh? If that ain't suspicious, nothin' is. I don't know what young women's comin' to. They ain't decent, I tell you. They ain't decent. That's what comes of Sunday dancin' an' all the rest. Young women nowadays are like a lot of animals. Such fast an' looseness I never saw...."

Saxon was white with anger, but while Sarah wandered on in her diatribe, Tom managed to wink privily and prodigiously at his sister and to implore her to help in keeping the peace.

"It's all right, kid sister," he comforted Saxon when they were alone. "There's no use talkin' to Sarah. Bill Roberts is a good boy. I know a lot about him. It does you proud to get him for a husband. You're bound to be happy with him..." His voice sank, and his face seemed suddenly to be very old and tired as he went on anxiously. "Take warning from Sarah. Don't nag. Whatever you do, don't nag. Don't give him a perpetual-motion line of chin. Kind of let him talk once in a while. Men have some horse sense, though Sarah don't know it. Why, Sarah actually loves me, though she don't make a noise like it. The thing for you is to love your husband, and, by thunder, to make a noise of lovin' him, too. And then you can kid him into doing 'most anything you want. Let him have his way once in a while, and he'll let you have yourn. But you just go on lovin' him, and leanin' on his judgement—he's no fool—and you'll be all hunky-dory. I'm scared from goin' wrong, what of Sarah. But I'd sooner be loved into not going wrong."

"Oh, I'll do it, Tom," Saxon nodded, smiling through the tears his sympathy had brought into her eyes. "And on top of it I'm going to do something else, I'm going to make Billy love me and just keep on loving me. And then I won't have to kid him into doing some of the things I want. He'll do them because he loves me, you see."

"You got the right idea, Saxon. Stick with it, an' you'll win out."

Later, when she had put on her hat to start for the laundry, she found Tom waiting for her at the corner.

"An', Saxon," he said, hastily and haltingly, "you won't take anything I've said... you know... —about Sarah... as bein' in any way disloyal to her? She's a good woman, an' faithful. An' her life ain't so easy by a long shot. I'd bite out my tongue before I'd say anything against her. I guess all folks have their troubles. It's hell to be poor, ain't it?"

"You've been awful good to me, Tom. I can never forget it. And I know Sarah means right. She does do her best."

"I won't be able to give you a wedding present," her brother ventured apologetically. "Sarah won't hear of it. Says we didn't get none from my folks when we got married. But I got something for you just the same. A surprise. You'd never guess it."

Saxon waited.

"When you told me you was goin' to get married, I just happened to think of it, an' I wrote to brother George, askin' him for it for you. An' by thunder he sent it by express. I didn't tell you because I didn't know but maybe he'd sold it. He did sell the silver spurs. He needed the money, I guess. But the other, I had it sent to the shop so as not to bother Sarah, an' I sneaked it in last night an' hid it in the woodshed."

"Oh, it is something of my father's! What is it? Oh, what is it?"

"His army sword."

"The one he wore on his roan war horse! Oh, Tom, you couldn't give me a better present. Let's go back now. I want to see it. We can slip in the back way. Sarah's washing in the kitchen, and she won't begin hanging out for an hour."

"I spoke to Sarah about lettin' you take the old chest of drawers that was your mother's," Tom whispered, as they stole along the narrow alley between the houses. "Only she got on her high horse. Said that Daisy was as much my mother as yourn, even if we did have different fathers, and that the chest had always belonged in Daisy's family and not Captain Kit's, an' that it was mine, an' what was mine she had some say-so about."

"It's all right," Saxon reassured him. "She sold it to me last night. She was waiting up for me when I got home with fire in her eye."

"Yep, she was on the warpath all day after I mentioned it. How much did you give her for it?"

"Six dollars."

"Robbery—it ain't worth it," Tom groaned. "It's all cracked at one end and as old as the hills."

"I'd have given ten dollars for it. I'd have given 'most anything for it, Tom. It was mother's, you know. I remember it in her room when she was still alive."

In the woodshed Tom resurrected the hidden treasure and took off the wrapping paper. Appeared a rusty, steel-scabbarded saber of the heavy type carried by cavalry officers in Civil War days. It was attached to a moth-eaten sash of thick-woven crimson silk from which hung heavy silk tassels. Saxon almost seized it from her brother in her eagerness. She drew forth the blade and pressed her lips to the steel.

It was her last day at the laundry. She was to quit work that evening for good. And the next afternoon, at five, she and Billy were to go before a justice of the peace and be married. Bert and Mary were to be the witnesses, and after that the four were to go to a private room in Barnum's Restaurant for the wedding supper. That over, Bert and Mary would proceed to a dance at Myrtle Hall, while Billy and Saxon would take the Eighth Street car to Seventh and Pine. Honeymoons are infrequent in the working class. The next morning Billy must be at the stable at his regular hour to drive his team out.

All the women in the fancy starch room knew it was Saxon's last day. Many exulted for her, and not a few were envious of her, in that she had won a husband and to freedom from the suffocating slavery of the ironing board. Much of bantering she endured; such was the fate of every girl who married out of the fancy starch room. But Saxon was too happy to be hurt by the teasing, a great deal of which was gross, but all of which was good-natured.

In the steam that arose from under her iron, and on the surfaces of the dainty lawns and muslins that flew under her hands, she kept visioning herself in the Pine Street cottage; and steadily she hummed under her breath her paraphrase of the latest popular song:

"And when I work, and when I work, I'll always work for Billy."

By three in the afternoon the strain of the piece-workers in the humid, heated room grew tense. Elderly women gasped and sighed; the color went out of the cheeks of the young women, their faces became drawn and dark circles formed under their eyes; but all held on with weary, unabated speed. The tireless, vigilant forewoman kept a sharp lookout for incipient hysteria, and once led a narrow-chested, stoop-shouldered young thing out of the place in time to prevent a collapse.

Saxon was startled by the wildest scream of terror she had ever heard. The tense thread of human resolution snapped; wills and nerves broke down, and a hundred women suspended their irons or dropped them. It was Mary who had screamed so terribly, and Saxon saw a strange black animal flapping great claw-like wings and nestling on Mary's shoulder. With the scream, Mary crouched down, and the strange creature, darting into the air, fluttered full into the startled face of a woman at the next board. This woman promptly screamed and fainted. Into the air again, the flying thing darted hither and thither, while the shrieking, shrinking women threw up their arms, tried to run away along the aisles, or cowered under their ironing boards.

"It's only a bat!" the forewoman shouted. She was furious. "Ain't you ever seen a bat? It won't eat you!"

But they were ghetto people, and were not to be quieted. Some woman who could not see the cause of the uproar, out of her overwrought apprehension raised the cry of fire and precipitated the panic rush for the doors. All of them were screaming the stupid, soul-sickening high note of terror, drowning the forewoman's voice. Saxon had been merely startled at first, but the screaming panic broke her grip on herself and swept her away. Though she did not scream, she fled with the rest. When this horde of crazed women debouched on the next department, those who worked there joined in the stampede to escape from they knew not what danger. In ten minutes the laundry was deserted, save for a few men wandering about with hand grenades in futile search for the cause of the disturbance.

The forewoman was stout, but indomitable. Swept along half the length of an aisle by the terror-stricken women, she had broken her way back through the rout and quickly caught the light-blinded visitant in a clothes basket.

"Maybe I don't know what God looks like, but take it from me I've seen a tintype of the devil," Mary gurgled, emotionally fluttering back and forth between laughter and tears.

But Saxon was angry with herself, for she had been as frightened as the rest in that wild flight for out-of-doors.

"We're a lot of fools," she said. "It was only a bat. I've heard about them. They live in the country. They wouldn't hurt a fly. They can't see in the daytime. That was what was the matter with this one. It was only a bat."

"Huh, you can't string me," Mary replied. "It was the devil." She sobbed a moment, and then laughed hysterically again. "Did you see Mrs. Bergstrom faint? And it only touched her in the face. Why, it was on my shoulder and touching my bare neck like the hand of a corpse. And I didn't faint." She laughed again. "I guess, maybe, I was too scared to faint."

"Come on back," Saxon urged. "We've lost half an hour."

"Not me. I'm goin' home after that, if they fire me. I couldn't iron for sour apples now, I'm that shaky."

One woman had broken a leg, another an arm, and a number nursed milder bruises and bruises. No bullying nor entreating of the forewoman could persuade the women to return to work. They were too upset and nervous, and only here and there could one be found brave enough to re-enter the building for the hats and lunch baskets of the others. Saxon was one of the handful that returned and worked till six o'clock.

CHAPTER XV

"Why, Bert!—you're squiffed!" Mary cried reproachfully.

The four were at the table in the private room at Barnum's. The wedding supper, simple enough, but seemingly too expensive to Saxon, had been eaten. Bert, in his hand a glass of California red wine, which the management supplied for fifty cents a bottle, was on his feet endeavoring a speech. His face was flushed; his black eyes were feverishly bright.

"You've ben drinkin' before you met me," Mary continued. "I can see it stickin' out all over you."

"Consult an oculist, my dear," he replied. "Bertram is himself to-night. An' he is here, arisin' to his feet to give the glad hand to his old pal. Bill, old man, here's to you. It's how-de-do an' good-bye, I guess. You're a married man now, Bill, an' you got to keep regular hours. No more runnin' around with the boys. You gotta take care of yourself, an' get your life insured, an' take out an accident policy, an' join a buildin' an' loan society, an' a buryin' association—"

"Now you shut up, Bert," Mary broke in. "You don't talk about buryin's at weddings. You oughta be ashamed of yourself."

"Whoa, Mary! Back up! I said what I said because I meant it. I ain't thinkin' what Mary thinks. What I was thinkin'.... Let me tell you what I was thinkin'. I said buryin' association, didn't I? Well, it was not with the idea of castin' gloom over this merry gatherin'. Far be it...."

He was so evidently seeking a way out of his predicament, that Mary tossed her head triumphantly. This acted as a spur to his reeling wits.

"Let me tell you why," he went on. "Because, Bill, you got such an all-fired pretty wife, that's why. All the fellows is crazy over her, an' when they get to runnin' after her, what'll you be doin'? You'll be gettin' busy. And then won't you need a buryin' association to bury 'em? I just guess yes. That was the compliment to your good taste in skirts I was tryin' to come across with when Mary butted in."

His glittering eyes rested for a moment in bantering triumph on Mary.

"Who says I'm squiffed? Me? Not on your life. I'm seein' all things in a clear white light. An' I see Bill there, my old friend Bill. An' I don't see two Bills. I see only one. Bill was never two-faced in his life. Bill, old man, when I look at you there in the married harness, I'm sorry—" He ceased abruptly and turned on Mary. "Now don't go up in the air, old girl. I'm onto my job. My grandfather was a state senator, and he could spiel graceful an' pleasin' till the cows come home. So can I.—Bill, when I look at you, I'm sorry. I repeat, I'm sorry." He glared challengingly at Mary. "For myself when I look at you an' know all the happiness you got a hammerlock on. Take it from me, you're a wise guy, bless the women. You've started well. Keep it up. Marry 'em all, bless 'em. Bill, here's to you. You're a Mohegan with a scalplock. An' you got a squaw that is some squaw, take it from me. Minnehaha, here's to you—to the two of you—an' to the papooses, too, gosh-dang them!"

He drained the glass suddenly and collapsed in his chair, blinking his eyes across at the wedded couple while tears trickled unheeded down his cheeks. Mary's hand went out soothingly to his, completing his break-down.

"By God, I got a right to cry," he sobbed. "I'm losin' my best friend, ain't I? It'll never be the same again never. When I think of the fun, an' scrapes, an' good times Bill an' me has had together, I could darn near hate you, Saxon, sittin' there with your hand in his."

"Cheer up, Bert," she laughed gently. "Look at whose hand you are holding."

"Aw, it's only one of his cryin' jags," Mary said, with a harshness that her free hand belied as it caressed his hair with soothing strokes. "Buck up, Bert. Everything's all right. And now it's up to Bill to say something after your dandy spiel."

Bert recovered himself quickly with another glass of wine.

"Kick in, Bill," he cried. "It's your turn now."

"I'm no hotair artist," Billy grumbled. "What'll I say, Saxon? They ain't no use tellin' 'em how happy we are. They know that."

"Tell them we're always going to be happy," she said. "And thank them for all their good wishes, and we both wish them the same. And we're always going to be together, like old times, the four of us. And tell them they're invited down to 507 Pine Street next Sunday for Sunday dinner.—And, Mary, if you want to come Saturday night you can sleep in the spare bedroom."

"You've told'm yourself, better'n I could." Billy clapped his hands. "You did yourself proud, an' I guess they ain't much to add to it, but just the same I'm goin' to pass them a hot one."

He stood up, his hand on his glass. His clear blue eyes under the dark brows and framed by the dark lashes, seemed a deeper blue, and accentuated the blondness of hair and skin. The smooth cheeks were rosy—not with wine, for it was only his second glass—but with health and joy. Saxon, looking up at him, thrilled with pride in him, he was so well-dressed, so strong, so handsome, so clean-looking—her man-boy. And she was aware of pride in herself, in her woman's desirableness that had won for her so wonderful a lover.

"Well, Bert an' Mary, here you are at Saxon's and my wedding supper. We're just goin' to take all your good wishes to heart, we wish you the same back, and when we say it we mean more than you think we mean. Saxon an' I believe in tit for tat. So we're wishin' for the day when the table is turned clear around an' we're sittin' as guests at your weddin' supper. And then, when you come to Sunday dinner, you can both stop Saturday night in the spare bedroom. I guess I was wised up when I furnished it, eh?"

"I never thought it of you, Billy!" Mary exclaimed. "You're every hit as raw as Bert. But just the same..."

There was a rush of moisture to her eyes. Her voice faltered and broke. She smiled through her tears at them, then turned to look at Bert, who put his arm around her and gathered her on to his knees.

When they left the restaurant, the four walked to Eighth and Broadway, where they stopped beside the electric car. Bert and Billy were awkward and silent, oppressed by a strange aloofness. But Mary embraced Saxon with fond anxiousness.

"It's all right, dear," Mary whispered. "Don't be scared. It's all right. Think of all the other women in the world."

The conductor clanged the gong, and the two couples separated in a sudden hubbub of farewell.

"Oh, you Mohegan!" Bert called after, as the car got under way. "Oh, you Minnehaha!"

"Remember what I said," was Mary's parting to Saxon.

The car stopped at Seventh and Pine, the terminus of the line. It was only a little over two blocks to the cottage. On the front steps Billy took the key from his pocket.

"Funny, isn't it?" he said, as the key turned in the lock. "You an' me. Just you an' me."

While he lighted the lamp in the parlor, Saxon was taking off her hat. He went into the bedroom and lighted the lamp there, then turned back and stood in the doorway. Saxon, still unaccountably fumbling with her hatpins, stole a glance at him. He held out his arms.

"Now," he said.

She came to him, and in his arms he could feel her trembling.

BOOK II

CHAPTER I

The first evening after the marriage night Saxon met Billy at the door as he came up the front steps. After their embrace, and as they crossed the parlor hand in hand toward the kitchen, he filled his lungs through his nostrils with audible satisfaction.

"My, but this house smells good, Saxon! It ain't the coffee—I can smell that, too. It's the whole house. It smells... well, it just smells good to me, that's all."

He washed and dried himself at the sink, while she heated the frying pan on the front hole of the stove with the lid off. As he wiped his hands he watched her keenly, and cried out with approbation as she dropped the steak in the fryin pan.

"Where'd you learn to cook steak on a dry, hot pan? It's the only way, but darn few women seem to know about it."

As she took the cover off a second frying pan and stirred the savory contents with a kitchen knife, he came behind her, passed his arms under her arm-pits with down-drooping hands upon her breasts, and bent his head over her shoulder till cheek touched cheek.

"Um-um-um-m-m! Fried potatoes with onions like mother used to make. Me for them. Don't they smell good, though! Um-um-m-m-m!"

The pressure of his hands relaxed, and his cheek slid caressingly past hers as he started to release her. Then his hands closed down again. She felt his lips on her hair and heard his advertised inhalation of delight.

"Um-um-m-m-m! Don't you smell good—yourself, though! I never understood what they meant when they said a girl was sweet. I know, now. And you're the sweetest I ever knew."

His joy was boundless. When he returned from combing his hair in the bedroom and sat down at the small table opposite her, he paused with knife and fork in hand.

"Say, bein' married is a whole lot more than it's cracked up to be by most married folks. Honest to God, Saxon, we can show 'em a few. We can give 'em cards and spades an' little casino an' win out on big casino and the aces. I've got but one kick comin'."

The instant apprehension in her eyes provoked a chuckle from him.

"An' that is that we didn't get married quick enough. Just think. I've lost a whole week of this."

Her eyes shone with gratitude and happiness, and in her heart she solemnly pledged herself that never in all their married life would it be otherwise.

Supper finished, she cleared the table and began washing the dishes at the sink. When he evinced the intention of wiping them, she caught him by the lapels of the coat and backed him into a chair.

"You'll sit right there, if you know what's good for you. Now be good and mind what I say. Also, you will smoke a cigarette.—No; you're not going to watch me. There's the morning paper beside you. And if you don't hurry to read it, I'll be through these dishes before you've started."

As he smoked and read, she continually glanced across at him from her work. One thing more, she thought—slippers; and then the picture of comfort and content would be complete.

Several minutes later Billy put the paper aside with a sigh.

"It's no use," he complained. "I can't read."

"What's the matter?" she teased. "Eyes weak?"

"Nope. They're sore, and there's only one thing to do 'em any good, an' that's lookin' at you."

"All right, then, baby Billy; I'll be through in a jiffy."

When she had washed the dish towel and scalded out the sink, she took off her kitchen apron, came to him, and kissed first one eye and then the other.

"How are they now. Cured?"

"They feel some better already."

She repeated the treatment.

"And now?"

"Still better."

"And now?"

"Almost well."

After he had adjudged them well, he ouched and informed her that there was still some hurt in the right eye.

In the course of treating it, she cried out as in pain. Billy was all alarm.

"What is it? What hurt you?"

"My eyes. They're hurting like sixty."

And Billy became physician for a while and she the patient. When the cure was accomplished, she led him into the parlor, where, by the open window, they succeeded in occupying the same Morris chair. It was the most expensive comfort in the house. It had cost seven dollars and a half, and, though it was grander than anything she had dreamed of possessing, the extravagance of it had worried her in a half-guilty way all day.

The salt chill of the air that is the blessing of all the bay cities after the sun goes down crept in about them. They heard the switch engines puffing in the railroad yards, and the rumbling thunder of the Seventh Street local slowing down in its run from the Mole to stop at West Oakland station. From the street came the noise of children playing in the summer night, and from the steps of the house next door the low voices of gossiping housewives.

"Can you beat it?" Billy murmured. "When I think of that six-dollar furnished room of mine, it makes me sick to think what I was missin' all the time. But there's one satisfaction. If I'd changed it sooner I wouldn't a-had you. You see, I didn't know you existed only until a couple of weeks ago."

His hand crept along her bare forearm and up and partly under the elbow-sleeve.

CHAPTER I

"Your skin's so cool," he said. "It ain't cold; it's cool. It feels good to the hand."

"Pretty soon you'll be calling me your cold-storage baby," she laughed.

"And your voice is cool," he went on. "It gives me the feeling just as your hand does when you rest it on my forehead. It's funny. I can't explain it. But your voice just goes all through me, cool and fine. It's like a wind of coolness—just right. It's like the first of the sea-breeze settin' in in the afternoon after a scorchin' hot morning. An' sometimes, when you talk low, it sounds round and sweet like the 'cello in the Macdonough Theater orchestra. And it never goes high up, or sharp, or squeaky, or scratchy, like some women's voices when they're mad, or fresh, or excited, till they remind me of a bum phonograph record. Why, your voice, it just goes through me till I'm all trembling—like with the everlastin' cool of it. It's it's straight delicious. I guess angels in heaven, if they is any, must have voices like that."

After a few minutes, in which, so inexpressible was her happiness that she could only pass her hand through his hair and cling to him, he broke out again.

"I'll tell you what you remind me of. Did you ever see a thoroughbred mare, all shinin' in the sun, with hair like satin an' skin so thin an' tender that the least touch of the whip leaves a mark—all fine nerves, an' delicate an' sensitive, that'll kill the toughest bronco when it comes to endurance an' that can strain a tendon in a flash or catch death-of-cold without a blanket for a night? I wanta tell you they ain't many beautifuler sights in this world. An' they're that fine-strung, an' sensitive, an' delicate. You gotta handle 'em right-side up, glass, with care. Well, that's what you remind me of. And I'm goin' to make it my job to see you get handled an' gentled in the same way. You're as different from other women as that kind of a mare is from scrub work-horse mares. You're a thoroughbred. You're clean-cut an' spirited, an' your lines...

"Say, d'ye know you've got some figure? Well, you have. Talk about Annette Kellerman. You can give her cards and spades. She's Australian, an' you're American, only your figure ain't. You're different. You're nifty—I don't know how to explain it. Other women ain't built like you. You belong in some other country. You're Frenchy, that's what. You're built like a French woman an' more than that—the way you walk, move, stand up or sit down, or don't do anything."

And he, who had never been out of California, or, for that matter, had never slept a night away from his birthtown of Oakland, was right in his judgment. She was a flower of Anglo-Saxon stock, a rarity in the exceptional smallness and fineness of hand and foot and bone and grace of flesh and carriage—some throw-back across the face of time to the foraying Norman-French that had intermingled with the sturdy Saxon breed.

"And in the way you carry your clothes. They belong to you. They seem just as much part of you as the cool of your voice and skin. They're always all right an' couldn't be better. An' you know, a fellow kind of likes to be seen taggin' around with a woman like you, that wears her clothes like a dream, an' hear the other fellows say: 'Who's Bill's new skirt? She's a peach, ain't she? Wouldn't I like to win her, though.' And all that sort of talk."

And Saxon, her cheek pressed to his, knew that she was paid in full for all her midnight sewings and the torturing hours of drowsy stitching when her head nodded with the weariness of the day's toil, while she recreated for herself filched ideas from the dainty garments that had steamed under her passing iron.

"Say, Saxon, I got a new name for you. You're my Tonic Kid. That's what you are, the Tonic Kid."

"And you'll never get tired of me?" she queried.

"Tired? Why we was made for each other."

"Isn't it wonderful, our meeting, Billy? We might never have met. It was just by accident that we did."

"We was born lucky," he proclaimed. "That's a cinch."

"Maybe it was more than luck," she ventured.

"Sure. It just had to be. It was fate. Nothing could a-kept us apart."

They sat on in a silence that was quick with unuttered love, till she felt him slowly draw her more closely and his lips come near to her ear as they whispered: "What do you say we go to bed?"

Many evenings they spent like this, varied with an occasional dance, with trips to the Orpheum and to Bell's Theater, or to the moving picture shows, or to the Friday night band concerts in City Hall Park. Often, on Sunday, she prepared a lunch, and he drove her out into the hills behind Prince and King, whom Billy's employer was still glad to have him exercise.

Each morning Saxon was called by the alarm clock. The first morning he had insisted upon getting up with her and building the fire in the kitchen stove. She gave in the first morning, but after that she laid the fire in the evening, so that all that was required was the touching of a match to it. And in bed she compelled him to remain for a last little doze ere she called him for breakfast. For the first several weeks she prepared his lunch for him. Then, for a week, he came down to dinner. After that he was compelled to take his lunch with him. It depended on how far distant the teaming was done.

"You're not starting right with a man," Mary cautioned. "You wait on him hand and foot. You'll spoil him if you don't watch out. It's him that ought to be waitin' on you."

"He's the bread-winner," Saxon replied. "He works harder than I, and I've got more time than I know what to do with—time to burn. Besides, I want to wait on him because I love to, and because... well, anyway, I want to."

CHAPTER II

Despite the fastidiousness of her housekeeping, Saxon, once she had systematized it, found time and to spare on her hands. Especially during the periods in which her husband carried his lunch and there was no midday meal to prepare, she had a number of hours each day to herself. Trained for years to the routine of factory and laundry work, she could not abide this unaccustomed idleness. She could not bear to sit and do nothing, while she could not pay calls on her girlhood friends, for they still worked in factory and laundry. Nor was she acquainted with the wives of the neighborhood, save for one strange old woman who lived in the house next door and with whom Saxon had exchanged snatches of conversation over the backyard division fence.

One time-consuming diversion of which Saxon took advantage was free and unlimited baths. In the orphan asylum and in Sarah's house she had been used to but one bath a week. As she grew to womanhood she had attempted more frequent baths. But the effort proved disastrous, arousing, first, Sarah's derision, and next, her wrath. Sarah had crystallized in the era of the weekly Saturday night bath, and any increase in this cleansing function was regarded by her as putting on airs and as an insinuation against her own cleanliness. Also, it was an extravagant misuse of fuel, and occasioned extra towels in the family wash. But now, in Billy's house, with her own stove, her own tub and towels and soap, and no one to say her nay, Saxon was guilty of a daily orgy. True, it was only a common washtub that she placed on the kitchen floor and filled by hand; but it was a luxury that had taken her twenty-four years to achieve. It was from the strange woman next door that Saxon received a hint, dropped in casual conversation, of what proved the culminating joy of bathing. A simple thing—a few drops of druggist's ammonia in the water; but Saxon had never heard of it before.

She was destined to learn much from the strange woman. The acquaintance had begun one day when Saxon, in the back yard, was hanging out a couple of corset covers and several pieces of her finest undergarments. The woman leaning on the rail of her back porch, had caught her eye, and nodded, as it seemed to Saxon, half to her and half to the underlinen on the line.

"You're newly married, aren't you?" the woman asked. "I'm Mrs. Higgins. I prefer my first name, which is Mercedes."

"And I'm Mrs. Roberts," Saxon replied, thrilling to the newness of the designation on her tongue. "My first name is Saxon."

"Strange name for a Yankee woman," the other commented.

"Oh, but I'm not Yankee," Saxon exclaimed. "I'm Californian."

"La la," laughed Mercedes Higgins. "I forgot I was in America. In other lands all Americans are called Yankees. It is true that you are newly married?"

Saxon nodded with a happy sigh. Mercedes sighed, too.

"Oh, you happy, soft, beautiful young thing. I could envy you to hatred—you with all the man-world ripe to be twisted about your pretty little fingers. And you don't realize your fortune. No one does until it's too late."

Saxon was puzzled and disturbed, though she answered readily:

"Oh, but I do know how lucky I am. I have the finest man in the world."

Mercedes Higgins sighed again and changed the subject. She nodded her head at the garments.

"I see you like pretty things. It is good judgment for a young woman. They're the bait for men—half the weapons in the battle. They win men, and they hold men—" She broke off to demand almost fiercely: "And you, you would keep your husband?—always, always—if you can?"

"I intend to. I will make him love me always and always."

Saxon ceased, troubled and surprised that she should be so intimate with a stranger.

"'Tis a queer thing, this love of men," Mercedes said. "And a failing of all women is it to believe they know men like books. And with breaking hearts, die they do, most women, out of their ignorance of men and still foolishly believing they know all about them. Oh, la la, the little fools. And so you say, little new-married woman, that you will make your man love you always and always? And so they all say it, knowing men and the queerness of men's love the way they think they do. Easier it is to win the capital prize in the Little Louisiana, but the little new-married women never know it until too late. But you—you have begun well. Stay by your pretties and your looks. 'Twas so you won your man, 'tis so you'll hold him. But that is not all. Some time I will talk with you and tell what few women trouble to know, what few women ever come to know.—Saxon!—'tis a strong, handsome name for a woman. But you don't look it. Oh, I've watched you. French you are, with a Frenchiness beyond dispute. Tell Mr. Roberts I congratulate him on his good taste."

She paused, her hand on the knob of her kitchen door.

"And come and see me some time. You will never be sorry. I can teach you much. Come in the afternoon. My man is night watchman in the yards and sleeps of mornings. He's sleeping now."

Saxon went into the house puzzling and pondering. Anything but ordinary was this lean, dark-skinned woman, with the face withered as if scorched in great heats, and the eyes, large and black, that flashed and flamed with advertisement of an unquenched inner conflagration. Old she was—Saxon caught herself debating anywhere between fifty and seventy; and her hair, which had once been blackest black, was streaked plentifully with gray. Especially noteworthy to Saxon was her speech. Good English it was, better than that to which Saxon was accustomed. Yet the woman was not American. On the other hand, she had no perceptible accent. Rather were her words touched by a foreignness so elusive that Saxon could not analyze nor place it.

"Uh, huh," Billy said, when she had told him that evening of the day's event. "So SHE'S Mrs. Higgins? He's a watchman. He's got only one arm. Old Higgins an' her—a funny bunch, the two of them. The people's scared of her—some of 'em. The Dagoes an' some of the old Irish dames thinks she's a witch. Won't have a thing to do with her. Bert was tellin' me about it. Why, Saxon, d'ye know, some of 'em believe if she was to get mad at 'em, or didn't like their mugs, or anything, that all she's got to do is look at 'em an' they'll curl up their toes an' croak. One of the fellows that works at the stable—you've seen 'm—Henderson—he lives around the corner on Fifth—he says she's bughouse."

"Oh, I don't know," Saxon defended her new acquaintance. "She may be crazy, but she says the same thing you're always saying. She says my form is not American but French."

"Then I take my hat off to her," Billy responded. "No wheels in her head if she says that. Take it from me, she's a wise gazabo."

"And she speaks good English, Billy, like a school teacher, like what I guess my mother used to speak. She's educated."

"She ain't no fool, or she wouldn't a-sized you up the way she did."

"She told me to congratulate you on your good taste in marrying me," Saxon laughed.

"She did, eh? Then give her my love. Me for her, because she knows a good thing when she sees it, an' she ought to be congratulating you on your good taste in me."

It was on another day that Mercedes Higgins nodded, half to Saxon, and half to the dainty women's things Saxon was hanging on the line.

"I've been worrying over your washing, little new-wife," was her greeting.

"Oh, but I've worked in the laundry for years," Saxon said quickly.

Mercedes sneered scornfully.

"Steam laundry. That's business, and it's stupid. Only common things should go to a steam laundry. That is their punishment for being common. But the pretties! the dainties! the flimsies!—la la, my dear, their washing is an art. It requires wisdom, genius, and discretion fine as the clothes are fine. I will give you a recipe for home-made soap. It will not harden the texture. It will give whiteness, and softness, and life. You can wear them long, and fine white clothes are to be loved a long time. Oh, fine washing is a refinement, an art. It is to be done as an artist paints a picture, or writes a poem, with love, holily, a true sacrament of beauty.

"I shall teach you better ways, my dear, better ways than you Yankees know. I shall teach you new pretties." She nodded her head to Saxon's underlinen on the line. "I see you make little laces. I know all laces—the Belgian, the Maltese, the Mechlin—oh, the many, many loves of laces! I shall teach you some of the simpler ones so that you can make them for yourself, for your brave man you are to make love you always and always."

On her first visit to Mercedes Higgins, Saxon received the recipe for home-made soap and her head was filled with a minutiae of instruction in the art of fine washing. Further, she was fascinated and excited by all the newness and strangeness of the withered old woman who blew upon her the breath of wider lands and seas beyond the horizon.

"You are Spanish?" Saxon ventured.

"No, and yes, and neither, and more. My father was Irish, my mother Peruvian-Spanish. 'Tis after her I took, in color and looks. In other ways after my father, the blue-eyed Celt with the fairy song on his tongue and the restless feet that stole the rest of him away to far-wandering. And the feet of him that he lent me have led me away on as wide far roads as ever his led him."

Saxon remembered her school geography, and with her mind's eye she saw a certain outline map of a continent with jiggly wavering parallel lines that denoted coast.

"Oh," she cried, "then you are South American."

Mercedes shrugged her shoulders.

"I had to be born somewhere. It was a great ranch, my mother's. You could put all Oakland in one of its smallest pastures."

Mercedes Higgins sighed cheerfully and for the time was lost in retrospection. Saxon was curious to hear more about this woman who must have lived much as the Spanish-Californians had lived in the old days.

"You received a good education," she said tentatively. "Your English is perfect."

"Ah, the English came afterward, and not in school. But, as it goes, yes, a good education in all things but the most important—men. That, too, came afterward. And little my mother dreamed—she was a grand lady, what you call a cattle-queen—little she dreamed my fine education was to fit me in the end for a night watchman's wife." She laughed genuinely at the grotesqueness of the idea. "Night watchman, laborers, why, we had hundreds, yes, thousands that toiled for us. The peons—they are like what you call slaves, almost, and the cowboys, who could ride two hundred miles between side and side of the ranch. And in the big house servants beyond remembering or counting. La la, in my mother's house were many servants."

Mercedes Higgins was voluble as a Greek, and wandered on in reminiscence.

"But our servants were lazy and dirty. The Chinese are the servants par excellence. So are the Japanese, when you find a good one, but not so good as the Chinese. The Japanese maidservants are pretty and merry, but you never know the moment they'll leave you. The Hindoos are not strong, but very obedient. They look upon sahibs and memsahibs as gods! I was a memsahib—which means woman. I once had a Russian cook who always spat in the soup for luck. It was very funny. But we put up with it. It was the custom."

"How you must have traveled to have such strange servants!" Saxon encouraged.

The old woman laughed corroboration.

"And the strangest of all, down in the South Seas, black slaves, little kinky-haired cannibals with bones through their noses. When they did not mind, or when they stole, they were tied up to a cocoanut palm behind the compound and lashed with whips of rhinoceros hide. They were from an island of cannibals and head-hunters, and they never cried out. It was their pride. There was little Vibi, only twelve years old—he waited on me—and when his back was cut in shreds and I wept over him, he would only laugh and say, 'Short time little bit I take 'm head belong big fella white marster.' That was Bruce Anstey, the Englishman who whipped him. But little Vibi never got the head. He ran away and the bushmen cut off his own head and ate every bit of him."

Saxon chilled, and her face was grave; but Mercedes Higgins rattled on.

"Ah, those were wild, gay, savage days. Would you believe it, my dear, in three years those Englishmen of the plantation drank up oceans of champagne and Scotch whisky and dropped thirty thousand pounds on the adventure. Not dollars—pounds, which means one hundred and fifty thousand dollars. They were princes while it lasted. It was splendid, glorious. It was mad, mad. I sold half my beautiful jewels in New Zealand before I got started again. Bruce Anstey blew out his brains at the end. Roger went mate on a trader with a black crew, for eight pounds a month. And Jack Gilbraith—he was the rarest of them all. His people were wealthy and titled, and he went home to England and sold cat's meat, sat around their big house till they gave him more money to start a rubber plantation in the East Indies somewhere, on Sumatra, I think—or was it New Guinea?"

And Saxon, back in her own kitchen and preparing supper for Billy, wondered what lusts and rapacities had led the old, burnt-faced woman from the big Peruvian ranch, through all the world, to West Oakland and Barry Higgins Old Barry was not the sort who would fling away his share of one hundred and fifty thousand dollars, much less ever attain to such opulence. Besides, she had mentioned the names of other men, but not his.

Much more Mercedes had talked, in snatches and fragments. There seemed no great country nor city of the old world or the new in which she had not been. She had even been in Klondike, ten years before, in a half-dozen flashing sentences picturing the fur-clad, be-moccasined miners sowing the barroom floors with thousands of dollars' worth of gold dust. Always, so it seemed to Saxon, Mrs. Higgins had been with men to whom money was as water.

CHAPTER III

Saxon, brooding over her problem of retaining Billy's love, of never staling the freshness of their feeling for each other and of never descending from the heights which at present they were treading, felt herself impelled toward Mrs. Higgins. SHE knew; surely she must know. Had she not hinted knowledge beyond ordinary women's knowledge?

Several weeks went by, during which Saxon was often with her. But Mrs. Higgins talked of all other matters, taught Saxon the making of certain simple laces, and instructed her in the arts of washing and of marketing. And then, one afternoon, Saxon found Mrs. Higgins more voluble than usual, with words, clean-uttered, that rippled and tripped in their haste to escape. Her eyes were flaming. So flamed her face. Her words were flames. There was a smell of liquor in the air and Saxon knew that the old woman had been drinking. Nervous and frightened, at the same time fascinated, Saxon hemstitched a linen handkerchief intended for Billy and listened to Mercedes' wild flow of speech.

"Listen, my dear. I shall tell you about the world of men. Do not be stupid like all your people, who think me foolish and a witch with the evil eye. Ha! ha! When I think of silly Maggie Donahue pulling the shawl across her baby's face when we pass each other on the sidewalk! A witch I have been, 'tis true, but my witchery was with men. Oh, I am wise, very wise, my dear. I shall tell you of women's ways with men, and of men's ways with women, the best of them and the worst of them. Of the brute that is in all men, of the queerness of them that breaks the hearts of stupid women who do not understand. And all women are stupid. I am not stupid. La la, listen.

"I am an old woman. And like a woman, I'll not tell you how old I am. Yet can I hold men. Yet would I hold men, toothless and a hundred, my nose touching my chin. Not the young men. They were mine in my young days. But the old men, as befits my years. And well for me the power is mine. In all this world I am without kin or cash. Only have I wisdom and memories—memories that are ashes, but royal ashes, jeweled ashes. Old women, such as I, starve and shiver, or accept the pauper's dole and the pauper's shroud. Not I. I hold my man. True, 'tis only Barry Higgins—old Barry, heavy, an ox, but a male man, my dear, and queer as all men are queer. 'Tis true, he has one arm." She shrugged her shoulders. "A compensation. He cannot beat me, and old bones are tender when the round flesh thins to strings.

"But when I think of my wild young lovers, princes, mad with the madness of youth! I have lived. It is enough. I regret nothing. And with old Barry I have my surety of a bite to eat and a place by the fire. And why? Because I know men, and shall never lose my cunning to hold them. 'Tis bitter sweet, the knowledge of them, more sweet than bitter—men and men and men! Not stupid dolts, nor fat bourgeois swine of business men, but men of temperament, of flame and fire; madmen, maybe, but a lawless, royal race of madmen.

"Little wife-woman, you must learn. Variety! There lies the magic. 'Tis the golden key. 'Tis the toy that amuses. Without it in the wife, the man is a Turk; with it, he is her slave, and faithful. A wife must be many wives. If you would have your husband's love you must be all women to him. You must be ever new, with the dew of newness ever sparkling, a flower that never blooms to the fulness that fades. You must be a garden of flowers, ever new, ever fresh, ever different. And in your garden the man must never pluck the last of your posies.

"Listen, little wife-woman. In the garden of love is a snake. It is the commonplace. Stamp on its head, or it will destroy the garden. Remember the name. Commonplace. Never be too intimate. Men only seem gross. Women are more gross than men.—No, do not argue, little new-wife. You are an infant woman. Women are less delicate than men. Do I not know? Of their own husbands they will relate the most intimate love-secrets to other women. Men never do this of their wives. Explain it. There is only one way. In all things of love women are less delicate. It is their mistake. It is the father and the mother of the commonplace, and it is the commonplace, like a loathsome slug, that beslimes and destroys love.

"Be delicate, little wife-woman. Never be without your veil, without many veils. Veil yourself in a thousand veils, all shimmering and glittering with costly textures and precious jewels. Never let the last veil be drawn. Against the morrow array yourself with more veils, ever more veils, veils without end. Yet the many veils must not seem many. Each veil must seem the only one between you and your hungry lover who will have nothing less than all of you. Each time he must seem to get all, to tear aside the last veil that hides you. He must think so. It must not be so. Then there will be no satiety, for on the morrow he will find another last veil that has escaped him.

"Remember, each veil must seem the last and only one. Always you must seem to abandon all to his arms; always you must reserve more that on the morrow and on all the morrows you may abandon. Of such is variety, surprise, so that your man's pursuit will be everlasting, so that his eyes will look to you for newness, and not to other women. It was the freshness and the newness' of your beauty and you, the mystery of you, that won your man. When a man has plucked and smelled all the sweetness of a flower, he looks for other flowers. It is his queerness. You must ever remain a flower almost plucked yet never plucked, stored with vats of sweet unbroached though ever broached.

"Stupid women, and all are stupid, think the first winning of the man the final victory. Then they settle down and grow fat, and state, and dead, and heartbroken. Alas, they are so stupid. But you, little infant-woman with your first victory, you must make your love-life an unending chain of victories. Each day you must win your man again. And when you have won the last victory, when you can find no more to win, then ends love. Finis is written, and your man wanders in strange gardens. Remember, love must be kept insatiable. It must have an appetite knife-edged and never satisfied. You must feed your lover well, ah, very well, most well; give, give, yet send him away hungry to come back to you for more."

Mrs. Higgins stood up suddenly and crossed out of the room. Saxon had not failed to note the litheness and grace in that lean and withered body. She watched for Mrs. Higgins' return, and knew that the litheness and grace had not been imagined.

"Scarcely have I told you the first letter in love's alphabet," said Mercedes Higgins, as she reseated herself.

In her hands was a tiny instrument, beautifully grained and richly brown, which resembled a guitar save that it bore four strings. She swept them back and forth with rhythmic forefinger and lifted a voice, thin and mellow, in a fashion of melody that was strange, and in a foreign tongue, warm-voweled, all-voweled, and love-exciting. Softly throbbing, voice and strings arose on sensuous crests of song, died away to whisperings and caresses, drifted through love-dusks and twilights, or swelled again to love-cries barbarically imperious in which were woven plaintive calls and madnesses of invitation and promise. It went through Saxon until she was as this instrument, swept with passional strains. It seemed to her a dream, and almost was she dizzy, when Mercedes Higgins ceased.

"If your man had clasped the last of you, and if all of you were known to him as an old story, yet, did you sing that one song, as I have sung it, yet would his arms again go out to you and his eyes grow warm with the old mad lights. Do you see? Do you understand, little wife-woman?"

Saxon could only nod, her lips too dry for speech.

"The golden koa, the king of woods," Mercedes was crooning over the instrument. "The ukulele—that is what the Hawaiians call it, which means, my dear, the jumping flea. They are golden-fleshed, the Hawaiians, a race of lovers, all in the warm cool of the tropic night where the trade winds blow."

Again she struck the strings. She sang in another language, which Saxon deemed must be French. It was a gayly-devilish lilt, tripping and tickling. Her large eyes at times grew larger and wilder, and again narrowed in enticement and wickedness. When she ended, she looked to Saxon for a verdict.

"I don't like that one so well," Saxon said.

Mercedes shrugged her shoulders.

"They all have their worth, little infant-woman with so much to learn. There are times when men may be won with wine. There are times when men may be won with the wine of song, so queer they are. La la, so many ways, so many ways. There are your pretties, my dear, your dainties. They are magic nets. No fisherman upon the sea ever tangled fish more successfully than we women with our flimsies. You are on the right path. I have seen men enmeshed by a corset cover no prettier, no daintier, than these of yours I have seen on the line.

"I have called the washing of fine linen an art. But it is not for itself alone. The greatest of the arts is the conquering of men. Love is the sum of all the arts, as it is the reason for their existence. Listen. In all times and ages have been women, great wise women. They did not need to be beautiful. Greater then all woman's beauty was their wisdom. Princes end potentates bowed down before them. Nations battled over them. Empires crashed because of them. Religions were founded on them. Aphrodite, Astarte, the worships of the night—listen, infant-woman, of the great women who conquered worlds of men."

And thereafter Saxon listened, in a maze, to what almost seemed a wild farrago, save that the strange meaningless phrases were fraught with dim, mysterious significance. She caught glimmerings of profounds inexpressible and unthinkable that hinted connotations lawless and terrible. The woman's speech was a lava rush, scorching and searing; and Saxon's cheeks, and forehead, and neck burned with a blush that continuously increased. She trembled with fear, suffered qualms of nausea, thought sometimes that she would faint, so madly reeled her brain; yet she could not tear herself away, sad sat on and on, her sewing forgotten on her lap, staring with inward sight upon a nightmare vision beyond all imagining. At last, when it seemed she could endure no more, and while she was wetting her dry lips to cry out in protest, Mercedes ceased.

"And here endeth the first lesson," she said quite calmly, then laughed with a laughter that was tantalizing and tormenting. "What is the matter? You are not shocked?"

"I am frightened," Saxon quavered huskily, with a half-sob of nervousness. "You frighten me. I am very foolish, and I know so little, that I had never dreamed... THAT."

Mercedes nodded her head comprehendingly.

"It is indeed to be frightened at," she said. "It is solemn; it is terrible; it is magnificent!"

CHAPTER IV

Saxon had been clear-eyed all her days, though her field of vision had been restricted. Clear-eyed, from her childhood days with the saloonkeeper Cady and Cady's good-natured but unmoral spouse, she had observed, and, later, generalized much upon sex. She knew the post-nuptial problem of retaining a husband's love, as few wives of any class knew it, just as she knew the pre-nuptial problem of selecting a husband, as few girls of the working class knew it.

She had of herself developed an eminently rational philosophy of love. Instinctively, and consciously, too, she had made toward delicacy, and shunned the perils of the habitual and commonplace. Thoroughly aware she was that as she cheapened herself so did she cheapen love. Never, in the weeks of their married life, had Billy found her dowdy, or harshly irritable, or lethargic. And she had deliberately permeated her house with her personal atmosphere of coolness, and freshness, and equableness. Nor had she been ignorant of such assets as surprise and charm. Her imagination had not been asleep, and she had been born with wisdom. In Billy she had won a prize, and she knew it. She appreciated his lover's ardor and was proud. His open-handed liberality, his desire for everything of the best, his own personal cleanliness and care of himself she recognized as far beyond the average. He was never coarse. He met delicacy with delicacy, though it was obvious to her that the initiative in all such matters lay with her and must lie with her always. He was largely unconscious of what he did and why. But she knew in all full clarity of judgment. And he was such a prize among men.

Despite her clear sight of her problem of keeping Billy a lover, and despite the considerable knowledge and experience arrayed before her mental vision, Mercedes Higgins had spread before her a vastly wider panorama. The old woman had verified her own conclusions, given her new ideas, clinched old ones, and even savagely emphasized the tragic importance of the whole problem. Much Saxon remembered of that mad preachment, much she guessed and felt, and much had been beyond her experience and understanding. But the metaphors of the veils and the flowers, and the rules of giving to abandonment with always more to abandon, she grasped thoroughly, and she was enabled to formulate a bigger and stronger love-philosophy. In the light of the revelation she re-examined the married lives of all she had ever known, and, with sharp definiteness as never before, she saw where and why so many of them had failed.

CHAPTER IV

With renewed ardor Saxon devoted herself to her household, to her pretties, and to her charms. She marketed with a keener desire for the best, though never ignoring the need for economy. From the women's pages of the Sunday supplements, and from the women's magazines in the free reading room two blocks away, she gleaned many ideas for the preservation of her looks. In a systematic way she exercised the various parts of her body, and a certain period of time each day she employed in facial exercises and massage for the purpose of retaining the roundness and freshness, and firmness and color. Billy did not know. These intimacies of the toilette were not for him. The results, only, were his. She drew books from the Carnegie Library and studied physiology and hygiene, and learned a myriad of things about herself and the ways of woman's health that she had never been taught by Sarah, the women of the orphan asylum, nor by Mrs. Cady.

After long debate she subscribed to a woman's magazine, the patterns and lessons of which she decided were the best suited to her taste and purse. The other woman's magazines she had access to in the free reading room, and more than one pattern of lace and embroidery she copied by means of tracing paper. Before the lingerie windows of the uptown shops she often stood and studied; nor was she above taking advantage, when small purchases were made, of looking over the goods at the hand-embroidered underwear counters. Once, she even considered taking up with hand-painted china, but gave over the idea when she learned its expensiveness.

She slowly replaced all her simple maiden underlinen with garments which, while still simple, were wrought with beautiful French embroidery, tucks, and drawnwork. She crocheted fine edgings on the inexpensive knitted underwear she wore in winter. She made little corset covers and chemises of fine but fairly inexpensive lawns, and, with simple flowered designs and perfect laundering, her nightgowns were always sweetly fresh and dainty. In some publication she ran across a brief printed note to the effect that French women were just beginning to wear fascinating beruffled caps at the breakfast table. It meant nothing to her that in her case she must first prepare the breakfast. Promptly appeared in the house a yard of dotted Swiss muslin, and Saxon was deep in experimenting on patterns for herself, and in sorting her bits of laces for suitable trimmings. The resultant dainty creation won Mercedes Higgins' enthusiastic approval.

Saxon made for herself simple house slips of pretty gingham, with neat low collars turned back from her fresh round throat. She crocheted yards of laces for her underwear, and made Battenberg in abundance for her table and for the bureau. A great achievement, that aroused Billy's applause, was an Afghan for the bed. She even ventured a rag carpet, which, the women's magazines informed her, had newly returned into fashion. As a matter of course she hemstitched the best table linen and bed linen they could afford.

As the happy months went by she was never idle. Nor was Billy forgotten. When the cold weather came on she knitted him wristlets, which he always religiously wore from the house and pocketed immediately thereafter. The two sweaters she made for him, however, received a better fate, as did the slippers which she insisted on his slipping into, on the evenings they remained at home.

The hard practical wisdom of Mercedes Higgins proved of immense help, for Saxon strove with a fervor almost religious to have everything of the best and at the same time to be saving. Here she faced the financial and economic problem of keeping house in a society where the cost of living rose faster than the wages of industry. And here the old woman taught her the science of marketing so thoroughly that she made a dollar of Billy's go half as far again as the wives of the neighborhood made the dollars of their men go.

Invariably, on Saturday night, Billy poured his total wages into her lap. He never asked for an accounting of what she did with it, though he continually reiterated that he had never fed so well in his life. And always, the wages still untouched in her lap, she had him take out what he estimated he would need for spending money for the week to come. Not only did she bid him take plenty but she insisted on his taking any amount extra that he might desire at any time through the week. And, further, she insisted he should not tell her what it was for.

"You've always had money in your pocket," she reminded him, "and there's no reason marriage should change that. If it did, I'd wish I'd never married you. Oh, I know about men when they get together. First one treats and then another, and it takes money. Now if you can't treat just as freely as the rest of them, why I know you so well that I know you'd stay away from them. And that wouldn't be right... to you, I mean. I want you to be together with men. It's good for a man."

And Billy buried her in his arms and swore she was the greatest little bit of woman that ever came down the pike.

"Why," he jubilated; "not only do I feed better, and live more comfortable, and hold up my end with the fellows; but I'm actually saving money—or you are for me. Here I am, with furniture being paid for regular every month, and a little woman I'm mad over, and on top of it money in the bank. How much is it now?"

"Sixty-two dollars," she told him. "Not so bad for a rainy day. You might get sick, or hurt, or something happen."

It was in mid-winter, when Billy, with quite a deal of obvious reluctance, broached a money matter to Saxon. His old friend, Billy Murphy, was laid up with la grippe, and one of his children, playing in the street, had been seriously injured by a passing wagon. Billy Murphy, still feeble after two weeks in bed, had asked Billy for the loan of fifty dollars.

"It's perfectly safe," Billy concluded to Saxon. "I've known him since we was kids at the Durant School together. He's straight as a die."

"That's got nothing to do with it," Saxon chided. "If you were single you'd have lent it to him immediately, wouldn't you?"

Billy nodded.

"Then it's no different because you're married. It's your money, Billy."

"Not by a damn sight," he cried. "It ain't mine. It's ourn. And I wouldn't think of lettin' anybody have it without seein' you first."

"I hope you didn't tell him that," she said with quick concern.

"Nope," Billy laughed. "I knew, if I did, you'd be madder'n a hatter. I just told him I'd try an' figure it out. After all, I was sure you'd stand for it if you had it."

"Oh, Billy," she murmured, her voice rich and low with love; "maybe you don't know it, but that's one of the sweetest things you've said since we got married."

The more Saxon saw of Mercedes Higgins the less did she understand her. That the old woman was a close-fisted miser, Saxon soon learned. And this trait she found hard to reconcile with her tales of squandering. On the other hand, Saxon was bewildered by Mercedes' extravagance in personal matters. Her underlinen, hand-made of course, was very costly. The table she set for Barry was good, but the table for herself was vastly better. Yet both tables were set on the same table. While Barry contented himself with solid round steak, Mercedes ate tenderloin. A huge, tough muttonchop on Barry's plate would be balanced by tiny French chops on Mercedes' plate. Tea was brewed in separate pots. So was coffee. While Barry gulped twenty-five cent tea from a large and heavy mug, Mercedes sipped three-dollar tea from a tiny cup of Belleek, rose-tinted, fragile as all egg-shell. In the same manner, his twenty-five cent coffee was diluted with milk, her eighty cent Turkish with cream.

"'Tis good enough for the old man," she told Saxon. "He knows no better, and it would be a wicked sin to waste it on him."

Little traffickings began between the two women. After Mercedes had freely taught Saxon the loose-wristed facility of playing accompaniments on the ukulele, she proposed an exchange. Her time was past, she said, for such frivolities, and she offered the instrument for the breakfast cap of which Saxon had made so good a success.

"It's worth a few dollars," Mercedes said. "It cost me twenty, though that was years ago. Yet it is well worth the value of the cap."

"But wouldn't the cap be frivolous, too?" Saxon queried, though herself well pleased with the bargain.

"'Tis not for my graying hair," Mercedes frankly disclaimed. "I shall sell it for the money. Much that I do, when the rheumatism is not maddening my fingers, I sell. La la, my dear, 'tis not old Barry's fifty a month that'll satisfy all my expensive tastes. 'Tis I that make up the difference. And old age needs money as never youth needs it. Some day you will learn for yourself."

"I am well satisfied with the trade," Saxon said. "And I shall make me another cap when I can lay aside enough for the material."

"Make several," Mercedes advised. "I'll sell them for you, keeping, of course, a small commission for my services. I can give you six dollars apiece for them. We will consult about them. The profit will more than provide material for your own."

CHAPTER V

Four eventful things happened in the course of the winter. Bert and Mary got married and rented a cottage in the neighborhood three blocks away. Billy's wages were cut, along with the wages of all the teamsters in Oakland. Billy took up shaving with a safety razor. And, finally, Saxon was proven a false prophet and Sarah a true one.

Saxon made up her mind, beyond any doubt, ere she confided the news to Billy. At first, while still suspecting, she had felt a frightened sinking of the heart and fear of the unknown and unexperienced. Then had come economic fear, as she contemplated the increased expense entailed. But by the time she had made surety doubly sure, all was swept away before a wave of passionate gladness. HERS AND BILLY'S! The phrase was continually in her mind, and each recurrent thought of it brought an actual physical pleasure-pang to her heart.

The night she told the news to Billy, he withheld his own news of the wage-cut, and joined with her in welcoming the little one.

"What'll we do? Go to the theater to celebrate?" he asked, relaxing the pressure of his embrace so that she might speak. "Or suppose we stay in, just you and me, and... and the three of us?"

"Stay in," was her verdict. "I just want you to hold me, and hold me, and hold me."

"That's what I wanted, too, only I wasn't sure, after bein' in the house all day, maybe you'd want to go out."

There was frost in the air, and Billy brought the Morris chair in by the kitchen stove. She lay cuddled in his arms, her head on his shoulder, his cheek against her hair.

"We didn't make no mistake in our lightning marriage with only a week's courtin'," he reflected aloud. "Why, Saxon, we've been courtin' ever since just the same. And now... my God, Saxon, it's too wonderful to be true. Think of it! Ourn! The three of us! The little rascal! I bet he's goin' to be a boy. An' won't I learn 'm to put up his fists an' take care of himself! An' swimmin' too. If he don't know how to swim by the time he's six..."

"And if HE'S a girl?"

"SHE'S goin' to be a boy," Billy retorted, joining in the playful misuse of pronouns.

And both laughed and kissed, and sighed with content. "I'm goin' to turn pincher, now," he announced, after quite an interval of meditation. "No more drinks with the boys. It's me for the water wagon. And I'm goin' to ease down on smokes. Huh! Don't see why I can't roll my own cigarettes. They're ten times cheaper'n tailor-mades. An' I can grow a beard. The amount of money the barbers get out of a fellow in a year would keep a baby."

"Just you let your beard grow, Mister Roberts, and I'll get a divorce," Saxon threatened. "You're just too handsome and strong with a smooth face. I love your face too much to have it covered up.—Oh, you dear! you dear! Billy, I never knew what happiness was until I came to live with you."

"Nor me neither."

"And it's always going to be so?"

"You can just bet," he assured her.

"I thought I was going to be happy married," she went on; "but I never dreamed it would be like this." She turned her head on his shoulder and kissed his cheek. "Billy, it isn't happiness. It's heaven."

And Billy resolutely kept undivulged the cut in wages. Not until two weeks later, when it went into effect, and he poured the diminished sum into her lap, did he break it to her. The next day, Bert and Mary, already a month married, had Sunday dinner with them, and the matter came up for discussion. Bert was particularly pessimistic, and muttered dark hints of an impending strike in the railroad shops.

"If you'd all shut your traps, it'd be all right," Mary criticized. "These union agitators get the railroad sore. They give me the cramp, the way they butt in an' stir up trouble. If I was boss I'd cut the wages of any man that listened to them."

"Yet you belonged to the laundry workers' union," Saxon rebuked gently.

"Because I had to or I wouldn't a-got work. An' much good it ever done me."

"But look at Billy," Bert argued "The teamsters ain't ben sayin' a word, not a peep, an' everything lovely, and then, bang, right in the neck, a ten per cent cut. Oh, hell, what chance have we got? We lose. There's nothin' left for us in this country we've made and our fathers an' mothers before us. We're all shot to pieces. We Can see our finish—we, the old stock, the children of the white people that broke away from England an' licked the tar outa her, that freed the slaves, an' fought the Indians, 'an made the West! Any gink with half an eye can see it comin'."

"But what are we going to do about it?" Saxon questioned anxiously.

"Fight. That's all. The country's in the hands of a gang of robbers. Look at the Southern Pacific. It runs California."

"Aw, rats, Bert," Billy interrupted. "You're takin' through your lid. No railroad can ran the government of California."

"You're a bonehead," Bert sneered. "And some day, when it's too late, you an' all the other boneheads'll realize the fact. Rotten? I tell you it stinks. Why, there ain't a man who wants to go to state legislature but has to make a trip to San Francisco, an' go into the S. P. offices, an' take his hat off, an' humbly ask permission. Why, the governors of California has been railroad governors since before you and I was born. Huh! You can't tell me. We're finished. We're licked to a frazzle. But it'd do my heart good to help string up some of the dirty thieves before I passed out. D'ye know what we are?—we old white stock that fought in the wars, an' broke the land, an' made all this? I'll tell you. We're the last of the Mohegans."

"He scares me to death, he's so violent," Mary said with unconcealed hostility. "If he don't quit shootin' off his mouth he'll get fired from the shops. And then what'll we do? He don't consider me. But I can tell you one thing all right, all right. I'll not go back to the laundry." She held her right hand up and spoke with the solemnity of an oath. "Not so's you can see it. Never again for yours truly."

"Oh, I know what you're drivin' at," Bert said with asperity. "An' all I can tell you is, livin' or dead, in a job or out, no matter what happens to me, if you will lead that way, you will, an' there's nothin' else to it."

"I guess I kept straight before I met you," she came back with a toss of the head. "And I kept straight after I met you, which is going some if anybody should ask you."

Hot words were on Bert's tongue, but Saxon intervened and brought about peace. She was concerned over the outcome of their marriage. Both were highstrung, both were quick and irritable, and their continual clashes did not augur well for their future.

The safety razor was a great achievement for Saxon. Privily she conferred with a clerk she knew in Pierce's hardware store and made the purchase. On Sunday morning, after breakfast, when Billy was starting to go to the barber shop, she led him into the bedroom, whisked a towel aside, and revealed the razor box, shaving mug, soap, brush, and lather all ready. Billy recoiled, then came back to make curious investigation. He gazed pityingly at the safety razor.

"Huh! Call that a man's tool!"

"It'll do the work," she said. "It does it for thousands of men every day."

But Billy shook his head and backed away.

"You shave three times a week," she urged. "That's forty-five cents. Call it half a dollar, and there are fifty-two weeks in the year. Twenty-six dollars a year just for shaving. Come on, dear, and try it. Lots of men swear by it."

He shook his head mutinously, and the cloudy deeps of his eyes grew more cloudy. She loved that sullen handsomeness that made him look so boyish, and, laughing and kissing him, she forced him into a chair, got off his coat, and unbuttoned shirt and undershirt and turned them in.

Threatening him with, "If you open your mouth to kick I'll shove it in," she coated his face with lather.

"Wait a minute," she checked him, as he reached desperately for the razor. "I've been watching the barbers from the sidewalk. This is what they do after the lather is on."

And thereupon she proceeded to rub the lather in with her fingers.

"There," she said, when she had coated his face a second time. "You're ready to begin. Only remember, I'm not always going to do this for you. I'm just breaking you in, you see."

With great outward show of rebellion, half genuine, half facetious, he made several tentative scrapes with the razor. He winced violently, and violently exclaimed:

"Holy jumping Jehosaphat!"

He examined his face in the glass, and a streak of blood showed in the midst of the lather.

"Cut!—by a safety razor, by God! Sure, men swear by it. Can't blame 'em. Cut! By a safety!"

"But wait a second," Saxon pleaded. "They have to be regulated. The clerk told me. See those little screws. There.... That's it... turn them around."

CHAPTER V

Again Billy applied the blade to his face. After a couple of scrapes, he looked at himself closely in the mirror, grinned, and went on shaving. With swiftness and dexterity he scraped his face clean of lather. Saxon clapped her hands.

"Fine," Billy approved. "Great! Here. Give me your hand. See what a good job it made."

He started to rub her hand against his cheek. Saxon jerked away with a little cry of disappointment, then examined him closely.

"It hasn't shaved at all," she said.

"It's a fake, that's what it is. It cuts the hide, but not the hair. Me for the barber."

But Saxon was persistent.

"You haven't given it a fair trial yet. It was regulated too much. Let me try my hand at it. There, that's it, betwixt and between. Now, lather again and try it."

This time the unmistakable sand-papery sound of hair-severing could be heard.

"How is it?" she fluttered anxiously.

"It gets the—ouch!—hair," Billy grunted, frowning and making faces. "But it—gee!—say!—ouch!—pulls like Sam Hill."

"Stay with it," she encouraged. "Don't give up the ship, big Injun with a scalplock. Remember what Bert says and be the last of the Mohegans."

At the end of fifteen minutes he rinsed his face and dried it, sighing with relief.

"It's a shave, in a fashion, Saxon, but I can't say I'm stuck on it. It takes out the nerve. I'm as weak as a cat."

He groaned with sudden discovery of fresh misfortune.

"What's the matter now?" she asked.

"The back of my neck—how can I shave the back of my neck? I'll have to pay a barber to do it."

Saxon's consternation was tragic, but it only lasted a moment. She took the brush in her hand.

"Sit down, Billy."

"What?—you?" he demanded indignantly.

"Yes; me. If any barber is good enough to shave your neck, and then I am, too."

Billy moaned and groaned in the abjectness of humility and surrender, and let her have her way.

"There, and a good job," she informed him when she had finished. "As easy as falling off a log. And besides, it means twenty-six dollars a year. And you'll buy the crib, the baby buggy, the pinning blankets, and lots and lots of things with it. Now sit still a minute longer."

She rinsed and dried the back of his neck and dusted it with talcum powder.

"You're as sweet as a clean little baby, Billy Boy."

The unexpected and lingering impact of her lips on the back of his neck made him writhe with mingled feelings not all unpleasant.

Two days later, though vowing in the intervening time to have nothing further to do with the instrument of the devil, he permitted Saxon to assist him to a second shave. This time it went easier.

"It ain't so bad," he admitted. "I'm gettin' the hang of it. It's all in the regulating. You can shave as close as you want an' no more close than you want. Barbers can't do that. Every once an' awhile they get my face sore."

The third shave was an unqualified success, and the culminating bliss was reached when Saxon presented him with a bottle of witch hazel. After that he began active proselyting. He could not wait a visit from Bert, but carried the paraphernalia to the latter's house to demonstrate.

"We've ben boobs all these years, Bert, runnin' the chances of barber's itch an' everything. Look at this, eh? See her take hold. Smooth as silk. Just as easy.... There! Six minutes by the clock. Can you beat it? When I get my hand in, I can do it in three. It works in the dark. It works under water. You couldn't cut yourself if you tried. And it saves twenty-six dollars a year. Saxon figured it out, and she's a wonder, I tell you."

CHAPTER VI

The trafficking between Saxon and Mercedes increased. The latter commanded a ready market for all the fine work Saxon could supply, while Saxon was eager and happy in the work. The expected babe and the cut in Billy's wages had caused her to regard the economic phase of existence more seriously than ever. Too little money was being laid away in the bank, and her conscience pricked her as she considered how much she was laying out on the pretty necessaries for the household and herself. Also, for the first time in her life she was spending another's earnings. Since a young girl she had been used to spending her own, and now, thanks to Mercedes she was doing it again, and, out of her profits, assaying more expensive and delightful adventures in lingerie.

Mercedes suggested, and Saxon carried out and even bettered, the dainty things of thread and texture. She made ruffled chemises of sheer linen, with her own fine edgings and French embroidery on breast and shoulders; linen hand-made combination undersuits; and nightgowns, fairy and cobwebby, embroidered, trimmed with Irish lace. On Mercedes' instigation she executed an ambitious and wonderful breakfast cap for which the old woman returned her twelve dollars after deducting commission.

She was happy and busy every waking moment, nor was preparation for the little one neglected. The only ready made garments she bought were three fine little knit shirts. As for the rest, every bit was made by her own hands—featherstitched pinning blankets, a crocheted jacket and cap, knitted mittens, embroidered bonnets; slim little princess slips of sensible length; underskirts on absurd Lilliputian yokes; silk-embroidered white flannel petticoats; stockings and crocheted boots, seeming to burgeon before her eyes with wriggly pink toes and plump little calves; and last, but not least, many deliciously soft squares of bird's-eye linen. A little later, as a crowning masterpiece, she was guilty of a dress coat of white silk, embroidered. And into all the tiny garments, with every stitch, she sewed love. Yet this love, so unceasingly sewn, she knew when she came to consider and marvel, was more of Billy than of the nebulous, ungraspable new bit of life that eluded her fondest attempts at visioning.

"Huh," was Billy's comment, as he went over the mite's wardrobe and came back to center on the little knit shirts, "they look more like a real kid than the whole kit an' caboodle. Why, I can see him in them regular manshirts."

Saxon, with a sudden rush of happy, unshed tears, held one of the little shirts up to his lips. He kissed it solemnly, his eyes resting on Saxon's.

"That's some for the boy," he said, "but a whole lot for you."

But Saxon's money-earning was doomed to cease ignominiously and tragically. One day, to take advantage of a department store bargain sale, she crossed the bay to San Francisco. Passing along Sutter Street, her eye was attracted by a display in the small window of a small shop. At first she could not believe it; yet there, in the honored place of the window, was the wonderful breakfast cap for which she had received twelve dollars from Mercedes. It was marked twenty-eight dollars. Saxon went in and interviewed the shopkeeper, an emaciated, shrewd-eyed and middle-aged woman of foreign extraction.

"Oh, I don't want to buy anything," Saxon said. "I make nice things like you have here, and I wanted to know what you pay for them—for that breakfast cap in the window, for instance."

The woman darted a keen glance to Saxon's left hand, noted the innumerable tiny punctures in the ends of the first and second fingers, then appraised her clothing and her face.

"Can you do work like that?"

Saxon nodded.

"I paid twenty dollars to the woman that made that." Saxon repressed an almost spasmodic gasp, and thought coolly for a space. Mercedes had given her twelve. Then Mercedes had pocketed eight, while she, Saxon, had furnished the material and labor.

"Would you please show me other hand-made things nightgowns, chemises, and such things, and tell me the prices you pay?"

"Can you do such work?"

"Yes."

"And will you sell to me?"

"Certainly," Saxon answered. "That is why I am here."

"We add only a small amount when we sell," the woman went on; "you see, light and rent and such things, as well as a profit or else we could not be here."

"It's only fair," Saxon agreed.

Amongst the beautiful stuff Saxon went over, she found a nightgown and a combination undersuit of her own manufacture. For the former she had received eight dollars from Mercedes, it was marked eighteen, and the woman had paid fourteen; for the latter Saxon received six, it was marked fifteen, and the woman had paid eleven.

"Thank you," Saxon said, as she drew on her gloves. "I should like to bring you some of my work at those prices."

"And I shall be glad to buy it... if it is up to the mark." The woman looked at her severely. "Mind you, it must be as good as this. And if it is, I often get special orders, and I'll give you a chance at them."

Mercedes was unblushingly candid when Saxon reproached her.

"You told me you took only a commission," was Saxon's accusation.

"So I did; and so I have."

"But I did all the work and bought all the materials, yet you actually cleared more out of it than I did. You got the lion's share."

"And why shouldn't I, my dear? I was the middleman. It's the way of the world. 'Tis the middlemen that get the lion's share."

"It seems to me most unfair," Saxon reflected, more in sadness than anger.

"That is your quarrel with the world, not with me," Mercedes rejoined sharply, then immediately softened with one of her quick changes. "We mustn't quarrel, my dear. I like you so much. La la, it is nothing to you, who are young and strong with a man young and strong. Listen, I am an old woman. And old Barry can do little for me. He is on his last legs. His kidneys are 'most gone. Remember, 'tis I must bury him. And I do him honor, for beside me he'll have his last long steep. A stupid, dull old man, heavy, an ox, 'tis true; but a good old fool with no trace of evil in him. The plot is bought and paid for—the final installment was made up, in part, out of my commissions from you. Then there are the funeral expenses. It must be done nicely. I have still much to save. And Barry may turn up his toes any day."

Saxon sniffed the air carefully, and knew the old woman had been drinking again.

"Come, my dear, let me show you." Leading Saxon to a large sea chest in the bedroom, Mercedes lifted the lid. A faint perfume, as of rose-petals, floated up. "Behold, my burial trousseau. Thus I shall wed the dust."

Saxon's amazement increased, as, article by article, the old woman displayed the airiest, the daintiest, the most delicious and most complete of bridal outfits. Mercedes held up an ivory fan.

"In Venice 'twas given me, my dear.—See, this comb, turtle shell; Bruce Anstey made it for me the week before he drank his last bottle and scattered his brave mad brains with a Colt's 44.—This scarf. La la, a Liberty scarf—"

"And all that will be buried with you," Saxon mused, "Oh, the extravagance of it!"

Mercedes laughed.

"Why not? I shall die as I have lived. It is my pleasure. I go to the dust as a bride. No cold and narrow bed for me. I would it were a coach, covered with the soft things of the East, and pillows, pillows, without end."

"It would buy you twenty funerals and twenty plots," Saxon protested, shocked by this blasphemy of conventional death. "It is downright wicked."

"'Twill be as I have lived," Mercedes said complacently. "And it's a fine bride old Barry'll have to come and lie beside him." She closed the lid and sighed. "Though I wish it were Bruce Anstey, or any of the pick of my young men to lie with me in the great dark and to crumble with me to the dust that is the real death."

She gazed at Saxon with eyes heated by alcohol and at the same time cool with the coolness of content.

"In the old days the great of earth were buried with their live slaves with them. I but take my flimsies, my dear."

"Then you aren't afraid of death?... in the least?"

Mercedes shook her head emphatically.

"Death is brave, and good, and kind. I do not fear death. 'Tis of men I am afraid when I am dead. So I prepare. They shall not have me when I am dead."

Saxon was puzzled.

"They would not want you then," she said.

"Many are wanted," was the answer. "Do you know what becomes of the aged poor who have no money for burial? They are not buried. Let me tell you. We stood before great doors. He was a queer man, a professor who ought to have been a pirate, a man who lectured in class rooms when he ought to have been storming walled cities or robbing banks. He was slender, like Don Juan. His hands were strong as steel. So was his spirit. And he was mad, a bit mad, as all my young men have been. 'Come, Mercedes,' he said; 'we will inspect our brethren and become humble, and glad that we are not as they—as yet not yet. And afterward, to-night, we will dine with a more devilish taste, and we will drink to them in golden wine that will be the more golden for having seen them. Come, Mercedes.'

"He thrust the great doors open, and by the hand led me in. It was a sad company. Twenty-four, that lay on marble slabs, or sat, half erect and propped, while many young men, bright of eye, bright little knives in their hands, glanced curiously at me from their work."

"They were dead?" Saxon interrupted to gasp.

"They were the pauper dead, my dear. 'Come, Mercedes,' said he. 'There is more to show you that will make us glad we are alive.' And he took me down, down to the vats. The salt vats, my dear. I was not afraid. But it was in my mind, then, as I looked, how it would be with me when I was dead. And there they were, so many lumps of pork. And the order came, 'A woman; an old woman.' And the man who worked there fished in the vats. The first was a man he drew to see. Again he fished and stirred. Again a man. He was impatient, and grumbled at his luck. And then, up through the brine, he drew a woman, and by the face of her she was old, and he was satisfied."

"It is not true!" Saxon cried out.

"I have seen, my dear, I know. And I tell you fear not the wrath of God when you are dead. Fear only the salt vats. And as I stood and looked, and as he who led me there looked at me and smiled and questioned and bedeviled me with those mad, black, tired-scholar's eyes of his, I knew that that was no way for my dear clay. Dear it is, my clay to me; dear it has been to others. La la, the salt vat is no place for my kissed lips and love-lavished body." Mercedes lifted the lid of the chest and gazed fondly at her burial pretties. "So I have made my bed. So I shall lie in it. Some old philosopher said we know we must die; we do not believe it. But the old do believe. I believe.

"My dear, remember the salt vats, and do not be angry with me because my commissions have been heavy. To escape the vats I would stop at nothing steal the widow's mite, the orphan's crust, and pennies from a dead man's eyes."

"Do you believe in God?" Saxon asked abruptly, holding herself together despite cold horror.

Mercedes dropped the lid and shrugged her shoulders.

"Who knows? I shall rest well."

"And punishment?" Saxon probed, remembering the unthinkable tale of the other's life.

"Impossible, my dear. As some old poet said, 'God's a good fellow.' Some time I shall talk to you about God. Never be afraid of him. Be afraid only of the salt vats and the things men may do with your pretty flesh after you are dead."

CHAPTER VII

Billy quarreled with good fortune. He suspected he was too prosperous on the wages he received. What with the accumulating savings account, the paying of the monthly furniture installment and the house rent, the spending money in pocket, and the good fare he was eating, he was puzzled as to how Saxon managed to pay for the goods used in her fancy work. Several times he had suggested his inability to see how she did it, and been baffled each time by Saxon's mysterious laugh.

"I can't see how you do it on the money," he was contending one evening.

He opened his mouth to speak further, then closed it and for five minutes thought with knitted brows.

"Say," he said, "what's become of that frilly breakfast cap you was workin' on so hard, I ain't never seen you wear it, and it was sure too big for the kid."

Saxon hesitated, with pursed lips and teasing eyes. With her, untruthfulness had always been a difficult matter. To Billy it was impossible. She could see the cloud-drift in his eyes deepening and his face hardening in the way she knew so well when he was vexed.

"Say, Saxon, you ain't... you ain't... sellin' your work?"

And thereat she related everything, not omitting Mercedes Higgins' part in the transaction, nor Mercedes Higgins' remarkable burial trousseau. But Billy was not to be led aside by the latter. In terms anything but uncertain he told Saxon that she was not to work for money.

"But I have so much spare time, Billy, dear," she pleaded.

He shook his head.

"Nothing doing. I won't listen to it. I married you, and I'll take care of you. Nobody can say Bill Roberts' wife has to work. And I don't want to think it myself. Besides, it ain't necessary."

"But Billy—" she began again.

"Nope. That's one thing I won't stand for, Saxon. Not that I don't like fancy work. I do. I like it like hell, every bit you make, but I like it on YOU. Go ahead and make all you want of it, for yourself, an' I'll put up for the goods. Why, I'm just whistlin' an' happy all day long, thinkin' of the boy an' seein' you at home here workin' away on all them nice things. Because I know how happy you are a-doin' it. But honest to God, Saxon, it'd all be spoiled if I knew you was doin' it to sell. You see, Bill Roberts' wife don't have to work. That's my brag—to myself, mind you. An' besides, it ain't right."

"You're a dear," she whispered, happy despite her disappointment.

"I want you to have all you want," he continued. "An' you're goin' to get it as long as I got two hands stickin' on the ends of my arms. I guess I know how good the things are you wear—good to me, I mean, too. I'm dry behind the ears, an' maybe I've learned a few things I oughtn't to before I knew you. But I know what I'm talkin' about, and I want to say that outside the clothes down underneath, an' the clothes down underneath the outside ones, I never saw a woman like you. Oh—"

He threw up his hands as if despairing of ability to express what he thought and felt, then essayed a further attempt.

"It's not a matter of bein' only clean, though that's a whole lot. Lots of women are clean. It ain't that. It's something more, an' different. It's... well, it's the look of it, so white, an' pretty, an' tasty. It gets on the imagination. It's something I can't get out of my thoughts of you. I want to tell you lots of men can't strip to advantage, an' lots of women, too. But you—well, you're a wonder, that's all, and you can't get too many of them nice things to suit me, and you can't get them too nice.

"For that matter, Saxon, you can just blow yourself. There's lots of easy money layin' around. I'm in great condition. Billy Murphy pulled down seventy-five round iron dollars only last week for puttin' away the Pride of North Beach. That's what ha paid us the fifty back out of."

But this time it was Saxon who rebelled.

"There's Carl Hansen," Billy argued. "The second Sharkey, the alfalfa sportin' writers are callin' him. An' he calls himself Champion of the United States Navy. Well, I got his number. He's just a big stiff. I've seen 'm fight, an' I can pass him the sleep medicine just as easy. The Secretary of the Sportin' Life Club offered to match me. An' a hundred iron dollars in it for the winner. And it'll all be yours to blow in any way you want. What d'ye say?"

"If I can't work for money, you can't fight," was Saxon's ultimatum, immediately withdrawn. "But you and I don't drive bargains. Even if you'd let me work for money, I wouldn't let you fight. I've never forgotten what you told me about how prizefighters lose their silk. Well, you're not going to lose yours. It's half my silk, you know. And if you won't fight, I won't work—there. And more, I'll never do anything you don't want me to, Billy."

"Same here," Billy agreed. "Though just the same I'd like most to death to have just one go at that squarehead Hansen." He smiled with pleasure at the thought. "Say, let's forget it all now, an' you sing me 'Harvest Days' on that dinky what-you-may-call-it."

When she had complied, accompanying herself on the ukulele, she suggested his weird "Cowboy's Lament." In some inexplicable way of love, she had come to like her husband's one song. Because he sang it, she liked its inanity and monotonousness; and most of all, it seemed to her, she loved his hopeless and adorable flatting of every note. She could even sing with him, flatting as accurately and deliciously as he. Nor did she undeceive him in his sublime faith.

"I guess Bert an' the rest have joshed me all the time," he said.

"You and I get along together with it fine," she equivocated; for in such matters she did not deem the untruth a wrong.

Spring was on when the strike came in the railroad shops. The Sunday before it was called, Saxon and Billy had dinner at Bert's house. Saxon's brother came, though he had found it impossible to bring Sarah, who refused to budge from her household rut. Bert was blackly pessimistic, and they found him singing with sardonic glee:

"Nobody loves a mil-yun-aire. Nobody likes his looks. Nobody'll share his slightest care, He classes with thugs and crooks. Thriftiness has become a crime, So spend everything you earn; We're living now in a funny time, When money is made to burn."

Mary went about the dinner preparation, flaunting unmistakable signals of rebellion; and Saxon, rolling up her sleeves and tying on an apron, washed the breakfast dishes. Bert fetched a pitcher of steaming beer from the corner saloon, and the three men smoked and talked about the coming strike.

"It oughta come years ago," was Bert's dictum. "It can't come any too quick now to suit me, but it's too late. We're beaten thumbs donn. Here's where the last of the Mohegans gets theirs, in the neck, ker-whop!"

"Oh, I don't know," Tom, who had been smoking his pipe gravely, began to counsel. "Organized labor's gettin' stronger every day. Why, I can remember when there wasn't any unions in California, Look at us now—wages, an' hours, an' everything."

"You talk like an organizer," Bert sneered, "shovin' the bull con on the boneheads. But we know different. Organized wages won't buy as much now as unorganized wages used to buy. They've got us whipsawed. Look at Frisco, the labor leaders doin' dirtier polities than the old parties, pawin' an' squabblin' over graft, an' goin' to San Quentin, while—what are the Frisco carpenters doin'? Let me tell you one thing, Tom Brown, if you listen to all you hear you'll hear that every Frisco carpenter is union an' gettin' full union wages. Do you believe it? It's a damn lie. There ain't a carpenter that don't rebate his wages Saturday night to the contractor. An' that's your buildin' trades in San Francisco, while the leaders are makin' trips to Europe on the earnings of the tenderloin—when they ain't coughing it up to the lawyers to get out of wearin' stripes."

"That's all right," Tom concurred. "Nobody's denyin' it. The trouble is labor ain't quite got its eyes open. It ought to play politics, but the politics ought to be the right kind."

"Socialism, eh?" Bert caught him up with scorn. "Wouldn't they sell us out just as the Ruefs and Schmidts have?"

"Get men that are honest," Billy said. "That's the whole trouble. Not that I stand for socialism. I don't. All our folks was a long time in America, an' I for one won't stand for a lot of fat Germans an' greasy Russian Jews tellin' me how to run my country when they can't speak English yet."

"Your country!" Bert cried. "Why, you bonehead, you ain't got a country. That's a fairy story the grafters shove at you every time they want to rob you some more."

"But don't vote for the grafters," Billy contended. "If we selected honest men we'd get honest treatment."

"I wish you'd come to some of our meetings, Billy," Tom said wistfully. "If you would, you'd get your eyes open an' vote the socialist ticket next election."

"Not on your life," Billy declined. "When you catch me in a socialist meeting'll be when they can talk like white men."

Bert was humming:

"We're living now in a funny time, When money is made to burn."

Mary was too angry with her husband, because of the impending strike and his incendiary utterances, to hold conversation with Saxon, and the latter, bepuzzled, listened to the conflicting opinions of the men.

"Where are we at?" she asked them, with a merriness that concealed her anxiety at heart.

"We ain't at," Bert snarled. "We're gone."

"But meat and oil have gone up again," she chafed. "And Billy's wages have been cut, and the shop men's were cut last year. Something must be done."

"The only thing to do is fight like hell," Bert answered. "Fight, an' go down fightin'. That's all. We're licked anyhow, but we can have a last run for our money."

"That's no way to talk," Tom rebuked.

"The time for talkin' 's past, old cock. The time for fightin' 's come."

"A hell of a chance you'd have against regular troops and machine guns," Billy retorted.

"Oh, not that way. There's such things as greasy sticks that go up with a loud noise and leave holes. There's such things as emery powder—"

"Oh, ho!" Mary burst out upon him, arms akimbo. "So that's what it means. That's what the emery in your vest pocket meant."

Her husband ignored her. Tom smoked with a troubled air. Billy was hurt. It showed plainly in his face.

"You ain't ben doin' that, Bert?" he asked, his manner showing his expectancy of his friend's denial.

"Sure thing, if you wont to know. I'd see'm all in hell if I could, before I go."

"He's a bloody-minded anarchist," Mary complained. "Men like him killed McKinley, and Garfield, an'—an' an' all the rest. He'll be hung. You'll see. Mark my words. I'm glad there's no children in sight, that's all."

"It's hot air," Billy comforted her.

"He's just teasing you," Saxon soothed. "He always was a josher."

But Mary shook her head.

"I know. I hear him talkin' in his sleep. He swears and curses something awful, an' grits his teeth. Listen to him now."

Bert, his handsome face bitter and devil-may-care, had tilted his chair back against the wall and was singing

"Nobody loves a mil-yun-aire, Nobody likes his looks, Nobody'll share his slightest care, He classes with thugs and crooks."

Tom was saying something about reasonableness and justice, and Bert ceased from singing to catch him up.

"Justice, eh? Another pipe-dream. I'll show you where the working class gets justice. You remember Forbes—J. Alliston Forbes—wrecked the Alta California Trust Company an' salted down two cold millions. I saw him yesterday, in a big hell-bent automobile. What'd he get? Eight years' sentence. How long did he serve? Less'n two years. Pardoned out on account of ill health. Ill hell! We'll be dead an' rotten before he kicks the bucket. Here. Look out this window. You see the back of that house with the broken porch rail. Mrs. Danaker lives there. She takes in washin'. Her old man was killed on the railroad. Nitsky on damages—contributory negligence, or fellow-servant-something-or-other flimflam. That's what the courts handed her. Her boy, Archie, was sixteen. He was on the road, a regular road-kid. He blew into Fresno an' rolled a drunk. Do you want to know how much he got? Two dollars and eighty cents. Get that?—Two-eighty. And what did the alfalfa judge hand'm? Fifty years. He's served eight of it already in San Quentin. And he'll go on serving it till he croaks. Mrs. Danaker says he's bad with consumption—caught it inside, but she ain't got the pull to get'm pardoned. Archie the Kid steals two dollars an' eighty cents from a drunk and gets fifty years. J. Alliston Forbes sticks up the Alta Trust for two millions en' gets less'n two years. Who's country is this anyway? Yourn an' Archie the Kid's? Guess again. It's J. Alliston Forbes'—Oh:

"Nobody likes a mil-yun-aire, Nobody likes his looks, Nobody'll share his slightest care, He classes with thugs and crooks."

Mary, at the sink, where Saxon was just finishing the last dish, untied Saxon's apron and kissed her with the sympathy that women alone feel for each other under the shadow of maternity.

"Now you sit down, dear. You mustn't tire yourself, and it's a long way to go yet. I'll get your sewing for you, and you can listen to the men talk. But don't listen to Bert. He's crazy."

Saxon sewed and listened, and Bert's face grew bleak and bitter as he contemplated the baby clothes in her lap.

"There you go," he blurted out, "bringin' kids into the world when you ain't got any guarantee you can feed em.

"You must a-had a souse last night," Tom grinned.

Bert shook his head.

"Aw, what's the use of gettin' grouched?" Billy cheered. "It's a pretty good country."

"It WAS a pretty good country," Bert replied, "when we was all Mohegans. But not now. We're jiggerooed. We're hornswoggled. We're backed to a standstill. We're double-crossed to a fare-you-well. My folks fought for this country. So did yourn, all of you. We freed the niggers, killed the Indians, an starved, an' froze, an' sweat, an' fought. This land looked good to us. We cleared it, an' broke it, an' made the roads, an' built the cities. And there was plenty for everybody. And we went on fightin' for it. I had two uncles killed at Gettysburg. All of us was mixed up in that war. Listen to Saxon talk any time what her folks went through to get out here an' get ranches, an' horses, an' cattle, an' everything. And they got 'em. All our folks' got 'em, Mary's, too—"

"And if they'd ben smart they'd a-held on to them," she interpolated.

"Sure thing," Bert continued. "That's the very point. We're the losers. We've ben robbed. We couldn't mark cards, deal from the bottom, an' ring in cold decks like the others. We're the white folks that failed. You see, times changed, and there was two kinds of us, the lions and the plugs. The plugs only worked, the lions only gobbled. They gobbled the farms, the mines, the factories, an' now they've gobbled the government. We're the white folks an' the children of white folks, that was too busy being good to be smart. We're the white folks that lost out. We're the ones that's ben skinned. D'ye get me?"

"You'd make a good soap-boxer," Tom commended, "if only you'd get the kinks straightened out in your reasoning."

"It sounds all right, Bert," Billy said, "only it ain't. Any man can get rich to-day—"

"Or be president of the United States," Bert snapped. "Sure thing—if he's got it in him. Just the same I ain't heard you makin' a noise like a millionaire or a president. Why? You ain't got it in you. You're a bonehead. A plug. That's why. Skiddoo for you. Skiddoo for all of us."

At the table, while they ate, Tom talked of the joys of farm-life he had known as a boy and as a young man, and confided that it was his dream to go and take up government land somewhere as his people had done before him. Unfortunately, as he explained, Sarah was set, so that the dream must remain a dream.

"It's all in the game," Billy sighed. "It's played to rules. Some one has to get knocked out, I suppose."

A little later, while Bert was off on a fresh diatribe, Billy became aware that he was making comparisons. This house was not like his house. Here was no satisfying atmosphere. Things seemed to run with a jar. He recollected that when they arrived the breakfast dishes had not yet been washed. With a man's general obliviousness of household affairs, he had not noted details; yet it had been borne in on him, all morning, in a myriad ways, that Mary was not the housekeeper Saxon was. He glanced proudly across at her, and felt the spur of an impulse to leave his seat, go around, and embrace her. She was a wife. He remembered her dainty undergarmenting, and on the instant, into his brain, leaped the image of her so appareled, only to be shattered by Bert.

"Hey, Bill, you seem to think I've got a grouch. Sure thing. I have. You ain't had my experiences. You've always done teamin' an' pulled down easy money prize-fightin'. You ain't known hard times. You ain't ben through strikes. You ain't had to take care of an old mother an' swallow dirt on her account. It wasn't until after she died that I could rip loose an' take or leave as I felt like it.

"Take that time I tackled the Niles Electric an' see what a work-plug gets handed out to him. The Head Cheese sizes me up, pumps me a lot of questions, an' gives me an application blank. I make it out, payin' a dollar to a doctor they sent me to for a health certificate. Then I got to go to a picture garage an' get my mug taken for the Niles Electric rogues' gallery. And I cough up another dollar for the mug. The Head Squirt takes the blank, the health certificate, and the mug, an' fires more questions. DID I BELONG TO A LABOR UNION?—ME? Of course I told'm the truth I guess nit. I needed the job. The grocery wouldn't give me any more tick, and there was my mother.

"Huh, thinks I, here's where I'm a real carman. Back platform for me, where I can pick up the fancy skirts. Nitsky. Two dollars, please. Me—my two dollars. All for a pewter badge. Then there was the uniform—nineteen fifty, and get it anywhere else for fifteen. Only that was to be paid out of my first month. And then five dollars in change in my pocket, my own money. That was the rule.—I borrowed that five from Tom Donovan, the policeman. Then what? They worked me for two weeks without pay, breakin' me in."

"Did you pick up any fancy skirts?" Saxon queried teasingly.

Bert shook his head glumly.

"I only worked a month. Then we organized, and they busted our union higher'n a kite."

"And you boobs in the shops will be busted the same way if you go out on strike," Mary informed him.

CHAPTER VII

"That's what I've ben tellin' you all along," Bert replied. "We ain't got a chance to win."

"Then why go out?" was Saxon's question.

He looked at her with lackluster eyes for a moment, then answered

"Why did my two uncles get killed at Gettysburg?"

CHAPTER VIII

Saxon went about her housework greatly troubled. She no longer devoted herself to the making of pretties. The materials cost money, and she did not dare. Bert's thrust had sunk home. It remained in her quivering consciousness like a shaft of steel that ever turned and rankled. She and Billy were responsible for this coming young life. Could they be sure, after all, that they could adequately feed and clothe it and prepare it for its way in the world? Where was the guaranty? She remembered, dimly, the blight of hard times in the past, and the plaints of fathers and mothers in those days returned to her with a new significance. Almost could she understand Sarah's chronic complaining.

Hard times were already in the neighborhood, where lived the families of the shopmen who had gone out on strike. Among the small storekeepers, Saxon, in the course of the daily marketing, could sense the air of despondency. Light and geniality seemed to have vanished. Gloom pervaded everywhere. The mothers of the children that played in the streets showed the gloom plainly in their faces. When they gossiped in the evenings, over front gates and on door stoops, their voices were subdued and less of laughter rang out.

Mary Donahue, who had taken three pints from the milkman, now took one pint. There were no more family trips to the moving picture shows. Scrap-meat was harder to get from the butcher. Nora Delaney, in the third house, no longer bought fresh fish for Friday. Salted codfish, not of the best quality, was now on her table. The sturdy children that ran out upon the street between meals with huge slices of bread and butter and sugar now came out with no sugar and with thinner slices spread more thinly with butter. The very custom was dying out, and some children already had desisted from piecing between meals.

Everywhere was manifest a pinching and scraping, a tightning and shortening down of expenditure. And everywhere was more irritation. Women became angered with one another, and with the children, more quickly than of yore; and Saxon knew that Bert and Mary bickered incessantly.

"If she'd only realize I've got troubles of my own," Bert complained to Saxon.

She looked at him closely, and felt fear for him in a vague, numb way. His black eyes seemed to burn with a continuous madness. The brown face was leaner, the skin drawn tightly across the cheekbones. A slight twist had come to the mouth, which seemed frozen into bitterness. The very carriage of his body and the way he wore his hat advertised a recklessness more intense than had been his in the past.

CHAPTER VIII

Sometimes, in the long afternoons, sitting by the window with idle hands, she caught herself reconstructing in her vision that folk-migration of her people across the plains and mountains and deserts to the sunset land by the Western sea. And often she found herself dreaming of the arcadian days of her people, when they had not lived in cities nor been vexed with labor unions and employers' associations. She would remember the old people's tales of self-sufficingness, when they shot or raised their own meat, grew their own vegetables, were their own blacksmiths and carpenters, made their own shoes—yes, and spun the cloth of the clothes they wore. And something of the wistfulness in Tom's face she could see as she recollected it when he talked of his dream of taking up government land.

A farmer's life must be fine, she thought. Why was it that people had to live in cities? Why had times changed? If there had been enough in the old days, why was there not enough now? Why was it necessary for men to quarrel and jangle, and strike and fight, all about the matter of getting work? Why wasn't there work for all?—Only that morning, and she shuddered with the recollection, she had seen two scabs, on their way to work, beaten up by the strikers, by men she knew by sight, and some by name, who lived in the neighhorhood. It had happened directly across the street. It had been cruel, terrible—a dozen men on two. The children had begun it by throwing rocks at the scabs and cursing them in ways children should not know. Policemen had run upon the scene with drawn revolvers, and the strikers had retreated into the houses and through the narrow alleys between the houses. One of the scabs, unconscious, had been carried away in an ambulance; the other, assisted by special railroad police, had been taken away to the shops. At him, Mary Donahue, standing on her front stoop, her child in her arms, had hurled such vile abuse that it had brought the blush of shame to Saxon's cheeks. On the stoop of the house on the other side, Saxon had noted Mercedes, in the height of the beating up, looking on with a queer smile. She had seemed very eager to witness, her nostrils dilated and swelling like the beat of pulses as she watched. It had struck Saxon at the time that the old woman was quite unalarmed and only curious to see.

To Mercedes, who was so wise in love, Saxon went for explanation of what was the matter with the world. But the old woman's wisdom in affairs industrial and economic was cryptic and unpalatable.

"La la, my dear, it is so simple. Most men are born stupid. They are the slaves. A few are born clever. They are the masters. God made men so, I suppose."

"Then how about God and that terrible beating across the street this morning?"

"I'm afraid he was not interested," Mercedes smiled. "I doubt he even knows that it happened."

"I was frightened to death," Saxon declared. "I was made sick by it. And yet you—I saw you—you looked on as cool as you please, as if it was a show."

"It was a show, my dear."

"Oh, how could you?"

"La la, I have seen men killed. It is nothing strange. All men die. The stupid ones die like oxen, they know not why. It is quite funny to see. They strike each other with fists and clubs, and break each other's heads. It is gross. They are like a lot of animals. They are like dogs wrangling over bones. Jobs are bones, you know. Now, if they fought for women, or ideas, or bars of gold, or fabulous diamonds, it would be splendid. But no; they are only hungry, and fight over scraps for their stomach."

"Oh, if I could only understand!" Saxon murmured, her hands tightly clasped in anguish of incomprehension and vital need to know.

"There is nothing to understand. It is clear as print. There have always been the stupid and the clever, the slave and the master, the peasant and the prince. There always will be."

"But why?"

"Why is a peasant a peasant, my dear? Because he is a peasant. Why is a flea a flea?"

Saxon tossed her head fretfully.

"Oh, but my dear, I have answered. The philosophies of the world can give no better answer. Why do you like your man for a husband rather than any other man? Because you like him that way, that is all. Why do you like? Because you like. Why does fire burn and frost bite? Why are there clever men and stupid men? masters and slaves? employers and workingmen? Why is black black? Answer that and you answer everything."

"But it is not right That men should go hungry and without work when they want to work if only they can get a square deal," Saxon protested.

"Oh, but it is right, just as it is right that stone won't burn like wood, that sea sand isn't sugar, that thorns prick, that water is wet, that smoke rises, that things fall down and not up."

But such doctrine of reality made no impression on Saxon. Frankly, she could not comprehend. It seemed like so much nonsense.

"Then we have no liberty and independence," she cried passionately. "One man is not as good as another. My child has not the right to live that a rich mother's child has."

"Certainly not," Mercedes answered.

"Yet all my people fought for these things," Saxon urged, remembering her school history and the sword of her father.

"Democracy—the dream of the stupid peoples. Oh, la la, my dear, democracy is a lie, an enchantment to keep the work brutes content, just as religion used to keep them content. When they groaned in their misery and toil, they were persuaded to keep on in their misery and toil by pretty tales of a land beyond the skies where they would live famously and fat while the clever ones roasted in everlasting fire. Ah, how the clever ones must have chuckled! And when that lie wore out, and democracy was dreamed, the clever ones saw to it that it should be in truth a dream, nothing but a dream. The world belongs to the great and clever."

"But you are of the working people," Saxon charged.

The old woman drew herself up, and almost was angry.

"I? Of the working people? My dear, because I had misfortune with moneys invested, because I am old and can no longer win the brave young men, because I have outlived the men of my youth and there is no one to go to, because I live here in the ghetto with Barry Higgins and prepare to die—why, my dear, I was born with the masters, and have trod all my days on the necks of the stupid. I have drunk rare wines and sat at feasts that would have supported this neighborhood for a lifetime. Dick Golden and I—it was Dickie's money, but I could have had it Dick Golden and I dropped four hundred thousand francs in a week's play at Monte Carlo. He was a Jew, but he was a spender. In India I have worn jewels that could have saved the lives of ten thousand families dying before my eyes."

"You saw them die?... and did nothing?" Saxon asked aghast.

"I kept my jewels—la la, and was robbed of them by a brute of a Russian officer within the year."

"And you let them die," Saxon reiterated.

"They were cheap spawn. They fester and multiply like maggots. They meant nothing—nothing, my dear, nothing. No more than your work people mean here, whose crowning stupidity is their continuing to beget more stupid spawn for the slavery of the masters."

So it was that while Saxon could get little glimmering of common sense from others, from the terrible old woman she got none at all. Nor could Saxon bring herself to believe much of what she considered Mercedes' romancing. As the weeks passed, the strike in the railroad shops grew bitter and deadly. Billy shook his head and confessed his inability to make head or tail of the troubles that were looming on the labor horizon.

"I don't get the hang of it," he told Saxon. "It's a mix-up. It's like a roughhouse with the lights out. Look at us teamsters. Here we are, the talk just starting of going out on sympathetic strike for the mill-workers. They've ben out a week, most of their places is filled, an' if us teamsters keep on haulin' the mill-work the strike's lost."

"Yet you didn't consider striking for yourselves when your wages were cut," Saxon said with a frown.

"Oh, we wasn't in position then. But now the Frisco teamsters and the whole Frisco Water Front Confederation is liable to back us up. Anyway, we're just talkin' about it, that's all. But if we do go out, we'll try to get back that ten per cent cut."

"It's rotten politics," he said another time. "Everybody's rotten. If we'd only wise up and agree to pick out honest men—"

"But if you, and Bert, and Tom can't agree, how do you expect all the rest to agree?" Saxon asked.

"It gets me," he admitted. "It's enough to give a guy the willies thinkin' about it. And yet it's plain as the nose on your face. Get honest men for politics, an' the whole thing's straightened out. Honest men'd make honest laws, an' then honest men'd get their dues. But Bert wants to smash things, an' Tom smokes his pipe and dreams pipe dreams about by an' by when everybody votes the way he thinks. But this by an' by ain't the point. We want things now. Tom says we can't get them now, an' Bert says we ain't never goin' to get them. What can a fellow do when everybody's of different minds? Look at the socialists themselves. They're always disagreeing, splittin' up, an' firin' each other out of the party. The whole thing's bughouse, that's what, an' I almost get dippy myself thinkin' about it. The point I can't get out of my mind is that we want things now."

He broke off abruptly and stared at Saxon.

"What is it?" he asked, his voice husky with anxiety. "You ain't sick... or... or anything?"

One hand she had pressed to her heart; but the startle and fright in her eyes was changing into a pleased intentness, while on her mouth was a little mysterious smile. She seemed oblivious to her husband, as if listening to some message from afar and not for his ears. Then wonder and joy transfused her face, and she looked at Billy, and her hand went out to his.

"It's life," she whispered. "I felt life. I am so glad, so glad."

The next evening when Billy came home from work, Saxon caused him to know and undertake more of the responsibilities of fatherhood.

"I've been thinking it over, Billy," she began, "and I'm such a healthy, strong woman that it won't have to be very expensive. There's Martha Skelton—she's a good midwife."

But Billy shook his head.

"Nothin' doin' in that line, Saxon. You're goin' to have Doc Hentley. He's Bill Murphy's doc, an' Bill swears by him. He's an old cuss, but he's a wooz."

"She confined Maggie Donahue," Saxon argued; "and look at her and her baby."

"Well, she won't confine you—not so as you can notice it."

"But the doctor will charge twenty dollars," Saxon pursued, "and make me get a nurse because I haven't any womenfolk to come in. But Martha Skelton would do everything, and it would be so much cheaper."

But Billy gathered her tenderly in his arms and laid down the law.

"Listen to me, little wife. The Roberts family ain't on the cheap. Never forget that. You've gotta have the baby. That's your business, an' it's enough for you. My business is to get the money an' take care of you. An' the best ain't none too good for you. Why, I wouldn't run the chance of the teeniest accident happenin' to you for a million dollars. It's you that counts. An' dollars is dirt. Maybe you think I like that kid some. I do. Why, I can't get him outa my head. I'm thinkin' about'm all day long. If I get fired, it'll be his fault. I'm clean dotty over him. But just the same, Saxon, honest to God, before I'd have anything happen to you, break your little finger, even, I'd see him dead an' buried first. That'll give you something of an idea what you mean to me.

"Why, Saxon, I had the idea that when folks got married they just settled down, and after a while their business was to get along with each other. Maybe it's the way it is with other people; but it ain't that way with you an' me. I love you more 'n more every day. Right now I love you more'n when I began talkin' to you five minutes ago. An' you won't have to get a nurse. Doc Hentley'll come every day, an' Mary'll come in an' do the housework, an' take care of you an' all that, just as you'll do for her if she ever needs it."

As the days and weeks pussed, Saxon was possessed by a conscious feeling of proud motherhood in her swelling breasts. So essentially a normal woman was she, that motherhood was a satisfying and passionate happiness. It was true that she had her moments of apprehension, but they were so momentary and faint that they tended, if anything, to give zest to her happiness.

Only one thing troubled her, and that was the puzzling and perilous situation of labor which no one seemed to understand, her self least of all.

"They're always talking about how much more is made by machinery than by the old ways," she told her brother Tom. "Then, with all the machinery we've got now, why don't we get more?"

"Now you're talkin'," he answered. "It wouldn't take you long to understand socialism."

But Saxon had a mind to the immediate need of things.

"Tom, how long have you been a socialist?"

"Eight years."

"And you haven't got anything by it?"

"But we will... in time."

"At that rate you'll be dead first," she challenged.

Tom sighed.

"I'm afraid so. Things move so slow."

Again he sighed. She noted the weary, patient look in his face, the bent shoulders, the labor-gnarled hands, and it all seemed to symbolize the futility of his social creed.

CHAPTER IX

It began quietly, as the fateful unexpected so often begins. Children, of all ages and sizes, were playing in the street, and Saxon, by the open front window, was watching them and dreaming day dreams of her child soon to be. The sunshine mellowed peacefully down, and a light wind from the bay cooled the air and gave to it a tang of salt. One of the children pointed up Pine Street toward Seventh. All the children ceased playing, and stared and pointed. They formed into groups, the larger boys, of from ten to twelve, by themselves, the older girls anxiously clutching the small children by the hands or gathering them into their arms.

Saxon could not see the cause of all this, but she could guess when she saw the larger boys rush to the gutter, pick up stones, and sneak into the alleys between the houses. Smaller boys tried to imitate them. The girls, dragging the tots by the arms, banged gates and clattered up the front steps of the small houses. The doors slammed behind them, and the street was deserted, though here and there front shades were drawn aside so that anxious-faced women might peer forth. Saxon heard the uptown train puffing and snorting as it pulled out from Center Street. Then, from the direction of Seventh, came a hoarse, throaty manroar. Still, she could see nothing, and she remembered Mercedes Higgins' words "THEY ARE LIKE DOGS WRANGLING OVER BONES. JOBS ARE BONES, YOU KNOW"

The roar came closer, and Saxon, leaning out, saw a dozen scabs, conveyed by as many special police and Pinkertons, coming down the sidewalk on her side of the street. They came compactly, as if with discipline, while behind, disorderly, yelling confusedly, stooping to pick up rocks, were seventy-five or a hundred of the striking shopmen. Saxon discovered herself trembling with apprehension, knew that she must not, and controlled herself. She was helped in this by the conduct of Mercedes Higgins. The old woman came out of her front door, dragging a chair, on which she coolly seated herself on the tiny stoop at the top of the steps.

In the hands of the special police were clubs. The Pinkertons carried no visible weapons. The strikers, urging on from behind, seemed content with yelling their rage and threats, and it remained for the children to precipitate the conflict. From across the street, between the Olsen and the Isham houses, came a shower of stones. Most of these fell short, though one struck a scab on the head. The man was no more than twenty feet away from Saxon. He reeled toward her front picket fence, drawing a revolver. With one hand he brushed the blood from his eyes and with the other he discharged the revolver into the Isham house. A Pinkerton seized his arm to prevent a second shot, and dragged him along. At the same instant a wilder roar went up from the strikers, while a volley of stones came from between Saxon's house and Maggie Donahue's. The scabs and their protectors made a stand, drawing revolvers. From their hard, determined faces—fighting men by profession—Saxon could augur nothing but bloodshed and death. An elderly man, evidently the leader, lifted a soft felt hat and mopped the perspiration from the bald top of his head. He was a large man, very rotund of belly and helpless looking. His gray beard was stained with streaks of tobacco juice, and he was smoking a cigar. He was stoop-shouldered, and Saxon noted the dandruff on the collar of his coat.

One of the men pointed into the street, and several of his companions laughed. The cause of it was the little Olsen boy, barely four years old, escaped somehow from his mother and toddling toward his economic enemies. In his right he bore a rock so heavy that he could scarcely lift it. With this he feebly threatened them. His rosy little face was convulsed with rage, and he was screaming over and over "Dam scabs! Dam scabs! Dam scabs!" The laughter with which they greeted him only increased his fury. He toddled closer, and with a mighty exertion threw the rock. It fell a scant six feet beyond his hand.

This much Saxon saw, and also Mrs. Olsen rushing into the street for her child. A rattling of revolver-shots from the strikers drew Saxon's attention to the men beneath her. One of them cursed sharply and examined the biceps of his left arm, which hung limply by his side. Down the hand she saw the blood beginning to drip. She knew she ought not remain and watch, but the memory of her fighting forefathers was with her, while she possessed no more than normal human fear—if anything, less. She forgot her child in the eruption of battle that had broken upon her quiet street. And she forgot the strikers, and everything else, in amazement at what had happened to the round-bellied, cigar-smoking leader. In some strange way, she knew not how, his head had become wedged at the neck between the tops of the pickets of her fence. His body hung down outside, the knees not quite touching the ground. His hat had fallen off, and the sun was making an astounding high light on his bald spot. The cigar, too, was gone. She saw he was looking at her. One hand, between the pickets, seemed waving at her, and almost he seemed to wink at her jocosely, though she knew it to be the contortion of deadly pain.

Possibly a second, or, at most, two seconds, she gazed at this, when she was aroused by Bert's voice. He was running along the sidewalk, in front of her house, and behind him charged several more strikers, while he shouted: "Come on, you Mohegans! We got 'em nailed to the cross!"

In his left hand he carried a pick-handle, in his right a revolver, already empty, for he clicked the cylinder vainly around as he ran. With an abrupt stop, dropping the pick-handle, he whirled half about, facing Saxon's gate. He was sinking down, when he straightened himself to throw the revolver into the face of a scab who was jumping toward him. Then he began swaying, at the same time sagging at the knees and waist. Slowly, with infinite effort, he caught a gate picket in his right hand, and, still slowly, as if lowering himself, sank down, while past him leaped the crowd of strikers he had led.

It was battle without quarter—a massacre. The scabs and their protectors, surrounded, backed against Saxon's fence, fought like cornered rats, but could not withstand the rush of a hundred men. Clubs and pick-handles were swinging, revolvers were exploding, and cobblestones were flung with crushing effect at arm's distance. Saxon saw young Frank Davis, a friend of Bert's and a father of several months' standing, press the muzzle of his revolver against a scab's stomach and fire. There were curses and snarls of rage, wild cries of terror and pain. Mercedes was right. These things were not men. They were beasts, fighting over bones, destroying one another for bones.

JOBS ARE BONES; JOBS ARE BONES. The phrase was an incessant iteration in Saxon's brain. Much as she might have wished it, she was powerless now to withdraw from the window. It was as if she were paralyzed. Her brain no longer worked. She sat numb, staring, incapable of anything save seeing the rapid horror before her eyes that flashed along like a moving picture film gone mad. She saw Pinkertons, special police, and strikers go down. One scab, terribly wounded, on his knees and begging for mercy, was kicked in the face. As he sprawled backward another striker, standing over him, fired a revolver into his chest, quickly and deliberately, again and again, until the weapon was empty. Another scab, backed over the pickets by a hand clutching his throat, had his face pulped by a revolver butt. Again and again, continually, the revolver rose and fell, and Saxon knew the man who wielded it—Chester Johnson. She had met him at dances and danced with him in the days before she was married. He had always been kind and good natured. She remembered the Friday night, after a City Hall band concert, when he had taken her and two other girls to Tony's Tamale Grotto on Thirteenth street. And after that they had all gone to Pabst's Cafe and drunk a glass of beer before they went home. It was impossible that this could be the same Chester Johnson. And as she looked, she saw the round-bellied leader, still wedged by the neck between the pickets, draw a revolver with his free hand, and, squinting horribly sidewise, press the muzzle against Chester's side. She tried to scream a warning. She did scream, and Chester looked up and saw her. At that moment the revolver went off, and he collapsed prone upon the body of the scab. And the bodies of three men hung on her picket fence.

Anything could happen now. Quite without surprise, she saw the strikers leaping the fence, trampling her few little geraniums and pansies into the earth as they fled between Mercedes' house and hers. Up Pine street, from the railroad yards, was coming a rush of railroad police and Pinkertons, firing as they ran. While down Pine street, gongs clanging, horses at a gallop, came three patrol wagons packed with police. The strikers were in a trap. The only way out was between the houses and over the back yard fences. The jam in the narrow alley prevented them all from escaping. A dozen were cornered in the angle between the front of her house and the steps. And as they had done, so were they done by. No effort was made to arrest. They were clubbed down and shot down to the last man by the guardians of the peace who were infuriated by what had been wreaked on their brethren.

It was all over, and Saxon, moving as in a dream, clutching the banister tightly, came down the front steps. The round-bellied leader still leered at her and fluttered one hand, though two big policemen were just bending to extricate him. The gate was off its hinges, which seemed strange, for she had been watching all the time and had not seen it happen.

Bert's eyes were closed. His lips were blood-flecked, and there was a gurgling in his throat as if he were trying to say something. As she stooped above him, with her handkerchief brushing the blood from his cheek where some one had stepped on him, his eyes opened. The old defiant light was in them. He did not know her. The lips moved, and faintly, almost reminiscently, he murmured, "The last of the Mohegans, the last of the Mohegans." Then he groaned, and the eyelids drooped down again. He was not dead. She knew that, the chest still rose and fell, and the gurgling still continued in his throat.

She looked up. Mercedes stood beside her. The old woman's eyes were very bright, her withered cheeks flushed.

"Will you help me carry him into the house?" Saxon asked.

Mercedes nodded, turned to a sergeant of police, and made the request to him. The sergeant gave a swift glance at Bert, and his eyes were bitter and ferocious as he refused.

"To hell with'm. We'll care for our own."

"Maybe you and I can do it," Saxon said.

"Don't be a fool." Mercedes was beckoning to Mrs. Olsen across the street. "You go into the house, little mother that is to be. This is bad for you. We'll carry him in. Mrs. Olsen is coming, and we'll get Maggie Donahue."

Saxon led the way into the back bedroom which Billy had insisted on furnishing. As she opened the door, the carpet seemed to fly up into her face as with the force of a blow, for she remembered Bert had laid that carpet. And as the women placed him on the bed she recalled that it was Bert and she, between them, who had set the bed up one Sunday morning.

And then she felt very queer, and was surprised to see Mercedes regarding her with questioning, searching eyes. After that her queerness came on very fast, and she descended into the hell of pain that is given to women alone to know. She was supported, half-carried, to the front bedroom. Many faces were about her—Mercedes, Mrs. Olsen, Maggie Donahue. It seemed she must ask Mrs. Olsen if she had saved little Emil from the street, but Mercedes cleared Mrs. Olsen out to look after Bert, and Maggie Donahue went to answer a knock at the front door. From the street came a loud hum of voices, punctuated by shouts and commands, and from time to time there was a clanging of the gongs of ambulances and patrol wagon's. Then appeared the fat, comfortable face of Martha Shelton, and, later, Dr. Hentley came. Once, in a clear interval, through the thin wall Saxon heard the high opening notes of Mary's hysteria. And, another time, she heard Mary repeating over and over. "I'll never go back to the laundry. Never. Never."

CHAPTER X

Billy could never get over the shock, during that period, of Saxon's appearance. Morning after morning, and evening after evening when he came home from work, he would enter the room where she lay and fight a royal battle to hide his feelings and make a show of cheerfulness and geniality. She looked so small lying there so small and shrunken and weary, and yet so child-like in her smallness. Tenderly, as he sat beside her, he would take up her pale hand and stroke the slim, transparent arm, marveling at the smallness and delicacy of the bones.

One of her first questions, puzzling alike to Billy and Mary, was:

"Did they save little Emil Olsen?"

And when she told them how he had attacked, singlehanded, the whole twenty-four fighting men, Billy's face glowed with appreciation.

"The little cuss!" he said. "That's the kind of a kid to be proud of."

He halted awkwardly, and his very evident fear that he had hurt her touched Saxon. She put her hand out to his.

"Billy," she began; then waited till Mary left the room.

"I never asked before—not that it matters... now. But I waited for you to tell me. Was it...?"

He shook his head.

"No; it was a girl. A perfect little girl. Only... it was too soon."

She pressed his hand, and almost it was she that sympathized with him in his affliction.

"I never told you, Billy—you were so set on a boy; but I planned, just the same, if it was a girl, to call her Daisy. You remember, that was my mother's name."

He nodded his approbation.

"Say, Saxon, you know I did want a boy like the very dickens... well, I don't care now. I think I'm set just as hard on a girl, an', well, here's hopin' the next will be called... you wouldn't mind, would you?"

"What?"

"If we called it the same name, Daisy?"

"Oh, Billy! I was thinking the very same thing."

Then his face grew stern as he went on.

"Only there ain't goin' to be a next. I didn't know what havin' children was like before. You can't run any more risks like that."

"Hear the big, strong, afraid-man talk!" she jeered, with a wan smile. "You don't know anything about it. How can a man? I am a healthy, natural woman. Everything would have been all right this time if... if all that fighting hadn't happened. Where did they bury Bert?"

"You knew?"

"All the time. And where is Mercedes? She hasn't been in for two days."

"Old Barry's sick. She's with him."

He did not tell her that the old night watchman was dying, two thin walls and half a dozen feet away.

Saxon's lips were trembling, and she began to cry weakly, clinging to Billy's hand with both of hers.

"I—I can't help it," she sobbed. "I'll be all right in a minute.... Our little girl, Billy. Think of it! And I never saw her!"

She was still lying on her bed, when, one evening, Mary saw fit to break out in bitter thanksgiving that she had escaped, and was destined to escape, what Saxon had gone through.

"Aw, what are you talkin' about?" Billy demanded. "You'll get married some time again as sure as beans is beans."

"Not to the best man living," she proclaimed. "And there ain't no call for it. There's too many people in the world now, else why are there two or three men for every job? And, besides, havin' children is too terrible."

Saxon, with a look of patient wisdom in her face that became glorified as she spoke, made answer:

"I ought to know what it means. I've been through it, and I'm still in the thick of it, and I want to say to you right now, out of all the pain and the ache and the sorrow, that it is the most beautiful, wonderful thing in the world."

As Saxon's strength came back to her (and when Doctor Hentley had privily assured Billy that she was sound as a dollar), she herself took up the matter of the industrial tragedy that had taken place before her door. The militia had been called out immediately, Billy informed her, and was encamped then at the foot of Pine street on the waste ground next to the railroad yards. As for the strikers, fifteen of them were in jail. A house to house search had been made in the neighborhood by the police, and in this way nearly the whole fifteen, all wounded, had been captured. It would go hard with them, Billy foreboded gloomily. The newspapers were demanding blood for blood, and all the ministers in Oakland had preached fierce sermons against the strikers. The railroad had filled every place, and it was well known that the striking shopmen not only would never get their old jobs back but were blacklisted in every railroad in the United States. Already they were beginning to scatter. A number had gone to Panama, and four were talking of going to Ecuador to work in the shops of the railroad that ran over the Andes to Quito.

With anxiety keenly concealed, she tried to feel out Billy's opinion on what had happened.

"That shows what Bert's violent methods come to," she said.

He shook his head slowly and gravely.

"They'll hang Chester Johnson, anyway," he answered indirectly. "You know him. You told me you used to dance with him. He was caught red-handed, lyin' on the body of a scab he beat to death. Old Jelly Belly's got three bullet holes in him, but he ain't goin' to die, and he's got Chester's number. They'll hang'm on Jelly Belly's evidence. It was all in the papers. Jelly Belly shot him, too, a-hangin' by the neck on our pickets."

Saxon shuddered. Jelly Belly must be the man with the bald spot and the tobacco-stained whiskers.

"Yes," she said. "I saw it all. It seemed he must have hung there for hours."

"It was all over, from first to last, in five minutes."

"It seemed ages and ages."

"I guess that's the way it seemed to Jelly Belly, stuck on the pickets," Billy smiled grimly. "But he's a hard one to kill. He's been shot an' cut up a dozen different times. But they say now he'll be crippled for life—have to go around on crutches, or in a wheel-chair. That'll stop him from doin' any more dirty work for the railroad. He was one of their top gun-fighters—always up to his ears in the thick of any fightin' that was goin' on. He never was leery of anything on two feet, I'll say that much for'm."

"Where does he live?" Saxon inquired.

"Up on Adeline, near Tenth—fine neighborhood an' fine two-storied house. He must pay thirty dollars a month rent. I guess the railroad paid him pretty well."

"Then he must be married?"

"Yep. I never seen his wife, but he's got one son, Jack, a passenger engineer. I used to know him. He was a nifty boxer, though he never went into the ring. An' he's got another son that's teacher in the high school. His name's Paul. We're about the same age. He was great at baseball. I knew him when we was kids. He pitched me out three times hand-runnin' once, when the Durant played the Cole School."

Saxon sat back in the Morris chair, resting and thinking. The problem was growing more complicated than ever. This elderly, round-bellied, and bald-headed gunfighter, too, had a wife and family. And there was Frank Davis, married barely a year and with a baby boy. Perhaps the scab he shot in the stomach had a wife and children. All seemed to be acquainted, members of a very large family, and yet, because of their particular families, they battered and killed each other. She had seen Chester Johnson kill a scab, and now they were going to hang Chester Johnson, who had married Kittie Brady out of the cannery, and she and Kittie Brady had worked together years before in the paper box factory.

Vainly Saxon waked for Billy to say something that would show he did not countenance the killing of the scabs.

"It was wrong," she ventured finally.

"They killed Bert," he countered. "An' a lot of others. An' Frank Davis. Did you know he was dead? Had his whole lower jaw shot away—died in the ambulance before they could get him to the receiving hospital. There was never so much killin' at one time in Oakland before."

"But it was their fault," she contended. "They began it. It was murder."

Billy did not reply, but she heard him mutter hoarsely. She knew he said "God damn them"; but when she asked, "What?" he made no answer. His eyes were deep with troubled clouds, while the mouth had hardened, and all his face was bleak.

To her it was a heart-stab. Was he, too, like the rest? Would he kill other men who had families, like Bert, and Frank Davis, and Chester Johnson had killed? Was he, too, a wild beast, a dog that would snarl over a bone?

CHAPTER X

She sighed. Life was a strange puzzle. Perhaps Mercedes Higgins was right in her cruel statement of the terms of existence.

"What of it," Billy laughed harshly, as if in answer to her unuttered questions. "It's dog eat dog, I guess, and it's always ben that way. Take that scrap outside there. They killed each other just like the North an' South did in the Civil War."

"But workingmen can't win that way, Billy. You say yourself that it spoiled their chance of winning."

"I suppose not," he admitted reluctantly. "But what other chance they've got to win I don't see. Look at 'us. We'll be up against it next."

"Not the teamsters?" she cried.

He nodded gloomily.

"The bosses are cuttin' loose all along the line for a high old time. Say they're goin' to beat us to our knees till we come crawlin' back a-beggin' for our jobs. They've bucked up real high an' mighty what of all that killin' the other day. Havin' the troops out is half the fight, along with havin' the preachers an' the papers an' the public behind 'em. They're shootin' off their mouths already about what they're goin' to do. They're sure gunning for trouble. First, they're goin' to hang Chester Johnson an' as many more of the fifteen as they can. They say that flat. The Tribune, an' the Enquirer an' the Times keep sayin' it over an over every day. They're all union-hustin' to beat the band. No more closed shop. To hell with organized labor. Why, the dirty little Intelligencer come out this morning an' said that every union official in Oakland ought to be run outa town or stretched up. Fine, eh? You bet it's fine.

"Look at us. It ain't a case any more of sympathetic strike for the mill-workers. We got our own troubles. They've fired our four best men—the ones that was always on the conference committees. Did it without cause. They're lookin' for trouble, as I told you, an' they'll get it, too, if they don't watch out. We got our tip from the Frisco Water Front Confederation. With them backin' us we'll go some."

"You mean you'll... strike?" Saxon asked.

He bent his head.

"But isn't that what they want you to do?—from the way they're acting?"

"What's the difference?" Billy shrugged his shoulders, then continued. "It's better to strike than to get fired. We beat 'em to it, that's all, an' we catch 'em before they're ready. Don't we know what they're doin'? They're collectin' gradin'-camp drivers an' mule-skinners all up an' down the state. They got forty of 'em, feedin' 'em in a hotel in Stockton right now, an' ready to rush 'em in on us an' hundreds more like 'em. So this Saturday's the last wages I'll likely bring home for some time."

Saxon closed her eyes and thought quietly for five minutes. It was not her way to take things excitedly. The coolness of poise that Billy so admired never deserted her in time of emergency. She realized that she herself was no more than a mote caught up in this tangled, nonunderstandable conflict of many motes.

"We'll have to draw from our savings to pay for this month's rent," she said brightly.

Billy's face fell.

"We ain't got as much in the bank as you think," he confessed. "Bert had to be buried, you know, an I coughed up what the others couldn't raise."

"How much was it?"

"Forty dollars. I was goin' to stand off the butcher an' the rest for a while. They knew I was good pay. But they put it to me straight. They'd been carryin' the shopmen right along an was up against it themselves. An' now with that strike smashed they're pretty much smashed themselves. So I took it all out of the bank. I knew you wouldn't mind. You don't, do you?"

She smiled bravely, and bravely overcame the sinking feeling at her heart.

"It was the only right thing to do, Billy. I would have done it if you were lying sick, and Bert would have done it for you an' me if it had been the other way around."

His face was glowing.

"Gee, Saxon, a fellow can always count on you. You're like my right hand. That's why I say no more babies. If I lose you I'm crippled for life."

"We've got to economize," she mused, nodding her appreciation. "How much is in bank?"

"Just about thirty dollars. You see, I had to pay Martha Skelton an' for the... a few other little things. An' the union took time by the neck and levied a four dollar emergency assessment on every member just to be ready if the strike was pulled off. But Doc Hentley can wait. He said as much. He's the goods, if anybody should ask you. How'd you like'm?"

"I liked him. But I don't know about doctors. He's the first I ever had—except when I was vaccinated once, and then the city did that."

"Looks like the street car men are goin' out, too. Dan Fallon's come to town. Came all the way from New York. Tried to sneak in on the quiet, but the fellows knew when he left New York, an' kept track of him all the way acrost. They have to. He's Johnny-on-the-Spot whenever street car men are licked into shape. He's won lots of street car strikes for the bosses. Keeps an army of strike breakers an' ships them all over the country on special trains wherever they're needed. Oakland's never seen labor troubles like she's got and is goin' to get. All hell's goin' to break loose from the looks of it."

"Watch out for yourself, then, Billy. I don't want to lose you either."

"Aw, that's all right. I can take care of myself. An' besides, it ain't as though we was licked. We got a good chance."

"But you'll lose if there is any killing."

"Yep; we gotta keep an eye out against that."

"No violence."

"No gun-fighting or dynamite," he assented. "But a heap of scabs'll get their heads broke. That has to be."

"But you won't do any of that, Billy."

"Not so as any slob can testify before a court to havin' seen me." Then, with a quick shift, he changed the subject. "Old Barry Higgins is dead. I didn't want to tell you till you was outa bed. Buried'm a week ago. An' the old woman's movin' to Frisco. She told me she'd be in to say good-bye. She stuck by you pretty well them first couple of days, an' she showed Martha Shelton a few that made her hair curl. She got Martha's goat from the jump."

CHAPTER XI

With Billy on strike and away doing picket duty, and with the departure of Mercedes and the death of Bert, Saxon was left much to herself in a loneliness that even in one as healthy-minded as she could not fail to produce morbidness. Mary, too, had left, having spoken vaguely of taking a job at housework in Piedmont.

Billy could help Saxon little in her trouble. He dimly sansed her suffering, without comprehending the scope and intensity of it. He was too man-practical, and, by his very sex, too remote from the intimate tragedy that was hers. He was an outsider at the best, a friendly onlooker who saw little. To her the baby had been quick and real. It was still quick and real. That was her trouble. By no deliberate effort of will could she fill the aching void of its absence. Its reality became, at times, an hallucination. Somewhere it still was, and she must find it. She would catch herself, on occasion, listening with strained ears for the cry she had never heard, yet which, in fancy, she had heard a thousand times in the happy months before the end. Twice she left her bed in her sleep and went searching—each time coming to herself beside her mother's chest of drawers in which were the tiny garments. To herself, at such moments, she would say, "I had a baby once." And she would say it, aloud, as she watched the children playing in the street.

One day, on the Eighth street cars, a young mother sat beside her, a crowing infant in her arms. And Saxon said to her:

"I had a baby once. It died."

The mother looked at her, startled, half-drew the baby tighter in her arms, jealously, or as if in fear; then she softened as she said:

"You poor thing."

"Yes," Saxon nodded. "It died."

Tear's welled into her eyes, and the telling of her grief seemed to have brought relief. But all the day she suffered from an almost overwhelming desire to recite her sorrow to the world—to the paying teller at the bank, to the elderly floor-walker in Salinger's, to the blind woman, guided by a little boy, who played on the concertina—to every one save the policeman. The police were new and terrible creatures to her now. She had seen them kill the strikers as mercilessly as the strikers had killed the scabs. And, unlike the strikers, the police were professional killers. They were not fighting for jobs. They did it as a business. They could have taken prisoners that day, in the angle of her front steps and the house. But they had not. Unconsciously, whenever approaching one, she edged across the sidewalk so as to get as far as possible away from him. She did not reason it out, but deeper than consciousness was the feeling that they were typical of something inimical to her and hers.

At Eighth and Broadway, waiting for her car to return home, the policeman on the corner recognized her and greeted her. She turned white to the lips, and her heart fluttered painfully. It was only Ned Hermanmann, fatter, bronder-faced, jollier looking than ever. He had sat across the aisle from her for three terms at school. He and she had been monitors together of the composition books for one term. The day the powder works blew up at Pinole, breaking every window in the school, he and she had not joined in the panic rush for out-of-doors. Both had remained in the room, and the irate principal had exhibited them, from room to room, to the cowardly classes, and then rewarded them with a month's holiday from school. And after that Ned Hermanmann had become a policeman, and married Lena Highland, and Saxon had heard they had five children.

But, in spite of all that, he was now a policeman, and Billy was now a striker. Might not Ned Hermanmann some day club and shoot Billy just as those other policemen clubbed and shot the strikers by her front steps?

"What's the matter, Saxon?" he asked. "Sick?"

She nodded and choked, unable to speak, and started to move toward her car which was coming to a stop.

"I'll help you," he offered.

She shrank away from his hand.

"No; I'm all right," she gasped hurriedly. "I'm not going to take it. I've forgotten something."

She turned away dizzily, up Broadway to Ninth. Two blocks along Ninth, she turned down Clay and back to Eighth street, where she waited for another car.

As the summer months dragged along, the industrial situation in Oakland grew steadily worse. Capital everywhere seemed to have selected this city for the battle with organized labor. So many men in Oakland were out on strike, or were locked out, or were unable to work because of the dependence of their trades on the other tied-up trade's, that odd jobs at common labor were hard to obtain. Billy occasionally got a day's work to do, but did not earn enough to make both ends meet, despite the small strike wages received at first, and despite the rigid economy he and Saxon practiced.

The table she set had scarcely anything in common with that of their first married year. Not alone was every item of cheaper quality, but many items had disappeared. Meat, and the poorest, was very seldom on the table. Cow's milk had given place to condensed milk, and even the sparing use of the latter had ceased. A roll of butter, when they had it, lasted half a dozen times as long as formerly. Where Billy had been used to drinking three cups of coffee for breakfast, he now drank one. Saxon boiled this coffee an atrocious length of time, and she paid twenty cents a pound for it.

The blight of hard times was on all the neighborhood. The families not involved in one strike were touched by some other strike or by the cessation of work in some dependent trade. Many single young men who were lodgers had drifted away, thus increasing the house rent of the families which had sheltered them.

"Gott!" said the butcher to Saxon. "We working class all suffer together. My wife she cannot get her teeth fixed now. Pretty soon I go smash broke maybe."

CHAPTER XI

Once, when Billy was preparing to pawn his watch, Saxon suggested his borrowing the money from Billy Murphy.

"I was plannin' that," Billy answered, "only I can't now. I didn't tell you what happened Tuesday night at the Sporting Life Club. You remember that squarehead Champion of the United States Navy? Bill was matched with him, an' it was sure easy money. Bill had 'm goin' south by the end of the sixth round, an' at the seventh went in to finish 'm. And then—just his luck, for his trade's idle now—he snaps his right forearm. Of course the squarehead comes back at 'm on the jump, an' it's good night for Bill. Gee! Us Mohegans are gettin' our bad luck handed to us in chunks these days."

"Don't!" Saxon cried, shuddering involuntarily.

"What?" Billy asked with open mouth of surprise.

"Don't say that word again. Bert was always saying it."

"Oh, Mohegans. All right, I won't. You ain't superstitions, are you?"

"No; but just the same there's too much truth in the word for me to like it. Sometimes it seems as though he was right. Times have changed. They've changed even since I was a little girl. We crossed the plains and opened up this country, and now we're losing even the chance to work for a living in it. And it's not my fault, it's not your fault. We've got to live well or bad just by luck, it seems. There's no other way to explain it."

"It beats me," Billy concurred. "Look at the way I worked last year. Never missed a day. I'd want to never miss a day this year, an' here I haven't done a tap for weeks an' weeks an' weeks. Say! Who runs this country anyway?"

Saxon had stopped the morning paper, but frequently Maggie Donahue's boy, who served a Tribune route, tossed an "extra" on her steps. From its editorials Saxon gleaned that organized labor was trying to run the country and that it was making a mess of it. It was all the fault of domineering labor—so ran the editorials, column by column, day by day; and Saxon was convinced, yet remained unconvinced. The social puzzle of living was too intricate.

The teamsters' strike, backed financially by the teamsters of San Francisco and by the allied unions of the San Francisco Water Front Confederation, promised to be long-drawn, whether or not it was successful. The Oakland harness-washers and stablemen, with few exceptions, had gone out with the teamsters. The teaming firm's were not half-filling their contracts, but the employers' association was helping them. In fact, half the employers' associations of the Pacific Coast were helping the Oakland Employers' Association.

Saxon was behind a month's rent, which, when it is considered that rent was paid in advance, was equivalent to two months. Likewise, she was two months behind in the installments on the furniture. Yet she was not pressed very hard by Salinger's, the furniture dealers.

"We're givin' you all the rope we can," said their collector. "My orders is to make you dig up every cent I can and at the same time not to be too hard. Salinger's are trying to do the right thing, but they're up against it, too. You've no idea how many accounts like yours they're carrying along. Sooner or later they'll have to call a halt or get it in the neck themselves. And in the meantime just see if you can't scrape up five dollars by next week—just to cheer them along, you know."

One of the stablemen who had not gone out, Henderson by name, worked at Billy's stables. Despite the urging of the bosses to eat and sleep in the stable like the other men, Henderson had persisted in coming home each morning to his little house around the corner from Saxon's on Fifth street. Several times she had seen him swinging along defiantly, his dinner pail in his hand, while the neighborhood boys dogged his heels at a safe distance and informed him in yapping chorus that he was a scab and no good. But one evening, on his way to work, in a spirit of bravado he went into the Pile-Drivers' Home, the saloon at Seventh and Pine. There it was his mortal mischance to encounter Otto Frank, a striker who drove from the same stable. Not many minutes later an ambulance was hurrying Henderson to the receiving hospital with a fractured skull, while a patrol wagon was no less swiftly carrying Otto Frank to the city prison.

Maggie Donahue it was, eyes shining with gladness, who told Saxon of the happening.

"Served him right, too, the dirty scab," Maggie concluded.

"But his poor wife!" was Saxon's cry. "She's not strong. And then the children. She'll never be able to take care of them if her husband dies."

"An' serve her right, the damned slut!"

Saxon was both shocked and hurt by the Irishwoman's brutality. But Maggie was implacable.

"'Tis all she or any woman deserves that'll put up an' live with a scab. What about her children? Let'm starve, an' her man a-takin' the food out of other children's mouths."

Mrs. Olsen's attitude was different. Beyond passive sentimental pity for Henderson's wife and children, she gave them no thought, her chief concern being for Otto Frank and Otto Frank's wife and children—herself and Mrs. Frank being full sisters.

"If he dies, they will hang Otto," she said. "And then what will poor Hilda do? She has varicose veins in both legs, and she never can stand on her feet all day an' work for wages. And me, I cannot help. Ain't Carl out of work, too?"

Billy had still another point of view.

"It will give the strike a black eye, especially if Henderson croaks," he worried, when he came home. "They'll hang Frank on record time. Besides, we'll have to put up a defense, an' lawyers charge like Sam Hill. They'll eat a hole in our treasury you could drive every team in Oakland through. An' if Frank hadn't ben screwed up with whisky he'd never a-done it. He's the mildest, good-naturedest man sober you ever seen."

Twice that evening Billy left the house to find out if Henderson was dead yet. In the morning the papers gave little hope, and the evening papers published his death. Otto Frank lay in jail without bail. The Tribune demanded a quick trial and summary execution, calling on the prospective jury manfully to do its duty and dwelling at length on the moral effect that would be so produced upon the lawless working class. It went further, emphasizing the salutary effect machine guns would have on the mob that had taken the fair city of Oakland by the throat.

And all such occurrences struck at Saxon personally. Practically alone in the world, save for Billy, it was her life, and his, and their mutual love-life, that was menaced. From the moment he left the house to the moment of his return she knew no peace of mind. Rough work was afoot, of which he told her nothing, and she knew he was playing his part in it. On more than one occasion she noticed fresh-broken skin on his knuckles. At such times he was remarkably taciturn, and would sit in brooding silence or go almost immediately to bed. She was afraid to have this habit of reticence grow on him, and bravely she bid for his confidence. She climbed into his lap and inside his arms, one of her arms around his neck, and with the free hand she caressed his hair back from the forehead and smoothed out the moody brows.

"Now listen to me, Billy Boy," she began lightly. "You haven't been playing fair, and I won't have it. No!" She pressed his lips shut with her fingers. "I'm doing the talking now, and because you haven't been doing your share of the talking for some time. You remember we agreed at the start to always talk things over. I was the first to break this, when I sold my fancy work to Mrs. Higgins without speaking to you about it. And I was very sorry. I am still sorry. And I've never done it since. Now it's your turn. You're not talking things over with me. You are doing things you don't tell me about.

"Billy, you're dearer to me than anything else in the world. You know that. We're sharing each other's lives, only, just now, there's something you're not sharing. Every time your knuckles are sore, there's something you don't share. If you can't trust me, you can't trust anybody. And, besides, I love you so that no matter what you do I'll go on loving you just the same."

Billy gazed at her with fond incredulity.

"Don't be a pincher," she teased. "Remember, I stand for whatever you do."

"And you won't buck against me?" he queried.

"How can I? I'm not your boss, Billy. I wouldn't boss you for anything in the world. And if you'd let me boss you, I wouldn't love you half as much."

He digested this slowly, and finally nodded.

"An' you won't be mad?"

"With you? You've never seen me mad yet. Now come on and be generous and tell me how you hurt your knuckles. It's fresh to-day. Anybody can see that."

"All right. I'll tell you how it happened." He stopped and giggled with genuine boyish glee at some recollection. "It's like this. You won't be mad, now? We gotta do these sort of things to hold our own. Well, here's the show, a regular movin' picture except for file talkin'. Here's a big rube comin' along, hayseed stickin' out all over, hands like hams an' feet like Mississippi gunboats. He'd make half as much again as me in size an' he's young, too. Only he ain't lookin' for trouble, an' he's as innocent as... well, he's the innocentest scab that ever come down the pike an' bumped into a couple of pickets. Not a regular strike-breaker, you see, just a big rube that's read the bosses' ads an' come a-humpin' to town for the big wages.

"An' here's Bud Strothers an' me comin' along. We always go in pairs that way, an' sometimes bigger bunches. I flag the rube. 'Hello,' says I, 'lookin' for a job?' 'You bet,' says he. 'Can you drive?' 'Yep.' 'Four horses!' 'Show me to 'em,' says he. 'No josh, now,' says I; 'you're sure wantin' to drive?' 'That's what I come to town for,' he says. 'You're the man we're lookin' for,' says I. 'Come along, an' we'll have you busy in no time.'

"You see, Saxon, we can't pull it off there, because there's Tom Scanlon—you know, the red-headed cop only a couple of blocks away an' pipin' us off though not recognizin' us. So away we go, the three of us, Bud an' me leadin' that boob to take our jobs away from us I guess nit. We turn into the alley back of Campwell's grocery. Nobody in sight. Bud stops short, and the rube an' me stop.

"'I don't think he wants to drive,' Bud says, considerin'. An' the rube says quick, 'You betcher life I do.' 'You're dead sure you want that job?' I says. Yes, he's dead sure. Nothin's goin' to keep him away from that job. Why, that job's what he come to town for, an' we can't lead him to it too quick.

"'Well, my friend,' says I, 'it's my sad duty to inform you that you've made a mistake.' 'How's that?' he says. 'Go on,' I says; 'you're standin' on your foot.' And, honest to God, Saxon, that gink looks down at his feet to see. 'I don't understand,' says he. 'We're goin' to show you,' says I.

"An' then—Biff! Bang! Bingo! Swat! Zooie! Ker-slambango-blam! Fireworks, Fourth of July, Kingdom Come, blue lights, sky-rockets, an' hell fire—just like that. It don't take long when you're scientific an' trained to tandem work. Of course it's hard on the knuckles. But say, Saxon, if you'd seen that rube before an' after you'd thought he was a lightnin' change artist. Laugh? You'd a-busted."

Billy halted to give vent to his own mirth. Saxon forced herself to join with him, but down in her heart was horror. Mercedes was right. The stupid workers wrangled and snarled over jobs. The clever masters rode in automobiles and did not wrangle and snarl. They hired other stupid ones to do the wrangling and snarling for them. It was men like Bert and Frank Davis, like Chester Johnson and Otto Frank, like Jelly Belly and the Pinkertons, like Henderson and all the rest of the scabs, who were beaten up, shot, clubbed, or hanged. Ah, the clever ones were very clever. Nothing happened to them. They only rode in their automobiles.

"'You big stiffs,' the rube snivels as he crawls to his feet at the end," Billy was continuing. "'You think you still want that job?' I ask. He shakes his head. Then I read'm the riot act 'They's only one thing for you to do, old hoss, an' that's beat it. D'ye get me? Beat it. Back to the farm for YOU. An' if you come monkeyin' around town again, we'll be real mad at you. We was only foolin' this time. But next time we catch you your own mother won't know you when we get done with you.'

"An'—say!—you oughta seen'm beat it. I bet he's goin' yet. Ah' when he gets back to Milpitas, or Sleepy Hollow, or wherever he hangs out, an' tells how the boys does things in Oakland, it's dollars to doughnuts they won't be a rube in his district that'd come to town to drive if they offered ten dollars an hour."

"It was awful," Saxon said, then laughed well-simulated appreciation.

"But that was nothin'," Billy went on. "A bunch of the boys caught another one this morning. They didn't do a thing to him. My goodness gracious, no. In less'n two minutes he was the worst wreck they ever hauled to the receivin' hospital. The evenin' papers gave the score: nose broken, three bad scalp wounds, front teeth out, a broken collarbone, an' two broken ribs. Gee! He certainly got all that was comin' to him. But that's nothin'. D'ye want to know what the Frisco teamsters did in the big strike before the Earthquake? They took every scab they caught an' broke both his arms with a crowbar. That was so he couldn't drive, you see. Say, the hospitals was filled with 'em. An' the teamsters won that strike, too."

"But is it necessary, Billy, to be so terrible? I know they're scabs, and that they're taking the bread out of the strikers' children's mouths to put in their own children's mouths, and that it isn't fair and all that; but just the same is it necessary to be so... terrible?"

"Sure thing," Billy answered confidently. "We just gotta throw the fear of God into them—when we can do it without bein' caught."

"And if you're caught?"

"Then the union hires the lawyers to defend us, though that ain't much good now, for the judges are pretty hostyle, an' the papers keep hammerin' away at them to give stiffer an' stiffer sentences. Just the same, before this strike's over there'll be a whole lot of guys a-wishin' they'd never gone scabbin'."

Very cautiously, in the next half hour, Saxon tried to feel out her husband's attitude, to find if he doubted the rightness of the violence he and his brother teamsters committed. But Billy's ethical sanction was rock-bedded and profound. It never entered his head that he was not absolutely right. It was the game. Caught in its tangled meshes, he could see no other way to play it than the way all men played it. He did not stand for dynamite and murder, however. But then the unions did not stand for such. Quite naive was his explanation that dynamite and murder did not pay; that such actions always brought down the condemnation of the public and broke the strikes. But the healthy beating up of a scab, he contended—the "throwing of the fear of God into a scab," as he expressed it—was the only right and proper thing to do.

"Our folks never had to do such things," Saxon said finally. "They never had strikes nor scabs in those times."

"You bet they didn't," Billy agreed "Them was the good old days. I'd liked to a-lived then." He drew a long breath and sighed. "But them times will never come again."

"Would you have liked living in the country?" Saxon asked.

"Sure thing."

"There's lots of men living in the country now," she suggested.

"Just the same I notice them a-hikin' to town to get our jobs," was his reply.

CHAPTER XII

A gleam of light came, when Billy got a job driving a grading team for the contractors of the big bridge then building at Niles. Before he went he made certain that it was a union job. And a union job it was for two days, when the concrete workers threw down their tools. The contractors, evidently prepared for such happening, immediately filled the places of the concrete men with nonunion Italians. Whereupon the carpenters, structural ironworkers and teamsters walked out; and Billy, lacking train fare, spent the rest of the day in walking home.

"I couldn't work as a scab," he concluded his tale.

"No," Saxon said; "you couldn't work as a scab."

But she wondered why it was that when men wanted to work, and there was work to do, yet they were unable to work because their unions said no. Why were there unions? And, if unions had to be, why were not all workingmen in them? Then there would be no scabs, and Billy could work every day. Also, she wondered where she was to get a sack of flour, for she had long since ceased the extravagance of baker's bread. And so many other of the neighborhood women had done this, that the little Welsh baker had closed up shop and gone away, taking his wife and two little daughters with him. Look where she would, everybody was being hurt by the industrial strife.

One afternoon came a caller at her door, and that evening came Billy with dubious news. He had been approached that day. All he had to do, he told Saxon, was to say the word, and he could go into the stable as foreman at one hundred dollars a month.

The nearness of such a sum, the possibility of it, was almost stunning to Saxon, sitting at a supper which consisted of boiled potatoes, warmed-over beans, and a small dry onion which they were eating raw. There was neither bread, coffee, nor butter. The onion Billy had pulled from his pocket, having picked it up in the street. One hundred dollars a month! She moistened her lips and fought for control.

"What made them offer it to you?" she questioned.

"That's easy," was his answer. "They got a dozen reasons. The guy the boss has had exercisin' Prince and King is a dub. King has gone lame in the shoulders. Then they're guessin' pretty strong that I'm the party that's put a lot of their scabs outa commission. Macklin's ben their foreman for years an' years—why I was in knee pants when he was foreman. Well, he's sick an' all in. They gotta have somebody to take his place. Then, too, I've been with 'em a long time. An' on top of that, I'm the man for the job. They know I know horses from the ground up. Hell, it's all I'm good for, except sluggin'."

"Think of it, Billy!" she breathed. "A hundred dollars a month! A hundred dollars a month!"

"An' throw the fellows down," he said.

It was not a question. Nor was it a statement. It was anything Saxon chose to make of it. They looked at each other. She waited for him to speak; but he continued merely to look. It came to her that she was facing one of the decisive moments of her life, and she gripped herself to face it in all coolness. Nor would Billy proffer her the slightest help. Whatever his own judgment might be, he masked it with an expressionless face. His eyes betrayed nothing. He looked and waited.

"You... you can't do that, Billy," she said finally. "You can't throw the fellows down."

His hand shot out to hers, and his face was a sudden, radiant dawn.

"Put her there!" he cried, their hands meeting and clasping. "You're the truest true blue wife a man ever had. If all the other fellows' wives was like you, we could win any strike we tackled."

"What would you have done if you weren't married, Billy?"

"Seen 'em in hell first."

"Than it doesn't make any difference being married. I've got to stand by you in everything you stand for. I'd be a nice wife if I didn't."

She remembered her caller of the afternoon, and knew the moment was too propitious to let pass.

"There was a man here this afternoon, Billy. He wanted a room. I told him I'd speak to you. He said he would pay six dollars a month for the back bedroom. That would pay half a month's installment on the furniture and buy a sack of flour, and we're all out of flour."

Billy's old hostility to the idea was instantly uppermost, and Saxon watched him anxiously.

"Some scab in the shops, I suppose?"

"No; he's firing on the freight run to San Jose. Harmon, he said his name was, James Harmon. They've just transferred him from the Truckee division. He'll sleep days mostly, he said; and that's why he wanted a quiet house without children in it."

In the end, with much misgiving, and only after Saxon had insistently pointed out how little work it entailed on her, Billy consented, though he continued to protest, as an afterthought:

"But I don't want you makin' beds for any man. It ain't right, Saxon. I oughta take care of you."

"And you would," she flashed back at him, "if you'd take the foremanship. Only you can't. It wouldn't be right. And if I'm to stand by you it's only fair to let me do what I can."

James Harmon proved even less a bother than Saxon had anticipated. For a fireman he was scrupulously clean, always washing up in the roundhouse before he came home. He used the key to the kitchen door, coming and going by the back steps. To Saxon he barely said how-do-you-do or good day; and, sleeping in the day time and working at night, he was in the house a week before Billy laid eyes on him.

Billy had taken to coming home later and later, and to going out after supper by himself. He did not offer to tell Saxon where he went. Nor did she ask. For that matter it required little shrewdness on her part to guess. The fumes of whisky were on his lips at such times. His slow, deliberate ways were even slower, even more deliberate. Liquor did not affect his legs. He walked as soberly as any man. There was no hesitancy, no faltering, in his muscular movements. The whisky went to his brain, making his eyes heavy-lidded and the cloudiness of them more cloudy. Not that he was flighty, nor quick, nor irritable. On the contrary, the liquor imparted to his mental processes a deep gravity and brooding solemnity. He talked little, but that little was ominous and oracular. At such times there was no appeal from his judgment, no discussion. He knew, as God knew. And when he chose to speak a harsh thought, it was ten-fold harsher than ordinarily, because it seemed to proceed out of such profundity of cogitation, because it was as prodigiously deliberate in its incubation as it was in its enunciation.

It was not a nice side he was showing to Saxon. It was, almost, as if a stranger had come to live with her. Despite herself, she found herself beginning to shrink from him. And little could she comfort herself with the thought that it was not his real self, for she remembered his gentleness and considerateness, all his finenesses of the past. Then he had made a continual effort to avoid trouble and fighting. Now he enjoyed it, exulted in it, went looking for it. All this showed in his face. No longer was he the smiling, pleasant-faced boy. He smiled infrequently now. His face was a man's face. The lips, the eyes, the lines were harsh as his thoughts were harsh.

He was rarely unkind to Saxon; but, on the other hand he was rarely kind. His attitude toward her was growing negative. He was disinterested. Despite the fight for the union she was enduring with him, putting up with him shoulder to shoulder, she occupied but little space in his mind. When he acted toward her gently, she could see that it was merely mechanical, just as she was well aware that the endearing terms he used, the endearing caresses he gave, were only habitual. The spontaneity and warmth had gone out. Often, when he was not in liquor, flashes of the old Billy came back, but even such flashes dwindled in frequency. He was growing preoccupied, moody. Hard times and the bitter stresses of industrial conflict strained him. Especially was this apparent in his sleep, when he suffered paroxysms of lawless dreams, groaning and muttering, clenching his fists, grinding his teeth, twisting with muscular tensions, his face writhing with passions and violences, his throat guttering with terrible curses that rasped and aborted on his lips. And Saxon, lying beside him, afraid of this visitor to her bed whom she did not know, remembered what Mary had told her of Bert. He, too, had cursed and clenched his fists, in his nights fought out the battles of his days.

One thing, however, Saxon saw clearly. By no deliberate act of Billy's was he becoming this other and unlovely Billy. Were there no strike, no snarling and wrangling over jobs, there would be only the old Billy she had loved in all absoluteness. This sleeping terror in him would have lain asleep. It was something that was being awakened in him, an image incarnate of outward conditions, as cruel, as ugly, as maleficent as were those outward conditions. But if the strike continued, then, she feared, with reason, would this other and grisly self of Billy strengthen to fuller and more forbidding stature. And this, she knew, would mean the wreck of their love-life. Such a Billy she could not love; in its nature such a Billy was not lovable nor capable of love. And then, at the thought of offspring, she shuddered. It was too terrible. And at such moments of contemplation, from her soul the inevitable plaint of the human went up: WHY? WHY? WHY?

Billy, too, had his unanswerable queries.

"Why won't the building trades come out?" he demanded wrathfuly of the obscurity that veiled the ways of living and the world. "But no; O'Brien won't stand for a strike, and he has the Building Trades Council under his thumb. But why don't they chuck him and come out anyway? We'd win hands down all along the line. But no, O'Brien's got their goat, an' him up to his dirty neck in politics an' graft! An' damn the Federation of Labor! If all the railroad boys had come out, wouldn't the shop men have won instead of bein' licked to a frazzle? Lord, I ain't had a smoke of decent tobacco or a cup of decent coffee in a coon's age. I've forgotten what a square meal tastes like. I weighed myself yesterday. Fifteen pounds lighter than when the strike begun. If it keeps on much more I can fight middleweight. An' this is what I get after payin' dues into the union for years and years. I can't get a square meal, an' my wife has to make other men's beds. It makes my tired ache. Some day I'll get real huffy an' chuck that lodger out."

"But it's not his fault, Billy," Saxon protested.

"Who said it was?" Billy snapped roughly. "Can't I kick in general if I want to? Just the same it makes me sick. What's the good of organized labor if it don't stand together? For two cents I'd chuck the whole thing up an' go over to the employers. Only I wouldn't, God damn them! If they think they can beat us down to our knees, let 'em go ahead an' try it, that's all. But it gets me just the same. The whole world's clean dippy. They ain't no sense in anything. What's the good of supportin' a union that can't win a strike? What's the good of knockin' the blocks off of scabs when they keep a-comin' thick as ever? The whole thing's bughouse, an' I guess I am, too."

Such an outburst on Billy's part was so unusual that it was the only time Saxon knew it to occur. Always he was sullen, and dogged, and unwhipped; while whisky only served to set the maggots of certitude crawling in his brain.

One night Billy did not get home till after twelve. Saxon's anxiety was increased by the fact that police fighting and head breaking had been reported to have occurred. When Billy came, his appearance verified the report. His coatsleeves were half torn off. The Windsor tie had disappeared from under his soft turned-down collar, and every button had been ripped off the front of the shirt. When he took his hat off, Saxon was frightened by a lump on his head the size of an apple.

"D'ye know who did that? That Dutch slob Hermanmann, with a riot club. An' I'll get'm for it some day, good an' plenty. An' there's another fellow I got staked out that'll be my meat when this strike's over an' things is settled down. Blanchard's his name, Roy Blanchard."

"Not of Blanchard, Perkins and Company?" Saxon asked, busy washing Billy's hurt and making her usual fight to keep him calm.

"Yep; except he's the son of the old man. What's he do, that ain't done a tap of work in all his life except to blow the old man's money? He goes strike-breakin'. Grandstand play, that's what I call it. Gets his name in the papers an makes all the skirts he runs with fluster up an' say: 'My! Some bear, that Roy Blanchard, some bear.' Some bear—the gazabo! He'll be bear-meat for me some day. I never itched so hard to lick a man in my life.

"And—oh, I guess I'll pass that Dutch cop up. He got his already. Somebody broke his head with a lump of coal the size of a water bucket. That was when the wagons was turnin' into Franklin, just off Eighth, by the old Galindo Hotel. They was hard fightin' there, an' some guy in the hotel lams that coal down from the second story window.

"They was fightin' every block of the way—bricks, cobblestones, an' police-clubs to beat the band. They don't dast call out the troops. An' they was afraid to shoot. Why, we tore holes through the police force, an' the ambulances and patrol wagons worked over-time. But say, we got the procession blocked at Fourteenth and Broadway, right under the nose of the City Hall, rushed the rear end, cut out the horses of five wagons, an' handed them college guys a few love-pats in passin'. All that saved 'em from hospital was the police reserves. Just the same we had 'em jammed an hour there. You oughta seen the street cars blocked, too—Broadway, Fourteenth, San Pablo, as far as you could see."

"But what did Blanchard do?" Saxon called him back.

"He led the procession, an' he drove my team. All the teams was from my stable. He rounded up a lot of them college fellows—fraternity guys, they're called—yaps that live off their fathers' money. They come to the stable in big tourin' cars an' drove out the wagons with half the police of Oakland to help them. Say, it was sure some day. The sky rained cobblestones. An' you oughta heard the clubs on our heads—rat-tat-tat-tat, rat-tat-tat-tat! An' say, the chief of police, in a police auto, sittin' up like God Almighty—just before we got to Peralta street they was a block an' the police chargin', an' an old woman, right from her front gate, lammed the chief of police full in the face with a dead cat. Phew! You could hear it. 'Arrest that woman!' he yells, with his handkerchief out. But the boys beat the cops to her an' got her away. Some day? I guess yes. The receivin' hospital went outa commission on the jump, an' the overflow was spilled into St. Mary's Hospital, an' Fabiola, an' I don't know where else. Eight of our men was pulled, an' a dozen of the Frisco teamsters that's come over to help. They're holy terrors, them Frisco teamsters. It seemed half the workingmen of Oakland was helpin' us, an' they must be an army of them in jail. Our lawyers'll have to take their cases, too.

"But take it from me, it's the last we'll see of Roy Blanchard an' yaps of his kidney buttin' into our affairs. I guess we showed 'em some football. You know that brick buildin' they're puttin' up on Bay street? That's where we loaded up first, an', say, you couldn't see the wagon-seats for bricks when they started from the stables. Blanchard drove the first wagon, an' he was knocked clean off the seat once, but he stayed with it."

"He must have been brave," Saxon commented.

"Brave?" Billy flared. "With the police, an' the army an' navy behind him? I suppose you'll be takin' their part next. Brave? A-takin' the food outa the mouths of our women an children. Didn't Curley Jones's little kid die last night? Mother's milk not nourishin', that's what it was, because she didn't have the right stuff to eat. An' I know, an' you know, a dozen old aunts, an' sister-in-laws, an' such, that's had to hike to the poorhouse because their folks couldn't take care of 'em in these times."

In the morning paper Saxon read the exciting account of the futile attempt to break the teamsters' strike. Roy Blanchard was hailed a hero and held up as a model of wealthy citizenship. And to save herself she could not help glowing with appreciation of his courage. There was something fine in his going out to face the snarling pack. A brigadier general of the regular army was quoted as lamenting the fact that the troops had not been called out to take the mob by the throat and shake law and order into it. "This is the time for a little healthful bloodletting," was the conclusion of his remarks, after deploring the pacific methods of the police. "For not until the mob has been thoroughly beaten and cowed will tranquil industrial conditions obtain."

That evening Saxon and Billy went up town. Returning home and finding nothing to eat, he had taken her on one arm, his overcoat on the other. The overcoat he had pawned at Uncle Sam's, and he and Saxon had eaten drearily at a Japanese restaurant which in some miraculous way managed to set a semi-satisfying meal for ten cents. After eating, they started on their way to spend an additional five cents each on a moving picture show.

At the Central Bank Building, two striking teamsters accosted Billy and took him away with them. Saxon waited on the corner, and when he returned, three quarters of an hour later, she knew he had been drinking.

Half a block on, passing the Forum Cafe, he stopped suddenly. A limousine stood at the curb, and into it a young man was helping several wonderfully gowned women. A chauffeur sat in the driver's sent. Billy touched the young man on the arm. He was as broad-shouldered as Billy and slightly taller. Blue-eyed, strong-featured, in Saxon's opinion he was undeniably handsome.

"Just a word, sport," Billy said, in a low, slow voice.

The young man glanced quickly at Billy and Saxon, and asked impatiently:

"Well, what is it?"

"You're Blanchard," Billy began. "I seen you yesterday lead out that bunch of teams."

"Didn't I do it all right?" Blanchard asked gaily, with a flash of glance to Saxon and back again.

"Sure. But that ain't what I want to talk about."

"Who are you?" the other demanded with sudden suspicion.

"A striker. It just happens you drove my team, that's all. No; don't move for a gun." (As Blanchard half reached toward his hip pocket.) "I ain't startin' anythin' here. But I just want to tell you something."

"Be quick, then."

Blanchard lifted one foot to step into the machine.

"Sure," Billy went on without any diminution of his exasperating slowness. "What I want to tell you is that I'm after you. Not now, when the strike's on, but some time later I'm goin' to get you an' give you the beatin' of your life."

Blanchard looked Billy over with new interest and measuring eyes that sparkled with appreciation.

"You are a husky yourself," he said. "But do you think you can do it?"

"Sure. You're my meat."

"All right, then, my friend. Look me up after the strike is settled, and I'll give you a chance at me."

"Remember," Billy added, "I got you staked out."

Blanchard nodded, smiled genially to both of them, raised his hat to Saxon, and stepped into the machine.

CHAPTER XIII

From now on, to Saxon, life seemed bereft of its last reason and rhyme. It had become senseless, nightmarish. Anything irrational was possible. There was nothing stable in the anarchic flux of affairs that swept her on she knew not to what catastrophic end. Had Billy been dependable, all would still have been well. With him to cling to she would have faced everything fearlessly. But he had been whirled away from her in the prevailing madness. So radical was the change in him that he seemed almost an intruder in the house. Spiritually he was such an intruder. Another man looked out of his eyes—a man whose thoughts were of violence and hatred; a man to whom there was no good in anything, and who had become an ardent protagonist of the evil that was rampant and universal. This man no longer condemned Bert, himself muttering vaguely of dynamite, end sabotage, and revolution.

Saxon strove to maintain that sweetness and coolness of flesh and spirit that Billy had praised in the old days. Once, only, she lost control. He had been in a particularly ugly mood, and a final harshness and unfairness cut her to the quick.

"Who are you speaking to?" she flamed out at him.

He was speechless and abashed, and could only stare at her face, which was white with anger.

"Don't you ever speak to me like that again, Billy," she commanded.

"Aw, can't you put up with a piece of bad temper?" he muttered, half apologetically, yet half defiantly. "God knows I got enough to make me cranky."

After he left the house she flung herself on the bed and cried heart-brokenly. For she, who knew so thoroughly the humility of love, was a proud woman. Only the proud can be truly humble, as only the strong may know the fullness of gentleness. But what was the use, she demanded, of being proud and game, when the only person in the world who mattered to her lost his own pride and gameness and fairness and gave her the worse share of their mutual trouble?

And now, as she had faced alone the deeper, organic hurt of the loss of her baby, she faced alone another, and, in a way, an even greater personal trouble. Perhaps she loved Billy none the less, but her love was changing into something less proud, less confident, less trusting; it was becoming shot through with pity—with the pity that is parent to contempt. Her own loyalty was threatening to weaken, and she shuddered and shrank from the contempt she could see creeping in.

She struggled to steel herself to face the situation. Forgiveness stole into her heart, and she knew relief until the thought came that in the truest, highest love forgiveness should have no place. And again she cried, and continued her battle. After all, one thing was incontestable: THIS BILLY WES NOT THE BILLY SHE HAD LOVED. This Billy was another man, a sick man, and no more to be held responsible than a fever-patient in the ravings of delirium. She must be Billy's nurse, without pride, without contempt, with nothing to forgive. Besides, he was really bearing the brunt of the fight, was in the thick of it, dizzy with the striking of blows and the blows he received. If fault there was, it lay elsewhere, somewhere in the tangled scheme of things that made men snarl over jobs like dogs over bones.

So Saxon arose and buckled on her armor again for the hardest fight of all in the world's arena—the woman's fight. She ejected from her thought all doubting and distrust. She forgave nothing, for there was nothing requiring forgiveness. She pledged herself to an absoluteness of belief that her love and Billy's was unsullied, unperturbed—severe as it had always been, as it would be when it came back again after the world settled down once more to rational ways.

That night, when he came home, she proposed, as an emergency measure, that she should resume her needlework and help keep the pot boiling until the strike was over. But Billy would hear nothing of it.

"It's all right," he assured her repeatedly. "They ain't no call for you to work. I'm goin' to get some money before the week is out. An' I'll turn it over to you. An' Saturday night we'll go to the show—a real show, no movin' pictures. Harvey's nigger minstrels is comin' to town. We'll go Saturday night. I'll have the money before that, as sure as beans is beans."

Friday evening he did not come home to supper, which Saxon regretted, for Maggie Donahue had returned a pan of potatoes and two quarts of flour (borrowed the week before), and it was a hearty meal that awaited him. Saxon kept the stove going till nine o'clock, when, despite her reluctance, she went to bed. Her preference would have been to wait up, but she did not dare, knowing full well what the effect would be on him did he come home in liquor.

The clock had just struck one, when she heard the click of the gate. Slowly, heavily, ominously, she heard him come up the steps and fumble with his key at the door. He entered the bedroom, and she heard him sigh as he sat down. She remained quiet, for she had learned the hypersensitiveness induced by drink and was fastidiously careful not to hurt him even with the knowledge that she had lain awake for him. It was not easy. Her hands were clenched till the nails dented the palms, and her body was rigid in her passionate effort for control. Never had he come home as bad as this.

"Saxon," he called thickly. "Saxon."

She stired and yawned.

"What is it?" she asked.

"Won't you strike a light? My fingers is all thumbs."

Without looking at him, she complied; but so violent was the nervous trembling of her hands that the glass chimney tinkled against the globe and the match went out.

"I ain't drunk, Saxon," he said in the darkness, a hint of amusement in his thick voice. "I've only had two or three jolts ... of that sort."

On her second attempt with the lamp she succeeded. When she turned to look at him she screamed with fright. Though she had heard his voice and knew him to be Billy, for the instant she did not recognize him. His face was a face she had never known. Swollen, bruised, discolored, every feature had been beaten out of all semblance of familiarity. One eye was entirely closed, the other showed through a narrow slit of blood-congested flesh. One ear seemed to have lost most of its skin. The whole face was a swollen pulp. His right jaw, in particular, was twice the size of the left. No wonder his speech had been thick, was her thought, as she regarded the fearfully cut and swollen lips that still bled. She was sickened by the sight, and her heart went out to him in a great wave of tenderness. She wanted to put her arms around him, and cuddle and soothe him; but her practical judgment bade otherwise.

"You poor, poor boy," she cried. "Tell me what you want me to do first. I don't know about such things."

"If you could help me get my clothes off," he suggested meekly and thickly. "I got 'em on before I stiffened up."

"And then hot water—that will be good," she said, as she began gently drawing his coat sleeve over a puffed and helpless hand.

"I told you they was all thumbs," he grimaced, holding up his hand and squinting at it with the fraction of sight remaining to him.

"You sit and wait," she said, "till I start the fire and get the hot water going. I won't be a minute. Then I'll finish getting your clothes off."

From the kitchen she could hear him mumbling to himself, and when she returned he was repeating over and over:

"We needed the money, Saxon. We needed the money."

Drunken he was not, she could see that, and from his babbling she knew he was partly delirious.

"He was a surprise box," he wandered on, while she proceeded to undress him; and bit by bit she was able to piece together what had happened. "He was an unknown from Chicago. They sprang him on me. The secretary of the Acme Club warned me I'd have my hands full. An' I'd a-won if I'd been in condition. But fifteen pounds off without trainin' ain't condition. Then I'd been drinkin' pretty regular, an' I didn't have my wind."

But Saxon, stripping his undershirt, no longer heard him. As with his face, she could not recognize his splendidly muscled back. The white sheath of silken skin was torn and bloody. The lacerations occurred oftenest in horizontal lines, though there were perpendicular lines as well.

"How did you get all that?" she asked.

"The ropes. I was up against 'em more times than I like to remember. Gee! He certainly gave me mine. But I fooled 'm. He couldn't put me out. I lasted the twenty rounds, an' I wanta tell you he's got some marks to remember me by. If he ain't got a couple of knuckles broke in the left hand I'm a geezer.—Here, feel my head here. Swollen, eh? Sure thing. He hit that more times than he's wishin' he had right now. But, oh, what a lacin'! What a lacin'! I never had anything like it before. The Chicago Terror, they call 'm. I take my hat off to 'm. He's some bear. But I could a-made 'm take the count if I'd ben in condition an' had my wind.—Oh! Ouch! Watch out! It's like a boil!"

Fumbling at his waistband, Saxon's hand had come in contact with a brightly inflamed surface larger than a soup plate.

"That's from the kidney blows," Billy explained. "He was a regular devil at it. 'Most every clench, like clock work, down he'd chop one on me. It got so sore I was wincin'... until I got groggy an' didn't know much of anything. It ain't a knockout blow, you know, but it's awful wearin' in a long fight. It takes the starch out of you."

When his knees were bared, Saxon could see the skin across the knee-caps was broken and gone.

"The skin ain't made to stand a heavy fellow like me on the knees," he volunteered. "An' the rosin in the canvas cuts like Sam Hill."

The tears were in Saxon's eyes, and she could have cried over the manhandled body of her beautiful sick boy.

As she carried his pants across the room to hang them up, a jingle of money came from them. He called her back, and from the pocket drew forth a handful of silver.

"We needed the money, we needed the money," he kept muttering, as he vainly tried to count the coins; and Saxon knew that his mind was wandering again.

It cut her to the heart, for she could not but remember the harsh thoughts that had threatened her loyalty during the week past. After all, Billy, the splendid physical man, was only a boy, her boy. And he had faced and endured all this terrible punishment for her, for the house and the furniture that were their house and furniture. He said so, now, when he scarcely knew what he said. He said "WE needed the money." She was not so absent from his thoughts as she had fancied. Here, down to the naked tie-ribs of his soul, when he was half unconscious, the thought of her persisted, was uppermost. We needed the money. WE!

The tears were trickling down her checks as she bent over him, and it seemed she had never loved him so much as now.

"Here; you count," he said, abandoning the effort and handing the money to her. "... How much do you make it?"

"Nineteen dollars and thirty-five cents."

"That's right... the loser's end... twenty dollars. I had some drinks, an' treated a couple of the boys, an' then there was carfare. If I'd a-won, I'd a-got a hundred. That's what I fought for. It'd a-put us on Easy street for a while. You take it an' keep it. It's better 'n nothin'."

In bed, he could not sleep because of his pain, and hour by hour she worked over him, renewing the hot compresses over his bruises, soothing the lacerations with witch hazel and cold cream and the tenderest of finger tips. And all the while, with broken intervals of groaning, he babbled on, living over the fight, seeking relief in telling her his trouble, voicing regret at loss of the money, and crying out the hurt to his pride. Far worse than the sum of his physical hurts was his hurt pride.

"He couldn't put me out, anyway. He had full swing at me in the times when I was too much in to get my hands up. The crowd was crazy. I showed 'em some stamina. They was times when he only rocked me, for I'd evaporated plenty of his steam for him in the openin' rounds. I don't know how many times he dropped me. Things was gettin' too dreamy....

"Sometimes, toward the end, I could see three of him in the ring at once, an' I wouldn't know which to hit an' which to duck....

"But I fooled 'm. When I couldn't see, or feel, an' when my knees was shakin an my head goin' like a merry-go-round, I'd fall safe into clenches just the same. I bet the referee's arms is tired from draggin' us apart....

"But what a lacin'! What a lacin'! Say, Saxon... where are you? Oh, there, eh? I guess I was dreamin'. But, say, let this be a lesson to you. I broke my word an' went fightin', an' see what I got. Look at me, an' take warnin' so you won't make the same mistake an' go to makin' an' sellin' fancy work again....

"But I fooled 'em—everybody. At the beginnin' the bettin' was even. By the sixth round the wise gazabos was offerin' two to one against me. I was licked from the first drop outa the box—anybody could see that; but he couldn't put me down for the count. By the tenth round they was offerin' even that I wouldn't last the round. At the eleventh they was offerin' I wouldn't last the fifteenth. An' I lasted the whole twenty. But some punishment, I want to tell you, some punishment.

"Why, they was four rounds I was in dreamland all the time... only I kept on my feet an' fought, or took the count to eight an' got up, an' stalled an' covered an' whanged away. I don't know what I done, except I must a-done like that, because I wasn't there. I don't know a thing from the thirteenth, when he sent me to the mat on my head, till the eighteenth.

"Where was I? Oh, yes. I opened my eyes, or one eye, because I had only one that would open. An' there I was, in my corner, with the towels goin' an' ammonia in my nose an' Bill Murphy with a chunk of ice at the back of my neck. An' there, across the ring, I could see the Chicago Terror, an' I had to do some thinkin' to remember I was fightin' him. It was like I'd been away somewhere an' just got back. 'What round's this comin'?' I ask Bill. 'The eighteenth,' says he. 'The hell,' I says. 'What's come of all the other rounds? The last I was fightin' in was the thirteenth.' 'You're a wonder,' says Bill. 'You've ben out four rounds, only nobody knows it except me. I've ben tryin' to get you to quit all the time.' Just then the gong sounds, an' I can see the Terror startin' for me. 'Quit,' says Bill, makin' a move to throw in the towel. 'Not on your life,' I says. 'Drop it, Bill.' But he went on wantin' me to quit. By that time the Terror had come across to my corner an' was standin' with his hands down, lookin' at me. The referee was lookin', too, an' the house was that quiet, lookin', you could hear a pin drop. An' my head was gettin' some clearer, but not much.

"'You can't win,' Bill says.

"'Watch me,' says I. An' with that I make a rush for the Terror, catchin' him unexpected. I'm that groggy I can't stand, but I just keep a-goin', wallopin' the Terror clear across the ring to his corner, where he slips an' falls, an' I fall on top of 'm. Say, that crowd goes crazy.

"Where was I?—My head's still goin' round I guess. It's buzzin' like a swarm of bees."

"You'd just fallen on top of him in his corner," Saxon prompted.

"Oh, yes. Well, no sooner are we on our feet—an' I can't stand—I rush 'm the same way back across to my corner an' fall on 'm. That was luck. We got up, an' I'd a-fallen, only I clenched an' held myself up by him. 'I got your goat,' I says to him. 'An' now I'm goin' to eat you up.'

"I hadn't his goat, but I was playin' to get a piece of it, an' I got it, rushin' 'm as soon as the referee drags us apart an' fetchin' 'm a lucky wallop in the stomach that steadied 'm an' made him almighty careful. Too almighty careful. He was afraid to chance a mix with me. He thought I had more fight left in me than I had. So you see I got that much of his goat anyway.

"An' he couldn't get me. He didn't get me. An' in the twentieth we stood in the middle of the ring an' exchanged wallops even. Of course, I'd made a fine showin' for a licked man, but he got the decision, which was right. But I fooled 'm. He couldn't get me. An' I fooled the gazabos that was bettin' he would on short order."

At last, as dawn came on, Billy slept. He groaned and moaned, his face twisting with pain, his body vainly moving and tossing in quest of easement.

So this was prizefighting, Saxon thought. It was much worse than she had dreamed. She had had no idea that such damage could be wrought with padded gloves. He must never fight again. Street rioting was preferable. She was wondering how much of his silk had been lost, when he mumbled and opened his eyes.

"What is it?" she asked, ere it came to her that his eyes were unseeing and that he was in delirium.

"Saxon!... Saxon!" he called.

"Yes, Billy. What is it?"

His hand fumbled over the bed where ordinarily it would have encountered her.

Again he called her, and she cried her presence loudly in his ear. He sighed with relief and muttered brokenly:

"I had to do it.... We needed the money."

His eyes closed, and he slept more soundly, though his muttering continued. She had heard of congestion of the brain, and was frightened. Then she remembered his telling her of the ice Billy Murphy had held against his head.

Throwing a shawl over her head, she ran to the Pile Drivers' Home on Seventh street. The barkeeper had just opened, and was sweeping out. From the refrigerator he gave her all the ice she wished to carry, breaking it into convenient pieces for her. Back in the house, she applied the ice to the base of Billy's brain, placed hot irons to his feet, and bathed his head with witch hazel made cold by resting on the ice.

He slept in the darkened room until late afternoon, when, to Saxon's dismay, he insisted on getting up.

"Gotta make a showin'," he explained. "They ain't goin' to have the laugh on me."

In torment he was helped by her to dress, and in torment he went forth from the house so that his world should have ocular evidence that the beating he had received did not keep him in bed.

It was another kind of pride, different from a woman's, and Saxon wondered if it were the less admirable for that.

CHAPTER XIV

In the days that followed Billy's swellings went down and the bruises passed away with surprising rapidity. The quick healing of the lacerations attested the healthiness of his blood. Only remained the black eyes, unduly conspicuous on a face as blond as his. The discoloration was stubborn, persisting half a month, in which time happened divers events of importance.

Otto Frank's trial had been expeditious. Found guilty by a jury notable for the business and professional men on it, the death sentence was passed upon him and he was removed to San Quentin for execution.

The case of Chester Johnson and the fourteen others had taken longer, but within the same week, it, too, was finished. Chester Johnson was sentenced to be hanged. Two got life; three, twenty years. Only two were acquitted. The remaining seven received terms of from two to ten years.

The effect on Saxon was to throw her into deep depression. Billy was made gloomy, but his fighting spirit was not subdued.

"Always some men killed in battle," he said. "That's to be expected. But the way of sentencin' 'em gets me. All found guilty was responsible for the killin'; or none was responsible. If all was, then they should get the same sentence. They oughta hang like Chester Johnson, or else he oughtn't to hang. I'd just like to know how the judge makes up his mind. It must be like markin' China lottery tickets. He plays hunches. He looks at a guy an' waits for a spot or a number to come into his head. How else could he give Johnny Black four years an' Cal Hutchins twenty years? He played the hunches as they came into his head, an' it might just as easy ben the other way around an' Cal Hutchins got four years an' Johnny Black twenty.

"I know both them boys. They hung out with the Tenth an' Kirkham gang mostly, though sometimes they ran with my gang. We used to go swimmin' after school down to Sandy Beach on the marsh, an' in the Transit slip where they said the water was sixty feet deep, only it wasn't. An' once, on a Thursday, we dug a lot of clams together, an' played hookey Friday to peddle them. An' we used to go out on the Rock Wall an' catch pogies an' rock cod. One day—the day of the eclipse—Cal caught a perch half as big as a door. I never seen such a fish. An' now he's got to wear the stripes for twenty years. Lucky he wasn't married. If he don't get the consumption he'll be an old man when he comes out. Cal's mother wouldn't let 'm go swimmin', an' whenever she suspected she always licked his hair with her tongue. If it tasted salty, he got a beltin'.

But he was onto himself. Comin' home, he'd jump somebody's front fence an' hold his head under a faucet."

"I used to dance with Chester Johnson," Saxon said. "And I knew his wife, Kittie Brady, long and long ago. She had next place at the table to me in the paper-box factory. She's gone to San Francisco to her married sister's. She's going to have a baby, too. She was awfully pretty, and there was always a string of fellows after her."

The effect of the conviction and severe sentences was a bad one on the union men. Instead of being disheartening, it intensified the bitterness. Billy's repentance for having fought and the sweetness and affection which had flashed up in the days of Saxon's nursing of him were blotted out. At home, he scowled and brooded, while his talk took on the tone of Bert's in the last days ere that Mohegan died. Also, Billy stayed away from home longer hours, and was again steadily drinking.

Saxon well-nigh abandoned hope. Almost was she steeled to the inevitable tragedy which her morbid fancy painted in a thousand guises. Oftenest, it was of Billy being brought home on a stretcher. Sometimes it was a call to the telephone in the corner grocery and the curt information by a strange voice that her husband was lying in the receiving hospital or the morgue. And when the mysterious horse-poisoning cases occurred, and when the residence of one of the teaming magnates was half destroyed by dynamite, she saw Billy in prison, or wearing stripes, or mounting to the scaffold at San Quentin while at the same time she could see the little cottage on Pine street besieged by newspaper reporters and photographers.

Yet her lively imagination failed altogether to anticipate the real catastrophe. Harmon, the fireman lodger, passing through the kitchen on his way out to work, had paused to tell Saxon about the previous day's train-wreck in the Alviso marshes, and of how the engineer, imprisoned under the overturned engine and unhurt, being drowned by the rising tide, had begged to be shot. Billy came in at the end of the narrative, and from the somber light in his heavy-lidded eyes Saxon knew he had been drinking. He glowered at Harmon, and, without greeting to him or Saxon, leaned his shoulder against the wall.

Harmon felt the awkwardness of the situation, and did his best to appear oblivious.

"I was just telling your wife—" he began, but was savagely interrupted.

"I don't care what you was tellin' her. But I got something to tell you, Mister Man. My wife's made up your bed too many times to suit me."

"Billy!" Saxon cried, her face scarlet with resentment, and hurt, and shame.

Billy ignored her. Harmon was saying:

"I don't understand—"

"Well, I don't like your mug," Billy informed him. "You're standin' on your foot. Get off of it. Get out. Beat it. D'ye understand that?"

"I don't know what's got into him," Saxon gasped hurriedly to the fireman. "He's not himself. Oh, I am so ashamed, so ashamed."

Billy turned on her.

"You shut your mouth an' keep outa this."

"But, Billy," she remonstrated.

"An' get outa here. You go into the other room."

"Here, now," Harmon broke in. "This is a fine way to treat a fellow."

"I've given you too much rope as it is," was Billy's answer.

"I've paid my rent regularly, haven't I?"

"An' I oughta knock your block off for you. Don't see any reason I shouldn't, for that matter."

"If you do anything like that, Billy—" Saxon began.

"You here still? Well, if you won't go into the other room, I'll see that you do."

His hand clutched her arm. For one instant she resisted his strength; and in that instant, the flesh crushed under his fingers, she realized the fullness of his strength.

In the front room she could only lie back in the Morris chair sobbing, and listen to what occurred in the kitchen. "I'll stay to the end of the week," the fireman was saying. "I've paid in advance."

"Don't make no mistake," came Billy's voice, so slow that it was almost a drawl, yet quivering with rage. "You can't get out too quick if you wanta stay healthy—you an' your traps with you. I'm likely to start something any moment."

"Oh, I know you're a slugger—" the fireman's voice began.

Then came the unmistakable impact of a blow; the crash of glass; a scuffle on the back porch; and, finally, the heavy bumps of a body down the steps. She heard Billy reenter the kitchen, move about, and knew he was sweeping up the broken glass of the kitchen door. Then he washed himself at the sink, whistling while he dried his face and hands, and walked into the front room. She did not look at him. She was too sick and sad. He paused irresolutely, seeming to make up his mind.

"I'm goin' up town," he stated. "They's a meeting of the union. If I don't come back it'll be because that geezer's sworn out a warrant."

He opened the front door and paused. She knew he was looking at her. Then the door closed and she heard him go down the steps.

Saxon was stunned. She did not think. She did not know what to think. The whole thing was incomprehensible, incredible. She lay back in the chair, her eyes closed, her mind almost a blank, crushed by a leaden feeling that the end had come to everything.

The voices of children playing in the street aroused her. Night had fallen. She groped her way to a lamp and lighted it. In the kitchen she stared, lips trembling, at the pitiful, half prepared meal. The fire had gone out. The water had boiled away from the potatoes. When she lifted the lid, a burnt smell arose. Methodically she scraped and cleaned the pot, put things in order, and peeled and sliced the potatoes for next day's frying. And just as methodically she went to bed. Her lack of nervousness, her placidity, was abnormal, so abnormal that she closed her eyes and was almost immediately asleep. Nor did she awaken till the sunshine was streaming into the room.

It was the first night she and Billy had slept apart. She was amazed that she had not lain awake worrying about him. She lay with eyes wide open, scarcely thinking, until pain in her arm attracted her attention. It was where Billy had gripped her. On examination she found the bruised flesh fearfully black and blue. She was astonished, not by the spiritual fact that such bruise had been administered by the one she loved most in the world, but by the sheer physical fact that an instant's pressure had inflicted so much damage. The strength of a man was a terrible thing. Quite impersonally, she found herself wondering if Charley Long were as strong as Billy.

It was not until she dressed and built the fire that she began to think about more immediate things. Billy had not returned. Then he was arrested. What was she to do?—leave him in jail, go away, and start life afresh? Of course it was impossible to go on living with a man who had behaved as he had. But then, came another thought, WAS it impossible? After all, he was her husband. FOR BETTER OR WORSE—the phrase reiterated itself, a monotonous accompaniment to her thoughts, at the back of her consciousness. To leave him was to surrender. She carried the matter before the tribunal of her mother's memory. No; Daisy would never have surrendered. Daisy was a fighter. Then she, Saxon, must fight. Besides—and she acknowledged it—readily, though in a cold, dead way—besides, Billy was better than most husbands. Better than any other husband she had heard of, she concluded, as she remembered many of his earlier nicenesses and finenesses, and especially his eternal chant: NOTHING IS TOO GOOD FOR US. THE ROBERTSES AIN'T ON THE CHEAP.

At eleven o'clock she had a caller. It was Bud Strothers, Billy's mate on strike duty. Billy, he told her, had refused bail, refused a lawyer, had asked to be tried by the Court, had pleaded guilty, and had received a sentence of sixty dollars or thirty days. Also, he had refused to let the boys pay his fine.

"He's clean looney," Strothers summed up. "Won't listen to reason. Says he'll serve the time out. He's been tankin' up too regular, I guess. His wheels are buzzin'. Here, he give me this note for you. Any time you want anything send for me. The boys'll all stand by Bill's wife. You belong to us, you know. How are you off for money?"

Proudly she disclaimed any need for money, and not until her visitor departed did she read Billy's note:

Dear Saxon—Bud Strothers is going to give you this. Don't worry about me. I am going to take my medicine. I deserve it—you know that. I guess I am gone bughouse. Just the same, I am sorry for what I done. Don't come to see me. I don't want you to. If you need money, the union will give you some. The business agent is all right. I will be out in a month. Now, Saxon, you know I love you, and just say to yourself that you forgive me this time, and you won't never have to do it again.

Billy.

Bud Strothers was followed by Maggie Donahue, and Mrs. Olsen, who paid neighborly calls of cheer and were tactful in their offers of help and in studiously avoiding more reference than was necessary to Billy's predicament.

In the afternoon James Harmon arrived. He limped slightly, and Saxon divined that he was doing his best to minimize that evidence of hurt. She tried to apologize to him, but he would not listen.

"I don't blame you, Mrs. Roberts," he said. "I know it wasn't your doing. But your husband wasn't just himself, I guess. He was fightin' mad on general principles, and it was just my luck to get in the way, that was all."

"But just the same—"

The fireman shook his head.

"I know all about it. I used to punish the drink myself, and I done some funny things in them days. And I'm sorry I swore that warrant out and testified. But I was hot in the collar. I'm cooled down now, an' I'm sorry I done it."

"You're awfully good and kind," she said, and then began hesitantly on what was bothering her. "You... you can't stay now, with him... away, you know."

"Yes; that wouldn't do, would it? I'll tell you: I'll pack up right now, and skin out, and then, before six o'clock, I'll send a wagon for my things. Here's the key to the kitchen door."

Much as he demurred, she compelled him to receive back the unexpired portion of his rent. He shook her hand heartily at leaving, and tried to get her to promise to call upon him for a loan any time she might be in need.

"It's all right," he assured her. "I'm married, and got two boys. One of them's got his lungs touched, and she's with 'em down in Arizona campin' out. The railroad helped with passes."

And as he went down the steps she wondered that so kind a man should be in so madly cruel a world.

The Donahue boy threw in a spare evening paper, and Saxon found half a column devoted to Billy. It was not nice. The fact that he had stood up in the police court with his eyes blacked from some other fray was noted. He was described as a bully, a hoodlum, a rough-neck, a professional slugger whose presence in the ranks was a disgrace to organized labor. The assault he had pleaded guilty of was atrocious and unprovoked, and if he were a fair sample of a striking teamster, the only wise thing for Oakland to do was to break up the union and drive every member from the city. And, finally, the paper complained at the mildness of the sentence. It should have been six months at least. The judge was quoted as expressing regret that he had been unable to impose a six months' sentence, this inability being due to the condition of the jails, already crowded beyond capacity by the many eases of assault committed in the course of the various strikes.

That night, in bed, Saxon experienced her first loneliness. Her brain seemed in a whirl, and her sleep was broken by vain gropings for the form of Billy she imagined at her side. At last, she lighted the lamp and lay staring at the ceiling, wide-eyed, conning over and over the details of the disaster that had overwhelmed her. She could forgive, and she could not forgive. The blow to her love-life had been too savage, too brutal. Her pride was too lacerated to permit her wholly to return in memory to the other Billy whom she loved. Wine in, wit out, she repeated to herself; but the phrase could not absolve the man who had slept by her side, and to whom she had consecrated herself. She wept in the loneliness of the all-too-spacious bed, strove to forget Billy's incomprehensible cruelty, even pillowed her cheek with numb fondness against the bruise of her arm; but still resentment burned within her, a steady flame of protest against Billy and all that Billy had done. Her throat was parched, a dull ache never ceased in her breast, and she was oppressed by a feeling of goneness. WHY, WHY?—And from the puzzle of the world came no solution.

In the morning she received a visit from Sarah—the second in all the period of her marriage; and she could easily guess her sister-in-law's ghoulish errand. No exertion was required for the assertion of all of Saxon's pride. She refused to be in the slightest on the defensive. There was nothing to defend, nothing to explain. Everything was all right, and it was nobody's business anyway. This attitude but served to vex Sarah.

"I warned you, and you can't say I didn't," her diatribe ran. "I always knew he was no good, a jailbird, a hoodlum, a slugger. My heart sunk into my boots when I heard you was runnin' with a prizefighter. I told you so at the time. But no; you wouldn't listen, you with your highfalutin' notions an' more pairs of shoes than any decent woman should have. You knew better'n me. An' I said then, to Tom, I said, 'It's all up with Saxon now.' Them was my very words. Them that touches pitch is defiled. If you'd only a-married Charley Long! Then the family wouldn't a-ben disgraced. An' this is only the beginnin', mark me, only the beginnin'. Where it'll end, God knows.

He'll kill somebody yet, that plug-ugly of yourn, an' be hanged for it. You wait an' see, that's all, an' then you'll remember my words. As you make your bed, so you will lay in it"

"Best bed I ever had," Saxon commented.

"So you can say, so you can say," Sarah snorted.

"I wouldn't trade it for a queen's bed," Saxon added.

"A jailbird's bed," Sarah rejoined witheringly.

"Oh, it's the style," Saxon retorted airily. "Everybody's getting a taste of jail. Wasn't Tom arrested at some street meeting of the socialists? Everybody goes to jail these days."

The barb had struck home.

"But Tom was acquitted," Sarah hastened to proclaim.

"Just the same he lay in jail all night without bail."

This was unanswerable, and Sarah executed her favorite tactic of attack in flank.

"A nice come-down for you, I must say, that was raised straight an' right, a-cuttin' up didoes with a lodger."

"Who says so?" Saxon blazed with an indignation quickly mastered.

"Oh, a blind man can read between the lines. A lodger, a young married woman with no self respect, an' a prizefighter for a husband—what else would they fight about?"

"Just like any family quarrel, wasn't it?" Saxon smiled placidly.

Sarah was shocked into momentary speechlessness.

"And I want you to understand it," Saxon continued. "It makes a woman proud to have men fight over her. I am proud. Do you hear? I am proud. I want you to tell them so. I want you to tell all your neighbors. Tell everybody. I am no cow. Men like me. Men fight for me. Men go to jail for me. What is a woman in the world for, if it isn't to have men like her? Now, go, Sarah; go at once, and tell everybody what you've read between the lines. Tell them Billy is a jailbird and that I am a bad woman whom all men desire. Shout it out, and good luck to you. And get out of my house. And never put your feet in it again. You are too decent a woman to come here. You might lose your reputation. And think of your children. Now get out. Go."

Not until Sarah had taken an amazed and horrified departure did Saxon fling herself on the bed in a convulsion of tears. She had been ashamed, before, merely of Billy's inhospitality, and surliness, and unfairness. But she could see, now, the light in which others looked on the affair. It had not entered Saxon's head. She was confident that it had not entered Billy's. She knew his attitude from the first. Always he had opposed taking a lodger because of his proud faith that his wife should not work. Only hard times had compelled his consent, and, now that she looked back, almost had she inveigled him into consenting.

But all this did not alter the viewpoint the neighborhood must hold, that every one who had ever known her must hold. And for this, too, Billy was responsible. It was more terrible than all the other things he had been guilty of put together. She could never look any one in the face again. Maggie Donahue and Mrs. Olsen had been very kind, but of what must they have been thinking all the time they talked with her? And what must they have said to each other? What was everybody saying?—over front gates and back fences,—the men standing on the corners or talking in saloons?

Later, exhausted by her grief, when the tears no longer fell, she grew more impersonal, and dwelt on the disasters that had befallen so many women since the strike troubles began—Otto Frank's wife, Henderson's widow, pretty Kittie Brady, Mary, all the womenfolk of the other workmen who were now wearing the stripes in San Quentin. Her world was crashing about her ears. No one was exempt. Not only had she not escaped, but hers was the worst disgrace of all. Desperately she tried to hug the delusion that she was asleep, that it was all a nightmare, and that soon the alarm would go off and she would get up and cook Billy's breakfast so that he could go to work.

She did not leave the bed that day. Nor did she sleep. Her brain whirled on and on, now dwelling at insistent length upon her misfortunes, now pursuing the most fantastic ramifications of what she considered her disgrace, and, again, going back to her childhood and wandering through endless trivial detail. She worked at all the tasks she had ever done, performing, in fancy, the myriads of mechanical movements peculiar to each occupation—shaping and pasting in the paper box factory, ironing in the laundry, weaving in the jute mill, peeling fruit in the cannery and countless boxes of scalded tomatoes. She attended all her dances and all her picnics over again; went through her school days, recalling the face and name and seat of every schoolmate; endured the gray bleakness of the years in the orphan asylum; revisioned every memory of her mother, every tale; and relived all her life with Billy. But ever—and here the torment lay—she was drawn back from these far-wanderings to her present trouble, with its parch in the throat, its ache in the breast, and its gnawing, vacant goneness.

CHAPTER XV

All that night Saxon lay, unsleeping, without taking off her clothes, and when she arose in the morning and washed her face and dressed her hair she was aware of a strange numbness, of a feeling of constriction about her head as if it were bound by a heavy band of iron. It seemed like a dull pressure upon her brain. It was the beginning of an illness that she did not know as illness. All she knew was that she felt queer. It was not fever. It was not cold. Her bodily health was as it should be, and, when she thought about it, she put her condition down to nerves—nerves, according to her ideas and the ideas of her class, being unconnected with disease.

She had a strange feeling of loss of self, of being a stranger to herself, and the world in which she moved seemed a vague and shrouded world. It lacked sharpness of definition. Its customary vividness was gone. She had lapses of memory, and was continually finding herself doing unplanned things. Thus, to her astonishment, she came to in the back yard hanging up the week's wash. She had no recollection of having done it, yet it had been done precisely as it should have been done. She had boiled the sheets and pillow-slips and the table linen. Billy's woolens had been washed in warm water only, with the home-made soap, the recipe of which Mercedes had given her. On investigation, she found she had eaten a mutton chop for breakfast. This meant that she had been to the butcher shop, yet she had no memory of having gone. Curiously, she went into the bedroom. The bed was made up and everything in order.

At twilight she came upon herself in the front room, seated by the window, crying in an ecstasy of joy. At first she did not know what this joy was; then it came to her that it was because she had lost her baby. "A blessing, a blessing," she was chanting aloud, wringing her hands, but with joy, she knew it was with joy that she wrung her hands.

The days came and went. She had little notion of time. Sometimes, centuries agone, it seemed to her it was since Billy had gone to jail. At other times it was no more than the night before. But through it all two ideas persisted: she must not go to see Billy in jail; it was a blessing she had lost her baby.

Once, Bud Strothers came to see her. She sat in the front room and talked with him, noting with fascination that there were fringes to the heels of his trousers. Another day, the business agent of the union called. She told him, as she had told Bud Strothers, that everything was all right, that she needed nothing, that she could get along comfortably until Billy came out.

A fear began to haunt her. WHEN HE CAME OUT. No; it must not be. There must not be another baby. It might LIVE. No, no, a thousand times no. It must not be. She would run away first. She would never see Billy again. Anything but that. Anything but that.

This fear persisted. In her nightmare-ridden sleep it became an accomplished fact, so that she would awake, trembling, in a cold sweat, crying out. Her sleep had become wretched. Sometimes she was convinced that she did not sleep at all, and she knew that she had insomnia, and remembered that it was of insomnia her mother had died.

She came to herself one day, sitting in Doctor Hentley's office. He was looking at her in a puzzled way.

"Got plenty to eat?" he was asking.

She nodded.

"Any serious trouble?"

She shook her head.

"Everything's all right, doctor... except..."

"Yes, yes," he encouraged.

And then she knew why she had come. Simply, explicitly, she told him. He shook his head slowly.

"It can't be done, little woman," he said

"Oh, but it can!" she cried. "I know it can."

"I don't mean that," he answered. "I mean I can't tell you. I dare not. It is against the law. There is a doctor in Leavenworth prison right now for that."

In vain she pleaded with him. He instanced his own wife and children whose existence forbade his imperiling.

"Besides, there is no likelihood now," he told her.

"But there will be, there is sure to be," she urged.

But he could only shake his head sadly.

"Why do you want to know?" he questioned finally.

Saxon poured her heart out to him. She told of her first year of happiness with Billy, of the hard times caused by the labor troubles, of the change in Billy so that there was no love-life left, of her own deep horror. Not if it died, she concluded. She could go through that again. But if it should live. Billy would soon be out of jail, and then the danger would begin. It was only a few words. She would never tell any one. Wild horses could not drag it out of her.

But Doctor Hentley continued to shake his head. "I can't tell you, little woman. It's a shame, but I can't take the risk. My hands are tied. Our laws are all wrong. I have to consider those who are dear to me."

It was when she got up to go that he faltered. "Come here," he said. "Sit closer."

He prepared to whisper in her ear, then, with a sudden excess of caution, crossed the room swiftly, opened the door, and looked out. When he sat down again he drew his chair so close to hers that the arms touched, and when he whispered his beard tickled her ear.

"No, no," he shut her off when she tried to voice her gratitude. "I have told you nothing. You were here to consult me about your general health. You are run down, out of condition—"

CHAPTER XV

As he talked he moved her toward the door. When he opened it, a patient for the dentist in the adjoining office was standing in the hall. Doctor Hentley lifted his voice.

"What you need is that tonic I prescribed. Remember that. And don't pamper your appetite when it comes back. Eat strong, nourishing food, and beefsteak, plenty of beefsteak. And don't cook it to a cinder. Good day."

At times the silent cottage became unendurable, and Saxon would throw a shawl about her head and walk out the Oakland Mole, or cross the railroad yards and the marshes to Sandy Beach where Billy had said he used to swim. Also, by going out the Transit slip, by climbing down the piles on a precarious ladder of iron spikes, and by crossing a boom of logs, she won access to the Rock Wall that extended far out into the bay and that served as a barrier between the mudflats and the tide-scoured channel of Oakland Estuary. Here the fresh sea breezes blew and Oakland sank down to a smudge of smoke behind her, while across the bay she could see the smudge that represented San Francisco. Ocean steamships passed up and down the estuary, and lofty-masted ships, towed by red-stacked tugs.

She gazed at the sailors on the ships, wondered on what far voyages and to what far lands they went, wondered what freedoms were theirs. Or were they girt in by as remorseless and cruel a world as the dwellers in Oakland were? Were they as unfair, as unjust, as brutal, in their dealings with their fellows as were the city dwellers? It did not seem so, and sometimes she wished herself on board, out-bound, going anywhere, she cared not where, so long as it was away from the world to which she had given her best and which had trampled her in return.

She did not know always when she left the house, nor where her feet took her. Once, she came to herself in a strange part of Oakland. The street was wide and lined with rows of shade trees. Velvet lawns, broken only by cement sidewalks, ran down to the gutters. The houses stood apart and were large. In her vocabulary they were mansions. What had shocked her to consciousness of herself was a young man in the driver's seat of a touring car standing at the curb. He was looking at her curiously and she recognized him as Roy Blanchard, whom, in front of the Forum, Billy had threatened to whip. Beside the car, bareheaded, stood another young man. He, too, she remembered. He it was, at the Sunday picnic where she first met Billy, who had thrust his cane between the legs of the flying foot-racer and precipitated the free-for-all fight. Like Blanchard, he was looking at her curiously, and she became aware that she had been talking to herself. The babble of her lips still beat in her ears. She blushed, a rising tide of shame heating her face, and quickened her pace. Blanchard sprang out of the car and came to her with lifted hat. "Is anything the matter?" he asked.

She shook her head, and, though she had stopped, she evinced her desire to go on.

"I know you," he said, studying her face. "You were with the striker who promised me a licking."

"He is my husband," she said.

"Oh! Good for him." He regarded her pleasantly and frankly. "But about yourself? Isn't there anything I can do for you? Something IS the matter."

"No, I'm all right," she answered. "I have been sick," she lied; for she never dreamed of connecting her queerness with sickness.

"You look tired," he pressed her. "I can take you in the machine and run you anywhere you want. It won't be any trouble. I've plenty of time."

Saxon shook her head.

"If... if you would tell me where I can catch the Eighth street cars. I don't often come to this part of town."

He told her where to find an electric car and what transfers to make, and she was surprised at the distance she had wandered.

"Thank you," she said. "And good bye."

"Sure I can't do anything now?"

"Sure."

"Well, good bye," he smiled good humoredly. "And tell that husband of yours to keep in good condition. I'm likely to make him need it all when he tangles up with me."

"Oh, but you can't fight with him," she warned. "You mustn't. You haven't got a show."

"Good for you," he admired. "That's the way for a woman to stand up for her man. Now the average woman would be so afraid he was going to get licked—"

"But I'm not afraid... for him. It's for you. He's a terrible fighter. You wouldn't have any chance. It would be like... like..."

"Like taking candy from a baby?" Blanchard finished for her.

"Yes," she nodded. "That's just what he would call it. And whenever he tells you you are standing on your foot watch out for him. Now I must go. Good bye, and thank you again."

She went on down the sidewalk, his cheery good bye ringing in her ears. He was kind—she admitted it honestly; yet he was one of the clever ones, one of the masters, who, according to Billy, were responsible for all the cruelty to labor, for the hardships of the women, for the punishment of the labor men who were wearing stripes in San Quentin or were in the death cells awaiting the scaffold. Yet he was kind, sweet natured, clean, good. She could read his character in his face. But how could this be, if he were responsible for so much evil? She shook her head wearily. There was no explanation, no understanding of this world which destroyed little babes and bruised women's breasts.

As for her having strayed into that neighborhood of fine residences, she was unsurprised. It was in line with her queerness. She did so many things without knowing that she did them. But she must be careful. It was better to wander on the marshes and the Rock Wall.

Especially she liked the Rock Wall. There was a freedom about it, a wide spaciousness that she found herself instinctively trying to breathe, holding her arms out to embrace and make part of herself. It was a more natural world, a more rational world. She could understand it—understand the green crabs with white-bleached claws that scuttled before her and which she could see pasturing on green-weeded rocks when the tide was low. Here, hopelessly man-made as the great wall was, nothing seemed artificial. There were no men here, no laws nor conflicts of men. The tide flowed and ebbed; the sun rose and set; regularly each afternoon the brave west wind came romping in through the Golden Gate, darkening the water, cresting tiny wavelets, making the sailboats fly. Everything ran with frictionless order. Everything was free. Firewood lay about for the taking. No man sold it by the sack. Small boys fished with poles from the rocks, with no one to drive them away for trespass, catching fish as Billy had caught fish, as Cal Hutchins had caught fish. Billy had told her of the great perch Cal Hutchins caught on the day of the eclipse, when he had little dreamed the heart of his manhood would be spent in convict's garb.

And here was food, food that was free. She watched the small boys on a day when she had eaten nothing, and emulated them, gathering mussels from the rocks at low water, cooking them by placing them among the coals of a fire she built on top of the wall. They tasted particularly good. She learned to knock the small oysters from the rocks, and once she found a string of fresh-caught fish some small boy had forgotten to take home with him.

Here drifted evidences of man's sinister handiwork—from a distance, from the cities. One flood tide she found the water covered with muskmelons. They bobbed and bumped along up the estuary in countless thousands. Where they stranded against the rocks she was able to get them. But each and every melon—and she patiently tried scores of them—had been spoiled by a sharp gash that let in the salt water. She could not understand. She asked an old Portuguese woman gathering driftwood.

"They do it, the people who have too much," the old woman explained, straightening her labor-stiffened back with such an effort that almost Saxon could hear it creak. The old woman's black eyes flashed angrily, and her wrinkled lips, drawn tightly across toothless gums, wry with bitterness. "The people that have too much. It is to keep up the price. They throw them overboard in San Francisco."

"But why don't they give them away to the poor people?" Saxon asked.

"They must keep up the price."

"But the poor people cannot buy them anyway," Saxon objected. "It would not hurt the price."

The old woman shrugged her shoulders.

"I do not know. It is their way. They chop each melon so that the poor people cannot fish them out and eat anyway. They do the same with the oranges, with the apples. Ah, the fishermen! There is a trust. When the boats catch too much fish, the trust throws them overboard from Fisherman Wharf, boat-loads, and boat-loads, and boat-loads of the beautiful fish. And the beautiful good fish sink and are gone. And no one gets them. Yet they are dead and only good to eat. Fish are very good to eat."

And Saxon could not understand a world that did such things—a world in which some men possessed so much food that they threw it away, paying men for their labor of spoiling it before they threw it away; and in the same world so many people who did not have enough food, whose babies died because their mothers' milk was not nourishing, whose young men fought and killed one another for the chance to work, whose old men and women went to the poorhouse because there was no food for them in the little shacks they wept at leaving. She wondered if all the world were that way, and remembered Mercedes' tales. Yes; all the world was that way. Had not Mercedes seen ten thousand families starve to death in that far away India, when, as she had said, her own jewels that she wore would have fed and saved them all? It was the poorhouse and the salt vats for the stupid, jewels and automobiles for the clever ones.

She was one of the stupid. She must be. The evidence all pointed that way. Yet Saxon refused to accept it. She was not stupid. Her mother had not been stupid, nor had the pioneer stock before her. Still it must be so. Here she sat, nothing to eat at home, her love-husband changed to a brute beast and lying in jail, her arms and heart empty of the babe that would have been there if only the stupid ones had not made a shambles of her front yard in their wrangling over jobs.

She sat there, racking her brain, the smudge of Oakland at her back, staring across the bay at the smudge of Ban Francisco. Yet the sun was good; the wind was good, as was the keen salt air in her nostrils; the blue sky, flecked with clouds, was good. All the natural world was right, and sensible, and beneficent. It was the man-world that was wrong, and mad, and horrible. Why were the stupid stupid? Was it a law of God? No; it could not be. God had made the wind, and air, and sun. The man-world was made by man, and a rotten job it was. Yet, and she remembered it well, the teaching in the orphan asylum, God had made everything. Her mother, too, had believed this, had believed in this God. Things could not be different. It was ordained.

For a time Saxon sat crushed, helpless. Then smoldered protest, revolt. Vainly she asked why God had it in for her. What had she done to deserve such fate? She briefly reviewed her life in quest of deadly sins committed, and found them not. She had obeyed her mother; obeyed Cady, the saloon-keeper, and Cady's wife; obeyed the matron and the other women in the orphan asylum; obeyed Tom when she came to live in his house, and never run in the streets because he didn't wish her to. At school she had always been honorably promoted, and never had her deportment report varied from one hundred per cent. She had worked from the day she left school to the day of her marriage. She had been a good worker, too. The little Jew who ran the paper box factory had almost wept when she quit. It was the same at the cannery. She was among the high-line weavers when the jute mills closed down. I And she had kept straight. It was not as if she had been ugly or unattractive. She had known her temptations and encountered her dangers. The fellows had been crazy about her. They had run after her, fought over her, in a way to turn most girls' heads. But she had kept straight. And then had come Billy, her reward. She had devoted herself to him, to his house, to all that would nourish his love; and now she and Billy were sinking down into this senseless vortex of misery and heartbreak of the man-made world.

No, God was not responsible. She could have made a better world herself—a finer, squarer world. This being so, then there was no God. God could not make a botch. The matron had been wrong, her mother had been wrong. Then there was no immortality, and Bert, wild and crazy Bert, falling at her front gate with his foolish death-cry, was right. One was a long time dead.

Looking thus at life, shorn of its superrational sanctions, Saxon floundered into the morass of pessimism. There was no justification for right conduct in the universe, no square deal for her who had earned reward, for the millions who worked like animals, died like animals, and were a long time and forever dead. Like the hosts of more learned thinkers before her, she concluded that the universe was unmoral and without concern for men.

And now she sat crushed in greater helplessness than when she had included God in the scheme of injustice. As long as God was, there was always chance for a miracle, for some supernatural intervention, some rewarding with ineffable bliss. With God missing, the world was a trap. Life was a trap. She was like a linnet, caught by small boys and imprisoned in a cage. That was because the linnet was stupid. But she rebelled. She fluttered and beat her soul against the hard face of things as did the linnet against the bars of wire. She was not stupid. She did not belong in the trap. She would fight her way out of the trap. There must be such a way out. When canal boys and rail-splitters, the lowliest of the stupid lowly, as she had read in her school history, could find their way out and become presidents of the nation and rule over even the clever ones in their automobiles, then could she find her way out and win to the tiny reward she craved—Billy, a little love, a little happiness. She would not mind that the universe was unmoral, that there was no God, no immortality. She was willing to go into the black grave and remain in its blackness forever, to go into the salt vats and let the young men cut her dead flesh to sausage-meat, if—if only she could get her small meed of happiness first.

How she would work for that happiness! How she would appreciate it, make the most of each least particle of it! But how was she to do it. Where was the path? She could not vision it. Her eyes showed her only the smudge of San Francisco, the smudge of Oakland, where men were breaking heads and killing one another, where babies were dying, born and unborn, and where women were weeping with bruised breasts.

CHAPTER XVI

Her vague, unreal existence continued. It seemed in some previous life-time that Billy had gone away, that another life-time would have to come before he returned. She still suffered from insomnia. Long nights passed in succession, during which she never closed her eyes. At other times she slept through long stupors, waking stunned and numbed, scarcely able to open her heavy eyes, to move her weary limbs. The pressure of the iron band on her head never relaxed. She was poorly nourished. Nor had she a cent of money. She often went a whole day without eating. Once, seventy-two hours elapsed without food passing her lips. She dug clams in the marsh, knocked the tiny oysters from the rocks, and gathered mussels.

And yet, when Bud Strothers came to see how she was getting along, she convinced him that all was well. One evening after work, Tom came, and forced two dollars upon her. He was terribly worried. He would like to help more, but Sarah was expecting another baby. There had been slack times in his trade because of the strikes in the other trades. He did not know what the country was coming to. And it was all so simple. All they had to do was see things in his way and vote the way he voted. Then everybody would get a square deal. Christ was a Socialist, he told her.

"Christ died two thousand years ago," Saxon said.

"Well?" Tom queried, not catching her implication.

"Think," she said, "think of all the men and women who died in those two thousand years, and socialism has not come yet. And in two thousand years more it may be as far away as ever. Tom, your socialism never did you any good. It is a dream."

"It wouldn't be if—" he began with a flash of resentment.

"If they believed as you do. Only they don't. You don't succeed in making them."

"But we are increasing every year," he argued.

"Two thousand years is an awfully long time," she said quietly.

Her brother's tired face saddened as he noted. Then he sighed:

"Well, Saxon, if it's a dream, it is a good dream."

"I don't want to dream," was her reply. "I want things real. I want them now."

And before her fancy passed the countless generations of the stupid lowly, the Billys and Saxons, the Berts and Marys, the Toms and Sarahs. And to what end? The salt vats and the grave. Mercedes was a hard and wicked woman, but Mercedes was right. The stupid must always be under the heels of the clever ones. Only she, Saxon, daughter of Daisy who had written wonderful poems and of a soldier-father on a roan war-horse, daughter of the strong generations who hall won half a world from wild nature and the savage Indian—no, she was not stupid. It was as if she suffered false imprisonment. There was some mistake. She would find the way out.

With the two dollars she bought a sack of flour and half a sack of potatoes. This relieved the monotony of her clams and mussels. Like the Italian and Portuguese women, she gathered driftwood and carried it home, though always she did it with shamed pride, timing her arrival so that it would be after dark. One day, on the mud-flat side of the Rock Wall, an Italian fishing boat hauled up on the sand dredged from the channel. From the top of the wall Saxon watched the men grouped about the charcoal brazier, eating crusty Italian bread and a stew of meat and vegetables, washed down with long draughts of thin red wine. She envied them their freedom that advertised itself in the heartiness of their meal, in the tones of their chatter and laughter, in the very boat itself that was not tied always to one place and that carried them wherever they willed. Afterward, they dragged a seine across the mud-flats and up on the sand, selecting for themselves only the larger kinds of fish. Many thousands of small fish, like sardines, they left dying on the sand when they sailed away. Saxon got a sackful of the fish, and was compelled to make two trips in order to carry them home, where she salted them down in a wooden washtubs.

Her lapses of consciousness continued. The strangest thing she did while in such condition was on Sandy Beach. There she discovered herself, one windy afternoon, lying in a hole she had dug, with sacks for blankets. She had even roofed the hole in rough fashion by means of drift wood and marsh grass. On top of the grass she had piled sand.

Another time she came to herself walking across the marshes, a bundle of driftwood, tied with bale-rope, on her shoulder. Charley Long was walking beside her. She could see his face in the starlight. She wondered dully how long he had been talking, what he had said. Then she was curious to hear what he was saying. She was not afraid, despite his strength, his wicked nature, and the loneliness and darkness of the marsh.

"It's a shame for a girl like you to have to do this," he was saying, apparently in repetition of what he had already urged. "Come on an' say the word, Saxon. Come on an' say the word."

Saxon stopped and quietly faced him.

"Listen, Charley Long. Billy's only doing thirty days, and his time is almost up. When he gets out your life won't be worth a pinch of salt if I tell him you've been bothering me. Now listen. If you go right now away from here, and stay away, I won't tell him. That's all I've got to say."

The big blacksmith stood in scowling indecisions his face pathetic in its fierce yearning, his hands making unconscious, clutching contractions.

"Why, you little, small thing," he said desperately, "I could break you in one hand. I could—why, I could do anything I wanted. I don't want to hurt you, Saxon. You know that. Just say the word—"

"I've said the only word I'm going to say."

"God!" he muttered in involuntary admiration. "You ain't afraid. You ain't afraid."

They faced each other for long silent minutes.

"Why ain't you afraid?" he demanded at last, after peering into the surrounding darkness as if searching for her hidden allies.

"Because I married a man," Saxon said briefly. "And now you'd better go."

When he had gone she shifted the load of wood to her other shoulder and started on, in her breast a quiet thrill of pride in Billy. Though behind prison bars, still she leaned against his strength. The mere naming of him was sufficient to drive away a brute like Charley Long.

On the day that Otto Frank was hanged she remained indoors. The evening papers published the account. There had been no reprieve. In Sacramento was a railroad Governor who might reprieve or even pardon bank-wreckers and grafters, but who dared not lift his finger for a workingman. All this was the talk of the neighborhood. It had been Billy's talk. It had been Bert's talk.

The next day Saxon started out the Rock Wall, and the specter of Otto Frank walked by her side. And with him was a dimmer, mistier specter that she recognized as Billy. Was he, too, destined to tread his way to Otto Frank's dark end? Surely so, if the blood and strike continued. He was a fighter. He felt he was right in fighting. It was easy to kill a man. Even if he did not intend it, some time, when he was slugging a scab, the scab would fracture his skull on a stone curbing or a cement sidewalk. And then Billy would hang. That was why Otto Frank hanged. He had not intended to kill Henderson. It was only by accident that Henderson's skull was fractured. Yet Otto Frank had been hanged for it just the same.

She wrung her hands and wept loudly as she stumbled among the windy rocks. The hours passed, and she was lost to herself and her grief. When she came to she found herself on the far end of the wall where it jutted into the bay between the Oakland and Alameda Moles. But she could see no wall. It was the time of the full moon, and the unusual high tide covered the rocks. She was knee deep in the water, and about her knees swam scores of big rock rats, squeaking and fighting, scrambling to climb upon her out of the flood. She screamed with fright and horror, and kicked at them. Some dived and swam away under water; others circled about her warily at a distance; and one big fellow laid his teeth into her shoe. Him she stepped on and crushed with her free foot. By this time, though still trembling, she was able coolly to consider the situation. She waded to a stout stick of driftwood a few feet away, and with this quickly cleared a space about herself.

A grinning small boy, in a small, bright-painted and half-decked skiff, sailed close in to the wall and let go his sheet to spill the wind. "Want to get aboard?" he called.

"Yes," she answered. "There are thousands of big rats here. I'm afraid of them."

He nodded, ran close in, spilled the wind from his sail, the boat's way carrying it gently to her.

"Shove out its bow," he commanded. "That's right. I don't want to break my centerboard.... An' then jump aboard in the stern—quick!—alongside of me."

She obeyed, stepping in lightly beside him. He held the tiller up with his elbow, pulled in on the sheet, and as the sail filled the boat sprang away over the rippling water.

"You know boats," the boy said approvingly.

He was a slender, almost frail lad, of twelve or thirteen years, though healthy enough, with sunburned freckled face and large gray eyes that were clear and wistful.

Despite his possession of the pretty boat, Saxon was quick to sense that he was one of them, a child of the people.

"First boat I was ever in, except ferryboats," Saxon laughed.

CHAPTER XVI

He looked at her keenly. "Well, you take to it like a duck to water is all I can say about it. Where d'ye want me to land you?"

"Anywhere."

He opened his mouth to speak, gave her another long look, considered for a space, then asked suddenly: "Got plenty of time?"

She nodded.

"All day?"

Again she nodded.

"Say—I'll tell you, I'm goin' out on this ebb to Goat Island for rockcod, an' I'll come in on the flood this evening. I got plenty of lines an' bait. Want to come along? We can both fish. And what you catch you can have."

Saxon hesitated. The freedom and motion of the small boat appealed to her. Like the ships she had envied, it was outbound.

"Maybe you'll drown me," she parleyed.

The boy threw back his head with pride.

"I guess I've been sailin' many a long day by myself, an' I ain't drowned yet."

"All right," she consented. "Though remember, I don't know anything about boats."

"Aw, that's all right.—Now I'm goin' to go about. When I say 'Hard a-lee!' like that, you duck your head so the boom don't hit you, an' shift over to the other side."

He executed the maneuver, Saxon obeyed, and found herself sitting beside him on the opposite side of the boat, while the boat itself, on the other tack, was heading toward Long Wharf where the coal bunkers were. She was aglow with admiration, the more so because the mechanics of boat-sailing was to her a complex and mysterious thing.

"Where did you learn it all?" she inquired.

"Taught myself, just naturally taught myself. I liked it, you see, an' what a fellow likes he's likeliest to do. This is my second boat. My first didn't have a centerboard. I bought it for two dollars an' learned a lot, though it never stopped leaking. What d 'ye think I paid for this one? It's worth twenty-five dollars right now. What d 'ye think I paid for it?"

"I give up," Saxon said. "How much?"

"Six dollars. Think of it! A boat like this! Of course I done a lot of work, an' the sail cost two dollars, the oars one forty, an' the paint one seventy-five. But just the same eleven dollars and fifteen cents is a real bargain. It took me a long time saving for it, though. I carry papers morning and evening—there's a boy taking my route for me this afternoon—I give 'm ten cents, an' all the extras he sells is his; and I'd a-got the boat sooner only I had to pay for my shorthand lessons. My mother wants me to become a court reporter. They get sometimes as much as twenty dollars a day. Gee! But I don't want it. It's a shame to waste the money on the lessons."

"What do you want?" she asked, partly from idleness, and yet with genuine curiosity; for she felt drawn to this boy in knee pants who was so confident and at the same time so wistful.

"What do I want?" he repeated after her.

Turning his head slowly, he followed the sky-line, pausing especially when his eyes rested landward on the brown Contra Costa hills, and seaward, past Alcatraz, on the Golden Glate. The wistfulness in his eyes was overwhelming and went to her heart.

"That," he said, sweeping the circle of the world with a wave of his arm.

"That?" she queried.

He looked at her, perplexed in that he had not made his meaning clear.

"Don't you ever feel that way?" he asked, bidding for sympathy with his dream. "Don't you sometimes feel you'd die if you didn't know what's beyond them hills an' what's beyond the other hills behind them hills? An' the Golden Gate! There's the Pacific Ocean beyond, and China, an' Japan, an' India, an'... an' all the coral islands. You can go anywhere out through the Golden Gate—to Australia, to Africa, to the seal islands, to the North Pole, to Cape Horn. Why, all them places are just waitin' for me to come an' see 'em. I've lived in Oakland all my life, but I'm not going to live in Oakland the rest of my life, not by a long shot. I'm goin' to get away... away...."

Again, as words failed to express the vastness of his desire, the wave of his arm swept the circle of the world.

Saxon thrilled with him. She too, save for her earlier childhood, had lived in Oakland all her life. And it had been a good place in which to live... until now. And now, in all its nightmare horror, it was a place to get away from, as with her people the East had been a place to get away from. And why not? The world tugged at her, and she felt in touch with the lad's desire. Now that she thought of it, her race had never been given to staying long in one place. Always it had been on the move. She remembered back to her mother's tales, and to the wood engraving in her scrapbook where her half-clad forebears, sword in hand, leaped from their lean beaked boats to do battle on the blood-drenched sands of England.

"Did you ever hear about the Anglo-Saxons?" she asked the boy.

"You bet!" His eyes glistened, and he looked at her with new interest. "I'm an Anglo-Saxon, every inch of me. Look at the color of my eyes, my skin. I'm awful white where I ain't sunburned. An' my hair was yellow when I was a baby. My mother says it'll be dark brown by the time I'm grown up, worse luck. Just the same, I'm Anglo-Saxon. I am of a fighting race. We ain't afraid of nothin'. This bay—think I'm afraid of it!" He looked out over the water with flashing eye of scorn. "Why, I've crossed it when it was howlin' an' when the scow schooner sailors said I lied an' that I didn't. Huh! They were only squareheads. Why, we licked their kind thousands of years ago. We lick everything we go up against. We've wandered all over the world, licking the world. On the sea, on the land, it's all the same. Look at Ivory Nelson, look at Davy Crockett, look at Paul Jones, look at Clive, an' Kitchener, an' Fremont, an' Kit Carson, an' all of 'em."

Saxon nodded, while he continued, her own eyes shining, and it came to her what a glory it would be to be the mother of a man-child like this. Her body ached with the fancied quickening of unborn life. A good stock, a good stock, she thought to herself. Then she thought of herself and Billy, healthy shoots of that same stock, yet condemned to childlessness because of the trap of the manmade world and the curse of being herded with the stupid ones.

She came back to the boy.

"My father was a soldier in the Civil War," he was telling her, "a scout an' a spy. The rebels were going to hang him twice for a spy. At the battle of Wilson's Creek he ran half a mile with his captain wounded on his back. He's got a bullet in his leg right now, just above the knee. It's been there all these years. He let me feel it once. He was a buffalo hunter and a trapper before the war. He was sheriff of his county when he was twenty years old. An' after the war, when he was marshal of Silver City, he cleaned out the bad men an' gun-fighters. He's been in almost every state in the Union. He could wrestle any man at the railings in his day, an' he was bully of the raftsmen of the Susquehanna when he was only a youngster. His father killed a man in a standup fight with a blow of his fist when he was sixty years old. An' when he was seventy-four, his second wife had twins, an' he died when he was plowing in the field with oxen when he was ninety-nine years old. He just unyoked the oxen, an' sat down under a tree, an' died there sitting up. An' my father's just like him. He's pretty old now, but he ain't afraid of nothing. He's a regular Anglo-Saxon, you see. He's a special policeman, an' he didn't do a thing to the strikers in some of the fightin'. He had his face all cut up with a rock, but he broke his club short off over some hoodlum's head."

He paused breathlessly and looked at her.

"Gee!" he said. "I'd hate to a-ben that hoodlum."

"My name is Saxon," she said.

"Your name?"

"My first name."

"Gee!" he cried. "You're lucky. Now if mine had been only Erling—you know, Erling the Bold—or Wolf, or Swen, or Jarl!"

"What is it?" she asked.

"Only John," he admitted sadly. "But I don't let 'em call one John. Everybody's got to call me Jack. I've scrapped with a dozen fellows that tried to call me John, or Johnnie—wouldn't that make you sick?—Johnnie!"

They were now off the coal bunkers of Long Wharf, and the boy put the skiff about, heading toward San Francisco. They were well out in the open bay. The west wind had strengthened and was whitecapping the strong ebb tide. The boat drove merrily along. When splashes of spray flew aboard, wetting them, Saxon laughed, and the boy surveyed her with approval. They passed a ferryboat, and the passengers on the upper deck crowded to one side to watch them. In the swell of the steamer's wake, the skiff shipped quarter-full of water. Saxon picked up an empty can and looked at the boy.

"That's right," he said. "Go ahead an' bale out." And, when she had finished: "We'll fetch Goat Island next tack. Right there off the Torpedo Station is where we fish, in fifty feet of water an' the tide runnin' to beat the band. You're wringing wet, ain't you? Gee! You're like your name. You're a Saxon, all right. Are you married?"

Saxon nodded, and the boy frowned.

"What'd you want to do that for. Now you can't wander over the world like I'm going to. You're tied down. You're anchored for keeps."

"It's pretty good to be married, though," she smiled.

"Sure, everybody gets married. But that's no reason to be in a rush about it. Why couldn't you wait a while, like me, I'm goin' to get married, too, but not until I'm an old man an' have been everywheres."

Under the lee of Goat Island, Saxon obediently sitting still, he took in the sail, and, when the boat had drifted to a position to suit him, he dropped a tiny anchor. He got out the fish lines and showed Saxon how to bait her hooks with salted minnows. Then they dropped the lines to bottom, where they vibrated in the swift tide, and waited for bites.

"They'll bite pretty soon," he encouraged. "I've never failed but twice to catch a mess here. What d'ye say we eat while we're waiting?"

Vainly she protested she was not hungry. He shared his lunch with her with a boy's rigid equity, even to the half of a hard-boiled egg and the half of a big red apple.

Still the rockcod did not bite. From under the stern-sheets he drew out a cloth-bound book.

"Free Library," he vouchsafed, as he began to read, with one hand holding the place while with the other he waited for the tug on the fishline that would announce rockcod.

Saxon read the title. It was "Afloat in the Forest."

"Listen to this," he said after a few minutes, and he read several pages descriptive of a great flooded tropical forest being navigated by boys on a raft.

"Think of that!" he concluded. "That's the Amazon river in flood time in South America. And the world's full of places like that—everywhere, most likely, except Oakland. Oakland's just a place to start from, I guess. Now that's adventure, I want to tell you. Just think of the luck of them boys! All the same, some day I'm going to go over the Andes to the headwaters of the Amazon, all through the rubber country, an' canoe down the Amazon thousands of miles to its mouth where it's that wide you can't see one bank from the other an' where you can scoop up perfectly fresh water out of the ocean a hundred miles from land."

But Saxon was not listening. One pregnant sentence had caught her fancy. Oakland just a place to start from. She had never viewed the city in that light. She had accepted it as a place to live in, as an end in itself. But a place to start from! Why not! Why not like any railroad station or ferry depot! Certainly, as things were going, Oakland was not a place to stop in. The boy was right. It was a place to start from. But to go where? Here she was halted, and she was driven from the train of thought by a strong pull and a series of jerks on the line. She began to haul in, hand under hand, rapidly and deftly, the boy encouraging her, until hooks, sinker, and a big gasping rockcod tumbled into the bottom of the boat. The fish was free of the hook, and she baited afresh and dropped the line over. The boy marked his place and closed the book.

"They'll be biting soon as fast as we can haul 'em in," he said.

But the rush of fish did not come immediately.

"Did you ever read Captain Mayne Reid?" he asked. "Or Captain Marryatt? Or Ballantyne?"

She shook her head.

"And you an Anglo-Saxon!" he cried derisively. "Why, there's stacks of 'em in the Free Library. I have two cards, my mother's an' mine, an' I draw 'em out all the time, after school, before I have to carry my papers. I stick the books inside my shirt, in front, under the suspenders. That holds 'em. One time, deliverin' papers at Second an' Market—there's an awful tough gang of kids hang out there—I got into a fight with the leader. He hauled off to knock my wind out, an' he landed square on a book. You ought to seen his face. An' then I landed on him. An' then his whole gang was goin' to jump on me, only a couple of iron-molders stepped in an' saw fair play. I gave 'em the books to hold."

"Who won?" Saxon asked.

"Nobody," the boy confessed reluctantly. "I think I was lickin' him, but the molders called it a draw because the policeman on the beat stopped us when we'd only teen fightin' half an hour. But you ought to seen the crowd. I bet there was five hundred—"

He broke off abruptly and began hauling in his line. Saxon, too, was hauling in. And in the next couple of hours they caught twenty pounds of fish between them.

That night, long after dark, the little, half-decked skiff sailed up the Oakland Estuary. The wind was fair but light, and the boat moved slowly, towing a long pile which the boy had picked up adrift and announced as worth three dollars anywhere for the wood that was in it. The tide flooded smoothly under the full moon, and Saxon recognized the points they passed—the Transit slip, Sandy Beach, the shipyards, the nail works, Market street wharf. The boy took the skiff in to a dilapidated boat-wharf at the foot of Castro street, where the scow schooners, laden with sand and gravel, lay hauled to the shore in a long row. He insisted upon an equal division of the fish, because Saxon had helped catch them, though he explained at length the ethics of flotsam to show her that the pile was wholly his.

At Seventh and Poplar they separated, Saxon walking on alone to Pine street with her load of fish. Tired though she was from the long day, she had a strange feeling of well-being, and, after cleaning the fish, she fell asleep wondering, when good times came again, if she could persuade Billy to get a boat and go out with her on Sundays as she had gone out that day.

CHAPTER VII

She slept all night, without stirring, without dreaming, and awoke naturally and, for the first time in weeks, refreshed. She felt her old self, as if some depressing weight had been lifted, or a shadow had been swept away from between her and the sun. Her head was clear. The seeming iron band that had pressed it so hard was gone. She was cheerful. She even caught herself humming aloud as she divided the fish into messes for Mrs. Olsen, Maggie Donahue, and herself. She enjoyed her gossip with each of them, and, returning home, plunged joyfully into the task of putting the neglected house in order. She sang as she worked, and ever as she sang the magic words of the boy danced and sparkled among the notes: OAKLAND IS JUST A PLACE TO START FROM.

Everything was clear as print. Her and Billy's problem was as simple as an arithmetic problem at school: to carpet a room so many feet long, so many feet wide, to paper a room so many feet high, so many feet around. She had been sick in her head, she had had strange lapses, she had been irresponsible. Very well. All this had been because of her troubles—troubles in which she had had no hand in the making. Billy's case was hers precisely. He had behaved strangely because he had been irresponsible. And all their troubles were the troubles of the trap. Oakland was the trap. Oakland was a good place to start from.

She reviewed the events of her married life. The strikes and the hard times had caused everything. If it had not been for the strike of the shopmen and the fight in her front yard, she would not have lost her baby. If Billy had not been made desperate by the idleness and the hopeless fight of the teamsters, he would not have taken to drinking. If they had not been hard up, they would not have taken a lodger, and Billy would not be in jail.

Her mind was made up. The city was no place for her and Billy, no place for love nor for babies. The way out was simple. They would leave Oakland. It was the stupid that remained and bowed their heads to fate. But she and Billy were not stupid. They would not bow their heads. They would go forth and face fate.—Where, she did not know. But that would come. The world was large. Beyond the encircling hills, out through the Golden Gate, somewhere they would find what they desired. The boy had been wrong in one thing. She was not tied to Oakland, even if she was married. The world was free to her and Billy as it had been free to the wandering generations before them. It was only the stupid who had been left behind everywhere in the race's wandering. The strong had gone on. Well, she and Billy were strong. They would go on, over the brown Contra Costa hills or out through the Golden Gate.

The day before Billy's release Saxon completed her meager preparations to receive him. She was without money, and, except for her resolve not to offend Billy in that way again, she would have borrowed ferry fare from Maggie Donahue and journeyed to San Francisco to sell some of her personal pretties. As it was, with bread and potatoes and salted sardines in the house, she went out at the afternoon low tide and dug clams for a chowder. Also, she gathered a load of driftwood, and it was nine in the evening when she emerged from the marsh, on her shoulder a bundle of wood and a short-handled spade, in her free hand the pail of clams. She sought the darker side of the street at the corner and hurried across the zone of electric light to avoid detection by the neighbors. But a woman came toward her, looked sharply and stopped in front of her. It was Mary.

"My God, Saxon!" she exclaimed. "Is it as bad as this?"

Saxon looked at her old friend curiously, with a swift glance that sketched all the tragedy. Mary was thinner, though there was more color in her cheeks—color of which Saxon had her doubts. Mary's bright eyes were handsomer, larger—too large, too feverish bright, too restless. She was well dressed—too well dressed; and she was suffering from nerves. She turned her head apprehensively to glance into the darkness behind her.

"My God!" Saxon breathed. "And you..." She shut her lips, then began anew. "Come along to the house," she said.

"If you're ashamed to be seen with me—" Mary blurted, with one of her old quick angers.

"No, no," Saxon disclaimed. "It's the driftwood and the clams. I don't want the neighbors to know. Come along."

"No; I can't, Saxon. I'd like to, but I can't. I've got to catch the next train to F'risco. I've ben waitin' around. I knocked at your back door. But the house was dark. Billy's still in, ain't he?"

"Yes, he gets out to-morrow."

"I read about it in the papers," Mary went on hurriedly, looking behind her. "I was in Stockton when it happened." She turned upon Saxon almost savagely. "You don't blame me, do you? I just couldn't go back to work after bein' married. I was sick of work. Played out, I guess, an' no good anyway. But if you only knew how I hated the laundry even before I got married. It's a dirty world. You don't dream. Saxon, honest to God, you could never guess a hundredth part of its dirtiness. Oh, I wish I was dead, I wish I was dead an' out of it all. Listen—no, I can't now. There's the down train puffin' at Adeline. I'll have to run for it. Can I come—"

"Aw, get a move on, can't you?" a man's voice interrupted.

Behind her the speaker had partly emerged from the darkness. No workingman, Saxon could see that—lower in the world scale, despite his good clothes, than any workingman.

"I'm comin', if you'll only wait a second," Mary placated.

And by her answer and its accents Saxon knew that Mary was afraid of this man who prowled on the rim of light.

Mary turned to her.

"I got to beat it; good bye," she said, fumbling in the palm of her glove.

She caught Saxon's free hand, and Saxon felt a small hot coin pressed into it. She tried to resist, to force it back.

"No, no," Mary pleaded. "For old times. You can do as much for me some day. I'll see you again. Good bye."

Suddenly, sobbing, she threw her arms around Saxon's waist, crushing the feathers of her hat against the load of wood as she pressed her face against Saxon's breast. Then she tore herself away to arm's length, passionate, queering, and stood gazing at Saxon.

"Aw, get a hustle, get a hustle," came from the darkness the peremptory voice of the man.

"Oh, Saxon!" Mary sobbed; and was gone.

In the house, the lamp lighted, Saxon looked at the coin. It was a five-dollar piece—to her, a fortune. Then she thought of Mary, and of the man of whom she was afraid. Saxon registered another black mark against Oakland. Mary was one more destroyed. They lived only five years, on the average, Saxon had heard somewhere. She looked at the coin and tossed it into the kitchen sink. When she cleaned the clams, she heard the coin tinkle down the vent pipe.

It was the thought of Billy, next morning, that led Saxon to go under the sink, unscrew the cap to the catchtrap, and rescue the five-dollar piece. Prisoners were not well fed, she had been told; and the thought of placing clams and dry bread before Billy, after thirty days of prison fare, was too appalling for her to contemplate. She knew how he liked to spread his butter on thick, how he liked thick, rare steak fried on a dry hot pan, and how he liked coffee that was coffee and plenty of it.

Not until after nine o'clock did Billy arrive, and she was dressed in her prettiest house gingham to meet him. She peeped on him as he came slowly up the front steps, and she would have run out to him except for a group of neighborhood children who were staring from across the street. The door opened before him as his hand reached for the knob, and, inside, he closed it by backing against it, for his arms were filled with Saxon. No, he had not had breakfast, nor did he want any now that he had her. He had only stopped for a shave. He had stood the barber off, and he had walked all the way from the City Hall because of lack of the nickel carfare. But he'd like a bath most mighty well, and a change of clothes. She mustn't come near him until he was clean.

When all this was accomplished, he sat in the kitchen and watched her cook, noting the driftwood she put in the stove and asking about it. While she moved about, she told how she had gathered the wood, how she had managed to live and not be beholden to the union, and by the time they were seated at the table she was telling him about her meeting with Mary the night before. She did not mention the five dollars.

Billy stopped chewing the first mouthful of steak. His expression frightened her. He spat the meat out on his plate.

"You got the money to buy the meat from her," he accused slowly. "You had no money, no more tick with the butcher, yet here's meat. Am I right?"

Saxon could only bend her head.

The terrifying, ageless look had come into his face, the bleak and passionless glaze into his eyes, which she had first seen on the day at Weasel Park when he had fought with the three Irishmen.

CHAPTER VII

"What else did you buy?" he demanded—not roughly, not angrily, but with the fearful coldness of a rage that words could not express.

To her surprise, she had grown calm. What did it matter? It was merely what one must expect, living in Oakland—something to be left behind when Oakland was a thing behind, a place started from.

"The coffee," she answered. "And the butter."

He emptied his plate of meat and her plate into the frying pan, likewise the roll of butter and the slice on the table, and on top he poured the contents of the coffee canister. All this he carried into the back yard and dumped in the garbage can. The coffee pot he emptied into the sink. "How much of the money you got left?" he next wanted to know.

Saxon had already gone to her purse and taken it out.

"Three dollars and eighty cents," she counted, handing it to him. "I paid forty-five cents for the steak."

He ran his eye over the money, counted it, and went to the front door. She heard the door open and close, and knew that the silver had been flung into the street. When he came back to the kitchen, Saxon was already serving him fried potatoes on a clean plate.

"Nothin's too good for the Robertses," he said; "but, by God, that sort of truck is too high for my stomach. It's so high it stinks."

He glanced at the fried potatoes, the fresh slice of dry bread, and the glass of water she was placing by his plate.

"It's all right," she smiled, as he hesitated. "There's nothing left that's tainted."

He shot a swift glance at her face, as if for sarcasm, then sighed and sat down. Almost immediately he was up again and holding out his arms to her.

"I'm goin' to eat in a minute, but I want to talk to you first," he said, sitting down and holding her closely. "Besides, that water ain't like coffee. Gettin' cold won't spoil it none. Now, listen. You're the only one I got in this world. You wasn't afraid of me an' what I just done, an' I'm glad of that. Now we'll forget all about Mary. I got charity enough. I'm just as sorry for her as you. I'd do anything for her. I'd wash her feet for her like Christ did. I'd let her eat at my table, an' sleep under my roof. But all that ain't no reason I should touch anything she's earned. Now forget her. It's you an' me, Saxon, only you an' me an' to hell with the rest of the world. Nothing else counts. You won't never have to be afraid of me again. Whisky an' I don't mix very well, so I'm goin' to cut whisky out. I've been clean off my nut, an' I ain't treated you altogether right. But that's all past. It won't never happen again. I'm goin' to start out fresh.

"Now take this thing. I oughtn't to acted so hasty. But I did. I oughta talked it over. But I didn't. My damned temper got the best of me, an' you know I got one. If a fellow can keep his temper in boxin', why he can keep it in bein' married, too. Only this got me too sudden-like. It's something I can't stomach, that I never could stomach. An' you wouldn't want me to any more'n I'd want you to stomach something you just couldn't."

She sat up straight on his knees and looked at him, afire with an idea.

"You mean that, Billy?"

"Sure I do."

"Then I'll tell you something I can't stomach any more. I'll die if I have to."

"Well?" he questioned, after a searching pause.

"It's up to you," she said.

"Then fire away."

"You don't know what you're letting yourself in for," she warned. "Maybe you'd better back out before it's too late."

He shook his head stubbornly.

"What you don't want to stomach you ain't goin' to stomach. Let her go."

"First," she commenced, "no more slugging of scabs."

His mouth opened, but he checked the involuntary protest.

"And, second, no more Oakland."

"I don't get that last."

"No more Oakland. No more living in Oakland. I'll die if I have to. It's pull up stakes and get out."

He digested this slowly.

"Where?" he asked finally.

"Anywhere. Everywhere. Smoke a cigarette and think it over."

He shook his head and studied her.

"You mean that?" he asked at length.

"I do. I want to chuck Oakland just as hard as you wanted to chuck the beefsteak, the coffee, and the butter."

She could see him brace himself. She could feel him brace his very body ere he answered.

"All right then, if that's what you want. We'll quit Oakland. We'll quit it cold. God damn it, anyway, it never done nothin' for me, an' I guess I'm husky enough to scratch for us both anywheres. An' now that's settled, just tell me what you got it in for Oakland for."

And she told him all she had thought out, marshaled all the facts in her indictment of Oakland, omitting nothing, not even her last visit to Doctor Hentley's office nor Billy's drinking. He but drew her closer and proclaimed his resolves anew. The time passed. The fried potatoes grew cold, and the stove went out.

When a pause came, Billy stood up, still holding her. He glanced at the fried potatoes.

"Stone cold," he said, then turned to her. "Come on. Put on your prettiest. We're goin' up town for something to eat an' to celebrate. I guess we got a celebration comin', seein' as we're going to pull up stakes an' pull our freight from the old burg. An' we won't have to walk. I can borrow a dime from the barber, an' I got enough junk to hock for a blowout."

His junk proved to be several gold medals won in his amateur days at boxing tournaments. Once up town and in the pawnshop, Uncle Sam seemed thoroughly versed in the value of the medals, and Billy jingled a handful of silver in his pocket as they walked out.

He was as hilarious as a boy, and she joined in his good spirits. When he stopped at a corner cigar store to buy a sack of Bull Durham, he changed his mind and bought Imperials.

"Oh, I'm a regular devil," he laughed. "Nothing's too good to-day—not even tailor-made smokes. An' no chop houses nor Jap joints for you an' me. It's Barnum's."

They strolled to the restaurant at Seventh and Broadway where they had had their wedding supper.

CHAPTER VII

"Let's make believed we're not married," Saxon suggested.

"Sure," he agreed, "—an' take a private room so as the waiter'll have to knock on the door each time he comes in."

Saxon demurred at that.

"It will be too expensive, Billy. You'll have to tip him for the knocking. We'll take the regular dining room."

"Order anything you want," Billy said largely, when they were seated. "Here's family porterhouse, a dollar an' a half. What d'ye say?"

"And hash-browned," she abetted, "and coffee extra special, and some oysters first—I want to compare them with the rock oysters."

Billy nodded, and looked up from the bill of fare.

"Here's mussels bordelay. Try an order of them, too, an' see if they beat your Rock Wall ones."

"Why not?" Saxon cried, her eyes dancing. "The world is ours. We're just travelers through this town."

"Yep, that's the stuff," Billy muttered absently. He was looking at the theater column. He lifted his eyes from the paper. "Matinee at Bell's. We can get reserved seats for a quarter.—Doggone the luck anyway!"

His exclamation was so aggrieved and violent that it brought alarm into her eyes.

"If I'd only thought," he regretted, "we could a-gone to the Forum for grub. That's the swell joint where fellows like Roy Blanchard hangs out, blowin' the money we sweat for them."

They bought reserved tickets at Bell's Theater; but it was too early for the performance, and they went down Broadway and into the Electric Theater to while away the time on a moving picture show. A cowboy film was run off, and a French comic; then came a rural drama situated somewhere in the Middle West. It began with a farm yard scene. The sun blazed down on a corner of a barn and on a rail fence where the ground lay in the mottled shade of large trees overhead. There were chickens, ducks, and turkeys, scratching, waddling, moving about. A big sow, followed by a roly-poly litter of seven little ones, marched majestically through the chickens, rooting them out of the way. The hens, in turn, took it out on the little porkers, pecking them when they strayed too far from their mother. And over the top rail a horse looked drowsily on, ever and anon, at mathematically precise intervals, switching a lazy tail that flashed high lights in the sunshine.

"It's a warm day and there are flies—can't you just feel it?" Saxon whispered.

"Sure. An' that horse's tail! It's the most natural ever. Gee! I bet he knows the trick of clampin' it down over the reins. I wouldn't wonder if his name was Iron Tail."

A dog ran upon the scene. The mother pig turned tail and with short ludicrous jumps, followed by her progeny and pursued by the dog, fled out of the film. A young girl came on, a sunbonnet hanging down her back, her apron caught up in front and filled with grain which she threw to the buttering fowls. Pigeons flew down from the top of the film and joined in the scrambling feast. The dog returned, wading scarcely noticed among the feathered creatures, to wag his tail and laugh up at the girl. And, behind, the horse nodded over the rail and switched on. A young man entered, his errand immediately known to an audience educated in moving pictures. But Saxon had no eyes for the love-making, the pleading forcefulness, the shy reluctance, of man and maid. Ever her gaze wandered back to the chickens, to the mottled shade under the trees, to the warm wall of the barn, to the sleepy horse with its ever recurrent whisk of tail.

She drew closer to Billy, and her hand, passed around his arm, sought his hand.

"Oh, Billy," she sighed. "I'd just die of happiness in a place like that." And, when the film was ended. "We got lots of time for Bell's. Let's stay and see that one over again."

They sat through a repetition of the performance, and when the farm yard scene appeared, the longer Saxon looked at it the more it affected her. And this time she took in further details. She saw fields beyond, rolling hills in the background, and a cloud-flecked sky. She identified some of the chickens, especially an obstreperous old hen who resented the thrust of the sow's muzzle, particularly pecked at the little pigs, and laid about her with a vengeance when the grain fell. Saxon looked back across the fields to the hills and sky, breathing the spaciousness of it, the freedom, the content. Tears welled into her eyes and she wept silently, happily.

"I know a trick that'd fix that old horse if he ever clamped his tail down on me," Billy whispered.

"Now I know where we're going when we leave Oakland," she informed him.

"Where?"

"There."

He looked at her, and followed her gaze to the screen. "Oh," he said, and cogitated. "An' why shouldn't we?" he added.

"Oh, Billy, will you?"

Her lips trembled in her eagerness, and her whisper broke and was almost inaudible "Sure," he said. It was his day of royal largess.

"What you want is yourn, an' I'll scratch my fingers off for it. An' I've always had a hankerin' for the country myself. Say! I've known horses like that to sell for half the price, an' I can sure cure 'em of the habit."

CHAPTER XVIII

It was early evening when they got off the car at Seventh and Pine on their way home from Bell's Theater. Billy and Saxon did their little marketing together, then separated at the corner, Saxon to go on to the house and prepare supper, Billy to go and see the boys—the teamsters who had fought on in the strike during his month of retirement.

"Take care of yourself, Billy," she called, as he started off.

"Sure," he answered, turning his face to her over his shoulder.

Her heart leaped at the smile. It was his old, unsullied love-smile which she wanted always to see on his face—for which, armed with her own wisdom and the wisdom of Mercedes, she would wage the utmost woman's war to possess. A thought of this flashed brightly through her brain, and it was with a proud little smile that she remembered all her pretty equipment stored at home in the bureau and the chest of drawers.

Three-quarters of an hour later, supper ready, all but the putting on of the lamb chops at the sound of his step, Saxon waited. She heard the gate click, but instead of his step she heard a curious and confused scraping of many steps. She flew to open the door. Billy stood there, but a different Billy from the one she had parted from so short a time before. A small boy, beside him, held his hat. His face had been fresh-washed, or, rather, drenched, for his shirt and shoulders were wet. His pale hair lay damp and plastered against his forehead, and was darkened by oozing blood. Both arms hung limply by his side. But his face was composed, and he even grinned.

"It's all right," he reassured Saxon. "The joke's on me. Somewhat damaged but still in the ring." He stepped gingerly across the threshold. "—Come on in, you fellows. We're all mutts together."

He was followed in by the boy with his hat, by Bud Strothers and another teamster she knew, and by two strangers. The latter were big, hard-featured, sheepish-faced men, who stared at Saxon as if afraid of her.

"It's all right, Saxon," Billy began, but was interrupted by Bud.

"First thing is to get him on the bed an' cut his clothes off him. Both arms is broke, and here are the ginks that done it."

He indicated the two strangers, who shuffled their feet with embarrassment and looked more sheepish than ever.

Billy sat down on the bed, and while Saxon held the lamp, Bud and the strangers proceeded to cut coat, shirt, and undershirt from him.

"He wouldn't go to the receivin' hospital," Bud said to Saxon.

"Not on your life," Billy concurred. "I had 'em send for Doc Hentley. He'll be here any minute. Them two arms is all I got. They've done pretty well by me, an' I gotta do the same by them.—No medical students a-learnin' their trade on me."

"But how did it happens" Saxon demanded, looking from Billy to the two strangers, puzzled by the amity that so evidently existed among them all.

"Oh, they're all right," Billy dashed in. "They done it through mistake. They're Frisco teamsters, an' they come over to help us—a lot of 'em."

The two teamsters seemed to cheer up at this, and nodded their heads.

"Yes, missus," one of them rumbled hoarsely. "It's all a mistake, an'... well, the joke's on us."

"The drinks, anyway," Billy grinned.

Not only was Saxon not excited, but she was scarcely perturbed. What had happened was only to be expected.

It was in line with all that Oakland had already done to her and hers, and, besides, Billy was not dangerously hurt. Broken arms and a sore head would heal. She brought chairs and seated everybody.

"Now tell me what happened," she begged. "I'm all at sea, what of you two burleys breaking my husband's arms, then seeing him home and holding a love-fest with him."

"An' you got a right," Bud Strothers assured her. "You see, it happened this way—"

"You shut up, Bud," Billy broke it. "You didn't see anything of it."

Saxon looked to the San Francisco teamsters.

"We'd come over to lend a hand, seein' as the Oakland boys was gettin' some the short end of it," one spoke up, "an' we've sure learned some scabs there's better trades than drivin' team. Well, me an' Jackson here was nosin' around to see what we can see, when your husband comes moseyin' along. When he—"

"Hold on," Jackson interrupted. "Get it straight as you go along. We reckon we know the boys by sight. But your husband we ain't never seen around, him bein'..."

"As you might say, put away for a while," the first teamster took up the tale. "So, when we sees what we thinks is a scab dodgin' away from us an' takin' the shortcut through the alley—"

"The alley back of Campbell's grocery," Billy elucidated.

"Yep, back of the grocery," the first teamster went on; "why, we're sure he's one of them squarehead scabs, hired through Murray an' Ready, makin' a sneak to get into the stables over the back fences."

"We caught one there, Billy an' me," Bud interpolated.

"So we don't waste any time," Jackson said, addressing himself to Saxon. "We've done it before, an' we know how to do 'em up brown an' tie 'em with baby ribbon. So we catch your husband right in the alley."

"I was lookin' for Bud," said Billy. "The boys told me I'd find him somewhere around the other end of the alley. An' the first thing I know, Jackson, here, asks me for a match."

"An' right there's where I get in my fine work," resumed the first teamster.

"What?" asked Saxon.

CHAPTER XVIII

"That." The man pointed to the wound in Billy's scalp. "I laid 'm out. He went down like a steer, an' got up on his knees dippy, a-gabblin' about somebody standin' on their foot. He didn't know where he was at, you see, clean groggy. An' then we done it."

The man paused, the tale told.

"Broke both his arms with the crowbar," Bud supplemented.

"That's when I come to myself, when the bones broke," Billy corroborated. "An' there was the two of 'em givin' me the ha-ha. 'That'll last you some time,' Jackson was sayin'. An' Anson says, 'I'd like to see you drive horses with them arms.' An' then Jackson says, 'let's give 'm something for luck.' An' with that he fetched me a wallop on the jaw—"

"No," corrected Anson. "That wallop was mine."

"Well, it sent me into dreamland over again," Billy sighed. "An' when I come to, here was Bud an' Anson an' Jackson dousin' me at a water trough. An' then we dodged a reporter an' all come home together."

Bud Strothers held up his fist and indicated freshly abraded skin.

"The reporter-guy just insisted on samplin' it," he said. Then, to Billy: "That's why I cut around Ninth an' caught up with you down on Sixth."

A few minutes later Doctor Hentley arrived, and drove the men from the rooms. They waited till he had finished, to assure themselves of Billy's well being, and then departed. In the kitchen Doctor Hentley washed his hands and gave Saxon final instructions. As he dried himself he sniffed the air and looked toward the stove where a pot was simmering.

"Clams," he said. "Where did you buy them?"

"I didn't buy them," replied Saxon. "I dug them myself."

"Not in the marsh?" he asked with quickened interest.

"Yes."

"Throw them away. Throw them out. They're death and corruption. Typhoid—I've got three cases now, all traced to the clams and the marsh."

When he had gone, Saxon obeyed. Still another mark against Oakland, she reflected—Oakland, the man-trap, that poisoned those it could not starve.

"If it wouldn't drive a man to drink," Billy groaned, when Saxon returned to him. "Did you ever dream such luck? Look at all my fights in the ring, an' never a broken bone, an' here, snap, snap, just like that, two arms smashed."

"Oh, it might be worse," Saxon smiled cheerfully.

"I'd like to know how. It might have been your neck."

"An' a good job. I tell you, Saxon, you gotta show me anything worse."

"I can," she said confidently.

"Well?"

"Well, wouldn't it be worse if you intended staying on in Oakland where it might happen again?"

"I can see myself becomin' a farmer an' plowin' with a pair of pipe-stems like these," he persisted.

"Doctor Hentley says they'll be stronger at the break than ever before. And you know yourself that's true of clean-broken bones. Now you close your eyes and go to sleep. You're all done up, and you need to keep your brain quiet and stop thinking."

He closed his eyes obediently. She slipped a cool hand under the nape of his neck and let it rest.

"That feels good," he murmured. "You're so cool, Saxon. Your hand, and you, all of you. Bein' with you is like comin' out into the cool night after dancin' in a hot room."

After several minutes of quiet, he began to giggle.

"What is it?" she asked.

"Oh, nothin'. I was just thinkin'—thinking of them mutts doin' me up—me, that's done up more scabs than I can remember."

Next morning Billy awoke with his blues dissipated. From the kitchen Saxon heard him painfully wrestling strange vocal acrobatics.

"I got a new song you never heard," he told her when she came in with a cup of coffee. "I only remember the chorus though. It's the old man talkin' to some hobo of a hired man that wants to marry his daughter. Mamie, that Billy Murphy used to run with before he got married, used to sing it. It's a kind of a sobby song. It used to always give Mamie the weeps. Here's the way the chorus goes—an' remember, it's the old man spielin'."

And with great solemnity and excruciating Batting, Billy sang:

"O treat my daughter kind-i-ly; An' say you'll do no harm, An' when I die I'll will to you My little house an' farm—My horse, my plow, my sheep, my cow, An' all them little chickens in the ga-a-rden.

"It's them little chickens in the garden that gets me," he explained. "That's how I remembered it—from the chickens in the movin' pictures yesterday. An' some day we'll have little chickens in the garden, won't we, old girl?"

"And a daughter, too," Saxon amplified.

"An' I'll be the old geezer sayin' them same words to the hired man," Billy carried the fancy along. "It don't take long to raise a daughter if you ain't in a hurry."

Saxon took her long-neglected ukulele from its case and strummed it into tune.

"And I've a song you never heard, Billy. Tom's always singing it. He's crazy about taking up government land and going farming, only Sarah won't think of it. He sings it something like this:

"We'll have a little farm, A pig, a horse, a cow, And you will drive the wagon, And I will drive the plow."

"Only in this case I guess it's me that'll do the plowin'," Billy approved. "Say, Saxon, sing 'Harvest Days.' That's a farmer's song, too."

After that she feared the coffee was growing cold and compelled Billy to take it. In the helplessness of two broken arms, he had to be fed like a baby, and as she fed him they talked.

"I'll tell you one thing," Billy said, between mouthfuls. "Once we get settled down in the country you'll have that horse you've been wishin' for all your life. An' it'll be all your own, to ride, drive, sell, or do anything you want with."

And, again, he ruminated: "One thing that'll come handy in the country is that I know horses; that's a big start. I can always get a job at that—if it ain't at union wages. An' the other things about farmin' I can learn fast enough.—Say, d'ye remember that day you first told me about wantin' a horse to ride all your life?"

Saxon remembered, and it was only by a severe struggle that she was able to keep the tears from welling into her eyes. She seemed bursting with happiness, and she was remembering many things—all the warm promise of life with Billy that had been hers in the days before hard times. And now the promise was renewed again. Since its fulfillment had not come to them, they were going away to fulfill it for themselves and make the moving pictures come true.

Impelled by a half-feigned fear, she stole away into the kitchen bedroom where Bert had died, to study her face in the bureau mirror. No, she decided; she was little changed. She was still equipped for the battlefield of love. Beautiful she was not. She knew that. But had not Mercedes said that the great women of history who had won men had not been beautiful? And yet, Saxon insisted, as she gazed at her reflection, she was anything but unlovely. She studied her wide gray eyes that were so very gray, that were always alive with light and vivacities, where, in the surface and depths, always swam thoughts unuttered, thoughts that sank down and dissolved to give place to other thoughts. The brows were excellent—she realized that. Slenderly penciled, a little darker than her light brown hair, they just fitted her irregular nose that was feminine but not weak, that if anything was piquant and that picturesquely might be declared impudent.

She could see that her face was slightly thin, that the red of her lips was not quite so red, and that she had lost some of her quick coloring. But all that would come back again. Her mouth was not of the rosebud type she saw in the magazines. She paid particular attention to it. A pleasant mouth it was, a mouth to be joyous with, a mouth for laughter and to make laughter in others. She deliberately experimented with it, smiled till the corners dented deeper. And she knew that when she smiled her smile was provocative of smiles. She laughed with her eyes alone—a trick of hers. She threw back her head and laughed with eyes and mouth together, between her spread lips showing the even rows of strong white teeth.

And she remembered Billy's praise of her teeth, the night at Germanic Hall after he had told Charley Long he was standing on his foot. "Not big, and not little dinky baby's teeth either," Billy had said, "... just right, and they fit you." Also, he had said that to look at them made him hungry, and that they were good enough to eat.

She recollected all the compliments he had ever paid her. Beyond all treasures, these were treasures to her—the love phrases, praises, and admirations. He had said her skin was cool—soft as velvet, too, and smooth as silk. She rolled up her sleeve to the shoulder, brushed her cheek with the white skin for a test, with deep scrutiny examined the fineness of its texture. And he had told her that she was sweet; that he hadn't known what it meant when they said a girl was sweet, not until he had known her. And he had told her that her voice was cool, that it gave him the feeling her hand did when it rested on his forehead. Her voice went all through him, he had said, cool and fine, like a wind of coolness. And he had likened it to the first of the sea breeze setting in the afternoon after a scorching hot morning. And, also, when she talked low, that it was round and sweet, like the 'cello in the Macdonough Theater orchestra.

He had called her his Tonic Kid. He had called her a thoroughbred, clean-cut and spirited, all fine nerves and delicate and sensitive. He had liked the way she carried her clothes. She carried them like a dream, had been his way of putting it. They were part of her, just as much as the cool of her voice and skin and the scent of her hair.

And her figure! She got upon a chair and tilted the mirror so that she could see herself from hips to feet. She drew her skirt back and up. The slender ankle was just as slender. The calf had lost none of its delicately mature swell. She studied her hips, her waist, her bosom, her neck, the poise of her head, and sighed contentedly. Billy must be right, and he had said that she was built like a French woman, and that in the matter of lines and form she could give Annette Kellerman cards and spades.

He had said so many things, now that she recalled them all at one time. Her lips! The Sunday he proposed he had said: "I like to watch your lips talking. It's funny, but every move they make looks like a tickly kiss." And afterward, that same day: "You looked good to me from the first moment I spotted you." He had praised her housekeeping. He had said he fed better, lived more comfortably, held up his end with the fellows, and saved money. And she remembered that day when he had crushed her in his arms and declared she was the greatest little bit of a woman that had ever come down the pike.

She ran her eyes over all herself in the mirror again, gathered herself together into a whole, compact and good to look upon—delicious, she knew. Yes, she would do. Magnificent as Billy was in his man way, in her own way she was a match for him. Yes, she had done well by Billy. She deserved much—all he could give her, the best he could give her. But she made no blunder of egotism. Frankly valuing herself, she as frankly valued him. When he was himself, his real self, not harassed by trouble, not pinched by the trap, not maddened by drink, her man-boy and lover, he was well worth all she gave him or could give him.

Saxon gave herself a farewell look. No. She was not dead, any more than was Billy's love dead, than was her love dead. All that was needed was the proper soil, and their love would grow and blossom. And they were turning their backs upon Oakland to go and seek that proper soil.

"Oh, Billy!" she called through the partition, still standing on the chair, one hand tipping the mirror forward and back, so that she was able to run her eyes from the reflection of her ankles and calves to her face, warm with color and roguishly alive.

"Yes?" she heard him answer.

"I'm loving myself," she called back.

"What's the game?" came his puzzled query. "What are you so stuck on yourself for!"

"Because you love me," she answered. "I love every bit of me, Billy, because... because... well, because you love every bit of me."

CHAPTER XIX

Between feeding and caring for Billy, doing the housework, making plans, and selling her store of pretty needlework, the days flew happily for Saxon. Billy's consent to sell her pretties had been hard to get, but at last she succeeded in coaxing it out of him.

"It's only the ones I haven't used," she urged; "and I can always make more when we get settled somewhere."

What she did not sell, along with the household linen and hers and Billy's spare clothing, she arranged to store with Tom.

"Go ahead," Billy said. "This is your picnic. What you say goes. You're Robinson Crusoe an' I'm your man Friday. Make up your mind yet which way you're goin' to travel?"

Saxon shook her head.

"Or how?"

She held up one foot and then the other, encased in stout walking shoes which she had begun that morning to break in about the house. "Shank's mare, eh?"

"It's the way our people came into the West," she said proudly.

"It'll be regular trampin', though," he argued. "An' I never heard of a woman tramp."

"Then here's one. Why, Billy, there's no shame in tramping. My mother tramped most of the way across the Plains. And 'most everybody else's mother tramped across in those days. I don't care what people will think. I guess our race has been on the tramp since the beginning of creation, just like we'll be, looking for a piece of land that looked good to settle down on."

After a few days, when his scalp was sufficiently healed and the bone-knitting was nicely in process, Billy was able to be up and about. He was still quite helpless, however, with both his arms in splints.

Doctor Hentley not only agreed, but himself suggested, that his bill should wait against better times for settlement. Of government land, in response to Saxon's eager questioning, he knew nothing, except that he had a hazy idea that the days of government land were over.

Tom, on the contrary, was confident that there was plenty of government hand. He talked of Honey Lake, of Shasta County, and of Humboldt.

"But you can't tackle it at this time of year, with winter comin' on," he advised Saxon. "The thing for you to do is head south for warmer weather—say along the coast. It don't snow down there. I tell you what you do. Go down by San Jose and Salinas an' come out on the coast at Monterey. South of that you'll find government land mixed up with forest reserves and Mexican rancheros. It's pretty wild, without any roads to speak of. All they do is handle cattle. But there's some fine redwood canyons, with good patches of farming ground that run right down to the ocean. I was talkin' last year with a fellow that's been all through there. An' I'd a-gone, like you an' Billy, only Sarah wouldn't hear of it. There's gold down there, too. Quite a bunch is in there prospectin', an' two or three good mines have opened. But that's farther along and in a ways from the coast. You might take a look."

Saxon shook her head. "We're not looking for gold but for chickens and a place to grow vegetables. Our folks had all the chance for gold in the early days, and what have they got to show for it?"

"I guess you're right," Tom conceded. "They always played too big a game, an' missed the thousand little chances right under their nose. Look at your pa. I've heard him tell of selling three Market street lots in San Francisco for fifty dollars each. They're worth five hundred thousand right now. An' look at Uncle Will. He had ranches till the cows come home. Satisfied? No. He wanted to be a cattle king, a regular Miller and Lux. An' when he died he was a night watchman in Los Angeles at forty dollars a month. There's a spirit of the times, an' the spirit of the times has changed. It's all big business now, an' we're the small potatoes. Why, I've heard our folks talk of livin' in the Western Reserve. That was all around what's Ohio now. Anybody could get a farm them days. All they had to do was yoke their oxen an' go after it, an' the Pacific Ocean thousands of miles to the west, an' all them thousands of miles an' millions of farms just waitin' to be took up. A hundred an' sixty acres? Shucks. In the early days in Oregon they talked six hundred an' forty acres. That was the spirit of them times—free land, an' plenty of it. But when we reached the Pacific Ocean them times was ended. Big business begun; an' big business means big business men; an' every big business man means thousands of little men without any business at all except to work for the big ones. They're the losers, don't you see? An' if they don't like it they can lump it, but it won't do them no good. They can't yoke up their oxen an' pull on. There's no place to pull on. China's over there, an' in between's a mighty lot of salt water that's no good for farmin' purposes."

"That's all clear enough," Saxon commented.

"Yes," her brother went on. "We can all see it after it's happened, when it's too late."

"But the big men were smarter," Saxon remarked.

"They were luckier," Tom contended. "Some won, but most lost, an' just as good men lost. It was almost like a lot of boys scramblin' on the sidewalk for a handful of small change. Not that some didn't have far-seein'. But just take your pa, for example. He come of good Down East stock that's got business instinct an' can add to what it's got. Now suppose your pa had developed a weak heart, or got kidney disease, or caught rheumatism, so he couldn't go gallivantin' an' rainbow chasin', an' fightin' an' explorin' all over the West. Why, most likely he'd a settled down in San Francisco—he'd a-had to—an' held onto them three Market street lots, an' bought more lots, of course, an' gone into steamboat companies, an' stock gamblin', an' railroad buildin', an' Comstock-tunnelin'.

CHAPTER XIX

"Why, he'd a-become big business himself. I know 'm. He was the most energetic man I ever saw, think quick as a wink, as cool as an icicle an' as wild as a Comanche. Why, he'd a-cut a swath through the free an' easy big business gamblers an' pirates of them days; just as he cut a swath through the hearts of the ladies when he went gallopin' past on that big horse of his, sword clatterin', spurs jinglin', his long hair flyin', straight as an Indian, clean-built an' graceful as a blue-eyed prince out of a fairy book an' a Mexican caballero all rolled into one; just as he cut a swath through the Johnny Rebs in Civil War days, chargin' with his men all the way through an' back again, an' yellin' like a wild Indian for more. Cady, that helped raise you, told me about that. Cady rode with your pa.

"Why, if your pa'd only got laid up in San Francisco, he would a-ben one of the big men of the West. An' in that case, right now, you'd be a rich young woman, travelin' in Europe, with a mansion on Nob Hill along with the Floods and Crockers, an' holdin' majority stock most likely in the Fairmount Hotel an' a few little concerns like it. An' why ain't you? Because your pa wasn't smart? No. His mind was like a steel trap. It's because he was filled to burstin' an' spillin' over with the spirit of the times; because he was full of fire an' vinegar an' couldn't set down in one place. That's all the difference between you an' the young women right now in the Flood and Crocker families. Your father didn't catch rheumatism at the right time, that's all."

Saxon sighed, then smiled.

"Just the same, I've got them beaten," she said. "The Miss Floods and Miss Crockers can't marry prize-fighters, and I did."

Tom looked at her, taken aback for the moment, with admiration, slowly at first, growing in his face.

"Well, all I got to say," he enunciated solemnly, "is that Billy's so lucky he don't know how lucky he is."

Not until Doctor Hentley gave the word did the splints come off Billy's arms, and Saxon insisted upon an additional two weeks' delay so that no risk would be run. These two weeks would complete another month's rent, and the landlord had agreed to wait payment for the last two months until Billy was on his feet again.

Salinger's awaited the day set by Saxon for taking back their furniture. Also, they had returned to Billy seventy-five dollars.

"The rest you've paid will be rent," the collector told Saxon. "And the furniture's second hand now, too. The deal will be a loss to Salinger's' and they didn't have to do it, either; you know that. So just remember they've been pretty square with you, and if you start over again don't forget them."

Out of this sum, and out of what was realized from Saxon's pretties, they were able to pay all their small bills and yet have a few dollars remaining in pocket.

"I hate owin' things worse 'n poison," Billy said to Saxon. "An' now we don't owe a soul in this world except the landlord an' Doc Hentley."

"And neither of them can afford to wait longer than they have to," she said.

"And they won't," Billy answered quietly.

She smiled her approval, for she shared with Billy his horror of debt, just as both shared it with that early tide of pioneers with a Puritan ethic, which had settled the West.

Saxon timed her opportunity when Billy was out of the house to pack the chest of drawers which had crossed the Atlantic by sailing ship and the Plains by ox team. She kissed the bullet hole in it, made in the fight at Little Meadow, as she kissed her father's sword, the while she visioned him, as she always did, astride his roan warhorse. With the old religious awe, she pored over her mother's poems in the scrap-book, and clasped her mother's red satin Spanish girdle about her in a farewell embrace. She unpacked the scrap-book in order to gaze a last time at the wood engraving of the Vikings, sword in hand, leaping upon the English sands. Again she identified Billy as one of the Vikings, and pondered for a space on the strange wanderings of the seed from which she sprang. Always had her race been land-hungry, and she took delight in believing she had bred true; for had not she, despite her life passed in a city, found this same land-hunger in her? And was she not going forth to satisfy that hunger, just as her people of old time had done, as her father and mother before her? She remembered her mother's tale of how the promised land looked to them as their battered wagons and weary oxen dropped down through the early winter snows of the Sierras to the vast and flowering sun-land of California: In fancy, herself a child of nine, she looked down from the snowy heights as her mother must have looked down. She recalled and repeated aloud one of her mother's stanzas:

"'Sweet as a wind-lute's airy strains Your gentle muse has learned to sing And California's boundless plains Prolong the soft notes echoing.'"

She sighed happily and dried her eyes. Perhaps the hard times were past. Perhaps they had constituted HER Plains, and she and Billy had won safely across and were even then climbing the Sierras ere they dropped down into the pleasant valley land.

Salinger's wagon was at the house, taking out the furniture, the morning they left. The landlord, standing at the gate, received the keys, shook hands with them, and wished them luck. "You're goin' at it right," he congratulated them. "Sure an' wasn't it under me roll of blankets I tramped into Oakland meself forty year ago! Buy land, like me, when it's cheap. It'll keep you from the poorhouse in your old age. There's plenty of new towns springin' up. Get in on the ground floor. The work of your hands'll keep you in food an' under a roof, an' the lend 'll make you well to do. An' you know me address. When you can spare send me along that small bit of rent. An' good luck. An' don't mind what people think. 'Tis them that looks that finds."

Curious neighbors peeped from behind the blinds as Billy and Saxon strode up the street, while the children gazed at them in gaping astonishment. On Billy's back, inside a painted canvas tarpaulin, was slung the roll of bedding. Inside the roll were changes of underclothing and odds and ends of necessaries. Outside, from the lashings, depended a frying pan and cooking pail. In his hand he carried the coffee pot. Saxon carried a small telescope basket protected by black oilcloth, and across her back was the tiny ukulele case.

"We must look like holy frights," Billy grumbled, shrinking from every gaze that was bent upon him.

"It'd be all right, if we were going camping," Saxon consoled. "Only we're not."

"But they don't know that," she continued. "It's only you know that, and what you think they're thinking isn't what they're thinking at all. Most probably they think we're going camping. And the best of it is we are going camping. We are! We are!"

At this Billy cheered up, though he muttered his firm intention to knock the block off of any guy that got fresh. He stole a glance at Saxon. Her cheeks were red, her eyes glowing.

CHAPTER XIX

"Say," he said suddenly. "I seen an opera once, where fellows wandered over the country with guitars slung on their backs just like you with that strummy-strum. You made me think of them. They was always singin' songs."

"That's what I brought it along for," Saxon answered.

"And when we go down country roads we'll sing as we go along, and we'll sing by the campfires, too. We're going camping, that's all. Taking a vacation and seeing the country. So why shouldn't we have a good time? Why, we don't even know where we're going to sleep to-night, or any night. Think of the fun!"

"It's a sporting proposition all right, all right," Billy considered. "But, just the same, let's turn off an' go around the block. There's some fellows I know, standin' up there on the next corner, an' I don't want to knock THEIR blocks off."

BOOK III

CHAPTER I

The car ran as far as Hayward's, but at Saxon's suggestion they got off at San Leandro.

"It doesn't matter where we start walking," she said, "for start to walk somewhere we must. And as we're looking for land and finding out about land, the quicker we begin to investigate the better. Besides, we want to know all about all kinds of land, close to the big cities as well as back in the mountains."

"Gee!—this must be the Porchugeeze headquarters," was Billy's reiterated comment, as they walked through San Leandro.

"It looks as though they'd crowd our kind out," Saxon adjudged.

"Some tall crowdin', I guess," Billy grumbled. "It looks like the free-born American ain't got no room left in his own land."

"Then it's his own fault," Saxon said, with vague asperity, resenting conditions she was just beginning to grasp.

"Oh, I don't know about that. I reckon the American could do what the Porchugeeze do if he wanted to. Only he don't want to, thank God. He ain't much given to livin' like a pig often leavin's."

"Not in the country, maybe," Saxon controverted. "But I've seen an awful lot of Americans living like pigs in the cities."

Billy grunted unwilling assent. "I guess they quit the farms an' go to the city for something better, an' get it in the neck."

"Look at all the children!" Saxon cried. "School's letting out. And nearly all are Portuguese, Billy, NOT Porchugeeze. Mercedes taught me the right way."

"They never wore glad rags like them in the old country," Billy sneered. "They had to come over here to get decent clothes and decent grub. They're as fat as butterballs."

Saxon nodded affirmation, and a great light seemed suddenly to kindle in her understanding.

"That's the very point, Billy. They're doing it—doing it farming, too. Strikes don't bother THEM."

"You don't call that dinky gardening farming," he objected, pointing to a piece of land barely the size of an acre, which they were passing.

"Oh, your ideas are still big," she laughed. "You're like Uncle Will, who owned thousands of acres and wanted to own a million, and who wound up as night watchman. That's what was the trouble with all us Americans. Everything large scale. Anything less than one hundred and sixty acres was small scale."

"Just the same," Billy held stubbornly, "large scale's a whole lot better'n small scale like all these dinky gardens."

Saxon sighed. "I don't know which is the dinkier," she observed finally, "—owning a few little acres and the team you're driving, or not owning any acres and driving a team somebody else owns for wages."

Billy winced.

"Go on, Robinson Crusoe," he growled good naturedly. "Rub it in good an' plenty. An' the worst of it is it's correct. A hell of a free-born American I've been, adrivin' other folkses' teams for a livin', a-strikin' and a-sluggin' scabs, an' not bein' able to keep up with the installments for a few sticks of furniture. Just the same I was sorry for one thing. I hated worse in Sam Hill to see that Morris chair go back—you liked it so. We did a lot of honeymoonin' in that chair."

They were well out of San Leandro, walking through a region of tiny holdings—"farmlets," Billy called them; and Saxon got out her ukulele to cheer him with a song.

First, it was "Treat my daughter kind-i-ly," and then she swung into old-fashioned darky camp-meeting hymns, beginning with:

"Oh! de Judgmen' Day am rollin' roan', Rollin', yes, a-rollin', I hear the trumpets' awful soun', Rollin', yes, a-rollin'."

A big touring car, dashing past, threw a dusty pause in her singing, and Saxon delivered herself of her latest wisdom.

"Now, Billy, remember we're not going to take up with the first piece of land we see. We've got to go into this with our eyes open—"

"An' they ain't open yet," he agreed.

"And we've got to get them open. "Tis them that looks that finds.' There's lots of time to learn things. We don't care if it takes months and months. We're footloose. A good start is better than a dozen bad ones. We've got to talk and find out. We'll talk with everybody we meet. Ask questions. Ask everybody. It's the only way to find out."

"I ain't much of a hand at askin' questions," Billy demurred.

"Then I'll ask," she cried. "We've got to win out at this game, and the way is to know. Look at all these Portuguese. Where are all the Americans? They owned the land first, after the Mexicans. What made the Americans clear out? How do the Portuguese make it go? Don't you see? We've got to ask millions of questions."

She strummed a few chords, and then her clear sweet voice rang out gaily:

"I's g'wine back to Dixie, I's g'wine back to Dixie, I's g'wine where de orange blossoms grow, For I hear de chillun callin', I see de sad tears fallin'—My heart's turned back to Dixie, An' I mus'go."

She broke off to exclaim: "Oh! What a lovely place! See that arbor—just covered with grapes!"

Again and again she was attracted by the small places they passed. Now it was: "Look at the flowers!" or: "My! those vegetables!" or: "See! They've got a cow!"

Men—Americans—driving along in buggies or runabouts looked at Saxon and Billy curiously. This Saxon could brook far easier than could Billy, who would mutter and grumble deep in his throat.

Beside the road they came upon a lineman eating his lunch.

CHAPTER I

"Stop and talk," Saxon whispered.

"Aw, what's the good? He's a lineman. What'd he know about farmin'?"

"You never can tell. He's our kind. Go ahead, Billy. You just speak to him. He isn't working now anyway, and he'll be more likely to talk. See that tree in there, just inside the gate, and the way the branches are grown together. It's a curiosity. Ask him about it. That's a good way to get started."

Billy stopped, when they were alongside.

"How do you do," he said gruffly.

The lineman, a young fellow, paused in the cracking of a hard-boiled egg to stare up at the couple.

"How do you do," he said.

Billy swung his pack from his shoulders to the ground, and Saxon rested her telescope basket.

"Peddlin'?" the young man asked, too discreet to put his question directly to Saxon, yet dividing it between her and Billy, and cocking his eye at the covered basket.

"No," she spoke up quickly. "We're looking for land. Do you know of any around here?"

Again he desisted from the egg, studying them with sharp eyes as if to fathom their financial status.

"Do you know what land sells for around here?" he asked.

"No," Saxon answered. "Do you?"

"I guess I ought to. I was born here. And land like this all around you runs at from two to three hundred to four an' five hundred dollars an acre."

"Whew!" Billy whistled. "I guess we don't want none of it."

"But what makes it that high? Town lots?" Saxon wanted to know.

"Nope. The Porchugeeze make it that high, I guess."

"I thought it was pretty good land that fetched a hundred an acre," Billy said.

"Oh, them times is past. They used to give away land once, an' if you was good, throw in all the cattle runnin' on it."

"How about government land around here?" was Billy'a next query.

"Ain't none, an' never was. This was old Mexican grants. My grandfather bought sixteen hundred of the best acres around here for fifteen hundred dollars—five hundred down an' the balance in five years without interest. But that was in the early days. He come West in '48, tryin' to find a country without chills an' fever."

"He found it all right," said Billy.

"You bet he did. An' if him an' father 'd held onto the land it'd been better than a gold mine, an' I wouldn't be workin' for a livin'. What's your business?"

"Teamster."

"Ben in the strike in Oakland?"

"Sure thing. I've teamed there most of my life."

Here the two men wandered off into a discussion of union affairs and the strike situation; but Saxon refused to be balked, and brought back the talk to the land.

"How was it the Portuguese ran up the price of lend?" she asked.

The young fellow broke away from union matters with an effort, and for a moment regarded her with lack luster eyes, until the question sank into his consciousness.

"Because they worked the land overtime. Because they worked mornin', noon, an' night, all hands, women an' kids. Because they could get more out of twenty acres than we could out of a hundred an' sixty. Look at old Silva—Antonio Silva. I've known him ever since I was a shaver. He didn't have the price of a square meal when he hit this section and begun leasin' land from my folks. Look at him now—worth two hundred an' fifty thousan' cold, an' I bet he's got credit for a million, an' there's no tellin' what the rest of his family owns."

"And he made all that out of your folks' land?" Saxon demanded.

The young man nodded his head with evident reluctance.

"Then why didn't your folks do it?" she pursued.

The lineman shrugged his shoulders.

"Search me," he said.

"But the money was in the land," she persisted.

"Blamed if it was," came the retort, tinged slightly with color. "We never saw it stickin' out so as you could notice it. The money was in the hands of the Porchugeeze, I guess. They knew a few more 'n we did, that's all."

Saxon showed such dissatisfaction with his explanation that he was stung to action. He got up wrathfully. "Come on, an' I'll show you," he said. "I'll show you why I'm workin' for wages when I might a-ben a millionaire if my folks hadn't been mutts. That's what we old Americans are, Mutts, with a capital M."

He led them inside the gate, to the fruit tree that had first attracted Saxon's attention. From the main crotch diverged the four main branches of the tree. Two feet above the crotch the branches were connected, each to the ones on both sides, by braces of living wood.

"You think it growed that way, eh? Well, it did. But it was old Silva that made it just the same—caught two sprouts, when the tree was young, an' twisted 'em together. Pretty slick, eh? You bet. That tree'll never blow down. It's a natural, springy brace, an' beats iron braces stiff. Look along all the rows. Every tree's that way. See? An' that's just one trick of the Porchugeeze. They got a million like it.

"Figure it out for yourself. They don't need props when the crop's heavy. Why, when we had a heavy crop, we used to use five props to a tree. Now take ten acres of trees. That'd be some several thousan' props. Which cost money, an' labor to put in an' take out every year. These here natural braces don't have to have a thing done. They're Johnny-on-the-spot all the time. Why, the Porchugeeze has got us skinned a mile. Come on, I'll show you."

Billy, with city notions of trespass, betrayed perturbation at the freedom they were making of the little farm.

"Oh, it's all right, as long as you don't step on nothin'," the lineman reassured him. "Besides, my grandfather used to own this. They know me. Forty years ago old Silva come from the Azores. Went sheep-herdin' in the mountains for a couple of years, then blew in to San Leandro. These five acres was the first land he leased. That was the beginnin'. Then he began leasin' by the hundreds of acres, an' by the hundred-an'-sixties. An' his sisters an' his uncles an' his aunts begun pourin' in from the Azores—they're all related there, you know; an' pretty soon San Leandro was a regular Porchugeeze settlement.

"An' old Silva wound up by buyin' these five acres from grandfather. Pretty soon—an' father by that time was in the hole to the neck—he was buyin' father's land by the hundred-an'-sixties. An' all the rest of his relations was coin' the same thing. Father was always gettin' rich quick, an' he wound up by dyin' in debt. But old Silva never overlooked a bet, no matter how dinky. An' all the rest are just like him. You see outside the fence there, clear to the wheel-tracks in the road—horse-beans. We'd a-scorned to do a picayune thing like that. Not Silva. Why he's got a town house in San Leandro now. An' he rides around in a four-thousan'-dollar tourin' car. An' just the same his front door yard grows onions clear to the sidewalk. He clears three hundred a year on that patch alone. I know ten acres of land he bought last year,—a thousan' an acre they asked'm, an' he never batted an eye. He knew it was worth it, that's all. He knew he could make it pay. Back in the hills, there, he's got a ranch of five hundred an' eighty acres, bought it dirt cheap, too; an' I want to tell you I could travel around in a different tourin' car every day in the week just outa the profits he makes on that ranch from the horses all the way from heavy draughts to fancy steppers.

"But how?—how?—how did he get it all?" Saxon clamored.

"By bein' wise to farmin'. Why, the whole blame family works. They ain't ashamed to roll up their sleeves an' dig—sons an' daughters an' daughter-in-laws, old man, old woman, an' the babies. They have a sayin' that a kid four years old that can't pasture one cow on the county road an' keep it fat ain't worth his salt. Why, the Silvas, the whole tribe of 'em, works a hundred acres in peas, eighty in tomatoes, thirty in asparagus, ten in pie-plant, forty in cucumbers, an'—oh, stacks of other things."

"But how do they do it?" Saxon continued to demand. "We've never been ashamed to work. We've worked hard all our lives. I can out-work any Portuguese woman ever born. And I've done it, too, in the jute mills. There were lots of Portuguese girls working at the looms all around me, and I could out-weave them, every day, and I did, too. It isn't a case of work. What is it?"

The lineman looked at her in a troubled way.

"Many's the time I've asked myself that same question. 'We're better'n these cheap emigrants,' I'd say to myself. 'We was here first, an' owned the land. I can lick any Dago that ever hatched in the Azores. I got a better education. Then how in thunder do they put it all over us, get our land, an' start accounts in the banks?' An' the only answer I know is that we ain't got the sabe. We don't use our head-pieces right. Something's wrong with us. Anyway, we wasn't wised up to farming. We played at it. Show you? That's what I brung you in for—the way old Silva an' all his tribe farms. Book at this place. Some cousin of his, just out from the Azores, is makin' a start on it, an' payin' good rent to Silva. Pretty soon he'll be up to snuff an' buyin' land for himself from some perishin' American farmer.

"Look at that—though you ought to see it in summer. Not an inch wasted. Where we got one thin crop, they get four fat crops. An' look at the way they crowd it—currants between the tree rows, beans between the currant rows, a row of beans close on each side of the trees, an' rows of beans along the ends of the tree rows. Why, Silva wouldn't sell these five acres for five hundred an acre cash down. He gave grandfather fifty an acre for it on long time, an' here am I, workin' for the telephone company an' putting' in a telephone for old Silva's cousin from the Azores that can't speak American yet. Horse-beans along the road—say, when Silva swung that trick he made more outa fattenin' hogs with 'em than grandfather made with all his farmin'. Grandfather stuck up his nose at horse-beans. He died with it stuck up, an' with more mortgages on the land he had left than you could shake a stick at. Plantin' tomatoes wrapped up in wrappin' paper—ever heard of that? Father snorted when he first seen the Porchugeeze doin' it. An' he went on snortin'. Just the same they got bumper crops, an' father's house-patch of tomatoes was eaten by the black beetles. We ain't got the sabe, or the knack, or something or other. Just look at this piece of ground—four crops a year, an' every inch of soil workin' over time. Why, back in town there, there's single acres that earns more than fifty of ours in the old days. The Porchugeeze is natural-born farmers, that's all, an' we don't know nothin' about farmin' an' never did."

Saxon talked with the lineman, following him about, till one o'clock, when he looked at his watch, said good bye, and returned to his task of putting in a telephone for the latest immigrant from the Azores.

When in town, Saxon carried her oilcloth-wrapped telescope in her hand; but it was so arranged with loops, that, once on the road, she could thrust her arms through the loops and carry it on her back. When she did this, the tiny ukulele case was shifted so that it hung under her left arm.

A mile on from the lineman, they stopped where a small creek, fringed with brush, crossed the county road. Billy was for the cold lunch, which was the last meal Saxon had prepared in the Pine street cottage; but she was determined upon building a fire and boiling coffee. Not that she desired it for herself, but that she was impressed with the idea that everything at the starting of their strange wandering must be as comfortable as possible for Billy's sake. Bent on inspiring him with enthusiasm equal to her own, she declined to dampen what sparks he had caught by anything so uncheerful as a cold meal.

"Now one thing we want to get out of our heads right at the start, Billy, is that we're in a hurry. We're not in a hurry, and we don't care whether school keeps or not. We're out to have a good time, a regular adventure like you read about in books.—My! I wish that boy that took me fishing to Goat Island could see me now. Oakland was just a place to start from, he said. And, well, we've started, haven't we? And right here's where we stop and boil coffee. You get the fire going, Billy, and I'll get the water and the things ready to spread out."

"Say," Billy remarked, while they waited for the water to boil, "d'ye know what this reminds me of?"

Saxon was certain she did know, but she shook her head. She wanted to hear him say it.

"Why, the second Sunday I knew you, when we drove out to Moraga Valley behind Prince and King. You spread the lunch that day."

"Only it was a more scrumptious lunch," she added, with a happy smile.

"But I wonder why we didn't have coffee that day," he went on.

"Perhaps it would have been too much like housekeeping," she laughed; "kind of what Mary would call indelicate—"

"Or raw," Billy interpolated. "She was always springin' that word."

"And yet look what became of her."

"That's the way with all of them," Billy growled somberly. "I've always noticed it's the fastidious, la-de-da ones that turn out the rottenest. They're like some horses I know, a-shyin' at the things they're the least afraid of."

Saxon was silent, oppressed by a sadness, vague and remote, which the mention of Bert's widow had served to bring on.

CHAPTER I

"I know something else that happened that day which you'd never guess," Billy reminisced. "I bet you couldn't.

"I wonder," Saxon murmured, and guessed it with her eyes.

Billy's eyes answered, and quite spontaneously he reached over, caught her hand, and pressed it caressingly to his cheek.

"It's little, but oh my," he said, addressing the imprisoned hand. Then he gazed at Saxon, and she warmed with his words. "We're beginnin' courtin' all over again, ain't we?"

Both ate heartily, and Billy was guilty of three cups of coffee.

"Say, this country air gives some appetite," he mumbled, as he sank his teeth into his fifth bread-and-meat sandwich. "I could eat a horse, an' drown his head off in coffee afterward."

Saxon's mind had reverted to all the young lineman had told her, and she completed a sort of general resume of the information. "My!" she exclaimed, "but we've learned a lot!"

"An' we've sure learned one thing," Billy said. "An' that is that this is no place for us, with land a thousan' an acre an' only twenty dollars in our pockets."

"Oh, we're not going to stop here," she hastened to say.

"But just the same it's the Portuguese that gave it its price, and they make things go on it—send their children to school... and have them; and, as you said yourself, they're as fat as butterballs."

"An' I take my hat off to them," Billy responded.

"But all the same, I'd sooner have forty acres at a hundred an acre than four at a thousan' an acre. Somehow, you know, I'd be scared stiff on four acres—scared of fallin' off, you know."

She was in full sympathy with him. In her heart of hearts the forty acres tugged much the harder. In her way, allowing for the difference of a generation, her desire for spaciousness was as strong as her Uncle Will's.

"Well, we're not going to stop here," she assured Billy. "We're going in, not for forty acres, but for a hundred and sixty acres free from the government."

"An' I guess the government owes it to us for what our fathers an' mothers done. I tell you, Saxon, when a woman walks across the plains like your mother done, an' a man an' wife gets massacred by the Indians like my grandfather an' mother done, the government does owe them something."

"Well, it's up to us to collect."

"An' we'll collect all right, all right, somewhere down in them redwood mountains south of Monterey."

CHAPTER II

It was a good afternoon's tramp to Niles, passing through the town of Haywards; yet Saxon and Billy found time to diverge from the main county road and take the parallel roads through acres of intense cultivation where the land was farmed to the wheel-tracks. Saxon looked with amazement at these small, brown-skinned immigrants who came to the soil with nothing and yet made the soil pay for itself to the tune of two hundred, of five hundred, and of a thousand dollars an acre.

On every hand was activity. Women and children were in the fields as well as men. The land was turned endlessly over and over. They seemed never to let it rest. And it rewarded them. It must reward them, or their children would not be able to go to school, nor would so many of them be able to drive by in rattletrap, second-hand buggies or in stout light wagons.

"Look at their faces," Saxon said. "They are happy and contented. They haven't faces like the people in our neighborhood after the strikes began."

"Oh, sure, they got a good thing," Billy agreed. "You can see it stickin' out all over them. But they needn't get chesty with ME, I can tell you that much—just because they've jiggerooed us out of our land an' everything."

"But they're not showing any signs of chestiness," Saxon demurred.

"No, they're not, come to think of it. All the same, they ain't so wise. I bet I could tell 'em a few about horses."

It was sunset when they entered the little town of Niles. Billy, who had been silent for the last half mile, hesitantly ventured a suggestion.

"Say... I could put up for a room in the hotel just as well as not. What d 'ye think?"

But Saxon shook her head emphatically.

"How long do you think our twenty dollars will last at that rate? Besides, the only way to begin is to begin at the beginning. We didn't plan sleeping in hotels."

"All right," he gave in. "I'm game. I was just thinkin' about you."

"Then you'd better think I'm game, too," she flashed forgivingly. "And now we'll have to see about getting things for supper."

They bought a round steak, potatoes, onions, and a dozen eating apples, then went out from the town to the fringe of trees and brush that advertised a creek. Beside the trees, on a sand bank, they pitched camp. Plenty of dry wood lay about, and Billy whistled genially while he gathered and chopped. Saxon, keen to follow his every mood, was cheered by the atrocious discord on his lips. She smiled to herself as she spread the blankets, with the tarpaulin underneath, for a table, having first removed all twigs from the sand. She had much to learn in the matter of cooking over a camp-fire, and made fair progress, discovering, first of all, that control of the fire meant far more than the size of it. When the coffee was boiled, she settled the grounds with a part-cup of cold water and placed the pot on the edge of the coals where it would keep hot and yet not boil. She fried potato dollars and onions in the same pan, but separately, and set them on top of the coffee pot in the tin plate she was to eat from, covering it with Billy's inverted plate. On the dry hot pan, in the way that delighted Billy, she fried the steak. This completed, and while Billy poured the coffee, she served the steak, putting the dollars and onions back into the frying pan for a moment to make them piping hot again.

"What more d'ye want than this?" Billy challenged with deep-toned satisfaction, in the pause after his final cup of coffee, while he rolled a cigarette. He lay on his side, full length, resting on his elbow. The fire was burning brightly, and Saxon's color was heightened by the flickering flames. "Now our folks, when they was on the move, had to be afraid for Indians, and wild animals and all sorts of things; an' here we are, as safe as bugs in a rug. Take this sand. What better bed could you ask? Soft as feathers. Say—you look good to me, heap little squaw. I bet you don't look an inch over sixteen right now, Mrs. Babe-in-the-Woods."

"Don't I?" she glowed, with a flirt of the head sideward and a white flash of teeth. "If you weren't smoking a cigarette I'd ask you if your mother knew you're out, Mr. Babe-in-the-Sandbank."

"Say," he began, with transparently feigned seriousness. "I want to ask you something, if you don't mind. Now, of course, I don't want to hurt your feelin's or nothin', but just the same there's something important I'd like to know."

"Well, what is it?" she inquired, after a fruitless wait.

"Well, it's just this, Saxon. I like you like anything an' all that, but here's night come on, an' we're a thousand miles from anywhere, and—well, what I wanta know is: are we really an' truly married, you an' me?"

"Really and truly," she assured him. "Why?"

"Oh, nothing; but I'd kind a-forgotten, an' I was gettin' embarrassed, you know, because if we wasn't, seein' the way I was brought up, this'd be no place—"

"That will do you," she said severely. "And this is just the time and place for you to get in the firewood for morning while I wash up the dishes and put the kitchen in order."

He started to obey, but paused to throw his arm about her and draw her close. Neither spoke, but when he went his way Saxon's breast was fluttering and a song of thanksgiving breathed on her lips.

The night had come on, dim with the light of faint stars. But these had disappeared behind clouds that seemed to have arisen from nowhere. It was the beginning of California Indian summer. The air was warm, with just the first hint of evening chill, and there was no wind.

"I've a feeling as if we've just started to live," Saxon said, when Billy, his firewood collected, joined her on the blankets before the fire. "I've learned more to-day than ten years in Oakland." She drew a long breath and braced her shoulders. "Farming's a bigger subject than I thought."

Billy said nothing. With steady eyes he was staring into the fire, and she knew he was turning something over in his mind.

"What is it," she asked, when she saw he had reached a conclusion, at the same time resting her hand on the back of his.

"Just been framin' up that ranch of ourn," he answered. "It's all well enough, these dinky farmlets. They'll do for foreigners. But we Americans just gotta have room. I want to be able to look at a hilltop an' know it's my land, and know it's my land down the other side an' up the next hilltop, an' know that over beyond that, down alongside some creek, my mares are most likely grazin', an' their little colts grazin' with 'em or kickin' up their heels. You know, there's money in raisin' horses—especially the big workhorses that run to eighteen hundred an' two thousand pounds. They're payin' for 'em, in the cities, every day in the year, seven an' eight hundred a pair, matched geldings, four years old. Good pasture an' plenty of it, in this kind of a climate, is all they need, along with some sort of shelter an' a little hay in long spells of bad weather. I never thought of it before, but let me tell you that this ranch proposition is beginnin' to look good to ME."

Saxon was all excitement. Here was new information on the cherished subject, and, best of all, Billy was the authority. Still better, he was taking an interest himself.

"There'll be room for that and for everything on a quarter section," she encouraged.

"Sure thing. Around the house we'll have vegetables an' fruit and chickens an' everything, just like the Porchugeeze, an' plenty of room beside to walk around an' range the horses."

"But won't the colts cost money, Billy?"

"Not much. The cobblestones eat horses up fast. That's where I'll get my brood mares, from the ones knocked out by the city. I know THAT end of it. They sell 'em at auction, an' they're good for years an' years, only no good on the cobbles any more."

There ensued a long pause. In the dying fire both were busy visioning the farm to be.

"It's pretty still, ain't it?" Billy said, rousing himself at last. He gazed about him. "An' black as a stack of black cats." He shivered, buttoned his coat, and tossed several sticks on the fire. "Just the same, it's the best kind of a climate in the world. Many's the time, when I was a little kid, I've heard my father brag about California's bein' a blanket climate. He went East, once, an' staid a summer an' a winter, an' got all he wanted. Never again for him."

"My mother said there never was such a land for climate. How wonderful it must have seemed to them after crossing the deserts and mountains. They called it the land of milk and honey. The ground was so rich that all they needed to do was scratch it, Cady used to say."

"And wild game everywhere," Billy contributed. "Mr. Roberts, the one that adopted my father, he drove cattle from the San Josquin to the Columbia river. He had forty men helpin' him, an' all they took along was powder an' salt. They lived off the game they shot."

"The hills were full of deer, and my mother saw whole herds of elk around Santa Rosa. Some time we'll go there, Billy. I've always wanted to."

"And when my father was a young man, somewhere up north of Sacramento, in a creek called Cache Slough, the tules was full of grizzliest He used to go in an' shoot 'em. An' when they caught 'em in the open, he an' the Mexicans used to ride up an' rope them—catch them with lariats, you know. He said a horse that wasn't afraid of grizzlies fetched ten times as much as any other horse An' panthers!—all the old folks called 'em painters an' catamounts an' varmints. Yes, we'll go to Santa Rosa some time. Maybe we won't like that land down the coast, an' have to keep on hikin'."

By this time the fire had died down, and Saxon had finished brushing and braiding her hair. Their bed-going preliminaries were simple, and in a few minutes they were side by side under the blankets. Saxon closed her eyes, but could not sleep. On the contrary, she had never been more wide awake. She had never slept out of doors in her life, and by no exertion of will could she overcome the strangeness of it. In addition, she was stiffened from the long trudge, and the sand, to her surprise, was anything but soft. An hour passed. She tried to believe that Billy was asleep, but felt certain he was not. The sharp crackle of a dying ember startled her. She was confident that Billy had moved slightly.

"Billy," she whispered, "are you awake?"

"Yep," came his low answer, "—an' thinkin' this sand is harder'n a cement floor. It's one on me, all right. But who'd a-thought it?"

Both shifted their postures slightly, but vain was the attempt to escape from the dull, aching contact of the sand.

An abrupt, metallic, whirring noise of some nearby cricket gave Saxon another startle. She endured the sound for some minutes, until Billy broke forth.

"Say, that gets my goat whatever it is."

"Do you think it's a rattlesnake?" she asked, maintaining a calmness she did not feel.

"Just what I've been thinkin'."

"I saw two, in the window of Bowman's Drug Store An' you know, Billy, they've got a hollow fang, and when they stick it into you the poison runs down the hollow."

"Br-r-r-r," Billy shivered, in fear that was not altogether mockery. "Certain death, everybody says, unless you're a Bosco. Remember him?"

"He eats 'em alive! He eats 'em alive! Bosco! Bosco!" Saxon responded, mimicking the cry of a side-show barker. "Just the same, all Bosco's rattlers had the poison-sacs cut outa them. They must a-had. Gee! It's funny I can't get asleep. I wish that damned thing'd close its trap. I wonder if it is a rattlesnake."

"No; it can't be," Saxon decided. "All the rattlesnakes are killed off long ago."

"Then where did Bosco get his?" Billy demanded with unimpeachable logic. "An' why don't you get to sleep?"

"Because it's all new, I guess," was her reply. "You see, I never camped out in my life."

"Neither did I. An' until now I always thought it was a lark." He changed his position on the maddening sand and sighed heavily. "But we'll get used to it in time, I guess. What other folks can do, we can, an' a mighty lot of 'em has camped out. It's all right. Here we are, free an' independent, no rent to pay, our own bosses—"

He stopped abruptly. From somewhere in the brush came an intermittent rustling. When they tried to locate it, it mysteriously ceased, and when the first hint of drowsiness stole upon them the rustling as mysteriously recommenced.

"It sounds like something creeping up on us," Saxon suggested, snuggling closer to Billy.

"Well, it ain't a wild Indian, at all events," was the best he could offer in the way of comfort. He yawned deliberately. "Aw, shucks! What's there to be scared of? Think of what all the pioneers went through."

Several minutes later his shoulders began to shake, and Saxon knew he was giggling.

"I was just thinkin' of a yarn my father used to tell about," he explained. "It was about old Susan Kleghorn, one of the Oregon pioneer women. Wall-Eyed Susan, they used to call her; but she could shoot to beat the band. Once, on the Plains, the wagon train she was in, was attacked by Indians. They got all the wagons in a circle, an' all hands an' the oxen inside, an' drove the Indians off, killin' a lot of 'em. They was too strong that way, so what'd the Indians do, to draw 'em out into the open, but take two white girls, captured from some other train, an' begin to torture 'em. They done it just out of gunshot, but so everybody could see. The idea was that the white men couldn't stand it, an' would rush out, an' then the Indians'd have 'em where they wanted 'em.

"The white men couldn't do a thing. If they rushed out to save the girls, they'd be finished, an' then the Indians'd rush the train. It meant death to everybody. But what does old Susan do, but get out an old, long-barreled Kentucky rifle. She rams down about three times the regular load of powder, takes aim at a big buck that's pretty busy at the torturin', an' bangs away. It knocked her clean over backward, an' her shoulder was lame all the rest of the way to Oregon, but she dropped the big Indian deado. He never knew what struck 'm.

"But that wasn't the yarn I wanted to tell. It seems old Susan liked John Barleycorn. She'd souse herself to the ears every chance she got. An' her sons an' daughters an' the old man had to be mighty careful not to leave any around where she could get hands on it."

"On what?" asked Saxon.

"On John Barleycorn.—Oh, you ain't on to that. It's the old fashioned name for whisky. Well, one day all the folks was goin' away—that was over somewhere at a place called Bodega, where they'd settled after comin' down from Oregon. An' old Susan claimed her rheumatics was hurtin' her an' so she couldn't go. But the family was on. There was a two-gallon demijohn of whisky in the house. They said all right, but before they left they sent one of the grandsons to climb a big tree in the barnyard, where he tied the demijohn sixty feet from the ground. Just the same, when they come home that night they found Susan on the kitchen floor dead to the world."

"And she'd climbed the tree after all," Saxon hazarded, when Billy had shown no inclination of going on.

"Not on your life," he laughed jubilantly. "All she'd done was to put a washtub on the ground square under the demijohn. Then she got out her old rifle an' shot the demijohn to smithereens, an' all she had to do was lap the whisky outa the tub."

Again Saxon was drowsing, when the rustling sound was heard, this time closer. To her excited apprehension there was something stealthy about it, and she imagined a beast of prey creeping upon them. "Billy," she whispered.

"Yes, I'm a-listenin' to it," came his wide awake answer.

"Mightn't that be a panther, or maybe... a wildcat?"

"It can't be. All the varmints was killed off long ago. This is peaceable farmin' country."

CHAPTER II

A vagrant breeze sighed through the trees and made Saxon shiver. The mysterious cricket-noise ceased with suspicious abruptness. Then, from the rustling noise, ensued a dull but heavy thump that caused both Saxon and Billy to sit up in the blankets. There were no further sounds, and they lay down again, though the very silence now seemed ominous.

"Huh," Billy muttered with relief. "As though I don't know what it was. It was a rabbit. I've heard tame ones bang their hind feet down on the floor that way."

In vain Saxon tried to win sleep. The sand grew harder with the passage of time. Her flesh and her bones ached from contact with it. And, though her reason flouted any possibility of wild dangers, her fancy went on picturing them with unflagging zeal.

A new sound commenced. It was neither a rustling nor a rattling, and it tokened some large body passing through the brush. Sometimes twigs crackled and broke, and, once, they heard bush-branches press aside and spring back into place.

"If that other thing was a panther, this is an elephant," was Billy's uncheering opinion. "It's got weight. Listen to that. An' it's comin' nearer."

There were frequent stoppages, then the sounds would begin again, always louder, always closer. Billy sat up in the blankets once more, passing one arm around Saxon, who had also sat up.

"I ain't slept a wink," he complained. "—There it goes again. I wish I could see."

"It makes a noise big enough for a grizzly," Saxon chattered, partly from nervousness, partly from the chill of the night.

"It ain't no grasshopper, that's sure."

Billy started to leave the blankets, but Saxon caught his arm.

"What are you going to do?"

"Oh, I ain't scairt none," he answered. "But, honest to God, this is gettin' on my nerves. If I don't find what that thing is, it'll give me the willies. I'm just goin' to reconnoiter. I won't go close."

So intensely dark was the night, that the moment Billy crawled beyond the reach of her hand he was lost to sight. She sat and waited. The sound had ceased, though she could follow Billy's progress by the cracking of dry twigs and limbs. After a few moments he returned and crawled under the blankets.

"I scared it away, I guess. It's got better ears, an' when it heard me comin' it skinned out most likely. I did my dangdest, too, not to make a sound.—O Lord, there it goes again."

They sat up. Saxon nudged Billy.

"There," she warned, in the faintest of whispers. "I can hear it breathing. It almost made a snort."

A dead branch cracked loudly, and so near at hand, that both of them jumped shamelessly.

"I ain't goin' to stand any more of its foolin'," Billy declared wrathfully. "It'll be on top of us if I don't."

"What are you going to do?" she queried anxiously.

"Yell the top of my head off. I'll get a fall outa whatever it is."

He drew a deep breath and emitted a wild yell.

The result far exceeded any expectation he could have entertained, and Saxon's heart leaped up in sheer panic. On the instant the darkness erupted into terrible sound and movement. There were trashings of underbrush and lunges and plunges of heavy bodies in different directions. Fortunately for their ease of mind, all these sounds receded and died away.

"An' what d'ye think of that?" Billy broke the silence.

"Gee! all the fight fans used to say I was scairt of nothin'. Just the same I'm glad they ain't seein' me to-night."

He groaned. "I've got all I want of that blamed sand. I'm goin' to get up and start the fire."

This was easy. Under the ashes were live embers which quickly ignited the wood he threw on. A few stars were peeping out in the misty zenith. He looked up at them, deliberated, and started to move away.

"Where are you going now?" Saxon called.

"Oh, I've got an idea," he replied noncommittally, and walked boldly away beyond the circle of the firelight.

Saxon sat with the blankets drawn closely under her chin, and admired his courage. He had not even taken the hatchet, and he was going in the direction in which the disturbance had died away.

Ten minutes later he came back chuckling.

"The sons-of-guns, they got my goat all right. I'll be scairt of my own shadow next.—What was they? Huh! You couldn't guess in a thousand years. A bunch of half-grown calves, an' they was worse scairt than us."

He smoked a cigarette by the fire, then rejoined Saxon under the blankets.

"A hell of a farmer I'll make," he chafed, "when a lot of little calves can scare the stuffin' outa me. I bet your father or mine wouldn't a-batted an eye. The stock has gone to seed, that's what it has."

"No, it hasn't," Saxon defended. "The stock is all right. We're just as able as our folks ever were, and we're healthier on top of it. We've been brought up different, that's all. We've lived in cities all our lives. We know the city sounds and thugs, but we don't know the country ones. Our training has been unnatural, that's the whole thing in a nutshell. Now we're going in for natural training. Give us a little time, and we'll sleep as sound out of doors as ever your father or mine did."

"But not on sand," Billy groaned.

"We won't try. That's one thing, for good and all, we've learned the very first time. And now hush up and go to sleep."

Their fears had vanished, but the sand, receiving now their undivided attention, multiplied its unyieldingness. Billy dozed off first, and roosters were crowing somewhere in the distance when Saxon's eyes closed. But they could not escape the sand, and their sleep was fitful.

At the first gray of dawn, Billy crawled out and built a roaring fire. Saxon drew up to it shiveringly. They were hollow-eyed and weary. Saxon began to laugh. Billy joined sulkily, then brightened up as his eyes chanced upon the coffee pot, which he immediately put on to boil.

CHAPTER III

It is forty miles from Oakland to San Jose, and Saxon and Billy accomplished it in three easy days. No more obliging and angrily garrulous linemen were encountered, and few were the opportunities for conversation with chance wayfarers. Numbers of tramps, carrying rolls of blankets, were met, traveling both north and south on the county road; and from talks with them Saxon quickly learned that they knew little or nothing about farming. They were mostly old men, feeble or besotted, and all they knew was work—where jobs might be good, where jobs had been good; but the places they mentioned were always a long way off. One thing she did glean from them, and that was that the district she and Billy were passing through was "small-farmer" country in which labor was rarely hired, and that when it was it generally was Portuguese.

The farmers themselves were unfriendly. They drove by Billy and Saxon, often with empty wagons, but never invited them to ride. When chance offered and Saxon did ask questions, they looked her over curiously, or suspiciously, and gave ambiguous and facetious answers.

"They ain't Americans, damn them," Billy fretted. "Why, in the old days everybody was friendly to everybody."

But Saxon remembered her last talk with her brother.

"It's the spirit of the times, Billy. The spirit has changed. Besides, these people are too near. Wait till we get farther away from the cities, then we'll find them more friendly."

"A measly lot these ones are," he sneered.

"Maybe they've a right to be," she laughed. "For all you know, more than one of the scabs you've slugged were sons of theirs."

"If I could only hope so," Billy said fervently. "But I don't care if I owned ten thousand acres, any man hikin' with his blankets might be just as good a man as me, an' maybe better, for all I'd know. I'd give 'm the benefit of the doubt, anyway."

Billy asked for work, at first, indiscriminately, later, only at the larger farms. The unvarying reply was that there was no work. A few said there would be plowing after the first rains. Here and there, in a small way, dry plowing was going on. But in the main the farmers were waiting.

"But do you know how to plow?" Saxon asked Billy.

"No; but I guess it ain't much of a trick to turn. Besides, next man I see plowing I'm goin' to get a lesson from."

In the mid-afternoon of the second day his opportunity came. He climbed on top of the fence of a small field and watched an old man plow round and round it.

"Aw, shucks, just as easy as easy," Billy commented scornfully. "If an old codger like that can handle one plow, I can handle two."

"Go on and try it," Saxon urged.

"What's the good?"

"Cold feet," she jeered, but with a smiling face. "All you have to do is ask him. All he can do is say no. And what if he does? You faced the Chicago Terror twenty rounds without flinching."

"Aw, but it's different," he demurred, then dropped to the ground inside the fence. "Two to one the old geezer turns me down."

"No, he won't. Just tell him you want to learn, and ask him if he'll let you drive around a few times. Tell him it won't cost him anything."

"Huh! If he gets chesty I'll take his blamed plow away from him."

From the top of the fence, but too far away to hear, Saxon watched the colloquy. After several minutes, the lines were transferred to Billy's neck, the handles to his hands. Then the team started, and the old man, delivering a rapid fire of instructions, walked alongside of Billy. When a few turns had been made, the farmer crossed the plowed strip to Saxon, and joined her on the rail.

"He's plowed before, a little mite, ain't he?"

Saxon shook her head.

"Never in his life. But he knows how to drive horses."

"He showed he wasn't all greenhorn, an' he learns pretty quick." Here the farmer chuckled and cut himself a chew from a plug of tobacco. "I reckon he won't tire me out a-settin' here."

The unplowed area grew smaller and smaller, but Billy evinced no intention of quitting, and his audience on the fence was deep in conversation. Saxon's questions flew fast and furious, and she was not long in concluding that the old man bore a striking resemblance to the description the lineman had given of his father.

Billy persisted till the field was finished, and the old man invited him and Saxon to stop for the night. There was a disused outbuilding where they would find a small cook stove, he said, and also he would give them fresh milk. Further, if Saxon wanted to test HER desire for farming, she could try her hand on the cow.

The milking lesson did not prove as successful as Billy's plowing; but when he had mocked sufficiently, Saxon challenged him to try, and he failed as grievously as she. Saxon had eyes and questions for everything, and it did not take her long to realize that she was looking upon the other side of the farming shield. Farm and farmer were old-fashioned. There was no intensive cultivation. There was too much land too little farmed. Everything was slipshod. House and barn and outbuildings were fast falling into ruin. The front yard was weed-grown. There was no vegetable garden. The small orchard was old, sickly, and neglected. The trees were twisted, spindling, and overgrown with a gray moss. The sons and daughters were away in the cities, Saxon found out. One daughter had married a doctor, the other was a teacher in the state normal school; one son was a locomotive engineer, the second was an architect, and the third was a police court reporter in San Francisco. On occasion, the father said, they helped out the old folks.

"What do you think?" Saxon asked Billy as he smoked his after-supper cigarette.

CHAPTER III

His shoulders went up in a comprehensive shrug.

"Huh! That's easy. The old geezer's like his orchard—covered with moss. It's plain as the nose on your face, after San Leandro, that he don't know the first thing. An' them horses. It'd be a charity to him, an' a savin' of money for him, to take 'em out an' shoot 'em both. You bet you don't see the Porchugeeze with horses like them. An' it ain't a case of bein' proud, or puttin' on side, to have good horses. It's brass tacks an' business. It pays. That's the game. Old horses eat more in young ones to keep in condition an' they can't do the same amount of work. But you bet it costs just as much to shoe them. An' his is scrub on top of it. Every minute he has them horses he's losin' money. You oughta see the way they work an' figure horses in the city."

They slept soundly, and, after an early breakfast, prepared to start.

"I'd like to give you a couple of days' work," the old man regretted, at parting, "but I can't see it. The ranch just about keeps me and the old woman, now that the children are gone. An' then it don't always. Seems times have been bad for a long spell now. Ain't never been the same since Grover Cleveland."

Early in the afternoon, on the outskirts of San Jose, Saxon called a halt.

"I'm going right in there and talk," she declared, "unless they set the dogs on me. That's the prettiest place yet, isn't it?"

Billy, who was always visioning hills and spacious ranges for his horses, mumbled unenthusiastic assent.

"And the vegetables! Look at them! And the flowers growing along the borders! That beats tomato plants in wrapping paper."

"Don't see the sense of it," Billy objected. "Where's the money come in from flowers that take up the ground that good vegetables might be growin' on?"

"And that's what I'm going to find out." She pointed to a woman, stooped to the ground and working with a trowel; in front of the tiny bungalow. "I don't know what she's like, but at the worst she can only be mean. See! She's looking at us now. Drop your load alongside of mine, and come on in."

Billy slung the blankets from his shoulder to the ground, but elected to wait. As Saxon went up the narrow, flower-bordered walk, she noted two men at work among the vegetables—one an old Chinese, the other old and of some dark-eyed foreign breed. Here were neatness, efficiency, and intensive cultivation with a vengeance—even her untrained eye could see that. The woman stood up and turned from her flowers, and Saxon saw that she was middle-aged, slender, and simply but nicely dressed. She wore glasses, and Saxon's reading of her face was that it was kind but nervous looking.

"I don't want anything to-day," she said, before Saxon could speak, administering the rebuff with a pleasant smile.

Saxon groaned inwardly over the black-covered telescope basket. Evidently the woman had seen her put it down.

"We're not peddling," she explained quickly.

"Oh, I am sorry for the mistake."

This time the woman's smile was even pleasanter, and she waited for Saxon to state her errand.

Nothing loath, Saxon took it at a plunge.

"We're looking for land. We want to be farmers, you know, and before we get the land we want to find out what kind of land we want. And seeing your pretty place has just filled me up with questions. You see, we don't know anything about farming. We've lived in the city all our life, and now we've given it up and are going to live in the country and be happy."

She paused. The woman's face seemed to grow quizzical, though the pleasantness did not abate.

"But how do you know you will be happy in the country?" she asked.

"I don't know. All I do know is that poor people can't be happy in the city where they have labor troubles all the time. If they can't be happy in the country, then there's no happiness anywhere, and that doesn't seem fair, does it?"

"It is sound reasoning, my dear, as far as it goes. But you must remember that there are many poor people in the country and many unhappy people."

"You look neither poor nor unhappy," Saxon challenged.

"You ARE a dear."

Saxon saw the pleased flush in the other's face, which lingered as she went on.

"But still, I may be peculiarly qualified to live and succeed in the country. As you say yourself, you've spent your life in the city. You don't know the first thing about the country. It might even break your heart."

Saxon's mind went back to the terrible months in the Pine street cottage.

"I know already that the city will break my heart. Maybe the country will, too, but just the same it's my only chance, don't you see. It's that or nothing. Besides, our folks before us were all of the country. It seems the more natural way. And better, here I am, which proves that 'way down inside I must want the country, must, as you call it, be peculiarly qualified for the country, or else I wouldn't be here."

The other nodded approval, and looked at her with growing interest.

"That young man—" she began.

"Is my husband. He was a teamster until the big strike came. My name is Roberts, Saxon Roberts, and my husband is William Roberts."

"And I am Mrs. Mortimer," the other said, with a bow of acknowledgment. "I am a widow. And now, if you will ask your husband in, I shall try to answer some of your many questions. Tell him to put the bundles inside the gate.. .. And now what are all the questions you are filled with?"

"Oh, all kinds. How does it pay? How did you manage it all? How much did the land cost? Did you build that beautiful house? How much do you pay the men? How did you learn all the different kinds of things, and which grew best and which paid best? What is the best way to sell them? How do you sell them?" Saxon paused and laughed. "Oh, I haven't begun yet. Why do you have flowers on the borders everywhere? I looked over the Portuguese farms around San Leandro, but they never mixed flowers and vegetables."

Mrs. Mortimer held up her hand. "Let me answer the last first. It is the key to almost everything."

But Billy arrived, and the explanation was deferred until after his introduction.

"The flowers caught your eyes, didn't they, my dear?" Mrs. Mortimer resumed. "And brought you in through my gate and right up to me. And that's the very reason they were planted with the vegetables—to catch eyes. You can't imagine how many eyes they have caught, nor how many owners of eyes they have lured inside my gate. This is a good road, and is a very popular short country drive for townsfolk. Oh, no; I've never had any luck with automobiles. They can't see anything for dust. But I began when nearly everybody still used carriages. The townswomen would drive by. My flowers, and then my place, would catch their eyes. They would tell their drivers to stop. And—well, somehow, I managed to be in the front within speaking distance. Usually I succeeded in inviting them in to see my flowers... and vegetables, of course. Everything was sweet, clean, pretty. It all appealed. And—" Mrs. Mortimer shrugged her shoulders. "It is well known that the stomach sees through the eyes. The thought of vegetables growing among flowers pleased their fancy. They wanted my vegetables. They must have them. And they did, at double the market price, which they were only too glad to pay. You see, I became the fashion, or a fad, in a small way. Nobody lost. The vegetables were certainly good, as good as any on the market and often fresher. And, besides, my customers killed two birds with one stone; for they were pleased with themselves for philanthropic reasons. Not only did they obtain the finest and freshest possible vegetables, but at the same time they were happy with the knowledge that they were helping a deserving widow-woman. Yes, and it gave a certain tone to their establishments to be able to say they bought Mrs. Mortimer's vegetables. But that's too big a side to go into. In short, my little place became a show place—anywhere to go, for a drive or anything, you know, when time has to be killed. And it became noised about who I was, and who my husband had been, what I had been. Some of the townsladies I had known personally in the old days. They actually worked for my success. And then, too, I used to serve tea. My patrons became my guests for the time being. I still serve it, when they drive out to show me off to their friends. So you see, the flowers are one of the ways I succeeded."

Saxon was glowing with appreciation, but Mrs. Mortimer, glancing at Billy, noted not entire approval. His blue eyes were clouded.

"Well, out with it," she encouraged. "What are you thinking?"

To Saxon's surprise, he answered directly, and to her double surprise, his criticism was of a nature which had never entered her head.

"It's just a trick," Billy expounded. "That's what I was gettin' at—"

"But a paying trick," Mrs. Mortimer interrupted, her eyes dancing and vivacious behind the glasses.

"Yes, and no," Billy said stubbornly, speaking in his slow, deliberate fashion. "If every farmer was to mix flowers an' vegetables, then every farmer would get double the market price, an' then there wouldn't be any double market price. Everything'd be as it was before."

"You are opposing a theory to a fact," Mrs. Mortimer stated. "The fact is that all the farmers do not do it. The fact is that I do receive double the price. You can't get away from that."

Billy was unconvinced, though unable to reply.

"Just the same," he muttered, with a slow shake of the head, "I don't get the hang of it. There's something wrong so far as we're concerned—my wife an' me, I mean. Maybe I'll get hold of it after a while."

"And in the meantime, we'll look around," Mrs. Mortimer invited. "I want to show you everything, and tell you how I make it go. Afterward, we'll sit down, and I'll tell you about the beginning. You see—" she bent her gaze on Saxon—"I want you thoroughly to understand that you can succeed in the country if you go about it right. I didn't know a thing about it when I began, and I didn't have a fine big man like yours. I was all alone. But I'll tell you about that."

For the next hour, among vegetables, berry-bushes and fruit trees, Saxon stored her brain with a huge mass of information to be digested at her leisure. Billy, too, was interested, but he left the talking to Saxon, himself rarely asking a question. At the rear of the bungalow, where everything was as clean and orderly as the front, they were shown through the chicken yard. Here, in different runs, were kept several hundred small and snow-white hens.

"White Leghorns," said Mrs. Mortimer. "You have no idea what they netted me this year. I never keep a hen a moment past the prime of her laying period—"

"Just what I was tellin' you, Saxon, about horses," Billy broke in.

"And by the simplest method of hatching them at the right time, which not one farmer in ten thousand ever dreams of doing, I have them laying in the winter when most hens stop laying and when eggs are highest. Another thing: I have my special customers. They pay me ten cents a dozen more than the market price, because my specialty is one-day eggs."

Here she chanced to glance at Billy, and guessed that he was still wrestling with his problem.

"Sahne old thing?" she queried.

He nodded. "Same old thing. If every farmer delivered day-old eggs, there wouldn't be no ten cents higher 'n the top price. They'd be no better off than they was before."

"But the eggs would be one-day eggs, all the eggs would be one-day eggs, you mustn't forget that," Mrs. Mortimer pointed out.

"But that don't butter no toast for my wife an' me," he objected. "An' that's what I've been tryin' to get the hang of, an' now I got it. You talk about theory an' fact. Ten cents higher than top price is a theory to Saxon an' me. The fact is, we ain't got no eggs, no chickens, an' no land for the chickens to run an' lay eggs on."

Their hostess nodded sympathetically.

"An' there's something else about this outfit of yourn that I don't get the hang of," he pursued. "I can't just put my finger on it, but it's there all right."

They were shown over the cattery, the piggery, the milkers, and the kennelry, as Mrs. Mortimer called her live stock departments. None was large. All were money-makers, she assured them, and rattled off her profits glibly. She took their breaths away by the prices given and received for pedigreed Persians, pedigreed Ohio Improved Chesters, pedigreed Scotch collies, and pedigreed Jerseys. For the milk of the last she also had a special private market, receiving five cents more a quart than was fetched by the best dairy milk. Billy was quick to point out the difference between the look of her orchard and the look of the orchard they had inspected the previous afternoon, and Mrs. Mortimer showed him scores of other differences, many of which he was compelled to accept on faith.

Then she told them of another industry, her home-made jams and jellies, always contracted for in advance, and at prices dizzyingly beyond the regular market. They sat in comfortable rattan chairs on the veranda, while she told the story of how she had drummed up the jam and jelly trade, dealing only with the one best restaurant and one best club in San Jose. To the proprietor and the steward she had gone with her samples, in long discussions beaten down their opposition, overcome their reluctance, and persuaded the proprietor, in particular, to make a "special" of her wares, to boom them quietly with his patrons, and, above all, to charge stiffly for dishes and courses in which they appeared.

Throughout the recital Billy's eyes were moody with dissatisfaction. Mrs. Mortimer saw, and waited.

"And now, begin at the beginning," Saxon begged.

But Mrs. Mortimer refused unless they agreed to stop for supper. Saxon frowned Billy's reluctance away, and accepted for both of them.

"Well, then," Mrs. Mortimer took up her tale, "in the beginning I was a greenhorn, city born and bred. All I knew of the country was that it was a place to go to for vacations, and I always went to springs and mountain and seaside resorts. I had lived among books almost all my life. I was head librarian of the Doncaster Library for years. Then I married Mr. Mortimer. He was a book man, a professor in San Miguel University. He had a long sickness, and when he died there was nothing left. Even his life insurance was eaten into before I could be free of creditors. As for myself, I was worn out, on the verge of nervous prostration, fit for nothing. I had five thousand dollars left, however, and, without going into the details, I decided to go farming. I found this place, in a delightful climate, close to San Jose—the end of the electric line is only a quarter of a mile on—and I bought it. I paid two thousand cash, and gave a mortgage for two thousand. It cost two hundred an acre, you see."

"Twenty acres!" Saxon cried.

"Wasn't that pretty small?" Billy ventured.

"Too large, oceans too large. I leased ten acres of it the first thing. And it's still leased after all this time. Even the ten I'd retained was much too large for a long, long time. It's only now that I'm beginning to feel a tiny mite crowded."

"And ten acres has supported you an' two hired men?" Billy demanded, amazed.

Mrs. Mortimer clapped her hands delightedly.

"Listen. I had been a librarian. I knew my way among books. First of all I'd read everything written on the subject, and subscribed to some of the best farm magazines and papers. And you ask if my ten acres have supported me and two hired men. Let me tell you. I have four hired men. The ten acres certainly must support them, as it supports Hannah—she's a Swedish widow who runs the house and who is a perfect Trojan during the jam and jelly season—and Hannah's daughter, who goes to school and lends a hand, and my nephew whom I have taken to raise and educate. Also, the ten acres have come pretty close to paying for the whole twenty, as well as for this house, and all the outbuildings, and all the pedigreed stock."

Saxon remembered what the young lineman had said about the Portuguese.

"The ten acres didn't do a bit of it," she cried. "It was your head that did it all, and you know it."

"And that's the point, my dear. It shows the right kind of person can succeed in the country. Remember, the soil is generous. But it must be treated generously, and that is something the old style American farmer can't get into his head. So it IS head that counts. Even when his starving acres have convinced him of the need for fertilizing, he can't see the difference between cheap fertilizer and good fertilizer."

"And that's something I want to know about," Saxon exclaimed. "And I'll tell you all I know, but, first, you must be very tired. I noticed you were limping. Let me take you in—never mind your bundles; I'll send Chang for them."

To Saxon, with her innate love of beauty and charm in all personal things, the interior of the bungalow was a revelation. Never before had she been inside a middle class home, and what she saw not only far exceeded anything she had imagined, but was vastly different from her imaginings. Mrs. Mortimer noted her sparkling glances which took in everything, and went out of her way to show Saxon around, doing it under the guise of gleeful boastings, stating the costs of the different materials, explaining how she had done things with her own hands, such as staining the doors, weathering the bookcases, and putting together the big Mission Morris chair. Billy stepped gingerly behind, and though it never entered his mind to ape to the manner born, he succeeded in escaping conspicuous awkwardness, even at the table where he and Saxon had the unique experience of being waited on in a private house by a servant.

"If you'd only come along next year," Mrs. Mortimer mourned; "then I should have had the spare room I had planned—"

"That's all right," Billy spoke up; "thank you just the same. But we'll catch the electric cars into San Jose an' get a room."

Mrs. Mortimer was still disturbed at her inability to put them up for the night, and Saxon changed the conversation by pleading to be told more.

"You remember, I told you I'd paid only two thousand down on the land," Mrs. Mortimer complied. "That left me three thousand to experiment with. Of course, all my friends and relatives prophesied failure. And, of course, I made my mistakes, plenty of them, but I was saved from still more by the thorough study I had made and continued to make." She indicated shelves of farm books and files of farm magazines that lined the walls. "And I continued to study. I was resolved to be up to date, and I sent for all the experiment station reports. I went almost entirely on the basis that whatever the old type farmer did was wrong, and, do you know, in doing that I was not so far wrong myself. It's almost unthinkable, the stupidity of the old-fashioned farmers. Oh, I consulted with them, talked things over with them, challenged their stereotyped ways, demanded demonstration of their dogmatic and prejudiced beliefs, and quite succeeded in convincing the last of them that I was a fool and doomed to come to grief."

"But you didn't! You didn't!"

Mrs. Mortimer smiled gratefully.

"Sometimes, even now, I'm amazed that I didn't. But I came of a hard-headed stock which had been away from the soil long enough to gain a new perspective. When a thing satisfied my judgment, I did it forthwith and downright, no matter how extravagant it seemed. Take the old orchard. Worthless! Worse than worthless! Old Calkins nearly died of heart disease when he saw the devastation I had wreaked upon it. And look at it now. There was an old rattletrap ruin where the bungalow now stands. I put up with it, but I immediately pulled down the cow barn, the pigsties, the chicken houses, everything—made a clean sweep. They shook their heads and groaned when they saw such wanton waste by a widow struggling to make a living. But worse was to come. They were paralyzed when I told them the price of the three beautiful O.I.C.'s—pigs, you know, Chesters—which I bought, sixty dollars for the three, and only just weaned. Then I hustled the nondescript chickens to market, replacing them with the White Leghorns. The two scrub cows that came with the place I sold to the butcher for thirty dollars each, paying two hundred and fifty for two blue-blooded Jersey heifers... and coined money on the exchange, while Calkins and the rest went right on with their scrubs that couldn't give enough milk to pay for their board."

Billy nodded approval.

"Remember what I told you about horses," he reiterated to Saxon; and, assisted by his hostess, he gave a very creditable disquisition on horseflesh and its management from a business point of view.

When he went out to smoke Mrs. Mortimer led Saxon into talking about herself and Billy, and betrayed not the slightest shock when she learned of his prizefighting and scab-slugging proclivities.

"He's a splendid young man, and good," she assured Saxon. "His face shows that. And, best of all, he loves you and is proud of you. You can't imagine how I have enjoyed watching the way he looks at you, especially when you are talking. He respects your judgment. Why, he must, for here he is with you on this pilgrimage which is wholly your idea." Mrs. Mortimer sighed. "You are very fortunate, dear child, very fortunate. And you don't yet know what a man's brain is. Wait till he is quite fired with enthusiasm for your project. You will be astounded by the way he takes hold. You will have to exert yourself to keep up with him. In the meantime, you must lead. Remember, he is city bred. It will be a struggle to wean him from the only life he's known."

"Oh, but he's disgusted with the city, too—" Saxon began.

"But not as you are. Love is not the whole of man, as it is of woman. The city hurt you more than it hurt him. It was you who lost the dear little babe. His interest, his connection, was no more than casual and incidental compared with the depth and vividness of yours."

Mrs. Mortimer turned her head to Billy, who was just entering.

"Have you got the hang of what was bothering you?" she asked.

"Pretty close to it," he answered, taking the indicated big Morris chair. "It's this—"

"One moment," Mrs. Mortimer checked him. "That is a beautiful, big, strong chair, and so are you, at any rate big and strong, and your little wife is very weary—no, no; sit down, it's your strength she needs. Yes, I insist. Open your arms."

And to him she led Saxon, and into his arms placed her. "Now, sir—and you look delicious, the pair of you—register your objections to my way of earning a living."

"It ain't your way," Billy repudiated quickly. "Your way's all right. It's great. What I'm trying to get at is that your way don't fit us. We couldn't make a go of it your way. Why you had pull—well-to-do acquaintances, people that knew you'd been a librarian an' your husband a professor. An' you had...." Here he floundered a moment, seeking definiteness for the idea he still vaguely grasped. "Well, you had a way we couldn't have. You were educated, an'... an'—I don't know, I guess you knew society ways an' business ways we couldn't know."

"But, my dear boy, you could learn what was necessary," she contended.

Billy shook his head.

"No. You don't quite get me. Let's take it this way. Just suppose it's me, with jam an' jelly, a-wadin' into that swell restaurant like you did to talk with the top guy. Why, I'd be outa place the moment I stepped into his office. Worse'n that, I'd feel outa place. That'd make me have a chip on my shoulder an' lookin' for trouble, which is a poor way to do business. Then, too, I'd be thinkin' he was thinkin' I was a whole lot of a husky to be peddlin' jam. What'd happen, I'd be chesty at the drop of the hat. I'd be thinkin' he was thinkin' I was standin' on my foot, an' I'd beat him to it in tellin' him he was standin' on HIS foot. Don't you see? It's because I was raised that way. It'd be take it or leave it with me, an' no jam sold."

"What you say is true," Mrs. Mortimer took up brightly. "But there is your wife. Just look at her. She'd make an impression on any business man. He'd be only too willing to listen to her."

Billy stiffened, a forbidding expression springing into his eyes.

"What have I done now?" their hostess laughed.

"I ain't got around yet to tradin' on my wife's looks," he rumbled gruffly.

"Right you are. The only trouble is that you, both of you, are fifty years behind the times. You're old American. How you ever got here in the thick of modern conditions is a miracle. You're Rip Van Winkles. Who ever heard, in these degenerate times, of a young man and woman of the city putting their blankets on their backs and starting out in search of land? Why, it's the old Argonaut spirit. You're as like as peas in a pod to those who yoked their oxen and held west to the lands beyond the sunset. I'll wager your fathers and mothers, or grandfathers and grandmothers, were that very stock."

Saxon's eyes were glistening, and Billy's were friendly once more. Both nodded their heads.

"I'm of the old stock myself," Mrs. Mortimer went on proudly. "My grandmother was one of the survivors of the Donner Party. My grandfather, Jason Whitney, came around the Horn and took part in the raising of the Bear Flag at Sonoma. He was at Monterey when John Marshall discovered gold in Sutter's mill-race. One of the streets in San Francisco is named after him."

"I know it," Billy put in. "Whitney Street. It's near Russian Hill. Saxon's mother walked across the Plains."

"And Billy's grandfather and grandmother were massacred by the Indians," Saxon contributed. "His father was a little baby boy, and lived with the Indians, until captured by the whites. He didn't even know his name and was adopted by a Mr. Roberts."

"Why, you two dear children, we're almost like relatives," Mrs. Mortimer beamed. "It's a breath of old times, alas! all forgotten in these fly-away days. I am especially interested, because I've catalogued and read everything covering those times. You—" she indicated Billy, "you are historical, or at least your father is. I remember about him. The whole thing is in Bancroft's History. It was the Modoc Indians. There were eighteen wagons. Your father was the only survivor, a mere baby at the time, with no knowledge of what happened. He was adopted by the leader of the whites."

"That's right," said Billy. "It was the Modocs. His train must have ben bound for Oregon. It was all wiped out. I wonder if you know anything about Saxon's mother. She used to write poetry in the early days."

"Was any of it printed?"

"Yes," Saxon answered. "In the old San Jose papers."

"And do you know any of it?"

"Yes, there's one beginning:

"'Sweet as the wind-lute's airy strains Your gentle muse has learned to sing, And California's boundless plains Prolong the soft notes echoing.'"

"It sounds familiar," Mrs. Mortimer said, pondering.

CHAPTER III

"And there was another I remember that began:

"'I've stolen away from the crowd in the groves, Where the nude statues stand, and the leaves point and shiver,'—

"And it run on like that. I don't understand it all. It was written to my father—"

"A love poem!" Mrs. Mortimer broke in. "I remember it. Wait a minute.... Da-da-dah, da-da-dah, da-da-dah, da-da—STANDS—

"'In the spray of a fountain, whose seed-amethysts Tremble lightly a moment on bosom and hands, Then drip in their basin from bosom and wrists.'

"I've never forgotten the drip of the seed-amethysts, though I don't remember your mother's name."

"It was Daisy—" Saxon began.

"No; Dayelle," Mrs. Mortimer corrected with quickening recollection.

"Oh, but nobody called her that."

"But she signed it that way. What is the rest?"

"Daisy Wiley Brown."

Mrs. Mortimer went to the bookshelves and quickly returned with a large, soberly-bound volume.

"It's 'The Story of the Files,'" she explained. "Among other things, all the good fugitive verse was gathered here from the old newspaper files." Her eyes running down the index suddenly stopped. "I was right. Dayelle Wiley Brown. There it is. Ten of her poems, too: 'The Viking's Quest'; 'Days of Gold'; 'Constancy'; 'The Caballero'; 'Graves at Little Meadow'—"

"We fought off the Indians there," Saxon interrupted in her excitement. "And mother, who was only a little girl, went out and got water for the wounded. And the Indians wouldn't shoot at her. Everybody said it was a miracle." She sprang out of Billy's arms, reaching for the book and crying: "Oh, let me see it! Let me see it! It's all new to me. I don't know these poems. Can I copy them? I'll learn them by heart. Just to think, my mother's!"

Mrs. Mortimer's glasses required repolishing; and for half an hour she and Billy remained silent while Saxon devoured her mother's lines. At the end, staring at the book which she had closed on her finger, she could only repeat in wondering awe:

"And I never knew, I never knew."

But during that half hour Mrs. Mortimer's mind had not been idle. A little later, she broached her plan. She believed in intensive dairying as well as intensive farming, and intended, as soon as the lease expired, to establish a Jersey dairy on the other ten acres. This, like everything she had done, would be model, and it meant that she would require more help. Billy and Saxon were just the two. By next summer she could have them installed in the cottage she intended building. In the meantime she could arrange, one way and another, to get work for Billy through the winter. She would guarantee this work, and she knew a small house they could rent just at the end of the car-line. Under her supervision Billy could take charge from the very beginning of the building. In this way they would be earning money, preparing themselves for independent farming life, and have opportunity to look about them.

But her persuasions were in vain. In the end Saxon succinctly epitomized their point of view.

"We can't stop at the first place, even if it is as beautiful and kind as yours and as nice as this valley is. We don't even know what we want. We've got to go farther, and see all kinds of places and all kinds of ways, in order to find out. We're not in a hurry to make up our minds. We want to make, oh, so very sure! And besides...." She hesitated. "Besides, we don't like altogether flat land. Billy wants some hills in his. And so do I."

When they were ready to leave Mrs. Mortimer offered to present Saxon with "The Story of the Files"; but Saxon shook her head and got some money from Billy.

"It says it costs two dollars," she said. "Will you buy me one, and keep it till we get settled? Then I'll write, and you can send it to me."

"Oh, you Americans," Mrs. Mortimer chided, accepting the money. "But you must promise to write from time to time before you're settled."

She saw them to the county road.

"You are brave young things," she said at parting. "I only wish I were going with you, my pack upon my back. You're perfectly glorious, the pair of you. If ever I can do anything for you, just let me know. You're bound to succeed, and I want a hand in it myself. Let me know how that government land turns out, though I warn you I haven't much faith in its feasibility. It's sure to be too far away from markets."

She shook hands with Billy. Saxon she caught into her arms and kissed.

"Be brave," she said, with low earnestness, in Saxon's ear. "You'll win. You are starting with the right ideas. And you were right not to accept my proposition. But remember, it, or better, will always be open to you. You're young yet, both of you. Don't be in a hurry. Any time you stop anywhere for a while, let me know, and I'll mail you heaps of agricultural reports and farm publications. Good-bye. Heaps and heaps and heaps of luck."

CHAPTER IV

Bill sat motionless on the edge of the bed in their little room in San Jose that night, a musing expression in his eyes.

"Well," he remarked at last, with a long-drawn breath, "all I've got to say is there's some pretty nice people in this world after all. Take Mrs. Mortimer. Now she's the real goods—regular old American."

"A fine, educated lady," Saxon agreed, "and not a bit ashamed to work at farming herself. And she made it go, too."

"On twenty acres—no, ten; and paid for 'em, an' all improvements, an' supported herself, four hired men, a Swede woman an' daughter, an' her own nephew. It gets me. Ten acres! Why, my father never talked less'n one hundred an' sixty acres. Even your brother Tom still talks in quarter sections.—An' she was only a woman, too. We was lucky in meetin' her."

"Wasn't it an adventure!" Saxon cried. "That's what comes of traveling. You never know what's going to happen next. It jumped right out at us, just when we were tired and wondering how much farther to San Jose. We weren't expecting it at all. And she didn't treat us as if we were tramping. And that house—so clean and beautiful. You could eat off the floor. I never dreamed of anything so sweet and lovely as the inside of that house."

"It smelt good," Billy supplied.

"That's the very thing. It's what the women's pages call atmosphere. I didn't know what they meant before. That house has beautiful, sweet atmosphere—"

"Like all your nice underthings," said Billy.

"And that's the next step after keeping your body sweet and clean and beautiful. It's to have your house sweet and clean and beautiful."

"But it can't be a rented one, Saxon. You've got to own it. Landlords don't build houses like that. Just the same, one thing stuck out plain: that house was not expensive. It wasn't the cost. It was the way. The wood was ordinary wood you can buy in any lumber yard. Why, our house on Pine street was made out of the same kind of wood. But the way it was made was different. I can't explain, but you can see what I'm drivin' at."

Saxon, revisioning the little bungalow they had just left, repeated absently: "That's it—the way."

The next morning they were early afoot, seeking through the suburbs of San Jose the road to San Juan and Monterey. Saxon's limp had increased. Beginning with a burst blister, her heel was skinning rapidly. Billy remembered his father's talks about care of the feet, and stopped at a butcher shop to buy five cents' worth of mutton tallow.

"That's the stuff," he told Saxon. "Clean foot-gear and the feet well greased. We'll put some on as soon as we're clear of town. An' we might as well go easy for a couple of days. Now, if I could get a little work so as you could rest up several days it'd be just the thing. I '11 keep my eye peeled."

Almost on the outskirts of town he left Saxon on the county road and went up a long driveway to what appeared a large farm. He came back beaming.

"It's all hunkydory," he called as he approached. "We'll just go down to that clump of trees by the creek an' pitch camp. I start work in the mornin', two dollars a day an' board myself. It'd been a dollar an' a half if he furnished the board. I told 'm I liked the other way best, an' that I had my camp with me. The weather's fine, an' we can make out a few days till your foot's in shape. Come on. We'll pitch a regular, decent camp."

"How did you get the job," Saxon asked, as they cast about, determining their camp-site.

"Wait till we get fixed an' I'll tell you all about it. It was a dream, a cinch."

Not until the bed was spread, the fire built, and a pot of beans boiling did Billy throw down the last armful of wood and begin.

"In the first place, Benson's no old-fashioned geezer. You wouldn't think he was a farmer to look at 'm. He's up to date, sharp as tacks, talks an' acts like a business man. I could see that, just by lookin' at his place, before I seen HIM. He took about fifteen seconds to size me up.

"'Can you plow?' says he.

"'Sure thing,' I told 'm.

"'Know horses?'

"'I was hatched in a box-stall,' says I.

"An' just then—you remember that four-horse load of machinery that come in after me?—just then it drove up.

"'How about four horses?' he asks, casual-like.

"'Right to home. I can drive 'm to a plow, a sewin' machine, or a merry-go-round.'

"'Jump up an' take them lines, then,' he says, quick an' sharp, not wastin' seconds. 'See that shed. Go 'round the barn to the right an' back in for unloadin'.'

"An' right here I wanta tell you it was some nifty drivin' he was askin'. I could see by the tracks the wagons'd all ben goin' around the barn to the left. What he was askin' was too close work for comfort—a double turn, like an S, between a corner of a paddock an' around the corner of the barn to the last swing. An', to eat into the little room there was, there was piles of manure just thrown outa the barn an' not hauled away yet. But I wasn't lettin' on nothin'. The driver gave me the lines, an' I could see he was grinnin', sure I'd make a mess of it. I bet he couldn't a-done it himself. I never let on, an away we went, me not even knowin' the horses—but, say, if you'd seen me throw them leaders clean to the top of the manure till the nigh horse was scrapin' the side of the barn to make it, an' the off hind hub was cuttin' the corner post of the paddock to miss by six inches. It was the only way. An' them horses was sure beauts. The leaders slacked back an' darn near sat down on their singletrees when I threw the back into the wheelers an' slammed on the brake an' stopped on the very precise spot.

"'You'll do,' Benson says. 'That was good work.'

"'Aw, shucks,' I says, indifferent as hell. 'Gimme something real hard.'

"He smiles an' understands.

"'You done that well,' he says. 'An' I'm particular about who handles my horses. The road ain't no place for you. You must be a good man gone wrong. Just the same you can plow with my horses, startin' in to-morrow mornin'.'

"Which shows how wise he wasn't. I hadn't showed I could plow."

When Saxon had served the beans, and Billy the coffee, she stood still a moment and surveyed the spread meal on the blankets—the canister of sugar, the condensed milk tin, the sliced corned beef, the lettuce salad and sliced tomatoes, the slices of fresh French bread, and the steaming plates of beans and mugs of coffee.

"What a difference from last night!" Saxon exclaimed, clapping her hands. "It's like an adventure out of a book. Oh, that boy I went fishing with! Think of that beautiful table and that beautiful house last night, and then look at this. Why, we could have lived a thousand years on end in Oakland and never met a woman like Mrs. Mortimer nor dreamed a house like hers existed. And, Billy, just to think, we've only just started."

Billy worked for three days, and while insisting that he was doing very well, he freely admitted that there was more in plowing than he had thought. Saxon experienced quiet satisfaction when she learned he was enjoying it.

"I never thought I'd like plowin'—much," he observed. "But it's fine. It's good for the leg-muscles, too. They don't get exercise enough in teamin'. If ever I trained for another fight, you bet I'd take a whack at plowin'. An', you know, the ground has a regular good smell to it, a-turnin' over an' turnin' over. Gosh, it's good enough to eat, that smell. An' it just goes on, turnin' up an' over, fresh an' thick an' good, all day long. An' the horses are Joe-dandies. They know their business as well as a man. That's one thing, Benson ain't got a scrub horse on the place."

The last day Billy worked, the sky clouded over, the air grew damp, a strong wind began to blow from the southeast, and all the signs were present of the first winter rain. Billy came back in the evening with a small roll of old canvas he had borrowed, which he proceeded to arrange over their bed on a framework so as to shed rain. Several times he complained about the little finger of his left hand. It had been bothering him all day he told Saxon, for several days slightly, in fact, and it was as tender as a boil—most likely a splinter, but he had been unable to locate it.

He went ahead with storm preparations, elevating the bed on old boards which he lugged from a disused barn falling to decay on the opposite bank of the creek. Upon the boards he heaped dry leaves for a mattress. He concluded by reinforcing the canvas with additional guys of odd pieces of rope and bailing-wire.

When the first splashes of rain arrived Saxon was delighted. Billy betrayed little interest. His finger was hurting too much, he said. Neither he nor Saxon could make anything of it, and both scoffed at the idea of a felon.

"It might be a run-around," Saxon hazarded.

"What's that?"

"I don't know. I remember Mrs. Cady had one once, but I was too small. It was the little finger, too. She poulticed it, I think. And I remember she dressed it with some kind of salve. It got awful bad, and finished by her losing the nail. After that it got well quick, and a new nail grew out. Suppose I make a hot bread poultice for yours."

Billy declined, being of the opinion that it would be better in the morning. Saxon was troubled, and as she dozed off she knew that he was lying restlessly wide awake. A few minutes afterward, roused by a heavy blast of wind and rain on the canvas, she heard Billy softly groaning. She raised herself on her elbow and with her free hand, in the way she knew, manipulating his forehead and the surfaces around his eyes, soothed him off to sleep.

Again she slept. And again she was aroused, this time not by the storm, but by Billy. She could not see, but by feeling she ascertained his strange position. He was outside the blankets and on his knees, his forehead resting on the boards, his shoulders writhing with suppressed anguish.

"She's pulsin' to beat the band," he said, when she spoke. "It's worsen a thousand toothaches. But it ain't nothin'... if only the canvas don't blow down. Think what our folks had to stand," he gritted out between groans. "Why, my father was out in the mountains, an' the man with 'm got mauled by a grizzly—clean clawed to the bones all over. An' they was outa grub an' had to travel. Two times outa three, when my father put 'm on the horse, he'd faint away. Had to be tied on. An' that lasted five weeks, an' HE pulled through. Then there was Jack Quigley. He blowed off his whole right hand with the burstin' of his shotgun, an' the huntin' dog pup he had with 'm ate up three of the fingers. An' he was all alone in the marsh, an'—"

But Saxon heard no more of the adventures of Jack Quigley. A terrific blast of wind parted several of the guys, collapsed the framework, and for a moment buried them under the canvas. The next moment canvas, framework, and trailing guys were whisked away into the darkness, and Saxon and Billy were deluged with rain.

"Only one thing to do," he yelled in her ear. "—Gather up the things an' get into that old barn."

They accomplished this in the drenching darkness, making two trips across the stepping stones of the shallow creek and soaking themselves to the knees. The old barn leaked like a sieve, but they managed to find a dry space on which to spread their anything but dry bedding. Billy's pain was heart-rending to Saxon. An hour was required to subdue him to a doze, and only by continuously stroking his forehead could she keep him asleep. Shivering and miserable, she accepted a night of wakefulness gladly with the knowledge that she kept him from knowing the worst of his pain.

At the time when she had decided it must be past midnight, there was an interruption. From the open doorway came a flash of electric light, like a tiny searchlight, which quested about the barn and came to rest on her and Billy. From the source of light a harsh voice said:

"Ah! ha! I've got you! Come out of that!"

Billy sat up, his eyes dazzled by the light. The voice behind the light was approaching and reiterating its demand that they come out of that.

"What's up?" Billy asked.

"Me," was the answer; "an' wide awake, you bet."

The voice was now beside them, scarcely a yard away, yet they could see nothing on account of the light, which was intermittent, frequently going out for an instant as the operator's thumb tired on the switch.

"Come on, get a move on," the voice went on. "Roll up your blankets an' trot along. I want you."

"Who in hell are you?" Billy demanded.

CHAPTER IV

"I'm the constable. Come on."

"Well, what do you want?"

"You, of course, the pair of you."

"What for?"

"Vagrancy. Now hustle. I ain't goin' to loaf here all night."

"Aw, chase yourself," Billy advised. "I ain't a vag. I'm a workingman."

"Maybe you are an' maybe you ain't," said the constable; "but you can tell all that to Judge Neusbaumer in the mornin'."

"Why you... you stinkin', dirty cur, you think you're goin' to pull me," Billy began. "Turn the light on yourself. I want to see what kind of an ugly mug you got. Pull me, eh? Pull me? For two cents I'd get up there an' beat you to a jelly, you—"

"No, no, Billy," Saxon pleaded. "Don't make trouble. It would mean jail."

"That's right," the constable approved, "listen to your woman."

"She's my wife, an' see you speak of her as such," Billy warned. "Now get out, if you know what's good for yourself."

"I've seen your kind before," the constable retorted. "An' I've got my little persuader with me. Take a squint."

The shaft of light shifted, and out of the darkness, illuminated with ghastly brilliance, they saw thrust a hand holding a revolver. This hand seemed a thing apart, self-existent, with no corporeal attachment, and it appeared and disappeared like an apparition as the thumb-pressure wavered on the switch. One moment they were staring at the hand and revolver, the next moment at impenetrable darkness, and the next moment again at the hand and revolver.

"Now, I guess you'll come," the constable gloated.

"You got another guess comin'," Billy began.

But at that moment the light went out. They heard a quick movement on the officer's part and the thud of the light-stick on the ground. Both Billy and the constable fumbled for it, but Billy found it and flashed it on the other. They saw a gray-bearded man clad in streaming oilskins. He was an old man, and reminded Saxon of the sort she had been used to see in Grand Army processions on Decoration Day.

"Give me that stick," he bullied.

Billy sneered a refusal.

"Then I'll put a hole through you, by criminy."

He leveled the revolver directly at Billy, whose thumb on the switch did not waver, and they could see the gleaming bullet-tips in the chambers of the cylinder.

"Why, you whiskery old skunk, you ain't got the grit to shoot sour apples," was Billy's answer. "I know your kind—brave as lions when it comes to pullin' miserable, broken-spirited bindle stiffs, but as leery as a yellow dog when you face a man. Pull that trigger! Why, you pusillanimous piece of dirt, you'd run with your tail between your legs if I said boo!"

Suiting action to the word, Billy let out an explosive "BOO!" and Saxon giggled involuntarily at the startle it caused in the constable.

"I'll give you a last chance," the latter grated through his teeth. "Turn over that light-stick an' come along peaceable, or I'll lay you out."

Saxon was frightened for Billy's sake, and yet only half frightened. She had a faith that the man dared not fire, and she felt the old familiar thrills of admiration for Billy's courage. She could not see his face, but she knew in all certitude that it was bleak and passionless in the terrifying way she had seen it when he fought the three Irishmen.

"You ain't the first man I killed," the constable threatened. "I'm an old soldier, an' I ain't squeamish over blood—"

"And you ought to be ashamed of yourself," Saxon broke in, "trying to shame and disgrace peaceable people who've done no wrong."

"You've done wrong sleepin' here," was his vindication. "This ain't your property. It's agin the law. An' folks that go agin the law go to jail, as the two of you'll go. I've sent many a tramp up for thirty days for sleepin' in this very shack. Why, it's a regular trap for 'em. I got a good glimpse of your faces an' could see you was tough characters." He turned on Billy. "I've fooled enough with you. Are you goin' to give in an' come peaceable?"

"I'm goin' to tell you a couple of things, old boss," Billy answered. "Number one: you ain't goin' to pull us. Number two: we're goin' to sleep the night out here."

"Gimme that light-stick," the constable demanded peremptorily.

"G'wan, Whiskers. You're standin' on your foot. Beat it. Pull your freight. As for your torch you'll find it outside in the mud."

Billy shifted the light until it illuminated the doorway, and then threw the stick as he would pitch a baseball. They were now in total darkness, and they could hear the intruder gritting his teeth in rage.

"Now start your shootin' an' see what'll happen to you," Billy advised menacingly.

Saxon felt for Billy's hand and squeezed it proudly. The constable grumbled some threat.

"What's that?" Billy demanded sharply. "Ain't you gone yet? Now listen to me, Whiskers. I've put up with all your shenanigan I'm goin' to. Now get out or I'll throw you out. An' if you come monkeyin, around here again you'll get yours. Now get!"

So great was the roar of the storm that they could hear nothing. Billy rolled a cigarette. When he lighted it, they saw the barn was empty. Billy chuckled.

"Say, I was so mad I clean forgot my run-around. It's only just beginnin' to tune up again."

Saxon made him lie down and receive her soothing ministrations.

"There is no use moving till morning," she said. "Then, just as soon as it's light, we'll catch a car into San Jose, rent a room, get a hot breakfast, and go to a drug store for the proper stuff for poulticing or whatever treatment's needed."

"But Benson," Billy demurred.

"I'll telephone him from town. It will only cost five cents. I saw he had, a wire. And you couldn't plow on account of the rain, even if your finger was well. Besides, we'll both be mending together. My heel will be all right by the time it clears up and we can start traveling."

CHAPTER V

Early on Monday morning, three days later, Saxon and Billy took an electric car to the end of the line, and started a second time for San Juan. Puddles were standing in the road, but the sun shone from a blue sky, and everywhere, on the ground, was a faint hint of budding green. At Benson's Saxon waited while Billy went in to get his six dollars for the three days' plowing.

"Kicked like a steer because I was quittin'," he told her when he came back. "He wouldn't listen at first. Said he'd put me to drivin' in a few days, an' that there wasn't enough good four-horse men to let one go easily."

"And what did you say?"

"Oh, I just told 'm I had to be movin' along. An' when he tried to argue I told 'm my wife was with me, an' she was blamed anxious to get along."

"But so are you, Billy."

"Sure, Pete; but just the same I wasn't as keen as you. Doggone it, I was gettin' to like that plowin'. I'll never be scairt to ask for a job at it again. I've got to where I savvy the burro, an' you bet I can plow against most of 'm right now."

An hour afterward, with a good three miles to their credit, they edged to the side of the road at the sound of an automobile behind them. But the machine did not pass. Benson was alone in it, and he came to a stop alongside.

"Where are you bound?" he inquired of Billy, with a quick, measuring glance at Saxon.

"Monterey—if you're goin' that far," Billy answered with a chuckle.

"I can give you a lift as far as Watsonville. It would take you several days on shank's mare with those loads. Climb in." He addressed Saxon directly. "Do you want to ride in front?"

Saxon glanced to Billy.

"Go on," he approved. "It's fine in front.—This is my wife, Mr. Benson—Mrs. Roberts."

"Oh, ho, so you're the one that took your husband away from me," Benson accused good humoredly, as he tucked the robe around her.

Saxon shouldered the responsibility and became absorbed in watching him start the car.

"I'd be a mighty poor farmer if I owned no more land than you'd plowed before you came to me," Benson, with a twinkling eye, jerked over his shoulder to Billy.

"I'd never had my hands on a plow but once before," Billy confessed. "But a fellow has to learn some time."

"At two dollars a day?"

"If he can get some alfalfa artist to put up for it," Billy met him complacently.

Benson laughed heartily.

"You're a quick learner," he complimented. "I could see that you and plows weren't on speaking acquaintance. But you took hold right. There isn't one man in ten I could hire off the county road that could do as well as you were doing on the third day. But your big asset is that you know horses. It was half a joke when I told you to take the lines that morning. You're a trained horseman and a born horseman as well."

"He's very gentle with horses," Saxon said.

"But there's more than that to it," Benson took her up. "Your husband's got the WAY with him. It's hard to explain. But that's what it is—the WAY. It's an instinct almost. Kindness is necessary. But GRIP is more so. Your husband grips his horses. Take the test I gave him with the four-horse load. It was too complicated and severe. Kindness couldn't have done it. It took grip. I could see it the moment he started. There wasn't any doubt in his mind. There wasn't any doubt in the horses. They got the feel of him. They just knew the thing was going to be done and that it was up to them to do it. They didn't have any fear, but just the same they knew the boss was in the seat. When he took hold of those lines, he took hold of the horses. He gripped them, don't you see. He picked them up and put them where he wanted them, swung them up and down and right and left, made them pull, and slack, and back—and they knew everything was going to come out right. Oh, horses may be stupid, but they're not altogether fools. They know when the proper horseman has hold of them, though how they know it so quickly is beyond me."

Benson paused, half vexed at his volubility, and gazed keenly at Saxon to see if she had followed him. What he saw in her face and eyes satisfied him, and he added, with a short laugh:

"Horseflesh is a hobby of mine. Don't think otherwise because I am running a stink engine. I'd rather be streaking along here behind a pair of fast-steppers. But I'd lose time on them, and, worse than that, I'd be too anxious about them all the time. As for this thing, why, it has no nerves, no delicate joints nor tendons; it's a case of let her rip."

The miles flew past and Saxon was soon deep in talk with her host. Here again, she discerned immediately, was a type of the new farmer. The knowledge she had picked up enabled her to talk to advantage, and when Benson talked she was amazed that she could understand so much. In response to his direct querying, she told him her and Billy's plans, sketching the Oakland life vaguely, and dwelling on their future intentions.

Almost as in a dream, when they passed the nurseries at Morgan Hill, she learned they had come twenty miles, and realized that it was a longer stretch than they had planned to walk that day. And still the machine hummed on, eating up the distance as ever it flashed into view.

"I wondered what so good a man as your husband was doing on the road," Benson told her.

"Yes," she smiled. "He said you said he must be a good man gone wrong."

CHAPTER V

"But you see, I didn't know about YOU. Now I understand. Though I must say it's extraordinary in these days for a young couple like you to pack your blankets in search of land. And, before I forget it, I want to tell you one thing." He turned to Billy. "I am just telling your wife that there's an all-the-year job waiting for you on my ranch. And there's a tight little cottage of three rooms the two of you can housekeep in. Don't forget."

Among other things Saxon discovered that Benson had gone through the College of Agriculture at the University of California—a branch of learning she had not known existed. He gave her small hope in her search for government land.

"The only government land left," he informed her, "is what is not good enough to take up for one reason or another. If it's good land down there where you're going, then the market is inaccessible. I know no railroads tap in there."

"Wait till we strike Pajaro Valley," he said, when they had passed Gilroy and were booming on toward Sargent's. "I'll show you what can be done with the soil—and not by cow-college graduates but by uneducated foreigners that the high and mighty American has always sneered at. I'll show you. It's one of the most wonderful demonstrations in the state."

At Sargent's he left them in the machine a few minutes while he transacted business.

"Whew! It beats hikin'," Billy said. "The day's young yet and when he drops us we'll be fresh for a few miles on our own. Just the same, when we get settled an' well off, I guess I'll stick by horses. They'll always be good enough for me."

"A machine's only good to get somewhere in a hurry," Saxon agreed. "Of course, if we got very, very rich—"

"Say, Saxon," Billy broke in, suddenly struck with an idea. "I've learned one thing. I ain't afraid any more of not gettin' work in the country. I was at first, but I didn't tell you. Just the same I was dead leery when we pulled out on the San Leandro pike. An' here, already, is two places open—Mrs. Mortimer's an' Benson's; an' steady jobs, too. Yep, a man can get work in the country."

"Ah," Saxon amended, with a proud little smile, "you haven't said it right. Any GOOD man can get work in the country. The big farmers don't hire men out of charity."

"Sure; they ain't in it for their health," he grinned.

"And they jump at you. That's because you are a good man. They can see it with half an eye. Why, Billy, take all the working tramps we've met on the road already. There wasn't one to compare with you. I looked them over. They're all weak—weak in their bodies, weak in their heads, weak both ways."

"Yep, they are a pretty measly bunch," Billy admitted modestly.

"It's the wrong time of the year to see Pajaro Valley," Benson said, when he again sat beside Saxon and Sargent's was a thing of the past. "Just the same, it's worth seeing any time. Think of it—twelve thousand acres of apples! Do you know what they call Pajaro Valley now? New Dalmatia. We're being squeezed out. We Yankees thought we were smart. Well, the Dalmatians came along and showed they were smarter. They were miserable immigrants—poorer than Job's turkey. First, they worked at day's labor in the fruit harvest. Next they began, in a small way, buying the apples on the trees. The more money they made the bigger became their deals. Pretty soon they were renting the orchards on long leases. And now, they are beginning to buy the land. It won't be long before they own the whole valley, and the last American will be gone.

"Oh, our smart Yankees! Why, those first ragged Slavs in their first little deals with us only made something like two and three thousand per cent. profits. And now they're satisfied to make a hundred per cent. It's a calamity if their profits sink to twenty-five or fifty per cent."

"It's like San Leandro," Saxon said. "The original owners of the land are about all gone already. It's intensive cultivation." She liked that phrase. "It isn't a case of having a lot of acres, but of how much they can get out of one acre."

"Yes, and more than that," Benson answered, nodding his head emphatically. "Lots of them, like Luke Scurich, are in it on a large scale. Several of them are worth a quarter of a million already. I know ten of them who will average one hundred and fifty thousand each. They have a WAY with apples. It's almost a gift. They KNOW trees in much the same way your husband knows horses. Each tree is just as much an individual to them as a horse is to me. They know each tree, its whole history, everything that ever happened to it, its every idiosyncrasy. They have their fingers on its pulse. They can tell if it's feeling as well to-day as it felt yesterday. And if it isn't, they know why and proceed to remedy matters for it. They can look at a tree in bloom and tell how many boxes of apples it will pack, and not only that—they'll know what the quality and grades of those apples are going to be. Why, they know each individual apple, and they pick it tenderly, with love, never hurting it, and pack it and ship it tenderly and with love, and when it arrives at market, it isn't bruised nor rotten, and it fetches top price.

"Yes, it's more than intensive. These Adriatic Slavs are long-headed in business. Not only can they grow apples, but they can sell apples. No market? What does it matter? Make a market. That's their way, while our kind let the crops rot knee-deep under the trees. Look at Peter Mengol. Every year he goes to England, and he takes a hundred carloads of yellow Newton pippins with him. Why, those Dalmatians are showing Pajaro apples on the South African market right now, and coining money out of it hand over fist."

"What do they do with all the money?" Saxon queried.

"Buy the Americans of Pajaro Valley out, of course, as they are already doing."

"And then?" she questioned.

Benson looked at her quickly.

"Then they'll start buying the Americans out of some other valley. And the Americans will spend the money and by the second generation start rotting in the cities, as you and your husband would have rotted if you hadn't got out."

Saxon could not repress a shudder.—As Mary had rotted, she thought; as Bert and all the rest had rotted; as Tom and all the rest were rotting.

"Oh, it's a great country," Benson was continuing. "But we're not a great people. Kipling is right. We're crowded out and sitting on the stoop. And the worst of it is there's no reason we shouldn't know better. We're teaching it in all our agricultural colleges, experiment stations, and demonstration trains. But the people won't take hold, and the immigrant, who has learned in a hard school, beats them out. Why, after I graduated, and before my father died—he was of the old school and laughed at what he called my theories—I traveled for a couple of years. I wanted to see how the old countries farmed. Oh, I saw.

CHAPTER V

"We'll soon enter the valley. You bet I saw. First thing, in Japan, the terraced hillsides. Take a hill so steep you couldn't drive a horse up it. No bother to them. They terraced it—a stone wall, and good masonry, six feet high, a level terrace six feet wide; up and up, walls and terraces, the same thing all the way, straight into the air, walls upon walls, terraces upon terraces, until I've seen ten-foot walls built to make three-foot terraces, and twenty-foot walls for four or five feet of soil they could grow things on. And that soil, packed up the mountainsides in baskets on their backs!

"Same thing everywhere I went, in Greece, in Ireland, in Dalmatia—I went there, too. They went around and gathered every bit of soil they could find, gleaned it and even stole it by the shovelful or handful, and carried it up the mountains on their backs and built farms—BUILT them, MADE them, on the naked rock. Why, in France, I've seen hill peasants mining their stream-beds for soil as our fathers mined the streams of California for gold. Only our gold's gone, and the peasants' soil remains, turning over and over, doing something, growing something, all the time. Now, I guess I'll hush."

"My God!" Billy muttered in awe-stricken tones. "Our folks never done that. No wonder they lost out."

"There's the valley now," Benson said. "Look at those trees! Look at those hillsides! That's New Dalmatia. Look at it! An apple paradise! Look at that soil! Look at the way it's worked!"

It was not a large valley that Saxon saw. But everywhere, across the flat-lands and up the low rolling hills, the industry of the Dalmatians was evident. As she looked she listened to Benson.

"Do you know what the old settlers did with this beautiful soil? Planted the flats in grain and pastured cattle on the hills. And now twelve thousand acres of it are in apples. It's a regular show place for the Eastern guests at Del Monte, who run out here in their machines to see the trees in bloom or fruit. Take Matteo Lettunich—he's one of the originals. Entered through Castle Garden and became a dish-washer. When he laid eyes on this valley he knew it was his Klondike. To-day he leases seven hundred acres and owns a hundred and thirty of his own—the finest orchard in the valley, and he packs from forty to fifty thousand boxes of export apples from it every year. And he won't let a soul but a Dalmatian pick a single apple of all those apples. One day, in a banter, I asked him what he'd sell his hundred and thirty acres for. He answered seriously. He told me what it had netted him, year by year, and struck an average. He told me to calculate the principal from that at six per cent. I did. It came to over three thousand dollars an acre."

"What are all the Chinks doin' in the Valley?" Billy asked. "Growin' apples, too?"

Benson shook his head.

"But that's another point where we Americans lose out. There isn't anything wasted in this valley, not a core nor a paring; and it isn't the Americans who do the saving. There are fifty-seven apple-evaporating furnaces, to say nothing of the apple canneries and cider and vinegar factories. And Mr. John Chinaman owns them. They ship fifteen thousand barrels of cider and vinegar each year."

"It was our folks that made this country," Billy reflected. "Fought for it, opened it up, did everything—"

"But develop it," Benson caught him up. "We did our best to destroy it, as we destroyed the soil of New England." He waved his hand, indicating some place beyond the hills. "Salinas lies over that way. If you went through there you'd think you were in Japan. And more than one fat little fruit valley in California has been taken over by the Japanese. Their method is somewhat different from the Dalmatians'. First they drift in fruit picking at day's wages. They give better satisfaction than the American fruit-pickers, too, and the Yankee grower is glad to get them. Next, as they get stronger, they form in Japanese unions and proceed to run the American labor out. Still the fruit-growers are satisfied. The next step is when the Japs won't pick. The American labor is gone. The fruit-grower is helpless. The crop perishes. Then in step the Jap labor bosses. They're the masters already. They contract for the crop. The fruit-growers are at their mercy, you see. Pretty soon the Japs are running the valley. The fruit-growers have become absentee landlords and are busy learning higher standards of living in the cities or making trips to Europe. Remains only one more step. The Japs buy them out. They've got to sell, for the Japs control the labor market and could bankrupt them at will."

"But if this goes on, what is left for us?" asked Saxon.

"What is happening. Those of us who haven't anything rot in the cities. Those of us who have land, sell it and go to the cities. Some become larger capitalists; some go into the professions; the rest spend the money and start rotting when it's gone, and if it lasts their life-time their children do the rotting for them."

Their long ride was soon over, and at parting Benson reminded Billy of the steady job that awaited him any time he gave the word.

"I guess we'll take a peep at that government land first," Billy answered. "Don't know what we'll settle down to, but there's one thing sure we won't tackle."

"What's that?"

"Start in apple-growin' at three thousan' dollars an acre."

Billy and Saxon, their packs upon the backs, trudged along a hundred yards. He was the first to break silence.

"An' I tell you another thing, Saxon. We'll never be goin' around smellin' out an' swipin' bits of soil an' carryin' it up a hill in a basket. The United States is big yet. I don't care what Benson or any of 'em says, the United States ain't played out. There's millions of acres untouched an' waitin', an' it's up to us to find 'em."

"And I'll tell you one thing," Saxon said. "We're getting an education. Tom was raised on a ranch, yet he doesn't know right now as much about farming conditions as we do. And I'll tell you another thing. The more I think of it, the more it seems we are going to be disappointed about that government land."

"Ain't no use believin' what everybody tells you," he protested.

"Oh, it isn't that. It's what I think. I leave it to you. If this land around here is worth three thousand an acre, why is it that government land, if it's any good, is waiting there, only a short way off, to be taken for the asking."

Billy pondered this for a quarter of a mile, but could come to no conclusion. At last he cleared his throat and remarked:

"Well, we can wait till we see it first, can't we?"

"All right," Saxon agreed. "We'll wait till we see it."

CHAPTER VI

They had taken the direct county road across the hills from Monterey, instead of the Seventeen Mile Drive around by the coast, so that Carmel Bay came upon them without any fore-glimmerings of its beauty. Dropping down through the pungent pines, they passed woods-embowered cottages, quaint and rustic, of artists and writers, and went on across wind-blown rolling sandhills held to place by sturdy lupine and nodding with pale California poppies. Saxon screamed in sudden wonder of delight, then caught her breath and gazed at the amazing peacock-blue of a breaker, shot through with golden sunlight, overfalling in a mile-long sweep and thundering into white ruin of foam on a crescent beach of sand scarcely less white.

How long they stood and watched the stately procession of breakers, rising from out the deep and wind-capped sea to froth and thunder at their feet, Saxon did not know. She was recalled to herself when Billy, laughing, tried to remove the telescope basket from her shoulders.

"You kind of look as though you was goin' to stop a while," he said. "So we might as well get comfortable."

"I never dreamed it, I never dreamed it," she repeated, with passionately clasped hands. "I... I thought the surf at the Cliff House was wonderful, but it gave no idea of this.—Oh! Look! LOOK! Did you ever see such an unspeakable color? And the sunlight flashing right through it! Oh! Oh! Oh!"

At last she was able to take her eyes from the surf and gaze at the sea-horizon of deepest peacock-blue and piled with cloud-masses, at the curve of the beach south to the jagged point of rocks, and at the rugged blue mountains seen across soft low hills, landward, up Carmel Valley.

"Might as well sit down an' take it easy," Billy indulged her. "This is too good to want to run away from all at once."

Saxon assented, but began immediately to unlace her shoes.

"You ain't a-goin' to?" Billy asked in surprised delight, then began unlacing his own.

But before they were ready to run barefooted on the perilous fringe of cream-wet sand where land and ocean met, a new and wonderful thing attracted their attention. Down from the dark pines and across the sandhills ran a man, naked save for narrow trunks. He was smooth and rosy-skinned, cherubic-faced, with a thatch of curly yellow hair, but his body was hugely thewed as a Hercules'.

"Gee!—must be Sandow," Billy muttered low to Saxon.

But she was thinking of the engraving in her mother's scrapbook and of the Vikings on the wet sands of England.

The runner passed them a dozen feet away, crossed the wet sand, never parsing, till the froth wash was to his knees while above him, ten feet at least, upreared a was of overtopping water. Huge and powerful as his body had seemed, it was now white and fragile in the face of that imminent, great-handed buffet of the sea. Saxon gasped with anxiety, and she stole a look at Billy to note that he was tense with watching.

But the stranger sprang to meet the blow, and, just when it seemed he must be crushed, he dived into the face of the breaker and disappeared. The mighty mass of water fell in thunder on the beach, but beyond appeared a yellow head, one arm outreaching, and a portion of a shoulder. Only a few strokes was he able to make are he was come pelted to dye through another breaker. This was the battle—to win seaward against the Creep of the shoreward hastening sea. Each time he dived and was lost to view Saxon caught her breath and clenched her hands. Sometimes, after the passage of a breaker, they enfold not find him, and when they did he would be scores of feet away, flung there like a chip by a smoke-bearded breaker. Often it seemed he must fail and be thrown upon the beach, but at the end of half an hour he was beyond the outer edge of the surf and swimming strong, no longer diving, but topping the waves. Soon he was so far away that only at intervals could they find the speck of him. That, too, vanished, and Saxon and Billy looked at each other, she with amazement at the swimmer's valor, Billy with blue eyes flashing.

"Some swimmer, that boy, some swimmer," he praised. "Nothing chicken-hearted about him.—Say, I only know tank-swimmin', an' bay-swimmin', but now I'm goin' to learn ocean-swimmin'. If I could do that I'd be so proud you couldn't come within forty feet of me. Why, Saxon, honest to God, I'd sooner do what he done than own a thousan' farms. Oh, I can swim, too, I'm tellin' you, like a fish—I swum, one Sunday, from the Narrow Gauge Pier to Sessions' Basin, an' that's miles—but I never seen anything like that guy in the swimmin' line. An' I'm not goin' to leave this beach until he comes back.—All by his lonely out there in a mountain sea, think of it! He's got his nerve all right, all right."

Saxon and Billy ran barefooted up and down the beach, pursuing each other with brandished snakes of seaweed and playing like children for an hour. It was not until they were putting on their shoes that they sighted the yellow head bearing shoreward. Billy was at the edge of the surf to meet him, emerging, not white-skinned as he had entered, but red from the pounding he had received at the hands of the sea.

"You're a wonder, and I just got to hand it to you," Billy greeted him in outspoken admiration.

"It was a big surf to-day," the young man replied, with a nod of acknowledgment.

"It don't happen that you are a fighter I never heard of?" Billy queried, striving to get some inkling of the identity of the physical prodigy.

The other laughed and shook his head, and Billy could not guess that he was an ex-captain of a 'Varsity Eleven, and incidentally the father of a family and the author of many books. He looked Billy over with an eye trained in measuring freshmen aspirants for the gridiron.

"You're some body of a man," he appreciated. "You'd strip with the best of them. Am I right in guessing that you know your way about in the ring?"

Billy nodded. "My name's Roberts."

CHAPTER VI

The swimmer scowled with a futile effort at recollection.

"Bill—Bill Roberts," Billy supplemented.

"Oh, ho!—Not BIG Bill Roberts? Why, I saw you fight, before the earthquake, in the Mechanic's Pavilion. It was a preliminary to Eddie Hanlon and some other fellow. You're a two-handed fighter, I remember that, with an awful wallop, but slow. Yes, I remember, you were slow that night, but you got your man." He put out a wet hand. "My name's Hazard—Jim Hazard."

"An' if you're the football coach that was, a couple of years ago, I've read about you in the papers. Am I right?"

They shook hands heartily, and Saxon was introduced. She felt very small beside the two young giants, and very proud, withal, that she belonged to the race that gave them birth. She could only listen to them talk.

"I'd like to put on the gloves with you every day for half an hour," Hazard said. "You could teach me a lot. Are you going to stay around here?"

"No. We're goin' on down the coast, lookin' for land. Just the same, I could teach you a few, and there's one thing you could teach me—surf swimmin'."

"I'll swap lessons with you any time," Hazard offered. He turned to Saxon. "Why don't you stop in Carmel for a while? It isn't so bad."

"It's beautiful," she acknowledged, with a grateful smile, "but—" She turned and pointed to their packs on the edge of the lupine. "We're on the tramp, and lookin' for government land."

"If you're looking down past the Sur for it, it will keep," he laughed. "Well, I've got to run along and get some clothes on. If you come back this way, look me up. Anybody will tell you where I live. So long."

And, as he had first arrived, he departed, crossing the sandhills on the run.

Billy followed him with admiring eyes.

"Some boy, some boy," he murmured. "Why, Saxon, he's famous. If I've seen his face in the papers once, I've seen it a thousand times. An' he ain't a bit stuck on himself. Just man to man. Say!—I'm beginnin' to have faith in the old stock again."

They turned their backs on the beach and in the tiny main street bought meat, vegetables, and half a dozen eggs. Billy had to drag Saxon away from the window of a fascinating shop where were iridescent pearls of abalone, set and unset.

"Abalones grow here, all along the coast," Billy assured her; "an' I'll get you all you want. Low tide's the time."

"My father had a set of cuff-buttons made of abalone shell," she said. "They were set in pure, soft gold. I haven't thought about them for years, and I wonder who has them now."

They turned south. Everywhere from among the pines peeped the quaint pretty houses of the artist folk, and they were not prepared, where the road dipped to Carmel River, for the building that met their eyes.

"I know what it is," Saxon almost whispered. "It's an old Spanish Mission. It's the Carmel Mission, of course. That's the way the Spaniards came up from Mexico, building missions as they came and converting the Indians."

"Until we chased them out, Spaniards an' Indians, whole kit an' caboodle," Billy observed with calm satisfaction.

"Just the same, it's wonderful," Saxon mused, gazing at the big, half-ruined adobe structure. "There is the Mission Dolores, in San Francisco, but it's smaller than this and not as old."

Hidden from the sea by low hillocks, forsaken by human being and human habitation, the church of sun-baked clay and straw and chalk-rock stood hushed and breathless in the midst of the adobe ruins which once had housed its worshiping thousands. The spirit of the place descended upon Saxon and Billy, and they walked softly, speaking in whispers, almost afraid to go in through the open ports. There was neither priest nor worshiper, yet they found all the evidences of use, by a congregation which Billy judged must be small from the number of the benches. Inter they climbed the earthquake-racked belfry, noting the hand-hewn timbers; and in the gallery, discovering the pure quality of their voices, Saxon, trembling at her own temerity, softly sang the opening bars of "Jesus Lover of My Soul." Delighted with the result, she leaned over the railing, gradually increasing her voice to its full strength as she sang:

"Jesus, Lover of my soul, Let me to Thy bosom fly, While the nearer waters roll, While the tempest still is nigh. Hide me, O my Saviour, hide, Till the storm of life is past; Safe into the haven guide And receive my soul at last."

Billy leaned against the ancient wall and loved her with his eyes, and, when she had finished, he murmured, almost in a whisper:

"That was beautiful—just beautiful. An' you ought to a-seen your face when you sang. It was as beautiful as your voice. Ain't it funny?—I never think of religion except when I think of you."

They camped in the willow bottom, cooked dinner, and spent the afternoon on the point of low rocks north of the mouth of the river. They had not intended to spend the afternoon, but found themselves too fascinated to turn away from the breakers bursting upon the rocks and from the many kinds of colorful sea life starfish, crabs, mussels, sea anemones, and, once, in a rock-pool, a small devilfish that chilled their blood when it cast the hooded net of its body around the small crabs they tossed to it. As the tide grew lower, they gathered a mess of mussels—huge fellows, five and six inches long and bearded like patriarchs. Then, while Billy wandered in a vain search for abalones, Saxon lay and dabbled in the crystal-clear water of a roak-pool, dipping up handfuls of glistening jewels—ground bits of shell and pebble of flashing rose and blue and green and violet. Billy came back and lay beside her, lazying in the sea-cool sunshine, and together they watched the sun sink into the horizon where the ocean was deepest peacock-blue.

She reached out her hand to Billy's and sighed with sheer repletion of content. It seemed she had never lived such a wonderful day. It was as if all old dreams were coming true. Such beauty of the world she had never guessed in her fondest imagining. Billy pressed her hand tenderly.

"What was you thinkin' of?" he asked, as they arose finally to go.

"Oh, I don't know, Billy. Perhaps that it was better, one day like this, than ten thousand years in Oakland."

CHAPTER VII

They left Carmel River and Carmel Valley behind, and with a rising sun went south across the hills between the mountains and the sea. The road was badly washed and gullied and showed little sign of travel.

"It peters out altogether farther down," Billy said. "From there on it's only horse trails. But I don't see much signs of timber, an' this soil's none so good. It's only used for pasture—no farmin' to speak of."

The hills were bare and grassy. Only the canyons were wooded, while the higher and more distant hills were furry with chaparral. Once they saw a coyote slide into the brush, and once Billy wished for a gun when a large wildcat stared at them malignantly and declined to run until routed by a clod of earth that burst about its ears like shrapnel.

Several miles along Saxon complained of thirst. Where the road dipped nearly at sea level to cross a small gulch Billy looked for water. The bed of the gulch was damp with hill-drip, and he left her to rest while he sought a spring.

"Say," he hailed a few minutes afterward. "Come on down. You just gotta see this. It'll 'most take your breath away."

Saxon followed the faint path that led steeply down through the thicket. Midway along, where a barbed wire fence was strung high across the mouth of the gulch and weighted down with big rocks, she caught her first glimpse of the tiny beach. Only from the sea could one guess its existence, so completely was it tucked away on three precipitous sides by the land, and screened by the thicket. Furthermore, the beach was the head of a narrow rock cove, a quarter of a mile long, up which pent way the sea roared and was subdued at the last to a gentle pulse of surf. Beyond the mouth many detached rocks, meeting the full force of the breakers, spouted foam and spray high in the air. The knees of these rocks, seen between the surges, were black with mussels. On their tops sprawled huge sea-lions tawny-wet and roaring in the sun, while overhead, uttering shrill cries, darted and wheeled a multitude of sea birds.

The last of the descent, from the barbed wire fence, was a sliding fall of a dozen feet, and Saxon arrived on the soft dry sand in a sitting posture.

"Oh, I tell you it's just great," Billy bubbled. "Look at it for a camping spot. In among the trees there is the prettiest spring you ever saw. An' look at all the good firewood, an'..." He gazed about and seaward with eyes that saw what no rush of words could compass. "... An', an' everything. We could live here. Look at the mussels out there. An' I bet you we could catch fish. What d'ye say we stop a few days?—It's vacation anyway—an' I could go back to Carmel for hooks an' lines."

Saxon, keenly appraising his glowing face, realized that he was indeed being won from the city.

"An' there ain't no wind here," he was recommending. "Not a breath. An' look how wild it is. Just as if we was a thousand miles from anywhere."

The wind, which had been fresh and raw across the bare hills, gained no entrance to the cove; and the beach was warm and balmy, the air sweetly pungent with the thicket odors. Here and there, in the midst of the thicket, severe small oak trees and other small trees of which Saxon did not know the names. Her enthusiasm now vied with Billy's, and, hand in hand, they started to explore.

"Here's where we can play real Robinson Crusoe," Billy cried, as they crossed the hard sand from highwater mark to the edge of the water. "Come on, Robinson. Let's stop over. Of course, I'm your Man Friday, an' what you say goes."

"But what shall we do with Man Saturday!" She pointed in mock consternation to a fresh footprint in the sand. "He may be a savage cannibal, you know."

"No chance. It's not a bare foot but a tennis shoe."

"But a savage could get a tennis shoe from a drowned or eaten sailor, couldn't hey" she contended.

"But sailors don't wear tennis shoes," was Billy's prompt refutation.

"You know too much for Man Friday," she chided; "but, just the same; if you'll fetch the packs we'll make camp. Besides, it mightn't have been a sailor that was eaten. It might have been a passenger."

By the end of an hour a snug camp was completed. The blankets were spread, a supply of firewood was chopped from the seasoned driftwood, and over a fire the coffee pot had begun to sing. Saxon called to Billy, who was improvising a table from a wave-washed plank. She pointed seaward. On the far point of rocks, naked except for swimming trunks, stood a man. He was gazing toward them, and they could see his long mop of dark hair blown by the wind. As he started to climb the rocks landward Billy called Saxon's attention to the fact that the stranger wore tennis shoes. In a few minutes he dropped down from the rock to the beach and walked up to them.

"Gosh!" Billy whispered to Saxon. "He's lean enough, but look at his muscles. Everybody down here seems to go in for physical culture."

As the newcomer approached, Saxon glimpsed sufficient of his face to be reminded of the old pioneers and of a certain type of face seen frequently among the old soldiers: Young though he was—not more than thirty, she decided—this man had the same long and narrow face, with the high cheekbones, high and slender forehead, and nose high, lean, and almost beaked. The lips were thin and sensitive; but the eyes were different from any she had ever seen in pioneer or veteran or any man. They were so dark a gray that they seemed brown, and there were a farness and alertness of vision in them as of bright questing through profounds of space. In a misty way Saxon felt that she had seen him before.

"Hello," he greeted. "You ought to be comfortable here." He threw down a partly filled sack. "Mussels. All I could get. The tide's not low enough yet."

Saxon heard Billy muffle an ejaculation, and saw painted on his face the extremest astonishment.

CHAPTER VII

"Well, honest to God, it does me proud to meet you," he blurted out. "Shake hands. I always said if I laid eyes on you I'd shake.—Say!"

But Billy's feelings mastered him, and, beginning with a choking giggle, he roared into helpless mirth.

The stranger looked at him curiously across their clasped hands, and glanced inquiringly to Saxon.

"You gotta excuse me," Billy gurgled, pumping the other's hand up and down. "But I just gotta laugh. Why, honest to God, I've woke up nights an' laughed an' gone to sleep again. Don't you recognize 'm, Saxon? He's the same identical dude say, friend, you're some punkins at a hundred yards dash, ain't you?"

And then, in a sudden rush, Saxon placed him. He it was who had stood with Roy Blanchard alongside the automobile on the day she had wandered, sick and unwitting, into strange neighborhoods. Nor had that day been the first time she had seen him.

"Remember the Bricklayers' Picnic at Weasel Park?" Billy was asking. "An' the foot race? Why, I'd know that nose of yours anywhere among a million. You was the guy that stuck your cane between Timothy McManus's legs an' started the grandest roughhouse Weasel Park or any other park ever seen."

The visitor now commenced to laugh. He stood on one leg as he laughed harder, then stood on the other leg. Finally he sat down on a log of driftwood.

"And you were there," he managed to gasp to Billy at last. "You saw it. You saw it." He turned to Saxon. "—And you?"

She nodded.

"Say," Billy began again, as their laughter eased down, "what I wants know is what'd you wanta do it for. Say, what'd you wants do it for? I've been askin' that to myself ever since."

"So have I," was the answer.

"You didn't know Timothy McManus, did you?"

"No; I'd never seen him before, and I've never seen him since."

"But what'd you wanta do it for?" Billy persisted.

The young man laughed, then controlled himself.

"To save my life, I don't know. I have one friend, a most intelligent chap that writes sober, scientific books, and he's always aching to throw an egg into an electric fan to see what will happen. Perhaps that's the way it was with me, except that there was no aching. When I saw those legs flying past, I merely stuck my stick in between. I didn't know I was going to do it. I just did it. Timothy McManus was no more surprised than I was."

"Did they catch you?" Billy asked.

"Do I look as if they did? I was never so scared in my life. Timothy McManus himself couldn't have caught me that day. But what happened afterward? I heard they had a fearful roughhouse, but I couldn't stop to see."

It was not until a quarter of an hour had passed, during which Billy described the fight, that introductions took place. Mark Hall was their visitor's name, and he lived in a bungalow among the Carmel pines.

"But how did you ever find your way to Bierce's Cove?" he was curious to know. "Nobody ever dreams of it from the road."

"So that's its name?" Saxon said.

"It's the name we gave it. One of our crowd camped here one summer, and we named it after him. I'll take a cup of that coffee, if you don't mind."—This to Saxon. "And then I'll show your husband around. We're pretty proud of this cove. Nobody ever comes here but ourselves."

"You didn't get all that muscle from bein' chased by McManus," Billy observed over the coffee.

"Massage under tension," was the cryptic reply.

"Yes," Billy said, pondering vacantly. "Do you eat it with a spoon?"

Hall laughed.

"I'll show you. Take any muscle you want, tense it, then manipulate it with your fingers, so, and so."

"An' that done all that'" Billy asked skeptically.

"All that!" the other scorned proudly. "For one muscle you see, there's five tucked away but under command. Touch your finger to any part of me and see."

Billy complied, touching the right breast.

"You know something about anatomy, picking a muscleless spot," scolded Hall.

Billy grinned triumphantly, then, to his amazement, saw a muscle grow up under his finger. He prodded it, and found it hard and honest.

"Massage under tension!" Hall exulted. "Go on—anywhere you want."

And anywhere and everywhere Billy touched, muscles large and small rose up, quivered, and sank down, till the whole body was a ripple of willed quick.

"Never saw anything like it," Billy marveled at the end; "an' I've seen some few good men stripped in my time. Why, you're all living silk."

"Massage under tension did it, my friend. The doctors gave me up. My friends called me the sick rat, and the mangy poet, and all that. Then I quit the city, came down to Carmel, and went in for the open air—and massage under tension."

"Jim Hazard didn't get his muscles that way," Billy challenged.

"Certainly not, the lucky skunk; he was born with them. Mine's made. That's the difference. I'm a work of art. He's a cave bear. Come along. I'll show you around now. You'd better get your clothes off. Keep on only your shoes and pants, unless you've got a pair of trunks."

"My mother was a poet," Saxon said, while Billy was getting himself ready in the thicket. She had noted Hall's reference to himself.

He seemed incurious, and she ventured further.

"Some of it was printed."

"What was her name?" he asked idly.

"Dayelle Wiley Brown. She wrote: 'The Viking's Quest'; 'Days of Gold'; 'Constancy'; 'The Caballero'; 'Graves at Little Meadow'; and a lot more. Ten of them are in 'The Story of the Files.'"

"I've the book at home," he remarked, for the first time showing real interest. "She was a pioneer, of course—before my time. I'll look her up when I get back to the house. My people were pioneers. They came by Panama, in the Fifties, from Long Island. My father was a doctor, but he went into business in San Francisco and robbed his fellow men out of enough to keep me and the rest of a large family going ever since.—Say, where are you and your husband bound?"

When Saxon had told him of their attempt to get away from Oakland and of their quest for land, he sympathized with the first and shook his head over the second.

CHAPTER VII

"It's beautiful down beyond the Sur," he told her. "I've been all over those redwood canyons, and the place is alive with game. The government land is there, too. But you'd be foolish to settle. It's too remote. And it isn't good farming land, except in patches in the canyons. I know a Mexican there who is wild to sell his five hundred acres for fifteen hundred dollars. Three dollars an acre! And what does that mean? That it isn't worth more. That it isn't worth so much; because he can find no takers. Land, you know, is worth what they buy and sell it for."

Billy, emerging from the thicket, only in shoes and in pants rolled to the knees, put an end to the conversation; and Saxon watched the two men, physically so dissimilar, climb the rocks and start out the south side of the cove. At first her eyes followed them lazily, but soon she grew interested and worried. Hall was leading Billy up what seemed a perpendicular wall in order to gain the backbone of the rock. Billy went slowly, displaying extreme caution; but twice she saw him slip, the weather-eaten stone crumbling away in his hand and rattling beneath him into the cove. When Hall reached the top, a hundred feet above the sea, she saw him stand upright and sway easily on the knife-edge which she knew fell away as abruptly on the other side. Billy, once on top, contented himself with crouching on hands and knees. The leader went on, upright, walking as easily as on a level floor. Billy abandoned the hands and knees position, but crouched closely and often helped himself with his hands.

The knife-edge backbone was deeply serrated, and into one of the notches both men disappeared. Saxon could not keep down her anxiety, and climbed out on the north side of the cove, which was less rugged and far less difficult to travel. Even so, the unaccustomed height, the crumbling surface, and the fierce buffets of the wind tried her nerve. Soon she was opposite the men. They had leaped a narrow chasm and were scaling another tooth. Already Billy was going more nimbly, but his leader often paused and waited for him. The way grew severer, and several times the clefts they essayed extended down to the ocean level and spouted spray from the growling breakers that burst through. At other times, standing erect, they would fall forward across deep and narrow clefts until their palms met the opposing side; then, clinging with their fingers, their bodies would be drawn across and up.

Near the end, Hall and Billy went out of sight over the south side of the backbone, and when Saxon saw them again they were rounding the extreme point of rock and coming back on the cove side. Here the way seemed barred. A wide fissure, with hopelessly vertical sides, yawned skywards from a foam-white vortex where the mad waters shot their level a dozen feet upward and dropped it as abruptly to the black depths of battered rock and writhing weed.

Clinging precariously, the men descended their side till the spray was flying about them. Here they paused. Saxon could see Hall pointing down across the fissure and imagined he was showing some curious thing to Billy. She was not prepared for what followed. The surf-level sucked and sank away, and across and down Hall jumped to a narrow foothold where the wash had roared yards deep the moment before. Without pause, as the returning sea rushed up, he was around the sharp corner and clawing upward hand and foot to escape being caught. Billy was now left alone. He could not even see Hall, much less be further advised by him, and so tensely did Saxon watch, that the pain in her finger-tips, crushed to the rock by which she held, warned her to relax. Billy waited his chance, twice made tentative preparations to leap and sank back, then leaped across and down to the momentarily exposed foothold, doubled the corner, and as he clawed up to join Hall was washed to the waist but not torn away.

Saxon did not breathe easily till they rejoined her at the fire. One glance at Billy told her that he was exceedingly disgusted with himself.

"You'll do, for a beginner," Hall cried, slapping him jovially on the bare shoulder. "That climb is a stunt of mine. Many's the brave lad that's started with me and broken down before we were half way out. I've had a dozen balk at that big jump. Only the athletes make it."

"I ain't ashamed of admittin' I was scairt," Billy growled. "You're a regular goat, an' you sure got my goat half a dozen times. But I'm mad now. It's mostly trainin', an' I'm goin' to camp right here an' train till I can challenge you to a race out an' around an' back to the beach."

"Done," said Hall, putting out his hand in ratification. "And some time, when we get together in San Francisco, I'll lead you up against Bierce—the one this cove is named after. His favorite stunt, when he isn't collecting rattlesnakes, is to wait for a forty-mile-an-hour breeze, and then get up and walk on the parapet of a skyscraper—on the lee side, mind you, so that if he blows off there's nothing to fetch him up but the street. He sprang that on me once."

"Did you do it!" Billy asked eagerly.

"I wouldn't have if I hadn't been on. I'd been practicing it secretly for a week. And I got twenty dollars out of him on the bet."

The tide was now low enough for mussel gathering and Saxon accompanied the men out the north wall. Hall had several sacks to fill. A rig was coming for him in the afternoon, he explained, to cart the mussels back to Carmel. When the sacks were full they ventured further among the rock crevices and were rewarded with three abalones, among the shells of which Saxon found one coveted blister-pearl. Hall initiated them into the mysteries of pounding and preparing the abalone meat for cooking.

By this time it seemed to Saxon that they had known him a long time. It reminded her of the old times when Bert had been with them, singing his songs or ranting about the last of the Mohicans.

"Now, listen; I'm going to teach you something," Hall commanded, a large round rock poised in his hand above the abalone meat. "You must never, never pound abalone without singing this song. Nor must you sing this song at any other time. It would be the rankest sacrilege. Abalone is the food of the gods. Its preparation is a religious function. Now listen, and follow, and remember that it is a very solemn occasion."

The stone came down with a thump on the white meat, and thereafter arose and fell in a sort of tom-tom accompaniment to the poet's song:

"Oh! some folks boast of quail on toast, Because they think it's tony; But I'm content to owe my rent And live on abalone.

"Oh! Mission Point's a friendly joint Where every crab's a crony, And true and kind you'll ever find The clinging abalone.

"He wanders free beside the sea Where 'er the coast is stony; He flaps his wings and madly sings—The plaintive abalone.

"Some stick to biz, some flirt with Liz Down on the sands of Coney; But we, by hell, stay in Carmel, And whang the abalone."

CHAPTER VII

He paused with his mouth open and stone upraised. There was a rattle of wheels and a voice calling from above where the sacks of mussels had been carried. He brought the stone down with a final thump and stood up.

"There's a thousand more verses like those," he said. "Sorry I hadn't time to teach you them." He held out his hand, palm downward. "And now, children, bless you, you are now members of the clan of Abalone Eaters, and I solemnly enjoin you, never, no matter what the circumstances, pound abalone meat without chanting the sacred words I have revealed unto you."

"But we can't remember the words from only one hearing," Saxon expostulated.

"That shall be attended to. Next Sunday the Tribe of Abalone Eaters will descend upon you here in Bierce's Cove, and you will be able to see the rites, the writers and writeresses, down even to the Iron Man with the basilisk eyes, vulgarly known as the King of the Sacerdotal Lizards."

"Will Jim Hazard come?" Billy called, as Hall disappeared into the thicket.

"He will certainly come. Is he not the Cave-Bear Pot-Walloper and Gridironer, the most fearsome, and, next to me, the most exalted, of all the Abalone Eaters?"

Saxon and Billy could only look at each other till they heard the wheels rattle away.

"Well, I'll be doggoned," Billy let out. "He's some boy, that. Nothing stuck up about him. Just like Jim Hazard, comes along and makes himself at home, you're as good as he is an' he's as good as you, an' we're all friends together, just like that, right off the bat."

"He's old stock, too," Saxon said. "He told me while you were undressing. His folks came by Panama before the railroad was built, and from what he said I guess he's got plenty of money."

"He sure don't act like it."

"And isn't he full of fun!" Saxon cried.

"A regular josher. An' HIM!—a POET!"

"Oh, I don't know, Billy. I've heard that plenty of poets are odd."

"That's right, come to think of it. There's Joaquin Miller, lives out in the hills back of Fruitvale. He's certainly odd. It's right near his place where I proposed to you. Just the same I thought poets wore whiskers and eyeglasses, an' never tripped up foot-racers at Sunday picnics, nor run around with as few clothes on as the law allows, gatherin' mussels an' climbin' like goats."

That night, under the blankets, Saxon lay awake, looking at the stars, pleasuring in the balmy thicket-scents, and listening to the dull rumble of the outer surf and the whispering ripples on the sheltered beach a few feet away. Billy stirred, and she knew he was not yet asleep.

"Glad you left Oakland, Billy?" she snuggled.

"Huh!" came his answer. "Is a clam happy?"

CHAPTER VIII

Every half tide Billy raced out the south wall over the dangerous course he and Hall had traveled, and each trial found him doing it in faster time.

"Wait till Sunday," he said to Saxon. "I'll give that poet a run for his money. Why, they ain't a place that bothers me now. I've got the head confidence. I run where I went on hands an' knees. I figured it out this way: Suppose you had a foot to fall on each side, an' it was soft hay. They'd be nothing to stop you. You wouldn't fall. You'd go like a streak. Then it's just the same if it's a mile down on each side. That ain't your concern. Your concern is to stay on top and go like a streak. An', d'ye know, Saxon, when I went at it that way it never bothered me at all. Wait till he comes with his crowd Sunday. I'm ready for him."

"I wonder what the crowd will be like," Saxon speculated.

"Like him, of course. Birds of a feather flock together. They won't be stuck up, any of them, you'll see."

Hall had sent out fish-lines and a swimming suit by a Mexican cowboy bound south to his ranch, and from the latter they learned much of the government land and how to get it. The week flew by; each day Saxon sighed a farewell of happiness to the sun; each morning they greeted its return with laughter of joy in that another happy day had begun. They made no plans, but fished, gathered mussels and abalones, and climbed among the rocks as the moment moved them. The abalone meat they pounded religiously to a verse of doggerel improvised by Saxon. Billy prospered. Saxon had never seen him at so keen a pitch of health. As for herself, she scarcely needed the little hand-mirror to know that never, since she was a young girl, had there been such color in her cheeks, such spontaneity of vivacity.

"It's the first time in my life I ever had real play," Billy said. "An' you an' me never played at all all the time we was married. This beats bein' any kind of a millionaire."

"No seven o'clock whistle," Saxon exulted. "I'd lie abed in the mornings on purpose, only everything is too good not to be up. And now you just play at chopping some firewood and catching a nice big perch, Man Friday, if you expect to get any dinner."

Billy got up, hatchet in hand, from where he had been lying prone, digging holes in the sand with his bare toes.

"But it ain't goin' to last," he said, with a deep sigh of regret. "The rains'll come any time now. The good weather's hangin' on something wonderful."

CHAPTER VIII

On Saturday morning, returning from his run out the south wall, he missed Saxon. After helloing for her without result, he climbed to the road. Half a mile away, he saw her astride an unsaddled, unbridled horse that moved unwillingly, at a slow walk, across the pasture.

"Lucky for you it was an old mare that had been used to ridin'—see them saddle marks," he grumbled, when she at last drew to a halt beside him and allowed him to help her down.

"Oh, Billy," she sparkled, "I was never on a horse before. It was glorious! I felt so helpless, too, and so brave."

"I'm proud of you, just the same," he said, in more grumbling tones than before. "'Tain't every married women'd tackle a strange horse that way, especially if she'd never ben on one. An' I ain't forgot that you're goin' to have a saddle animal all to yourself some day—a regular Joe dandy."

The Abalone Eaters, in two rigs and on a number of horses, descended in force on Bierce's Cove. There were half a score of men and almost as many women. All were young, between the ages of twenty-five and forty, and all seemed good friends. Most of them were married. They arrived in a roar of good spirits, tripping one another down the slippery trail and engulfing Saxon and Billy in a comradeship as artless and warm as the sunshine itself. Saxon was appropriated by the girls—she could not realize them women; and they made much of her, praising her camping and traveling equipment and insisting on hearing some of her tale. They were experienced campers themselves, as she quickly discovered when she saw the pots and pans and clothes-boilers for the mussels which they had brought.

In the meantime Billy and the men had undressed and scattered out after mussels and abalones. The girls lighted on Saxon's ukulele and nothing would do but she must play and sing. Several of them had been to Honolulu, and knew the instrument, confirming Mercedes' definition of ukulele as "jumping flea." Also, they knew Hawaiian songs she had learned from Mercedes, and soon, to her accompaniment, all were singing: "Aloha Oe," "Honolulu Tomboy," and "Sweet Lei Lehua." Saxon was genuinely shocked when some of them, even the more matronly, danced hulas on the sand.

When the men returned, burdened with sacks of shellfish, Mark Hall, as high priest, commanded the due and solemn rite of the tribe. At a wave of his hand, the many poised stones came down in unison on the white meat, and all voices were uplifted in the Hymn to the Abalone. Old verses all sang, occasionally some one sang a fresh verse alone, whereupon it was repeated in chorus. Billy betrayed Saxon by begging her in an undertone to sing the verse she had made, and her pretty voice was timidly raised in:

"We sit around and gaily pound, And bear no acrimony Because our ob—ject is a gob Of sizzling abalone."

"Great!" cried the poet, who had winced at ob—ject. "She speaks the language of the tribe! Come on, children—now!"

And all chanted Saxon's lines. Then Jim Hazard had a new verse, and one of the girls, and the Iron Man with the basilisk eyes of greenish-gray, whom Saxon recognized from Hall's description. To her it seemed he had the face of a priest.

"Oh! some like ham and some like lamb And some like macaroni; But bring me in a pail of gin And a tub of abalone.

"Oh! some drink rain and some champagne Or brandy by the pony; But I will try a little rye With a dash of abalone.

"Some live on hope and some on dope And some on alimony. But our tom-cat, he lives on fat And tender abalone."

A black-haired, black-eyed man with the roguish face of a satyr, who, Saxon learned, was an artist who sold his paintings at five hundred apiece, brought on himself universal execration and acclamation by singing:

"The more we take, the more they make In deep sea matrimony; Race suicide cannot betide The fertile abalone."

And so it went, verses new and old, verses without end, all in glorification of the succulent shellfish of Carmel. Saxon's enjoyment was keen, almost ecstatic, and she had difficulty in convincing herself of the reality of it all. It seemed like some fairy tale or book story come true. Again, it seemed more like a stage, and these the actors, she and Billy having blundered into the scene in some incomprehensible way. Much of wit she sensed which she did not understand. Much she did understand. And she was aware that brains were playing as she had never seen brains play before. The puritan streak in her training was astonished and shocked by some of the broadness; but she refused to sit in judgment. They SEEMED good, these light-hearted young people; they certainly were not rough or gross as were many of the crowds she had been with on Sunday picnics. None of the men got drunk, although there were cocktails in vacuum bottles and red wine in a huge demijohn.

What impressed Saxon most was their excessive jollity, their childlike joy, and the childlike things they did. This effect was heightened by the fact that they were novelists and painters, poets and critics, sculptors and musicians. One man, with a refined and delicate face—a dramatic critic on a great San Francisco daily, she was told—introduced a feat which all the men tried and failed at most ludicrously. On the beach, at regular intervals, planks were placed as obstacles. Then the dramatic critic, on all fours, galloped along the sand for all the world like a horse, and for all the world like a horse taking hurdles he jumped the planks to the end of the course.

Quoits had been brought along, and for a while these were pitched with zest. Then jumping was started, and game slid into game. Billy took part in everything, but did not win first place as often as he had expected. An English writer beat him a dozen feet at tossing the caber. Jim Hazard beat him in putting the heavy "rock." Mark Hall out-jumped him standing and running. But at the standing high back-jump Billy did come first. Despite the handicap of his weight, this victory was due to his splendid back and abdominal lifting muscles. Immediately after this, however, he was brought to grief by Mark Hall's sister, a strapping young amazon in cross-saddle riding costume, who three times tumbled him ignominiously heels over head in a bout of Indian wrestling.

"You're easy," jeered the Iron Man, whose name they had learned was Pete Bideaux. "I can put you down myself, catch-as-catch-can."

Billy accepted the challenge, and found in all truth that the other was rightly nicknamed. In the training camps Billy had sparred and clinched with giant champions like Jim Jeffries and Jack Johnson, and met the weight of their strength, but never had he encountered strength like this of the Iron Man. Do what he could, Billy was powerless, and twice his shoulders were ground into the sand in defeat.

CHAPTER VIII

"You'll get a chance back at him," Hazard whispered to Billy, off at one side. "I've brought the gloves along. Of course, you had no chance with him at his own game. He's wrestled in the music halls in London with Hackenschmidt. Now you keep quiet, and we'll lead up to it in a casual sort of way. He doesn't know about you."

Soon, the Englishman who had tossed the caber was sparring with the dramatic critic, Hazard and Hall boxed in fantastic burlesque, then, gloves in hand, looked for the next appropriately matched couple. The choice of Bideaux and Billy was obvious.

"He's liable to get nasty if he's hurt," Hazard warned Billy, as he tied on the gloves for him. "He's old American French, and he's got a devil of a temper. But just keep your head and tap him—whatever you do, keep tapping him."

"Easy sparring now"; "No roughhouse, Bideaux"; "Just light tapping, you know," were admonitions variously addressed to the Iron Man.

"Hold on a second," he said to Billy, dropping his hands. "When I get rapped I do get a bit hot. But don't mind me. I can't help it, you know. It's only for the moment, and I don't mean it."

Saxon felt very nervous, visions of Billy's bloody fights and all the scabs he had slugged rising in her brain; but she had never seen her husband box, and but few seconds were required to put her at ease. The Iron Man had no chance. Billy was too completely the master, guarding every blow, himself continually and almost at will tapping the other's face and body. There was no weight in Billy's blows, only a light and snappy tingle; but their incessant iteration told on the Iron Man's temper. In vain the onlookers warned him to go easy. His face purpled with anger, and his blows became savage. But Billy went on, tap, tap, tap, calmly, gently, imperturbably. The Iron Man lost control, and rushed and plunged, delivering great swings and upper-cuts of man-killing quality. Billy ducked, side-stepped, blocked, stalled, and escaped all damage. In the clinches, which were unavoidable, he locked the Iron Man's arms, and in the clinches the Iron Man invariably laughed and apologized, only to lose his head with the first tap the instant they separated and be more infuriated than ever.

And when it was over and Billy's identity had been divulged, the Iron Man accepted the joke on himself with the best of humor. It had been a splendid exhibition on Billy's part. His mastery of the sport, coupled with his self-control, had most favorably impressed the crowd, and Saxon, very proud of her man boy, could not but see the admiration all had for him.

Nor did she prove in any way a social failure. When the tired and sweating players lay down in the dry sand to cool off, she was persuaded into accompanying their nonsense songs with the ukulele. Nor was it long, catching their spirit, ere she was singing to them and teaching them quaint songs of early days which she had herself learned as a little girl from Cady—Cady, the saloonkeeper, pioneer, and ax-cavalryman, who had been a bull-whacker on the Salt Intake Trail in the days before the railroad.

One song which became an immediate favorite was:

"Oh! times on Bitter Creek, they never can be beat, Root hog or die is on every wagon sheet; The sand within your throat, the dust within your eye, Bend your back and stand it—root hog or die."

After the dozen verses of "Root Hog or Die," Mark Hall claimed to be especially infatuated with:

"Obadier, he dreampt a dream, Dreampt he was drivin' a ten-mule team, But when he woke he heaved a sigh, The lead-mule kicked e-o-wt the swing-mule's eye."

It was Mark Hall who brought up the matter of Billy's challenge to race out the south wall of the cove, though he referred to the test as lying somewhere in the future. Billy surprised him by saying he was ready at any time. Forthwith the crowd clamored for the race. Hall offered to bet on himself, but there were no takers. He offered two to one to Jim Hazard, who shook his head and said he would accept three to one as a sporting proposition. Billy heard and gritted his teeth.

"I'll take you for five dollars," he said to Hall, "but not at those odds. I'll back myself even."

"It isn't your money I want; it's Hazard's," Hall demurred. "Though I'll give either of you three to one."

"Even or nothing," Billy held out obstinately.

Hall finally closed both bets—even with Billy, and three to one with Hazard.

The path along the knife-edge was so narrow that it was impossible for runners to pass each other, so it was arranged to time the men, Hall to go first and Billy to follow after an interval of half a minute.

Hall toed the mark and at the word was off with the form of a sprinter. Saxon's heart sank. She knew Billy had never crossed the stretch of sand at that speed. Billy darted forward thirty seconds later, and reached the foot of the rock when Hall was half way up. When both were on top and racing from notch to notch, the Iron Man announced that they had scaled the wall in the same time to a second.

"My money still looks good," Hazard remarked, "though I hope neither of them breaks a neck. I wouldn't take that run that way for all the gold that would fill the cove."

"But you'll take bigger chances swimming in a storm on Carmel Beach," his wife chided.

"Oh, I don't know," he retorted. "You haven't so far to fall when swimming."

Billy and Hall had disappeared and were making the circle around the end. Those on the beach were certain that the poet had gained in the dizzy spurts of flight along the knife-edge. Even Hazard admitted it.

"What price for my money now?" he cried excitedly, dancing up and down.

Hall had reappeared, the great jump accomplished, and was running shoreward. But there was no gap. Billy was on his heels, and on his heels he stayed, in to shore, down the wall, and to the mark on the beach. Billy had won by half a minute.

"Only by the watch," he panted. "Hall was over half a minute ahead of me out to the end. I'm not slower than I thought, but he's faster. He's a wooz of a sprinter. He could beat me ten times outa ten, except for accident. He was hung up at the jump by a big sea. That's where I caught 'm. I jumped right after 'm on the same sea, then he set the pace home, and all I had to do was take it."

"That's all right," said Hall. "You did better than beat me. That's the first time in the history of Bierce's Cove that two men made that jump on the same sea. And all the risk was yours, coming last."

"It was a fluke," Billy insisted.

And at that point Saxon settled the dispute of modesty and raised a general laugh by rippling chords on the ukulele and parodying an old hymn in negro minstrel fashion:

CHAPTER VIII

"De Lawd move in er mischievous way His blunders to perform."

In the afternoon Jim Hazard and Hall dived into the breakers and swam to the outlying rocks, routing the protesting sea-lions and taking possession of their surf-battered stronghold. Billy followed the swimmers with his eyes, yearning after them so undisguisedly that Mrs. Hazard said to him:

"Why don't you stop in Carmel this winter? Jim will teach you all he knows about the surf. And he's wild to box with you. He works long hours at his desk, and he really needs exercise."

Not until sunset did the merry crowd carry their pots and pans and trove of mussels up to the road and depart. Saxon and Billy watched them disappear, on horses and behind horses, over the top of the first hill, and then descended hand in hand through the thicket to the camp. Billy threw himself on the sand and stretched out.

"I don't know when I've been so tired," he yawned. "An' there's one thing sure: I never had such a day. It's worth livin' twenty years for an' then some."

He reached out his hand to Saxon, who lay beside him.

"And, oh, I was so proud of you, Billy," she said. "I never saw you box before. I didn't know it was like that. The Iron Man was at your mercy all the time, and you kept it from being violent or terrible. Everybody could look on and enjoy—and they did, too."

"Huh, I want to say you was goin' some yourself. They just took to you. Why, honest to God, Saxon, in the singin' you was the whole show, along with the ukulele. All the women liked you, too, an' that's what counts."

It was their first social triumph, and the taste of it was sweet:

"Mr. Hall said he'd looked up the 'Story of the Files,'" Saxon recounted. "And he said mother was a true poet. He said it was astonishing the fine stock that had crossed the Plains. He told me a lot about those times and the people I didn't know. And he's read all about the fight at Little Meadow. He says he's got it in a book at home, and if we come back to Carmel he'll show it to me."

"He wants us to come back all right. D'ye know what he said to me, Saxon t He gave me a letter to some guy that's down on the government land—some poet that's holdin' down a quarter of a section—so we'll be able to stop there, which'll come in handy if the big rains catch us. An'—Oh! that's what I was drivin' at. He said he had a little shack he lived in while the house was buildin'. The Iron Man's livin' in it now, but he's goin' away to some Catholic college to study to be a priest, an' Hall said the shack'd be ours as long as we wanted to use it. An' he said I could do what the Iron Man was doin' to make a livin'. Hall was kind of bashful when he was offerin' me work. Said it'd be only odd jobs, but that we'd make out. I could help'm plant potatoes, he said; an' he got half savage when he said I couldn't chop wood. That was his job, he said; an' you could see he was actually jealous over it."

"And Mrs. Hall said just about the same to me, Billy. Carmel wouldn't be so bad to pass the rainy season in. And then, too, you could go swimming with Mr. Hazard."

"Seems as if we could settle down wherever we've a mind to," Billy assented. "Carmel's the third place now that's offered. Well, after this, no man need be afraid of makin' a go in the country."

"No good man," Saxon corrected.

"I guess you're right." Billy thought for a moment. "Just the same a dub, too, has a better chance in the country than in the city."

"Who'd have ever thought that such fine people existed?" Saxon pondered. "It's just wonderful, when you come to think of it."

"It's only what you'd expect from a rich poet that'd trip up a foot-racer at an Irish picnic," Billy exposited.

"The only crowd such a guy'd run with would be like himself, or he'd make a crowd that was. I wouldn't wonder that he'd make this crowd. Say, he's got some sister, if anybody'd ride up on a sea-lion an' ask you. She's got that Indian wrestlin' down pat, an' she's built for it. An' say, ain't his wife a beaut?"

A little longer they lay in the warm sand. It was Billy who broke the silence, and what he said seemed to proceed out of profound meditation.

"Say, Saxon, d'ye know I don't care if I never see movie pictures again."

CHAPTER IX

Saxon and Billy were gone weeks on the trip south, but in the end they came back to Carmel. They had stopped with Hafler, the poets in the Marble House, which he had built with his own hands. This queer dwelling was all in one room, built almost entirely of white marble. Hailer cooked, as over a campfire, in the huge marble fireplace, which he used in all ways as a kitchen. There were divers shelves of books, and the massive furniture he had made from redwood, as he had made the shakes for the roof. A blanket, stretched across a corner, gave Saxon privacy. The poet was on the verge of departing for San Francisco and New York, but remained a day over with them to explain the country and run over the government land with Billy. Saxon had wanted to go along that morning, but Hafler scornfully rejected her, telling her that her legs were too short. That night, when the men returned, Billy was played out to exhaustion. He frankly acknowledged that Hafler had walked him into the ground, and that his tongue had been hanging out from the first hour. Hafler estimated that they had covered fifty-five miles.

"But such miles!" Billy enlarged. "Half the time up or down, an' 'most all the time without trails. An' such a pace. He was dead right about your short legs, Saxon. You wouldn't a-lasted the first mile. An' such country! We ain't seen anything like it yet."

Hafler left the next day to catch the train at Monterey. He gave them the freedom of the Marble House, and told them to stay the whole winter if they wanted. Billy elected to loaf around and rest up that day. He was stiff and sore. Moreover, he was stunned by the exhibition of walking prowess on the part of the poet.

"Everybody can do something top-notch down in this country," he marveled. "Now take that Hafler. He's a bigger man than me, an' a heavier. An' weight's against walkin', too. But not with him. He's done eighty miles inside twenty-four hours, he told me, an' once a hundred an' seventy in three days. Why, he made a show outa me. I felt ashamed as a little kid."

"Remember, Billy," Saxon soothed him, "every man to his own game. And down here you're a top-notcher at your own game. There isn't one you're not the master of with the gloves."

"I guess that's right," he conceded. "But just the same it goes against the grain to be walked off my legs by a poet—by a poet, mind you."

They spent days in going over the government land, and in the end reluctantly decided against taking it up. The redwood canyons and great cliffs of the Santa Lucia Mountains fascinated Saxon; but she remembered what Hafler had told her of the summer fogs which hid the sun sometimes for a week or two at a time, and which lingered for months. Then, too, there was no access to market. It was many miles to where the nearest wagon road began, at Post's, and from there on, past Point Sur to Carmel, it was a weary and perilous way. Billy, with his teamster judgment, admitted that for heavy hauling it was anything but a picnic. There was the quarry of perfect marble on Hafler's quarter section. He had said that it would be worth a fortune if near a railroad; but, as it was, he'd make them a present of it if they wanted it.

Billy visioned the grassy slopes pastured with his horses and cattle, and found it hard to turn his back; but he listened with a willing ear to Saxon's argument in favor of a farm-home like the one they had seen in the moving pictures in Oakland. Yes, he agreed, what they wanted was an all-around farm, and an all-around farm they would have if they hiked forty years to find it.

"But it must have redwoods on it," Saxon hastened to stipulate. "I've fallen in love with them. And we can get along without fog. And there must be good wagon-roads, and a railroad not more than a thousand miles away."

Heavy winter rains held them prisoners for two weeks in the Marble House. Saxon browsed among Hafler's books, though most of them were depressingly beyond her, while Billy hunted with Hafler's guns. But he was a poor shot and a worse hunter. His only success was with rabbits, which he managed to kill on occasions when they stood still. With the rifle he got nothing, although he fired at half a dozen different deer, and, once, at a huge cat-creature with a long tail which he was certain was a mountain lion. Despite the way he grumbled at himself, Saxon could see the keen joy he was taking. This belated arousal of the hunting instinct seemed to make almost another man of him. He was out early and late, compassing prodigious climbs and tramps—once reaching as far as the gold mines Tom had spoken of, and being away two days.

"Talk about pluggin' away at a job in the city, an' goin' to movie' pictures and Sunday picnics for amusement!" he would burst out. "I can't see what was eatin' me that I ever put up with such truck. Here's where I oughta ben all the time, or some place like it."

He was filled with this new mode of life, and was continually recalling old hunting tales of his father and telling them to Saxon.

"Say, I don't get stiffened any more after an all-day tramp," he exulted. "I'm broke in. An' some day, if I meet up with that Hafler, I'll challenge'm to a tramp that'll break his heart."

"Foolish boy, always wanting to play everybody's game and beat them at it," Saxon laughed delightedly.

"Aw, I guess you're right," he growled. "Hafler can always out-walk me. He's made that way. But some day, just the same, if I ever see 'm again, I'll invite 'm to put on the gloves.. .. though I won't be mean enough to make 'm as sore as he made me."

After they left Post's on the way back to Carmel, the condition of the road proved the wisdom of their rejection of the government land. They passed a rancher's wagon overturned, a second wagon with a broken axle, and the stage a hundred yards down the mountainside, where it had fallen, passengers, horses, road, and all.

"I guess they just about quit tryin' to use this road in the winter," Billy said. "It's horse-killin' an' man-killin', an' I can just see 'm freightin' that marble out over it I don't think."

CHAPTER IX

Settling down at Carmel was an easy matter. The Iron Man had already departed to his Catholic college, and the "shack" turned out to be a three-roomed house comfortably furnished for housekeeping. Hall put Billy to work on the potato patch—a matter of three acres which the poet farmed erratically to the huge delight of his crowd. He planted at all seasons, and it was accepted by the community that what did not rot in the ground was evenly divided between the gophers and trespassing cows. A plow was borrowed, a team of horses hired, and Billy took hold. Also he built a fence around the patch, and after that was set to staining the shingled roof of the bungalow. Hall climbed to the ridge-pole to repeat his warning that Billy must keep away from his wood-pile. One morning Hall came over and watched Billy chopping wood for Saxon. The poet looked on covetously as long as he could restrain himself.

"It's plain you don't know how to use an axe," he sneered. "Here, let me show you."

He worked away for an hour, all the while delivering an exposition on the art of chopping wood.

"Here," Billy expostulated at last, taking hold of the axe. "I'll have to chop a cord of yours now in order to make this up to you."

Hall surrendered the axe reluctantly.

"Don't let me catch you around my wood-pile, that's all," he threatened. "My wood-pile is my castle, and you've got to understand that."

From a financial standpoint, Saxon and Billy were putting aside much money. They paid no rent, their simple living was cheap, and Billy had all the work he cared to accept. The various members of the crowd seemed in a conspiracy to keep him busy. It was all odd jobs, but he preferred it so, for it enabled him to suit his time to Jim Hazard's. Each day they boxed and took a long swim through the surf. When Hazard finished his morning's writing, he would whoop through the pines to Billy, who dropped whatever work he was doing. After the swim, they would take a fresh shower at Hazard's house, rub each other down in training camp style, and be ready for the noon meal. In the afternoon Hazard returned to his desk, and Billy to his outdoor work, although, still later, they often met for a few miles' run over the hills. Training was a matter of habit to both men. Hazard, when he had finished with seven years of football, knowing the dire death that awaits the big-muscled athlete who ceases training abruptly, had been compelled to keep it up. Not only was it a necessity, but he had grown to like it. Billy also liked it, for he took great delight in the silk of his body.

Often, in the early morning, gun in hand, he was off with Mark Hall, who taught him to shoot and hunt. Hall had dragged a shotgun around from the days when he wore knee pants, and his keen observing eyes and knowledge of the habits of wild life were a revelation to Billy. This part of the country was too settled for large game, but Billy kept Saxon supplied with squirrels and quail, cottontails and jackrabbits, snipe and wild ducks. And they learned to eat roasted mallard and canvasback in the California style of sixteen minutes in a hot oven. As he became expert with shotgun and rifle, he began to regret the deer and the mountain lion he had missed down below the Sur; and to the requirements of the farm he and Saxon sought he added plenty of game.

But it was not all play in Carmel. That portion of the community which Saxon and Billy came to know, "the crowd," was hard-working. Some worked regularly, in the morning or late at night. Others worked spasmodically, like the wild Irish playwright, who would shut himself up for a week at a time, then emerge, pale and drawn, to play like a madman against the time of his next retirement. The pale and youthful father of a family, with the face of Shelley, who wrote vaudeville turns for a living and blank verse tragedies and sonnet cycles for the despair of managers and publishers, hid himself in a concrete cell with three-foot walls, so piped, that, by turning a lever, the whole structure spouted water upon the impending intruder. But in the main, they respected each other's work-time. They drifted into one another's houses as the spirit prompted, but if they found a man at work they went their way. This obtained to all except Mark Hall, who did not have to work for a living; and he climbed trees to get away from popularity and compose in peace.

The crowd was unique in its democracy and solidarity. It had little intercourse with the sober and conventional part of Carmel. This section constituted the aristocracy of art and letters, and was sneered at as bourgeois. In return, it looked askance at the crowd with its rampant bohemianism. The taboo extended to Billy and Saxon. Billy took up the attitude of the clan and sought no work from the other camp. Nor was work offered him.

Hall kept open house. The big living room, with its huge fireplace, divans, shelves and tables of books and magazines, was the center of things. Here, Billy and Saxon were expected to be, and in truth found themselves to be, as much at home as anybody. Here, when wordy discussions on all subjects under the sun were not being waged, Billy played at cut-throat Pedro, horrible fives, bridge, and pinochle. Saxon, a favorite of the young women, sewed with them, teaching them pretties and being taught in fair measure in return.

It was Billy, before they had been in Carmel a week, who said shyly to Saxon:

"Say, you can't guess how I'm missin' all your nice things. What's the matter with writin' Tom to express 'm down? When we start trampin' again, we'll express 'm back."

Saxon wrote the letter, and all that day her heart was singing. Her man was still her lover. And there were in his eyes all the old lights which had been blotted out during the nightmare period of the strike.

"Some pretty nifty skirts around here, but you've got 'em all beat, or I'm no judge," he told her. And again: "Oh, I love you to death anyway. But if them things ain't shipped down there'll be a funeral."

Hall and his wife owned a pair of saddle horses which were kept at the livery stable, and here Billy naturally gravitated. The stable operated the stage and carried the mails between Carmel and Monterey. Also, it rented out carriages and mountain wagons that seated nine persons. With carriages and wagons a driver was furnished The stable often found itself short a driver, and Billy was quickly called upon. He became an extra man at the stable. He received three dollars a day at such times, and drove many parties around the Seventeen Mile Drive, up Carmel Valley, and down the coast to the various points and beaches.

"But they're a pretty uppish sort, most of 'em," he said to Saxon, referring to the persons he drove. "Always MISTER Roberts this, an' MISTER Roberts that—all kinds of ceremony so as to make me not forget they consider themselves better 'n me. You see, I ain't exactly a servant, an' yet I ain't good enough for them. I'm the driver—something half way between a hired man and a chauffeur. Huh! When they eat they give me my lunch off to one side, or afterward. No family party like with Hall an' HIS kind. An' that crowd to-day, why, they just naturally didn't have no lunch for me at all. After this, always, you make me up my own lunch. I won't be be holdin' to 'em for nothin', the damned geezers. An' you'd a-died to seen one of 'em try to give me a tip. I didn't say nothin'. I just looked at 'm like I didn't see 'm, an' turned away casual-like after a moment, leavin' him as embarrassed as hell."

Nevertheless, Billy enjoyed the driving, never more so than when he held the reins, not of four plodding workhorses, but of four fast driving animals, his foot on the powerful brake, and swung around curves and along dizzy cliff-rims to a frightened chorus of women passengers. And when it came to horse judgment and treatment of sick and injured horses even the owner of the stable yielded place to Billy.

"I could get a regular job there any time," he boasted quietly to Saxon. "Why, the country's just sproutin' with jobs for any so-so sort of a fellow. I bet anything, right now, if I said to the boss that I'd take sixty dollars an' work regular, he'd jump for me. He's hinted as much.—And, say! Are you onta the fact that yours truly has learnt a new trade. Well he has. He could take a job stage-drivin' anywheres. They drive six on some of the stages up in Lake County. If we ever get there, I'll get thick with some driver, just to get the reins of six in my hands. An' I'll have you on the box beside me. Some goin' that! Some goin'!"

Billy took little interest in the many discussions waged in Hall's big living room. "Wind-chewin'," was his term for it. To him it was so much good time wasted that might be employed at a game of Pedro, or going swimming, or wrestling in the sand. Saxon, on the contrary, delighted in the logomachy, though little enough she understood of it, following mainly by feeling, and once in a while catching a high light.

But what she could never comprehend was the pessimism that so often cropped up. The wild Irish playwright had terrible spells of depression. Shelley, who wrote vaudeville turns in the concrete cell, was a chronic pessimist. St. John, a young magazine writer, was an anarchic disciple of Nietzsche. Masson, a painter, held to a doctrine of eternal recurrence that was petrifying. And Hall, usually so merry, could outfoot them all when he once got started on the cosmic pathos of religion and the gibbering anthropomorphisms of those who loved not to die. At such times Saxon was oppressed by these sad children of art. It was inconceivable that they, of all people, should be so forlorn.

One night Hall turned suddenly upon Billy, who had been following dimly and who only comprehended that to them everything in life was rotten and wrong.

"Here, you pagan, you, you stolid and flesh-fettered ox, you monstrosity of overweening and perennial health and joy, what do you think of it?" Hall demanded.

"Oh, I've had my troubles," Billy answered, speaking in his wonted slow way. "I've had my hard times, an' fought a losin' strike, an' soaked my watch, an' ben unable to pay my rent or buy grub, an' slugged scabs, an' ben slugged, and ben thrown into jail for makin' a fool of myself. If I get you, I'd be a whole lot better to be a swell hog fattenin' for market an' nothin' worryin', than to be a guy sick to his stomach from not savvyin' how the world is made or from wonderin' what's the good of anything."

"That's good, that prize hog," the poet laughed. "Least irritation, least effort—a compromise of Nirvana and life. Least irritation, least effort, the ideal existence: a jellyfish floating in a tideless, tepid, twilight sea."

"But you're missin' all the good things," Billy objected.

"Name them," came the challenge.

Billy was silent a moment. To him life seemed a large and generous thing. He felt as if his arms ached from inability to compass it all, and he began, haltingly at first, to put his feeling into speech.

"If you'd ever stood up in the ring an' out-gamed an' out-fought a man as good as yourself for twenty rounds, you'd get what I'm drivin' at. Jim Hazard an' I get it when we swim out through the surf an' laugh in the teeth of the biggest breakers that ever pounded the beach, an' when we come out from the shower, rubbed down and dressed, our skin an' muscles like silk, our bodies an' brains all a-tinglin' like silk.. .."

He paused and gave up from sheer inability to express ideas that were nebulous at best and that in reality were remembered sensations.

"Silk of the body, can you beat it?" he concluded lamely, feeling that he had failed to make his point, embarrassed by the circle of listeners.

"We know all that," Hall retorted. "The lies of the flesh. Afterward come rheumatism and diabetes. The wine of life is heady, but all too quickly it turns to—"

"Uric acid," interpolated the wild Irish playwright.

"They's plenty more of the good things," Billy took up with a sudden rush of words. "Good things all the way up from juicy porterhouse and the kind of coffee Mrs. Hall makes to...." He hesitated at what he was about to say, then took it at a plunge. "To a woman you can love an' that loves you. Just take a look at Saxon there with the ukulele in her lap. There's where I got the jellyfish in the dishwater an' the prize hog skinned to death."

A shout of applause and great hand-clapping went up from the girls, and Billy looked painfully uncomfortable.

"But suppose the silk goes out of your body till you creak like a rusty wheelbarrow?" Hall pursued. "Suppose, just suppose, Saxon went away with another man. What then?"

Billy considered a space.

"Then it'd be me for the dishwater an' the jellyfish, I guess." He straightened up in his chair and threw back his shoulders unconsciously as he ran a hand over his biceps and swelled it. Then he took another look at Saxon. "But thank the Lord I still got a wallop in both my arms an' a wife to fill 'em with love."

Again the girls applauded, and Mrs. Hall cried:

"Look at Saxon! She blushing! What have you to say for yourself?"

"That no woman could be happier," she stammered, "and no queen as proud. And that—"

She completed the thought by strumming on the ukulele and singing:

"De Lawd move in or mischievous way His blunders to perform."

"I give you best," Hall grinned to Billy.

"Oh, I don't know," Billy disclaimed modestly. "You've read so much I guess you know more about everything than I do."

"Oh! Oh!" "Traitor!" "Taking it all back!" the girls cried variously.

Billy took heart of courage, reassured them with a slow smile, and said:

"Just the same I'd sooner be myself than have book indigestion. An' as for Saxon, why, one kiss of her lips is worth more'n all the libraries in the world."

CHAPTER X

"There be hills and valleys, and rich land, and streams of clear water, good wagon roads and a railroad not too far away, plenty of sunshine, and cold enough at night to need blankets, and not only pines but plenty of other kinds of trees, with open spaces to pasture Billy's horses and cattle, and deer and rabbits for him to shoot, and lots and lots of redwood trees, and... and... well, and no fog," Saxon concluded the description of the farm she and Billy sought.

Mark Hall laughed delightedly.

"And nightingales roosting in all the trees," he cried; "flowers that neither fail nor fade, bees without stings, honey dew every morning, showers of manna between-whiles, fountains of youth and quarries of philosopher's stones—why, I know the very place. Let me show you."

She waited while he pored over road-maps of the state. Failing in them, he got out a big atlas, and, though all the countries of the world were in it, he could not find what he was after.

"Never mind," he said. "Come over to-night and I'll be able to show you."

That evening he led her out on the veranda to the telescope, and she found herself looking through it at the full moon.

"Somewhere up there in some valley you'll find that farm," he teased.

Mrs. Hall looked inquiringly at them as they returned inside.

"I've been showing her a valley in the moon where she expects to go farming," he laughed.

"We started out prepared to go any distance," Saxon said. "And if it's to the moon, I expect we can make it."

"But my dear child, you can't expect to find such a paradise on the earth," Hall continued. "For instance, you can't have redwoods without fog. They go together. The redwoods grow only in the fog belt."

Saxon debated a while.

"Well, we could put up with a little fog," she conceded, "—almost anything to have redwoods. I don't know what a quarry of philosopher's stones is like, but if it's anything like Mr. Hafler's marble quarry, and there's a railroad handy, I guess we could manage to worry along. And you don't have to go to the moon for honey dew. They scrape it off of the leaves of the bushes up in Nevada County. I know that for a fact, because my father told my mother about it, and she told me."

A little later in the evening, the subject of farming having remained uppermost, Hall swept off into a diatribe against the "gambler's paradise," which was his epithet for the United States.

"When you think of the glorious chance," he said. "A new country, bounded by the oceans, situated just right in latitude, with the richest land and vastest natural resources of any country in the world, settled by immigrants who had thrown off all the leading strings of the Old World and were in the humor for democracy. There was only one thing to stop them from perfecting the democracy they started, and that thing was greediness.

"They started gobbling everything in sight like a lot of swine, and while they gobbled democracy went to smash. Gobbling became gambling. It was a nation of tin horns. Whenever a man lost his stake, all he had to do was to chase the frontier west a few miles and get another stake. They moved over the face of the land like so many locusts. They destroyed everything—the Indians, the soil, the forests, just as they destroyed the buffalo and the passenger pigeon. Their morality in business and politics was gambler morality. Their laws were gambling laws—how to play the game. Everybody played. Therefore, hurrah for the game. Nobody objected, because nobody was unable to play. As I said, the losers chased the frontier for fresh stakes. The winner of to-day, broke to-morrow, on the day following might be riding his luck to royal flushes on five-card draws.

"So they gobbled and gambled from the Atlantic to the Pacific, until they'd swined a whole continent. When they'd finished with the lands and forests and mines, they turned back, gambling for any little stakes they'd overlooked, gambling for franchises and monopolies, using politics to protect their crooked deals and brace games. And democracy gone clean to smash.

"And then was the funniest time of all. The losers couldn't get any more stakes, while the winners went on gambling among themselves. The losers could only stand around with their hands in their pockets and look on. When they got hungry, they went, hat in hand, and begged the successful gamblers for a job. The losers went to work for the winners, and they've been working for them ever since, and democracy side-tracked up Salt Creek. You, Billy Roberts, have never had a hand in the game in your life. That's because your people were among the also-rans."

"How about yourself?" Billy asked. "I ain't seen you holdin' any hands."

"I don't have to. I don't count. I am a parasite."

"What's that?"

"A flea, a woodtick, anything that gets something for nothing. I batten on the mangy hides of the workingmen. I don't have to gamble. I don't have to work. My father left me enough of his winnings.—Oh, don't preen yourself, my boy. Your folks were just as bad as mine. But yours lost, and mine won, and so you plow in my potato patch."

"I don't see it," Billy contended stoutly. "A man with gumption can win out to-day—"

"On government land?" Hall asked quickly.

Billy swallowed and acknowledged the stab.

"Just the same he can win out," he reiterated.

"Surely—he can win a job from some other fellow? A young husky with a good head like yours can win jobs anywhere. But think of the handicaps on the fellows who lose. How many tramps have you met along the road who could get a job driving four horses for the Carmel Livery Stabler And some of them were as husky as you when they were young. And on top of it all you've got no shout coming. It's a mighty big come-down from gambling for a continent to gambling for a job."

"Just the same—" Billy recommenced.

"Oh, you've got it in your blood," Hall cut him off cavalierly. "And why not? Everybody in this country has been gambling for generations. It was in the air when you were born. You've breathed it all your life. You, who 've never had a white chip in the game, still go on shouting for it and capping for it."

"But what are all of us losers to do?" Saxon inquired.

"Call in the police and stop the game," Hall recommended. "It's crooked."

Saxon frowned.

"Do what your forefathers didn't do," he amplified. "Go ahead and perfect democracy."

She remembered a remark of Mercedes. "A friend of mine says that democracy is an enchantment."

"It is—in a gambling joint. There are a million boys in our public schools right now swallowing the gump of canal boy to President, and millions of worthy citizens who sleep sound every night in the belief that they have a say in running the country."

"You talk like my brother Tom," Saxon said, failing to comprehend. "If we all get into politics and work hard for something better maybe we'll get it after a thousand years or so. But I want it now." She clenched her hands passionately. "I can't wait; I want it now."

"But that is just what I've been telling you, my dear girl. That's what's the trouble with all the losers. They can't wait. They want it now—a stack of chips and a fling at the game. Well, they won't get it now. That's what's the matter with you, chasing a valley in the moon. That's what's the matter with Billy, aching right now for a chance to win ten cents from me at Pedro cussing wind-chewing under his breath."

"Gee! you'd make a good soap-boxer," commented Billy.

"And I'd be a soap-boxer if I didn't have the spending of my father's ill-gotten gains. It's none of my affair. Islet them rot. They'd be just as bad if they were on top. It's all a mess—blind bats, hungry swine, and filthy buzzards—"

Here Mrs. Hall interferred.

"Now, Mark, you stop that, or you'll be getting the blues."

He tossed his mop of hair and laughed with an effort.

"No I won't," he denied. "I'm going to get ten cents from Billy at a game of Pedro. He won't have a look in."

Saxon and Billy flourished in the genial human atmosphere of Carmel. They appreciated in their own estimation. Saxon felt that she was something more than a laundry girl and the wife of a union teamster. She was no longer pent in the narrow working class environment of a Pine street neighborhood. Life had grown opulent. They fared better physically, materially, and spiritually; and all this was reflected in their features, in the carriage of their bodies. She knew Billy had never been handsomer nor in more splendid bodily condition. He swore he had a harem, and that she was his second wife—twice as beautiful as the first one he had married. And she demurely confessed to him that Mrs. Hall and several others of the matrons had enthusiastically admired her form one day when in for a cold dip in Carmel river.

They had got around her, and called her Venus, and made her crouch and assume different poses.

Billy understood the Venus reference; for a marble one, with broken arms, stood in Hall's living room, and the poet had told him the world worshiped it as the perfection of female form.

"I always said you had Annette Kellerman beat a mile," Billy said; and so proud was his air of possession that Saxon blushed and trembled, and hid her hot face against his breast.

The men in the crowd were open in their admiration of Saxon, in an above-board manner. But she made no mistake. She did not lose her head. There was no chance of that, for her love for Billy beat more strongly than ever. Nor was she guilty of over-appraisal. She knew him for what he was, and loved him with open eyes. He had no book learning, no art, like the other men. His grammar was bad; she knew that, just as she knew that he would never mend it. Yet she would not have exchanged him for any of the others, not even for Mark Hall with the princely heart whom she loved much in the same way that she loved his wife.

For that matter, she found in Billy a certain health and rightness, a certain essential integrity, which she prized more highly than all book learning and bank accounts. It was by virtue of this health, and rightness, and integrity, that he had beaten Hall in argument the night the poet was on the pessimistic rampage. Billy had beaten him, not with the weapons of learning, but just by being himself and by speaking out the truth that was in him. Best of all, he had not even known that he had beaten, and had taken the applause as good-natured banter. But Saxon knew, though she could scarcely tell why; and she would always remember how the wife of Shelley had whispered to her afterward with shining eyes: "Oh, Saxon, you must be so happy."

Were Saxon driven to speech to attempt to express what Billy meant to her, she would have done it with the simple word "man." Always he was that to her. Always in glowing splendor, that was his connotation—MAN. Sometimes, by herself, she would all but weep with joy at recollection of his way of informing some truculent male that he was standing on his foot. "Get off your foot. You're standin' on it." It was Billy! It was magnificently Billy. And it was this Billy who loved her. She knew it. She knew it by the pulse that only a woman knows how to gauge. He loved her less wildly, it was true; but more fondly, more maturely. It was the love that lasted—if only they did not go back to the city where the beautiful things of the spirit perished and the beast bared its fangs.

In the early spring, Mark Hall and his wife went to New York, the two Japanese servants of the bungalow were dismissed, and Saxon and Billy were installed as caretakers. Jim Hazard, too, departed on his yearly visit to Paris; and though Billy missed him, he continued his long swims out through the breakers. Hall's two saddle horses had been left in his charge, and Saxon made herself a pretty cross-saddle riding costume of tawny-brown corduroy that matched the glints in her hair. Billy no longer worked at odd jobs. As extra driver at the stable he earned more than they spent, and, in preference to cash, he taught Saxon to ride, and was out and away with her over the country on all-day trips. A favorite ride was around by the coast to Monterey, where he taught her to swim in the big Del Monte tank. They would come home in the evening across the hills. Also, she took to following him on his early morning hunts, and life seemed one long vacation.

CHAPTER X

"I'll tell you one thing," he said to Saxon, one day, as they drew their horses to a halt and gazed down into Carmel Valley. "I ain't never going to work steady for another man for wages as long as I live."

"Work isn't everything," she acknowledged.

"I should guess not. Why, look here, Saxon, what'd it mean if I worked teamin' in Oakland for a million dollars a day for a million years and just had to go on stayin' there an' livin' the way we used to? It'd mean work all day, three squares, an' movie' pictures for recreation. Movin' pictures! Huh! We're livin' movie' pictures these days. I'd sooner have one year like what we're havin' here in Carmel and then die, than a thousan' million years like on Pine street."

Saxon had warned the Halls by letter that she and Billy intended starting on their search for the valley in the moon as soon as the first of summer arrived. Fortunately, the poet was put to no inconvenience, for Bideaux, the Iron Man with the basilisk eyes, had abandoned his dreams of priesthood and decided to become an actor. He arrived at Carmel from the Catholic college in time to take charge of the bungalow.

Much to Saxon's gratification, the crowd was loth to see them depart. The owner of the Carmel stable offered to put Billy in charge at ninety dollars a month. Also, he received a similar offer from the stable in Pacific Grove.

"Whither away," the wild Irish playwright hailed them on the station platform at Monterey. He was just returning from New York.

"To a valley in the moon," Saxon answered gaily.

He regarded their business-like packs.

"By George!" he cried. "I'll do it! By George! Let me come along." Then his face fell. "And I've signed the contract," he groaned. "Three acts! Say, you're lucky. And this time of year, too."

CHAPTER XI

"We hiked into Monterey last winter, but we're ridin' out now, b 'gosh!" Billy said as the train pulled out and they leaned back in their seats.

They had decided against retracing their steps over the ground already traveled, and took the train to San Francisco. They had been warned by Mark Hall of the enervation of the south, and were bound north for their blanket climate. Their intention was to cross the Bay to Sausalito and wander up through the coast counties Here, Hall had told them, they would find the true home of the redwood. But Billy, in the smoking car for a cigarette, seated himself beside a man who was destined to deflect them from their course. He was a keen-faced, dark-eyed man, undoubtedly a Jew; and Billy, remembering Saxon's admonition always to ask questions, watched his opportunity and started a conversation. It took but a little while to learn that Gunston was a commission merchant, and to realize that the content of his talk was too valuable for Saxon to lose. Promptly, when he saw that the other's cigar was finished, Billy invited him into the next car to meet Saxon. Billy would have been incapable of such an act prior to his sojourn in Carmel. That much at least he had acquired of social facility.

"He's just teen tellin' me about the potato kings, and I wanted him to tell you," Billy explained to Saxon after the introduction. "Go on and tell her, Mr. Gunston, about that fan tan sucker that made nineteen thousan' last year in celery an' asparagus."

"I was just telling your husband about the way the Chinese make things go up the San Joaquin river. It would be worth your while to go up there and look around. It's the good season now—too early for mosquitoes. You can get off the train at Black Diamond or Antioch and travel around among the big farming islands on the steamers and launches. The fares are cheap, and you'll find some of those big gasoline boats, like the Duchess and Princess, more like big steamboats."

"Tell her about Chow Lam," Billy urged.

The commission merchant leaned back and laughed.

"Chow Lam, several years ago, was a broken-down fan tan player. He hadn't a cent, and his health was going back on him. He had worn out his back with twenty years' work in the gold mines, washing over the tailings of the early miners. And whatever he'd made he'd lost at gambling. Also, he was in debt three hundred dollars to the Six Companies—you know, they're Chinese affairs. And, remember, this was only seven years ago—health breaking down, three hundred in debt, and no trade. Chow Lam blew into Stockton and got a job on the peat lands at day's wages. It was a

Chinese company, down on Middle River, that farmed celery and asparagus. This was when he got onto himself and took stock of himself. A quarter of a century in the United States, back not so strong as it used to was, and not a penny laid by for his return to China. He saw how the Chinese in the company had done it—saved their wages and bought a share.

"He saved his wages for two years, and bought one share in a thirty-share company. That was only five years ago. They leased three hundred acres of peat land from a white man who preferred traveling in Europe. Out of the profits of that one share in the first year, he bought two shares in another company. And in a year more, out of the three shares, he organized a company of his own. One year of this, with bad luck, and he just broke even. That brings it up to three years ago. The following year, bumper crops, he netted four thousand. The next year it wan five thousand. And last year he cleaned up nineteen thousand dollars. Pretty good, eh, for old broken-down Chow Lam?"

"My!" was all Saxon could say.

Her eager interest, however, incited the commission merchant to go on.

"Look at Sing Kee—the Potato King of Stockton. I know him well. I've had more large deals with him and made less money than with any man I know. He was only a coolie, and he smuggled himself into the United States twenty years ago. Started at day's wages, then peddled vegetables in a couple of baskets slung on a stick, and after that opened up a store in Chinatown in San Francisco. But he had a head on him, and he was soon onto the curves of the Chinese farmers that dealt at his store. The store couldn't make money fast enough to suit him. He headed up the San Joaquin. Didn't do much for a couple of years except keep his eyes peeled. Then he jumped in and leased twelve hundred acres at seven dollars an acre."

"My God!" Billy said in an awe-struck voice. "Eight thousan', four hundred dollars just for rent the first year. I know five hundred acres I can buy for three dollars an acre."

"Will it grow potatoes?" Gunston asked.

Billy shook his head. "Nor nothin' else, I guess."

All three laughed heartily and the commission merchant resumed:

"That seven dollars was only for the land. Possibly you know what it costs to plow twelve hundred acres?"

Billy nodded solemnly.

"And he got a hundred and sixty sacks to the acre that year," Gunston continued. "Potatoes were selling at fifty cents. My father was at the head of our concern at the time, so I know for a fact. And Sing Kee could have sold at fifty cents and made money. But did he? Trust a Chinaman to know the market. They can skin the commission merchants at it. Sing Kee held on. When 'most everybody else had sold, potatoes began to climb. He laughed at our buyers when we offered him sixty cents, seventy cents, a dollar. Do you want to know what he finally did sell for? One dollar and sixty-five a sack. Suppose they actually cost him forty cents. A hundred and sixty times twelve hundred... let me see... twelve times nought is nought and twelve times sixteen is a hundred and ninety-two... a hundred and ninety-two thousand sacks at a dollar and a quarter net... four into a hundred and ninety-two is forty-eight, plus, is two hundred and forty—there you are, two hundred and forty thousand dollars clear profit on that year's deal."

"An' him a Chink," Billy mourned disconsolately. He turned to Saxon. "They ought to be some new country for us white folks to go to. Gosh!—we're settin' on the stoop all right, all right."

"But, of course, that was unusual," Glunston hastened to qualify. "There was a failure of potatoes in other districts, and a corner, and in some strange way Sing Kee was dead on. He never made profits like that again. But he goes ahead steadily. Last year he had four thousand acres in potatoes, a thousand in asparagus, five hundred in celery and five hundred in beans. And he's running six hundred acres in seeds. No matter what happens to one or two crops, he can't lose on all of them."

"I've seen twelve thousand acres of apple trees," Saxon said. "And I'd like to see four thousand acres in potatoes."

"And we will," Billy rejoined with great positiveness. "It's us for the San Joaquin. We don't know what's in our country. No wonder we're out on the stoop."

"You'll find lots of kings up there," Gunston related. "Yep Hong Lee—they call him 'Big Jim,' and Ah Pock, and Ah Whang, and—then there's Shima, the Japanese potato king. He's worth several millions. Lives like a prince."

"Why don't Americans succeed like that?" asked Saxon.

"Because they won't, I guess. There's nothing to stop them except themselves. I'll tell you one thing, though—give me the Chinese to deal with. He's honest. His word is as good as his bond. If he says he'll do a thing, he'll do it. And, anyway, the white man doesn't know how to farm. Even the up-to-date white farmer is content with one crop at a time and rotation of crops. Mr. John Chinaman goes him one better, and grows two crops at one time on the same soil. I've seen it—radishes and carrots, two crops, sown at one time."

"Which don't stand to reason," Billy objected. "They'd be only a half crop of each."

"Another guess coming," Gunston jeered. "Carrots have to be thinned when they're so far along. So do radishes. But carrots grow slow. Radishes grow fast. The slow-going carrots serve the purpose of thinning the radishes. And when the radishes are pulled, ready for market, that thins the carrots, which come along later. You can't beat the Chink."

"Don't see why a white man can't do what a Chink can," protested Billy.

"That sounds all right," Gunston replied. "The only objection is that the white man doesn't. The Chink is busy all the time, and he keeps the ground just as busy. He has organization, system. Who ever heard of white farmers keeping books? The Chink does. No guess work with him. He knows just where he stands, to a cent, on any crop at any moment. And he knows the market. He plays both ends. How he does it is beyond me, but he knows the market better than we commission merchants.

"Then, again, he's patient but not stubborn. Suppose he does make a mistake, and gets in a crop, and then finds the market is wrong. In such a situation the white man gets stubborn and hangs on like a bulldog. But not the Chink. He's going to minimize the losses of that mistake. That land has got to work, and make money. Without a quiver or a regret, the moment he's learned his error, he puts his plows into that crop, turns it under, and plants something else. He has the savve. He can look at a sprout, just poked up out of the ground, and tell how it's going to turn out—whether it will head up or won't head up; or if it's going to head up good, medium, or bad. That's one end. Take the other end. He controls his crop. He forces it or holds it back with an eye on the market. And when the market is just right, there's his crop, ready to deliver, timed to the minute."

The conversation with Gunston lasted hours, and the more he talked of the Chinese and their farming ways the more Saxon became aware of a growing dissatisfaction. She did not question the facts. The trouble was that they were not alluring. Somehow, she could not find place for them in her valley of the moon. It was not until the genial Jew left the train that Billy gave definite statement to what was vaguely bothering her.

"Huh! We ain't Chinks. We're white folks. Does a Chink ever want to ride a horse, hell-bent for election an' havin' a good time of it? Did you ever see a Chink go swimmin' out through the breakers at Carmel?—or boxin', wrestlin', runnin' an' jumpin' for the sport of it? Did you ever see a Chink take a shotgun on his arm, tramp six miles, an' come back happy with one measly rabbit? What does a Chink do? Work his damned head off. That's all he's good for. To hell with work, if that's the whole of the game—an' I've done my share of work, an' I can work alongside of any of 'em. But what's the good? If they's one thing I've learned solid since you an' me hit the road, Saxon, it is that work's the least part of life. God!—if it was all of life I couldn't cut my throat quick enough to get away from it. I want shotguns an' rifles, an' a horse between my legs. I don't want to be so tired all the time I can't love my wife. Who wants to be rich an' clear two hundred an' forty thousand on a potato deal! Look at Rockefeller. Has to live on milk. I want porterhouse and a stomach that can bite sole-leather. An' I want you, an' plenty of time along with you, an' fun for both of us. What's the good of life if they ain't no fun?"

"Oh, Billy!" Saxon cried. "It's just what I've been trying to get straightened out in my head. It's been worrying me for ever so long. I was afraid there was something wrong with me—that I wasn't made for the country after all. All the time I didn't envy the San Leandro Portuguese. I didn't want to be one, nor a Pajaro Valley Dalmatian, nor even a Mrs. Mortimer. And you didn't either. What we want is a valley of the moon, with not too much work, and all the fun we want. And we'll just keep on looking until we find it. And if we don't find it, we'll go on having the fun just as we have ever since we left Oakland. And, Billy... we're never, never going to work our damned heads off, are we?"

"Not on your life," Billy growled in fierce affirmation.

They walked into Black Diamond with their packs on their backs. It was a scattered village of shabby little cottages, with a main street that was a wallow of black mud from the last late spring rain. The sidewalks bumped up and down in uneven steps and landings. Everything seemed un-American. The names on the strange dingy shops were unspeakably foreign. The one dingy hotel was run by a Greek. Greeks were everywhere—swarthy men in sea-boots and tam-o'-shanters, hatless women in bright colors, hordes of sturdy children, and all speaking in outlandish voices, crying shrilly and vivaciously with the volubility of the Mediterranean.

"Huh!—this ain't the United States," Billy muttered. Down on the water front they found a fish cannery and an asparagus cannery in the height of the busy season, where they looked in vain among the toilers for familiar American faces. Billy picked out the bookkeepers and foremen for Americans. All the rest were Greeks, Italians, and Chinese.

At the steamboat wharf, they watched the bright-painted Greek boats arriving, discharging their loads of glorious salmon, and departing. New York Cut-Off, as the slough was called, curved to the west and north and flowed into a vast body of water which was the united Sacramento and San Joaquin rivers.

Beyond the steamboat wharf, the fishing wharves dwindled to stages for the drying of nets; and here, away from the noise and clatter of the alien town, Saxon and Billy took off their packs and rested. The tall, rustling tules grew out of the deep water close to the dilapidated boat-landing where they sat. Opposite the town lay a long flat island, on which a row of ragged poplars leaned against the sky.

"Just like in that Dutch windmill picture Mark Hall has," Saxon said.

Billy pointed out the mouth of the slough and across the broad reach of water to a cluster of tiny white buildings, behind which, like a glimmering mirage, rolled the low Montezuma Hills.

"Those houses is Collinsville," he informed her. "The Sacramento river comes in there, and you go up it to Rio Vista an' Isleton, and Walnut Grove, and all those places Mr. Gunston was tellin' us about. It's all islands and sloughs, connectin' clear across an' back to the San Joaquin."

"Isn't the sun good," Saxon yawned. "And how quiet it is here, so short a distance away from those strange foreigners. And to think! in the cities, right now, men are beating and killing each other for jobs."

Now and again an overland passenger train rushed by in the distance, echoing along the background of foothills of Mt. Diablo, which bulked, twin-peaked, green-crinkled, against the sky. Then the slumbrous quiet would fall, to be broken by the far call of a foreign tongue or by a gasoline fishing boat chugging in through the mouth of the slough.

Not a hundred feet away, anchored close in the tules, lay a beautiful white yacht. Despite its tininess, it looked broad and comfortable. Smoke was rising for'ard from its stovepipe. On its stern, in gold letters, they read Roamer. On top of the cabin, basking in the sunshine, lay a man and woman, the latter with a pink scarf around her head. The man was reading aloud from a book, while she sewed. Beside them sprawled a fox terrier.

"Gosh! they don't have to stick around cities to be happy," Billy commented.

A Japanese came on deck from the cabin, sat down for'ard, and began picking a chicken. The feathers floated away in a long line toward the mouth of the slough.

"Oh! Look!" Saxon pointed in her excitement. "He's fishing! And the line is fast to his toe!"

The man had dropped the book face-downward on the cabin and reached for the line, while the woman looked up from her sewing, and the terrier began to bark. In came the line, hand under hand, and at the end a big catfish. When this was removed, and the line rebaited and dropped overboard, the man took a turn around his toe and went on reading.

A Japanese came down on the landing-stage beside Saxon and Billy, and hailed the yacht. He carried parcels of meat and vegetables; one coat pocket bulged with letters, the other with morning papers. In response to his hail, the Japanese on the yacht stood up with the part-plucked chicken. The man said something to him, put aside the book, got into the white skiff lying astern, and rowed to the landing. As he came alongside the stage, he pulled in his oars, caught hold, and said good morning genially.

"Why, I know you," Saxon said impulsively, to Billy's amazement. "You are.. .."

Here she broke off in confusion.

"Go on," the man said, smiling reassurance.

"You are Jack Hastings, I 'm sure of it. I used to see your photograph in the papers all the time you were war correspondent in the Japanese-Russian War. You've written lots of books, though I've never read them."

"Right you are," he ratified. "And what's your name?"

Saxon introduced herself and Billy, and, when she noted the writer's observant eye on their packs, she sketched the pilgrimage they were on. The farm in the valley of the moon evidently caught his fancy, and, though the Japanese and his parcels were safely in the skiff, Hastings still lingered. When Saxon spoke of Carmel, he seemed to know everybody in Hall's crowd, and when he heard they were intending to go to Rio Vista, his invitation was immediate.

"Why, we're going that way ourselves, inside an hour, as soon as slack water comes," he exclaimed. "It's just the thing. Come on on board. We'll be there by four this afternoon if there's any wind at all. Come on. My wife's on board, and Mrs. Hall is one of her best chums. We've been away to South America—just got back; or you'd have seen us in Carmel. Hal wrote to us about the pair of you."

It was the second time in her life that Saxon had been in a small boat, and the Roamer was the first yacht she had ever been on board. The writer's wife, whom he called Clara, welcomed them heartily, and Saxon lost no time in falling in love with her and in being fallen in love with in return. So strikingly did they resemble each other, that Hastings was not many minutes in calling attention to it. He made them stand side by side, studied their eyes and mouths and ears, compared their hands, their hair, their ankles, and swore that his fondest dream was shattered—namely, that when Clara had been made the mold was broken.

On Clara's suggestion that it might have been pretty much the same mold, they compared histories. Both were of the pioneer stock. Clara's mother, like Saxon's, had crossed the Plains with ox-teams, and, like Saxon's, had wintered in Salt Intake City—in fact, had, with her sisters, opened the first Gentile school in that Mormon stronghold. And, if Saxon's father had helped raise the Bear Flag rebellion at Sonoma, it was at Sonoma that Clara's father had mustered in for the War of the Rebellion and ridden as far east with his troop as Salt Lake City, of which place he had been provost marshal when the Mormon trouble flared up. To complete it all, Clara fetched from the cabin an ukulele of boa wood that was the twin to Saxon's, and together they sang "Honolulu Tomboy."

Hastings decided to eat dinner—he called the midday meal by its old-fashioned name—before sailing; and down below Saxon was surprised and delighted by the measure of comfort in so tiny a cabin. There was just room for Billy to stand upright. A centerboard-case divided the room in half longitudinally, and to this was attached the hinged table from which they ate. Low bunks that ran the full cabin length, upholstered in cheerful green, served as seats. A curtain, easily attached by hooks between the centerboard-case and the roof, at night screened Mrs. Hastings' sleeping quarters. On the opposite side the two Japanese bunked, while for'ard, under the deck, was the galley. So small was it that there was just room beside it for the cook, who was compelled by the low deck to squat on his hands. The other Japanese, who had brought the parcels on board, waited on the table.

"They are looking for a ranch in the valley of the moon," Hastings concluded his explanation of the pilgrimage to Clara.

"Oh!—don't you know—" she cried; but was silenced by her husband.

"Hush," he said peremptorily, then turned to their guests. "Listen. There's something in that valley of the moon idea, but I won't tell you what. It is a secret. Now we've a ranch in Sonoma Valley about eight miles from the very town of Sonoma where you two girls' fathers took up soldiering; and if you ever come to our ranch you'll learn the secret. Oh, believe me, it's connected with your valley of the moon.—Isn't it, Mate?"

This last was the mutual name he and Clara had for each other.

She smiled and laughed and nodded her head.

"You might find our valley the very one you are looking for," she said.

But Hastings shook his head at her to check further speech. She turned to the fox terrier and made it speak for a piece of meat.

"Her name's Peggy," she told Saxon. "We had two Irish terriers down in the South Seas, brother and sister, but they died. We called them Peggy and Possum. So she's named after the original Peggy."

Billy was impressed by the ease with which the Roamer was operated. While they lingered at table, at a word from Hastings the two Japanese had gone on deck. Billy could hear them throwing down the halyards, casting off gaskets, and heaving the anchor short on the tiny winch. In several minutes one called down that everything was ready, and all went on deck. Hoisting mainsail and jigger was a matter of minutes. Then the cook and cabin-boy broke out anchor, and, while one hove it up, the other hoisted the jib. Hastings, at the wheel, trimmed the sheet. The Roamer paid off, filled her sails, slightly heeling, and slid across the smooth water and out the mouth of New York Slough. The Japanese coiled the halyards and went below for their own dinner.

"The flood is just beginning to make," said Hastings, pointing to a striped spar-buoy that was slightly tipping up-stream on the edge of the channel.

The tiny white houses of Collinsville, which they were nearing, disappeared behind a low island, though the Montezuma Hills, with their long, low, restful lines, slumbered on the horizon apparently as far away as ever.

As the Roamer passed the mouth of Montezuma Slough and entered the Sacramento, they came upon Collinsville close at hand. Saxon clapped her hands.

"It's like a lot of toy houses," she said, "cut out of cardboard. And those hilly fields are just painted up behind."

They passed many arks and houseboats of fishermen moored among the tules, and the women and children, like the men in the boats, were dark-skinned, black-eyed, foreign. As they proceeded up the river, they began to encounter dredges at work, biting out mouthfuls of the sandy river bottom and heaping it on top of the huge levees. Great mats of willow brush, hundreds of yards in length, were laid on top of the river-slope of the levees and held in place by steel cables and thousands of cubes of cement. The willows soon sprouted, Hastings told them, and by the time the mats were rotted away the sand was held in place by the roots of the trees.

"It must cost like Sam Hill," Billy observed.

CHAPTER XI

"But the land is worth it," Hastings explained. "This island land is the most productive in the world. This section of California is like Holland. You wouldn't think it, but this water we're sailing on is higher than the surface of the islands. They're like leaky boats—calking, patching, pumping, night and day and all the time. But it pays. It pays."

Except for the dredgers, the fresh-piled sand, the dense willow thickets, and always Mt. Diablo to the south, nothing was to be seen. Occasionally a river steamboat passed, and blue herons flew into the trees.

"It must be very lonely," Saxon remarked.

Hastings laughed and told her she would change her mind later. Much he related to them of the river lands, and after a while he got on the subject of tenant farming. Saxon had started him by speaking of the land-hungry Anglo-Saxons.

"Land-hogs," he snapped. "That's our record in this country. As one old Reuben told a professor of an agricultural experiment station: 'They ain't no sense in tryin' to teach me farmin'. I know all about it. Ain't I worked out three farms?' It was his kind that destroyed New England. Back there great sections are relapsing to wilderness. In one state, at least, the deer have increased until they are a nuisance. There are abandoned farms by the tens of thousands. I've gone over the lists of them—farms in New York, New Jersey, Massachusetts, Connecticut. Offered for sale on easy payment. The prices asked wouldn't pay for the improvements, while the land, of course, is thrown in for nothing.

"And the same thing is going on, in one way or another, the same land-robbing and hogging, over the rest of the country—down in Texas, in Missouri, and Kansas, out here in California. Take tenant farming. I know a ranch in my county where the land was worth a hundred and twenty-five an acre. And it gave its return at that valuation. When the old man died, the son leased it to a Portuguese and went to live in the city. In five years the Portuguese skimmed the cream and dried up the udder. The second lease, with another Portuguese for three years, gave one-quarter the former return. No third Portuguese appeared to offer to lease it. There wasn't anything left. That ranch was worth fifty thousand when the old man died. In the end the son got eleven thousand for it. Why, I've seen land that paid twelve per cent., that, after the skimming of a five-years' lease, paid only one and a quarter per cent."

"It's the same in our valley," Mrs. Hastings supplemented. "All the old farms are dropping into ruin. Take the Ebell Place, Mate." Her husband nodded emphatic indorsement. "When we used to know it, it was a perfect paradise of a farm. There were dams and lakes, beautiful meadows, lush hayfields, red hills of grape-lands, hundreds of acres of good pasture, heavenly groves of pines and oaks, a stone winery, stone barns, grounds—oh, I couldn't describe it in hours. When Mrs. Bell died, the family scattered, and the leasing began. It's a ruin to-day. The trees have been cut and sold for firewood. There's only a little bit of the vineyard that isn't abandoned—just enough to make wine for the present Italian lessees, who are running a poverty-stricken milk ranch on the leavings of the soil. I rode over it last year, and cried. The beautiful orchard is a horror. The grounds have gone back to the wild. Just because they didn't keep the gutters cleaned out, the rain trickled down and dry-rotted the timbers, and the big stone barn is caved in. The same with part of the winery—the other part is used for stabling the cows. And the house!—words can't describe!"

"It's become a profession," Hastings went on. "The 'movers.' They lease, clean out and gut a place in several years, and then move on. They're not like the foreigners, the Chinese, and Japanese, and the rest. In the main they're a lazy, vagabond, poor-white sort, who do nothing else but skin the soil and move, skin the soil and move. Now take the Portuguese and Italians in our country. They are different. They arrive in the country without a penny and work for others of their countrymen until they've learned the language and their way about. Now they're not movers. What they are after is land of their own, which they will love and care for and conserve. But, in the meantime, how to get it? Saving wages is slow. There is a quicker way. They lease. In three years they can gut enough out of somebody else's land to set themselves up for life. It is sacrilege, a veritable rape of the land; but what of it? It's the way of the United States."

He turned suddenly on Billy.

"Look here, Roberts. You and your wife are looking for your bit of land. You want it bad. Now take my advice. It's cold, hard advice. Become a tenant farmer. Lease some place, where the old folks have died and the country isn't good enough for the sons and daughters. Then gut it. Wring the last dollar out of the soil, repair nothing, and in three years you'll have your own place paid for. Then turn over a new leaf, and love your soil. Nourish it. Every dollar you feed it will return you two. Lend have nothing scrub about the place. If it's a horse, a cow, a pig, a chicken, or a blackberry vine, see that it's thoroughbred."

"But it's wicked!" Saxon wrung out. "It's wicked advice."

"We live in a wicked age," Hastings countered, smiling grimly. "This wholesale land-skinning is the national crime of the United States to-day. Nor would I give your husband such advice if I weren't absolutely certain that the land he skins would be skinned by some Portuguese or Italian if he refused. As fast as they arrive and settle down, they send for their sisters and their cousins and their aunts. If you were thirsty, if a warehouse were burning and beautiful Rhine wine were running to waste, would you stay your hand from scooping a drink? Well, the national warehouse is afire in many places, and no end of the good things are running to waste. Help yourself. If you don't, the immigrants will."

"Oh, you don't know him," Mrs. Hastings hurried to explain. "He spends all his time on the ranch in conserving the soil. There are over a thousand acres of woods alone, and, though he thins and forests like a surgeon, he won't let a tree be chopped without his permission. He's even planted a hundred thousand trees. He's always draining and ditching to stop erosion, and experimenting with pasture grasses. And every little while he buys some exhausted adjoining ranch and starts building up the soil."

"Wherefore I know what I 'm talking about," Hastings broke in. "And my advice holds. I love the soil, yet to-morrow, things being as they are and if I were poor, I'd gut five hundred acres in order to buy twenty-five for myself. When you get into Sonoma Valley, look me up, and I'll put you onto the whole game, and both ends of it. I'll show you construction as well as destruction. When you find a farm doomed to be gutted anyway, why jump in and do it yourself."

"Yes, and he mortgaged himself to the eyes," laughed Mrs. Hastings, "to keep five hundred acres of woods out of the hands of the charcoal burners."

CHAPTER XI

Ahead, on the left bank of the Sacramento, just at the fading end of the Montezuma Hills, Rio Vista appeared. The Roamer slipped through the smooth water, past steamboat wharves, landing stages, and warehouses. The two Japanese went for'ard on deck. At command of Hastings, the jib ran down, and he shot the Roomer into the wind, losing way, until he called, "Let go the hook!" The anchor went down, and the yacht swung to it, so close to shore that the skiff lay under overhanging willows.

"Farther up the river we tie to the bank," Mrs. Hastings said, "so that when you wake in the morning you find the branches of trees sticking down into the cabin."

"Ooh!" Saxon murmured, pointing to a lump on her wrist. "Look at that. A mosquito."

"Pretty early for them," Hastings said. "But later on they're terrible. I've seen them so thick I couldn't back the jib against them."

Saxon was not nautical enough to appreciate his hyperbole, though Billy grinned.

"There are no mosquitoes in the valley of the moon," she said.

"No, never," said Mrs. Hastings, whose husband began immediately to regret the smallness of the cabin which prevented him from offering sleeping accommodations.

An automobile bumped along on top of the levee, and the young boys and girls in it cried, "Oh, you kid!" to Saxon and Billy, and Hastings, who was rowing them ashore in the skiff. Hastings called, "Oh, you kid!" back to them; and Saxon, pleasuring in the boyishness of his sunburned face, was reminded of the boyishness of Mark Hall and his Carmel crowd.

CHAPTER XII

Crossing the Sacramento on an old-fashioned ferry a short distance above Rio Vista, Saxon and Billy entered the river country. From the top of the levee she got her revelation. Beneath, lower than the river, stretched broad, flat land, far as the eye could see. Roads ran in every direction, and she saw countless farmhouses of which she had never dreamed when sailing on the lonely river a few feet the other side of the willowy fringe.

Three weeks they spent among the rich farm islands, which heaped up levees and pumped day and night to keep afloat. It was a monotonous land, with an unvarying richness of soil and with only one landmark—Mt. Diablo, ever to be seen, sleeping in the midday azure, limping its crinkled mass against the sunset sky, or forming like a dream out of the silver dawn. Sometimes on foot, often by launch, they cries-crossed and threaded the river region as far as the peat lands of the Middle River, down the San Joaquin to Antioch, and up Georgiana Slough to Walnut Grove on the Sacramento. And it proved a foreign land. The workers of the soil teemed by thousands, yet Saxon and Billy knew what it was to go a whole day without finding any one who spoke English. They encountered—sometimes in whole villages—Chinese, Japanese, Italians, Portuguese, Swiss, Hindus, Koreans, Norwegians, Danes, French, Armenians, Slavs, almost every nationality save American. One American they found on the lower reaches of Georgiana who eked an illicit existence by fishing with traps. Another American, who spouted blood and destruction on all political subjects, was an itinerant bee-farmer. At Walnut Grove, bustling with life, the few Americans consisted of the storekeeper, the saloonkeeper, the butcher, the keeper of the drawbridge, and the ferryman. Yet two thriving towns were in Walnut Grove, one Chinese, one Japanese. Most of the land was owned by Americans, who lived away from it and were continually selling it to the foreigners.

A riot, or a merry-making—they could not tell which—was taking place in the Japanese town, as Saxon and Billy steamed out on the Apache, bound for Sacramento.

"We're settin' on the stoop," Billy railed. "Pretty soon they'll crowd us off of that."

"There won't be any stoop in the valley of the moon," Saxon cheered him.

But he was inconsolable, remarking bitterly:

"An' they ain't one of them damn foreigners that can handle four horses like me.

"But they can everlastingly farm," he added.

And Saxon, looking at his moody face, was suddenly reminded of a lithograph she had seen in her childhood It was of a Plains Indian, in paint and feathers, astride his horse and gazing with wondering eye at a railroad train rushing along a fresh-made track. The Indian had passed, she remembered, before the tide of new life that brought the railroad. And were Billy and his kind doomed to pass, she pondered, before this new tide of life, amazingly industrious, that was flooding in from Asia and Europe?

At Sacramento they stopped two weeks, where Billy drove team and earned the money to put them along on their travels. Also, life in Oakland and Carmel, close to the salt edge of the coast, had spoiled them for the interior. Too warm, was their verdict of Sacramento and they followed the railroad west, through a region of swampland, to Davisville. Here they were lured aside and to the north to pretty Woodland, where Billy drove team for a fruit farm, and where Saxon wrung from him a reluctant consent for her to work a few days in the fruit harvest. She made an important and mystifying secret of what she intended doing with her earnings, and Billy teased her about it until the matter passed from his mind. Nor did she tell him of a money order inclosed with a certain blue slip of paper in a letter to Bud Strothers.

They began to suffer from the heat. Billy declared they had strayed out of the blanket climate.

"There are no redwoods here," Saxon said. "We must go west toward the coast. It is there we'll find the valley of the moon."

From Woodland they swung west and south along the county roads to the fruit paradise of Vacaville. Here Billy picked fruit, then drove team; and here Saxon received a letter and a tiny express package from Bud Strothers. When Billy came into camp from the day's work, she bade him stand still and shut his eyes. For a few seconds she fumbled and did something to the breast of his cotton work-shirt. Once, he felt a slight prick, as of a pin point, and grunted, while she laughed and bullied him to continue keeping his eyes shut.

"Close your eyes and give me a kiss," she sang, "and then I'll show you what iss."

She kissed him and when he looked down he saw, pinned to his shirt, the gold medals he had pawned the day they had gone to the moving picture show and received their inspiration to return to the land.

"You darned kid!" he exclaimed, as he caught her to him. "So that's what you blew your fruit money in on? An' I never guessed!—Come here to you."

And thereupon she suffered the pleasant mastery of his brawn, and was hugged and wrestled with until the coffee pot boiled over and she darted from him to the rescue.

"I kinda always been a mite proud of 'em," he confessed, as he rolled his after-supper cigarette. "They take me back to my kid days when I amateured it to beat the band. I was some kid in them days, believe muh.—But say, d'ye know, they'd clean slipped my recollection. Oakland's a thousan' years away from you an' me, an' ten thousan' miles."

"Then this will bring you back to it," Saxon said, opening Bud's letter and reading it aloud.

Bud had taken it for granted that Billy knew the wind-up of the strike; so he devoted himself to the details as to which men had got back their jobs, and which had been blacklisted. To his own amazement he had been taken back, and was now driving Billy's horses. Still more amazing was the further information he had to impart. The old foreman of the West Oakland stables had died, and since then two other foremen had done nothing but make messes of everything. The point of all which was that the Boss had spoken that day to Bud, regretting the disappearance of Billy.

"Don't make no mistake," Bud wrote. "The Boss is onto all your curves. I bet he knows every scab you slugged. Just the same he says to me—Strothers, if you ain't at liberty to give me his address, just write yourself and tell him for me to come a running. I'll give him a hundred and twenty-five a month to take hold the stables."

Saxon waited with well-concealed anxiety when the letter was finished. Billy, stretched out, leaning on one elbow, blew a meditative ring of smoke. His cheap workshirt, incongruously brilliant with the gold of the medals that flashed in the firelight, was open in front, showing the smooth skin and splendid swell of chest. He glanced around—at the blankets bowered in a green screen and waiting, at the campfire and the blackened, battered coffee pot, at the well-worn hatchet, half buried in a tree trunk, and lastly at Saxon. His eyes embraced her; then into them came a slow expression of inquiry. But she offered no help.

"Well," he uttered finally, "all you gotta do is write Bud Strothers, an' tell 'm not on the Boss's ugly tintype.—An' while you're about it, I'll send 'm the money to get my watch out. You work out the interest. The overcoat can stay there an' rot."

But they did not prosper in the interior heat. They lost weight. The resilience went out of their minds and bodies. As Billy expressed it, their silk was frazzled. So they shouldered their packs and headed west across the wild mountains. In the Berryessa Valley, the shimmering heat waves made their eyes ache, and their heads; so that they traveled on in the early morning and late afternoon. Still west they headed, over more mountains, to beautiful Napa Valley. The next valley beyond was Sonoma, where Hastings had invited them to his ranch. And here they would have gone, had not Billy chanced upon a newspaper item which told of the writer's departure to cover some revolution that was breaking out somewhere in Mexico.

"We'll see 'm later on," Billy said, as they turned northwest, through the vineyards and orchards of Napa Valley. "We're like that millionaire Bert used to sing about, except it's time that we've got to burn. Any direction is as good as any other, only west is best."

Three times in the Napa Valley Billy refused work. Past St. Helena, Saxon hailed with joy the unmistakable redwoods they could see growing up the small canyons that penetrated the western wall of the valley. At Calistoga, at the end of the railroad, they saw the six-horse stages leaving for Middletown and Lower Lake. They debated their route. That way led to Lake County and not toward the coast, so Saxon and Billy swung west through the mountains to the valley of the Russian River, coming out at Healdsburg. They lingered in the hop-fields on the rich bottoms, where Billy scorned to pick hops alongside of Indians, Japanese, and Chinese.

"I couldn't work alongside of 'em an hour before I'd be knockin' their blocks off," he explained. "Besides, this Russian River's some nifty. Let's pitch camp and go swimmin'."

So they idled their way north up the broad, fertile valley, so happy that they forgot that work was ever necessary, while the valley of the moon was a golden dream, remote, but sure, some day of realization. At Cloverdale, Billy fell into luck. A combination of sickness and mischance found the stage stables short a driver. Each day the train disgorged passengers for the Geysers, and Billy, as if accustomed to it all his life, took the reins of six horses and drove a full load over the mountains in stage time. The second trip he had Saxon beside him on the high boxseat. By the end of two weeks the regular driver was back. Billy declined a stable-job, took his wages, and continued north.

Saxon had adopted a fox terrier puppy and named him Possum, after the dog Mrs. Hastings had told them about. So young was he that he quickly became footsore, and she carried him until Billy perched him on top of his pack and grumbled that Possum was chewing his back hair to a frazzle.

They passed through the painted vineyards of Asti at the end of the grape-picking, and entered Ukiah drenched to the skin by the first winter rain.

"Say," Billy said, "you remember the way the Roamer just skated along. Well, this summer's done the same thing—gone by on wheels. An' now it's up to us to find some place to winter. This Ukiah looks like a pretty good burg. We'll get a room to-night an' dry out. An' to-morrow I'll hustle around to the stables, an' if I locate anything we can rent a shack an' have all winter to think about where we'll go next year."

CHAPTER XIII

The winter proved much less exciting than the one spent in Carmel, and keenly as Saxon had appreciated the Carmel folk, she now appreciated them more keenly than ever. In Ukiah she formed nothing more than superficial acquaintances. Here people were more like those of the working class she had known in Oakland, or else they were merely wealthy and herded together in automobiles. There was no democratic artist-colony that pursued fellowship disregardful of the caste of wealth.

Yet it was a more enjoyable winter than any she had spent in Oakland. Billy had failed to get regular employment; so she saw much of him, and they lived a prosperous and happy hand-to-mouth existence in the tiny cottage they rented. As extra man at the biggest livery stable, Billy's spare time was so great that he drifted into horse-trading. It was hazardous, and more than once he was broke, but the table never wanted for the best of steak and coffee, nor did they stint themselves for clothes.

"Them blamed farmers—I gotta pass it to 'em," Billy grinned one day, when he had been particularly bested in a horse deal. "They won't tear under the wings, the sons of guns. In the summer they take in boarders, an' in the winter they make a good livin' coin' each other up at tradin' horses. An' I just want to tell YOU, Saxon, they've sure shown me a few. An' I 'm gettin' tough under the wings myself. I'll never tear again so as you can notice it. Which means one more trade learned for yours truly. I can make a livin' anywhere now tradin' horses."

Often Billy had Saxon out on spare saddle horses from the stable, and his horse deals took them on many trips into the surrounding country. Likewise she was with him when he was driving horses to sell on commission; and in both their minds, independently, arose a new idea concerning their pilgrimage. Billy was the first to broach it.

"I run into an outfit the other day, that's stored in town," he said, "an' it's kept me thinkin' ever since. Ain't no use tryin' to get you to guess it, because you can't. I'll tell you—the swellest wagon-campin' outfit; anybody ever heard of. First of all, the wagon's a peacherino. Strong as they make 'em. It was made to order, upon Puget Sound, an' it was tested out all the way down here. No load an' no road can strain it. The guy had consumption that had it built. A doctor an' a cook traveled with 'm till he passed in his checks here in Ukiah two years ago. But say—if you could see it. Every kind of a contrivance—a place for everything—a regular home on wheels. Now, if we could get that, an' a couple of plugs, we could travel like kings, an' laugh at the weather."

CHAPTER XIII

"Oh! Billy! it's just what I've been dreamin' all winter. It would be ideal. And... well, sometimes on the road I 'm sure you can't help forgetting what a nice little wife you've got... and with a wagon I could have all kinds of pretty clothes along."

Billy's blue eyes glowed a caress, cloudy and warm; as he said quietly:

"I've ben thinkin' about that."

"And you can carry a rifle and shotgun and fishing poles and everything," she rushed along. "And a good big axe, man-size, instead of that hatchet you're always complaining about. And Possum can lift up his legs and rest. And—but suppose you can't buy it? How much do they want?"

"One hundred an' fifty big bucks," he answered. "But dirt cheap at that. It's givin' it away. I tell you that rig wasn't built for a cent less than four hundred, an' I know wagon-work in the dark. Now, if I can put through that dicker with Caswell's six horses—say, I just got onto that horse-buyer to-day. If he buys 'em, who d'ye think he'll ship 'em to? To the Boss, right to the West Oakland stables. I 'm goin' to get you to write to him. Travelin', as we're goin' to, I can pick up bargains. An' if the Boss'll talk, I can make the regular horse-buyer's commissions. He'll have to trust me with a lot of money, though, which most likely he won't, knowin' all his scabs I beat up."

"If he could trust you to run his stable, I guess he isn't afraid to let you handle his money," Saxon said.

Billy shrugged his shoulders in modest dubiousness.

"Well, anyway, as I was sayin' if I can sell Caswell's six horses, why, we can stand off this month's bills an' buy the wagon."

"But horses!" Saxon queried anxiously.

"They'll come later—if I have to take a regular job for two or three months. The only trouble with that 'd be that it'd run us pretty well along into summer before we could pull out. But come on down town an' I'll show you the outfit right now."

Saxon saw the wagon and was so infatuated with it that she lost a night's sleep from sheer insomnia of anticipation. Then Caswell's six horses were sold, the month's bills held over, and the wagon became theirs. One rainy morning, two weeks later, Billy had scarcely left the house, to be gone on an all-day trip into the country after horses, when he was back again.

"Come on!" he called to Saxon from the street. "Get your things on an' come along. I want to show you something."

He drove down town to a board stable, and took her through to a large, roofed inclosure in the rear. There he led to her a span of sturdy dappled chestnuts, with cream-colored manes and tails.

"Oh, the beauties! the beauties!" Saxon cried, resting her cheek against the velvet muzzle of one, while the other roguishly nuzzled for a share.

"Ain't they, though?" Billy reveled, leading them up and down before her admiring gaze. "Thirteen hundred an' fifty each, an' they don't look the weight, they're that slick put together. I couldn't believe it myself, till I put 'em on the scales. Twenty-seven hundred an' seven pounds, the two of 'em. An' I tried 'em out—that was two days ago. Good dispositions, no faults, an' true-pullers, automobile broke an' all the rest. I'd back 'em to out-pull any team of their weight I ever seen.—Say, how'd they look hooked up to that wagon of ourn?"

Saxon visioned the picture, and shook her head slowly in a reaction of regret.

"Three hundred spot cash buys 'em," Billy went on. "An' that's bed-rock. The owner wants the money so bad he's droolin' for it. Just gotta sell, an' sell quick. An' Saxon, honest to God, that pair'd fetch five hundred at auction down in the city. Both mares, full sisters, five an' six years old, registered Belgian sire, out of a heavy standard-bred mare that I know. Three hundred takes 'em, an' I got the refusal for three days."

Saxon's regret changed to indignation.

"Oh, why did you show them to me? We haven't any three hundred, and you know it. All I've got in the house is six dollars, and you haven't that much."

"Maybe you think that's all I brought you down town for," he replied enigmatically. "Well, it ain't."

He paused, licked his lips, and shifted his weight uneasily from one leg to the other.

"Now you listen till I get all done before you say anything. Ready?"

She nodded.

"Won't open your mouth?"

This time she obediently shook her head.

"Well, it's this way," he began haltingly. "They's a youngster come up from Frisco, Young Sandow they call 'm, an' the Pride of Telegraph Hill. He's the real goods of a heavyweight, an' he was to fight Montana Red Saturday night, only Montana Red, just in a little trainin' bout, snapped his forearm yesterday. The managers has kept it quiet. Now here's the proposition. Lots of tickets sold, an' they'll be a big crowd Saturday night. At the last moment, so as not to disappoint 'em, they'll spring me to take Montana's place. I 'm the dark horse. Nobody knows me—not even Young Sandow. He's come up since my time. I'll be a rube fighter. I can fight as Horse Roberts.

"Now, wait a minute. The winner'll pull down three hundred big round iron dollars. Wait, I 'm tellin' you! It's a lead-pipe cinch. It's like robbin' a corpse. Sandow's got all the heart in the world—regular knock-down-an'-drag-out-an'-hang-on fighter. I've followed 'm in the papers. But he ain't clever. I 'm slow, all right, all right, but I 'm clever, an' I got a hay-maker in each arm. I got Sandow's number an' I know it.

"Now, you got the say-so in this. If you say yes, the nags is ourn. If you say no, then it's all bets off, an' everything all right, an' I'll take to harness-washin' at the stable so as to buy a couple of plugs. Remember, they'll only be plugs, though. But don't look at me while you're makin' up your mind. Keep your lamps on the horses."

It was with painful indecision that she looked at the beautiful animals.

"Their names is Hazel an' Hattie," Billy put in a sly wedge. "If we get 'em we could call it the 'Double H' outfit."

But Saxon forgot the team and could only see Billy's frightfully bruised body the night he fought the Chicago Terror. She was about to speak, when Billy, who had been hanging on her lips, broke in:

"Just hitch 'em up to our wagon in your mind an' look at the outfit. You got to go some to beat it."

"But you're not in training, Billy," she said suddenly and without having intended to say it.

"Huh!" he snorted. "I've been in half trainin' for the last year. My legs is like iron. They'll hold me up as long as I've got a punch left in my arms, and I always have that. Besides, I won't let 'm make a long fight. He's a man-eater, an' man-eaters is my meat.

I eat 'm alive. It's the clever boys with the stamina an' endurance that I can't put away. But this young Sandow's my meat. I'll get 'm maybe in the third or fourth round—you know, time 'm in a rush an' hand it to 'm just as easy. It's a lead-pipe cinch, I tell you. Honest to God, Saxon, it's a shame to take the money."

"But I hate to think of you all battered up," she temporized. "If I didn't love you so, it might be different. And then, too, you might get hurt."

Billy laughed in contemptuous pride of youth and brawn.

"You won't know I've been in a fight, except that we'll own Hazel an' Hattie there. An' besides, Saxon, I just gotta stick my fist in somebody's face once in a while. You know I can go for months peaceable an' gentle as a lamb, an' then my knuckles actually begin to itch to land on something. Now, it's a whole lot sensibler to land on Young Sandow an' get three hundred for it, than to land on some hayseed an' get hauled up an' fined before some justice of the peace. Now take another squint at Hazel an' Hattie. They're regular farm furniture, good to breed from when we get to that valley of the moon. An' they're heavy enough to turn right into the plowin', too."

The evening of the fight at quarter past eight, Saxon parted from Billy. At quarter past nine, with hot water, ice, and everything ready in anticipation, she heard the gate click and Billy's step come up the porch. She had agreed to the fight much against her better judgment, and had regretted her consent every minute of the hour she had just waited; so that, as she opened the front door, she was expectant of any sort of a terrible husband-wreck. But the Billy she saw was precisely the Billy she had parted from.

"There was no fights" she cried, in so evident disappointment that he laughed.

"They was all yellin' 'Fake! Fake!' when I left, an' wantin' their money back."

"Well, I've got YOU," she laughed, leading him in, though secretly she sighed farewell to Hazel and Hattie.

"I stopped by the way to get something for you that you've been wantin' some time," Billy said casually. "Shut your eyes an' open your hand; an' when you open your eyes you'll find it grand," he chanted.

Into her hand something was laid that was very heavy and very cold, and when her eyes opened she saw it was a stack of fifteen twenty-dollar gold pieces.

"I told you it was like takin' money from a corpse," he exulted, as he emerged grinning from the whirlwind of punches, whacks, and hugs in which she had enveloped him. "They wasn't no fight at all. D 'ye want to know how long it lasted? Just twenty-seven seconds—less 'n half a minute. An' how many blows struck? One. An' it was me that done it. Here, I'll show you. It was just like this—a regular scream."

Billy had taken his place in the middle of the room, slightly crouching, chin tucked against the sheltering left shoulder, fists closed, elbows in so as to guard left side and abdomen, and forearms close to the body.

"It's the first round," he pictured. "Gong's sounded, an' we've shook hands. Of course, seein' as it's a long fight an' we've never seen each other in action, we ain't in no rush. We're just feelin' each other out an' fiddlin' around. Seventeen seconds like that. Not a blow struck. Nothin'. An' then it's all off with the big Swede. It takes some time to tell it, but it happened in a jiffy, in fess In a tenth of a second. I wasn't expectin' it myself. We're awful close together. His left glove ain't a foot from my jaw, an' my left glove ain't a foot from his. He feints with his right, an' I know it's a feint, an' just hunch up my left shoulder a bit an' feint with my right. That draws his guard over just about an inch, an' I see my openin'. My left ain't got a foot to travel. I don't draw it back none. I start it from where it is, corkscrewin' around his right guard an' pivotin' at the waist to put the weight of my shoulder into the punch. An' it connects!—Square on the point of the chin, sideways. He drops deado. I walk back to my corner, an', honest to God, Saxon, I can't help gigglin' a little, it was that easy. The referee stands over 'm an' counts 'm out. He never quivers. The audience don't know what to make of it an' sits paralyzed. His seconds carry 'm to his corner an' set 'm on the stool. But they gotta hold 'm up. Five minutes afterward he opens his eyes—but he ain't seein' nothing. They're glassy. Five minutes more, an' he stands up. They got to help hold 'm, his legs givin' under 'm like they was sausages. An' the seconds has to help 'm through the ropes, an' they go down the aisle to his dressin' room a-helpin' 'm. An' the crowd beginning to yell fake an' want its money back. Twenty-seven seconds—one punch—n' a spankin' pair of horses for the best wife Billy Roberts ever had in his long experience."

All of Saxon's old physical worship of her husband revived and doubled on itself many times. He was in all truth a hero, worthy to be of that wing-helmeted company leaping from the beaked boats upon the bloody English sands. The next morning he was awakened by her lips pressed on his left hand.

"Hey!—what are you doin'?'" he demanded.

"Kissing Hazel and Hattie good morning," she answered demurely. "And now I 'm going to kiss you good morning.. .. And just where did your punch land? Show me."

Billy complied, touching the point of her chin with his knuckles. With both her hands on his arm, she shored it back and tried to draw it forward sharply in similitude of a punch. But Billy withstrained her.

"Wait," he said. "You don't want to knock your jaw off. I'll show you. A quarter of an inch will do."

And at a distance of a quarter of an inch from her chin he administered the slightest flick of a tap.

On the instant Saxon's brain snapped with a white flash of light, while her whole body relaxed, numb and weak, volitionless, sad her vision reeled and blurred. The next instant she was herself again, in her eyes terror and understanding.

"And it was at a foot that you struck him," she murmured in a voice of awe.

"Yes, and with the weight of my shoulders behind it," Billy laughed. "Oh, that's nothing.—Here, let me show you something else."

He searched out her solar plexus, and did no more than snap his middle finger against it. This time she experienced a simple paralysis, accompanied by a stoppage of breath, but with a brain and vision that remained perfectly clear. In a moment, however, all the unwonted sensations were gone.

"Solar Plexus," Billy elucidated. "Imagine what it's like when the other fellow lifts a wallop to it all the way from his knees. That's the punch that won the championship of the world for Bob Fitzsimmons."

Saxon shuddered, then resigned herself to Billy's playful demonstration of the weak points in the human anatomy. He pressed the tip of a finger into the middle of her forearm, and she knew excruciating agony. On either side of her neck, at the base, he dented gently with his thumbs, and she felt herself quickly growing unconscious.

"That's one of the death touches of the Japs," he told her, and went on, accompanying grips and holds with a running exposition. "Here's the toe-hold that Notch defeated Hackenschmidt with. I learned it from Farmer Burns.—An' here's a half-

Nelson.—An' here's you makin' roughhouse at a dance, an' I 'm the floor manager, an' I gotta put you out."

One hand grasped her wrist, the other hand passed around and under her forearm and grasped his own wrist. And at the first hint of pressure she felt that her arm was a pipe-stem about to break.

"That's called the 'come along.'—An' here's the strong arm. A boy can down a man with it. An' if you ever get into a scrap an' the other fellow gets your nose between his teeth—you don't want to lose your nose, do you? Well, this is what you do, quick as a flash."

Involuntarily she closed her eyes as Billy's thumb-ends pressed into them. She could feel the fore-running ache of a dull and terrible hurt.

"If he don't let go, you just press real hard, an' out pop his eyes, an' he's blind as a bat for the rest of his life. Oh, he'll let go all right all right."

He released her and lay back laughing.

"How d'ye feel?" he asked. "Those ain't boxin' tricks, but they're all in the game of a roughhouse."

"I feel like revenge," she said, trying to apply the "come along" to his arm.

When she exerted the pressure she cried out with pain, for she had succeeded only in hurting herself. Billy grinned at her futility. She dug her thumbs into his neck in imitation of the Japanese death touch, then gazed ruefully at the bent ends of her nails. She punched him smartly on the point of the chin, and again cried out, this time to the bruise of her knuckles.

"Well, this can't hurt me," she gritted through her teeth, as she assailed his solar plexus with her doubled fists.

By this time he was in a roar of laughter. Under the sheaths of muscles that were as armor, the fatal nerve center remained impervious.

"Go on, do it some more," he urged, when she had given up, breathing heavily. "It feels fine, like you was ticklin' me with a feather."

"All right, Mister Man," she threatened balefully. "You can talk about your grips and death touches and all the rest, but that's all man's game. I know something that will beat them all, that will make a strong man as helpless as a baby. Wait a minute till I get it. There. Shut your eyes. Ready? I won't be a second."

He waited with closed eyes, and then, softly as rose petals fluttering down, he felt her lips on his mouth.

"You win," he said in solemn ecstasy, and passed his arms around her.

CHAPTER XIV

In the morning Billy went down town to pay for Hazel and Hattie. It was due to Saxon's impatient desire to see them, that he seemed to take a remarkably long time about so simple a transaction. But she forgave him when he arrived with the two horses hitched to the camping wagon.

"Had to borrow the harness," he said. "Pass Possum up and climb in, an' I'll show you the Double H Outfit, which is some outfit, I'm tellin' you."

Saxon's delight was unbounded and almost speechless as they drove out into the country behind the dappled chestnuts with the cream-colored tails and manes. The seat was upholstered, high-backed, and comfortable; and Billy raved about the wonders of the efficient brake. He trotted the team along the hard county road to show the standard-going in them, and put them up a steep earthroad, almost hub-deep with mud, to prove that the light Belgian sire was not wanting in their make-up.

When Saxon at last lapsed into complete silence, he studied her anxiously, with quick sidelong glances. She sighed and asked:

"When do you think we'll be able to start?"

"Maybe in two weeks... or, maybe in two or three months." He sighed with solemn deliberation. "We're like the Irishman with the trunk an' nothin' to put in it. Here's the wagon, here's the horses, an' nothin' to pull. I know a peach of a shotgun I can get, second-hand, eighteen dollars; but look at the bills we owe. Then there's a new '22 Automatic rifle I want for you. An' a 30-30 I've had my eye on for deer. An' you want a good jointed pole as well as me. An' tackle costs like Sam Hill. An' harness like I want will cost fifty bucks cold. An' the wagon ought to be painted. Then there's pasture ropes, an' nose-bags, an' a harness punch, an' all such things. An' Hazel an' Hattie eatin' their heads off all the time we're waitin'. An' I 'm just itchin' to be started myself."

He stopped abruptly and confusedly.

"Now, Billy, what have you got up your sleeve?—I can see it in your eyes," Saxon demanded and indicted in mixed metaphors.

"Well, Saxon, you see, it's like this. Sandow ain't satisfied. He's madder 'n a hatter. Never got one punch at me. Never had a chance to make a showin', an' he wants a return match. He's blattin' around town that he can lick me with one hand tied behind 'm, an' all that kind of hot air. Which ain't the point. The point is, the fight-fans is wild to see a return-match. They didn't get a run for their money last time. They'll fill the house. The managers has seen me already. That was why I was so long. They's three hundred more waitin' on the tree for me to pick two weeks from last night if you'll say the word. It's just the same as I told you before. He's my meat. He still thinks I 'm a rube, an' that it was a fluke punch."

"But, Billy, you told me long ago that fighting took the silk out of you. That was why you'd quit it and stayed by teaming."

"Not this kind of fightin'," he answered. "I got this one all doped out. I'll let 'm last till about the seventh. Not that it'll be necessary, but just to give the audience a run for its money. Of course, I'll get a lump or two, an' lose some skin. Then I'll time 'm to that glass jaw of his an' drop 'm for the count. An' we'll be all packed up, an' next mornin' we'll pull out. What d'ye say? Aw, come on."

Saturday night, two weeks later, Saxon ran to the door when the gate clicked. Billy looked tired. His hair was wet, his nose swollen, one cheek was puffed, there was skin missing from his ears, and both eyes were slightly bloodshot.

"I 'm darned if that boy didn't fool me," he said, as he placed the roll of gold pieces in her hand and sat down with her on his knees. "He's some boy when he gets extended. Instead of stoppin' 'm at the seventh, he kept me hustlin' till the fourteenth. Then I got 'm the way I said. It's too bad he's got a glass jaw. He's quicker'n I thought, an' he's got a wallop that made me mighty respectful from the second round—an' the prettiest little chop an' come-again I ever saw. But that glass jaw! He kept it in cotton wool till the fourteenth an' then I connected.

"—An', say. I 'm mighty glad it did last fourteen rounds. I still got all my silk. I could see that easy. I wasn't breathin' much, an' every round was fast. An' my legs was like iron. I could a-fought forty rounds. You see, I never said nothin', but I've been suspicious all the time after that beatin' the Chicago Terror gave me."

"Nonsense!—you would have known it long before now," Saxon cried. "Look at all your boxing, and wrestling, and running at Carmel."

"Nope." Billy shook his head with the conviction of utter knowledge. "That's different. It don't take it outa you. You gotta be up against the real thing, fightin' for life, round after round, with a husky you know ain't lost a thread of his silk yet—then, if you don't blow up, if your legs is steady, an' your heart ain't burstin', an' you ain't wobbly at all, an' no signs of queer street in your head—why, then you know you still got all your silk. An' I got it, I got all mine, d'ye hear me, an' I ain't goin' to risk it on no more fights. That's straight. Easy money's hardest in the end. From now on it's horsebuyin' on commish, an' you an' me on the road till we find that valley of the moon."

Next morning, early, they drove out of Ukiah. Possum sat on the seat between them, his rosy mouth agape with excitement. They had originally planned to cross over to the coast from Ukiah, but it was too early in the season for the soft earth-roads to be in shape after the winter rains; so they turned east, for Lake County, their route to extend north through the upper Sacramento Valley and across the mountains into Oregon. Then they would circle west to the coast, where the roads by that time would be in condition, and come down its length to the Golden Gate.

All the land was green and flower-sprinkled, and each tiny valley, as they entered the hills, was a garden.

"Huh!" Billy remarked scornfully to the general landscape. "They say a rollin' stone gathers no moss. Just the same this looks like some outfit we've gathered. Never had so much actual property in my life at one time—an' them was the days when I wasn't rollin'. Hell—even the furniture wasn't ourn. Only the clothes we stood up in, an' some old socks an' things."

Saxon reached out and touched his hand, and he knew that it was a hand that loved his hand.

"I've only one regret," she said. "You've earned it all yourself. I've had nothing to do with it."

"Huh!—you've had everything to do with it. You're like my second in a fight. You keep me happy an' in condition. A man can't fight without a good second to take care of him. Hell, I wouldn't a-ben here if it wasn't for you. You made me pull up stakes an' head out. Why, if it hadn't been for you I'd a-drunk myself dead an' rotten by this time, or had my neck stretched at San Quentin over hittin' some scab too hard or something or other. An' look at me now. Look at that roll of greenbacks"—he tapped his breast—"to buy the Boss some horses. Why, we're takin' an unendin' vacation, an' makin' a good livin' at the same time. An' one more trade I got—horse-buyin' for Oakland. If I show I've got the savve, an' I have, all the Frisco firms'll be after me to buy for them. An' it's all your fault. You're my Tonic Kid all right, all right, an' if Possum wasn't lookin', I'd—well, who cares if he does look?"

And Billy leaned toward her sidewise and kissed her.

The way grew hard and rocky as they began to climb, but the divide was an easy one, and they soon dropped down the canyon of the Blue Lakes among lush fields of golden poppies. In the bottom of the canyon lay a wandering sheet of water of intensest blue. Ahead, the folds of hills interlaced the distance, with a remote blue mountain rising in the center of the picture.

They asked questions of a handsome, black-eyed man with curly gray hair, who talked to them in a German accent, while a cheery-faced woman smiled down at them out of a trellised high window of the Swiss cottage perched on the bank. Billy watered the horses at a pretty hotel farther on, where the proprietor came out and talked and told him he had built it himself, according to the plans of the black-eyed man with the curly gray hair, who was a San Francisco architect.

"Goin' up, goin' up," Billy chortled, as they drove on through the winding hills past another lake of intensest blue. "D'ye notice the difference in our treatment already between ridin' an' walkin' with packs on our backs? With Hazel an' Hattie an' Saxon an' Possum, an' yours truly, an' this high-toned wagon, folks most likely take us for millionaires out on a lark."

The way widened. Broad, oak-studded pastures with grazing livestock lay on either hand. Then Clear Lake opened before them like an inland sea, flecked with little squalls and flaws of wind from the high mountains on the northern slopes of which still glistened white snow patches.

"I've heard Mrs. Hazard rave about Lake Geneva," Saxon recalled; "but I wonder if it is more beautiful than this."

"That architect fellow called this the California Alps, you remember," Billy confirmed. "An' if I don't mistake, that's Lakeport showin' up ahead. An' all wild country, an' no railroads."

"And no moon valleys here," Saxon criticized. "But it is beautiful, oh, so beautiful."

CHAPTER XIV

"Hotter'n hell in the dead of summer, I'll bet," was Billy's opinion. "Nope, the country we're lookin' for lies nearer the coast. Just the same it is beautiful... like a picture on the wall. What d'ye say we stop off an' go for a swim this afternoon?"

Ten days later they drove into Williams, in Colusa County, and for the first time again encountered a railroad. Billy was looking for it, for the reason that at the rear of the wagon walked two magnificent work-horses which he had picked up for shipment to Oakland.

"Too hot," was Saxon's verdict, as she gazed across the shimmering level of the vast Sacramento Valley. "No redwoods. No hills. No forests. No manzanita. No madronos. Lonely, and sad—"

"An' like the river islands," Billy interpolated. "Richer in hell, but looks too much like hard work. It'll do for those that's stuck on hard work—God knows, they's nothin' here to induce a fellow to knock off ever for a bit of play. No fishin', no huntin', nothin' but work. I'd work myself, if I had to live here."

North they drove, through days of heat and dust, across the California plains, and everywhere was manifest the "new" farming—great irrigation ditches, dug and being dug, the land threaded by power-lines from the mountains, and many new farmhouses on small holdings newly fenced. The bonanza farms were being broken up. However, many of the great estates remained, five to ten thousand acres in extent, running from the Sacramento bank to the horizon dancing in the heat waves, and studded with great valley oaks.

"It takes rich soil to make trees like those," a ten-acre farmer told them.

They had driven off the road a hundred feet to his tiny barn in order to water Hazel and Hattie. A sturdy young orchard covered most of his ten acres, though a goodly portion was devoted to whitewashed henhouses and wired runways wherein hundreds of chickens were to be seen. He had just begun work on a small frame dwelling.

"I took a vacation when I bought," he explained, "and planted the trees. Then I went back to work an' stayed with it till the place was cleared. Now I 'm here for keeps, an' soon as the house is finished I'll send for the wife. She's not very well, and it will do her good. We've been planning and working for years to get away from the city." He stopped in order to give a happy sigh. "And now we're free."

The water in the trough was warm from the sun.

"Hold on," the man said. "Don't let them drink that. I'll give it to them cool."

Stepping into a small shed, he turned an electric switch, and a motor the size of a fruit box hummed into action. A five-inch stream of sparkling water splashed into the shallow main ditch of his irrigation system and flowed away across the orchard through many laterals.

"Isn' tit beautiful, eh?—beautiful! beautiful!" the man chanted in an ecstasy. "It's bud and fruit. It's blood and life. Look at it! It makes a gold mine laughable, and a saloon a nightmare. I know. I... I used to be a barkeeper. In fact, I've been a barkeeper most of my life. That's how I paid for this place. And I've hated the business all the time. I was a farm boy, and all my life I've been wanting to get back to it. And here I am at last."

He wiped his glasses the better to behold his beloved water, then seized a hoe and strode down the main ditch to open more laterals.

"He's the funniest barkeeper I ever seen," Billy commented. "I took him for a business man of some sort. Must a-ben in some kind of a quiet hotel."

"Don't drive on right away," Saxon requested. "I want to talk with him."

He came back, polishing his glasses, his face beaming, watching the water as if fascinated by it. It required no more exertion on Saxon's part to start him than had been required on his part to start the motor.

"The pioneers settled all this in the early fifties," he said. "The Mexicans never got this far, so it was government land. Everybody got a hundred and sixty acres. And such acres! The stories they tell about how much wheat they got to the acre are almost unbelievable. Then several things happened. The sharpest and steadiest of the pioneers held what they had and added to it from the other fellows. It takes a great many quarter sections to make a bonanza farm. It wasn't long before it was 'most all bonanza farms."

"They were the successful gamblers," Saxon put in, remembering Mark Hall's words.

The man nodded appreciatively and continued.

"The old folks schemed and gathered and added the land into the big holdings, and built the great barns and mansions, and planted the house orchards and flower gardens. The young folks were spoiled by so much wealth and went away to the cities to spend it. And old folks and young united in one thing: in impoverishing the soil. Year after year they scratched it and took out bonanza crops. They put nothing back. All they left was plow-sole and exhausted land. Why, there's big sections they exhausted and left almost desert.

"The bonanza farmers are all gone now, thank the Lord, and here's where we small farmers come into our own. It won't be many years before the whole valley will be farmed in patches like mine. Look at what we're doing! Worked-out land that had ceased to grow wheat, and we turn the water on, treat the soil decently, and see our orchards!

"We've got the water—from the mountains, and from under the ground. I was reading an account the other day. All life depends on food. All food depends on water. It takes a thousand pounds of water to produce one pound of food; ten thousand pounds to produce one pound of meat. How much water do you drink in a year? About a ton. But you eat about two hundred pounds of vegetables and two hundred pounds of meat a year—which means you consume one hundred tons of water in the vegetables and one thousand tons in the meat—which means that it takes eleven hundred and one tons of water each year to keep a small woman like you going."

"Gee!" was all Billy could say.

"You see how population depends upon water," the ax-barkeeper went on. "Well, we've got the water, immense subterranean supplies, and in not many years this valley will be populated as thick as Belgium."

Fascinated by the five-inch stream, sluiced out of the earth and back to the earth by the droning motor, he forgot his discourse and stood and gazed, rapt and unheeding, while his visitors drove on.

"An' him a drink-slinger!" Billy marveled. "He can sure sling the temperance dope if anybody should ask you."

"It's lovely to think about—all that water, and all the happy people that will come here to live—"

"But it ain't the valley of the moon!" Billy laughed.

CHAPTER XIV

"No," she responded. "They don't have to irrigate in the valley of the moon, unless for alfalfa and such crops. What we want is the water bubbling naturally from the ground, and crossing the farm in little brooks, and on the boundary a fine big creek—"

"With trout in it!" Billy took her up. "An' willows and trees of all kinds growing along the edges, and here a riffle where you can flip out trout, and there a deep pool where you can swim and high-dive. An' kingfishers, an' rabbits comin' down to drink, an', maybe, a deer."

"And meadowlarks in the pasture," Saxon added. "And mourning doves in the trees. We must have mourning doves—and the big, gray tree-squirrels."

"Gee!—that valley of the moon's goin' to be some valley," Billy meditated, flicking a fly away with his whip from Hattie's side. "Think we'll ever find it?"

Saxon nodded her head with great certitude.

"Just as the Jews found the promised land, and the Mormons Utah, and the Pioneers California. You remember the last advice we got when we left Oakland' "Tis them that looks that finds.'"

CHAPTER XV

Ever north, through a fat and flourishing rejuvenated land, stopping at the towns of Willows, Red Bluff and Redding, crossing the counties of Colusa, Glenn, Tehama, and Shasta, went the spruce wagon drawn by the dappled chestnuts with cream-colored manes and tails. Billy picked up only three horses for shipment, although he visited many farms; and Saxon talked with the women while he looked over the stock with the men. And Saxon grew the more convinced that the valley she sought lay not there.

At Redding they crossed the Sacramento on a cable ferry, and made a day's scorching traverse through rolling foot-hills and flat tablelands. The heat grew more insupportable, and the trees and shrubs were blasted and dead. Then they came again to the Sacramento, where the great smelters of Kennett explained the destruction of the vegetation.

They climbed out of the smelting town, where eyrie houses perched insecurely on a precipitous landscape. It was a broad, well-engineered road that took them up a grade miles long and plunged down into the Canyon of the Sacramento. The road, rock-surfaced and easy-graded, hewn out of the canyon wall, grew so narrow that Billy worried for fear of meeting opposite-bound teams. Far below, the river frothed and flowed over pebbly shallows, or broke tumultuously over boulders and cascades, in its race for the great valley they had left behind.

Sometimes, on the wider stretches of road, Saxon drove and Billy walked to lighten the load. She insisted on taking her turns at walking, and when he breathed the panting mares on the steep, and Saxon stood by their heads caressing them and cheering them, Billy's joy was too deep for any turn of speech as he gazed at his beautiful horses and his glowing girl, trim and colorful in her golden brown corduroy, the brown corduroy calves swelling sweetly under the abbreviated slim skirt. And when her answering look of happiness came to him—a sudden dimness in her straight gray eyes—he was overmastered by the knowledge that he must say something or burst.

"O, you kid!" he cried.

And with radiant face she answered, "O, you kid!"

They camped one night in a deep dent in the canyon, where was snuggled a box-factory village, and where a toothless ancient, gazing with faded eyes at their traveling outfit, asked: "Be you showin'?"

They passed Castle Crags, mighty-bastioned and glowing red against the palpitating blue sky. They caught their first glimpse of Mt. Shasta, a rose-tinted snow-peak rising, a sunset dream, between and beyond green interlacing walls of canyon—a landmark destined to be with them for many days. At unexpected turns, after mounting some steep grade, Shasta would appear again, still distant, now showing two peaks and glacial fields of shimmering white. Miles and miles and days and days they climbed, with Shasta ever developing new forms and phases in her summer snows.

"A moving picture in the sky," said Billy at last.

"Oh,—it is all so beautiful," sighed Saxon. "But there are no moon-valleys here."

They encountered a plague of butterflies, and for days drove through untold millions of the fluttering beauties that covered the road with uniform velvet-brown. And ever the road seemed to rise under the noses of the snorting mares, filling the air with noiseless flight, drifting down the breeze in clouds of brown and yellow soft-flaked as snow, and piling in mounds against the fences, ever driven to float helplessly on the irrigation ditches along the roadside. Hazel and Hattie soon grew used to them though Possum never ceased being made frantic.

"Huh!—who ever heard of butterfly-broke horses?" Billy chaffed. "That's worth fifty bucks more on their price."

"Wait till you get across the Oregon line into the Rogue River Valley," they were told. "There's God's Paradise—climate, scenery, and fruit-farming; fruit ranches that yield two hundred per cent. on a valuation of five hundred dollars an acre."

"Gee!" Billy said, when he had driven on out of hearing; "that's too rich for our digestion."

And Saxon said, "I don't know about apples in the valley of the moon, but I do know that the yield is ten thousand per cent. of happiness on a valuation of one Billy, one Saxon, a Hazel, a Hattie, and a Possum."

Through Siskiyou County and across high mountains, they came to Ashland and Medford and camped beside the wild Rogue River.

"This is wonderful and glorious," pronounced Saxon; "but it is not the valley of the moon."

"Nope, it ain't the valley of the moon," agreed Billy, and he said it on the evening of the day he hooked a monster steelhead, standing to his neck in the ice-cold water of the Rogue and fighting for forty minutes, with screaming reel, ere he drew his finny prize to the bank and with the scalp-yell of a Comanche jumped and clutched it by the gills.

"'Them that looks finds,'" predicted Saxon, as they drew north out of Grant's Pass, and held north across the mountains and fruitful Oregon valleys.

One day, in camp by the Umpqua River, Billy bent over to begin skinning the first deer he had ever shot. He raised his eyes to Saxon and remarked:

"If I didn't know California, I guess Oregon'd suit me from the ground up."

In the evening, replete with deer meat, resting on his elbow and smoking his after-supper cigarette, he said:

"Maybe they ain't no valley of the moon. An' if they ain't, what of it? We could keep on this way forever. I don't ask nothing better."

"There is a valley of the moon," Saxon answered soberly. "And we are going to find it. We've got to. Why Billy, it would never do, never to settle down. There would be no little Hazels and little Hatties, nor little... Billies—"

"Nor little Saxons," Billy interjected.

"Nor little Possums," she hurried on, nodding her head and reaching out a caressing hand to where the fox terrier was ecstatically gnawing a deer-rib. A vicious snarl and a wicked snap that barely missed her fingers were her reward.

"Possum!" she cried in sharp reproof, again extending her hand.

"Don't," Billy warned. "He can't help it, and he's likely to get you next time."

Even more compelling was the menacing threat that Possum growled, his jaws close-guarding the bone, eyes blazing insanely, the hair rising stiffly on his neck.

"It's a good dog that sticks up for its bone," Billy championed. "I wouldn't care to own one that didn't."

"But it's my Possum," Saxon protested. "And he loves me. Besides, he must love me more than an old bone. And he must mind me.—Here, you, Possum, give me that bone! Give me that bone, sir!"

Her hand went out gingerly, and the growl rose in volume and key till it culminated in a snap.

"I tell you it's instinct," Billy repeated. "He does love you, but he just can't help doin' it."

"He's got a right to defend his bones from strangers but not from his mother," Saxon argued. "I shall make him give up that bone to me."

"Fox terriers is awful highstrung, Saxon. You'll likely get him hysterical."

But she was obstinately set in her purpose. She picked up a short stick of firewood.

"Now, sir, give me that bone."

She threatened with the stick, and the dog's growling became ferocious. Again he snapped, then crouched back over his bone. Saxon raised the stick as if to strike him, and he suddenly abandoned the bone, rolled over on his back at her feet, four legs in the air, his ears lying meekly back, his eyes swimming and eloquent with submission and appeal.

"My God!" Billy breathed in solemn awe. "Look at it!—presenting his solar plexus to you, his vitals an' his life, all defense down, as much as sayin': 'Here I am. Stamp on me. Kick the life outa me.' I love you, I am your slave, but I just can't help defendin' my bone. My instinct's stronger'n me. Kill me, but I can't help it."

Saxon was melted. Tears were in her eyes as she stooped and gathered the mite of an animal in her arms. Possum was in a frenzy of agitation, whining, trembling, writhing, twisting, licking her face, all for forgiveness.

"Heart of gold with a rose in his mouth," Saxon crooned, burying her face in the soft and quivering bundle of sensibilities. "Mother is sorry. She'll never bother you again that way. There, there, little love. See? There's your bone. Take it."

She put him down, but he hesitated between her and the bone, patently looking to her for surety of permission, yet continuing to tremble in the terrible struggle between duty and desire that seemed tearing him asunder. Not until she repeated that it was all right and nodded her head consentingly did he go to the bone. And once, a minute later, he raised his head with a sudden startle and gazed inquiringly at her. She nodded and smiled, and Possum, with a happy sigh of satisfaction, dropped his head down to the precious deer-rib.

"That Mercedes was right when she said men fought over jobs like dogs over bones," Billy enunciated slowly. "It's instinct. Why, I couldn't no more help reaching my fist to the point of a scab's jaw than could Possum from snappin' at you. They's no explainin' it. What a man has to he has to. The fact that he does a thing shows he had to do it whether he can explain it or not. You remember Hall couldn't explain why he stuck that stick between Timothy McManus's legs in the foot race. What a man has to, he has to. That's all I know about it. I never had no earthly reason to beat up that lodger we had, Jimmy Harmon. He was a good guy, square an' all right. But I just had to, with the strike goin' to smash, an' everything so bitter inside me that I could taste it. I never told you, but I saw 'm once after I got out—when my arms was mendin'. I went down to the roundhouse an' waited for 'm to come in off a run, an' apologized to 'm. Now why did I apologize? I don't know, except for the same reason I punched 'm—I just had to."

And so Billy expounded the why of like in terms of realism, in the camp by the Umpqua River, while Possum expounded it, in similar terms of fang and appetite, on the rib of deer.

CHAPTER XVI

With Possum on the seat beside her, Saxon drove into the town of Roseburg. She drove at a walk. At the back of the wagon were tied two heavy young work-horses. Behind, half a dozen more marched free, and the rear was brought up by Billy, astride a ninth horse. All these he shipped from Roseburg to the West Oakland stables.

It was in the Umpqua Valley that they heard the parable of the white sparrow. The farmer who told it was elderly and flourishing. His farm was a model of orderliness and system. Afterwards, Billy heard neighbors estimate his wealth at a quarter of a million.

"You've heard the story of the farmer and the white sparrow'" he asked Billy, at dinner.

"Never heard of a white sparrow even," Billy answered.

"I must say they're pretty rare," the farmer owned. "But here's the story: Once there was a farmer who wasn't making much of a success. Things just didn't seem to go right, till at last, one day, he heard about the wonderful white sparrow. It seems that the white sparrow comes out only just at daybreak with the first light of dawn, and that it brings all kinds of good luck to the farmer that is fortunate enough to catch it. Next morning our farmer was up at daybreak, and before, looking for it. And, do you know, he sought for it continually, for months and months, and never caught even a glimpse of it." Their host shook his head. "No; he never found it, but he found so many things about the farm needing attention, and which he attended to before breakfast, that before he knew it the farm was prospering, and it wasn't long before the mortgage was paid off and he was starting a bank account."

That afternoon, as they drove along, Billy was plunged in a deep reverie.

"Oh, I got the point all right," he said finally. "An' yet I ain't satisfied. Of course, they wasn't a white sparrow, but by getting up early an' attendin' to things he'd been slack about before—oh, I got it all right. An' yet, Saxon, if that's what a farmer's life means, I don't want to find no moon valley. Life ain't hard work. Daylight to dark, hard at it—might just as well be in the city. What's the difference? Al' the time you've got to yourself is for sleepin', an' when you're sleepin' you're not enjoyin' yourself. An' what's it matter where you sleep, you're deado. Might as well be dead an' done with it as work your head off that way. I'd sooner stick to the road, an' shoot a deer an' catch a trout once in a while, an' lie on my back in the shade, an' laugh with you an' have fun with you, an'... an' go swimmin'. An' I 'm a willin' worker, too. But they's all the difference in the world between a decent amount of work an' workin' your head off."

Saxon was in full accord. She looked back on her years of toil and contrasted them with the joyous life she had lived on the road.

"We don't want to be rich," she said. "Let them hunt their white sparrows in the Sacramento islands and the irrigation valleys. When we get up early in the valley of the moon, it will be to hear the birds sing and sing with them. And if we work hard at times, it will be only so that we'll have more time to play. And when you go swimming I 'm going with you. And we'll play so hard that we'll be glad to work for relaxation."

"I 'm gettin' plumb dried out," Billy announced, mopping the sweat from his sunburned forehead. "What d'ye say we head for the coast?"

West they turned, dropping down wild mountain gorges from the height of land of the interior valleys. So fearful was the road, that, on one stretch of seven miles, they passed ten broken-down automobiles. Billy would not force the mares and promptly camped beside a brawling stream from which he whipped two trout at a time. Here, Saxon caught her first big trout. She had been accustomed to landing them up to nine and ten inches, and the screech of the reel when the big one was hooked caused her to cry out in startled surprise. Billy came up the riffle to her and gave counsel. Several minutes later, cheeks flushed and eyes dancing with excitement, Saxon dragged the big fellow carefully from the water's edge into the dry sand. Here it threw the hook out and flopped tremendously until she fell upon it and captured it in her hands.

"Sixteen inches," Billy said, as she held it up proudly for inspection. "—Hey!—what are you goin' to do?"

"Wash off the sand, of course," was her answer.

"Better put it in the basket," he advised, then closed his mouth and grimly watched.

She stooped by the side of the stream and dipped in the splendid fish. It flopped, there was a convulsive movement on her part, and it was gone.

"Oh!" Saxon cried in chagrin.

"Them that finds should hold," quoth Billy.

"I don't care," she replied. "It was a bigger one than you ever caught anyway."

"Oh, I 'm not denyin' you're a peach at fishin'," he drawled. "You caught me, didn't you?"

"I don't know about that," she retorted. "Maybe it was like the man who was arrested for catching trout out of season. His defense was self defense."

Billy pondered, but did not see.

"The trout attacked him," she explained.

Billy grinned. Fifteen minutes later he said:

"You sure handed me a hot one."

The sky was overcast, and, as they drove along the bank of the Coquille River, the fog suddenly enveloped them.

"Whoof!" Billy exhaled joyfully. "Ain't it great! I can feel myself moppin' it up like a dry sponge. I never appreciated fog before."

Saxon held out her arms to receive it, making motions as if she were bathing in the gray mist.

"I never thought I'd grow tired of the sun," she said; "but we've had more than our share the last few weeks."

"Ever since we hit the Sacramento Valley," Billy affirmed. "Too much sun ain't good. I've worked that out. Sunshine is like liquor. Did you ever notice how good you felt when the sun come out after a week of cloudy weather. Well, that sunshine was just like a jolt of whiskey. Had the same effect. Made you feel good all over. Now, when you're swimmin', an' come out an' lay in the sun, how good you feel. That's because you're lappin' up a sun-cocktail. But suppose you lay there in the sand a couple of hours. You don't feel so good. You're so slow-movin' it takes you a long time to dress. You go home draggin' your legs an' feelin' rotten, with all the life sapped outa you. What's that? It's the katzenjammer. You've been soused to the ears in sunshine, like so much whiskey, an' now you're payin' for it. That's straight. That's why fog in the climate is best."

"Then we've been drunk for months," Saxon said. "And now we're going to sober up."

"You bet. Why, Saxon, I can do two days' work in one in this climate.—Look at the mares. Blame me if they ain't perkin' up already."

Vainly Saxon's eye roved the pine forest in search of her beloved redwoods. They would find them down in California, they were told in the town of Bandon.

"Then we're too far north," said Saxon. "We must go south to find our valley of the moon."

And south they went, along roads that steadily grew worse, through the dairy country of Langlois and through thick pine forests to Port Orford, where Saxon picked jeweled agates on the beach while Billy caught enormous rockcod. No railroads had yet penetrated this wild region, and the way south grew wilder and wilder. At Gold Beach they encountered their old friend, the Rogue River, which they ferried across where it entered the Pacific. Still wilder became the country, still more terrible the road, still farther apart the isolated farms and clearings.

And here were neither Asiatics nor Europeans. The scant population consisted of the original settlers and their descendants. More than one old man or woman Saxon talked with, who could remember the trip across the Plains with the plodding oxen. West they had fared until the Pacific itself had stopped them, and here they had made their clearings, built their rude houses, and settled. In them Farthest West had been reached. Old customs had changed little. There were no railways. No automobile as yet had ventured their perilous roads. Eastward, between them and the populous interior valleys, lay the wilderness of the Coast Range—a game paradise, Billy heard; though he declared that the very road he traveled was game paradise enough for him. Had he not halted the horses, turned the reins over to Saxon, and shot an eight-pronged buck from the wagon-seat?

South of Gold Beach, climbing a narrow road through the virgin forest, they heard from far above the jingle of bells. A hundred yards farther on Billy found a place wide enough to turn out. Here he waited, while the merry bells, descending the mountain, rapidly came near. They heard the grind of brakes, the soft thud of horses' hoofs, once a sharp cry of the driver, and once a woman's laughter.

"Some driver, some driver," Billy muttered. "I take my hat off to 'm whoever he is, hittin' a pace like that on a road like this.—Listen to that! He's got powerful brakes.—Zocie! That WAS a chuck-hole! Some springs, Saxon, some springs!"

Where the road zigzagged above, they glimpsed through the trees four sorrel horses trotting swiftly, and the flying wheels of a small, tan-painted trap.

CHAPTER XVI

At the bend of the road the leaders appeared again, swinging wide on the curve, the wheelers flashed into view, and the light two-seated rig; then the whole affair straightened out and thundered down upon them across a narrow plank-bridge. In the front seat were a man and woman; in the rear seat a Japanese was squeezed in among suit cases, rods, guns, saddles, and a typewriter case, while above him and all about him, fastened most intricately, sprouted a prodigious crop of deer- and elk-horns.

"It's Mr. and Mrs. Hastings," Saxon cried.

"Whoa!" Hastings yelled, putting on the brake and gathering his horses in to a stop alongside. Greetings flew back and forth, in which the Japanese, whom they had last seen on the Roamer at Rio Vista, gave and received his share.

"Different from the Sacramento islands, eh?" Hastings said to Saxon. "Nothing but old American stock in these mountains. And they haven't changed any. As John Fox, Jr., said, they're our contemporary ancestors. Our old folks were just like them."

Mr. and Mrs. Hastings, between them, told of their long drive. They were out two months then, and intended to continue north through Oregon and Washington to the Canadian boundary.

"Then we'll ship our horses and come home by train," concluded Hastings.

"But the way you drive you oughta be a whole lot further along than this," Billy criticized.

"But we keep stopping off everywhere," Mrs. Hastings explained.

"We went in to the Hoopa Reservation," said Mr. Elastings, "and canoed down the Trinity and Klamath Rivers to the ocean. And just now we've come out from two weeks in the real wilds of Curry County."

"You must go in," Hastings advised. "You'll get to Mountain Ranch to-night. And you can turn in from there. No roads, though. You'll have to pack your horses. But it's full of game. I shot five mountain lions and two bear, to say nothing of deer. And there are small herds of elk, too.—No; I didn't shoot any. They're protected. These horns I got from the old hunters. I'll tell you all about it."

And while the men talked, Saxon and Mrs. Hastings were not idle.

"Found your valley of the moon yet?" the writer's wife asked, as they were saying good-by.

Saxon shook her head.

"You will find it if you go far enough; and be sure you go as far as Sonoma Valley and our ranch. Then, if you haven't found it yet, we'll see what we can do."

Three weeks later, with a bigger record of mountain lions and bear than Hastings' to his credit, Billy emerged from Curry County and drove across the line into California. At once Saxon found herself among the redwoods. But they were redwoods unbelievable. Billy stopped the wagon, got out, and paced around one.

"Forty-five feet," he announced. "That's fifteen in diameter. And they're all like it only bigger. No; there's a runt. It's only about nine feet through. An' they're hundreds of feet tall."

"When I die, Billy, you must bury me in a redwood grove," Saxon adjured.

"I ain't goin' to let you die before I do," he assured her. "An' then we'll leave it in our wills for us both to be buried that way."

CHAPTER XVII

South they held along the coast, hunting, fishing, swimming, and horse-buying. Billy shipped his purchases on the coasting steamers. Through Del Norte and Humboldt counties they went, and through Mendocino into Sonoma—counties larger than Eastern states—threading the giant woods, whipping innumerable trout-streams, and crossing countless rich valleys. Ever Saxon sought the valley of the moon. Sometimes, when all seemed fair, the lack was a railroad, sometimes madrono and manzanita trees, and, usually, there was too much fog.

"We do want a sun-cocktail once in a while," she told Billy.

"Yep," was his answer. "Too much fog might make us soggy. What we're after is betwixt an' between, an' we'll have to get back from the coast a ways to find it."

This was in the fall of the year, and they turned their backs on the Pacific at old Fort Ross and entered the Russian River Valley, far below Ukiah, by way of Cazadero and Guerneville. At Santa Rosa Billy was delayed with the shipping of several horses, so that it was not until afternoon that he drove south and east for Sonoma Valley.

"I guess we'll no more than make Sonoma Valley when it'll be time to camp," he said, measuring the sun with his eye. "This is called Bennett Valley. You cross a divide from it and come out at Glen Ellen. Now this is a mighty pretty valley, if anybody should ask you. An' that's some nifty mountain over there."

"The mountain is all right," Saxon adjudged. "But all the rest of the hills are too bare. And I don't see any big trees. It takes rich soil to make big trees."

"Oh, I ain't sayin' it's the valley of the moon by a long ways. All the same, Saxon, that's some mountain. Look at the timber on it. I bet they's deer there."

"I wonder where we'll spend this winter," Saxon remarked.

"D'ye know, I've just been thinkin' the same thing. Let's winter at Carmel. Mark Hall's back, an' so is Jim Hazard. What d'ye say?"

Saxon nodded.

"Only you won't be the odd-job man this time."

"Nope. We can make trips in good weather horse-buyin'," Billy confirmed, his face beaming with self-satisfaction. "An' if that walkin' poet of the Marble House is around, I'll sure get the gloves on with 'm just in memory of the time he walked me off my legs—"

"Oh! Oh!" Saxon cried. "Look, Billy! Look!"

Around a bend in the road came a man in a sulky, driving a heavy stallion. The animal was a bright chestnut-sorrel, with cream-colored mane and tail. The tail almost swept the ground, while the mane was so thick that it crested out of the neck and flowed down, long and wavy. He scented the mares and stopped short, head flung up and armfuls of creamy mane tossing in the breeze. He bent his head until flaring nostrils brushed impatient knees, and between the fine-pointed ears could be seen a mighty and incredible curve of neck. Again he tossed his head, fretting against the bit as the driver turned widely aside for safety in passing. They could see the blue glaze like a sheen on the surface of the horse's bright, wild eyes, and Billy closed a wary thumb on his reins and himself turned widely. He held up his hand in signal, and the driver of the stallion stopped when well past, and over his shoulder talked draught-horses with Billy.

Among other things, Billy learned that the stallion's name was Barbarossa, that the driver was the owner, and that Santa Rosa was his headquarters.

"There are two ways to Sonoma Valley from here," the man directed. "When you come to the crossroads the turn to the left will take you to Glen Ellen by Bennett Peak—that's it there."

Rising from rolling stubble fields, Bennett Peak towered hot in the sun, a row of bastion hills leaning against its base. But hills and mountains on that side showed bare and heated, though beautiful with the sunburnt tawniness of California.

"The turn to the right will take you to Glen Ellen, too, only it's longer and steeper grades. But your mares don't look as though it'd bother them."

"Which is the prettiest way?" Saxon asked.

"Oh, the right hand road, by all means," said the man. "That's Sonoma Mountain there, and the road skirts it pretty well up, and goes through Cooper's Grove."

Billy did not start immediately after they had said good-by, and he and Saxon, heads over shoulders, watched the roused Barbarossa plunging mutinously on toward Santa Rosa.

"Gee!" Billy said. "I'd like to be up here next spring."

At the crossroads Billy hesitated and looked at Saxon.

"What if it is longer?" she said. "Look how beautiful it is—all covered with green woods; and I just know those are redwoods in the canyons. You never can tell. The valley of the moon might be right up there somewhere. And it would never do to miss it just in order to save half an hour."

They took the turn to the right and began crossing a series of steep foothills. As they approached the mountain there were signs of a greater abundance of water. They drove beside a running stream, and, though the vineyards on the hills were summer-dry, the farmhouses in the hollows and on the levels were grouped about with splendid trees.

"Maybe it sounds funny," Saxon observed; "but I 'm beginning to love that mountain already. It almost seems as if I d seen it before, somehow, it's so all-around satisfying—oh!"

Crossing a bridge and rounding a sharp turn, they were suddenly enveloped in a mysterious coolness and gloom. All about them arose stately trunks of redwood. The forest floor was a rosy carpet of autumn fronds. Occasional shafts of sunlight, penetrating the deep shade, warmed the somberness of the grove. Alluring paths led off among the trees and into cozy nooks made by circles of red columns growing around the dust of vanished ancestors—witnessing the titantic dimensions of those ancestors by the girth of the circles in which they stood.

Out of the grove they pulled to the steep divide, which was no more than a buttress of Sonoma Mountain. The way led on through rolling uplands and across small dips and canyons, all well wooded and a-drip with water. In places the road was muddy from wayside springs.

"The mountain's a sponge," said Billy. "Here it is, the tail-end of dry summer, an' the ground's just leakin' everywhere."

"I know I've never been here before," Saxon communed aloud. "But it's all so familiar! So I must have dreamed it. And there's madronos!—a whole grove! And manzanita! Why, I feel just as if I was coming home... Oh, Billy, if it should turn out to be our valley."

"Plastered against the side of a mountain?" he queried, with a skeptical laugh.

"No; I don't mean that. I mean on the way to our valley. Because the way—all ways—to our valley must be beautiful. And this; I've seen it all before, dreamed it."

"It's great," he said sympathetically. "I wouldn't trade a square mile of this kind of country for the whole Sacramento Valley, with the river islands thrown in and Middle River for good measure. If they ain't deer up there, I miss my guess. An' where they's springs they's streams, an' streams means trout."

They passed a large and comfortable farmhouse, surrounded by wandering barns and cow-sheds, went on under forest arches, and emerged beside a field with which Saxon was instantly enchanted. It flowed in a gentle concave from the road up the mountain, its farther boundary an unbroken line of timber. The field glowed like rough gold in the approaching sunset, and near the middle of it stood a solitary great redwood, with blasted top suggesting a nesting eyrie for eagles. The timber beyond clothed the mountain in solid green to what they took to be the top. But, as they drove on, Saxon, looking back upon what she called her field, saw the real summit of Sonoma towering beyond, the mountain behind her field a mere spur upon the side of the larger mass.

Ahead and toward the right, across sheer ridges of the mountains, separated by deep green canyons and broadening lower down into rolling orchards and vineyards, they caught their first sight of Sonoma Valley and the wild mountains that rimmed its eastern side. To the left they gazed across a golden land of small hills and valleys. Beyond, to the north, they glimpsed another portion of the valley, and, still beyond, the opposing wall of the valley—a range of mountains, the highest of which reared its red and battered ancient crater against a rosy and mellowing sky. From north to southeast, the mountain rim curved in the brightness of the sun, while Saxon and Billy were already in the shadow of evening. He looked at Saxon, noted the ravished ecstasy of her face, and stopped the horses. All the eastern sky was blushing to rose, which descended upon the mountains, touching them with wine and ruby. Sonoma Valley began to fill with a purple flood, laying the mountain bases, rising, inundating, drowning them in its purple. Saxon pointed in silence, indicating that the purple flood was the sunset shadow of Sonoma Mountain. Billy nodded, then chirruped to the mares, and the descent began through a warm and colorful twilight.

On the elevated sections of the road they felt the cool, delicious breeze from the Pacific forty miles away; while from each little dip and hollow came warm breaths of autumn earth, spicy with sunburnt grass and fallen leaves and passing flowers.

They came to the rim of a deep canyon that seemed to penetrate to the heart of Sonoma Mountain. Again, with no word spoken, merely from watching Saxon, Billy stopped the wagon. The canyon was wildly beautiful. Tall redwoods lined its entire length. On its farther rim stood three rugged knolls covered with dense woods of spruce and oak. From between the knolls, a feeder to the main canyon and likewise fringed with redwoods, emerged a smaller canyon. Billy pointed to a stubble field that lay at the feet of the knolls.

"It's in fields like that I've seen my mares a-pasturing," he said.

They dropped down into the canyon, the road following a stream that sang under maples and alders. The sunset fires, refracted from the cloud-driftage of the autumn sky, bathed the canyon with crimson, in which ruddy-limbed madronos and wine-wooded manzanitas burned and smoldered. The air was aromatic with laurel. Wild grape vines bridged the stream from tree to tree. Oaks of many sorts were veiled in lacy Spanish moss. Ferns and brakes grew lush beside the stream. From somewhere came the plaint of a mourning dove. Fifty feet above the ground, almost over their heads, a Douglas squirrel crossed the road—a flash of gray between two trees; and they marked the continuance of its aerial passage by the bending of the boughs.

"I've got a hunch," said Billy.

"Let me say it first," Saxon begged.

He waited, his eyes on her face as she gazed about her in rapture.

"We've found our valley," she whispered. "Was that it?"

He nodded, but checked speech at sight of a small boy driving a cow up the road, a preposterously big shotgun in one hand, in the other as preposterously big a jackrab-bit. "How far to Glen Ellen?" Billy asked.

"Mile an' a half," was the answer.

"What creek is this?" inquired Saxon.

"Wild Water. It empties into Sonoma Creek half a mile down."

"Trout?"—this from Billy.

"If you know how to catch 'em," grinned the boy.

"Deer up the mountain?"

"It ain't open season," the boy evaded.

"I guess you never shot a deer," Billy slyly baited, and was rewarded with:

"I got the horns to show."

"Deer shed their horns," Billy teased on. "Anybody can find 'em."

"I got the meat on mine. It ain't dry yet—"

The boy broke off, gazing with shocked eyes into the pit Billy had dug for him.

"It's all right, sonny," Billy laughed, as he drove on. "I ain't the game warden. I 'm buyin' horses."

More leaping tree squirrels, more ruddy madronos and majestic oaks, more fairy circles of redwoods, and, still beside the singing stream, they passed a gate by the roadside. Before it stood a rural mail box, on which was lettered "Edmund Hale." Standing under the rustic arch, leaning upon the gate, a man and woman composed a pieture so arresting and beautiful that Saxon caught her breath. They were side by side, the delicate hand of the woman curled in the hand of the man, which looked as if made to confer benedictions. His face bore out this impression—a beautiful-browed countenance, with large, benevolent gray eyes under a wealth of white hair that shone like spun glass. He was fair and large; the little woman beside him was daintily wrought. She was saffron-brown, as a woman of the white race can well be, with smiling eyes of bluest blue. In quaint sage-green draperies, she seemed a flower, with her small vivid face irresistibly reminding Saxon of a springtime wake-robin.

Perhaps the picture made by Saxon and Billy was equally arresting and beautiful, as they drove down through the golden end of day. The two couples had eyes only for each other. The little woman beamed joyously. The man's face glowed into the benediction that had trembled there. To Saxon, like the field up the mountain, like the mountain itself, it seemed that she had always known this adorable pair. She knew that she loved them.

"How d'ye do," said Billy.

"You blessed children," said the man. "I wonder if you know how dear you look sitting there."

That was all. The wagon had passed by, rustling down the road, which was carpeted with fallen leaves of maple, oak, and alder. Then they came to the meeting of the two creeks.

"Oh, what a place for a home," Saxon cried, pointing across Wild Water. "See, Billy, on that bench there above the meadow."

"It's a rich bottom, Saxon; and so is the bench rich. Look at the big trees on it. An' they's sure to be springs."

"Drive over," she said.

Forsaking the main road, they crossed Wild Water on a narrow bridge and continued along an ancient, rutted road that ran beside an equally ancient worm-fence of split redwood rails. They came to a gate, open and off its hinges, through which the road led out on the bench.

"This is it—I know it," Saxon said with conviction. "Drive in, Billy."

A small, whitewashed farmhouse with broken windows showed through the trees.

"Talk about your madronos—"

Billy pointed to the father of all madronos, six feet in diameter at its base, sturdy and sound, which stood before the house.

They spoke in low tones as they passed around the house under great oak trees and came to a stop before a small barn. They did not wait to unharness. Tying the horses, they started to explore. The pitch from the bench to the meadow was steep yet thickly wooded with oaks and manzanita. As they crashed through the underbrush they startled a score of quail into flight.

"How about game?" Saxon queried.

Billy grinned, and fell to examining a spring which bubbled a clear stream into the meadow. Here the ground was sunbaked and wide open in a multitude of cracks.

Disappointment leaped into Saxon's face, but Billy, crumbling a clod between his fingers, had not made up his mind.

"It's rich," he pronounced; "—the cream of the soil that's been washin' down from the hills for ten thousan' years. But—"

He broke off, stared all about, studying the configuration of the meadow, crossed it to the redwood trees beyond, then came back.

"It's no good as it is," he said. "But it's the best ever if it's handled right. All it needs is a little common sense an' a lot of drainage. This meadow's a natural basin not yet filled level. They's a sharp slope through the redwoods to the creek. Come on, I'll show you."

CHAPTER XVII

They went through the redwoods and came out on Sonoma Creek. At this spot was no singing. The stream poured into a quiet pool. The willows on their side brushed the water. The opposite side was a steep bank. Billy measured the height of the bank with his eye, the depth of the water with a driftwood pole.

"Fifteen feet," he announced. "That allows all kinds of high-divin' from the bank. An' it's a hundred yards of a swim up an' down."

They followed down the pool. It emptied in a riffle, across exposed bedrock, into another pool. As they looked, a trout flashed into the air and back, leaving a widening ripple on the quiet surface.

"I guess we won't winter in Carmel," Billy said. "This place was specially manufactured for us. In the morning I'll find out who owns it."

Half an hour later, feeding the horses, he called Saxon's attention to a locomotive whistle.

"You've got your railroad," he said. "That's a train pulling into Glen Ellen, an' it's only a mile from here."

Saxon was dozing off to sleep under the blankets when Billy aroused her.

"Suppose the guy that owns it won't sell?"

"There isn't the slightest doubt," Saxon answered with unruffled certainty. "This is our place. I know it."

CHAPTER XVIII

They were awakened by Possum, who was indignantly reproaching a tree squirrel for not coming down to be killed. The squirrel chattered garrulous remarks that drove Possum into a mad attempt to climb the tree. Billy and Saxon giggled and hugged each other at the terrier's frenzy.

"If this is goin' to be our place, they'll be no shootin' of tree squirrels," Billy said.

Saxon pressed his hand and sat up. From beneath the bench came the cry of a meadow lark.

"There isn't anything left to be desired," she sighed happily.

"Except the deed," Billy corrected.

After a hasty breakfast, they started to explore, running the irregular boundaries of the place and repeatedly crossing it from rail fence to creek and back again. Seven springs they found along the foot of the bench on the edge of the meadow.

"There's your water supply," Billy said. "Drain the meadow, work the soil up, and with fertilizer and all that water you can grow crops the year round. There must be five acres of it, an' I wouldn't trade it for Mrs. Mortimer's."

They were standing in the old orchard, on the bench where they had counted twenty-seven trees, neglected but of generous girth.

"And on top the bench, back of the house, we can grow berries." Saxon paused, considering a new thought "If only Mrs. Mortimer would come up and advise us!—Do you think she would, Billy?"

"Sure she would. It ain't more 'n four hours' run from San Jose. But first we'll get our hooks into the place. Then you can write to her."

Sonoma Creek gave the long boundary to the little farm, two sides were worm fenced, and the fourth side was Wild Water.

"Why, we'll have that beautiful man and woman for neighbors," Saxon recollected. "Wild Water will be the dividing line between their place and ours."

"It ain't ours yet," Billy commented. "Let's go and call on 'em. They'll be able to tell us all about it."

"It's just as good as," she replied. "The big thing has been the finding. And whoever owns it doesn't care much for it. It hasn't been lived in for a long time. And—Oh, Billy—are you satisfied!"

"With every bit of it," he answered frankly, "as far as it goes. But the trouble is, it don't go far enough."

CHAPTER XVIII

The disappointment in her face spurred him to renunciation of his particular dream.

"We'll buy it—that's settled," he said. "But outside the meadow, they's so much woods that they's little pasture—not more 'n enough for a couple of horses an' a cow. But I don't care. We can't have everything, an' what they is is almighty good."

"Let us call it a starter," she consoled. "Later on we can add to it—maybe the land alongside that runs up the Wild Water to the three knolls we saw yesterday."

"Where I seen my horses pasturin'," he remembered, with a flash of eye. "Why not? So much has come true since we hit the road, maybe that'll come true, too.

"We'll work for it, Billy."

"We'll work like hell for it," he said grimly.

They passed through the rustic gate and along a path that wound through wild woods. There was no sign of the house until they came abruptly upon it, bowered among the trees. It was eight-sided, and so justly proportioned that its two stories made no show of height. The house belonged there. It might have sprung from the soil just as the trees had. There were no formal grounds. The wild grew to the doors. The low porch of the main entrance was raised only a step from the ground. "Trillium Covert," they read, in quaint carved letters under the eave of the porch.

"Come right upstairs, you dears," a voice called from above, in response to Saxon's knock.

Stepping back and looking up, she beheld the little lady smiling down from a sleeping-porch. Clad in a rosy-tissued and flowing house gown, she again reminded Saxon of a flower.

"Just push the front door open and find your way," was the direction.

Saxon led, with Billy at her heels. They came into a room bright with windows, where a big log smoldered in a rough-stone fireplace. On the stone slab above stood a huge Mexican jar, filled with autumn branches and trailing fluffy smoke-vine. The walls were finished in warm natural woods, stained but without polish. The air was aromatic with clean wood odors. A walnut organ loomed in a shallow corner of the room. All corners were shallow in this octagonal dwelling. In another corner were many rows of books. Through the windows, across a low couch indubitably made for use, could be seen a restful picture of autumn trees and yellow grasses, threaded by wellworn paths that ran here and there over the tiny estate. A delightful little stairway wound past more windows to the upper story. Here the little lady greeted them and led them into what Saxon knew at once was her room. The two octagonal sides of the house which showed in this wide room were given wholly to windows. Under the long sill, to the floor, were shelves of books. Books lay here and there, in the disorder of use, on work table, couch and desk. On a sill by an open window, a jar of autumn leaves breathed the charm of the sweet brown wife, who seated herself in a tiny rattan chair, enameled a cheery red, such as children delight to rock in.

"A queer house," Mrs. Hale laughed girlishly and contentedly. "But we love it. Edmund made it with his own hands even to the plumbing, though he did have a terrible time with that before he succeeded."

"How about that hardwood floor downstairs?—an' the fireplace?" Billy inquired.

"All, all," she replied proudly. "And half the furniture. That cedar desk there, the table—with his own hands."

"They are such gentle hands," Saxon was moved to say.

Mrs. Hale looked at her quickly, her vivid face alive with a grateful light.

"They are gentle, the gentlest hands I have ever known," she said softly. "And you are a dear to have noticed it, for you only saw them yesterday in passing."

"I couldn't help it," Saxon said simply.

Her gaze slipped past Mrs. Hale, attracted by the wall beyond, which was done in a bewitching honeycomb pattern dotted with golden bees. The walls were hung with a few, a very few, framed pictures.

"They are all of people," Saxon said, remembering the beautiful paintings in Mark Hall's bungalow.

"My windows frame my landscape paintings," Mrs. Hale answered, pointing out of doors. "Inside I want only the faces of my dear ones whom I cannot have with me always. Some of them are dreadful rovers."

"Oh!" Saxon was on her feet and looking at a photograph. "You know Clara Hastings!"

"I ought to. I did everything but nurse her at my breast. She came to me when she was a little baby. Her mother was my sister. Do you know how greatly you resemble her? I remarked it to Edmund yesterday. He had already seen it. It wasn't a bit strange that his heart leaped out to you two as you came drilling down behind those beautiful horses."

So Mrs. Hale was Clara's aunt—old stock that had crossed the Plains. Saxon knew now why she had reminded her so strongly of her own mother.

The talk whipped quite away from Billy, who could only admire the detailed work of the cedar desk while he listened. Saxon told of meeting Clara and Jack Hastings on their yacht and on their driving trip in Oregon. They were off again, Mrs. Hale said, having shipped their horses home from Vancouver and taken the Canadian Pacific on their way to England. Mrs. Hale knew Saxon's mother or, rather, her poems; and produced, not only "The Story of the Files," but a ponderous scrapbook which contained many of her mother's poems which Saxon had never seen. A sweet singer, Mrs. Hale said; but so many had sung in the days of gold and been forgotten. There had been no army of magazines then, and the poems had perished in local newspapers.

Jack Hastings had fallen in love with Clara, the talk ran on; then, visiting at Trillium Covert, he had fallen in love with Sonoma Valley and bought a magnificent home ranch, though little enough he saw of it, being away over the world so much of the time. Mrs. Hale talked of her own Journey across the Plains, a little girl, in the late Fifties, and, like Mrs. Mortimer, knew all about the fight at Little Meadow, and the tale of the massacre of the emigrant train of which Billy's father had been the sole survivor.

"And so," Saxon concluded, an hour later, "we've been three years searching for our valley of the moon, and now we've found it."

"Valley of the Moon?" Mrs. Hale queried. "Then you knew about it all the time. What kept you so long?"

"No; we didn't know. We just started on a blind search for it. Mark Hall called it a pilgrimage, and was always teasing us to carry long staffs. He said when we found the spot we'd know, because then the staffs would burst into blossom. He laughed at all the good things we wanted in our valley, and one night he took me out and showed me the moon through a telescope. He said that was the only place we could find such a wonderful valley. He meant it was moonshine, but we adopted the name and went on looking for it."

"What a coincidence!" Mrs. Hale exclaimed. "For this is the Valley of the Moon."

"I know it," Saxon said with quiet confidence. "It has everything we wanted."

"But you don't understand, my dear. This is the Valley of the Moon. This is Sonoma Valley. Sonoma is an Indian word, and means the Valley of the Moon. That was what the Indians called it for untold ages before the first white men came. We, who love it, still so call it."

And then Saxon recalled the mysterious references Jack Hastings and his wife had made to it, and the talk tripped along until Billy grew restless. He cleared his throat significantly and interrupted.

"We want to find out about that ranch acrost the creek—who owns it, if they'll sell, where we'll find 'em, an' such things."

Mrs. Hale stood up.

"We'll go and see Edmund," she said, catching Saxon by the hand and leading the way.

"My!" Billy ejaculated, towering above her. "I used to think Saxon was small. But she'd make two of you."

"And you're pretty big," the little woman smiled; "but Edmund is taller than you, and broader-shouldered."

They crossed a bright hall, and found the big beautiful husband lying back reading in a huge Mission rocker. Beside it was another tiny child's chair of red-enameled rattan. Along the length of his thigh, the head on his knee and directed toward a smoldering log in a fireplace, clung an incredibly large striped cat. Like its master, it turned its head to greet the newcomers. Again Saxon felt the loving benediction that abided in his face, his eyes, his hands—toward which she involuntarily dropped her eyes. Again she was impressed by the gentleness of them. They were hands of love. They were the hands of a type of man she had never dreamed existed. No one in that merry crowd of Carmel had prefigured him. They were artists. This was the scholar, the philosopher. In place of the passion of youth and all youth's mad revolt, was the benignance of wisdom. Those gentle hands had passed all the bitter by and plucked only the sweet of life. Dearly as she loved them, she shuddered to think what some of those Carmelites would be like when they were as old as he—especially the dramatic critic and the Iron Man.

"Here are the dear children, Edmund," Mrs. Hale said. "What do you think! They want to buy the Madrono Ranch. They've been three years searching for it—I forgot to tell them we had searched ten years for Trillium Covert. Tell them all about it. Surely Mr. Naismith is still of a mind to sell!"

They seated themselves in simple massive chairs, and Mrs. Hale took the tiny rattan beside the big Mission rocker, her slender hand curled like a tendril in Edmund's. And while Saxon listened to the talk, her eyes took in the grave rooms lined with books. She began to realize how a mere structure of wood and stone may express the spirit of him who conceives and makes it. Those gentle hands had made all this—the very furniture, she guessed as her eyes roved from desk to chair, from work table to reading stand beside the bed in the other room, where stood a green-shaded lamp and orderly piles of magazines and books.

As for the matter of Madrono Ranch, it was easy enough he was saying. Naismith would sell. Had desired to sell for the past five years, ever since he had engaged in the enterprise of bottling mineral water at the springs lower down the valley. It was fortunate that he was the owner, for about all the rest of the surrounding land was owned by a Frenchman—an early settler. He would not part with a foot of it. He was a peasant, with all the peasant's love of the soil, which, in him, had become an obsession, a disease. He was a land-miser. With no business capacity, old and opinionated, he was land poor, and it was an open question which would arrive first, his death or bankruptcy.

As for Madrono Ranch, Naismith owned it and had set the price at fifty dollars an acre. That would be one thousand dollars, for there were twenty acres. As a farming investment, using old-fashioned methods, it was not worth it. As a business investment, yes; for the virtues of the valley were on the eve of being discovered by the outside world, and no better location for a summer home could be found. As a happiness investment in joy of beauty and climate, it was worth a thousand times the price asked. And he knew Naismith would allow time on most of the amount. Edmund's suggestion was that they take a two years' lease, with option to buy, the rent to apply to the purchase if they took it up. Naismith had done that once with a Swiss, who had paid a monthly rental of ten dollars. But the man's wife had died, and he had gone away.

Edmund soon divined Billy's renunciation, though not the nature of it; and several questions brought it forth—the old pioneer dream of land spaciousness; of cattle on a hundred hills; one hundred and sixty acres of land the smallest thinkable division.

"But you don't need all that land, dear lad," Edmund said softly. "I see you understand intensive farming. Have you thought about intensive horse-raising?"

Billy's jaw dropped at the smashing newness of the idea. He considered it, but could see no similarity in the two processes. Unbelief leaped into his eyes.

"You gotta show me!" he cried.

The elder man smiled gently.

"Let us see. In the first place, you don't need those twenty acres except for beauty. There are five acres in the meadow. You don't need more than two of them to make your living at selling vegetables. In fact, you and your wife, working from daylight to dark, cannot properly farm those two acres. Remains three acres. You have plenty of water for it from the springs. Don't be satisfied with one crop a year, like the rest of the old-fashioned farmers in this valley. Farm it like your vegetable plot, intensively, all the year, in crops that make horse-feed, irrigating, fertilizing, rotating your crops. Those three acres will feed as many horses as heaven knows how huge an area of unseeded, uncared for, wasted pasture would feed. Think it over. I'll lend you books on the subject. I don't know how large your crops will be, nor do I know how much a horse eats; that's your business. But I am certain, with a hired man to take your place helping your wife on her two acres of vegetables, that by the time you own the horses your three acres will feed, you will have all you can attend to. Then it will be time to get more land, for more horses, for more riches, if that way happiness lie."

Billy understood. In his enthusiasm he dashed out:

"You're some farmer."

Edmund smiled and glanced toward his wife.

"Give him your opinion of that, Annette."

Her blue eyes twinkled as she complied.

"Why, the dear, he never farms. He has never farmed. But he knows." She waved her hand about the booklined walls. "He is a student of good. He studies all good things done by good men under the sun. His pleasure is in books and wood-working."

"Don't forget Dulcie," Edmund gently protested.

"Yes, and Dulcie." Annette laughed. "Dulcie is our cow. It is a great question with Jack Hastings whether Edmund dotes more on Dulcie, or Dulcie dotes more on Edmund. When he goes to San Francisco Dulcie is miserable. So is Edmund, until he hastens back. Oh, Dulcie has given me no few jealous pangs. But I have to confess he understands her as no one else does."

"That is the one practical subject I know by experience," Edmund confirmed. "I am an authority on Jersey cows. Call upon me any time for counsel."

He stood up and went toward his book-shelves; and they saw how magnificently large a man he was. He paused a book in his hand, to answer a question from Saxon. No; there were no mosquitoes, although, one summer when the south wind blew for ten days—an unprecedented thing—a few mosquitoes had been carried up from San Pablo Bay. As for fog, it was the making of the valley. And where they were situated, sheltered behind Sonoma Mountain, the fogs were almost invariably high fogs. Sweeping in from the ocean forty miles away, they were deflected by Sonoma Mountain and shunted high into the air. Another thing, Trillium Covert and Madrono Ranch were happily situated in a narrow thermal belt, so that in the frosty mornings of winter the temperature was always several degrees higher than in the rest of the valley. In fact, frost was very rare in the thermal belt, as was proved by the successful cultivation of certain orange and lemon trees.

Edmund continued reading titles and selecting books until he had drawn out quite a number. He opened the top one, Bolton Hall's "Three Acres and Liberty," and read to them of a man who walked six hundred and fifty miles a year in cultivating, by old-fashioned methods, twenty acres, from which he harvested three thousand bushels of poor potatoes; and of another man, a "new" farmer, who cultivated only five acres, walked two hundred miles, and produced three thousand bushels of potatoes, early and choice, which he sold at many times the price received by the first man.

Saxon receded the books from Edmund, and, as she heaped them in Billy's arms, read the titles. They were: Wickson's "California Fruits," Wickson's "California Vegetables," Brooks' "Fertilizers," Watson's "Farm Poultry," King's "Irrigation and Drainage," Kropotkin's "Fields, Factories and Workshops," and Farmer's Bulletin No. 22 on "The Feeding of Farm Animals."

"Come for more any time you want them," Edmund invited. "I have hundreds of volumes on farming, and all the Agricultural Bulletins... . And you must come and get acquainted with Dulcie your first spare time," he called after them out the door.

CHAPTER XIX

Mrs. Mortimer arrived with seed catalogs and farm books, to find Saxon immersed in the farm books borrowed from Edmund. Saxon showed her around, and she was delighted with everything, including the terms of the lease and its option to buy.

"And now," she said. "What is to be done? Sit down, both of you. This is a council of war, and I am the one person in the world to tell you what to do. I ought to be. Anybody who has reorganized and recatalogued a great city library should be able to start you young people on in short order. Now, where shall we begin?"

She paused for breath of consideration.

"First, Madrono Ranch is a bargain. I know soil, I know beauty, I know climate. Madrono Ranch is a gold mine. There is a fortune in that meadow. Tilth—I'll tell you about that later. First, here's the land. Second, what are you going to do with it? Make a living? Yes. Vegetables? Of course. What are you going to do with them after you have grown them? Sell. Where?—Now listen. You must do as I did. Cut out the middle man. Sell directly to the consumer. Drum up your own market. Do you know what I saw from the car windows coming up the valley, only several miles from here? Hotels, springs, summer resorts, winter resorts—population, mouths, market. How is that market supplied? I looked in vain for truck gardens.—Billy, harness up your horses and be ready directly after dinner to take Saxon and me driving. Never mind everything else. Let things stand. What's the use of starting for a place of which you haven't the address. We'll look for the address this afternoon. Then we'll know where we are—at."—The last syllable a smiling concession to Billy.

But Saxon did not accompany them. There was too much to be done in cleaning the long-abandoned house and in preparing an arrangement for Mrs. Mortimer to sleep. And it was long after supper time when Mrs. Mortimer and Billy returned.

"You lucky, lucky children," she began immediately. "This valley is just waking up. Here's your market. There isn't a competitor in the valley. I thought those resorts looked new—Caliente, Boyes Hot Springs, El Verano, and all along the line. Then there are three little hotels in Glen Ellen, right next door. Oh, I've talked with all the owners and managers."

"She's a wooz," Billy admired. "She'd brace up to God on a business proposition. You oughta seen her."

Mrs. Mortimer acknowledged the compliment and dashed on.

"And where do all the vegetables come from? Wagons drive down twelve to fifteen miles from Santa Rosa, and up from Sonoma. Those are the nearest truck farms, and when they fail, as they often do, I am told, to supply the increasing needs, the managers have to express vegetables all the way from San Francisco. I've introduced Billy. They've agreed to patronize home industry. Besides, it is better for them. You'll deliver just as good vegetables just as cheap; you will make it a point to deliver better, fresher vegetables; and don't forget that delivery for you will be cheaper by virtue of the shorter haul.

"No day-old egg stunt here. No jams nor jellies. But you've got lots of space up on the bench here on which you can't grow vegetables. To-morrow morning I'll help you lay out the chicken runs and houses. Besides, there is the matter of capons for the San Francisco market. You'll start small. It will be a side line at first. I'll tell you all about that, too, and send you the literature. You must use your head. Let others do the work. You must understand that thoroughly. The wages of superintendence are always larger than the wages of the laborers. You must keep books. You must know where you stand. You must know what pays and what doesn't and what pays best. Your books will tell that. I'll show you all in good time."

"An' think of it—all that on two acres!" Billy murmured.

Mrs. Mortimer looked at him sharply.

"Two acres your granny," she said with asperity. "Five acres. And then you won't be able to supply your market. And you, my boy, as soon as the first rains come will have your hands full and your horses weary draining that meadow. We'll work those plans out to-morrow Also, there is the matter of berries on the bench here—and trellised table grapes, the choicest. They bring the fancy prices. There will be blackberries—Burbank's, he lives at Santa Rosa—Loganberries, Mammoth berries. But don't fool with strawberries. That's a whole occupation in itself. They're not vines, you know. I've examined the orchard. It's a good foundation. We'll settle the pruning and grafts later."

"But Billy wanted three acres of the meadow," Saxon explained at the first chance.

"What for?"

"To grow hay and other kinds of food for the horses he's going to raise."

"Buy it out of a portion of the profits from those three acres," Mrs. Mortimer decided on the instant.

Billy swallowed, and again achieved renunciation.

"All right," he said, with a brave show of cheerfulness. "Let her go. Us for the greens."

During the several days of Mrs. Mortimer's visit, Billy let the two women settle things for themselves. Oakland had entered upon a boom, and from the West Oakland stables had come an urgent letter for more horses. So Billy was out, early and late, scouring the surrounding country for young work animals. In this way, at the start, he learned his valley thoroughly. There was also a clearing out at the West Oakland stables of mares whose feet had been knocked out on the hard city pave meets, and he was offered first choice at bargain prices. They were good animals. He knew what they were because he knew them of old time. The soft earth of the country, with a preliminary rest in pasture with their shoes pulled off, would put them in shape. They would never do again on hard-paved streets, but there were years of farm work in them. And then there was the breeding. But he could not undertake to buy them. He fought out the battle in secret and said nothing to Saxon.

At night, he would sit in the kitchen and smoke, listening to all that the two women had done and planned in the day. The right kind of horses was hard to buy, and, as he put it, it was like pulling a tooth to get a farmer to part with one, despite the fact that he had been authorized to increase the buying sum by as much as fifty dollars. Despite the coming of the automobile, the price of heavy draught animals continued to rise. From as early as Billy could remember, the price of the big work horses had increased steadily. After the great earthquake, the price had jumped; yet it had never gone back.

"Billy, you make more money as a horse-buyer than a common laborer, don't you?" Mrs. Mortimer asked. "Very well, then. You won't have to drain the meadow, or plow it, or anything. You keep right on buying horses. Work with your head. But out of what you make you will please pay the wages of one laborer for Saxon's vegetables. It will be a good investment, with quick returns."

"Sure," he agreed. "That's all anybody hires any body for—to make money outa 'm. But how Saxon an' one man are goin' to work them five acres, when Mr. Hale says two of us couldn't do what's needed on two acres, is beyond me."

"Saxon isn't going to work," Mrs. Mortimer retorted.

"Did you see me working at San Jose? Saxon is going to use her head. It's about time you woke up to that. A dollar and a half a day is what is earned by persons who don't use their heads. And she isn't going to be satisfied with a dollar and a half a day. Now listen. I had a long talk with Mr. Hale this afternoon. He says there are practically no efficient laborers to be hired in the valley."

"I know that," Billy interjected. "All the good men go to the cities. It's only the leavin's that's left. The good ones that stay behind ain't workin' for wages."

"Which is perfectly true, every word. Now listen, children. I knew about it, and I spoke to Mr. Hale. He is prepared to make the arrangements for you. He knows all about it himself, and is in touch with the Warden. In short, you will parole two good-conduct prisoners from San Quentin; and they will be gardeners. There are plenty of Chinese and Italians there, and they are the best truck-farmers. You kill two birds with one stone. You serve the poor convicts, and you serve yourselves."

Saxon hesitated, shocked; while Billy gravely considered the question.

"You know John," Mrs. Mortimer went on, "Mr. Hale's man about the place? How do you like him?"

"Oh, I was wishing only to-day that we could find somebody like him," Saxon said eagerly. "He's such a dear, faithful soul. Mrs. Hale told me a lot of fine things about him."

"There's one thing she didn't tell you," smiled Mrs. Mortimer. "John is a paroled convict. Twenty-eight years ago, in hot blood, he killed a man in a quarrel over sixty-five cents. He's been out of prison with the Hales three years now. You remember Louis, the old Frenchman, on my place? He's another. So that's settled. When your two come—of course you will pay them fair wages—and we'll make sure they're the same nationality, either Chinese or Italians—well, when they come, John, with their help, and under Mr. Hale's guidance, will knock together a small cabin for them to live in. We'll select the spot. Even so, when your farm is in full swing you'll have to have more outside help. So keep your eyes open, Billy, while you're gallivanting over the valley."

CHAPTER XIX

The next night Billy failed to return, and at nine o'clock a Glen Ellen boy on horseback delivered a telegram. Billy had sent it from Lake County. He was after horses for Oakland.

Not until the third night did he arrive home, tired to exhaustion, but with an ill concealed air of pride.

"Now what have you been doing these three days?" Mrs. Mortimer demanded.

"Usin' my head," he boasted quietly. "Killin' two birds with one stone; an', take it from me, I killed a whole flock. Huh! I got word of it at Lawndale, an' I wanta tell you Hazel an' Hattie was some tired when I stabled 'm at Calistoga an' pulled out on the stage over St. Helena. I was Johnny-on-the-spot, an' I nailed 'm—eight whoppers—the whole outfit of a mountain teamster. Young animals, sound as a-dollar, and the lightest of 'em over fifteen hundred. I shipped 'm last night from Calistoga. An', well, that ain't all.

"Before that, first day, at Lawndale, I seen the fellow with the teamin' contract for the pavin'-stone quarry. Sell horses! He wanted to buy 'em. He wanted to buy 'em bad. He'd even rent 'em, he said."

"And you sent him the eight you bought!" Saxon broke in.

"Guess again. I bought them eight with Oakland money, an' they was shipped to Oakland. But I got the Lawndale contractor on long distance, and he agreed to pay me half a dollar a day rent for every work horse up to half a dozen. Then I telegraphed the Boss, tellin' him to ship me six sore-footed mares, Bud Strothers to make the choice, an' to charge to my commission. Bud knows what I 'm after. Soon as they come, off go their shoes. Two weeks in pasture, an' then they go to Lawndale. They can do the work. It's a down-hill haul to the railroad on a dirt road. Half a dollar rent each—that's three dollars a day they'll bring me six days a week. I don't feed 'em, shoe 'm, or nothin', an' I keep an eye on 'm to see they're treated right. Three bucks a day, eh! Well, I guess that'll keep a couple of dollar-an '-a-half men goin' for Saxon, unless she works 'em Sundays. Huh! The Valley of the Moon! Why, we'll be wearin' diamonds before long. Gosh! A fellow could live in the city a thousan' years an' not get such chances. It beats China lottery."

He stood up.

"I 'm goin' out to water Hazel an' Hattie, feed 'm, an' bed 'm down. I'll eat soon as I come back."

The two women were regarding each other with shining eyes, each on the verge of speech when Billy returned to the door and stuck his head in.

"They's one thing maybe you ain't got," he said. "I pull down them three dollars every day; but the six mares is mine, too. I own 'm. They're mine. Are you on?"

CHAPTER XX

"I'm not done with you children," had been Mrs. Mortimer's parting words; and several times that winter she ran up to advise, and to teach Saxon how to calculate her crops for the small immediate market, for the increasing spring market, and for the height of summer, at which time she would be able to sell all she could possibly grow and then not supply the demand. In the meantime, Hazel and Hattie were used every odd moment in hauling manure from Glen Ellen, whose barnyards had never known such a thorough cleaning. Also there were loads of commercial fertilizer from the railroad station, bought under Mrs. Mortimer's instructions.

The convicts paroled were Chinese. Both had served long in prison, and were old men; but the day's work they were habitually capable of won Mrs. Mortimer's approval. Gow Yum, twenty years before, had had charge of the vegetable garden of one of the great Menlo Park estates. His disaster had come in the form of a fight over a game of fan tan in the Chinese quarter at Redwood City. His companion, Chan Chi, had been a hatchet-man of note, in the old fighting days of the San Francisco tongs. But a quarter of century of discipline in the prison vegetable gardens had cooled his blood and turned his hand from hatchet to hoe. These two assistants had arrived in Glen Ellen like precious goods in bond and been receipted for by the local deputy sheriff, who, in addition, reported on them to the prison authorities each month. Saxon, too, made out a monthly report and sent it in.

As for the danger of their cutting her throat, she quickly got over the idea of it. The mailed hand of the State hovered over them. The taking of a single drink of liquor would provoke that hand to close down and jerk them back to prison-cells. Nor had they freedom of movement. When old Gow Yum needed to go to San Francisco to sign certain papers before the Chinese Consul, permission had first to be obtained from San Quentin. Then, too, neither man was nasty tempered. Saxon had been apprehensive of the task of bossing two desperate convicts; but when they came she found it a pleasure to work with them. She could tell them what to do, but it was they who knew how do. Prom them she learned all the ten thousand tricks and quirks of artful gardening, and she was not long in realizing how helpless she would have been had she depended on local labor.

Still further, she had no fear, because she was not alone. She had been using her head. It was quickly apparent to her that she could not adequately oversee the outside work and at the same time do the house work. She wrote to Ukiah to the energetic widow who had lived in the adjoining house and taken in washing. She had promptly closed with Saxon's offer. Mrs. Paul was forty, short in stature, and weighed two hundred pounds, but never wearied on her feet. Also she was devoid of fear, and, according to Billy, could settle the hash of both Chinese with one of her mighty arms. Mrs. Paul arrived with her son, a country lad of sixteen who knew horses and could milk Hilda, the pretty Jersey which had successfully passed Edmund's expert eye. Though Mrs. Paul ably handled the house, there was one thing Saxon insisted on doing—namely, washing her own pretty flimsies.

"When I 'm no longer able to do that," she told Billy, "you can take a spade to that clump of redwoods beside Wild Water and dig a hole. It will be time to bury me."

It was early in the days of Madrono Ranch, at the time of Mrs. Mortimer's second visit, that Billy drove in with a load of pipe; and house, chicken yards, and barn were piped from the second-hand tank he installed below the house-spring.

"Huh! I guess I can use my head," he said. "I watched a woman over on the other side of the valley, packin' water two hundred feet from the spring to the house; an' I did some figurin'. I put it at three trips a day and on wash days a whole lot more; an' you can't guess what I made out she traveled a year packin' water. One hundred an' twenty-two miles. D'ye get that? One hundred and twenty-two miles! I asked her how long she'd been there. Thirty-one years. Multiply it for yourself. Three thousan', seven hundred an' eighty-two miles—all for the sake of two hundred feet of pipe. Wouldn't that jar you?"

"Oh, I ain't done yet. They's a bath-tub an' stationary tubs a-comin' soon as I can see my way. An', say, Saxon, you know that little clear flat just where Wild Water runs into Sonoma. They's all of an acre of it. An' it's mine! Got that? An' no walkin' on the grass for you. It'll be my grass. I 'm goin' up stream a ways an' put in a ram. I got a big second-hand one staked out that I can get for ten dollars, an' it'll pump more water'n I need. An' you'll see alfalfa growin' that'll make your mouth water. I gotta have another horse to travel around on. You're usin' Hazel an' Hattie too much to give me a chance; an' I'll never see 'm as soon as you start deliverin' vegetables. I guess that alfalfa'll help some to keep another horse goin'."

But Billy was destined for a time to forget his alfalfa in the excitement of bigger ventures. First, came trouble. The several hundred dollars he had arrived with in Sonoma Valley, and all his own commissions since earned, had gone into improvements and living. The eighteen dollars a week rental for his six horses at Lawndale went to pay wages. And he was unable to buy the needed saddle-horse for his horse-buying expeditions. This, however, he had got around by again using his head and killing two birds with one stone. He began breaking colts to drive, and in the driving drove them wherever he sought horses.

So far all was well. But a new administration in San Francisco, pledged to economy, had stopped all street work. This meant the shutting down of the Lawndale quarry, which was one of the sources of supply for paving blocks. The six horses would not only be back on his hands, but he would have to feed them. How Mrs. Paul, Gow Yum, and Chan Chi were to be paid was beyond him.

"I guess we've bit off more'n we could chew," he admitted to Saxon.

That night he was late in coming home, but brought with him a radiant face. Saxon was no less radiant.

"It's all right," she greeted him, coming out to the barn where he was unhitching a tired but fractious colt. "I've talked with all three. They see the situation, and are perfectly willing to let their wages stand a while. By another week I start Hazel and Hattie delivering vegetables. Then the money will pour in from the hotels and my books won't look so lopsided. And—oh, Billy—you'd never guess. Old Gow Yum has a bank account. He came to me afterward—I guess he was thinking it over—and offered to lend me four hundred dollars. What do you think of that?"

"That I ain't goin' to be too proud to borrow it off 'm, if he IS a Chink. He's a white one, an' maybe I'll need it. Because, you see—well, you can't guess what I've been up to since I seen you this mornin'. I've been so busy I ain't had a bite to eat."

"Using your head?" She laughed.

"You can call it that," he joined in her laughter. "I've been spendin' money like water."

"But you haven't got any to spend," she objected.

"I've got credit in this valley, I'll let you know," he replied. "An' I sure strained it some this afternoon. Now guess."

"A saddle-horse?"

He roared with laughter, startling the colt, which tried to bolt and lifted him half off the ground by his grip on its frightened nose and neck.

"Oh, I mean real guessin'," he urged, when the animal had dropped back to earth and stood regarding him with trembling suspicion.

"Two saddle-horses?"

"Aw, you ain't got imagination. I'll tell you. You know Thiercroft. I bought his big wagon from 'm for sixty dollars. I bought a wagon from the Kenwood blacksmith—so-so, but it'll do—for forty-five dollars. An' I bought Ping's wagon—a peach—for sixty-five dollars. I could a-got it for fifty if he hadn't seen I wanted it bad."

"But the money?" Saxon questioned faintly. "You hadn't a hundred dollars left."

"Didn't I tell you I had credit? Well, I have. I stood 'm off for them wagons. I ain't spent a cent of cash money to-day except for a couple of long-distance switches. Then I bought three sets of work-harness—they're chain harness an' second-hand—for twenty dollars a set. I bought 'm from the fellow that's doin' the haulin' for the quarry. He don't need 'm any more. An' I rented four wagons from 'm, an' four span of horses, too, at half a dollar a day for each horse, an' half a dollar a day for each wagon—that's six dollars a day rent I gotta pay 'm. The three sets of spare harness is for my six horses. Then... lemme see... yep, I rented two barns in Glen Ellen, an' I ordered fifty tons of hay an' a carload of bran an' barley from the store in Glenwood—you see, I gotta feed all them fourteen horses, an' shoe 'm, an' everything.

"Oh, sure Pete, I've went some. I hired seven men to go drivin' for me at two dollars a day, an'—ouch! Jehosaphat! What you doin'!"

"No," Saxon said gravely, having pinched him, "you're not dreaming." She felt his pulse and forehead. "Not a sign of fever." She sniffed his breath. "And you've not been drinking. Go on, tell me the rest of this... whatever it is."

"Ain't you satisfied?"

"No. I want more. I want all."

"All right. But I just want you to know, first, that the boss I used to work for in Oakland ain't got nothin' on me. I 'm some man of affairs, if anybody should ride up on a vegetable wagon an' ask you. Now, I 'm goin' to tell you, though I can't see why the Glen Ellen folks didn't beat me to it. I guess they was asleep. Nobody'd a-overlooked a thing like it in the city. You see, it was like this: you know that fancy brickyard they're gettin' ready to start for makin' extra special fire brick for inside walls? Well, here was I worryin' about the six horses comin' back on my hands, earnin' me nothin' an' eatin' me into the poorhouse. I had to get 'm work somehow, an' I remembered the brickyard. I drove the colt down an' talked with that Jap chemist who's been doin' the experimentin'. Gee! They was foremen lookin' over the ground an' everything gettin' ready to hum. I looked over the lay an' studied it. Then I drove up to where they're openin' the clay pit—you know, that fine, white chalky stuff we saw 'em borin' out just outside the hundred an' forty acres with the three knolls. It's a down-hill haul, a mile, an' two horses can do it easy. In fact, their hardest job'll be haulin' the empty wagons up to the pit. Then I tied the colt an' went to figurin'.

"The Jap professor'd told me the manager an' the other big guns of the company was comin' up on the mornin' train. I wasn't shoutin' things out to anybody, but I just made myself into a committee of welcome; an', when the train pulled in, there I was, extendin' the glad hand of the burg—likewise the glad hand of a guy you used to know in Oakland once, a third-rate dub prizefighter by the name of—lemme see—yep, I got it right—Big Bill Roberts was the name he used to sport, but now he's known as William Roberts, E. S. Q.

"Well, as I was sayin', I gave 'm the glad hand, an' trailed along with 'em to the brickyard, an' from the talk I could see things was doin'. Then I watched my chance an' sprung my proposition. I was scared stiff all the time for maybe the teamin' was already arranged. But I knew it wasn't when they asked for my figures. I had 'm by heart, an' I rattled 'm off, and the top-guy took 'm down in his note-book.

"'We're goin' into this big, an' at once,' he says, lookin' at me sharp. 'What kind of an outfit you got, Mr. Roberts?'"

"Me!—with only Hazel an' Hattie, an' them too small for heavy teamin'.

"'I can slap fourteen horses an' seven wagons onto the job at the jump,' says I. 'An' if you want more, I'll get 'm, that's all.'

"'Give us fifteen minutes to consider, Mr. Roberts,' he says.

"'Sure,' says I, important as all hell—ahem—me!—'but a couple of other things first. I want a two year contract, an' them figures all depends on one thing. Otherwise they don't go.'

"'What's that,' he says.

"'The dump,' says I. 'Here we are on the ground, an' I might as well show you.'

"An' I did. I showed 'm where I'd lose out if they stuck to their plan, on account of the dip down an' pull up to the dump. 'All you gotta do,' I says, 'is to build the bunkers fifty feet over, throw the road around the rim of the hill, an' make about seventy or eighty feet of elevated bridge.'

"Say, Saxon, that kind of talk got 'em. It was straight. Only they'd been thinkin' about bricks, while I was only thinkin' of teamin'.

"I guess they was all of half an hour considerin', an' I was almost as miserable waitin' as when I waited for you to say yes after I asked you. I went over the figures, calculatin' what I could throw off if I had to. You see, I'd given it to 'em stiff—regular city prices; an' I was prepared to trim down. Then they come back.

"'Prices oughta be lower in the country,' says the top-guy.

"'Nope,' I says. 'This is a wine-grape valley. It don't raise enough hay an' feed for its own animals. It has to be shipped in from the San Joaquin Valley. Why, I can buy hay an' feed cheaper in San Francisco, laid down, than I can here an' haul it myself.'

"An' that struck 'm hard. It was true, an' they knew it. But—say! If they'd asked about wages for drivers, an' about horse-shoein' prices, I'd a-had to come down; because, you see, they ain't no teamsters' union in the country, an' no horseshoers' union, an' rent is low, an' them two items come a whole lot cheaper. Huh! This afternoon I got a word bargain with the blacksmith across from the post office; an' he takes my whole bunch an' throws off twenty-five cents on each shoein', though it's on the Q. T. But they didn't think to ask, bein' too full of bricks."

Billy felt in his breast pocket, drew out a legal-looking document, and handed it to Saxon.

"There it is," he said, "the contract, full of all the agreements, prices, an' penalties. I saw Mr. Hale down town an' showed it to 'm. He says it's O.K. An' say, then I lit out. All over town, Kenwood, Lawndale, everywhere, everybody, everything. The quarry teamin' finishes Friday of this week. An' I take the whole outfit an' start Wednesday of next week haulin' lumber for the buildin's, an' bricks for the kilns, an' all the rest. An' when they're ready for the clay I 'm the boy that'll give it to them.

"But I ain't told you the best yet. I couldn't get the switch right away from Kenwood to Lawndale, and while I waited I went over my figures again. You couldn't guess it in a million years. I'd made a mistake in addition somewhere, an' soaked 'm ten per cent. more'n I'd expected. Talk about findin' money! Any time you want them couple of extra men to help out with the vegetables, say the word. Though we're goin' to have to pinch the next couple of months. An' go ahead an' borrow that four hundred from Gow Yum. An' tell him you'll pay eight per cent. interest, an' that we won't want it more 'n three or four months."

When Billy got away from Saxon's arms, he started leading the colt up and down to cool it off. He stopped so abruptly that his back collided with the colt's nose, and there was a lively minute of rearing and plunging. Saxon waited, for she knew a fresh idea had struck Billy.

"Say," he said, "do you know anything about bank accounts and drawin' checks?"

CHAPTER XXI

It was on a bright June morning that Billy told Saxon to put on her riding clothes to try out a saddle-horse.

"Not until after ten o'clock," she said "By that time I'll have the wagon off on a second trip."

Despite the extent of the business she had developed, her executive ability and system gave her much spare time. She could call on the Hales, which was ever a delight, especially now that the Hastings were back and that Clara was often at her aunt's. In this congenial atmosphere Saxon Burgeoned. She had begun to read—to read with understanding; and she had time for her books, for work on her pretties, and for Billy, whom she accompanied on many expeditions.

Billy was even busier than she, his work being more scattered and diverse. And, as well, he kept his eye on the home barn and horses which Saxon used. In truth he had become a man of affairs, though Mrs. Mortimer had gone over his accounts, with an eagle eye on the expense column, discovering several minor leaks, and finally, aided by Saxon, bullied him into keeping books. Each night, after supper, he and Saxon posted their books. Afterward, in the big morris chair he had insisted on buying early in the days of his brickyard contract, Saxon would creep into his arms and strum on the ukelele; or they would talk long about what they were doing and planning to do. Now it would be:

"I'm mixin' up in politics, Saxon. It pays. You bet it pays. If by next spring I ain't got a half a dozen teams workin' on the roads an' pullin' down the county money, it's me back to Oakland an' askin' the Boss for a job."

Or, Saxon: "They're really starting that new hotel between Caliente and Eldridge. And there's some talk of a big sanitarium back in the hills."

Or, it would be: "Billy, now that you've piped that acre, you've just got to let me have it for my vegetables. I'll rent it from you. I'll take your own estimate for all the alfalfa you can raise on it, and pay you full market price less the cost of growing it."

"It's all right, take it." Billy suppressed a sigh. "Besides, I 'm too busy to fool with it now."

Which prevarication was bare-faced, by virtue of his having just installed the ram and piped the land.

"It will be the wisest, Billy," she soothed, for she knew his dream of land-spaciousness was stronger than ever. "You don't want to fool with an acre. There's that hundred and forty. We'll buy it yet if old Chavon ever dies. Besides, it really belongs to Madrono Ranch. The two together were the original quarter section."

"I don't wish no man's death," Billy grumbled. "But he ain't gettin' no good out of it, over-pasturin' it with a lot of scrub animals. I've sized it up every inch of it. They's at least forty acres in the three cleared fields, with water in the hills behind to beat the band. The horse feed I could raise on it'd take your breath away. Then they's at least fifty acres I could run my brood mares on, pasture mixed up with trees and steep places and such. The other fifty's just thick woods, an' pretty places, an' wild game. An' that old adobe barn's all right. With a new roof it'd shelter any amount of animals in bad weather. Cook at me now, rentin' that measly pasture back of Ping's just to run my restin' animals. They could run in the hundred an' forty if I only had it. I wonder if Chavon would lease it."

Or, less ambitious, Billy would say: "I gotta skin over to Petaluma to-morrow, Saxon. They's an auction on the Atkinson Ranch an' maybe I can pick up some bargains."

"More horses!"

"Ain't I got two teams haulin' lumber for the new winery? An' Barney's got a bad shoulder-sprain. He'll have to lay off a long time if he's to get it in shape. An' Bridget ain't ever goin' to do a tap of work again. I can see that stickin' out. I've doctored her an' doctored her. She's fooled the vet, too. An' some of the other horses has gotta take a rest. That span of grays is showin' the hard work. An' the big roan's goin' loco. Everybody thought it was his teeth, but it ain't. It's straight loco. It's money in pocket to take care of your animals, an' horses is the delicatest things on four legs. Some time, if I can ever see my way to it, I 'm goin' to ship a carload of mules from Colusa County—big, heavy ones, you know. They'd sell like hot cakes in the valley here—them I didn't want for myself."

Or, in lighter vein, Billy: "By the way, Saxon, talkin' of accounts, what d'you think Hazel an' Hattie is worth?—fair market price?"

"Why?"

"I 'm askin' you."

"Well, say, what you paid for them—three hundred dollars."

"Hum." Billy considered deeply. "They're worth a whole lot more, but let it go at that. An' now, gettin' back to accounts, suppose you write me a check for three hundred dollars."

"Oh! Robber!"

"You can't show me. Why, Saxon, when I let you have grain an' hay from my carloads, don't you give me a check for it? An' you know how you're stuck on keepin' your accounts down to the penny," he teased. "If you're any kind of a business woman you just gotta charge your business with them two horses. I ain't had the use of 'em since I don't know when."

"But the colts will be yours," she argued. "Besides, I can't afford brood mares in my business. In almost no time, now, Hazel and Hattie will have to be taken off from the wagon—they're too good for it anyway. And you keep your eyes open for a pair to take their place. I'll give you a check for THAT pair, but no commission."

"All right," Billy conceded. "Hazel an' Hattie come back to me; but you can pay me rent for the time you did use 'em."

"If you make me, I'll charge you board," she threatened.

CHAPTER XXI

"An' if you charge me board, I'll charge you interest for the money I've stuck into this shebang."

"You can't," Saxon laughed. "It's community property."

He grunted spasmodically, as if the breath had been knocked out of him.

"Straight on the solar plexus," he said, "an' me down for the count. But say, them's sweet words, ain't they—community property." He rolled them over and off his tongue with keen relish. "An' when we got married the top of our ambition was a steady job an' some rags an' sticks of furniture all paid up an' half-worn out. We wouldn't have had any community property only for you."

"What nonsense! What could I have done by myself? You know very well that you earned all the money that started us here. You paid the wages of Gow Yum and Chan Chi, and old Hughie, and Mrs. Paul, and—why, you've done it all."

She drew her two hands caressingly across his shoulders and down along his great biceps muscles.

"That's what did it, Billy."

"Aw hell! It's your head that done it. What was my muscles good for with no head to run 'em,—sluggin' scabs, beatin' up lodgers, an' crookin' the elbow over a bar. The only sensible thing my head ever done was when it run me into you. Honest to God, Saxon, you've been the makin' of me."

"Aw hell, Billy," she mimicked in the way that delighted him, "where would I have been if you hadn't taken me out of the laundry? I couldn't take myself out. I was just a helpless girl. I'd have been there yet if it hadn't been for you. Mrs. Mortimer had five thousand dollars; but I had you."

"A woman ain't got the chance to help herself that a man has," he generalized. "I'll tell you what: It took the two of us. It's been team-work. We've run in span. If we'd a-run single, you might still be in the laundry; an', if I was lucky, I'd be still drivin' team by the day an' sportin' around to cheap dances."

Saxon stood under the father of all madronos, watching Hazel and Hattie go out the gate, the full vegetable wagon behind them, when she saw Billy ride in, leading a sorrel mare from whose silken coat the sun flashed golden lights.

"Four-year-old, high-life, a handful, but no vicious tricks," Billy chanted, as he stopped beside Saxon. "Skin like tissue paper, mouth like silk, but kill the toughest broncho ever foaled—look at them lungs an' nostrils. They call her Ramona—some Spanish name: sired by Morellita outa genuine Morgan stock."

"And they will sell her?" Saxon gasped, standing with hands clasped in inarticulate delight.

"That's what I brought her to show you for."

"But how much must they want for her?" was Saxon's next question, so impossible did it seem that such an amazement of horse-flesh could ever be hers.

"That ain't your business," Billy answered brusquely. "The brickyard's payin' for her, not the vegetable ranch. She's yourn at the word. What d'ye say?"

"I'll tell you in a minute."

Saxon was trying to mount, but the animal danced nervously away.

"Hold on till I tie," Billy said. "She ain't skirt-broke, that's the trouble."

Saxon tightly gripped reins and mane, stepped with spurred foot on Billy's hand, and was lifted lightly into the saddle.

"She's used to spurs," Billy called after. "Spanish broke, so don't check her quick. Come in gentle. An' talk to her. She's high-life, you know."

Saxon nodded, dashed out the gate and down the road, waved a hand to Clara Hastings as she passed the gate of Trillium Covert, and continued up Wild Water canyon.

When she came back, Ramona in a pleasant lather, Saxon rode to the rear of the house, past the chicken houses and the flourishing berry-rows, to join Billy on the rim of the bench, where he sat on his horse in the shade, smoking a cigarette. Together they looked down through an opening among the trees to the meadow which was a meadow no longer. With mathematical accuracy it was divided into squares, oblongs, and narrow strips, which displayed sharply the thousand hues of green of a truck garden. Gow Yum and Chan Chi, under enormous Chinese grass hats, were planting green onions. Old Hughie, hoe in hand, plodded along the main artery of running water, opening certain laterals, closing others. From the work-shed beyond the barn the strokes of a hammer told Saxon that Carlsen was wire-binding vegetable boxes. Mrs. Paul's cheery soprano, lifted in a hymn, doated through the trees, accompanied by the whirr of an egg-beater. A sharp barking told where Possum still waged hysterical and baffled war on the Douglass squirrels. Billy took a long draw from his cigarette, exhaled the smoke, and continued to look down at the meadow. Saxon divined trouble in his manner. His rein-hand was on the pommel, and her free hand went out and softly rested on his. Billy turned his slow gaze upon her mare's lather, seeming not to note it, and continued on to Saxon's face.

"Huh!" he equivocated, as if waking up. "Them San Leandro Porchugeeze ain't got nothin' on us when it comes to intensive farmin'. Look at that water runnin'. You know, it seems so good to me that sometimes I just wanta get down on hands an' knees an' lap it all up myself."

"Oh, to have all the water you want in a climate like this!" Saxon exclaimed.

"An' don't be scared of it ever goin' back on you. If the rains fooled you, there's Sonoma Creek alongside. All we gotta do is install a gasolene pump."

"But we'll never have to, Billy. I was talking with 'Redwood' Thompson. He's lived in the valley since Fifty-three, and he says there's never been a failure of crops on account of drought. We always get our rain."

"Come on, let's go for a ride," he said abruptly. "You've got the time."

"All right, if you'll tell me what's bothering you."

He looked at her quickly.

"Nothin'," he grunted. "Yes, there is, too. What's the difference? You'd know it sooner or later. You ought to see old Chavon. His face is that long he can't walk without bumpin' his knee on his chin. His gold-mine's peterin' out."

"Gold mine!"

"His clay pit. It's the same thing. He's gettin' twenty cents a yard for it from the brickyard."

"And that means the end of your teaming contract." Saxon saw the disaster in all its hugeness. "What about the brickyard people?"

"Worried to death, though they've kept secret about it. They've had men out punchin' holes all over the hills for a week, an' that Jap chemist settin' up nights analyzin' the rubbish they've brought in. It's peculiar stuff, that clay, for what they want it for, an' you don't find it everywhere. Them experts that reported on Chavon's pit made one hell of a mistake. Maybe they was lazy with their borin's. Anyway, they slipped up on the amount of clay they was in it. Now don't get to botherin'. It'd come out somehow. You can't do nothin'."

"But I can," Saxon insisted. "We won't buy Ramona."

"You ain't got a thing to do with that," he answered. "I 'm buyin' her, an' her price don't cut any figure alongside the big game I 'm playin'. Of course, I can always sell my horses. But that puts a stop to their makin' money, an' that brickyard contract was fat."

"But if you get some of them in on the road work for the county?" she suggested.

"Oh, I got that in mind. An' I 'm keepin' my eyes open. They's a chance the quarry will start again, an' the fellow that did that teamin' has gone to Puget Sound. An' what if I have to sell out most of the horses? Here's you and the vegetable business. That's solid. We just don't go ahead so fast for a time, that's all. I ain't scared of the country any more. I sized things up as we went along. They ain't a jerk burg we hit all the time on the road that I couldn't jump into an' make a go. An' now where d'you want to ride?"

CHAPTER XXII

They cantered out the gate, thundered across the bridge, and passed Trillium Covert before they pulled in on the grade of Wild Water Canyon. Saxon had chosen her field on the big spur of Sonoma Mountains as the objective of their ride.

"Say, I bumped into something big this mornin' when I was goin' to fetch Ramona," Billy said, the clay pit trouble banished for the time. "You know the hundred an' forty. I passed young Chavon along the road, an'—I don't know why—just for ducks, I guess—I up an' asked 'm if he thought the old man would lease the hundred an' forty to me. An' what d 'you think! He said the old man didn't own it. Was just leasin' it himself. That's how we was always seein' his cattle on it. It's a gouge into his land, for he owns everything on three sides of it.

"Next I met Ping. He said Hilyard owned it an' was willin' to sell, only Chavon didn't have the price. Then, comin' back, I looked in on Payne. He's quit blacksmithin'—his back's hurtin' 'm from a kick—an' just startin' in for real estate. Sure, he said, Hilyard would sell, an' had already listed the land with 'm. Chavon's overpastured it, an' Hilyard won't give 'm another lease."

When they had climbed out of Wild Water Canyon they turned their horses about and halted on the rim where they could look across at the three densely wooded knolls in the midst of the desired hundred and forty.

"We'll get it yet," Saxon said.

"Sure we will," Billy agreed with careless certitude. "I've ben lookin' over the big adobe barn again. Just the thing for a raft of horses, an' a new roof'll be cheaper 'n I thought. Though neither Chavon or me'll be in the market to buy it right away, with the clay pinchin' out."

When they reached Saxon's field, which they had learned was the property of Redwood Thompson, they tied the horses and entered it on foot. The hay, just cut, was being raked by Thompson, who hallo'd a greeting to them. It was a cloudless, windless day, and they sought refuge from the sun in the woods beyond. They encountered a dim trail.

"It's a cow trail," Billy declared. "I bet they's a teeny pasture tucked away somewhere in them trees. Let's follow it."

A quarter of an hour later, several hundred feet up the side of the spur, they emerged on an open, grassy space of bare hillside. Most of the hundred and forty, two miles away, lay beneath them, while they were level with the tops of the three knolls. Billy paused to gaze upon the much-desired land, and Saxon joined him.

CHAPTER XXII

"What is that?" she asked, pointing toward the knolls. "Up the little canyon, to the left of it, there on the farthest knoll, right under that spruce that's leaning over."

What Billy saw was a white scar on the canyon wall.

"It's one on me," he said, studying the scar. "I thought I knew every inch of that land, but I never seen that before. Why, I was right in there at the head of the canyon the first part of the winter. It's awful wild. Walls of the canyon like the sides of a steeple an' covered with thick woods."

"What is it?" she asked. "A slide?"

"Must be—brought down by the heavy rains. If I don't miss my guess—" Billy broke off, forgetting in the intensity with which he continued to look.

"Hilyard'll sell for thirty an acre," he began again, disconnectedly. "Good land, bad land, an' all, just as it runs, thirty an acre. That's forty-two hundred. Payne's new at real estate, an' I'll make 'm split his commission an' get the easiest terms ever. We can re-borrow that four hundred from Gow Yum, an' I can borrow money on my horses an' wagons—"

"Are you going to buy it to-day?" Saxon teased.

She scarcely touched the edge of his thought. He looked at her, as if he had heard, then forgot her the next moment.

"Head work," he mumbled. "Head work. If I don't put over a hot one—"

He started back down the cow trail, recollected Saxon, and called over his shoulder:

"Come on. Let's hustle. I wanta ride over an' look at that."

So rapidly did he go down the trail and across the field, that Saxon had no time for questions. She was almost breathless from her effort to keep up with him.

"What is it?" she begged, as he lifted her to the saddle.

"Maybe it's all a joke—I'll tell you about it afterward," he put her off.

They galloped on the levels, trotted down the gentler slopes of road, and not until on the steep descent of Wild Water canyon did they rein to a walk. Billy's preoccupation was gone, and Saxon took advantage to broach a subject which had been on her mind for some time.

"Clara Hastings told me the other day that they're going to have a house party. The Hazards are to be there, and the Halls, and Roy Blanchard...."

She looked at Billy anxiously. At the mention of Blanchard his head had tossed up as to a bugle call. Slowly a whimsical twinkle began to glint up through the cloudy blue of his eyes.

"It's a long time since you told any man he was standing on his foot," she ventured slyly.

Billy began to grin sheepishly.

"Aw, that's all right," he said in mock-lordly fashion. "Roy Blanchard can come. I'll let 'm. All that was a long time ago. Besides, I 'm too busy to fool with such things."

He urged his horse on at a faster walk, and as soon as the slope lessened broke into a trot. At Trillium Covert they were galloping.

"You'll have to stop for dinner first," Saxon said, as they neared the gate of Madrono Ranch.

"You stop," he answered. "I don't want no dinner."

"But I want to go with you," she pleaded. "What is it?"

"I don't dast tell you. You go on in an' get your dinner."

"Not after that," she said. "Nothing can keep me from coming along now."

Half a mile farther on, they left the highway, passed through a patent gate which Billy had installed, and crossed the fields on a road which was coated thick with chalky dust. This was the road that led to Chavon's clay pit. The hundred and forty lay to the west. Two wagons, in a cloud of dust, came into sight.

"Your teams, Billy," cried Saxon. "Think of it! Just by the use of the head, earning your money while you're riding around with me."

"Makes me ashamed to think how much cash money each one of them teams is bringin' me in every day," he acknowledged.

They were turning off from the road toward the bars which gave entrance to the one hundred and forty, when the driver of the foremost wagon hallo'd and waved his hand. They drew in their horses and waited.

"The big roan's broke loose," the dryer said, as he stopped beside them. "Clean crazy loco—bitin', squealin', strikin', kickin'. Kicked clean out of the harness like it was paper. Bit a chunk out of Baldy the size of a saucer, an' wound up by breakin' his own hind leg. Liveliest fifteen minutes I ever seen."

"Sure it's broke?" Billy demanded sharply.

"Sure thing."

"Well, after you unload, drive around by the other barn and get Ben. He's in the corral. Tell Matthews to be easy with 'm. An' get a gun. Sammy's got one. You'll have to see to the big roan. I ain't got time now.—Why couldn't Matthews a-come along with you for Ben? You'd save time."

"Oh, he's just stickin' around waitin'," the driver answered. "He reckoned I could get Ben."

"An' lose time, eh? Well, get a move on."

"That's the way of it," Billy growled to Saxon as they rode on. "No savve. No head. One man settin' down an' holdin his hands while another team drives outa its way doin what he oughta done. That's the trouble with two-dollar-a-day men."

"With two-dollar-a-day heads," Saxon said quickly. "What kind of heads do you expect for two dollars?"

"That's right, too," Billy acknowledged the hit. "If they had better heads they'd be in the cities like all the rest of the better men. An' the better men are a lot of dummies, too. They don't know the big chances in the country, or you couldn't hold 'm from it."

Billy dismounted, took the three bars down, led his horse through, then put up the bars.

"When I get this place, there'll be a gate here," he announced. "Pay for itself in no time. It's the thousan' an' one little things like this that count up big when you put 'm together." He sighed contentedly. "I never used to think about such things, but when we shook Oakland I began to wise up. It was them San Leandro Porchugeeze that gave me my first eye-opener. I'd been asleep, before that."

They skirted the lower of the three fields where the ripe hay stood uncut. Billy pointed with eloquent disgust to a break in the fence, slovenly repaired, and on to the standing grain much-trampled by cattle.

"Them's the things," he criticized. "Old style. An' look how thin that crop is, an' the shallow plowin'. Scrub cattle, scrub seed, scrub farmin'. Chavon's worked it for eight years now, an' never rested it once, never put anything in for what he took out, except the cattle into the stubble the minute the hay was on."

In a pasture glade, farther on, they came upon a bunch of cattle.

"Look at that bull, Saxon. Scrub's no name for it. They oughta be a state law against lettin' such animals exist. No wonder Chavon's that land poor he's had to sink all his clay-pit earnin's into taxes an' interest. He can't make his land pay. Take this hundred an forty. Anybody with the savve can just rake silver dollars offen it. I'll show 'm."

They passed the big adobe barn in the distance.

"A few dollars at the right time would a-saved hundreds on that roof," Billy commented. "Well, anyway, I won't be payin' for any improvements when I buy. An I'll tell you another thing. This ranch is full of water, and if Glen Ellen ever grows they'll have to come to see me for their water supply."

Billy knew the ranch thoroughly, and took short-cuts through the woods by way of cattle paths. Once, he reined in abruptly, and both stopped. Confronting them, a dozen paces away, was a half-grown red fox. For half a minute, with beady eyes, the wild thing studied them, with twitching sensitive nose reading the messages of the air. Then, velvet-footed, it leapt aside and was gone among the trees.

"The son-of-a-gun!" Billy ejaculated.

As they approached Wild Water; they rode out into a long narrow meadow. In the middle was a pond.

"Natural reservoir, when Glen Ellen begins to buy water," Billy said. "See, down at the lower end there?—wouldn't cost anything hardly to throw a dam across. An' I can pipe in all kinds of hill-drip. An' water's goin' to be money in this valley not a thousan' years from now.—An' all the ginks, an' boobs, an' dubs, an' gazabos poundin' their ear deado an' not seein' it comin.—An' surveyors workin' up the valley for an electric road from Sausalito with a branch up Napa Valley."

They came to the rim of Wild Water canyon. Leaning far back in their saddles, they slid the horses down a steep declivity, through big spruce woods, to an ancient and all but obliterated trail.

"They cut this trail 'way back in the Fifties," Billy explained. "I only found it by accident. Then I asked Poppe yesterday. He was born in the valley. He said it was a fake minin' rush across from Petaluma. The gamblers got it up, an' they must a-drawn a thousan' suckers. You see that flat there, an' the old stumps. That's where the camp was. They set the tables up under the trees. The flat used to be bigger, but the creek's eaten into it. Poppe said they was a couple of killin's an' one lynchin'."

Lying low against their horses' necks, they scrambled up a steep cattle trail out of the canyon, and began to work across rough country toward the knolls.

"Say, Saxon, you're always lookin' for something pretty. I'll show you what'll make your hair stand up... soon as we get through this manzanita."

Never, in all their travels, had Saxon seen so lovely a vista as the one that greeted them when they emerged. The dim trail lay like a rambling red shadow cast on the soft forest floor by the great redwoods and over-arching oaks. It seemed as if all local varieties of trees and vines had conspired to weave the leafy roof—maples, big madronos and laurels, and lofty tan-bark oaks, scaled and wrapped and interwound with wild grape and flaming poison oak. Saxon drew Billy's eyes to a mossy bank of five-finger ferns. All slopes seemed to meet to form this basin and colossal forest bower.

Underfoot the floor was spongy with water. An invisible streamlet whispered under broad-fronded brakes. On every hand opened tiny vistas of enchantment, where young redwoods grouped still and stately about fallen giants, shoulder-high to the horses, moss-covered and dissolving into mold.

At last, after another quarter of an hour, they tied their horses on the rim of the narrow canyon that penetrated the wilderness of the knolls. Through a rift in the trees Billy pointed to the top of the leaning spruce.

"It's right under that," he said. "We'll have to follow up the bed of the creek. They ain't no trail, though you'll see plenty of deer paths crossin' the creek. You'll get your feet wet."

Saxon laughed her joy and held on close to his heels, splashing through pools, crawling hand and foot up the slippery faces of water-worn rocks, and worming under trunks of old fallen trees.

"They ain't no real bed-rock in the whole mountain," Billy elucidated, "so the stream cuts deeper'n deeper, an' that keeps the sides cavin' in. They're as steep as they can be without fallin' down. A little farther up, the canyon ain't much more'n a crack in the ground—but a mighty deep one if anybody should ask you. You can spit across it an' break your neck in it."

The climbing grew more difficult, and they were finally halted, in a narrow cleft, by a drift-jam.

"You wait here," Billy directed, and, lying flat, squirmed on through crashing brush.

Saxon waited till all sound had died away. She waited ten minutes longer, then followed by the way Billy had broken. Where the bed of the canyon became impossible, she came upon what she was sure was a deer path that skirted the steep side and was a tunnel through the close greenery. She caught a glimpse of the overhanging spruce, almost above her head on the opposite side, and emerged on a pool of clear water in a clay-like basin. This basin was of recent origin, having been formed by a slide of earth and trees. Across the pool arose an almost sheer wall of white. She recognized it for what it was, and looked about for Billy. She heard him whistle, and looked up. Two hundred feet above, at the perilous top of the white wall, he was holding on to a tree trunk. The overhanging spruce was nearby.

"I can see the little pasture back of your field," he called down. "No wonder nobody ever piped this off. The only place they could see it from is that speck of pasture. An' you saw it first. Wait till I come down and tell you all about it. I didn't dast before."

It required no shrewdness to guess the truth. Saxon knew this was the precious clay required by the brickyard. Billy circled wide of the slide and came down the canyon-wall, from tree to tree, as descending a ladder.

"Ain't it a peach?" he exulted, as he dropped beside her. "Just look at it—hidden away under four feet of soil where nobody could see it, an' just waitin' for us to hit the Valley of the Moon. Then it up an' slides a piece of the skin off so as we can see it."

"Is it the real clay?" Saxon asked anxiously.

"You bet your sweet life. I've handled too much of it not to know it in the dark. Just rub a piece between your fingers.—Like that. Why, I could tell by the taste of it. I've eaten enough of the dust of the teams. Here's where our fun begins. Why, you know we've been workin' our heads off since we hit this valley. Now we're on Easy street."

"But you don't own it," Saxon objected.

"Well, you won't be a hundred years old before I do. Straight from here I hike to Payne an' bind the bargain—an option, you know, while title's searchin' an' I 'm raisin' money. We'll borrow that four hundred back again from Gow Yum, an' I'll borrow all I can get on my horses an' wagons, an' Hazel and Hattie, an' everything that's worth a cent. An' then I get the deed with a mortgage on it to Hilyard for the balance. An' then—it's takin' candy from a baby—I'll contract with the brickyard for twenty cents a yard—maybe more. They'll be crazy with joy when they see it. Don't need any borin's. They's nearly two hundred feet of it exposed up an' down. The whole knoll's clay, with a skin of soil over it."

"But you'll spoil all the beautiful canyon hauling out the clay," Saxon cried with alarm.

"Nope; only the knoll. The road'll come in from the other side. It'll be only half a mile to Chavon's pit. I'll build the road an' charge steeper teamin', or the brickyard can build it an' I'll team for the same rate as before. An' twenty cents a yard pourin' in, all profit, from the jump. I'll sure have to buy more horses to do the work."

They sat hand in hand beside the pool and talked over the details.

"Say, Saxon," Billy said, after a pause had fallen, "sing 'Harvest Days,' won't you?"

And, when she had complied: "The first time you sung that song for me was comin' home from the picnic on the train—"

"The very first day we met each other," she broke in. "What did you think about me that day?"

"Why, what I've thought ever since—that you was made for me.—I thought that right at the jump, in the first waltz. An' what'd you think of me?

"Oh, I wondered, and before the first waltz, too, when we were introduced and shook hands—I wondered if you were the man. Those were the very words that flashed into my mind.—IS HE THE MAN?"

"An' I kinda looked a little some good to you?" he queried. "*I* thought so, and my eyesight has always been good."

"Say!" Billy went off at a tangent. "By next winter, with everything hummin' an' shipshape, what's the matter with us makin' a visit to Carmel? It'll be slack time for you with the vegetables, an' I'll be able to afford a foreman."

Saxon's lack of enthusiasm surprised him.

"What's wrong?" he demanded quickly.

With downcast demurest eyes and hesitating speech, Saxon said:

"I did something yesterday without asking your advice, Billy."

He waited.

"I wrote to Tom," she added, with an air of timid confession.

Still he waited—for he knew not what.

"I asked him to ship up the old chest of drawers—my mother's, you remember—that we stored with him."

"Huh! I don't see anything outa the way about that," Billy said with relief. "We need the chest, don't we? An' we can afford to pay the freight on it, can't we?"

"You are a dear stupid man, that's what you are. Don't you know what is in the chest?"

He shook his head, and what she added was so soft that it was almost a whisper:

"The baby clothes."

"No!" he exclaimed.

"True."

"Sure?"

She nodded her head, her cheeks flooding with quick color.

"It's what I wanted, Saxon, more'n anything else in the world. I've been thinkin' a whole lot about it lately, ever since we hit the valley," he went on, brokenly, and for the first time she saw tears unmistakable in his eyes. "But after all I'd done, an' the hell I'd raised, an' everything, I... I never urged you, or said a word about it. But I wanted it... oh, I wanted it like ... like I want you now."

His open arms received her, and the pool in the heart of the canyon knew a tender silence.

Saxon felt Billy's finger laid warningly on her lips. Guided by his hand, she turned her head back, and together they gazed far up the side of the knoll where a doe and a spotted fawn looked down upon them from a tiny open space between the trees.

www.ingramcontent.com/pod-product-compliance
Lightning Source LLC
Chambersburg PA
CBHW080811020826
48982CB00017B/916

* 9 7 8 1 7 8 1 3 9 3 3 9 0 *